Maeve Binchy was born in County Dublin and was educated at the Holy Child convent in Killiney and at University College, Dublin. After a spell as a teacher in various girls' schools, she joined the *Irish Times*, for whom she still writes occasional columns. Her first novel, *Light a Penny Candle*, was published in 1982, and since then she has written more than a dozen novels and short story collections, each one of them bestsellers. Several have been adapted for cinema and television, most notably *Circle of Friends* in 1995, and *Tara Road* which is soon to be released. Maeve Binchy was awarded the Lifetime Achievement award at the British Book Awards in 1999. She is married to the writer and broadcaster Gordon Snell. Visit her website at www.maevebinchy.com.

By Maeve Binchy

Light a Penny Candle
Echoes
London Transports
Dublin 4
The Lilac Bus
Firefly Summer
Silver Wedding
Circle of Friends
The Copper Beech
The Glass Lake
Evening Class
Tara Road
Scarlet Feather
Quentins
Nights of Rain and Stars

Aches & Pains (non-fiction)

Three No. 1 Bestsellers

Maeve Binchy

The Glass Lake
Scarlet Feather
Quentins

ORION

This omnibus edition first published in Great Britain in 2005
by Orion, an imprint of the Orion Publishing Group Ltd,
Orion House, 5 Upper St Martin's Lane, London WC2H 9EA

ISBN 0 75287 264 8

A CIP catalogue record for this book is available
from the British Library

Typeset by Deltatype Ltd, Birkenhead, Merseyside

Printed in Great Britain by Clays Ltd, St Ives plc

www.orionbooks.co.uk

Contents

The Glass Lake

To my dearest Gordon
with the greatest gratitude for everything
and with all my love

1

1952

Kit had always thought that the Pope had been *at* her mother and father's wedding. There was a picture of him in their house – a different Pope, a dead one – and the writing underneath said that Martin McMahon and Helen Healy had prostrated themselves at his feet. It had never occurred to her to look for him in the wedding picture. Anyway, it was such an awful photograph, with all those people in embarrassing coats and hats standing in a line. If she'd thought about it at all, Kit might have assumed that the Pope had left before the picture was taken, got on the mail boat in Dun Laoghaire and gone back to Rome.

That was why it was such a shock when Mother Bernard explained that the Pope could never ever leave the Holy See; not even a war would make him leave the Vatican.

'But he went to weddings, didn't he?' Kit said.

'Only if they were in Rome.' Mother Bernard knew it all.

'He was at my parents' wedding,' Kit insisted.

Mother Bernard looked at the little McMahon girl, a mop of black curly hair and bright blue eyes. A great wall climber, an organiser of much of the devilment that went on in the school yard, but not until now a fantasist.

'I don't think so, Katherine,' the nun said, hoping to stop it there.

'But he *was*.' Kit was stung. 'They have a framed picture of him on the wall saying that he was there.'

'That's the Papal Blessing, you eejit,' said Clio. 'Everyone has them ... they're ten-a-penny.'

'I'll thank you not to speak of the Holy Father in those terms, Cliona Kelly.' Mother Bernard was most disapproving.

Neither Kit nor Clio listened to the details of the Concordat that made the Pope an Independent Ruler of his own tiny state. With her face down on the desk and hidden by the upright atlas, Kit hissed abuse towards her best friend. 'Don't you *ever* call me an eejit again, or you'll be sorry.'

Clio was unrepentant. 'Well, you *are* an eejit. The Pope coming to your parents' wedding. *Your* parents of all people!'

'And why shouldn't he be at their wedding if he were let out?'

'Oh, I don't know.'

Kit sensed something was not being said. 'What would be wrong with their wedding, for example?'

Clio was avoiding the matter. 'Shush, she's looking.' She was right.

'What did I just say, Cliona Kelly?'

'You said that the Holy Father's name was Pacelli, Mother. That he was called that before he was called Pius the Twelfth.'

Mother Bernard reluctantly agreed that this was what she had been saying.

'How did you know that?' Kit was full of admiration.

'Always listen with half your mind to something else,' Clio said.

Clio was very blonde and tall. She was great at games; she was very quick in class. She had lovely, long hair. Clio was Kit's best friend, and sometimes she hated her.

Clio's younger sister Anna often wanted to walk home with them, but this was greatly discouraged.

'Go away, Anna. You're a pain in the bottom,' Clio said.

'I'll tell Mam you said bottom out loud on the road,' Anna said.

'Mam has better things to do than to listen to stupid tall tales. Go *away*.'

'You just want to be skitting and laughing with Kit . . .' Anna was stung by the harshness of her dismissal. 'That's all you do all the time. I heard Mam say . . . I don't know what Clio and Kit are always skitting and laughing about.'

That made them laugh even more. Arm in arm they ran off and left Anna, who had the bad luck to be seven and have no friends of her own.

There were so many things they could do on the way home from school. That was the great thing about living in a place like Lough Glass, a small town on the edge of a big lake. It wasn't *the* biggest lake in Ireland but it was a very large one. You couldn't see across to the other side except on a clear day and it was full of little creeks and inlets. Parts of it were clogged up with reeds and rushes. They called it the Glass Lake, which wasn't a real translation. Lough Glass really meant the green lake, all the children knew that. But sometimes it did look like a mirror.

They said that if you went out on St Agnes' eve and looked in the lake at sunset, you could see your future. Kit and Clio didn't go in for that kind of thing. The future? The future was tomorrow or the next day, and anyway there were always too many half-cracked girls and fellows, old ones nearly twenty, pushing each other out of the way to try to see. As if they could see anything except reflections of themselves and each other!

Sometimes, on the way home from school, Clio and Kit would call to McMahon's pharmacy to see Kit's father, with the hope of being offered a barley sugar from the jar. Or they would go to the wooden pier that jutted out into the lake to see the fishermen coming in with their catch. They might go up to the golf course and see could they find any lost balls, which they could sell to golfers.

They rarely went to each other's houses. There was a danger in going home, a danger of being asked to do their homework. To avoid this for as long as possible, the girls dallied on their way back from school.

There was never much to look at in the post office; the same things had been in the window for years: pictures of stamps, notices about post office savings stamps and books, the rates on letters going to America. They wouldn't delay long there. Mrs Hanley's, the drapery shop, sometimes had nice Fair Isle jumpers and the occasional pair of shoes you might like. But Mrs Hanley didn't like schoolgirls gathering around the window in case it put other people off. She would come out and shoo them away like hens.

'That's right. Off with you. Off with you,' she would say, sweeping them ahead of her.

Then they would creep past Foley's bar with the sour smell of porter coming out, and on past Sullivan's garage, where old Mr Sullivan might be drunk and shout at them, calling attention to their presence. This would be dangerous because McMahon's pharmacy was right across the road and someone would surely be alerted by the shouting. They could look in Wall's hardware in case there was anything exciting like a pair of new sharp shears, or across the road in the Central Hotel, where you might see visitors coming out if you were lucky. Usually you just saw Philip O'Brien's awful father glowering at everyone. There was the meat shop, which made them feel a bit sick. They could go into Dillon's and look at birthday cards and pretend they were going to buy, but the Dillons never let them read the comics or magazines.

Kit's mother would have found them a million things to do if they went home to McMahons'. She could show them how to make shortbread, and Rita the maid would watch too. She might get them to plant a window box, or show them how to take cuttings that would grow. The McMahons didn't have a proper garden like the Kellys did, only a yard at the back. But it was full of plants climbing out of barrels and up walls. Kit's mother had shown them how to do calligraphy and they had written, 'Happy Feast Day' for Mother Bernard. It was in lovely writing that looked as if a monk had done it. Mother Bernard still kept it in her prayer book. Or sometimes she would show them her collection of cigarette cards and the gifts she was going to get when she had a book filled with them.

But Clio often asked things like, 'What does your mother *do* all day, that she has so much time to spend with us?' It seemed like a criticism. As if Mother should be doing something more important, like going out to tea with people the way Mrs Kelly did. Kit didn't want to give Clio the chance to find fault, so she didn't often invite her home.

The thing they liked doing most was going to see Sister Madeleine, the hermit who lived in a very small cottage by the lake. Sister Madeleine had great fun being a hermit, because everyone worried about her and brought her food and firewood. No one could remember when she had come to live in the old abandoned cottage at the water's edge. People were vague about what community Sister Madeleine had belonged to at one time, and why she had left. But nobody doubted her saintliness.

Sister Madeleine saw only good in people and animals. Her bent figure was to be seen scattering crumbs for the birds, or stroking the most snarling and bad-tempered dog. She had a tame fox, which came to lap up a saucer of bread and milk in the evenings, and she was rarely without splints to mend a broken wing of a bird she had found on her travels.

Father Baily and Mother Bernard, together with Brother Healy from the boys' school, had decided to make Sister Madeleine welcome rather than regard her with suspicion. As far as could be worked out, she believed in the one true God, and did not object to the way any of them interpreted His will. She attended Mass quietly at the back of the church on Sundays, setting herself up as no rival pulpit.

Even Doctor Kelly, Clio's father, said that Sister Madeleine knew as much as he did about some things: childbirth, and how to console the dying. Kit's father said that in olden days she might have been thought a Wise Woman or even a witch. She certainly knew how to make poultices and use the roots and berries that grew in abundance around her little home. She never spoke about other people so everyone knew that their secrets were safe.

'What will we bring her?' Kit asked. Nobody ever went to Sister Madeleine empty-handed.

'She always says not to be bringing her things.' Clio was practical.

'Yes, she *says* that.' Kit still thought they should bring something.

'If we went to your dad's shop he'd give us something.'

'No, he might say we should go straight home,' Kit said. That was a possibility they couldn't risk. 'We could pick some flowers.'

Clio was doubtful. 'Yeah, but isn't her place full of flowers?'

'*I* know!' Kit had a sudden inspiration. 'Rita's making jam. We'll take a pot of it.'

That would, of course, mean going home; Rita was the maid at the McMahons'. But the jam was cooling on the back window; they could just lift a pot of it. This seemed by far the safest way of getting a gift for Sister Madeleine the Hermit without having to run the gauntlet of a home interrogation.

The McMahons lived over the chemist's shop in the main street of Lough Glass. You could get in up the front stairs beside the shop, or else go around the back. There was nobody about when Kit slipped into the yard and climbed the back steps. Clothes were hanging on the line, but Rita wasn't in sight. Kit tiptoed to the window where the jams sat in containers of every sort and shape. She took one of the more common jars. It would be less likely to be missed.

With a shock, she saw a figure through the window. Her mother was sitting at the table, perfectly still. There was a faraway look on her face. She hadn't heard Kit, nor did she seem even aware of her surroundings. To Kit's dismay she saw that tears were falling down her mother's face and she wasn't even bothering to wipe them.

She moved quietly away.

Clio was waiting at the back. 'Were you spotted?' she asked.

'No.' Kit was short.

'What's wrong?'

4

'Nothing's wrong. You always think something's wrong when nothing ever is.'

'Do you know, Kit, you're becoming as bad a pain in the bottom as awful Anna is. God, you're lucky you haven't any sisters,' Clio said with feeling.

'I have Emmet.'

But they both knew Emmet was no problem. Emmet was a boy, and boys didn't hang around wanting to be part of your secrets. Emmet wouldn't be seen dead with girls. He went his own way, fought his own battles, which were many because he had a speech impediment, and the other boys mimicked his stutter. 'Emm ... Emm ... Emmemm ... Emmet,' they called him. Emmet always answered back. 'At least I'm not the school dunce,' he would say, or, 'At least I don't have the smell of pigs on my boots.' The trouble was, it took him a long time to say these telling things and his tormentors had often gone away.

'What's annoying you?' Clio persisted, as they walked down the lane towards the lake.

'I suppose someone will marry you eventually, Clio. But it'll have to be someone very patient, maybe stone deaf even.' There was no way that Kit McMahon was going to let her best friend Clio worm out of her the fact that it had been very shocking to see her mother sitting crying like that.

Sister Madeleine was pleased to see them.

Her face was lined from walking in all weathers; her hair was hidden under a short dark veil. It was a cross between a veil and a head scarf really. You could see some grey hair at the front, unlike the nuns at school, who had no hair at all. Theirs was all cut off and sold for wigs.

Sister Madeleine was very old. Kit and Clio didn't know exactly how old, but very old. She was older than their parents, they thought. Older than Mother Bernard. Fifty, or sixty or seventy. You wouldn't know. Clio had once asked her. They couldn't remember exactly what Sister Madeleine had said, but she certainly hadn't answered the question. She had a way of saying something else entirely, which was a little bit connected with what you had asked, so that you didn't feel you had been rude, but which wasn't anywhere near telling you.

'A pot of jam,' said Sister Madeleine with excitement, as if she were a child getting a bicycle as a surprise. 'Isn't that the nicest thing we could have ... will we all have tea?'

It was exciting having tea there, not boring like at home. There was an open fire and a kettle hanging on a hook. People had given Sister Madeleine little stoves and cookers in the past, but she had always passed them on to someone less fortunate. She managed to insult nobody by this recycling of gifts, but you knew that if you gave her anything for her own comfort, like a rug or some cushions, it would end up in the caravan of a travelling family or someone who needed it more. The people of Lough Glass had got used to giving the hermit only what she could use in her own daily life.

The place was so simple and spare it was almost as if nobody lived there. No possessions, no pictures on the walls, only a cross made out of some simply carved wood. There were mugs, and a jug of milk that someone must have brought her during the day. There was a loaf of bread that had been baked by another friend. She cut slices and spread the jam as if it were a feast that she was preparing.

Clio and Kit had never enjoyed bread and jam like it before. Little ducks walked in the door in the sunlight; Sister Madeleine put down her plate so that they could pick at her crumbs. It was always peaceful there; even restless Clio didn't need to be jumping up and moving about.

'Tell me something you learned at school today. I love facts for my mind,' Sister Madeleine said.

'We learned that Kit McMahon thought the Pope came to her mother and father's wedding,' Clio said. Sister Madeleine never corrected anyone or told them that they were being harsh or cruel, but often people seemed to realise it themselves. Clio felt she had said the wrong thing. 'Of course, it's a mistake anyone could make,' she said grudgingly.

'Maybe one day the Pope will come to Ireland,' Sister Madeleine said.

They assured her this could never happen. It was all to do with a treaty. The Pope had to promise to stay inside the Vatican and not to go out conquering Italy like popes used to do years ago. Sister Madeleine listened with every sign of believing them.

They told Sister Madeleine news about Lough Glass, about old Mr Sullivan up at the garage coming out in the middle of the night in his pyjamas chasing angels. He said he had to catch as many as he could before the dawn, and he kept knocking on people's doors asking were there any angels hiding inside.

Sister Madeleine was interested in that. She wondered what he could have dreamed that was so convincing.

'He's as mad as a hatter,' Clio explained.

'Well, we are all a bit mad, I expect. It's that stops us being too much alike, you know, like peas in a pod.'

They helped her wash and tidy away the remains of tea. As Kit opened the cupboard she saw another pot of jam exactly the same as the one she had brought. Perhaps her mother had been here today. If so, Sister Madeleine had not told them, any more than she told anyone about the visits from Clio and Kit.

'You have some jam already,' Kit said.

Sister Madeleine just smiled.

Tea in the McMahon household had been at a quarter past six for as long as Kit could remember. Dad closed the pharmacy at six, but never on the dot. There was always someone who had come for a cough bottle, or a farmer in for marking fluids for cattle or sheep. It would never do to rush people out the door. A chemist's, after all, was a place you came when you were contemplating some of the greater mysteries of life, like your health or the welfare of someone in the family. It was not a visit that was taken lightly.

Kit had often heard her mother asking why she couldn't work in the shop. It would be sensible, she had pleaded. People would like to deal with a woman when they were buying sanitary napkins, or aids for breast feeding, and then there was the cosmetics side of things. Travellers from the various cosmetic companies were paying more and more visits to country pharmacies to sell their wonders. There wasn't a week when someone from Ponds, Coty, Dawn, or Max Factor didn't call.

Martin McMahon had very little interest in such things. 'Give me what you think,' he'd say, and take an order of expensive bath soaps and assorted lipsticks.

They were badly displayed, often fading in the window and never sold. Kit's mother had said that the women of Lough Glass were like women everywhere: they would like to look their best. These cosmetic companies would give short training courses to tell the chemists' assistants how best to display the products, how the women customers should use them for best advantage. But Kit's father was adamant. They didn't want to be pushing paints and powders on people who couldn't afford them, selling magic potions promising eternal youth . . .

'I wouldn't do that,' Helen McMahon had argued often. 'I'd only learn how to make the best of them and give them advice.'

'They don't want advice,' her husband said. 'They don't want temptation either. Don't they look fine the way they are . . . And anyway, would I want people to think that I had to have my wife out working for me, that I can't earn a living for her and my children?' Father would always laugh when he said this and make a funny face.

He loved a joke and he could do card tricks and make coins disappear. Mother didn't laugh as much, but she smiled at Father and usually agreed with him. She didn't complain like Clio's mother did when he worked late, or when he went with Doctor Kelly to Paddles' bar.

Kit thought that Mother would have liked to work in the pharmacy, but she realised that for people such as they were it would have been unsuitable for Father to have let her work there. Only people like Mrs Hanley, who was a widow and ran the drapery, or Mona Fitz, who was the postmistress because she wasn't married, or Mrs Dillon whose husband was a drunk, worked in businesses. It was the way things were in Lough Glass, and everywhere.

Kit couldn't get the vision of her mother's tears out of her mind as they went home from Sister Madeleine's. She walked up the stairs slowly, almost unwilling to go in and discover what was wrong. Perhaps there was some very bad news. But what could it be?

Dad was fine; he was there closing up the chemist's. Emmet was home safely from rolling around in the dirt or whatever he did after school. So there couldn't be anything wrong with the family. With a sense of walking on eggshells Kit went into the kitchen, where they all ate their meals. Everything was normal. Mother's eyes might have been a bit bright, but that was only if you were looking for something. She wore a different dress; she must have changed.

Mother always looked so gorgeous, almost like a Spaniard. Someone had sent them a postcard from Spain of a dancer, where the dress was of real material, not just a photograph. Kit always thought it looked just like Mother, with her long hair swept up in a roll, and her big dark eyes.

Dad was in great form, so there couldn't have been a row or anything. He was laughing and telling them about old Billy Sullivan coming in for some tonic wine. He had been barred from every other establishment that sold alcohol, and suddenly he had discovered his salvation in the shape of tonic wine. Dad did a great imitation of Mr Sullivan trying to appear sober.

'I suppose that's why he saw the angels, due to the drink,' Kit said.

'God knows what he'll see after the Emu Burgundy,' her father said ruefully. 'I've had to tell him that's the last of the stock, that you can't get it any more.'

'That's a lie,' said Emmet.

'I know it is, son, but it's tell a lie or have the poor fellow lying on the road, roaring up to the skies.'

'Sister Madeleine says that we're all a bit mad; it's what makes us different from other people,' Kit said.

'Sister Madeleine is a saint,' Mother said. 'Did you go to see her yet, Rita, about the other thing?'

'I will, Mrs McMahon, I will,' Rita said, and put the big dish of macaroni cheese on the table.

Even though they ate in the kitchen, Mother always insisted that everything was elegantly served. They had coloured place mats instead of a table cloth, and there was a big raffia mat for the casserole dish. It was decorated with sprigs of parsley, one of Mother's touches for making food look nice.

'Wouldn't it all taste the same no matter the way it looked, Mam?' Rita used to say at one time.

'Let's have it looking nice anyway,' Mother would say gently, and now it was second nature for Rita to cut tomatoes into triangles and slice hard-boiled eggs thinly. Even though the Kellys ate in a separate dining room, Kit knew that their meals were not served as graciously as they were in *her* home. It was another thing that made her feel her mother was special.

Rita was made part of the family, unlike the Kellys' maid. Emmet loved Rita, and was always very curious about her comings and goings. 'What other thing?' Emmet asked.

'Helping me with reading.' Rita spoke out clearly before Emmet could be asked not to be nosy. 'I never learned it properly at school, you see. I wasn't there often enough.'

'Where were you?' Emmet was envious. It was so wonderful to be able to say casually that you skipped school.

'Usually looking after a baby, or saving the hay, or making the turf.' Rita spoke in a matter of fact way. She didn't sound bitter about the book learning missed, the years of childminding, growing old before her time, culminating in going out to mind other people's children and clean their houses for them.

*

Not long after tea, Mr Sullivan saw devils everywhere. In the fading light he noticed them creeping with pitchforks into the houses along the street, including the chemist's. Maybe they had gone in through the floorboards and through cracks in the wall. Kit and Emmet listened, giggling, from the top of the stairs to their father remonstrating with Mr Sullivan, while issuing orders out of the corner of his mouth.

'You're all right Billy. There isn't a devil here except yourself and myself.'

'Helen, ring Peter will you.'

'Now sit down, Billy, here, and we'll talk the thing out, man to man.'

'Helen, let him know how bad it is.'

'Billy, listen to me. Am I a man who'd let fellows with pitchforks into my house?'

'As quick as he bloody well can, with any kind of tranquilliser he can get into a syringe.'

They sat on the stair top and waited until Clio's father arrived. The cries, and shouts of panic, and the hunt for devils stopped. They heard Dr Kelly saying to their father that it was the County Home now. Billy was a danger to himself and everyone else.

'What'll happen to the business?' Dad asked.

'One of those fine sons he threw out will come back and learn to run it for him. At least the uncle sent the boys to school. They may be able to turn it into something rather than the doss house it is,' said Dr Kelly, who did not share Sister Madeleine's view that we were all different and that's what made us special.

Emmet was sitting with his chin in his hands. His stutter always came back when he was frightened. 'Are they going to lock him up?' he said, his eyes big and round. It took him ten attempts to get his tongue around the word 'lock'.

Kit thought suddenly that if she had been given a wish now, at this very moment, it would have been that Emmet's stutter would go. Sometimes it would be that she had long blonde hair like Clio, or that her mother and father might be friends with each other like Dr Kelly and Mrs Kelly were. But tonight it would have been Emmet's speech.

When Mr Sullivan had been taken away, Dad and Clio's father went for a drink. Mother went back inside without a word. Kit saw her moving around the sitting room, picking up objects and putting them down, before going to the bedroom and closing the door.

Kit knocked.

'Come in, sweetheart.' Mother was sitting at the dressing table brushing her hair. She looked like a princess when her hair was down.

'Are you all right, Mam? You seem a bit sad.'

Mother put her arm around Kit and drew her towards her. 'I am fine, just fine. What makes you think I'm sad?'

Kit didn't want to tell about seeing her through the kitchen window. 'Your face.'

'Well, I suppose I *am* sad about some things, like that poor fool being tied up and taken off to a mental home for the rest of his life because he

couldn't drink in moderation. And about Rita's selfish, greedy parents who
had fourteen children and let the older ones rear the younger ones until
they could send them out as skivvies and then take half their wages from
them ... Otherwise, I'm fine.' Kit looked at her mother's reflection in the
mirror doubtfully. 'And are you fine, my little Kit?'

'Not really. Not completely fine.'

'What would you like that you haven't got?'

'I'd like to be quicker,' Kit said. 'I'd like to understand things
immediately, the way Clio does, and to have fair hair, and to be able to
listen to one thing while saying another. And be taller.'

'I don't suppose you'd believe me if I told you that you were twenty times
more beautiful than Clio, and much more intelligent.'

'Oh Mam, I'm not.'

'You are, Kit. I swear it. What Clio has is style. I don't know where she
got it, but she knows how to make the most of everything she has. Even at
twelve she knows what looks well on her and how to smile. That's all it is.
It's not beauty, not like you have, and you have my cheek bones, remember.
Clio only has Lilian's.'

They laughed together, grown-ups in a conspiracy of mockery. Mrs Kelly
had a plump face and no cheek bones at all.

Rita went to Sister Madeleine on Thursdays, her half day. If anyone else
called, Sister Madeleine would say, 'Rita and I are reading a bit of poetry.
We often do that on a Thursday.' It was such a tactful way of telling them
that this was Rita's time, people began to recognise it as such.

Rita would bake some scones, or bring a half an apple tart. They would
have tea together and bend over the books. As the weeks went on and the
summer came, Rita began to have new confidence. She could read without
putting her finger under the words; she could guess the harder words from
the sense of the sentence. It was time for the writing lessons. Sister
Madeleine gave Rita a fountain pen.

'I couldn't take that, Sister. It was given to you as a gift.'

'Well, if it's mine, can't I do what I like with it?' Sister Madeleine rarely
kept anything that she had been given for more than twenty-four hours.

'Well, could I have a loan of it then, a long loan?'

'I'll lend it to you for the rest of your life,' Sister Madeleine said.

There were no boring headline copy books; instead, Rita and Sister
Madeleine wrote about Lough Glass and the lake and changing seasons.

'You could write to your sister in America soon,' Sister Madeleine said.

'Not a real letter, not to a person.'

'Why not? That's as good as any letter she'll get from these parts, I tell
you.'

'Would she want to hear all this about home?'

'She'll be so full of happiness to hear about home you'd nearly hear her
thanking you across the Atlantic Ocean.'

'I never got a letter. I wouldn't want them to be thinking above in
McMahons' that I was in the class of having people writing to me.'

'She could write to you here.'

'Would the postman bring letters to you, Sister Madeleine?'

'Ah, Tommy Bennet is the most decent man in the world. He delivers letters to me three times a week. Comes down here on his bicycle whatever the weather, and has a cup of tea.'

Sister Madeleine didn't add that Tommy never came without some contribution to the store cupboard. Nor that she had been instrumental in getting his daughter quickly and quietly into a home for unmarried mothers and keeping the secret safe from the interested eyes and ears of Lough Glass.

'And you'd get enough post for that?' Rita asked in wonder.

'People are very kind. They often write to me,' Sister Madeleine said with the same sense of wonder.

*

Clio and Kit had learned to swim when they were very young. Dr Kelly had stood waist deep in the water to teach them. As a young medical student he had once pulled three dead children from the Glass Lake, children who had drowned in a couple of feet of water because nobody had taught them how to swim. It had made him very angry. There was something accepting and dumb about people who lived on the edge of a hazard and yet did nothing to cope with it.

Like those fishermen over in the West of Ireland who went out in frail boats to fish in the roaring Atlantic. They all wore different kinds of jumpers so they would know whose family it was when a body was found. Each family had its own stitch. Complicated and perverse, Dr Kelly thought. Why hadn't they taught the young fishermen to swim?

As soon as the young Kellys and McMahons could walk they were taken to the lake shore. Other families followed suit; the doctor was a figure of great authority. Young Philip O'Brien from the hotel learned, and the Hanley girls. Of course, old Sullivan from the garage told the doctor to keep his hands off other people's children, so Stevie and Michael probably couldn't swim to this day.

Peter Kelly had been in other countries where lakes like this one had been tourist attractions. Scotland, for example. People came to visit places just because there was a lake there. And in Switzerland, where he and Lilian had spent their honeymoon, lakes were all important. But in Ireland in the early fifties, nobody seemed to see their potential.

People thought he was mad when he bought a small rowing boat jointly with his friend Martin McMahon. Together they rowed and fished for perch, bream and pike. Big ugly fish all of them, but waiting for them on the ever-changing waters of their lake was a restful pastime.

The men had been friends since they were boys. They knew the beds of reeds and rushes where the moorhens sheltered and where sometimes even the swans hid from view. They occasionally had company on the lake as they went out to fish, since a few local people shared their enthusiasm; but normally the only boats you saw on Lough Glass were those carrying animal foodstuff or machinery from one side to the other.

Farms had been divided up so peculiarly that often a farmer had bits of land so far apart that the journey across the water could well be the shortest route. Yet another strange thing about Ireland, Peter Kelly often said, those inconvenient things that weren't laid on us by a colonial power we managed to do for ourselves by incessant family feuds and differences. Martin was of a sunnier disposition. He believed the best of people; his patience was never-ending. There was no situation that couldn't be sorted out by a good laugh. The only thing Martin McMahon ever feared was the lake itself.

He used to warn people, even visitors who came into his chemist's shop, to be careful as they went along the paths by the lake shore. Clio and Kit were old enough to take a boat out alone now, they had proved it a dozen times, but Martin still felt nervous. He admitted it to Peter over a pint in Paddles' bar. 'Jesus, Martin! You're turning into an old woman.'

Martin didn't take it as an insult. 'I suppose I am. Let me look for any secondary signs: I haven't developed breasts or anything, but I don't need to shave as often ... You could be right, you know.'

Peter looked affectionately at his friend. Martin's bluster was hiding a real concern. 'I've watched them, Martin. I'm as anxious as you are that they don't run into trouble ... but they aren't such fools when they're out on the water as they seem to be on dry land. We've drilled that into them. Watch them yourself and you'll see.'

'I will. They're going out tomorrow. Helen says we have to let them go and not wrap them in cotton wool.'

'Helen's right,' Peter said sagely, and they debated whether or not to have another pint. As always on these occasions they made a huge compromise by ordering a half pint. So predictable that Paddles had it ready for them when they got around to ordering it.

'Mr McMahon, will you please tell Anna to go home,' Clio begged Kit's father. 'If I tell her, it only starts a row.'

'Would you like to go for a walk with me?' Kit's father suggested.

'I'd like to go in the boat.'

'I know you would, but they're big, grown-up girls now, and they want to be having their own chats. Why don't you and I go and see if we could find a squirrel?' He looked at the girls in the boat. 'I know I'm a fusser. I just came down to be sure you were all right.'

'Of course we're all right.'

'And you'll take no chances? This is a dangerous lake.'

'Daddy, *please!*'

He went off, and they saw Anna grumbling and following him.

'He's very nice, your father,' said Clio, fitting the oars properly into the oar locks.

'Yes, when you think of the fathers we might have got,' Kit agreed.

'Mr Sullivan up in the home.' Clio gave an example.

'Tommy Bennet, the bad-tempered postman.'

'Or Paddles Burns, the barman with the big feet ...'

They laughed at their lucky escapes.

'People often wonder why your father married your mother, though,' Clio said.

Kit felt a bile of defence rise in her throat. 'No, they don't wonder that. *You* might wonder it. *People* don't wonder it at all.'

'Keep your hair on. I'm only saying what I heard.'

'Who said what? Where did you hear it?' Kit's face was hot and angry. She could have pushed her friend Clio into the dark lake and held her head down when she surfaced. Kit was almost alarmed at the strength of her feeling.

'Oh, people say things . . .' Clio was lofty.

'Like what?'

'Like your mother was a different sort of person, not a local person . . . you know.'

'No, I don't know. Your mother isn't from here either, she's from Limerick.'

'But she used to come here on holidays. That made her sort of from here.'

'My mother came here when she met Dad, and that makes her from here too.' There were tears in Kit's eyes.

'I'm sorry,' Clio said. She really did sound repentant.

'What are you sorry about?'

'For saying your mother wasn't from here.'

Kit felt she was sorry for more, for hinting at a marriage that was less than satisfactory. 'Oh, don't be stupid Clio. No one cares what you say about where my mother is from, you're so boring. My mother's from Dublin and that's twenty times more interesting than being from old Limerick.'

'Sure,' said Clio.

The sunlight went out of the day. Kit didn't enjoy the first summer outing on the lake. She felt Clio didn't either, and there was a sense of relief when they each went home.

Rita got two weeks' holiday every July.

'I'll miss going to Sister Madeleine,' she told Kit.

'Imagine missing lessons,' Kit said.

'Ah, it's what you don't have, you see. Everyone wants what they don't have.'

'What would you really like to do in the holidays?' Kit asked.

'I suppose not to have to go home. It's not a home like this one. My mother'd hardly notice whether I was there or not, except to ask me for money.'

'Well, don't go.'

'What else would I do?'

'Could you stay here and not work?' Kit suggested. 'I'd bring you a cup of tea in the mornings.'

Rita laughed. 'No, that wouldn't work. But you're right, I don't have to go home.' Rita said she would discuss it with Sister Madeleine. The hermit might have an idea.

The hermit had a great idea. She thought that Mother Bernard in the convent would simply love someone to come and help her spring clean the parlour for a few hours a day, maybe even give it a lick of paint. And in return, Rita could stay in the school and some of the nuns would give her a hand with the lessons.

Rita had a great holiday, she said, the best in her life.

'You mean it was nice, staying with the nuns?'

'It was lovely. You don't know the peace of the place and the lovely singing in the chapel, and I had a key and could go to the town to dances or to the pictures. And I got all my food and hours of help at my books.'

'You won't leave us, will you, Rita?' Kit felt a shadow of change fall over them.

Rita was honest. 'Not while you're young and the way you are. Not till Emmet's grown up a bit.'

'Mam would die if you left, Rita. You're part of the family.'

'Your mother understands, honestly she does. She and I often talk about trying to take your chance in life; she encourages me to better myself. She knows it means I hope to be doing better than scrubbing floors.'

Kit's eyes felt full of tears suddenly. 'It's not safe when you talk like that. I want things always to be the same, not to change.'

Rita said, 'That's not going to be the way it is. Look at the way Farouk stopped being a kitten and is a cat now; we wanted him to be a kitten for ever. And look at the way those little ducklings in Sister Madeleine's grew up and sailed away. And your mother wants you and Emmet to be young and nice like you are, but you'll grow up and leave them. It's the way of things.'

Kit wished it wasn't the way of things, but she feared that Rita was right.

'Will you come out in the boat with me, Mam?' Kit asked.

'Lord no, my love. I'd not have time for that. Go on yourself with Clio.'

'I'm sick of Clio. I'd like you to come. I want to show you places you haven't been.'

'No Kit, it's not possible.'

'But what do you *do* in the afternoons, Mam? What do you do that's more important than coming out in the boat?'

It was only in the school holidays that Kit was aware of how her mother's pattern of living differed from other people's. Clio's mother was always getting a bus or a lift to the big town to look at curtain material or to try on clothes, or to have coffee in one of the smart shops with friends. Mrs Hanley and Mrs Dillon were working in their shops; Philip O'Brien's mother went up to the church and cleaned the brasses or arranged the flowers for Father Baily. There were mothers who went to Mother Bernard and helped make things for the various sales of work, bazaars and functions that were held regularly to aid the Order's work on the missions.

Mother did none of these things. She spent time in the kitchen with Rita, helping, experimenting, improving the cooking, much more than other people's mothers spent with maids. Mother arranged leaves and branches as decoration in their sitting room and framed pictures of the lake so that one whole wall had two dozen different views of Lough Glass. If people came in they were amazed to see the collection.

But people didn't often come in.

And Mother's work was swift and efficient. She had a lot of time on her own . . . all the time in the world to come out with Kit in the boat. 'Tell me,' Kit asked again. 'What *do* you like doing if you won't come out with me?'

'I live my life the best I can,' her mother said. And Kit felt a shock at the faraway look that came over Helen McMahon's face as she said it.

'Dad, why do you and Mam sleep in different rooms?' Kit asked.

She picked a time when the chemist's was empty, when they would not be disturbed. Her father stood in his white coat behind the counter, his glasses pushed back on his head, his round, freckled face full of concentration. Kit was only allowed to sit on the high stool if she didn't distract him.

'What?' he said absently.

She began again, but he interrupted. 'I heard you, but why do you ask?'

'I was just asking, Dad.'

'Did you ask your mother?'

'Yes.'

'And?'

'And she said it was because you snored.'

'So now you know.'

'Yes.'

'Any more questions Kit, or can I get on with earning my living and making up compounds?'

'Why did you and Mam get married?'

'Because we loved each other, and still love each other.'

'How did you know?'

'You *know*, Kit, that's it. I'm afraid it's not very satisfactory, but that's the only way I can explain it. Like, I saw your mother at a friend's house in Dublin, and I thought, isn't she lovely and nice and fun and wouldn't it be great if she'd go out with me. And she did, over and over, and then I asked her to marry me and she said yes.' He seemed to be telling it from the heart.

But Kit wasn't convinced. 'And did Mam feel the same?'

'Well, darling child. She must have felt the same. I mean, there was nobody with a great big stick saying you *must* marry this young chemist from Lough Glass who loves you to distraction. Her parents were dead; she didn't do it to please anyone, because I was a safe bet or anything.'

'Were you a safe bet, Daddy?'

'I was a man with a steady job. In 1939, with the world on the edge of the war and everyone very confused by everything, a man with a good job was always a safe bet. Still is.'

'And were you surprised that she said yes?'

'No, darling, I wasn't surprised, not at that stage. We loved each other, you see. I know it's not like the pictures, or the things you youngsters giggle about, but that's what it was for us.'

Kit was silent.

'What is it Kit? Why are you asking all this?'

'Nothing, Daddy. You know the way you get to wondering, that's all.'

'I know the way *you* get to wondering,' he said.

And he left it there, so Kit didn't even have to think any more about what Clio had said. Clio had told her that she had overheard a conversation in her home where someone had said that Martin McMahon had a job keeping that wife of his tied to Lough Glass and the miracle of the whole thing being why she had ever come here in the first place.

'I'm only telling you,' Clio had said, 'because you and I are best friends and I think you ought to know.'

'Sister Madeleine?'

'Yes, Kit.'

'Do you know the way people tell you everything?'

'Well, they tell me things Kit, because I haven't much to tell them, you see. What with gathering sticks and picking flowers and saying my prayers, there isn't much to tell.'

'Do people tell you their secrets, like, their sins even?'

Sister Madeleine was shocked. 'No, Kit McMahon. Don't you know as well as I do that the only one we'd tell our sins to is an anointed priest of God, who has the power to act between God and man.'

'Secrets then?'

'What are you saying to me at all? Chook, chook, chook . . . will you look at the little bantams. Brother Healy was so kind. He gave me a clutch of eggs and they all hatched out beside the fire . . . It was like a miracle.' She knelt on the floor to direct the little chickens away from some perilous journey they were about to make and back into the box of straw she had prepared for them.

Kit would not be put off. 'I came by myself today because . . .'

'Yes, I missed Clio. She's a grand friend for you, isn't she?'

'She is and she isn't, Sister Madeleine. She told me that people were talking about my father and mother . . . and I wondered . . . I wanted to know maybe if you . . .'

Sister Madeleine straightened up. Her lined, weather beaten face was in a broad smile, as if she was willing the anxiety away from Kit. 'Aren't you the grown-up woman of twelve years of age, and don't you know that everyone talks about everyone else? That's what people *do* in a village . . . You're not going to get all upset over that, are you?'

'No, but . . .'

Sister Madeleine seized the word No. 'There, I knew you weren't. You see, it's a funny thing when people go miles and miles away to big cities where they know nobody and nobody knows them. The whole thing is turned around. It's then they *want* people to be all interested in them and their doings. We are funny sorts of people, the human race . . .'

'It's just that . . .' Kit began desperately. She didn't want to discuss the human race. She wanted Sister Madeleine to tell her that everything was all right, that her mother wasn't unhappy or wild or bad, or whatever it was that Clio was suggesting. But she didn't get far.

Sister Madeleine was in full flight. 'I knew you'd agree with me, and one of the funniest things – animals are much more simple. I don't know why the Lord thought that we were so special. We're not nearly as loving and good as the animal kingdom.'

The old dog, Whiskers, that Sister Madeleine had rescued when someone had tried to drown him in a bag, looked up when she said this. Whiskers seemed to understand when she was saying something good about animals. It was as if the tone of her voice changed. He gave a sort of gurgle to show he approved. 'Whiskers agrees with me. And how's Farouk, that fine noble cat of yours?'

'He's fine, Sister Madeleine. Why don't you come and see him?'

'Sure you know me. I'm not one to be visiting people's houses. All I want to know is that he's well and happy, and stalking around Lough Glass as if he owned it.'

There they were, talking about Farouk and Whiskers and the human race, and it would be rude now to go back to the reason why Kit had walked down the leafy lane to see Sister Madeleine on her own.

'How are things, Kit?'

'Fine, Mrs Kelly.'

Lilian Kelly stood back to look more attentively at her daughter's friend. The child was very handsome, with the great head of dark curly hair and those unexpected blue eyes. She would probably be a beauty like her mother.

'And tell me, have you and Clio had a falling out?'

'A falling out?' Kit's blue eyes were too innocent. She repeated the phrase with wonder, as if she hadn't a clue what the words meant.

'Well, it's just that up to now you've been like Siamese twins, joined at the hip. But in the last few weeks you don't seem to be going within a donkey's roar of each other, and that seems a pity, seeing that it's the summer holidays.' She paused, waiting.

But she was getting nothing from Kit. 'We didn't have a row, honestly Mrs Kelly.'

'I know. That's what Clio said.' Kit was anxious to be away. 'Nobody listens to their own mother, so maybe you might listen to me instead. You and Clio need each other. This is a small place; you'll always be glad to have a friend here. Whatever silliness this is it doesn't *matter*, it'll soon be over. Now you know where we live. Come on up to the house this evening, will you?'

'Clio knows where *I* live too, Mrs Kelly.'

'God protect me from two such stubborn women. I don't know what's going to happen to the next generation . . .' Mrs Kelly sighed and went off good-naturedly. Kit watched her go. Clio's mother was large and square and wore sensible clothes. Today she had on a cotton dress with white cuffs and collar and a small daisy print, and she was carrying a shopping basket. She was like the picture of a mother in a story book.

Not like Kit's own mother, who was very thin, and who wore bright greens or crimson or royal blue, and whose clothes were sort of floaty looking. She looked much more like a dancer than a mother.

Kit sat on the wooden pier.

Their boat was tied up beside her, but there was an iron-hard rule that no one took the boat out alone. Someone had been drowned in the lake because she went out alone. It was ages ago, but people still talked about it. Her body wasn't found for a year, and during that year her soul used to haunt the lake calling out, 'Look in the reeds, look in the reeds.' Everyone knew this. It was enough to frighten the most foolhardy, even the boys, from going out on their own.

Kit watched enviously as she saw some of the older boys from the Brothers' school untying a boat, but she would not go back up and pretend to Clio that everything was all right. Because it wasn't.

The days seemed very long. There was nobody to talk to. It didn't seem fair to go down to Sister Madeleine on her own. It had been the place that she and Clio always went to, and that one time she had gone to try to find out things, Sister Madeleine must have known what she was after. Rita was always working, or else she had her head in a book. Emmet was too young for any conversation. Daddy was busy and Mother . . . Mother. Mother expected Kit to be less clingy, less worried. It had been very easy when Clio was around. Perhaps Mrs Kelly was right and they did need each other.

But she was *not* going to go up to that house.

She heard footsteps behind her and felt the spring of the wooden pier as someone walked along. It was Clio. She had two milk chocolate biscuits; their favourites.

'I wouldn't go to your house, and you wouldn't come to mine. This is neutral ground, all right?' she said.

Kit paused. 'Sure,' she shrugged.

'We can just go on as we were before the fight.' Clio wanted it defined.

'There wasn't a fight,' Kit reminded her.

'Yeah, I know. But I said something stupid about your mother.' There was a silence. Clio went on to fill it. 'The truth is, Kit, that I was jealous. I'd *love* to have a mother who looks like a film star.'

Kit reached out and took one of the Club Milk biscuits. 'Now you're here, we can take out the boat,' she said.

The row that had never been was over.

During the holidays Brother Healy came up to the convent for his annual discussion with Mother Bernard. They had many things to discuss, and they got on well together when discussing them. There was the school curriculum for the year, the difficulty of getting lay teachers who would have the same sense of dedication; the terrible problem they shared about children being wild and undisciplined, preferring the goings-on on the cinema screen to real life as it should be lived in Ireland. They co-ordinated their timetables so that the girls should be released from school at one time and the boys at another, leaving less chance for the two sexes to meet each other and get involved in unnecessary familiarity.

Brother Healy and Mother Bernard were such old friends now that they could even indulge in the odd little grumble, about the length of Father Baily's sermons for example. The man was inclined to be hypnotised by the sound of his own voice, they thought. Or the excessive love the children had for that difficult Sister Madeleine. It was somehow highly irritating that this odd woman, who came from a deeply confused and ill-explained background, should have taken such an unexpected place in the hearts and minds of Lough Glass's children, who would do anything for her. They were eager to save stamps, collect silver paper, and gather sticks for her fire. The boys had been outraged when Brother Healy had stamped on a spider. There had been a near mutiny in the classroom. And these were the same lads who would have pulled the wings off flies for sport a few years ago.

Mother Bernard said that Sister Madeleine was altogether too tolerant for this world; she seemed to have a good word to say for everyone, including the enemies of the Church. She had told some of the impressionable girls that Communists might have their own very reasonable belief in dividing wealth equally. That had been a headache, Mother Bernard said, and one that she could have done without.

And it wasn't only the children who were under her spell, Brother Healy said in an aggrieved tone. Oh no, no. A man who should know better, like Martin McMahon the chemist. Brother Healy had heard with his own ears the man suggesting to Mrs Sullivan, whose poor Billy had been carried off screaming, that she should go to Sister Madeleine for some advice about a nice soothing drink to make her sleep.

'Next stop will be black magic altogether,' said Mother Bernard, nodding feverishly in agreement.

And of course, if Martin minded his business and paid a bit of attention to that fancy wife of his, he'd be better off. Brother Healy might have gone too far now in uncharitable gossip. He knew it and so did Mother Bernard. They both began to shuffle their papers together and end the meeting.

It would remain unsaid that Helen McMahon, with her disturbing good looks, walked too much alone, beating at the hedges with a blackthorn stick, her eyes and mind far, far away from Lough Glass and the people who lived there.

It was a Wednesday, and Martin McMahon closed his shop with a sigh of relief. The flypaper was thick with dead bluebottles. He must remove it quickly before Kit or Emmet came in with a lecture about them being God's creatures and how unfair of him to lure them to their death.

He was relieved that Kit and Clio Kelly seemed to have got over whatever childish squabble it had been that kept them apart for a few weeks. Girls were so intense at that age, it was impossible to know their minds. He had asked Helen if they should interfere, try to bring the children together, but Helen had said to let it run its course. And she had been right about everything.

When Helen said something, it was always likely to happen. She had said that Emmet would be able to cope with his stutter, that he would laugh away the mimicry and criticism. She had been right. She had said Rita was a bright girl when everyone else had thought the child mentally deficient. Helen had known that Billy Sullivan was drinking behind his garage doors when no one else knew. And Helen had told him all those years ago that she could never love him totally, but she would love him as much as she was able to. Which wasn't nearly enough, but he knew it was that or nothing.

He had first met her when she was pining for someone else, and she had been open with him. It would not be fair to encourage his attentions, she had said, when her mind was so committed elsewhere. He had agreed to wait around. He had made more and more excuses to be in Dublin, to invite her out. Gradually, they became close. She never spoke of the man who had left her to marry some girl with money.

Little by little, the colour returned to her cheeks. He invited her down here to see his place . . . his lake, his people . . . and she came and walked with him around the shores.

'It might not be the greatest love the world has ever known for you . . . but it will for me,' he said.

She said it was the most beautiful proposal that a man could make. She would accept, she said. She sighed as she said it.

Helen had told him that she would stay with him, and if she ever left she would tell him why, and it would have to be for a very good reason. She said that it was dangerous to try to know somebody too well. People should have their own reserves, she said, the places they went in their minds, where no one else should follow.

He had agreed with her, of course. It was the price he paid for getting her as his wife. But he wished she didn't go off so often and so far in her mind, and he dearly wished she didn't wander around the lake in all kinds of weather. She assured him that she loved to do this; it brought her peace to see the lake in its changing seasons. She knew all kinds of things about its nesting creatures. She felt at home there; she knew all the people around.

Once she had told him that it would be lovely to have a little cottage like Sister Madeleine's and have the lake water lap up to your door.

He had laughed at that. 'Isn't it hard enough to squash the whole family into this place? How would we fit in the hermit's cottage?' he had asked.

'I didn't mean the whole family. I was thinking of going there by myself.' Her eyes had been far away that day. He hadn't followed her train of thought; it had been too unsettling.

Martin let himself in his own front door beside the chemist's shop. It led straight upstairs to what they called their house, even though Kit had complained that they were the only people she knew who had a house without a downstairs.

Rita was setting the table. 'The mistress won't be here, Sir. She said to say she'll see you after your game of golf.'

He was disappointed and it showed.

'Women have to have their time off, too,' Kit said defensively.

'Of course they do,' he said, over-jovially. 'And it's a Wednesday, so everyone except Rita has an afternoon off. I'm going to playa round of golf with Clio's father. I'm feeling in powerful form. I'm going to beat him into the ground today. I can see a few pars coming up, and a birdie and an eagle and ... maybe an albatross.'

'Why are they all called after birds?' Emmet wanted to know.

'I suppose because the ball soars like a bird, or it should anyway ... Come on, I'll be mother,' he said, and began to ladle out the lamb stew.

He realised that he had been saying this more and more recently. He wondered why on earth Helen had not said she was going out. Where on earth could she be?

From the golf course you got fine views of the lake. People said it was one of the most attractive courses in Ireland. Not as rugged as the great championship courses on the coast, but very varied, with rolling parkland and many clusters of trees ... And always the lake, dark blue today with hardly any shadows on it.

Peter Kelly and Martin McMahon stopped to rest and look down from the eighth green upon the high ground. It wasn't a busy golf course; they were holding nobody up. There was always time to stand and look down on Lough Glass and its lake.

'The tinkers are back, I see.' Peter pointed out the coloured roofs of caravans on the far shore of the lake.

'They're like the seasons, aren't they? Always coming back the same way and at the same time.'

'Desperate life to inflict on the children, though. Some of them come up to get bits of machinery out of them or with dog bites. You'd pity them,' said the doctor.

'They come in to me, too, only the very odd time. Often I tell them they know more than I do,' Martin laughed. He had indeed said that between the travellers and old Madeleine there was a very good second line of defence as regards medicine in Lough Glass.

'Some of them are very fine-looking people.' Peter peered into the distance, where two women walked by the water's edge. Martin looked too, and then they both moved at the same time to go back to line up their shots. It was as if they both thought one of the women looked very like Helen McMahon, but neither of them wanted to say it.

Clio told Kit that there was a woman among the travellers who told fortunes. And that she knew everything that was going to happen. But Mother Bernard would kill you stone dead if you went anywhere near her.

'What would Sister Madeleine say?' Kit wondered.

This was a good idea. Sister Madeleine wasn't black and white about things. Happily they scampered off down the lane to consult her. She thought it might well be possible; some people *did* have a gift.

'How much silver do you think she'd need to cross her palm? Would a threepence do?' Kit wondered.

'I'd say she'd want more. What would you say, Sister Madeleine?' Clio was excited. It was her birthday next week. Maybe they might get enough money before the caravans left. How marvellous to know the future.

To their disappointment, Sister Madeleine didn't seem at all in favour of it. She never told anyone *not* to do anything; she didn't use words like foolish or unwise; she never spoke of sin or things being wrong. She just looked at them with her eyes burning from her brown, lined face and her look said everything. 'It's not safe to know the future,' she said.

And in the silence that followed both Clio and Kit felt themselves shiver. They were glad when Whiskers stood up and gave a long unexplained yowl at nothing in particular.

Rita made her quiet way down the narrow road to Sister Madeleine's cottage. She carried her poetry book and the warm shortbread that was just out of the oven. To her surprise, she heard voices. Usually the hermit was alone when she called for her lessons.

She was about to move away, but Sister Madeleine called out. 'Come on in, Rita. We'll have a cup of tea together.'

It was the tinker woman who told fortunes. Rita knew her immediately, because she had been to her last year. She had given her half a crown and had heard that her life would change. She would have seven times by seven times the land that her father had owned. That meant she would have nearly fifty acres. The woman had seen that she would have a life with book learning, and she would marry a man who was at this moment across the sea. She also saw that the children of the marriage would be difficult – it wasn't clear whether in their health or their disposition. She said that Rita, when she died, would be buried in a big cemetery, not in the churchyard in Lough Glass.

It had been very exciting to go to the woman, who told fortunes only by the lake shore. She had said she didn't like doing it near the camps, near her own people. They didn't approve of her doing it. She said it was because she was too good. Listening to her, Rita had believed that this might be true. Everything had been said with a great, calm certainty. And the bits about the book learning had begun to come true.

Rita had been struck then and now how like the mistress she was. If you saw them in a poor light you'd swear that the tinker woman and Mrs McMahon were sisters. She wondered what she was doing here with Sister Madeleine, but she would never know.

'Rita and I read poetry together.' Sister Madeleine made the only gesture she would ever make towards an introduction. The woman nodded as if she only expected as much; she was sure that everything else she had seen in the future was true also.

And suddenly, with a slight sense of alarm, so was Rita. There was a man across the sea who would marry her; she would have fifty acres of land, and money in her own right. She would have children and they would not be easy. She thought about her tombstone, far away in a city with lots of other crosses nearby.

The woman slipped silently away.

' "My dark Rosaleen",' said Sister Madeleine. 'Read it nice and slowly to me. I'll close my eyes and make pictures of it all.'

Rita stood in the sunlight by the little window with pots of geraniums people had brought for the hermit and, with the bantam chicks around her feet, she read:

> My Dark Rosaleen!
> My own Rosaleen!
> Shall glad your heart, shall give you hope,
> Shall give you health, and help, and hope,
> My Dark Rosaleen!

'Wasn't that beautiful!' Sister Madeleine spoke of the poem. Rita laughed aloud with pleasure, sheer pleasure that she had read without stumbling. 'That was beautiful, Rita. Don't ever tell me you couldn't read a poem,' she said.

'Do you know what I was thinking, Sister?'

'No. What were you thinking? Your mind was far away. Poetry does that to you.'

'I was just thinking that if young Emmet were to come to you. . .'

'Emmet McMahon?'

'Yes. Maybe you could cure his stutter, getting him to read sonnets and everything.'

'I can't cure a stutter.'

'You could make him read. He's too shy to read at school. He's fine with his friends, but he hates it when Brother Healy comes to him in class. He was the same when he was in Babies. He got red in the face with fright.'

'He'd have to *want* to come. Otherwise, it'd only be a torture to him.'

'I'll tell him the kind of magic you do.'

'I think we should talk less about magic, you know. People might take you seriously.'

Rita understood at once. There were people in Lough Glass who were suspicious of Sister Madeleine, the hermit. They thought she might not come in a direct line from God. It had been whispered that people who believed in herbs and cures from the olden times might be getting their power from the very opposite of God. The Devil hadn't been mentioned, but the word had stood hovering in the air.

*

Dan O'Brien stood at his door looking up and down the street. Business in the Central Hotel was never so pressing that he couldn't find several opportunities during the day to come out and survey the main thorough-fare. Like many towns in Ireland, Lough Glass consisted of one long street. The church was in the middle, the Brothers at one end and the convent strategically placed far at the other, giving the children as little chance of accidental meetings as possible. In between, there were the shops, houses and businesses of his neighbours, fronting on to the same street as he did himself.

You could learn a lot by standing at your own door. Dan O'Brien knew that Billy Sullivan's two boys had come back from their uncle's once their father had been locked away. The fiction was that they had been visiting, helping the uncle out with the farm. Everyone knew, of course, that Kathleen had sent them there to avoid the drunken rages and the unsettled atmosphere in the family house. It was hard on children like that.

The lads were not to blame for the life they were born into. They were handsome little fellows, too, the very image of Billy himself before his face had turned fleshy from the drink and he had coarsened beyond recognition. They would be company for poor Kathleen, anyway. Stevie must be about sixteen, and Michael was the same age as his own lad, Philip.

Philip didn't like him. He said that Michael Sullivan was tough, was always ready for a fight.

'So would you be if you had been brought up with an old man like his,' Dan O'Brien said. 'Not everyone is as lucky as you are, Philip.' Philip had looked at him doubtfully. But then, the young were never satisfied with what they got.

Dan watched as the summer afternoon took its leisurely course. There was never much of a sense of urgency in Lough Glass. Even a Fair Day had a relaxed air about it. But when the weather was warm like this, people seemed to move at half speed.

He saw young Clio Kelly and Kit McMahon, arm-in-arm, practising the steps of some dance along the footpath, oblivious to anyone else. It only seemed a few months since those two had skipping ropes, and here they were getting ready for the ballroom. They were twelve, the same age as Philip – an unsettled age.

And as he watched, he saw Mother Bernard from the convent walking in a stately manner, accompanied by one of the younger nuns. Her face was one line of disapproval. Even in the holidays, her charges should not behave like that, treating the public road as a place for silly dancing.

They sensed her coming, and changed their antics rapidly.

Dan smiled to himself at the contrite appearance of the two rascals. He would like to have had a daughter, but his wife was not well enough to face another pregnancy after Philip was born.

'Haven't we the son? Isn't that enough for you?' Mildred had said. As there were going to be no more children, there was no more lovemaking. That was obvious, Mildred had said.

Dan O'Brien sighed, as he often did. Imagine being a man with a normal married life, like ... well, like anyone really. His eye fell on Martin McMahon, crossing the road to Sullivan Motors. A man with a spring in his step and a very attractive wife. Imagine being able to take a woman like Helen McMahon upstairs and draw the curtains and ...

Dan decided not to think about it any more. It was too frustrating.

Mother Bernard and Brother Healy were discussing the autumn retreat. Sometimes the priests who came to do the Mission weren't at all suitable to face the children in a school. But this year they heard that there was a very famous priest coming to Lough Glass, a Father John, who gave sermons that were attended by hundreds of people at a time. They travelled to hear him, or that's what Father Baily had told them.

'I wonder can he keep order with a crowd of hooligans.' Brother Healy had his doubts. Famous preachers could be a bit ethereal for his liking.

'Or realise when those girls are making a fool of him.' Mother Bernard had an eagle eye for mischief makers.

'I don't know why we're even debating it, Mother Bernard. These decisions are never left to *us*, the people who know about how things should be done.'

They often asked each other why they bothered discussing things, but in their hearts they knew that they loved discussing things. As educators of Lough Glass's young they were united in facing the problems of the uncaring world.

Secretly Mother Bernard thought that Brother Healy had life easy. Boys were so simple and straightforward. They weren't devious, like girls. Brother Healy thought that it must be a very easy number just to have little girls in a uniform. They didn't write terrible words in the bicycle shed and beat each other black and blue in the yard. But neither of them had much faith that Father John, preacher extraordinary, would keep the minds and attention of the children of this lakeland town.

The day before school reopened the children were all down by the lake enjoying the last hours of freedom, and even though they groaned about the awfulness of going back to the dreaded classroom the next day, quite a few of them were relieved that the long summer was over.

Philip O'Brien from the hotel was particularly pleased. It had been very hard to fill the hours. If he stayed in the hotel his father was inclined to say that he should wash the glasses or empty the ashtrays.

Emmet McMahon was looking forward to showing off his new confidence. A few weeks with Sister Madeleine had done wonders. He had even asked her if she could do the poems in his school book, in case they might make sense like the ones in her book. As if you read them with your heart.

'Why doesn't Brother Healy teach them like that?' he asked Sister Madeleine.

But she had no explanation. She seemed insistent that Brother Healy *did* teach them like that. It was very unsatisfactory.

Clio Kelly didn't want to go back to school. She was fed up with school. She knew enough now; she wanted to go to a stage school in London and learn to dance and sing, and be discovered by a kind old man who owned a theatre.

Anna her younger sister would be quite happy when lessons started. Anna was in disgrace at home. She claimed she had seen the ghost. She said she saw the woman crying. She couldn't exactly hear what the words were, but she thought it was, 'Look in the reeds, look in the reeds.' Her father had been unexpectedly cross with her and accused her of looking for notice.

'But I *did* see her,' Anna had wept.

'No, you did *not* see her. And you are not to go around saying you did. This is a hysterical enough place already without you adding to it. It's dangerous and foolish to let simple people think that an educated girl like you should give in to such foolishness.'

Even her mother had been unsympathetic. And Clio had a horrible smirk of superiority, as if she was saying to her family, 'Now wasn't I right about how awful Anna is.'

Kit McMahon was pleased to be going back to school. She had made a promise that this year she would work very hard. It had been a promise made during the only good conversation she had had with her mother for as long as she could remember.

It was the day she got her first period. Mother had been marvellous, and said all the right things, like wasn't it great she was a woman now, and that this was a fine time to be a woman in Ireland. There was so much freedom and so many choices.

Kit expressed some doubt about this. Lough Glass wasn't a place that inspired you with a notion of wild and free, and she wondered how very unlimited were the options that lay ahead of her. But Mother had been serious. When the next decade came, when they got to the 1960s, there'd be nothing a woman couldn't do. Even this year people were beginning to accept that a woman could run things.

Look at poor Kathleen Sullivan over there across the road, filling tractors with fuel, supervising the man from the oil company when he came to restock. A few years ago they wouldn't have taken an order from a woman, preferring to deal with any man, even one as obviously incapable as Billy Sullivan.

'But it all depends on being ready for it, Kit. Will you promise me whatever happens that you'll work hard at school?'

'Yes, yes of course.' Kit was impatient. Why did it always have to come back to this in the end? But there was something in Mother's face that made this sound different.

'Sit here beside me and hold my hand, and promise me that you'll remember this day. It's an important day for you, let's mark it by something else. Let's make it the day you promised your mother that you'd prepare yourself for the world properly.' Kit had looked at her blankly. 'I know it sounds like the old refrain ... but if only I were your age again ... if only

... I would work so hard. Oh Kit, if I'd known . . .' Her mother's face was anguished.

Kit was very alarmed. 'Known what? What is it, Mam? What didn't you know?'

'That being educated makes you free. Having a career, a place, a position, you can do what you want.'

'But you did what you wanted, didn't you? You married Dad, and you had us?' Kit knew her own face must be white because she saw her mother's expression change.

Her mother stroked her cheek. 'Yes, yes of course I did.' She was soothing, like she was when she told Emmet there were no demons in the dark, when she encouraged Farouk the cat to come out from a hidey place behind the sofa.

'So why did you wish . . . ?'

'I don't wish it for myself, I wish it for you . . . so that you'll always be able to choose, so that you won't have to do things because there's nothing else to do.'

Mother was holding her hand. 'Will you tell me something truly?' Kit had asked.

'Of course I will.'

'Are you happy? I often see you looking sad. Is this where you want to be?'

'I love you, Kit and I love Emmet, with all my heart. Your father is the kindest and best man in the whole world. That is the truth. I would never lie to him and I don't lie to you either.' Mother was looking at her; she wasn't half-looking out the window with her mind abstracted, as she often did.

Kit felt a wave of relief flood over her. 'So you're not sad and worried then?'

'I said I wouldn't lie to you and I won't. Sometimes I do get sad and a bit lonely in this little town. I don't love it as much as your father does; he was brought up here and knows every stone of it. I sometimes feel I might go mad if I have to see Lilian Kelly every day, and listen to Kathleen Sullivan whingeing about how hard life is in the garage, or Mildred O'Brien saying that the dust in the air is making her feel sick . . . but then, you know that . . . you get annoyed with Clio and with school.' Mother had treated her as an equal. Mother had told her the truth. 'So do you believe me now, Kit?'

'Yes, I do,' Kit said. And she did.

'And will you remember, whatever happens, that your passport to the world is to have your own career and that's the only way you are free to choose what you want to do.'

It had been a great conversation. She felt much better about everything now. At the back of her mind, she had one nagging worry. Why had Mother said twice, not once, *whatever happens*? It was as if Mother could see the future. Like Sister Madeleine seemed to do. Like the gypsy woman down by the lake.

But Kit had put it out of her mind. There was too much to think of, and wasn't it great that she had got her periods before Clio. That was a real triumph.

Dr Kelly called as Martin was closing the shop. 'I am the living embodiment of temptation. Will you come down to Paddles' with me and have a pint? I need your advice.'

In another town the local doctor and chemist might be expected to drink at the hotel, which would have a better class bar, but O'Brien's was so dismal and gloomy that Martin and Peter much preferred to bypass it in favour of Paddles' earthier but more cheerful atmosphere. They settled into a snug.

'My advice?' Martin held his head on one side quizzically. He didn't think there was any real excuse other than a need for a companion.

'It's young Anna. She has me worried. She keeps saying that everyone has a down on her, and that she really did see a woman down at the lake crying . . .'

'At that age they're so full of drama . . .' Martin was consoling.

'I know. God, don't I know. But you know the way you sense when someone's telling the truth?'

'Well, you don't think she saw a ghost?'

'No, but I think she saw something.'

Martin was nonplussed. He didn't know what he was expected to say. 'Do you remember her?'

'Remember who?'

'Bridie Daly, or Brigid Daly, or whatever her name was? The one who drowned.'

'How would I remember her? Weren't we only kids?'

'What did she look like?'

'I haven't a clue. When was it? It was way back.'

'It was in 1920.'

'Peter, we were only eight.'

'Was she dark with long hair? It's just that Anna is so positive.'

'And what are you thinking?'

'I was wondering was there someone dressing up to frighten the kids.'

'Well if there was they've succeeded, and the kid's father, it seems, too.'

Peter laughed. 'Yes, you're right. I suppose it's nonsense. I just didn't like to think of someone deliberately setting out to upset them. Anna has many faults, God knows, but I think she did see something that worried her.'

'And what did she say the woman looked like?'

'You know children . . . they have to relate it to someone they know. She said she looked like your Helen.'

The senior girls in the convent were going to have a special session of their own with Father John. That meant that the twelve to fifteen-year-olds would hear something the younger ones would not.

Anna Kelly was very curious. 'Is it about babies?' she asked.

'Probably,' Clio said loftily.

'I know about babies,' Anna said defiantly.

'I wish I'd known enough about them to suffocate you while you still were one,' Clio spoke from the heart.

'You and Kit think you're terrific. You're just stupid,' Anna said.

'Yeah, I know. We can't see ghosts and we don't get nightmares . . . it's desperate.'

They shook her off eventually and went to sit on the low wall of Sullivan's Motor Works. It was a good vantage point to survey Lough Glass and no one could say they were causing trouble if they just sat still.

'Isn't it a wonder that Emmet is so normal. I mean, for a boy and everything,' Clio said in admiration. Privately Kit thought that Anna Kelly might not be so irritating if Clio had ever spoken to her younger sister with anything other than disdain.

'Emmet's just born that way,' Kit said. 'I never remember him getting into trouble or anything. I suppose they didn't roar at him much because of his stammer. That must have been it.'

'They didn't roar at Anna enough,' Clio said darkly. 'Listen, what do you think he'll really talk to us about? Do you think it might be about doing *it*?'

'I'd die if he did.'

'I'll die if he doesn't,' Clio said, and they pealed with enough laughter to bring Philip O'Brien's father to his usual position at the door of his hotel to view them with disapproval.

Whatever Father John, the Missioner, had intended to talk about to the senior girls in Lough Glass convent was never known, because it happened that his visit coincided with a huge argument that raged through the senior school, about whether Judas was or was not in Hell. Mother Bernard was not considered a satisfactory arbiter on the matter. The girls were persistent that the visiting Missioner give a ruling.

There was a very strong view that Judas must be in Hell. 'Hadn't Our Lord said that it were better for that man if he hadn't ever been born?'

'Now that *must* mean he was in Hell.'

'It could mean that for thousands of years his name would be connected with traitor and betrayer and that was his punishment for betraying Our Lord. Couldn't it?'

'No, it couldn't, because that would only be name calling. Sticks and stones could break your bones but words would never hurt you.'

Father John looked at their young faces, heated and red with excitement. He hadn't come across such fervour in a long time. 'But Our Lord couldn't have chosen him as a friend, knowing that he was going to betray him and that he'd be sent to Hell. That would mean Our Lord was setting a trap for Judas.'

'He didn't have to betray him, he just did it for the money.'

'But what would they want with money? They just went around as a gang.'

'But it was over. Judas knew it was coming to an end, that's why he did it.'

Father John was used to girls shuffling with embarrassment and asking was French kissing a venial or a mortal sin, and accepting whichever he said it was. He was not normally faced with such cosmic questions and debates on the nature of Free Will and Predestination.

He tried to answer as best he could with what was, after all, fairly inconclusive evidence. He said he thought that, as in all things, the benefit of the doubt must be extended, and that perhaps in his infinite mercy Our Lord had seen fit . . . and to remember that one never knew the heart of a sinner, and the words that passed between man and his maker at the moment of death.

Loosening his collar a little, he asked Mother Bernard afterwards about their extraordinary preoccupation. 'Was there any case of anyone local who perhaps ended their own life?'

'No, no. Nothing like that. You know the way girls get something into their heads.' Mother Bernard sounded wise and certain.

'Yes, but this is very intense. Are you sure?'

'Years and years ago, long before any of them were born, there was an unfortunate woman who found herself in a certain condition, Father, and is believed to have taken her own life. I think the ignorant people had a story about her ghost or some such nonsense. Maybe they are thinking of that.' Mother Bernard's lips were pursed with disapproval for having to mention a suicide and an out of wedlock pregnancy to a visiting priest.

'That could be it, all right. There are two little girls, two of the younger ones in the front row, a very fair girl and a very dark one, who seem most het up about it, and whether or not people who take their own lives should be buried in Holy Ground.'

Mother Bernard sighed. 'That will be Cliona Kelly and Mary Katherine McMahon. Those two would argue with you that blackbirds were white, I'm afraid.'

'Well, it's good to be forewarned,' said Father John, as he went back into the convent chapel and told the girls very firmly that, since taking your own life was taking away a gift that God had given you, it was a sin against Hope – one of the two great sins against Hope – despair. And that anyone who did so was not fit to be buried in a Christian burial ground.

'Not even if her poor mind . . .' began the blonde girl in the front pew.

'Not even if her poor mind,' Father John said firmly.

He was worn out from it, and he had the boys' school to do still. Serious warnings on the evils of drink and self abuse.

Father John sometimes wondered whether any of it did any good at all. But he reminded himself that thinking along those lines was almost a sin against Hope. He must be careful of it.

2

'You don't have proper cousins,' Clio said to Kit, as they lay on the two divan beds in Clio's room.

'Oh God, what are you picking on me for *now*?' Kit groaned. She was reading a magazine article telling you how to soften your hands.

'You never have families of cousins coming to stay.'

'Why would they come to stay? Don't all the other McMahons live just a few miles away?' Kit sighed. Clio could be very tiresome sometimes.

'We have cousins coming from Dublin always, and aunts and things.'

'And you're always saying you hate it.'

'I like Aunt Maura.'

'That's only because she gives you a shilling every time she comes to stay.'

'You've no aunts.' Clio was persistent.

'Oh Clio, will you shut up. Of course I've aunts, what is Aunty Mary and what's Aunty Margaret . . . ?'

'They're just married to your father's brothers.'

'Well, there's Daddy's sister in the convent in Australia. She's an aunt. You can't expect her to be coming and staying and giving us a shilling, can you?'

'Your mother has no people.' Clio lowered her voice. 'She's a person with no people of her own at all.' There was something in the way she said it which made it obvious that she was repeating it like a parrot from something she had heard.

'What do you mean?' Kit was angry now.

'Just what I said.'

'Of course she has people. She has us, a family, here.'

'It's peculiar, that's all.'

'It's *not* peculiar, it's just you are always picking on my mother for some reason. I thought you said you were giving that up.'

'Keep your shirt on.'

'No, I won't. And I'm going home.' Kit flounced off the bed.

Clio was alarmed. 'I didn't mean it.'

'Then why did you say it? What kind of booby goes round saying things she doesn't mean?'

'I was only saying . . .'

'What *were* you saying?' Kit's eyes flashed.

'I don't know what I was saying.'

'Neither do I.' Kit ran lightly out of the room and down the stairs.

'Are you off so soon?' Clio's mother was in the hall. Mrs Kelly always knew when there had been a row. 'I was going to offer you some shortbread,' she said. Many a skirmish had been avoided by the timely appearance of food.

But not today.

'I'm sure Clio would love it, but I have to go back home,' Kit said.

'Surely not yet!'

'My mother might be a bit lonely. You see, she is a person who has no people of her own.' Kit was as near to insolent as she could get away with. A dark red flush around Mrs Kelly's cheeks and neck showed her she had been right. She left, pulling the door gently behind her. With a smile she realised that there would be little shortbread for Clio. Good, Kit thought in satisfaction. I hope her mother eats the face off her.

Mother wasn't at home. She had gone to Dublin on the day excursion, Rita said.

'What did she want to do that for?' Kit grumbled.

'Wouldn't we all love to go to Dublin on a day excursion,' Rita said.

'I wouldn't ... we have no people there,' Kit said.

'There's millions of people in Dublin,' Emmet said.

'Thousands,' Kit corrected him absently.

'Well then?' Emmet said.

'Right.' Kit let it go. 'What did you read with Sister Madeleine?'

'It's all William Blake now. Somebody gave her a book of his poems and she loves them.'

'I don't know anything he wrote except "Tyger, Tyger".'

'Oh, he wrote lots. That's the only one in the school book, but he wrote thousands and thousands.'

'Maybe dozens and dozens,' Kit corrected. 'Maybe. Say me one.

'I don't remember them.'

'Oh go on. You say them over and over.'

'I know the one about the piper ...' Emmet went to the window and stood, as he had stood in Sister Madeleine's cottage, looking out the window.

> '"Pipe a song about a Lamb!"
> So I piped with merry cheer.
> "Piper, pipe that song again;"
> So I piped: he wept to hear.'

He looked so proud of himself. It was a difficult word to say, *piper*, at the best of times, and coming so often in the one sentence. Sister Madeleine must be a genius to have cured his stutter like that.

Kit didn't notice that her father had come in as Emmet was speaking, but the boy hadn't faltered; his confidence was extraordinary. And as they sat there in the September evening, she felt a shiver over her. It was as if

Mother didn't belong to this family at all, as if all there was was Emmet, and Dad, and Rita and herself.

And that mother wouldn't come back.

Mother came back, cold and tired. The heating had broken down on the train; the train itself had broken down twice.

'How was Dublin?'

'It was noisy, and crowded and everyone seemed to be rushing.'

'That's why we all live here.' Father was delighted.

'That's why we all live here,' Mother said flatly.

Kit watched the flames in the fire. 'I think I'll be a hermit when I grow up,' she said suddenly.

'You wouldn't want this lonely kind of a life. It's only for odd people like myself.'

'Are you odd, Sister Madeleine?'

'I'm very peculiar. Isn't that a funny word, "peculiar"? I was saying it with Emmet the other day; we were wondering where it came from.'

It reminded Kit that Clio said it was peculiar her mother had no family. 'Did you get hurt when people spoke badly about your family when you were young?'

'No child, not ever.'

'How did you make yourself not worry?'

'I suppose I thought if anyone would try to pull down my family they would just be wrong.' Kit was silent. 'As they would be if they said anything about your family.'

'I know.' But the little voice was doubtful.

'Your father is the most respected man in three counties; he's so kind to the poor and he's like a second doctor in the town. Your mother is as gentle and loving a soul as it was ever my good fortune to meet. She has a poet's heart and she loves beauty . . .' The silence lay between them, so Sister Madeleine spoke again. Her face was hard to read; you wouldn't know what she was thinking. She spoke slowly, deliberately. 'Of course, people often say things out of jealousy, because they're not secure in themselves. Because they worry they lash out, like a man with a stick might hit a hedge and take all the lovely heads off the flowers and not knowing why he did it . . .' Sister Madeleine's voice was hypnotic. It was as if she knew all about Clio. Maybe Clio had been here and told her. Who could know? 'And often a fellow who beat the heads off the flowers with a stick would be sorry he did it but he wouldn't know how to say that.'

'I know,' Kit said. She was pleased to know that Sister Madeleine thought her mother had a poet's heart and was a good and gentle soul. And she'd forgive Clio in her own good time.

Provided, of course, Clio apologised properly.

'I'm very sorry,' Clio said.

'That's all right,' Kit said.

'No, it's not. I don't know why I did it, why I keep doing it. I suppose I just want to be one better than you or something. I don't like myself, that's the truth.'

'And I don't like myself sulking,' said Kit.

Their families were relieved. It was always unsettling when Kit and Clio had a falling out. Like thunder in the air, and the hint of a bad storm ahead.

*

Sometimes it was harder to break the news of a death that was meaningless than one which would cause huge grief. Peter Kelly paused for breath before he went to tell Kathleen Sullivan that her husband had finally succumbed to the liver disease that had been threatening him as seriously as the brain deterioration which had given him his place in the County Home. He knew there would be no conventional words of grief or consolation. But it was never simple.

Kathleen Sullivan took the information with a stony face. Her elder son, Stevie, a dark, good-looking boy who had felt his father's fist once too often, and left of his own volition for the uncle's farm, just shrugged. 'He died a long time ago, Doctor,' he said.

The younger boy, Michael, looked confused. 'Will there be a funeral?' he asked.

'Yes, of course,' the doctor said.

'We'll have no funeral,' Stevie said unexpectedly. 'No mourning or making a mockery of the whole thing.'

His mother looked startled. 'There'll *have* to be a funeral,' she began.

They all seemed to be looking at the doctor for the solution. As he so often felt, Peter Kelly wondered what kind of social structure had made him the fount of all wisdom in such matters.

Stevie, a boy of sixteen maybe, looked him in the eye. 'You're not a hypocrite, Dr Kelly. You wouldn't want a charade.' There was something strong about the boy's face, and determined. Maybe six or seven years of his childhood robbed from him had been a good training for life as well as a high price to pay. The lad should not have to take part in a sham ceremony.

'I think the whole thing can be arranged very quietly at the Home. That is often done in such cases, and just the family attend a Mass there. Father Baily will arrange it, I know.'

Kathleen Sullivan looked at him gratefully. 'You're very good, Doctor. I just wish it had all been different.' Her face was set and hard as she spoke. 'I can't go to anyone for sympathy or anything because they'll all say it was for the best, and we're all well rid of him.'

'I know what you mean, Kathleen.' Peter Kelly *did*, only too well, and if he didn't have any suitable words of comfort, no one else in Lough Glass would be able to find them. 'You could always call on Sister Madeleine,' he said. 'She'll be the very one to comfort you at a time like this.'

He sat in his car after he left the house, and watched while Kathleen Sullivan, now wearing her coat and head scarf, followed his advice. He saw her heading down towards the boreen that led to the lake. As he drove home he passed Helen McMahon walking with her hair blowing in the wind. The wind was cold and she wore a woollen dress but had no coat. She looked flushed and excited.

He stopped the car. 'Will I drive you back, take the weight off your legs?' he asked.

She smiled at him, and he realised again how very beautiful she was. Sometimes he forgot, and didn't really see the beauty that had broken all their hearts in Dublin. The girl with the perfect face, who had chosen Martin McMahon of all people to be her consort.

'No, Peter, I love to walk on an evening like this . . . it's so free. Do you see the birds over the lake? Aren't they magnificent?'

She looked magnificent. Her eyes were bright, her skin was glowing. He had forgotten that for a slight woman she had such a voluptuous figure; her breasts seemed to strain at the blue wool dress. With a shock he realised that Helen McMahon was pregnant.

'Peter, *what* is it?'

'You keep asking me that.' He was irritated with Lilian. 'What is what?'

'You haven't said a word all evening. You just keep staring into the fire.'

'I have things on my mind.'

'Obviously you have. I was just asking what things.'

'Are you some kind of Grand Inquisitor? Can I not even think now without your permission?' he snapped.

He saw the tears jump into Lilian's eyes and her plump face pucker. It was very unjust of him. They had the kind of relationship where each would ask the other how they felt and what they were thinking. It was monstrous of him to behave like this.

He admitted it.

'I only asked because you looked worried.' Lilian was almost mollified.

'I'm wondering did I do the right thing over Kathleen Sullivan, telling her to have the funeral above in the Home,' said Peter Kelly, and listened with part of his mind to some of his wife's views on the subject while he tried to work out the implications of Helen McMahon's pregnancy. In the pit of his stomach was the feeling that all was not as it should be.

There was no reason why Martin and Helen should not try for a late baby. Helen must be thirty-seven or thirty-eight, an age when most women around here would think nothing of having children. But Peter Kelly was uneasy. Just scraps of conversation floating around in the air coming back to disturb him: Clio saying that Kit McMahon's parents slept in different rooms, something Martin said one night down in Paddles' place about the old days, some reference to making love as if it were all in the past, something Helen had said when Emmet was a toddler, about there being no younger brothers and sisters for him. It all made a crazy jigsaw in his head. And he realised that it had to be crazy because just suppose, suppose for the sake of argument, that all these jumbled ideas spelled out the truth.

Who on earth could be the father of Helen McMahon's child if it were not her husband?

*

Martin heard footsteps on the stairs. He got up and came to the sitting room door. 'Helen?'

'Yes, love.'

'I was looking for you. Did you hear about poor Billy Sullivan?'

'Yes, Dan told me. I suppose it's a blessing in a way. He was never going to get better.'

'Should we go in, do you think?' Martin was always a good neighbour.

'No, Kathleen's not there, only the two lads. I called on my way back.'

'You were out late . . .'

'I was just walking. It's a lovely night. They say their mother went down to Sister Madeleine. That was a good idea. She always knows what to say.'

'Were you in the hotel then?'

Helen looked surprised. 'Lord, no. What would I go in there for?'

'You said Dan told you about Billy Sullivan.'

'Doesn't Dan stand there at the door telling the dogs in the street bits of information . . . No, I told you, I was walking. Down by the lake.'

'Why do you want to walk by yourself? Why won't you let me walk with you?'

'You know why. I want to think.'

'But what is there to think about?' He looked blank, bewildered.

'There's so much to think about that my mind is overflowing . . .'

'And are they good, the things you think about?' He sounded almost fretful of the answer, as if he regretted asking.

'We must talk . . . we have to talk . . .' Helen looked to the door as if to see were they out of earshot.

Martin was alarmed. 'There's nothing to talk about. I just wanted to know were you happy, that's all.'

Helen sighed. A heavy sigh. 'Oh Martin, how many times have I told you. I was neither happy nor unhappy, there was nothing you could have done – it would have been like asking you to change the weather . . .'

He looked at her, crestfallen. His face showed that he knew he should not have asked.

'But it's all different now. It's all changed. And we have always been honest with each other – that's more than many other couples . . .' She spoke as if giving him crumbs of comfort.

'More than that, surely?' His voice was full of hope.

'Of course more than that – but because I never lied to you, I would always tell you if there was something important.'

Martin moved away, putting up his hands as if to ward off any explanation that she was about to begin. Her face was agonised. He was unable to bear it.

'No, my love, I was wrong. Haven't you every right to walk by yourself? By the lake, or anywhere. What am I doing cross-questioning you? I'm turning into an old Mother Bernard before my time, that's what I'm doing.'

'I want to tell you everything . . .' Her face was empty.

'Now, hasn't enough happened tonight with that poor man across the road going to meet his maker . . .'

'*Martin* . . .' she interrupted.

But he wasn't going to talk. He took her hands and drew her across the room towards him. When she was right beside him be put his arms around her very tight. 'I love you, Helen,' he said over and over into her hair.

And she murmured, 'I know. I know, Martin, I know.'

Neither of them saw Kit in the shadow pass the door, wait for a moment and then go on to her own room. She lay in bed without sleeping for a long time that night. She couldn't decide whether what she had seen was very good or very bad.

At least it didn't look as if her mother was wild and fancy free, or whatever Clio was constantly hinting at.

Hallowe'en was a Friday. Kit wondered could they have a party.

Mother seemed against it. 'We don't know what we'll be doing,' she said in a fussed sort of way.

'But of course we know what we'll be doing.' Kit was stung by the unfairness of this. 'It's a Friday. We'll be having scrambled eggs and potatoes like every Friday, and I only asked for a few friends to come in . . .'

Mother looked quite different when she spoke. She seemed to underline every word as if she were giving a message or reading a notice, rather than having a normal conversation. 'Believe me, I *do* know what I'm saying. We do not know what we will be doing on Hallowe'en. This is not the time to be thinking of Hallowe'en parties. There will be parties again, but not now.'

It was very final. It was also very frightening.

'Are there really ghosts on Hallowe'en?' Clio asked Sister Madeleine.

'You know there aren't ghosts,' Sister Madeleine said.

'Well, spirits.'

'There are spirits around us all the time.' Sister Madeleine was being remarkably cheerful about it, as if she wouldn't indulge in Clio Kelly's wish to be dramatic.

'Are you afraid of spirits?' Clio persisted. She wanted to get a bit of terror into the conversation somehow.

'No child, I'm not. How could you be afraid of someone's spirit? A spirit is a friendly thing. It's the life that was in them once – the memory of it – that stays around a place . . .'

This was more promising. 'Are there spirits round here, round the lake?'

'Of course there are – the people who loved the place and who lived here.'

'And died here?'

'And died here, of course.'

'Would Bridie Daly's spirit be here?'

'Bridie Daly?'

'The woman who said, "Look in the reeds." The woman who was going to have a baby without being married.' Clio sounded too eager, too gossipy, for Sister Madeleine.

She looked at them thoughtfully. 'And are you girls having a party for Hallowe'en?' she asked.

Kit said nothing.

Clio grumbled, 'Kit was going to have one and then it was all cancelled.' 'I only said I might.' Kit was mutinous.

'Well, it's stupid to say you might and then give no explanation,' Clio said.

Sister Madeleine looked at Kit sympathetically. The child was distressed about something. The Hallowe'en party was not the right distraction to have made. 'Have you ever seen a tame fox?' she asked them, with the air of a conspirator.

'You can't have a tame fox, can you?' Clio knew everything.

'Well, you can't have one that you'd trust with the ducklings and the chickens,' Sister Madeleine agreed. 'But I have a lovely little fellow I could show you. He's in a box in my bedroom. I can't let him out but you can come in with me and see.'

Her bedroom! The girls looked at each other in delight. No one knew what was behind the closed door. Forgotten now were bodies in the lake, spirits of the dead, and the intransigence of cancelling a hallowe'en party. In they went and Sister Madeleine closed the door behind them.

There was a simple bed with a small iron headboard, and a smaller bed-end made the same way. It was covered in a snow-white bedspread. On the wall was a cross, not a crucifix, just a plain cross. There was a small chest of drawers which had no mirror, just a comb and a pair of rosary beads.

There was a chair, and a *prie-dieu* facing the cross. This is where Sister Madeleine must say her prayers.

'You have it very tidy,' Clio said eventually, trying to think of some compliment and finding this the only thing she could say in honesty about a place which had the comfort of a prison cell.

'Here he is,' cried Sister Madeleine, and pulled out a cardboard box with straw in it. Sitting in the middle was a tiny fox cub with his head on one side.

'Isn't he gorgeous!' Clio and Kit spoke in one voice. They reached out awkwardly as if to stroke him.

'Will he bite?' Clio asked.

'He might nip a little, but he's so small his little teeth wouldn't hurt you.' Any other grown-up in the world would have said not to touch him.

'Will he live here for ever?' Kit wanted to know.

'He broke his leg, you see. I was mending it . . . it's not the kind of thing you can take to the vet. Mr Kenny would not thank you for bringing up a fox to him.' Sister Madeleine knew that even the warm feelings of Lough Glass she enjoyed would not extend towards her harbouring a fox. Foxes were rodents; they killed people's chickens and geese, and little turkeys. If a baby fox were to be cured, then you wouldn't get any branch of the medical profession or establishment to help you. They looked admiringly at the little piece of wood tied to the tiny leg. 'He'll soon be able to walk and run, and then we'll send him off to whatever life awaits him.' Sister Madeleine looked

at the little pointed face that stared trustingly up at her and stroked his
small soft head.

'How can you let him go?' Kit breathed. 'I'd keep him for ever.'

'His place is out there. You can't keep anything that wants to go; it's in
his nature to be free.'

'But you could make him into a pet . . .'

'No, that wouldn't work. Anything or anyone who is meant to be free will
go.'

Kit shivered. It was as if Sister Madeleine was looking into the future.

Helen went slowly down the stairs and into the pharmacy. She gave a wan
little smile.

'It's like the shoemaker's children never being shod . . . I can't find an
aspirin up in the bathroom,' she said.

He ran to get a glass of water and put out two little tablets for her. His
hand lay over hers for a moment. She smiled the same feeble attempt to
respond to him.

'You look washed out, love . . . did you not sleep?' Martin McMahon
spoke very fondly.

'I didn't actually. I kept walking around. I hope I didn't wake the house.'

'You should have come in to me. I'd have fixed you something to make
you sleep.'

'Ah, I don't like calling you in the middle of the night. It's bad enough
not wanting you in my bedroom, I don't want to be raising your hopes.'

'The hopes are always there, Helen. Maybe some day?' His face looked
eager. She was silent. 'Or some night?' he smiled.

'I have to talk to you, Martin.'

He looked concerned; immediately he felt her forehead.

'What is it, love? A fever?'

'No, no, it's not that.'

His eyes were wide with distress. 'Well, tell me about it, and don't be
putting the heart across me . . .'

'Not here – it's all too long and confused and . . . I have to get out of
here . . .' She was flushed now, her earlier pallor gone.

'Will we get Peter?'

'No we will not get Peter,' she snapped. 'I want to talk to you by yourself.
Will you come out for a walk with me?'

'Now? But aren't we going upstairs to have the meal that's on the table
for us?' He was utterly bewildered by her.

'I told Rita that you and I would not be having our meal today, I made
you a few sandwiches.' She had a neat packet wrapped in greaseproof paper.
'I have to talk to you.' Her voice was not menacing, but yet Martin seemed
to fear her words.

'Listen, love, I'm a working man, I can't go off wandering where the
fancy takes me,' he said.

'It's early closing today.'

'But I have . . . I have a hundred things to do – will we bring those sandwiches upstairs and have them with Rita? Wouldn't that be grand?'

'I don't want to talk in front of Rita . . .'

'You know, I don't think you should be talking at all – come on, now and I'll settle you into your bed, and we'll have no more of this nonsense.' His voice was the same as when he was taking a splinter out of a child's finger, or painting iodine on to a cut knee. He was soothing and full of encouragement.

Helen's eyes filled with tears.

'Oh, Martin, what am I going to do with you?' she asked.

He patted her hand. 'You're going to smile at me. There is nothing on this earth that is not made better by a good smile.'

She forced a smile and he dusted away the tear-drops.

'What did I tell you?' he said, triumphantly. He was still holding her hand, and they looked like a happy couple sharing a secret, a life together and maybe a loving moment when the door opened and Lilian Kelly came in followed by her sister Maura, who had come on a visit as she did every year around this time.

'Well, isn't this the way to live, like a courting couple in the middle of all the potions and the bottles,' Lilian laughed.

'Hello Helen, and there isn't a pick on you this year as well.' Maura was a plump woman like her sister, bustling and enthusiastic, a great golfer. She worked for a horse trainer and it had been said that she had hopes of him. The hopes had not materialised. Maura must be forty now, but always cheerful and full of activity.

They pulled up the two tall chairs that Martin McMahon kept for customers to use, and an ashtray was produced as both Lilian and Maura smoked the Gold Flakes, waving them around as they gestured or exclaimed at whatever was being said.

Martin noticed Helen back away a little from the smoke. 'Will I open the door a bit?' he suggested.

She gave him a grateful look.

'You'll freeze us all to death, Martin.'

'It's just that Helen's a bit . . .' he was protective.

'Aren't you well?' Lilian was sympathetic.

'I'm fine, just a bit nauseous today, I don't know why.'

'Would it be the oldest reason in the book, do you think?' Lilian was arch.

Helen looked at her levelly. 'I don't think so,' she said with a faint smile.

She stood in the street, gulping the cold air. It was chilly even for the end of October, and there was a mist coming up from the lake. Still, it brought more colour to her cheeks.

'Listen, we called because we're going to treat ourselves to lunch at the Central. Ah come on, Helen. It's early closing day – Peter'll come down too, to make an occasion out of it. You will come, won't you?'

Helen looked at her husband. A few moments ago, he had been pleading that he had hundreds of things to do. He couldn't take the time off on early closing day to be alone with her. And yet now there was the chance of an outing with a group, he was obviously dying to go.

'Well, I don't know, I really don't know . . .' he said.

Helen said not a word to help him decide.

'We don't do this kind of thing very often.' Lilian Kelly was trying to be persuasive.

'Martin, I insist.' Maura seemed eager too. 'Come on now, it'd be my treat, all of you. Let me do this – I'd love it.' She beamed at them all.

'Helen, what do you think?' He was as eager as a boy. 'Will we be devils?'

Lilian and Maura almost clapped their hands with enthusiasm.

'You go, Martin, please. I can't I'm afraid. I have to go . . .' Helen waved her hand vaguely in a direction that could have meant anywhere.

Nobody questioned why she wouldn't come, or where she was going.

The Brothers had a half day on Wednesday, the convent did not. Emmet McMahon went to see Sister Madeleine and read the *Lays of Ancient Rome* with her; over and over he told the story about how Horatius kept the bridge. She closed her eyes and said she could see it all: those brave young men fighting off the enemy hordes, just three of them, and then being flung into the Tiber. Emmet began to see it too, and he spoke it with great confidence.

'"Oh, Tiber! Father Tiber! To whom the Romans pray" . . .' He interrupted himself. 'Why did the Romans pray to a river?'

'They thought it was a God.'

'They must have been mad.'

'I don't know,' Sister Madeleine speculated. 'It was a very powerful river, rushing and foaming, and it was their livelihood in many ways . . . a bit like God to them I suppose.' Sister Madeleine found nothing surprising.

'Can you show me the little fox you showed Kit?' he asked.

'Certainly, but tell me more about those brave Romans first. I love to hear about them.'

And Emmet McMahon, who had not been able to say his own name in public with any hope of finishing it, stood and declaimed the verses of Lord Macaulay as if it was his mission in life.

'Aunt Maura'll be at home when I get back,' Clio said.

'That's nice for you,' Kit said.

'Yes. She said she'd teach us golf. Would we learn?'

Kit considered it. It would be a very grown-up thing to do, certainly. It would put them in a different class from those who just collected golf balls. But Kit felt a resistance. She wondered why. Possibly because her mother didn't play. Mother had never shown any interest in the game at all. It seemed a bit disloyal somehow for Kit to learn, as if she didn't agree with her mother's choice.

'I'll think about it,' she said eventually.

'With you that means no,' Clio said.

'Why do you say that?'

'Because I know you very well.' Clio spoke menacingly.

Kit resolved to discuss the golf with her mother that evening; if Mam encouraged her to go ahead, she would. That would show Clio Kelly that she wasn't always right.

'Don't give me very much, Rita. I had a meal that you wouldn't give to a condemned man there was so much on the plate,' Martin McMahon said ruefully.

'Why did you eat all that, Daddy?' Emmet asked.

'We went on an outing to the hotel as a treat.'

'How much did it cost?' Emmet wondered.

'I don't know, to tell you the truth. Clio's Auntie Maura paid for all of us.'

'Did Mother enjoy it?' Kit was pleased there had been an outing.

'Ah. Your mother wasn't able to come with us.'

'Where is Mother now?'

'She'll be back later.'

Kit wished she was there now, she wanted to talk about the golf to her. Why did everyone think it was so normal for Mother not to be around any more?

Clio came around after tea. 'Well, what did you decide?'

'Decide?'

'About golf. Aunt Maura wants to know.'

'No she doesn't. *You* want to know.' Kit knew that and said it very definitely.

'Well, she *would* want to know.'

'I haven't decided yet.'

'What'll we do then?' Clio looked around Kit's bedroom, waiting for inspiration, or an invitation to look at the dance steps of the cha-cha-cha which they had nearly mastered. The pattern of where the feet should go was worse than geometry with Mother Bernard.

'I don't know,' Kit said. She wanted to hear Mother's light step on the stair.

There was a silence. 'Are we having a fight?' Clio asked.

Kit was full of remorse. She nearly told her best friend that she was just worried because Mother wasn't home. Nearly, but she didn't.

'Clio didn't stay long.' Kit's father was drawing the curtains in the sitting room.

'No, she didn't.'

'Another fight?'

'No, she asked that too,' Kit said.

'Good, that's a relief.'

'Daddy? Where's Mother?'

'She'll be back, love, she likes people not to be policing her.'

'But *where* is she?'

'I don't know, love. Come on now, and stop pacing the room like a caged animal.'

Kit sat down and looked at the patterns in the fire. She saw houses and castles, and big fiery mountains. The same pattern never appeared twice. She looked at her father from time to time.

He sat with a book on his lap, but never turned a page.

In the kitchen Rita sat beside the range. The Aga was a comfort on a windy night like this. She thought of people who had no home, like the Old Woman of the Roads in the poem. They had a framed print from the Cuala Press of the poem by Padraic Colum up on the wall. It was a great thing to have a bit of comfort.

She wondered about the tinker women travelling on and on in those damp caravans, about Sister Madeleine who didn't know where the next crust was going to come from, but it never worried her. Someone would bring her wood for the fire, or potatoes to cook.

And Rita thought about the Mistress.

What would have her, a fine young woman with a family that adored her, wandering about down by the lake on a cold windy night like this, instead of sitting by the fire in her own room with the thick velvet curtains drawn.

'People are funny, Farouk,' Rita said to the cat.

Farouk leaped up on the windowsill and looked out over the back yards of Lough Glass, as if he, too, might have been out wandering, had he the mind.

Emmet was in bed, Father was straining, listening for the sound of the door. Kit felt the tick tock of the clock going through her, almost shaking her body. Why did they have a clock with such a loud sound, or maybe it had just got louder. Kit hadn't remembered it like this before, dominating the whole house.

Wouldn't it have been wonderful if Mother was there teaching her some game. Mother said you could learn any game from a book. There was no such thing as having a head for that sort of thing or having a good card sense, you did it for yourself.

Soon they would hear the door opening and Mother's light step running up the stair. Father would never ask her what kept her out so late . . . even though this was surely later than she had ever been out before.

Perhaps he should ask her, Kit thought with a surge of impatience. It wasn't normal; it wasn't what Clio would call normal.

And then they heard the sound at the door downstairs. Kit felt the colour return to her face. She and her father exchanged conspiratorial glances of relief, the relief that would not be mentioned when Mother came in. But the door didn't open. It wasn't Mother. It was somebody rattling the door trying to turn the handle and then resorting to knocking. Kit's father ran down to answer it.

It was Dan O'Brien from the hotel, and his son Philip. They were wet and windblown.

Kit watched them from the top of the stairs. It felt as if everything was moving very slowly.

'Martin, I'm sure everything's all right,' Dan began.

'What is it, man? Tell me. Speak, God damn you.' Father was in a panic, wanting the words which Mr O'Brien didn't seem able to say.

'I'm sure it's all fine, the children are home, aren't they . . . ?'

'What is it, Dan?'

'It's the boat, your boat . . . your boat, Martin. It's cut loose and it's upside down drifting. There's fellows pulling it in. I said I'd run up and see . . . make sure the children were at home.' Dan O'Brien seemed relieved to see the two faces peering down at him. Emmet had come from his bed in his pyjamas and sat huddled on the top of the stairs.

'Well, sure, it's only a boat . . . and there's maybe not much damage.' He stopped.

Martin McMahon was holding him by the lapels of his jacket. 'Was there anybody in the boat . . . ?'

'Martin now, aren't the children there behind you . . .'

'Helen?' Martin almost sobbed out the word.

'Helen? Sure what would Helen be doing down there at that time of night? Martin, it's a quarter to ten. Have you taken leave of your senses?'

'Helen . . .' Father cried, and ran out in the rain, leaving the door open.

'Helen . . .' they heard him cry as he ran down the one street of Lough Glass towards the lake.

That was the bit that was all very slow, the bit that Kit heard with the words taking ages to come out of Father's mouth and Mr O'Brien's, even though they looked as if they were shouting. And even when Father ran, his legs seemed to be going up and down the way they showed the slow motion bits in athletics at Pathé News when you saw people doing the high jump or the long jump.

Then things returned to normal speed and Kit saw Emmet's frightened face looking up at her.

'What's happened?' he began, but he couldn't get the word out, his lips kept circling the start of happened and he seemed as if he would choke before he said it.

And at the same time, Rita had run to close the hall door, which was banging in and out, while Philip O'Brien stood looking foolish, unable to help.

'Either come in or go out,' Rita snapped at the boy.

He came in and followed her up the stairs.

'There was nobody there,' he said to Kit. 'I mean your mother wasn't in it or anything. They all thought that it was you kids tricking and trick-acting with the boat.'

'Well, it wasn't me,' Kit said in a voice that felt as if it was coming from somewhere else.

'Where's Daddy?' Emmet couldn't get that word out either; Emmet who could read every poem in the Primary Cert Primer.

'He's gone to bring Mother home,' Kit said. And she listened to the words to see what they meant. They sounded safe. She said them again. 'That's where he's gone. To bring Mother home.'

*

They had flashlights down at the lake.

Sergeant O'Connor was there, and Peter Kelly, and the two Sullivan boys from the garage.

They were bending over the boat when they heard the sound of running feet and noises in Martin McMahon's throat. 'It's not Helen. Tell me you haven't found Helen in the lake.' His eyes went from one to another, the semicircle of men he had known all his life. Young Stevie Sullivan looked away; the tears pouring down a man's face were too naked to look at.

'Please, tell me?' Martin said again.

Peter Kelly pulled himself together. With his arm around the shaking man he moved him away from the group. 'Now Martin, will you catch hold of yourself. What brought you running down here anyway?'

'Dan came to the house, he said the boat . . .'

'God blast that great interfering Dan O'Brien into the pit of hell. What did he have to go upsetting you for . . .'

'Is she . . . ?'

'Martin, there's nothing here, man. Nothing except a boat that wasn't tied up. It was blown out into the lake . . . That's all there is.'

Martin stood trembling beside his old friend. 'She didn't come home, Peter. I sat there saying she's never been as late as this. I wanted to come looking for her. If only I'd come. But she wanted to be left alone; she said she felt like a prisoner unless she could walk on her own.'

'I know, I know.' Dr Kelly was listening and patting the man's shaking shoulders, but he was looking around him too.

In the trees the oil lamps shone through the windows of the caravans. The travellers might have a fire built in a sheltered spot. He could make out their shapes; they stood, watchful, silent, observing the confusion and drama on the lake's edge.

'I'll bring you up there out of the wind,' Peter Kelly said. 'They'll give you somewhere to shelter, till we make sure that everything . . .' His voice trailed away as if he sensed the uselessness of his words.

Peter Kelly had always been in two minds about the travelling people. He knew for a fact that they took poultry from nearby farms; there weren't enough rabbits in those trees to keep them in food. He knew that some of the boys could be troublesome if they came into Paddles' bar. But to be fair, they were often provoked into anger by locals.

Peter wished they could see that the travelling life didn't offer much opportunity to the children of their group. The youngsters could barely read and write. They never stayed long enough anywhere for any education to sink in if they were welcomed in the school, which wasn't always the case. They had little need of his services. They coped with birth, illness and death in their way. And their way often had more fortitude and dignity than the other way. He had never approached them for a favour before.

'Could you give this man something to throw around his shoulders?' he asked a group of unsmiling men.

The men parted and from behind came a woman with a big rug and a cup of something that had steam coming from it. They sat Martin

McMahon on a fallen tree nearby. 'Do you want any help?' said one of the dark men.

'I'd be grateful if you could bring more light down to the shore,' Peter said simply. And he knew that for the rest of his life he would not be able to remove the image of his friend, sitting on a log wrapped in a rug, while the whole encampment lit up with the blazing torches made from dipping tar-covered sticks into the fire.

And then there was the procession down to the edge of the lake.

Martin hugged himself in the rug and moaned. Over and over he said, 'She's not in the lake, she'd have let me know. Helen never told me a lie. She said she wouldn't do anything without letting me know.'

The clock was ticking and there was a little whir between each tick. Kit had never noticed that before. But then she had never sat at the foot of the grandfather clock before, leaning against it, holding her brother in her arms, while Philip O'Brien sat on the bit of stairs that went up further still, up to the attic where Rita slept.

Rita sat on a chair in the doorway of the kitchen. Once or twice or maybe more often, she got up and said, 'I'll throw another log on the fire. They'll need that when they get back.'

Someone had sent for Clio. She came through the door and up the stairs. They had left the key in the door. She saw the little tableau. 'My mother said I should come down to you straight away,' she said. They waited for Kit to reply. Kit said nothing. 'She said this was where I should be.'

Something exploded in Kit's mind.

How dare Clio talk about herself, it was always *I, I, I*. It was the place *she* should be, *she* came straight down. She knew she must not speak, not until this huge wave of rage passed over. If she opened her mouth now she would hurl abuse at Clio Kelly, order her out of the house.

'Kit, say something.' Clio stood awkward on the stairs.

'Thanks, Clio,' she gulped. Please may she not say something terrible, something for which she would be apologising for the rest of her life.

Emmet sensed the odd silence. 'Mummy . . .' he began, but he couldn't get beyond the first M.

Clio looked at him sympathetically. 'Oh Emmet, your stammer has come back,' she said.

Philip stood up. 'There's probably enough people here, Clio. Could you go home now,' he said.

Clio snapped at him.

'He's right, Clio.' Kit found her voice very calm and clear. 'Thank you very much for coming, but Philip was asked to keep the place sort of clear, for when everyone's coming back.'

'I want to be here when everyone comes back.' Clio seemed like a spoiled child.

There was the *I* again, Kit noticed. 'You're a wonderful friend. I knew you'd understand,' Kit said. And Clio went down the stairs.

The clock ticked on with its new whir, and none of them said anything at all.

'There's not going to be anything until the light of day,' said Sergeant O'Connor, shaking his head.

'We just can't leave it and go home.' Peter Kelly's face ran with sweat, or tears, or rain, it was impossible to tell.

'Be sensible, man. You'll have half the people here as your patients and the other half up the graveyard if they go on. There's nothing to be found, I tell you. Go on, tell the tinkers to go home, will you.'

'Don't call them tinkers, Sean.' But Peter Kelly knew it was neither the time nor the place to try to impose some sensitivity on to Sergeant Sean O'Connor.

'What'll I call them, Household Cavalry? Apache Indians?'

'Come on, they've been a great help . . . they've no reason to be friends to any of us . . . they're doing their best . . .'

'They look like savages with those torches. They make my flesh creep.'

'If it helped to find her . . .' Peter began.

'Oh she'll be found all right, but it won't make any difference to anyone whether it's tonight or next Tuesday week.'

'You're very sure?' Peter said.

Sean O'Connor had a simple direct way of getting to the truth of things, and tonight it left no area for doubt or hope. 'Sure, wasn't the poor woman out of her wits?' the sergeant said. 'Didn't you see her night and day, wandering around here, half talking to herself? It's only a mystery that she didn't do it sooner.'

A tall dark woman brought Martin McMahon a cup from her caravan.

'Drink this,' she said. It was like an order.

He sipped it and made a face. 'What is it? I thought it was tea,' he said.

'I wouldn't give you anything to harm you,' she said. Her voice was low; he barely heard it above the wind, and the calling all around the lake's edge.

'Thank you indeed,' he said, and drank what tasted like Bovril with something sharp in it. It could have been anything; he didn't care.

'Be calm,' the woman said to him. 'Try not to shake and tremble, it may well be all right.'

'They think my wife . . .' he said.

'I know, but she wouldn't. She wouldn't go anywhere without telling you,' said the woman in her low voice that he had to strain to hear.

He turned to thank her, to tell her that he knew this was true, but she had slipped back into the shadows.

He heard Sergeant O'Connor calling off the search for the night. He saw his friend Peter coming to take him home. Martin McMahon knew he must be strong for their children.

Helen would have wanted that.

Rita heard them coming.

She knew by the shufflings and low voices down at the hall door there was no good news to tell. She ran into the kitchen to put on the kettle.

Philip O'Brien stood up. It wasn't often he was in charge, but he knew he was in charge now. 'Your father will be all wet from the rain,' he said. Kit was wordless. 'Is there an electric fire in their bedroom? He might want to change.'

'In whose bedroom?' she spoke from far away.

'In your parents' room.'

'They have different rooms.'

'Well, in his room then.'

She flashed Philip a grateful look. Clio would always use an opportunity like this to comment on how strange it was that Kit's mother and father did not sleep in the same bed. Philip was being a great help. 'I'll go and plug it in,' she said. It took her away from the top of the stairs; she didn't have to see her father's face when he came up. She didn't want to have to look at it.

Emmet wouldn't know how bad things were. He wouldn't know that Mother and Father were unhappy, and that Mother might not be coming back. Might be gone.

She wanted the moment on her own.

The room was cold as she found the one-bar electric fire and plugged it in the socket in the wall just above the yellow skirting board. Everything seemed very clear somehow. She could see the pattern on the carpet and the way the fringe of the bedspread hung unevenly, more to one side than the other.

Maybe if Daddy was very wet he might put on his dressing gown. He wouldn't if there were other people there, and Kit had heard Clio's father's voice, and people like Father Baily and Philip's father were outside. No, he would wear a jacket. She walked past the top of the bed towards the big chair where her father's tweed sports coat hung as it always had.

It was then she saw the letter on the pillow. A big white envelope with the word *Martin* on it.

Over Daddy's bed hung the picture of the Pope, the Pope that Kit had always believed was a guest at their wedding. Time seemed to stand still as she looked at it. The Pope had small round glasses. They looked like a little boy's spectacles that were much too small for him. He had a white fur trim around his garment, a bit like the frill Santa Claus wore when they went up to Clery's in Dublin for a Christmas treat. He had his hands raised as if to give a blessing.

She read the words very slowly: Martin McMahon and Mary Helena Healy humbly prostrate at the feet of your holiness, beg the apostolic blessing on the occasion of their marriage, 20th June 1939. And there was a kind of raised seal beneath.

She looked at it as if she had never seen it before. It was as if by memorising every single detail she could somehow control what was about to happen now.

And for some reason she never understood, she bent down and

unplugged the electric fire. It was as if she wanted it to be thought she had never entered the room.

Kit stood with the letter in her hand. Her mother had left a message. She had explained why she had done what she did. For no reason, the words of the priest who had come to give their retreat came back to her. The priest who said that your life wasn't yours to take, it was a gift from God and that those who threw it back in God's face had no place being mourned by the faithful. And had no place in the burial grounds of God's family on earth. She could see his face. And she acted as an automaton. She slipped the envelope deep in the pocket of her blue tunic and went to the stairs to greet the party that was coming up, and to face her father's terrible smile.

'Now there's no sign of an accident. We're not to worry about a thing. Your mother could walk in that door as right as rain. Any minute now.' Nobody spoke. 'Any minute at all,' said Kit's father, with hope written all over his face.

Rita built up the fire in the sitting room, and hunted Farouk from his important looking place in front of the grate. People stood about, awkward, embarrassed, not sure what to say next.

Except Clio's father. Dr Kelly always knew what to say. Kit looked at him with gratitude; he was being the host. 'Do you know everyone's frozen solid from standing on the coldest spot in Ireland. Now I hear that Rita has the kettle on. Philip, will you run round to your father's hotel like a good lad, and ask the barman for a bottle of Paddy and we'll have a hot whiskey for ourselves, everyone.'

'There's going to be no money changing hands at a time like this.' Philip's father, Mr O'Brien, had a funeral face on him.

Dr Kelly hastened to make things more cheerful. 'Well that's very good of you, Dan. And we have a lemon and some cloves, and that'll put the heat into all of us. I'm prescribing it as a doctor now, mind you, so you all have to take heed.' Sergeant O'Connor kept saying he wouldn't have a drink, but yet he waited as they were poured out. 'Sean, it's for your own good. Drink it,' Dr Kelly said.

'I don't want to drink this man's whiskey, I have to ask was there a note . . . ?'

'*What?*' Dr Kelly looked at the sergeant in horror.

'You know what I mean. I have to ask it sometime. This is the time.'

'This is *not* the time,' Clio's father whispered.

But not quietly enough for Kit. She turned away as if she hadn't been listening.

She heard the sergeant speak in a lower tone. 'Jesus God, Peter. If there *is* a note, isn't it as well we know?'

'Don't you ask him, I'll do it.'

'It's important. Don't let him . . .'

'Don't tell me what's important or not. Don't tell me what I'm to do or not do . . .'

'We're all on edge . . . don't take offence.'

'I'll take as much offence as will suit me. Drink that whiskey for God's sake, and try not to open your mouth until you've something to say.'

Kit saw Sergeant O'Connor redden, and she felt sorry for him. It was like getting a telling off at school. Then she saw Clio's father move through the people to get to her father. Surreptitiously she moved nearer to them.

'Martin ... Martin, my old friend ...'

'What is it, Peter? What is it? You don't know anything you're not saying?'

'I don't know anything I wouldn't say.' Peter Kelly looked wretched. 'But listen to me. Would there be a question at all that Helen went off somewhere on her own? Like ... Dublin, to see anyone ... you know ...'

'She'd tell me. She's never gone anywhere without telling me. That's the way it is between us.'

'Where would she leave a note if you weren't here to tell?'

'A note ... a message ...' Martin McMahon finally understood what his friend was struggling to say. 'No, no,' he said.

'I know. Jesus Christ, don't I know. But that ignorant bosthoon Sean O'Connor says he can't go on looking until he's made sure ...'

'How dare he even suggest ...'

'Where, Martin? Let's just rule it out for him ...'

'I suppose in the bedroom ...' Kit saw them walk into her father's bedroom, the cold room with the picture of the Pope over the bed. She stood with her hand at her throat, and realised that they were both watching her. 'Kit love, will you go back inside out of the cold, and sit by the fire with Emmet.'

'Yes,' she said. She watched as they went into her father's bedroom, and then she slipped into the kitchen.

Rita was busy pouring the whiskey into glasses that had cloves and lemon juice and sugar. 'It's too like a party for my taste,' she grumbled.

'Yes.' Kit stood beside the range. 'I know.'

'Should we put Emmet to bed do you think? Would your mother like that if she came home?'

'I think she would.' Neither of them noticed the if.

'Will you get him, or will I?'

'Could you go, Rita, then I'll go and sit with him?'

Rita carried the tray of whiskies out of the kitchen, and with a quick move Kit lifted the handle and opened the mouth of the range. The flames inside licked up at her as she threw in the envelope that said *Martin*, the letter that would mean her mother could not be buried in consecrated ground.

For a whole week every day was like the day before. Peter Kelly got a friend to come and work in the pharmacy, with instructions to bother Mr McMahon only when really necessary. It seemed that Lough Glass put off having problems that only the chemist could cure.

Clio's mother and her aunt were in and out of the McMahon house all the time. They were very polite to Rita. They kept saying that they didn't want to interfere, but they happened to have a pound of ham, or an apple tart, or an excuse to take the children up to their house. And the days seemed to fit into a sort of mad pattern.

They all slept with their doors open. Only Mother's door was closed. Every night Kit dreamed that her mother had come back, and said, 'I was in my room all the time, you never looked.'

But they did look. Everyone had looked in Mother's room. Including Sergeant O'Connor in case there were any clues that she had gone away.

There had been all kinds of questions. How many suitcases were there? Were any of them missing? What had Mother been wearing? Only a jacket, not an overcoat, not a raincoat. And the drawers were opened as well as the wardrobe. Were any clothes missing?

Kit felt very proud that everything was so tidy, so neat.

She felt that maybe Sergeant O'Connor would tell his wife that Mrs McMahon had beautiful sprigs of lavender in the drawers of nightdresses and slips. That her shoes were all polished and neat in a line under her dresses in the old wardrobe. That the brushes on the dressing table had silver handles matching the mirror. And most of all she was pleased that she had done what her mother would have wanted.

Yes, surely it was what Mother would have wanted.

There was hardly any time to think, but from time to time Kit stole into her own room to try and work it out. Was it possible that Mother, who always knew what she was doing, wanted that letter found? Should she have read it? Suppose there had been a last wish in it. But then it had not been addressed to her and if there were something for Daddy . . .

Kit felt young and frightened. But she knew she must have done the right thing. She had burned the note. Now when they found Mother's body it could be buried in the right place, and they could all go and put flowers on the grave.

There were divers in the lake, men who wore suits of rubber. Kit had not been allowed to go down and watch, but Clio told her. Clio was being very nice. Kit couldn't remember why she ever got annoyed with her.

'They want you to come up and stay with me,' Clio said over and over.

'I know and it's nice of you all, but . . . Daddy, you know. I don't like to leave Daddy alone.'

Clio understood. 'Would it help or be worse if I were to stay here?' she asked.

'It would be different, and we're trying to make things feel a bit the same, I think.'

Clio nodded in agreement. 'Can I do anything? I'd do anything to help.'

'I know you would.' And Kit did know.

'Well, think then.'

'Tell me what people say, tell me if there are things they wouldn't say in front of us . . .'

'Anything, even if it's not what you want to hear?'

'Yes.'

So Clio brought her all the gossip of Lough Glass, and Kit got a picture of the investigation. People had been asked if they had seen Mrs McMahon on the bus or at the train station, in the nearby town, out in the road looking for a lift, or in anyone else's car. The guards were ruling out the possibility of her having left the town alive and well.

'Wouldn't it be great if she had just lost her memory?' Clio said. 'If she were found in Dublin and didn't know who she was.'

'Yes,' Kit said flatly. She knew that this would not happen. She knew that Mother had not left Lough Glass that night. Because Mother had written a note to say why she was taking her own life.

'It could have been an accident,' Clio said, trying to put the minority view.

All Lough Glass was saying it had been coming for a long time. The poor woman was unbalanced, there was no way she would have taken the boat out on a night like that except to end her life.

'Of course it was an accident,' Kit said, eyes blazing.

When Mother's body was found it would be buried properly thanks to the good work Kit had done in thinking fast. It must always be considered an accident. Mother must never become a name like Bridie Daly, a ghost to frighten children, a voice calling in the reeds.

'If she's in heaven, she could see us now,' Clio said, looking at the ceiling.

'Of course she's in heaven,' Kit said, putting aside the fear that sometimes bubbled up to the surface that Mother might be in hell, suffering the torture of the damned for all eternity.

The callers to the house were legion.

Everyone in Lough Glass had something to offer: a word of comfort or hope, a special prayer or a story of someone who was missing for three weeks and had been found.

Sister Madeleine didn't call. But she never went visiting people. After a week, Kit went down the lane to the hermit's cottage. For the first time she went with no gift.

'You knew her, Sister Madeleine ... why did she do it?'

'I suppose she thought she knew how to manage a boat ...' To the hermit it was simple.

'But we *never* take the boat out alone. She never did before ...'

'She must have wanted to that night. It was a very beautiful night. The clouds kept racing across the moon like smoke from a fire. I stood at the window and watched for a long time ...'

'You didn't see Mother?'

'No child, I saw nobody.'

'She wouldn't be in hell, Sister Madeleine, would she?'

The nun put down the toasting fork and looked at Kit in amazement. 'You can't mean that you seriously think that for a moment?' she said.

'Well, it's a sin against Hope, isn't it? It's despair, the one sin that can't be forgiven.'

'Where did you hear that?'

'At school, I suppose. And at Mass, and at the retreat.' Kit was trying to draw up some kind of reinforcement.

'You heard nothing of the sort. But what makes you think that your poor mother took her own life?'

'She must have, Sister, she must have. She was so unhappy.'

'We're all unhappy, everyone's a bit unhappy.'

'No, but she really was, you don't know . . .'

Now Sister Madeleine was firm. 'I *do* know. I know a lot. Your mother would not have done such a thing.'

'But . . .'

'No buts, Kit. Please believe me, I know people. And suppose, just suppose, your mother did feel that there was no point in going on, I know as sure as we are both sitting here that she would have left a note to tell your father and you and your brother what had happened to make her feel this way, and to ask your forgiveness . . .' There was a silence. 'And there was no note,' Sister Madeleine said.

The silence between them was stifling. Kit was tempted to speak. Sister Madeleine would not tell, she would advise what to do. But it would be the end of everything if she told.

Kit said nothing. Sister Madeleine said it again. 'Since there was no note, then there was no way that your mother took her own life. Believe me, Kit, and sleep peacefully in your bed tonight.'

'Yes, Sister Madeleine,' said Kit, with a pain in her chest that she felt would be there for ever.

The sergeant was at their house that evening. He was talking to Rita in the kitchen. The conversation ended when Kit came in.

She looked from one to the other. 'Is there any news?'

'Nothing. Nothing new.' Rita spoke.

'I was just asking Rita if she was sure that you had all looked everywhere . . .'

'I assure you that if the mistress had left any account of her plans, whatever they might have been . . . it would have been a great relief to this family, and there is no way anyone would have kept it to themselves.'

The child looked pale to the point of fainting.

His voice softened. 'I'm sure that's right, Rita. We've all got our job to do. You have to swill out the pots, I have to ask hard questions in places where there's grief.' His tread was heavy as he went down the stairs to the street.

'Swilling pots, huh,' Rita said.

Her indignation made Kit smile. 'He has a great way of putting things,' she said.

'As if we didn't hunt the house high and low for a letter from the poor mistress.'

'And suppose we had found one . . . ?'

'Wouldn't it have stopped them all asking bosthoons at the bus office and the railway station did they see the mistress all dolled up in a head scarf . . . ? If there had been a letter, wouldn't the poor master be at rest instead of wandering like a lost soul?'

Kit sat very still. Rita didn't know everything. Rita was wrong. If the letter had been shown, Mother would be buried outside the walls of the cemetery. Like Bridie Daly.

Now when they found Mother's body it could be buried with honour. When they found it.

Brother Healy told the boys that young Emmet was coming back to class. 'If there's one mention or murmur out of anyone of you about *Mem Mem Memmet*, or the lad's stutter I'll knock your heads sideways off of your necks in a way that no one will ever fix them straight again.' He had a ferocious look about him.

'Would you think it's definite, Brother, that she's drowned?' asked Philip O'Brien, the young lad from the hotel.

'I think we can assume that, O'Brien, and we'll go on saying the three Hail Marys that her body will be found.'

'It's nine days now, Brother,' Philip said.

'Yes, but bodies have been found after a longer time than that . . . it's a deep lake, our lake. That's why you're all being warned about it night and day.'

'Brother, what would happen if . . . ?' said Michael Sullivan. The boy was about to ask what condition the body would be in. Would it have begun to deteriorate? The kind of thing boys of that age would love to discuss.

'Kindly open your Carty's Irish History, page fourteen,' he roared. Not for the first time he wished he taught the gentle girls up at Mother Bernard's school. The nun had told him they were organising a daily rosary in the school chapel for Kit McMahon's mother. Girls were a pleasure to teach. He had said it over and over. There was no comparison with what he had in front of him day in and day out.

Martin McMahon ate hardly anything. He said he got a scalding feeling once the food was swallowed. It was like a lump in his chest all day. But he was adamant that the children had their proper meals.

'I don't feel like a whole dinner,' Emmet had said.

'You need to keep your strength up, boy. Eat it up. Rita's made a grand spread for us.'

'And don't you need your strength, Daddy?' Emmet asked.

There was no answer.

Kit brought a cup of Bovril into the sitting room later on, and two fingers of soft buttered toast. She and Rita had decided that he might be able to manage this.

'Please, Father,' she urged. 'Please. What'll I do if you get sick? Then we'll have no one at all to be able to tell us what to do.' Her father obediently tried to swallow the spoonfuls. 'Would it be better . . .' she began. His eyes lifted slowly to know what she was going to say. Her father was moving like a man with a heavy weight attached to him. 'Would it have been better if Mother had left a note do you think . . . ?'

'Oh, a million times better . . .' he said. 'Then we'd know why . . . and what . . . she did.'

'It could have been an accident, something she didn't know was going to happen?'

'Yes, yes it could . . .'

'But even if it wasn't . . . It would be better to know . . . ?'

'Anything on earth would be better than this, Kit. Than wondering and worrying and wishing I had done something different. Even if they found Mother's body and we could bury her in a grave and go to pray there, then surely that would be better than this . . . ?'

She knelt beside him, her small hand on his. 'They'll have to find her body won't they, if she's in the lake . . . ?'

'It's a deep lake, it's a treacherous lake . . . They might not find her body for a very long time . . .'

'But the people who are looking . . . every day . . .'

'They'll be looking no more. The sergeant told me that they're going to have to call off the search.' His face was desolate.

'Father, you couldn't do any more . . . I know there was nothing you should have done. Mother told me. She told me she loved you and that she'd never hurt you.'

'Your mother was a saint, she was an angel. You'll always remember that, won't you Kit?'

'I'll always remember it,' Kit promised him.

She went through another night of broken sleep, of waking with a start to hear her mother say, 'It wasn't your letter . . . You should have left it the way it was . . .' Then she would see as clearly as if it were really in the room a picture of the grave with a simple wooden cross outside the churchyard walls. And the goats and sheep would walk over the grave of the woman who had not been allowed to have a Christian burial.

'They've called off the dragging of the lake.' Philip O'Brien's mother rarely left the hotel, but she knew all the business of the town.

'Does that mean that Kit's mother mightn't be drowned?' he asked with some hope. Kit had been white-faced for so long and there were big black lines under her eyes.

'No, it just means that she's very deep.' Mildred O'Brien spoke with no great emotion. She had not been close to Helen McMahon; she had found the woman a bit distant and hard to fathom.

'What will they do for a funeral then?' Philip asked. He didn't like the way his parents looked at each other.

'There might not be a funeral anyway,' his father said.

'Why not, if they found her body?'

'Ah, well. It doesn't do to be speaking ill of the dead,' said Dan O'Brien, in his most pious voice. 'But of course, if there was a sort of shadow over how she got into the lake, then the Church has to be very careful . . .' He could sense that Philip was about to speak again, so he headed him off. 'No need at all to be talking along those lines to the unfortunate McMahon children. It was none of their doing.'

The matter was closed.

*

Clio was being a good friend. She wasn't asking questions that couldn't be answered as she so often had in the past. She was coming up with no farfetched solutions. She was just there. And sometimes didn't talk at all. It was very comforting. In the old days it had often been Clio who came up with ideas of what they might do, or where their outings might take them. But nowadays she waited until Kit gave her the lead.

'I'd like to go for a walk down by the lake,' Kit said.

'Would you like me to come with you?' Clio was gentle. A while back she'd have tossed her head and given all the reasons why it might be a bad idea.

'If you've got the time.'

'I have the time,' Clio said.

They walked the main street together. Kit wanted to leave in her schoolbag and tell Rita that she would be late. Since the day of the disappearance, neither she nor Emmet had ever been half a minute later than their expected time of arrival. They knew too well the agony of waiting.

'Where will I say you are?' Rita asked.

'Say I'm with Clio, that's all.'

'Above in her house, is it?'

'Yes, with Clio.' Kit was impatient to be gone.

At the garage they saw Michael Sullivan with his friend Kevin Wall. They were two of the tougher pupils at the Brothers. Normally they would have shouted and jeered at Clio and Kit, but these weren't normal times. Kit saw Michael begin to form some comment and then choke it back; the McMahons were not fair game for shouts and taunts. Not after what had happened to them.

'Hello,' he said lamely.

His elder brother Stevie looked up from under the bonnet of a car. 'Get into the house and leave those girls alone,' he shouted.

He was good-looking in a way, hard to see because he had such filthy overalls on, and his hair was all grease from either the car or Brylcreem. Clio had once said that if somebody dressed Stevie Sullivan up properly he could pass as anybody.

He had a nice smile.

'It's okay,' Kit called. 'He only said "Hello".'

'That must be the first civil word he said to anybody.' Stevie was back into the car again.

Kit and Clio looked at each other and shrugged. It was nice to be defended and protected by a great, grown-up sixteen-year-old, but not when there wasn't any need. Michael Sullivan could be such a pain, and very rude, like asking what colour their knickers were. But to be honest, all he had said was a simple 'Hello'.

They walked past the hotel, nodding to Philip's father who stood at his doorway.

'It's dark for you girls to be heading down to the lake,' he said as he saw them turn down the small road.

'It's just for some fresh air. Everyone knows where we are,' Clio called back to him.

They walked companionably along the road that Kit's mother must have walked every day or night of her life.

'Going round the block' was what she called the walk. She either turned down at the hotel and came back up by the garda station, or else she did it the other way round. On finer days and on longer evenings she walked all the way around to the woods and the travellers' camp at one end of the lake, or else she might go in the other direction to Sister Madeleine's cottage and further. It was as if she had been looking for something. Something she couldn't find in the house over the pharmacy or in Lough Glass.

And it wasn't as if it was trying to get away from work. Helen McMahon had worked with Rita at the sewing machine, putting new linings on the curtains, turning the sheets so that the same bits didn't get all the wear. Rita and Helen McMahon made jam and marmalade; they bottled fruit and they made pickles. The kitchen shelves in McMahons' looked as if people were working on them day and night.

When she walked by the lake, it was not to escape work. It must have been so that she never had to sit down and think. What had she seen in those dark waters that was better to look at than touring the length of the street like the other women did?

Clio's mother would know every item to wear in the one clothes shop, P. Hanley, Drapery. Mrs Kelly often called in, even if she wasn't buying anything, to admire new soft cardigans, or blouses with embroidery on the collar. Other mothers would go into Joseph Wall and Son Hardware Merchants and look at new kitchen beaters, and baking tins.

But Kit's mother had no interest in these things. The paths and lanes and woods of the lake were the only places that seemed to gladden her heart.

'I wonder what took her down here all the time,' Kit said eventually as they came to the wooden pier where the boats were moored.

'She was happy here, you said that yourself,' Clio replied. Kit gave her a grateful glance. Clio was being so unexpectedly nice, saying the right thing always instead of the wrong thing. It was as if somebody had told her how to behave. Clio began to speak hesitantly. 'Kit, . . . you know my Aunt Maura . . . ?'

'Yes?' Kit was watchful again. Was this some of Clio's old style coming to the surface again? Was she going to boast of her nice settled normal family, her plump cheerful aunt who had wanted them all to play golf, something Kit had been going to discuss with her mother four long weeks ago?

'Well, she's gone back to Dublin you know . . .'

'Yes, I know . . .'

'And before she went she gave me some money. She said I was to get you a treat, and I'd know what treat to get . . .'

'Yes, well . . .' Kit was at a loss.

'But I don't know, Kit. I don't know.'

'It was kind of her . . .'

'She said it wouldn't cure anything, but it might distract us. Sweets, new socks, or a record ... whatever I thought you'd like ...'

'I'd like a record,' Kit said suddenly.

'Well, that's great ... We could go to the town on Saturday and get one.'

'Is there enough money for that?' Kit was taking the bus fare into account, and the lemonade and biscuits they would have afterward.

'Yes, there's plenty ... She gave me three pounds.'

'Three pounds!' They both stood in the wind, awed by the huge amount of money. Kit's eyes filled with tears. Clio's Aunt Maura must have thought that things were very bad indeed if she gave that much money to distract them.

'Stevie?'

'What is it?'

'Stevie, I want to tell you something.'

'I'm busy.'

'You're always busy, you never have time for anything except the cars.'

'Well, isn't that what I have to give my time to, not let everyone go on thinking that if you give your money into Sullivan's it'll be spent on drink instead of on spare parts, like the way it used to be.'

'Promise not to bite the head off of me.'

'No, I won't promise that. It might well be a thing that your head has to be bitten off for.'

'Then I won't tell you.' Michael was definite now.

'Thanks be to God,' said Steve Sullivan. He had enough on his mind. He had to get cleaned up and dressed; he had a date to meet a girl for the first time. Deirdre Hanley had agreed to go to the pictures with him. She was seventeen, a whole year older, and she would expect him to make advances. Stevie Sullivan was anxious to do it right. It was a relief not to have to waste time biting his brother's head off over some misdemeanour that would undoubtedly come to light with a stormy visit from Brother Healy to his mam.

'What time will you be home?' Mrs Hanley, the draper, felt there was something that didn't sit right on this outing.

'Aw, Mam. How many times do I have to tell you? Won't I be back on the bus.'

'Yes, and I'll be looking out to see you getting off it,' her mother said in a heavy warning tone.

Deirdre nodded meekly. There would be no problem about that. Stevie would drive her in his car for a bit of a court, she imagined, and then pick up the bus a mile out of Lough Glass. Her mother could be as suspicious as she liked; there was no way she could be caught. Deirdre wiped off the lipstick she had been rehearsing; she wouldn't let them see her leave the house too dolled up. That would definitely make them think she was on a different kind of outing than the one she had said.

Meeting a group of girls in the cinema in the town.

*

'Come with me to Paddles'.'

'No, Peter.'

'Martin, she's not going to come back, she's not going to come in that door you know. I know it.'

'No, I must stay here.'

'For ever, Martin? For ever and ever? Is that what Helen would have wanted for you?'

'You didn't know her.' Martin was flustered.

'I knew her well enough to know that she would want you to try and behave as normal, not turn yourself into a hermit.' There was silence. 'We have one hermit in the place already. Lough Glass wouldn't be able to afford two.' Peter Kelly was rewarded with a watery smile.

'I was wrong, Peter. You did know her. Did she ever ... was there ever ... ?'

'She never told me anything. She never asked me anything that you should know about ... I swear it. Like I have sworn it for twenty-eight days to you. You ask me every single day, and every single day I say the same thing.'

'Do I ask you every day? Every day?' Martin McMahon looked pitiful.

'No, I exaggerate. You may have missed out a few.'

'I'll not come for a pint until they find her body, Peter.'

'Then I will be drinking alone for some considerable time, won't I?' The doctor looked resigned.

'Why do you say that?' The words seemed bleak and full of horror.

Peter Kelly wiped his brow. 'Jesus, Martin, it's only her body. Her soul, her spirit, has gone long ago, soared way up over us all. You know that, man, you know it. Won't you admit it?'

Martin wept, his shoulders shook.

Peter stood beside him, unwilling to reach out. Theirs had not been a friendship where a man held another man through a storm of tears. Eventually the shaking stopped.

Martin looked up, his face tear-stained and red. 'I suppose I won't admit it because I keep hoping ... Let's go to Paddles'.'

Emmet told Sister Madeleine that he couldn't concentrate on poetry. It all seemed to remind him of ... of ... well, what had happened.

'Well, that's all right, isn't it?' Sister Madeleine said. 'You wouldn't want to forget your mother.'

'But I don't seem to be able to say it, feel it, the way I used to ...' His stutter was as bad as it had ever been. Sister Madeleine never gave any sign that he was taking any extra time.

'Well, don't say it at all.' To Sister Madeleine everything was simple.

'Don't I have to? Isn't this a lesson?'

'Not a real lesson. More a chat. It's you reading to me because my old eyes can't see to read all that well by the candle and firelight.'

'Are you very old, Sister Madeleine?'

'No, not very old. Much older than you, much older than your mother.' Sister Madeleine was the only person who ever mentioned Mother; everyone else avoided the subject.

'Do you know what happened to Mummy?' he said hesitantly.

'No child, I don't.'

'But you sit here all the time and look out at the lake . . . you might have seen her falling out of the boat . . . maybe?'

'No Emmet, I didn't. Nobody saw her, it was dark remember . . .'

'Would it have been terrible . . . like choking . . . ?' He couldn't ask this to anyone else . . . they would have hushed him up . . . or soothed him down.

Sister Madeleine appeared to give the matter some thought. 'No, I think it would have been very peaceful, you know, a lot of dark water just falling over, like silk or velvet, sweeping you away . . . I don't think it would have been very frightening . . .'

'And would she have been sad . . . ?'

'I don't think so. She might have been worried about you and about Kit . . . Mothers always worry, you know, about silly things like people wearing warm, dry socks and doing their homework and having enough to eat . . . All mothers I have known worried about those kinds of things . . . but not, not when she was drowning . . .' If Sister Madeleine noticed that Emmet's stutter had gone she gave no sign. 'No, no, of course not, but just hoping that you'd all be all right, that you'd carry on . . . that kind of thing, I'd imagine.'

'Imagine her thinking of that . . .' His voice was shaking.

Sister Madeleine looked at him expectantly, as if she were waiting for him to say something else, something positive. And right on cue Emmet McMahon said, 'Well, she needn't have been worrying. Of course we can carry on.'

Father Baily gritted his teeth when he saw the McMahons at Mass on Sunday. He was fast running out of words of consolation for the family. There were just so many times a priest could explain about things being God's will to a bereaved family.

And the more he heard the less he could accept it as the will of God. It was much more the will of that poor disturbed woman Helen McMahon, who had come to Confession to him and knelt in the dark, telling him that her heart was heavy. What kind of way was that to confess sins? Father Baily felt that he had often given the woman absolution when she had not really sought it, when there was no contrition, no firm purpose of amendment.

He couldn't recall now what she had to tell.

If only people knew how similar and unremarkable their sins were to a confessor. But what did stand out was that she seemed to think she was not in control of her life. She accused herself of feeling distant, detached, of being an outsider instead of a participator. But she had not followed his suggestions of joining the sodality, getting herself on the flower-arranging committee, or cooking for the sales of work.

After Mass he greeted his parishioners by name.

'There you are, Dan. Cold day, isn't it?'

'It is Father. Perhaps you'll come and have something to warm you up in the hotel?'

'Well, I'd love to, but I have a few sick calls to make after my breakfast.'

Father Baily would have liked nothing better than to sit in the obscurity of the back room of the Central Hotel and have three brandies to keep out the cold. But a breakfast table had been set up by his houskeeper, and then he had to go up to Mother Bernard's convent to see an elderly nun, out to a farm in the back of beyond to bring the Blessed Sacrament to a farmer who had not thought to cross the door of a church until he got a diagnosis of terminal cancer and now wanted the Church to come to him.

And everywhere he went, people asked him what would happen when Helen McMahon's body was found. Always he had been vague and hopeful, committing himself to nothing, saying that the poor woman must always be in everyone's prayers.

He made a great point of shaking the hand of Martin McMahon warmly. 'Good man Martin, a tower of strength, that's what you are. I pray every day that you'll get the grace you need ...' The man looked pale and wretched. Father Baily wondered what good his prayers were doing.

'Thank you, Father.'

'And Kit and Emmet. Good, good.' The words were meaningless, he knew it. But what could he give in the way of comfort? The only merciful thing was the woman had left no note. When they found the body, the coroner would surely be discreet enough to talk of accidents and misadventure. They could bury Helen McMahon in the churchyard where she belonged.

Sister Madeleine was at Mass, too, quietly in the back of the church, a grey cloak wrapped around her thin shoulders.

'Will you come back and have your Sunday dinner with us?' Kit said to her suddenly.

'Thank you child, but no. I'm not much good at going to people's houses.'

'We need you,' Kit said simply.

'You have each other.'

'Yes, but it's not enough these days. It's gone on too long. We just sit and look at each other.'

'Wouldn't you ask one of your friends, Clio ... young Philip O'Brien from the hotel ...'

'You're my friend. Please come.'

'Thank you. That would be very nice,' said Sister Madeleine.

Rita carved the meat, a big piece of beef from Hickeys.

'I never saw so much meat in my life.' Sister Madeleine was full of wonder.

'It's not extravagant. It's for today, then cold tomorrow, and mince on Tuesday, and there's often enough for rissoles on a Wednesday.' Rita was proud of the way she ran the house.

Sister Madeleine looked around the kitchen where they sat at the table, a home with a tragedy hanging over it so heavily you could almost see it there in the air.

'The travellers are still looking, you know,' she said. They all seemed to sit up startled, shocked that a visitor was mentioning what everyone else wanted to avoid. 'They go all around the lake. If there's anything to be seen they'll see it.'

There was a total silence. The McMahons were not able to respond when someone spoke about the subject uppermost in their minds. Sister Madeleine waited. She never minded silences; she didn't rush to fill them with words.

'That's good of them ... to take such an interest,' Martin said eventually.

Sister Madeleine appeared not to notice his unease. 'Helen was always very courteous to them on her walks, she knew their names and the names of their children. She often asked them about their ways, the language they spoke.' Kit looked at her, amazed. She had never known this about her mother. And yet Sister Madeleine spoke with sincerity: she wasn't making up a story to console them, to wrap the dead up in soothing phrases. 'They know the need for a funeral,' Sister Madeleine said. 'They have wonderful funerals for their own people. They travel all over the country to be there. It's a way of saying goodbye, of finding a resting place up in the churchyard.'

'That's if ...' Kit began.

Sister Madeleine interrupted: 'That's if they find her ... but they will ... either the travellers or someone else, and then you'll be able to pray at her grave ...' Sister Madeleine's tone was firm.

She was having no dealings with the idea that Helen McMahon would be buried outside the walls of the churchyard. A grave without a tombstone. Marking her as someone who had taken her own life.

That night Kit sat with her father.

'It's so long now ... it's over a month ... Would there be any of Mother left to bury?'

'I asked Peter Kelly that, Kit, the other night in Paddles' bar. He said we mustn't think of that, we must think your mother's spirit and soul left her that night, and what's left of the body doesn't matter.'

'I suppose he's right.'

'I suppose he is, Kit, I suppose he is.'

Mother Bernard was called out of class.

The conversation in the classroom rose to a high level. There was great excitement anyway because Deirdre Hanley, a senior girl, had been seen in a hedge with Stevie Sullivan, sort of wrapped around him, not just kissing mind, but more, much more. They were so anxious for more details that they didn't notice Mother Bernard coming back and were startled by the crack of her voice, like a whip across the classroom.

'I expected big, grown-up girls of your age to be able to continue with your work. But I was wrong. Very, very wrong.' They had crept shamefacedly back to their places. Mother Bernard's face was white. She must be very angry indeed. 'This time, however, I shall put you on your honour. Each girl is to take out her composition book and write one full page about Advent. The season of waiting, the preparation for Christmas.' They looked at each other in despair. A whole page about Advent. What was there to say about it except that it went on for ever and was nearly as bad as Lent? 'And there shall be no blots, and no big spaces between words. This will be a work of which we will all be proud.' Mother Bernard spoke with menace in her tones.

They picked up their pens, knowing that this time she meant it. There would be no more news about Deirdre Hanley at this time.

'Katherine McMahon, could you come with me for a moment,' Mother Bernard said to Kit.

Brother Healy had told Kevin Wall that he would be a very fortunate lad if he were to see the day out without feeling the weight of a stick on both his hands. The boy looked fearful, but not fearful enough. He busied himself making pellets out of blotting paper soaked in ink.

Brother Healy was called to the door.

'I'll be back in five minutes. Is that clear?' he roared at his class. And then went to find young Emmet McMahon and tell him what he had to tell him.

No training could prepare you for this kind of job. Brother Healy sighed to himself as his cassock swished down the corridors to the room where second class were sitting with Brother Doyle, not knowing what lay ahead.

By nightfall everyone in Lough Glass knew.

A body had been found in the reeds. It was already badly decomposed. There wasn't any way that anyone would have to identify it.

Dr Kelly had gone to his friend Martin McMahon. Everyone heard and said that there was no way he should look on something that bore no relation to what his wife had been. The state pathologist had come from Dublin; he had agreed. It would take some days, they were told.

A section of the lake had been cordoned off. People told each other how they had heard the ambulance coming. As if an ambulance would be any use after a month, but still, what other way could the poor woman's body have been brought to the morgue in the hospital?

Everyone had a story to tell about the McMahon family.

Kathleen Sullivan from the garage said that the lights were on in that house all night. None of them must have gone to bed. Clio Kelly said that things were much different there now, more normal. They had all stopped speaking in funny tight voices. Mrs Hanley from the draper's said she had gone to pay her condolences and that very pushy maid of theirs hadn't let her in, had said the family were suffering from nervous exhaustion.

Mrs Dillon in the newsagent's said that she had a great demand for Mass cards, because now that there was a body and there was going to be a funeral, everyone wanted to show their respect by having a Mass said for the repose of the soul of Helen McMahon.

Sergeant Sean O'Connor had to say that the men who came down from Dublin from garda headquarters were as nice a pair of fellows as he had ever come across.

They told him that he had completed all the paperwork very well, and that he wasn't to worry himself over the length of time it took to find the body. This was wild country around here. 'Indian country,' one of them suggested. They didn't know how a man could live in such a place, with nothing going on. Sean O'Connor didn't like this, he felt it was a bit disparaging, but they told him that Dublin was full of drawbacks too.

And they stayed with him in Paddles' bar until an unconscionable time in the morning, nodding to the rest of Lough Glass who were drinking late.

'You know everyone in the place,' one of the guards said to him.

'Indeed I do, and all about them.'

'Did you know the deceased?'

'Of course I did.'

'Why did she do it do you think?'

'Well, we don't know if she did.' Sean O'Connor had a caution that no number of pints could dislodge.

'No, we don't know she did, but we think she did. What drove her to it, do you think?'

'She wasn't right for here. She didn't settle; she sort of floated along the surface. Maybe she was too good-looking for the place.'

'Had she a fellow at all?'

'God, you couldn't have a fellow in Lough Glass if you were a married woman. If you're a single woman it's hard enough with every eye in the place watching you . . .'

'So she wasn't crossed in love, no hint of a baba or anything . . .'

'No.' Sergeant O'Connor was suddenly alert. 'They didn't find anything like that, did they?'

'No.' The young Dublin guard was cheerful. 'No, I'd say it was all far too late to discover anything like that, even if it had existed. Will we have another, do you think?'

Philip O'Brien called to the McMahon house to know if Kit would like him to sit with her for a bit. 'You know, like the night she got lost,' he said.

Kit's eyes filled with tears. That was such a nice way of putting it. Mother had got lost.

'Thanks very much, Philip,' she said, and reached out and stroked his cheek. 'You're very kind and good. But I think we'd . . .'

He interrupted her. 'I know. I just wanted you to know I was always here down the road, like.' He went down the stairs again, and felt the spot on his face where Kit McMahon had stroked him.

It was oddly peaceful in the house, better than it had been for a month. They knew the formalities would take some days, but the funeral would be next weekend. They had something they could do for Mother now. They could give her a good farewell.

'Are you sorry they found her, Father? Did you hope she might have been alive somewhere, kidnapped even?' Kit asked.

'No, no. I knew that wasn't going to be the case.'

'So it's better that she's found?'

'Yes, it's much better. It's bad enough to have Mother dead, without leaving her for ever in the lake. This way we can go to her grave.' There was a long silence. 'It was a terrible accident, Kit, you know that,' her father said.

'I know,' said Kit. And she looked into the flames, big red and gold flames licking upwards.

They were right in thinking that the formalities would not be long drawn out. Since Doctor Kelly, who was the local doctor, had identified the body, there had been only brief consultations with the pathologist. There was no question of foul play or of anyone else being involved.

Nor was they any mention of taking a life while of unsound mind. If there was doubt about the advanced state of decomposition of the body, it was never aired publicly. Helen McMahon had only been in the lake a month, but it was winter time, the fish in that part of the lake . . . well, there was no need for details.

And who else could it have been? Nobody from these parts had disappeared. The coroner spoke of the great need to clear the inland waterways of Ireland. Too many tragic accidents had happened among the reeds and overgrown parts of lakes.

And then the body of Helen McMahon was released for burial.

On the day of the funeral, Clio arrived at their house. 'I brought you a mantilla,' she said.

'What's that?'

'It's like a black lace veil, a bit like a handkerchief. It's what Spanish people and posh Catholics everywhere wear on their heads when they don't want hats and when headscarfs aren't right.'

'Is it for me to wear at the Church?'

'If you'd like to. It's a present from Auntie Maura.'

'She's very nice, isn't she?' Usually Kit found something to criticise about Clio's aunt.

Clio seemed pleased. 'She is, and she always knows what to do.'

Kit nodded. It was true. Rita had told her last night that Mrs Kelly's sister had come to advise her about the food to serve. She had suggested a big ham, and to ask Mr Hickey at the butcher's to cook it for them. Rita had said they'd never do that, but Clio's aunt had been firm. Theirs was good custom, always at the shop. The Hickeys would be happy to do something to help. Let them bring it up on Sunday afternoon, when it was needed, before the people came back from the churchyard.

Rita said it was a great help. She didn't want to be mounting guard on a huge pot and smelling the whole house with it. She could concentrate now on asking people to bake home-made bread, and asking Mr O'Brien from the hotel to lend them three dozen glasses.

And yet Kit felt somehow that it was disloyal to Mother to say that Clio's Aunt Maura was being a great help. Mother hadn't liked her; she had never said so, but Kit was sure of it. But it was idiotic to think that Mother would want her to carry on a distance that was never even spoken of.

Would Mother like Kit to wear the mantilla? Kit stood still, wondering if Mother had thought about her funeral at all, before she had gone and done what she did. When she was writing the letter, had she paused to think about how Lough Glass would bury her?

A surge of anger passed across Kit.

'Are you okay?' Clio looked worried.

'Yes, I'm fine.'

'Aunt Maura said I wasn't to hang around you in case you wanted to be by yourself.' Clio looked uncertain, her big blue eyes full of concern.

Kit was covered in guilt. This was her best friend, who couldn't do more for her. Why was she always being so prickly and defensive towards her? 'I'd love you to stay,' she said. 'I need you. It would be great to have you there.' Clio's smile lit up the room. 'Do you have a mantilla too?'

'No, Aunt Maura said it was just for you.' Kit put it on. 'It looks terrific. Your mother would have been proud of you.'

And then for the first time in front of her friend Kit let herself go and wept.

The hymns at a funeral were always sad. But on this wet winter afternoon, when the wind whipped up the lake and the church was cold and draughty, Father Baily thought that they had never seemed sadder.

Perhaps it was the round simple face of Martin McMahon, bewildered and unbelieving. Maybe the two children, the girl in a Spanish type veil, the boy who had a speech difficulty which was cured and had got as bad as ever again.

Father Baily looked around the church.

The cast was assembled as usual. The choir sang 'I'll sing a hymn to Mary'. They sang the first verse and the whole congregation joined in for the second.

> 'O, lily of the valley,
> O mystic flower what tree
> What flower e'en the fairest
> Is half as fair as thee . . .'

Between the coughs and splutters they sang, eyes misted with tears for the woman who had died out on their lake.

When he had been saying his Office the previous night, Father Baily had thought about Helen McMahon's death. Suppose she had taken her own life? But he had told himself firmly that God did not expect him to act as judge, jury and executioner. He was merely the priest to say the funeral mass and to commit her body to its resting place. It was 1952. It wasn't the Middle Ages. Let her rest in peace.

The Sullivans stood together, Kathleen and her two sons. Stevie was busy catching the eye of Deirdre Hanley from the drapery shop. Kathleen glared at him. A church was not the place to make eyes at a girl. A funeral was not the time. Michael was kicking the front of his shoe, trying to get some of the loose bits off. She gave him a sharp jab to get him to stop.

Michael had been a worry to her for a while. He kept moping about and asking her strange questions to which there were no answers. Like, if you knew something that other people didn't know, what should you say? Or, suppose everybody else thought one thing and you knew another thing, were you meant to tell them the other thing? Kathleen Sullivan had scant patience with such imponderables. Last weekend she had told Michael she hadn't a notion of what he was talking about, and would he please consult his older brother. She was certain it must be about sex in some shape or form, and Stevie would give him the basic information he needed. At any rate, he seemed to be less agitated now. She hoped that Stevie had spoken with some kind of authority. She didn't at all like the glances he was giving that big bold strap of a Hanley girl, who was far too old for him, and a forward madam if ever there was one.

Kevin Wall thought that it must be desperate to have your mother all eaten up by fish. That's what had happened to Emmet McMahon's mother. And all on the night that he and Michael Sullivan had gone out on the lake. They might have been near to it happening. Michael had been very worried. He said they should tell people that it was they who had taken the boat out that night. Kevin had been against it. They'd get the arses beaten off them, he said. Michael, who didn't have a father to beat the arse off him, said maybe they shouldn't have guards and everyone looking for Emmet McMahon's mother when she hadn't gone near the boat. They had been playing in it and rowing up and down by the pier when it slipped away from them and they couldn't reach it. It had been blown into the middle of the lake and then the waves had overturned it. Kevin said it didn't matter one way or the other, but Michael had been all frightened.

He said with guards involved they could all end in gaol. Anyway, it had all turned out fine. Kevin had been right, after all, to say nothing. Michael Sullivan was half mad. Of course, his father had died in an asylum. Not that Kevin would mention that.

Maura Hayes and her sister Lilian stood in good dark coats and their sober velour hats. Peter blew his nose loudly many times during the Requiem Mass. Young Clio and Anna stood beside them for the final hymn.

'Kit is holding up very well,' Lilian said approvingly to her daughter. 'Isn't she very composed that she doesn't cry.'

'She's cried a lot. Maybe all her tears are gone,' Clio said.

Lilian looked at her in surprise. Clio was not always so sensitive. Perhaps the child had more feeling than Lilian had realised.

As the crowds came out into the biting cold wind, Stevie Sullivan managed to be near Deirdre Hanley. 'Will you come to my house . . . you know, after this?'

'Your house? You must be mad!' she said.

'My mother's going to be across the road in McMahon's.'

'Yes, so's mine.'

'So, we'll see from the window when they're all leaving and you can slip home.'

'See from where?' She ran her tongue across her lips.

'My bedroom ...'

'You're joking!'

'A bed's just like a sofa, isn't it?' he said.

'And better than a car seat,' said Deirdre.

At the grave, Kit spoke to Sister Madeleine. 'Will her soul be at peace now?' she asked.

'Her soul has always been at peace,' said Sister Madeleine. 'It's the rest of us will be at peace because we are seeing her laid to rest.' In her mind Kit saw the white envelope with the word *Martin* on it. Sister Madeleine took her arm and held it tight. 'I beg you think only of what your mother would want of you, to be a strong young woman looking always to the future and not to the past.' Kit stared at Sister Madeleine in amazement. Her mother had indeed wanted that for her, said it in almost those words. 'That's what you must think of now. That's how you make her feel at peace, knowing that you did what she wanted you to do.'

Kit looked around and saw all the people of Lough Glass preparing to say a decade of the Rosary for Helen McMahon. Kit had made this possible. She had burned the letter that would have meant her mother being put in an unmarked grave outside the place where Christians were fit to lie.

She held her shoulders back.

'I'm doing the best I can, Sister,' she said and reached for her father's big cold hand and Emmet's small trembling one, as they stood at the grave in the rain.

3

Helen McMahon reached for another cigarette. She needed to calm herself. She needed to think.

She did not believe that Martin could have reacted this way. She had fulfilled every promise that she had ever made him, telling him that she could not love him fully, as she knew there would be no forgetting Louis Gray. She had said that she would be faithful to Martin and live with him and be as good a wife as she could possibly be, if he allowed her freedom to walk and think and escape from the stifling boredom of a small town.

She had sworn she would not leave him without telling him exactly why. She had written it all out, painstakingly, in a letter. And put it on his bed before she left. She had told him about the child. About how she had met Louis again, how he had said it had been a mistake ever to have left her. They must try for their chance of happiness.

She would take nothing. Nothing that Martin had given her.

It had taken her a week to write that letter, the week before she left. She said he could say whatever he liked, and she would go along with it. That she had gone away with Louis. That she was visiting relatives. That she was ill and needed some treatment. It was all she could give him, the choice to cover her departure with whatever story he wanted.

It wasn't much to give him in terms of dignity or face-saving when you considered how much she was taking.

She had given him the address and phone number of an organisation that rescued Irish girls in trouble in London. There was a grim irony about it. That's what she was in many ways, an Irish girl in trouble. She had said she would be there every day from four to six. She had said she would wait to hear what he wanted to say.

They had arrived on the afternoon of October 30th, tired and wet, she still nauseous with her pregnancy. She had sat by the phone as she had promised for four days. There had been no call.

She had said that she would not get in touch with him, she would wait until he had decided what to do. Her letter had been very firm on that point. She would give him time, all the time he wanted to digest the news and to respond to it as he saw fit. Twenty times she had tried to tell him and on every occasion he had smiled his foolish loving smile, or made a silly child's joke.

The only way she could let him know the serious nature of her decision was to write it to him. And now, in spite of her impatience to know his reaction and what he planned to tell the children, she was sitting here in agony. But fairness meant that she must keep her word. Now she couldn't telephone ... she could not write again.

The days of her new life, the life she had run to with Louis Gray, the man she had always loved, were nightmare days.

She had steeled her heart for the tearful call from Martin begging her to return.

She had prepared explanations for the accusations that she was a monster to leave her children. She was having another child now, her responsibility was to the future. She knew he would not lower himself to get the children to beseech her to come back. He would not use them as pawns. If he were reasonable and calm, she might be able to give him advice.

She had rehearsed how she would tell him that people would forget in time, the way they had forgotten about so many other people who had left Lough Glass for this reason or that. There would be questions for a few weeks, then the interest would die down. He would not be a figure of scandal or of pity and scorn.

And she owed him this ... she would co-operate with anything he wanted her to do.

And she waited for four days and four nights without hearing anything at all.

'Ring him,' Louis had urged.

'No.' She was adamant.

'Jesus, Helena, it's Monday night. You've been gone since Wednesday. He'll have us both in a madhouse with these tactics.'

'They're not tactics, Louis. Martin isn't like that.'

She looked at him, his thick dark hair, his handsome face white with worry. He wore a slate blue jacket exactly the colour of his eyes. He was the most handsome man she had ever met in her life. After she had seen him nobody else counted.

She still could not believe that he had come back for her. She believed him when he said it had all been a mistake, his own greedy mistake to run away with a rich woman. Helen knew it was true.

His face had lines on it now. They made him more handsome than ever, but they were lines of sadness. And what was so wonderful was that he was so grateful she had forgiven him, that she had put behind her his desertion and betrayal.

'I don't deserve you,' he had said a thousand times since he had come back to find her. 'I wouldn't blame you if you sent me away,' he had said.

Send him away?

Louis Gray, the man she had wanted since she was twenty-three? The man she had still wanted on the day she married Martin McMahon when she was twenty-five? The man she had thought of with her eyes tightly closed every time that Martin made love to her.

Send him away?

She would have wandered the world looking for him had she thought that there was a chance to get him back.

But he had come to look for *her*. He had come secretly to Lough Glass, to beg her to believe that his eyes were open now. There was just one love in the world for everyone, Louis had said. He had been so wrong to think that he could create the same thing with another woman.

It appeared that Helen might have been wrong to try and create it with Martin McMahon, kindly, honourable, and dull chemist in Lough Glass. Then it was clear to both of them that they had to seize it and run. The stolen hours in the spring and summer around the woods of Lough Glass had been proof that the magic was there. The discovery that Helen was pregnant had been the spur they needed.

They were like teenage lovers in their excitement about the adventure ahead, irresponsible, uncaring about the world around them as they hid from the inquisitive eyes of the small town. Would they disguise themselves when they went to London? It would be just their luck to meet someone from Lough Glass – Lilian over on a secret expedition to have her facial hair dealt with, Mrs Hanley to look at exotic lingerie for her drapery shop. They giggled with each other at the madness of it all, yet when they did arrive Helen had gone immediately to the hairdresser to have her hair cut. It was more than an effort to disguise herself; it was also the start of a new life.

Helen watched her long dark curls fall to the ground and she felt the wasted years slipping away. She looked younger, stronger now. And Louis loved it. That was the important thing. Not that anyone would find them in this part of London. Irish visitors would go to Piccadilly or Oxford Street, or Camden Town to see their relations. They wouldn't come to this street in Earl's Court.

They had been so lucky to find the flat. It was a room, really, in a tall house which the landlady was in the process of doing up. But so far she had only got around to doing up one floor. She certainly hadn't got around to this room, and by the time she would manage to include that in her plans for making the place more elegant Helen and Louis would be far away, in a house more suitable for a family.

They would be living with their child. In the meantime, this was their home, a room in Earl's Court, London SW5. Helen had to keep saying it over and over to herself. A City so big that you had to tell people whether you were north or south or east or west in it. You had to give your area a number as well as a name.

After thirteen long years in Lough Glass, a place with one street that had little laneways off down to the lake ... This was heady excitement.

It was a small room certainly, with a sofa that turned into a bed. There were few adornments: a couple of pictures of Alice Springs left by the previous tenants, who had been Australian, a small table and two wooden chairs. The carpet was threadbare, and the paper that lined the chest of drawers was grimy and smelled of must. The sink had a rust mark where the tap had dripped and the little shelf beside it, which did as dressing table and draining board, had a torn piece of oilcloth. But it was their home, the home she had always wanted to live in with Louis Gray.

Four days away from their previous life, Helen had forgotten the carved furniture in her bedroom: the mahogany wardrobes that had belonged to Martin's parents, the graceful dressing table with its ball and claw legs. They were part of something that was far behind. Or that should have been far behind if Martin had played his part in the bargain.

Louis was very certain what was happening. 'I don't blame the man, truly I don't. We made him suffer, now he's making us sweat. It's what I'd do if someone stole you away from me.' He hunkered on the floor beside her and looked up at her.

Helen didn't want to argue it any further. She had lived for thirteen years with Martin McMahon. It was not in his character to let people sweat, to make them suffer. What she had most feared was that he would telephone her and cry. That he would promise to be better, different, kinder, stronger ... whatever she wanted him to be. 'I suppose he *got* the letter?' she said suddenly.

'You said you left it where he couldn't miss it.'

'I know I did ...'

'And no one else would have taken it ... it *was* addressed to him?'

'No one else would have taken it.' Helen had been over this ground before. It wasn't helping her and it was beginning to irritate Louis. She forced it out of her mind. 'I love you, Louis,' she said.

'And I love you, Helena.'

He had always called her that. It was special between them. She remembered helping Kit with her history homework – the island where Napoleon spent his exile. Saint Helena. Like my name, she had said.

'You're Helen.' Kit had corrected her sharply as if there was something dangerous about Mother having a different name. It was as if the child had known.

'Will you take me out on the town?' she smiled at him. She hoped her eyes didn't look as old and tired as they felt from inside.

'Now you're talking,' he said. He got their raincoats and handed her the red square she wore to cover her hair. She tied it like the gypsy woman had tied hers. Jaunty, cheerful. 'You are so beautiful,' he said.

She bit her lip. She had dreamed so often that he would come back for her. It was impossible to take it in now that he had.

They went down the stairs, past the bathroom they shared with three other flats. There were rules on the wall, in a plastic frame so that the writing could not fade with the steam. Hot water from the geyser had to be paid for. The place was to be left as you would like to find it. Sponge bags were not to be left in the bathroom.

Helen's thoughts never went back to the big comfortable bathroom over McMahon's pharmacy, where the thick towels were warmed by the radiator, where there was a woolly mat to keep chilly feet warm.

'This is great fun,' Helen said as she ran down the stairs lightly. She saw from his smile that she was doing the right thing. Louis Gray loved life to be easy, to be free from furrowed brows.

Ivy looked out from her flat near the door. She was a small, wiry woman with short pepper-and-salt hair turning grey. She had a lined face but a bright smile. It was hard to know whether she was nearer forty or fifty. She wore cotton overalls with tiny pink and purple flowers on them. She had the look of someone who had always worked very hard and who could take on any task. Certainly, she found the business of being a landlord to many varied tenants no strain. She had a glass-fronted door with a thick curtain so that she could observe the comings and goings of her tenants.

'Off out to enjoy yourselves?' she said.

Helen didn't resent Ivy Brown's questions. They weren't like the enquiries back in Lough Glass. 'Going for a walk by the lake, Mrs McMahon?' 'Off on your own again, Helen?' 'And where have you been this afternoon?' She hated every greeting from Mrs Hanley of the draper's, from Dan O'Brien of the Central Hotel, from Lilian Kelly the doctor's wife, with the eyes that knew too much.

Ivy Brown was different. She only checked the stairs so that Australian youngsters wouldn't bring in a dozen more tenants to sleep on the floor, or that no one sublet so that some could use the room by day and some by night depending on the shifts they worked.

'He's taking me out to see a bit of London, Mrs Brown.' She flung her head back and laughed at the pleasure of it all.

'Call me Ivy, dear. Otherwise we're all Mrs Gray and Mrs Brown, a bit gloomy,' Ivy laughed.

Louis stepped forward to shake her hand, to make the change from acquaintance to friend. 'Louis and Helena Gray,' he said.

Helen felt a thrill as he said it. Like a sixteen-year-old, not a middle-aged runaway wife, expecting someone else's child.

'Lena Gray,' said Ivy Brown thoughtfully. 'That's a lovely name. Sounds like a film star. You *could* be a film star, love, and all.'

They walked hand in hand down to Earl's Court Road, and on the Old Brompton Road. Everywhere seemed to be commemorating somewhere or something important. Baron's Court . . . and the places named after battles – Waterloo, and Trafalgar. The places sounded noble and dignified somehow, especially if you had lived for years in a place where people talked about Paddles' Lane, meaning the narrow boreen down to the lake behind a bar run by a man who had great big feet.

'We'll be very happy here,' she said, smiling at Louis and squeezing his arm.

'I know we will,' he said. A shopkeeper was bringing in the unsold fruit and vegetables that he had on display outside on the pavement. A flower fell on the ground. Louis picked it up. 'Is this any use to you?' he asked the shopkeeper. 'Or shall I give it to my beautiful wife?' His smile was infectious.

'That's not your wife, mate.' The man said, his tired face breaking into a smile.

'Oh yes she is, this is Lena Gray, my wife.' Louis seemed outraged.

'Nah, never. Give her the carnation, but she's not your wife. You're having too good a time.'

They laughed like children as they ran from him up the street and found an Italian restaurant.

At the table Louis took her hand. 'Promise me something?'

'Anything on earth, you know that.'

'Promise we won't become like couples that have nothing left to say to each other. Promise?' His eyes were troubled.

'I'll always have something to say to you, but you may not always want to listen.' He had tired of listening before and gone away, leaving her weeping for him alone in Dublin. It was in her eyes.

'You are *my* Lena, like Ivy said, Lena Gray. It's a film star's name . . . You are full of glamour and beauty, my love . . . Think of yourself now as Lena . . . as exciting as living a new life.' His eyes burned and she knew that if she were to keep him, there must be no more talk of one-horse towns, or of being provincial. She would indeed become Lena Gray, woman enough to hold a man like Louis . . . with no fear of becoming dull and old.

For this whole week they said they would give themselves a honeymoon. No looking for work, no harsh realities of the living they would have to earn. They'd start that *next* Monday, 10 November.

There would be plenty of time for that.

Louis was a salesman. There was nothing he could not sell. He would not have references, of course. Well, he had worked for this company in Ireland, and been highly regarded. Highly regarded until he had run off with the daughter of the family. That was that. They had gone to Spain. The details were never clear, and they had never been asked for. There had been years of movement since then, vaguely accounted for, never probed. And Lena Gray would not probe for them now.

Louis had been paid some money to leave the girl, the only child of that family, alone. Naturally, he had refused it. And then when the fire had run out of the relationship, when he had seen what a mistake he had made, he took it to give himself a start in life. The start was never discussed too much either.

It had involved going to America and working there, but without a visa, and then there was a time in Greece.

He would have come back for Helen, the girl he truly loved, but he had thought it would not have been fair. Her children were babies; she was trying to make a new start for herself. He would not come for her until he could prove he loved her and wanted her for the rest of his life.

He had known she was in Lough Glass, of course. And apparently he had come once or twice just to look at her from afar. He would not have spoken to her this year had he not seen her look so unhappy. He saw her on a winter's day last January walking by the lake, tears or rain on her face, hitting away the nettles and bramble. And he had spoken to her.

She had looked at him wildly as if he had come straight out of a dream, and then thrown herself into his arms. He had been mad to have waited so long, he accused himself. But Lena said no, it was perfect. If he had come for her earlier, she would never have been able to leave.

But now the children would be old enough ... if not to understand, at least to make their own lives without her. They would be better without her if the truth were told. There was no life living with a mother who had no joy in her heart, no hope and no wish to see the next day dawn. Kit was able to fend for herself ... She had been trained over the months that her mother was planning to leave. And Emmet – she had done as much as she could for the boy, helped his stutter by taking him to Sister Madeleine, the old hermit woman whose clear eyes seemed to see everything and know what was going on in every heart.

And she had even done what she could for the maid, Rita, encouraging her to work towards an education so that she could be a better companion for the children when ... after ... well, when it all happened.

Martin would survive. She had always known that. He had married her knowing that she loved another man. She had given him her promise that she would not leave him without a full explanation. Yes, of course it should have been face to face. But he was so emotional. He would have cried. He would have done something entirely inappropriate, like kneeling and begging her to stay, like threatening to kill himself, maybe?

No, he was too level-headed for that. But he would accept it. He was realist enough to know that it had always been on the cards. It was just so odd, so strange that he hadn't responded.

Louis was telling her where they would go the next day. He would take her on a train to the seaside. There was nothing as wonderful as to walk on a beach in winter where there was no one but themselves. They might go to Brighton, and see the two great piers jutting out into the sea. They would go to the Pavilion, and walk in the little Lanes looking at the tiny shops, each with its own magic.

His face was alive with the excitement of showing her all these places. 'You will never forget it,' he said.

'I never forget anything I do with you,' she said simply, and she saw his eyes water because what she said was so obviously true.

Lena Gray never forgot Brighton. That was where she began to lose her child. The feeling was a dragging one, a downward pain, a bit like a period. But she decided to ignore it. They had walked hand in hand as had been promised, and laughed at the grey clouds and run from the white-flecked dark waters.

They said that when the child was four they would take him – or her – back here and they would all play on the beach in the summer. They would stay in the same hotel. They would be rich and happy; their child would want for nothing.

Lena ignored that dragging cramp in her stomach.

At Brighton railway station on the way back she felt a dampness but decided not to go to the Ladies to investigate. Some superstition made her feel that if she didn't acknowledge it here in Brighton, where they had been so happy, it would go away.

By the time they got to Victoria she was in no doubt.

'Something's wrong,' she said to Louis.

'Can you make it home?' He had fear in his eyes.

'I don't know.'

'It's only whatever number of stops on the District Line,' he said.

It passed in a nightmare haze. She remembered being put on the bed and Ivy's face very near her.

'You're all right, love. Hang on. Hang on. Stay as still as you can.' Louis was over by the window biting his hand. 'The doctor's coming. He won't be a minute now ... Hold my hand.'

'I was going to tell you ...' Lena wept. They had been told very specifically that this was a house where no children would be allowed.

The pain was sharp. The journey up and down to the bathroom intolerable. There seemed to be blood everywhere, even on Ivy's flowered overall.

Then a doctor's face, a kind man, old, tired. Lena mixed him up with the greengrocer who had given them the flower last week, some week. Maybe everyone in England looked the same.

Questions about the number of weeks pregnant, about any complications earlier on in the pregnancy. What had her doctor said then.

'There was no doctor,' Lena said.

'She's from Ireland, you see,' Ivy explained.

'They have doctors there too,' said the man with the tired face.

'Don't tell Peter,' she said. 'Don't tell Peter and Lilian, whatever you do.' She gripped the doctor's hand. Her eyes were wild.

'No, no,' he soothed. And to Louis standing by the window, 'Who are Peter and Lilian?'

'I don't know. People back in ... back in the place she came from.'

'Your wife has lost a lot of blood ...' the doctor began.

'Will she be all right?'

'Yes, she will. She doesn't need to be taken into hospital. We've done everything. I'll give her a sedative ... You have children already?'

'No,' Louis said.

'Yes,' said Lena.

There was a silence.

'From a previous marriage, she has,' Louis said.

'Poor lamb,' Ivy said.

'I'll send a nurse in the morning. I'll come again tomorrow on my way home from the surgery.'

'Thank you, doctor.' Lena's voice was weak.

The doctor supported her head as she drank the sedative. 'The worst is over, Mrs Gray,' he said kindly. 'The best is ahead.'

'What did you call me?' She was drowsy.

76

'You'll sleep now.' He spoke in a low voice to Ivy, technical matters: towels, buckets, water, keeping the room warm.

When they had gone Louis came and held her hand. There were tears running down his face. 'I'm so sorry, Lena ... Oh Lena, I'm so sorry this should happen.'

'Do you still want me? Do you still want me to stay with you, even though there is no baby now, no family for us?' Her face was white and anxious.

'Oh my love. Of course I do ... more than ever my love ... Now that there are only the two of us we need each other more than ever. Nothing will separate us. Nothing.'

Lines seemed to fall from Lena's face and she slept holding his hand under her cheek. He sat there for a long time stroking her hair. All he could hear was her even breathing. Not the hiss of the oil heater that Ivy had brought in. Not the traffic out in the London streets below.

She found it a funny world for a couple of days. She kept expecting Rita to come in with tea and scones, but it turned out to be Ivy with Bovril and biscuits. She found herself waiting for the children to come home from school. And then Louis would come in the door again beaming with yet another treat. A little glass of tonic wine on a tray with two chocolates wrapped up in silver paper. Or a magazine for her to read with a card pinned inside saying, 'I love you.' Or a dish of chopped-up chicken he had got from the restaurant on the corner when he had told them his wife was sick in bed.

'You've got a good one there,' Ivy said sagely about Louis when he had gone running off on yet another errand.

'Don't I know it?' The colour was coming back to Lena's cheeks.

'Other fellow a sod, was he?' Ivy asked sympathetically.

'Other fellow?' Lena was bewildered.

'Your first husband ... You know you said, he said the night the doctor was here ...'

'Oh no. No, Ivy. He wasn't a sod. No, not at all.'

Ivy felt she had put her foot in it. 'Well, you never know. Takes all sorts ...' she said vaguely. Then, as if to show comradeship she said, 'My first husband was no loss. I don't care who knows it.'

'I'm glad.' Lena was glad. Ivy was so kind to her.

'You and your first husband been split up long then?'

'Not long.' Lena drew down the shutters on the conversation.

How could she tell this woman that she had left Martin McMahon just nine days ago. How would Ivy, or anyone, understand that two weeks ago Lena Gray had gone to Mass in Lough Glass with her husband Martin and her children, and people had thought that she was Helen McMahon.

By Sunday Lena had colour in her cheeks.

'How long have I been in bed?' she asked Ivy.

'It happened on Thursday, love. You're not ready to get up yet.'

'But I have to. We're meant to be looking for jobs tomorrow.'

'Not a chance of it. Not for another week at least.'

'You don't understand . . .'

'No. *You* don't understand. I told the doctor I'd keep an eye on you. Letting you go down to the Employment Exchange isn't keeping an eye on you.'

'I have to, Ivy. Truly. Louis may not get a job at once, I can do anything . . .'

'I'm sure you can, but not this week. Believe me.'

'I need to.' Lena spoke the words she didn't want to. 'I need to, for the rent. You must have the rent.' She was thinking of the treats Louis had bought, the reckless disregard for money that had to be paid to Ivy. He would probably say that she was a good soul, she'd not push them for it, not for a week . . .

But Lena had her pride. She would not let this kind woman think that they were the type of people who would skip a week's payment. Even if she had to drag herself out.

Ivy bit her lip. 'One week's not going to come between us,' she said.

'No.' Lena was adamant.

'Well then, let Louis earn it, love. I'm not taking any money you get out of your bed to make, and that's a promise.'

They heard his foot on the stair. Lena looked up alarmed. 'Not a word please, Ivy.'

'As long as you know my word is law.' Her frown was terrifying but they laughed together.

'What are you two conspiring about?' Louis came in with his arms full of newspapers.

'*Louis*, did you buy the whole shop?' Lena looked in dismay at the selection.

'Had to, my darling. This isn't for pleasure, this is my research. I've got to find a job tomorrow, or had you forgotten? I have to take care of my beautiful sick wife, and pay my wicked landlady . . .' He looked mischievously from one to another.

Ivy spoke first. 'The circumstances have changed. I wouldn't mind letting you have a couple of weeks' credit.'

Louis leaned over and patted Ivy on the hand. 'You're a good true friend to us, even though you've only known us a week. I don't want you to think that we're just unreliable Paddies who come in and take advantage of your hospitality. We'll pay, Ivy. We want to be here a long time.'

Ivy stood up from the chair beside the bed. 'I'll leave you to it then. You're a lucky girl, Lena. You got yourself a real man.'

'Don't I know it.' She smiled up at him.

'And any references or anything . . . I'd be happy . . .' Ivy said.

'That's so good of you.' His eyes were warm with gratitude. 'People are very good,' he said as he spread the papers across the bed.

Lena stroked his dark hair. 'Isn't she so kind, it would break your heart . . . Imagine poor Ivy thinking *she* could give you a reference.'

'I'll be very glad to take her up on it,' he said. He was serious.

'Ivy! A landlady running a rooming house?' Lena was astonished.

'Well, who else will say I'm reliable?'

'But Louis . . . in business, in a company . . . you can't say you have a reference from Ivy . . .'

Louis sighed. 'It won't *be* business, darling. It won't be a matter of talking to sales directors, or marketing managers. You *know* that. It'll be whatever I can get. Ivy will be very useful if I want a job as a hotel porter, or in a bar. She can say she's known me for five years, not ten days.'

Lena looked at him aghast. 'You can't take a job like that, Louis . . . I won't have it. It was never meant to be this way.'

'It was always meant to be this way,' he said, holding both her hands. 'It's just that I was the fool who didn't see it. And you gave me the second chance.'

She cried for a long time.

She cried over the lost baby. And the dreams of Louis having a fine living, dreams which were based on nothing. She cried because she heard the church bells ring somewhere in west London and she thought of her children going to Mass and she had absolutely no idea what Martin had told them about her. She cried because she knew she was a bad mother, the worst kind of mother. One who could leave her own children. No wonder God had taken this much-wanted child away from her.

'I'll make it all right, believe me.' His eyes had tears in them too.

'Louis, tell me something . . .'

'Anything, my love. Anything.'

'Is God very angry with us . . . Is that why this happened?' She touched her stomach as she spoke. 'Is it a punishment, a warning?'

'Of course it isn't.' He was utterly certain.

'But you're not all that well up on God. You've not gone to Mass all the time,' She was doubtful.

'No. But I know he's there, and he's the God of Love. He said that himself, didn't he? He said that was the greatest of the commandments, that you should have love for each other and for God.'

'Yes, but I think he meant that we should . . .'

'You think he meant . . . You think he meant . . . Now, now, now. What way is this to go on? When you're happy you think he meant great things for us. When you are low you think he meant punishments and all this doom and gloom . . .' He held his head on one side and smiled at her. 'What kind of faith have you at all, that you start giving everyone bad motives. This was an accident. The doctor said it. Brought on by stress maybe . . . and he hadn't an idea how much stress . . . Listen love, you can't start thinking that God is lined up against us. He was one of the things meant to be on our side.'

'I know.' She felt better. He was very reassuring.

'So?'

'So, I'll stop attacking him and laying it all at his door.'

'Excellent. Now a great big blow, then help me find a job.'

She blew her nose, wiped her eyes, and looked through the Situations Vacant advertisements with a heart that was much less heavy.

'I'll go to Mass myself next Sunday,' she said in a half mutter. 'That way God will know I haven't given up on him.'

'God knows that,' Louis said. 'If you didn't give up on me who treated you really badly you won't give up on God.'

It was a strangely endless week.

On Monday Louis came home despondent. There were any number of building jobs, he said. Half of Ireland seemed to be over in London signing on with subcontractors, using a different name for each job. But he hadn't the build, the experience or the liking to swing a pickaxe or carry a hod. It had been a wasted day.

He was determined to be cheerful. 'Now, stop looking so upset. Don't get out of that bed. Listen to me. This is just Day One. Day Two will be fine. If you're going to look so mournful then it makes it worse for me. I can't come home and tell you the truth; I'll only have to be making up lies.'

She saw the reason in what he said. She lay awake Monday night while he slept beside her, but she didn't let him know how anxious she was.

Day Two was fine. Louis came home elated. He had got a job and would start tomorrow. As a hall porter in a big hotel, not far away on the underground. He would begin at eight a.m. and work days for the first two weeks, but there was the possibility of nights after that. Which was great.

'Why is it great?' Lena wanted to know.

Because then of course he could use some of the days for going for interviews for other jobs, the ones for which they felt he was more suited. Meanwhile, wasn't that great? The rent was secure. It had only taken him twenty-four hours to find honourable employment.

Lena couldn't smile. She forced her face, but it wouldn't go into the right position. 'I can't bear you having to do this,' she said.

'Jesus Christ, won't it be hard enough to do the bloody thing without having to listen to you being so negative,' he burst out, Lena looked at him, stricken. But he was quick to apologise. 'Forgive me, forgive me. I didn't mean to lash out at you. It was a long day. I'm nearly forty. They sort of implied I might be too old for a job like this. It was hard, darling; I didn't mean to take it out on you.'

The reconciliation was as sweet as ever.

They had always known there would be things like this to trip them up along the way. The main thing was to recognise them, admit them. They were both so sorry.

On Wednesday night Louis had funny stories about the hotel. The head porter was a crook, the manager was hopelessly ineffectual, the receptionist had a moustache and she was a woman, the guests he had talked to were mainly American GI soldiers serving in the various bases in Britain, nice fellows, kids a lot of them. The day had seemed long, but it was interesting.

Lena took a huge interest and learned all their names. On Thursday night

Louis told her the head porter had tried to take a tip that should have belonged to Louis, but the Scots lady had insisted.

'It's for the nice wee man with the blue eyes,' she had said.

The head porter had smiled good-naturedly in front of the Scottish lady, but out of the corner of his mouth he had hissed to Louis, 'I have my eye on you.'

'What did you say?' Lena showed great enthusiasm.

'I said that I had my eye on his job. That silenced him.'

Lena pealed with laughter.

Louis would be out of there, gone to something worthy of him in days, or weeks at the very worst.

On Friday Louis was tired, but he had a pay packet. They got paid every Friday, and his three days' work paid the rent. They handed it to Ivy in an envelope.

'I think you're well enough to go out and celebrate,' she said. 'My treat. A couple of pints in a place that a friend of mine runs.'

They went on a red bus. Lena's legs felt weak still, but she was buoyed up by the outing. Ivy pointed out places to her as the bus went through the London traffic, and Louis pointed out other places. She felt like a child on a birthday treat.

Ivy showed her a big office where she had worked during the war, and areas that had been bombed. She said that this was a great eel shop and that was a very honourable pawnbroker in case they fell on a really bad time, and to be sure to say that Ivy had recommended him. Louis showed her restaurants and hotels and theatres. He knew all the names, but he didn't have a little story go to with each one like Ivy did. This was part of Louis' past, places she didn't enquire about but was grateful to be shown. They got to a big noisy pub where Ivy knew a lot of the clientele.

'Very far from home for a local,' Louis said.

'Ah love, I used to work here, but we won't go into all that now.'

'Certainly.' Louis squeezed Lena's hand. This was more like it. Going out on a raffish adventure where things mustn't be said ... this was the kind of thing they liked.

They sat at a table, the three of them. A lot of people came over and were introduced as Doris and Henry and Nobby and Steve and the landlord was called Ernest. A small man with a lot of tattoos up his arm. He made it his business to come to the table several times.

Lena and Louis noticed this because, unlike the pubs at home, there wasn't table service. You had to go up to the bar to get your pint refilled.

But not Ivy.

Their glasses of bitter and Louis' pint were refilled by the guvnor, as people called him. Lena saw no money change hands. They had just enough to buy a drink themselves and offered, but the offer was waved away.

'Ernest will look after us,' Ivy said firmly. 'He likes to do that.'

During the evening Lena saw Ivy's eyes follow the small wizened man as he moved behind the bar and greeted customers. From time to time his eyes sought out Ivy's and he smiled.

Some of the customers asked, 'How's Charlotte then?' and Ernest always said 'Gone to her mother's like every Friday.'

Lena knew why Ivy visited on Fridays only. She wondered how long it had been going on. Ivy might tell her some time. But then again, she might not. This was not Lough Glass, where everyone's life was discussed inside out until it had no meaning any more.

Tonight in Paddles' bar they would be saying . . .

Suddenly she realized with a start that she didn't know *what* they would be saying. Had Martin said she had gone on a visit? Had he said she was sick? No. Surely Peter Kelly would need to have been involved in that.

But what had he told the children? She felt her face redden with rage that he hadn't told her what story he was going to give Kit and Emmet. She had urged him to tell them the truth if he could bear it, and to let them write to her. But that had obviously not been done.

Ivy was talking to Ernest, the two of them sitting together like a long-married couple while she picked pieces of fluff from the sleeve of his jacket.

Lena felt Louis' eyes on her. She smiled, shaking away memories of Lough Glass. 'What are you thinking about?' he asked her.

'I was thinking how I'm well enough to get a job now . . . and next week I'll take us all out for a celebration,' she said.

'I don't want you to have to work.'

'I don't want you to either, but it's only for a while. Then we'll have careers and a home like real people . . .' she smiled brightly.

It was one of the many lies she told him.

On Saturday Lena dressed herself up and went to Millar's Employment Agency. She stood outside and took three very deep breaths. She drew in the cold London air right down to her toes. This could be the start of many fruitless interviews. What would they want with her? A woman with no shorthand. No typing speeds to speak of. No references. She was too old to be an office junior. She was too ill equipped to be an office senior.

At the desk sat a woman in a cardigan, sucking a pencil. She had a pleasant smile and a vague expression on her face. She was a gentle woman, not at all the sort of person you might have expected to come across in an employment agency.

She pushed a form across the desk and Lena filled it in with a shaking hand. At almost every category she felt she sounded like a loser. *Be confident* she told herself. So she didn't have any real experience or any written reference, but she had more than some of the local school leavers had: she had the ability to think on her own, to take the initiative. She smiled encouragingly at the woman in the cardigan, with her hair like a bird's nest, in order to hide her own feelings of dread. At least this wasn't the kind of woman who would laugh at her and order her out of the office, implying that she had been wasting valuable time.

'There, I think that's everything,' she said with a bright smile. Lena dug her nails into her palms as she watched the woman read slowly through the completed form. She willed herself not to explain, not to apologise.

'It's rather hard to see . . . well to know what exactly you could . . . where we might . . .'

Lena put on her most confident face. 'Oh, I know I'm not the run of the mill clerical or secretarial appointment,' she said, hardly believing the sound of her own voice. 'But I *was* hoping that there might be something where my particular skills, more mature qualities might be useful.'

'Like what, exactly?' The woman at the other side of the desk was more embarrassed than she was, Lena realised.

'Excuse me, what is your name?' Lena asked.

'Miss Park. Jessica Park.'

'Well, Miss Park, you know maybe the kind of firm that wants someone who can try anything, not a young woman on her way up through some kind of ladder. Somewhere that I could turn my hand to anything, to answering the phone, doing the filing, making the tea, keeping the place nice, thinking up new ideas . . .' Lena looked around the dingy office of Millar's Employment Agency, waving her hands to illustrate her point.

'I know what you mean. Every office wants someone like you,' said Miss Park wistfully. At that point the phone rang and immediately after two girls came in saying they just wanted leaflets, and the phone rang again.

It had given Lena time to think. When Jessica Park was free again she decided to speak her thoughts. 'For example, here in this office,' she said, hoping that the shake in her voice was not obvious. 'I can see you're very busy. Perhaps this is just the kind of place I might be useful.'

Jessica Park was not a decision maker; she seemed alarmed. 'Oh no, I don't think so . . .' she began.

'Well why not? You seem very overworked. I could do some of the more routine stuff. You know, keep the files . . .'

'But I don't know anything about you . . .'

'You know everything about me.' She indicated the form.

'I don't run the place . . . Mr Millar will need . . .'

'Why don't I start now? You can see whether I'm any good or not, and then you can ask Mr Millar.'

'I don't know, I'm sure . . .'

Lena paused. It was hard to tell what age Jessica Park was. She might have been forty or forty-five. But she could equally have been thirty-five, a woman who had taken no care of herself and aged beyond her years.

Lena decided to choose this option. 'Well, Jessica. I'll call you that because I can see you're younger than I am . . . Why don't we give it a try? Nothing to lose, nothing to pay if it doesn't work out.'

'Jessie actually, and I'm a little older than you,' Jessie admitted. 'But all right. Just so long as we don't get into any trouble.'

'What trouble can we get into? Look, I'll find a chair and sit beside you.'

Before Jessica could change her mind, Lena was installed. She sharpened pencils, tidied up the desk and rearranged the enrolment forms so that there was a carbon paper attached to each one and a second sheet below.

'I never thought of that,' Jessie said in wonder.

'Of course you did,' said Lena. 'It's just you're too busy to have time for it.' Lena answered the phone with a cheerful 'Millar's Employment Agency, how can we help you?' which was a vast improvement on Jessie's tentative 'Hello.'

She said that she would really like to become familiar with the filing system. That way she could be of the greatest assistance. Jessie gave her vague outlines and left her to it. Lena's eyes raked through the lists until she found what she wanted. It wasn't long before she tracked down the section that she was really interested in.

The situations vacant in Sales and Marketing. The kinds of jobs that Louis Gray might be able to apply for, once they knew what was wanted and where to go.

'You mean you just walked in and said they needed you?' Louis was amazed.

'More or less,' Lena laughed, hardly daring to believe it had worked. There was no need to tell him how frightened she had been.

Mr Millar had said that Miss Park was intelligent to have picked a mature woman from the many people she saw, and to suggest her. Jessie had been delighted with the unexpected praise. Lena would start on Monday.

She said nothing to Louis about her real reason for taking the job, and the possible gold mine it might turn out to be for them. She wanted to call these firms herself in her role as employment agency and arm herself with the information.

Then Louis could apply on his own behalf.

It was all working out for the best. Lena thought she would be able to talk to God without bitterness at Mass next day.

Ivy was so sorry but she didn't know where there were Roman Catholic churches. She was always seeing them. She'd ask. She said there *was* a great big one in Kilburn, Quex Road it was. Always huge crowds going in and out of it on a Sunday. That might be the place.

'Kilburn ... Would it be a bit Irish for us? ... Would people know us?' she asked Louis.

'No,' he said. 'There's hardly anyone from Lough Grass emigrated since you've left.'

'No, no of course not. But you ... Would people know *you*?'

'It doesn't matter if they know me, love. It's you who's on the run. Anyway, am I coming?'

'I'd like you to, if you wouldn't hate it. Just to give thanks.'

'Well, I've a lot to give thanks for. Of course I'll come.'

It was such an adventure going to Mass in London. Finding the right bus, remembering which direction to take it. Crossing Kilburn High Road and following the crowd with head scarves and collars turned up against the cold. There were a few Polish people, and Italians too.

They knew nobody.

Lena compared it to the Sunday journey to Mass in Lough Glass. Good morning Mrs Hanley, Mr Foley, Dan, Mildred, Mr Hickey, Mother Bernard, Mrs Dillon, Hello Lilian, Hello Peter. How nice to see you again,

Maura. How are you Kathleen? Stevie? You were exhausted before you got up to the church. And then when you got there you recognised everyone's cough and splutter. And you knew what Father Baily would say before he said it.

The familiar Latin words washed over her. It must be terrible being a Protestant. You couldn't have the same service all over the world. You wouldn't understand Protestants in Africa or Germany. Being a Catholic was so safe. And indeed if you were like Louis, so simple. It was a God of Love up there looking down.

Lena felt peaceful and happy as they came out into the cold wind. Just by the church was a kiosk that sold newspapers.

'They're all the Irish provincial ones, or religious ones,' Louis said. 'I'll get a real paper from the man over here and we'll go and have a Sunday drink. Okay?'

Lena nodded her encouragement, but she looked at the headlines all the same. There were all the papers from home: the *Kerryman*, the *Cork Weekly Examiner*, the *Wexford Free Press*, the *Connaught Tribune*. And among them the paper that was delivered to the pharmacy each Friday. They looked at it for the times of the cinema, the property for sale, for news of fellow county men and women who had done well in civil service examinations, postings overseas, who had married or celebrated a golden wedding.

She was about to look away when she saw there, on the front page, a picture of the lake in Lough Glass and some of the boats. Underneath it was the heading 'Search Called Off For Missing Lough Glass Woman.'

With her eyes widening in disbelief she read that Helen McMahon, wife of noted Lough Glass pharmacist, Martin McMahon, had last been seen walking by the treacherous lake waters on Wednesday, 29 October. Divers and volunteers had searched the reed-infested water of the lake that gave Lough Glass its name, but nothing had been found. A boat had been seen upside down and it was assumed that Mrs McMahon must have taken it out and failed to cope with the sudden squalls that blow up in that region.

'Are you going to buy it?' asked the man who sold the papers. Helen handed him half a crown and began to walk away, still clutching the paper. 'Hey, they're dear, but not that dear,' he called after her with her change.

But she didn't hear. 'Louis,' she called, her voice roaring in her own ears. 'Louis, oh my God . . .'

They lifted her to her feet, everyone suggesting something different – air, brandy, whiskey, water, tea, walk her around, sit her down.

The man trying to give her change kept insisting that it be put into her handbag.

Eventually, his arms supported her along the road. Half walking, half being carried, she knew they were hastening to somewhere they could be alone. He kept saying that they should get a doctor.

'Believe me, there is nothing more to lose. Just get me somewhere away from people.'

'Please, darling, please.' There were mainly Irish accents in the bar, but they were far away. They were all concentrated on their own business. They had no interest in the man and woman who sat with the untouched brandy between them while they read unbelievingly the account of the search for Helen McMahon.

'He can't have got the whole town out, guards, detectives from Dublin Castle.' Louis was shaking his head.

'He mustn't have got the note,' Helen said. 'He must have thought I was really in the lake . . . Oh my God. Oh my God, what have I done?'

'But we've been over this a hundred times already. Where did you put the note?'

'In his room.'

'And how could he not see it? How, tell me?'

'Suppose he didn't go in there?'

'Lena, have sense. He must have gone in there. They got the guards, for God's sake. The guards would have gone in there even if he didn't.'

'He couldn't do all this, bring all this horror on the children, let them think I was lying dead in the bottom of the lake like poor Bridie Daly.'

'Who was she?'

'It doesn't matter. Martin wouldn't have done this, not to the children.'

'Well then, how could he *not* have got the note?' Louis' face was anguished and he kept looking back at the account in case the article might go away.

'The maid. You say she wouldn't have kept it?'

'No, not a chance.'

'To blackmail you, or anything?'

'We're talking about Rita. No, that's not possible.'

'The children then. Suppose one of them opened it. Suppose they didn't want to believe you'd gone. You know how strange children can be. Hid the note and pretended none of it was true.'

'No.' She spoke simply.

'How can you be so sure?'

'I know them, Louis. They're my children. First, they wouldn't open it if it was addressed to Martin . . . But if they did . . . if they did . . .'

'Suppose they did. Just suppose it.'

'If Emmet opened it he would show it to his father. If Kit opened it she would have phoned me in London. She would have telephoned the moment we arrived. She would have demanded that I come home.'

There was a silence.

It seemed to have gone on for ever, when Louis spoke. 'Will you accept that he read it?'

'I find it *very* hard to think he could have unleashed all this . . .' She waved at the newspaper.

'It might have been his only way of coping, you know.'

There was another silence.

'I'll have to know, Louis.'

'What do you mean?'

'I must telephone him.' She almost went as if to stand up now. He looked at her in alarm.

'And say what? What would you say?'

'Tell them to stop looking in the lake. Tell my children I'm alive . . .'

'But you're not going back to them. You're *not*, are you?'

The longing in his eyes was almost too much to bear. 'You *know* I'm not going back, Louis.'

'Then think. Think for a moment.'

'What is there to think about? You read it yourself, all that stuff about what I was wearing when I left. I'm a missing person, like you hear about on the news. They think I'm in the lake . . .' Her voice became almost hysterical. 'They might even have a funeral, for God's sake.'

'Not without a body, they can't.'

'But they'll have me presumed dead. I can't be presumed dead. Not for my children. They *must* know their mother is alive and well and happy, not in the mud and the reeds at the bottom of the lake in Lough Glass.'

'It's not *your* fault they think that.'

'What do you mean it's not my fault? I left them.'

'It's *his* fault,' Louis said slowly.

'How do you say that?'

'That's what *he* told them. You gave him a choice of what he could say. This is what he said.'

'But he can't say that. It's preposterous. He can't tell them their mother is dead. I want to see them. I want to meet them, watch them grow up.'

Louis looked at her sadly. 'Did you ever think he would let you do that?'

'Of course I did.'

'That he would forgive you and say, "There there, you have a nice life with Louis in London, and from time to time come home to Lough Glass and we'll all kill the fatted calf."'

'No, not like that.'

'But like what then? Think, Lena. Think. This is Martin's way. It might be the best way.'

She leaped to her feet. 'To tell two innocent children that I'm dead because he can't face telling them I left him!'

'Maybe he thinks that it'd be better for them. You're always saying it's a mass of whispers that place. Maybe the sympathy over a dead mother is better than the gossip over one that ran away.'

'I don't believe any of this. I'm going to ring him, Louis. I have to.'

'That's so unfair of you. You told the poor bastard that the one thing you'd do for him was let him sort it out whatever way he wanted. You'd give him that dignity. Wasn't that what you wrote?'

'I don't know the exact words.'

'Was it or wasn't it?'

'I didn't have carbon paper,' she snapped.

'But we went over it often enough.'

'That's what I told him,' she agreed. 'But I must know. I must know do they really . . .' All the fight had gone out of her.

'Suppose they do think you're dead, Lena. Think, I beg you. Might not that be the best for the little girl and the little boy. If you phone now you'll have to go home and explain everything. Martin will be in deep trouble. You'll make it so much worse for him. Think of all the harm you might do.'

'I must know,' she said, tears falling down her face.

'Right. We'll ring them.'

'What?'

'I'll ring,' he said. 'I'll say I want to speak to you, find out what I'm told.'

'You can't.'

'I'll get change,' he said. His face was in a grim line as he went to the bar. Lena drank the entire brandy in one gulp. It felt like swallowing nettles.

They didn't phone from the bar, there was too much noise, but just along the road they came to a public box.

'What will you say?' Lena asked for the tenth time.

Louis had said little, but now as they heard the phone ringing he held her face in one hand and said, 'I'll say what's right. Trust me. I'll wait to see what he says first.'

She gripped his hand tight and leaned very close so that she could hear.

'Lough Glass three double nine.' It was Kit's voice.

Lena raised the hand that held Louis' hand to her lips to bite back the words. Then the operator came on the line. 'A call from London for you . . . Go ahead, caller.'

'Hello.' Louis spoke in a slightly altered voice. 'Is that McMahons'?'

'Yes, this is McMahons' in Lough Glass.'

'Is Mr McMahon there please?'

'No, I'm sorry. He's out at the moment . . .' Lena's eyes widened. Martin should be well back from Mass by now. They should have started their lunch. The house had gone to pieces since she left. Then she remembered this was a house in mourning, a house where everyone professed to think she was drowned.

'When will he return?'

'May I ask who's calling, please?' Lena smiled proudly. Only twelve and already practical and efficient. Don't give information until you get information.

'My name's Smith. I'm a commercial representative. I've been to your parents' chemist's in the nature of business calls.'

'This is our home, not the chemist's,' Kit explained.

'I know, I'm sorry to intrude on you. Might I have a word with your mother?' Lena squeezed his hand so hard it hurt him. Her eyes were enormous. What was the child going to say?

It seemed an age before she answered.

What did she want Kit to say? Something like, 'There's been a lot of confusion over where my mother is, but it will all be sorted out before Christmas.'

'You're ringing from London?' Kit said.

'That's right, yes.'

'Then you won't have heard. There's been a terrible accident. My mother was drowned.' There was a pause as she struggled to get her breath again.

Louis said nothing. His face was white. Then, in a choked voice, he said, 'I'm very sorry.'

'Yes, I know you would be.' The voice was very small.

Lena had often fantasised about her children talking to Louis. She knew they would like each other. Somehow she had felt it would turn out to be all right. But that was before this. Before this terrible turn in events.

'So where is your father now?' he asked.

'He's having lunch with friends of ours. They're trying to take his mind off things a bit.'

That would be the Kellys, thought Lena.

'And why did *you* not go?' Louis sounded genuinely caring. The lump in Lena's throat was enormous.

'I thought someone should be here in case there was any news, you know . . .'

'What kind of news?'

'Well, they haven't found . . . in case they found Mummy's body,' said Kit. Louis' face was working but he couldn't speak. 'Are you still there?' she asked.

'Yes . . . yes,'

'Will I ask my father to ring you?'

'No, no. It was just a call, in case I was going to be passing that way. Please don't tell him and disturb him. I'm so sorry to have intruded . . . at such a time . . .'

'It was an accident,' Kit said. 'They had prayers for the repose of her soul at Mass today.'

'Yes, I'm sure. I'm sure.'

'So that she'd be at peace,' Kit explained. 'So I won't say you rang?'

'No. No. And is your little brother managing all right?'

'How did you know I had a brother?'

'I think your father and mother said it when I was in the shop.'

'I bet she did. She was always talking about us.' Kit's voice was near tears. 'It was only the winds you know. It would have been all right but for the winds.' There was a silence. The silences had eaten up a lot of the three minutes.

'Do you want further time, caller?' asked the operator.

'No, thank you. We have finished,' Louis said.

And across the distance on that wet November Sunday they heard Kit's voice saying 'Goodbye' and again, hesitantly, in case she hadn't signed off properly, 'Goodbye now.'

They hung up and held each other tight in the phone box as the rain lashed against the window. And anyone who came hoping to make a call saw the anguish between them and went away. Nobody could ask a couple who had obviously had such bad news to leave a phone box and go out into the real world.

'I could kill him,' Louis said, when they were at home sitting in this half world of disbelief.

89

'If he did it on purpose.'

'Let's go through it again.'

Louis would ask, 'How could he *not* know?' And always it was unanswerable.

They couldn't sleep, even though they needed to. They both had jobs to go to in the morning.

Once Louis asked in a wide-awake voice, 'Did he think people wouldn't want to buy his bloody cough bottles if they thought his wife had run away, but they would if she had drowned?'

'Don't ask me. I don't know him at all.'

'You lived with him for thirteen years of your life.'

She was silent. Then an hour later she asked, 'What did Kit mean about the winds . . . what winds?'

'I suppose the night we left.'

'I don't remember any winds.'

'Neither do I, but then . . .'

He didn't need to say any more. They would have noticed neither thunderstorm nor snow on the night they began their new life.

She had crossed to the far side of the lake before the gypsy camp where Louis was waiting with his car, well, his friend's car. His friend had known nothing of the plan, only that Louis needed transport for the day. They had driven to Dublin and taken the tram to Dun Laoghaire. They were the first people on the boat. And they had talked all night from Holyhead to Euston, and laughed over their breakfast in a Lyon's Corner House.

And all this time, every day and night since then, people in Lough Glass had assumed that Helen McMahon was at the bottom of their lake.

Louis was right. Martin's bitterness must have been greater than any of them could ever have realised.

Jessie had a mother who was poorly. She had been poorly for a long time. Nothing that you could put your finger on. Lena learned this in a lot of detail on her first full day at work, on that first Monday.

'Why don't you pop back and see her at lunchtime?' Lena suggested.

'Ooh, I couldn't do that.' Jessie was very timid.

'Why ever not? I'm here, aren't I? I can hold the fort.'

'No. I wouldn't like to.'

'Jessie, I'm not going to take your job. I'm your assistant. I'm not going to go out and leave the place wide open to the public. If anything comes in that I can't handle I'll ask them to see Miss Park later on. What's the sense of us both sitting here when you're worried about your mother?'

'But suppose Mr Millar comes in?'

'I could say that you have gone to investigate better stationery. You *could* too, on your way. There's a big place on the corner. Why don't you see if they have any discounts for bulk buy? We do get a lot of envelopes at a time. They should give us a reduction.'

'Yes . . . I could do that.' Jessie was riddled with doubt.

'Please go,' Lena insisted. 'Isn't this why I was hired, to be a nice sensible mature woman who can keep things ticking over? Let me earn my wages.'

'Will you be all right?'

'I'll be fine. I've lots to do.' Lena felt her smile was nailed onto her face. If only Jessie Park knew how much she did have to do, how many decisions she had to make if she could just get a little peace to make them.

While she was pretending to keep down a real job, Lena Gray was going to have to decide today whether or not to telephone Lough Glass and say that Helen McMahon was alive and well. Hours of conversation with Louis had not convinced her. She couldn't write her own obituary and move out of the lives of Kit and Emmet.

Even if the baby she had been carrying had continued to live within her, she would still have had to face the fact that she had somehow allowed her son and daughter to believe that she was dead. It was no use railing against Martin and his weakness of character. She wanted some time to think. Time on her own, where she had access to a telephone.

That's why it was so important to get poor Jessie out of the office.

Lena delayed looking up the job opportunities for Louis. After all, a lot depended on what she did now. If she were to telephone home and tell the news that she was alive and well, then it might change everything. It might mean that she and Louis would not be starting their life as planned here, in London. It might mean that she would have to return home and face the consequences of everything she had done.

So it would be folly to try to set up interviews for him when she did not even know whether they would still be here. She tried to imagine the scene of Louis escorting her back to Lough Glass.

Her imagination let her down. She could not begin to run the conversation that would take place between the three of them, Martin, Louis and herself in the sitting room. There were no words, no explanations. She thought of the children holding her, clutching her. Of Kit saying 'I *knew* you weren't dead. I just *knew* it.' Of Emmet with his stutter getting worse until every word seemed to choke him.

She thought of Rita being discreet, and baffled, in the background. She thought of the false conversation with Peter and Lilian. Of Maura, Lilian's sister, being determinedly cheerful and saying that life was short and they should all rejoice in the good fortune that had resulted from all this instead of dwelling on the bad side.

All the time she tried to imagine a role for Louis and couldn't find one. His smile, his charm, his love for her would all be so inappropriate.

She knew she would have to go alone. And she supposed she would have to go. You couldn't tell two innocent children the news that their mother was not dead without telling it to their faces. She didn't even think about talking to Martin. The years of respect for him had just vanished. She could not believe that anyone could have behaved in such a way over a blow to his pride.

She must really not have known Martin at all.

*

Jessie left, and took her incessant chatter with her. Lena hoped for some time on her own. But the lunch hour was one of the busiest times in Millar's Employment Agency. All those already in jobs which they hoped to change used their lunch break to seek details and to register for other posts.

Lena was rushed off her feet. Perhaps it was all for the best, she thought, as the wire trays filled up with application forms and personal details. Perhaps she would not have been able to work anything out even if she did have the free time. Twice she had lifted a telephone receiver and twice she had replaced it. If she had spoken to Martin in the pharmacy she would not have been able to control her anger with him. Maybe she should wait until the children were home from school.

Or should she go through someone else? But who?

Not the Kellys. Never the Kellys. Now, if Sister Madeleine had had a telephone. Lena smiled at the notion of a modern instrument like a telephone in the hermit's little cottage.

'You're smiling, that's good,' Jessie said to her.

'Do you mean I don't always smile?' Lena pulled herself together.

'You look a different woman today from the one that was here on Saturday. I thought you had something bad happen to you over the weekend.' Jessie looked eager to hear.

But Lena was well able for her. 'No, divil a bit of it. Now, how was your Mum? Glad to see you?'

'Well, it was a good thing I *did* go back.' Jessie began another lengthy tale of her mother's difficulty in digesting her food.

Up to this, Lena had thought that Mrs Hanley in the drapery at Lough Glass was the only woman in the world whose food passed through a hundred different stages, all of them fascinating to herself, before it was digested. Now she realized that Mrs Hanley had a sister-figure in West London.

Lena had thirteen years' experience in moulding her face into an expression of interest in awful Mrs Hanley's gullet. It was no problem to assume acceptable interest in the digestive tract of Jessie Park's mother. Her hands were busy putting new and clearer labels on the files; her mind was hundreds of miles away by a winter lake in Ireland.

She knew when she saw Louis' face that there would be no conversation about it tonight. This was not a man who would sit down to work out yet again the best way to tell her children that she was still alive.

He was tired and drawn from his long day. His hands were chapped and his shoulders ached. 'Do we have the money for a hot bath, or is it madness?' he asked.

His eyes were like huge dark smudges in his face, his smile as lopsided and heartbreaking as she had ever known. She felt such a rush of love and protection for him that it nearly took her breath away. She would work from dusk to dawn and then to dusk again to look after him, to take away his tiredness.

And she knew that he would do that for her, too.

Remember how he had nearly died of anguish over her miscarriage, how he had sat holding her hand and stroking her brow, leaving only to get some treat. Her eyes filled with tears. This was her man, her great love.

She was so lucky. So few people really had the love of their lives with them. Most people yearned for lost chances. For opportunities missed. It would be a stupid woman who would give away one moment of this time by fretting and agonising and trying to redefine the past.

She would think about it herself. She would not waste one precious minute of her time with Louis in what he would think was re-going over old ground.

'I think this company can run to a hot bath for one of the workers,' she said, eyes bright and dancing. 'But on one condition.'

'What's that?'

'That I get to come into the bathroom and rub your back.'

'Ivy'll be shocked, goings-on in the bathroom.'

'Back rubbings isn't goings-on . . .'

'It might lead to it, though. Mightn't it?' He looked at her eagerly.

'Oh, I'd say it most certainly will,' she said – her way of telling him that she felt able to make love again. And not just able . . . eager, to a degree that startled her.

'We'll splash out on a bath then,' said Louis happily, taking up his towel and sponge bag and reaching for a sixpence from the saucer of coins that they called Spending Money.

There was no mention of the crisis in Lough Glass that night.

Lena woke at five in the morning and couldn't get back to sleep. Perhaps we'll talk about it. Perhaps the time will be right, she told herself. But as she thought, she knew she was deceiving herself. As far as Louis Gray was concerned, her life in Lough Glass was over. In some ways, the way it was seen to be over seemed the best solution. He was busy planning their new life. He did not want to be dragged back to her old life.

The faces of Kit and Emmet were as clear as if they were thrown by projection on to the wall opposite the bed: Kit pushing her hair out of her eyes, face wet from rain and tears at the lake, her expression grim and set; Emmet, his eyes bewildered, raising his hand to his throat as he often did when he stammered, in an effort to force the words out.

She couldn't let them believe she was dead. She would find a way to tell them.

She didn't find a way on Tuesday.

Mr Millar called at the agency.

His visits always made Jessie very nervous. 'I don't know what he thinks he's at, coming spying,' she hissed to Lena.

'It *is* his business,' Lena said mildly. 'He just wants to make sure it's going well, see if there's anything we need, that sort of thing.'

Jessie was doubtful. 'If he thought it was all going well and we were running it properly, then he wouldn't need to come in at all,' she said, biting her lip.

Lena forced herself to laugh even though her mind was far from the subject. 'Come on now, Jessie. Let's look on the bright side. Because it *is* going well, he likes to be here and to be a part of it. Did you ever think of it that way?'

Jessie never had. 'I suppose it's being married and all that makes you so confident, Lena,' she said.

Lena swallowed. Imagine they thought she was confident. She was as weak as a kitten, if only they knew. 'Let's make him very welcome when he comes in today, and get him involved in it rather than waiting until he's gone to make our plans.'

'I wonder . . .' Jessie didn't want to rock the boat.

'Let's try it anyway,' Lena said.

'I was wondering, Mr Millar, do you think that we might have some chairs and a little table so that clients could sit down while they're waiting?'

'I don't know about that,' he said. He was a tall, bald man with an egg-like head and face, and an expression of permanent surprise.

'You know, if we made them feel that this was a place where they could drop in . . . almost a social occasion rather than standing in a line queueing like they might at a post office or a bank.'

'But what would be the advantage to us?'

Jessie began to cringe, but Lena knew that the man just wanted to know. He wasn't dismissing the suggestion.

'Miss Park was pointing out to me – you know she's being marvellous at showing me the ropes – well, she was saying that so much of our business is actually repeat business. Someone will come again if they got a good placing the first time.'

'Yes, but armchairs . . .'

'Oh I don't mean anything very grand, Mr Millar. I think what Miss Park had in mind was the feeling that Millar's was a sort of place they could trust, a place they felt at home in.' Her smile was bright and confident.

And he was nodding. 'It's a good idea, Miss Park. Yes it is. I wonder where we'd get that kind of furniture.'

'You wouldn't need to spend too much, Mr Millar. You'd need to look around a bit.' He looked at a loss. 'The real person to do this, of course, is Miss Park. She's wonderful at finding exactly the right thing.' Jessie looked up. She gave the impression of someone who had never been able to find the right thing: the right cardigan, hairstyle, expression on her face. But Lena sailed past that. 'You know, these second-hand places. I bet with a bit of hunting there'd be great bargains there. Suppose after her lunch hour . . . That is, I mean if . . . What do you think . . . ?'

Even Jessie's slow uptake got the message this time. Lena was trying to get her time off so that she could spend it with her mother. 'If I were to have a little extra time?' she began, like a dog begging to be whipped.

'It would pay for itself over and over,' Lena finished for her.

'Well, if you wouldn't mind, Miss Park?' He was doubtful about everything. Fortunately, Jessie's naturally apologetic manner stood her in good stand. She didn't sound too eager for the whole endeavour.

'I suppose I could . . .' she began.

Then Mr Millar became eager. 'We could have a couple of ashtrays,' he ventured. 'An old umbrella stand even, for weather like this.'

'A table with all our information on it, rather than having them read it at the counter, taking up time.' Lena remembered to curb the enthusiasm before they might get carried away and abandon the whole project as being unrealistic.

'Yes, and as Miss Park said, it wouldn't have to cost a lot.'

Mr Millar went away happy. Delighted, in fact, with his visit.

Jessie looked at Lena as if she had braved a lion in a den. 'I don't know how you think of things, I really don't. And you always make *me* look so good.' She was like a spaniel in her gratitude.

'You *are* good,' Lena said. 'You were very good to find me and let me work here.'

'It was the best thing I ever did in my life,' Jessie said happily.

Lena patted her on the hand. 'Right. Now don't find the furniture too quickly. Not for a couple of weeks anyway. Gives you more time to get home without it all being a huge rush.'

Lena realised she had been acting all day.

Acting since she got up and told Louis that she had slept so well and happily in his arms. When she told Ivy she was just sweeping the office and making the tea because she didn't want to seem to have a better job than Louis had. She had been acting a whole series of little charades to clients who phoned, to job seekers who came in, promising everyone that huge opportunities existed.

Was this what it was going to be like from now on?

There had been so many years of acting already in Lough Glass. Assuming an interest in the new lumber jackets that Mrs Hanley had got in, individually boxed, in the drapery. Forcing her face to smile at Lilian Kelly's stream of consciousness about people she didn't know who lived in big houses in the country. Telling the Hickeys that the round steak was good and the rib steak was inclined to be a bit tough, but that naturally if you didn't pay for sirloin then you didn't get sirloin.

Acting at home she felt Martin's eyes on her. Knowing that he would ask, as he so often did, 'Are you happy?' 'Are things all right?' And trying not to give him her answer in a scream.

The only time she hadn't acted was with her children. And yet she had been able to put on her coat and leave them. Leave them to follow Louis Gray.

She had thought it would turn out so differently. A new life, the life she had always wanted. A new baby, hers and Louis'. And look what had happened. She had lost the baby, her family back home thought that she was dead and she was still acting.

She longed to be in the small spare cabin where Sister Madeleine lived. To be able to talk as she had talked there, where there was no advice, critical or otherwise, but the very talking helped. Somehow, if she could talk this over in front of the old hermit, things would become clearer.

But this was dangerous fantasy. Imagining telling a nun that you were tempted to please your fancy man by putting off the moment you told your children that you were not dead. It would be beyond anyone's belief.

Lena sighed and settled her face into a position that might be acceptable to a young woman called Dawn, who wanted a job as a hotel receptionist.

'I've gone for lots of interviews, but they take one look at me and say I wouldn't do,' she said in an aggrieved tone.

Dawn looked like a tart. Her blonde hair was dark at the roots, her nails were dirty and her lipstick was a big red gash across her face.

'You're too glamorous,' Lena told her. 'You give the wrong impression. They want something safe-looking in a hotel. Why don't you change your appearance a bit? Come on, it's worth it . . .'

The girl listened, fascinated. No one had ever taken such an interest in her before. 'Like what way change myself, Mrs Gray?' Her eyes were bright and eager.

Lena looked at her thoughtfully and gave her considered advice. Nothing appeared as criticism. Everything sounded positive. 'Getting a job is like auditioning for a part. It's like being an actress. Now, Dawn, we'll see if we can get you the role you want.'

Dawn gave her a look of gratitude bordering on love as she left to see to nails, hair, and outfit, before coming in tomorrow for a dress rehearsal. 'This is a terrific agency,' she said from the door. 'It's more than an agency really, it's a place you'd want to come back to.'

Lena, Jessie and Mr Millar looked at each other, delighted.

They were on their way.

Louis ran up the stairs excitedly. 'They want me to do the desk tonight,' he said.

'The desk?'

'Yes. Someone called in sick, they have nobody. So I'm promoted from porter to night manager.'

'Will you have to work all night?'

'Yup. That's what we night managers do. Now, that's not too bad in terms of climbing the ladder, is it?' He was like a glowing handsome puppy dog looking for praise.

Lena looked at him as dispassionately as she could. No wonder the hotel saw him as a person who could stand behind a desk welcoming late guests, coping with any problems that might arise. It was amazing that they had let him wear a porter's uniform at all. He was obviously a man who should have higher status.

'You'll be exhausted.'

'Ah, but I'll have tomorrow off,' he said. 'And I thought maybe you might have a diplomatic flu and stay here to keep me company.'

'You'll need to sleep.'

'I'll sleep better if my arms were around you.'

'We'll see.' She smiled at him.

It was not the time to tell him she was devastated that he would not be here tonight to discuss with her finally what she must do. And how to give the children the good news. She knew that it was not the time to tell him that she had no intention of taking a day off from her job.

Instead she smiled as they found him a shirt that would be up to his new position.

'Will you miss me? Will you be lonely?'

'Yes to the first, no to the second. I'll put my feet up, maybe go out and explore the neighbourhood.'

'And you won't do anything ... you know, you won't make any decisions?'

He was asking her not to ring home. She knew that. 'Not a decision in the world,' Lena said. 'Not until you and I talk about them, and make them together.'

He seemed relieved. And then he was off, his quick light step running down the stairs so soon after he had come up them.

Lena lit a cigarette and inhaled deeply. Now, for the first time since she had woken this morning, she was on her own. With time to think and no other calls on her time. But it didn't seem right somehow. The walls of the room, with their pink and orange paper, seemed to be closing in on her. She remembered the Count of Monte Cristo and how the walls of his cell moved a little every day. This must be happening in her room. There was definitely less distance between the table and the window than there had been before. By the time she had finished her cigarette she knew she could not stay there a minute longer.

'I don't want you to think I'm going to be a dropper-in.'

'No, love. Don't say that. I can always do with the company.' Ivy had been doing the football pools. She gave it a great deal of time every week. When she won, it was going to change her life. She would buy a big hotel by the seaside, install a full-time manager, and she would live like a lady in a flat of her own on the top floor. 'Isn't that right, Hearthrug?' she asked the old cat. The cat purred happily in anticipation.

Lena stroked his old grizzled head. 'They're a great comfort, cats. I was very fond of Farouk at home, though he was truly the cat that walked by itself.' Her eyes seemed far away.

'Was that when you were a little girl?'

'No, no. Just back home,' Lena said. It was the first time she had let down the guard. She realised that Ivy had noticed.

Ivy said nothing but busied herself making the tea. There was no need to explain. Lena felt the same ease that she felt in Sister Madeleine's cottage, though two places more different would be hard to find.

Sister Madeleine on this winter night would be sitting by her fire, speaking with some one of Lough Glass's citizens. It might be Rita planning her future; it might be Paddles, the man who had run a bar for thirty-seven years without ever having a drink in it. Perhaps it was Kathleen Sullivan, the mournful widow who ran the garage and seemed to despair over every aspect of it, including her two strapping sons. And there would be some animal sitting on a sack: a fox, a dog, a turkey that had been saved from becoming Christmas Dinner because it had the good luck to wander to the hermit's house.

And there would be no questioning, no trying to defend the indefensible.

As it was here in Earl's Court in the busy room where there was hardly a square inch of the wallpaper showing. The wall was covered with shelves of knick knacks and there were pictures of outings long ago. A big mirror was almost useless as a looking glass since so many letters and postcards had been wedged into its frame. There were vases of coloured glass, gnomes, little egg cups and souvenir ashtrays. And yet the place had the same feel. A place where you could be yourself.

And where no one would demand any explanation that you might not be ready to give.

Very simply, as if it had been intended, Lena Gray began to tell Ivy Brown the story. The tea was poured, the packet of biscuits opened. And when it got to the bit about Sunday, the discovery of the newspaper, the phone call home, Ivy stood up and without a word produced two small glasses and a bottle of brandy. Lena opened her handbag and showed the cutting. At no stage did Ivy's small quizzical face look anything but sympathetic. It registered no shock, no disbelief, not even as they smoothed out the newspaper page and read of the death that had distressed everyone so much. Ivy seemed to take it all in, and to realise the enormity without resorting to panic.

Sister Madeleine never reached out and touched you. She gave warmth and support without the clasp or the embrace. Ivy Brown was the same. She stood across at the far side of her sitting room and leaned against the chest of drawers that held all her records.

Her arms were crossed. She looked like the kind of picture you would see in a newspaper to illustrate the British housewife. All that was needed was to have her hair in curlers. Her floral pinny was tied tightly around her small frame, her face set in a grim line as she listened to the tale unfolding. The waves of solidarity and support were almost tangible. If she had held a weeping Lena close to her breast, she couldn't have radiated more concern.

'Well, love,' she said after a long pause. 'You've made up your mind, haven't you?'

'No.' Lena was surprised. She had never been so much at sea.

'You have, Lena.' Ivy was very sure.

'Why do you say that? What have I decided to do?'

'You're not going to phone them, love. That's it, isn't it? You're not going to do a thing. You're going to let them think you're dead.'

They talked for what must have been hours.

Lena told of how Louis had loved her and left her. How he had come back. How this was the life she had dreamed of. She painted a picture of Martin McMahon that she hoped was fair. Until Sunday she would have spoken with admiration and deep affection. There would have been guilt, even though she had kept her part of the bargain to the letter.

But the letter was it.

His reaction had killed any feeling that she ever had for him. The man was a monster, a victim of small town respectability. They went through it bit by bit, like she had done with Louis. The possibility of the letter not getting to him. The eventual knowledge that this must not be a reasonable thing to suppose.

But with Ivy it was not a strain to talk. She didn't have to fear upsetting her at every turn. And in the end Ivy was as unshaken as she had been at the outset.

Louis Gray was the love of Lena's life. She had waited for him for thirteen years, and now they were together. Ivy and Lena both knew that nothing would be done that would jeopardise this.

'But my children?' Lena's voice was shaky. It was as if she knew that tears were not far away.

'What can you give them by going back?' Ivy asked. The silence between them was not a hostile one. Lena tried to think. She could hold them, and stroke them. But that would be taking, not giving. She might shame them. And then she would leave them again anyway. 'Why do you have to leave them twice?' Ivy asked. 'Wasn't once hard enough?'

'If they drag the lake and don't find a body, they'll know I'm not dead. They'll start looking.' As she spoke, Lena knew she had begun to make up her mind. She was, in fact, only hunting for flaws or danger areas in the plan.

'You said it was a deep lake.'

'Yes, yes.'

'So there may well have been people who drowned there and were never found.'

'Yes, that's true.'

'You love him, Lena. Let him know you're not going back to your other life. Let him be very sure. He doesn't want you wavering or dithering.'

'He left me to waver and dither for half a lifetime.'

'Yes. But you forgave him. You ran off with him. Don't end up losing them all.'

'Maybe I only ran after a dream.'

'It seems substantial enough. Don't lose him, Lena. There'll be too many waiting to catch him if you let him fall from your grasp.' She seemed to speak with great authority.

'Do you know all this because you did it?'

'No, love. I know it because I didn't do it.' Lena looked at her blankly. 'Ernest, in the pub. He may not be a looker like your Louis is, but he's the man I loved, and still do.'

'Ernest? That we met on Friday?'

'Ernest that I've met every Friday for years now.'

'Why do you meet him on Fridays?'

'Because it's what makes the week have a bit of purpose for me, and because his cow of a wife goes to her mother on Fridays.'

'And what happened?'

'I hadn't the guts. I wasn't brave enough.' Again the silence was an easy one. Ivy refilled their brandy glasses. 'I worked in the pub with him. I'd just started when the war broke out. Ron, that's my husband, he was called up. Anyway, it was a good time then. It sounds silly to say we all enjoyed the war, but you know what I mean. Folk were very friendly. You didn't know whether anyone would be here next week. It made for a lot of shortcuts. I might never have got to know Ernest if it hadn't been for the time. You see, there were air raid warnings, and we went down to shelters, and we all listened to the radio in the pub. It was very close, like people being wrecked together after a ship goes down.'

Ivy smiled at the memory of it all. 'He had two children and Charlotte was all eyes of course, suspecting things before they even began. And there was lots of chat about our brave boys fighting at the front and the tarts of wives having a great time running around. Everyone got the drift of it; it made things very unpleasant.'

'And did you love Ron at all?'

'No. Not like I knew love when I met Ernest. You see, girls just got married then. And I wasn't a raving beauty, as you can see. I didn't get many offers. I was glad to take Ron. I was twenty-nine, nearly thirty, when we married. He was ten years older. He wanted everything just so. He liked a nice clean house, a good meal on the table. He didn't ever want to go out. When we didn't have children he didn't seem all that put out. I think he thought they'd mess up the house. I went and got myself tested and all, but he wouldn't. I said we might adopt and he said he wouldn't raise another man's son.'

'Oh Ivy, I'm so sorry.'

'Yes. Well it was no worse than a lot of people had. And from what you say people in your Lough Glass put up with whatever hand they were dealt too.'

'Absolutely. All of them except me.'

'Well, I had your chance and didn't take it. That's why I know what I'm talking about.'

'Ernest?' Lena asked.

'Yes. He said we should go off together. But I was guilty. I was dead guilty. There I was, my husband out fighting for his country. Ernest with a wife and family. I was afraid. Afraid he'd regret it, that I wouldn't be woman enough for him. Afraid that Ron would have a breakdown. I didn't go, you see.'

'And what happened in the pub?'

'The pub. Yes. There was more action there than there was out at the Front, I tell you. Charlotte seemed to know all about it by radar. She knew when he had asked me to go with him, and when I said no. She picked her time perfectly. She said that she'd like me to leave and not darken the door again while she was on the premises. I left that day.'

'What did you do?'

'I went back to our flat and I cleaned it until it shone. When Ron came home from the war he had less to say than before he went. He was very discontented. The country didn't appreciate the soldiers, he said. There was no pleasing him. And then the lovely Charlotte wrote to him and told him that she thought he ought to know. It drove him over the top. He said I was filth and I was disgusting and he didn't want to know. There's a nice depressing story for you, isn't it love?'

'What are you telling me?'

'I'm telling you I have my Friday nights.'

'And Ron?'

'He left. It was strange really. He just said he wanted to hear no more about it. He moved out that very week, the week he heard from Charlotte.'

'And did you want him to stay?'

'At the time I suppose I did. I was frightened. I had no one, I had nothing to show for my life. But of course he had to go, he hated me, and I didn't even know him. I moved here to this flat. It was as different to the place we had together as you could imagine. I cleaned the house, and I did cleaning in other houses. I got the money together and when the house went on the market I got a mortgage and bought it.'

'Wasn't that wonderful?' Lena's eyes shone with admiration.

'Cold comfort as they say. Believe me, Lena, very cold. When I think of what I could have had.'

'And did you think . . . will she . . . suppose she . . .'

'It's too late, love. I made my decision. I let go of my chance.'

There was a silence.

'I know what you're telling me,' Lena said eventually.

'You have him, you love him, you've always loved him. If you ring them at home, you'll have lost everything.'

'So I have to fake being dead?'

'You never pretended to be dead. You left a letter telling what you did. You can't be blamed for what they think.'

'Kit and Emmet?' Lena's face was white.

'This way they'll remember you with love, not hate.'

'I don't think I can do it.'

'I've seen you look at him. You'll do it,' said Ivy.

Louis was back in high good humour at seven-thirty in the morning. 'So you're going to take the day off and spoil me?' he asked, head on one side, looking at her with the half smile she loved so much.

'Better than that,' Lena said to him. 'I'm going to drag you into bed with me now, and love you to death, then let you sleep peacefully for the day.'

He was about to complain. But she had already taken off her blouse slowly in the way he liked to see her undress. 'You're a very bossy lady,' he said. She had started to unbutton his shirt.

He was asleep before she left the flat.

'You always look so bright and cheerful, Mrs Gray,' said Mr Millar approvingly. She looked up at him from her desk, pleased.

She had crept from her bed so as not to wake Louis; she had dressed in the bathroom; she had run along through the rush hour crowds on wet streets. Her mind was racing at the enormity of allowing her children to think of her ever more as having drowned in the lake beside their home. She had miscarried a child.

And yet this man thought she looked bright and cheerful.

Back in Lough Glass people always thought she looked tired. 'Have you had the flu, Mrs McMahon?' they might ask in Hickey's the butcher's. 'Do you need a tonic at all?' Peter Kelly had boomed so often. 'You look pale, Helen my love,' Martin must have said a hundred times a year.

But here, in the midst of terrible confusion but with the man she loved, they all told her she looked blooming and happy. It must prove something.

'It's a very nice place to work, Mr Millar, and it's great to be in at the start of such new changes with you and Miss Park.'

Lena Gray had brightened up their office and their lives. She could see this in their faces and it made her feel better than ever.

The days passed. Sometimes they flew by, and Lena wondered how it could be time to close, she could hardly remember having reached lunch time. Other days time went so slowly she wondered was the world coming to an end and had everything slowed down. She roamed the second-hand shops and auction rooms of London and found wonderful wall hangings and Indian bedspreads to drape the shabby furniture in the flat. She bought a briefcase, a leather one with brass locks, for Louis. She polished it until it shone.

'Not really essential for a hall porter,' he said ruefully.

'Come on out of that. How many times have they asked you to do night manager. Your portering days are drawing to a close.'

And indeed they did.

Soon Louis was working on the night desk three times a week. And it didn't seem fitting for the guests to meet someone they had known in the administration to appear carrying their bags.

One evening Lena went with him to see where he worked.

'I can imagine you much better if I see it,' she said.

He hadn't wanted it at first. 'It's very hard to explain why,' he said. 'I sort of play a role at work, you know. I'm not my real self.'

'Neither am I,' Lena agreed.

And he had let her come.

Mr Williams the manager had been impressed with the handsome dark-haired woman that the Irishman had produced. 'No wonder he has been keeping you hidden,' Mr Williams said.

Lena knew just how to reply. 'Ah, that's very flattering of you, Mr Williams, but it's all my fault. I'm still so unfamiliar with London.' She was throwing herself at his mercy, saying she was a country person who didn't understand the big city.

Not flirting, that would have been crass.

It was exactly the right course to take. Mr Williams, a large bluff man, became protective and gallant. 'I hope you have both taken to the place. Louis is a very valued employee.'

'Oh, we intend to make a good life here, I assure you. London has so much to offer.'

'I'm surprised you can leave this attractive wife and work here at night.'

Lena spoke quickly. 'It wouldn't be my choice, Mr Williams. But I know that if Louis wants to work his way to working on the desk in the day time he has to put in his hours at the more antisocial end of things as well.' They all smiled. This was not a couple who groaned or complained. But it was a couple who intended to move upwards.

It was not long before Louis Gray was offered a position on the desk as an assistant manager. He was unfailingly courteous to those who had worked with him as porters. Particularly the head porter, who had been so difficult when he came first.

The Christmas lights were going up in London. Lena forced her mind away from the trains of thought that brought her down the road to Hickey's to order the turkey. There would be no decorations above McMahon's pharmacy this year.

As she had guessed, Ivy did not refer to the conversation they had had together on the wet Tuesday night when Lena had decided against ringing Lough Glass. If Ivy understood how strange and hard the decision had been she gave no sign, just little gestures of friendship. A pot of homemade jam that someone had given her, a couple of records that she didn't play any more. Lena knew that these were a gift because she had heard Louis say how much he loved 'Singing in the Rain'.

Ivy made no mention of Christmas. She must have known it would be a time of tension and drama for the young couple on the second floor. Sometimes Lena wondered about the kind of Christmases Louis had spent during the long years of their separation. But part of the promise and the plan had been that they would not talk about the past.

He would not ask about sleeping with her husband. She would not ask him about the times and the people and the places she knew nothing of.

It worked very well. They had their own little world. Sometimes he came to Sunday Mass with her, sometimes not. It was easier when he didn't go with her. Then she could buy the paper and read about what was happening in Lough Glass and the places for fifty miles around it. She read of land bought and sold, of children born, and of people buried.

And on Sunday, 21 December, when she went to the big church in Quex Road Kilburn to pray that God would help her sort out how to make Christmas a good Christmas for Louis and herself, Lena made a deal with God. She said to Him that He had always loved sinners, and shown them mercy and that if her only sin had been to run away with Louis then God might see it with a more forgiving eye.

'So,' Lena said, 'I don't cheat, I don't steal, I don't lie, apart from the one big one that we are husband and wife. I don't say bad things about people, I don't blaspheme, I don't miss Mass.' She had no way of knowing if God went along with the deal. But then, even if you weren't living in mortal sin you often didn't know whether God was going along with the deal either. You had to try to interpret His answers in your heart. It was hard sometimes. Especially in a big strange church with a lot of coughing and sneezing. It was a cold December day.

Lena went to the kiosk and bought the paper that told her of home. She read that her body had been found in the lake. That a verdict of death by misadventure had been returned. And that a large crowd had attended her funeral at the parish church in Lough Glass. Through her tears she saw that the chief mourners had been the late woman's husband Martin McMahon of the Lough Glass pharmacy, her daughter Mary Katherine and her son Emmet John. Their mother was dead and buried now in the churchyard. Someone else's bones had been found. And identified as hers.

Lena thought suddenly, and knew somehow, God had acted for her. Perhaps He had answered her prayers. Lena had no decision to make now. Now she could never go home.

4

Lilian Kelly brought up the subject again. 'Peter, I wish you'd put it more clearly to Martin. Tell him to bring the lot of them here for their Christmas dinner.'

'I suggested it . . .'

'Ah, you only suggested it . . . Tell them it would be the right thing to do. And that girl of theirs in the kitchen, too, if he's worried about her. She can help Lizzie here. Lizzie'd be glad of it. They don't want to be sitting looking at each other in that house after all that happened there.'

'Nothing happened there, Lilian,' Peter Kelly said. He was reading a medical journal as always, and seemed to give little attention to his wife.

Lilian appealed to her sister Maura, who had come to join them for the Christmas holiday. 'Come on, Maura. Tell him they can't sit there looking at each other . . .'

'But they're going to have to some time,' Maura said. 'Maybe they should get used to it rather than running away.'

Peter looked up, surprised. 'That's what Martin said himself.'

'Well then.'

In the hotel Dan O'Brien asked Mildred did she think they should ask the McMahons in for their Christmas dinner.

'We don't want to be imposing on them.'

'It wouldn't be imposing, it would be a kindness.' Dan didn't relish the thought of yet another empty celebration with his wife and son, and little conversation. At least the presence of the McMahons might force some talk around his dinner table.

'I think they're going to have their own kind of a meal, you know, to make things seem normal,' Philip suggested. He too would have loved Kit sitting at his table and to have stood to serve her, but he knew it wouldn't happen.

'Well, there you are then,' said Mildred O'Brien. She had never liked that arty Helen McMahon, and everyone knew that there was something suspicious about her death. Note or no note, there were a lot of people in Lough Glass who thought she had ended her own life.

Mrs Hanley in the drapery was having severe trouble with her daughter Deirdre. 'You want to go *where* on Christmas Day?' she asked.

'Out for a walk, visiting graves, you know.'

'No, I don't know. Whose graves?'

'People who died, Mam. That's what's done on Christmas Day. They go and say prayers for the dear departed.'

'You have no dear departed at the moment. Except yourself might be heading that way if you're not careful.'

'You're a selfish, unfeeling person.'

'Tell me, who would you pray for if you went out on Christmas Day . . . just one.'

'Well, I could pray up at the graveyard for Stevie Sullivan's father.'

'He's not buried there, he's buried in a madhouse thirty miles away!' Deirdre Hanley's mother was triumphant.

'Well, for Kit McMahon's mother.'

'She's barely buried. Come on out of that, Deirdre, you want to go out to get up to no good with someone, and when I find out who it is there'll be trouble I tell you.'

'Who could get up to no good in this town?' Deirdre asked with a sigh.

'You could. And I have my eye on you. Is it that young fellow, Dan O'Brien's son?'

'Philip O'Brien!' There was genuine horror and revulsion in Deirdre Hanley's voice.

Mrs Hanley knew she had to look elsewhere for a suspect.

Sister Madeleine refused invitations for Christmas Day, but it was said that she had more on her table than most of the people in Lough Glass. They tactfully found out what others were bringing so that items would not be duplicated.

Rita said she'd just take her a loaf of bread. 'At least I know you'll eat that. You'll be giving the plum pudding to the gypsies and the slices of turkey to the little fox or whatever you have nowadays.'

'I have a big lame goose,' said Sister Madeleine. 'And it would be very undiplomatic of me to feed her something as nearly related as a turkey. But you're right, I love the bread.'

'It'll be very hard above in the house there on Thursday,' Rita said.

'No harder than any other day.' Sister Madeleine was surprisingly unsympathetic.

'But you know, thinking back on other Christmas Days . . .'

'It's better that she's safely buried. It does give people a sort of peace, you know.'

'Would you mind where you were buried yourself, Sister Madeleine?'

'No, not at all. But then, I'm as odd as two left shoes. You know that.'

'Is there anything I should do, do you think?'

'No, I don't believe in putting on an act. Whatever's going to happen will happen.'

'I wish they'd talk about her.'

'They might at Christmas.'

*

'Brother Healy! Always good to see you. They tell me that the Christmas Crib down at St John's has to be seen to be believed.' Mother Bernard was loftily gracious.

'All the work of that young criminal Kevin Wall. Apparently the hermit gave him greenery and hay and all kinds of things. The Lord moves in mysterious ways, Mother Bernard.'

'And isn't it a good thing that the Lord directed them where to find the body of poor Helen McMahon in time to have her buried in Holy Ground before Christmas?' The nun spoke as if it were another tiresome problem that God had conveniently tidied up and got out of the way before the Christmas season.

But Brother Healy knew what she meant. 'Lord have mercy on her. It was indeed,' he said. Teachers hear more than they are meant to, and he had heard a lot of speculation, mainly in the school yard.

There was some complicated story that young Wall had taken out the McMahons' boat and that this meant that Emmet's mother had not drowned from it. And then there were rumours that she might have been having a romance with one of the gypsies. Maybe she had run away with him. Or they were hiding her in their caravans.

Nothing you'd want to burden Sean O'Connor with up at the Garda Station, but all the same, it was great when that body had been found. Mother Bernard was right, it had been good of the Lord to direct them to find Helen McMahon and finish her troubled life off as every life should be finished, with hymns being sung and Father Baily accompanying the coffin to the churchyard.

'What does Emmet think about Santa Claus?' Clio asked on Christmas Eve.

'He thinks like we all think.'

'No, I mean, would he be expecting something . . . Your father mightn't remember.'

'It was always Mam that did it.' Kit was defensive in the recall of her mother's good deeds.

'Oh!' Clio was surprised.

'It's all right. He knows, but I'll do it for him anyway. Something beside the chimney.'

'And who'll do it for you?'

'Dad might leave me some soap from the chemist's.' She sounded doubtful.

There were so many things that Mother used to do, things that everyone took for granted. At Christmas time she used to fill the house with holly boughs; Father used to laugh and say it was like living in a forest. He would never say that again. Mother used to go to town and buy presents ages before Christmas and there was never a trace of them around the house. Kit still didn't know how she had got the bicycles home with her the year of the bikes, or how she had hidden the record player last year. Was it only last year when everything had been all right?

And Mother knew the right kind of clothes to get Rita, always something brand new in a box from the big town. Kit and Father didn't even know what size Rita was and couldn't go looking or measuring or anything. Mother always had boxes of crackers stored somewhere, and long paper chains that criss-crossed the kitchen. Kit wondered should she look for them. They weren't in the kitchen cupboards. Perhaps they were in Mother's room, her little secret surprise.

But they were in mourning. Maybe they wouldn't have a Christmas tree even. They would have to have a crib, with the straw in it. That hadn't to do with celebrating, that had to do with welcoming baby Jesus. Kit sighed with the weary burden of it all.

Clio thought it was still about the Christmas stockings. 'We could do them for you, you know, my mother and father could. They'd be glad to do something,' Clio said, her eyes full of tears.

Kit shook her head. 'No, I'll manage it, thanks very much all the same. The Santa Claus bit isn't the worst bit, let me tell you.'

'What is the worst bit?'

'She won't know how I turn out. She'll never know.'

'She'll know from heaven.'

'Yes,' Kit said. The silence lay between them. Despite the comforting words that Father Baily had intoned over the coffin, Kit knew that her mother had not been met by the angels and let into paradise. She had committed the great sin against Hope, for which there is no forgiveness.

Kit's mother was in Hell.

*

'Christmas Eve can be hell on earth,' Ivy said to Lena. 'Everyone running round doing their last-minute shopping. It's as if Christmas comes on people by surprise, as if they hadn't known for weeks it was on its way.'

'We work until lunchtime, though I don't know why. Nobody wants to come to look for a job on Christmas Eve.'

'Probably Mr Millar and Jessie Park have nowhere to go,' Ivy said shrewdly.

'I'm sure you're right.' Lena realised that this was indeed true.

Some people's lives just revolved around their work. In the hotel where Louis worked they stayed open for Christmas mainly because the staff had nowhere else to go. Mr Williams had told them there would be a big staff meal at four o'clock. He would be honoured if Lena would join them. It had indeed been an answer to all her problems. There would be no false re-creating of a Christmas scene for the two of them. The flat had been nicely decorated but it would make things much easier for her if they had a duty dinner to attend.

'And what will you do for the day?' Lena looked into Ivy's face as she spoke and she knew the other woman was lying.

'Oh, don't let me begin. I have to go here, there and everywhere. I'm like a doctor on Christmas Day . . . too many obligations from the past.'

Lena nodded sympathetically. It was better that way.

*

'Isn't this a barbarous country that they don't open the pubs on Christmas Day?' Peter Kelly said to Kit's father as they walked home from Mass.

'Aren't you the one who's always saying it's the number of pubs that has us in the state we're in, as a nation?'

'Ah yes, but that's a different argument entirely.'

'Would you like to come in then and have something sociable?' Kit thought her father looked wretched. A morning of having people sympathise all over again had taken its toll.

Dr Kelly seemed to sense this too. 'Not at all. You've enough of chat, go back to the family.'

'Yes.' The word hung there, empty and sad.

They took off their coats and blew on their fingers.

'That smells very nice, Rita.'

'Thank you, sir.'

They sat down together, the four of them, as they had done since Helen had left that day two months before. Martin sat in the seat that Helen had used, and Kit had moved to her father's place. Emmet had moved up one, and Rita sat in the place that Emmet used to have.

When Helen McMahon had been alive they still ate in the kitchen, but Rita had taken her meal at the end of the table, or sometimes she had just served and eaten her own meal later. It might appear that the departure of the Mistress had somehow equalised things more, had done away with the class distinctions, but this was not Mother's fault, and Kit wanted that known, defined in some way.

'You could always have had your Christmas dinner with us Rita, do you know that? I mean, it was just that you'd be standing up making gravy and everything . . .'

'Of course I know that,' Rita said.

'Rita doesn't need to be told such a thing.' Her father sounded sharp.

'But Daddy, in a way people *have* to say things. Sister Madeleine says that we don't often say the most important things, we say little silly ones.'

'True for her, true for her,' Father nodded. He looked very old, Kit thought. He nodded like an old man would nod and repeat things. They were silent for a while after that, as if none of them knew what to say.

Rita spoke eventually. 'Will I serve it, sir, dish it up for you . . . for us all?'

'Yes, please, Rita. That would be fine.' Father's face looked wretched; he had great dark hollows under his eyes. He must not have slept at all last night, remembering like they had all remembered all the Christmas Eves before, when there was so much to do. This one had seemed unbearably long.

'Well, we have grapefruit first,' Rita said. 'The mistress taught me to cut it with a jagged edge you see, so that it looks a bit like an ornament or something . . . and to put a glacé cherry on top of each one divided into four like a flower . . . and a bit of angelica pretending to be the stem of the flower. The mistress said it didn't hurt to make things look nice . . . Presentation is what she called it.'

They all studied the grapefruit, trying to think of something to say about it.

There was a lump in Kit's throat. 'No one else in Lough Glass or anywhere else would be having anything as nice as this,' she said in a voice that sounded unnatural in her own ears. It was as if she were reading lines from a play.

'Oh, that's right, that's right,' her father said. 'Nobody else would have a dinner like this, we always said so . . .' He didn't quite finish the sentence because it was obvious that he realised that nobody else was having a dinner under such circumstances. Everywhere else behind the closed curtains of Lough Glass people were eating and drinking, they were planning an afternoon laughing or arguing or sleeping in front of the fire. They weren't sitting bolt upright trying to swallow sections of a grapefruit so bitter it stuck on their tongues and made their eyes water again.

And when the turkey came to the table they all looked away from Father's face. Mother used to say that it was well he had chosen to be a chemist and not a surgeon or the population here would have been wiped out. Mother had taught herself to carve, and did it deftly. Rita had not liked to usurp her position.

'Isn't this grand?' Father said with a death head grin on his face trying to cheer them up. 'This is the grandest turkey we ever had.' They said that every year too, and talked about the Hickey family going to the turkey market five miles away and picking the best, the plumpest and youngest birds. There was a silence. 'Isn't it grand, Emmet?' Poor Father was waving the carving knife, trying to smile and spread cheer. He didn't realise he looked like a butcherous murderer in a film, or in one of the mobile theatres that came to the town every two years.

Emmet looked at him mutely.

'Say something, lad. Your mother wouldn't want you to be moping there and all of you sitting in silence; she'd like there to be a bit of a chat. It's Christmas Day, and we're all here and you have the memory of a great mother to keep with you for the rest of your lives. Isn't that grand?'

Emmet looked at his father's red face. 'It's not grand at all, Daddy,' he said. 'It's ttt-ttt-errible.' His stutter was as bad as it had ever been before.

'We have to pretend that things are all right, Emmet son,' he said. 'Don't we, Kit? Don't we, Rita?'

They looked at him wordlessly.

Then Kit said, 'Mother wouldn't pretend. I don't think she'd have said things were grand if they weren't.'

They could hear the clock on the landing ticking. In other houses people would barely hear a word anyone else was saying, but in this house they could hear the purring of the old cat, the ticking of a clock and the gurgling sounds of saucepans still simmering on the Aga cooker beside them.

Father's face was grim, grey and grim. Kit looked at him in anguish. Father must still be turning in his bed at night wondering why Mother had left that night and got drowned.

For the hundredth time she wondered had she done the right thing in burning that letter. And yet again she told herself that she had. Think of what would have happened when Mother's body had been found if her daughter had not acted in the way she had? And Father must have heard, too, the story that fool Kevin Wall had told about how he took the McMahon boat out on the night that Mother had drowned. As if anyone would believe Kevin Wall even if he told you today was Christmas Day.

Father was speaking again. 'I'm going to start by telling the truth just like your mother did . . .' His voice broke. 'And the truth is that it's *not* all right,' he said through his tears. 'It's terrible. I miss her so much I can't be comforted by the thought of seeing her in heaven later on. I'm so lonely for her . . .' His shoulders heaved. The mood changed. Kit and Emmet left their places to go and put their arms around him. They crowded together for what seemed a long time. Rita sat at her place. She was like the background. Like the kitchen curtains, like old Farouk asleep on the stool beside the Aga. Like the grey wet rain outside.

And then they stopped, and it was as if a thunderstorm had cleared the air. They spoke with lighter voices; the tightrope of pretence had been taken away. Wasn't it extraordinary that Sister Madeleine had more or less foretold to her that this would happen?

Into the midst of this came a sharp shrill sound. It was the telephone ringing. On Christmas Day, a day when nobody made any calls except for an emergency.

*

In the Dryden Hotel they made a great effort to have a cheerful Christmas for the staff. A lot of them had been there a long time. Most had weathered the war years with loyalty and, as James Williams knew, there were many who had no real homes to go to.

A Christmas tree that had been set up in the hall to establish a festive mood for guests was now in the dining room, and everyone had a role, including spouses. Lena's job was to do place cards.

Louis gave her the list. 'They want artistic writing,' he explained. 'It's a mad idea, but you did volunteer.'

'No, I think it's a good idea. It'll be a souvenir of the day,' she said. She asked him to bring her a sheaf of Dryden Hotel notepaper, so that she could stick the name on top of each card. 'It's more like an invitation then,' she said, and painstakingly wrote out the names. Barry Jones, Antonio Bari, Michael Kelly, Gladys Wood . . . Each one with great attention and little holly leaves and berries drawn as an order.

At the start they were shy, awkward to be allowed to sit down at the tables instead of serving at them or sweeping up under them. But James Williams kept circulating the bowl of punch and soon the inhibitions went. By the time they were carving the turkey some of them had already pulled the Christmas crackers which were meant for the plum pudding stage. There was a roar of conversation from the twenty-nine strangely assorted people sitting around the table.

Lena slipped away to the ladies' room and just beside the door she saw

MAEVE BINCHY

the little booth for the telephone. It was five-thirty in the afternoon. This time last year she had been down by the lake with the children, walking off the effects of the dinner. That's what she would have called it, but escaping the stifling walls of the house is what it would have been. Martin had looked at her eagerly, but she had advised him to have a little sleep by the fire. At the time she had felt guilty denying her husband the simple pleasure of a walk with his own wife on Christmas Day.

Now she felt no pity, only rage with the man she had begged to play fair. If it had not been for Martin she could have spoken to Kit and to Emmet this Christmas, sent them presents, told them that she loved them, planned for them to come and see her at Easter.

Anger rose in her throat. She could feel it. Before she realised what she was doing she was in the phone box and dialling the operator. She gave the number and waited.

The operator came back. 'It appears that Lough Glass is a small place, caller, with a manual exchange. Unless the call is in the nature of an emergency it cannot be put through on Christmas Day.'

'It *is* an emergency,' she said in a tight voice.

She heard the clicks and the sounds, the long ringing as the phone rang in the post office on the corner of Lakeview Road and the main street. It seemed to ring endlessly. Lena wondered that Mrs Hanley next door hadn't come in and answered it. She was as nosy as anyone in the town. Surely she wondered who could be ringing for what emergency.

But eventually the slow feet of Mona Fitz must have moved themselves to the phone. Lena heard her halting voice and the sense of outrage that she had been woken from her sleep.

The number of the house was given.

'It's only emergency calls on Christmas Day,' Mona said.

Lena clenched her fists with impatience. What trouble was it to the stupid woman just to plug the bloody piece of equipment into one of the row of holes in front of her. She could have it done and finished with by the time she went into all this tiresome explanation and cross questioning.

'That's what the caller says; it *is* an emergency.'

'Very well, so.'

Lena could imagine her putting on her glasses to direct the call a few yards down the street.

A few rings and she heard Martin reply. 'Hello,' he said, his voice hesitant and doubtful. Did he know that she would ring on Christmas Day? That he couldn't keep her from her children for ever just by pretending she was dead. Was he frightened now, and in an agony wondering how he was going to explain the whole terrible mess that he had created? 'Hello,' Martin said again. 'Who's that?'

The whole terrible mess. It could be undone in a moment. But so would Lena's life. The life that had only just begun. She said nothing and clicked the bar in the cradle that held the receiver. She could hear the operator in London saying 'Are you there, caller? Your number has been reached . . .'

She could hear Mona Fitz saying, 'What kind of emergency is this if there's no one on the line?'

She heard Martin saying 'Hello, Hello, Who is it?'

Then Mona spoke to Martin. I wouldn't have let this happen for the world, Martin, but it's a man from England, from London. They said it was an emergency.'

'A man . . . ?' Martin sounded startled, but not guilty. He didn't sound like a man who was trying to hush everything up. But then she didn't know him at all.

'No, Martin. I think I was only speaking to the operator . . . Hold on till I see is he still there.'

Lena listened. She heard Martin and Mona and the operator discuss the fact that someone had definitely phoned that number. 'It's all right, I have the number the caller was phoning from. I'll get them back,' he said.

She hung up, shaking from head to toe. *Why* had she done anything so stupid? Now they would call the hotel, and ask who had phoned Lough Glass in Ireland. Louis would be furious. The coins in her hand were hot and sweaty.

Then, as she knew it would, the phone rang. She lifted the receiver at the first sound. 'Were you trying to call Lough Glass in the Irish Republic?'

'No,' Lena said, she tried to put a Cockney accent into her voice.

'But someone from that number was calling Lough Glass . . .'

'No, I said I was calling *Loughrea* . . .' she said.

The operator got back to the others. 'It was the wrong place,' he said.

'I don't know how you got mixed up with Lough Glass and Loughrea,' Mona grumbled.

'That's all right then,' said Martin.

'Caller, do you want to give me the Loughrea number then?' The operator was a man who had to work on Christmas Day and did not seem to be enjoying it.

Lena said nothing. In the background she heard her daughter asking who was on the phone.

'It's nothing Kit. It's someone trying to phone Loughrea.' She couldn't hear what Kit said, but whatever it was, Martin laughed. Had she said, 'That's a roundabout way to do it?'

'Caller?' The operator was impatient now.

'Listen, I've changed my mind. It's too late,' she said.

'Thanks a million,' said the young man.

'So I'll hang up now.' Lena was anxious that there should be no further checking on the number.

'Yes, Madam.'

'And you are not going to call back?' She wanted to make sure it was safe to leave the booth.

'No, Madam. Goodbye, Madam.' She stood in the box feeling dizzy. She hadn't been buried a week and her daughter was already able to laugh about things. She took deep breaths until she had the strength to walk back to the festivities.

'Are you all right?' It was James Williams who asked the question. 'You've been gone a long time.'

'I'm fine ... Did I miss anything?' she asked.

Louis was the centre of a laughing group. Gladys Wood, whose name she had carefully written out, had a paper hat at a rakish angle and her arm around Louis' neck.

'Read my fortune to me again,' she shouted happily.

'It says you will meet a dark handsome man,' Louis read obediently from the little piece of paper that Gladys had found in her Christmas cracker.

'I've met him,' screamed Gladys.

'Oh dear,' whispered James Williams. His benevolent smile of the owner glad to see the staff enjoying themselves was a little strained.

'A little over-excited.' Lena was amazed at her own power of speech. She had thought that after the incident on the telephone she might not be able to talk at all.

'For 364 days a year that woman works in the still room, quiet as a mouse. Christmas, regular as clockwork, she gets drunk. And spends the rest of the year apologising for it.'

'Will she get sick, do you think?' Lena asked, in a detached professional way, as if she were asking the time of a train.

'Very probably, I fear.'

'Do you think someone should take her out, just in case?' Lena was looking at Louis' jacket. It had been her Christmas present to him, and had cost a lot of money. She didn't want to see it ruined.

'Yes, I wonder could I prevail on you ...'

'Well, I don't think I am exactly the person who should approach her. After all, it is my husband she is manhandling. Perhaps it might be thought I had a special interest in seeing her escorted from the room.'

'You are truly wonderful, Mrs Gray,' he said, flicking his fingers for Eric the head porter.

'Lena,' she corrected him.

'Lena,' he smiled, and ordered Eric to get one of the girls to march Miss Wood out to the ladies' room and to stay with her. Right now.

Louis ran a finger around his collar and smiled at them ruefully.

He could have escaped earlier, Lena thought with a flash of annoyance. But then, women always went for Louis, he was used to it. It made him smile, and she had to remember to smile about it too.

*

'What are you going to make as a New Year resolution?' Clio was eager to know.

'I haven't thought, what with everything.'

Clio *had* thought. 'I'm going to get good-looking, really good-looking, mind.'

'But you are good-looking, aren't you?'

'No I'm not. I'm like a picture in a children's book. The Dish Ran Away With The Spoon,' Clio said tragically.

Kit giggled. 'Which are you, the dish or the spoon?'

'I'm like both of them.'

'Oh, don't be silly, Clio, you can't be like both. One's thin, one's fat.'

'But they both have awful dull expressions, no character, faces like the moon.'

'And how are you going to get character?'

'I'm going to read books and look at what beautiful people get themselves up like.'

'Do you mean clothes? We haven't any money for clothes.'

'No. Just their faces, their way of going on.'

'We're not allowed to wear make-up.'

'Stop finding fault. That's *my* resolution. I'll look smashing when I'm thirteen.'

'Sure, *be* good-looking. Who's stopping you?'

'You are, Kit, you're always so ... I don't know, so shruggy.'

Kit was contrite. 'What ways are you going to learn? Maybe I could learn them too.'

'I know about putting vaseline on your eyelashes. It makes them grow. And I think we should suck in our cheeks a bit to give us interesting shapes in our faces,' said Clio.

They puckered their faces in and laughed at the results.

'There must be more to it than that,' Kit said.

'We'll learn.' Clio was determined.

'It looks as if we're going to kiss someone.'

'We should practise that, too.'

'On who, for heaven's sake?'

'On anyone who turns up.'

'You can't be serious.'

'Of course I am. How else will we know if we're doing it right?'

'Like who?' Kit was practical.

'You could kiss Philip O'Brien; he's always ogling you ...'

'And who would you kiss?'

'Stevie Sullivan, maybe.' Clio smiled archly.

'But isn't he always kissing Deirdre Hanley?' Kit was surprised that Clio should choose someone so busy.

'She's old. She'll go off in looks. Men often turn to younger women.'

'She's only sixteen.'

'Yes, well. In 1953 she'll be seventeen and she'll go on and on, just getting older.'

'Do you like Stevie?'

'No. But he's good-looking.'

'And is Philip O'Brien good-looking?'

'No, but he's keen on you.' Clio had the world sorted out.

There was snow in January. Anna Kelly threw a snowball at Emmet McMahon. In the time-honoured ritual he scooped a handful of snow and pushed it down her neck as she screamed with excitement. He laughed too.

'Are you over it now?' Anna asked.

'Over it?'

'Your mammy being dead?'

'No, I'm not over it. I've sort of got used to it, I suppose.'

'Can I play with you and Kevin Wall?' she asked.

'No, Anna. I'm sorry, but you're a girl.'

'But that's not fair.'

'It's the way it is.' Emmet was philosophical.

'Kit and Clio won't let me play with them, they're girls.'

'But they're old girls.'

'Are they horrible to you like they are to me?' Anna hoped Emmet was a victim too.

'No, they're not horrible at all.'

'I wish I was really really old. Like twenty. Then I'd know what to do.'

'What would you do?' Emmet was interested.

Anna was a funny little thing in her scarlet coat and pixie hood and red excited face. 'I'd come back here and take Clio and Kit out on the lake and hold them both under the water and drown them,' she said triumphantly. Then she remembered. 'Oh Emmet,' she said. Emmet said nothing. 'Emmet, I'm so sorry.'

He was walking away. Anna ran after him. 'I'm so stupid. That's why nobody will play with me. I just want you to know I forgot. That's all. I just forgot.'

Emmet turned. 'Yes, well. It was *my* mother and I didn't forget.' He began to stammer at the words 'forget' and 'mother'. Anna had tears running down her face.

At that moment Stevie Sullivan came out of his garage. 'Hey, leave her alone, Emmet. She's only a baby. Don't make her cry.'

Emmet turned on his heel and went into his house.

Anna turned her tear-stained face to Stevie. 'I have no friends,' she said.

'Yeah, that's a problem,' said Stevie, looking idly down the road towards Hanley's drapery in case he might catch sight of his enthusiastic friend Deirdre taking a little stroll down the snow-covered street of Lough Glass with plans for another meeting.

*

James Williams took a personal interest in training Louis Gray to be the person that most customers met first when they arrived at the Dryden. He made sure that the handsome Irishman was well dressed and smartly turned out.

'I can get my shirts done in the hotel laundry,' Louis told Lena proudly. 'That'll save you washing and ironing.'

It certainly saved time and space. But in a way she had enjoyed doing it for him. It was part of playing husband and wife. Back in Lough Glass she had never done the ironing. Rita had done it as a matter of course. Sometimes now she wondered how *had* she spent her days in a home where she had no role.

And Louis told of more and more successes.

This was a place and a time where people just wanted proof that you could do a job and had the ability to get on with others. The war had changed everything. There was no need for written certificates and coming up through some traditional profession.

Lena knew that Louis was not exaggerating when he said that being on that desk was being at the heart of the whole hotel. Everyone in the Dryden had to consult him about some aspect of the way the place ran. The housekeeper and the chambermaids checked about the times that the different rooms should be made up. He would talk to the chef about the possibility of placing a copy of the menu on a stand in the hall. This way, when visitors were going out they might be persuaded to come back again for their lunch.

It was Louis who suggested that the porters wear name badges.

'I know who I am, thank you,' said Eric, the head porter, who had always regretted having allowed Louis to be taken on and to rise so far above him.

Louis never acknowledged any resentment. Perhaps he didn't even see it. 'Of course you do, Eric. And so do the regulars. But what about the one-off Americans? They'll want to know the name of the good guy who welcomed them to the Dryden.'

Eric saw the reason for it, but did not notice any increase in his tips. In fact, most of the dollars that changed hands went towards Louis Gray. Americans *did* appreciate the personal service, the way he remembered their names, how he could give them good suggestions of where to go and how to spend the holidays.

Nobody ever called Louis a manager; he was Mr Gray on the desk. People were urged to consult him on everything and Louis never let them down.

'I'd never get another job nearly as good as this. I must make myself as indispensable as I can possibly be here,' he said, and Lena knew he was right. Not even the most glowing reference would give Louis an entrée to any similar position at another hotel. He had no written qualifications, but he would always get by on charm once installed.

Her mind went sometimes to his previous lives in Spain and in Greece. Even back in the early days in Dublin as a travelling salesman, which was how she had first met him, he was never impatient with people or seeming anxious to be out of their company but always restless to do more or get more out of whatever was going. That was an extraordinary mixture in one man. He looked so alive with the lopsided, small-boy smile.

Month by month his wages increased and so did his perks, a lot of this due to Lena. She had seen that there was a small storeroom behind the front desk. Little by little the place was transformed. All the old boxes, broken bicycles and legless chairs were moved out. In their place came old tables beginning to show too much wear in bedrooms or reception rooms. Louis found an umbrella stand and a row of brass coat hooks on a mahogany stand. No longer did he have to put his coat in the crowded area where staff garments were pushed. And yet no one could question it. He was giving himself no lordly airs. He was only taking over a disused room. Making the place tidier, in fact.

Louis noted with pleasure that people who were senior to him in status in the hotel took him very seriously, but he moved cautiously.

'I can't just go in there to that room and close the door, when I'm meant to be on the desk,' he said to Lena.

'Have you any friend in maintenance, someone who could put a pane of glass in the top of it? Like Ivy's door. You could even have a curtain, a net curtain. Then you could see when you were wanted outside. It would give you the option of being in or out.'

And it worked.

James Williams, if he noticed the expansionist tendencies of the new clerk on the desk, must have approved of them because nothing was said. And no one entered Louis Gray's territory without knocking.

The months passed. Their love grew stronger. Lena was sure of that. There was nothing they could not talk about. They spoke of her children and how she had done the best thing for them. He praised her for her courage. 'You're like a heroine, a real-life heroine,' he would tell her. And he meant it. As he stroked her hair and took her face in his hands he said she was like a lioness, and there was nothing she could not do.

Sometimes Lena wondered whether there might be other people in London living new lives like she was. Perhaps there were hundreds of thousands of them, people who left one way of living and took up another. It wasn't as hard as it sounded. After all, here she was with a new husband – in the eyes of the world anyway – a new home, a new job, a new look. Few people from Lough Glass would recognise the tailored, trim figure hastening through the streets of London as Helen McMahon, wife of Martin the cheerful local chemist. If they saw her bending over files and encouraging young applicants for jobs in large companies they would be amazed. Mrs McMahon, so private a person, someone who didn't engage in long chats, yet here she was urging these girls to make the best of themselves, telling them the sky was the limit, begging them to take more night classes, increase their speeds, improve their image. How would Mrs McMahon of Lough Glass know such things and get people to believe her?

When she looked back on her life there, thirteen years of living in the small community by the lake, Lena realised that there was so much she *could* have done. She could have suggested that she work with Mrs Hanley and brighten up her dowdy shop, get in the kind of clothes that the women of Lough Glass would have enjoyed wearing, colourful garments for the children; she would have suggested training one of the Hanley daughters as a dressmaker so that alterations could be done on the premises.

Or Mildred O'Brien in the hotel? Look at all the things she could have done to help the Central Hotel out of the last century, things that she was doing now with Louis for the Dryden.

If she had persuaded Martin to let her work in the pharmacy, she could have done the kind of windows and displays she was doing here in an employment agency where there was so little scope. Think what she might have done if she had all those soaps and cosmetics to work on. She could have lined the windows with greenery and draped them with fancy materials and papers so that no one could resist coming in.

But Martin wouldn't hear of it. No wife of mine is going to have to go out to work. He used to say it with his face bursting with pride, as if by standing alone hour after hour in that dreary pokey place he was somehow making her into a queen, someone who wouldn't have to raise a hand.

A lot of the time she had felt grateful to him, Martin the undemanding husband who had taken her to a peaceful place by a big beautiful lake when her heart was broken and yearning for Louis who had left her. Martin, who had asked her no questions and promised her escape from anxiety and a restful life.

But now she felt totally different about him. No longer could she see his jokes as kindly meant and his funny faces as loving attempts to entertain her. Now she saw everything about him as a deep and destructive insecurity, a wish to trap her, keep her like a caged bird. A man who could not face up to the fact that his wife had left him for another man, but who had carried on a charade . . . even to the point of getting his friend Peter to identify a totally different body as hers.

What kind of people were these? They were barbarians. She had given birth to two children in a land of barbarians.

Lena ached for her children. Although she talked a little about them to Louis, it was only skimming the surface. She could not let him know how large a part of her mind they occupied. Louis was in many ways a child himself; he would not want to share this part of her with Kit and Emmet. She loved and needed him so much, it would be an act of folly to weep and cling to him and tell him how much she missed her children. It would be to tell him that he was not enough for her, that the decision to go with him had involved too much sacrifice. And that was not true.

Old Sister Madeleine had once said to her that in the end people do what they want to do. Even not doing something is a decision. So she had decided to leave her children. She must remember that and face it, even though she could not have foreseen that Martin would go through this grotesque charade, letting them think she was dead. She had made the choice to leave them. She must have wanted to be with Louis more than with them.

It was a harsh fact to face but Lena felt stronger for admitting it to herself. She must plunge herself into her new life and live it without regret. Live it in as full a way as possible, do all the things that she always had the power to do but never the chance. Sometimes she wondered would they be surprised back in Lough Glass to know just how very much she was doing. And to know that there were not enough hours in the day for all she had to do, that she was nearly running Millar's Employment Agency on her own.

Neither Mr Millar nor Jessie Park had contributed one single idea to her entire reorganisation programme. But they were easy to lead and quick to agree that business had doubled. Bigger and better-known bureaux had come to have a look at them. There had even been a feature about their new-look offices in a local paper. Lena had kept very much in the background.

'Please, Mrs Gray, you would be an adorment to the picture,' Mr Millar begged.

Lena had prepared for this. She had given Jessie a voucher to a hairdresser and the loan of a smart jacket to replace the old fuzzy cardigan.

'No, no truly. You are the ones who run it,' Lena said, refusing to pose for the press picture.

After all, she *was* meant to be dead. There was no use having her photograph in a newspaper. Who knew who might see it?

'You're looking pale,' Ivy said to her one day.

'I don't know what it is, but I don't feel great, certainly,' Lena agreed.

'Are you pregnant?' Ivy asked.

'No, not that.' Lena spoke sharply.

She saw Ivy look at her thoughtfully. Those small buttons of eyes understood everything. They probably understood that Louis and Lena would not have a child. The matter had been brought up and discussed. But both their careers were starting out so well here. Perhaps they should not think of it for the moment. Lena smiled wryly at the idea of putting things off for the moment. She was thirty-nine years of age. Next year she would be forty. The moment had probably passed already. The child that she had begun to lose in Brighton was her last. The two she had in Ireland were lost to her. She was a woman with no children. A career woman, as they were beginning to call themselves in the London of 1953.

'Suppose I were to send you a lot of business, could we come to a deal?' Lena asked Grace at the hairdresser's.

Grace had once come to Millar's looking for a secretarial job. She was so elegant looking and had such a way with customers that Lena realised she would be lost in an office. Her sympathetic personality was much more suited to a post where she would meet the public. Grace West, a tall handsome young woman whose mother was from Trinidad, had been anxious to get what they called an office job – it would be such a step up. She had been doubtful at first about hairdressing. A lot of West Indian girls did that. It wouldn't be seen as a great success.

'Yes, but when you're running the place, then you'll be a success,' Lena had said.

Grace did not do people's hair, she made the appointments, she kept the till, she strolled around in her elegant suits, advising and admiring.

'A little more conditioner on Mrs Jones, I think,' she would say. 'Why not give Miss Nixon an extra rinse with a little squeeze of fresh lemon?' Customers thought they were getting special attention. They loved it.

'What's the deal?' Grace pretended to be resigned. She was standing behind the chair as Lena got her usual Friday shampoo and set. Only the best hairdresser in the salon was allowed to touch Mrs Gray's wavy dark hair.

The others didn't see that no money changed hands. Grace knew how to pay her debts. Lena Gray had got her this position by advising her every step of the way. They had almost rehearsed the interview line by line.

'A lot of the girls who come in to us ... they haven't an idea how to present themselves.'

'Who are you telling?' Grace remembered how self-deprecating and humble she had been until Lena taught her how to make her height, her colour and her startling stylish good looks into an asset.

'You were always a looker,' Lena said. 'No, they come in with frightened faces and no make-up, or else looking like something from a music hall. Suppose I sent you at least ten a week, would you throw in a free make-up lesson as well?'

'Ten a week? You'd never get that.' Grace's eyes were wide in disbelief.

'That would be the deal. If I get less, you don't have to give the discount.'

'What kind of make-up lesson? In a classroom?'

'No. Just telling them what would suit them. You don't sell them anything, just tell them how to put it on so it doesn't look as if it was laid on with a garden trowel.'

Grace laughed. 'You have such funny ways of putting things.'

'What do you think? Is it worth your while?'

'Of course it is. Some day, when you're famous, I'll say that I helped you on in your career, like you did for me.'

'Famous. I doubt it.'

'I don't. I see that Mr Millar handing over to you. I see big interviews in the papers ...' Grace was excited.

'No. I don't see that at all.' Lena spoke quietly.

Whatever happened, there would be no interviews with her in any paper. Not now.

*

Clio was a month older than Kit, so for the whole month of May she was thirteen. 'There's many a country I could get married in,' she said loftily.

'Ah, wouldn't that be a very foolish thing to do all the same,' Sister Madeleine said. They were arranging the blossoms that the girls had brought in a series of jars along the windowsill.

'Isn't it good to get married early?' Clio asked. It seemed to be her one superiority, having reached an age where technically, in some far-off land, she might be able to be a bride.

'No, not good at all.' Sister Madeleine was adamant.

'But if that's what you're going to do eventually, why not do it soon?' Clio asked.

'Because you might marry the wrong person, you eejit,' Kit said.

'You could do that any time,' Clio said.

They looked at Sister Madeleine for another view. 'It's all a matter of luck anyway,' she said, poking.

'Well of course it was different for you, since you had a vocation. There was no luck about that. You had the call from God,' Clio said.

There was a silence.

'Would you like to have been married at all, Sister Madeleine, do you think?' Kit asked.

'Oh I was.' Sister Madeleine looked at them with her clear blue eyes, smiling as if they should have known this.

They looked at her open-mouthed.

'Married?' said Kit.

'To a man?' asked Clio.

'It was a long time ago,' Sister Madeleine said, as if that explained everything. The goose came in the door at that moment, waddling and looking from side to side foolishly. 'Well, would you look at Bernadette.' Sister Madeleine's face creased into a smile, as if a friend had come in for tea. 'You're welcome in, Bernadette. The girls here will get you a bit of cornmeal in a nice dish now.'

Clio and Kit would hear no more about Sister Madeleine's marriage.

'She did say married?'

'Yes, I heard her.'

'To a man. Not just to Christ or anything.'

'No. She agreed with that. She said it was long ago.'

They sat down on mossy stone by the lakeside.

'She couldn't have been married. Not sleeping with a man and all.'

'Well she said it, didn't she?'

'I wonder does anyone else know,' Clio said.

'I'm not going to tell anyone, are you?' Kit said suddenly.

Clio seemed disappointed. It would have been a great thing to tell. 'She didn't say to keep it a secret.'

'No Clio, but she sort of trusted us, didn't she?'

Clio thought about it. This way there was some importance attached to the momentous piece of information they had just been given. If they were guardians of a huge and privileged piece of information that no one else knew, then Clio Kelly could just about keep it to herself. 'I suppose so.'

'Imagine her telling us. You and me,' Kit said in wonder.

Clio liked that. 'She knows we wouldn't let each other down,' she said.

They walked home companionably and came up from the lake by Paddles' bar. Paddles was standing at his door. 'When will you ladies be old enough to frequent my premises?' he asked.

They giggled. 'Ah, it'll be a few years yet, Paddles,' Clio said.

'Well, the place will be honoured, Miss Kelly, when you're ready for us.'

They clutched each other with laughter the whole way home. Imagine, whatever age you were, wanting to go into Paddles' bar!

'Maybe you could have your thirteenth birthday there. We could send out invitations. Miss Kit McMahon will be launched into society at Paddles' bar on 2 June 1953.'

They laughed so much they had to hold onto the wall of the Central Hotel to stop themselves falling.

'You're having great fun.' Philip was very envious.

'We're planning Kit's birthday party,' Clio said.

'Are you having a party?' Philip brightened up.

'Of course not. She's in mourning,' Clio snapped. 'But that's no reason why we couldn't have a laugh over it.'

*

Everyone in London was getting ready for the Coronation. There would be bunting on the houses in the street. Ivy was getting hers ready. She had some since the end of the war, kept as a sort of souvenir from the really memorable days down in the King's Head.

'It'll be a great day,' she told Lena.

'I suppose so.'

'Sorry, I keep forgetting you're not all that interested, being Irish and all.'

'No, it's not that. Of course I'm interested. I keep forgetting it . . . I'm working so hard these days.'

'Don't I see it. You're home later every night.'

'Well, so's Louis . . .'

'Don't work too hard, love.' Ivy's face was full of concern.

And she was right of course. Lena did stay later and later at the agency, writing letters to large companies explaining the kind of screening techniques they used, how Millar's did not just send *any* applicant for any job. She also had a mailing list of schools and secretarial colleges. A Millar's girl would get much more than a list of job opportunities. She would get career advice and more intelligent women would assess her potential, giving young applicants the necessary confidence to prepare them for interviews and for their early working career.

Mention was made of the low-price hairdressing and make-up services and of the fashion suggestions. Business was increasing at a great rate. Mr Millar had doubled her salary in six months. Lena had insisted on a similar rise for Jessie Park.

'We're a team, Mr Millar. I couldn't work without Jessie,' she had said.

Mr Millar's eyes were sharp. He saw the changed image and new confidence of Miss Park, who had been the most mouselike of employees. If Lena Gray could do this for the woman that she had outstripped a hundredfold and still remain loyal and supportive then she was indeed a treasure and must be humoured. Anyway, profits were looking very good. He could afford to pay Jessie as well.

He had met Mrs Gray's husband once, a strikingly handsome Irishman. A hotel manager, it appeared. She was very quiet and uninformative about her private life. Which made a refreshing change to the daily detail they got from Jessie Park.

'Mr Millar,' Lena said. 'Miss Park and I were wondering should we do a special window display for the Coronation?'

'But what would we say in our window?'

Jessie looked at them eagerly. Jessie didn't look so gormless these days; she had a smartly fastened blouse with a modern cameo brooch. Instead of a picture it said 'Millar's' in the blue and gold which had become the company colours.

The cushions on the new chairs were blue and gold, as was the decoration on their stationery, the fresh paint on the exterior, the frames for the pictures on the walls. Jessie used to wear floppy, open-necked blouses until Lena had thought up this smart new uniform for them, a white blouse, a blue skirt and a gold-looking scarf. Jessie's new hairstyle and the occasional application of make-up had transformed her.

Lena had even suggested that with an increased wage packet Jessie might pay someone to look after her mother on an occasional evening, and she could get accustomed to having some free time. It was such a relief to hear Jessie talking about how much she had enjoyed *Singing in the Rain*. Lena and Mr Millar would have listened to every song and every line of the dialogue over and over rather than revert to Mrs Park's eating difficulties.

The old Jessie would have agreed with Mr Millar that she didn't know she was sure, but today Jessie spoke up. 'In a way, Mr Millar, our very colours are royal, you know. A nice blue and gold display in the window, with a picture of the new Queen . . .'

'Yes, that's a great idea.' Lena said. 'We could put something like "Welcome to a New Elizabethan Age . . . from Millar's, who look to a great future for all of us" . . .'

They loved it. They were so excited. A lump came to Lena's throat at their eagerness. Were the English much more simple and less critical than the Irish? Or was it that she had never been able to play any part in the town where she had withered away for thirteen years?

'Do you think they should get a television in the hotel for the coronation?' Louis asked.

'You mean they haven't got one? Not one in the whole place?'

'No. It sort of prides itself on being quiet.'

'It'll pride itself on being empty before long.' He looked at her in surprise. This wasn't the usual way Lena spoke. It was too sharp. 'Nothing's wrong. Maybe I'm just tired.'

'Very well. I'll know not to ask in future,' Louis said. He had a funny tight look around his lips.

'Louis!' she cried in alarm. 'Oh Louis, please don't sulk.'

'Sulk? Me! I'm not sulking. You're the one who bit the head off me.' He was really hurt.

'I'm sorry. It's all my fault.' There was silence. 'Louis, I had a rotten day.'

'Mine wasn't great either.'

She reached for him, but he pulled away. 'Louis, please talk to me about the television set. I'm very interested, honestly. Truly, truly I am.' She was beseeching him now.

'No, Helena. It's all right. This time the Dryden Hotel will have to manage without your advice.'

She pleaded with him again. 'I spoke quickly. I'm sorry. You often do too when you're tired. It doesn't mean anything, not between us. Does it?'

'No. Of course not.' He was frosty.

She bit her lip. She would do whatever it took to get him back to the way he had been before she had so stupidly snapped at him. Did it need more apology or was it best to change the subject? She decided to move on. 'We've been having all kinds of debates about how to celebrate the day, too,' she began cheerfully.

'How interesting.' Louis spoke with a deliberate sneer. She had never seen his face curl up like that.

'Love?' She felt her face redden.

'No, go on. Tell me more tales of Mr Millar and Jessie Park. I mean, these are really interesting people now. Not just dross like the poor fools that try to earn a living in the Dryden Hotel.'

'I must have sounded sharper than I meant to. I can't tell you how sorry I am.' Lena hung her head.

She hoped he would come over and put his arms around her, say that it didn't matter, that they were both over tired. Maybe he might say they would go out to the little Italian restaurant and they would be closer because of it. But he was a long time coming over to her and she began to doubt that this would happen.

She heard his hand on the door handle and looked up. 'Where are you going, Louis?' she asked.

'Out.'

'But where out?'

'You told me, Helena, that the thing that drove you mad all those years in Lough Glass was when people kept asking you where you were going. Just out. Isn't that enough?'

'No, it's not enough. We love each other . . . Don't go.'

'We don't want to stifle each other.'

'I won't stifle you. Please.' She was begging now.

Had Martin begged her this way? Louis came towards her and took both her hands in his. 'Listen, my love. We're annoyed with each other. Let's cool off.'

'Let me go out too, if you want to. That's what grown-ups do. We're grown-ups, remember.'

His smile was so loving, so much a part of him, it almost hurt her to see it. She felt almost paralysed. Did she want to flounce out before him? Could she plead with him once more? She said nothing. Not a word. He released her hands, and she heard the door close behind him. She would not cry. She would not go down to Ivy for consolation. But she would go out.

She bought an apple and a piece of cheese at the corner shop, and walked on towards Millar's Employment Agency. She let herself in, and looked around her with pleasure. This, at least, had been an achievement, something to show for her months in London. The little glass-covered noticeboard with carefully edited letters from satisfied customers; the blue and gold motif everywhere; the cushions covered by Jessie's mother, who had now found a role in life; the gold painted tray with the blue mugs where coffee was served to all who came in.

Lena sat down at her desk and took out her files. Exactly what she needed. A few hours on her own to sort things through. This was the time she hardly ever had to herself so anxious was she to run home and have everything ready for Louis.

Louis. She would not think about him because it made her shake with rage at the injustice of it all.

The time flew past. She could hardly believe that it was eleven. She felt her heart jump. This was later than she had intended to stay. He would be long home by now, and there might be more words if she were to say she had gone in to the agency. But she couldn't pretend to have been wandering around London on her own all this time.

As she ran up the stairs she rehearsed what she would say, but first she would see what mood he was in. That was the secret. Respond to him, don't fire off herself. She opened the door and the flat was empty. Louis had not come back yet. When he'd said he was going out, he'd meant it.

Her eyes were closed when he came in, but she was wide awake. It was twenty past three. He slipped quietly into the bed beside her. He did not reach for her, which was his automatic gesture whenever he got into bed.

Where could he have been until this time of the morning? He was too proud to go back to his place of work; he wouldn't have gone back to catch up on things like Lena had done. Which meant that he must have been in someone's house. Someone he knew well enough to entertain him until all hours in the morning. She made her breathing sound even, as if she were asleep.

Lena Gray could swear that she slept not a wink that night.

Her head was full of pictures, but none of them were dreams. She pictured her daughter Kit. It would be her birthday on 2 June, the day of the Coronation. She would be thirteen years of age, a girl whose mother was dead. If only she had been able to write to her. Suppose Martin had let them think that she was far away and never coming back, but that she could still write them letters.

And as the light came up on London, and the yellow blinds on their window started to turn a pale colour rather than seeming black like the night, Lena knew that was what she would do. She would write a letter to her daughter. Pretending to be someone else. The thought of it made her feel exhilarated. Nobody seeing her get up and dress would have thought that this was a woman who had not slept all night. Louis was surprised, she could see that.

'Less angry with the world today?' he asked, head on one side waiting for her to apologise yet again. But he got no apology.

'Weren't we like a pair of Kilkenny cats last night?' she said, marvelling at it.

Louis paused. This wasn't what he had expected. 'What made us like that do you think?'

'As you said, crowding each other out . . .' She was anxious to be gone; it was written all over her.

So now naturally he wanted her to stay. 'I didn't mean that it was bad crowding out . . .' he began. It was as near to a climb down as she would get.

'No, no. Of course not. See you this evening.'

'I didn't wake you when I came back.'

'Lord no. I was asleep. Out like a light.' She kissed him quickly on the forehead, and he pulled her back to his lap.

'We don't kiss like that. That's for old people.'

'True, true,' she laughed, and responded to him, but she pulled away firmly. 'Let's not start anything we can't continue . . . See you tonight, hey? hey?' She laughed at him suggestively.

'You're a terrible tease,' he said.

They were happy again. But it wasn't at the forefront of her mind. Her brain was racing with ways she could write to her daughter.

Mr Millar was at work before her.

'You remind me of a story about the Little People,' he said to Lena.

'What Little People?'

'I don't know . . . They used to come and do the work at night for some fairy prince, spin and weave or something and . . . Do you know it?'

'I think I've heard of it all right, but why do I remind you of it?'

'I think someone must have come in at night and done all your work. The basket is full of letters written and notes made.'

'I came in for an hour or two last night.'

'I don't know what lucky good fairy brought you here.' He took off his glasses and polished them. 'My brother used to laugh at me, and say I had no business sense. Now, in a few short months he wants to buy into the business. What do you think of that?'

'What do *you* think of it, Mr Millar?' Lena knew that there was little love lost between the brothers.

'I'm happier doing it without his help really, Mrs Gray. That is, if you're going to stay.'

During the morning, her thoughts went back to the conversations she had had with Kit about a previous life. They had of their nature been sparse. You didn't tell a daughter that you only married because you were on the rebound and that your every waking thought was so filled with the memory of Louis Gray it didn't really matter *what* you did. Had she spoken of the girls she was in digs with when she was at secretarial college? Possibly. It was so hard to remember. But if she couldn't remember then maybe Kit wouldn't either.

She would write the letter and see how it looked.

Dear Kit,

You will find it strange to get a letter from someone you do not know. But a while back I read in an Irish newspaper about the death of your mother and I wanted to write and offer sympathy. I do not know your father because your mother and I were friends long long ago when we were very young, well before she met him. Sometimes she used to write to me about you all, and the life you lived in Lough Glass. I even remember the date you were born, and know that you will be thirteen very shortly.

Your mother was so pleased with her little girl, she wrote and told me about all the dark hair you had as a baby, and determined little fists. I don't want to write to you at home in case it makes your father sad. Your mother told me that there was a sort of second postal system in Lough Glass and that people often write care of this nun.

If you would like to write to me, and to know more things about your mother as a girl when we were all only about four or five years older than you are now, then let me know.

I hope I might hear from you, but if not I will understand. At your age you will have more important things to do than writing to strangers in London.

Warm wishes for a happy birthday from your mother's old friend,
Lena Gray

When she put the letter into the red pillar box on the corner of the street, Lena left her hand for a long time on the mouth where the letters drop in. It was like reaching out her hand and touching her daughter.

Tommy Bennet helped to sort the letters at the post office. Mona Fitz was very interested in the origin of a lot of them. She could comment when the Hanleys got a few dollars in a fat letter from America. Sometimes she examined the mail that arrived for Sister Madeleine. For a woman who said she had retreated from the world, she was still using quite a lot of the world's services. Like the postal system.

Tommy Bennet deflected any comment. Sister Madeleine was a saint as far as he was concerned. She had done the impossible and made things all right when Tommy's fifteen-year-old daughter came home with the most feared news in any Irish village, the news of an unexpected pregnancy. He had wept at Sister Madeleine's fireplace. And somehow the hermit had made it all right. A friend had been found and his daughter went to live with her. Another friend had been found somewhere else who adopted the baby. And Sister Madeleine had found a third friend who gave the girl a job. Nobody in Lough Glass knew the secret. Nor even suspected there was anything unusual about the girl's long absence.

Tommy delivered three letters to the hermit's cottage on a warm sunny morning in late May. One contained a five-pound note, to be put to good causes. She gave the note to Tommy.

'Give it where it should be given.'

'I don't like you trusting me to dole out all that money. I mightn't give it away right.'

'What would I be doing with it? You know where it is needed,' she insisted.

Tommy always felt a hundred feet tall; Sister Madeleine thought he was a man of responsibility. Nobody else much did. His wife thought he was lazy, Mona Fitz the postmistress thought he was soft. His own daughter, whose life he had saved, thought him old-fashioned and strict, and knew nothing of her father's role in her good fortune.

'I'll leave you in peace to read your other letters, Sister.'

'Put on a pot of tea for us both, it's a thirsty walk up and down that lane.' Sister Madeleine shooed the collection of animals in front of her and sat on the little three legged stool to read the letter addressed to her.

Dear Sister,

I am a friend of the late Helen McMahon, and would like to correspond with her daughter Kit.

For a variety of reasons I do not wish to write to her at her house. I have said to the child that I do not wish to make Martin McMahon sad to see reminders of his dead wife coming to his home, but the truth is that I was part of Helen's life when she loved another man. This would make it inappropriate for me to resurrect such memories for him.

I shall write nothing disturbing to the girl, and you are at liberty to read my letters in case you think the effect will be unsettling. I am sending what I hope will be the first of many letters to you. I am marking the corner of the envelope KM so that you will know they are for her. And perhaps you might send some message to say whether this is acceptable to you.

Yours sincerely,

Lena Gray

It was neatly typed. There was an address in West London. And it said in capital letters PLEASE ENSURE THAT YOU WRITE c/o MRS IVY BROWN. Sister Madeleine looked out over the lake for a long time. When Tommy made the tea and brought it out to her he stood for quite a while looking at the small woman entirely lost in thought.

'Clio, you're great with dogs. Will you go and see if you can find Ambrose for me,' Sister Madeleine said later that day.

'Where's he gone, Sister?'

'I couldn't say truthfully, but he's lying low somewhere and you've always been able to make dogs come to you.'

Clio headed off, pleased to be singled out.

Kit looked after her jealously. 'I'm better with cats really, myself,' she said.

'Don't I know it,' Sister Madeleine agreed. 'The cats nearly talk to you, Kit McMahon. Even half-wild cats.' She gave Kit the letter.

There were very few words, but Kit knew it was something to be opened at home alone. And probably not something to be shared with Clio. Nor, since it had been addressed to Sister Madeleine's home, something to be shared with her father.

She must have read the letter forty times. She knew every line of it off by heart. Mother had told this woman all about her, about her little fists, her dark hair. She might have told her more. The letter was typed, which made it easy to read. But it looked like a business letter that would come to the pharmacy.

She sounded nice, but a bit standoffish too. Was it Mrs Gray or Miss Gray? Did she want to know more? Kit felt reassured because Sister Madeleine had said that Mother had in the past mentioned this woman was a friend.

'I didn't know Mother had any friends,' Kit had said.

'Your mother was a friend to everyone,' Sister Madeleine had said.

'She was, I know she was.' Kit's eyes were shining. 'People liked her a lot, didn't they?'

'Very much so.' The old nun nodded in agreement.

'But you didn't know her well, she didn't come here all that often, did she?' Kit was eager to hear more good about her mother. 'But you don't have to meet people often to know them.' That was true. You sort of knew immediately who you liked and who you didn't. 'What did you and Mother talk about when she came here?'

'Oh, this and that.' There was seal of confession on anyone's conversations with Sister Madeleine.

'But she didn't talk about this Lena Gray?' Kit's face was troubled.

'She mainly talked about you, about you and Emmet.' Helen McMahon on her infrequent visits spoke with such love about her children that it was inconceivable she could have drowned herself and left them behind.

Sister Madeleine had always believed that.

It took Kit two weeks to think of something to write back. She began once or twice. But it always seemed wrong, it seemed like a school essay, or else too friendly for someone she hardly knew. She wondered what Mother would have done. Mother would have thought about it for a bit, not rushed in.

That's what Kit would do, too.

*

'I've given your address, Ivy, in case I get any post,' Lena said.

'Well, it's your address too, isn't it?' Ivy was mystified.

'No, I mean your flat.'

'I see.'

'No you don't.'

'Are you going to tell me then?'

'It's just that I want to get a letter from Ireland now and then that I'd prefer Louis didn't know about.'

'Be very careful, Lena.'

'No. It's nothing like love letters ...'

There was a silence between them.

'But it's from Ireland?'

'Yes. It's a kind of lifeline to my daughter ...'

'Who thinks you're dead?'

'Yes. I'm not pretending to be me, I'm pretending to be someone else. Another me.'

'I wouldn't, love. I really wouldn't.'

'I've done it.'

'You're not still sulking about the television in the hotel?' Louis asked.

'Of course not. I was never sulking in fact, I was being bad tempered. *You* were the one who was sulking. Let's get the memory of the row right.' Her eyes laughed and there was nothing but ease and pleasure between them.

'Right, so you'll come and watch it down there . . .'

'Certainly not. If I'm going to be in London for a big historic occasion like this, I'm going to watch it on the street.'

'You'll have to queue all night with rugs and a flask.'

'No, of course I won't. Ivy and Jessie have found a corner.'

'And what about me? What about Mr Millar and Jessie's mother, and the rest of the cast?'

'You have to work, you've told me a dozen times. Ivy doesn't want to go to Ernest's pub because the horrible Charlotte will be there. Mrs Park will be parked on a potty at a neighbour's looking at their television. Mr Millar will be with his brother whom he hates . . . Now, does that answer the interrogation?' she asked jokily.

'I love you,' Louis said suddenly.

'I should hope so. Didn't I run away with you?' she said.

'And I didn't run away with you too?'

But it wasn't an equal running away.

'Of course you did,' Lena said gently. 'We ran like silver fish across the sea.'

*

'Did Mother have a best friend like I have Clio?' Kit asked.

'Well, she had Clio's mum of course.' But they both knew that wasn't true. Mother hadn't liked Lilian Kelly.

'I mean before. Before she met you.'

'She had the girls in the digs. She spoke of them a bit.'

'What were they called, Daddy?'

'It's so long ago, love, I can't remember. There was Dorothy I think, and a Kathleen maybe . . .'

'Would she have been called Lena?'

'I don't know. Why?'

'I just wondered what people shorten their names to. Might the short name for Kathleen be Lena?' She looked flushed and eager.

Martin McMahon gave it some thought. She seemed to want it to be that way. 'I think it might have been all right. It certainly is a way of shortening the name,' he said. Kit nodded, satisfied. As he did so often Martin McMahon wished he knew what was going on in his daughter's mind.

Boys were so much simpler. He went fishing with Emmet many evenings on the lake. At first Emmet had been unwilling to touch the boat, but

Martin had persevered. 'We have no idea what happened that night, but we know one thing. Your mother would want you to grow up as part of this lake that she loved so much. She wouldn't want you to stay away from it.'

'But the boat, Daddy . . .'

'The boat is part of the lake, son. We won't ever know what happened in that boat and how your poor mother got dragged away. She'd surely want yourself and myself to go out in it and love the place as she did.'

It had been the right thing to say. His son went with him happily on the lake. And it seemed that Emmet enjoyed his fishing trips catching perch and pike.

The boy never noticed that his father's eyes were dead as he rowed.

*

'No letters for you to my flat, Lena.'

'No? Well, there you go.'

'You're getting lots of London expressions,' Ivy said.

'If I'm going to live in London then I'd better learn to talk like Londoners,' Lena said.

'I thought you might be thinking of going back across the sea.'

'No, there's not any chance of that.'

'But the lifelines . . . ?' Ivy persisted.

'Probably just as you said. Very dangerous, very foolish.'

'Take that hard look off your face, Lena Gray. I'm your friend . . . I never said it was dangerous or foolish, I just told you to take care.'

'You're a great friend, Ivy.'

'When I get the chance to be, but that's not at the moment, so let it lie.' Ivy went back into her room on the ground floor. She didn't ask Lena in. She knew the time for intimacy was not now.

Jessie Park was worried whether her mother might be able to make the bathroom in her neighbour's house during the Coronation.

'She gets very excited you know, when things are emotional.' Lena listened patiently. 'Oh Lena. I know I'm wittering on a bit and I'm always telling you my woes, but I just don't know where to turn and you're always so calm, so practical.'

Lena looked at her kindly. It was a huge compliment to be called calm and practical, a woman like she was, on the run, living a false life with a man who might leave her again as he had done before.

Here she was in this great strange city, heartbroken that she had heard nothing from Kit and fearing that the letter had frightened the child. Yet Jessie thought she was as strong as an oak tree. 'Let's see,' she said. 'Didn't you tell me that flat was all on one level? There won't be any stairs.'

'I know, Lena, but she moves so very slowly. Suppose she had a little accident?' Jessie bit her lip.

'I saw some pads in a chemist's last week. She could wear those and then there'd be no problem.' Lena was bright and positive.

Jessie thanked her so profusely that it almost brought tears to Lena's eyes.

It was so easy to solve a little problem for someone else when they asked, and so hard to sort out your own ...

In the Dryden Hotel all the preparations had gone ahead for the Coronation Day. The chairs had been arranged in a semicircle in the drawing room just as Lena had suggested to Louis, and he had advised the hotel.

'Your lovely wife will not be with us for the day?' James Williams said with disappointment. He thought that Lena would have added a touch of class to the proceedings.

'Sadly no. She is needed in her own work.'

'I'm not surprised. I'm sure she is excellent in that employment agency. Perhaps she might be able to find places for us as they become vacant.'

'Ah, yes. Of course she's always looking for the perfect position for her husband,' Louis joked.

'I'd be sorry to lose you, Louis. You'd never take anything without letting us discuss a salary and conditions.'

'Mr Williams, I wouldn't even want you to think I was speaking seriously.'

'And although I have asked you a dozen times to call me James you never will.'

'I am very happy here.'

'And is your wife happy in London? She doesn't yearn for somewhere else?'

'What makes you ask that, Mr Williams.' Louis' eyes had narrowed.

'I don't know. Something she said at Christmas, about everyone on earth should be forced to work in London for a time. I thought there was a message in those words.'

'She's my wife, and I never heard a message like that.' The words were perfectly polite but James Williams decided not to pursue it any further.

*

'Wouldn't it be great to go to England for the Coronation?' Clio said.

'Where would we stay?'

'Aunt Maura has friends there. *She's* going to go.'

'Would she take us if we asked her?' Kit wondered.

'No, probably not. It's still termtime and they'd say we're too young.'

'I'd love to go anywhere,' Kit said.

'I know. So would I. By the time they let us we'll be too old.' Clio was glum and resigned about it.

'Philip O'Brien's going to Belfast with his mother,' Kit revealed.

'Yeah, but imagine going anywhere with Philip's mother.'

'He's all right though. I like him.'

'You're going to marry him. I can see it.' Clio was definite.

'You're always saying that. I haven't a notion of it. Why do you keep saying it?'

'Because he fancies you.'

'Well?'

'It doesn't matter that you don't fancy him. People always end up marrying people that fancy them.'

'That couldn't work out.' Kit fought it.

'No, I mean women do, girls do.'

'Why? I thought we were the ones meant to do the choosing and refusing and all that.'

'No, that's only in books and films. In real life we marry people who want to marry us.'

'All women do that?'

'Yes. Honestly.'

Kit thought about it. 'Your mother? My mother?'

'Yes. Yes, definitely.'

'And nobody fancied your Aunt Maura?'

'That's different. She told me that she wasted time on a man who didn't fancy her. That was her mistake.'

'But was it a mistake?' Kit wanted to know. 'You always said she was very happy, happier than anyone we know.'

'Yes, I know I did say that, but that's the way we see it. Maybe inside she's desperately unhappy.'

'What about Sister Madeleine, who says she was married *and* is a nun?'

'I'll never understand that,' said Clio. 'Not till the day I die.'

*

'What are you thinking about?' Lena asked.

Louis smiled at her lazily. 'I was thinking how beautiful you are,' he said.

'No you weren't.'

'Then why ask me?'

'I don't know. I suppose I sometimes want to know what goes on in your handsome head. We had a cat at home called Farouk. I used to look at him and wonder what could be going on in his head.'

'And am I like Farouk – a cat?'

'Not nearly as handsome, I'm afraid.'

'I don't like you saying "at home". Lough Glass is not your home. Your home is with me. It has always in some way been with me.'

She looked at him for a moment or two. A few weeks back she would have rushed in, begged, pleaded, said that she had been using only a form of words. But the night that he had left in the petty sulk, the night she knew she needed to write to her daughter, everything had changed. She didn't wish to tie him to her with humble words of apology; it could be no love if it was bought at such a price.

'Well, tell me, do you agree?' He was challenging her.

'No, my love, I don't. It wasn't where I wanted to be but I was there for thirteen damn years and other people called it my home and it was where I lived. So if I mention in passing that a cat who lived there with me, a fine handsome cat called Farouk lived at home with me . . . I don't think it's a slip of the tongue that is going to make or break us.'

He looked at her with admiration.

With a sudden flash of regret, she realised that if she had behaved like this years ago he might never have left her in the first place. But if he had stayed ... what about Kit and Emmet? Would they have been the same people? Or different people? Or not existed at all?

No price was worth paying for them not to have existed at all.

'I'm going to have a perm for the Coronation,' Jessie Park said.

'Great idea,' Lena said.

'Mr Millar has invited us both around to his brother's house this evening,' Jessie spoke with reverence.

'Yes. I hope you'll go and tell me about it. I have to meet Louis, I think he's a bit let down that I won't be with him all day ...' She saw Jessie's face crumble.

'Oh Lena, do you have to? Please come to Mr Millar's. You can be with Louis any night. This is special.'

Lena looked at her fondly. Although she still called him Mr Millar, Jessie had very fond thoughts about her employer. Lena had seen her looking at him in a way that had nothing to do with the employment agency. 'No, honestly. I would if I could, but this is something I have to do. Anyway, you'll have more fun without me. I'd only be a gooseberry.'

'He doesn't see me in that way at all.' Jessie's face was long and sad.

'How do we know what way men see things? You'd need a fleet of interpreters to work out what they're thinking ... but it's better you go on your own. You'll get to know him more than if I were there.'

'Do you think so? Do you think it will be all right?'

'Certainly it will. It's not as if he were a stranger, a man you only met at a party or somewhere. You and he have so much in common, shared so much already ...' Lena was full of encouragement.

'But I never know what to say when you're not there,' Jessie looked flustered.

'Maybe this is the time to begin.'

'I hope I'll look all right. Do you think it's worth having a perm?'

'Oh indeed I do, and anyway it will cost half nothing. Grace owes us. We've been sending so much business her way, she practically runs the salon on the people we refer.'

Jessie left for the salon cheerfully, full of plans. Lena picked up the phone. 'Grace, do me a favour. When Jessie makes a booking give her everything, I mean every single thing. I'll sort it out with you later. Nails, facial, colour ... anything you think.'

'She's never going to look for a new job?'

'Better than that,' Lena said, 'she's looking for romance.'

*

Deirdre Hanley called to the pharmacy. 'I came to know if you'd be needing an assistant or anything, Mr McMahon,' she said.

'Are you going to study pharmacy, Deirdre?' Martin McMahon was surprised.

'No, but I wouldn't need to for working here, would I?'

'Well, to be any help to me you would really.' He spoke mildly.

She was a restless girl, Mrs Hanley's daughter. A child who had always been loud in her impatience for the day when she could leave Lough Glass. Sometimes she had even said it to Helen and found, Martin feared, only too sympathetic an audience.

'But isn't it all a matter of trying to get people to buy make-up and all?' she asked.

'I think there's a bit more to it than that, Deirdre. But were you going to train as a beautician? Is that it?'

'You wouldn't need much training, Mr McMahon. All you'd need is to talk one of the cosmetic companies into giving you a bit of a course, then you push their stuff, tell people it's great. You know the sort of thing.'

'And you'd like to do that in Lough Glass?'

'Yeah, why not?'

'But do you think . . . Suppose we were able to find a place for you here, which I don't think is possible . . . Do you think you'd be happy doing that?'

'Mr McMahon, you have to do something from dawn to dusk to justify your existence. That's what it's all about,' Deirdre Hanley said.

'And you'd like your existence here in Lough Glass?' He'd had nothing but despair from this child about her home town. What had changed her? Deirdre looked across the road at Sullivan's garage. It was only a glance, but Martin McMahon remembered having seen her with Stevie Sullivan on a few occasions. Usually down by the lake or away from the public eye. 'What would your mother like you to do?' he asked suddenly.

'She'd like me to get out of here. She says she doesn't know why but she thinks it would be the best thing for me.'

'Go, Deirdre. You'd be much more exciting to him if you were an out of town girl.'

'Mr McMahon, imagine you knowing all about women and life and everything,' said Deirdre in amazement.

'I know,' Martin McMahon said goodnaturedly. 'Isn't it extraordinary all right!'

'Will the pair of you come into the chemist's with me, do you think?' he asked the children that night.

'Now?' Emmet asked in surprise. Once the door had been locked their father hardly ever opened it again, unless it was an emergency for someone.

'No, I meant in the future,' he said.

'Would you like us to?' Kit asked.

'Only if you want to, or one of you wants to. It's long hours and you'd need to enjoy the work.'

'I thought I might be an actress,' Kit said.

'And I thought I'd be a priest out on the Missions,' Emmet said.

'Oh well then, it's all settled.' He looked from one to the other. 'Father Emmet . . . out in Nigeria . . . with his long white soutane, saving souls, and then back to catch the first night of Katherina McMahon in the Abbey

Theatre. It'll be a busy life for me. I suppose I'd better take Deirdre Hanley in to help me.'

'Deirdre Hanley?' Emmet and Kit said in a voice of disbelief.

'She came looking for a job today, to help out.'

'You wouldn't want her, Daddy,' Kit said.

'I don't have to be a priest, it was just an idea.' Emmet rushed in.

'And I mightn't get accepted as an actress, to be honest . . .'

'So you might fall back on the chemist's; like if all else failed.'

'Exactly,' said Kit.

'Children are marvellous,' Martin McMahon said to the air around him. 'Who'd be without them.'

*

On the morning of 2 June Lena woke eagerly. Her daughter was thirteen today. She hoped Martin would mark the day for her, make it special, cheerful.

She got an urge to ring him and whisper encouragement down the phone. She longed to cry, and tell him that it was very hard to live without her children, but she knew this was a fanciful thing to indulge herself. She had a life to live. A life of her own. And here she was in London on the day of the Coronation.

Everyone was listening to the wireless from the moment they got up. It was as if they feared the whole thing might be cancelled. They wanted to know every detail. The newspapers were full of the splendour of the day and a minute by minute itinerary of how the procession would go to Westminster Abbey, and a step-by-step guide to the ceremony.

Lena looked around her with delight at the crowds who were determined to enjoy the great day. Less than ten years ago they had been in the middle of a terrible war. Thirteen years ago, the day her child was born, the day that Martin had wept for joy at her bedside to say they had a beautiful daughter . . . there had been fear and panic in these streets in London.

In a way Lena thought the English didn't have enough celebrations; they didn't have St Patrick's Day, and Corpus Christi Processions, and the Blessings of the Boats, and pilgrimages to Croagh Patrick and all the things that give people a chance to take a day off and think about something else. It was heartening to see them all smile and talk to strangers. She made her way to the corner that Ivy had managed to secure by knowing the family that owned a small shop there. The children had been out since long before dawn guarding the places for them. There were little wooden stools and picnic baskets, and flags and bunting.

For a moment Lena felt as if she were outside herself looking at it from somewhere else. She didn't feel part of the great excitement and anticipation. The knowledge that the young Queen was going to pass feet away didn't fill her with awe. But neither was it foreign to her. These were as much her people as were those who lived in the main street of Lough Glass.

She was as much at home here as she would be anywhere in the world.

They settled into their vantage point and heard the news about Everest.

Britain had conquered the highest mountain in the world; the excitement knew no bounds. The roar became louder as the carriages came into view, the horses gleaming and decorated with magnificent brocades and livery. And then the smiling but slightly anxious face of Princess Elizabeth, as they still referred to her, waving her gloved hand, eagerly responding to all the love and welcome from the pavements.

She seemed to look straight at them, they all said it, Ivy, Jessie, everyone all around. And Lena thought it too. She looked back and waved at the woman who was going to be crowned. A woman who still had her little boy and girl. She felt tears spring into her eyes.

A man beside her clutched her arm. It's a great day, love, isn't it? You'll be able to tell your children about this.'

Lena squeezed his arm back. 'Great day, great day,' she stumbled.

*

'Do you always know what to do, Sister Madeleine?'

'No, Kit, I hardly ever know what to do.'

'But you don't worry about it.'

'No, that's true. I don't.'

'Is that why you weren't good at being married?'

'I never said I wasn't good at being married.'

'No, but you can't have been, otherwise you'd still be married, wouldn't you, not a nun?'

'Oh, you think I left a marriage and went into a convent, is that it?'

'But isn't that what you told us, Clio and myself?' Poor Kit was wishing she hadn't brought it up. The nun's blue eyes were interested and alive, but giving nothing away. 'I mean we didn't just imagine it, did we?'

'I did have a husband once, but he left me. He went away far across the world.'

'Did you have a fight?' Kit was sympathetic.

'No, not at all. I thought everything was fine. He wasn't happy, he said.' She looked out over the lake as she remembered it.

'And did the nuns take you then because he wasn't coming back any more?'

'Oh no. Not for a long time. I sat in the house polishing it and cleaning it and growing the flowers in the garden and telling everyone he was coming back soon ...'

'Where was all this, Sister Madeleine?'

'Oh, far away from here. But anyway, the weeks passed and the months and one day I asked myself what I was doing, and God made a little voice in me say that all I was doing really was minding possessions, keeping silver clean and polishing glass ... I surely should be doing something else.'

'So what did you do?'

'I sold it all, and I put the money in the bank for my husband, and I wrote a letter to a friend of his and said I was going to join a convent, and that if ever he came back everything was there for him.'

'And did he come back, Sister Madeleine?'

'I don't know, Kit. I don't think so.' She was very calm. Not sad or confused.

'So you were a nun?'

'For a while. Then one day I asked myself in the convent what I was doing. Polishing tables in the parlour, and polishing pews in the church and the marble around the base of the altar. And I heard the little voice from God again.'

'What did it say this time?' Kit scarcely dared to believe that Sister Madeleine was telling her all this.

'It said the same thing. It said that I was spending my time polishing and cleaning possessions. They weren't mine admittedly, they belonged to the convent, but still it didn't seem a good thing to be doing.'

'So you left and came here?'

'Yes. That was it, more or less.'

'And you couldn't hear a voice from God saying that you're wrapped up in possessions here because you haven't any.' Kit looked around the spare house and marvelled at how it had all turned out.

'Yes, I think it was the right thing to do. I hope so.'

'But it was God talking, wasn't it?'

'Of course it was, but God is always talking to us. The thing is to be sure and hear the bit that He wants us to hear.'

'Like when making up your mind you think one thing is right and then you think the other is.' Kit seemed to know the problem of indecision.

'Exactly, Kit. You have to listen carefully and work out what is actually being said, what God wants you to do.'

'And is it an actual voice, like you and me talking?'

'No. It's more a feeling.'

'So if I wasn't sure whether to do something or not . . . I'd just wait and see which feeling was the stronger.'

'It usually works.' Kit closed her eyes. 'But you can't force it, Kit. It's not like a fairy granting you three wishes or anything.' Kit stared out over the lake. It was so calm, not a ripple. A perfect June day. 'Write to her, Kit,' Sister Madeleine said.

'What?' Kit started in alarm.

'You're wondering whether to write to your mother's friend or not. It can't do any harm. Write to her.'

*

'Lena?'

'Ivy!'

Ivy hadn't seen Louis was there too. 'Did you think of coming down to the pub on Friday? Ernest was asking about you both the other day.'

'Hey, that would be good,' Louis said. 'But can we never buy a drink there? That's the only thing that bothers me about it. Tell Ernest, he'd understand.'

'The only thing Ernest can do for me, Louis, is to buy my friends a few beers. He loves to do it, give him the chance.'

'Oh, I'm easily turned into a kept man,' Louis said, continuing up the stairs.

Ivy called up after them, 'I have that leaflet you wanted, Lena . . . you know, about those evening classes . . .'

Louis groaned. 'She's not taking up more activities, is she? Don't encourage her, Ivy. Please, if you love me don't encourage her.'

'They're not for me, silly. They're for the clients. Right, Ivy, I'll come down later and have a look at them with you.' Her voice was calm, she looked as if nothing had happened. But inside she was churning.

A letter from her daughter.

Ivy was waiting, the letter in her hand. 'It's a child's writing, Lena. You wrote to the children.'

'You knew that.'

'I didn't know they'd write back. I'm frightened for you, I really am.'

'I'm frightened, too.' They looked at each other for a long moment.

Then Ivy pulled out a chair. 'Sit down and read it. I'll get us both a drink.'

Lena began to read.

Dear Miss Gray,

Or maybe it's Mrs Gray, you didn't say. I took a long time to answer because I was thinking. I almost felt afraid. I don't know what I was afraid of. I think I am worried that you'll tell me something sad about my mother, like that she wrote to you and said she didn't love us or she was unhappy in Lough Glass.

So I wanted you to know she had a great time here, a really good time. We have a terrific home, and Daddy is so good to everyone, and was best of all to Mother because he didn't fuss her. He knew she liked to walk by herself, and even if he was lonely he let her go. Sometimes he would stand at the kitchen window at the back of the house where it looks down over the lake and he'd say, 'Look there's your mother walking by the lake, she loves the lake in Lough Glass.' And she had a lot of friends here, the Kellys were great friends of all ours, and my mother knew everyone in the town, and they all still talk about her. So I thought I'd tell you that, in case you were going to tell Emmet and myself that mother didn't have a good time or had any complaints. So that you would know what it was like.

I haven't told Emmet about your letter because he's very young and doesn't really understand anything at all. It's not much of a letter but I wanted to explain.

Yours faithfully,

Kit McMahon

Lena looked at Ivy. Her face was empty, as if someone had reached in and taken all the life and feeling out of it. Ivy wondered if Lena were going to faint, she had never seen such a deathly white.

'Oh my God, Ivy,' she said. 'My God. What have I done? Oh Ivy, what on God's earth have I done?'

'It's all right, it's all right,' Ivy soothed.

'I have destroyed so many lives. Oh I wish I were at the bottom of the lake like they all think. That's where I deserve to be.'

'*Stop it!*' Ivy spoke in a voice that Lena had never heard her use. 'Stop it this minute. I can't abide that kind of self pity. Think. You have a man upstairs who loves you and who is the love of your life. And now you have a chance to set the record straight, to make amends to this child.'

'How can I make amends? How can I ever undo all this?'

'Tell her Helen McMahon was as happy as a sandboy. Tell her a pack of lies, let her have some good thoughts about her mother. You can do that.'

'It would all be a lie. I can't write my daughter lies.'

'Well you sure as hell can't write her the truth, can you?' Ivy said, refilling the glasses.

*

Clio's Aunt Maura brought them both Coronation mugs. She had a great time in London, she said. Very exciting. Everyone was in such a good mood.

She was always very kind to Kit, and managed to say the right thing much more often than Mrs Kelly did. 'You look lovely, Kit, you're so tall and strong-looking too. Your mother would be proud of you.' Mrs Kelly always said 'your poor mother', as if Mother was someone to be pitied. 'She had a great love for this place, she knew every fern and reed that grew by the lake,' Clio's Aunt Maura said, and Kit agreed. Mrs Kelly would have steered clear of any mention of the lake, a difficult thing to do in Lough Glass.

And it was true that Mother knew all the plants. Kit had heard that from Lena Gray, Mother's friend in London. Kit had been asked to call her Lena, not Miss or Mrs. The woman typed such long, interesting letters about Mother that Kit would love to have shown them to Dad. Surely it would cheer up his sad heart to read about how much Mother loved the place, sunset over the lake in the evenings, and the little clumps of primroses and cowslips in the spring. But she knew that Lena Gray was right; these were thoughts that somehow didn't concern anyone else.

And Kit's heart was full to think that her mother had loved her so much she had written all these things about her to a woman in England. It was so strange that Mother had never mentioned her. How private Mother must have been to have kept this great friendship all to herself.

*

Lena kept all her letters from Kit in Ivy's flat. 'It's not that I don't trust Louis,' she told Ivy.

'I know, love.' Ivy did know.

'It's such a comfort to me,' Lena said.

'I know, love, I know.'

'But you're warning me again about something, aren't you?'

'Don't tell her too much. Don't get too close to her.'

141

*

'Sister Madeleine?'

'Yes, Kit.'

'Do I ask too many questions?'

'Not at all. It's good to ask questions. People don't have to answer them any more fully than they want to.'

'So, I was wondering . . .' she paused. It was as if she didn't want to know the answer. 'I was wondering did my mother use you as a letter box too?'

'Why do you ask that, child?'

'Well, you see her friend, Lena . . . she sort of said that she and mother were writing to each other all the time, and I never saw any letters coming from England up at home. We'd have noticed the stamp, you see.'

'I know, I know.' Sister Madeleine was thoughtful. But she had not said yes or no.

'So did she, do you think?'

'Did she what, Kit?'

'Did she get letters addressed to her through you?'

'Well, of course, there could be lots of ways . . . Everyone does things differently.' Sister Madeleine was sliding away without refusing to answer.

'How do you mean?' Kit was trying her best.

'About people being different? It's a thing that could keep you thinking every day of your life how different we all are. And how different the animals are from each other. Like how do the little ducks know they can swim, and the little sparrows know they can fly. And people have such different ways of looking at things.

'Take your mother now. She knew every name of every child over there in the gypsy camp, and they all knew her, yet they lived such different lives. They would have done anything for your mother.'

'So, you mean she could have had letters addressed there?'

'Neither you nor I would ask them, would we, Kit? It's like what we've always said, people are special. They have their own lives in their souls to live. And I wouldn't tell anyone about our conversations or who writes letters to whom. And you wouldn't tell Clio about what I told you, all about my cleaning those possessions, because we know that it doesn't have to come up. Not that we're making secrets or anything – there's just no need to know . . .'

'I know.' Kit knew that she would never know whether this was the letter box for Lena Gray and Mother. But she was sure it was. Now only one problem. If Lena was so nice and such a close friend, why couldn't Father have known about it?

Mother Bernard welcomed Rita to the convent with pleasure. 'Are you sure that you want to do this, Rita? We love your excellent work here, of course, but I wonder are we taking advantage of you.'

'No, Mother. It is a pleasure. I love to clean your beautiful things. I get lodgings like the Queen of England wouldn't have . . .'

'I can't see her coming to a convent in Lough Glass on her travels, mind you.' Mother Bernard, of course, disapproved of the new Queen of England thinking herself the head of a church. Any church.

'Well, it's her loss, Mother, I tell you that. And I don't want to go back to my family. They don't need me and they only upset me. Also . . .' She paused.

'Do you have a young man in Lough Glass, possibly?' Mother Bernard was coy.

'No, not a fear of it, Mother. No, what I was going to say, I don't like to be too far from Emmet and Kit. My heart goes out to them.'

'Kit seems to be managing very well, better than I would have thought.'

'Yes, of the three of them she does seem to have found some kind of peace. It's as if she had a secret. Maybe she prays to her mother, do you think?'

Mother Bernard didn't want to go as far as this.

Although it would be a sin against charity to go around repeating it, Mother Bernard was one of the very sizeable number who believed that Helen McMahon might well have ended her own life, and would therefore not be in a place where anyone might pray to her with any hope of an answer.

5

Maura was very reassuring to her sister Lilian Kelly. 'They're all terrible between thirteen and sixteen ... it's their glands ... it's to do with nature ...'

'Nobody has a nature like Clio. I'll swing for her before it's over, I really will.'

'No, no. I see it everywhere. It's their bodies you see. They're all ready to breed and raise families, but society won't let them, and so it's a very confused time ...'

'All we need is for them to be breeding all round us. That's the only thing she hasn't done yet.' Lilian Kelly's mouth was grim.

Clio was a handful. The odd thing was that Kit, the motherless girl who had been restless and wild herself, seemed to have settled down. Clio's blonde good looks had caught the attention of many a young man, but her parents had been strict. There would be no outings of that sort until the summer she left school. Lessons were important. Fun could come later.

Maura came down almost every weekend. She said it was no distance from Dublin. She loved seeing them all. And as the months and indeed years went by the weekends had fallen into a pattern. There would be a supper up at Kellys' on a Friday night. And the next day spent playing golf. Martin McMahon had been assured by his friend the doctor that exercise was essential for a man in his forties. They would have dinner in the golf club on a Saturday night.

Martin had to be persuaded that it was a good thing to leave his children to their own devices some of the time. 'I'm sure Helen would want you to encourage them to be independent,' Maura had said. And that had settled it. Martin McMahon liked the easy way that she mentioned his dead wife. So many people dropped their voices when they mentioned her. If they mentioned her at all.

But while every other girl fought with a mother, Kit McMahon developed a friendship that became closer and closer with her mother's friend, Lena. Lena's typed letters arrived at Sister Madeleine's cottage week after week, pages and pages of conversation and memory and reaction to things that Kit wrote to her.

Sister Madeleine mentioned the letters once. And only once. 'She writes long letters, your mother's friend?'

Kit had paused for a moment. 'I'd show them to you, Sister Madeleine, but ... it's hard to say ... it's kind of ... not exactly a secret but you'd get the feeling she's only writing to me.'

'Oh, child. Don't think for a moment that I'd want to read what she says ... She tells you good things about your mother ...'

'Marvellous things, they must have known every single thing about each other. But then, they wrote to each other a lot. You know that because they must have written through here.' Sister Madeleine looked into the fire and said nothing. 'I feel so much better about Mother. I know her properly, what she was like as a child and everything. It's like finding her diary or something ...'

'That's a great blessing for you,' Sister Madeleine said, and she watched the little flame catch the wood.

*

Lena had a ritual about reading the letters.

It was in Ivy's flat at the kitchen table, surrounded by the cluttered shelves, the walls on which there wasn't an inch of free space so great was the festooning of postcards, scarves, ornaments and posters.

She would sip her small brandy and be transported to a world of breezes on the lake, end of term exams, Father Baily being an hour late because he had forgotten that the clocks went on.

She read about her own son getting his tonsils out, and eating only jelly and ice cream, and how Rita had done her secretarial course but fortunately hadn't left to go to Dublin and get a good job; she was working in the office of Sullivan's Garage across the road.

Lena read of people she had disliked for thirteen years whom she now found fascinating.

The Hickeys weren't speaking to each other, it appeared. If anyone went into the butcher's and asked for three lamb chops Mrs Hickey would repeat the phrase in the tones of a Christian Martyr and then Mr Hickey would go and chop them. The days when she would talk to the customers and shout in to her husband were gone. Kit wrote that it was better than going to a play just to go in and watch them. Sometimes she begged Rita to let her go and do the shopping just for the sheer fun of it.

She read about Philip O'Brien being so nice, and his mother being so awful. How Clio was fighting with her mother too, and how Deirdre Hanley wasn't in the door of Hanley's drapery before she and her mother had a row.

'I sometimes think that if my mother had lived we would have had a fight too. Otherwise it wouldn't be natural.'

Lena's hands shook as she read this. She wrote page after page about it.

Your mother always spoke of you so lovingly, you were so strong, so full of courage. You would never have fought, you would have seen her for all she was, her weaknesses as well ...

Then she stopped and tore the pages up. She mustn't give herself away. She had been so careful for these years. She must not throw it all away now.

*

Rita kept the accounts for Stevie Sullivan.

His mother, a mournful woman, felt that there was something not entirely appropriate about this. There was that maid of the McMahons coming across the road and putting on airs as she did. She decided she would set the relationship off on a correct footing.

'I'm glad you're going to be with us in the mornings, Rita.'

'Thank you, Mrs Sullivan.'

'And I thought maybe I'd leave a little ironing a couple of days a week...' Rita looked at her politely. But said nothing. 'To do in your own time, of course.'

'What was that you said, Mrs Sullivan?'

Kathleen knew when she was beaten. She began to retreat. 'If there's time, of course...'

'That's always the problem, isn't it? Your son is paying me to work three hours a morning. I hope we'll be able to get all his books and correspondence dealt with in that time. It's certainly going to be a challenge, isn't it?'

'And then you'll go back to domestic work across the road?' It was a barb.

But Rita pretended not to see it. 'I've always felt McMahons' was my home in many ways. I wouldn't dream of leaving Mr McMahon until his children are reared.'

In Paddles' bar Peter Kelly asked Martin about Rita's job.

'She seems to be doing very well.' Martin was proud of Rita. 'She's cleaned it up for a start.'

'I know, didn't I see it. Fresh paint, shelves, filing cabinets, in old Sullivan's! Could you believe it?'

'I'd say she has a hard time with Kathleen.'

'Everyone has a hard time with Kathleen,' said Peter Kelly. 'But on the other hand, she wasn't dealt much of a hand herself, and she's got a handful in those two boys.'

'Stevie's a bit of a lad, isn't he?'

'We'll have to lock up our daughters, Martin. Stevie Sullivan knows a lot more than you and I knew when we were nineteen.'

'And the young lad, Michael, a hooligan. Himself and young Wall were found drinking the dregs of empty bottles behind Shea's the other night. Little pups.'

But Peter Kelly was not as outraged as he might have sounded. He was very tolerant of what other people in Lough Glass regarded as the criminal side of young people. He couldn't see that it was all that very bad for Clio to have gone out in her mother's black satin slip to the pictures on a summer night, but Lilian still hadn't recovered from the outrage.

'It's a great blessing that Maura comes down so regularly,' he confided to

Martin. 'Lilian would be at Clio's throat a lot of the time if we didn't have company to be pleasant in front of, so to speak...'

Martin's face brightened up. 'She's great company, Maura. I'm surprised that she's able to find so much time to visit, but it's grand to see her.'

Peter Kelly sipped his pint thoughtfully. He knew very well why Maura found so much time to come and visit. He wondered would Martin McMahon ever realise that he was the main attraction.

Rita realised it, however. She spoke about it to Sister Madeleine.

'I thought that might be the way the land was lying all right.'

'How on earth would you know, Sister? You don't go visiting ... How do you know things?'

'I just feel them.'

Sister Madeleine knew that Kit mentioned how her father laughed when Clio's aunt was around, and that the golf had become a regular feature of the weekends. When Emmet came to read his poetry with her, he sometimes mentioned Anna Kelly's aunt. She liked poetry too apparently, and had often asked him to read for her because she had forgotten her glasses.

'And is she a kind woman?' Sister Madeleine asked.

'Very, I'd say.'

'Well, maybe he should ask her to supper, don't you think?'

'I was wondering about that, with the Kellys, would you say?'

'Oh, I'd say so, the first time anyway.'

... and next week we've asked the Kellys and Clio's Aunt Maura to supper. It's a mad idea really, but Rita said that Dad was getting too many meals up in their house, and not giving any in return. I said that Dad paid for meals in O'Brien's Hotel or up at the golf club, but Rita said hadn't he got his own home to entertain them in. So that's it. Not us mind you, not Emmet and me, or Clio and Anna or anything ... just grown-ups. There'll be soup and roast lamb and trifle. And wine. Dad's delighted. I'm in two minds. You might think this is very silly but I feel it's a bit disloyal. You see, when Mother was here she could have cooked a meal for the Kellys and their Aunt Maura any time she wanted to. Mother was such a terrific cook. It seems silly all of us struggling to make a dinner when she could have done it so easily. But she didn't. Perhaps she didn't like the Kellys. It's so hard to know. I have this feeling that if she *had* liked them then she would have had this dinner ...

Lena felt her eyes mist over. How little escaped the quick mind of a child. She had neither liked nor disliked the Kellys; they represented all that was safe and dull about Lough Glass. She had deliberately held herself from confiding in them from a wish to stay separate and free, as if she knew Louis would come back one day and take her away.

And now she had left the legacy of that indifference with this innocent girl who thought so well of her that even after her death she didn't want to do anything to compromise her memory.

Lena wrote immediately.

I don't know if you're right about the Kelly family. Helen always spoke of them in her letters as people she liked. She said you and Clio had such a stormy friendship – sometimes it was till death do us part, other times worst enemies. I know she didn't want to play golf with them, but she sometimes felt guilty about depriving your father of it. She used to urge him apparently, but he'd say no, not without her.

So it's good now that he does play. I hope the dinner party goes well. I'd love to be a fly on the wall.

'What'll happen if he marries again?' Ivy asked one day.

'Who?'

'Your ex. Martin.'

'Oh, he won't marry again.' Lena was surprised at the question.

'From all you tell me I know these characters better than Mrs Dale's Diary . . . there's this Maura appearing a lot.'

'He wouldn't marry Maura.' Lena smiled at the thought.

'Well, why not? Everyone thinks you're dead, he's free to marry. Wouldn't it be sensible?'

'Martin wasn't sensible when it came to love. If he had been sensible he'd have married Maura in the first place and none of this mess would have happened.'

'And Kit and Emmet would never have existed.'

'It might have been better. They're only existing for me in a limbo.'

'What's wrong, love?'

'I don't know, Ivy. I don't know.'

But Lena did know what was wrong.

Louis had been restless. He had been nearly five years in one place. He felt it was time to move on. He said they should go somewhere warm, like the south of Spain.

A lot more British people were going there these days. They could get a partnership there. There wasn't much he didn't know about the business. They could make a killing. Live in a proper climate.

'What about my job?' Lena had asked.

'It's only a job, darling. You went in there the first day and stayed . . .'

'So did you,' she countered. 'But we both stayed because we got on, made something of the jobs.'

'Lena, there are millions of jobs.'

'They're our jobs, they're our careers. You practically run the Dryden, I practically run Millar's.'

'So? We're not married to them,' Louis had said.

'Nor to each other,' she had replied.

It was a bit of a problem, the marriage business. Technically Helen McMahon was dead. If she went to get a birth certificate, then a corresponding death certificate might be produced. Better not to risk it and unearth the Lord knew how many problems.

That's what they had said. But there was a part of Lena that thought Louis had taken the whole thing very calmly. If he had really loved her with the deep love he claimed, he would have made some more determined attempts to marry her.

Jessie Park and Mr Millar had a long romance. It was assisted throughout by the best efforts of Lena Gray. Often on a Saturday Mr Millar, Jessie and Lena had lunch together. Then Lena would excuse herself early and leave them to chat.

They made the big decisions about the business at these meetings. Lena would take notes and type them up on Mondays. Business at the agency was booming; they needed to take on someone else. Probably someone young, they thought. Young and glamorous looking.

'What about Dawn Jones?' Lena had suggested. 'She's between jobs. We couldn't get much more glamorous than her.'

'Would Dawn find us lively enough?' Jessie wondered. 'She usually likes places with lots going on.'

'Lots going on with us,' Mr Millar said, missing the point.

'I think Dawn's a bit tired of getting pawed by people,' Lena said. 'She might well be glad of a spell in a more responsible setting.'

Dawn Jones had been one of their earliest success stories. She had arrived for an interview looking like a tart about to set out for Soho: heavy make-up, low-cut sweater and nicotine-stained fingers. 'None of my sisters ever had an office job. I'd love to say I worked in an office,' Dawn had begged.

Her innocence and enthusiasm had appealed to Jessie and Lena. Tactfully they had advised her about dressing differently and she had been given a new hair do in Grace West's salon. Her typing speeds were adequate; it had not proved difficult to place the lovely Dawn in any office. The problem was that it had proved difficult to persuade many of her employers and colleagues to keep their hands off her. There was something about Dawn even in a neat navy twin set and pale blue skirt that suggested excitement and adventure.

She had done a spell in the Dryden, in Mr Williams' office. Louis had said she was sweet but silly. Nothing you could put a finger on, but just not someone you'd trust to take a message or type up a report. Dawn had left the Dryden after three months and James Williams had got a pleasant middle-aged woman, motherly, efficient, much more what was needed. An excellent reference had been provided for Dawn, but everywhere it was the same story. She was too sexy to be taken seriously.

Lena wondered if this might be to their advantage. Young girls loved someone to follow, a role model they could identify with. She and Jessie were too old and settled; if they saw Dawn in Millar's they might think that secretarial work was much more glittering than they had believed.

Jim Millar said yes, he saw the point, and Jessie said she thought Jim was absolutely right. So Dawn was approached.

'I'm not sure, Mrs Gray, really. I don't know. Would I be right here, do you think?' Dawn looked doubtfully around the office.

'We're doing a face lift, Dawn. And having journalists and photographers come in and everything.'

Lena knew she had won the battle. She sent a press release to the local newspapers and to the trade magazines. And with it she sent a description of Dawn Jones, who had left her job in a model agency to join Millar's. The model agency had been a brief interlude and one on which Dawn had not wanted to dwell. There were many definitions of modelling, it appeared. Still, it gave her the necessary glamour to attract the interest of the press.

And if they came and took pictures of Dawn then they had to mention Millar's also, the agency where there was an emphasis on grooming and presentation as well as on typing and shorthand speeds. It was just the right approach and resulted in a great many enquiries for the agency.

Jessie and Jim were delighted.

'It's going so well I can hardly believe it.' Jessie was breathless.

'What would I do without my two girls?' said Jim Millar looking at them both with pride.

'Do you think he's fond of me, Lena?' Jessie asked in a whisper when Mr Millar had left.

'Of course he is, of course he is,' Lena was reassuring.

'I wish I knew what to do, I'm so inexperienced at all this sort of thing . . . You'd know, Lena.'

'No, I'm pretty hopeless too,' Lena said. She felt she spoke the truth. She had no idea how to cope with the kind of passion that Louis had for her until recently. She would have given anything on earth to know.

'But you're so . . . well, so terrific looking and you've got such a gorgeous husband. I was wondering, had you any hints or anything . . . ?' Jessie's big pale eyes were full of innocence and hope.

'I think he's a man who takes his time over things but makes the right decision in the end,' Lena said.

'Suppose someone else comes along?' Jessica was biting her lower lip.

'No, not for Mr Millar, believe me.'

And Jessie did because Lena looked so authoritative. If only she knew, Lena thought, if only she knew where she was asking advice about love and marriage.

Dawn was delighted with all the publicity. 'You've really done me a good turn, Mrs Gray,' she said, 'and I like working here with women actually. I didn't think I would. They're sort of more reasonable than men, aren't they?'

'Some of them are, I suppose,' Lena tried to hide her smile. Dawn was proving a good choice. They had even included her name in the brochure they sent out, just in order to use her picture.

Lena was proud of all they had achieved, and she couldn't help talking about it to Louis. He was still in poor form but at least he had stopped mentioning Spain.

'You're putting a lot of effort into that place,' Louis said to her.

'So are you, in the Dryden. It's the kind of people we are.' She sat on the floor with her head in his lap. She loved the evenings they had together; the shabby flat was in no way small and shabby to her.

'What's the point?' Louis said waving around him. 'Working our guts out to keep four walls in a kip like this?'

'It isn't a kip.' Lena was indignant.

'Well it's hardly the Camino Real,' he said, his mouth turned down. He was playing with her hair as she spoke, idly twisting the strands around.

Louis touched a lot. He wasn't a man to sit in his own space and make statements across a table, he always had a hand on her arm or neck, or was stroking her cheek.

'What's the Camino Real?' she asked.

'It's just a phrase ... like the kind of names hotels would have, but in Spain ... where we could easily work ...' She was silent. 'Easily,' he said again, his big dark eyes pleading at her.

She felt a rising panic in her throat. She must keep the conversation away from Spain. Lena would have given up so much else, so much that was far more important. She could arrange for Kit to write to her anywhere, that wasn't the problem. The problem was that if Louis went to Spain he would go alone. She could not get a passport. Lena Gray did not exist.

*

'Do you think we should get drunk?' Clio asked Kit.

'Now?' They were walking up to school for the last frantic weeks of revision before the exams.

'Well, not this minute but soonish. It's an experience we haven't yet had.'

'How soonish? Should we turn round and go back to Paddles' or maybe ask Mr and Mrs O'Brien to make us a few cocktails before class?'

'You make a jeer out of everything,' Clio complained.

'I do not.' Kit was indignant. 'I'm prepared to do anything, you know I am. But I think it might be poor timing to get plastered just coming up to the exams. Suppose it took a hold of us like those old fellows with runny eyes and red noses waiting for Foley's to open.'

Clio giggled. Sometimes Kit could be very funny. But then sometimes for no reason she flared up and took offence. There were certain subjects that made her very touchy. Clio was dying to ask her whether she thought that Aunt Maura might be going to get engaged to Kit's father, and if she would like the idea of having a stepmother and of their being cousins. But this was territory she mustn't venture into.

She would love to know whether Aunt Maura and Mr McMahon ... well ... courted a bit. And if they got married, would they do it properly in bed. Normally these were things you could talk about with a best friend, but with Kit McMahon there were so many areas that were off limits.

'Have you ever been drunk, properly out of your mind drunk?' Kit asked Stevie Sullivan.

'Why do you ask?' he said. He was handsome even when covered in grease and wearing filthy overalls. But unreliable of course. Everyone knew that.

'It's just that you've done most things. Clio and I are thinking of getting drunk when we finish our exams and I was looking for suggestions. Like what's cheap and quick and wouldn't make us too sick?'

'You're asking the wrong one. I don't know.'

'I bet you do,' Kit insisted.

'No truly, we had too much of that in this house when I was young.'

Kit had forgotten. She felt ashamed that she hadn't remembered the alcoholic father who saw animals and all kinds of things emerging from walls when he was in the horrors. But she decided against apologising. She hated people saying thoughtless things about drownings or people gone missing and then being covered with confusion. She disliked the embarrassment and the apologies more than the original mistake.

'Yes, I suppose that makes sense.' she said in a matter of fact way.

'It does to me, but not to Michael. He'd drink it off a sore foot as they say.'

'God, who are they, the people who say that?' Kit recoiled at the thought.

'The kind of low people I mix with, Kit McMahon,' he said and left her.

There was always a keen rivalry between Mother Bernard and Brother Healy about the Leaving Certificate results. They were published in the local newspaper so that all could see and compare. Brother Healy always said that the odds were weighted in favour of Mother Bernard. Girls did all those easy subjects like art and domestic science. It was not so difficult for Mother Bernard to build up a frightening total of passes and honours amongst her pupils.

But the nuns were adamant that she had a harder route to go. Many of the small farmers were anxious for their daughters only to learn the basic skills that would turn them into acceptable farmers' wives. When the time came they were suspicious of girls learning French and Latin. They would have preferred classes in buttermaking and poultry raising and in many ways they had a point. Why raise the expectations of a girl who was going to leave her father's house and move into one fairly similar a parish away?

'And have you a very bright crop this year, Brother Healy?' Mother Bernard asked courteously but disguising her deep interest to know the lie of the land and assess her own chances in this year's contest.

'Dunderheads, Mother Bernard. Dunces and idle blocks of wood . . . and you . . . you have the crème de la crème this time I expect?'

'Empty vessels I'm afraid, Brother. Empty vessels with nothing tinkling inside except jazz music.'

'This jazz is a great distraction to them all right.' agreed Brother Healy.

Wise though they were about the ways of the youth of Lough Glass they were not sound on its musical taste. Jazz was not the enemy within that it had been a previous generation. The noise tinkling in the hearts of the young people of Lough Glass was the early sound of rock and roll.

*

'Peter, will you speak to Clio?'

'No, Lilian. To be frank, I won't.'

'Well, that's a nice thing to say, you won't speak to your own daughter.'

'She's only my daughter, my own daughter, and I'm only asked to speak to her when some dreadful thing has happened for which some terrible punishment is to be meted out. As it happens . . . as it happens, Lilian, I've had a very bad day, a horrible day. And I'm not going to speak to either of my own daughters or even my own wife, I'm going down to Paddles' for a pint with my friend Martin. Right?'

'Well, sorry for existing, and running your house and minding your children, both of whom are turning into juvenile delinquents.'

'Let them turn, they'll turn back again when they see there's no future in it.' Peter Kelly was out the door. He knew Anna's offence had something to do with cosmetics and perfume. He suspected that Clio's had something to do with getting her ears pierced like a gypsy without asking permission. It was too trivial. He banged out of the house and down the road towards the privacy and peace of Paddles'.

There wasn't much peace in Paddles', as it happened. Mr Hickey was singing away in a corner.

'If I've told you once, John, I've told you a dozen times. This is not a singing house,' Paddles remonstrated with him.

'Oh bollocks, Paddles. You wouldn't know a singing house if you saw one.'

'Well I see *this* one and what's more I run it, and you're getting no more drink in it unless you cut out that caterwauling this instant,' Paddles said.

'Are you barring me? Do my ears deceive me or do I hear you barring me – John J. Hickey, High Class Victualler, barred from your pathetic premises?'

'You heard me, John,' Paddles said.

'Well, I'd deem it an *honour* to be barred from such a dump. An honour I will wear proudly.' He staggered to the door. 'And an honour not to have a drink with the scum who frequent it.' Mr Hickey smiled pleasantly around at all his neighbours, friends and clients before stepping out briefly into the fresh air that he would encounter on the way to Foley's bar.

Martin and Peter exchanged glances.

'That was a good day's work, Paddles,' Peter said approvingly.

'Can't you frighten him, Dr Kelly? Tell him his liver's packing up. It probably is,' Paddles said.

'No, I can't, Paddles. I'm in a poor position to be telling him that, seeing as I've seen him across this bar every night since time began. And you're in an equally poor position Paddles, seeing that you sell him the drink. It's a strange world where no one takes any responsibility.'

Paddles had moved away, grumbling, to serve the other end of the bar when the door flew open and Mrs Hickey stood there carrying something very alarming on a tray.

'What's that, Mrs Hickey?' Paddles' voice sounded less than confident.

'Ah Paddles, this is a sheep's head. I thought you'd like to see it, and maybe the rest of the clientele might like to have a look at it too . . .'

There was an uneasy murmuring around the premises, a low dark pub, very basic in its design and decor, and not a place where ladies came at all, not to mention carrying a large sheep's head on a white butcher's tray.

'Yes, well thank you, Mrs Hickey. Thank you indeed.'

'I'll just take it round so everyone can see it properly,' she said. She had a very mad glint in her eye. No one wished to upset her or even enter into conversation with her. They nodded and muttered vague sounds of approval as the object was carried around for their inspection. 'This is the way John looks when he comes home from here each evening; he has the features and colour of a sheep's head. I thought you should not be denied the pleasure of seeing this for yourself.'

'Well, John isn't actually here himself at the moment . . .' Paddles began uneasily. 'But when we see him . . . well . . .' his voice trailed away.

'No need to mention it at all,' Mrs Hickey said airily. 'Just wanted you all to be aware of everything that's going on.'

'Thank you, Mrs Hickey,' said Paddles gravely, in the tone of voice that implied the show was over.

'Would you live anywhere else?' Martin asked Peter Kelly when Mrs Hickey and her tray were safely off the premises.

Peter Kelly had come in about to inveigh against the kind of society they lived in, people who had told him that a baby's death was all for the best, all for the best because you see she hadn't got a father. It had upset him greatly that a pious morality should be so inverted that it could think a bastard child better dead than surviving to be a child raised with love in a small mountain cottage. But there was Martin, peaceable, easy going and finding everything about Lough Glass comic and delightful. He couldn't impose his misery on his friend.

'You're right, Martin,' he said after an effort. 'It's got everything here except a three-ring circus. Maura says there's more life here than in the whole of Dublin.'

Kit came home and found Rita whitewashing the yard. 'Will I help you? Is there another brush?'

'Aren't you meant to be studying?' Rita said.

'Oh God, Rita, not you too. Here, I'll go from this end.'

'Take off your school uniform first, anyway.' Kit did that immediately, standing in her bra and knickers. 'I didn't mean that,' Rita laughed. 'I meant get some old clothes.'

'No, what's the point? By the time I'm upstairs and changed and downstairs you'll have finished. And who'll see me anyway except Farouk?'

The old cat looked at them sleepily and indifferently. It was hard to get Farouk interested in anything.

The grey-streaked walls transformed before their very eyes, the yard was soon the bright gleaming colour it had been before the damp and spatters changed it to its messy state every year.

'I don't know why we bother sometimes,' Kit said. 'It just gets mucky again and no one sees it but us.'

'Your mother always said that that made it even more important that it was kept nice,' Rita said.

'Did she?' Kit laid down her brush for a moment.

'Yes, she said you had to have pride in a place for its own sake, not for what the neighbours saw or didn't see.'

'She liked nice surroundings, didn't she?'

'Yes, she did.'

'Wasn't it sad she didn't have a garden like the Kellys do? It must have been hard stuck in the side of the street here with only a yard.'

'She said the lake was her garden,' Rita said. She was unselfconscious, she didn't stop and put her hand over her mouth as if suddenly remembering that Helen McMahon had died in the lake. 'She said no one could have a better garden on their doorstep.'

'I didn't inherit that from her. I couldn't care less about my surroundings,' Kit said.

'You will when you have a place of your own,' Rita promised. 'Now, get some clothes on before Sergeant O'Connor comes over the wall and arrests you for indecent exposure.'

*

Lena looked around her little home and tried to be objective. Why did Louis say it was a kip? Why did he say they hadn't much to show for their years of hard work?

Ivy's house had improved considerably since they had gone to live there. The outside was painted and the railings had been repaired. So many of London's railings had disappeared during the war, wrenched up to form part of the war effort. Lena had never known that before. The hall was carpeted now and the banisters had been replaced. In fact the only flat that had not been given an overhaul was the one that she and Louis lived in.

And they had beautified it themselves, done it up with pictures and rugs and wall hangings. To Lena it was a haven, the place where she made passionate love to the man who was the centre of her life, where she cooked him little meals and talked to him and looked out at the sky of London . . . She felt the freedom of the place everywhere she looked. True, it was small. But they didn't entertain people; they didn't want to. Louis was out so late, his hours were getting worse and worse. It was the same everywhere, once you got some responsibility, you found your life was no longer your own.

But Lena loved it here. She loved the undemanding friendship of Ivy Brown, she would never find anyone to share her post secrets with such glee. She loved being around the corner from the agency. She could even dash home at lunch time and put a flower and a love letter and maybe a sticky almond bun for him to find if he came home early on a split shift.

And Louis loved this place too. He had shopped with her in markets for outlandishly coloured bedspreads, and for the mirror with a cherub on the side of it that looked as decadent as you could get. Why had he said it was a dump, a kip, and that they had nothing to show for their time here? He liked Ivy and it was near the tube station. Perhaps it just wasn't smart enough for his image of how they should live. A flat without a bathroom. But suppose, suppose one of the other flats in the house came free … suppose.

But it was silly to think that. Most of the people in the house were settled. She must not start chasing rainbows.

But there was a God or a fate or something, Lena told herself. Three days later Ivy told her that the New Zealanders on the second floor were leaving.

'Homesick, they say.' Ivy shook her head doubtfully. 'You couldn't be homesick for out there surely.' Anyway, they'd given her a month's rent and they were moving out now. 'You can help me choose the tenants,' Ivy offered. 'After all, they'll be your neighbours. You want to have people you'll get along with.'

'How did they leave it?' Lena asked.

'Come and have a look.' Ivy picked the key of her rack and they went upstairs.

It had high ceilings and big windows. This was never a place that Louis Gray could dismiss and run down. Not if they furnished it properly. 'How much does it cost?' Lena asked.

'I never offered it to you … I thought you were saving for a place of your own to buy,' Ivy said.

'No, no nothing like that.' Lena would not let Ivy know that the savings were very little. They spent what they had. She would have to make economies to rent this place but it would be worth it.

'Does he know?' Ivy asked.

'Of course not, I only knew myself ten seconds ago.'

'Let me get it spruced up a bit before you show it.'

'What will you do?'

'What do you think?' They stood looking at it, minds full of ideas. 'Ernest can send me a few chippies over from the pub, you know, meant to be doing a day's work for the Brewery but out on six other jobs at the same time.'

'A big cupboard in the bedroom maybe.'

'To hang all Louis Gray's jackets in and lay out his nice shoes.' Ivy was teasing her.

'Don't say a word against him.'

'I wouldn't dare,' Ivy said. 'Listen, give me a week, then I'll show it to the pair of you and see what you think. If you change your mind, that's no problem. I'll let it anyway.'

'I'd say he'll love it,' Lena said, her heart full of hope again. This might chase the notion of Spain out of his mind. For a while anyway.

And he did love it. He was so excited by the proportion of the rooms, better than the Dryden, he told Ivy. He waltzed Lena around the big empty rooms and said that at last they'd have space for a proper life in London. He bought a bottle of champagne and the three of them drank the health of the new home.

'I can't wait to move in,' Louis said. He was eager and excited like a child, he moved around the room touching the walls, the door handles ... stroking them almost. 'Now we're making something of ourselves,' he said, as pleased as punch.

There was a hoteliers' conference in Scarborough.

'That's a place I've always wanted to go,' said Lena.

'I'll tell you about it.'

'Will I not see it with you?' Lena had been about to take a few days off from the agency.

'No spouses, I'm afraid.'

'Tell me about it then,' she said with a great smile.

She was choosing fabric for the curtains of the new flat when she ran into James Williams in Selfridges.

'More blue and gold for your agency?' he asked. He had remembered.

'No, just browsing.'

'You're looking fit and well.' He always eyed her rather over-appreciatively she thought.

'Thank you, James.' She smiled her routine smile acknowledging the compliment.

'Enjoy Scarborough,' he said.

'Will you be there too?' she said, her voice coming somehow through the icy feeling in her throat.

'No, I have no excuse, unfortunately. They do some work, but mainly it's a thank you to a lot of these guys who work so hard and such highly unsocial hours. Gives them a chance to entertain their wives properly without having to count the pennies.'

'And do all wives go?'

'Yes. They're not going to pass on a trip like that. Enjoy it anyway.'

'I will,' she said. And held the counter to steady herself.

*

It's probably all in my mind, *Kit wrote*, but I have this feeling that Dad and Clio's Aunt Maura are walking out. I know that's a very old-fashioned expression, but I can't think what else to call it. And there's nobody I could say it to. They've had a couple of meals in O'Brien's Hotel. Philip told me their heads were very close, but Philip is always talking about people's heads being close. It's sort of on his mind.

But would you think at their age they might really and truly be thinking of getting married? I know it wouldn't come to anything like that without Dad discussing it with us, but I was very keen to know what you thought.

This time the answer came to Kit very quickly. It must have been by return of post. It was a very short letter.

> Kit, write and tell me. Do you think Maura would make your father happy? He has had a hard life. He deserves happiness. Then tell me would you and Emmet like it or would it make you upset to see another woman walking around where your mother did, in her room. When you tell me these things I'll write and tell you what I think.

Kit wrote:

> How did you know Mother had a separate room? I never told you that. I can't believe she would have told you. Please let me know.

Lena paced her office. She must never write quickly again. That's how mistakes happened. But it was all right. It could be covered.

> How observant you are, Kit, *Lena wrote*.
> Your mother did indeed tell me that she had a separate room. She said she didn't sleep well at night with anyone else in the room. She didn't need to ask me to tell it to nobody, since I spoke to nobody about her. Our correspondence was a sort of secret life, in a way like yours and mine is. Other people might think it sad, pathetic even. But I don't. And I hope you don't. Your mother never did. You have no idea how lonely I felt when her letters ceased. Tell me you understand.

> I understand, *Kit wrote*. But I don't know why you said you read in a paper that Mother died. You must have known at once when she stopped writing to you.

> I only said that in the first letter, *Lena explained*, so that I could get on to introduce myself to you. Perhaps you might not have wanted to write, to stay in touch, out of loyalty to your mother. I didn't want to tell about our letter writing.

> It's all so confusing, *Kit wrote*. You're such a mystery woman, I know nothing about you, nothing at all. And yet you know everything about me. Did you tell my mother about yourself? Did she destroy your letters? There was nothing found when she left. Nothing at all that would make us know of you.

> I'll tell you anything you like, *Lena wrote*. Just make a list of questions and I'll try to answer them.

She knew it was risky. She was getting in too deep. She would have to invent a persona for Lena, a past that had never existed. She feared what questions would be asked.

In fact, there were no searching questions. It was as if Kit had decided it would be impolite. Instead, there was something much more heartbreaking, something Lena could never have foreseen. And yet, of course, it was the normal response of a friend. Kit wanted her to come to Ireland.

> Can you come and see us? You have plenty of money. And if you want it all to be a secret still you could just stay in O'Brien's Hotel.

There were ways in which Kit hoped she wouldn't come. Maybe she would be a disappointment to meet. Perhaps she would have a funny cockney accent from living in England. Perhaps she wouldn't be nearly as nice to talk to as to write to.

But it was getting to be silly now, and if Lena was Mother's age she must be in her middle forties, too old really for having a life writing to a teenage girl in Ireland about events long ago. Lena sounded very normal, and she had a husband who was a hotelier. And she worked in a big employment agency somewhere. And she lived in some woman called Mrs Brown's house.

And maybe she was made like Miss Havisham. Anyway, if she came Kit would know.

> Dear Sister Madeleine,
> You have been acting as a postbox for me for years. I want to thank you for your discretion and lack of curiosity. Kit McMahon speaks of you with such admiration and devotion I wonder if I could ask you a great favour. Kit has suggested that I come to Lough Glass. For a great variety of reasons I do not want to do so. It would not be good for her or for anyone. But I am not thinking about myself first in this instance, I am really thinking of others. From what Kit tells me you can always come up with some solution to a seemingly impossible situation. If there is any way you could help Kit to see that it would be a good thing for us not to meet in Lough Grass or at all I would be for ever in your debt.
> I don't want to invent a string of lies, I just know you will believe me when I say it would not be for the best.
> Yours in despair, dear Sister Madeleine,
> Lena Gray

> My dear child,
> I have always believed that there is a life of the imagination which suffers when it is mixed with reality. Two worlds can be kept separate. Lives can live in parallels and never meet. I wish you peace and happiness and the knowledge that you have friends, and have always had them, here.
> Yours sincerely in Jesus Christ,
> Madeleine

'She knows, doesn't she?' Lena handed the letter to Ivy.
'I expect so,' Ivy said. 'What now?'
'She won't tell,' Lena said. 'That much I know for certain.'

*

'Are you doing a line with Philip O'Brien?' Clio demanded to know.

'God, Clio. I wish I had a different friend. I've been saying it for ever, of course I'm not doing a line with Philip. Whatever that means.'

'He's always here. Hanging around. Or else you're in there,' Clio grumbled.

'Well, we do live beside each other.'

'Has he kissed you?'

'Shut up.'

'We swore to tell each other everything. I told you about the spin the bottle at the party.'

'I told you about everything. It's just that there's not anything to tell.'

'So he *did* kiss you, but because you and he are in love you can't tell me, is that it?'

Kit couldn't stop giggling. 'That's not it, okay? He sort of kissed me, but he missed because I didn't know it was happening, and I looked the other way and he got my chin. And he said sorry, and I said sorry and we tried again, and it seemed a bit awkward. So you know every single thing. Now, will you leave me alone.'

'When did all this happen?' Clio wasn't satisfied.

'Oh, Clio. It was a day last week . . .'

'And you never told me.'

'I'll tell you what I will tell you. Stevie Sullivan's got a new girl.'

'No!' Now this did seem a matter of interest and some disappointment to Clio.

'Yes. An American girl staying at O'Brien's Hotel. Her parents came here to look for their roots. They're up in the graveyard most of the time, and she went across the road and got talking to Stevie.'

'I bet she did.'

'She's gorgeous looking, according to Philip. And anyway, Stevie came over to the hotel and she said to her Mom and Pop that he was taking her to meet a gang of kids across the lake, and they said fine. And there was no gang of kids at all of course. It was just Stevie putting on the act.'

'Well, she'll be gone soon,' Clio said grimly. 'Once the parents have found their roots they'll be out of here like bats from hell. And it'll be Bye Bye from Mr Stevie Sullivan's little new pal.'

'It's another Careers talk this afternoon,' Kit groaned.

'Yeah, hopeless,' Clio said. 'I suppose they have to tell us what's available.'

'Nothing's available except nursing and teaching, and that's only if you get called.'

'And I'd hate both of those,' Clio said.

'Mother Bernard's mad keen for you to be a doctor,' Kit said.

'That's because she wants to say that a doctor came out of the convent here, and because she'd like me to have my head down studying for seven years.'

'So what *are* you going to do?'

'I'm going to do a B.A. Aunt Maura says its a great stepping stone.'

'Where will it make you step?'

'Into the arms of a rich husband, I hope.'

'You don't want that.'

'No, I want him sexy as well, and experienced. I don't want him missing my mouth and hitting me on the chin with his nose.'

'Is it a wonder that nobody'd tell you anything, Clio?'

'But you're getting very secretive altogether,' Clio said, with narrowing eyes.

'What about now?'

'You go down to Sister Madeleine's when I'm not with you, for one thing.'

'Yes.'

'And then there's this face-bashing with Philip. And you're going off mysteriously to study.'

'Well, I do study. We are doing our Leaving in three months' time, if you haven't forgotten.'

'And are you studying now?'

'Yes.'

'You haven't any books, you only have paper . . .'

'I'm making notes.'

'Let's see.' Clio snatched the writing case and unzipped it. Inside she saw a stamped envelope and a half written letter. 'No you're not studying, you're writing letters . . . love letters.'

'Give it to me.' Kit's face was white with anger.

'Let me read . . .'

'*Give it to me, Clio.*'

Clio was reading 'Dearest . . . dearest what, I can't read his name.'

With a cry Kit lunged at her. 'You are such a selfish, greedy person. You have no manners, you have no decency.'

'No manners, no decency,' Clio mocked, holding the letter high.

But Kit gave her a totally unexpected punch in the stomach that winded her. Then Kit grabbed the letter and ran out of the classroom.

She met Mother Bernard in the corridor. 'Ladies are rarely seen running, Mary Katherine.'

'I know. Sorry, Mother. I was running to the library to do more revision.'

'Right. But just walk briskly. Do you feel all right? You look flushed.'

'I'm fine, Mother.' Kit escaped before the groaning lie should be discovered and further explanations sought.

'Emmet, will you deliver a note up to Kellys' for me.'

'No.'

'I'll pay you.'

'How much? Threepence?'

'I was going to say a penny.'

'I won't do it for a penny.'

'You're a horrible, horrible person.'

'Okay. I won't do it at all.'

'When I think of all I do for you.' Kit was stung.

'What exactly do you do for me?'

'I protect you.'

'Who do you protect me from?'

'From people shouting at you.'

'Oh, don't be silly, Kit. You don't protect me. People shout at everyone.'

'I always speak nicely about you. I even think nicely about you.'

'Well, why shouldn't you? I'm not that bad. Why should you be giving out about me?'

'Everyone else gives out about their sisters and brothers. I don't.'

'Who gives out?'

'Clio does. Stevie does. Patsy Hanley gives out about Deirdre.'

'Well,' Emmet shrugged as if these were people with crosses to bear.

'Oh all right. Be as rotten as everyone else. I used to think you were special.'

'What did you want delivered?'

'A note to Clio.'

'Why couldn't you walk up with it yourself? You and Clio have a path worn to each other's houses.'

'I'm not talking to her.'

'So it's a note making it all up?'

'No it's not. It's a note saying how bad she is, and how she pokes her horrible nose everywhere it isn't wanted.'

'That'll only make things worse.' Emmet was philosophical.

'Yes, but I don't care. They couldn't be bad enough between us as far as I'm concerned.'

'But then you'll go and apologise or she will, and it will all be back where it was.' Emmet had seen these fights ebb and flow over the years.

'I don't think so this time.'

'That's what you always say,' Emmet said. 'You'll forgive her or she'll forgive you, and things will be the same for a while.'

Kit thought about it. He was quite right. That was the way the pattern always had been. But not this time. No, Clio had almost snatched her secret from her.

Out of nothing but sheer pique she had nearly found out that Mother's friend Lena was writing these letters. And if Clio discovered that then it would all have been over. In some way Kit knew that it had to be secret to continue. She wished that Lena had been able to say something sensible about why she couldn't come to Lough Glass. It sounded like a load of excuses.

'So what happens now?' Emmet asked. He was wondering whether to bring his price down.

But life was full of surprises. 'I'll tell you what happens next,' Kit said cheerfully tucking her arm into his. 'I am going to buy you an ice cream, how about that?'

'What do I have to do for it?' Emmet asked suspiciously.

'Nothing, nothing at all. Just admit that you have the best sister in these parts for miles.'

'I suppose I do really,' Emmet said thoughtfully. And together they ran up towards the shop before Kit might change her mind.

*

'Sweetheart?' Louis rang Lena at the agency.

'The very person,' she said, and the smile came into her voice.

'You know this conference?'

'Oh, yes.' Did it sound casual enough, she wondered? Did it give any telltale hint that she had been thinking about nothing else for weeks?

'The rules have changed.'

'In what way?'

'We are allowed to take spouses, partners, whatevers.' A great silence. 'So . . .'

'So Louis?'

'So, isn't that great? Pack your glad rags and we'll have a ball.'

'I can't.'

'You what?'

'I can't, love. You know that. I've arranged to babysit Mrs Park, and to keep the office open. No, there are too many people. I can't back out.'

'We'll never have anything like this again. You can't turn it down.'

'If I'd known earlier I wouldn't have set all this up.'

'Well, I didn't bloody know earlier.'

Oh how she would love to have gone on a train journey, all expenses paid, to Yorkshire. She would have taken out a map and wondered were they passing places like the Wash and the Humber.

They would have stayed, for the first time since the time of the miscarriage, that terrible visit to Brighton, in a hotel together. They would have had free time, time to talk and relax together. She could have looked well for him, and been happy. She could have sparkled in front of other people and made him proud of her. The tight knot in her stomach would have gone because he would have wanted her.

She had allowed a silence to fall between them. She heard him grumble. 'Are you making your mind up, or is that it?'

'Why *didn't* you tell me earlier?' she asked.

'Because I didn't know earlier,' he said, as if explaining to an idiot or a child.

'James Williams knew earlier,' Lena said.

'What do you mean?'

'I met him. And he asked me was I going. I said there were no spouses; he said he thought there were.'

'And he was right,' Louis cried triumphantly. 'He was the one who said from the start that this was the way it should be.'

Lena felt very very tired. What would someone else have done in her shoes? A cleverer woman? Would she have dropped everything and gone,

gone with him, stormed her way back into his heart again? Or would she have allowed herself to be persuaded slowly, played hard to get?

'I can't go, Louis,' she said. Because she had thought she would be alone for the weekend Lena had set up so many activities to distract her that she was going to be busy every second of the time. Now she realised with bitter irony it would be impossible to unpick them. There were too many people depending on her. Louis believed she was sulking and trying to make a point about staying behind. She decided it would be best not to apologise or explain too much. Just to let him know that she would have loved the trip. 'Let me take you to lunch on the Friday,' she suggested.

'I don't know. If you've time to go gallivanting off to lunch with men like me, why haven't you got time to come to Scarborough?'

'Because, you idiot, I thought you couldn't take me. Come on, let's have a lunch like people do in the movies.' She had persuaded him.

But as Lena sat in her office and studied her face in the mirror of her compact she saw with alarm that she must look many many years older than she was. There was a tight drawn look, a near-permanent frown. Her hair seemed dull and her eyes lifeless. No wonder he had asked someone else to Scarborough. Someone who had let him down at the last moment. No, no. She would not allow herself to think that way. But what a dreary wife she would look.

'Jessie,' she said suddenly standing up. 'I have to go out on business. See you after lunch.'

She knew her voice sounded raspy and tinny. She saw Dawn and the two other assistants look up in surprise. Mrs Gray always spoke gently and moved smoothly from place to place. She didn't grab up a handbag and scamper out the way she had today.

Dawn looked after her in amazement. 'What's happened to her?' she asked.

Jessica didn't like office gossip, and especially not about Lena. 'Carry on, Dawn,' she said briskly.

But inside in the inner sanctum she confessed to Jim Millar that she thought Lena Gray was working too hard. 'She's looking after my mum while you and I go out; she's coming in to deal with workmen here ... carpenters she found herself. She's got the girls doing overtime so that we'll have the whole new filing system set up by Monday ... I don't know.'

'What's that handsome husband of hers going to think if she's working in here all hours of the day and night?'

'I think he's going away on some conference or other.'

'Maybe that's what has her on edge,' said Jim Millar.

'Grace, can you squeeze me in?'

'Sure thing. Come to the end cubicle.' Grace started to take out the shampoo.

'Not you yourself ... you're the manager ... I meant one of the girls.'

'They're all busy, I'm glad to say.' Grace's sing-song voice never sounded anything other than cheerful, yet Lena knew she had a hard life. The man Grace loved had two children by other women. They were not spoken of.

'I feel so awful. I look old and sad and no use to anyone.'

'Tired maybe?' Grace suggested.

'We know what tired means.' They laughed. It was a polite way of saying that age was showing.

'Work, is it?' Grace asked as her firm fingers massaged Lena's scalp.

'No,' Lena muttered into the towel as she leaned over the basin. 'No, work runs itself.'

'Me too,' Grace said. 'Funny isn't it? Men make such a big deal about work. To women like you and me it's nothing. Nothing at all.'

'He has someone else,' Lena said as she sat and looked at herself turbanned with a towel.

'No, I'm sure that's not so,' Grace said.

'I'm sure it is.'

'I'll give you a hot oil treatment, make your hair shinier, and I'll look out some nice make-up for you.'

'It won't get him back.'

'Perhaps he has not gone.'

'I think he has . . . you know the way you know these things.'

Grace had massaged in the warm olive oil and replaced the towel with another one. 'Has he *said* he has someone else?'

'No, of course not.'

'Well then . . .'

'I didn't ask him,' Lena confessed.

'No of course you didn't,' Grace grinned.

'But I can't stop thinking about it . . . all the time, everywhere: at home, at work, in bed, even here. And I'm going to find out, I really am. I can't sleep until I know.'

'Not much sign of sleep recently.' Grace gently touched the dark shadows under Lena's eyes. Lena wanted to cry and hold the woman close to her. But it was a public place, and she had years and years of experience at hiding her feelings.

'Think of something nice. Think of something you really know is constant and true . . .'

'My daughter,' Lena said.

'Grace looked up startled. In all the time they had known each other the previous life had not been discussed. Only Ivy knew the whole story.

'How old is she?' Graced asked gently.

'Soon to be seventeen.'

'That's a great age. They're lovely at seventeen. And can you talk to her?'

'No, not directly.'

'Why?'

'She thinks I'm dead,' Lena said. And wondered had anyone in the world ever felt so lonely before.

'Well, well, don't you look a treat,' he said in the restaurant.

And indeed she did. Grace had worked miracles.

'Have to send you off with a good memory of me,' she said smiling at him.

'I wish it weren't only the memory.'

'So do I, but honestly it's only a weekend . . . there'll be others.' She was determined to make a virtue out of it now that it had to be done this way.

His eyes were on her, she could feel them without looking up. 'You look so alive,' he said.

'Thank you, Louis.'

'Let's have a glass of wine and go home, hey?'

'What! We've only just arrived.'

'We can be home in a few minutes. I can't go away to the wilds and leave unfinished business behind me.' He wanted her now. She could still arouse him, make him desire her.

Lena smiled. 'Well, I said let's have lunch like people do in the movies, but this is even better,' she said, and went ahead of him out of the restaurant.

They ran like youngsters down the road, and if Ivy heard them come in she didn't come out to make conversation.

When they got into the flat he held her very tight. 'There's no other woman in the world for me except you, Lena,' he said. 'Oh God, I need you so much. I can't tell you how much I need you.'

Afterwards she helped Louis pack his case.

'I'm a very understanding man,' he said, as she folded his shirts.

'And tell me, Louis Gray, how is that?' She was determined to laugh and be happy with him. No letting him go away with the memory of a grousing, sulking woman at home.

'My wife doesn't do her duty, her conjugal duty, and accompany me on a works' outing.' His smile across the case was heartbreaking.

'Aha, but I'm *not* your wife, Louis.'

'Well, whose fault is that? I must be the only man in the world teamed up with a woman who is officially dead. I'd marry you tomorrow if I could. You know that.'

'Do I?' She couldn't help the question.

'Well, if you don't know you'll never know.' He reached into the shelf of the cupboard where they kept his underwear. As he took out his folded underpants, vests and socks, two packets of condoms remained deliberately on the shelf.

'Not much point in taking those if I can't take you,' he said.

'None at all,' Lena laughed.

But her laugh was hollow. There were many chemists' where such things could be bought between here and Scarborough.

I suppose it's because I'm so involved in an employment agency that I wonder about what you'll do when you leave school, *Lena wrote to Kit*. You see, girls get such a poor start because nobody gives them any proper career advice at all. You don't talk much about the future, and I am very interested in what you are going to decide to do.

You never say whether you'd like to be taken on in the pharmacy or not, or whether you want to go to university.

She didn't expect a reply so soon.

It's funny you should ask that question just then, but I've been thinking I'd love to do hotel management. Now there are things for this and against. The main thing against is this boy, Philip O'Brien. I've told you all about him. He's very nice, but he sort of likes me more than I like him. I'm not the kind of girl people fancy much, so it's quite nice . . . but I wouldn't want him to get the notion that I was going to enrol in Cathal Brugha Street, the hotel school, just to follow him, or be with him.

Lots of times he has talked about us running the hotel together in Lough Glass, and honestly, Lena, if you saw it you'd prefer to be in partnership with the Draculas running their castle.

I do know it, Lena thought grimly, and I never heard a better description. The letter went on.

Your husband is in a hotel. Maybe I could come and work in that for summer experience . . . if you could put in a word for me.

Lena sat for a while with the letter in her hand. It was a grotesque thought that Louis might all unknowingly start a relationship with her daughter. A beautiful, dark-haired girl with dancing eyes. Almost seventeen years old, a prize for any man who might think he was growing old. What a cruel fate to allow a situation where mother and daughter would be seduced by the same man. Where daughter and mother would share Louis Gray as a first lover.

Kit could never come to London. Kit could never meet her. She only had Ivy's address, with Ivy's name. There were no names on bells that would identify their flat suppose Kit were to come. Kit didn't know the name of Millar's Employment Agency. She didn't know the name of the hotel where Louis worked. The name Dryden had not been allowed to appear in any letter.

She knew Louis' name of course, but that was all.

Lena wrote:

The problem is, Kit, that everything has changed here. The hotel industry has changed. Louis never had any real written qualifications, so he's moving. He's going into marketing. Everyone seems to think that's where the future lies. He is in Scarborough at the moment trying to sort out his future . . . so he'd be no use to you at all. I miss him a lot I can tell you. The weekend seems very long . . .'

Kit read the letter. She read it over and over. It was obvious that Lena and Louis had had a row. They might even be going to separate, divorce possibly. It was England after all, where such things could happen.

She wished she had a phone number, she could ring her and say something helpful. But what could she say, Kit McMahon, almost seventeen and studying for her Leaving Certificate? Kit who knew nothing about men except that she really didn't want Philip O'Brien to go on kissing her. Imagine her being able to say something helpful to Lena Gray, who was so confident and ran a huge agency and had a handsome husband.

Many times in her letters she had said things that made Kit know Louis was handsome. Like he had a new jacket, or how well he had looked in the car they had been lent that time, or the night he had worn the dinner jacket for the formal function. Kit knew that Lena Gray must be beautiful too. It was clear to see that Louis Gray would want to have a beautiful wife.

On Saturday Lena played gin rummy with Mrs Park.

'I wish I had more people to play cards with. The days are very long,' she said.

'Why don't you move to the little close I was telling you about before? They have a dining room where everyone has their lunch, then you all go back to your own flats in the evening. That way there are plenty of people to play cards with all afternoon.'

Was she imagining it, or did Mrs Park look wistful. 'Oh well, we'll wait and see,' she said.

'Oh, that's not like you, Mrs Park. A fine decisive woman like yourself. Surely you must make up your own mind.'

'Lena, you don't understand. You don't have children of your own. Jessie is very dependent on me. She loves to come home and make my lunch. Her day is built around it. She might think I didn't need her . . .'

'Oh, I don't know, Mrs Park,' she said. 'From what Jessie tells me I know she'd love to think you had more of a life of your own.'

'But what about her life?'

'I could involve her in more social outings if I thought you were able to take care of yourself more. I don't like to ask her to socialise when I think she feels she should go home to you.'

'I'm not sure that you're right.' Mrs Park was doubtful.

'I think I am, but then I may not be. Why don't you test it out, suggest it to Jessie when she comes home.'

'And you'd be able to get her to go out a bit and meet people?'

'I would, Mrs Park, truly I would.'

'You're very kind, Lena Gray, but you don't understand how it is between a mother and daughter. You want the very best for your girl. It's like that from the moment they're born. Nothing can ever get in the way of it.'

'I'm sure you're right, Mrs Park,' said Lena Gray, with a forced smile on her face.

*

Ivy moved her curtain. Lena stopped at the door.

'All right, Florence Nightingale? Are you going to come in and have a chat?'

'You don't need to cheer me up,' Lena said.

'No, selfish, I don't. But maybe I want to be cheered up myself,' Ivy said.

'You!' Lena raised her eyes to heaven.

'Yes, me.' Ivy's mouth was in a tight line. Perhaps for once she was in low spirits. Lena went in and sat down. 'It's Charlotte,' Ivy said.

'Charlotte? What's she done now?' Lena had scant patience with the dog-in-the-manger wife. Charlotte did not appear to want Ernest for herself, and yet she would let no one else have him.

'She's gone and got cancer, that's what,' Ivy said.

'No!'

'Yes. That's what he said. He left an hour ago. On the way back to the hospital. She won't come out, Lena.'

Lena looked at her blankly. It was one of those very rare times when she didn't know what to say. Part of her wanted to be glad, glad that the unknown woman who had stood between Ivy and happiness would no longer be there. But she couldn't rejoice in another woman's cancer. 'Where had she got it, Ivy?'

'Everywhere.'

'And an operation?'

'No use.'

'How is Ernest taking it?'

'Hard to know. He was very quiet. He just said he wanted to sit here. We hardly said anything.' Ivy looked up at her pitifully, her eyes were red from crying. 'Do you know, Lena. I've been sitting here thinking; it may be that there's nothing to say.' Lena looked bewildered. She didn't follow what Ivy meant. 'We left it too long, too late.'

'But you're always so close, every Friday of the year ... nearly.'

'Fooling ourselves probably. When Charlotte's gone it will all be gone. Mark my words.'

'No, I won't mark your words. What a silly expression.'

'It's only a saying,' Ivy said. 'You say lots of things that mean half nothing too, Irish things.'

'Well, what were you trying to say?' Lena's voice was more gentle.

'I suppose I'm saying that it only lasted because it was impossible. Now that this bloody illness might make it possible he's off like a bat out of hell.'

Lena saw the pain in her friend's face. 'Listen, of course he's upset. He's guilty too, and relieved, and guilty about being relieved. He's a mass of feeling, why pick out the worst one to dwell on?'

'If you've loved someone for as long as I have you can read them like a book.'

'You can read them wrong sometimes,' Lena said.

She might have been wrong herself about Louis. She might have imagined this whole thing about him being interested in someone else, asking some other woman to go on the trip with him and then being left suddenly in the lurch. It was possible after all.

And look at how he had been so loving yesterday afternoon before he went on the train. And remember how excited he was about the new apartment. And how he'd miss her and find it hard to sleep without her in the bed where she was meant to be. It was possible, wasn't it, that she might have been working too hard and seeing dangers where there were none.

Maybe somebody outside could see better. Like Grace for example.

'Had you thought he might have been telling the truth?' Grace had asked. 'That he really didn't know spouses were invited.'

'No, I hadn't thought that,' Lena had replied. 'Which shows how very deeply I mistrust him.' And Grace had tried to give her a hope that she was brushing aside.

Just as she was doing now to Ivy. Trying to convince her that the love of a lifetime had not been wasted. 'Do you know, Ivy, women are wonderful. I wish the world was run by women.'

'It is,' said Ivy, with a trace of her former self returning.

Lena woke with a headache on Sunday morning. She would so love to have been waking in Scarborough in Louis' arms. What was it that James Williams had said when he was describing it to her . . . just a little holiday to thank the employees for putting in such antisocial hours . . . a chance for them to be with their wives in nice surroundings.

She must have been insane to have arranged all these million things to do. Minding Mrs Park, supervising carpenters that she had hijacked from Ernest's pub to do finishing touches to the new flat in Ivy's house and to the office. She must have been crazy to offer those girls extra money to come in on Sunday and set the place up properly.

The day seemed very long. She kept thinking of other things. Like what they were doing on a sunny Sunday in Lough Glass. She knew so much more about the place now than when she lived there. She could write a book about the people of the small lakeside community just based on Kit's letters. She wondered about Jessie and Jim Millar. Maybe this weekend would be the one where they would make up their minds. Or rather, Jim would. Jessie's mind was already made up. She thought about Ivy and her love for the strange dour Ernest. She thought of the woman Charlotte whom she had never met, lying in a hospital bed which she would never leave. Did this woman believe in God and that he was going to take her to heaven?

But then did anyone believe in God, Lena wondered.

How could Martin McMahon, a man she could have sworn had a firm personal faith in a God who was all powerful, possibly contemplate a bigamous marriage with Maura Hayes?

He knew she was alive, Martin knew that he had a living wife.

Lena shook her head in disbelief at the thought of him standing in the church in Lough Glass while Father Baily pronounced him and Maura man and wife, having asked anyone to say if they knew any reason why they shouldn't be joined together.

Possibly Kit was imagining it all. The child might be lonely. Well, she must be lonely otherwise she wouldn't pour her heart and soul out like that in letters. Maybe she hoped for a pleasant placid unchallenging stepmother to replace the mother she had loved so much. The mother who was taken from her by her father's arrogance and vanity.

As these thoughts went through her head Lena worked on, organising the new shelf space, encouraging the girls to fill it in the correct manner. Never again would they be confused about application forms, leaflets, documentation. This was a very professional set up.

She had even thought of a picnic for them, and as they all sat down to eat at three-thirty Lena said that she thought they had done brilliantly.

'But you're paying us until six, we'd better eat up quickly,' Dawn said.

Beautiful Dawn, who could have been a cover girl with her flawless skin and her shining hair. She looked years younger than she must be.

'No, you've worked like slaves, you all get paid until six, but relax, let's enjoy the feeling that we set up a great office.' Lena raised her cup of coffee from the blue and gold mugs, the mugs that were used to give clients coffee when they came to call and discuss work.

They tidied up and finished the sandwiches she had brought for them, and the shortbread biscuits. And she gave them each an envelope. 'Go out and enjoy what little there is of the weekend,' she said.

They ran like children released from school. They were hardly more than that, the two younger ones. Dawn hung back for a moment. 'That was fun, Mrs Gray, I did enjoy it. Nobody could ever had told me that a while back ... that I'd enjoy working on a Sunday, but I did.'

'Don't run yourself down, Dawn. You could be a business tycoon if you wanted,' Lena laughed at her.

'No, I'm not cut out for it. Finding me a nice rich husband, that's what I'll start doing soon.'

'Marriage isn't the only goal.'

'How can *you* say that, Mrs Gray? You've got a gorgeous husband.'

'What?' Lena had forgotten for a moment that of course Dawn had worked in the Dryden some time back. She would have known Louis then. 'That's true, Dawn, I've been very lucky.'

'He's lucky too,' Dawn said. She looked as if she were going to say more but changed her mind. Lena waited. 'Very lucky too,' Dawn said. Then she went out into the warm London air.

Lena sat at her desk and wondered whether Louis could possibly have had any kind of fling with Dawn Jones. Maybe he had even asked her to go to this conference with him and she had changed her mind.

Dawn Jones, born in 1932, would have been a golden-haired moppet when Lena went up the aisle to her loveless marriage. It wasn't possible. Then she took a deep breath. No, it wasn't possible. This was the way to go mad. The sure-fire way to end up in a mental hospital.

Louis loved her, he told her that. He would be home to her tonight. Dawn was a brainless child. Louis probably hardly met her when she was in the Dryden, she had worked for James Williams. It was only because she was so tired and had so much on her mind. The phone rang shrilly beside her as she sat in the empty office. It was Jessie.

'Oh Jessie . . . well, it all went very well. Tell Jim that the place is fantastic, and the carpenters took all the rubbish away with them so you'd never know there had been any work done at all.' She was eager to give the good news.

'Lena, Lena, we're getting married,' Jessie cried. 'Jim asked me to do him the honour of becoming his wife. Those were his words, Lena. Isn't it wonderful?'

Unaccountably, two tears came down Lena's face. 'It's wonderful news, Jessie. I'm so happy for you,' she said as the tears splashed into one of the blue and gold ashtrays.

'We're going round to tell Mother tonight, but I wanted you to be the very first to know.'

Lena said that she thought it was the most marvellous thing she had ever heard. She sat quite still for a long time after the call. She had an almost uncontrollable urge to ring her daughter.

But fortunately she just managed to resist it.

After an age she stood up from her chair, cleaned the ashtray, packed the picnic things in her basket and locked up the offices. She walked very slowly down the road with its Sunday evening crowds beginning to gather for whatever festivities they had in mind. She went home and lay on her bed to wait for Louis.

At eleven o'clock he burst into the flat. 'Oh God, I missed you, Lena. Lena, I love you,' he said and he launched himself at her like an over-affectionate puppy dog. 'I brought you a rose,' he said.

It was all done up with a fern and a safety pin, as if it were a corsage. It didn't matter *where* he got it; he might have found it, or bought it, or stood for ages while it was being made up. Someone could have left it on the train.

He had brought it for her. He smelled of the sea and she loved him. Nothing else mattered at all.

*

'Kit, you know that friend of yours and Clio's, this Mother Madeleine?' Clio's Aunt Maura spoke hesitantly.

'Yes, she's Sister Madeleine, Miss Hayes.'

'I was wondering, would you mind if I went to see her?'

'About us, do you mean?' Kit and Clio had not been speaking for twenty days. It was the longest silence ever between them. Most of the town seemed to be aware of it.

But Clio's aunt laughed. 'No, not at all about you. About me. I gather she's a very fine person at sorting things out.'

'Yes, but some things can't be sorted out.' Kit was very adamant about that. And Sister Madeleine was about the only person in the place who hadn't urged her to make it up with Clio.

'It's just that I didn't want to be moving in on her if you thought it was your territory . . .'

Kit looked at the woman with new respect. 'No, no. Everyone sort of talks to her, and she tells nothing on, it's like the seal of confession.'

'So, if I went to see her it would just be considered like a passer by dropping in?'

'That's very nice of you Miss Hayes, to ask, I mean.'

'I wouldn't want to tread on your toes. And do you think you might ever feel like calling me Maura?'

'I'd be happy to,' said Kit. And indeed she was, more than happy. It would be great.

Imagine saying it in front of Mrs Kelly. Better still, imagine saying it in front of Clio.

'Sister Madeleine, I'm Maura Hayes.'

'Of course you are. Haven't I often seen you at Mass on a Sunday with Dr Kelly.'

'I hear nothing but good about you, Sister.'

'I'm blessed to live in such a warm place, Maura. Would you join me in a cup of tea and some nice scones? Rita up in McMahons' is a gifted cook and she often leaves me a batch of these in case someone drops by.'

'A fine girl indeed, Sister. Maybe she should better herself.'

'I know, I know. It's a problem.'

They both knew the problems. Rita would not leave the McMahons until the place was settled. The question was now which would mention that a solution might be in sight.

The hermit decided to make it easy for Maura Hayes. 'Of course, you're a regular visitor here to these parts yourself,' she said.

'I do come down often. My sister has such a happy home here herself.'

'And one day you might make a happy home yourself.'

'There are many who might say I was far too old to be considering any such thing.'

'I wouldn't say that, Maura. I've never been a great advocate of young marriages myself. They don't seem to work somehow. The danger, of course, in leaving it late is that you mightn't be able to replace what had gone before. That would only be a danger if you were trying to replace it with the same thing. I wouldn't imagine you'd be trying to do that.'

'No indeed. If it were to happen I'm sure it would be a very different variety.'

'Well then . . . I feel very sure it would work very well.' The kettle that had been moved to the centre of the fire began to hiss and splutter. The old nun lifted it away deftly.

By the time they had finished their tea a lot had been straightened out. Without confidences being broken or anyone named by name, Maura understood that if Martin McMahon were to be enthusiastic about a union there would be no opposition with the house. The daughter Kit would be going to Dublin to study hotel management. The son Emmet was, like all boys, hardly aware of his surroundings. The maid Rita was only looking for an excuse to leave the family in good hands so that she could go and live in

Dublin. There was a chance of a position in a car hire company. Warmly recommended by Sullivans of Lough Glass, she would be sure to get the position and start a fuller life.

'I wouldn't ever be anything like as special as Helen,' Maura said in a small voice.

'No, of course not.'

Maura ached to ask what she was really like, what had she talked about, had she ever said what made her soul so tormented and so far away as she paced the length and breadth of Lough Glass. But there would be no point. The nun would just look away across the lake, the lake where Helen had met her death, and would speak distantly. It's hard to know what anyone's like, she might say. Maura would not ask. Instead she said, 'If it does work out, and Martin and I do make a life together, do you think that Helen McMahon would have been pleased rather than upset about it?'

The nun's eyes seemed very far away, as if she was thinking of something much further away than the lake. There was a long silence. Then, 'I think she would be very pleased,' she said slowly.

*

They moved flat two weeks after Scarborough. Louis was loving and enthusiastic about it all. He didn't mention Spain any more. He said no more about England being finished and men of vision getting out while the going was good. He was so much the old Louis that the days and nights of bleak despair almost disappeared.

Almost, but not quite. He was still out very late. And he resented it terribly if Lena asked him why.

'Sweetheart, is it clocking in and clocking out at home as well as at work?' he said impatiently.

And of course she had been wrong about that weekend. Lots of people had said to her it was a pity she wasn't there, the whole thing had been an innocent mix up. And she must have been mad to think there was anything between him and Dawn Jones. Dawn worked beside her day in and day out, putting in extra hours coming up to the official opening of the new premises. If Louis telephoned, Dawn would say 'Oh hello, Mr Gray, I'll get her for you now.' Unless she had been trained in the Royal Shakespeare Company, she wouldn't have been able to do that and hide a liaison. Lena felt she had been foolishly suspicious, yet she knew that this was not the same Louis who had run with her to London so eagerly and without a care.

This was a man who did not feel caught up with her to the exclusion of all others as he had once been, as she still was. Sometimes he stayed on a bit in the Dryden because a few of them were having a drink in the pub around the corner. It didn't do to be seen imbibing on your own premises.

'You were having a drink rather than coming home?' Lena had said. But she had only said it once in that hurt tone.

'Jesus Christ, Lena. If I tell you where I am you get offended, and if I don't tell you where I am you get offended. Shall we go down to some ironmonger now and get a ball and chain welded on. It would save us a lot of trouble.'

'Don't be an idiot,' she said in a voice disguising her terror. She had seen real annoyance and impatience in his eyes.

The new premises were opened in May, and there was the expected publicity. Yet again Dawn was photographed and Lena managed to stay out of the limelight, but this time there was something she could offer in return.

'Mr Millar, our managing director, and Miss Park, our senior executive, are going to be married later this year,' she told the reporters who attended the opening ceremony for Millar's new-look agency.

Nobody except her own colleagues would notice that she wasn't properly acknowledged. Some of the clients, maybe. Louis would know why, so would Ivy.

Grace did ask. 'Are you on the run, by any chance?' she asked, when the papers were published telling everyone's life story except Lena's, and showing every face except that of the woman who made the agency what it was.

'Sort of,' Lena said. 'Not the law, we're all right there, I think.'

'A man then.'

'Well, yes. I more ran to one than from one.'

'But there was one, and a daughter?'

'Yes, and a handsome boy.'

'I hope he's worth it . . . your Louis.'

'Grace, you know he isn't. Stop having silly hopes like that.' And they collapsed in giggles.

I miss the laughing more than anything else, *Clio wrote.*

I don't miss the secrets and the plans. Those are separate, and different anyway. I should never have looked at your letter, and the truth is that I didn't see who it was to. But I shouldn't have looked. I was trying to see if it was Philip and if you were holding out on me. If ever we do get to be friends again I swear I will always regard letters as sacred. Also, I don't want to spend any more time persuading you to come to university with me. I know you won't, and it's your life. I'm not much of a friend, I know, a bit bossy, and I'm very ashamed about that letter. But I'm lonely and I miss you, and I can't study properly and I was wondering whether you thought it might be worth patching it up.

Love Clio

Dear Clio,

Okay. But remember something. We don't *have* to be friends. There's no law saying that we must walk for ever two by two in this town or anywhere. I'm glad you got in touch. I'm sick to death of Lonny Donegan. Have you anything better to play?

Love Kit

Emmet delivered the letter to the Kellys' house.

'They're mad, aren't they?' Anna Kelly said to him.

'Stone mad,' Emmet agreed.

'They go to the same school, sit in the same classroom and they use us as postmen.'

'It must have been a big row,' Emmet said in wonder.

'Don't you know what it was?'

'No, Kit never said.'

'Clio's never talked of anything else. Apparently, Kit dropped some letter and Clio picked it up and gave it back to her and accidentally looked to see who she was writing to. And Kit lost her head altogether.'

'And who was she writing to that was so secret?' Emmet asked.

'A fellow called Len,' said Anna, proud to be the bearer of such important news.

'Thanks Emmet, you're a pal.'

'No,' said Emmet, 'I'm an eejit.'

'Why do you say that?'

'I felt such a fool. I didn't know you have a fellow called Len. Anna Kelly had to tell me.'

'What fellow called Len?' Kit was mystified.

'The one you wrote the letter to, the one that you let fall.'

Kit looked at him levelly. 'Was Clio at home when you went there?'

'No, just Anna.'

'I'll give you anything if you go and get it back.'

'No, Kit. This is silly, you're going mad.'

'I may be, but I'll give you sixpence.'

'You haven't got sixpence.'

'I'll give you the sixpence out of the bottom of the Infant of Prague statue and then I'll put it back when I get my pocket money.'

'Why do you want it back?'

'Please, Emmet. Please.'

'You're old. You're not meant to be like this.'

'I know, but it's the way I am. I'll do anything for you. Any time you want something for the rest of your life ... I'll do it.'

'Will you?' He seemed doubtful.

'I'll remember this day, remember this act you did for me.'

'And you'll do anything at all?' Emmet weighed it up.

'Yes. Hurry.'

'If she's back?'

'Then it doesn't count, so go off as quick as you can.'

'Are you a bit of a doormat?' Anna Kelly asked Emmet.

'No, I did a great deal,' Emmet said.

'What was it?'

'She's going to do me any favour I want ever in life.'

'That's soft. She won't.' Anna laughed.

'She will. Kit's as straight as a die,' Emmet said, pocketing the letter and going home.

At school next day Mother Bernard told the sixth years that she had now counted exactly twenty-three working days for intensive revision, prayer to the Holy Spirit and little else. The Leaving Certificate would soon be upon them with all its attendant anxieties. She wanted to hear nothing of silliness or divilment until the examination was over.

At break Clio said, 'I hear you sent a letter up and then thought better of it.'

'Your information service is as good as ever,' Kit said.

'Why, Kit? Why did you change your mind?'

'You don't know what I said.'

'Yes I do. Anna read it, she steamed it open and told me. I've brought you "Che sera sera" as a peace offering.'

'You're such a liar, Clio. You lie about everything.'

Clio's face reddened. 'No I don't. I have it in my schoolbag.'

'You said you didn't see who it was to, but you did.'

'Only the name . . .'

'You said I dropped it on the floor. You didn't say you snatched it.'

'Bloody Anna.'

And for the first time Kit smiled. 'All right, you dishonest old fraud, give me the record and come round this evening and we'll go for a walk.'

'We're meant to be studying!' Clio could hardly believe the long row was over.

'Well, study then. I'm going for a walk.'

'And you'll tell me everything,' Clio said.

'I'll tell you nothing,' Kit promised.

Martin had not asked Maura Hayes to marry him. He just couldn't say the words. They were like lines from a play. He knew that every woman deserved to be proposed to, but he was afraid it would come out wrong. He was afraid that the echo of years ago would sound through what he said without his intending it to.

He was hoping that somehow it could all be agreed to and organised without having to ask. She was so understanding and undemanding. She cheered him up and made him laugh. She loved to go walking with him, but she didn't choose the routes that Helen had walked so ceaselessly by the lake. Instead, she found new places to go, a sheltered glen where you saw the mountains in the far distance, and just a shimmering line of the lake on one side. Sometimes she packed a flask of coffee and a slice of Fullers cake that she had brought down from Dublin. It was companionable and close, something Martin had never known in a marriage.

He had spoken to both his children separately, told them that his friendship with Maura Hayes was special. Both had said they were enthusiastic.

Kit in particular. 'Dad, you don't have to explain to us that she's not

Mother. We *know* that. And she's very nice. I always liked her much more than Clio's mother.'

Peter Kelly drank a pint each night with Martin in Paddles' bar. The solidarity was huge, but the subject was never broached. Both men knew that when there was something to be said, then it would be said.

And yet something in his heart, some unfinished business, prevented Martin McMahon from doing what he knew was the honourable and right thing to do. It depressed him that he seemed to be a weak man, unsure and dithering. There were so many areas of his life where he was sure and confident: in the pharmacy, where he gave advice and consolation as well as compound medicines; as a father, for the past years his children had been able to trust him and talk to him. Even, possibly, as a friend.

But not as a suitor to this good woman who deserved more from him. 'I wonder are you wasting your time with me, Maura,' he said to her.

'I wouldn't say any time spent with you was wasted.' She was calm, unflustered.

'I am not what you hoped.'

'You are what you are.'

He looked at her fondly. It was the night before the Leaving Certificate started. She had been so helpful to Kit, explaining to her that examinations were all about showing what you *did* know rather than fearing you would be caught out in what you didn't know.

Kit had found it not only useful but a revelation. 'I never knew that,' she said truthfully.

'Well, that's the system,' Maura had said, going over an old examination paper. 'Look, here when it says as an essay title "The place I love most in Ireland" or here it says, "My earliest memory" . . . Now you were telling me that you know all about Glendalough and you were hoping to get a subject like "A place of historic interest". You could always turn either of those titles to your advantage . . .'

Maura suggested she have tea and a chocolate biscuit to take with her to bed.

Martin and Maura sat in the large sofa, side by side. He had never sat there with Helen. She had perched on the window seat, or gone to read in a narrow high-backed chair that had been gradually moved to a position of less importance over the years. Helen's bedroom had now become a store room. The signs of her presence had lessened but her spirit was still there.

Martin reached for Maura's hand. 'It's not fair on you, Maura. I'm not ready, you see.'

'Did I ask you to be ready . . . for anything?'

She leaned over and kissed him, the kind of kisses they had, gentle and lingering. This was not an area where he compared her to Helen. Helen had never reached to kiss him in her whole life. Helen had just accepted his love. He never knew whether it pleased her or not. There had been no sign of great delight, and certainly none of revulsion. But it had been a passive thing. Never had she raised her hand to stroke his cheek even.

He clung to Maura. 'Is it fair to ask you to give me some more time?' he murmured into her neck. She smelled of Elizabeth Arden Blue Grass soap and talcum powder. He felt himself aroused to hold her longer and to know her body more. But this would be the final betrayal. If he were to have Maura Hayes it must be as a wife and a life companion. Not as a quick coupling on their sofa.

She seemed to know this, and pulled gently away. 'Have all the time you want, Martin,' she said. 'What else am I doing that you're keeping me from?'

Just then they heard a foot on the stair, and Kit knocked at the door. 'I just wanted to tell you I can't sleep. The tea didn't work.'

'Would you like to come in and talk?' Maura was courteous, not directive.

'Well, what I'd really like to do is to walk up to Sister Madeleine's for a half hour or so.' Kit always said where she was going. The history of going out for a walk and not returning was too heavy in this house for anyone to make unexplained journeys.

'I don't know. Isn't it a bit late?' Martin sounded worried.

'Sister Madeleine is probably the best place on earth to go,' Maura said. 'That woman is able to make everything seem reasonable.'

Kit flashed her a grateful look and ran down the stairs.

'I wish I could find the same kind of consolation in Sister Madeleine that everyone else does.' Martin had never been able to confide in the old, lined woman whom most of Lough Glass seemed to hold in such respect.

'That's probably because Helen used to go there so much. You are afraid that she knows too much and might think you were coming to find out something for yourself.'

'That's quite true.' Martin was surprised.

'Well, I wouldn't worry about that side of it. Whatever she has been told or not told seems to be totally secret.' Maura gathered her cardigan and handbag. 'I'll be off now, Martin. I don't want Lilian and Peter thinking I'm up to no good.' She had a brave smile on her face. If Maura Hayes was hurt to the heart that Martin could make no commitment she was not going to show it. She waved to him as he stood at the door, then watched Kathleen Sullivan's curtains twitch. At least she would be able to report the doctor's foolish sister-in-law had left the widower's home at a reasonably respectable time.

'Tell me now why the exam is so important to you,' Sister Madeleine asked.

'Oh Sister Madeleine, you must be the only person in Ireland who doesn't know that the Leaving is the making or breaking of you. My whole life depends on it.'

'I'd hardly say that.'

'Well, it *does*. If I get it, I get into Cathal Brugha Street Training College and do Hotel Management for two whole years and then I have a career. Otherwise I'm finished, my life is over.'

'I suppose you could always go back to school for another year.' The suggestion was a mild one.

'Another year at school with Mother Bernard, with all those horrible girls in Fifth Year laughing and mocking you, with Clio gone off to Dublin to university. I'd die, Sister Madeleine, die ... and anyway I want to be something, be someone. Not just for myself.'

'Who for?'

'Well, for Daddy, so he wouldn't look foolish down in Paddles' bar with Dr Kelly. And ... well, for my mother really.'

'I know.' Sister Madeleine did know.

'I told her I'd amount to something. You know ... long ago.'

'And you have and will.'

'But these are kind of milestones, markers along the way, these exams.'

'Your mother told you that?'

'No. Lena, her friend, you know ... who writes here. She told me.'

'You pay a lot of heed to this friend?'

'Yes. You see, she knew Mother very well ... it's almost like ...'

'It must be.'

'I wish she'd come over here ... I did suggest it,' Kit said.

'Maybe she prefers to live in her own world.'

'I'll have to wait until I go over to see her then.'

'Yes, but that may be a while. In the meantime you can stay friends with her by writing.'

'It mightn't be all that time, Sister Madeleine. After the Leaving I think I'm going to London.'

'You are?' The nun seemed startled.

'Yes. Daddy said I could have a holiday.'

'But London! On your own?'

'It wouldn't be on my own, it would be with Clio and others from our class. Mother Bernard's arranging that we can stay in a convent in London, then none of our parents will get frightened and think we're going to join the white slave traffic.'

'My goodness. And what will you do?'

'Well, I'm going to see Lena.'

'And will you tell her that you're coming to visit?'

'No. I think I'll turn up and surprise her.'

Sister Madeleine's eyes seemed further away than usual as she looked across the calm lake. Eventually she spoke. 'Well, we'll have to make sure that you get your Leaving Certificate then. I'll say special prayers for you tonight.'

'Will you kneel down and say a Rosary?' Kit was eager to know how much support she could count on.

'Now, Kit. You're a grown-up woman of seventeen. You know God just wants to listen to a request and hear the reasons why it should be granted. He doesn't want a great numerical totting up of Hail Marys. *That's* not how the system works.'

Kit knew that Sister Madeleine was absolutely right, but she was sure that this was the kind of talk that made Father Baily, Brother Healy and Mother

Bernard suspicious of the hermit. It was the kind of talk that at another time might have had her burned at the stake.

As Kit went off home by the lake Sister Madeleine took out her writing paper.

> Dear Lena Gray,
>
> I am writing to let you know that Kit McMahon is hoping to go to London, when the Leaving Certificate examination is over . . . she wants to surprise you with a visit. I feel that surprises lose their excitement after a certain age, and thought that perhaps you might like to be prepared for such an eventuality.
>
> If there is anything I can do for you please let me know. I have tried to suggest a relationship based entirely on letters but I am afraid she is too drawn to you and your memories of her mother, as well as your insights about her own future, to let matters rest there.
>
> She is a very determined young woman . . . just like her mother.
>
> Yours sincerely in Jesus Christ,
>
> Madeleine

'She doesn't know which flat I live in,' Lena said to Ivy.

'No, but all she has to do is ask anyone on the stairs,' Ivy said.

'She'll ask *you*. You'll say we're away.'

'Yes, but she'll come back when she thinks you'll be back.'

'I'll write and say we're going away for the summer.'

'You can't keep running away from her.'

'I can't *meet* her, we know that.'

'Could you dye your hair, wear sunglasses?' Ivy was serious.

'I'm her mother, for God's sake.'

'I'm *trying* to help.' Ivy was aggrieved. Things were hard for her. Ernest spent every evening at the hospital, where Charlotte was sinking fast. He called at Ivy's flat for a drink on the way home each night. A drink and a long recounting of the guilt he felt in his life at how poorly he had treated his wife. It was increasingly hard to bear.

Lena was full of shame at having spoken so harshly. 'I'm terrified, that's why I'm snapping at you. You're the only friend I have in the world.'

'I'm *not* your only friend . . . you have dozens of friends. You have Louis, and all those people at work who dote on you and depend on you. You have a daughter who loves you even if she doesn't know who you are . . . Don't tell me about having few friends.'

'Oh, Ivy. Do you know what I'd love to do for you? I'd love to take you to Ireland for a holiday.'

'So, take me,' Ivy challenged.

'I can't, you know that. They'd see me, they'd find out.'

'Yes. I imagine they have armed guards posted at the airport and the ferries, waiting for you,' Ivy scoffed. 'After all, they do that when anyone drowns in a lake, is found and buried.' Ivy sounded bitter.

'We could go some day. I'm too frail these days. Everything's coming apart,' Lena said.

'Don't crack up on me, Lena. Charlotte only has another week at the most.'

*

'Can I come to London?' Anna Kelly asked.

'Daddy, don't even let her think of talking like that,' Clio protested.

'Shush, Clio. Anna, when you get your Leaving Certificate of course you can go to London. In three years' time.'

'But Daddy, wouldn't this be a heaven-sent opportunity? My big sister could look after me and my mind would get broader by travel, and I'd be in no danger.'

'Don't waste your breath, Anna,' Clio warned.

'None of the others would mind. I asked Kit McMahon and Jane Wall and Eileen Hickey who are going and they said they didn't care.'

'Of course they don't care. You aren't their rotten sister.' Clio was incensed.

Aunt Maura spoke unexpectedly. 'I hope you won't go, Anna,' she said.

'Why is that?' Anna was suspicious.

'Well you see, I'll be coming down for the golf tournament and we need to have caddies, but everyone in the club is taken up and Martin McMahon and I were wondering whether you and Emmet might do it for us.'

'No, I don't think . . .'

'It's awfully well paid,' said Aunt Maura. 'And much more fun in a way than trailing around London in the heat with a lot of people who aren't your real friends. I know I'm only trying to persuade you because Martin and I would like our own families to be there to support us, but there'll be lots of parties, and a dance with a lot of young people.'

'I was never allowed to a dance when I was her age.' Clio was stung.

'The world is changing since you were young, Clio,' Anna said.

For a fraction of a second Clio's eyes met those of her Aunt Maura. There was a hint of a smile. Clio knew that her aunt had succeeded where no one else could have in putting an end to Anna's bleating. Although Anna Kelly was only fourteen, she was showing alarming tendencies of getting her own way in everything she suggested.

'Do you think they're ever going to do anything about it or are they going to go on mooning about for ever?' Lilian asked her husband.

'I don't know,' Peter Kelly said mildly.

'Well you must know. He's your friend.'

'She's your sister,' he countered.

'There are things you can't say to sisters if they are old and still spinsters,' Lilian explained.

'Yes, and there are things you can't say to friends if they are old and have been through a lot,' Dr Peter Kelly said.

*

'It's nice to see you down here so regularly, Maura,' Sister Madeleine said.

'Well, Sister, I'll come for as long as I think he likes me to be here.'

'He likes you to be here.'

'But would you know? I'm not being rude to you, but would you?'

'I think I would, Maura. From what people say.'

Maura realised that people did say a lot and Sister Madeleine listened a lot. She probably did know.

'You're such a kind person I wish there was something I could do for you.'

Sister Madeleine looked at her thoughtfully. 'There is something I would like done, but it's very, very complicated, and I could never tell you why.'

'I wouldn't need to know why.'

'No, God bless you, I don't think you would. Well, I'll ask you and it may not be possible, but if you could . . .'

'Please ask, Sister. It would be a great pleasure to do anything for you, anything at all.'

'You know there's talk of Clio and Kit and a few of the girls in Sixth Year going to London after the Leaving Cert . . .'

'Don't I know it. They talk of so little else.'

'Yes well, what I was wondering was could you persuade Kit and Clio not to go?'

'But why on earth? I'm sorry, I forgot . . .' Maura paused. After a while she said, 'I think it would be very, very difficult.'

'I was afraid of that.'

'And is there a good reason?'

'A very good reason.'

'I can't think what I could do. I can't tell them London is full of typhoid fever. I can't offer to take them to France or anything, I've just managed to prevent Anna from trying to go with them by offering her a job as my caddy in the golf tournament.' There was a silence. 'Is there no one else?' Maura asked.

'No one I could ask,' the hermit said.

Maura felt a surge of pride that she was among the very few who could be approached. 'I believe Mother Bernard up in the convent is organising it, maybe if she told . . .'

'No. Sadly she'd need every detail and these are impossible to give.' There was another silence.

'I'm really trying but I can't think of any single thing that would distract them, not at this stage.'

'Thank you for trying anyway. I know you are.'

'What will you do now?'

'I suppose I'll pray that the Lord will sort things out, and that you won't puzzle too much about what may seem like a very odd request.'

'I will put it right out of my mind and forget it was ever mentioned.' Maura Hayes smiled.

And Sister Madeleine reached over and took her hand. This was a truly kind woman who would make an excellent wife and companion for poor Martin McMahon if ... if ... well, if things were different.

*

Charlotte died in hospital on a Thursday morning.

Ivy wanted to come to the hospital to be with Ernest, but he said no. 'I'll just stay in the waiting room away from everyone in case you need me,' Ivy had pleaded.

'No, love. Honestly. Don't cause a fuss. Don't let's make trouble at this stage for everyone. Stay at home. I'll come to you later in the day.'

Thursday passed and Ernest never came. Ivy rang the pub around closing time. She spoke to a barman she knew. 'He's with his family in the front snug, Ivy. It's probably best I don't tell him you rang.'

'Absolutely,' Ivy said. She sat in her little room awake all night. She was sure he would come at some stage, when everyone else had gone home.

At three o'clock she heard a taxi drawing up at the door. She moved the curtain and looked out, but the taxi was not Ernest, it was a woman in a white cotton polo-necked sweater, with very blonde hair, very red lips and very high heels. She had got out of the taxi to kiss Louis Gray goodbye properly with a great deal of squeaking and lifting one leg at a time as she embraced him. She was oblivious to his shushing sounds as he paid the taxi and urged the driver to take her away as quickly as possible.

'Will I go to the funeral with you?' Lena asked.

'What?'

'You'll need someone to go with. You can hardly be up there in mourning with the family. I thought you'd need a friend as a sort of disguise.'

'Lord, Lena, you're great.'

'So I'll go with you then. When is it?'

'Love, we're not going, whenever it is. It would not be, as Ernest has put it, appropriate. Can you imagine Ernest knowing a big word like appropriate?'

'But of course we can go. Anyone can go to a funeral.'

'In Ireland maybe. Not here.'

'They don't sell tickets, do they? We'll go.'

'He doesn't want us. Why push?'

'All right, all right. Maybe she has relatives, maybe it will be small. Maybe he's right not to want you there.'

'He doesn't want me *anywhere*. That's what I'm mourning, not bloody Charlotte,' Ivy said.

*

'Are you definite about doing hotel management?' Philip O'Brien asked.

'Sure I am, Philip. You know that.'

'So we'll be together in Dublin.'

'At classes yes, but not exactly together. I'm staying in the hostel in Mountjoy Square. It's just around the corner. I'd say it's a bit grim.'

'I'm staying with my aunt and uncle and I *know* that will be grim.' Philip was glum these days. He had agreed unwillingly when Kit had said she didn't want to get into kissing and groping and all that because of exams.

'It might distract me,' she had lied to him.

The day the Leaving Certificate finished Philip came back. 'It won't distract you now,' he said, eager as the two Jack Russell terriers that terrorised people in the Central Hotel.

So Kit had to give him a different excuse. 'It's an odd time for a girl, being seventeen. Please be understanding. I promise I don't fancy anyone else, but I really and truly don't want to get involved at the moment.'

'But aren't you fond of me?' Philip would ask.

'Very fond of you.'

'So then?' He was eternally hopeful.

'So then you'll understand.'

'And are you waiting for me and am I waiting for you? Just tell me,' Philip had begged.

'Let's say we're not hunting for anyone else, but if someone else turned up for you it wouldn't be a betrayal or anything. I'd quite understand,' she had said.

'And for you, Kit?'

'I won't have time for anyone else to turn up. I'm so busy.'

'No you're not. You're on holiday.'

'I'm going to London. Who could turn up in London?'

'You're only going to London for ten days.'

'Then I'll be back. Philip, *please*.'

And because he didn't want to be tiring, he stopped. And they went to the pictures just on their own, and sometimes with Emmet, sometimes with Clio. Because as Clio said, Anna was so awful and such a troublemaker, the only thing to do was to let her come to places where she couldn't do much harm, like at the cinema, a place where nobody had to talk to her.

*

Dear Kit,

I am so eager to hear the result of your exams. It will be so exciting to plan your course in hotel management. Do tell me more about it. And what are you going to do for the holidays? I'll be away a lot travelling, but your letters may be forwarded to me, so I can reply from wherever I am. It's a pity I won't be in London during the summer because, unlike everyone else, I actually enjoy the city when all the visitors come. If you have Sister Madeleine praying for you, and your father's nice friend, Maura Hayes, rooting for you, and if you've done all the work you say you did, I'm sure you don't need me on the case as well. But I do keep my fingers crossed for you.

Love as always,
Lena

*

'London could be very crowded during the summer,' Maura Hayes said to Kit the day after she got this letter from Lena.

'I'd say it's nice when it's full of tourists, holiday like,' Kit said.

'Not the best time to see it in a way.'

'Oh don't join all the others who say not to go, please, Maura.'

'I'm not saying not to go . . .'

'What are you saying?' Kit asked.

'I don't know,' Maura answered truthfully, and for some reason it made both of them laugh helplessly. Martin McMahon came in to the kitchen and asked what the joke was. 'If I were to go through the whole conversation there wouldn't be a laugh in it,' said Maura, wiping her eyes.

'They'd lock us up,' Kit agreed.

Rita was finishing the ironing. She had heard the whole exchange and all she could understand was that it was really time Mr McMahon made a move. Miss Hayes was a very nice person. He would never find anyone who got on so well with his children.

Mother Bernard got a phone call in the school. It was from a lady in London. She wanted to know when the results of the Leaving Certificate were expected.

'They arrived today.' Mother Bernard sounded pleased. It had been a very good result as far as she was concerned. The lady wanted to enquire about the successes and failures.

'And to whom am I speaking?' Mother Bernard wouldn't reveal that the Wall girl and young Hickey had done so badly, not to any stranger on the phone.

'I am a distant relation of Cliona Kelly.'

If Mother Bernard thought it odd that this woman had not called the Kelly family she said nothing. Instead, she listed with pride the number of Honours Cliona Kelly had got in her examination.

'And her friend, Kit McMahon?'

'Mary Katherine McMahon did very well also. The whole standard was very high.'

'And I believe the girls are coming on a visit to London, to your sister house?'

'That is so, but . . .'

'I was going to write a letter there to whoever you would suggest . . . perhaps arranging to meet Cliona. Can you tell me what date they are arriving?'

'Mother Lucy is in charge of the London house and our girls for the duration of their stay. They will be arriving on 9 August for nine full days . . . And you are?'

'Thank you so much, Mother Bernard.' The connection was broken. Mother Bernard looked at the receiver. How did this woman know she was Mother Bernard?

*

At Mass on Sunday Mother Bernard was talking to the Kellys. 'Your relation rang up from England to enquire about Cliona's Leaving results,' she said.

'England?' said Peter Kelly.

'Relation?' said Lilian.

'That's what she said.' Mother Bernard sounded defensive.

What could she mean, they asked each other on the way home. 'Getting a bit dozy maybe,' Lilian suggested.

'She seems sharp enough.' Peter was thoughtful.

'Let's hope she lasts out for Anna's time anyway.' Lilian was always practical.

. . . and so I am off on a tour, leaving 8 August. I told you I'd be out of London for about two weeks. Still, it's a great opportunity for me. Hope your summer plans are going well, and that you have everything ready for your new life in Dublin.

Again, I want to say how great it was to hear from you so quickly. Thank you so much for writing on the day you got your results. I kept crossing my fingers and got on with my work. I drank your health last night with my friend, Ivy Brown.

It's so exciting to be on your way at last.

'What will I do if Louis comes in?' Ivy asked.

'He won't.' Lena was grim. 'As you very well know. He hasn't been in much.'

'He never stays out all night.' Ivy was aghast.

'No, but if Kit comes to look for me, it won't be at night. They won't clash.'

'And what about you? Suppose she sees you on the street?'

'There's eight million people in this city.'

'Not in this road, there aren't.'

'She doesn't think I'm hiding on her, she doesn't know I'm me. Relax, Ivy.'

'*You're* not relaxed.'

'Well that's because my daughter's going to be in the same city and I want to see her.'

'I have an awful feeling about it, I really do.'

'Nonsense, Ivy. Just let me spend the evenings in your back kitchen, that's all.'

'How do you know she'll come looking for you?'

'I know.'

*

The boat journey was marvellous fun. They met a great crowd of Irish builders who had been back home for their summer holidays. It was with some relief that they were making the return journey to England and freedom.

'Why are they all singing about how wonderful Ireland is if they're leaving it?' Kit asked.

'That's the point of Irish songs. They're only good if you sing them while you're abroad.' Clio was very knowledgeable.

'Imagine! We're abroad,' Kit said.

'Nearly.' Clio was being lofty.

'We're in the middle of the Irish Sea. That's abroad. We're beyond the three-mile limit.'

The men asked them to come and listen while they sang the 'Rose of Tralee'. It was always good to have beautiful girls listening when you sang that song.

'We really are going to London,' whispered Clio. 'We'll see real teddy boys, real coffee bars, everything.'

'I know,' said Kit. 'I know.' She was thinking about how she would find her mother's friend, Lena, the woman who knew much more about her mother than anyone. She would go to her house and ask Mrs Brown where she was. Then she would go and surprise her.

If ever they had thought Mother Bernard was bad they soon realised that compared to Mother Lucy, she was a wild and free soul. Mother Lucy assumed that they would all want to see cultural sights only, and that evenings would be spent playing table tennis and making cocoa once the Rosary had been said in the convent chapel.

Although they enjoyed the visits to Westminster Abbey and the Tower of London, the Planetarium and Madame Tussaud's, the girls were bleakly disappointed with their escorted tour. It was tantalising being so near and yet so far.

'We could always escape,' Jane Wall said.

'Is it worth the bloody trouble?' Clio asked. 'It will be painted as black as sin. They'll think at home we did the divil and all, and all just for a cup of coffee in Soho.'

'Your aunt rang again, Cliona,' Mother Lucy said on the third night.

'My aunt?' Clio was alarmed. 'There isn't anything wrong, is there?'

'No, she just wanted to know your movements, if you had any free time on your own.'

Clio shrugged at Kit. 'Why on earth did she want to know that?' she said.

'I don't know. I think she may have wanted to take you out somewhere, she was very anxious to be filled in on your timetable.'

It was a mystery. Aunt Maura, in London.

'Is she going to ring again?' Clio wanted to know.

'I'm not sure. But if she does want to take you out then I assume it will be in order.'

Clio's eyes met Kit's and began to dance. 'If she does ring again, then it would be nice to see her,' Clio said in her fawning voice.

'Yes, well, of course.'

'Maura's not in London. She's back in Lough Glass playing golf,' Kit whispered later.

'I know, but it must be some glorious mistake sent by God and St Patrick and St Jude, the patron saint of hopeless cases. Go out and ring and leave a message for me.'

'Where?'

'Anywhere, phone box in the street. They'll think you're in the bathroom.'

Kit found a red phone box and put the money in. 'May I speak to Cliona Kelly? It's her aunt.' She asked the little sister who minded the door.

In a moment Kit was put through to Cliona in the recreation room. 'Hello,' she whispered, terrified that it was all going to be unmasked.

'Oh Aunt Maura, how nice of you to call. Mother and Father were so much hoping you would get in touch.'

Kit listened wordlessly to the easy flow of Clio's lies. They would so much love to meet Aunt Maura at five o'clock tomorrow. No, no, Mother Lucy would be happy to let Kit and herself out for just a few hours.

'Aren't you lucky,' said Jane Wall. 'Imagine your aunt being in London.'

'I know,' said Clio. 'Makes you believe in fate.'

'What will we do?' Clio asked. 'Where will we go?'

'You go where you like. I'm going off on my own.'

'Oh Kit, you can't. We can go on our own, but together.'

'You're the one who said it was ludicrous grown-up women like us being tied up in a convent.'

'Well it is of course, but it doesn't mean you're going to get into some kind of mood and go off and leave me. I got you this free time. After all, it is my aunt who is in London.'

'You know as well as I there is no aunt in London. It is some kind of mistake that poor sister at the door made.'

'It's still me that got it.'

'No it isn't. I was the one who went out to a phone box.'

'Where are you going?' Clio demanded.

'I'm not telling you. I'm going nowhere. I'm just trying to be free.'

'We can be free together, and have a bit of fun.'

'No we can't. Stop whingeing, Clio. Do what you like. We'll meet at ten and then you can tell me everything.'

'I hate you at times.'

'I know, I hate you at times, too, but a lot of the time we get on quite well,' Kit said.

'I can't imagine why,' Clio grumbled.

Kit had the map and she knew where to catch the underground to Earl's Court. But first she had to shake Clio. 'You've been talking about Soho since we were fifteen. You just get on a bus and get out at . . .'

'You're meeting someone, I know that's what you're doing,' Clio said.

'Clio, already you're eating into the bit of free time we have. Will you get the bus or will you not?'

When she was sure that the bus had gone out of view carrying Clio aboard, Kit ran down the steps of the station and took the Circle Line. At least she would see the house where Lena and Louis Gray lived. She would leave a note and maybe talk to this Mrs Brown. Once or twice she had asked in letters who Mrs Brown was, but there had never been a real explanation. Kit felt a surge of excitement well up in her throat. In twenty minutes she would be there.

Kit had thought it would be a more fashionable street. Somehow she had always seen it as a place with big houses that had drives leading up to them. She thought that Mrs Brown might be an aunt, or a relative anyway. A rich woman whom they partly looked after. But this was definitely the road. And number 27 was definitely the place she had been writing letters for almost four years.

Lena had never said the place was elegant, but neither had she said it was so ordinary. The paint was peeling on several of the doors and nearby the railings were rusty. There were dustbins in the street and in basements. It wasn't the kind of place that this friend of Mother's should be living in.

Kit looked at her own reflection in a window. She had dressed carefully, in her best tartan skirt, and a yellow blouse. She wore a tartan scarf around her neck, a present from Maura. She had put on lipstick, of course, as soon as she left the convent gate. Over her shoulder she wore a black shoulder bag. Her long dark curly hair was tied up with a smart black ribbon. She thought Lena would think she had made an effort, that is if Lena were there. Anyway, this Mrs Brown would tell her that Kit was a smart girl.

With a feeling of anxiety that was near dread, something she couldn't understand, Kit McMahon knocked on the door of number 27.

Louis had come in to Millar's at lunchtime. 'Quick half pint?' he asked Lena.

Jessie Park always liked to see Louis Gray; he had such distinction and good looks. She wagged her finger at him. 'You don't come to see us nearly often enough,' she said with mock severity. Jessie had certainly improved over the years. Her hair was no longer the wild bird's nest of hair. She wore a smart grey dress with a blue and gold scarf; her nails were painted. She looked a perfectly acceptable London business woman.

'You look very lovely today, Jessie,' he said.

Her blush and smile were predictable. Lena had seen the same response on the faces of so many women since she had been with Louis. A response to flattery. An innocent pleasure at being appreciated and admired.

Lena excused herself from the clients. This was important. Louis never came to see her at work. A sudden fear come to her. Had Kit arrived? Had she met Louis? Then she told herself this was impossible. She had checked in the convent where the girls were staying. There would be no chance of Kit being released during the daytime; the educational programme was too intense.

They walked side by side to the pub nearby, and she sat at the table while he bought them a drink.

'Remember you tried to make me get this week off,' he said.

'Yes.' She had begged him, beseeched, offered to take them to any hotel, offered to go where he'd choose. But he had said it was impossible, he was needed at the hotel. He had become annoyed about it also, claiming that Lena never accepted that he, too, had responsibilities at work. She had dropped it.

'You go alone if you need a holiday so badly,' he had said.

But Lena couldn't leave number 27 knowing that Kit McMahon was on her way there to give her a surprise. She couldn't risk that Kit might meet Louis and learn everything.

His smile was as warm as ever. 'My love . . . Wasn't it well that you didn't let me weaken and take a little holiday?'

'Why was that?' She forced her voice to be up and bright.

'They're sending me to Paris,' he said triumphantly.

'To Paris?' Her heart was like a stone.

'Not for ever. Just for ten days. To see how this French hotel is run. It's an exchange. A Frenchman is coming here. Won't that set their pulses racing at the Dryden?'

'Not as much as you do.' It was an automatic response, but oddly it came out wrong. It sounded bitter, it sounded like an accusation.

'So I'm off.'

'You're off?'

'Well, you can hardly come with me, can you?' he asked.

'I suppose I *could* get some time . . .'

'You don't have a passport,' Louis said. His glance was very level. Of course Lena didn't have a passport. How could a dead woman get a passport? He could go abroad for ever without her.

'When do you go?' she asked.

'I thought today,' he said.

Lena's head felt very heavy, as if it was a great weight to lift up and look him in the eye. 'Do you love me at all, Louis?' she asked.

'I love you very much,' he said. There was silence, 'You believe me?' he asked.

'I don't know.' Her voice was bleak. She saw the impatience in his face. This was what he hated, but she was too tired, too weary to care. And he was going anyway, whether she was light and cheerful, or heavy and gloom laden.

'Well, you should know,' he said. 'Why would I stay if I didn't love you. I'm here, aren't I?'

'That's right.' She was resigned.

'Lena, don't make me go with this big draggy feeling of guilt about it. It's an opportunity, it's a chance, it's what we want. You are making squeaks just like a wife now. It's not like you.'

'No, you're right. It's much more like me to be jolly and full of smiles and turn a blind eye to what's happening.'

'And what *is* happening?' His voice was very cold.

'What's happening is that you are treating me like dirt. You are coming in all hours of the night . . .'

'Oh, God, no. Not a scene in a public place.' He put his head in his hands.

'What's happening is that you know you can do anything you bloody well like. You don't have to marry me because I'm dead. You don't have to take me abroad because I'm dead and buried already. Did you think of that, did you?' Her laugh had a hysterical tinge.

'Jesus, Lena, get a hold of yourself.' He looked around him, alarmed.

'I've got a hold of myself all right, but I have no hold on you, none at all.'

Now he was angry. 'Nor should you have. We don't believe in all that business of tying each other down. We've been through this. Love isn't about making rules – thou shalt not do this or do that . . .'

'And love certainly isn't about going off to France with whatever bit of stuff you're sleeping with nowadays.'

'Lena, you're disgusting. Ring the Dryden, ask them am I doing an exchange, ask them.'

'Give me credit for something, for some bloody bit of dignity. Do you *think* I'd lower myself to make a call like that to check on you?'

'See, you have it every way now. You want proof, I give you proof, you won't take it.'

'Go to Paris. I'm sick of you, Louis, go there and stay there.'

'I just might,' he said. 'And if I do . . . you sent me.'

The afternoon was stifling. Jessie looked at her several times, but always Lena waved away any question or sympathy.

'Not bad news, was it?' Dawn asked.

'Absolutely not. Louis is going to France, I may join him there at the weekend.'

'Aren't you a lucky couple,' Dawn said in genuine admiration.

At six o'clock, with a great sense of relief, she put her cover on her typewriter, locked her files into her drawer, and left the office. Louis would be out of the flat by now. He would have gone straight home and packed his things. The only problem was how much he had packed. Enough for ten days in France, or enough for a longer time away from her. And as he had said, it was she who had sent him.

She put off the evil moment of arriving home, and went to a pub.

'You're too good-looking to drink alone,' the barman said as Lena bought her gin and tonic.

'Chat me up at your peril,' she said to him.

He laughed but he moved away smartly. There was something about her eye that made him know she wasn't joking.

Ivy made tea for the strikingly attractive Irish girl in her fresh yellow blouse and tartan skirt. She was a younger version of Lena, with the same shiny curly hair, and big dark eyes.

'I thought you'd be different, Mrs Brown. I've been sending you letters for years, I didn't know you'd be . . .' she paused.

'I'd be what?' Ivy had a mock threatening look.

'Well, young and kind of fun. I got the impression you were old and sort of making people be quiet in front of you.'

'Is that what Lena wrote about me?'

'No. She wrote nothing about you; she wrote always about me. I know so little of her life here, but all about her time with my mother. And she's so interested in everything I do, it makes me a bit selfish in my letters, I'm afraid . . .'

'She loves to hear from you, I do know that.'

'What a pity she isn't here.'

Kit sounded so bereft Ivy found herself swallowing. 'Yes . . . well, you can't have let her know you were coming. I'm sure she'd have stayed.'

'I wanted it to be a surprise.'

'And didn't you know she was going away? She didn't tell you?'

'Yes, she did. But you know this is very odd, I got the feeling that she might not be going, that it wasn't really definite. I thought she might still be here.'

'And now you've had a wasted journey.'

'No it's not, I've met you. I know where she lives. She's the only person who ever made sense of anything about my mother to me. They were great friends. And I can see why. Lena's such a letter writer, she makes it like a conversation.'

'Yes, I'm sure,' Ivy said.

'I don't suppose you could show me their flat. You know, I bet she wouldn't mind.'

'No love, I'd better not. People rent from me and they have absolute privacy. It wouldn't be right.'

'But you have all the keys hanging on the wall here.'

'Yes, but that's only for an emergency.'

'Am I not an emergency?'

'No, darling. You're just someone she'll be heartbroken to miss, and she'll say . . .' Ivy's voice broke off. Behind Kit there was a hammering on the door.

'Sorry love, just a moment . . .' Ivy leaped to the door with a speed Kit wouldn't have suspected her capable of. Just before Ivy pulled the door behind her Kit saw a very handsome man in an open-necked white shirt and grey flannels standing there. He looked like a film star.

'Ivy . . .' he began.

'I'll talk to you further down the corridor if that's all right.'

'Hey, where's the fire?' Kit saw him being dragged out of view.

She looked around Ivy's amazing room. Every inch of wall was covered with pictures and posters, programmes, beer mats and little clippings from magazines. You could never get bored in this room, Kit thought, it would be a comforting place to stay. But she must not wear out her welcome. She would have to leave when she finished the tea. She could write a letter to Lena, and leave it.

The voices outside seemed to be raised. The handsome man, whoever he was, did not seem to meet with Ivy's approval. 'Listen here, let me leave the box in here out of the way. You don't want people falling over it, breaking their necks and suing you, do you?'

'I'll take it in later. I said, it's all right.'

But he would hear nothing of it. A big wooden chest was pushed in the door and then the man looked up and saw Kit. 'Well for heavens sake,' he said.

'Hello,' she smiled.

Ivy seemed very anxious to get him out. 'So if that's everything,' she said.

'I'll give you my key, Ivy, hang it up there with the others. The box will be collected later.'

'Fine, fine,' Ivy cut across him. 'Yes, I understand everything. Safe journey.'

'And who's this?' His smile was so warm.

'That's a friend of mine. Her name is Mary Katherine . . .'

Kit opened her mouth amazed.

'Lovely to meet you, Mary . . .' he said.

'And you?' She had an upward lilt on the words as if asking him to give his name.

There was a hoot from the street. 'Your taxi won't wait for ever,' Ivy said.

And he was gone. They spoke in the hall and through the glass door. Kit could see the man was trying to kiss Ivy on the cheek and noticed she recoiled from him.

'Who is *he*? He's gorgeous.'

'He is trouble, Kit. A lot of trouble.'

'Why did you call me Mary Katherine?'

'Your mother . . .' Ivy began, and managed to change the sentence by going on, '. . . your mother's friend always said that this was your baptismal name and that this was how you were known at school.'

'Imagine you all knowing about me over in London.' Kit clasped her hands with pleasure.

Ivy hadn't the heart to shoo her out. The girl had nowhere else to go. And if Lena wasn't home by now she probably would be late. They had an agreement, anyway, that Lena would not pause at her door.

'Kit, sweetheart, will you hold on a moment? I have to leave something upstairs. I'll be right back.' Ivy ran up the stairs with a pencil and paper. *She's here*, she wrote, and slipped it under the door. Then she came down the stairs two at a time. Kit hadn't moved. She hadn't read the label on the box that Louis had left, the label saying that it was to be collected, the label giving his own name.

'We'll have another cup of tea,' Ivy said.

'If you're sure I'm not keeping you.'

'No my love, I'm happy with the company.' And since Lena was going to come home to a life without Louis it would be good if at least there were details for her about the visit from her child.

The hall door opened. Ivy looked up. There was something about her glance that made Kit look too, the sense of anxiety, the frown. All she could see was the outline of a dark-haired woman through the glass door. The curtain obscured a better view.

'It's all right,' Ivy called in a high unnatural voice. 'I've left a note in your room. No need to come in.' She couldn't hear what was being said outside. It sounded a bit strangled. 'I'll come up and talk to you later. I have a visitor just now.' It was said like the lines from a very bad actress.

Kit never knew afterwards what made her do it, but she went to the door. She had a feeling it was Lena, home unexpectedly. The woman who was about to go up the stairs turned as the door opened.

There she stood. A woman in a cream dress with a cream jacket, loose over her shoulders, a long blue and gold scarf around her neck. Her dark curly hair was like a frame around her face.

Kit gave a cry that sounded strangled in her throat. The moment lasted for ever. The woman on the stairs, Ivy Brown in the doorway behind and Kit with her hand to her throat.

'Mother!' she cried. 'Mother!'

Nobody said anything.

'Mother,' Kit said again.

Lena stretched out her hand – but Kit backed away.

'You didn't die – you ran away. You're not drowned – you just left us – you left us.'

She was white as she looked at the figure on the stairs.

'You let us think you were dead,' she cried in horror, and with her eyes full of tears made for the front door out into the street.

6

Ivy reached her as she got to the traffic lights. 'Please,' she begged. 'Please come back.'

Kit's face was ashen; all the life and vitality had gone from her. This was not the bright girl who had sat chatting in Ivy's room a few minutes before. But then, she was a girl who had seen a ghost.

'I beg you to come back.' Ivy reached out but Kit shrank back. 'It's been a terrible shock. Don't stay here in the street.'

'I must go ... I must go.' Kit looked around her wildly at the traffic swirling in every direction, the big red buses so unfamiliar, people who looked different from the people back home. The thud and pound of a London evening.

Ivy didn't touch, didn't grab her wrist; she was afraid that Kit would break free and run headlong into the traffic.

'Your mother loves you so much,' Ivy said, hoping it was the right thing.

'My mother is dead,' Kit flared.

'No, no.'

'She's *dead*, she drowned in the lake ... she drowned herself. I know that ... I'm the only one who knows it. She can't be here ... she drowned herself...' Kit's voice had the high tinge of hysteria.

Ivy realised it was time to take control. She put a small, wiry arm around Kit's shoulders. 'I don't care *what* you say, you can't be allowed to be alone. I'm taking you back with me now.' And she half led, half supported the girl back to number 27 and in the door of her own flat.

Lena wasn't there. It was as the place had been not ten minutes ago, the walls covered in their idiotic decorations. Kit sat on the same chair where she had been sitting when she had heard the woman on the stairs and gone out to investigate.

What had drawn her there? Suppose she had not gone? Her head felt very strange, as if the top of it had turned into paper. Then she heard a roaring in her ears and felt the floor rise up towards her. Everywhere it seemed there were voices shouting, shouting from a distance.

Then she felt something jabbing at her face and a strange terrible smell that nearly choked her. Ivy's face came into focus, big now and anxious, very near her. She had a small bottle in her hand.

'Don't speak, just sniff it.'

'What? What?'

'It's smelling salts, *sal volatile* they call it . . . You fainted.'

'I never faint,' Kit said indignantly.

'You're fine now. Here, let me help you on to the sofa.'

'Where is she?' Kit asked. The whole thing had come back to her with all its enormity.

'She's upstairs. She won't come down until I tell her.'

'I don't want to see her.'

'Shush, shush . . . all right. Put your head between your knees for a bit to get the blood back.'

'I don't want . . .'

'Did you hear me? I said I won't get her until you're ready.'

'I won't be ready.'

'Right. Now for a cup of very sweet tea.'

'I don't take sugar . . .' Kit began.

'You do today,' Ivy said in a voice that was not going to be argued with. The strong sweet tea began to bring back some of the colour.

Eventually Kit spoke. 'Was she here from the start? From the very beginning, when we thought she was dead?'

'She'll tell you herself.'

'No.'

'More tea . . . another biscuit . . . *please* Kit, it's what we did in the war when people had a shock. It worked then; it will work now.' The woman was trying so hard.

She had a lined face, and bright eyes like buttons. She looked a little like a friendly inquisitive monkey that Kit had seen in the zoo. Was that the time they had gone with Mother, or was it the next year when Father had brought Emmet and herself as a treat, as something to take their minds off the tragedy that had happened to them all?

She had been about to refuse the second cup but suddenly she realised that it was the only thing this woman had to give; so she took it.

'How did she know to come to you?' Kit asked.

'What do you mean?'

'Were you friends already?'

'I rent flats, rooms. That's all.'

'But you're friends now.'

'Yes, we're friends now.'

'Why?' Kit asked. Her face was full of misery and incomprehension.

'Why? Because she's such a great person. Who wouldn't be friends with her?' Ivy was brisk and cheerful and deliberately misunderstanding the question. She wasn't going to attempt to answer that one.

They could hear the clock ticking on Ivy's wall, and outside the muffled sound of traffic. There were footsteps on the stairs, but it was not Lena. It was the couple from the third floor going out. Kit and Ivy strained to see through the net curtain.

When they heard the hall door click Ivy said almost triumphantly, 'I told you she said she wouldn't come down until you wanted to see her here.'

A silence.

'Or to go up to her even?'

'I can't.'

'Take your time.'

'No, not any time.'

There was another silence then Ivy asked 'Do you mind if I go up and tell her that you're all right? No, I *promise* I won't fetch her downstairs. It's just that she'll want to know.'

'What does she care whether we're all right or not?' Kit said.

'Please Kit, don't let me leave her sitting there not knowing. I won't be a minute.' Kit said nothing. 'Don't run away.'

'I'm not the one that ran away,' Kit said.

'She'll tell you.'

'No.'

'When you want to hear,' Ivy said and was gone.

Kit went to the door after she heard Ivy's footsteps go upstairs.

This was the room where her letters had arrived for all those years, letters to Lena Gray, saying private secret things about her mother, talking about the grave and the flowers they had planted around it. She had told this Lena secrets she had told no one, and all the time she had been deceived. A wave of anger and shame rose in her. She would not leave it like this, slip quietly away from this house and pretend that it hadn't happened. Mother was alive, Father must be told, and Emmet and everyone.

It was almost too huge to grapple with. She felt dizzy once more, as if she was about to faint again. But she steeled herself. She would go up the stairs and speak to her mother. She would find out what had happened and why. Why her mother had left them all like that to come here and live in this place in London, letting them hunt for her in the lake.

Kit went out and climbed the stairs. She would knock at doors until she found them. But she didn't need to.

She heard Ivy's voice on the first floor. 'I'll go back down to her, Lena. The child has had such a shock she shouldn't be on her own.' Then Ivy saw Kit on the stairs. She stood aside silently to let the girl walk into the room.

'Kit?' Her mother was sitting in a chair with a small rug around her shoulders. She was shivering; Ivy had obviously put it around her. She had a glass of water in her hand.

Ivy closed the door softly behind her and they were alone.

Mother and daughter.

'Why did you do it?' Kit said. Her eyes were hard and her voice was cold. 'Why did you let us think you were dead?'

'I had to.' Lena's voice was flat.

'You didn't have to. If you wanted to go away from us, from Daddy and Emmet and me, you could have gone . . . you could have told us you were going, not have us hunting for you, praying for you . . . and thinking you were in hell.' Kit's voice was breaking up with the emotion of what she was saying.

Lena said nothing. Her eyes were wide in horror. Everything had turned out in the worst possible way. Her daughter had found her. She was filled with loathing and contempt. Must Lena speak now? Tell the girl that it was her father who had done the real betrayal? Or should she protect him? Let Kit think that she had at least one trustworthy parent instead of being saddled with two who had let her down?

The girl was so fiery and strong. And Lena knew the secrets of her heart from her letters. Now she would never hear any more. It was as bad a pain as the open cupboard which had once held Louis Gray's suits.

Lena indicated a chair but the girl would not sit down. Instead, she looked around the room, her face working, trying to get control of herself possibly. Lena's eyes followed her, wondering how she saw the place, wishing she could read the thoughts that were darting around inside Kit's head.

She took a breath as if to speak, and then changed her mind. She went over to one of the windows and pulled back the heavy curtain to look at the street beneath. Again it was as if she was struggling to work something out before she trusted herself to speak.

Lena sat there, eyes enormous, hand shaking as she laid down her glass of water. Everything seemed to have gone into slow motion. 'Say something,' Lena said.

Kit's voice was steady. 'Why should I say *anything*? What have I got to say? You're the one who should say something.'

'Will you listen?'

'Yes.'

'I made a decision. I loved another man . . . it was such a powerful love I left you and Emmet and my life with you.'

'And where is he, the man you loved so much?' There was a sneer in Kit's voice.

'He's not here,' Lena said.

'But *why* did you pretend to be dead?' The voice had a false calm as if she were holding on by a thread.

'I didn't pretend to be dead. That's something that came about by mistake.'

'Oh listen to me,' the temper broke, 'now listen to me. Since I've been twelve I thought you were dead. My brother and I go up to your grave; you are prayed for every year on your anniversary. Daddy's face is so sad when he speaks about you it would make a stone statue cry . . . and here you are in this place . . . because you loved some other man . . . a man who doesn't love you . . .

'. . . and you say it's only a mistake that people think you're dead . . . you must be mad, mad.'

Kit's anger somehow galvanised Lena. She flung the rug from her shoulder and stood up to face her daughter. 'I was no part of this conspiracy to pretend I was dead. I told your father that I was leaving him. I said that he must choose how to explain it to his neighbours and friends, that this was the least I could give him, some dignity . . .

'I didn't make any demands . . . I wasn't in a position to do so . . . I just said I hoped he'd let me see you over the years.'

'You did *not* tell Daddy you were leaving. You didn't tell him. I don't care what kind of lies you tell yourself, you're not going to lie to me. I'm the one who heard him crying night after night in his room. I'm the one who walked with him by the lake all the time they were still looking for you.

'I was there when the body came back and he was so pleased and he said that you'd rest easy in your grave. Don't tell me that Daddy knows all about this . . . this set up. He doesn't.' They were standing a few feet from each other, faces angry and upset.

'He must be a much better actor than I gave him credit for if he fooled you as well.' Lena had a great bitterness in her voice. 'And I will never forgive myself for what I have done to you and Emmet, but he has his share in the blame. I told him. He knows. I left him a letter.'

'*What?*'

'I left him a long letter telling him everything, asking for nothing, not even understanding.'

Kit backed away. 'A letter. Oh my God!' She held her hand to her throat. Her face had gone white. Kit McMahon had never fainted before this day, and now she thought she was about to do so again. She staggered as the floor started its climb towards her but she forced back the dizziness and nausea.

'I know that you're not going to believe me,' Lena said.

'Yes, I do believe you.' Kit's voice was strangled.

'You knew?' Lena said.

'I found it . . . and I put it in the Aga.'

'You *what?*'

'I burned it.'

'You burned it? A letter addressed to someone else? In the name of God, why did you do that? Jesus Christ, why did you do that?'

'I wanted you to be buried in the churchyard,' Kit said simply. 'If they knew you'd committed suicide they wouldn't let you.'

'But I *didn't* commit suicide. Oh God, why did you have to interfere?'

'I thought you had . . .'

'*What* made you think that? What right had you to decide what to do? I can't believe this, I really can't believe it.'

'Everyone was looking for you. There were people out with lights and Sergeant O'Connor . . . and the boat turned upside down . . .'

'But for Christ's sake . . . if you had *given* your father the letter . . .'

'But you had been so strange . . . so wild, don't you remember . . . that's what we thought.'

'That's what *you* thought, what *you* took it on yourself to think.'

'Quite a lot of people thought it, as it happens.'

'How do you know?'

'You hear whispers.'

'And what about the inquest . . . the put-up job between your father and Peter Kelly, identifying some other unfortunate as me?'

'They thought it was you, that's what we all thought.'

'But who *was* it? Whose body is in my grave?'

Kit looked at her, stricken. 'I don't know. It could have been someone who drowned a long time ago.'

Lena dismissed this. 'Imagine. He would have done *anything* to hide the fact that I'd left him.'

Kit was very quiet. 'Father doesn't know you left him. Thanks to me, Father thinks you're dead.'

Lena looked at her and let the horror of this sink in. For years and years Martin really *had* thought she had drowned herself in the lake on his doorstep. How could this grotesque thing have happened?

'And does he know why . . . or did he suspect that I was about to leave him and that's why I took my life?'

'No, he doesn't think you took your life. He thinks that you drowned accidentally. He may be one of the few, but he thinks that. He told Emmet and me over and over.'

Lena reached for a packet of cigarettes. Automatically she stretched the pack towards Kit. Kit shook her head. The room that had heard such shouting was now so silent that the striking of the match sounded like a whip cracking.

After an eternity Kit said, 'I'm sorry for burning the letter. It seemed like the only thing to do at the time.'

Another long silence and Lena said: 'You don't know how sorry I am to have left you, but at the time . . . at the time . . .' Lena sat down, but Kit still stood.

'You could have come back to us, told us you were alive, that it had been a mistake.' Lena said nothing. 'I mean, I couldn't have unburned the letter, and anyway I didn't know I should have. But you didn't want to, did you? You didn't mind leaving us there thinking . . . thinking . . .'

'I was trapped,' Lena said. 'I promised your father . . .'

'You *made* the trap,' Kit said. 'And don't talk of what you promised Daddy. Presumably you promised you'd love, honour and obey him when you got married. You didn't think much of that promise.'

'Sit down, please, Kit.'

'No, I won't sit down. I don't feel like sitting down.'

'You look very pale . . . you look ill.'

'People at home don't say ill, we say sick. You're forgetting words even . . .'

'Kit, sit down. You and I may not have much time to talk . . . this may be our only chance.'

'I don't want a cosy chat.'

'I don't want a cosy chat either.' But Kit sank into a chair gratefully, her legs were feeling very wobbly. 'What's the very worst part of it?' Lena asked eventually.

'What you did to Daddy.'

There was a silence. And then Lena said very gently, 'Or what *you* did to him?'

'No, that is not fair. I'm not going to take the blame for this.'

'I'm not asking you to take the blame, I'm just asking you to talk to me
... tell me what we should do now ...'

'How can I talk to you? I haven't seen you since I was a child of twelve ...
I don't know who you are. I don't know anything about you.' Kit seemed to
shrink away from her.

Lena hardly dared to speak. Anything she said seemed to upset the child
further. She sat there waiting. Eventually she could bear it no longer. 'You
do know about me ... we have been writing to each other for years ...'

Kit's eyes were cold. 'No, you're wrong ... you know all about me. You
know things nobody else on earth knows. I told them all to you in good
faith. I know nothing about you. Nothing but lies.'

'I wrote the truth,' Lena cried. 'I wrote that your mother loved you and
was so proud of you ... didn't I tell you that ... all the time?'

'It was lies, you didn't say my mother had left ... run away and left us
there to think she was dead.'

Lena's eyes flashed. 'And you certainly didn't write saying that you had
burned the letter of explanation.'

'I didn't do that because I wanted to protect her reputation.'

Lena noted with pain that she spoke of her mother in the third person.
As if, in any real sense, her mother was dead.

And would always remain so.

'You seemed fond of me in your letters,' Lena tried. 'And I am that
person who wrote. All the things I told you were true. I work in the
employment agency, Louis works in the hotel ...'

'I don't care about any of that. You can't think that any of that has any
interest for me. I want to go now.'

'Don't go, I beg you. You can't go out there in London all alone with this
terrible news.'

'I've had terrible news before. I survived.' The girl's voice was bitter.

'Just sit for a while. I won't talk if it annoys you. But I don't want you to
be alone after this shock.'

'You didn't care about the shock before ... when you went away.' Kit
had her hand against her mouth, fist clenched as if she were willing back the
tears.

Lena knew she must make no gesture to hold her, to touch her. Kit was
poised to leave. The only thing keeping her in this room was her attempt to
gather the strength and courage to leave it. She was fighting back the tears.
Her face was working and she was almost biting her knuckles in her efforts
not to give way.

Lena sat very still. She didn't stare at Kit, she rested her head on her hand
and looked out the window to the outside world where people were living
ordinary lives.

Kit raised her head and looked at her.

Mother had always been like this. Able to sit still for ages on end. When
they sat by the lake and everyone else was running here and there and
pointing things out, Mother would sit there composed and peaceful, not
needing to speak or to move. And at night when they sat at the fire, Father

would do card tricks or teach them tongue twisters and riddles, or he would play Ludo with them. And Mother just sat there looking at the flames, sometimes her hand on Farouk's neck stroking him, saying nothing but being peaceful.

It had all seemed so safe then. Why had this man come in and taken Mother away from them? The anger against the man who had broken up their lives took over from the tears. Kit was able to speak.

'Does he know about us?' she asked eventually.

'Does who know?' Lena seemed genuinely startled.

'The man ... Louis, whatever his name is?'

'Yes, his name is Louis. Yes, he knows about you, of course he does.'

'And he still took you away?' Kit's voice was full of distaste.

'I went willingly. I wanted to go. You must realise how much I must have wanted to go ... how else could I have left you?'

Kit put her hands over her ears. 'I don't want to hear what you wanted. I don't want to think about you wanting. It makes me sick to think about it.' Her face was red and upset. It was hard enough for a girl to think about her mother mating with her father let alone think about wanting anyone else.

Lena realised this. 'I only said it because I wanted to take the blame,' she said.

'Blame!' The word from Kit sounded like a snort.

Lena feared that Kit might leave, that suddenly she might get up and go out that door without turning her head. 'What are we going to do?' she asked again.

'I don't know what you mean.'

'Are you going to tell Emmet and ... well, your father that ... that things are not the way they thought?'

'You've always known things weren't the way we thought.'

'Kit, please ... you know this was not my intention. It's what you did that brought this about.'

'So what are you asking me?' Kit's voice was cold.

There was a long pause. Then Lena raised her head and looked her daughter in the eye. 'I suppose I'm asking whether you want me alive or dead.'

There was another pause, then Kit said slowly: 'I think since you've wanted to be dead as far as we're concerned for the last five years ... you should stay dead.' She stood up to leave the room; and for Lena it was like the lid closing on her coffin.

Ivy saw the girl go down the stairs and walk towards the hall door. Her face looked more composed now. She didn't look as if she needed anyone to support her, help her through the traffic. She looked as if she could manage by herself. But her face was very dead. There was something empty and cold about her expression which had not been there before.

Ivy longed to go up to Lena. She wanted more than anything to comfort the woman who had lost her lover and her daughter in one day. But she knew better than to approach her. Lena knew where she lived. When she was ready she would come downstairs. Not before.

Kit found a café. It had a juke box and a group of girls her own age played record after record. How wonderful to be like that. To live in ordinary homes. Their mothers hadn't run away and pretended to be dead. None of these girls had ever come across a ghost. They had enough money to have play after play.

They talked of the fellows they were going out with. Two of them were black girls with London accents. Imagine this whole kind of life went on, people of different colours and dozens of cafés in the same street, and nobody knowing everyone on the street like at home.

And this is where Mother had been living since the day she drowned.

Mother alive. What would Emmet say? He'd be so delighted. Daddy. What would Father say when he heard? And then the black heavy weight again. But they couldn't hear. They couldn't hear now. It would be too much hurt and unhappiness after all these years.

And it was all Kit's fault.

So often over the past years she had wondered guiltily if she had done the right thing by burning that letter. But she had always told herself that God would know she had done it for the best of motives. She wanted Mother to have a burial place with everyone else. Not like a criminal outside the walls. She had done it for love of Mother. But who would care now or understand that she had meant it for the best? She had created the most terrible situation for everyone.

Kit felt the coffee scald her throat.

The best thing was that no one should ever know. That was the way that . . . she . . . wanted it. Kit didn't think of her as Mother . . . not this thin woman who sat in the elegant apartment and talked about wanting Louis . . . and needing him or whatever it was she said. Why should Emmet be put through everything Kit had been through? And Father. What would it do to Father to think his beloved Helen who he had cried over so much had left him because she wanted this man called Louis?

And where *was* this Louis anyway? If she was so crazy about him, why wasn't he there or any sign of him? Kit remembered that man who had come into Ivy's. The handsome dark-haired man like an actor. But that couldn't have been Louis; he was going away somewhere. He was leaving a big crate of his belongings to be collected. That wasn't Mother's Louis. Anyway, he was far too young. Too young to be Mother's fancy man.

Someone touched her arm. She looked up, startled. Surely Mother or Mrs Brown couldn't have followed her here.

But it was a boy of about eighteen. 'Are you on your own?' he asked.

'Yes,' Kit looked at him cautiously.

'Would you like to join us?' He waved over at a table where the group was sitting. They smiled encouragingly.

'No, thank you . . . thank you very much . . .'

'Come on, can't have you sitting on your own when there's music playing,' the boy said.

Kit looked at him doubtfully. They were just singing and clapping to the music. As she and Clio would have done with them had things been different. She couldn't sit with them laughing, pretending that nothing was wrong. But neither could she sit with her thoughts going round and round like a red hot circle in a groove, with no solution.

'Thank you,' she smiled at him.

He looked pleased to have brought such a pretty, well-dressed girl to their table. She smiled brightly and nodded at their names. She must have told them she was Kit because that's what they called her when she said she had to go, and ran from the café to catch a bus back to the convent.

Clio was walking up and down grumbling. 'You're late,' she said.

'No, you're early.' It was the way they had always been. Yet the last time Kit had seen Clio she hadn't known this awful fact. The fact that Mother had never died; she had run away. And that Kit had helped her to continue the deception by burning the letter.

'What did you do?' Clio was still sulking that they hadn't gone to do the town together.

'Mainly a coffee bar,' Kit shrugged.

'That's all? I saw lots of places.'

'Good for you.'

'Did you get talking to people?' Clio's eyes were piggy for information.

'Yeah, a whole group. They played the juke box.'

'And were there fellows?'

'Mainly fellows.' Kit's mind was miles away. Miles from Clio and from the coffee bar.

'What were they like?'

'They were okay. What about you?' Kit knew she must make things seem normal.

But Clio obviously had found no satisfying adventures in London on her own. 'I just looked here and there. What were their names?'

'Who?'

'The fellows you met.'

'I can't remember.' Kit obviously couldn't.

Clio looked alarmed as they walked up the steps to the convent door. 'Kit, you didn't have sexual intercourse with any of them, did you?' Clio asked suddenly.

'Jesus, why would you say that?' Clio never failed to surprise her.

'Well, you look different,' Clio said. 'And you know you can always tell someone who's done it from someone who hasn't.'

'Sorry to disappoint you, but I didn't. We didn't get round to it in the coffee bar. Maybe too many people there or something.'

'Oh shut up, Kit. It's just that you've changed. I don't know what it is, but I know you so well and something happened.'

'It wasn't the loss of my virginity on a coffee table, I can tell you that.'

'What was it?'

'It was nothing. It was being in a strange city and not really a part of it, I suppose.'

That was the right thing to say. Clio bought it. She had felt her outing a miserable failure. It was consoling to think that Kit McMahon had found nothing to do either. But odd that she looked as if something had happened, as if she had been in an accident or something.

Kit hardly slept all night. She sat and looked out the window as the dawn came up over London. She wondered if her mother was worrying the same way. No, she was probably with this Louis that she had wanted so much. Again, Kit wondered was it possible that Louis might have been the handsome man who was leaving his belongings to collect later.

Then a thought came from nowhere, with the force and pain of a sharp cold wind. Suppose Louis had gone, and Mother knew that she was now proven to be alive, then Mother might come home after all. She might come back to Lough Glass after all those years and try to take up life again. Come back as a ghost to poor Father who thought she was a dead saint. And to Emmet who had been so young when she had drowned. And to stop Maura Hayes from getting married to Father. Of course Maura Hayes could never marry Father now.

And no one would ever forgive Mother.

Alternately Kit's face burned with a feverish heat and felt ice cold. By morning light she was far too unwell to join them on the excursion, which that day was a walking tour of Dickens' London.

Mother Lucy was worried. 'Do you often get such a reaction?' she asked. The girl had a high temperature certainly.

'I'll be fine if I can lie in bed for a while. In a nice dark room,' Kit had said.

'I'll call in on you every hour or so,' Mother Lucy said.

'That'll put a stop to your gallop,' Clio said.

'I've no gallop. You are such a pain, Clio. Such an awful one-track pain.'

'If I find your coffee shop will I tell them you'll be back for more?' Clio was annoyed that Kit wasn't coming with them. Things were much funnier when Kit was there, but she really did look as if she had caught some illness or disease.

Kit lay in the small narrow bed in the dormitory that held eight girls. Eight English girls slept here during term time. The girls from Lough Glass slept here this week. All of them could go to sleep on these pillows without having barbed wire coils of fear around their heart.

Kit lay with her eyes open in the dark room, and every time the nun put her head around the door she pretended to be asleep. This way there was no need for more speculation about what might have caused her fever.

Lena had not slept. By six o'clock she knew there wasn't a chance of closing her eyes. She got up and dressed and went downstairs. She pushed a note under Ivy's door. *I'll talk to you tonight,* she wrote. There was no need to say anything else. Ivy would know how grateful she was to be left alone last night. Ivy knew she wasn't closing her out, excluding her from a life which she had once invited her to join.

At Millar's Lena began to write a letter to her daughter. She wrote and wrote, tearing up the pages, ripping them from her typewriter. She tried to write by hand but that didn't work either. When the door rattled and Dawn Jones came in, Lena had given up. There were no words to say any of the million things that should be said. She had torn the rejected letters into tiny fragments. Therapeutic almost, reducing them to confetti-sized pieces from which no clue could be read.

No one would ever know that the calm Mrs Gray had spent a night in anguish. That in one day she had found her daughter, lost her again, and been abandoned by the man she had lived with as man and wife for five years. She had nothing to live for, yet she was going to live through this day. The thoughts that had chased around in her head all through the wakeful hours had convinced her that her daughter was right. She must remain dead. She had caused enough harm and hurt already.

But what had come to her in a sudden and unwelcome flash had been the fear that perhaps Kit would change her mind. When the initial horror and revulsion had passed by, when her own guilt at the part she had played – the tragic and well meaning gesture of burning a letter to avoid the disgrace of public suicide – then she might change her view. She might think that her duty lay in revealing that she had found Lena, that it was her duty to tell Emmet his mother was alive, and then to tell Martin.

Lena's guilt at what had happened to Martin knew no bounds. She had misjudged him utterly. For years the man had lived in the shadow of her death, her possible suicide. Kit had said the town was full of whispers. He had survived it, brought them up to revere her memory. He could not be exposed now as what he was, a man whose wife had run off with another man, and had allowed the explanation of her death by drowning to be accepted.

Martin deserved more dignity. He deserved some happiness. Kit must be warned never to relent.

During the night Lena had thought that she would find the words if she were at her desk, the desk where she had so often written long letters to the daughter of a supposedly dead friend. Letters that would never be written or answered again.

But it had not been possible to write the words.

And there was Dawn, fresh as a daisy. 'Well, I thought I was an early bird ... but no, you're here before me again.' Dawn's voice was like the chirrup of a bird. She looked like a little canary or a budgie in her blue and gold outfit, her shining hair and her perfect make-up.

Lena felt old and tired. 'Dawn, I may have to take some time off today. I wonder, could you get your pad and come in to me until I list some of my work that you and Jessie may have to divide between you.'

'Certainly, Mrs Gray.' Dawn listened attentively.

Lucky Dawn, thought Lena. Dawn who had slept a full night's sleep and had a dozen admirers. Her only decisions after work today would be who to go out with.

Lena went back to number 27. She knocked on Ivy's door. 'Ivy, when you have a minute can you come upstairs with me?'

She was so frail looking, Ivy was alarmed. 'Shall I take you to the doctor?' she asked.

'No. Just a helping hand up the stairs would be nice.'

Ivy took Lena's clothes as she undressed and got into her bed, the big bed that she and Louis had shared but which was far too wide and empty for her now. She folded the clothes and laid them on a chair, then handed her a nightdress as if she were a lady's maid. Lena slipped it over her head. Her face was lined deep with pain and tiredness.

Neither of them had spoken.

Then Ivy said, 'She's a very beautiful girl, Lena. She's a lovely daughter for you to have . . .'

She couldn't have said anything more guaranteed to open the barrier that was holding back the tears. Lena had not cried since it all began, but hearing Ivy Brown praise the beauty and warmth of the daughter she had lost for ever let it all out. She cried like a baby for what seemed an age. And only after a very long time was she persuaded to blow her nose and tell Ivy the depth of the tragedy . . . the wrong that in all innocence her daughter had done by ensuring that Helen McMahon could never go back and see her family again.

*

'You didn't enjoy it all that much, did you?' Martin McMahon said.

'Oh I did, Daddy, and it was a lot of money and everything . . .'

'That doesn't matter. We sometimes spend a lot on things that don't work out. Was it a bit schoolish, is that it?'

'No it was fine, I told you. I sent you cards; we saw everything.'

'Where did you like best?' Emmet asked.

Kit looked at him suddenly. He reminded her of her mother saying, 'What was the worst thing?' She swallowed and tried to find something to say that would satisfy him. 'I think I liked the Tower of London best,' she said.

'And this fever you got?' Her father was still anxious.

'It was only a temperature for a day or two . . . you know the way nuns fuss.'

'Clio was telling Peter about it. She said you were in bed two days.'

'Clio is worse than the nuns, Daddy.'

'Don't let poor Mother Bernard hear you say that, after all the effort she put into educating the pair of you.' Her father had been satisfactorily sidetracked.

Trust Clio to make it into a big, big deal.

'There you are, Kit McMahon.' That was Father Baily's normal greeting to people. He more or less gave them permission to exist by saying it.

'Here I am, Father,' said Kit mischievously.

He looked at her sharply to see if she was making fun of him, but couldn't prove it. 'And tell me, what did you all make of London?'

'It was interesting, Father. We were lucky to have been given such an opportunity.' She spoke primly as if she were a little girl reciting what she had been told to say.

Clio giggled.

'A fine place in its own way,' Father Baily said. 'If you look at it for what it is, there isn't a thing you could criticise about it.'

Kit wondered how you could look at London as if it were something other than it was, but decided this was not the time to argue it with the elderly priest. 'Were you ever there yourself, Father?' she asked.

'I passed through it twice on the way to the Holy City,' he said.

'Were there coffee shops at that time?' Clio asked.

'We hadn't much time to spend in coffee shops,' Father Baily said.

'Just as well,' Clio hissed as they left. 'Think what he might have seen if he had been given the time to visit them.'

'Wasn't it a great coincidence your being in London at the same time as our school trip?' Mother Bernard said to Maura Hayes.

'What's that, Mother?'

'You know, Clio and Kit going out to meet you from the convent ... Mother Lucy was telling me about it.'

'Ah, Mother Lucy ...' She was at a loss but didn't want to let the nun realise.

'What a coincidence!' Mother Bernard said again.

'Wasn't it?' Maura said, her brow darkening.

'Oh Clio, a word please.'

'Yes, Aunt Maura?'

'Was there some confusion in Mother Bernard's mind, or did anyone tell her I was in London when you were?'

'I swear I didn't. I swear it,' Clio said.

'Well who did, Clio?'

'I haven't a clue. But some daft nun over there said our aunt phoned so we kind of used the heaven-sent opportunity...' Clio giggled. 'You couldn't turn your back on a heaven-sent chance like that, could you?'

'And where did you and Kit go on the heaven sent opportunity?'

'I don't know where Kit went, she was most mysterious. I had a dull time actually, looked in shop windows and went in and out of cafés and bars pretending I was looking for someone.'

'And did you not enquire about this sudden aunt who was asking for you?'

Clio shrugged. 'Nope, I just thought it was a bit of rare good luck. But I was wrong.'

*

Orla Dillon, now Orla Reilly, was in her mother's shop. 'Why can't I help you, Mammy? You used always complain that I didn't help.'

'That was when you were living here. Now you live with your husband and I'd like you to go back to him.'

'God, Mammy. You'd need to get out of that house from time to time. I told him you needed a bit of a hand in the shop.'

'Well, you told him wrong. And who is minding the baby?'

'His mother. Give her something to do, Mrs Reilly, the old rip.'

'I've said it once and I won't say it again, there's no work for you here, Orla.'

'Mammy, please.'

'You should have thought of this before all the other business.' Her mother's face was hard. Orla's shotgun wedding had not been a matter of pleasure to her family.

Clio and Kit were reading the magazines. They usually managed to read about five for every one they bought. Clio had been following the whole conversation between Orla and her mother. 'Marriage isn't all it's cracked up to be,' she whispered to Kit.

'What?' Kit said.

'You're miles away,' Clio said. It was like talking to the side of a wall talking to Kit McMahon these days. She just had no interest in anything.

The prospectus from St Mary's Catering College in Cathal Brugha Street arrived. It lay unopened on the hall table for three days.

'Aren't you going to open it, Kit?' Rita asked. 'It will have all the details about your uniforms and everything.'

'I will, of course,' Kit said.

But she didn't.

'Catering?' Mrs Hanley in the drapery said. 'Catering, well I'm sure that's very nice. You're not going to university, then, like Clio?'

'No, Mrs Hanley. I'd love to learn the hotel business. It's meant to be a very good course. You learn to cook and do accounts and all kinds of things.'

'Is your father disappointed you're not going to university? I know he had his heart set on it.'

Kit looked at Mrs Hanley. 'Had he? You know he never said. He never said a word about that. Maybe I should go home and ask him. I never knew that till you said it this minute.'

'Well now, I may be mistaken, and you wouldn't want to go round upsetting people.' Mrs Hanley looked alarmed.

Kit's eyes were blazing with annoyance. She didn't know that Mrs Hanley was so ashamed that her daughter Deirdre was working in a low class kind of café in Dublin – not even waiting tables properly, just clearing up after people with a broom and a cloth – she did everything she could to belittle the opportunities and futures of others from Lough Glass.

Mrs Hanley didn't know that the red-faced angry girl in front of her had hardly heeded her words and their meaning. It was just the trigger of mentioning her father that had set off the storm.

Kit slept badly at night and concentrated not at all during the day. What if her mother were to write from England or, worse still, arrive? Suppose that the nice safe future that her father seemed about to embark on was going to blow away in front of their eyes?

'Emmet, you smell of drink,' Kit said.

'Oh, do I? I thought it would have gone by now.'

'You thought what?'

'You won't tell?'

'Did I ever tell?'

'Well, Michael Sullivan and Kevin Wall and I . . . we had a cocktail.'

'I don't believe this.'

'Yes, we made it from all the bottles outside Foley's. We poured it into a jug and shook it.'

'You are mad, Emmet. Quite mad.'

'Actually, it was awful. And it was mainly watery stout, there was hardly anything left in the whiskey and brandy bottles.'

'What a shame,' Kit said.

'But anyway, thanks for telling me, I'll wash my teeth.'

'Why on earth did you do it?' Kit asked.

'It was something to do. Sometimes it's kind of lonely here. Wouldn't you say that's true?'

Kit looked at Emmet and bit her lip. Should she tell him?

'How are you, Kit?' Stevie Sullivan called.

'Not well,' Kit said.

'I hate to hear of a good-looking girl not being in good form.' Stevie smiled a crooked attractive smile.

It cut no ice with Kit McMahon. 'I'd be a lot better if you could stop your brother arranging cocktail parties in the back yard of Foley's and Paddles',' she said.

'What are you all of a sudden? Pioneer Total Abstinence Society? Father Matthew Apostle of Temperance?' Stevie asked.

'I'm someone who'd prefer my own brother not to come home stinking of booze,' she said.

'Okay,' Stevie nodded.

'What do you mean, Okay?'

'I mean, Okay, I'll stop it.'

'Thanks,' she said, and let herself in the door. As she climbed the stairs Kit asked herself why she had reacted so strongly to something that was only a kid's game. They hadn't been really drunk. It was pretending to be grown-up.

But she told herself that it was for her father. Daddy had enough behind him. And enough ahead of him. Because Kit now thought this was too big a secret to keep. She wouldn't be able to hide it as she had hidden the burning of the letter. It would all come out now, everything, and their lives would all be ruined.

She dreamed that Mother was home, and that they were all having tea in the kitchen. 'Don't be too hard on Kit,' Mother was saying and they all sat grouped together with Rita standing behind them. Kit seemed to be the outcast far away across the table. And in her dream she heard Maura crying noisy sobs.

'I have a lovely present for you to start your new career, Kit.' Mrs Hanley handed Kit a flat box.

'That's very nice of you, Mrs Hanley.'

'Open it and see do you like it.'

It was a lemon-coloured, short-sleeved jumper, something Kit would never have worn. But under a jacket it might look all right.

'It's beautiful, Mrs Hanley. That's very kind of you.'

'I spoke a bit out of turn the other day. You were a good girl not to take any notice of me.'

Kit looked at her blankly. She hadn't an idea what the woman was talking about. Everything was so odd these days, and she could hardly remember anything she had done since she came back from London. It all seemed suspended somehow, unreal.

*

The days and nights were endless in London for Lena. She slept or tried to sleep curled up in a little corner of the great bed that they had shared so happily.

In the office she worked on like a machine . . . there was no purpose to the working day for her any more. No plans for an evening meal with Louis, no running home at lunchtime to catch him on his split shifts so that they could have an hour together.

Impossible to believe that her birthday would come and go, and nobody would know. Louis in France would have forgotten. Kit in Ireland would not remember. Everyone else in Ireland thought she was dead. Maybe Ivy knew but she would be tactful enough to realise that this year there was nothing to celebrate.

Sometimes on Saturday lunchtimes when they closed the agency doors Lena congratulated herself that she had survived another week. Perhaps this is what the rest of her life would be like, unless of course her daughter could bear the strain no longer. Unless she was unmasked as living, alive if not well, in London. Living in the empty bed of a man who had left her, just as she had left her own husband.

Some days were harder than others. There was a widow who came in looking for part-time work saying she had to be home at four o'clock in the afternoon when her son got back from school.

'He's thirteen, you see, and they really need their mothers at that age,' she confided to Lena.

To her surprise Mrs Gray's eyes filled with tears. 'Yes, I expect they do,'

she said earnestly. 'Let's try everything until we get you something suitable.'
And Lena threw herself into the task. It was as if she could somehow reach
out to Emmet by helping this woman to see her son.

She thought about Emmet a lot. Perhaps he might be less hard of heart,
less quick to condemn than Kit had been. After all, he was blameless in
every way. He had burned no note of explanation. Was there a way she
could write to him, tell him she was alive? Or was this the way madness lay?

And then there was Martin. Martin whom she had so sorely misjudged.
Was it better, as Kit had said, that she remain dead? But suppose that Kit
was not constant in her intentions? Might she not give in and admit
everything? Would it be fairer to Martin to tell him now, tell him herself,
rather than let him hear it second hand?

She had given him her promise that she would never leave him without
explanation, but he had not known. Was she only telling him because Louis
had gone? Or would he think that this was the case?

Like mice, the thoughts scurried around in her head while she was awake.

And when she slept she dreamed often that Louis had come back. She
would wake cold and cramped and realise it was not true. One night she
dreamed she went back to Lough Glass: that she got off a bus outside the
Mercy Convent and walked through the town, past the Lakeview Road
which led up to the Kellys' house, past the Post Office where Mona Fitz
closed the door in her face. Tommy the postman tried to come out and talk
to her but Mona called him back; and the curtains in the Garda Station
across the road twitched as they saw her but nobody came out to greet her.
Mrs Hanley had Early Closing written on the shop so as to avoid meeting
her.

And a sullen crowd stood in the doorways of Foley's bar. Sullivan's garage
was deserted, Wall's hardware people turned the other way; Father Baily
hastened up Church Road so as not to have to see her, so she tried to come
back up the street on the other side in case there would be someone to meet
her; but at Paddles' the doors were closed and Mrs Dillon didn't speak. Dan
and Mildred O'Brien in the Central Hotel avoided her eye.

And then she was at the pharmacy. 'I'm home,' she called up the stairs.
But there was no reply. Rita, dressed in black, came to the top of the stairs.
'I'm afraid you can't come in Mam, the Mistress is dead,' Rita said
solemnly. 'I am the Mistress,' Lena cried in her dream. 'I know, Mam, but
you can't come in.'

At that she woke up sweating. It was true. There was no life of any sort
ahead for her. She might as well be dead.

Lena missed the letters terribly. There was no point in looking in to Ivy
hopefully. There would never be a letter from Kit again. Never a letter
overflowing with news to her mother's friend.

Kit missed the letters. There was nobody to sound off to, no one to tell
about all the things that lay ahead, the catering college, the dog-like
devotion of Philip O'Brien, the increasing bossiness of Clio. The Lena Gray
she had written to would have been able to come up with some course of

action about everything, everything, of course, except what was really wrong.

It was a great lacking, the letters. Not having Sister Madeleine slip her the envelope with the English stamp which she would take home and read in her room. Now the knowledge that these letters were all lies made them worthless. She could hardly bear to think of what they had said. She didn't believe Lena Gray any more. About anything.

There was a postcard from Philip. He was in Killarney.

Dear Kit,

I have a holiday job here in this hotel that you see on the front of the card. Imagine having a picture of your hotel on the card. How boastful.

I can't wait to start the course, can you? We'll be so much ahead of the others, after all we're going out together. They'll all have to find new friends.

Love,

Philip

Dear Kit,

Your father tells me that you will be in the Mountjoy Square Hostel, which I am sure will be excellent for you while you are studying in Catering College.

I also realise that some of the greatest joys of coming to Dublin centre around the sense of freedom you have from home, and everything connected with your own place. I would like you to know that I have a very comfortable flat in Rathmines. If ever you would like to come and see me I would be delighted. But most of all I want you to know that I shall not be sitting at home waiting for you. I leave work at five-thirty and very often when the weather is good I go on the golf course an hour after that time. Often I go to the cinema, or to the houses of friends. Sometimes people come to my flat for supper.

I tell you this so that you will know I am not trying to seek for company, nor am I trying to keep an eye on you while you are in Dublin. But this is my phone number just in case you'd like to come for a meal some time.

Yours affectionately,

Maura

Dear Michael Sullivan,

This is from a well wisher. You have been observed drinking the dregs from bottles outside various public houses in Lough Glass.

This must now cease.

Immediately.

Otherwise Sergeant O'Connor will be informed.

And Father Baily.

And most important your brother who will beat the shit out of you.

You have been warned.

Dear Philip,

Whatever else we are doing when we get to Dublin we are not going out together. I want you to know this from the very start so that there will be no misunderstanding.

Love (but only if you take it in the right spirit),

Kit

'They want me to start soon in Dublin, Stevie,' Rita said.

'Oh Jesus! You run everything here like a dream.'

'It's nearly time.'

'But your woman hasn't moved in with Martin yet.'

'If you are speaking of Miss Hayes, they are very close friends. But you are right there is no engagement . . . as yet.'

'I thought you'd stay with me and keep the garage afloat.'

'Your mother doesn't approve of me, Stevie.'

'Don't mind her. I don't.'

'It's not pleasant to be asked to empty the rubbish, scrub the pots, take in the washing . . .'

'But come off it, Rita, you don't *do* any of those things. She just asks you, you refuse. It's a game.'

'Not to me it isn't.'

'I don't believe this. There's another reason . . . you've been offered a better job?'

'No, not really.'

'What do you mean?'

'I've come from nothing, I've made myself acceptable. I want to be somewhere that I *am* accepted.'

'I pay you well.'

'If I went on the streets I'd be paid even better. Money isn't everything.'

'Okay, I've been working my arse off here. I agree I don't have time to be polite to people.'

'You're quite polite to customers, Stevie. And to the people who might get you a Ford agency.'

He looked stricken. 'That's true.'

'And to girls who catch your eye, and to people you want credit from, or those you think might be in the way of buying a new car.'

'You've had your eyes open.'

'Yes, and I don't particularly like everything that I see.'

'Jesus, Rita, I'm ashamed. That's all I can say.'

'Funnily, I think you mean it,' Rita said.

'So will everything be all right now? I've learned my lesson, and I'll be as good as gold.' He smiled his heartbreaking smile.

'You're only a kid, Stevie. That won't work with me.' Rita laughed at him.

'So what do I have to do?'

'Nothing, really. Just a nice reference and I'll be off tonight. Everything's in apple-pie order.'

'You're never walking out on me.'

'More on your mother.'

'She's nothing to do with this.'

'Then she has no business in your office.'

'Who taught you to be so tough?'

'Mrs McMahon, the Lord have mercy on her.'

'I doubt if he will, she drowned herself.'

'You've a big mouth, Stevie Sullivan.'

'I'll give you a lot more money. Stay, Rita. Please.'

'No, thanks all the same.'

'Who will I get?'

'An older woman, even older than me.'

'How old are you, Rita? You're only a girl.'

'I'm a good five years older than you.'

'That's nothing these days.'

'Get someone older. And someone who'll frighten the bejaysus out of your mother.'

'What'll I say in the reference you want from me?'

'I have it written here,' Rita smiled at him.

'I can't believe this, Rita. I really can't,' Martin McMahon said to her.

'It's time for me to go, sir.'

'Is there anything I can say to make you stay?'

'Everything you did here was always for my good, but I could find you someone, sir. Someone to work in my place.'

'There's no one that could equal you, Rita.'

'What I was going to suggest was a young cousin of mine. She might just work mornings, do the cleaning, ironing and wash the vegetables . . . you'll probably be able to make your own arrangements and maybe want the house run in a different way.' It was as near as she could come to telling him that it was time he married Maura.

*

Maura Hayes opened the letter. It was typed and post-marked Lough Glass.

You may think this is an extraordinary letter, Mrs Hayes, and if you are offended by it then my judgement has been wrong.

Maura hastened to see who it was from. The signature 'Rita Moore' meant nothing. Then she understood. The girl who had worked in Martin's house was telling her that she was leaving. That there were two vacancies. Housekeeper, and in the office across the road.

'Is there an understanding between you and young Kit McMahon?' Dan O'Brien asked his son the night before the course began in the Cathal Brugha Street College of Catering.

'What do you mean?'

'You know what I mean.'

'No I don't, actually,' Philip said.

'Well, actually, for your information, I meant do you and she intend to be boyfriend and girlfriend?'

'And suppose we did?'

'Suppose you did, I want to warn you that she could be a bit flighty like her mother, and I wouldn't want to think that you'd have your name up with someone like that.'

'Thank you, Father.'

'Don't take that tone with me.'

'What tone?'

'Mildred, speak to him.'

'There isn't any point, is there? He's determined to be like all the modern youth today.'

'Sister Madeleine,' said Kit. 'There *was* a thing I was going to say about the letters from London.'

'What's that now?'

'I think my mother's friend will write to me in Dublin now, at the hostel.'

'Yes, of course . . .'

'I just didn't want you to think I took things for granted, or was keeping things secret from you.'

'No, of course not . . . and often things that sound complicated are quite simple.' Sister Madeleine was light-hearted about her alternative postal service. 'Anyway, Kit, when you're as old as I am and half talking to the birds and the foxes and the butterflies that come in at the end of the summer, you're not sure what you know and what you only dream . . .'

'Does everyone have a secret, do you think?'

'Certainly. Some are more important than others, of course.'

Kit looked at her. There was one more thing she wanted to ask. It was hard to know how to put it. 'Suppose you knew something . . . something that should actually stop something . . .' The nun's eyes were very blue and gave nothing away. 'I was wondering if that were to happen to someone . . . should that someone try to change what was going to happen, you know, by saying everything, or would it be better to let things go ahead?'

'A very hard question, all right.' Sister Madeleine was sympathetic.

'But you'd need to know more before you could answer it . . . is that it?'

'No, no. Not at all. *I* couldn't answer a question like that for anyone else. They'd have to find the solution all on their own. They'd know it in their hearts anyway.'

'They might know what they *want* but that needn't be the right thing.'

'If it was the right thing that helped people and made them happy . . .' Sister Madeleine paused.

Not for the first time the thought crossed Kit's mind that the hermit had an easy, simplistic view of the laws of God that might not be found totally acceptable to the more official wings of the Church.

*

Lena bought the paper every week. She read it from cover to cover, wishing there was more about Lough Glass and less about the surrounding countryside and villages in the area.

She read it first in fear. Fear that news of a great local scandal might be revealed. And then as the weeks went on she realised that Kit had not broken down under the strain of the knowledge she had come by. There were not going to be stories unmasking the great mistake that had been made in identifying a body all those years ago.

Lena read how two Lough Glass students had been accepted in St Mary's College of Catering. Kit was described as daughter of Martin McMahon, the well-known pharmacist and his late wife, Mrs Helen McMahon.

She read of the new drainage scheme, the improved roads and the campaign for street lighting. She saw a picture of a bus shelter and read the outraged correspondence when it had been defaced.

And one day, most unexpectedly, she read that Martin McMahon, pharmacist of Lough Glass, and Miss Maura Hayes were to marry. She sat still for a very long time. Then she read it again.

Kit McMahon must be a strong girl to be able to take that in her stride. At her age she could allow her father to make a bigamous marriage. She knew that her mother was alive and she would have the courage to stand in a church and watch a wedding ceremony that she knew was a sham. She must be very courageous indeed to face the wrath of the Church or the State if it ever came to light.

Either that or she must hate her mother and have forced herself to believe that she was really dead.

Kit knew it was the right thing to do. She had no doubts at all. Sister Madeleine was right; you followed your conscience.

But she did have one worry. Suppose Lena . . . found out. Suppose Lena wanted to spoil things. She might come at the last moment. It would be unforgivable if Kit were to let her father's day be ruined, and have him and Maura made into a laughing stock. But she couldn't write and ask a favour now.

She had left that day knowing she was doing the right thing. Her mother didn't exist for them any more in the way she once had. She couldn't go crawling now, begging, pleading, asking her not to come back and haunt the happiness that had been so slow to come to this family. She would have to hope and pray that Lena would never hear about the wedding. How could she hear? She didn't know anyone who lived in Lough Glass. It wasn't going to be on the news or anything.

It was hard to pray in conventional terms about this. Kit said big swooping prayers which skirted the issue of God's law on marriage.

God was out for the best too, wasn't he?

Lena thought about it for a long time.

Martin holding the hand of Maura Hayes and saying the words that couples said all over the world. Martin taking Maura home to his bed.

Maura presiding at the table in the kitchen . . . going to Kit's graduation, buying Emmet's clothes.

She smoked late into the night. But what was another sleepless night? She had had so many of them.

By morning she had made up her mind. At lunch time she took a bus to one of the smarter shopping streets and spent two hours choosing a dress. She had it wrapped for postage and took it to a post office. She addressed it to Kit McMahon, First Year Hotel Management Student, St Mary's College of Catering, Cathal Brugha Street, Dublin. And before she had time to change her mind she put in a note, 'I thought you might like this to wear at the wedding. L'

And she left the parcel into their hands so that she could have no second thoughts.

She didn't tell Ivy, not about the dress, nor even about the wedding. Somehow it was better if it wasn't spoken about. It made her own position less vulnerable, less lonely.

She dreamed about the children every night. Emmet looking for her everywhere – behind rocks on a beach, behind trees in a wood, calling always, 'I know you're there, please come out, come back, come back.' And of Kit wearing the dress, and standing stonily at the church gate. 'You can't come in, you must not come to the wedding, you're buried over there. Remember this and go away.'

*

Maura Hayes gave a lot of thought to the wedding.

It would be small but not hole-in-the-corner. It should be held in Dublin, far from the eyes of a too-interested Lough Glass. Lilian would be her matron of honour, and Peter the best man. Or was that the wrong way? After all, Peter had been best man at Martin's first wedding, when he had married Helen with all the hope that had been involved there. But if it weren't Peter who else would it be? Martin had no other close friend in Lough Glass or anywhere. It would be deliberate and wrong to exclude Peter.

Maura would wear a cream-coloured suit and a blue hat with a cream ribbon.

Maura's wedding plans came as a surprise to her Dublin friends, who hadn't somehow thought of sensible, golfing Maura as a likely bride. They heard of this kind widower, a pharmacist in a small country town, with two children whom Maura liked very much and who as far as she could tell seemed pleased that she was marrying their father. They learned with amazement that Maura had already found herself a job in this town. There was a position as a bookkeeper/administrator in a fast growing motor business. It was two steps from her front door.

And her sister was married to the local doctor, and there was great golf. Her colleagues and friends were grudgingly pleased on her behalf. Father Baily from Lough Glass would attend as a guest, but the couple would be married by a priest that Maura knew in her own parish in Dublin. There would be about twenty people to lunch in a restaurant.

Maura had studied the earlier wedding pictures, the ones taken in 1939. On that occasion there had been sixty people. Maura recognised the brother and sisters of Martin, a dispersed, silent family who met only at funerals and weddings.

They would not be included in this guest list. It would look like asking for a present a second time round. She saw her sister Lilian, young and innocent looking, Peter stern as the best man. She saw the bridesmaid, a girl called Dorothy, and her eyes stayed long on the beautiful face of Helen Healy, the woman that Martin McMahon had loved with a wild and unreasonable love.

He had told her all about it one day by the lake. He had been truthful and fair, to everyone, to Helen, to himself and to Maura. He said she was something that filled his mind like a sandstorm.

Maura's eyes searched the face. What had she been thinking that day while she stood for the photographs? Had she hoped that the years with a kind, good man like Martin would smooth out the hurt of a man who had left her, a man she had loved and hoped to marry? The face was oval, the eyes were big and dark, the smile was sweet. But surely even someone who didn't know the whole story could see that this was not the normal expression of a bride on her wedding day? This was someone looking out way beyond the camera to something no one else could see.

Maura put aside her reflections, and went back to her list. The O'Briens from the hotel were invited, mainly to get over their sense of grievance at the wedding not being held in their premises. Young Philip who was at the catering college with Kit might come too. Maura would ask Kit. It was foolish to assume that all young people liked each other just because they grew up next door.

Ivy called Millar's Agency.

'I'm afraid she's with a client, Mrs Brown,' Dawn said. 'Can any of the rest of us help you?'

'No, darling, tell her it's Ivy. It'll only take thirty seconds.'

'But, Mrs Brown, I know you're a friend and everything, but she is with a very senior businessman, someone who might be able to put a lot of business her way. I don't know whether she'd thank me or indeed thank you for being interrupted.'

'She'll thank us,' Ivy said.

'Mrs Gray, Mrs Ivy Brown is most persistent. May I put her through for a short moment?'

'Thank you, yes, Dawn.' Lena's voice was unruffled.

Ivy knew that Dawn would be listening. 'Oh Lena, sorry to interrupt you, but Mr Tyrone turned up looking for his key. I told him I had given it to you.'

'And so you did.' Lena's voice was bright.

'So I suppose I should mention to Mr Tyrone when you might be back.'

'Tonight. Eight o'clock at the very earliest, and thank you so much for calling, Ivy.' Lena hung up.

But Ivy remained on the line until she heard the click showing that Dawn had hung up also. She smiled to herself grimly. They had never had to use a code before. How quick Lena was on the uptake. Together they had giggled about how handsome Louis was, that he really did look like a film star. Tyrone Power possibly.

Ivy would not give young Dawn the satisfaction of knowing that Mrs Gray's erring husband was back. And particularly Ivy did not want to let Dawn or anyone know how eagerly and willingly Lena would take him back.

Eight o'clock. That meant she must be going to the hairdresser.

Grace was philosophical. 'Of course I don't think you're silly. I think you're right. Look as well as you can ... that way if he stays you'll be glad you made the effort. If he doesn't you'll think you look so damn good anyway you'll have no trouble getting any other man.'

'I don't want any other man, of course,' said Lena.

'Of course,' Grace agreed. 'That's the problem. That's the meaning of the universe, isn't it?'

Ivy had been upstairs and tidied round. She had polished the table by the window and put a glass bowl of gold roses in the centre of it. She had ironed some of Lena's blouses and put fresh sheets on the bed. She had thrown out the remains of old, hastily grabbed meals, the packets of slightly stale biscuits, and installed instead some fresh bread, ham and tomatoes. And a bottle of wine. Something that would not look as if she had been expecting Louis, but which gave no appearance of desperation either.

Ivy hadn't prayed much in recent years, but she found herself offering up a little wish all day that Louis' return would be glorious. That this time he would find something that would make him stay.

There was a café across the street, a place where workmen had heavy-duty sandwiches and big cups of tea. Louis Gray sat there, out of it because of his clothes and his suntan, but still acceptable because of his easy way with people, his need to know about the chances of a horse in the following day's races. Out of the corner of his eye he watched number 27.

He had been there for an hour. Ivy said that Lena would be back at eight. Lena would not know he was coming home. When he saw her coming he excused himself from a conversation on form, and slipped across the road. He wanted to catch her as she went up the stairs.

He saw her legs disappearing around the corner. 'Lena,' he called softly.

She looked around, glowing and confident. A woman that any man would stop to look at. Her hair, which never ceased to amaze him, was shining, her make-up perfect. No other woman returning home after a long working day looked like this. He went up and stood close to her. She smelled as fresh as a daisy, her eyes were big and dancing with interest and surprise. 'Well, well, well,' Lena said slowly.

'You didn't call into Ivy.'

'I don't every night, no.' They were speaking like old friends.

'Can I come in?' He pointed upwards at their flat.

'Well, Louis, it's your home. Of course you can come in.' How had she learned to be such an actress? She marvelled at her own skills.

'I gave my key back to Ivy. She said you had it.'

'As indeed I have.' Lena knew that Ivy would have returned the key in her absence. And as she went in to the newly cleaned flat her heart filled with love for the good woman downstairs. Everything was perfect for the reconciliation, for the promises, the assurances, the night of love. And there on the mantelpiece where no one could miss it, in a small glass dish was Louis' key. Lena went straight over to it, picked it up and handed it to him.

'I brought some champagne,' Louis said.

'That's nice.' Lena had steeled herself, drilled herself all day, to be calm.

'I thought if you'd let me come home it would be a celebration, and if you wouldn't then I could drink it to console myself.' He smiled his boyish smile.

Lena smiled back. In a way it was no different to her going to the hairdressers and having a facial. As Grace had said, if Louis stayed then it would be a celebration, if not, a consolation. Very much the same thing.

'Let's celebrate then,' she said, and she turned her face a little to one side as he came to take her in his arms. She didn't want him to see how much she hungered to hold him so tight that she would squeeze the breath from him. She wanted to kiss his lips, his eyes, his neck, to take his clothes off slowly and walk with him into the bedroom. But this way she would seem too eager.

He moved her face to kiss her lips. 'I'm a fool, Lena,' he said.

'No more than most of us,' she said.

'This is my home. I knew that five minutes after I left it.'

'And now you're back,' she said.

'Don't you want to know . . . to hear?'

'Oh no, I do most certainly *not* want to know . . . Now, are you going to pour me a glass of champagne or is this all just an empty promise?'

'There'll be no more empty promises, Lena,' he said. 'I'll love you for ever and I'll never leave again.'

*

Kit had been helpful. 'What would you like me to wear?' she had asked Maura.

'Oh, Kit, whatever you like. Whatever you think would be nice for later.'

'No, it's your day, you should have a say in it,' Kit had said. Maura's eyes had filled with tears. She tried to say something but the words wouldn't come. 'And Daddy's,' Kit had added. 'But men don't really notice things of importance. Tell me if there's anything I can do that would help to make it nice for you.'

'The fact that you are happy your father is marrying me makes it very nice for me,' Maura said, having found her voice at last.

'And Emmet too, Maura. It's just that he's hopeless at saying it.'

'A boy remembers a mother in a different way, I suppose.'

'No, that's not so, he was only nine when it happened. And anyway I was always the one who was closer to her. I understood her more, he was still a baby in many ways. He just saw her as "there's my mummy" ... He didn't know her as a person, as I did.'

'I hope she'd be pleased that Martin's marrying again. You see, I'm such a different person, it would be no question of trying to be a second Helen.'

'I'm sure she would,' Kit said.

Kit asked herself how was it that she was allowing a marriage to go ahead that was sinful. There was a bit in the service which asked if anyone knew any impediment to this couple being joined together. And when the priest asked this, Kit, who knew that her father had a living wife, would say nothing. She had after all asked Sister Madeleine, and Sister Madeleine had said to do what she thought was right.

It was a huge responsibility, but she would do it.

Kit settled into the College of Catering with great ease.

The very first week she met a girl called Frankie Barry with dancing eyes and a sense of rebellion. Frankie was going to go to America eventually and travel coast to coast, managing a hotel here and there along the way.

'Would we be able to do that, do you think?' Kit was doubtful.

'Certainly we will. Aren't we going to do the City and Guilds Exams? That's the highest qualification in the world,' said Frankie confidently.

Kit was pleased about this. There would be no fear of ending up jobless after two and a half years and having to go meekly into the Central Hotel and work with Philip's awful parents and maybe marry him just to keep everyone quiet.

Philip was enjoying the college too. He showed her proudly how he had sewed on his own name tapes. 'Aren't you the little treasure?' Kit had teased him. 'A prize for any girl.' But he had flushed and she felt ashamed. Wouldn't it be wonderful if he fancied Frankie. She tried to bring them together, but it didn't work. Frankie had a flat with two other girls, Philip lived in his uncle's house, Kit was in the hostel.

Dublin was filled with things to do. The problem was to choose. She arranged to go and meet Rita. Philip was waiting patiently for her after the lecture as she knew he would be.

'No, Philip. I have arranged to meet someone, honestly.'

'Who?'

'I beg your pardon?'

'I mean, is it anyone I know?' Philip realised that he had been too proprietorial.

'It is actually. It's Rita Moore.'

'Rita, your maid from Lough Glass?'

'Yes.' Kit didn't like the snobbish way he said it; it was very like his mother.

'I mean you're meeting her in a café ... and everything,' he said, astounded by the democracy of it all.

'No, of course not ... I'm going to sit down at a table and ask her to serve me and then eat on my own.'

'I only asked.'

'And you were told,' Kit said shortly.

Rita wanted all the news, and details of how Peggy the daily who came for a few hours was doing her job.

'Will Miss Hayes make any changes, do you think?'

'I hope so,' Kit said. 'I mean I'd like her to make it into her place, you know, not just moving into our place.'

'She's going to ask me to the wedding,' Rita said.

'I know. What are you going to wear?'

'I saw a suit in Clery's. It's the very thing. And I might get shoes to match. It's a sort of light green. What'll you wear yourself, Kit?'

'I don't know. Daddy gave me money to buy an outfit. I haven't seen anything I like yet.'

Next morning at the college Kit was told that there was a parcel for her.

When she saw that it was from London she took it to the ladies' cloakroom where, heart bearing like a hammer, she opened it. What could Lena Gray be doing now? What awful secret was there here that was going to upset them all?

She unpacked the grey and white silk dress in amazement and read the note. The dress didn't look like much, but that wasn't important; what was important was the note.

I thought you might like something to wear at the wedding. L.

She read it over and over.

What it meant was that she was giving her blessing to the wedding. Helen McMahon was saying that the marriage could go ahead and she would not interfere. Tears came down Kit's face, tears of pure relief.

She looked at the dress again. It was silk, maybe even pure silk. It must have cost a fortune. She would try it on tonight and then she would think of what she would write.

That is if she *did* write.

But you'd have to write to thank for something like this. Which was probably what Lena wanted.

Clio's hostel was near the university. There were girls from all over Ireland there, some of them from very posh families. Most of them had never heard of Lough Glass. Lots of them had been to boarding schools and knew each other. It wasn't as easy as Clio had thought to make friends. And it was the same at lectures. In some magical way other people seemed to know each other.

Clio found her first days at University College, Dublin much less fun than she had hoped they would be. For the first time in her life she was a little bit lonely. For the first time she realised she was a very small fish in a pond so big she couldn't even see the edges.

She cheered herself up with the thought that however bad it was for her it must be worse for Kit with all those awful hotel people from everywhere. And down at the other end of O'Connell Street, miles away from where all the action was.

Kit went out to supper with Philip O'Brien. She invited *him* and said it was her treat.

'What's this about?' Philip was suspicious.

'I want to talk to you properly and if I am your guest then I think you've invited me out, like asking someone out.'

'Well you're asking *me* out, isn't that the same?' he grumbled.

'You know it isn't,' Kit said firmly.

He was tall, Philip, and his freckles seemed to suit him more, his hair had stopped standing up at odd angles, he didn't have that slightly puzzled look he had as a youngster. He had a sense of humour. In most ways he was the perfect friend. Apart from one way, and that's what Kit wanted to talk about.

'I'm going to have spaghetti,' she said looking at the menu.

'It's probably tinned,' Philip said.

'Good. I loved tinned spaghetti. It's much easier to eat.'

'Don't let them hear you saying that in the training college. They'll think we're a couple of yahoos.'

'That's exactly what I wanted to talk to you about,' Kit said.

'What? Spaghetti?'

'No, the word you said, a couple of yahoos . . .'

'A lot of them are from Dublin or from big cities. They think everyone from a place like Lough Glass would be a yahoo.'

'I'm not talking about the word yahoo, it's the word *couple* that worried me.'

'It is what you call two people,' Philip was aggrieved.

'It's not what you call us. I have my whole life to live and things to worry about. I can't find myself sliding into a sort of pairing with you as well as everything else.'

'I don't see what's so terrible . . .' he began.

'It's not terrible, it's just something that has to be agreed between two people, not assumed by one and the other go along without thinking.'

'Will you be my girlfriend?' Philip asked.

'No, Philip.'

'Why?'

'Because I want to be me, I want to be without a boyfriend.'

'For ever?'

'No, not for ever, but until I meet one, and it might be you, and we both agree.'

'But you have met me.' Philip was very confused now.

'Philip, I'm your friend, not your girlfriend. And if you say *but you are a girl*, I'll stick my fork in your eyes.'

'I'll always want you as my girlfriend,' he said simply. 'You can go off with whoever you like, but I'll always be there for you in Lough Glass with the hotel, and maybe we might even get married.'

'Philip, you're eighteen. Nobody get's married at eighteen.' The waitress was standing there.

'People who love each other get married at eighteen,' Philip said, ignoring the girl poised with her little order book.

'They don't unless they're pregnant,' Kit said with spirit.

'We could get pregnant. That would be a great idea,' Philip said.

'Jesus!' said the waitress. 'I'll come back when you've something less dramatic on your mind, like what you're going to have for your supper.'

'Are they a terrible crowd of hicks down there?' Clio asked. She and Kit were having coffee in Grafton Street.

'Stop talking about down there. It would take me less time to walk to my college than you to yours.'

'Yeah, but what are they like?'

'Very nice mainly. It's quite hard work. You have to concentrate a bit, but I suppose I'll get the hang of it.'

'And what will you do in the end, I mean where will it take you?'

'Christ, how do I know, Clio? I've only been in it a week. How about you? Where's B.A. going to take you?'

'Aunt Maura said it's a great basis for meeting people.'

'Maura says she never said that.'

'I wish you wouldn't talk to her behind my back about things I told you. She *is* my aunt you know.'

'And she's going to be my stepmother.' They both laughed. They were squabbling like they did when they were seven years of age.

'Maybe we'll always go on like this,' Clio said.

'Oh yes. When we're old ladies holidaying in the south of France, fighting about our deck chairs in the sun and our poodles,' Kit agreed.

'You getting away from Philip O'Brien, crotchety old owner of the Central Hotel.'

'Why don't you see me as the owner of a string of hotels of my own?'

'It's not what women do,' Clio said.

'And what about you? Will you have married some suitable fellow from First Arts?'

'God no. There's no one suitable there. I'll be looking amongst the lawyers and the medics.'

'A doctor's wife? Clio, you'd never have the patience. Look at what your mother has to put up with.'

'A *surgeon*'s wife, a *specialist*'s wife ... I'm planning this properly,' Clio said. Then she asked, 'What are you wearing anyway?'

'A sort of grey and white dress,' Kit said.

'What material?'

'Silk, sort of silk.'

'No! Where did you get it?'

'In a small shop on a side street.' Kit was evasive.

'You're not exactly killing yourself then, are you?'

'It's quite nice. It looks weddingy.' Kit defended the dress.

'Grey and white, it sounds like a postulant nun to me.'

'Well, let's wait and see, will we?'

'Does it feel funny your father getting married again?' Anna Kelly asked Emmet as they met at the sweet counter of Dillon's grocery.

'What do you mean funny?' Emmet asked. Anna was pretty. She had blonde curly hair and a gorgeous smile. They were going to be sort of related after the wedding.

'Well, will you call her Mummy?' Anna wanted to know.

'Lord no. We call her Maura already.'

'And will she sleep in your father's room or your mother's room?' Anna wanted to know all the details.

'I don't know. I didn't ask. Daddy's, I suppose. That's what married people do.'

'Why didn't your mother then?'

'She had a cold, she didn't want to give it to Daddy.'

'A cold? The whole time?'

'That's what I was told,' Emmet said. He spoke without guile.

Something changed in Anna. 'Yes, well, some people do,' she agreed, and companionably they discussed the relative merits of Cleeves toffees, which were flatter, and Scots Clan, which were more chunky but dearer.

Mrs Dillon watched them. At least these two didn't look likely to pocket half the display when no one was looking, but you couldn't be too careful.

Maura hadn't wanted an engagement ring. 'We're too mature for that,' she said to Martin.

'We're not old, don't say that.'

'I didn't say old, I meant we didn't have to get engaged ... We had an understanding in the real sense of the word.'

'I don't know how you waited so long and were so understanding when I was such a ditherer,' Martin said.

'Shush, we've been through that before. You had much more to sort out than I did.' Maura could afford to be generous now she told herself. Her months and months of coping with Martin's indecision were over. He was now deeply committed to their marriage. He would make it work, he would make her happy. He knew these things were possible. And as for Maura herself, she could hardly believe her good fortune in having chased the ghost of the beautiful, restless-looking woman who was her predecessor. Martin and Maura could walk by the lake of an autumn evening now without pausing, stricken, to remember that this was where Helen's life had ended.

'I want the wedding day to be the best day in the world for you.'

'It will,' Maura said.

'Then let me get you some jewel if you won't have a diamond

engagement ring. I want you to have more than a plain wedding ring. Would you like a diamond brooch, do you think?' His face was eager to please her.

'No, my love. Truly.'

'There are jewels of Helen's in a box. You know that. Suppose I were to bring them to a jeweller in the town and ask him to make something completely different, then you wouldn't worry about cost.' He was able to speak of Helen naturally now, without his face contorting.

'No, Martin. Those belong to Kit. She must have them some day. When she's twenty-one, maybe. Three years' time. You must give them to her. She should wear them with pleasure. Don't have them altered for me. I have enough.'

'They're all there somewhere. I never even looked at them.'

'Fine. Let's leave them for Kit's twenty-first.' Maura had looked at them, though. She had fingered them sadly. A marcasite brooch, a locket, a diamante clip, a pair of earrings that might have been real rubies and might not.

But mostly she had noticed two rings, an engagement ring and a wedding ring. Helen McMahon had not taken those with her on the night she went out in the boat on the lake. Maura wondered whether Sergeant Sean O'Connor or the detectives from Dublin had enquired about that at the time. It surely must have been a pointer to the state of mind of someone, who might have been thought to end their own life, if they had carefully removed valuable jewellery and left it behind.

'Are you asking Stevie Sullivan to the wedding?' Clio asked her Aunt Maura.

'No. There was a lot of debate about that. He is my future boss, that would mean a yes, but then think of his mother and that means a no. And he is a neighbour but think of his terrible little brother.'

'He is a single man and quite good looking,' Clio added.

'Yes, but he also has a reputation for disappearing from public functions with young ladies in tow.' Maura knew the whole world of Lough Glass now. 'Martin and I added it up and it came out against asking him.'

'Imagine you working for him, Aunt Maura. He came from nothing.'

'Imagine you using an expression like that ... a young girl like you.' Maura's eyes were cold. Clio realised too late that she often misjudged her aunt. Aunt Maura didn't have the same cosy, gossipy way of looking at the world as her own mother did. There was very little gossip, and absolutely no feeling that some people were acceptable and some were not.

The week before the wedding gifts poured into the chemist's shop. And even more important for Maura and Martin were the accompanying notes wishing them well. People said that it was good to see two such nice people finding happiness. Maura was a known visitor to the town in recent years, and as a child had grown up only a few miles away. It wasn't as if Martin McMahon was looking outside for a stranger.

As he had before.

Mona from the post office gave some Belleek china. She said she thought there was something gracious about it which would suit the new Mrs McMahon. Mildred O'Brien chose a small set of silver coffee spoons. The Walls sent a glass bonbon dish with a silver handle. The Hickeys, who had been intending to send meat as they always did if the event was being held in Lough Glass, stirred themselves and sent something which looked suspiciously like a pram rug.

Paddles sent four bottles of brandy and four bottles of whiskey, on the grounds that the groom and the bride's brother-in-law would consume that amount easily in any given year. There was an embroidered sampler from Mother Bernard and the community, a history of the county from Brother Healy and the Brothers' school, a set of saucepans from Mrs Hickey in the drapery and from Sister Madeleine a great clump of white heather and a tub to plant it in. She said that, although it was superstitious to believe that white heather was lucky, at least it might be nice to have this as a symbol of their marriage, and that when it grew every year it would remind them of their good fortune in coming together.

Kit looked at the heather thoughtfully. Sister Madeleine knew that this was not a marriage in the eyes of God and yet she was going along with it.

Sometimes Kit felt the world was tilting.

*

'You never tell me anything about Lough Glass,' Louis said to Lena on Saturday morning.

'I used to, my love, but you said it was very trivial.'

'Well, some of it was ... you know, the petty things ... but I'm not totally insensitive. I know you must think about the children and about Martin.'

'From time to time,' Lena agreed.

'Well, don't shut me out ... I mean, I am interested in everything that concerns you. I do love you.' He sounded defensive.

'I know.'

'How do you know?' He seemed to doubt the rather flat tone of voice.

'I know because you came back,' she said. Again it was as if she was saying something by rote. In fact she was repeating his own words to her. *Why would I come back to you if I didn't love you?*

'Well that's all right then.' But Louis was watchful. Lena didn't seem herself this morning.

'What do you think the place is like now?'

Lena looked at him for a long moment. She debated for a wild moment whether to tell him that her husband was marrying Maura Hayes at 11 a.m. and that she had spent a week's salary on a dress for her daughter Kit to wear at the ceremony. She wondered was it possible that, if she were to fill him in on the important areas of her own life, he would be able to feel involved with her to such a degree that he could put aside all the many distractions of his world. But the moment ended. She knew it would not be possible. She would not get the reaction she hoped for. Instead, she would get blame and recrimination for having hidden the fact that she had written to her daughter for years and then met the girl in London.

'Oh, I expect it will be like any other day,' she said. 'Any ordinary Saturday in Lough Glass.'

*

Stevie Sullivan said since he'd be in Dublin anyway he'd drive the bride to the church, and drive them both to the reception.

'We can't accept that Stevie . . .' Martin began to protest.

'Jesus, Martin, isn't it a grand easy wedding present. Let me do it for you.'

Stevie was a handsome young man now of twenty-one, with his long dark hair falling over his eyes and his tanned skin. When Stevie was a boy he had often heard part of his father's drunken rages include the possibility that his mother had lain down with the tinkers . . . how else could she have produced such an unlikely looking son for him. Stevie had heard her reply that since it had been such a hellish thing to have to lie down for her husband she was unlikely to repeat the experience with anyone else, tinker or no tinker. His own experience of sex had made him think that his mother must have missed out a lot on life if this had been her attitude. But it was a view he kept to himself.

'Anyway, you can rely on me, Maura. You wouldn't want to be having any truck with these Dublin fellows.'

She was grateful. It would be good to have a friendly face beside her as she set off to the church. She had packed the possessions that she needed from her flat in Dublin and brought them in advance to Lough Glass. The flat had been painted and let to a young couple who had already moved in. Maura had hoped that in the future Kit and Clio might be able to share the flat. It would be handy for them; it had two bedrooms, it was central. But she thought that they might not be temperamentally suited to sharing a flat. There was an edge between them that did not suggest a real friendship, more a wishing to score off each other. She wouldn't suggest the idea until they had made up their minds more about life.

Stevie wore a dark suit, that could almost have been a uniform, when he came to the hotel to collect Maura.

'You look lovely, Maura,' he said.

He was the first to see her and, even though he was little more than a child, still she was pleased. A flush came over her face and neck. 'Thank you Stevie.'

'I'm pleased to see my staff know how to kit themselves out,' he said.

Kit and Clio stood side by side in the big church.

Clio hadn't ceased to gripe about the dress since she arrived. '*What* kind of a shop did you say it was, that shop?'

'Oh I told you, in a side street.'

'You're lying in your teeth.'

'Why would I lie?'

'Because that's the way you're made.'

'Ask anyone. Ask Daddy. Ask Maura.'

'You lied to them too. This is a really good smart dress. It cost a fortune. Did you steal it?'

'You have a very diseased mind. Will you shut up and let me enjoy my father's wedding.'

At that moment they saw the small congregation turning around. Maura Hayes was walking up the church with her brother. Martin McMahon stood beaming at the altar rails.

'She looks great,' Clio whispered. 'That's a terrific outfit.'

'She probably stole it. Most of us did,' Kit said loftily.

Stevie was outside the church holding open the door of the car. 'I didn't know he was coming,' Philip said to Clio.

'Oh, he gets anywhere,' Clio said. 'If you have a brass neck and flash good looks like that, the world is open to you.'

Philip seemed disappointed by this. 'Is that his car?' he asked.

'Yes,' Clio still sounded scornful. 'Part of the Sullivan Motor Service is to realise that there will be times in people's lives, functions, when they'll need a bit of class. Stevie's ahead of the game.'

'Do women like him?'

'Yes, but only in a very obvious kind of way. I mean, I personally wouldn't touch him with a barge pole. He's been with every maid and skivvy from here to Lough Glass and back.'

'Slept with them, you mean?' Philip's eyes were round.

'So I hear.'

'And none of them got ... um ... pregnant?'

'Apparently not. Or if they did, we didn't hear.'

Maura had chosen the hotel well. There was a sherry reception in a big bright room with chintzy covered couches and chairs. The waitresses moved around efficiently, making sure that glasses were well filled. When they went in to sit down the late autumn sun was slanting in the windows on the group.

The seating plan had been carefully thought out. Kit and Emmet sat on either side of Rita. The O'Briens were divided up so that they could not glare at each other. Lilian Kelly was put beside two of Maura's work colleagues so that she could talk about shops in Dublin and the races.

There was a grapefruit cocktail, then chicken and ham, and ice cream with hot chocolate sauce. The wedding cake was small, one tier.

'There won't be any need to keep a tier for the christening,' Mildred O'Brien explained to her neighbour who nodded, bewildered.

The speeches were very simple. Peter Kelly said how this was the happiest day for a long time. And how great it was that his good friend had found a partner for the rest of his life. Everyone clapped.

Martin thanked everyone for their support in coming to wish them well. He said it was particularly gratifying that Maura had so many friends already in Lough Glass, and it would in many senses for her be like coming home. They thought the speeches were over but Maura McMahon stood up. A little ripple went through the group. Women so rarely spoke in public. Brides never.

'I would like to add my thanks to Martin, and to say this is the happiest day of my life. But I want to thank most of all Kit and Emmet McMahon for their generosity in sharing their father with me. They are the children of Martin and Helen, they will always be that. I hope the memory of their mother will never fade. For them or for any of us. Without Helen McMahon Kit and Emmet would not have existed. Without Helen, Martin would not have known his years of happiness in a first marriage, I thank her for all she gave to us, I hope her spirit knows what a feeling of warmth there is towards her this day. And I assure you all that I will do my very best to make Martin as happy as he deserves to be. He is a truly good man.'

There was a silence as people took in the depth of feeling in her words. Then they clapped and clapped and raised their glasses. And the pianist in the corner began to tinkle so that a few songs could be called for. Maura had checked. There had been no singing at Martin and Helen's wedding.

Stevie Sullivan stood outside the door. Maura had not changed her outfit. The wedding dress and jacket were quite suitable for travelling. The cases were packed and had been put in the back of the car.

'You're looking fairly irresistible, Kit,' Stevie said.

'Better resist me, though,' Kit said. 'I believe you're taking them to the train.'

'That's not what I heard,' he said.

'But aren't you going to take them off to start their honeymoon?'

'Right in one.'

'So?'

'So, it's not the station, it's the airport.'

'The *airport*?' Kit had thought they were going to Galway.

'They're going to London,' Stevie said. 'Didn't they tell you?'

7

Ivy could hardly believe it when she saw the letter with the Irish stamp and the foreign-looking postmark that nobody could read. She twitched her curtain as Lena ran downstairs on her way to work.

Lena scarcely dared to hope. She sat down in Ivy's kitchen and read it. It was one page. It had no beginning, no greeting. But then neither had her note to Kit.

Thank you very much for the beautiful dress. It looked very well and was much admired. It arrived at the college over a week ago but I waited until now to write.

So that I could tell you the ceremony has taken place. It all went very well and they have gone to London today. I thought it was Galway that they were going to, but apparently it's the Regent Palace Hotel, London.

I know London is a huge city but I thought you would want to know. Just in case.

Once more, thank you for the dress.

Kit

Lena sat holding the letter.

'Is it bad news?' Ivy asked.

'No. Not bad news, no.'

'Well, is she speaking to you?'

'No, not really speaking to me. Not yet, no.'

'Oh come on, Lena. Don't make me beg . . . What is it?'

'It's a sort of contact, sort of warning me of something . . . but I haven't told you the whole background. Can I do that some long, lonely evening?'

'There'll be plenty of those ahead of us,' Ivy agreed.

When she got to the agency she found Jessie Park waiting in her office for her. Jessie was a changed person to the tired, flustered woman in the cardigan that Lena had discovered the first day. Now a trim short woman of forty-seven, Jessie exuded confidence. Her mother played racing demon with the other tenants in the sheltered accommodation and seemed to have forgotten her digestive problems.

They had set the date; they were going to have a small wedding. Just eight people to sit down to a lunch in a hotel. Could Lena be one of the witnesses? Jim Millar's brother would be the other. And they would love

Lena's Louis to come as a guest to the wedding of course. Lena embraced her and said how happy she was. She very much hoped that Louis would be free. His hours were difficult. She said all the right things. But her mind was far away.

She was breathing up a prayer of thanks to Kit for having warned her about Martin and Maura being in London. Suppose for example that Jessie's wedding lunch had been in the Regent Palace Hotel? There had been stranger coincidences. To be forewarned was very useful indeed.

She knew that Louis wouldn't want to go to the wedding.

'Darling heart, don't I get enough of this every day at work?' he said smiling at her despairingly and holding his hands out as if to show that it was raining weddings on him every time he moved.

The Dryden did a very scant wedding business indeed. But Lena didn't make an issue out of it. 'I know. Just to let you know that you're welcome and they'd love if you could get away. That's all.'

'Can you get me out of it?' He seemed pleased.

'Easily,' she said.

She saw the little tension lines around his eyes relax. Perhaps Louis Gray didn't like the idea of going to weddings with her, watching other people making promises for a future together. And Louis was in such good form these days, so light-hearted and happy. It would be ludicrous to make a fuss over his attending the function. It would of its very nature be as dry as dust. Louis would hate it.

Because she hadn't forced him or complained, he was even more loving than ever. And he called unexpectedly at the office one day with a bottle of champagne for the happy couple.

'I'm so sorry I can't be there,' he said. There was a real regret in his eyes and voice.

Lena listened to him and even she felt that there were ways in which Louis Gray *was* sorry he wouldn't be attending.

Jim Millar and Jessie Park were of course delighted with him. 'He's a great man, that husband of yours. I'm sure he's a top businessman,' Jim Millar said.

'I think they value him a lot at the Dryden,' Lena agreed.

'I'm surprised he doesn't run his own hotel,' Jessie said.

'He may one day,' Lena said. But she didn't think that far ahead. She had discovered that you got by better taking life in short bursts.

She dressed in front of Louis. He lay making admiring sounds from the bed. It was one of his late mornings.

'You're far too glamorous for that crowd,' he said. 'Let's you and me go off somewhere and dazzle the world.'

'I'll see you later,' she blew him a kiss.

'Come home sober,' he called after her.

'I think that's fairly likely,' she laughed.

The wedding luncheon ended nice and early as everyone had known it would. Mrs Park was brought back to her new friends; Jessie and Jim caught the train for St Ives. They were going back to Cornwall, where their romance had begun. Lena assured them she had many things to do.

Without her realising it, her feet took her towards the Regent Palace. She stopped and studied hard her appearance in a shop window mirror. She was wearing a cream-coloured suit with lilac trim. Her hat was in velvet to match the trim. She had a large black bag, black gloves and very high heeled court shoes. She wore a fair amount of well-applied make-up. Surely she could not look like the woman in the dirndl skirts and loose flowing dresses that they had known years ago.

Her eyes might give her away. People often recognised others by the eyes alone. She stopped in Boots and bought a pair of sunglasses. 'Not much call for those these days,' said the young girl selling them.

'I'm going to rob a bank,' Lena explained.

'Want anyone to help you carry it all away?' the girl said. Louis was right about the English. They were dying to talk; it was just that they needed someone to start them off.

Lena studied herself in the sunglasses. That was just the trick. She positioned herself in the lounge of the Regent Palace. She had no other plans for the rest of the day, she would wait here until she saw them going in or coming out.

James Williams couldn't believe it. He had thought that the well-dressed woman in sunglasses was Louis Gray's wife. There weren't many with that hair and those legs. But what on earth was she doing sitting in the foyer of a huge hotel like this? It was almost as if she were waiting to pick someone up. But perhaps she was just waiting to meet that handsome, if feckless, husband.

James Williams wondered whether Mrs Gray had any idea of her husband's popularity with the ladies. He declined to listen to whispers in his own hotel, thinking it beneath him. But he would have to be deaf not to have known that Louis Gray had gone off with some rich, spoiled young American to Paris not long ago. Possibly Mrs Gray put up with it.

He looked over at the elegant figure sitting in front of a drink, which she was studying through sunglasses. Perhaps she might even be here consoling herself. It was an attractive thought, but James Williams had a meeting in one of the conference rooms.

When he came down through the hall again he saw she was still there. 'What's the lady drinking?' he asked a waiter.

'She's refused other drinks that were offered.'

'She won't from me, I know her.' He learned it was gin and orange. He ordered one for both of them and just as the tray arrived he appeared at her table. '*Really*, Mr Williams,' she said.

'*Really*, Mrs Gray.' It was always their joke to be so formal.

'Were you waiting here by any chance hoping I'd turn up?' He was playful, flattering, flirtatious.

'No, I'm sorry to disappoint you. I just came in to take the weight off my feet,' she said.

'Just came in? Wasn't I lucky!'

'Just this minute,' Lena Gray said. He looked at her with interest. She had been in this lounge for over two hours. What on earth was making her lie to him like this?

They talked away, Lena and James, about the world in general and hotels in particular. At no stage did either of them mention Louis Gray, who was the only person they had in common. They had another round and another.

Three gins and oranges with him, and perhaps more before he arrived. James was wondering if by the most amazing good fortune he had got lucky with this attractive Irishwoman. Her voice was not slurred. He couldn't see her eyes because of the ridiculous glasses, but she said she had an eye infection and needed to wear them. He thought there was something a little odd and lightheaded about her behaviour, and at one stage she stood up and excused herself very suddenly. She didn't go to the ladies' as he expected, she went instead to stand by the gates of the lift. She stood quite near a middle-aged couple who were carrying a lot of shopping - typical out-of-town tourists and shoppers. If it hadn't been so ridiculous James Williams would have thought that the elegant Lena Gray had gone over to eavesdrop what they were saying.

It was five years since she had seen them. Her head was slightly dizzy. She must remember this moment.

Martin was still in a bulky suit. It looked new, this one, but it had not been made by a tailor. He was forty-five, a year older than Louis, but he could have been ten or fifteen years older. His stance was the same, slightly stooped. His good natured smile was there. His arms were full of bags, from British Home Stores, C & A, and even Liberty's. Was anything different? He looked happy, he looked like he used to when he had been playing with the children or had pushed the boat out on the lake. He looked less anxious to please.

And Maura Hayes. Maura, whom she hated to meet because she was the jovial sister of Lilian, the woman who made it very difficult to refuse an invitation. Was she older or younger than Lilian? Had she been told? Had she ever listened? She looked flushed and happy.

'I'd love a cup of tea,' Lena heard her say. 'Is that a real country hick thing to want?'

'And this from the city sophisticate working in Dublin all those years?' he said laughing. 'But I imagine that they'll have no difficulty in bringing a tray to the room.'

'Do you think so?' She looked as if all her problems had been solved at a stroke.

'This isn't the Central Hotel in Lough Glass, you know,' he said.

She was so near she could touch them, the ghost of the wife they had thought was dead. Her appearance would destroy so many lives. Filled with the self-pity that gin can often bring, Lena started to weep. Perhaps it would have been better if she had died in the lake that night.

She looked flushed when she came back. James Williams leaned across the table. 'If you're in no hurry home . . . ?' he asked. His tone was polite, it was not remotely like a proposition.

'If I'm not, Mr Williams . . . ?'

'Then I was wondering what we might do . . .' He was walking on eggshells now; her voice had got shaky, there seemed to be glistening tears on her face.

'I was wondering if you might like me to give you a lift in a taxi . . . perhaps?'

'To where?'

'To wherever you'd like to go next. Somewhere for another drink possibly? A bite to eat? Home to your doorstep? To the Dryden Hotel?'

'Anywhere you say.' She took off her glasses and looked at him. She had been crying, but her eyes did not look infected. She was very upset. 'You're a very intelligent man, James Williams, very smooth, very polished. I'm no match for you. I think I'm so capable and in control, but I'm only a poor country hick. That's the word I heard two people using a few minutes ago. That's what I am, a hick.'

'No. No,' he protested. 'Please tell me. What can I offer you?'

'A chance to go now while I still have two legs to carry me to the door,' she said.

She put on her sunglasses. She was a very attractive woman. If ever he saw anyone who needed a strong shoulder to cry on over something it was Lena Gray.

After she had cried she would feel grateful to him. He considered it for a moment. But only a moment. 'Off we go then, I'll find you a taxi.' His hand lightly on her arm he steered her out into the traffic of Piccadilly Circus.

'I see you didn't take my advice,' Louis said as Lena stumbled in the door.

'What advice wash that?' Lena couldn't get the words out.

'I thought I said you should stay sober, and you said there was no question but that you would.' He looked at her quizzically.

She had flung off her shoes and her hat was at an awkward angle on her head. 'Yesh,' she smiled at him. 'That's what I thought. But I wash wrong.'

'You're a sweetheart,' he said. And peeled off her good suit, hung it carefully on a hanger and steered her to bed.

Twice in the night she got up to be sick.

If Louis heard he made no sound. He lay breathing gently. He never dreamed, or at least he couldn't remember his dreams. A man who had so much to remember, why did none of it come out in dreams?

Lena had dreamed incessantly of James Williams and what might have happened if she had accepted the offer he was so definitely making. She shuddered to think she had been so near to saying yes.

Louis was on an early shift. 'I didn't wake you,' he wrote in a note. 'Your lovely little snores sounded as if they deserved to be allowed to continue. See you tonight.'

She had never felt worse. *Why* did people drink too much if this is how it left them feeling next morning? She wasn't at all sure that she could make the office.

She called in on Ivy.

'How did the wedding go?' Ivy said, pouring coffee.

'They seemed to be happy, buying lots of stuff in Oxford Street and going back to the hotel to have tea served in the bedroom.'

'You went on their honeymoon with them?' Ivy asked, shocked.

'No, that was something else. Ivy, do you think I should have something like a prairie oyster?'

'A what?'

'It's to cure a hangover.'

'What is it?'

'You're the one with the contacts in the pub.'

'Not any more,' Ivy said.

'Well, I need to know. Would Ernest know?'

'I expect he would.'

'What's his number?'

'Lena, you're mad. It's only nine-thirty in the morning.'

'Yes, I'm half an hour late for work already. I can't go in like this or I'd collapse. Give me his home number or I'll ring directory enquiries.'

'I've always said you're *mad*.'

'Hello Ernest, it's Lena Gray.'

'Yes?' he sounded cautious.

'You do remember me?'

'Well, yes.'

'Ernest, very simply, what's a prairie oyster? It's got something to do with raw eggs and nothing to do with oysters, am I right?'

'A raw egg in a glass, a tablespoon of sherry, some Lea and Perrins, shake like mad and swallow in one.'

'Thank you, Ernest.'

'Have you got all the ingredients?'

'Yes, I think so. Thanks.'

'Will she be all right, do you think?'

'Who?'

'Ivy. I presume she's been over-indulging.'

Lena paused for a moment. Perhaps this was a way to get Ivy back with Ernest. 'I do hope so, Ernest. She doesn't tell you, but it's all hitting her very badly.'

'Could you – um – tell her . . . ?'

'Yes?'

'Tell her . . . to take care.'

'Maybe *you* should tell her yourself, Ernest.'

'It's difficult.'

'No, it's not. These things are easy.'

'But she's always pissed drunk.'

'No, she's not, last night was special. It was some kind of anniversary between you both. I don't know exactly. But whatever it was it hit her hard.' Lena hardly dared to lift her eyes to meet Ivy's.

'Yeah well, it's about this time of year that she and I . . . But you don't want to bother.'

'It's none of my business. All I know is that she won't hear a word against you, Ernest. I have tried, God help me I've tried to say a few, but she won't listen.'

'You're a very good friend, Lena. Even with you being Irish and not understanding any of our ways,' he said.

'Thank you, Ernest,' she said humbly and hung up.

'I'll kill you here and now in my own kitchen,' Ivy said.

'No, get two eggs, sherry, worcester sauce, and a saucer to put on top of the glass.'

'Why?'

'So that it won't all fall out when I shake it.'

'No, I mean why should I do any of this for you?'

'Because I think I may have saved your great romance for you. Hurry, Ivy. I might be about to die.'

'Was it a great wedding?' Dawn asked.

'Simply lovely,' Lena said.

'I was hoping I might be asked.'

'There were very few of us there. Honestly, it was only a handful.'

'Was your husband there, Mrs Gray?'

'No. Louis wasn't able to go, sadly.'

Dawn went back to her work.

Lena looked over at her blonde head bent over the papers at her desk. Dawn was a spectacular looking girl. Lena and Jessie had arranged that she take public speaking lessons and it had been a wise investment. Now Dawn could stand up in front of any gathering of school leavers. Lena knew that the students would listen to the words that came from a slim young glamour girl only a few years older than themselves. If Dawn talked about the need to get good typing speeds, exact shorthand symbols and office routine then they would accept it. Such advice coming from Jessie or herself would carry little weight.

Lena felt her head heavy and she had an inexplicable thirst. She must have drunk six glasses of water by lunchtime. Is this the way all heavy drinkers felt? The regulars in Paddles' and Foley's back in Lough Glass? The regulars in Ernest's bar? Did they all have to rehydrate themselves the next morning? What a pointless exercise it was. She would never get drunk again.

'Ernest is coming around tonight,' Ivy said.

'Great stuff. Have you said "Thank you, Lena"?'

'No, I haven't. I've said I wonder why I am now cast in the role of a screaming alcoholic.'

'You could be a reformed alcoholic. Men love that,' Lena suggested.

'I'm actually pleased,' Ivy said.

'I know you are.'

'But I don't want to put too much hope in it.'

'No, of course not.' Lena lay down on her bed and drifted off to sleep.

When she woke Louis was standing beside her. 'How's my poor drunk?' he said, full of sympathy and love.

'I'm so sorry Louis, was I disgusting?'

'No, you were sweet, you were like a floppy bunny. You couldn't sit or stand or anything...' He handed her a cup of tea which she drank thirstily.

'And what was I saying?' She was ninety per cent sure she hadn't mentioned the Regent Palace Hotel, the journey to spy on the newly married couple.

'Nothing too intelligible, great difficulty in pronouncing words with an S in them.' He stroked her forehead. 'More tea, then I'll scramble you some eggs ... that's all you'll be able for. Trust Uncle Louis.'

Lena closed her eyes. How strange it all was. Here she was lying in bed while Louis Gray got her a cup of tea. A couple of miles away Maura Hayes was lying in bed while Martin also arranged for tea to be served.

Lena let her mind wander back to the way they looked ... Martin and Maura. At ease with each other, that was definite, like people who had been friends and loved each other for years and had only just realised it. Martin wasn't straining and struggling to please her as he would have been with Helen. Maura was making no effort to concentrate.

They were well matched.

Lena wondered whether there was any passion between them. There must be some sexual love. They would hardly enter into a relationship unless they had planned to consummate it.

But she found herself unable to imagine it.

She could hardly remember her own coupling with Martin. Sex had always meant Louis, from the very first time she had known him and known he was for her. It didn't make her uneasy, thinking about Martin and Maura making love on their London honeymoon, nor about Maura sleeping beside Martin in the bedroom that Helen McMahon had abandoned early in their marriage.

It was just that she couldn't imagine it at all.

Jessie and Jim came back from their honeymoon. They were anxious that the wedding party had been a success.

'I think everyone enjoyed it,' Jessie said.

'Oh yes, it was wonderful,' Lena assured her.

'My brother didn't say much about it, but then he's a silent man,' said Jim Millar.

This was an understatement. He had been almost wordless through the ceremony and the lunch that followed it.

'My mother enjoyed it, though?' Jessie was hoping it had been the great social event that she wanted to remember it as.

'It was a wonderful day,' Lena said. 'A marvellous happy occasion. We won't ever forget it.'

She was rewarded by the relief and pleasure in Jessie's eyes, and in Jim's when she looked at him triumphantly.

The truth was that Lena had hardly any memory whatsoever of anything that day except standing beside Martin and Maura as they waited to go upstairs.

Ivy grumbled from time to time that Ernest had taken a very strong stance about things like sherry trifle. He said it could be the beginning of the slippery slope. But it seemed a small price to pay to have him back in her life.

He called regularly. Sometimes Lena spoke to him. 'I owe you a great debt of gratitude,' he said once conspiratorially. 'I always thought that Ivy was a woman who could take care of herself, run her own life. I never knew she'd gone to pieces.'

*

The months passed in Lough Glass as they did everywhere else, and people were so accustomed to seeing Martin McMahon and his wife Maura walking together exchanging affectionate smiles that the memory of Helen had faded from the forefront of every mind.

'She's a lot dumpier than her predecessor,' Mildred O'Brien said, looking out the hotel window at the McMahons striding along with Rusty, their red setter puppy. Mildred had never liked Helen when she was alive, but she didn't seem to be pleased either with the second Mrs McMahon.

Dan sighed. 'She doesn't have Helen's way with her, that's true,' he said, thinking back wistfully on the slow swish of Helen McMahon's skirt as she walked down the lane behind the hotel, her hair tumbling down her back, her eyes restless.

Maura went from time to time to see Sister Madeleine. Once she brought a pane of glass and some putty. 'At least you won't give this away,' she said, knocking out the broken window with a hammer and collecting the shattered glass on old newspapers.

'Don't be too sure of it. There are plenty of people worse off than I am,' said the hermit.

'This is the first window I've ever put in. You wouldn't destroy my faith in myself by taking it out to give to some ne'er do well.'

'You sound very happy, Maura.'

'I am, thank God, very happy indeed. And what's more, I'm blessed in those two children.'

'You wouldn't be if you weren't so good to them.'

'I was wondering . . .' Maura lined the window frame with the putty as she spoke. 'I was wondering whether you'd put my mind at rest over something . . .'

'My own mind is so confused, Maura, I'm never one to set myself up as an adviser to other people's minds.'

'It's just, you know, dreams, and superstitions, and sort of thinking you see things . . .'

'Go on.'

'Would that be real at all, or would it be just from being over tired?'

'Would you tell me a bit more and maybe I'd know the drift.'

'It sounds very silly.'

'Things always do.' Madeleine went to the fire to move in the old black kettle over the flames.

Maura eased the glass into place. 'There now, isn't that a dream,' she said, standing back to admire the slightly crooked window, which was a great deal better than the cracked frame with several pieces out of it which had been there before.

'It's beautiful, Maura. Thank you from the bottom of my heart,' said Sister Madeleine, looking at it with admiration.

'I've put in an extra bit of putty at the top, where there was a bit of a gap on the top corner. I don't think you'd see it.' Maura bit her lip looking at it.

'I only see a lovely clean shiny window keeping out the wind and rain. Thank you again, Maura.' The tea was poured. 'And what did you see or dream that disturbed you.'

'It's so odd. But it was when we were in London . . . A woman came and stood beside us, just as close as I am to you.'

'Yes?'

'And I was absolutely sure it was Helen.'

They were having dinner at the golf club as they did every Saturday. It was such an easy foursome and sometimes they were joined by other couples. The talk turned to the hermit.

'She won't let me listen to her chest,' Peter Kelly said. 'I don't think she has any truck with modern medicine; you have to be a mystic or a gypsy for her to take any notice.'

'She's warm enough in there, the place is quite snug,' Maura said.

'Ah yes, it's warm all right, but what's she inhaling? Turf smoke, and her bedding could be damp. Still, you might as well be talking to the wall, she was always full of cracked notions. She'll live and die by them.'

'I tried to give her a preparation for chilblains last year and she thanked me and said they'd go in their own time.' Martin shook his head about her.

'But I think she's fairly sound in her own head,' Maura said.

'She certainly cured Emmet's stutter,' Martin agreed.

'And she calmed Clio down when she was behaving like someone bound for the gallows,' Lilian added.

'She doesn't encourage foolish fantasies. She's as practical as Mother Bernard in many ways,' Maura said.

They talked about Mother Bernard and her drive to build a new wing on the convent; her fundraising activities had Lough Glass demented.

Maura's mind wandered away from the conversation.

She thought of the way the nun had been so adamant it couldn't have been Helen McMahon she had seen in London. What it undoubtedly must be was the imagination playing tricks. Like a tree can take on the image of a dangerous bogey man if you're frightened, like a shadow on the window pane can look like an intruder rather than a branch waving. So it was when Maura had been thinking of Helen she would automatically think any woman of the same age and size might be she.

'I wasn't thinking about her, you see,' Maura had countered.

'How was she dressed?'

'She had dark glasses and a little hat. Purple feathers. It was *so* like her, Sister Madeleine.' The nun threw back her head and laughed away Maura's anxieties. 'Well now, don't you believe me?'

'Helen McMahon in sunglasses? Indoors? And in a hat? In all the years I saw her here she never wore a hat . . .'

'But suppose . . .'

'You see, even though you weren't thinking of her consciously, you must have been on another level. That's why you transposed her features on to a totally different stranger standing beside you.' Sister Madeleine had beamed at the obvious explanation.

And of course Maura knew she must be right.

*

They learned a lot in the catering college, but there was still some free time. Often Kit went to the cinema with Frankie, who was always planning some devilment and great at negotiating late passes from the hostel for her friend Kit.

Frankie was cheerful and casual. She didn't have the hothouse intensity of Clio, nor did she criticise with such outrage if Kit didn't do exactly what she wanted. She invited Kit for a weekend to Cork to stay with her family. Kit would love to have gone but it was at the end of the month and she had spent most of her allowance. She didn't have the train fare. Frankie shrugged. Another time. It was a relief. Kit thought of all the cross questioning and analysis that she would have got from Clio.

There were some parties in flats, some of them marvellous with people singing and laughing way into the night, some of them messy evenings that shouldn't have been parties at all because they were just excuses for groping. Kit and Frankie thought that it was badly behaved to go in search of groping to a public place. This was a private matter, they said, and clucked at each other pretending to be nuns until they fell about laughing.

'What do you do all the time? I never see you,' Clio complained. Kit tried to explain but nothing she said met with any approval. 'It sounds awful,' Clio said dismissively.

'Then you're just as well out of it.' Kit was unconcerned. 'But I would like to meet you for coffee now and then. We are meant to be friends.'

Clio shut up sounding like a fourteen-year-old. 'Let's go to Bewley's in Grafton Street tomorrow.'

'Have you gone all the way yet?' Clio asked Kit.

'Are you out of your mind?' Kit asked.

'Does that mean out of my mind, yes, or out of my mind, no?' Clio had an infectious grin. That was why their fights had never lasted long when they were young. They didn't have fights now. They were much too old for that sort of silliness.

'The answer is No, as you know very well,' Kit said.

'Me neither.' Clio was sheepish.

'I didn't ask, remember that. I am mature enough to think it's people's own business.'

'I wonder, are we just the odd ones out? Like, is everyone else doing it and being mature and not telling?' Clio sounded very unsure.

'Well, we know Deindre Hanley does it with everyone she sees. We know that Orla Dillon from the newsagent's at home was stupid enough to do it with that man from the mountains and is married to him now, which is about as bad as could happen.'

'I don't mean people like that,' Clio said. 'I mean people like us.'

'Well, they are like us. They come from Lough Glass.'

'No, you know, middle-class-people, upper-class people.'

'Clio, you sound like Margaret Rutherford in a film.' Kit pealed with laughter.

'I'm being serious. How would we know?'

'We wouldn't. We'd have to work it out for ourselves.'

'There must be some way of knowing.' Clio looked very agitated.

Kit looked at her with interest. 'Why, is it important?'

'It's very important.'

'Well, I suppose people like us do if we want to and don't if we don't want to.'

'We don't if we're afraid we'll go to hell, or people might talk about us and give us a bad name.'

'I don't think it's simple as that.'

'Simple? I've spelled out every possibility for you, every eventuality.'

'What do you want?'

'It's just that Michael O'Connor, you know the fellow I was telling you about . . .'

Kit did know. A tall, unattractive Commerce student with a very irritating laugh, a brother of Kevin O'Connor in her own Catering College . . . sons of a very wealthy family, each with their own car in Dublin – something unheard of as regards luxury . . . Clio had spoken several times about Michael O'Connor.

'Yes, what about Michael?'

'He says everyone does it, and that I'm only being a foolish provincial. Out of step with the world.'

'Well, do you want to or do you not?'

'I don't want to lose him.'

'If he likes you he'll hang around.'

'That's only the Mother Bernard school of philosophy, Kit. They don't hang around nowadays.'

'And do you like him?'

'Yes, of course I do.'

'Why? Does he make you laugh? Does he understand the same things?'

'Not particularly. But I like being with him. I like being his girl.' Clio sometimes looked very babyish Kit thought. Not like someone studying for a degree at University.

'And does he say it's goodbye unless you have sex with him?'

'He calls it making love.'

'Whatever it's called.'

'Well, he doesn't quite say that, but you'd know that's what's meant.'

'It's blackmail.'

'He says you can't love someone properly without . . .'

'I bet he does.' Kit sounded sarcastic.

Clio's eyes flashed. 'He also says his brother Kevin did it with you.'

'He *what*?'

Clio looked alarmed at the emphatic response. 'That's what he said, after some party apparently.'

Kit got up from the table, her face red with rage. 'I have some advice for you, Clio . . . Take it if you like, or ignore it. That is a great big lie. His stupid ox of a brother did try to take the knickers off me one night and I refused, because whenever I lose my virginity it will not be with one of those pig ignorant O'Connors, with their stupid laughs and their lies and thinking they're God-all-bloody-mightys in their cars going vroom-vroom.'

The people at the other tables looked up with great interest as the handsome dark-haired girl with the long black curly hair and the smart red jacket flung some coins on the table and stormed out of the restaurant. It wasn't every day that you overheard a conversation that covered lies and virginity and knickers and God-all-bloody-mighty.

Dublin was changing.

*

A hundred times Lena thought of an excuse to send Kit a short letter, a postcard even. But she always dismissed it as being too flimsy. The girl would shy away again if she were to attempt to contact her. After all, Kit's note had only been a belated thank you letter for the dress and a warning about the presence of Martin and Maura in her city. It had not been a letter with any warmth or wish to rekindle a friendship.

But there might be something. Some possible excuse she could find that would give her a reason. Lena raked the local newspaper for any item of interest, something that might reasonably trigger a communication. She saw an item about the difficulties of getting employment in the hotel industry. She cut it out and pasted it on a sheet of paper. Then she added the Millar's

Agency brochure on 'opportunities in the hotel trade' and posted them to Kit at her college.

Kit was in her second year now. It would be time for her to think about positions and jobs. Surely she could not take offence at this.

Lena wrote the note over and over until she was satisfied with it. She made sure that the address was still the same, care of Ivy Brown. She wanted neither Louis nor her office colleagues to know of this correspondence with Ireland. In the end the note she wrote said:

> Thought this might be of some interest to you and your fellow students.
> Hope the course is going well.
> Sincerest wishes for your success and happiness

And she signed it L.

*

It was Maura who noticed that there was something the matter with Emmet.

He didn't want any fuss, he said. Anyway, he was playing in a match. Brother Healy wouldn't take kindly to his crying off.

'I'll get Peter to have a look at you, if you don't mind,' Maura insisted.

'I'm quite grown up really, Maura. I'd know if there was anything wrong with me.' They looked each other in the eye. This was their first confrontation.

Emmet was a handsome boy, slim and sometimes frail-looking. He was a wiry hurler and much in demand on the team. Maura knew that missing a match wasn't something that would be countenanced except in the case of dire emergency. But the boy had aches and pains, his skin looked sallow and the whites of his eyes were yellow.

She wasn't going to back down. 'I know you are an adult, Emmet, believe me I do. And if it were a matter of asking you to come up and wait in the surgery and waste time and make it all official I wouldn't try to force it on you. But Peter is my brother-in-law. Is it all right if I ask him to look at you, just look, this evening?'

Emmet grinned. 'You're too reasonable, Maura. That's the problem.'

Peter Kelly said that Emmet McMahon had acute jaundice. It could be cured at home. A darkened room, a lot of barley water, a heavy dose of those M and B tablets, examination of the urine which was as red as port wine.

Maura came across twice a morning from her job in Stevie Sullivan's. His father came up twice a morning from the chemist's below. Anna Kelly was off school recovering from measles. She called in too and read to him.

'What would you like? You wouldn't like *Desirée*, it's a great story about Napoleon's girlfriend.'

'No, I'd prefer something else if you wouldn't mind, poetry maybe.'

'Will I do some from our text book? It could be revision for the exams.'

'No, the only good thing about all this is not having to think of revision or school. Do you know any funny poems?'

'Not by heart, no,' Anna said. They seemed to be at a loss. 'I have a book of funny poems at home though ... Ogden Nash ... would that do?'

'Well, if you're passing.'

'I'll go and get it,' she offered.

'I don't want to waste all your time off.' He was solicitous.

'No, heavens no. Anyway, you're the one with the bad sickness, I only had measles.'

Emmet felt important that he had a serious illness, and was flattered that Anna had gone all the way up to Lakeview Road to get the book.

They loved Ogden Nash. The house rang to the sound of their laughter as they read to each other.

When Kit came back from Dublin she found them there together day after day - her brother Emmet with the yellow skin and the yellowed eyes, Anna Kelly with the dark brown rash of fading measles spots. They looked quite companionable together.

Kit debated for a long time about writing to Lena. The brochure had to be acknowledged. But did Lena not have a right to know that her son had been very ill and had recovered. Of course she had forfeited any rights when she went away. But if she had been able to have the letter she left delivered, then she would at least have had some knowledge of her children and their wellbeing. If the letter had been delivered rather than burned, then Father and Maura could never have married.

It was always the same circle of thoughts. Kit never got any further in her understanding of them. You just had to make it all fit in with the way things were rather than wishing and wondering.

> Thank you very much for the brochures, *she wrote eventually*. It's interesting the range of opportunities that are on offer in Britain. We do the same examinations here so anyone from our college would be qualified. We hear all the time of the huge opportunities which will come our way as soon as tourism in Ireland begins to take off properly, but it is very interesting to read about the specialisation that is already happening over in England.
>
> Emmet is now recovering from a bad bout of jaundice. He was well looked after and cared for, and he should be back in school in two weeks.
>
> I just thought you would want to know.
>
> I too send you kind wishes,
>
> Kit

Lena read about her only son lying in bed with jaundice, which after all was a form of hepatitis.

She felt jealous. Jealous of Maura Hayes, who got to bring him beef tea and chicken broth, who made a little gauze cover for his jug of lemon barley water. Lena would have done all that and more. She could have stroked his forehead and changed his pyjamas. She would have sat and told him stories and read poetry to him. Her mind was far away thinking about it.

Louis touched her hand. She always arranged that they had a relaxed breakfast together. Real coffee, a warmed roll and honey. She set the table nicely with a pink cloth. It helped to give him a good start to the day.

'And what were *you* dreaming about?' he asked.

'I was thinking that my son has jaundice . . . and I hope he'll be all right,' she said before she could check herself.

'How on earth do you know that?' He looked alarmed.

But she had recovered. 'You asked me what I was dreaming about. That's what I dreamed.' Her smile was reassuring.

He looked sympathetic. 'I don't go on about it because there's no point in speculating. But I *do* know how hard it is for you.'

'I know, Louis. I know you know.'

'It's a pity we never had a child, you and I.'

'Yes, it is.' Her voice was dead.

'But still, you must think of the boy and girl . . . I know that.' It was as if he was forgiving her, excusing her for harking back to her son and daughter.

'From time to time, yes.'

'You're not sorry ever that you left . . . ?' He knew what the answer was going to be.

She paused before she said it. His face had a flicker of anxiety but then it creased into a great smile. 'You know, Louis, that I loved you all my life. Any time away from you was wasted time . . . How can you ask me do I regret doing anything that meant I had the chance to be with you?'

He seemed moved. Did he ever feel any guilt at having jilted her, abandoned her all those years ago? About being so constantly unfaithful to her now. He said over and over that she was the only woman with the power to hold him. But that could easily mean she was the only woman foolish enough to stay with him through such a series of humiliations. Was that what he considered holding him?

Years ago, when she had told Martin McMahon that she couldn't marry him because she still loved the memory of another man, he had said in a puzzled way that surely this wasn't love, it was infatuation. At the time it had irritated her terribly. It was so silly to try to define things by words, she had said. What did one person mean by infatuation or obsession and another mean by love? The whole thing couldn't be tidied away with neat little labels.

She still believed that. She looked at the line of Louis Gray's jaw and the shadow of his eyelashes, and wondered what a different turn her life might have taken if she had been able to forget him when he had gone away and left her the first time, if she had been able to say no when he came back to collect her.

'What would you like to do this weekend?' he asked her.

What she would *really* like to have done was to have flown to Dublin, put on her headscarf and dark glasses, got the train and bus to Lough Glass, let herself in to the house and gone to her son's room. She would like to have come in, during the afternoon when he might be asleep, and touched his forehead, whispered to him that his mother loved him and knew all about him – every heartbeat – then she would have kissed him. And when he awoke he would remember it all, but as if it were a dream.

She would have gone down to Sister Madeleine's cottage and thanked her for being a lifeline for so long. She would have told the old nun that she had found happiness. Then she would meet Kit and walk a bit by the lake. It would make her so free. It was such a fanciful idea. And she knew it was dangerous to think of it even for a few moments. It was to contemplate betraying even more people than she'd betrayed already.

'Do you know where I'd love to go? I'd love to go to Oxford or Cambridge and stay the night.' She sounded like an eager child.

He thought about it. 'Well, they're not far on a train, certainly.'

'And then we could take a tour and see the way they live their lives there...'

'And we could be up for one of them in the boat race because we'd been there,' he said, entering into the spirit of it.

They picked Oxford. He'd enquire at work about a nice hotel. It was easy to be the only woman in the world who could hold Louis Gray. All you had to do was walk around with your eyes closed and your mind open. Oxford and Cambridge were two places he had never gone on business trips. They would be safe places to go to.

*

'How's the young lad?' Stevie asked.

'Over the worst of it. He's as yellow as a duck's foot but he's on the mend.' Maura spoke with relief and concern. She had been worried by the illness.

'That's good. Listen Maura. I'll be out for a few hours this afternoon. In fact, I mightn't be back at all. It's all under control, isn't it?'

'The *business* is, Stevie, yes.'

'What on earth do you mean by that?'

What she had meant was that Stevie Sullivan's private life was in no way under control. Maura McMahon had eyes in her head. She knew about the pretty little Orla Dillon from the newsagent's shop. Orla who had married in great haste a couple of years back and lived with her husband's family in a faraway parish.

Orla had been spotted with Stevie a couple of times in places which were, to say the least of it, unwise. She had telephoned this morning. Even though she gave another name, Maura knew her voice. Obviously an afternoon meeting was planned.

'I don't mean anything, Stevie.' She lowered her glance.

'Great. Well, I'll be off then. The two young lads are okay on the forecourt, and take the phone off the hook if you look back in on Emmet...' He stood at the door swinging his car keys, a tall handsome young man. Far too intelligent and full of promise to get into a messy situation with that Dillon girl, and all her in-laws from the back of the mountains.

'I know I'm not your mother...' she began.

'Thank God you're not, Maura. A younger classier smarter person entirely...'

She looked after him in despair.

His mother indeed was unlikely to give him any constructive advice. She was a sour woman, hardened by the life she had led, but unable to realise that its quality had improved. She passed her time by making jibes at Maura. She would have thought the pharmacist would be able to support a wife himself. And she managed to mention many a time that the first Mrs McMahon never saw any need to burden herself with a job outside the home. Maura took no notice. Kathleen Sullivan was a pity. That's what people said about her, she was a poor pity.

She couldn't have been more than fifteen minutes across the road. Long enough to change her stepson's pyjama jacket, to give him a wet flannel to wipe his forehead, neck and hands, and a bar of Kit Kat as a treat. He was well on the road to recovery. She let herself out quietly and didn't even pause to go into Martin in the chemist's.

As soon as she went into the office she saw the safe door open. Things were knocked from every shelf, and the desk drawers were upside down on the floor. Maura had often heard of people saying they were rooted to the ground by a shock, and she realised it was a good description. Her feet were not able to move. Not until she heard the sounds of groaning ... a faint sound coming from beyond the door into the Sullivans' house. It was then that her feet began to move and she ran to find Kathleen Sullivan lying on the floor, her two hands raised for help. She had been savagely beaten, her face and hair were covered in blood. Somebody had attacked her in a frenzy, and had very nearly killed her.

They all praised Maura for being so level-headed, but she pushed away the praise. It was easy: she had her husband in the chemist's shop a few yards away, her brother-in-law at the other end of a telephone. If anything, she blamed herself for having left the office. Had she been there Kathleen might not have been attacked.

'Don't say that,' Martin whispered. 'It might have been you. God, Maura. Suppose it had been you...'

She had been tactful, too, about Stevie's absence. He had told her that he had a meeting. It was with financial advisers, she assumed. No, not the bank, not the accountants. He would be back.

She insisted on staying on the premises until he returned. Kathleen had been taken by ambulance to the hospital in the town. She had lost a great deal of blood and needed to be examined for broken bones. Her wounds were too deep to be stitched without anaesthetic.

Peter's face had been grim. 'You don't look all that well yourself, Maura. Go back across the road home,' he suggested.

'That's what I keep telling her.'

She knew she must keep the shrill note out of her voice, lest it sound like a tinge of hysteria. 'Let me stay, please. I was minding the place for Stevie Sullivan. I want to be here when he gets back.'

Sergeant O'Connor said he'd stay too.

'Ah Sean, can't you go back to the station for God's sake? I'll tell Stevie to call when he gets back.'

'No, I'll wait too.' Sean's face was set.

'I can tell you what's missing . . .'

'I'm waiting too, Maura.'

'We'll have a bit of a wait.'

'Is it young Dillon?'

'I've no idea who Stevie's meeting . . . He said . . .'

'Okay Maura, leave it.' The sergeant sounded weary. 'Only, if it's Orla Dillon, I hear they usually go to an empty house up behind the churchyard.'

'How would you hear things like that?'

'It's my job.'

'It's not. It's a gossip's job, a scandalmonger's job.'

'Would I be wasting my time going up there, would you say?'

'You're not going to get me to say . . .'

'No, it was short-cuts I was thinking of really. Like, it would mean we'd all get home hours earlier.'

'Well then . . .'

Sean stood up and took out the keys of the Garda car.

Nobody knew where they could have come from. There hadn't been any other burglaries in the area. There were no clear fingerprints.

Could it have been a professional gang? Sean O'Connor didn't think so. Professionals might have left the place in such a mess but wouldn't have missed so many car documents that could have easily translated into money, registration certificates, endorsed cheques and even number plates. It hadn't the hallmark of an organised gang.

Kathleen Sullivan, recovering in hospital, couldn't remember how many there had been amongst her assailants. Sometimes she thought it had only been one, a big fellow with coarse black eyebrows and a smell of sweat off him. Other times she thought it must have been two, because something hit her from around the back and the dark-faced fellow was in front of her.

'It could have been the desk,' the sergeant suggested. She had hit her head on that.

Yes, but it hadn't risen up to hit her.

She felt there were two. Whoever it was hadn't come in a car, the lads who filled up with petrol knew that. They could account for who had been in and out. None of them had left to go into the house. It must have been someone who came in the back, someone watching who had seen Maura cross the road to the pharmacy. Someone who hadn't expected to find Kathleen in the office.

What *had* she been doing in the office anyway? There was no need to ask. Everyone from Maura to Stevie to Sergeant O'Connor knew that she had pounced on the opportunity of Maura going back across the road to come and have a rummage around, probably in Maura's handbag too. Not to take anything mind, but to get information . . . find out how much there was in a post office book, see the age on a driving licence, know what kind of letters she carried.

They didn't even bother to ask Kathleen why she was in there. Which was a relief to the older woman as she lay in the hospital recovering from her injuries and accepting the sympathy of Lough Glass.

'I shouldn't have gone across the road,' Maura said to Stevie.

'I shouldn't have been where I was,' he grinned.

'They mightn't have gone for me, fine strong woman that I am,' she said. Her voice was still shaky.

'My life is bad enough, Maura. If they did have a go at you, I'd have to be looking at Martin McMahon for the rest of my life. I wouldn't have liked that. Just as the man has got a bit of a life for himself at last.'

Maura smiled with pleasure at that remark. 'Did you know Helen?'

'Not really. Who know her? She was, as they say, a looker, but even with my enthusiasm for ladies I think I probably felt a bit young for her.'

'I pity the woman you marry, Stevie Sullivan.'

'No you don't. People who say that have an insane urge to be part of the excitement.'

'Aren't you full of yourself! Will we start the clean up tonight? Sean is finished with everything.'

'Oh God no. Let's not go within a mile of it. Will you come down to Paddles' and I'll buy you a drink to help us recover?'

'No, Paddles doesn't like females. They upset the even tenor of his ways.'

Stevie laughed. 'The Central then?'

'No honestly, I'll go back across the road. Poor Emmet doesn't know what's happening. Come with me there. Martin would be delighted.'

'I will. My legs are a bit shaky.' A lot of Stevie's shakes had to do with the fright he got when the love nest was so suddenly interrupted by the sergeant. He thought he was going to have to deal with all Orla Dillon's in-laws, and it would not have been an engagement which he would have come out of alive.

He needed a drink. Anywhere.

Anna Kelly was sitting beside Emmet's bed. She wore a white cardigan over a pale blue dress. Her blonde hair, like Clio's, was shiny and the colour of corn.

Stevie hadn't realised that she was such an attractive little thing. 'Well, well. Lucky Emmet. His own little Florence Nightingale,' he said admiringly.

'We're playing Old Maid,' Anna explained.

'Never a fear that you'll be that, Anna,' Stevie smiled.

'Oh I don't know, it could be worse. Imagine marrying anyone from round here.'

'You don't only have to choose from round here,' her Aunt Maura said.

'You did,' Anna said.

'Yes, but that was when I was mature, shall we say, and knew that this is where I wanted to be. Now Emmet, I was coming in, in case you were lonely ... but you're not.'

'Have they caught them?' Emmet's eyes were eager and bright.

'Not yet,' Stevie said. 'But don't worry, they're not hanging around. The guards think they have gone off out the back again, the way they got in. Up the lane and out by the church. They're halfway between here and Dublin now.'

'Why did they choose *your* place?' Anna asked.

'Fastest growing car business in the land,' Stevie said.

Anna looked at her aunt to confirm this.

'You don't think I'd be working there otherwise,' Maura said. 'Come on, Stevie. I'll get you that drink I promised you.'

They went into the sitting room. Martin was on the phone to Kit. The robbery had been reported on the news. She had heard Lough Glass mentioned and wanted to know was everyone all right.

'Talk to her,' he gestured eagerly to Maura.

'Oh Maura,' Kit burst into tears. 'I was so afraid something might have happened to you. Thank God it was only batty old Kathleen.'

Maura held the receiver for a while before replacing it. She was hardly able to speak with the emotion she felt that her stepdaughter should cry over her possible safety. It was more than she had ever hoped for. That, and the look of relief and love in Martin's eyes as he poured them all a large brandy. Purely medicinal of course.

Sister Madeleine poured out a cup of tea for Mrs Dillon. 'It's a hard world to understand, all right,' she said.

'I came to you, Sister Madeleine, because you know all about the wickedness that goes on and you're not above in a pulpit preaching about it and forgiving people or not forgiving them as the case may be.' Mrs Dillon from the newsagent's and confectioner's nodded her head vigorously as she spoke. This was serious praise for the hermit.

Sister Madeleine accepted the high regard. She didn't say that it wasn't actually her position to forgive sins or to ascend a pulpit. It was easier to let people think they had a second line of approach. An alternative confession, if you liked to put it that way.

The woman was very worried about the behaviour of her daughter Orla. 'Maybe she should never have married into that clan,' Mrs Dillon said. 'But Father Baily was very anxious that it should be done as quickly as possible not to give scandal, or "any more scandal" as he put it.' Madeleine murmured and sighed as she always did and people always took great comfort from it. No blame was being attributed. That was why people loved to come and see her. It was more soothing than anything. But when advice was being sought, she let you work it out.

'I fear that Orla may be neglecting her child and that I will not stand for.' Mrs Dillon's head bobbed up and down. 'But Sister Madeleine, you can't talk to young people these days. They're not afraid like we were.'

'She might be afraid of her husband's brothers, though,' Sister Madeleine said eventually. 'If you were to hint that they had been drinking somewhere and that a rumour had come to their ears. You might find that that would work wonders.'

Mrs Dillon left, thanking the nun as if she had performed a miracle. This is exactly what she would do. That was precisely the route to take. Neither of them commented on the fact that it was a trick, a lie even. It would work.

Alone now Sister Madeleine poured a saucer of milk for the blinded kitten that some children had brought her. The vet had said that it would be kinder to have put the animal to sleep but Sister Madeleine said that she would care for it, point it at the food and keep it safe from anything that might be a danger. It was a frail little thing, trembling as well it might after all that had happened to it in its short life. But she was rewarded with the purring when it realised that its face had been pointed towards something as comforting as bread and milk.

Then she heard the sound. It was a rough, gasping breath. And very near her door. At first she thought it was an animal; once a deer had come right up to the water's edge in front of her cottage. But there was a grunt as well.

Sister Madeleine never felt fear. When the big form loomed up at the doorway she was calm, calmer than the man with the bushy eyebrows and blood-streaked arm, a man who had been in some fight and had been injured. He had very wild eyes and he was more startled to see her than she him. He had thought that the cottage was empty.

'Don't move and you won't get hurt,' he shouted at her.

Sister Madeleine stood without stirring; her hand was at her neck fingering the simple cross she wore on a chain. Her hair was pulled as always into a short grey veil. Her clothes marked her out as a nun. Not one that lived in a convent perhaps, but with the grey skirt and cardigan, the sensible laced shoes, she could be nothing else. The most nun-like thing about her was the fact that when asked not to move she stayed so utterly still. Her eyes never left his face.

After what seemed like a very long time his face began to crumple. 'Help me, Sister. Please help me,' he said. And the tears began to pour down his face.

Very gently, so as not to frighten him, Sister Madeleine moved towards him, and motioned him to a chair. 'Sit down, friend' she said, in a slow calm voice. 'Sit down and let me look at your poor arm.'

'At least it's not the tinkers,' Sean O'Connor said to his wife.

'Why should it be the unfortunate tinkers?' she defended them.

'That's what I'm saying. No one can say it was them. They've all gone off on some outing or to some horsefair – whatever it is they do.'

'If you talked to them more instead of frightening the daylights out of them you'd know what they do,' said Maggie O'Connor.

'Jesus, isn't it hard to say anything to anyone these days without being taken up wrong,' said Sean O'Connor, feeling very hard done by.

They had no idea who had robbed Sullivan's and battered Kathleen so severely. It looked to be the work of a madman. But how had a madman got away so skilfully?

'It's no concern of anyone else's,' Sister Madeleine said as she washed the man's wound.

He kept asking her to look out the door, fearing that she would run off and tell someone that he was there. 'Don't get out of where I can see you,' he said, his great frown darkening even further.

'I have to get more water,' Sister Madeleine spoke simply, without fear or any sense of making excuses. 'It comes from the pump outside and then I have to boil it.' He lay back in the chair. There was something about her that made him feel she wouldn't turn him in.

'I'm in trouble,' he said eventually.

'I'm sure you are.' She said it mildly as if he had said he was from Donegal or from Galway, a matter of no huge concern. She said that the wound didn't need to be stitched as far as she could see. If she bandaged it up the skin would probably knit together. 'You might like to give yourself a bit of a splash out at the pump there. Mind your poor arm of course, try not to wet it . . . but it would make you more comfortable before we had tea.'

'Tea?' He couldn't believe it.

'I was going to put a lot of sugar in it, it gives you energy when you've had an accident.'

'It wasn't an accident.'

'Well, whatever it was. And I have some nice fresh bread that Mrs Dillon brought . . .'

'People come here?' He was alert and watchful.

'Not at night. Go on now.' She was gentle and firm at the same time.

Soon he was sitting, half-washed and more relaxed, at her table swallowing cup after cup of sugared tea. He had gulped slices of warm buttered bread. 'You're a good woman,' he said eventually.

'No, I'm the same as anyone else.'

'You wouldn't want to let people like me come in and take a loan of you like this. Some of them wouldn't be decent men like I am.'

If she were hiding a smile he didn't see it. 'No, I generally find people are generous and decent if you let them be.'

He pounded on the table with his spoon in agreement. 'That's exactly it, but people *don't* let them be. That's where you're right.'

'Would you care to sleep the night here by the fire? There's a rug and a cushion.'

His big face almost crumpled. 'You don't understand . . . you see.'

'I don't have to understand. The fire is there if you'd like to stay rather than going out into the wind.'

'Well, you see, Sister. There's a possibility that people would come looking for me.'

'Not in my house, not in the night they wouldn't.'

'I wouldn't sleep easy. I really wouldn't.'

She sighed and took him to the door. 'Do you see in a straight line from here a big tree on its own away from the others?'

'Yes,' he squinted into the night.

'There's a tree-house up there. Steps in the trunk and up there a secret tree-house. Children made it a long time ago.'

'And would they want it now?'

'They're grown up and away from it now.'

It was the talk of the town. For days Mona Fitz said that her heart was in her mouth because those kind of gangs came back and did post offices; she had read of this happening. Wall's hardware put padlocks on every door. If the gang had made their getaway down the back lane they might have seen all the pickings that lay waiting for them in Wall's. They could come back again another day.

Dan and Mildred O'Brien in the Central Hotel were depressed. The place was bad enough, they said, without having the reputation of a town where there were armed robberies. And of course it was written up in the local press.

*

There was extensive coverage in the paper that Lena bought every week. She read the details of what seemed a violent and senseless crime. Without having to be told she could sense the towns relief that Maura McMahon had been on an errand of mercy and was not in her customary position. Reading between the lines she knew that Kathleen Sullivan would have been snooping.

It was not news that gave her any pleasure to read, but at least it provided an excuse to write again to Kit.

> I read with concern about the events in the garage across the road from where you live. I just wanted you to know how sympathetic I feel and how I hope everyone has recovered from the shock. I do not wish you to feel that you always have to acknowledge every note I write to you. But when I feel such an urge to let you know how very involved and concerned I am, I'm sure you will forgive me for writing.

She signed it 'Lena'.

*

'Kit, I was going to sort of say that you and I were going off together for a weekend,' Clio said on the phone.

'Why were you going to sort of say that?'

'Because I'm going off for a weekend.'

'And ...'

'You know the way Aunt Maura's always poking her nose into things and asking am I all right ...'

'Yes.' Kit didn't mind it as it happened. Maura only asked enough to make sure that they had enough money, entertainment, sources of clean

256

clothes. She didn't question them about their friends. But then of course, Clio was probably up to no good and felt threatened by even the simplest request for information.

'So I thought I'd say you and I had gone to Cork. It's the kind of thing we might do.'

'It's nothing like the kind of thing we might do.'

'Well, will you go along with it?'

'When for?'

'Weekend after next.'

'Where *are* you going, Clio?'

'I don't know exactly.'

'You do. You're going off to lose your virginity with that terrible Michael O'Connor, aren't you?'

'Kit, really!'

'Aren't you?'

'Well, possibly.'

'Oh, you're such an eejit.'

'Sorry, Sister Mary Katherine, I didn't realise I was talking to a fully professed nun.'

'I didn't mean it, I mean him.'

'Just because you don't like his brother . . .'

'I don't like him and neither do you, Clio. You only like that they're rich.'

'That's not true. I've met his family and I like them. I don't care whether they're wealthy or not.'

'I've met a bit of their family in that fellow Kevin and I don't like him at all. I especially don't like what he's been saying about me. I wish I could get back at him . . . I'll think of a way.'

'Oh, don't make such a drama out of it,' Clio complained. 'They're very nice really. They have this elder sister Mary Paula. You never saw anything like her clothes, you wouldn't believe it. And she's been everywhere . . . hotels in Switzerland, France . . . everywhere.'

'Did she train . . . ? As a hotel manager?'

'No, I think it was just experience. She was in this great skiing place.'

'Lots of opportunities for skiing jobs in Ireland,' Kit said sarcastically.

'Oh stop condemning them all. Listen, what are you doing that weekend anyway?'

'As it happens I *am* going to Cork to stay with Frankie,' Kit said. 'But you can't come, either of you.'

'That's all right, I'll just say I'm going there and that will provide some kind of smoke screen. What's her second name?'

'Who?'

'Frankie!'

'I don't know, I never asked.'

'Oh don't be such a pain and a pig, Kit . . . I'll make up a name. God, you're so uncooperative. Sometimes I think you're getting as mad as your mother.' There was a silence.

Kit hung up.

*

Frankie and Kit laughed all the way down to Cork on the train.

A fat old man bought them fizzy orange drinks and chocolate biscuits. He said he loved to see young girls eat and drink and laugh.

'That's all he's going to see,' Frankie whispered to Kit.

'We can't take another one. Stop, Frankie, you're going too far.' Kit felt guilty as the man looked at them excitedly, hoping for something ... possibly a squeeze ... in return for his heavy investment.

'It's his choice,' Frankie said.

They got a bus to the town where she lived in County Cork. It was bigger than Lough Glass but not much. Frankie's father ran a pub. He said that when he had a daughter a hotel manager and a son a solicitor he was going to retire, sell the pub, and that was his plan. Frankie's mother said he would never retire. He would be carried out of the pub with his arm still up in the position of pulling pints. He had done it since he was eighteen years old; he knew no other life.

They were happy, easy-going people. Much less full of nonsense and questions about her background than the Kellys would have been, but somehow less stylish and elegant than her mother would have made her house for a guest. Kit wondered why she thought of her mother suddenly. The house in Lough Glass had been run by Maura for a sizeable time now. Why did she think of it as her mother's place still?

She wondered if she should write to Lena again, but there wasn't a reason. She was not going to start a correspondence all over again. Not after all the lies. All the deception.

Frankie's brother Paddy came home from Dublin too. He had got a lift from a fellow who had a hopeless car; he wasn't in until nearly midnight.

'Oh good,' he said when he saw Kit. 'A nice bird for the weekend.'

'Not really,' Kit said loftily.

'You know what I mean. It was a term of admiration,' he said.

'Oh well, thank you then,' she said good-naturedly.

Paddy was a law student. He attended lectures in the Four Courts, he said. And that was the bit that had some freedom about it, the rest was being apprenticed to his mother's brother which was like being a galley slave.

'He's not that bad, is he?' Frankie defended her uncle.

'Easy now, you don't have to work for him ... still, it's a good training.'

They sat companionably in Frankie's father's pub. Paddy was drinking half pints of stout, the girls were drinking bitter lemon. A few regulars, who didn't feel it necessary to observe the licensing hours, were sitting around with the air of people who had a perfect right to be there and wouldn't cause any trouble just as long as they were left in peace.

Paddy told the girls about some of the work he had to do.

Debt collecting was the side of it he hated most. It meant going into houses where women with children in their arms tried to explain why money hadn't been paid by a man who was not there to make the explanation himself.

You saw all of life in a solicitor's office, he said. They had people with no lights on bicycles, applications for publicans' licences, a woman who had choked eating a piece of poultry that had not been properly carved. Now they'd better watch out for that sort of thing when they were hotel managers, because she had got quite a lot of compensation, as it happened.

And there was a claim for damages from a woman who had got a big scar on her face. It diminished her chances of marriage so she would get a lump sum.

'Is it only women who get that money for disfigurement, or is it men as well?'

'Only women in terms of losing marriage prospects,' Paddy said cheerfully. 'Men could get married if they had faces criss-crossed with scars; it wouldn't affect their chances at all.'

'That's very unfair, isn't it?' Kit said. 'It sort of says that women can only get married if they look all right.'

'It's true,' Paddy said. 'And this woman is entitled to big compensation. What does a woman have to offer anyway except her appearance and her reputation?'

Frankie laughed. 'That's straight from the nuns,' she said.

'Well, it's case law as it happens,' Paddy said. 'If you take a woman's reputation away falsely, you have to pay.'

'Tell me more about that,' said Kit, her eyes shining with excitement. 'Tell me all about that, I'm fascinated.'

They had great fun during the weekend writing the letter. Paddy said that the more threatening you made it the greater the chance of there being a craven response.

'We're looking for high compensation here,' he said. 'That fellow is the son of Fingers O'Connor. He's very well known; he wouldn't want any scandal getting out. He'll pay all right.'

'I don't expect him to pay,' Kit said. 'I just want to terrify him.'

'Anyway, you're not a real solicitor,' Frankie said.

'He won't know that if we use the office stationery,' Paddy said.

Kit sent a postcard to Lena. It was a picture of the Blarney Stone in Cork, the place you were meant to kiss and then you got the gift of the gab for ever, or so they told the tourists.

> Having a nice weekend here with friends. Thank you for your enquiry about the drama in Lough Glass. It's all passed over now, though nobody has a clue who did it or why.
> Look after yourself,
> Kit

'Who do you know in London?' Frankie asked as Kit posted the card.

'Oh, just a woman I got to know. She's been very good about writing. This seemed an interesting place to send her a card from.'

'Sure, and you don't have to say too much on a card,' Frankie agreed. After Clio, Frankie was a very restful friend.

He lived very peaceably in the tree house. It was a quiet place, but he liked the sound of the lake lapping below, and the call of the birds. The nun was a very reasonable woman. She said she was an outcast herself in her way and she understood. He had tried to tell her that first night, but she wouldn't listen. Then the next day he knew she had heard because her face was different.

'Where is the other man?' she had asked him. 'The people of the village had said there were at least two, maybe even a gang.'

He became very agitated when he heard this. Now they would be definitely after him and maybe with tracker dogs. He told her he had done it on his own. He had needed money and he had waited in the lane until that woman had left. How was he to know that the old one was going to creep in as soon as she was out of the place? And the screaming and roaring . . . well, he had to hit her just to shut her up. He hadn't intended it to be so hard.

'What's your name?' Sister Madeleine had asked him.

This conversation was carried on the whole length of a tree. The man sat in the tree house, wrapped in the rug she had given him, Sister Madeleine sat on a tree trunk.

'You're asking me to give my name?' he said in disbelief.

'I have to call you something. I'm Madeleine,' she said.

'I'm Francis,' he said. 'Francis Xavier Byrne.' There was a silence. She thought of the day he had been baptised and someone had considered this was a fine, fitting name.

'And where do you live . . . usually, that is, Francis?'

'I live . . . I live . . .' he stopped. She was still. 'I used to live in a home, Sister Madeleine, but I got out of it. The trouble was I needed money. I hated the home . . . they should never call it that. This place is more of a home than that was.'

'Then stay here,' she said simply.

'You mean that? After what I did?'

'I'm not a judge and a jury, I'm just another person living on the same earth,' she said.

He spent most of the day sleeping in his treehouse.

Sergeant O'Connor came later that day. He said they were searching the area. 'You'd tell us if you saw or heard anything, wouldn't you?' He looked at the woman's unsettling eyes.

'Well, sure I never go up to the town at all, Sergeant. And who do I see but friends dropping in?'

'Well, if you saw anything unusual you'd tell your friends, wouldn't you?' He was in some doubt as she looked back at him directly.

'You see all there is to be seen here, Sean. Just a two-room cottage.' The door of her simple bedroom was open, with its white coverlet and its cross on the wall. Was it his imagination or had she always kept that door closed before? It was almost as if she was showing him that nobody was harboured here.

Sean knew he was becoming tired and fanciful about this. 'I'll leave you on your own, Sister. God, I nearly stepped on that little cat of yours. Is it sick?'

'It's blind, poor little thing.' Sister Madeleine picked it up and stroked it.

'Not much of a life for a cat if it can't see where it's going. I'm surprised you wouldn't do the right thing and let it be put to sleep,' he said.

'We don't always know what the right thing is,' Sister Madeleine said.

'No? Well, the right thing if any group of men turn up here is to let us know where to find them and not to be making them tea and sandwiches.'

'Is it a gang? It's not one person then?' Her face was bland.

'It's a gang. I'll be seeing you, Sister.' He was thoughtful as he walked away. He looked around him, but there was no sign of a boat in or out, no blood around the place, and the one thing they did know was that one of them, or maybe indeed the only one, was bleeding like a stuck pig.

Sister Madeleine smiled and stroked the kitten. She was glad that she had thought of burning all the torn bits of shirt and sheet that she had used to mop up the blood.

She sat for a long time looking at the lake, wondering was she doing the right thing. Usually she was fairly clear about what to do, you did what hurt nobody. But this man had beaten poor Kathleen Sullivan and might have killed her. Was he a dangerous person who should be handed over? She didn't think so, but for the first time in a long time a shadow of indecision came across Sister Madeleine's mind.

'All the yellow look has gone off you now,' Anna said proudly to Emmet, as if it had been entirely her own doing.

'I know. I don't look so like a rat.'

'You never looked like a rat.' Anna ruffled his hair. 'You're very good-looking actually.' There was a pause. 'As it happens,' Anna added so that he would be sure.

'Yeah, of course.'

'I wouldn't say it otherwise.'

'It's just that I'd like to look . . . well okay, if I were to be a bit around with you.'

'What do you mean, a bit around?'

'Well you know, the pictures, or a walk or something.'

'Are you asking me to do a line with you?' Her eyes were dancing, she seemed eager.

'You know my stutter is inclined to come back at moments of high emotion and drama like this,' he said.

'Oh, is that what we're in the middle of?' Anna held her head on one side and looked at him quizzically.

'Very much so,' Emmet said. He was making fun of himself in case she might ridicule him. Everything depended on what she said now.

'Well, it would be very inconvenient,' Anna said after a time.

'How's that?'

'If your stutter came back when you were trying to say I was beautiful or something . . . Too many stammers over the bb-bb-bb would have me very uneasy . . .'

'Why might I say you were beautiful?' He still didn't want to believe that she might be taking him seriously enough.

'Because I said you were very good-looking. It might have been a nice way to return the compliment.' Again her smile was arch. But he thought he read enthusiasm in it.

'You're very beautiful, Anna,' he said.

'There now, not a stutter or a hestitation. Perhaps it's not a moment of high drama or emotion at all.'

She blew him a kiss and he heard her feet running down the stairs and out onto the street.

Emmet McMahon hugged himself. He had never felt so happy in his life.

Emmet was almost ready to go back to school but he still looked a little shaken. Maura decided to suggest a family holiday, a week in one of the big seaside resorts which would be quiet now that the summer was over.

She looked up prices and presented Martin with the idea. 'Maybe we could even get Kit to come for a long weekend. She has the Monday off anyway. Suppose she was to take the Friday as well?'

Maura was so enthusiastic about her new family and this was hard to resist. 'I'd say she'd love it,' Martin said. 'But aren't you going to have great difficulty in prising young Romeo away from the scenes of his conquest?' They had been observing discreetly the romance of Emmet and Anna from a distance and without comment.

'Aha, but suppose the object of desire is coming with us?' Maura laughed. 'Peter and Lilian say it's just the sort of thing they could do with too . . . and there are these two little houses side by side. It will be like magic,' Maura said.

Emmet was very sorry but he didn't really want to leave Lough Glass. With an earnest face he spoke of having to do his revision and get back to school. He had no idea how transparent he was being. Anyone could have seen that he didn't want to leave the place where Anna Kelly lived.

Martin teased him a bit. 'It would be a great rest, you know, probably the last time anyone will ever pay for a holiday for you and order you not to work,' he said.

'I know Dad, and it's very kind . . . but just at the moment . . .' He looked embarrassed refusing the generosity.

'Oh, go on, Emmet, if you don't want to go she won't take me.' Martin often pretended that he had no standing at all in the family.

'Oh, I have to take you. I promised Peter and Lilian when we all arranged the trip that I would *make* you take a rest and I've got the time off myself from Stevie, and *you* can have that nice young fellow who did relief before for you . . .'

'Oh, are the Kellys going?' Emmet said eagerly.

'Yes indeed they are, and I'm sure Anna'll be very disappointed you're not going to be there.'

'Maybe it would be a disappointment for you then, if I didn't come,' he said to Maura.

'Yes, it would have been a bit of a disappointment, all right,' Maura admitted.

His face was radiant at this stage. 'Maybe I'll just stroll up to the Kellys' and discuss it a bit,' he said.

'Put on your jacket,' his father said. 'You're not totally cured yet.'

'Oh but I am. I'm absolutely better.'

'I was very surprised when Clio said she'd come with us,' Lilian Kelly said to her husband.

'Don't look a gift horse in the mouth.' Peter Kelly was glad that his elder daughter had shown an interest in going to a quiet holiday resort, off-season.

'It won't be glittering,' he had said, in case there should be any misunderstanding.

'You can get a bellyful of glitter,' Clio said mysteriously.

Philip heard about the trip. 'I might be there as it happens at that time.'

'No you won't,' Kit said. 'It never crossed your mind to be there at that time. If you turn up I shall take it as definite proof that you followed me.'

'I only do it for your own good.' He was defensive.

'What?'

'Follow you.'

'You dared to follow me. Where did you follow me?'

'To the station when you were going to Cork.'

'To Cork? You followed me to Cork!' Her face was white with rage.

'No, only to the station. To make sure you weren't going off with that great ape . . .'

'What great ape? Not that I'm not entitled to go off with any great ape, but which one do you mean?'

'I mean Kevin O'Connor. He told us all he slept with you and that you were mad to do it again . . . I knew it wasn't true, but I didn't think he'd talk like that unless he had some hopes.' Philip was very upset.

'Why are you telling me all this filth and madness?' Kit shouted at him.

'You asked.'

'I did not ask. I just asked you not to follow us to the seaside. I had no idea about all this rake of lies . . . I was thinking about getting a solicitor's letter written to that Kevin O'Connor . . . There's a crime saying you did when you didn't . . . By God he'll suffer from this . . . I thought it was just Clio exaggerating.'

'Well, don't tell him . . .'

'Yes I *will* tell him, you weak, yellow coward . . . That ape is going to be sorry he ever met me.'

*

Clio and Kit walked along the beach. It was a lovely time of the year to come. Just too cool for anyone to expect them to be spartan enough to try out the cold Atlantic waters; warm enough to walk easily on the damp, firm sand without any sense of discomfort.

'Before you tell me all about it in glorious technicolour I have to tell you something about that family,' Kit said.

'What makes you think I'm going to tell you anything at all? You were so unhelpful about the weekend,' Clio grumbled.

'And I'm going to be even more unhelpful now,' Kit said with some pleasure.

'Tell me.'

'I'm going to sue his brother.' She stood away to observe fully the reaction on Clio's face.

'Sue him? What in the name of God for?'

'For impugning unchastity to a woman, that what it's called.'

'What?'

'I told you, he tells people like his own brother that he has had sexual relations with me. That is not true. I am an unmarried woman; to imply I had sexual relations is implying I am unchaste. It is diminishing my marriage prospects. He'll have to pay for that.'

'Jesus,' Clio began.

'And it's not only you. Stop panicking, you're not the only one who heard. He told Philip O'Brien too, which is like putting it on the six-thirty news on Radio Eireann.' Kit's eyes blazed at the injustice of it all.

'And will it go to court?'

'Oh, I hope so.'

'Oh, God. When?'

'Well, if he doesn't apologise and pay full costs and give me a sum of money to compensate for my reputation being taken away . . .'

'Your reputation hasn't been taken away.'

'Yes it has. If his awful brother tells you . . . if he tells Philip . . . What's that but taking away a reputation?'

'No Kit, don't do it. I beg you.'

'It's too late. It's done.'

'You've sued him? You've sued Michael O'Connor's brother?'

'I've sent him a solicitor's letter.'

'You can't. You're not old enough. You have to be twenty-one.'

'No I don't.'

'It's posted?'

'Yeah, nothing to it. He says they're three-a-penny.'

'That can't be true. I never heard of it. You never heard it until this time.'

'No, solicitor's letters about anything, I mean. They told me I had to be prepared to go through with it if he said that I was a tramp and all. So I said I'm a virgin, I can prove that, so he's a liar.'

Clio was sitting on a rock looking greener than the seaweed around her.

'You've ruined everything for me and Michael, ruined it.'

'Not at all, quite the contrary. You can warn Michael that if Kevin challenges this I'm going the whole distance to fight him. I'm very, very interested in having sex with someone, when the time comes and I will not have that great, drunken, ignorant ape who I wouldn't sleep with if he were the last man on earth and I was about to die wondering . . . going around saying he did it with me. You can tell him that. I'd actually enjoy it.'

'Kit, your father, Aunt Maura . . . what would everyone say?'

'They'd say that I was terrific and I set a high store by myself. Now, tell me about your weekend with Michael.'

The Kellys and McMahons had rented two adjoining lodges. There were three bedrooms in each. There were little verandahs on the front that looked out on the long strand. They saw Emmet and Anna walking very close together but not hand in hand. That took place when they were around the corner and out of the verandah's view.

They saw Clio and Kit talking intensely.

'They seem to have remained friends in spite of all the ups and downs,' Lilian Kelly said.

'They seem to, all right,' said Maura, who watched the way the two girls spoke. It wasn't the easy laughter of girls finding everything funny, it was much more intense than that.

The rains came and the tree-house was very damp. It needed a firmer roof. Tommy Bennet the postman was a helpful man.

'Do you know what would be a great ease to me, Tommy, is a couple of sheets of lino or tarpaulin, something that would keep that rain out of a caravan.'

'Now, Sister, I've told you a thousand times they could buy and sell us, those tinkers.'

'I'm not talking about the travelling people across the lake who are good friends to this community, but about another friend who has a caravan. You often ask if there's anything you could do for me. This is something I couldn't thank you enough for.'

'Say no more.' Tommy Bennet hated these people taking advantage of the kind nun. 'I'll have it for you in a day or two.' As he left the house he put on his cape. The rain was lashing against the door. 'Ah, would you look at that,' he said. 'The poor little kitten is half drowned in a big dish of water.'

'What? Where?' Sister Madeleine ran out in the rain, mindless of getting wet.

There it was, panting and struggling for life but obviously nearly gone. 'Let me finish her off in the barrel, poor little thing. She's not going to make it.' Tommy had a kind heart.

'No!' Sister Madeleine cried.

'Ah, look at it, Sister. It's gasping for breath, it's dying. Be kind to it. We can't will it back to life. Be fair to it, Sister. It was blind anyway, always hitting into things, maybe we should have let it go at the start.'

Tears were mixed with rain on Sister Madeleine's face. 'Drown it then, Tommy,' she said and turned away.

It only took a few seconds for the small wet limbs to stop moving.

'There, Sister. All at peace now,' he said.

He wondered at the nun. She took the body and put it into a box that had once held Cornflakes. 'I'll bury her later,' she said. Other animals had died – she had the place surrounded with little crosses, she knew what foxes and tame hares and elderly dogs lay under each simple marker. Why was there such a fuss about a poor blind kitten that everyone had said she was mad to have kept in the first place? He wasn't to know that she saw the kitten as an omen, some kind of sign that she hadn't always done the right thing.

'I've stopped saying my prayers, but you're the kind of woman that would bring you back to them,' said Francis Xavier Byrne as he chewed the lamb chops down to the bone.

The young Hickey boy had been so grateful for a reference that Sister Madeleine had written him he had agreed to do anything for her. 'Just the odd bit of meat, whenever you think there's some your parents don't need. I don't want you to take from their earnings,' she had said. He understood that he wasn't to tell them about it either. 'Is it for the gypsies?' he had asked. 'It's for someone who needs meat to make them strong,' she had said.

'We could always say a prayer together, Francis,' she said.

'What would we pray for?'

'We could give thanks that Kathleen Sullivan will be out of hospital and back in her house again.'

'I don't have all that sympathy for her, to be honest. She came at me herself like a demon out of hell.'

'Well you were attacking her and robbing her son's premises. Just because you stay here I don't want you to think that I approve of everything you do.'

'But you know why I did it.'

'Do I?'

'You know I didn't mean to do it. I needed something to keep going. I couldn't be cooped up. You said yourself that you hated the feeling of being cooped up.'

'I didn't rob and steal and hit people to get out of it.'

'You didn't need to, Sister,' he said.

And again the sureness came back that she was doing the right thing. When the blind kitten died, Sister Madeleine wondered had it been a message from God that she might not always be right in her feelings, that the loudest voice she heard in her mind might just be her own.

'Do you know I think you got a suntan even in this weather,' Stevie said admiringly to Anna Kelly.

'Well, they always say it's the wind that tans you,' she said smiling.

'Only one more year and then you'll be a free woman,' he said, looking up and down the tall blonde girl with the perfect teeth and the bright smile.

Anna liked the admiration. 'Free from school, but not what you'd call free, Stevie Sullivan,' she said.

'And what would I call free?'

'Oh something much racier than me altogether,' she said.

She went home pleased with herself. It wasn't bad to have the two best-looking fellows in Lough Glass interested in her. Not that she'd pay any attention to Stevie. Everyone knew what he had been up to.

They were old enough now to have a flat in Dublin. Everyone thought that Kit and Clio would share. Everyone in Lough Glass, that was. Except perhaps Maura.

'Won't you be lonely in a little bedsitter of your own?' Martin worried about his daughter.

'No, Dad, and it's so near College and everything . . .'

'But if you were to share with Clio . . . you could both afford somewhere nicer.'

'We'd do no work . . . we'd be laughing and talking all the time . . . Anyway, we have different friends in Dublin.'

Maura glanced at him and Martin let the matter drop.

Frankie helped Kit to move into her little room.

'I wish there was room for you in our place,' she said. 'But I was the last one in so I can't throw any of the others out.'

'No, I mean it, I like being on my own.'

And mainly Kit did like being by herself. She could study when she wanted to and if she needed friends she could go to Frankie's flat or to see Clio who had also got a place on her own. But Michael O'Connor spent a lot of time there. Clio's need to be without flatmates had a lot to do with Michael O'Connor's idea of entertainment. Not that she would ever let on to them back home.

'Now, isn't that fine?' Frankie admired that way she had tacked a brightly coloured bedspread to the wall and fitted lino on to the little shelf where the kitchen things assembled by Maura were arranged.

Frankie's brother Paddy, the law student, had helped them too. 'I pretended I was delivering a summons,' he said.

'You'll get fired one day.' Kit was amazed at how casually Paddy took his job.

'Nephew of the boss! Not a chance,' he said cheerfully.

'Oh well then,' Kit laughed at him.

'Hey, why don't I just put in an appearance in the office, show them I'm alive, and then take you girls to beans and chips?'

He made it sound a great outing. Kit and Frankie said it was the best offer they had had all week.

He was back in fifteen minutes, racing up the stairs waving a paper and so excited that he could hardly speak. 'You won't believe it! He's paid, he's paid. I have the cheque here for you!'

'What, what?'

'Fingers O'Connor. A cheque from him in absolute settlement. He fell for it . . . he's paid what we asked for . . .'

The girls looked at him in disbelief. 'But isn't it illegal . . . I mean it's not a real demand . . . from a real solicitor.' Kit said.

'Could you get struck off the rolls before you get on to them?' Frankie wondered.

'No, it's all legitimate . . . look at what he's written . . .' The letter was addressed to Paddy.

Dear Mr Barry

I am sure I can rely on your discretion in this matter. The statement attributed to my son Kevin is agreed to be entirely false, and shall never be repeated. I am enclosing a cheque made payable to Miss McMahon, who has my son's assurances that no further statement of this nature shall ever be made concerning her character or behaviour to any other person.

If there are legal fees above and beyond this I shall be happy to pay them. Please mark any correspondence in this matter *Strictly Private*.

I look forward to hearing from you.

Yours sincerely,

Francis Fingleton O'Connor

They whooped with delight when Paddy finished reading it out.

'Can we keep it, do you think?' Kit said.

'You can . . . you earned it by being reported as unchaste.'

'I'll take you out to something better than beans and chips,' Kit said.

'We have to cash it first,' Frankie said.

'Fingers' cheque won't bounce,' Paddy said.

'What will you do about fees? You can't get your office to send him a bill when they don't know they've sent him this.' Kit hardly dared to think it was true.

'Oh, I'll write him a generous letter and say that since he paid so promptly and that since you are a personal friend of mine I will not charge any fee. That leaves me in the clear.'

'You're terrific, Paddy,' Kit said.

He looked embarrassed. His freckled face reddened and he didn't know how to take the compliment.

'What's this about a slap-up meal?' he said.

'Anywhere you like,' Kit said. Paddy Barry's letter had got her the kind of sum of money she would never have dreamed of. The whole year's allowance for pocket money that she got from her father.

Weren't these old-fashioned laws about women's reputations absolutely marvellous.

*

'Hi, Philip, it's Kit.'

'Yes?' His voice sounded fearful. What was she going to throw at him now?

'I'm going to take you out on the town for a great night out,' she said.

'You are?'

'Where would you like to go?'

'Don't make fun of me, Kit. Please.'

'I swear I want to take you on a treat. Suppose someone asked you, what would you say? Don't think what I'd like, what you'd like.'

'I'd like to go to the pictures first to *Mon Oncle*, the French one, you know, like *Monsieur Hutlot's Holiday* we saw, then I'd like to go to Jammet's, for just a main course, not a full meal. I'd love to see the way they serve it.'

'Done,' said Kit. 'Where'll we meet? Let's look up the times at the cinema.'

'Why, Kit?'

'Because you're my friend.'

'No. Why really?'

'Because thanks to you I got a fortune from awful Kevin O'Connor. A fortune.'

'How much?'

'You'll never know, you'll have your night out and that's it.'

Kit went to Switzers in Grafton Street and bought a lace nightdress for Clio. She gave it to her in a box all wrapped in tissue.

'What's this?' Clio was suspicious.

'The ape paid, the big bad ape, he ran for cover. I owe it to you.'

'They all think you're cracked, you know. A screw loose is what they say.'

'Good. Then I won't have to be bridesmaid.'

'Stop making jokes. What did he say when he gave you the money?'

'He said nothing. It was all done through solicitors with mutual assurances of confidentiality'.

'So how much did you get?'

'You heard me, assurances of confidentiality.'

'I'm your friend. I'm the one who put you on the track.'

'You get a nightie. Enjoy it, though how you could, I do not know.'

'You're no authority on anything.'

'I know. Don't you keep reminding me.'

'Why can't Emmet come up to Dublin for a weekend? – I'll show him the ropes,' Kit asked.

'We might all go together some time,' Maura suggested.

'No, I'd love to show my little brother Dublin. Go on, Maura. Let me feel a big important person,' Kit pleaded. Maura's smile was so warm and nice Kit felt a heel.

Maura gave in at once. Emmet was to come to town.

Philip lived in a flat now so there would be a bed for Emmet there. 'Only if you don't hang on and spy, and follow and do all those awful things,' Kit said.

'I told you, that phase of my life is over,' Philip said. He was much nicer now. The night at Jammet's, Dublin's poshest restaurant, had been a huge success. Philip had discussed wines with the waiters as if he were a regular visitor.

'What are you going to do to entertain him?' Philip asked.

'I warned you, no spying,' Kit threatened.

'What do I care what you do?' Philip asked. 'Even if my future brother-in-law is shown none of his capital city I'll say nothing.'

'That's the boy,' Kit said approvingly.

*

The postcard of the Blarney Stone from Kit had been a breakthrough as far as Lena was concerned.

There was no reason for it. It wasn't thanking her for anything . . . not in any real sense. And Kit had asked her to look after herself. The girl who had run from her in disgust all those months ago had softened enough to ask her to take care. It was a ray of hope. Lena kept these letters carefully in a drawer in Ivy's kitchen. Sometimes she took them out to read them again. The last one was definitely full of promise.

Lena waited until she left London to send Kit a card. She and Dawn went to talk to sixth formers in four different cities. It meant spending the night in Birmingham. Lena bought a postcard of the Bull Ring and addressed it.

I'm here spreading the good news of our agency to schoolgirls. Very exhausting but satisfying all the same. I think maybe I should have been a school teacher. All I know is that I was extremely foolish to have had no career for so long. Have you got a date for your exams? And I'd be so interested to know about your brother's too, of course.

I hope you are well and happy.

Lena

She debated putting love but decided against it.

'Are you sending a card to Mr Gray?' Dawn asked her.

'Hardly, Dawn. I'll be home to him tomorrow night.'

'He's so nice, Mr Gray. Great fun and everything . . . he was the life and soul at the Dryden.'

'I forgot you knew him then.'

Lena had forgotten. Dawn had been with her so long in Millar's she had almost forgotten the tempestuous, short-lived series of appointments they had found for her in offices and hotels, and where there always was some incident of Dawn being highly fancied by the most unsuitable men in the company. As far as she knew that hadn't happened in the Dryden. James Williams was not the type.

'Did you like Mr Williams?' she asked Dawn.

'I can't say I remember him, Mrs Gray.' Dawn's big blue eyes were unaware of a lot of people who had passed through her life.

'Oh, well. It's a long time back now.'

'That's true.'

Dawn looked around the dining room in the hotel. They were the centre of many appreciative glances, the blonde girl and the dark handsome woman. Nobody could quite place what they were doing there. They looked too respectable to approach and yet surely Dawn's eyes promised a lot of fun.

Lena smiled to herself to think how the great James Williams would feel to be so instantly forgotten by a pretty little secretary like Dawn Jones.

But then with the familiar turn of her heart she remembered that Dawn hadn't forgotten Louis Gray or what fun he had been. The life and soul of the Dryden Hotel was how she put it.

Back in the office she found herself looking speculatively at the blonde girl that she had thought was such an asset to Millar's Employment Agency. She had, of course, been quite right in insisting that a young attractive girl would sell the whole idea better than any other approach from a different generation. She must beat down this absurd and dangerous suspicion. She could not be jealous of every single woman who had ever worked with Louis.

Pausing to pick up some papers in an outer office she heard Dawn talking to Jennifer the receptionist on the desk.

'. . . Honestly she was so nice, and she's done so much for me. Sometimes I feel guilty, dead guilty about her husband.'

Dawn noticed Jennifer staring horrified over her shoulder and she met Lena's smile. 'Oh, Mrs Gray . . .' Dawn's face reddened. Lena said nothing, just stood there with the smile nailed on her face. 'Mrs Gray, you know what I mean. It was all a bit of fun, nobody meant anything by it.'

'I know indeed, Dawn . . . a bit of fun is what it was.'

'And you're not upset . . . ?'

'About Louis having a bit of fun . . . heavens, what do you take me for?' she said, and left them.

She barely got to the bathroom basin in time to throw up. Louis and this girl, this girl whom he knew had been sent to his hotel by Lena. Lena rinsed her face and reapplied her make up. She returned to her desk and managed to avoid Dawn for the rest of the day.

That evening she went to Jessie's office and said she would like to dismiss Dawn Jones.

'I missed you when you were in Birmingham,' Louis said that night to her.

'I wasn't away for long.'

'No, but any time is long.'

'It was hard work,' she said. 'Dawn and I were almost hoarse at the end of it.'

'Dawn?' he said.

She looked at him. He probably didn't remember Dawn. Truthfully. The bit of fun had been so passing, so fleet, that it had not stayed in his mind.

'Dawn Jones, remember she used to work for James Williams once?'

'Oh yes.' Now he did remember. 'And how did she get on there . . . with you?'

'Fine, just fine. I think she's leaving the agency though.'

'Oh is she? Why's that?'

'I'm not really sure,' Lena said, turning off the light.

*

Rita was well established now in the car-hire company in Dublin. She was walking out with one of her colleagues. He came from Donegal, far far away. She thought of the gypsy who had said she would marry a man from far away. She hoped this was the man. His name was Timothy and one day soon he was going to introduce her to his mother.

Rita had told him she didn't come from important stock. Not from any people you could speak of. Her father and mother had lost interest in her when she had gone as a girl to be a maid at the McMahons'. She didn't want Timothy to have any false impressions.

Timothy told her that nothing mattered less. He said that all that old nonsense was changing in Ireland and about time too. Once or twice Rita wondered whether she should ask Kit if she might meet Timothy. It would give her a bit of standing if a lovely, confident young hotel management student appeared as her friend.

But Kit had enough to do and Rita would not abuse their friendship. One day she would meet Timothy and that would be fine.

Emmet went up to Kellys' to tell Anna about his trip to Dublin. Kit was going to meet him off the train and he would stay with Philip O'Brien, who had improved beyond all measure, apparently. They were going to the pictures and on a little train out to Bray to the amusements. And Kit had a friend who was a law student who was going to take them to see a prison and a tattooist.

It was going to be a fantastic weekend, everything he'd want to do. He hated leaving Lough Glass and Anna of course, but then she'd had so many outings recently . . . there was a school trip here and a careers talk there and he had not really seen her for ages.

Lilian Kelly opened the door. 'Hello, Emmet,' she said, surprised. There was something about her voice that alerted Emmet. He said nothing, just grinned. 'I thought Anna was with you,' she said.

It was awkward telling Father and Maura that she didn't need any money to entertain Emmet in Dublin. Kit would've liked to have bought them presents too with her unexpected windfall. But she thought it would cause too much trouble if she explained it.

She waved and he saw her. 'Come on, we'll get the bus back. Quick, to the front seat,' she said taking his hand and they ran together to board the bus for the city centre.

'Imagine you knowing Dublin so well.' He seemed wistful.

'Well, you will too next year, won't you?'

'Yes.' His voice sounded a bit down. But perhaps he was just tired after the journey.

'I'll show you my flat first,' Kit said, determined she wouldn't start looking for problems where none existed.

Emmet said he thought it was great. Imagine all this whole place of her very own. Kit was touched by that.

It was so small even her bedroom in Lough Glass was bigger than the area where she slept, sat, ate, studied and washed at a sink. But it was very central, there were no bus fares, she was even so near one of the cinemas that she could look out of her window and see whether the queues were lessening.

'We could go to a dance, seeing it's Friday night,' Kit said. 'And I'd be happy to bring you to one of the places we go, but they're very hot and sweaty. And honestly, as it's your first night I thought we might go somewhere less noisy.'

'That would be nice,' he said.

He *did* sound flat. Kit was *not* imagining it.

'What do you think of an Indian restaurant?' she suggested. 'There's one up in Leeson Street. It's great, and I've been there a couple of times so I know what to order. And then we'll meet Philip and he'll take you home.'

He said it sounded great. They walked together through O'Connell Street, past crowds of people.

'I've never been here at night,' Emmet said.

'No. It's changed completely.' They stopped and looked at the Liffey flowing under O'Connell Bridge.

'It's not smelly,' Emmet said. 'People are always saying it is.'

'It is a bit, to be honest, in the summer time, but not now,' Kit agreed.

They went past Trinity College, and Kit pointed out students coming and going through the main gate.

'Are they very posh? English and upper class?' Emmet asked.

'I don't think so. I used to think that, but apparently it's just lots of foreigners and people who aren't Catholics ... but ordinary just the same.'

'It's cracked, Catholics not being allowed to go there. Brother Healy says it's right, he says that for years when we wanted to they wouldn't let us in.'

They walked up Grafton Street and looked at all the expensive things in the windows. They went by St Stephen's Green all dark and shadowy now at night and then up to Leeson Street.

'There's a student pub here on the corner. This is where we'll meet Philip afterwards,' Kit explained.

'I'm glad he's not coming to dinner with us,' Emmet said unexpectedly.

'Yes, well he has improved, but not so much as you'd want him round all the time. It's just his parents are so awful it rubs off on him, you know.'

They went into the Indian restaurant and Kit picked a corner table. She advised Emmet about the menu.

'Suppose you have the mutton and I have the Kofta Curry – that's meat balls.'

He nodded. His eyes were fixed on the menu as if he were trying to summon up the courage to say something. 'This is quite dear, Kit. Are you sure we can afford it?' he asked.

'No problem,' she said.

'But all this and the pictures tomorrow and the tattoo parlour.'

'That won't cost any money. Honestly Emmet, don't worry.' She put her hand to pat his as reassurance and, to her horror, his eyes filled with tears. 'Oh Emmet, what's wrong?' she cried.

'Kit, I want you to do me a big favour. Will you do something for me, it's a huge thing?'

'What is it?'

'Promise first.'

'I can't promise until I know. That's not fair. I'll try, you know I will.'

'You have to promise . . .'

'What *is* it?'

'It's Anna. She's keen on Stevie Sullivan and he's taking her out. They're doing a line. She doesn't want me any more.'

'It's only a crush. She'll get over him.'

'No, they meet all the time, she's crazy about him.'

'He's too old for her. Much too old.'

'I know, but that makes him more interesting than ever.'

'But he can't feel the same about her, can he?'

'Yes, he's crazy about her, too.'

'What about Doctor and Mrs Kelly? I bet they're furious.'

'Yes, but all this makes it even more . . . I don't know . . . dramatic.'

'What can I do . . . tell me what kind of favour could I possibly do you? Hypnotise her? Kidnap Stevie Sullivan?' Kit looked at him mystified to know what role he could see for her in all this.

'You're not bad-looking, Kit. Fellows are always saying that you look terrific. Could you sort of set yourself at him and get him. Distract him from Anna . . . then she'd come back to me.'

Her first instinct was to laugh. Kit McMahon, a Mata Hari who could attract the desire of any man away from a little blonde beauty like Anna Kelly!

Then she saw his face and she didn't laugh. Emmet was near breaking point. And he really believed she could do it. Poor, poor Emmet. Imagine feeling so strongly as this.

Kit had never loved anyone to the extent that she would admit it so openly, so wretchedly. She didn't know anyone who could, except in books. Then, with a shock, she realised the only other person who had loved so foolishly and recklessly that she didn't consider anyone else was Helen McMahon. Their mother. She looked at her brother, stricken.

'Will you do it for me, please, Kit?' he begged.

'I'll try,' she said.

The least she could do for him was to try.

8

Paddy Barry apologised profusely. The man he had been going to visit in prison had been released.

'It was very bad luck,' he said over and over.

'Good luck for him, I suppose,' Kit had said.

'Yes, but bad for your brother.'

'I don't mind,' Emmet said. 'Is the tattooist still there?'

Paddy's cheerful freckled face lit up. 'Emmet boy, he is still there and we're going to meet him this morning.'

'There's no question of any of us getting things done on our arms, is there?' Kit regarded Paddy with some awe and anxiety. Anyone who could trick Fingers O'Connor into such craven submission was a force to be reckoned with.

'I might have a very small anchor done myself . . . I'll see,' Paddy said. 'No obligation on the rest of you, of course.'

'Does it hurt?' Emmet asked.

'Excruciating, I believe,' Paddy said.

The tattooist was a very small man with an anxious face. 'Any friends of Mr Barry's are welcome here,' he said looking doubtfully at Kit and Emmet.

'See, I told you.' Paddy was triumphant.

It had never been clear what particular service Paddy Barry had done for the tattooist. Kit didn't really want to know. She felt it may not have been on the right side of the law that he was learning to uphold. It had something to do with giving him a warning about smuggled cigarettes from sailors. Whatever it had been, it had been a matter deserving great gratitude.

'Would you all like tea?' the tattooist offered, and provided it out of grimy enamel mugs.

He showed the needles and the fluids and a book of designs, as well as letters from satisfied clients.

Kit looked at Emmet. This had been a brilliant idea. She could hardly recognise the troubled face that had sat opposite her last night in the Indian restaurant as Emmet toyed with his food and begged her support.

They had agreed that Kit would give it her best. But in her own time and in her own way. Emmet must not keep enquiring how it was going, he must make no efforts to help. They had shaken hands on it and he had cheered up in time to meet Philip in the pub.

Philip had wanted to come to the tattooist as well, but Kit had said that the thing was sufficiently like a circus already ... they didn't want to have to sell tickets for the visit. What about lunch, Philip had wondered. That was no use either. Emmet and Kit were meeting Rita and her boyfriend.

'Rita who worked for you?' Philip said.

'The very same.'

'What would you have to say to each other?' he asked. It was uncanny the way he sounded like his mother. You really could hear Mildred O'Brien in some of the things he said.

'We have lots to say to each other,' Kit explained. 'Rita brought us up.'

Philip had felt the reproof and regretted his attitude, but it was too late. He wouldn't be able to see Kit and Emmet until the evening when they would meet for the pictures.

Kit brought her mind back to the conversation taking place in the tattoo parlour. Emmet seemed to be costing a small heart with a four letter word inside it.

'Don't consider it for two seconds, Emmet,' she said.

'It would be discreet,' the tattooist said.

'And a sign of how much I cared,' Emmet said.

'You wouldn't want to commit yourself to one name at too early a stage, though.' Paddy Barry was wise in the ways of the world.

'I'll never want any other name,' Emmet said in a voice that chilled Kit to hear.

'This is my friend Timothy,' Rita said, and introduced the man from the car-hire firm.

Rita looked well. She had her hair cut smartly and she was wearing make-up. She wore a bright uniform jacket, as did Timothy. They worked Saturdays so were only free for a short lunch hour. Rita asked Kit all about the people in Lough Glass and Timothy told Emmet about the cars.

'Not a sign of his stammer. Isn't it wonderful?' Rita said when she knew she couldn't be overheard by Emmet.

'It comes and goes when he's upset,' Kit said.

'Well, it's probably not too often that happens. And Maura's running the house all right with Peggy?'

'Nothing to the way you did,' Kit laughed.

They both knew that was only a politeness. Maura McMahon managed their home magnificently.

'Is this the real thing?' Kit jerked her head towards Timothy.

'I hope so, Kit, he's very good to me. He's mentioned marriage several times.' Rita looked pleased and proud.

'Can I come to the wedding?' Kit whispered.

'Of course you can, but it may not be for a while. We have to save a bit first. Perhaps I'll be at yours before then.'

'I doubt it,' Kit said. 'I'm not great with the fellows at all.'

'Too choosy more like it, you have them all admiring you.'

Kit hoped this was true. If she could just get Stevie Sullivan to admire her for a bit, that would honour her promise to Emmet. She wondered would it involve going the whole way. Kit swallowed nervously at the thought of it. Surely nobody could be expected to do that just for a childish promise to a brother?

'I often meet Clio on a Sunday,' Kit said to Emmet. 'Would you like that or not?'

His eyes lit up. Even the thought of being close to Anna's sister was a delight. 'And don't forget, her family know nothing of her meeting Stevie . . .'

'So why don't we let her get caught, make more trouble for her? Clio would help with that.'

'No, you don't understand.' Emmet's face had the tight, tense look again. 'She came and told me honestly, she made me promise as a friend that I'd not tell tales on her.'

'And you promised?'

'I did, of course,' Emmet said.

'Heigh Ho,' said Kit.

'I hope my mother doesn't hear you've had Emmet up here for a weekend,' Clio grumbled on the phone when Kit rang.

'You can be sure she will. They hear everything in Lough Glass,' Kit said.

'She'll think I should be having the dreadful Anna.'

'Well, why not? It would be nice for her.' Kit was being very cunning. Perhaps it was an opportunity to get Anna away from Lough Glass and Stevie.

'We've always said that she and Emmet are two different species. Are they still in love with each other, by the way?'

'Hard to say,' Kit lied. 'You know boys don't talk much about that sort of thing.'

'Anyway, she's working very hard. Horrible little sneak that she is, she'll get much more honours in her Leaving than I did. Apparently she's off studying all the time.'

Kit nodded glumly. She knew about all this studying and what form it took.

Clio couldn't stay long, she said as soon as she arrived. She was going to Michael O'Connor's house. It was his sister's birthday and there was a family lunch party for them.

'They're very family-conscious,' she said proudly to Kit. Clio loved being included in the O'Connor rituals. 'Mary Paula is allowed to choose what she wants for lunch and it's made in one of the hotels and then served in the house.'

'Will there be champagne?' Emmet wanted to bring news home to Anna when he saw her as a friend.

'No, I don't think so. Mr O'Connor has probably had to make a few economies recently. He had to pay out unexpected sums of money.'

Clio glared at Kit, who giggled. It was as far as Clio would go; she would not risk the story getting home. It would reflect no credit on the beloved O'Connor family.

Philip and Kit said that Emmet would have to be on the train in good time. It got crowded early and there were a lot of people going home after spending a Sunday in Dublin. They went to have chips in a café first.

The girl at the cash desk in a bright-green, tent-like dress looked familiar. All three of them looked at her with interest and then they spoke at the same time.

'It's Deirdre,' said Kit.

'Deirdre Hanley,' said Philip.

'And she's pregnant,' said Emmet.

Deirdre was delighted to see them. 'Imagine you lot being old enough to go out on your own,' she said. 'I'll get them to give you bigger helpings.' She called to the man in the white apron, 'Gianni, these are friends of mine, huge helpings.'

'*Molto grande*,' Gianni cried enthusiastically.

'That's my Gianni,' she said proudly to Kit. 'He owns the place.'

'He's very nice-looking,' Kit said admiringly.

'Yes, he's not bad,' Deirdre said.

'Emmet came up for the weekend. Philip and I are doing Hotel Management.' Kit felt that Deirdre might not be up to date with all the details of their lives.

'You're in Patsy's year, Emmet, aren't you?' Deirdre said. Patsy was the entirely different younger sister. All the mistakes that Mrs Hanley considered she had made with her eldest were being righted in her second daughter. Patsy was watched like a hawk.

'That's right, I often see her,' Emmet said. He hardly noticed Patsy Hanley if the truth were told, but he was being polite.

'When did you and Gianni get married?' Kit asked. It was something she had never heard at home, and Mrs Hanley was great with news and information. Surely the eventual settling down of her troublesome daughter with an Italian who ran his own restaurant was worthy of mention.

'We didn't actually get married,' Deirdre said. 'You see, there's this business . . . Gianni has a first marriage which has to be annulled. It will, of course, but it all takes time.'

'I know, I know,' Kit nodded sympathetically. She wished she hadn't mentioned the word.

But Deirdre didn't seem at all put out. 'So the bambino may well be able to come to the wedding,' she laughed.

Emmet and Philip were amazed at the fast conversation that was taking place.

Gianni came to shake hands with them. 'Deirdre tells me everyone in Lough Glass is old and old-fashioned,' he said stroking the bump on her stomach . . . 'but this is not so.'

'Not at all,' gasped Philip.

As they went to the station Kit said to Emmet, 'Maybe you shouldn't necessarily mention . . .'

'About Deirdre? I wasn't going to,' he said.

'No, indeed. Wiser not,' Philip said.

But Kit knew that Mildred and Dan O'Brien would be told.

*

'Isn't Slough a funny word?' Lena said to Louis, shuffling some papers around. Normally she took very little work home; he hated to see her working.

'Why is it funny?'

'I thought it was pronounced *sluff,* you know, like enough, like to slough something off . . .'

'And what made you think of it?'

'I have to go there on Saturday to talk to a couple of schools.'

'Dawn going with you?'

'No, she left. Remember?'

'Oh that's right.' He hadn't remembered. But at least it meant that Dawn hadn't contacted him and said that she had been fired because of her past.

Dawn had more style than that, Lena thought regretfully. The girl was a loss to them. They were grooming Jennifer, but she didn't have the same appeal.

'I'm going on my own . . . but you're off that day . . . why don't you come with me?'

'Much as I'd love to wander round a few girls' schools, I don't think it's really my scene.'

'No, it's only a couple of hours for me . . . then we could go and stay somewhere.'

'It's all buses and trains,' he grumbled. He would love to have had a car.

'There must be nice places . . . we deserve a bit of a treat, a night out, a night away. The two of us.'

'All right, I'll look into it. I'll ask James, he knows everywhere and everything.'

Louis sounded a little restless these days. She had hoped that the mention of a change in their routine would brighten him up, but it seemed just another wearying chore. She wished that her location had been somewhere more glamorous than Slough.

She had forgotten how unpredictable Louis was. Next day he telephoned the office. 'James knows the perfect place. He's lending us the car, it will be a great weekend.'

'Where are you off to?' Grace asked.

'I don't know. Louis found a hotel. We're spending tonight there and tomorrow.'

'A real holiday,' Grace said admiringly.

'The nearest we get,' Lena said.

'Why don't you go abroad?' Grace wanted to know.

'Too many complications.'

'Still, Buckinghamshire is nice.'

'I hope so.' Lena sounded a little unsure of herself.

'And you look lovely as always.'

'Ah Grace . . .' Lena caught her eye in the mirror.

'Look at yourself, woman.' Grace was impatient. 'You're fantastic. Slim as a reed . . . gorgeous. But you're not if you don't believe it.'

'Sound advice, Miss West,' Lena said laughing, a real laugh and banishing all the strain from her eyes.

They had dinner at the elegant country hotel where James Williams had got them a fifty per cent reduction for bed and breakfast. A wine-bucket came to the table as soon as they sat down.

'We haven't ordered anything yet,' Louis said.

'It has been ordered for you,' said the waiter. James Williams had wanted them to have a good weekend.

There was a small dance floor; a pianist and a saxophone player made music for the diners. Sometimes there were only two or three couples dancing. Louis and Lena held each other and danced to the music. They were a handsome couple. Anyone looking at them would have thought it might be an anniversary or an illicit weekend. They didn't look like an ordinary married couple having a night out.

Lena was tired and aching next morning after a long night of love. She would have liked nothing better than to have lain on in their hotel bedroom and enjoyed a luxurious breakfast served in bed, but she had work to do.

She slipped out quietly so as not to wake Louis. He lay with his arm behind his head, his long lashes casting a shadow on his face. He was so handsome and she loved him so very much. Nothing he had done or might have done could ever change that.

When she got back to the hotel by taxi after two exhausting but hopefully profitable sessions he was waiting in the coffee lounge.

'You should have told me,' he said. 'I'd have driven you. The car was for both of us, but I had no idea where your schools were.' Of course if he had really wanted to know he could have phoned Millar's. 'Come on,' he said. 'We're off. I've planned a trip.'

They drove through the English countryside past farms and villages. Louis and Lena never compared the English countryside to the places they knew back home. It meant too much of a journey into what was over, what was best forgotten.

'Where are we going?' she asked.

'You'll see,' he said and he placed his hand on her knee. He looked so right driving James Williams' car. Louis Gray was a man born to style and gracious living, no matter what his original circumstances had been.

She saw the name of the village of Stoke Poges.

'But isn't this where . . . ?' she began.

'Yes . . . I wanted you to see the family's pride and joy.'

'What!'

' "The curfew tolls the knell of parting day . . . er . . ." Elegy Written in a Country Churchyard, by my ancestor Thomas Gray,' he said and parked outside the gate of an absurdly picturesque churchyard.

'But you're not a relation of that Gray . . .' she laughed, half believing he might be.

'Of course I am.'

'You never said.'

'You never asked me.'

'But not seriously!'

'We are who we say. I'm upset you don't believe me,' he said.

'But Louis, you're not from these parts . . . you're from Wicklow . . . you're not from Buckinghamshire in England.'

She knew scant details of his background. His father had died when he was young . . . he had older brothers and sisters who had all left home . . . gone abroad to work. They had not stayed in touch, he had not sought them out. Because Lena had no family herself she always thought that people would rate a family highly. Not Louis. He spoke little of his childhood, he neither blamed it nor harked back to it. It was now that mattered, he said. Now, not the past.

They walked to the poet's tomb, they stroked the flat top of his grave. They read the poem to each other, remembering little bits of it from what they had learned off by heart at school.

'. . . and leaves the world to darkness and to me,' read Lena.

'That's it, Uncle Thomas,' Louis said.

'He wasn't a relative really?'

'We are what we think we are,' Louis said.

'I love you, Lena,' Louis said later that night. He had woken up and found her sitting in her dressing gown by the window smoking and looking out into the night.

'Why do you say that to me?' she asked.

'Because it's true. And sometimes you look sad, as if you had forgotten that it's true.'

*

Stevie Sullivan's mother, Kathleen, was discharged from hospital and came back to Lough Glass.

'Don't end up getting her cups of tea, Maura,' Peter Kelly advised his sister-in-law. 'They can well afford to get a woman in to do it.'

'Who knows better than I what they can afford?' Maura answered. She did the books and knew exactly how well the motor business was working for the Sullivans, thanks entirely to the flair and hard work of Stevie. If he gave his full mind to it she didn't dare to think how successful he would be.

He toured farms and explained to farmers that might be slow in making decisions the wisdom of improving their farm machinery and their pick-up trucks before they had been run into the ground. Then he did up their original vehicles and sold them on to others. Nowhere did he break the law or indeed break faith in his clients. His success came from knowing how to suggest, rather than waiting for business to fall into his lap.

'Do you think we should arrange for someone to come in and look after your mother?' she asked Stevie.

'Oh I don't know, Maura. She mightn't want it. You know she'd say she's the class that should be serving people rather than having people serve her.'

'You've changed all that, you're in a different set-up now.'

'Yes, I know that you know it, my mother might not.'

'Let her benefit from it. I know a friend of Peggy's that could come in.'

'Set it up, Maura. That is, if you haven't already.'

She smiled at him. They liked each other. 'No word yet on who did it?' Maura knew that Stevie had been talking to Sergeant O'Connor earlier on that day.

'No, they seem to have gone off in a flying saucer, whoever they were. Maybe it's for the best, Sean says. He says it might make her worse than she is already if she had to identify them . . . Pretty relaxed attitude to detecting crime, if you ask me.'

'Very human attitude as well,' Maura said. 'He may be kind but he's not a fool, Sean O'Connor.'

'I know that, he gets inspired about lots of things. I know nobody gave him a hint.' Stevie stared hard at Maura, as if trying to get her to admit that she had ratted on his being with Orla Dillon.

'He knew chapter and verse, Stevie. I wouldn't have told him but he knew already, and where to find you.'

'He knew how to frighten the wits out of me, too,' Stevie said ruefully.

'Yes, well,' Maura pursed her lips.

'But by amazing chance, Orla's mother came up with the same argument at the same time. Beware the mountain men. Orla's so afraid of the troop of brothers-in-law coming for her with scythes and hatchets she won't raise her eyes to greet me. So that little episode is over.' He looked for a moment like a small boy who has been told he can't play football that afternoon. His lower lip stuck out mutinously.

'I'm sure you'll find other distractions,' Maura said unsympathetically.

'I suppose so,' Stevie said. There was no reason to tell Maura McMahon that her sister's daughter, her own little niece, Anna Kelly, had proved to be a very great distraction indeed.

'You can't stay here for ever, Francis,' Sister Madeleine said.

He sat shivering by her fire. With damp sacking hung ineffectually around it, the tree-house was no protection to the start of a wet winter in Lough Glass. 'Where would I go, Sister?' he asked. His face was thin and white. He had a hacking cough.

She had asked young Emmet McMahon for a cough bottle from his father; and, to her irritation, Martin McMahon had sent back a message saying that it was going to he a harsh winter and he would very much prefer if Sister Madeleine went to visit Dr Kelly and had herself and her chest looked at and listened to. She had got lozenges, but still Francis coughed and barked and looked like a man that should really be in a hospital bed.

'Sleep in my bed, Francis,' she said.

'But you, Sister?'

'I'll sleep by the fire.'

'I can't. I'm too dirty and shabby and bad. Your bed is snow white.' But he craved a night in the warmth and peace.

She knew that. 'I'll give you some hot water to wash.'

'No, you often do that. But there's too much of me.'

'Suppose I put a kind of cloth on the bed, in it even, like that you could wrap yourself in.'

'And something for under my head, Sister.'

She found an old bedspread which she warmed by the fire, and put some tea towels on her immaculate pillow slips. He was asleep in minutes, breathing coarsely and with a gurgle, as would a man with a chest infection. She sat at the open door watching him for a long time. Francis Xavier Byrne, somebody's son. A man not right in the head, who should be allowed some freedom like the wild animals. He should not be chained up and fenced in. He couldn't do any harm here, and he was learning to trust again. Soon, when he was better, she would give him his bus fare and he would go far away.

Kathleen Sullivan was better now, they said. Back from the hospital with a woman going in and out to look after her. Surely a loving God wouldn't want to work out any revenge on poor Francis, that man sleeping there in his fitful turning sleep, shivering and coughing as he tossed in her bed.

She would have to work something out about the bag of possessions, as he called it. Normally he never left it out of his hand. Tonight it was laid casually in her simple wooden chair. He was learning to trust; he couldn't be handed over now. She would make it clear that he would have to return whatever money he stole from Sullivan's garage. She would be responsible for doing it herself.

'What did you eat at the Indian restaurant?' Maura asked Emnet.

'I can't remember, Maura. I'm sorry.'

'Was it fish or meat ... or what?'

'I don't know. Meat, I think.'

'Lord, and that girl saving her money to take you to a special meal.' Maura shook her head in mock despair.

'We had Knickerbocker Glory in Cafollas,' he said, desperate to sound as if he had been appreciative.

'Good, at least we know what remains in the mind,' Maura laughed.

'It's just we were talking rather a lot and I ate without thinking.'

'I know, I know.' She was sympathetic. There was something bothering Emmet McMahon, but she wasn't going to find it out.

She thought it might be the absence of Anna Kelly, but yet Emmet went out as soon as meals were over, so perhaps he was meeting her then. She hoped they weren't going to get too serious, and debated whether she should discuss it with her sister, Lilian. But Lilian had a poor track record as regards coping with either of her daughters' emotional adventures. Maura thought that, as so often in life, the best thing to say was nothing.

'Hello, Emmet.'

Anna Kelly had never looked so lovely. She wore a green coat with a white angora scarf around her neck. She was flushed and excited looking, her blonde hair held up by a green clip in a ponytail. She looked like a film star. Yet here she was in Lough Glass. Anna Kelly, who only a few weeks ago had been happy to kiss him and let him stroke her. Now she said that this couldn't go on any more, but that she did want very much to be friends. She didn't know how very very hard that was for him.

But it would gain him nothing if he were to sulk. 'Hello, Anna, how are things?' he said cheerfully.

'Awful ... it's like living in a German prisoner-of-war camp,' Anna grumbled.

'Oh, why's that?'

'Where am I going, what am I doing, where will I be, who am I meeting, what time will I be back?' Anna groaned. 'Jesus, Mary and Joseph it would make you want to throw yourself into the lake.' There was a silence. 'Oh Emmet, I'm so sorry,' Anna said.

'Sorry for what?' He was cold.

'What I said ... like your mother and everything.'

'My mother drowned in a boating accident on the lake, she didn't throw herself in because people kept asking her questions,' he said.

Her face was dark red.

He longed to reach out and hold her close to him, tell her that of course he knew that was what people had said and that he understood her embarrassment and that it didn't matter one little bit. But he had been told they were no longer close, they were just friends. So he kept his hands in his pockets instead of reaching out for her. And he looked away.

She laid her hand on his arm. 'Emmet?' she said in a small voice.

'Yes?' She had been going to ask him a favour; he knew that tone of voice. But her eyes met his and something in Anna Kelly's mind told her this was not the time to ask a favour.

'Nothing, nothing at all.'

'Well, okay then. I'll see you, I expect.' His heart ached to tell her that he would always be here, whatever she wanted. But it would be wrong. Anna hated people who were weak, she had told him that. She liked the strong things about him. So he had to be strong now.

He saw Kevin Wall and shouted to him.

Kevin was pleased to see him. 'What about your one?' he said, jerking his head back to where Anna stood forlorn on the road.

'Oh Anna, she and I were just having a chat.'

'I thought you were soft on her.'

'Don't be mad, Kevin. She's only a friend,' said Emmet McMahon, and walked off with his school mate without a backward glance.

*

Kit was doing her practical work in a Dublin hotel where they took a serious interest in the trainees. One week she was on the reception desk, and the next in the bar. Then she could be waiting tables, or supervising chambermaids. It wasn't easy, but she knew that it wouldn't be from the outset.

'You must be mad,' Clio said when she came to call one day.

'You say that about every single thing I do.'

'Why be different this time?' Clio was sitting up at a high stool at the bar. 'Do I get free drinks for knowing the bar woman?' she asked hopefully.

'Not a chance,' Kit said.

'Okay, I'll buy one then. Can I have a gin and lime?'

'Gin! Clio, you're not serious.'

'Why not! Are you an apostle of Temperance masquerading as a barmaid?'

'No, it's just that we don't drink gin.'

'You don't. I do.'

'As you wish. The customer is always right.' Kit turned and filled the optic measure. In the mirror she saw Clio's face. Clio was biting her lip; she looked very unhappy. Kit carefully put the ice lumps in with her silver tongs and pushed the lime bottle and the jug of water toward her friend. 'Help yourself . . .' she said with a smile.

'Will you have one too?' Clio asked.

'Thanks, Clio. I'll have a Club Orange.'

They drank companionably for a few moments. 'Aunt Maura is becoming a bit nosy,' Clio said eventually.

'Ah, she's only making conversation, asking us what we're doing,' Kit defended her stepmother.

'I think she knows about me and Michael.'

'Well of course she does, you never stop talking about him.'

'No, I mean about the other bit, about sleeping with him and everything.'

'How could she know that?'

'I don't know.' Clio bit her lip again.

'Well, stop looking at me. I didn't tell her.'

'No, I know that.' Clio *did* know that much.

'What makes you think she knows?'

'She says things like . . . oh, I don't know, awful cautionary tales about lack of respect, and girls not needing to do more than they want to . . . to keep men.'

'Well, you're not doing more than you want to,' Kit said briskly. 'According to yourself you're only doing what you love doing.'

'Yes, that's true, but it's not something you'd say to Aunt Maura . . . and apparently she knew Michael's father.'

'Well, isn't that good? They love knowing people and who people are.'

'I get the feeling she didn't like him.'

'Oh?'

'And when I was in Michael's house, Mr O'Connor said he sort of remembered her.'

'But not enthusiastically?'

'No, kind of furtively, if you know what I mean.'

'Maybe they had a romance.'

'I doubt it. Michael's mother and father have been married for ever.'

'I'm sure you're imagining it,' Kit said, trying to console her.

'I wish we were young again. Things were easier then.'

'You're not even twenty. A lot of people think that's still young.'

'No, you know what I mean. It's easy for you, Kit. It always has been. You'll marry Philip O'Brien and run the Central and boot awful old Mildred and Dan down into some kind of cottage and be the real queen bee of everything.'

'As long as I remember you, you've been saying that, and I've been saying I won't. Why won't you believe me?'

'Because we all do the same as our parents in the end. Your mother was glamorous and could have gone anywhere and done anything and yet she married your nice, safe father and came to live in a one-horse town like Lough Glass for security; you'll do the same.'

'And what about you? Do you love Michael, Clio?'

'I don't know. I honestly don't know. What's love?'

'I wish I knew that too,' Kit spoke absently. She wondered was there any truth in what Clio said, that people did what their mothers did. If so, there was a stormy future ahead of Kit.

Kevin O'Connor brought some friends into the bar of the hotel where Kit was working. As she served them one of his companions put a familiar hand on her bottom.

Kit tensed up immediately and looked him straight in the eye. 'Remove your hand,' she said, in a staccato voice like shots from a gun.

The boy dropped his arm immediately.

Kevin O'Connor looked at her, horrified. 'Kit, I'm sorry, I swear ... I mean ... I swear ... Matthew, why don't you fuck off out of here if you can't treat a woman with respect.'

Matthew, the offender, looked at his friend Kevin in open amazement. This was not the response he had expected. 'I was only being friendly,' he blustered.

'Leave the company,' Kevin O'Connor ordered.

'Jesus, O'Connor, you're an ignorant bollocks,' he said, aggrieved.

'If there is one more word of that language, nobody will be served,' Kit said. She was confident and secure. Not only did Kevin respect her but he made sure that his loudmouthed and ignorant friends did so too.

'Sorry, Kit,' he said to her sheepishly, as a bewildered Matthew left the hotel.

'That's all right, Kevin. Thank you.' She gave him a warm smile, and he looked pleased. She felt cheap, practising on him this way, but she had to do something to rehearse for Stevie Sullivan.

Dear Kit,

Your card about working in a bar was most entertaining. I found this book on cocktails to send you in case there might be anything in it that would be of use. It does seem a very odd thing to send you. I suppose in other circumstances someone in my position would be warning you of the evils of drink rather than sending you a book detailing ways to make even stronger concoctions. But then these are very unusual circumstances by any standards and I want to thank you for everything. It makes a huge difference.

Love Lena

Kit read the letter that came with the cocktail book a dozen times. She wondered what exactly Lena was thanking her for. For not blowing the whole situation wide open? But that was in Kit's interest, in her father's and for peace in general. Why did it make a huge difference? Her mother had left them, chosen another life. What difference could it make to get the odd card from Kit?

Possibly Lena too missed the happy carefree correspondence when she and Kit wrote as friends. Kit certainly missed it. There were so many things she would have written to Lena, had she continued to be the friend she had once been.

And not the mother who had lied to her.

'Stevie? It's Kit McMahon.' She had rung deliberately when she knew Maura would have gone across the road to have lunch with Father.

'Oh sorry, Kit, you just missed her. She'll be back at two.'

'No, it was you I wanted.'

'Great. You've saved enough to get a car?'

'No, not work. Pleasure, I'm afraid.' She could see him smiling lazily and leaning against something as he held the phone with his shoulder raised and looked for his packet of cigarettes at the same time. 'Would you like to come to a dance in Dublin next Saturday?' she asked.

'Say that again.'

If she had been keen on him, if she had waited in panic for his reaction, she would never have been able to do it. But because she was so casual she was playing it just right.

'What kind of dance?'

'Aren't you choosy?'

'Wouldn't you be if somebody phoned you out of the blue with a notion like this?' He was laughing, and playing for time.

'Yes, I would be.' Kit was being fair. 'It's one of those dances where we all pay for our own ticket in the Gresham on a Saturday night, tables you know, and a great band.'

'I've not been to one of those,' Stevie said.

'No, neither have I, and we got up a party but we're a couple of fellows short and I was wondering . . .'

'Why don't you ask Philip O'Brien? He'd go like a shot.'

'If I asked him he'd think I fancied him.'

'And what about me? What might I think?'

'Oh God, Stevie, you've known me long enough to say yes or no.'

'Would I like it?'

'You might love it. Loads of great girls, music, drink even. Wouldn't you love it?'

'And I'd be getting you out of a problem.'

'Not just that. I think you'd like the people going. I think they'd like you too, you're great fun.'

She tried to remember whether he was or not. He always seemed so jaded and cynical and eyeing people up and down. But he did have a kind of laughing way with him.

'Okay, it's a deal,' he said.

'Thanks, Stevie.' She told him where they were going to meet and how much it was going to cost.

'And do I say anything about this to your stepmother or not?'

'I leave this entirely to you whether you do or not.'

'May I put this another way, do you intend to tell her?'

'I'll probably mention sooner or later that we organised a party, but I don't believe in burdening people with every detail of life, do you?'

'I get your drift,' he said.

Kit hung up and let out a breath of relief. 'Well, Emmet. Your old sister is beginning to deliver the promise for you,' she said to herself. This at least would mean that the awful little Anna Kelly would be at a loose end for Saturday night. But she wouldn't tell Emmet yet, she didn't want him rushing in too early and ruining it all.

Stevie Sullivan hung up and looked at the phone in surprise. That McMahon girl was remarkably attractive nowadays. Imagine her asking him to make up a party. He had always wanted to go to one of those Dublin dressy-up affairs. It would mean telling Anna Kelly that the pictures were off. But he'd tell her nicely and she'd understand.

Anna Kelly didn't sound very understanding. 'I just got permission from my parents to go into the big town for the pictures. I told them a whole group of us were going.'

'Well, go then. I have to go to Dublin for work,' Stevie said.

'No, if I go it'll waste an outing I could have had with you.' Why didn't he understand?

'Well, I'm sorry too.' He gave her his lopsided grin, but it didn't work.

'You couldn't change it, I suppose,' she pleaded. Stevie looked impatient, and Anna caught the mood. 'No, I'm being silly, of course you can't. Okay, another night, right?'

'Right,' Stevie smiled. It was easy in the end if you were just nice to girls. That's what lots of people didn't understand.

'I could go to the pictures with you this weekend if you liked, Emmet . . .'

'Thanks, Anna, but no.'

'Are you sulking?'

'Absolutely not. Remember I said I wouldn't sulk. You said you and I were to be friends, that's what I'm doing.' His smile was bright.

'Well, friends go to the pictures,' Anna complained.

'That's what I said to you, but you said no, it would interfere with what there was between you and Stevie.' Again his glance was innocent.

'Yes, but as it happens Stevie is not going to be here this weekend. He's got to go to Dublin on business.'

Emmet smiled warmly. Kit had begun to do her stuff for him. 'But he'll be back of course,' he said in false consolation.

'Yes, of course he'll be back,' Anna snapped. 'But I thought that since . . .'

'You weren't asking me to come just because you were at a loose end suddenly?' Emmet shook his head in disbelief. 'We're friends, you and I. That wouldn't be the action of a friend. Just using somebody.'

She turned and walked away very fast.

'I could get all the things in that bag back to the garage for you, Francis.' Sister Madelaine was being helpful.

'I don't want to give them back, Sister.' He clutched his bag tightly.

'But it would be for the best.' Her voice was gentle.

'They're mine now. They're all I have to help me get away and make a new life.'

'If we gave them back then they might stop looking for you, and you wouldn't have to live up in the tree-house . . .' her voice trailed away. She knew when she was talking to someone who wasn't listening.

'It's all I have,' he said again, and held the bag close to him.

'What are we going to do with you?' she asked the air around her.

'You said you'd look after me.' He was plaintive now.

'I know I did, and I will.' Sister Madeleine felt less confident than she usually did.

It had always been right to do the things she had done in the past. There had not been a moment of doubt about any of these.

But recently . . . perhaps she had not been right to save the little blind kitten that everyone else said should have been put to sleep painlessly. Had its life been worth it? Certainly its slow painful death made her think not. Had she been right to keep this mentally ill man here for so long living in her tree-house? Should she have just tended his arm that first night and sent a message so that he could be taken into custody? But for Sister Madelaine any uncertainty was impossible. She had to believe in what she was doing and that it was for the best, otherwise her life had no centre.

'Very well, I won't force you, obviously,' she said.

'Will you still be nice to me?' He had the mind of a child.

'Yes, of course I will.' She dipped a metal mug into the pot over the fire and gave him soup. 'Will you want to go and look around . . . for a new life?' she asked him.

'Yes I will, soon,' he said.

'Perhaps I should cut your hair for you, make you look more . . .' Sister

Madeleine paused. What was the word she was looking for? Normal? Non-criminal?

But he nodded eagerly. 'Please Sister, that would be good.'

She tied a cloth around his neck as if she were running a barber's shop and trimmed his hair, his eyebrows and his beard. He looked far less frightening, far more ordinary, nearly normal in fact.

'When you go out, Francis, if they see you with that bag they still might put two and two together.'

'I could leave it here, Sister, for a bit.'

'You'll be back then?'

'Well, I will. I'll come back and tell you when I get settled. I think I'll just take the money.'

'Francis, might you not be better to . . . ?'

'I'll trust you, Sister, like you trusted me. You were never afraid of me, I'd not be afraid of you either.'

She gave him her hand even though her heart was troubled.

'That's right Francis, you can trust me. In a world full of people you don't know about, you can rely on me.' And she was rewarded by the big and foolish smile of a slow child. A child in a big, strong, man's body.

*

'I wish we had a car,' Louis grumbled as they were getting dressed.

'Let's get one then.'

'Easy to say.' He spent a time fixing his tie.

'Easy to do. We haven't bought a house, we've no mortgage, no children. What are we saving for?'

'We're not saving much,' he said.

Which in Louis' case was true. But he didn't know how carefully Lena put away money. How her account in the Building Society was mounting, how shares in Millar's were increasing every year.

'Well, let's see how much you could afford a month,' Lena began.

'Not much.'

'I'll see if I can raise a deposit. You know, get it a bit as a perk from my work.'

'Could you?' Louis looked at her, his eyes were alight.

For a man so clever at deceiving, at attracting people, and knowing what a customer in a hotel might want, he was remarkably innocent and naive about other things. It didn't even occur to him to enquire why Mr Millar might give her a car allowance since she lived five minutes away from her job and went there on foot every morning.

'Yes, it's a possibility, isn't it?' he agreed.

'So this is the last time we head out for the home counties by train,' she laughed.

'I love you, Lena,' he said and came across to kiss her as she sat at a smaller mirror in a poorer light fixing her earrings. He hadn't noticed that there was new colour in her hair, but he did think she looked well.

Grace's salon had come up trumps again.

The taxi driver at the station said he knew the road. 'That's where the nobs live,' he said.

'Great,' Louis said. 'We wouldn't want to be going anywhere downmarket.' He had such an infectious way with him.

The driver, in his shabby coat and his nicotine-stained fingers, who would never be allowed inside the gates of these houses unless he was driving a taxi, seemed pleased and enthusiastic. That was Louis all over: he made other people glad that he was around.

James Williams was divorced, Lena knew. But he had a friend, a lady who had great designs on being the next Mrs Williams, Louis had said.

'Will she?' Lena had wanted to know.

'No, I think he's too clever for that,' Louis had smiled.

Lena smiled too. How innocent of Louis to admit to her that a clever man avoided marriage, commitment of any kind. As if she didn't know already that this was his view.

James Williams was delighted to see them. A kiss on each cheek for Lena. 'You look younger every day.'

'You're too kind.'

'No, I mean it. Come in, come in and meet everyone . . . Laura, come here and meet Lena Gray.'

Laura was hard as nails. Shiny red lipstick, shiny metallic black hair, a satin blouse with a sheen and a tight black shiny skirt. Her shoes were patent leather high heels. She looked as if she had been polished and burnished. 'The famous Mrs Gray,' she said, looking Lena up and down.

'Ah no, it's my husband who's the famous one in the hotel business.'

'James always brings your name into the conversation . . . if I didn't know better I'd think he fancied you . . .'

James Williams had turned to welcome Louis.

Lena looked at Laura long and hard. 'But you know better.'

'Oh, I know better.' She paused. Her eyes flickered over towards Louis and away again. Lena thought she was going to say that she realised Lena had a very fanciable man of her own. But she wasn't looking at it from that point of view. 'I know better, because if James had fancied you he'd have done something about it.'

'And what's your second name, Laura?'

'Why on earth do you ask?' Laura looked at her as if Lena had committed the greatest social *faux pas* of all time.

But Lena had not been idle in her years of dealing with people through Millar's Agency. She was not easily put down. 'Because it wasn't given to me,' she said, in the coolest tones possible.

Their eyes held each other.

'Evans,' she said eventually.

Did James Williams sense the mood? Or was it by pure coincidence that he turned and placed an arm on each of their shoulders. 'Now let me take my two favourite ladies to meet the rest of the guests.'

Lena didn't look at Laura, but she knew that in this unexpected and unimportant battle that had suddenly flamed up she, Lena, had most definitely won.

They had never been to a party like this before, but Lena knew how it was going to turn out. She could see from the outset the two women who would vie for Louis' attention. And she knew now that Angela would win.

Let them fight it out. Let him ply one with plates of tiny cocktail sausages on coloured sticks, let him fill the other's glass. Let him laugh, delighted, into both their eager faces. That was part of the fun. This was probably the only fun.

Lena pretended the party was a conference. She told the stockbrokers and their wives that she worked in an employment agency. She refused to give business cards; it was a party in someone's house. But she did say the name Millar's so often that nobody would have forgotten it. She advised them about their daughters, their mature, unmarried, own hopeless office staff, none of whom could spell 'sincerely' or 'faithfully' so all letters had to end simply 'yours'.

And as she moved, talking animatedly but not stridently, she knew people were interested in her. A groomed, handsome woman, in charge of her own life, unaware or possibly indifferent to the fact that her handsome husband was being overtly flirtatious with two of the other guests. And Lena knew that the eyes of James Williams were on her all night.

And that Laura Evans, who might never be Laura Williams, was drinking far too much and far too quickly. Already there was a stain down the shiny cream satin blouse, a stain that looked ugly and out of character with the elegant woman who should have been acting as a hostess for James tonight.

It was only when everyone had gone that Laura seemed to remember any hostess duties. 'Better clear up all this mess,' she grumbled, staggering towards a table with glasses on it.

'Leave it Laura. It'll all be done.'

'I don't mind. I do stay here. I don't want the place looking like bedlam.' She looked at Lena to make sure the part about staying here wasn't lost.

'Yes, well. Everyone's staying here . . .' James was easy. 'Let's have a last drink and a post mortem.'

But Laura was having none of it. She lurched towards the glasses and missed her footing, then fell, spilling dregs of wine and splintering some of the glasses on the floor.

'Now will you leave it, Laura?' James was exasperated, as you might be with a small child, but not angry.

'I'll pick them up, let me.'

'Maybe it'd be better to wait for the daylight,' Lena suggested mildly. 'Easier to see all the little bits of glass then, than in the artificial light.'

'I can see perfectly well,' Laura said and fell, cutting herself on both palms on the broken glass.

Lena took her to the kitchen and silently picked the particles of glass from Laura's hands. Then she dabbed the cuts with TCP. 'There, you're fine now,' she said eventually.

'Stop being so bloody patronizing,' Laura said.

'She means, thank you very much,' James said.

'I meant stop being so bloody patronizing,' Laura said.

'Those look very slight, but they can sting a lot,' Lena said, referring to the marks on Laura's hands.

'You're a proper pain in the arse,' Laura said, flouncing to the door. 'No wonder he never made a move on you, Lena Gray. You were too po-faced. You'd have frozen him out of it.'

'Good night, Laura,' James Williams said coldly.

They sat by the fire, the three of them. They talked about the party, the neighbours, the things people had said about *Room at the Top*. Some had thought it very vulgar, others had said it was realistic about England at last. They talked about Cliff Richard and Yves St Laurent. 'Would many of the guests have met either of them?' Louis asked his boss respectfully.

Nobody visiting this house had ever been within an ass's roar of either Cliff Richard, or Yves St Laurent, who had shortened skirts again. But she said nothing. It was part of Louis' charm to look innocent and vulnerable when it mattered.

What she found a little uneasy making was the way James Williams caught her eye. It was as if he understood not only the crassness of Laura Evans who would, after tonight, never become Mrs Laura Williams, but also the naiveté of Louis Gray, who would never in a million years be as smart as his wife, Lena.

It was an awkward moment. Lena let her glance fall to the floor. 'Well, do you think . . . ?' Louis suggested.

'You must be exhausted, James . . . how lovely to have met all your friends,' Lena said.

He showed them up the stairs to the room, the big guest room with a bathroom of its own adjoining. It was more elegant than anywhere they had ever stayed. The sound of snoring came from an open door, and a glance showed Laura Evans asleep on a bed, one shoe on the floor, the other dangling. It was unlikely that James Williams would sleep beside her.

When the door was closed, Louis reached for Lena as she had known he would. There was nothing that excited him so much as knowing that two women had left that party unwillingly. Both of them would have given anything to have been with Louis Gray that night. Lena knew that this would make Louis desire her very much indeed.

'You're beautiful,' he whispered into her ear.

'I love you,' she said truthfully.

'You're a queen among the women here tonight,' he said.

Lena closed her eyes. Well at least she wasn't lying drunk and snoring like Laura Evans, the woman who had hopes of the host, and she hadn't gone home to her own house as had done the ladies Louis had found attractive. She was here, sober and not looking her forty-five years. Yes, she was certainly queen for the night.

*

'I was wondering, that is *we* were wondering, if you'd do us the honour of being a witness.'

'In a case, a court case?'

'In a registry office, you dolt. I'm asking you to be my bridesmaid.'

'You're getting married?' Lena looked at her, astounded.

'Well, I did all the things you told me to.'

'Oh, Ivy, I'm so happy for you. When did you decide this?'

'Last night.'

'And is Ernest all delighted too?'

'Of course he's not, let's not ask for the moon. But he says it's what we should do. And it's most certainly what I want to do. Always wanted to do.' Her eyes were very bright.

'Isn't that great!' Lena hugged her tight and over her friend's shoulder, as she saw the walls with all their postcards, clippings, cuttings and little pictures, she thought how much Ivy deserved good luck and happiness.

*

'There you are, Mona.' Martin McMahon handed her bottle of tablets across the counter.

Mona Fitz from the post office was on a mild blood pressure medication. Martin could have prescribed for almost everyone in the town even if Peter wasn't here, he knew their complaints and symptoms so intimately.

'These keep me alive, Martin.' Mona was very dramatic.

'Indeed they do,' he nodded gravely.

That's the way she liked to play it. No point in telling her how slight their strength and how unimportant it would be if one or indeed several days were missed. Tablet-taking and spooning from a bottle had almost magic powers. No one knew this better than the local pharmacist.

'Tommy's cut heal up all right?' he enquired about the postman who had ordered a lot of bandages and sticking plaster, as well as disinfectant.

'I didn't know he had one,' Mona said.

Martin McMahon often wished he hadn't made some harmless remark. It could lead to endless speculation. He could see Mona Fitz looking puzzled.

'He could have hurt his leg but he never said a word. I might be wrong, I'm often wrong about things.' He looked apologetic.

But Mona was having none of it. 'Of course you're not, Martin. Would we all be able to take our pills and bottles from you if you were wrong about things?' Her tone was most reproving indeed. And she went off puzzling why Tommy Bennet would have needed to buy bandages.

The house seemed oddly empty when Francis Ryan had left. Sister Madeleine felt no need to build up the fire that evening. When she went out of her door there was no cause to look up and over at the tree-house with a friendly wave. When people brought a cake or bread she knew that this time she would have to walk over to the travellers to make sure that it got a proper home. Francis Xavier Ryan could eat an entire loaf of bread from which she had cut one slice for herself.

In a bizarre way, even though he was disturbing and a worry, he was company for her. The nights strangely now seemed very long. She prayed that he would make his way all right. That he would come back in some months for the rest of his things. To tell her that he was well settled now, under another name, working for a farmer. Or maybe as a chopper of wood in a big monastery where the monks would be kind to him. Better, he might write and say that she could give back the bag of items taken from Sullivan's garage. He couldn't write, of course. But someone would do a letter for him. Some kind person who was looking after him now as she had looked after him.

Philip had come home for the night; he had brought all his washing with him on the bus.

'You look like Dick Whittington,' Kit had said.

'Don't you bring your washing home?'

'I most certainly do not, I wash it myself.'

'You're a woman.'

'That's very true, but even if I were a man I would too.'

'You only say that because you're not,' Philip said.

'Not true.'

'Or to fight with me,' he said glumly.

'Now that's certainly not true.' She laid her hand on his arm. 'I think you're terrific. You got rid of all this lovey-dovey bit and we've been great friends, you and I, haven't we?'

'I only got rid of the lovey-dovey bit on the outside,' Philip said sadly.

For a moment he reminded her of her brother Emmet and the way he talked about Anna Kelly. Wouldn't it be extraordinary to feel so strongly about someone as that? She was brisk with Philip. 'Nonsense. It's gone totally,' she said.

'It's not, Kit. It's there and aches a lot of the time, like a nagging toothache; it keeps asking me questions.'

'What does it ask?' She couldn't be harsh or flippant with him. He was far too like Emmet.

'Things like . . . why didn't you ask me to join this group for the dance you're setting up for Saturday?' His disappointment was naked.

'*I'm* not really setting it up, it's other people too.'

'If you wanted me there you'd have asked.'

'Well, you're going home.' She was anxious not to have him hurt.

'I'm only going home so as not to be around. If you asked me to the dance I'd not be going home.'

She wanted desperately not to disappoint him. But she couldn't have him there while she was making her play for Stevie Sullivan, that would be even worse. 'It'll all work out all right in the end, Philip,' she said.

'It better had,' Philip said. 'It sure as anything isn't working out well now.'

It was dark when Philip got off the bus in Lough Glass. He didn't know why he had come home. His mother was bound to complain that they saw so little of him. His father was going to tell him that he had chosen the world's worst trade, that the hotel business was over. Kit was in Dublin organising a gathering of her friends of which he apparently wasn't one.

The porter in the hotel welcomed him in a half-hearted way. Philip knew that was the way Jimmy would greet anyone. The boss's son, a regular customer, a new American visitor; the half shrug and grunt and weary sigh would be your welcome to O'Brien's Central Hotel.

'I'll leave my things here for a bit and go down and have a walk by the lake,' Philip said, a heavy unwillingness to go into his family home coming on him suddenly.

'Suit yourself,' said Jimmy.

Philip went down the lane to the lakeside. He looked back up at the hotel. One of the best frontages in Ireland, they should be doing much much more than they were. He sighed, and walked along moodily by the shore, watching the winds whip up the lake into what looked like waves. He often thought about Kit's mother, dying here alone that night. He had tried to mention it to Kit to show he understood, that he wasn't just an insensitive hulk like so many men. But she never wanted to talk about it.

Without realising it, Philip's walk had taken him towards Sister Madeleine's cottage. He knew the hermit, of course, like everyone did. But he had not been one to go in and give her his confidences. He was about to turn away when he saw her standing at the door. She clutched a shawl around her thin shoulders, and there was something about the way she hugged herself to make Philip think she was in distress.

He debated slipping away. After all, she had not seen him. She had chosen to live this strange hermit existence. There was probably nothing wrong at all, just his imagination. But something made him call out. 'Are you all right, Sister Madeleine?'

She squinted out into the dark. 'Who is that? It's so dark.'

'Philip O'Brien,' he called back.

'Isn't that grand, the very person,' she said. Philip's heart sank, she wanted him to do some errand. 'Would you like a cup of tea? It hardly seems worth making one for myself.'

It was an odd thing to say. She lived by herself. For heaven's sake, she must always be making cups of tea on her own. Still, it would be welcome; he was stiff and tired after the journey. He followed her in. 'How's the kitten, the little blind one?' he asked. He remembered Kit had told him that the hermit had insisted she could give it a good life.

'It died. Drowned there in three inches of water outside my door.' Her voice was curiously flat and dead.

'Oh, I'm sorry.'

'It should have died the first day, the vet was right.'

'Maybe it had a nice life.'

'No, it had a stupid life, hitting its poor little head on things.'

Philip had no idea how to contribute to the conversation, so he said nothing, just settled himself on the three-legged stool to await tea.

She cut him a slice of currant bread and spread it with butter. 'You're an earnest fellow, Philip. It's the kind of thing that will stand to you in the future.'

'I hope *something* will stand to me in the future.' He was morose.

'So life isn't good?'

'I want to marry Kit MacMahon,' he said suddenly. 'Not now, but in a couple of years' time maybe. And I've always known that. I've known it since way back the night her mother died, and that's years ago.'

'Yes,' Sister Madeleine said looking into the fire.

'But being patient isn't enough. She must like someone else and she hasn't told me.'

'Why do you think that?' The old nun's voice was gentle.

He explained about the dance. If there hadn't been someone else special she wouldn't have kept Philip out so deliberately. 'I just don't know who it is,' he said, his face sad and resigned.

'There might be nobody.'

'No, her mind's very caught up with somebody.'

'I'm going to tell you something ... I know Kit does have problems on her mind ... and something which takes up a lot of her attention, but I assure you it's not another boy. You have no rival. She's just not ready to think about men yet.' Her eyes were very bright and very blue. They almost bored through him. He believed her and he trusted her. His heart felt light. 'Go on back to the hotel, Philip. Your mother and father will be looking out for you.'

'They know I'm back, I left my stuff with Jimmy. Bundle of fun, Jimmy. A hundred thousand welcomes to Lough Glass written in his face.'

'If you had Jimmy's life you might have a few less welcomes written in your face too.' She spoke in general tones. He would never know what she had learned of Jimmy's life, but it made him feel a small wave of sympathy. It can have been no picnic working for the O'Briens, chopping wood, filling coal scuttles in rain and heat.

'You're very good for people, you know,' he said as he left.

'I used to think so, Philip. Nowadays I'm not so sure.' She shivered although she was in no draught.

'Goodbye and thank you ... thank you again.'

She made no reply. She was sitting looking into the fire. He pulled the door after him and fastened the latch. He walked back along the lake shore with a smarter step. Kit didn't love anyone else. She would have told the hermit, they were great friends altogether. This was very good news, very good news indeed.

On that Saturday in November Martin McMahon told his wife Maura that they were going to get a new car. He had been discussing it with Stevie Sullivan but it was a surprise until now.

'That's the one the great spit-and-polish job was being done on.' Maura was delighted. 'I can tell you we're not getting anything half looked at. Stevie was under the bonnet and lying under the chassis examining every inch of it.'

'You're the best husband that ever lived,' she said.

'I wasn't always a good husband.' There was a shadow on his face.

She could see him almost physically struggling. She laid her hand on his arm. 'Wherever Helen's soul is today it's at peace, Martin. We've told each other that so often ... and we believe it. None of us can look back on any year, any hour even, and not wish that we had done something differently. But remember, we worked all this out. Time spent regretting is time wasted.'

He nodded. She could see the shadow beginning to lessen.

*

Lena Gray was explaining to Jim and Jessie Millar that she would be buying the car through the firm.

'But of course you can have a car,' Mr Millar said. 'Haven't I asked you a dozen times to take something out of this firm that you built up to be what it is.'

'I won't use it, Jim. It's for my husband, so I want to pay for it.'

'No, the principle is still the same.'

'You don't take things out of the firm for your own personal use. I will not either.'

*

Kit arranged that they should have a little party in Frankie's flat. The girls would provide some wine, and cheese on biscuits. Later on at the hotel the boys would pay for drinks, so this sort of evened it out.

'They're not coming back for coffee,' Frankie explained very firmly. 'The landlady here has her hand on the phone to all of our mothers if a fellow comes into the house after ten o'clock.'

The others agreed. Bringing guys back to a flat afterwards was asking for it. It was cheap.

Clio heard about the party and came down to challenge Kit.

'Why was I excluded?' she asked.

'You weren't included, that's a totally different thing. This is just friends to do with catering.'

'Kevin O'Connor is going,' Clio said.

'Yes. It may have escaped your notice and probably everyone else's but he *is* meant to be in catering, you know.'

'Well, it may have escaped your notice that I happen to be going out with his brother,' Clio said.

'Clio, you and Michael can afford to go to the Gresham to a dance every night they have one,' Kit said.

'I wish I knew what you were planning to do with your life, Kit McMahon,' Clio said.

'So do I,' Kit agreed fervently.

*

The Blue Lagoon was showing in the town. It would have been great to go with Anna, but Emmet knew he mustn't weaken. He saw Patsy Hanley walking disconsolately down the main street of Lough Glass. 'Would you like to go to the pictures tonight?' he said quickly before he could change his mind.

Patsy blushed with pleasure. 'Me? Just me, like a date?'

'Sure.'

'I'd love that,' she said and scampered home to get organised.

Anna Kelly had intended to go to *The Blue Lagoon* with some of the girls from her class, but fortunately for her pride she heard that Patsy Hanley was going to go with Emmet. They would all be on the same bus.

She wouldn't let anyone see her being a wallflower. She would stay at home. In fact, she would stay at home alone because her mother and father would be having dinner at a golf club. Anna felt this was a very bad way of spending a Saturday night.

Philip sat with his father and mother in the dining room. The walls were a mournful brown; the table cloths were stained with the memory of too many sauce bottles. The lighting was poor, and the service was slow.

Philip knew that this was not a hotel that would tempt anyone to make a return visit; it was not the place that would invite a business traveller to come back with his family. It was going to be a long uphill road to transform it. He had hoped he would have had Kit McMahon at his side. And perhaps that hope was not so farfetched. Sister Madeleine had been very confident and sure when she spoke. She had extraordinary piercing eyes; you believed everything they said, and she had assured him that Kit McMahon had no other love.

Philip sat trying to work out what other problems Kit might have that took up her time and attention. His parents looked at him without much pleasure.

'You're gone for weeks on end and then not a word out of you when you come home,' his mother complained.

'You know, son, if you're ever going to make any kind of a fist out of the hotel business you're going to have to be outgoing, greet people,' said Philip's father Dan O'Brien, who had never been known to begin any conversation except with a list of moans and complaints.

'You're right,' he said agreeably. 'I'm luckier than a lot of the others, I have a hotel in my family where I can learn.'

They looked at him suspiciously, in case he was making fun of them, but could see no sign of it.

Philip nailed a smile to his face and wondered whether any other young man of his age was having such an appalling Saturday night.

*

'Who'll be first?' Frankie wondered as they admired the table.

It looked very festive with its coloured candles and paper napkins, and plates of food. They had speared an orange with little cocktail sticks, each one bearing a cube of cheese and a portion of pineapple. They had stuffed hard-boiled eggs, where the yolks had been taken out, mixed with mayonnaise, and put back. There were bottles of beer and glasses of red and white wine.

'I bet you it'll be that Kevin O'Connor,' Kit grumbled.

'I don't think he's all that bad,' Frankie said. 'You have him actually crawling on the ground he's so afraid of you, and still you won't be civil to him.'

'He has been very uncivil to me indeed in the past,' Kit said. 'It's hard to forget that sort of thing.'

'You have to forget,' Frankie shrugged. She almost shrugged herself out of her strapless taffeta dress and made a note not to raise her shoulders again.

'Do you, though?' Kit was wondering.

'Do you what?'

'Do you have to forget?'

'Jesus, Kit, of course you do, otherwise wars would be going on for ever and women would be committing suicide over fellows they loved.'

'But what's the point of anything if it can be forgotten, wiped out, start again?' Kit asked.

'Listen, we're having a party, not a debate,' Frankie said. 'Who do you hope to end up with tonight?'

'I don't know. Maybe the fellow from my own home town. He's very good looking, Stevie.' Kit said this partly to put the glamorous Frankie in the position of knowing that Stevie was out of bounds, partly to convince herself. In her heart she knew that Stevie was cheap and obvious.

The doorbell rang. 'Here we go,' said Frankie, bouncing off to answer it. She came back in, eyes rolling up to heaven and followed by the most handsome man that any of them were ever likely to see in a long time.

In his dinner jacket, his hair longish but clean and shiny, with his outdoor look from working all weathers, fitter than any of the college sportsmen, and with a smile that would stop a hundred women in their tracks, Stevie Sullivan was like something that had stepped down from a poster outside a cinema.

'Well, don't you look great!' Kit said before she could help herself.

'You beat me to it,' he said. His eyes were warm and admiring on her bare shoulders and the peach-coloured silk dress with its halter neckline.

Kit had been worried about not wearing a bra, but the girl in the shop had assured her it was so well formed in the bodice that no other undergarments were needed. She thought she felt Stevie Sullivan's eyes examining the bodice as if he were making the assessment too, but then she was sure she imagined it.

The doorbell rang again at that moment and several more guests arrived. One was Kevin O'Connor. He made straight for Kit. 'I just want to say that Matthew is here, but he's under observation from all of us. Anything untoward and he'll be sent home. Just so that you understand.'

'Matthew?' Kit said, confused.

'Yes, who made the unfortunate mistake and behaved in a manner that was unseemly when you were working in the bar. That's him over there at the door. I said I'd come in and clear it with you. He's replacing Harry, you see.'

'It's all right. He may stay,' Kit said regally. 'As long as everything is under control.'

'You have my word on that,' Kevin assured her.

'My God, Kit McMahon, don't you have Dublin brought down to size,' Stevie said admiringly.

'Ah you don't know the half of it, Stevie.' She tucked her arm companionably in his and brought him around to introduce him. She saw from the looks that he was getting that she wasn't alone in her admiration. Stevie Sullivan dressed up and in a place like this was a knock-out. Far too good for Clio's horrible little sister. Suddenly Kit remembered the purpose of the whole evening. She must distract him from Anna, so that Anna would go back humbly to Emmet. She must dazzle the eyes out of him at this dance. It mightn't work but she was certainly going to give it her best try.

*

It was the usual Saturday night in the golf club and the Kellys and the McMahons were finishing their dinner as they did so many weekends. It seemed impossible to believe that this had not always been the way things were.

They talked about the children. Clio wasn't studying that much, they knew. When she came home for visits it was always to sleep. 'I don't think she sleeps at all in Dublin.' Lilian worried about her elder daughter. Maura McMahon worried about where Clio slept, but this was not the time nor the place to bring up such a subject.

'Apparently Kit is going to a dance tonight,' Peter Kelly said. 'Clio was on the phone full of envy about it all.'

'That's right. They were having a party in some girls' flat first. I think it was the College of Catering people.' Martin was always a peacemaker.

'Oh, I'm sure. Anyway, Clio said that if she could get a lift home she'd come tonight.'

'That would be nice,' Maura said, a little insincerely. She found her niece trying and unrestful. There was always some hidden tension there.

'I left a plate of sandwiches out for her,' Lilian said fussing. 'Anna's not going to eat ever again she says; she has this belief that she's as fat as a pig. Lord they can be very hard to cope with sometimes.'

'I see young Philip's home,' Martin said. 'They could have come down together for the company.'

'Oh she's full of some boy with a posh car. He might drive her.' Lilian sounded worried.

'Will he want to stay?' Peter asked.

'That wasn't mentioned. And you know Clio, she'd snap your head off if you asked a question. We'll have to wait and see. I did leave out some clean sheets and pillow cases in case.'

Maura said nothing. She knew the boy in the posh car was the son of Fingers O'Connor.

Francis Fingleton O'Connor was a legendary hotelier who had made a fortune through his four strategically placed hotels in Ireland. But he was even more legendary for his belief that he was attractive to all women, and that all a woman needed to make her feel feminine and desired was a grope and a feel, and a few suggestive remarks. Maura had met him on more than one occasion through her work, and had disliked him intensely. She had kept her hostility until she was sure she was not observed and then had told him that his attentions were unwelcome, in such a firm tone that even Fingers O'Connor understood. But about this, as about so many things, she kept her own counsel.

Kit had mentioned that a son of his, Kevin, was in Cathal Brugha Street with her. An unpleasant lout, Kit had said. Maura told no tales, but was glad to hear it. Clio, on the other hand, seemed very involved with the boy's brother. Maura felt sure it was the lure of the car and the lifestyle.

She brought up the subject of Emmet; there would be no dissension here surely. 'He's gone to the pictures tonight. Aren't they all getting very grown up, all four of them with their own lives to live,' Maura said admiringly.

She thought that the Kellys didn't seem particularly confident that their daughters were leading their own lives very well. One was coming back discontentedly from Dublin to sleep for hour after hour. The other was sitting at a kitchen table on her own refusing to go to the pictures or to eat. And both of them such beautiful girls, Maura thought.

For the first time for a long time she thought of Helen McMahon. Her beauty had brought her nothing but tragedy.

*

'They're too old to get married,' Louis said about Ivy and Ernest. His tone was dismissive.

'Why not if they want to?' Lena knew that Louis would take this line. She had prepared herself for it, and was determined not to sound defensive.

'Ah come on, it's ridiculous. Everyone knows they've been at it for years, why doesn't he move in or she move in, not all this Love, Honour and Obey bit?'

'It's a sign, that's all.' She knew she was short.

'It's a sign of nothing.'

'Not to people like us,' she said as if it was obvious. 'We don't need things like that, you and I . . . because I think we know, but other people often do need them. You're usually so tolerant of the things people do that we don't understand . . . Why can't you be glad for Ivy and Ernest that they're making a bit of a thing out of it?' It was exactly the right tone.

'Well yes, when you look at it like that . . .' It was as if he felt a burden, a threat, lifted from him. 'Hey, let's buy them a bottle and go down straight. Make a bit of a party of it, remind them that it's their last Saturday as free people.' He was all smiles now. He would charm them to bits.

Lena was right. Louis was the life and soul of the party. He had invited all the tenants to come in and wish the happy couple well. Each one had brought a little gift. Ernest and Ivy were overcome with the emotion of it all.

'How did you know?' Ivy whispered to one of the New Zealanders.

'Mr Gray told us. He wanted it to be a bit of a celebration,' she said.

'You've got a good man there,' Ivy said to Lena.

'Yes,' Lena said.

Ivy looked at her sharply. 'Deep down he's full of heart,' Ivy insisted. Ivy, who knew how unfaithful he was, how hard she tried to entertain him. Ivy, who alone knew that they were not married, could be fooled by this little gesture of goodwill.

Lena felt that life was all an act. 'I know,' she said, in a voice that had no life in it. She felt that she had stepped outside herself and that she was watching this whole scene without being a part of it. It was she who had thought of having a celebration to mark Ivy's happiness. She had swallowed her own feelings of jealousy and envy at Ivy's sudden rush of luck in the security of her man. Ivy deserved this, and Lena was glad for her neighbour and friend's moment of happiness.

Louis had felt it was meaningless and foolish for people of this age to marry and that as an empty symbol it was laughable. But once Lena had been able to rid him of any residual guilt he changed and turned it into a triumphal party.

She watched the others looking at Louis, animated, handsome and the centre of attention. He was a sham, she thought angrily, he was a fraud and a con trick. Why had she wasted her life on him? Why was she not back in Lough Glass where she belonged with her family, with her children who needed her?

What was she *doing* in this ridiculous house in London, working her guts out for an employment agency up the road, drinking a toast to Ivy and Ernest in a roomful of people she hardly knew? This was a Saturday night, she should be at home in Lough Glass.

A terrible emptiness took hold of her. At home in Lough Glass doing what?

*

Michael O'Connor and Clio drove through the night to Lough Glass.

'You do know we can't sleep together at home,' Clio said.

'So you keep saying.'

'No, so I keep insisting. I wouldn't have to if you didn't just take it as a joke.'

'Peace, peace. We start the night in separate places and then you creep along to me. Right?'

'No, Michael, not right. This is the house that I was born in and grew up in. My parents are there with ears sharpened waiting for every creak of the floorboards.'

'We'll find a way around them.'

'No!' She sounded very angry.

He pulled the car into the side of the road. 'What's this, what are we fighting about?' he asked.

'About the fact that I did say to you before we left Dublin that this wasn't on. I didn't want you to be under any false impression.' She looked very troubled and very young. Her blonde curls looked babyish and her lower lip was trembling like any toddler's.

He softened. 'Okay, okay. I take your point.'

'But will you take it when you're in the spare room, Michael?' she asked.

'I don't know. It depends on how eager I feel.'

'Unless you know that it doesn't matter how eager you feel, we're not going any further. We stop right here,' she said.

'Oh, really, and what would you do in the middle of nowhere?'

'I'd either get out and hitch or I'd come back to Dublin with you.' She sounded more confident than she felt.

'Aw to hell, we're halfway there. I'll drive you to Loughwhatsit and then go back to civilisation.'

'It's too much to ask.'

'The lady must be obeyed.'

'Honestly, Michael.'

'No, I want to see your place anyway. I have to report on whether my girlfriend is my social equal.' She assumed he was joking and laughed. 'I'm deadly serious,' Michael said. 'My father keeps asking me what class of a girl Maura Hayes's niece is. I think your aunt was quite a goer.'

'A goer?'

'A flier.'

'Aunt Maura? You have to be joking.'

'That's what he says, or sort of doesn't say. A real party girl.'

'Is that good or bad?'

'It's great. Like you, a party girl, full of fun.' He gave her a squeeze and then reminded himself that this was not the place or time. 'No point in getting myself going, especially if nothing lovely lies ahead for me.'

They drove through the dark Irish countryside, through small villages, and past farmhouses with lights in the windows, past herds of cattle looking at them over hedges. Past wayside shrines to Our Lady of Lourdes. But they spoke of none of these things they passed. They had little conversation, Clio realised; it was not a life that involved much sitting down together and chatting about the way of the world.

But then they had something much more important, they had a very passionate love life. Most people weren't lucky enough to have that. Ever. Clio knew now how hard it was to define love in poems or in paintings or in music. It was all about ... well, closeness, being intimate. That kind of thing was impossible to describe.

She looked at Michael's face as he drove. She wondered was he thinking something on the same lines. She placed her hand on his leg.

'We're very lucky, aren't we?' Clio said.

'No, we're bloody not ... your parents are there waiting like grizzly bears to catch us.'

'They're not at home yet, they'll be up in the golf club,' Clio said.

Michael's face brightened. 'Maybe we'd have time before they got back,' he said.

Clio looked at her watch. It was ten o'clock, they were half an hour from Lough Glass, but her mother and father rarely left the golf club before midnight. 'Drive faster,' she said, and was rewarded by Michael's whoop of delight.

Sister Madeleine was restless. Yet again the evening seemed long and lonely to her. This was something she must not allow to happen. She had craved to be away from the ceaseless chatter and business of other people's lives. She had always been proud to live comfortably with her own thoughts. But maybe that was in the days when she had faith in her own thoughts. Recently she was less and less sure of everything, and when the certainty had gone a lot of other things went too.

The shadows of evening over the lake seemed a little menacing now: the creaks and sounds in the trees around, the rustle in the undergrowth. She could see the limits of the travellers' camp in the woods. They had a fire and they would make her welcome but she would cast a quietness on them. She would change their mood. She looked through the trees up at Lough Glass, and saw the lights of the one long street. In those houses were settled people, not travellers, not hermits like herself. She knew most of their stories, their secrets. There was hardly a home where they wouldn't reach out a hand and pull her warmly into the house.

But there was something holding Sister Madeleine back. If she went calling, if she gave up this life of independence, she would be lost. She told herself that she was being full of fancies. She tried to imagine that she was one of the many who filed to her little cottage for advice. What would she have said?

'The great trouble with most of us is that we think too much about ourselves, that's what makes our problems seem so much more important than they are. Now if you were to think about someone else . . .' Very good advice, but the only person she could think of was poor Francis with his scattered wits wandering somewhere in the night. She wished she could believe he was settled and safe. He had been gone for three days. She shivered as she tried to imagine where he was laying his head this Saturday night. She wished it was still on the settle bed beside the open fire in her little cottage.

*

There was a buzz of conversation in Frankie's flat. The party was going well. Frankie and Kit looked at each other in delight. It was working better than they had hoped. It would be magic when they got to the ballroom. Kevin O'Connor was standing beside Matthew, the one-time foul-mouthed friend, as if he were a bodyguard. Kit had to stifle her amusement. Boys were so young really compared to girls. Those two were behaving as if they were Emmet's age.

Thinking about Emmet she realised she had been neglecting the night's mission. It wasn't enough to lure Stevie to Dublin for just one Saturday night, she must try and let him think she was interested in him so that he would forget Anna and concentrate all his attentions on her.

Really, those Kelly girls were very tiresome, Kit said to herself. Clio had behaved like a wounded deer just because she wasn't included, but it would have been impossible to have her. The whole of Lough Glass would know that Kit McMahon had behaved disgracefully with Stevie Sullivan, which was what she was now about to do.

She smeared a little Vaseline over her lipstick to make her mouth look shinier and moved over to where he was standing talking cars, relaxed, at ease, as if he spent every Saturday night in the company of people in evening dresses and dinner jackets. He was far more comfortable there than some of the guests. Kit decided that he might not be as rough a diamond as she had thought, or perhaps he was just a very good actor.

'We're thinking about who'll go in whose car down to the Gresham,' she said. 'Do you have room for a few in yours?'

'Sure,' he smiled easily.

Kevin was beside her blustering. 'I'll take you, Kit. I've got the Morris tonight, plenty of room, we can get four in the back.'

'I have to help Frankie as hostess and sort of be in charge,' Kit smiled at him sweetly. Kevin beamed back idiotically. He seemed to have been forgiven, welcomed back to the fold. She laid her hand on Kevin's arm. 'Why don't you be a sweetheart and get Matthew in the front seat where you can keep an eye on him and take those four girls over there?'

Kevin was delighted to oblige. Kit did rapid mental arithmetic and saw to it that Stevie was driving her and her alone. When they locked the door of the flat behind them, Paddy and Frankie had been installed in one of the other cars, Stevie and Kit were left together.

'So nobody wanted to come with us?' He looked at her playfully.

'That's the way it turned out,' she said.

He opened the door of a very smart car indeed.

'What is it?' she asked in wonder.

'It's an E-type,' said Stevie casually.

'Well now, if they'd seen this we'd have been killed in the rush,' she said.

'No good, Kit, if they just want you for the car. They have to want you for yourself,' he said.

He was easy company, semi-flirting, more admiring really. She found it easy to play her role.

'Ah, I'd say you have no trouble in that department,' she said.

'What department?'

'The department where they want you for yourself. Queuing up from what I hear.'

'Come on out of that, you're the girl next door, remember. You never saw any queues form at the garage.'

'I saw enough,' Kit laughed.

He looked at her and she smiled quite deliberately, like people did in films. It felt corny inside but he liked it. 'You've certainly changed since those days,' he said.

'Have I? I feel just the same.'

'No you don't. You were a silly giggling schoolgirl with Clio. You laughed at everything and everyone.'

'And now I'm all morose, is that it?' Again she looked up at him from under her eyelashes. Kit wondered was she overdoing this.

Stevie wasn't a fool, he must know what she was trying on, and despise her. But apparently not. 'That's a nice crowd of friends you have,' he said. 'Yes ... that's the great thing about Dublin, isn't it? There's a chance to meet so many more people than at home. Is the big blond guy your boyfriend?' He was very direct.

'Why do you ask?' She had raised her eyebrows. Surely he'd tell her to stop play-acting.

'He seemed very attentive.'

'He's in my year at the Catering College.'

'Is he that O'Connor, of the hotels?' How quick he was. He had learned Kevin's name and put two and two together.

'That's it,' she said. She had an urge to tell him that Kevin O'Connor was a great ignorant loudmouth who had told all his friends that he had slept with her, and paid dearly for it. That he was afraid out of his life of her now. That he would probably run one at least, if not all, of his father's hotels into the ground by the time he had finished with them. She wanted to tell him about Matthew and how he had been allowed in only if he kept his hands to himself and a clean tongue in his mouth.

But that wasn't part of the game. The game had to do with making him just a little jealous. Letting him think she was rushed off her feet. So she said none of these interesting facts about Kevin. But then, going out with a fellow like Stevie wasn't like going out with a friend.

'So he's the one, is he?'

'Frankie's brother, the law student? No just a pal but as you said, he's attentive. I think that describes it well.'

'And young Philip O'Brien from the hotel attentive as well! Lord, you're notching them up, Kit McMahon.'

'Oh no. Philip's just a friend.'

'And why wasn't he at tonight's do?'

'I think he had to go home,' Kit lied. She felt sure he could see through her like glass.

'Well, I'm glad you asked me. I'm having a good time,' said Stevie. He swung the car around and parked in a place that looked as if it were reserved for visiting celebrities. Hardly anyone visiting tonight would have a smarter car, so a judicious discussion with a porter made sure that it was all organised.

Then, with his hand under her elbow, Stevie Sullivan led Kit into the hotel where the others in their party were gathered, looking open-mouthed at the car that Stevie had parked so casually.

'That's some motor,' Kevin O'Connor said, the envy oozing from his every pore.

'Oh, I don't know, they're a bit flash. I think you're just paying for all that chrome. You say you have a Morris? I thing they're the best thing on the road these days, fast too if you need it.'

Kevin was appeased. 'Yeah, sure. That's what I thought.' They came nearer to the ballroom and they heard the music of the band.

'Kit, can I book you for the first dance?' Kevin said.

It was loud rock and roll. It wasn't a seducing number. Nothing she would need to concentrate on with Stevie. 'That would be great, Kevin,' she said in a low breathy voice. Kevin straightened his bow tie and led her by the hand onto the floor.

Men are such idiots, Kit said to herself. And for some reason a vision of her mother flashed in front of her.

*

'Are these the bright lights of Lough Glass coming up ahead?' Michael O'Connor asked Clio.

'You're not going to make me defensive about my home town,' she laughed at him.

'No, it must be very deep and important coming from a place of the size of this,' said Michael O'Connor.

'Okay, so you were born in Dublin, but your father wasn't, nor your mother. Everyone came from a place like this, it's just a question of when,' Clio said.

'I love you when you're angry, Miss Kelly.'

'I'm not angry,' Clio said.

'Good, so you're going to be real nice to me . . .'

'Yes, but we'll have to be quick.'

They parked the car in the drive. As she had expected, her parents' car was not there. They would be another hour at the golf club.

She opened the door and saw Michael O'Connor's eyes take in the house. It was comfortable and she felt no sense that it was not worthy of them. Her mother spent a lot of time and money choosing furnishing fabrics. The hall had an antique mirror and two old tables of elegant design. There was a light in the kitchen.

Clio saw the glum figure of her younger sister sitting reading at the kitchen table. 'Oh shit,' said Clio. 'It's Anna.'

'What does that mean?' Michael asked, peering over her shoulder.

'What you've guessed it means,' said Clio with her mouth a hard line.

Anna looked up from her book. 'Oh hello,' she said. 'I thought it was them, back from tombstone city a bit early.'

'Why aren't you out?' Clio snapped. 'It's a Saturday night.'

'Why aren't *you* out?' Anna retorted.

Michael just stood there.

'I am out,' Clio said foolishly. 'I'm out from Dublin.'

'Great.' Anna went back to her book.

'Anna, this is Michael O'Connor, a friend of mine from Dublin. This is my younger sister, Anna, who's at school.'

'But not at the moment,' Anna said. 'At the moment I'm committing what is apparently the worst crime in the book, I'm in my own house sitting here reading my own book, and for some reason I have offended my big sister greatly by doing this.'

'Oh shut up Anna. You're a pain in the arse,' said Clio.

'Well, I think I should be . . .' Michael was anxious to be far away from this kitchen.

'No, heavens, you must have a drink, a coffee or something. You can't drive me all this way and just . . .'

'Well it looks as if I have driven you all this way and then just . . .' he said. And there was a look of real annoyance on his face.

'Perhaps, Anna, if I could ask you to go to your own room and read, Michael and I could . . . um . . . talk here with more comfort?' Clio didn't hold out much hope.

'There are six chairs.' Anna looked around as if to reassure herself. 'And there's the drawing room and the dining room. I don't remember anyone saying that when I read a book I had to be confined to my own room.'

'Jesus,' Clio said to her, with a look that would have weakened a lesser sister.

'It's been great,' said Michael icily.

'Listen, come back. I'm sorry.'

'Come back for what exactly? For repartee in the kitchen? No, I'll just drive back to Dublin. It's what I love to do on a Saturday, drive to the middle of nowhere and back.' She heard the bang of the car door and he was gone.

With a look of murder in her eyes Clio returned to the kitchen.

Emmet had thought *The Blue Lagoon* a bit soppy and sentimental, but Patsy Hanley had liked it. She giggled a lot when she talked about it afterwards and said 'you know' and 'I forgot what I was going to say' a lot. Maybe she was shy and that was why she talked so much. Emmet knew how hard it was to mean to say one thing and have another come out. But really Patsy was hard going. If it had been Anna . . .

If only it had been Anna. They could have talked about it properly . . . Anna was so bright, she had such imagination. Her mind went everywhere.

As he sat on the bus beside Patsy, who was prattling on about the film, he thought of Anna. She wasn't going out with that greasy Stevie, that was good. But had he been right to pass up the chance of taking her out tonight? Was it wise to take Patsy and make her jealous? Why did life have to be such a series of games?

When the bus stopped outside Paddles' bar, Emmet and Patsy walked together along the street in Lough Glass. 'Wouldn't it be great if there was a place to go for coffee or ice cream here?' Patsy said.

'Yeah.' Emmet didn't think he could take any more of Patsy and was quite relieved that there wasn't anywhere to go. They passed the Central

Hotel and looked at it without enthusiasm. 'It's a real mausoleum isn't it?' said Emmet.

'A what?' Patsy asked.

Emmet dug his hands into his pockets.

'Were you at the pictures?' called Philip O'Brien.

'It was terrific, *The BLue Lagoon*,' said Patsy.

Philip was always nice to Emmet McMahon. One day Emmet would be his brother-in-law; he wanted them to have a history of being friends. 'Anna Kelly not with you?' he asked conversationally. He thought Emmet would be pleased to know that he, Philip, a much older man, would even know who his friends were.

He was unprepared for the glower he got from Emmet. 'No, she's not,' he said with his stammer returning. He struggled out the words that people were free to come and go as they wanted to and then marched off with a red face. Patsy Hanley shrugged at Philip and followed. She didn't know what was wrong either.

'Well, I'm home,' Emmet said gruffly as they got to McMahon's pharmacy.

'Aren't you going to escort me home?' Patsy said. 'You *did* ask me to the pictures.'

Emmet had opened the door, but he realised that it was just pure annoyance and bad temper on his part to dart into his house. Of course he should have walked her across to her house over Hanley's drapery. 'Sorry,' he muttered.

They walked through the quiet town. There was never much sound coming from Foley's bar up at this end; all the activity seemed to be down at Paddles' place.

Mrs Hanley was waiting. 'I thought the bus should be in about now,' she said. She had no mention of allowing her second daughter follow the path of Deirdre and be regarded as an easy conquest. 'Come on in, Emmet. I'll give you a cup of drinking chocolate,' she said.

'No, really, thanks, Mrs Hanley.'

'Ah come on up, can't you. I've chocolate biscuits.'

Emmet went up. There would be nobody at home. His father and Maura were at the golf club and he didn't want to be alone thinking about Anna. This was more companionable.

Kit discovered that Stevie was a great dancer. She wanted to ask him where he had learned. She had learned at special lessons, an optional class provided by Mother Bernard on Friday afternoons up at the convent. They had mocked the teacher at the time but always looked back in gratitude.

But Stevie now. All his life spent in overalls, tinkering with engines. Living with that awful moaning mother of his and a wild young brother. Where had he found time and interest to make himself so smart and so skilled? When they danced to 'Smoke Gets in Your Eyes' he laid his cheek against hers. Kit moved slightly away but only very slightly, so that he could follow.

'Do you know something?' Stevie said.

'No. What?' Kit was giggly and coy. It seemed to be working.

'The words of that song are utterly ridiculous. It's about some guy who had laughing friends deride him . . . listen . . .' They listened to the words. It was as he said. 'What kind of a shower of friends would they be?' Stevie asked.

Kit agreed with him. She was about to give her views then she remembered her role. She was here to make him fall for her. What that involved was not having views yourself but talking entirely about the boy.

'Do you have friends?' she asked looking up at him.

'You know bloody well I don't have friends. Haven't you known me all my life? What time have I for friends? Where would I find them?' He sounded bitter.

'I don't know you all my life,' she came back with spirit. 'I hardly know you at all. You're a different man tonight, a person I don't know at all. For all I know you could have friends in Hollywood or the South of France. You look the part.' She realised she sounded angry.

But he took it as admiration. 'Thank you,' he said. She longed to talk to him. But there was no time. 'And have you many friends?' he asked as they stood on the dance floor. They didn't even bother returning to the table where the wine and the others were, they knew they would be dancing again.

'Not all that many really.' Kit was thoughtful.

'I thought you and Clio were still Siamese twins.'

'No, not at all. She's not here tonight, for example.'

'Anna says you're as thick as thieves.'

'Anna!' There was the word. This is what she must get back to – outsmarting Anna. 'Anna knows nothing.' She put all the scorn in the world into her voice.

'She's brighter than you think, she's got a mind of her own,' he defended her.

Kit knew that this was true. Anna was bright and imaginative. She remembered that from when Emmet had been so sick and she had come to mind him. She mustn't protest too much. 'She's pretty, mind you,' Kit said in a coquettish way that felt horribly alien. 'I can see that people would think she was a little attractive, but bright . . . I don't think so.'

'She's only pretty in a schoolgirl way,' Stevie said. Then the band began to play 'A Fool Such As I' and he held her close to him for the slow swaying number. He held himself back from her to look at her face, flushed, eyes sparkling. 'Now you, Kit McMahon, you are seriously good-looking,' he said.

She understood in those seconds why people had found him so sexy and attractive, why even married women had gone off with him and taken terrible risks. But of course he would be a ridiculous person to fall for, Kit told herself. Thank heavens she was only doing this ludicrous charade as a favour for her little brother. She reminded herself of this again as his arms tightened around her when they danced.

*

'You behaved like a spoiled brat,' Clio said to Anna. 'I want you to know that I will never forgive you for this as long as I live.'

'Did I spoil your plans?' Anna asked.

'You were extremely discourteous to a friend who kindly drove me the whole way from Dublin.'

'And was about to drive you upstairs to bed if only little sister hadn't been here to guard your reputation.'

'Don't you dare even suggest such a thing.' Clio was white with rage.

'I think we're quits,' Anna said calmly. 'You don't mention my bad manners, I don't mention your intentions.' She went back to her book.

Clio saw it was *Wuthering Heights*. 'Poseur, affected show off ... pretending you read books like that for pleasure ...'

'But I do,' Anna said. 'There's real passion in this book, not just gropes and feels in motor cars. And anyway, aren't you the one studying English for a degree? I thought you would read a book a day, a classic I mean, for pleasure.'

'I could stab you with the bread knife and pretend it was an intruder that did it,' Clio said.

'Yes, but it wouldn't be worth it,' Anna said, going back to her reading.

Martin McMahon was annoyed when they got home. The door was open. 'That's very careless of Emmet,' he grumbled. 'Leaving a door swinging open on the street.'

'Maybe he's just gone upstairs,' Maura said.

'Let me check the chemist's.' Martin always feared that someone might break in, in search of his medicines and drugs.

Maura went up the stairs without him. There didn't seem to be any sign of Emmet, but the light was on in the kitchen, so Maura went in there.

But it wasn't Emmet who sat there. It was a tramp, she thought first, a man with a torn coat that had been wet through. His shoes looked as if they had let in water and he was unshaven, and wild-looking even though he was asleep with his head lolling to one side.

Maura's hand flew to her throat. 'Oh my God!' she said before she could stop herself. Her voice woke the man and he leapt to his feet. Maura saw that his eyes were wild and she clutched her throat in terror. 'Please,' she said. 'Please.'

The man stood up unsteadily. He looked around him for something that would serve as a weapon.

Maura knew with relief that the knives were at the very back of a drawer. He wouldn't find one easily. She was surprised at how rationally her mind was able to work. She prayed that Martin would come up the stairs, and then she prayed at the same time that he wouldn't. The man was like a wild animal who would see himself trapped by two people and flail even more dangerously. 'I won't hurt you,' she said.

He gave a strangled cry, a sound that wasn't any words. But at the same time he picked up one of the kitchen chairs and lunged at Maura.

She moved away from him leaving him the doorway free to make his exit. Please, please God, may Martin not be coming up the stairs. 'Go now. Run away, I'll say nothing,' she said in a voice a bit above a whisper. He looked at her, confused, and seemed to come after her again. She fell on her knees trying to avoid him.

When Martin came in and stood frozen in shock, blocking the doorway, he saw the tableau of his wife kneeling, cowering in terror from a wild man about to batter her with a chair. 'Get off, get off her,' roared Martin, flinging himself on the man with the wild eyes.

The man raised the chair and beat Martin with it as Maura dragged herself to her feet to come and pull him off. Only the sound of Emmet's voice as he ran up the stairs shouting, 'What's wrong, what's wrong, what's happening?' broke the remorseless series of blows.

Now that there were three of them, the man with the wet coat, the straggly hair and wild, mad eyes realised he might be outnumbered. Grabbing up a soaking wet bag, he pushed his way past Emmet and down the stairs.

'Daddy, Daddy,' Emmet stuttered out the words in his grief.

'Get Peter,' Maura said. 'Phone him this minute.' Then she ran out the door and down the stairs.

'Maura, come back,' Emmet cried.

'He's not going to get away . . . he's not going to do this to Martin and get away.' In seconds she was at the door and looking out on the dark quiet street of Lough Glass. 'Help!' she called. 'Help! Get help, there's a man running down the road. Stop him, stop him. He's attacked Martin.'

Almost at once lights went on, doors opened. Maura saw young Michael Sullivan come out of the garage across the road, and the Walls in the hardware shop followed.

'Which way?' called Mr Wall.

'He's gone down towards the Brothers.' The Walls started to shout too and roused the Hickeys over their meat shop and by the time the noise came to Foley's pub there were people out in the street running after the figure they saw staggering and stumbling away.

When Sergeant Sean O'Connor arrived on the scene the man with the wild eyes and the words that were hard to understand was firmly held. Held, it had to be said, by the after-hours drinkers from Foley's bar and some who had crossed the street from after-hours drinking at Paddles' place. But such niceties as the licensing laws were unimportant now.

'It's one of the knackers, bloody tinkers, always the same,' said Mrs Dillon from the newsagent's shop. She hadn't known such excitement in years as to witness the capture of a criminal just outside her door.

'It's not,' said Paddles.

Sergeant Sean O'Connor was indifferent as to who the man was. He moved him firmly into the Garda car under the efficient arm lock of the young garda who was with him. The sergeant was giving the impression that the fun was over. 'You'll all be on your way home now,' he said mildly, looking at the two open licensed premises beckoning warmly if illegally in the night.

People shuffled around noncommittally.

'Is Martin McMahon all right?' asked Dan O'Brien who had run from the hotel to see the cause of the commotion.

'The doctor is with him now, he won't want a flood of people in on top of him. So I won't detain any of you from your beds,' said Sean O'Connor, taking his prisoner into custody.

'It's not very deep, Maura.' Peter Kelly knelt on the floor beside his friend Martin.

'But he's unconscious.'

'That's because he hit his head falling down . . .'

'Has he concussion?'

'I don't know. We'll get him to hospital.'

'My God, Peter, what'll we do? I will kill that madman with my own bare hands if Martin's badly hurt.'

'No, his pulse is fine. He's going to be fine.'

'Do you mean that? Or is it just to make me feel better?'

'Maura, he'll be grand.'

'Can he hear me?' she asked.

'No, I wouldn't think so. No, not now. But he'll come around, he'll be fine.'

Just in case Maura knelt beside him and kissed his bloodstained face. 'You're going to be fine, Martin. I've seen Peter's eyes, he means it. And I love you, I love you with all my heart. You make me sing with happiness.'

Emmet McMahon and Peter Kelly exchanged glances. They weren't meant to hear such a declaration of love. It was very private and neither of them would ever refer to it again.

It was a long night in the cell. Sean O'Connor got dry clothes for the dirty and shivering man in his charge. He even gave him a cup of tea, though his heart wasn't in it. He had seen the blood on the floor of McMahon's kitchen and was still awaiting news from the hospital about Martin's condition.

The man was deranged and made little sense. He spoke a lot about his sister. Or was it his sister? She'd want to know where he was and what had happened to him. Mostly he rambled and moved from sentence to sentence without finishing the first. His words were confused. He needed to be in a psychiatric home, Sean O'Connor guessed. Perhaps he had even come from one. As he left the cell he saw the man curl up to sleep on the bench-style bed. He was mumbling names over and over. None of them made any sense to Sergeant O'Connor.

Lilian was still up when Peter Kelly got back from the hospital.

'It's all right,' he reassured her from the door. 'It's all right. He's regained consciousness, they're testing him for concussion, and he's had a lot of X-rays. No, he'll be fine.'

Lilian let out her breath in relief. 'And Maura?'

'Insisted on staying in there in the hospital with him. Brought Emmet with her. They found them beds.'

'Was it necessary?'

'It was what she wanted to do,' Peter said, pouring himself a brandy.

'I had some tea ready.'

'I'm past tea,' Peter said. He sat down at the kitchen table. 'The girls in? Did Clio come home?'

'Yes, both of them like vipers. You could cut the atmosphere. They had some huge row which was still simmering.'

'What else is new?' Peter sounded weary.

'Who was he? Was it one of the tinkers?'

'No it *wasn't*. Why do people automatically blame them?'

'Because they're different, that's why. What *was* he then?'

'God knows ... some tramp who came in.'

'There aren't any tramps in Lough Glass. Anyway, how did he get in?'

'Emmet left the door open. The poor lad is nearly dead with grief. He thinks it was all his fault. That's why Maura brought him with her.'

They were silent. Lilian was thinking that Maura seemed to get on much better with her two stepchildren than she, Lilian, did with her natural children. She looked at Peter and wondered had he anything of the same thoughts running through his mind.

Kevin O'Connor danced with Kit. 'Eventually I was able to prise you away from the lounge lizard,' he said.

'Whatever else he is he isn't that,' Kit said.

'Oh really? He looks as if he'd stepped straight from the pages of a glossy magazine ... with all the shine intact. Years of escorting ladies through crowded dance floors.'

'No, years of working long hours getting rust out of cars, tuning engines, selling tractors . . .'

'How do you know all that?'

'He's the boy next door, he's from Lough Glass.'

'Jesus, half of Dublin seems to be from that one-horse town. Clio as well. Well, it sure breeds fine-looking women.' His arms tightened a little around her.

Kit was about to pull away when she saw Stevie Sullivan looking at her over Frankie's shoulder. She didn't pull away, instead she smiled up at Kevin. 'Any tighter and I'll put my knee up with a sudden jerk,' she said, still smiling sweetly.

'You'll what . . . ?' he looked alarmed.

'You won't be able to walk for a week,' Kit said, her face never changing. She could see Stevie watching them with interest, but with no idea of what was being said.

It wasn't all that difficult to get men to fancy you if you tried, Kit decided.

The dance was over at midnight. All Saturday night dances in Dublin had to end then; it was so that they wouldn't go on into the Sabbath Day. The National Anthem was played and they went for their coats. Kevin O'Connor and his friend Matthew wondered casually if people might like to come around to their flat for a beer or a coffee. And to play records. Matthew managed to put such a leer of suggestiveness into the words *play records* that nobody was in any doubt about what he meant.

'I'll drive you back to the hostel,' Stevie suggested to Kit.

'It's not a hostel actually, it's a bedsit,' Kit said.

'Well, if I'd have known that, then I might have had somewhere to lay my weary head,' he smiled at her.

'Oh no, no weary heads, only my own,' Kit was relaxed. This was surely going well.

'I might have tried to persuade you,' he smiled.

'I wouldn't have counted on it. No, better to have made your own arrangements.'

'Mine are simple, I drive back to the ranch, now.'

'Now, at this time?'

'No rest for the self-employed.'

'But tomorrow's Sunday.'

'What other day do I have of meeting farmers, when they come in to Mass, telling them all about new equipment?'

'You're really determined to make that place a success, aren't you?'

'Well, it would make a nice change from the way it was handed to me, I can tell you that.' His voice sounded bitter for a second.

'Your mother must be very proud of you . . .'

'You know my mother, she's proud of nothing . . . oh God, that reminds me . . . could you hang on till I make a phone call.' They were just coming out of the hotel door but he searched his pockets for change and headed to the phone. He turned back to say, 'I totally forgot that my mother's staying with her sister . . . and I'm meant to be responsible for that young hooligan, Michael.'

'How can you be responsible for him from here?'

'A good question. But I said I'd phone him at midnight to check that he was home and I'd kick the arse off him if he wasn't.'

Kit laughed. He didn't have to tell her who he was phoning, but somehow it was a relief. Stevie Sullivan must have had a lot of telephone numbers that he could call. Even this late on a Saturday night.

She watched the dancers leaving and the hotel wind down. Kit thought that it had been about as successful as it could possibly have been. She had definitely taken his mind off that baby-faced Anna. Anna would go back to Emmet for consolation. It was all going according to the plan.

Stevie was walking over to her, but there was something different about his face. 'Hey, let's sit down for a minute.' He indicated a group of chairs.

'But aren't we going to go? They're cleaning up.'

'It'll only take a minute . . .'

'Was Michael not there?' She knew something had happened.

'No, he was there all right, but . . .'

'But what?'

'But he said that there had been an accident, that your father had got hurt.'

'Oh my God, a car crash, the new car. They weren't used to it.'

'No, nothing like that, an intruder. But he's fine, your father. He's in hospital, but he'll be out in a day or two, truly.'

Kit thought of scatty young Michael Sullivan and didn't put very much faith in his judgement. Kit's face was white with anxiety, she felt lightheaded, as if she were going to faint. Father in an accident with an intruder . . . what did it mean?

'Please, I tell you, it's going to be all right.' She didn't even have to say it; Stevie had realised. 'No, I didn't take Michael's word for it, I went back through the exchange to Mona Fitz in the post office. There was some kind of madman, they caught him. He hit your father but it's going to be all right . . .'

'It might have been the same people who hit your mother.'

'Yes, it might.'

'I feel sick.' Kit said.

'It's all right, go home and get on a nice warm coat and I'll drive you back to him.'

'Will you?' She looked at him trustingly. All flirtatious behaviour was long forgotten now. He put his arm around her shoulder and walked her to the car. 'Maybe I'm only delaying you. I'll go like this,' she said.

'No, you can't go like that, not into a hospital. You'll frighten the wits out of them.' Yes, he was right. 'And another thing, I couldn't drive all those miles beside you dressed in that get up. It would be more than flesh and blood could bear to keep my hands off you.'

'Then I'll get changed,' she said, her tone was muted.

And he seemed sorry to have made the remark. Kit was worried about her father, it had been a coarse sort of thing to say. 'I'm sorry, Kit,' he said simply. 'Sometimes I'm very rough, I disgust myself.'

'No, it doesn't matter,' she said. They were talking like friends, real friends who knew each other very well. He sat in the car while she went in to change.

She hung up the dress that had worked such wonders and looked at her pale face in the mirror. It all seemed very childish and unimportant now. She wished she knew more about what had happened. Wasn't it lucky that Stevie had phoned home. She had never known that he was the kind of fellow who would actually mind his younger brother. There were a lot of things she hadn't known about him until tonight.

The towns and the fields, the woods, the crossroads and the farmhouses slipped past in the night. Kit felt it was all so unreal.

'Try to sleep,' Stevie said. 'There's a rug there, you could put it under your head like a cushion.' She sat, still and frightened in her black polo-necked sweater and her black and red skirt. She had taken a jacket and a warm woolly scarf too but she didn't need them. The luxurious car was very warm.

'Did Mona Fitz say any more?' she asked.

'No, I didn't keep her on the phone, I thought it was better just to head out there.'

'Much better,' she said. Her voice was small.

'You'll be fine,' Stevie said.

'I know.'

'These things don't happen,' he said.

She looked at him. His face was very handsome in the moonlight. 'What things?'

'There's some fairness in the world,' Stevie Sullivan said. 'I mean, they wouldn't let you lose your mother *and* your father. He's got to be all right.'

*

Sergeant Sean O'Connor woke with a start. It was seven-thirty in the morning. He had suddenly made sense of all the jumble of names, and of the man talking about his sister. He went in to the cell, kicked the bed, and the man sat up, alarmed.

'Tell me about Sister,' he said.

'What, what?'

'Sister Madeleine. Did you hurt her? Did you lay a hand on her? If you touched her I'll have you beaten to death in this station and then give myself up.'

'No, no.' The man was frightened.

'I'm going down to her house this minute, and you'd better pray to your God that you didn't harm her. That woman is a living saint.'

'No, no,' The man was like an animal crouched and frightened. 'She was good to me. I stayed with her. She hid me, you see. She hid me in her house, first up a tree in the tree-house, and then in her own cottage. I wouldn't hurt Sister Madeleine, she's the only person who was ever good to me.'

He parked the Garda car outside Paddles' bar and walked down the narrow path to the hermit's cottage. He stopped outside the window and peered in. The small bent figure was lifting her heavy black kettle from the hook over the fire. That at least was good timing. They could talk over tea.

She was pleased to see him. 'This is a real treat for me now. I was thinking wouldn't I love a friendly soul to come in and have something to eat and drink with me. Not to be doing it on my own.'

'But don't you choose to live on your own? Aren't you a solitary person?' His eyes were narrow as he looked at her.

'Ah, there's solitude and solitude.' A silence fell between them. Eventually the hermit said, 'Is there anything troubling you, Sean?'

'Is there anything troubling *you*, Sister Madeleine?'

Her eyes seemed to see through him, right across the corner of the lake and up to the prison cell where the frightened madman had lain on his bunk bed babbling her name. 'You found Francis, Sean, is that it?'

'I don't know what his bloody name is, but he said he'd stayed here, that you looked after him.'

'I did what I had to.'

'Shelter a lunatic?'

'Well, I couldn't let him off on his own, he was wounded. And anyway he was frightened.'

'What was he frightened of?'

'That you'd catch him, and punish him.'

'But he hadn't done anything yet, had he?'

'The garage, Kathleen Sullivan . . . you *know* all this, Sean.'

And suddenly it all clicked together in Sean O'Connor's head. 'You knew he had beaten that woman and still you hid him. You harboured a criminal.'

'That's being too harsh.'

'For God's sake, he's put two people in the county hospital. What do you call that, peace and light?'

'Two people?'

'Yeah. He beat Martin McMahon senseless last night.'

Sister Madeleine's hands went up over her face, her shoulders shook. 'The poor man,' she said. 'The poor, poor man.'

Sergeant Sean O'Connor sat there, grim-faced. He would like to have believed that the poor man she was feeling such sympathy for was Martin McMahon, coming innocently up his own stairs into his kitchen and seeing his wife being attacked.

But he feared it was the disturbed mind of the prisoner in his cell, the man she called Francis. 'Tell me about Francis,' he said wearily.

'You won't hurt him?'

'No. We'll get him looked after.'

'You promise?'

Sean gave a wave of impatience. Why did he have to do deals with people over something as basic as this? 'Did he tell you where he came from, Sister?' he said slowly and deliberately.

'He said he'd come back when he got settled. Come back for his things.'

'How long has he been gone?'

'Only three days.'

'Well, he didn't get far, up to the main street of the town, it seems. Into the kitchen of the McMahons to beat them all with a chair.'

'I can't believe it,' she said.

'Where did you think he was going?'

'I didn't know. He said he wanted to be free.' She looked very upset.

Sean O'Connor forced himself to lower his tone and be gentle. 'And how long was he here altogether, would you say?'

'I suppose about six weeks . . . who can tell? Time has no meaning.'

'Immediately after the garage, and Kathleen being taken to hospital, would it?'

'I expect it must have been.' Her voice was very flat.

'And you never thought of telling us he was here?'

'Never.'

'You have a strange sense of responsibility to the community, if I may say so, Sister Madeleine.'

'I felt he couldn't do any harm while he was here.' Her eyes were clear in their sincerity.

'True, but he sure did the very moment he left you.'

'I didn't know.' There was another long silence. 'I'll get you his things,' Sister Madeleine said. She produced a blue carrier bag with money, cheques, motor registration books and the few cheap ornaments he had taken from the office in Sullivan Motors.

Sean O'Connor looked through them in disbelief. 'We've had half the country searching for all this.' She said nothing. 'How did you hide him? People come in and out. I've been in and out myself, for God's sake!'

'He lived in the tree-house during the day,' she said simply, as if it were a perfectly natural thing to do.

The sergeant stood up. 'It wasn't the right thing to do, Sister. He's not a fox or a rabbit, or a poor little duck with a broken wing. He's a man, a disturbed man who injured people badly, who could have killed them. You did him no service by giving him this Alice in Wonderland place to live.'

'He was happy here,' she said. Sean O'Connor didn't trust himself to speak. He was afraid he would lose his temper and say something he would regret. 'Sean?'

'Yes, Sister?'

'Can I come and see him? Up in the station?' There was a long pause. 'It couldn't do any harm, it might possibly do some good.'

Stevie Sullivan had left Kit at the door of the hospital.

'Aren't you coming in?'

'No, I'd be in the way. He's all right, I tell you. I wouldn't leave you to face things if he weren't.'

'Thank you very very much, Stevie. You've been wonderful to me.'

'Glad I was there,' he said. She didn't want him to leave. And she felt he didn't want her to go. 'I'll see you later in the day,' he said.

'When you've talked the Mass-goers into buying tractors,' she said with an attempt at a watery smile.

'That's the girl,' he said, and drove the E-type out of the hospital grounds in a flourish.

'Your mother and brother are with him. He's talking now,' the nurse said.

Kit got a shock for a moment. The wild idea that Lena had flown over from London to be at his side crossed her mind. Then she realised. 'He's going to be all right?' she said, searching the nurse's face.

'Oh, definitely,' the nurse said. 'Come on and I'll bring you up there.'

Maura and Emmet jumped up with shock and delight to see her. She went straight to her father. He was on a drip; there was a lot of bruising and bandaging around his head. 'I look worse than I am, Kit,' he said.

'You look grand to me,' she said and put her head on his bed and burst into tears.

They knew that he was in no danger but they wanted to stay nearby. The hospital provided beds for them all. Kit lay under her rug and tried to sleep. Her mind was too full of images. There was the dance. The shock of Father's face with the bruises and cuts. There was Emmet crying that it was his fault, if only he had closed the door. There was Maura holding Father's hand with such love in her eyes that Kit almost had to look away.

And there was Stevie Sullivan's handsome face as he leaned out of the car, still in his dinner jacket but his white shirt open at the neck. 'I'll see you later in the day,' he had said. Later in the day.

Finally she fell into a sort of sleep.

When they got back to Lough Glass, they all hesitated before going up the stairs to the scene of all the violence the night before.

Sergeant O'Connor had said that the place would be tidied up a bit for them. And so it was. The broken chair had been removed. Someone had washed the blood from the sisal floor covering. There was a dark damp stain but at least it didn't look like blood. The place seemed grey and empty.

Maura opened a note that had been left through the door. 'That's very kind,' she exclaimed. Philip O'Brien from the hotel had invited them to come and have breakfast when they returned. They wouldn't be in the mood to cook anything for themselves. 'Will we do that?' she asked Emmet and Kit. 'It would give us energy to face the day.' They knew she wanted to, so they agreed.

Philip hadn't expected Kit to be home. He was delighted to see her. 'You missed the dance then?' he said with barely hidden delight.

'No, I heard afterwards,' Kit said.

'And how did you get down?'

'You're very good to ask us to breakfast, Philip,' Kit said quickly.

Maura was agreeing, and soon the smell of bacon and sausages came from the kitchen. They sat by the window. Morning had come up and the lake looked very beautiful.

'Don't you have a wonderful view?' Kit said to keep the conversation going, and away from both her father's injuries and how she had got back from Dublin.

'Yes . . . I suppose like everyone here we get used to it. It's only because you and I have been in Dublin we appreciate it.' Philip was trying to find a common bond with her, something which marked the two of them out as sharing something special. Even if it was something as ordinary as both living in Dublin.

'That's right, Philip,' she said kindly. 'In fact, if you were to cut down some of those bushes over there it would be really terrific, like a kind of panorama.'

He had been suggesting that to his parents for over six months, but as always they resisted change. He smiled at Kit, a warm smile of recognition. They were indeed kindred spirits. And perhaps he had been right to believe

Sister Madeleine that she was not taken up with anyone else. After all, the party or dance or whatever it was couldn't have been that special if she had been able to leave it so quickly.

'I'll leave you to get on with your breakfast without having to make conversation all the time,' he said to them all, and Kit flashed him a grateful look.

As he left he heard Kit say to Maura, 'Philip is the kindest man at any crisis. I always remember that.'

If Maura realised what previous crisis Kit might be thinking of she said nothing. 'I promised your father that we'd go on as normal, but this isn't exactly normal, is it? A real hotel breakfast with lashings of everything.'

They heard the sound of relief and happiness in her voice, the delight that their father would soon be well and home to them.

Sister Madeleine walked quietly along the lake shore. She did not come up by Paddles' bar, nor by O'Brien's hotel. She waited until she had passed the Garda station. This way she would meet fewer people.

The small grey figure stood humbly by the desk. She had a packet. 'He likes a bit of soda bread, Sean,' she said diffidently.

'I'll make a note of it,' he said flatly.

'Maybe we could both have a cup of tea and I could serve it to him. It would be like old times.'

'You're not going into the cell with him.' Sean O'Connor was appalled. 'Whatever way he was when he was with you, he's like a caged animal now, he hits out at everyone.'

'I'll be all right,' she said.

He handed her two mugs of tea and put the buttered bread on a tray. He had never called the man by his name. 'Listen, you,' he called into the cell. 'I've brought a friend of yours. She wants to come in and sit with you, the Lord knows why. If you touch her, you'll get such a pasting you'll have to be scraped off the walls.'

The man seemed not to understand, then he saw Sister Madeleine. His eyes filled with tears. 'You came to take me home,' he said.

'I came to bring you breakfast,' she said.

They sat in the cell, the nun and the wild man, sipping tea and eating thick slices of buttered bread. Sean O'Connor watched them from a distance. They talked about the trees by the lake, and the way a bit of the tree-house had fallen down in the wind. Sister Madeleine spoke about the birds going away for the winter, and how they would be back next year. They always came back, too.

She called him by his name. She said the word Francis so gently and with such respect that Sean felt ashamed of having called him *you*.

Francis replied, coherently now; you could understand his words. He asked about the old dog, he asked did she have trouble getting wood for the fire. He said he had got very wet and had wanted to sit by a fire.

'And did you go far when you left me?' Her voice was low and interested.

There wasn't a trace of hectoring him or doing an investigation, but she knew that the sergeant was listening.

'I slept in the fields, Sister. It was cold and wet. I couldn't find anywhere, I got a pain in my head.'

'And why didn't you come back to me? There was always a home for you with me.'

'I'll go back now,' he said eagerly. Like a child.

'And at night did you have to sleep in the rain?'

'I found a barn one night, but there were animals in it and I was afraid. And another night I was under a tree. I didn't go far. I was tired of walking.'

'But you found a kitchen and a range to sit at in the town, didn't you? In a house?'

'Yes.' He hung his head.

'And why did you hit the good people . . . they wouldn't have hurt you.'

'They were going to get me locked up again,' he said.

'You hurt Mr McMahon. He's a very good man. He's the one who got you the bandage and the throat sweets and you hurt him.'

'I was frightened,' he said.

'Poor Francis, don't be frightened.' She held his hand. 'Fright is only in our heads.'

'Is it, Sister?'

'Yes, it is. I know that, I feel it in my own head.'

'Am I not coming home with you?'

'No, you'll be taken where people can look after your head and take a lot of the fright out of it. I wasn't good at doing that.' She stood up.

'Don't go,' he pleaded.

'I must. I have a lot of things to do.'

'My bag of things, it's in your house.'

'Sergeant O'Connor has it. He found it when he came to tell me you were here.'

It was a slight bending of the truth, Sean O'Connor observed. He hadn't found it, the hermit had gone to find it for him, but he understood. She had to leave Francis with the belief that she had been faithful to him.

'Will you come to see me?' he asked.

'I'll be thinking about you, and praying for you. I'll think about you every single day, Francis Xavier Byrne, so I will. Wherever I am.'

'You'll be in your cottage, won't you? For when I get better.'

'I'll be thinking of you wherever I am,' she said.

After Mass everyone crowded around the McMahons; the whole place had heard the story of the night before. The good wishes to Martin were overpowering.

Through the crowd Kit caught sight of Stevie Sullivan. Dressed now in his brown belted coat and wearing a tweed cap, he looked a different person. He was talking to a group of men. It was a few minutes to opening time. They would walk together down Church Road and turn into the main street, then they would move to Foley's bar or O'Shea's, or even Paddles', to do the kind of deals that he had told her about.

He wouldn't appreciate her coming over to join him now. Their eyes met. She smiled and waved but made no move to join him. He excused himself for a minute from his group and moved over to her.

'He was fine?'

'Exactly as you said. Go on back to business, no rest for the self-employed! And thanks again, Stevie. I'll never forget.'

She could feel his eyes still on her as she moved back to Maura. There was a hooting of a car horn. Peter and Lilian Kelly had come to take them to lunch.

'I wanted to go back in to see Martin,' Maura protested.

'I've been on to the hospital. He's having a doze, better let him rest. You can go in during the afternoon. Come on, all of you pile in.'

'Seven of us in one car?' Maura laughed at the idea.

'Why do you think doctors have station wagons?'

Emmet and Anna looked at each other in a guarded way. 'Did you like the pictures, Emmet?' Anna asked finally.

'Yes, but it's rather gone out of my mind now with everything that happened since,' Emmet said.

Anna was instantly sympathetic. 'Yes, that was stupid of me. It must have been an awful shock. Were you frightened?' There was a lot of warmth in her voice.

Kit could see Emmet responding. Stevie Sullivan had been right about one thing. Anna Kelly was a bright little thing, not just a pretty face under a mop of blonde curls.

After lunch at the Kellys, Kit went up to Clio's room. 'What's wrong, Clio?' she asked.

'What do you mean? Don't come this nanny bit with me. What should be wrong?'

'You look very fed up.'

'Well, I am fed up. My best friend doesn't invite me to her party. Then Michael gave me a lift home last night and bloody Anna was down there behaving like some kind of dervish spitting fire at us, and he had to go back to Dublin without ... well, you know, without coming up here.'

'Jesus, Clio. You were never going to go to bed with him in your own house.'

'There would have been time before the others came home from the golf club.'

'You must have been off your head. Thank God Anna was there. You must be losing your marbles.'

'I've probably lost my boyfriend.'

'Well, he can't be much of a loss if he's only staying round because of the pouncing.'

'It's not just pouncing. He could pounce on anyone in Ireland. It's me he likes, and also pouncing on me.' Clio seemed very aggrieved.

'Well then, he'll wait until you're free to pounce, which would appear to be most of the time.'

'God, you sound like Mother Bernard.'

'No, I'm not. I'm just hoping you don't get caught. Honestly, I'm out for your good,' Kit said spiritedly.

Clio was a little reassured. 'Yes well, maybe you are. I don't know, Kit. I don't. It's so bloody confused. Do I ring him and say sorry about this little hiccup, or does that look pleading and pathetic? Would it be better to say nothing and hope he'll come back?'

'Lord, isn't that the question!' Kit had been pondering exactly the same problem about Stevie Sullivan. She must leave the next move to him, but suppose he didn't make one? What then?

'Remember in the old days we used always to go down to Sister Madeleine and ask her about things like this.'

'Not exactly like this,' Kit said.

'No, but she always had some sort of answer,' Clio said.

It was an idea. Kit decided that when Maura went to see Father this afternoon she would go down on her own and talk to the hermit.

There was something different about the place. A lot of the old boxes that had held various animals in their different degrees of convalescence were gathered in front of the door. Inside the house had changed too. Almost all the few possessions that Sister Madeleine had were laid out on her kitchen table. An old kettle, the three cups, the tin that held biscuits or cake.

The little can that she had scalded to keep the milk in was there, a few plates, one or two little boxes. Sister Madeleine was in the bedroom looking around.

'Are you all right, Sister?' Kit called.

'Who is that?' The voice sounded flat and dead, not like the usual enthusiasm that greeted any caller.

'Kit McMahon.'

'I'm so sorry, Kit.' Sister Madeleine stretched out both her hands. 'To the end of my life I'll pray for you and your family that you'll get over this, and understand.'

'But he's going to be fine, Sister Madeleine. I saw him last night and this morning. He'll be out of hospital in two days.'

'That's good, surely. That's good.' The whole place had changed. Sister Madeleine looked unbelievably as if she were packing, as if she were closing up her cottage and going to move somewhere else. 'He was a poor man out of his mind, you know. He should have been in a mental hospital. They'll put him back in one.'

'I know, I know. Clio's father told us.'

'He didn't know what he was doing. It doesn't make it better on your poor father, or poor Kathleen Sullivan ... but that's the only way we can look at it. His mind wasn't right.'

'Was it the same man who hit Mrs Sullivan and stole the things from the garage?'

'Yes, didn't Sergeant O'Connor tell you?'

'No, no. He told us nothing ...'

'He will, everyone will know.'

'But where was he between? That was ages ago, months ago.'

'He was here, Kit. Here in your tree-house.'

'*What?*' Kit couldn't believe it.

'I minded him because he was sick, you know. Just like the poor Gerald there with his broken wing.' She indicated a bird that normally lived in a box but was struggling to walk outside.

'He was here all the time?' Kit asked.

'That's what I'm so sorry about.' Sister Madeleine's eyes were full of tears. 'While he was here he was safe, he couldn't harm anyone or come to any harm himself. But he wanted to go, and I never keep anyone if they want to go.' She looked up at the sky, remembering birds that had flown off when their time had come.

'Oh, Sister Madeleine.'

'And if I hadn't kept him, minded him, been good to him, then things would have been different. He wouldn't have hurt your father, he would have been in a hospital now, the Sullivans would have had their money back . . . why did I have to interfere?' She sounded many years older and much more frail. She wasn't sure of herself any more . . . there was a long pause.

'You did what you thought was right,' Kit said.

'Even though it meant your father ending up in hospital. Suppose he had killed him. Suppose your poor father was dead. It would all have been my fault.'

'It didn't happen.'

'You have no hatred for me for playing God? For thinking I knew better than everyone else?'

'None. I could never hate you. Look at all you did for me – for all of us.'

'I used to have good judgement. Not any more.'

'You don't usually talk about yourself . . .'

'There was no need to when things were going well. Now I must stop this life. I knew it really when that little kitten drowned a slow painful death. I caused that . . . my wish to know better.' Her once piercing eyes seemed dim.

'What are you going to do?' Kit spoke in a whisper.

'I'm going away. To somewhere where people will look after me, where I can be safe and obey rules and not be allowed all the freedom to make wrong decisions.'

'Where will that be?'

'A convent. I know a place where they take in people like me. I could clean floors and help in the garden or the kitchen, and have my meals and a little cell.'

'But you said you hated being with people and living to rules.'

'That was then, this is now.'

'How will you make arrangements, will you ring them or write to them?'

'No, Kit. I'll just go on the bus.'

'You *can't* go away, Sister Madeleine. People love you here.'

'Not after this, they won't. The person who sheltered the villain who attacked Kathleen and said not a word, then let him loose to attack Martin McMahon. Love turns to scorn very quickly.'

'Please don't go.'

'I have to go, Kit. I'm just so glad you came in to say goodbye.'

'But there'd be a procession of people coming to say goodbye if they really thought you were going. In fact, they wouldn't let you go.' Kit's eyes were blazing.

'If you want to be my friend, Kit, you won't tell them.'

'Have you any money, any cash to tide you over?'

'Yes, your mother sends me English five pound notes from time to time. She doesn't say it's from her, but I know. It just says *For Emergencies* and this is an emergency.'

'People will be so hurt, Sister. They've come down here time after time, they've told you their life stories and you leave without saying goodbye.'

'It's the best.'

'No, it's not. What about Emmet? You taught him to speak, to read, to love poetry. What about Rita, when she comes back to Lough Glass and comes to see you, she'll find an empty cottage . . . ? I know Maura thinks the world of you, she wouldn't blame you for what happened to Father. And I heard awful Mrs Dillon, who never said a nice word about anyone, saying you should be canonised . . . you can't walk out on everyone.'

But Kit's words were in vain. 'When are you going, Sister?' she asked.

'This evening, on the six o'clock bus. I have a lot to do, Kit. May God bless you, and guide you.' She paused and then spoke again. 'May your mother find peace and fulfilment in the life she has. Is it a good life?'

'Only sort of,' Kit said.

'It must have been what she wanted.' Sister Madeleine's eyes were still misty.

'I could tell you all the story if you stayed . . .' Kit pleaded.

'No, I don't want to hear a story of someone else. People should tell their own story. God go with you always, Kit McMahon.' She turned away.

Kit ran out of the cottage in tears. She ran by the lakeside until she came to the path that went up by the hotel. Looking into the neglected grounds and gardens of the Central Hotel she saw Philip sitting in the old summer-house. It was rotting and needed great repairs and a coat of paint. He wore his thick coat, but still it must have been a cold place to sit and read.

'Can I come and join you?' she asked.

He closed his book. She saw it was one of their text books. 'Will you be warm enough?' He was kind, out for her good.

'Imagine you reading this. That bonehead Kevin O'Connor hasn't even opened it.'

'He doesn't need to with his hotels,' Philip said.

'No. Life's not fair, is it?'

'Were you down with Sister Madeleine?'

'Yes, how did you know?'

'Well, you came in the side way. Where else would you have been walking on a Sunday afternoon?'

'She's leaving,' Kit said. And she told him the whole story.

*

There was a wide bit of road outside Paddles' bar. The bus came in about ten to six. The small figure of Sister Madeleine came up the lane. She carried a bag, a torn bag held together with twine. Somebody must have brought it to her once as a way of carrying something. It was one of the few things she had not been able to pass on to anyone else.

A lot of people stood around, many many more than would have been travelling on the bus. Or indeed going into Paddles bar. Or knocking on the back door of Mrs Dillon's to ask her to give them a tin of beans or a packet of Gold Flake on the quiet. They had come to see if it was true that the hermit was leaving.

Clio was there, and Anna. Michael Sullivan, Patsy Hanley, Kevin Wall standing beside Emmet. Patsy Hanley eyed them speculatively as she sucked her finger, and tried to take in all that was going on. There were some older people too, Tommy Bennet the postman, and Jimmy the porter from the hotel. They stood silently shuffling as if waiting for someone to say something. Something that would stop the hermit from leaving town.

Sister Madeleine seemed to be unaware of the people standing around.

Tommy Bennet stepped forward. 'Where are you going to, Sister? I'd be glad to pay the fare.'

'It's nine shillings, Tommy,' Sister Madeleine said in a low voice. She didn't want the name of the place she was heading for to be said aloud.

'But you'll be back, Sister,' he said, paying the fare and accepting the ticket for the hermit.

Shadowy forms in the background meant that other people were there too to see the departure.

She can pay you with the money that came from Sullivan's garage, someone called. And there was a half laugh. Kit looked around her in disbelief. These were the people who loved Sister Madeleine. How could they have turned on her like this?

The driver, who was not from around this part of the world, shivered. There was something happening here that he didn't understand, but he didn't like it. He saw various youngsters come and shake the hand of the small woman who was most probably a nun. He saw a lot of others hang back, and look at the scene as if they were watching a play.

Just before they heard the Angelus begin to ring out at six o'clock the conductor was in the bus, and had the driver ready to move. He looked hastily up and down the long main street of Lough Glass. He didn't want to miss any stragglers by leaving too early, but he felt a wish to be gone. The bus went down the dark street.

And nobody at all waved goodbye.

9

James Williams had been debating for a long time whether he should invite Mrs Gray to lunch. If he telephoned to make an arrangement she would certainly say no. He could hardly run into her casually again.

He decided to call at the agency. To say that he had been passing. He would say that he had found himself in the area and wondered if he could tear her away from her work for an hour. If she said no, then he would find another opportunity. He wanted to talk to her very much indeed, and lunch seemed the right time to do it.

The place was much bigger and smarter than he had been led to believe. Why did Louis live in a run-down street in Earl's Court if his wife ran a place as prestigious as this? And run it she did, there was no doubt about it.

She was well guarded from the casual passerby. He was offered an appointment. If he could wait for half an hour, Mrs Millar might be free. There wouldn't be a chance of seeing Mrs Gray he was told. Several times.

'But it's only for a moment,' he begged, putting on a mock despairing face.

'In what connection?' the receptionist said.

'I am so anxious to take Mrs Gray out to lunch,' he said with his practised charm. 'I wonder could I ask you to go in and intercede on my behalf.'

'Does she know you, Mr Williams?'

'Ah yes, she does. But that alone might not make her say yes.' He looked suitably humble and hopeful, and sat in the blue and gold waiting room admiring the professionalism that had been brought to bear on this place. It was all a credit to Lena. Millar had made nothing of it for years, and there was no other explanation for its success since Lena's arrival.

Lena came through the door. 'James, what a surprise,' she said, both hands out to meet him. He thought she looked thinner than when he had seen her last. And a little pale. Perhaps it was the dark red outfit that took the colour from her face.

She was very smart in a red check dress and jacket, her shoes were black and red ... she was the role model for every young office worker. If they could look as good and confident as this at Mrs Gray's age ... then life would have been very satisfactory.

'It's twelve forty-five, I was passing the door ...'

'You never pass doors,' Lena said, laughing at him.

'I'd never pass yours. Say yes, a little lunch, I'll have you back well before two.'

'I should think so too. We don't take long lunch breaks at Millar's, not like your world, James.'

She hadn't revealed what his world was; neither did he.

They made small talk, polite banter. Each accusing the other of knowing much more about wines than they claimed. Then the fish had been ordered, and the chat was over. A little silence fell between them.

'Have you any idea why I wanted to see you?' James asked.

Lena was thoughtful. He had lost his air of mock gallantry now, he seemed more serious. She decided not to be flippant. 'Something about Louis, I imagine.'

'Yes. It's not easy. Do you have any idea what it is?'

'No. Has he been unreliable? Not turning up?' Her eyes were troubled.

'No, no. On the contrary, he has been working almost too many hours. Surely you must have noticed that.'

'Well, he's away from home many hours, that's true certainly.' She spoke without bitterness, with a sort of resignation.

'And has he said anything at all to you about a new post?'

'No, nothing at all.' She looked up at him, bewildered. Louis always discussed work with her – his wilder ideas from which she had to turn him so gently and tactfully that he thought it was he who had made the decision; his disputes and indignations with fellow workers . . . they had talked them through, often late into the night. Lena would bring about a situation where Louis would see that confrontation would be a loser's game. Diplomacy meant playing at being careful.

But what new position could there be? He was manager of the Dryden. It must be somewhere else. There was no higher he could go where he was. God, had he entered into negotiations without telling her? Was there some plan afoot to go to Scotland? Had he decided not to consult her in case she threw obstacles in his path?

She looked at James Williams' face and tried to read it. He could read hers easily. It was absolute ignorance of any new position, and the huge hurt that went with being left out in the cold.

But James Williams had a face that was hard to understand. A gently flirtatious smile seemed to be coming back to play about his lips. The admiring, distant stance that he always had with her had replaced what looked like being a serious discussion. 'Well, I suppose he's absolutely right not to drag boring old hotel politics home with him . . .' His smile was broad.

But Lena thought he had deliberately decided to change the direction of the conversation. 'What post exactly?'

'In hotels there are always debates, discussions, worrying about this post and that . . . it obsesses us, it's surprising we have any time to look after clients . . .'

Lena looked at him with respect. James Williams was very smooth. Look at how effortlessly he moved away from the topic once he realised that Lena knew nothing of any new position. She would play the same game and help him to change the subject.

'Tell me about Laura Evans, that friend of yours we met when we came to stay.' Lena said. She heard the question almost echoing in her ears, and could hardly believe she had asked it.

'Laura?' he said, in well-bred disbelief that she should have brought the name up.

She did not let her glance drop from his. 'That's right.' She was bright, eager, interested.

'Oh, I think she's fine. I haven't seen her for some time,' he said.

'I see,' said Lena.

He laid his hand on hers. It was a long moment. 'It's a funny old life,' he said.

'How do you mean?'

'You could have met someone like me, I could have met someone like you.'

Now Lena decided to be the one who changed the direction. 'Ah, but the world is very small. We *did* meet eventually. Now, let's pay great attention to this very decorated dish of plaice I see coming towards us.'

Her eyes were bright in her face, which he realised was indeed thinner and more drawn than before. James Williams wondered what it would be like to be loved so passionately and uncomplainingly by a woman like Lena Gray.

The afternoon seemed very long, which was rare. Normally the time flew by.

'I told you twice already we went to Julio's and I had Plaice Florentine. Now, can you get on with your work and let me get on with mine.' She rarely snapped at people.

Jennifer, her secretary, looked up startled. 'Was it bad news, Mrs Gray?' she asked.

'Why on earth do you think it was bad news? Now, might I add that at Millar's we actually publish guidelines for our clients. We advise office workers not to interrogate their employers about their private lives, especially having been advised to get on with their work.'

She knew she had behaved badly. Why could she not have spent two minutes saying that Mr Williams was a friend of hers and her husband's outside work, and said that they had a delicious lunch in a place where the waiters called you Signora? That way Jennifer, who was only being friendly, would have gone happily back to her desk. Why could Lena not have pretended to be calm as she did so often?

Because she didn't feel bloody calm, that was why.

'I won't be having lunch with you on Saturday, I'm a witness at Ivy's marriage,' Lena told Jim and Jessie Millar.

'That's nice, a wedding's great,' Jessie said, looking back affectionately at her own wedding day.

Lena shuddered, remembering.

'You're looking tired,' Jim Millar said. 'Perhaps we're working you too hard. Take a few days off for your friend's wedding.'

'No, Jim. I'm better working,' Lena said.

'You *are* tired, I said only the other day you were, and Jessie was saying it too.'

Tired meant old. People didn't know that's what they were saying but that was it all the same. Well, she was in her forties, well into her forties. What could she expect to look but old. This wedding was probably the last time she would dress up and put on the style. After this she would wear sedate clothes, dove greys, navy with a little touch of white. Mother of the bride outfits.

With a lurch she realised she would not be there at Kit's wedding, no matter what kind of outfit she wore. Plump, generous, spirited Maura Hayes would go to Dublin with her sister Lilian and buy something suitable, something that would see her through other social events during the years that followed. Unexpected tears came to her eyes.

'Are you all right, Lena?' Jessie was concerned.

'I'm fine, never better,' Lena said with a smile that was much too bright.

'What'll we give Ivy and Ernest?' Louis asked. He was home just for an hour. It was all go at the Dryden these days. They had a function again tonight, he needed to be there to oversee it.

'You shouldn't have come all the way back,' Lena said, solicitous that he was rushing too much.

'I wanted to see you, say hello, anyway.'

'Well, will it be a late do?'

'Makes no sense my coming back, darling. I won't be out of it until four, and then start again at eight. No, better that I sleep there.'

The old familiar dull thud came in her heart. 'Sure,' she said brightly.

Louis stood there smiling at her. He had taken his shirt off and he patted his stomach. 'Terrible middle-aged spread . . . I'm pathetic,' he said.

'Come on, flat as a board . . . you'd think you were playing tennis all day, you're so fit.' She loved to praise him, and see the light dance back into his eyes.

'Oh, I don't know, I don't think I'd cut much of a figure on the beach . . .'

'Let's go to a beach somewhere for our holidays next year,' she said suddenly.

He looked caught unawares. 'Who knows where we'll be next year?' he said.

'Exactly. We could go somewhere smashing. I'll start looking up brochures.'

'Yeah, well, we'll talk about that later. Now let's think what we'll give love's young dream downstairs.'

She wished he didn't make such fun of their ages. When she and Louis got married some day they too would be old. *When* they got married.

He was fastening his clean shirt and looking critically at his face in the mirror. She knew with a certainty that they would never marry. Why had she kept this foolish notion, like a child's toy, in her mind? She also knew that he was about to start an adventure tonight. Or perhaps he was in the middle of one. She knew the signs by now.

'I thought we'd get them a mirror, a nice antique mirror,' she said. She heard her voice as if it was coming down a tunnel.

Louis smiled at her. 'Would there be room for it on the wall, with all Ivy's rubbish?'

'Oh yes. They're doing the place up, haven't you noticed?'

'No, I didn't see any difference.' He hadn't been in to Ivy's since the night he had taken over her little celebration for them.

'I think they'd like it.'

'Sure, get it then, as long as it's not too dear.'

He wouldn't pay a penny towards it, nor would he ever know that her real present to Ivy had been an outfit, a maroon velvet suit, and a hat to match. She had arranged a facial and a hair do at Grace's salon. She had spent maybe ten times the cost of the mirror already.

Was Louis mean? He had always seemed the very spirit of generosity. When he had hardly sixpence left he would spend the coins he had on a bunch of violets. She couldn't bear to think of Louis as mean. Anything else but that.

'And you're all clear to come to the wedding on Saturday?' she said.

'Yes, I wouldn't miss a good feed and booze up. Funny he's not having it in his own pub.'

'No, that wouldn't be good for the people who remembered Charlotte, or for his sons ... more tactful to have it elsewhere.'

'But a bloody railway station! Really, Lena.' He was so scornful, so full of ridicule. And yet she knew he wouldn't say anything of the sort. He would tell Ivy and Ernest that it had been an inspired thing to have a party in a pub by one of the big railway stations and then leave for a honeymoon. His pity and ridicule wouldn't be seen publicly. The public Louis was a man you couldn't fault.

'We have to be at the Register Office at twelve,' she said.

'I know, I know. I'll be there. I've arranged a split shift.'

'You mean you have to go back to work after it?'

'Some of us have to work,' he said, hurt.

She remembered James Williams saying that he worked almost too hard. She felt very uneasy. 'I met James Williams today,' she said suddenly.

Was it her imagaination or did he look wary. 'And what did he have to report?'

'Not much, mainly wine conversation, fish conversation. The fact that Laura Evans has gone the route of all other ladies before her, and probably after her.'

'She was a drunken tramp,' Louis said. 'I can't think why a man like that bothered with her.'

'Perhaps he was lonely.'

'With all that money! You saw his house. How could he be lonely?'

Lena didn't agree at all. But he was on the point of leaving, she didn't want an atmosphere, a silly row over something that mattered not at all.

'Why was James talking about fish and wine anyway?'

'We were in a restaurant. He brought me to lunch, he was passing by.'

'When was James ever passing by?'

'Funny, that's just what I said to him.'

'So what was it then?' He really did look ill at ease.

But she was light. 'Well, that's what I'd like to know. He looked as if he were going to tell me something, and then he seemed to decide against it.'

'What kind of thing?'

'I haven't an idea. Maybe he has a new Laura Evans installed. Who knows? He went back to talking about fish and wine and all.'

'And did neither of you talk about me at all?' His voice was light, but he was poised. She could sense it.

'Only to tell me that you work all the hours God sends.'

He came over and put both hands on her shoulders. He kissed her on the forehead. It was a solemn sort of thing to do, like a ceremony, or someone acting in a play. 'See you at the wedding tomorrow,' he said.

'Try to get some sleep,' she said to his back as he ran lightly down the stairs.

She went into Ivy as she had promised.

'Is he out or in?' Ivy asked.

'Out.'

'Good, I have you for longer then.' Again Ivy took out the wine-coloured velvet suit. Again she thanked and blessed her good friend Lena. 'Without you, none of this would have happened. None of it,' she said in a choked voice.

'Give over, you'll have me crying now.'

'Ernest's out with some of the lads, we can have a drink, you and I.'

'Don't tell me you're *still* meant to be on the wagon?' Lena laughed.

'Ah yes, but wait till I get my lines, as they say. When I'm a Mrs again, then I'll introduce alcohol slowly back into our lives.' They raised a glass to the future.

'And what are your plans, Lena? You who sort out everyone else's lives.'

'I don't know. Louis and I were talking about going to the seaside for a holiday next year.'

'Imagine. That would be great!' Ivy was very impressed.

'It's not definite yet, of course.'

'No, of course.'

Lena longed to cry on her friend's shoulder, to tell her that she thought there was something serious afoot. Something which James Williams was about to tell her and had chickened out at the last moment. Something she had read in Louis' eyes when she had spoken of the holiday next year. And when he had come and put his hands on her shoulders.

She couldn't think what it might be. What could be worse than the affairs he had hidden from her over the years? But this was the night before Ivy's wedding. This was no time to sit and drink and cry that there ain't no good in men.

'Do you think it's silly having the few drinks near the station?' Ivy asked.

'No, I think it's brilliant. You said Ernest doesn't want a big formal sit-down thing. This way it's a nice familiar set-up that we all know and like. I've been in and arranged the sandwiches.' She had also arranged a small wedding cake but that was to be a surprise.

'When I married Ron,' Ivy said, 'I had a girl called Elsie as my bridesmaid. I haven't an idea where she is. I don't know what happened to her.'

'I don't know what's become of my bridesmaid first time round either,' Lena said. 'I suppose she came to my funeral. I forgot to check.' Her smile was a little watery.

Ivy always felt uneasy when she joked about the events of long ago. To her it was unfathomable that someone should have to pretend to be dead instead of getting divorced properly. 'But I'll never forget you, Lena. I mean it. You're truer than any friend I ever had.'

'I think this port is making you weepy,' Lena said. 'I think I'm going to have to side with your husband and keep you off it altogether.'

'My husband,' Ivy said in wonder. 'Imagine, tomorrow I'll be Ernest's wife.'

'It's all you deserve,' said Lena.

Her heart felt like a cold, heavy stone.

*

The letter from Kit was three pages long. Lena's first reaction was anxiety. Why was she saying so much, was there something that had to be told . . . but as she skimmed it quickly it seemed to carry no terrible message.

Kit wrote about the man called Francis Xavier Byrne who had been the one responsible for the events in Sullivan's Garage and how Sister Madeleine had harboured him as if he was a runaway fox.

She wrote very simply about how her father had been beaten but had recovered well.

I know you'd be glad to hear Maura looked after him so well that he's as good as new again, and back making jokes and laughing like always.

I tell you this because if you just read about it in the paper that you get you might think it was worse than it was. It's strange that you read news of Lough Glass still. I don't know what kind of things to tell you about the place.

The Hickeys have extended their shop. Mr Hickey has taken the pledge and Mrs Hickey says that this means with the money they save they'll own a fleet of butchers' shops all over the country. Sister Madeleine's house stands empty, the door swinging open. I went to see it last week. There were rabbits inside and a couple of very tame-looking birds. I expect they thought she was coming back to feed them. The worst thing is that people say she was never any good, that she was more superstitious than saintly. I always liked her anyway and I'm not going to change.

Clio feels the same. I don't see a great deal of Clio these days. She's very much 'in love' as she says with an awful fellow called Michael O'Connor, whose father owns a lot of hotels. He's very rich. His brother is in our class at Cathal Brugha Street and is even worse. I'm not 'in love' with anyone yet.

Stevie Sullivan in the garage turned out to be much better than he looked as if he was going to be. His brother is still a monster though.

Some things haven't changed. Father Baily is the same, and Mother Bernard and Brother Healy. They were always like that I suppose and always will be. Farouk is the same, he doesn't mind Dad and Maura's dog, he just ignores it ands walks loftily out of the room if the dog comes in. I don't know why I'm telling you all these things. I suppose I thought if you go every week to buy the newspaper you must still care about what's going on.

All the very best to you.

Kit

Kit was pleased that she had written. She didn't know why she had changed the nature of her usual curt little notes. It was as if she felt somehow that Lena Gray must be lonely and it didn't cost much to write a few lines.

Kit,

I can't tell you how much I love to know what's going on. Anything you have time and energy to write is interesting. I'm deliberately making this a short note so that you will not think I am burdening you down with correspondence.

And you were quite right in thinking that I would be glad to hear how well Maura looked after your father. I was very glad indeed to hear that and to know of his recovery.

Love from Lena

Lena did not sleep. At two a.m. she was wider awake than she often was in the middle of the day. She got up and made herself some tea. It didn't work. She had read that you should do some physical work like cleaning silver. That one was easy; they didn't have any silver. The flat was tidy. She always kept it immaculate so that he would never say they lived in a pokey place. She wandered around, restless, opening cupboards and drawers. They were all tidy.

It reminded her of the time those years ago when she had been about to leave Lough Glass.

She had spent so long leaving everything so that it would be perfect. She wanted Rita to be able to dispose of her clothes for her. She had even got all her shoes mended so that they could be given away. How was she to know that they would think she was dead? Why had Kit taken it into her head to burn the letter?

She looked at the wardrobe where Louis' clothes were kept. They hung there, the jackets she had bought for him, the shirts that she took to the Chinese laundry each week, the shoes that she polished until they shone. 'Oh nonsense, I'm doing my own,' she had said the first time he protested, and he hadn't protested again.

Of course she had done too much for him. But if she had done any less it would have ended long ago. Long before now. She felt a chill. Why did she think it was ending now?

The phone was on the landing, the public telephone that any of the tenants could use. If she spoke in a low voice no one would hear her. No one would know her shame. She dialled the Dryden Hotel. A voice answered. She knew it was the night porter. 'I just wanted to enquire about tonight's function,' she said.

'I beg your pardon?'

'Just a quick question. What time do you expect it to be over?' she asked.

'I'm sorry, Madam. There's no function tonight,' the voice said.

'Thank you, thank you very much,' she said.

She saw the dawn come over the city. She knew how to do small miracles with make-up, but not major miracles. Nothing would hide black hollows in her face, nothing that would give a shine and sparkle to haunted eyes.

She remembered hearing a coal miner, who had managed to hack his way out of a pit disaster, saying on the radio: 'I tried to think of something else, not the big thing. I wouldn't allow myself to believe that I might be dead, so I thought about the garden shed I was building, and I went through all the wood I'd need and the nails and the roofing. It saw me through.'

That's what she would do, Lena decided. She would throw herself so much into Ivy's wedding that there would be no time to think that her own life might be about to end.

She made a pot of tea, and toast with honey and brought it down to Ivy.

'I don't believe you.' Ivy's delight was so great she didn't notice the hollows and lines in the face of her bridesmaid. And on a wedding day people only look at the bride. 'You're going to have every single thing you want today,' Lena said, her smile so wide it made her face ache.

She walked up to the Grace West Beauty Salon and handed Ivy over to their care. 'I'll be back for you at ten thirty,' she promised.

'I think Louis Gray will be glad to see me off your hands. I'm taking up so much of your time,' Ivy said.

'Oh don't mind about Louis.'

Grace gave Lena a sharp look. 'Do you want anything? A bit of a comb out, eyeshadow,' she asked Lena quietly.

'No, it goes deeper than that.' Her voice to Grace was bleak.

'You've been there before and back,' Grace said.

'Not this time.' They had moved away from Ivy's hearing.

'I don't believe you, I'd bet you five to one.'

'I'm not a gambling woman ...' Lena's voice was flat.

'Oh yes you are, you gambled on that man of yours.'

'If I did I lost.'

Grace said nothing.

'By the way, Ivy doesn't know,' Lena said.

'Nobody knows,' Grace said. 'You're just overtired, imagining things.'

'Yes, sure.'

She went home and dressed. She made no telephone call to the Dryden to discover whether there had been a split shift or not. She put the film in her camera, she prepared four envelopes of rice in case other people might like to throw it as well.

She emptied the wastepaper baskets into a paper bag so that she could bring it down and put it into the dustbin. There she found a printed paper with the times and prices of flights to Ireland. It was crumpled up and thrown away. But it was not something she had ever had. So many times she had thought of flying there, but she had never gone so far as getting a brochure with the times of the plane departures.

Louis couldn't have been thinking of going to Ireland without letting her know. It couldn't possibly mean that his latest fling might be someone from Ireland. That would be too hurtful to imagine. Or someone that he was taking to Ireland on a magic trip. Some girl that he was going to impress with his fairytale ways in the Emerald Isle. She left it in the basket, just where it was, and straightened up her back. This day was going to be very long and very hard.

And now it was almost time to go and collect Ivy.

Ernest was nervous too, and his friend Sammy was no help. Just a stream of jokes in rapid fire delivery. Nothing reassuring. Nothing to calm the nervous Ernest down and tell him that it was a few words said at whatever volume he wished to say them.

'I feel such a fool in front of all these people,' Ernest complained.

Lena wanted to smack him very hard.

There were going to be sixteen people there altogether. All friends who wished them well. His two sons had accepted that Ivy would now be his wife. They would be there. He had nothing to do, nothing to organise, all he had to do was be bloody grateful that Ivy saw fit to marry him.

Lena wondered was she becoming very anti-men. But that was not so. Mr Millar was an angel. James Williams was a gentleman. Martin had been a sort of saint. Peter Kelly had been a good and loyal friend. There was so many around her who were giving. And Ernest wasn't all that bad, he was gruff and inarticulate, he didn't have the silver tongue of Louis Gray.

Louis, who would come and join them and lie his way into their hearts. When the day was over they would remember him and the lovely mirror he had given and the jokes he had told and how he had made people happy.

She saw that Sammy was perspiring heavily: the man really was nervous. These were timid people, she remembered; people who feared ritual and occasion. They didn't realise that they controlled it, and they could run it. They thought it controlled them.

'Well, are we ready for the road?' she asked the two men. 'The taxi is outside the door.' She had arranged that too. And paid for it in advance.

Otherwise they might have been searching the streets of London for one when they were all assembled.

'The bride?' Sammy said, as if he had only just thought of her as an essential part of the undertaking.

'Is in the bedroom. She'll come out when we're all set to go.' Lena went to fetch her. 'You look absolutely lovely,' she said. 'You never ever looked better.'

Ivy's lined face lit up with pleasure. Her hat was at an angle, her cream and maroon scarf was tied jauntily. She looked years younger, the kind of lady you might see coming out of the Ritz Hotel.

Ernest and Sammy looked at her in awe. That was Lena's reward, the pure undisguised surprise and delight that their Ivy had smartened up so well. And the slight fear that they might not look her equal.

'Where's Louis?' Ivy said. As almost anyone who had ever met Louis always said.

'He'll meet us there, he has to get away specially.' She linked Ivy's arm and escorted her out to the taxi. 'Caxton Hall please,' she said at the top of her voice, so that nobody could be in any doubt where they were heading.

Louis slipped in beside Lena just before the ceremony. He smelled of lavender soap. Of course, they could have lavender soap at the Dryden. He smiled at her warmly. 'You look gorgeous,' he said appreciatively. The tan and cream outfit had cost a lot, but she could wear it for giving lectures, for meeting important new clients. For the many work engagements that stretched ahead of her as her future. 'Sweet little hat,' he whispered.

The function might have been cancelled. And he might have had to stay and work on late anyway so that it seemed a waste of time to come home. Don't ask, Lena told herself. Leave yourself that escape route. You can always think it. If you ask then you'll know. 'How was the function?' she asked before she could stop herself.

'Don't ask,' he sighed rolling his eyes to heaven. 'Interminable, I suppose that's the best way to sum it up.'

'What was it, a conference, a golden wedding or what?'

'A crowd of salesmen on the piss.'

'Still, it's good for the hotel.'

'I'm getting a bit sick of doing things so that the hotel will make money.'

She looked at him. This was her cue to soothe him, persuade him to stay, tell him what a good position it was, how highly they thought of him . . . how unwise it would be to make any move.

This time she did it differently. 'Well, you should move, Louis.'

'What?'

They were whispering, waiting for the little group to assemble itself. Lena should be up beside Ivy. 'Don't let them use you, take advantage of you, there must be some new positions coming up. You should think about them seriously.'

He was staggered. 'But I thought you would . . .'

'Never assume you know what I'm going to do or think . . . which reminds me, I'm meant to be a witness here.'

With perfect timing, at the arrival of the registrar she went to stand beside Ivy and Ernest and Sammy, and take part in a ceremony which felt a million miles away. Like a little pinpoint down there on earth. Far below where her mind had gone to try and take in the whole situation.

Once the formal bit was over, Ernest and Sammy relaxed to the extent that Lena thought that the couple might never leave on their honeymoon. The pints were bought, the brandies and gingers. Plates of sandwiches circulated in the corner of the pub that had been reserved for them. Passers-by came to wish them luck and were offered a sandwich and even a drink for their trouble. Then the little cake came in and Lena photographed them cutting it.

She took some time to pose this picture. It would be the one on the wall. She straightened Ivy's hat and Ernest's tie. She even got them to put their hands together on the knife so that it looked like a real wedding picture.

'I'm surprised you didn't have her in white with half a dozen trainbearers,' Louis said under his breath.

Lena flashed him a smile as if he had said something warm and encouraging instead of sneering. Ivy was very quick on the uptake; she would notice if Lena glowered.

Then they asked the barman to take a group picture, and the bride and groom ran in a shower of rice across the station. They were going to spend three nights in a town thirty miles and one hour from London. Their friends waved them goodbye from the platform. The pubs were closed now, the little group wandered back through the barrier.

The goodbyes were lengthy, Sammy wanted everyone to come to a drinking club he knew down in the City, but their heart wasn't in it. Lena knew that she could have invited them back to the flat, a couple of bottles of wine would have kept the party going until opening time. But she had no intention of doing it. Not for Ernest's two sullen sons, not for Sammy and the handful of people who couldn't organise anything for themselves.

With huge regret she said she had to go back to work and she dragged Louis away with her.

'You don't really have to go back to work,' he said.

'No, but you do. I wanted to get you out of it without having the lot of them descend on the Dryden.'

'I don't have to go back to work,' he said.

'You said you had a split shift, didn't you?'

He looked at her searchingly to see was he being tested. 'My God, of course I did.' He hit his forehead.

'Well now, who's a good secretary to you then?' She was playful.

'I work too hard, Lena,' he said.

'I know you do.' She was insincere but he wouldn't know it.

'Maybe you're right. Maybe I should leave the place.'

'Not in the middle of a Saturday split shift. Wait till there's something better on offer. You could do any job.' They had walked as far as a tube station by now.

'Where are you going?' he asked.

'Well, if you have to go to work, so will I. It's no fun without you at home.'

'Do you really think that?' He looked troubled.

'Come on, handsome, you know I do.' She kissed him on the nose and looked around once to find him still standing at the top of the steps looking after her as if there were things to be said but he hadn't said them.

Lena picked up the post. It always seemed a luxury to her to have a postal delivery on a Saturday. Imagine if there had been such a thing in Lough Glass. Mona Fitz and poor Tommy Bennet would have had a fit if anyone had suggested it.

She divided it up expertly, marvelling as she often did at the way the business had blossomed. When she came here first the mail was hardly worth talking about and there had been only Jessie sitting bewildered and confused with overstuffed drawers full of papers that would take hours to sort out. If she had done nothing else in the years of life in London then at least she had built this monument to working women, their needs and hopes and chances.

She made herself a cup of tea, took off her wedding hat with its little tan feather, and her shoes. She sat back in her office chair and wondered what she would like to do now. She decided she would like to write to Kit. She must be careful, she thought. It was fragile, the peace between them; she must not rush the fences and destroy it again.

But this was the first time today that she had asked herself what she, Lena, would like to do. And she was going to do it. After hours of encouraging Ivy, calming Ernest, making conversation to Ernest's sons, taking pictures, throwing rice, smiling at everyone, telling Louis that she knew he had to go back to work, she bloody *deserved* to do what she wanted to do.

She wrote to her daughter about the wedding she had just come from. About how well Ivy had looked and how nervous the groom had been, about the people in the pub who had all joined in and the passers-by who had waved as the happy couple got on to the train. She wrote light-heartedly and read through it many times to make sure that there was no tell-tale sign of bitterness or self pity. Nowhere in the three closely typed pages had she mentioned Louis Gray.

It was as if he did not exist.

*

'Hello, Maura, it's Kit.'

'Oh, Kit. I'm so sorry, your father's just gone down to Paddles' with Peter. He'll be so sorry you wasted your money on the phone.'

'Will you come on out of that, wicked stepmother. I didn't waste my money. Didn't I get to talk to you?'

'We're all fine here, he's back to his old self again. And Emmet's cheerful too, head down studying hard. You won't know this house when you get back at Christmas.'

'Is Emmet there, Maura?'

'No, love, you've missed him too. He's gone to the pictures with Anna. They seem to be pals again, really, they're as bad as you and Clio used to be. How's Clio, by the way?'

'I don't see her that much, Maura, but she's fine.'

'Ask her to ring home a bit more, will you? I feel ashamed telling Lilian that you ring twice a week, it's like I'm boasting.'

'So you should, you're much nicer than Lilian,' Kit said.

'Stop that. Do you want me to give them any messages?'

'Yes. Tell Father that his only daughter was distraught to hear he was out drinking his skull off, and tell Emmet I'm keeping my promise.'

'I don't suppose I'm going to be told what promise.'

'No, but he'll know.'

'You're a great girl, Kit.'

'And you're not the worst either.'

'Clio, will we go out for chips?'

'Lord, who stood *you* up that you have to phone me as a last resort?'

'Did you go to special classes in how to be charming, or did you just read a book?'

'Sorry, I'm in bad form.'

'Would chips help?'

'When did they not?'

'This is Philip. Kit, I was wondering would you like to go to the pictures. Normally like, you know the way people often go together.'

'I know the way people go to the pictures, Philip. But I can't, I've just said I'd meet Clio for chips.'

'Oh.' He sounded very disappointed.

'Come with us if you like,' she offered.

'Won't you want to giggle and laugh?'

'No, we're too old for that now. Come with us.'

'It would make life so much easier if you fancied Kevin O'Connor,' Clio said.

'I told you what I felt about him, I even told him by solicitor's letter, for God's sake. There's no use going after that particular fantasy.'

'A person can wish,' Clio said.

'I told Philip O'Brien he could join us, he seemed a bit at a loose end.'

'Of course he's at a loose end until he can take you to the Happy Ring House and buy you a miserable small diamond and chain you to his side.'

Kit laughed. 'Where on earth is Michael? What has he done to bring on all this fit of the miseries?'

'He wants me to go to England with him for Christmas and New Year. His sister's having a big party or something.'

'Well, isn't that great.'

'They're not letting me go.'

'Oh ask them nicely, Clio.'

'No, it's a brick wall. And Aunt Maura is in it too, up to her eyes in it.'

'But you're grown up. They'll have to see that.'

'They don't see it. It's just an ultimatum. We expect you to come home to us for Christmas and New Year, Clio, like any nice girl from any nice family would do.' Her face was full of tragedy.

'He won't take anyone else,' Kit consoled her.

'But it makes me such a fool. The one time he does see my home it's got that mongrel Anna sitting hissing insults at him in the kitchen. Now he hears that they're such gaolers they won't let me accept a perfectly reasonable generous invitation to a friend's house.'

'Have you told him that you're not allowed go?'

'No, I'm too ashamed. I'll pretend to be sick or something, or I may just go.'

'You won't do that.' Kit knew Clio well enough to realise that she wouldn't defy her family this way.

'No, I want to have some kind of family left to present him with when we get engaged.'

'You really will get engaged, the Happy Ring House and all?' Kit was surprised.

'Oh eventually, not yet. Not the Happy Ring House.'

Philip came in.

'We're talking about the future,' Kit said.

'Shut up,' Clio said.

'I knew you'd have things to giggle about,' Philip said defensively.

'Giggle?' Clio said. 'I haven't giggled in years. Will we have double chips?'

'Yes, and cappucino,' Kit said.

'I want your advice.' Philip had never asked their advice before, he had always offered it. They leaned forward, interested. 'The floor in the golf club is banjaxed,' he said eventually. Clio and Kit looked at each other mystified. 'Banjaxed completely,' he confirmed. 'So you see, they won't be able to have their New Year's Eve Dinner Dance there, and I thought . . . well I thought I'd try to have it in our hotel. In the Central.'

'In the Central?' cried Clio and Kit in such disbelief that Philip felt defensive.

'At least the floor isn't subsiding,' he said, hurt.

'No of course it isn't.' Kit felt they should look less astounded. 'But a dance, a dinner dance.'

'The dining room is very big,' Philip said. It was indeed, a great gloomy barn of a place. Kit had only eaten there once, the day Philip had invited them for breakfast. Despite all Maura's praise it had seemed a cheerless kind of room. 'And the band could be up in the bay window. We could have the curtains pulled back and if there was a moon the lake would look great.'

'They might all freeze to death watching it though,' Clio said.

'Philip would get proper heating,' Kit said.

He gave her a grateful look. 'Yes, but I've only a few weeks. We'll have to tell the committee in the Golf Club that it can be done, and that it will be right . . .'

'They might take a bit of convincing,' Clio said.

'It's your father, Clio and yours, Kit. They're kind of the ones who could make it happen.' The girls were silent. In neither home had much good ever been spoken of the Central Hotel. 'And there's no floor, remember that.'

'They might mend their floor rather than go somewhere different,' Clio said.

'No, there's going to be a court case and all about their floor. The fellows that put it in gave them a guarantee and now it's falling to bits . . .'

'What do your parents say?' Kit cut through all the inessentials.

'They don't know yet.'

'They'll say no,' Clio said.

'Well, they will *at first*, but they might say yes later.'

'Six weeks after the dance is over.' Clio saw no good in anything or anyone in Lough Glass.

'So we must make them see it would be a great thing,' Philip said.

'Who's this *we*?' Kit asked suspiciously.

'Well, you, Kit. You could help me, I mean you're nearly qualified too, and you got such good marks . . . and if they hear you saying it could be done they'd believe you more than they would just me. No one ever thinks their own children grow up.'

Kit was thoughtful. There was a danger of being drawn into something which was doomed from the start. Who wanted to lock horns with Mr and Mrs O'Brien?

Philip looked so full of hope.

And wouldn't it be wonderful if it worked? A real glittering dance on their doorstep. A dance where she and Stevie Sullivan could whirl around together under coloured lights. Where Emmet could get together with Anna Kelly again. Where Philip could show his gloomy parents that he was indeed a grown-up man with ideas of his own.

'Well?' he said, hardly daring to let out his breath.

'I can hear the tinkle of trays of very small stones,' Clio murmured to her.

'I think it's a great idea, Philip,' cried Kit. 'And this will solve all our problems too, Clio.'

'How's that?' Clio was suspicious.

'If there was a great dance that we'd all be helping at, a great smashing gala affair . . . then you could ask the magnificent Michael to come to that instead of you going to England . . .'

'It wouldn't work . . .'

'Yes, it would,' Kit warmed to the idea. 'And I'd ask the awful dreadful Kevin too just to make a party out of it. Oh, stop looking at me like that, Philip. You know I can't stand Kevin, it's only to be sociable and make it good for Clio.'

Clio was beginning to see the possibilities. 'Where would they stay . . . ?' she asked.

'At the hotel,' Kit said.

'I'm not sure if they'd think . . .'

'The hotel will be terrific . . .' Kit insisted.

'It's only a few weeks,' Philip said in a panic.

'Then we've got to work very hard. On everybody.'

'Everybody?'

'Yes, Clio's got to tell her parents and I've got to tell mine, and we'll get your father enthusiastic and awful Mrs Hickey, she's a great organiser.'

'She's not in the golf club though, is she?' Clio found a flaw.

'No, but she'd love to be in that crowd so she'll work like the devil.'

'When will we start?' Philip's eyes were shining now.

'This weekend. We'll all go home on the train on Friday night. They won't know what's hit them.'

'I don't think Dan would be able to take on the golf club dinner dance,' Kit's father said. 'Haven't you always said yourself that the place smells of stale gravy?'

'We've got a few weeks to get that smell out of the place,' Kit said. 'Oh go on, Father, be enthusiastic. It's people like you and Clio's father we need to push it that way.'

'I'm not the leading social light in the town . . .'

'No, but you could bring all the golf club crowd with you . . . otherwise it'll all be in the big town, in some well-known place and the poor old Central will never get a chance to show what it can do.'

'You've always said that the best thing it could do was fall to the ground.' Martin was shaking his head at the complete change of attitude.

'But I've grown up a bit. I want something that will be good for Lough Glass. And for Philip. He's been my friend for years.'

Maura intervened. 'It would be much handier, Martin, if it could be here . . . and wouldn't it be lovely if we were all there. Emmet's keen to go, and Clio and Anna . . . it would be a family outing for us rather than just the four oldies up in the club.'

'And you can't be in the club anyway, because of the floor,' Kit said.

'Well, I'd be very glad to give Dan and Mildred the turn . . . but do they want to . . . ? I mean they never want to do anything new.'

'If they thought that all you lot were coming . . . the quality . . . they'd agree.'

'We're not the quality,' Martin said.

'No, but we're as near as it gets in Lough Glass,' Kit sighed.

'Will we help them, Philip, Kit and Clio?' Emmet asked Anna.

'I don't want to do anything to help Clio. I'll take part in anything at all that might lead to her downfall,' Anna said.

'You don't mean that.'

'Oh but I do. Just because you get on with Kit doesn't mean it's the normal thing to do.'

'I know.' Emmet did know. Very few people had a sister as marvellous as Kit. Someone who promised to help him and did. She had been very successful indeed at distracting Stevie Sullivan's attention away from Anna Kelly.

Emmet thought that Kit was reasonably good-looking. Of course, being her brother it was hard to look at things objectively; but he couldn't understand why Stevie would feel drawn to her instead of the beautiful Anna.

But whatever Kit was doing it was working. 'I hope it's not an awful bore for you,' he had said to Kit.

'No,' Kit had assured him. 'I'm quite enjoying it actually. But don't assume it's working totally. I wouldn't rush in there to Anna, you know.'

'You're right,' he said sagely. And he had been cautious.

He could see that Anna was still hanging around hoping that Stevie would be available, but he always seemed to be in Dublin these days, she grumbled.

'Never mind, I'm sure he'll be around at Christmas,' Emmet was encouraging.

'Yes? Well, I hope so.'

'So you'll help in the dance ... it's a place you could go with him.'

Anna hadn't thought of that. It was indeed a heaven-sent opportunity, a glittering dance on their doorstep. She began to think of what she would wear. 'You're very kind, Emmet. I really appreciate it, what with you fancying me and all that.'

'That's all right.' Emmet was courteous. 'After all, you fancied me too for a while. Maybe we might get back to the way we were, but I understand that's not the situation at present.'

'You deserve someone terrific,' Anna said. 'Someone much more worthy of you than Patsy Hanley.'

'Patsy's quite nice to talk to when you know her,' Emmet lied.

Clio knew just how to play it. She wouldn't plead with her parents to support the Central's bid to get into the big time in terms of entertainment. Instead, she put on the look of an early Christian martyr.

'Clio, sweetheart, please cheer up. We were looking forward to your coming home, now you just sit there as if the world were coming to an end.'

'It *is* as far as I'm concerned, Daddy.'

'We can't leave you off there to England with people we don't know.'

'So you said. I gave in, you've won. But I'm not expected to be happy about it.'

'We all have a life to live, Clio. Your mother is very upset by you.'

'And I'm very upset by her and by you. These are facts, Daddy.'

'You'll have a good Christmas here.'

'Sure.'

'And perhaps your friend Michael would come here and see you, see us all.'

'I can't invite him *here*; nothing ever happens in Lough Glass. You'd have to give a person a reason for driving from Dublin.'

That night in Paddles' Peter Kelly heard about the plans that were afoot.

'I suppose we should support them,' Martin McMahon said.

'God, this might be the direct answer from God that we were looking for.' Dr Kelly seemed very pleased. 'Count us in, Martin, and if this doesn't put a smile on Clio's face nothing will.'

Clio didn't sound enthusiastic.

'I thought you'd be pleased,' her father said, disappointed.

'Yes, but it probably won't happen. You know all the old golf club fuddy duddies won't think the Central is good enough for their precious party on New Year's Eve.'

'It's not, it's a terrible hotel ... you and Kit have always been to the forefront of saying what a desperate place it is.' He was bewildered now.

'Things will always be desperate while old people don't make any move to change them,' Clio said.

'Yes, I know that's your view. We've ruined everything for you, but what are your lot doing? Tell me that, except sitting around complaining and sulking.'

'I'd help Philip get the hotel into good shape if his awful old parents and everyone else's awful old parents didn't go round shaking their shaggy locks and saying that things should just stay as they were.'

Peter Kelly ran his hand over his rapidly balding head. 'It's very nice of you to refer to my shaggy locks,' he said, hoping to coax a smile out of her.

Clio gave a watery smile. 'You're not the worst, Daddy.'

'And you all would like us to have the dinner dance there ... even though we're crumbling old geriatrics ...'

'Yes. The rest of us would be normal,' she said.

'I hope you have a daughter yourself one day and you'll know how much you'd love her to praise you instead of always finding fault,' he said, in a rare mood of admitting his affection for her. Normally they had a jokey, sparring relationship.

'I'm sure I'll be a terrific mother when the time comes,' Clio said.

But she spoke with a slightly hollow note. She was five days late with her period; she fervently hoped the time to be a mother hadn't come yet.

'They won't come here,' Philip's father said, sniffing.

'They've had many a year when they could come, but they preferred their great ugly concrete barn of a golf club,' Mildred said.

Philip gritted his teeth. He would *not* lose his temper. Part of a hotelier's training was to remain outwardly calm when inwardly seething. They had been told that often enough. He had to practise it often enough in the various establishments where he had done his practical work.

'They have nowhere else to go,' he said.

'And we'd put ourselves out for one year, then they'd go back next year to their old shed out there.' His mother felt very keenly the fact that she was not part of the Lough Glass golfing set. The fact that she didn't play the game seemed to her irrelevant.

'It could be such a success that they'd want it here next time, and so would other people.'

'How would they know?' Dan O'Brien asked. 'That it had been a success, if it was a success?'

'We'd take photographs. Send them to the papers, magazines even.'

'You'd be off back to Dublin and we'd be left with the work of it.'

'No. I'd come back, every weekend, and I'll be home for the Christmas holidays.'

'And what would you know . . .' his father began.

Philip sounded weary but he knew that Kit and Clio were having similar arguments in their families. 'I don't know everything, but we're hoteliers, Father. All three of us, isn't that right, Mother? And if we're ever going to get a chance to do something different, a bit exciting . . . isn't this one being handed to us on a plate?' He didn't know why, or what words he had used, but it worked.

They looked at each other, a flicker of life and enthusiasm in their eyes. You would have to be quick to see it, but it was there. 'How will we heat the place?' his father asked, and Philip knew the battle had been won.

They had a little committee, and they met in the hotel. Kit took the minutes of the meeting in a big notebook; then she would type the notes up afterwards and give everyone a copy so that they would all know what they had agreed to do. They sat in the freezing cold breakfast room, a square unattractive place only marginally touched by the small smoky fire that sent all its heat up the chimney.

They were very businesslike, even though dressed in their outdoor clothes to keep warm: Kit in her navy duffel coat and white angora scarf; Clio in her grey flannel coat with its peach-coloured blouse showing at the neck – she had read that peach gave a good glow to the face – Anna in her tartan jacket; Patsy Hanley belted into her navy gaberdine coat that was too small for her and also not smart enough. She made a resolve to tell her mother that there was no point in being the daughter of the drapery if you ended up the least well-dressed girl in Lough Glass. Emmet in his thick wool polo-neck sweater and belted brown jacket. Michael Sullivan with his long dark hair below the collar of his grey overcoat. Not as good-looking as his elder brother, but one day, when the pimples were gone and his face and shoulders filled out, he might well turn into the same kind of heartbreaker.

The young people of Lough Glass determined that their New Year's Eve would be the kind of success they saw when they went to the pictures. The kind of happening that other people had and that they would have to create themselves if it were to come to Lough Glass.

Philip decided that he had to wear indoor clothes as some kind of act of faith in his hotel. It might be seen to be letting the side down if he too were dressed in a kind of lifeboatman's outfit that would make the place tolerable.

He was doing quite well as chairman . . . he seemed to know at the outset that he should never think of it as His hotel or His dinner dance, but as theirs.

'Have any of us ever been to anything up in the golf club?' he asked.

Nobody had. That was the first priority; they were to find out what aspects of the place had been good, and what had needed improvements. Everyone had a specific job to do. Even Patsy Hanley, whose mother wouldn't have been there – Philip was able to find her a responsibility.

Patsy was to discover what kind of facilities they had in the ladies cloakroom: were there mirrors, how many lavatories, did they hang their coats on a rail or did they have a lady who gave them cloakroom tickets? Would it be better to use one of the Hotel bedrooms for this purpose? Patsy was to come back with her report on Sunday afternoon.

'How will I find it all out?' she asked.

'Research,' Philip said.

'You'd be in the way of asking people things. You're good at chatting to people,' Emmet said. He noticed Anna Kelly jerk up her head as he did so. Then Emmet himself would be in charge of what the gentlemen would require. He would ask his father and Dr Kelly and Father Baily and anyone who went to the Golf Club.

Clio was going to come back with her ideas on decoration. It was very important, the first look of a place. Her ideas would be put to the group and they would vote on what they could do and what might be beyond them. Clio was flattered that people thought her ideas might be beyond them. She made up her mind to look at magazines and study the thing properly.

Michael Sullivan and Kevin Wall were deputed to find out how the front of the hotel could be altered so that it looked more splendid. Michael, because the garage had improved its appearance and secured troughs of plants and flowers to smarten it up; Kevin because his brother was a jobbing builder, and the materials would naturally be bought from Wall's. They were to come back with an estimate.

Anna Kelly was to concentrate on curtains and lighting. Hers were to be practical suggestions, the matter of image was left to Clio. 'How will I know what we should do with curtains until I know what the artistic designer has dreamed up for the whole hotel?' Anna was being heavily sarcastic.

Philip didn't appear to see it. 'Ah, but that's the hard part, Anna. Whatever you come up with will have to be sheer genius, there's no question of there being any money to coordinate anything with anything else ... you're on your own.' Anna seemed pleased by this.

Kit looked at Philip with admiration. He did seem to have the thing under control, and he was far more diplomatic than she would ever have believed. 'What will I do?' she heard herself asking, almost too eagerly. After all, she had been the moving force behind it. 'Will I just keep the notes?'

'Kit and I will do the food,' Philip said. 'We are the trained folk, after all, and we want them to have a meal they'll never forget.'

'They'll never forget the night, anyway,' Kevin Wall said. 'Most of them will be taken to the county hospital with frostbite.'

'My father's going to tell us by Sunday just how much he can afford to spend on storage heaters and radiators.' Philip was unperturbed. 'Will we meet here at three o'clock?'

And they went their ways, each with a dream. Clio, with great relief that motherhood did not seem to be imminent, was in high good humour. She thought about the New Year's Eve dance. She would see that at least one of the Central's terrifyingly plain rooms would be properly done up, one that would be away from prying eyes.

Patsy Hanley left happy. Emmet McMahon had made much of her in front of that stuck-up Anna Kelly.

Kevin Wall and Michael Sullivan wouldn't have admitted it to anyone, but they were flattered to be part of something new. It hadn't been long ago since they were regarded as the young thugs that would have to be kept away from any function rather than invited in to help run it.

Philip was pleased with how it had gone. They were all offering to help. If it failed it would be a group failure, and Kit in particular would be at his side, win or lose.

Emmet McMahon knew that this dance would be the great opportunity to let Anna Kelly come back to him on his terms in his own town.

Kit McMahon and Anna Kelly looked over at the garage where Stevie was talking to a client. Neither of them would interrupt him during working hours. Both of them had huge hopes of him when the dance came to town on New Year's Eve.

*

Lena did not know how she had managed to survive the days after Ivy's wedding. How had she gone on acting normally to everyone? Someone had told her that chickens did this; if you cut off their heads they still ran around for a while, just as if they still had a head and everything was normal. Nobody said what happened then. They probably just fell over and died.

There had been so many discoveries in the past week. Things she had not set out to discover. And did not want to know. She knew that he must be about to leave the Dryden. That he was going to leave her and go far away. Sometimes she suspected that he was going to Ireland. He came in so rarely, often to pick up mail which had suddenly started arriving at the flat rather than at the hotel. She never remembered him getting any letters at home before. There were references to Ireland in the conversation. Not the Ireland of long ago that they knew . . . but today's Ireland. He never stayed the night. She never asked for details of functions or late shifts. It was as if they were both waiting. Waiting for the day when he would tell her.

Lena felt very frail, the thread that was holding her together was so fragile it could easily break. When she saw the envelope from Kit so soon after she had written, her heart turned over with fear. Please may her daughter not say anything scathing to her. Not just now, not at this point. Please may Kit not write dismissively about her long and now much regretted letter describing Ivy's wedding. Suppose Kit were to say that she did not wish to hear tittle-tattle about these people she didn't know. Suppose Kit wrote to say that she wanted no more letters, that she wanted to snap the lifeline that was all Lena had.

Please, God ... Lena said as she opened the envelope.

She realised it was a long time since she had asked a God for something. Why should it work now?

> Dear Lena,
>
> That sounds a great wedding. It was like seeing a film, I could imagine everyone, especially the terrible Best Man.
>
> I realise how much I have missed your letters from the time when you were just Lena, my mother's friend. And I missed writing to you, though these days there's hardly time to breathe, let alone write. You'll never believe what we're going to do, sit down before you read this ... we're going to try and have a glittering fabulous New Year's Gala at O'Brien's hotel ...

Hardly daring to believe her luck Lena read with shining eyes the tale of the hotel's transformation and the committee hard at work.

> Even Clio is taking part, Kit wrote, it's only because these terrible O'Connors that she is so taken with are going to be there. She thought they were going to be in London and miss it but once the almighty Michael said he was going to be present then it all had Clio's blessing.

Lena hugged herself and laughed aloud to read this. She could hear Kit's voice ... just as she had been at nine, ten, eleven, twelve ... always complaining about Clio's airs and graces, and yet always involved with her as well. The letter sparkled with life and enthusiasm. In the last paragraph it changed its tone.

> You didn't mention that Louis was at the wedding. Don't feel that he can't be mentioned or anything, I wouldn't want you to think that he has to be cut out of what you tell me.

It ended, 'Warmest wishes always, Kit.'

She *couldn't* tell Kit about Louis. All she had left in the world was Kit, and Lena was going to be some kind of person in the girl's eyes, not a worn-out, thrown-aside fool, which was actually what she was.

She read over and over and over her daughter's plans for the hotel. Some of them ludicrous, some of them well within anyone's power. She wondered how much money she had: she would love to have invested it there and then in a refurbishment programme for the Central Hotel, Lough Glass. After all, hotels were doing very well in Ireland. Their time was coming.

Lena had reason to know this very well.

*

'We'll have to come home again next weekend,' Kit told Philip.

'I can't ask you all to do that.'

'It's only Clio and myself. The others are there already.' They sat companionably in the summer-house which they had agreed to paint and surround with fairy lights for the occasion.

'Well, it's taking you away from whatever keeps you both in Dublin.' He was a bit different. He was so much nicer than when he had assumed that they were like foreign princes and princesses, promised to each other from birth.

'Oh, better for Clio to come home, let me tell you. That eejit she is stuck on values her much more when she makes a move out of Dublin instead of waiting on his every move.'

'And what about you?'

'I told you. I have no romances. Hand on heart, there's nothing to keep me in Dublin.'

And she spoke the truth. Stevie Sullivan was home running his business every weekend. She made no move to contact him, but she was there like a sentinel in case he might make any step in the direction of Anna Kelly.

The O'Connor hotels all had a Christmas programme. It was becoming quite a smart thing for a family to go and stay in one of their hotels. Everything done for you, wonderful atmosphere, people said. Those who said it didn't have the *real* spirit of Christmas were almost always those who didn't have the money to afford it.

'Will you be helping out at one of them?' Kit asked Kevin O'Connor.

'Jesus, no. I have enough work to do all term without taking that lot on in my holidays,' he said.

Again Kit wondered how two boys could have been brought up in such a way that they seemed to have no interest at all in what was after all going to be their inheritance.

'So where will it be then?'

'My sister in England has a new fellow, a fiancé I think ... Oh heavy, heavy secrecy ... but I gather the ring's being bought and we're all to go over there.'

'Is he English?'

'I don't know. I suppose so.' The O'Connors knew very little of each other's business.

'Do your father and mother approve?'

'I'd say they're so relieved that Mary Paula's getting hitched they don't care ...'

'I'm sure that's not so ...'

'But it is. She's getting very long in the tooth.'

'How old exactly?'

'Wait till I see. It's always a grey area, but she must be nearly thirty. We're the two youngest by a lot, Michael and I.'

'Little afterthoughts ... how sweet,' Kit said.

'Do you have a big family?'

'Just one brother.' Kit had told him before but he hadn't remembered.
'Oh, very posh. Like Protestants, small families.'
'Clio has only two in her family also.'
'Yea, Michael told me there's a really frightful sister.'
'She is a bit of a pain all right,' Kit agreed. 'Good-looking though. Do you like Mary Paula, the one in England?'
'I hardly remember her,' said Kevin O'Connor. 'She was okay, she always had friends round the place. I think she thought we were dead boring. She's only keen on us going over to England for this party so that she can field a team.'
'You're not all mad keen to go then, are you?'
'No. I'm not particularly. Why? Are you arranging another party?' He moved closer to her.
'In a way I am. It's going to be fabulous, we've taken over Philip's hotel. Everyone will stay there.'
'But that's in the arse end of the world.' His enthusiasm died.
'It's in my home town, and Clio's, and Stevie's and Philip's. It's a beautiful old Georgian house, not a big ugly modern concrete block. We're going to have a *fantastic* New Year there. I *was* going to ask you, but if you're so dismissive . . .'
'I'm not dismissive . . .' He was full of contrition now.
'Yes, well, maybe it's too late . . .'
'Will Michael be going . . . will there be a crowd from Dublin?'
'I've no idea whether Michael will be going or not; presumably if he answers Clio the way you answered me, he won't. But don't worry, we'll have plenty who will.'
'No, you got the wrong end of the stick . . .'
'Listen, our New Year's Eve dinner dance can well do without the O'Connor brothers . . . just know that . . .'
He blustered for a while then went away to make a phone call. Kit smiled to herself. She didn't even need to listen to know who he was calling and with what advice.
'Listen, Michael. Kevin here. Did Clio say anything to you about a big dance in this godforsaken place they live in? No? Well, ask her. And for God's sake be nice about it. Say you do want to go. We'll be staying in a hotel, it won't be like last time . . .' He paused. 'Mary Paula won't give a damn. We'll stay for New Year, that will be enough. Anyway, this will be a lot of fun.'

'We must get Spot Prizes,' Philip said to Kit.
'Of course we must. Let's ask Anna to collect them.'
'Why Anna?'
'She's good-looking, she's kind of charming. People won't say no to her.'
'You're good-looking, they wouldn't say no to you either,' he said.
'Jesus Christ. Philip, I've got enough to do . . . let Anna loose on them. Anyway she's there the whole time, I'm not. Make it a point of honour that

she gets a lot, say it out in front of everyone that she'll have a hard job extracting them. She'll kill herself.'

'You don't like her, do you?'

Kit looked at him thoughtfully. She must be careful not to let anyone get this idea. 'I'm still inclined to think of her as Clio's awful little sister at times. But usually I think she's terrific, that's why I suggested she'd be a good one to wheedle the prizes out of people.'

'Stevie Sullivan thinks she's the bee's knees,' Philip said.

'Go on, he's years older than she is.'

'That's what I hear, anyway,' Philip said. He looked like his mother when he spoke like that: prissy, mouth pursed, a real village gossip.

'I hear Stevie Sullivan fancies everything that moves,' she said. 'But let that not detain us. We have a banquet to organise.'

She took his arm companionably and Philip straightened up with pride. Everything was going his way at last. He had been right to take things slowly and not rush in foolishly. Here he was in Dublin with Kit's arm in his, making plans for his hotel, their hotel. It was exactly as he had hoped.

'The O'Connor boys will be coming down to stay over New Year, I gather.' Maura spoke in the very over-casual voice she used when she was anxious about something. She was standing at the door of Kit's bedroom.

'That's right, they're going to stay in the hotel. Quite a few from Dublin are coming: Philip's giving us a special price.'

'He should give it to you free after all you're doing.' Maura had seen the frenzied activity.

'It'll be great, everyone's really putting their hearts into it,' Kit said.

'The O'Connors?' Maura said.

'Yes?'

'Clio's going out with one of them, isn't she?'

'Oh you know Clio, half of Dublin admires her.'

'It's not just idle curiosity, Kit. I never ask you about your friends or Clio's.'

'You do ask about the O'Connors, though,' Kit said.

'Yes, that's perfectly true, I do. And I'll tell you why.' Maura's face had got a little pink. She stood in the doorway slightly at a loss.

'Oh come on in, Maura, sit down.' Kit moved her notes and folders from a chair to make room.

'In the olden days I used to know their father, and I never liked him, but that's not the reason. Poor Mildred O'Brien is like a wet week and look at how well Philip's turned out.'

'Yes, I know.' Kit waited.

'Well, I was in Dublin last week . . .'

'You didn't tell me . . .'

'I just went for an examination, tests . . .'

'Oh Maura!' Kit was stricken.

'No, please Kit. This is *why* I didn't tell you. I'm a middle-aged woman, all kinds of bits and parts of me aren't working any more. I thought it best to go quietly . . .'

'And what did they find?'

'They didn't find anything yet, and probably may not find anything at all . . . let me finish . . .'

'What were they looking for . . . ?'

'They were looking at my womb; I may have to have a hysterectomy. Apparently it's a great operation; you feel better than you ever felt after it, but it's a long way down the road. I didn't intend to tell you any of this, I haven't even told your father.'

'You must let us share, we're your family.'

'I know, and was ever anyone more grateful for the family they got than I am. But believe me that's not what I was going to say . . . you've wormed all this out of me. Now can I tell you what I wanted to?'

'Yes, go on . . .'

'When I was in Vincent's, it was just overnight you know, who did I meet but Francis O'Connor, the father of the twins.'

'Fingers? Was he in hospital?'

'Or visiting someone . . . Anyway, he was the last person I wanted to meet, I can tell you. And he was full of chat and wanting to take me off to the Shelbourne for coffee.'

'Well, look at the antics you get up to from your sickbed in Dublin.'

'I tried to get away from him but he insisted that we sit and have a chat over old times . . .'

'And?' Kit waited.

'And Kit . . . he's a very vulgar man, he always was and always will be . . . but he said, well he as good as said, he implied . . .' Kit waited. 'I can't remember his words exactly, I suppose I sort of deliberately didn't want to remember them, or to be talking to him at all, I had my own worries . . .' She paused.

'Poor Maura,' Kit said sympathetically.

'And he sort of said, he as good as said . . .'

'Oh come on, what did he say, Maura?'

It did the trick. It shocked Maura into saying something at last. 'He said his two sons were having their way with you and Clio, and they'd been invited down here for a week for more of it after Christmas, and he's very annoyed because he wanted them all to go to England to one of his other children who's just got engaged to someone, and is coming home to run one of his hotels . . .'

'He said *what*?'

Kit's face was white with rage. 'Now, Maura. I'm going to tell you something that will cheer you up greatly. I am a virgin, I have never been to bed with anybody, but if the survival of the human race depended on it I wouldn't go to bed with that great misshapen oaf, Kevin O'Connor.'

Maura was startled by the strength of Kit's reaction. 'I wish I hadn't said anything . . .' she began.

'Oh, but I'm glad you did, very glad.' Kit's eyes flashed with anger.

'Perhaps we should leave it . . .' Maura knew she had opened floodgates.

'No, I can't leave it. They made an undertaking, those disgusting creepy O'Connors. They signed a legal document promising not to tell any more of these lies, and now they've bloody broken it.'

'They signed a what?' Maura was horrified.

'I sent Kevin O'Connor a solicitor's letter because he imputed unchastity to a woman, and he apologised and his father did and they paid me compensation for the slight on my reputation, and for casting aspersions on my virtue and possibly minimising my marriage chances.'

Maura's eyes were wide in disbelief. 'Kit, you're making this up.'

'I'll show you the letter from Fingers,' she said smiling broadly.

'A solicitor's letter! You consulted a law firm?' Maura felt weak at the shock.

'Yes, well, to be strictly honest, it was Paddy Barry – you know Frankie's brother – but it was on real solicitor's paper and it looked legal . . . anyway it frightened them to death and they paid up.' Kit grinned with pleasure remembering it.

'You got a friend . . . a student . . . to demand money with menaces from the O'Connors. I can't believe I'm hearing this.'

'Look what he said . . . look what Kevin O'Connor said! He said I was anyone's, that I'd do it with anyone and I'd done it with him. He told his brother, he told Philip O'Brien, he could have taken an advertisement in the *Evening Herald* for all I know . . . and I'm meant to ignore that and say it's just his little way of having fun.'

Maura had never seen Kit so angry. 'No, of course not . . . but . . .'

'But nothing Maura . . . there are no buts in this . . . his father who paid out good money obviously thinks it's a tale worth telling and trots it out to my stepmother . . . after all his undertakings . . .' She looked very determined.

'What are you going to do?' Maura asked anxiously.

'I may ask my lawyer to remind him of his obligations,' Kit sounded lofty.

'You and your lawyer will get caught,' Maura warned.

'Right. I think you are right actually. I tell him I'm approaching him personally before placing it all in the hands of solicitors again.' Kit smiled at the challenge ahead. Her enthusiasm and sense of outrage was infectious.

Maura began to share it. 'I agree it is appalling that he should be allowed to say such things about you and Clio.' Maura's eyes met Kit's for a long moment.

'I'm fighting my own battles on this one Maura,' Kit said. 'Clio can fight hers.'

And Maura knew without having to be told that her sister's daughter would not be sending any solicitor's letters.

She marked the envelope *Strictly Confidential*.

Dear Mr O'Connor,

My solicitor would probably disapprove of my contacting you personally but I am doing so because of family connections. You will remember the letter you sent to me (copy enclosed) and the undertaking it contains. Unfortunately grave news has reached me that you spoke in the very terms that caused my having to seek legal redress in the first place, and you addressed these remarks to my stepmother, Mrs Maura McMahon (née Hayes).

I demand that you write a letter to my stepmother at once retracting every word that you said in this regard, and that you also give me your assurance that I do not have to have recourse to further legal action.

Normally I would have taken such action, but my friend Cliona Kelly is friendly with your son Michael, and I would not wish to make trouble between the families.

I look forward to hearing from you tomorrow,

Yours faithfully,

Mary Katherine McMahon

'Kevin?'

'Is that you, Pa?'

'Turn off that bloody rock and roll and you'd know who was on the phone. Do you do any work or do you just fill your head with that jungle music?'

'You don't often ring me, Pa,' Kevin said uneasily.

'No, is it any wonder? You know this girl Mary Katherine . . . ?'

'Who?'

'The McMahon girl from Lough Glass.'

'Kit, yes. What about her?'

'What about her, what about her? Didn't I have to pay out good money to shut her up when you said you'd ridden her more often than Roy Rogers rode Trigger . . . ?'

'Yes, but that's all over now, Pa. You know I told you there was a misunderstanding.'

'I tell you there was a misunderstanding . . . is she cracked, off her head or something . . . ?'

'No, she's not, she's terrific. Why do you ask?' There was a silence. 'What is it, Pa? We apologised, well, I apologised and you paid and Kit accepted it and that was that. And we're quite friendly now . . .'

'Yes. Right.' Fingers O'Connor saw that the blame must be entirely his. He had thought it would make that nice plump Maura Hayes more pliable. What a mistake it had been. 'And this girl and her friend . . . are they the half-wits you're going to cancel the whole arrangements for Christmas to go and see, down in Bally-mac-flash or whatever it's called?'

'Lough Glass, and it's only for the New Year. Ma told you. We'll be in London for Christmas.'

'I can't wait,' said his father and hung up.

*

'Kit, it's Maura. I can't talk long, I'm ringing from work.'

'Hello, Maura. Tell Stevie that the labourer is worthy of her hire, you're entitled to the odd phone call.'

'He's out of the office. Kit, I got the most extraordinary letter from Fingers O'Connor.'

Kit giggled. 'I thought you would. I got one too.'

'Kit you didn't, you didn't . . .'

'That's it, Maura, I didn't. And I'm damned if that madman of a son of his is going to say I did . . .'

'Clio?'

'Hello, Michael.'

'Can I come round and see you?'

'No, I've got loads to do. I'm trying to work out a plan for decorating a big barn of a room.'

'Is this down in the hotel in Lough Glass?'

'Yes, how did you know?' She had said nothing to Michael about it yet, she wanted to be sure it was going to work before she began to persuade him.

'Kevin told me, and my dad.'

'Yeah, it should be great.'

'Why didn't you ask me?' Michael was aggrieved.

'You're going to be away in England, staying with Mary Paula, remember?'

'I don't have to, Kevin's not going.'

'Well, then.'

'Well, what? Why didn't you ask me?'

'You didn't seem to rate Lough Glass very highly when you were there last.'

'That's because everything went wrong and your sister was behaving like an alsatian with distemper.'

Clio laughed. 'That's good. I'll remember that.'

'Can I come then? To Lough Glass?'

'I'd love it if you would. I didn't want you to be bored, that's all.'

'And Clio, another thing . . . you know Kit?'

'Of course I do. I've known her since I was six months old.'

'I might not have been right about her and Kevin being at it like knives.'

'I know you weren't right.'

'Maybe we'd better not say that she was, you know?'

'I never said she was. Jesus, you didn't say it, did you?'

'This is becoming more like a police state,' said Michael.

Peter Kelly and Martin were in Paddles' bar.

'I see that Fingers O'Connor has bought a new hotel . . . that'll be his fifth,' Dr Kelly said.

'I wonder how he got a name like that.' Martin McMahon was thoughtful.

'It's not a good one for a businessman, sounds as if he's into shady deals.'

'But these names stick. Do you remember Arse Armstrong?'

They laughed like boys.

'Where is he now? Didn't he join the priesthood?'

'Oh I think Arse is a bishop or something out in Africa. Maybe he wears a long white frock. You wouldn't know the reason for the nickname.'

'Well, however Fingers got the name, it seems that everything he touches turns to gold. Our Clio seems very friendly with his son. We haven't met him yet, but apparently he's coming down here for all the Versailles Ball activity up in Dan O'Brien's.'

Martin McMahon smiled. 'Isn't it great that they all come home and seem so wrapped up in it? Our house is draped high and low in recipes and table decorations . . .'

'You're lucky, we have branches of trees in ours,' said Peter Kelly.

'God, what's that for?'

'Search me. *Decor* is the word Clio uses. Still, I'm happy she's not gone gallivanting with young O'Connor. Maura always gives me the impression that the father was a bit wild and his sons could be the same.'

'Ah, Clio's well able to look after herself,' said Martin McMahon.

'I hope so. God, it's one thing I couldn't bear, some fellow taking advantage of one of my girls. I'd kill them, you know, not that I'm a violent man.'

'When am I going to see you, Kit?'

'Well, Stevie, aren't you looking at me now?'

'I am for two minutes, then you'll be off down to your committee meeting in Dan O'Brien's mausoleum.'

'Never to be called that again . . . all is changed, changed utterly.'

'That's not fair, I haven't read Yeats.'

'At least you knew it was Yeats.'

'So where'll we go and when?'

'You could take me out to dinner in the Castle Hotel.'

'You're joking!'

'I'll pay for myself.'

'It's not the money. What would we want to go to the Castle Hotel for?'

'To see what competition we have.'

'But that's ludicrous. It's an ordinary Saturday night, it's not a New Year's Eve Ball, you'll not be comparing like with like.'

'I'd consider it research, Stevie . . .'

'Oh yeah?'

'And great fun . . .' She smiled up at him. 'I'll never forget how well you looked that night in Dublin.'

'You don't want me to put on a monkey suit?'

'No, but you're super when you're dressed up.'

'Will you dress up too? I haven't forgotten that nice backless number.'

'No, I haven't got any backless things down here, and anyway we don't want . . .' she paused.

'You're right, we don't want . . . but let's go there anyway. It's research, remember . . .'

'If we're caught . . .' Kit said.

'Yes, and we don't need to be.' They both recognised the need for their outings to be secret.

The committee meeting on Sunday went well.

Everyone had brought news of some sort. Kevin Wall and Michael Sullivan had technical details to blind everyone, but the estimates about the cost of labour were depressing.

'We can't afford that,' Philip said firmly.

'It's a pity, though, the front would look very well if we had all these shrubs in containers and a new sign painted.' Clio was keen that the place should not look like a hick town when the guests approached.

'We could plant things ourselves, I suppose,' Michael Sullivan suggested.

'In what?' they asked. They were not dismissive, they wanted to know.

'Barrels,' Michael Sullivan said.

And that was agreed. Everyone would get at least two barrels. They divided up the public houses between them so that the same people would not be asked over and over. This was regarded as men's work. They would dig shrubs and greenery from the lakeside.

'Are we allowed to?' Anna Kelly asked.

'We'll ask later,' Emmet said.

Clio had a friend who went to the College of Art: she could do a new sign. She would have to be paid for the materials. Kevin Wall said they could get the paint from the hardware shop. No one asked in too great detail how this would be negotiated with his father. They agreed that Kevin would deliver the paint to Clio's house and the friend would come down and paint it before Christmas.

Anna Kelly had drawings of the curtains. They would be looped back from the window and tied with red and white ribbons. Huge bunches of holly would be pinned to the ribbons. Anna said that the frames needed to be painted white. She would organise a painting team if there were volunteers. She had ideas for the lighting too, wine bottles with candles in them. They must be high on the mantelpieces in places where they couldn't be knocked over. Each bottle would have a spray of holly attached to it. The main centre lights should not be on at all; in fact, Philip should have the bulbs taken out of them in case they should be switched on accidentally.

Everyone was pleased with Anna's industry. Kit watched her accept the praise. She was strikingly pretty, much more glamorous than Clio. Kit must remember the way she looked at people, it was minx-like. She half looked and then looked away. It made her seem shy and vulnerable when in fact she was nothing of the sort. Kit noted every glance and filed it for further use.

Patsy Hanley had none of those skills but she read eagerly from her notebook that in a gathering where there might be sixty or more ladies, they would need at least five lavatories. This caused some gloom.

'You see, they'll all want to go at the same time,' Patsy explained. 'That's what I found out.'

'Why can't they go like everyone else, when it's time?' complained Kevin Wall.

'Because you can't have them hopping about holding on, it would spoil the atmosphere,' Patsy said.

'We're going to have to get new facilities some time,' Philip said. 'Leave that with me.'

'You'll never get your father to agree to five toilets in the next few weeks.' Kit was concerned.

'No, but that's my problem. Patsy's done the research, we're grateful for it.'

Emmet gave the good news that men were much less fussy. Two cabinets and a urinal would be fine. He also had learned that men loved a place where there could be pints as well, so maybe the bar would broaden itself out a bit for the night, and have a couple of extra barmen on there to serve ... the money would be taken in pints ... otherwise Emmet had learned they might all be slipping out to Paddles' or across to O'Shea's.

'They don't do that up in the club,' Clio said.

'No, that's because the club is as deserted as the bog of Allen,' Emmet said.

Anna Kelly looked at him admiringly. Emmet noticed and reddened with pleasure.

Clio spoke about the hotel's image. She was glad that the new sign had been agreed, and thought that some money might be diverted to have a light which would illuminate it.

'But doesn't everyone know where it is? It's not as if anyone would be looking for the Central,' Kevin said.

Philip agreed with Clio. 'It's a statement, isn't that what you mean?' he said.

'That's exactly what I mean.' Clio was mollified. She thought that a lot of the sombre, dark brown pictures in the halls should be replaced with garlands of Ivy. There were miles of it by the lake, nothing would make a better decoration. And that the guests should be greeted in the vestibule with a glass of warmed wine with cinnamon in it. Something to make them feel welcome.

'I hope I'm not venturing into Kit's territory here,' she said tentatively. 'I know you're in charge of food and drink ... but it is part of the image. The statement.'

'Perfect,' said Kit with gritted teeth.

And it was a good idea. In one stroke Clio had managed to conquer the very worst bits of the hotel, the ugly entrance way, the hideous sepia pictures in their ugly frames, and also give an illusion of warmth by offering a warm drink.

'And now the food.' Philip pointed at Kit.

She drew a deep breath. Her idea was to have a buffet. She knew it would meet with huge resistance from the diners and wanted to try it out on the audience here. It would be self-service where you could come back to the table again and have seconds or even third helpings. She showed them her costings. It would be less than for a traditional sit-down supper. For one thing you would save on waitresses. You wouldn't need as many experienced people to attend tables, and serve. Anyone could clear. 'Kids from the convent could clear,' she explained.

'Or from the Brothers,' Kevin Wall said.

'Yes, possibly.' Kit had her doubts.

She said that at a formal meal there would be soup or melon, and then always chicken and ham. There would have to be potatoes, gravy and two other vegetables, it would be a lot more work than preparing a buffet.

'But will they think they've had a dinner?' Emmet wanted to know.

'They'll have had three helpings, some of them,' Kit assured him.

'But suppose everything gets finished, suppose they all eat the chicken in wine sauce and no one eats the cold tongue, what then?' Patsy Hanley spoke with the intensity of someone who would never have eaten cold tongue but feared with her luck it might be all that was left on when her turn came.

Patiently Kit pleaded her case. As she had suspected they all objected. 'But that's what all the places in Dublin are beginning to do,' she said.

'It might be too Dublinish for people round here,' Anna said.

The others nodded; they were much more conservative around here than up in the capital city.

'They have it in the Castle Hotel,' Kit said.

'Are you sure?' Philip would be convinced by anything they did in the Castle Hotel.

'Yes, I was there last night,' she said. If she claimed to have visited the planet Mars they wouldn't have been more surprised.

'You never were.' Clio was green with envy.

'Yes, and they find it works very well. I was watching, it actually looked much more lavish than it is, if you know what I mean . . .' She was anxious to define how the buffet would work for them but they were looking at her open-mouthed.

'You went to dinner out in the Castle Hotel!' Philip said.

'Yes, to look,' Kit feigned surprise. 'We said we'd do research, didn't we?'

'Yes, but the cost of it.'

'It wasn't too bad. I didn't have anything to drink, that's where they make the profit. Oh, and coffee's extra. I didn't have any of that. They serve it in their drawing room, you see, to get you out of the place so that they can clear up.'

'You never went in by yourself and sat down to have dinner in the Castle Hotel.' Anna Kelly's eyes were narrow with suspicion.

Kit smiled at her. 'But look at all you've done, Anna. All those spot prizes you've been promised and all the bottles with the holly and candles.' Kit looked admiringly at the chianti bottle decorated as an example of how things could be done.

'How did you get out there?' Philip asked.

Kit caught Emmet's eye. He was even quicker than she had hoped. 'The point is, were they the kind of people who'd be coming here or were they lords and ladies and things?'

'They weren't lords and ladies. I talked to the waitresses. They were kind of middle-class people like the ones who'd be coming to our do.'

Philip was so pleased with her calling it Our Do that he forgot to worry about who had driven her the fifteen miles to the Castle Hotel.

'Let's make a list of their possible objections. Come on, everyone say what they think's wrong with a buffet and we'll see does it sound reasonable.'

As they began their list Kit glanced over at Emmet again. He was looking at her with awe. Things must be really moving if Kit and Stevie Sullivan had gone to the Castle Hotel. Soon Anna wasn't going to have a look-in. She would come back to him and everything would be the way it was.

'How are you, Martin?'

'Oh come in, Stevie.'

'No, I won't, I'm rushing. Listen, has Kit gone back yet?'

'No, she's going down on the six o'clock bus. Why, did you want to see her?'

'It's just that I have to take a car to Dublin, so I wondered did she want a lift.'

'Well, I'm sure she'd love it, you'll have a full car. Clio and Philip are going back too.'

'It's only a sports car, a two-seater. I thought I'd ask Kit since she was a neighbour's child.' His smile was winning. Maura was at the top of the stairs.

'I think they all travel as a team, Stevie. They're all so involved in this dinner dance they're organising.'

His eyes met Maura's. She knew exactly what he was offering. And on Kit's behalf she was refusing it. He was going to have to get Maura McMahon on his side.

It was a long journey back to Dublin. The bus to the town, the train to Kingsbridge station and then a bus back to O'Connell Bridge.

'Will we go and have chips?' Philip said hopefully.

'I'm too tired, Philip.' Kit looked tired and pale.

'Wouldn't it be great if we had a car?' he said.

'You will, one day. Wait till we make your hotel into the In Place in all of Ireland.'

He hated her calling it his hotel. It had been their place and their do earlier on. But he knew better than to give any hint of it. 'Kevin O'Connor's father's bought another place.'

'That's because his daughter's getting married. He's bought a hotel for her husband. It's like a game for him . . . they're not people we want to be like.'

Philip waved her goodbye as he got his bus one way and Kit ran lightly down O'Connell Street in the other direction.

Stevie Sullivan was parked outside her door in a small red sports car.

'I don't believe you,' she said.

'I got an urge for a Chinese meal. Come on, get in.' She got into the car and they drove to a restaurant.

'Aren't you very fussy about your food. Imagine a good ham sandwich in Lough Glass wouldn't do you.'

'Not a bit, I fancied sweet and sour chicken, and if you've been out with the lovely Kit McMahon in the Castle Hotel one night, you somehow want more of the same the next night.'

The Chinese restaurant was fairly basic and simple. Kit looked around her. 'Better not let them know in the Castle Hotel that you think this is more of the same,' she said.

'I want you, Kit,' he said.

'You can't have me, it's as simple as that.'

'That's very harsh.'

'The way you put it is harsh, and demanding also.' She realised she was speaking to him as a real person, there was no simpering and playacting involved.

'What way should it have been put?' He was being serious also. Not falsely flirtatious. Not the Stevie Sullivan she had watched for years around her home town.

'Well, it's a question of people wanting each other, isn't it? One doesn't say *I want you* implying *I mean to have you*, as if you were a cowboy taking your head of cattle, or your ranch, or your woman from the saloon ... that's not the way things should be done.'

'Okay, but I don't believe in a lot of fancy phrases either. I drove all the way up here to tell you that I want you, I want to be with you. I want to be with you properly, not just kissing and stroking each other in a car like last night.'

'Was it only last night? it seems ages ago.' She looked at him with surprise.

'Yes, it seems a lot longer to me too,' he said.

She lifted her eyes and looked at him. His face was absolutely sincere. She could see that. But then this was the whole secret of Stevie Sullivan's charm. Everyone thought he was utterly sincere. Anna Kelly, Deirdre Hanley, Orla Dillon, dozens and dozens more that she could name, hundreds that she had never heard of.

He probably was sincere at the time. He just wasn't exclusive. That was his winning streak. He meant it, he meant it with everybody.

'I didn't mean to feel this way,' he said to her.

'No,' she agreed.

'It isn't at all what I thought would happen.'

'No, indeed.'

'Kit, stop yessing and noing and three bags fulling. Do you feel the same or don't you?' He was angry.

'I'm very fond of you ...' she began.

'Fond!' he snorted.

'I was going to say unless I was very fond of you I wouldn't have been so warm and loving to you last night ...'

'I don't believe this,' he said.

'What don't you believe?'

'I don't believe you're sitting here cool as a cucumber explaining your behaviour, explaining it as if I were someone who had demanded an explanation. We held on to each other last night because we wanted to, and wanted to do a lot more. Why can't you be honest enough to admit it?' His eyes were hurt and his face very upset.

But then this must be new for him. Everyone else, including that little baby-face Anna still in her gym slip, had probably gone along with his line of persuasion so easily. It must be strange if you were the great Stevie Sullivan. It must be strange and unpleasant to find yourself refused. Especially if you have just driven up from Lough Glass to Dublin, overtaking the bus and the train and then to be refused. But refuse she would.

'Why are we fighting?' she asked him.

'Because you are being so prissy and dishonest.'

'Prissy maybe, it's just the way the words come out, but dishonest, no.'

'You sit there and say I mean nothing to you.'

'I didn't say that.'

'I've told you what I feel. I need you.'

'No, you don't.'

'Don't bloody tell me what I need and what I don't need.'

'I'm trying to say, without being cheap and vulgar, that anyone, just *anyone* would do.'

'And I'm trying not to sound cheap and vulgar either that you are a right prick tease.'

Her coat was on the back of her chair, Kit began to put her arms back into it. 'I'll go now, and let you finish your meal.' Her face was white. She was shaking with anger. At the words he had used, at the fact that she had let Emmet down – he would be back to Anna Kelly within twenty-four hours. And at the fact that she wanted him so much. She *did* need him. She would like nothing more than for him to go back with her to her little bedsitter tonight.

How had it all gone so terribly wrong?

He put his head in his hands. 'Don't go,' he mumbled.

'I'd better.' Her voice was shaky now and he looked up.

He saw her lip trembling and reached out his hand for hers. 'I'm very, very sorry. I wish more than anything I could have the last minute back so that I wouldn't say that. I'm so sorry.'

'It's all right, I know. I know.'

'No you don't know, Kit,' he said, and she saw he had tears in his eyes. 'You don't know. I've never felt like this before. I want you so much I can't bear it.' She looked at him, distressed. 'Listen. This is the worst thing that could have happened. I just meant to go to a dance with you, to have a little fling if you felt like it. I didn't mean all this.'

'All what?' She marvelled at how calm her voice was.

'All the way I feel. I suppose it's love, I haven't ever loved anyone before

. . . but I'm so eager to see you and to know what you'll say . . . and to touch you and see you laugh . . .' his words came tumbling out. 'Is that it, do you think?' he asked her.

'Is that what?'

'Is that love? I didn't love anyone up to now, so it's hard to recognise.'

'I don't know,' she said truthfully. 'If that's truly the way you feel then it might be.'

'And you?'

She had forgotten her coat now; now they talked as equals. 'I suppose it's the same, I didn't mean this to happen either. I thought, I thought . . .'

'What did you think? You started it, you asked me to the dance.'

'I know.' She was guilt-ridden. She could never tell him why she had done that. They were much too far in for that ever to come to the surface.

'So what did you hope? What did you think would happen?'

'That you'd be a nice man to join our party . . . which you certainly were . . . but I didn't expect that I'd get so close to you, so involved.'

'You won't say *love*.'

'I haven't loved anybody either,' she said. 'So I don't know.'

'Aren't we a real pair of cold zombies. Most people of our age have loved dozens of people.'

'Or what they say is love,' Kit said.

'Or what they think is love,' Stevie said. There was a silence. 'I'm sorry for what I said.' He spoke eventually.

'And I'm sorry for saying anyone would do; that was coarse.' She was apologetic.

'I'm not hungry any more.' He pushed his plate away.

'Me neither.'

He was cheery and apologetic to the Chinese waiter, who seemed impassive about the whole business.

'They must be mystified by us, coming from as far away as they do,' Kit said.

'Anyone would be mystified by us,' Stevie said. He helped her into the tiny, low car.

He dropped her at the door and leaned over to kiss her cheek. 'I'll see you again during the week, I hope.' He looked at her, his face a question.

'I'd love that if you're going to be up here again.'

'I'll be here tomorrow night, for example.'

Her voice was still shaky; she didn't know whether to make a little joke or not. 'Lord, you'll have the road worn out with all that travelling up and down.'

'I'm not going back tonight, I'll wait until tomorrow night.'

'And who'll mind the little shop?'

'Your stepmother. And we'll start with a clean slate tomorrow.' He looked like an eager nervous schoolboy. He reminded her of her brother Emmet when he was struggling and hoping that the right words would come out. Not like the great Stevie Sullivan.

'A shiny clean slate,' she said.

'I love you, Kit,' he said, and turned the car and was gone.

Kit lay awake all night. There was a church clock that struck every quarter of an hour. She wondered why it hadn't driven her mad before. She got up and made herself some tea. She looked around the room: small, untidy, but full of character, her good dresses hanging on hooks on the wall because the wardrobe wasn't big enough. Shelves of books, a little home-made desk with a small red lamp. She had blue and white pillow cases. It would have been a lovely warm friendly place to have brought Stevie Sullivan back for the night.

As the clock chimed on and Kit sat hugging her knees, she wondered why she had been so adamant. It wasn't such a big deal. She had been the one making it so. Look at Clio, the skies hadn't fallen on her. She sat there, confused and lonely. She wondered could she ever tell Lena about it. She might. Lena had been through all this kind of thing, she would know what it felt like.

*

Lena always organised the office party. That way she could keep control of it. It would be dangerous to leave it to one of the younger, giddier girls or even Jennifer. They would pick an entirely unsuitable place with a wrong atmosphere.

Lena always found a restaurant with atmosphere, somewhere that Italian, Greek or Spanish waiters could join in the fun but where there would be no silliness.

She had seen office parties go so wrong. She had heard stories from the girls who had moved on from perfectly satisfactory posts only because they had been compromised or done the wrong thing at the annual office party.

'Lord, I'm so sensible,' Lena said to Grace.

'You look too good to be sensible.' Lena looked at Grace's reflection in the mirror. They had been friends for too long to let Grace lie without being caught. The look of reproach was enough. Grace began to backtrack. 'Too thin of course, too tired, but still good.'

'I'm a scrawny old turkey, Grace. I used to see them in Lough Glass - they were survivors. They looked so woebegone and bedraggled at Christmas no one would kill them. They escaped the oven year after year.'

'So will you,' Grace said tenderly.

'Not this year. No, the time comes for every old turkey, even if the bones only make soup.'

'Will you and Louis join us for Christmas dinner?' Ivy asked her on the stairs.

'You're very good, Ivy.'

'That means no.' Ivy looked at her shrewdly.

'Why do you say that?'

'Because I know you so well.'

'It doesn't mean no, it means I don't know.' There was a silence. 'It sounds very rude.'

'No, love, it sounds very sad.'

'That's exactly what it is, Ivy, very sad.' Lena walked up the stairs with a heavy tread.

Jessie Millar was spending the evening with her mother. Every Thursday she went around to Mrs Park while Jim went to the Rotary Club. Every weekend they took her mother out to Sunday lunch.

Jessie's life had changed in so many ways for the better the day that Lena Gray had walked in her door. She would do anything to help Lena through what was obviously some huge crisis. But Lena was so private she would freeze you out if you dared suggest that anything was wrong.

'I suppose it's her husband,' Jessie said to her mother.

'It usually is,' Mrs Park nodded sagely.

'I have to do something. I have to tell her that I'd do anything.'

'Well, if it is her husband, what could you do, Jessica? Go and meet him and say "You're upsetting Mrs Gray, desist this minute"?'

'No, but I could give her some comfort.'

Mrs Park shook her head. 'You could only tell her you were sorry for her. She's a proud, confident woman, she wouldn't want that.'

'She comes to see you from time to time, do you get any hint of anything . . . ?'

The old woman was thoughtful. It was true that Lena Gray found time to call and see her at least once a month. She always brought some small useful gift, an airtight biscuit tin, a foot cushion, a cover for the *Radio Times*. It was amazing that such a busy career woman as Lena should make the time to visit her. But then Mrs Park remembered that when she was young they used to say if you want something done ask a busy man. Woman, in this case.

'She never talks about herself at all,' Mrs Park said eventually.

'I know, but what do you think?'

'I think she has children, grown up children of her own from a previous marriage.'

'Oh, that couldn't be possible,' Jessie said.

'Why not?'

'Well, if she has, where are they? No normal woman would have children and leave them.'

'I wish it was an office lunch, not a dinner,' Jennifer complained.

'The lunch would go on all day . . .' Jessie said.

'Yes, I know. Wouldn't it be marvellous, everyone going mad, and we'd get to know other tables having lunch . . .'

That was exactly what Lena had been trying to avoid, Jessie realised. At least at a dinner there was some end to the evening. People had to go for trains and buses. They weren't left high and dry and drunk at five o'clock waiting for the pubs to open and to carry on the foolishness.

'We're lucky we don't have to pay for our party,' squeaked the new receptionist. 'In the last place we all had to contribute.'

'Lena set that up years ago when she first came. She was always making little savings on this and that in a tin called Office Party.' Jessie remembered it with affection.

'Has she been here for years and years?' asked the receptionist.

'Eight or nine years, that's all. But of course I can hardly remember what it was like before she came.'

'So you never knew her when she was young?' Jennifer said.

'Not really young, no.' Jessie shifted on her feet, annoyed by the dismissive ways of youth.

'I'd say she was a stunner,' Jennifer said. 'She must have been to get that dream boat she married.'

Jessie felt they were on dangerous ground now and wanted to move.

'Yes, I'm sure she had the pick of the bunch,' she said, in a tone that was bringing the conversation to an end.

'We can't persuade you to change your mind, Louis?' James Williams said.

'No, James. Many, many thanks for everything. I came here with nothing nearly a decade ago and I have the world at my feet now.'

'The Dryden didn't give you that. You built it yourself. We'll be very sorry to lose you.'

'Well, you know I'll see you over the season. I won't be off until we've New Year's Eve well over us.'

'That's good of you, that's certainly a relief.'

'Come on, I wouldn't do that to you.'

'And I imagine Lena is delighted to be going back to Ireland . . . I think her heart was always there despite her great success here.' The enquiry was made with a bland face and innocent eyes.

Louis Gray took a deep breath. 'Ah James, now there's something I have to tell you about that . . .'

For weeks she had taken work home and listened for his key in the door. At the sound she would slip off her glasses, which made her older than ever, and sweep away the paperwork from evidence. She would get up to greet him, fresh and fragrant as she always was. Sometimes she would suggest he had a bath and that she'd bring him a drink.

She never asked where he had been or why he was so late. She knew that he would tell her one evening. Some warning had told her it would be tonight.

Habits die hard. She put on her best cream blouse and her pencil slim red skirt. She put a red glass necklace around her throat and then replaced it with a red scarf. The scarf hid more of the lines, and anyway, the red necklace had been bought in Brighton when he had said that one day he would buy her rubies.

She sat at her table for three hours.

But her eyes were too tired and her head too heavy to concentrate on any of the work she had brought home. Instead she waited and waited for the sound of his step on the stair. She had a bottle of wine in the fridge, and she had coffee at the ready. This was going to be a long night, they would need both.

When he came in she stood up. Her feet seemed stuck to the ground, she didn't go towards him as she normally did. Instead her hand flew to her throat and fiddled with the red scarf.

'I'm sorry I'm late,' he said.

It had become an automatic greeting. Usually she said, 'Well it's great to see you now.' Tonight she said nothing. She just looked at him, She knew her eyes were wide and staring as if she had never seen him before. She tried to relax the muscles of her face, but nothing would obey her.

'Lena,' he said. She still looked. 'Lena, I have something to tell you.'

Ivy and Ernest were looking at television downstairs, but Ivy's glance always went to her net-curtained door to see who went in and out. It was a habit that she could not give up, even nowadays when her tenants were respectable settled people who would not do a moonlight flit.

She saw Louis Gray come home, late as usual. But tonight he had paused on the stairs, where he thought he was unobserved. She saw him take deep breaths like someone gasping for oxygen. Then, as if he were still unable to catch enough air, he sat down on the step and let his head drop down to his feet. He must be feeling faint, she thought. Her instinct was to go out to see what was wrong. Perhaps he had been taken ill.

But then she remembered the cold, dead look in Lena's face earlier in the day. This was the end of the road for them, Ivy knew it now. Eventually Louis recovered himself and went on up the stairs. Ernest was happily looking at the television set.

'I'll get you a cup of tea,' Ivy said. She was restless now; she couldn't concentrate.

'God, it's great to be spoiled,' Ernest said.

It only seemed such a short time since Ivy had envied the young couple upstairs, the handsome young husband and wife who couldn't wait to get their hands on each other. She felt life had passed her by, and she felt foolish and dull in the light of their passion and love. Now she ached to give Lena, who had been such a good friend, a share of the peace and security she had with the man she had always loved.

She sat at the table. He had guided her there with his arms on her shoulders. She fought the urge to hold on to him and plead, assure him that it didn't matter, he could have this other woman, whoever she was. Even if she was Irish and he had been looking at a hotel in Ireland with her. He could continue seeing her as much as he liked just as long as he didn't leave home, didn't leave Lena, his wife. Because she was his wife. He had said so over and over.

In everyone's eyes they were man and wife. So that is what they were. But the words didn't come. She sat and waited.

'I never wanted this to happen, Lena,' he said.

She smiled at him, a vague half-smile, like the one she used when she was at work. All it involved was a small readjustment of the muscles. She wondered why people didn't teach it at school. It made you look such a good listener, alert, interested, receptive.

'We have always been utterly honest with each other.' He reached for her hand. Her hand was cold, but so was his. It must be taking something from him too.

'Yes, of course,' she said.

What did she *mean* by this? Honest with each other, of course they hadn't. He had betrayed her with who knew how many women. He had told her lie after lie about his activities. She had lied to him about Kit and the lifeline she had established to her daughter and the life of Lough Glass. And yet they sat in a flat in west London and pretended that they had always been honest with each other.

'So, because of that I have to tell you . . . that I've found somebody else. Somebody I really love.'

'But you really love me,' she said in a small voice.

'I know, I know. Lena, what I have for you is something special that will never change.'

'We've loved each other all our lives,' she said. It was not argumentative, or defensive. She was just stating a fact.

'That's what I'm saying. Nobody could or indeed will replace what you and I had. It was strong and good and important.'

She looked at him. These were mere lines he had learned for a play.

'But . . . ?' she said, helping him on to the next bit.

'But . . . I've met this girl . . .' The silence must have only been for a few seconds. But after what seemed a long time he said '. . . I didn't want it to happen, I wanted us to go on the way we were . . . but you don't know when these things happen, you don't invite them in, they just . . .' He was at a loss for words.

'Happen?' suggested Lena. She was not being ironic. She just wanted it to get to the bit where he said he was leaving. All the rest of it was unnecessary torture.

'Happen . . .' he repeated, unaware he had used the word so often himself. 'And in the beginning it was just a bit of fun . . . you know, harmless . . . and then we knew . . . we knew that this was meant to be.'

'Meant to be . . .' she repeated his words again, without any intonation except that of someone trying to grasp their importance.

'Yes, she never really loved anyone before . . . and she took some time to realise that it was . . .'

'And you, Louis?'

'Well, I had and did so it was both easier for me and more difficult, if you know what I mean . . .' She nodded dumbly.

'So?' said Lena.

'So, it developed, and we got further into it and it got to the stage where it was too late to go back . . .'

'Too late?'

'Yes, we both know now that this is what we want . . . and what we must take. She had no one to tell but her parents . . . I have to tell you.'

She looked at his face, sad to be causing such hurt to another. His handsome, loved face. And suddenly she knew why he was telling her, why he wasn't just rushing off and coming back to be forgiven when it didn't work out. The realisation went right through her body causing her to shake.

'She's pregnant, isn't she?'

'Well, this was something . . . something that we are both very glad about now.'

His chin was up, he was defiant. He was challenging her to say anything that might diminish his love.

'You're glad?' She was holding her throat.

'We're very proud and happy. I always wanted a child . . . Lena, you've had children. You know what it's like to have been there, seen a young person who is part of you . . . a new generation. I'm getting old, I want a son . . . or a daughter. I want to settle down, be someone in my own land instead of always on the run. You know that. You and I always felt that.'

Her head felt very clear suddenly, like a fog lifting. She looked at him in disbelief. What was she meant to know, what were he and she meant to be agreeing? That she had left her husband and children for him, her children who she loved and missed every day of those years. She had been pregnant with his child and lost it. She had wanted another child: Louis had said the time was wrong.

Now that her childbearing years were over he had discovered that he wanted to be a father. And he expected her to understand all this. Possibly even be glad for him. Louis Gray must be a man without any sensitivity at all. He must be lacking in any real brain as well. Perhaps he was a bit simple. Maybe that lopsided smile and those deep eyes were empty, meaningless things, not an indication of a loving soul.

Could it be true that he was only a shell and she hadn't seen it until now?

'Say something please, Lena, say something.' His voice seemed very far away.

'What would you like me to say?'

'I suppose, impossible though it is, I'd like you to say that you understand.'

'That I understand?'

'And that you forgive me, even.'

She still felt this strange clearness, and the very odd sensation that she was looking at him through the wrong end of a telescope, that he was miles away, and that his voice was far off.

'Very well,' she said.

'What?'

'That's what I'll say.'

'You'll say what?'

'What you'd like me to say. I understand what has happened, and I forgive you.'

'But you don't mean that. You don't really, you're only saying what I asked you to.'

'Come now, you can't have everything. How do we know what people mean? You said this morning as you were leaving, "Love you". You said that to me this morning. And you didn't mean it.' She was quite calm.

'But I did in a way.'

Yes, in a way he had meant it. 'So maybe I mean this in a way.'

'But, Lena, you do realise it's over between us? I mean, I told Mary Paula, I told her I was telling you tonight. We're getting married in the New Year.'

'Married?' she said.

'Yes, here in London. I've had to get a letter of freedom, would you believe, from a priest.'

'A letter of freedom?'

'You know, to say that I haven't been married to anyone else.'

'Imagine,' she said.

'Are you all right, Lena?'

'Yes. What did you say her name was?'

'Mary Paula O'Connor. Her father's a hotelier. They're opening a new place in Ireland. I'm going to manage it.'

'Mary Paula O'Connor? Daughter of Fingers O'Connor?'

'Yes, I didn't think you'd have heard of him.'

'And will his family all be coming over for the wedding?'

'They're coming this Christmas.' He was at perfect ease telling her these facts of his new life. Was he mad, clinically mad? That he didn't realise that he was speaking of the ruined splinters of her life.

'And are you going tonight?'

'Once we've talked.'

'We've talked, haven't we?' She was polite and distant.

'But I won't be back. You know sometimes in the past I went and came back . . . ?'

'Did you?'

'You know I did. I want it to be clear now how sad I am to stand here and tell you this . . . you've been so good, so understanding, and in many ways you gave up so much for me . . .'

'We gave up things for each other, didn't we?' She was bright and helpful.

'Yes we did, that's true.'

It was *not* true, Lena wanted to roar at him. Louis Gray had given up nothing. He had come to her when he was penniless, alone in the world, and had run through all his other options. How *dare* he end what they had in this welter of invention.

'So I suppose you'd better pack.'

'I don't think . . .'

'Or would you prefer to come back tomorrow and take things when I'm at work?'

'Wouldn't that be better . . . then you could sort of . . .'

'Sort of what?'

'Well, lay out what you want rid of and what you want to keep.'

'Well, I would imagine you'll take your clothes and things. I mean I wouldn't want those.'

'I'll leave all the things we got together, like pictures and books and bits of furniture.'

'Yes, I don't imagine you'd want those.'

'And of course I'll leave you the car.'

'No, I gave you the car as a present, Louis.'

'It's an office car.'

'No, I bought it for you.'

There were tears in his eyes. 'You must keep it.'

'No, truly. I walk to work.'

There was a silence. 'And I'll leave the key here,' he said. 'When I'm going.'

'Or you could leave it with Ivy.'

'No, that would mean explaining.'

'Well, someone will have to explain to Ivy. She'd like to say goodbye, she's very fond of you.'

'I think it would be best if I left it on the mantelpiece.'

'Well, you must do what you think . . .'

'I can't just go like this.'

'Why not?'

'We haven't talked anything out . . . explained.'

'We have.'

He was about to say more, she knew his face so well. He wanted to ask her to reassure him, tell him that she didn't think too badly of him, say that it had been great while it lasted, that she had found someone she loved too, that she was going to move to a new city, a new life . . . But he said nothing.

'I hope you'll be . . .' he stopped.

'I hope so too,' she said, agreeing with him.

He walked out the door.

She stared in front of her for a long time. What she hoped was that she would be dead by the time that Louis Gray married Mary Paula O'Connor, the girlfriend who was going to have his son.

Ivy saw Louis Gray leaving. His face was white and stained with tears.

She didn't sleep well, thinking of the woman upstairs. No matter how many times she told herself that she should go up to Lena she always answered herself with the fact that Lena Gray had survived on being able to put a brave face on things. It was up to Lena, and only her, when she let that face drop.

There was a letter from Kit next day.

Ivy was pleased. This meant she had an excuse to intercept Lena on the way out. The woman's face shocked her. It was as if someone had reached in and taken the life out of it.

'Thanks, Ivy.' Lena put the letter in her handbag. Even her voice was dead.

'You know where I am,' Ivy said.

'Indeed I do.'

Ivy stood at the door and watched her go up the street. There was no life in her step. She stopped at the traffic lights and leaned her head against the lamp post.

In the office there was the usual excitement on the day of the office party. People had brought in clothes to dress up in after work.

'I'm going to have a big lunch this time,' Jennifer confided. 'There was that year I got a bit tiddly and silly. This time I'm going to lay down a base for all that wine.'

'Good idea,' Lena nodded approvingly.

'A Mr James Williams left a message asking you to ring him, Mrs Gray.'

'Thank you,' said Lena.

'My mother sent you her love, I was there last night,' Jessie said.

'That's very kind of her. Is she keeping well?'

All the answers were adequate, but they were lifeless. By lunchtime everyone in the office had decided that Mrs Gray was sickening for flu. There had been a lot of it going about.

'It would be a shame if she missed the party,' Jennifer said.

Last year Louis Gray had turned up to collect her. He had only stayed five minutes, but long enough to make everyone feel they wished they knew him better.

She worked alone all morning, wanting no calls, no interruptions.

The receptionist came into her office. 'Mr Williams phoned again. I told him that I had given you the message. Was that right?'

'Absolutely. Thank you, dear.' It was a pleasant remark, but dismissing her.

'They're wondering are you ill, Mrs Gray,' the girl said suddenly.

'I don't know. I *hope* not, thank you for asking.' Her smile was strained.

Then there was a phone call from Ivy. There were some names that always got through to Mrs Gray; this was one. 'Lena, it's only Ivy. Sorry to interrupt, but just thought I'd tell you that Mr Tyrone has been and gone, in case you wanted to rest your weary head or anything.'

'Oh, thank you, Ivy. You must be psychic. I've got a load of stuff to finish up here, but I might well do that in the mid-afternoon.'

'Give you a bit of energy for your office party.'

'I think I'm coming down with a flu thing. I might have to cry off that.'

'I'll put a hot water bottle in your bed around four o'clock.'

'Bless you, Ivy.'

'And you, dear Lena.'

She sent out for some Beechams Powders and asked for a mug of tea and a lemon drink.

'Anything to eat at all?' Jennifer was very sympathetic.

'No, but be a dear and try and keep people away from me. I'm trying hard to get through all this in case I have to take a couple of days off with flu.'

Jennifer seemed relieved that there was some physical explanation. She had looked at Lena several times that day and thought that her face was so drawn and abstracted that Mrs Gray might be about to have some kind of mental breakdown. It was great to think it might only be flu.

She was very methodical. In her clear handwriting she attached a note to every one of the files that had to be dealt with. Here she suggested a letter offering a sizeable reduction in consultancy fees to one client who was a good friend of the agency; there she suggested no allowances at all to another who was a late payer. She arranged that they cancelled every one of her own public appearances and lectures for the next two months. There were reminders and notes from her own diary. Bills that should be paid, Christmas gifts that had been given in the past and would be expected now.

Then she dictated a long memo to Jessie incorporating a lot of what she had done.

About three o'clock she came and told them that she had been trying to fight it but she had to give in now to what seemed like a bad flu germ. 'I'll keep away from you all in the hopes of not spreading it any further,' she said.

They all tut-tutted and said she looked dreadful.

'Shall I come round and see you'll be all right?' Jessie asked.

'No, no. I'll be well looked after.'

They saw the elegant Mrs Gray, whose eyes were blurred and hollowed. None of them had ever remembered her taking a day off work in all their time there. It was such a pity that she would miss the party.

Lena was well known in the bank. 'Sorry for leaving it towards closing time,' she said to the young manager.

'Good customers like you are allowed all kinds of leniencies,' he said.

'Right, I'd like to take up a little of your time. You see, I'm going away for a few weeks, I need to withdraw quite an amount of cash from my own account for myself.'

'There's no problem there, Mrs Gray.'

'And I want to leave instructions that I won't be countersigning cheques for the office for the next few weeks.'

'Mr and Mrs Millar will be the only signatories needed.'

'I have typed you a letter to that effect.'

'Always efficient,' he murmured admiringly.

'Yes, I hope so, but on this occasion I haven't yet informed Mr and Mrs Millar of my intention to take some time off because I don't know how much time it might take me ... to get well ...'

'Are you going to have an operation?'

'No, no. Just an illness I have to shake off. So I want everything to go smoothly in my absence.'

'Certainly ... I quite understand.' He didn't understand anything at all, but he knew the woman who had been running that agency almost single-handed was giving him some kind of message. She was trying to tell him that she would be back at the helm sometime, and that he wasn't to give the Millars their head to run the agency into the ground.

A very complicated request for a banker.

It was good to see women doing so well but they were, no matter what anyone said, hard to understand.

'I suppose you're not in a drinking mood.' Ivy looked hopeful.

'Not a chance, Ivy. But come up and talk to me for a bit, will you?'

They went into the flat and Lena looked at the mantelpiece. There was the key in a little glass dish. The dish was new. It was good too, cut glass, probably one of the only presents he had ever bought for her. Beside it was a card. A plain white card with the words *Thank you* written on it.

She tore the card in two, and gave the dish to Ivy. 'Would you like that?'

'I can't take that.'

'It's you or the dustbin.'

'Well, it's a nice thing, sure I'll have it. I'll leave it downstairs till you want it back.'

'That'll be a time,' Lena said. She opened the wardrobe and took out her two suitcases.

'Lena, no. Not you too,' Ivy cried.

'Just for a while. I'll be back, Louis won't.'

'Of course he will. He always comes back.'

'No.'

'Don't go. Where are you going anyway just before Christmas? You haven't any friends anywhere. Stay with me, stay here.'

'I'll be back, I swear.'

'I need you at Christmas. Ernest and I need you.'

'No, you're just afraid I'll kill myself. I did think of it last night, but I'm through that now. I won't.'

'One day you'll look back on this . . .' Ivy began.

'I know.' She was folding her clothes neatly and putting her shoes into bags. Years of taking short trips to give talks and lectures had made packing second nature.

'Where are you going?'

'I don't know.'

'You wouldn't let *me* walk out saying I didn't know where I was going. Come on, be fair, why should I let you?'

'I'll ring you.'

'When? Tonight?'

'No, in a few days.'

'I'm not letting you go.'

'Ivy, you mean well, but . . .'

'Don't but Ivy me . . . See how bloody good I am! I'm not asking you one question about your private life, I didn't come upstairs last night after he left, even though I saw him go. You'll never have such a friend as me anywhere, don't throw it back in my face.'

'I'll ring you tonight.'

'And give me an answer about where you're staying?'

'I swear.'

'All right, you can go then.'

'Why aren't you begging me to stay?'

'You need to be out of these four walls . . . they still have Louis' memory written over them. If I knew when you were coming back I'd repaper the rooms.'

Lena managed a weak smile. 'No need to go that far.'

'I would if I thought he really wasn't coming back. I don't want him to come and put his imprint on a whole new set of wallpaper.'

'No. Truly, he's getting married.'

Ivy didn't dare to meet Lena's eyes. She looked at the floor. 'Right, then,' she sort of mumbled. 'New wallpaper. A small print, do you think, or maybe regency stripes?'

'Stripes,' Lena said remembering the huge sunflowers and birds of paradise on Ivy's own walls.

'Tonight before midnight. All right?'

'Yes, Mother,' Lena said.

She went to Victoria Station. She couldn't think why. It was that or Euston.

Euston would take her to Ireland. She knew it would be dangerous to go, she must only go to Ireland when she was calm, prepared, ready for whatever might happen. She saw the destinations of the trains. In half an hour there was a train to Brighton, that's where she would go. She would walk along that pier, and the beach and the promenade. She would feel the rain in her face and she would remember their plans and hopes when she was carrying his child. And maybe she might make some sense out of what had happened and plan what to do with the rest of her life.

For so many of the girls who had gone through Millar's she had been the crossroad, she had made them face decicions, take control of their lives, create a destiny for themselves. Now the legendary Mrs Gray would take herself in hand.

She sat in a café and watched the pre-Christmas crowds swelling around. There were people on their way to and from office parties. There were shoppers up from the country for the day. There were businessmen going home after a day's work. Every one of them had a life to lead, a life with hopes and disappointments.

When she opened her handbag to get her purse and pay for her coffee she saw with a shock Kit's letter to her, unopened. Never before had her daughter written a letter which had not been enjoyed as soon as she could find the time. But today had been a day like no other. It would not have been possible to lose herself in Kit's world until she had escaped from her own. Here in the anonymity of this huge railway station, this was the right place to read it.

My dear Lena,

I didn't think I would be sad to read about Louis, that you think it's

379

over and that he may go away. Once this was the news I wanted to hear. I wanted you to be punished, and for him to leave you alone like you left us. But I don't feel that any more. I would much much prefer to think that he was there and that you had a good life together.

Perhaps it's not true that he's thinking of going away. It's very hard to know what men are thinking. Not that I'm any kind of authority but I do know that hours and hours are spent in Frankie's flat, in cafés and after lectures talking about men and what they are thinking and what they're planning . . . and it seems to turn out in the end that they're not thinking about anything or planning anything. I just tell you that in case it's some comfort.

Lena sat in the station café as the world moved about its business on either side of her . . . tears fell down her face, she didn't even wipe them away, she just read on.

Kit wrote of the dance, the endless difficulties put in their way by Dan and Mildred O'Brien, the fear that the guests would all spend so long in Paddles' before they arrived that there would be no bar business for the Central and that everyone would be drunk and disorderly.

And Kit wrote about Stevie Sullivan, about his childhood, what it had been like to have no shoes because his father had drunk the money that had been set aside to buy them. Stevie Sullivan wore the best of leather shoes now and always would. Stevie didn't drink alcohol, he didn't gamble, he worked hard and of course, as everyone knew, had a been a bit foolish in the past.

But one of the terrible things about a small Irish town was the way your past hung around for ever. No one was allowed to make a fresh start. People still said he was old Billy Sullivan's boy, a drunkard's son. They said he was a wild boy who had been with all the girls in the parish. Wasn't it strange that they couldn't see how he had changed?

And as Lena read she heard the echo loud and clear. Kit thought of Stevie Sullivan in exactly the same protective and excusing way as she had thought of Louis Gray. She was blind to any criticism of him. She was her mother's daughter and she was about to follow exactly the same path.

Lena sat for a long time in the café and then with heavy limbs got up and took a train to the south coast of England.

'Ivy?'
'Where are you, Lena?'
'In a nice place in Brighton. Quiet, warm.'
'What's its telephone number?'
'Now listen . . .'
'Just tell me. I won't ring you, just tell me for me, not for you.'
She read it from the wall beside the phone.
'I had a Mr James Williams round here looking for you.'
'You didn't tell him?'
'What do you think? But he said most specially that if you were in touch

to say he was very lonely for Christmas and he would love it if you could . . .'

'Right Ivy . . . you're very good.'

'Have you anyone to talk to?'

'I don't need anyone. I'm so tired.'

'All right. When will you ring me again?' She fixed a day, three days ahead. 'And this James Williams . . . ?'

'Will have to find someone else to play Santa Claus for him.'

'He looked very nice,' Ivy said.

'Goodnight, Ivy.'

'Goodnight, pet. I wish you were upstairs.'

'Louis, a minute.'

Louis looked up from all his plans of the O'Connor visit. They were being a very troublesome group, constantly changing their plans. Firstly there were going to be five of them, then four and now two, and then five for Christmas and only three for New Year. It had played hell with the booking schedules, as if he weren't nervous enough meeting Mr O'Connor.

He hadn't yet been filled in about the forthcoming event. He might not be overjoyed to meet his future son-in-law for the second time and hear such news. But Mary Paula had assured him that she lived her own life. She was very much her own person, and had been for years. She was twenty-eight years of age, a grown-up.

Louis wished that things were different, that he was nearer to her age than to her father's, that he had been able to prove himself at the new hotel before he proved himself able to father a child. Still, he would believe Mary Paula that it would sort itself out.

'Sorry, James,' he said. 'I seem to be pulled in a hundred ways today.'

James Williams looked stern and unsmiling. 'Lena's not at work today.'

'I beg your pardon?'

'And she's not at home, I went round to ask the landlady.'

'James, I don't understand . . .'

'Where is she, Louis?'

'I have no idea. I spoke to her last night, I told her everything, I went round this morning, took my things, left my key as we arranged.'

'What did she say?'

'I don't think it's any of your business, actually.'

'I think it is if my manager decides to take another job and move to another country, and then says *oops, I forgot to tell her* when I ask how his wife is taking it.'

'She's *not* my wife, I told you yesterday.'

'She bloody is your wife, if you lived with her for years and told everyone she was.'

'You don't know the story. Lena wasn't free to marry.'

'Wasn't she lucky, the way things turned out.'

'Look, I don't know what's brought all this on.'

'I'll tell you what's brought it on – the behaviour of a man who has acted like a selfish bastard. You've thought of nobody but yourself, Louis, all the time ... self, self, self.'

'I'm not going to stay here and listen to this.'

'No, you're bloody right you're not. You can take your cards and leave today.'

'On what grounds?'

'On the grounds that I couldn't look at your face while you worked out your notice.'

'You can't be serious, James.'

'Never more so.'

'You'd let your personal feelings and the fact that you have always been attracted to Lena stand in the way of normal business behaviour?'

'You've had your reference, Louis, you've had the build-up that got you the new job, and made you an acceptable son-in-law for this Irish tycoon, now get out of here.'

Louis' handsome face was very hard and cold. 'It won't do you any good, all this posturing. Lena won't think any better of you. She thinks you're a cold, dull fish already, now she'll think you're just a petty one.'

'By this afternoon, Louis.' James Williams turned and left.

It took a lot of time and ingenuity but Louis Gray had many contacts and friends in the hotel business. He found a suite in another hotel, somewhere he could entertain the O'Connors in style. He would turn the whole business to his advantage, say that he had left the Dryden to concentrate on them properly.

Now of course he would have to organise a whole Christmas and New Year programme for them. He must think what to do. For a wild moment he thought of asking Lena, she was always great about ideas and thinking up the right thing for the right occasion.

Wasn't it absurd that she had come to his mind just like that? But it was only natural, they had been together for so long it was obvious that they should still automatically think of consulting each other. He wondered whether James Williams was right about her having disappeared from work and from the flat in Earl's Court.

It was improbable; Lena had seemed so calm. As if she had known this was all inevitable. And the one sure and certain thing was that in any time of crisis you'd find Lena at her desk in that bloody agency. She was more married to Millar's than she ever would be to a man.

All the shops in Brighton were full of Christmas gifts. Lena looked in the windows at things she would like to have bought for her daughter. She had a handbag full of money. She could have bought the necklace and earrings set in a little musical box. She could have got her that smart coat which would have done so much for her colouring. The manicure set in the genuine leather case. The overnight case with the smart two-tone trim – it would be ideal for going up and down between Dublin and Lough Glass.

But why was she torturing herself? She would not send anything to her daughter.

This was a Christmas when she would give no presents and get none. When she would have to stay far from a church lest the sound of carols make her weep. She must not listen to the radio in case the programmes of goodwill and celebration pointed out too clearly what she had lost.

The waves were high and crashing on to the big beach.

Was this the beach she had walked with Louis when she was expecting his child? It seemed like a different age, and two different people. When she was here that time she had been waiting for the letter of abuse, and the torrent of rage and blame from Martin. She didn't know that they were dragging the lake in Lough Glass looking for her.

If she had the time all over again . . . ?

But it was an empty speculation. She wouldn't have the time all over again. It was useless to work out what she would have done. She must think what to do now. She walked, the spray and salt air in her face, her hair wet and curling in the damp. She didn't see anyone glance at her and wonder why a handsome woman should walk so ceaselessly, hands deep in pockets, unaware of the world around her, the weather, the season of the year.

Then she found a shelter and sat down to write to Kit. She wrote on pages of a notebook. Not her usual style of letter. And she didn't read it over as she normally would have done. Back at the guest house she got an envelope and stamp and went out to find a pillar box. She felt a little better, as if she had spoken to a good friend.

*

Kit's heart gave a jump when she saw the envelope with her mother's writing on it laid on the hall table upstairs. Surely her father had recognised it. That was the way Mother had always written. But apparently not.

It was the day before Christmas Eve. Kit and Philip had just come back from Dublin. Maura had decorated the house. It wasn't the same as Mother used to do. Mother would have had all leaves and ivy and holly. Maura had bought paper decorations and tinsel.

The house looked very festive. There were lots of Christmas cards on the mantelpiece and around the mirror. Maura sent and received many more than Helen McMahon had ever known.

Kit felt a rush of anxiety. Why had her mother been so rash as to write here? She was anxious to be alone to read the letter, but they were welcoming her home. Emmet had carried up her luggage, including the dress box with the extravagant new dress bought on the compensation money. She had spent a fortune on it, and didn't want anyone to see it before the dance in case there might be question of it being somewhat revealing.

She had told Clio that it was a bargain, marked down in a pre-Christmas sale.

'There are no pre-Christmas sales,' Clio had said sagely. 'You are turning into a mysterious and very sinister liar.'

Maura was offering soup to take the chill off her, her father was eager to tell her all the news and how the golf club committee had thrown themselves behind the great New Year's Eve dance. But Kit couldn't wait to be away from them. Eventually she decided that the bathroom was her only hope of peace and quiet. Sitting on the side of the bath she read:

My dear Kit,
This is to wish you a very happy Christmas this year and every Christmas.

I was so pleased with the letter you wrote to me. I read it in a railway station. All around there were people living their own lives, making journeys to see people or escape from people and I just sat there and read your letter over and over.

It's good to know that Stevie was able to rise above his childhood and triumph over all the bad things that happened to him in his youth. It must have made him very strong. Of course the same goes for you. You had a lot happen to you in your youth that shouldn't have happened and you coped with it. You coped with the death of a mother, and the rumours about that death. You thought your mother had committed suicide and was in hell. You met a ghost. You survived that.

In many ways I think you are well suited for each other. Of course like every mother I worry for you. But perhaps I don't have the right to have those feelings. Maybe they were forfeited a long time ago.

It was kind of you to say that perhaps Louis was not thinking of going. But in fact he has gone. He is going to get married to someone else. Somebody much younger and they will have a child. So that part of my life is over now.

I just wanted to reassure you that I will make no more trouble for all the people I have hurt so much already. You may worry that since Louis has left me I might become like a ship without a rudder. So I wanted you to set your heart at ease. I will disturb nothing that has been done.

I tell you this because I know it will cross your mind and also because I have an ache, a yearning to go back to Lough Glass and to see the dance that you have all been preparing. I had this feeling I could watch from the outside. So in a way I am writing this to tell myself that I must not go. May it be a great success for you all.

Peace, Kit. Peace and goodwill. Isn't that what we are all looking for when all is said and done?
Your loving mother,
Lena

Kit sat in the bathroom looking at the letter in disbelief. This wasn't the kind of letter Lena wrote. The sentences were all wrong. Short jerky phrases, ramblings about sitting in railway stations. Lena had addressed this letter to the pharmacy, she had signed it your loving mother.

Louis had left her, he was getting married to another woman. Lena was not able to cope.

Kit behaved normally. She was sure that nobody knew there was a thing wrong. She wrapped gifts, she delivered Christmas cards by hand, she spent hours in the Central Hotel, she kept her voice and smile polite for Philip's parents, she made lists and timetables. She listened to Clio's ramblings and complaints about Anna, about her parents, about Aunt Maura, about Michael not ringing to say goodbye before he left for London.

Her only hope was to work as hard as she could. When it was all over she would think what she could do to help Lena. But now there was nothing she could say or do or write that would help. She felt very much alone.

On Christmas Eve she lay awake for a long time and wondered about her mother lying in bed alone in that flat in London. She wished she could telephone her. But it would be easier to contact the planet Mars than to make a phone call from Lough Glass at Christmas-time to someone in London.

And suppose Lena were so disturbed that she let everything be revealed. Suppose the phone call unhinged her and that she told Maura and Father that she was alive ... suppose Emmet were to hear.

Kit lay in her bed and wished she could tell someone. The only person she could tell was Stevie Sullivan.

But it wasn't her secret to tell.

The feeling of anxiety remained with her on Christmas Day and for no reason Kit found herself crying just at the wrong time. They were all getting ready to go up to Kellys' for a sherry and present-giving.

Everyone wanted to go, Maura to see her sister, Father to see his friend Peter, Emmet to see the beloved Anna ... only Kit didn't want to go.

But go she must. 'I'll follow you up there,' she called as she heard them getting ready to leave. She needed just a little time to compose herself, get herself ready for the Kellys.

She splashed cold water on her face and left the house. Her heart was like lead on this Christmas morning.

'Hey, wait for me.' Stevie Sullivan had seen Kit leaving her house and he ran after her. She turned around to look at him. His smile was broad, his delight to see her was written all over his face. 'You didn't call to say happy Christmas,' he accused her.

'I thought I'd see you at Mass.'

'Oh, I was at the back of the church, humble you know, not putting myself forward.'

'Talking, doing deals I imagine,' she mocked him.

He looked at her closely. 'You've been crying,' he said.

'Does it show? I couldn't bear the third degree from Clio.'

'Only to me, I know every little bit of your face. Why were you crying, Kit?'

'I can't tell you.'

'Is there anything I can do?'

'No thank you, Stevie, No.'

'Will you ever tell me?'

'I might some day.'

'You'll have forgotten.'

'No, I'll never forget why I'm crying today.'

'Michael and Kevin are having the time of Reilly over in London,' Clio said. 'He rang last night.' Clio was pleased at this.

'What's she like, the sister?' Kit asked.

'I don't know, I only met her the once.'

'And the fellow she's marrying?'

'Oh, he's as old as the hills apparently. Michael says he could be her father.'

'But nice?'

'Apparently.'

'Is he a sugar daddy sort?'

'No, the total reverse, he hasn't a penny, according to Michael.'

'But he's going to be admitted to the ranks?'

'Yes, apparently he's a dynamo in the hotel industry over in London.'

'Why isn't he rich then?' Kit wondered.

'Search me,' Clio said. 'But she's very stuck on him. Michael thinks that she might be pregnant.'

'No!' Kit's eyes were round with excitement.

'Well, the marriage is very speedy apparently, speedier than one would have thought.'

'What's his name?' Kit didn't care very much but anything was better than answering Clio's questions.

'Louis. There, isn't that romantic? Louis Gray.'

On the day after Christmas, Kit asked Stevie to drive her into the big town.

'Nothing will be open,' he said, puzzled.

'That doesn't matter.'

'Of course it matters. What's the point of going into Tombstone City in the rain? Why don't we stay here in the rain?'

'Please Stevie, I don't ask much.'

He considered this. It was true, she didn't ask him favours. 'Okay, fine,' he said.

He didn't ask her why she wanted all the change to make a phone call from a hotel in the town. He sat and had a pint in the hotel bar and looked at her from a distance as she stood in the phone booth at the far end of the hall. Kit McMahon was running her hand through her hair and talking earnestly. Stevie realised the point of the journey through the rain was so that she could phone someone whom it would have been impossible to phone from home. She could have used the phone in the Central Hotel but it would still have meant going through Mona Fitz.

He wouldn't ask her. She would tell him when she was ready.

'Ivy Brown?'

'Yes, yes, who is this?'

'Mrs Brown, I'm Kit McMahon. I met you once, do you know who I am?'

'Yes, yes, of course I do.' Ivy sounded worried. 'Is anything wrong?'

'Could I talk to Lena do you think . . . ? I got the number from Directory Enquiries . . .'

'But love, she's not here . . .' Ivy said.

'Look, Ivy, I *have* to talk to her, I have to. I have some terrible news I want to give her.'

'I think she'd had all the bad news she can take.'

'I know who he's marrying, he's marrying someone else, the bastard. The bastard out of hell.'

'Kit, stop . . .'

'I won't stop. I've no money, Ivy. I can't leave here, we have a huge thing I'm up to my neck in. I can't walk out on it, but I have to talk to Lena. You must tell me where she is.'

'She was in Brighton, but she rang me from a coin box in London. She said she'd be away for a few days and she'd ring me on New Year's Day.'

'Where?'

'She wouldn't say.'

They had bookings for one hundred and fifty-eight people. The most the golf club had ever catered for was eight-six. Philip O'Brien told Kit that he hadn't slept since Christmas Eve, not more than two hours at a time.

'It'll be great,' Kit said.

'You're not sure, you're only encouraging me, you're only being nice.'

'Jesus, Philip, you really piss me off at times. I'm saying what I mean, why do you accuse me of just being nice?'

'Because your mind is miles away,' he said. 'Since Christmas Day you've been thinking of something else entirely.' Kit was silent. 'Isn't that right?' Philip asked.

'I have a lot on my mind, that's true, but I do think the dinner will be great.'

'Will you tell me what's worrying you?'

'Why?'

'I might be able to help,' Philip said.

'I don't know,' she hesitated. 'I don't know if I'll tell you.' Why did she feel that she might be able to tell wild Stevie Sullivan all about her mother and the tragedies of her life, but that she wouldn't be able to explain them to good loyal Philip O'Brien?

'I'll always be here,' he said.

'You're a great and good friend,' she said truthfully.

'Tell me again it won't be a disaster,' he said.

'Philip, it'll have them talking about it for a year. Now, back to business.' She took out her clipboard and got back to the countdown.

They agreed that they would have big tables, set for anything from sixteen to twenty. And even though there would be guests from Dublin, the O'Connor brothers, Matthew (who was going to be watched by Kevin O'Connor all night in case anything untoward happened) Frankie, and more, the committee would all have to keep hawk-like eyes out in case anything went wrong.

Kit was to be in charge of the food and training the group of girls from the convent in their waitress duties. Philip was responsible for the entire drink side of things, the opening and pouring of wine, the pulling of pints, the trays of alcohol being brought with speed to tables. Emmet was in charge of furniture. They had identified this as a possible problem, chairs and tables too close together, not leaving access for waiters, people wanting to join up with other tables. Emmet would appear miraculously when people started heaving and dragging things.

Anna was in charge of decoration. If bits of holly separated themselves from curtains, from the wine bottles holding candles, it was Anna who must replace them. She was to be forever vigilant and move around from table to table. Anna liked this. Stevie Sullivan was not going to be sitting at their table. This would give her a chance to mingle.

Patsy was to keep an eye on the ladies' room, make sure there were tissues and clean soaps. One of the downstairs rooms had been transformed with pink drapes and pink and white striped regency-style coverings on the furniture and artistic floral sprays. The two new lavatories that had been badly needed for the hotel were installed and functioning. The job had been done by Kevin Wall's brother, who had worked even on Christmas Eve to get everything finished.

Philip's parents had severe doubts about the expenditure, but they were so pleased by the attention the hotel was getting from Lough Glass and the entire surrounding countryside they didn't protest too much. 'It's about time that people took us seriously as a hotel,' Mildred sniffed, when she heard more and more bookings coming in from landowners whose patronage they had never known before.

'I always said that this place would be recognised for what it was in the end,' Dan O'Brien assured her, giving absolutely no credit to his son and his son's friends who had made the whole thing possible.

Clio had no specific responsibility: it was generally agreed that she should look after the guests from Dublin, keep everything going smoothly at the table, and cover for the fact that the others would be coming and going all night.

'We won't just dance with people at our own table, will we?' Anna asked.

Kit couldn't bear to see the look on Emmet's face. 'No, I think it should be open plan,' Kit said. Of course it was going to be open plan. Stevie Sullivan had booked a table for some of his customers. There were going to be more men than women in the party.

In the afternoon Kit and Philip looked around. 'We've done it,' she said.

The tables were so festive, and the walls draped in greenery looked as if the whole place was out of doors. They would light the candles just before the people arrived. The convent school girls had come to show their uniform, every single one of them in white blouses and navy skirts and each wearing an embroidered badge with the letters CHL for Central Hotel

Lough Glass. Kit had seen to it that those with hair flopping over their faces wore hair slides or ribbons.

She had rehearsed over and over what to do in the case of accidents. If somebody let a plate fall there was to be no giggling and no fussing; dustpans and brushes were under some tables hidden by the long tablecloths. She asked them all to repeat the names of the dishes and drummed it into them – Hors d'oeuvres – say it after me, no, say it again, each one of you.

'What are these starters called?'

'Hors d'oeuvres.'

'That's much better.'

'Go home now,' Philip said. 'You all look terrific and be back here looking just like that at 6.30.'

They were giggling as they left.

Kit shouted at them suddenly. 'What are the starters called?'

'Hors d'oeuvres,' the six girls chanted.

'And what are the main courses?'

'Chicken with tarragon, or beef in red wine.'

'Great. What are the desserts?'

'Sherry trifle or apple tart and ice cream.'

'Can people come back to the tables as often as they like?'

'Yes, as much as they want.'

'Don't giggle as you say that,' Kit said. 'They want to feel welcome, they don't want to feel stupid.' The girls looked at her respectfully. 'Philip and I spend all our time at college learning this kind of thing.' Kit wanted to take some of the harm out of her direction.

'You're getting it all for free,' Philip added.

The girls smiled from one to the other. He would never be able to thank Kit for all her support over this.

'I got you a little corsage,' he said. 'It's in the fridge to keep it nice and fresh. Just to thank you, from one friend to another.'

'You're a dear good friend,' she said, and put her arms around his neck to hug him.

He felt her breasts against him and it was all he could do not to hold her to him tightly and kiss her on the lips. 'So are you,' he said in a voice that struggled to be casual.

The Dublin contingent came in three cars around six o'clock. The bar was bright and welcoming. Philip had the first round of mulled wine ready for them to sample. 'If it lays you lot out then we'll know not to serve it to the real people,' he said.

Kevin O'Connor looked at him with interest. This wasn't the mousy Philip he knew at college. This hotel was certainly not the dump Michael had said it was when he drove past it before. It was an elegant, creeper-covered building, with a lot of attractive greenery in barrels around the entrance. The decorations for the New Year's Eve celebrations were stylish.

Their rooms were much more comfortable than he had been led to believe. Kevin was sharing a room with his friend Matthew. He had promised to watch Matthew's behaviour. And anyway there was no point in sharing with his twin; Michael O'Connor would be entertaining Clio Kelly as the night went on. Kevin wondered how his brother had got so lucky with the Lough Glass girl *he* had chosen.

'Hell of a nice place this, Philip,' Kevin said. The others agreed.

'Thank you.' Philip seemed confident. He had kept his parents off the scene, saying that they should be there to greet guests in the bar at seven thirty when it all began. But not before. He felt a surge of excitement like he had never known before. It was all going to happen. Tonight his career and his long-term plan of marrying Kit McMahon were all taking off.

Kit had asked her father and Maura to be among the early arrivals.

'I was hoping I might have a pint in Paddles' with Peter,' Martin said.

'No, have it in the bar.'

'It's a bit of a gloomy place . . .' he began.

'Wait until you see it tonight,' Kit promised.

Maura looked very well: she had on a black dress with black chiffon sleeves. 'I hate wearing my coat over it but I suppose I'd freeze walking down without it . . .'

'It's only a few yards,' Kit said. 'You look so nice it's a pity to spoil it.'

'Put on your coat, Maura, like a good woman, and don't be catching pneumonia.'

'Lilian's wearing a stole, but I always look like a washerwoman in one.' Maura's face seemed disappointed.

'Father, can I ask you something?' Martin looked a little surprised. 'Do you remember the little fur stole that Mother had, it was like a little cape?'

'Yes, I think I do, why?'

'You probably don't remember because she hardly ever wore it. It's in my wardrobe in a box, in case I'd ever wear it. I don't think it suits me. Why don't we give it to Maura to wear?' It was a risk, she knew this. They had never mentioned anything of Mother's before.

'That's very nice of you, Kit but I really don't think . . .'

'Let me get it . . . I can, can't I, Father?'

'Child, it's yours and I'd be delighted if Maura would like it. Delighted.'

Kit was back in a moment. It was in tissue paper in a box. There was a faint whiff of mothballs. The little cape had a fastener in the front. It was old-fashioned, dated almost, but it might look smart on Maura. Kit draped it around her stepmother's shoulders and stepped back to look at the effect. 'It's *lovely* on you . . . come and look in a mirror.'

It was indeed splendid. It could have been made for Maura around the shoulders but the fastener didn't meet. 'This needs to be held together with some black ribbon,' Kit said quick as a flash. 'I have some in a drawer.'

When she came back her father and Maura were holding hands, and there were tears in Maura's eyes. She hoped nothing had gone wrong. 'I was just saying that perhaps I shouldn't wear it. Someone might remember Helen wearing it on some other occasion . . .'

'I never saw Helen wear it, not in all my life.'

'Did you buy it for her, Father?'

'I don't remember that I did. No, she must have had it already, but I can't ever recall seeing it on her anywhere. I'd love you to wear it, Maura dear.'

'It might have been special to her.' Maura was still doubtful.

'No, it couldn't have been or else she'd have . . .' Kit stopped, horrified. She nearly said she would have taken it with her to London.

'Or else . . . ?' Maura looked at her.

'Or else we'd have seen her wear it . . . Here, let me thread this ribbon in, you're the belle of the ball.'

'When are *you* going to put on your dress?'

'I have it down at the hotel, I didn't want to put it on until I'm through in the kitchen.'

'Does the chef not mind you taking over?'

'I don't think by any stretch of the imagination you could call Con Daly a chef . . . a cook is even stretching it a bit. He's so relieved that we're all there, he's nearly licking our shoes with gratitude.'

Emmet came in wanting his bow tie tied. 'A girlfriend should be doing this for you,' Maura said as she tied it expertly.

'Oh, I've no time to be interested in girls for a few years yet,' Emmet said.

Kit caught his eye and smiled.

'Very sensible,' Martin McMahon said. 'The country would be in a better state if everyone thought the same.'

'I'll see you down there.' Kit ran off.

Stevie Sullivan knocked from an upstairs window. 'Will you come on up here and help me dress?'

'Sadly, no,' she called back. 'I'm on duty five minutes ago, and the battle orders are very strict. I made most of them myself.'

'You're not exactly gussied up yourself,' he said, disappointed.

She was wearing her duffel coat and her hair, still in big loose rollers, was under a headscarf. 'Gussied up . . . what a marvellous phrase . . . see you later.'

He watched from the window as she ran into the hotel: you wouldn't recognise the Central with its smart barrels of greenery, its trimmed creeper, its glittering new sign, perfectly illuminated by some fixture which also showed the old oak tree to its best.

Funny that Kit didn't see the naked longing in Philip O'Brien's face. She was not an unkind girl, she wouldn't play games with him. She simply didn't see that the young son of the hotel was head over heels in love with her.

Kit slipped into the kitchen. She didn't want to join the loud voices that were coming from the bar, she could hear Matthew booming away. She must remember to warn Kevin that very strict control should be exercised over Matthew.

The kitchen was too hot: she opened a window but the draught blew things from a shelf. 'Hold the back door open with a chair,' she ordered.

'I'll do it, that's the very thing,' said Con Daly in his spotless whites.

There had been a time when Con always looked as if somebody had spilled the contents of thirty-five dinner plates over him.

The young waitresses were standing in a little group, giggling with excitement. Kit frowned. How many times had she tried to tell them ... but then when she and Clio were young they did nothing but laugh and giggle for about three years. Suppose they had been asked to help in the O'Briens.

'Listen,' she said to the girls. 'I know you think we're all quite old and probably mad, but I want to tell you what we're doing. We're trying to show that we can be as good and better than the grown-ups. And the grown-ups think we're still children ... so we need to look desperately polished. We need to be able to pronounce starters.'

'Hors d'oeuvres.'

'We need to know what tarragon is ...'

'It's a herb in the sauce,' they said.

'But most of all we want them to think you are real waitresses, not schoolgirls. For some reason laughing and enjoying yourselves makes you look amateur, I don't know why, so I can't let you do it. We can all laugh our heads off when it's over. And Philip has said that if there's no laughing there's going to be an extra four shillings each for all of you.' This was serious money. They looked at each other in disbelief. 'But that's everyone. One giggler and nobody gets the four shillings extra. Okay?'

They nodded, faces solemn, afraid to meet each other's eyes.

'Great,' Kit said. 'Now, what else was I going to do?'

'Get dressed, I think,' said one of the girls. The others reddened but managed not to laugh. Kit had them well frightened into earning their extra wage.

She took the scarlet dress from its hanger. Philip had told her she could change in his room. He had tidied it and left around it all kinds of things that would make her think better of him. Books he hadn't read, clean towels and a kind of soap that he never used but was expensive.

The dress fitted perfectly. It was an off the shoulder model so there would be no bra. But again it was so perfectly moulded that there would be no need. As she stood in her half slip and washed herself at Philip's handbasin, Kit studied her face in the mirror. Her heart was not in tonight's festivities. If only she had been able to ring Lena and talk to her.

She was tired from all the work involved. She looked pale, she thought. She must be sure not to waste tonight's opportunities. That's what it had been about. She mustn't grant an inch to poisonous little Anna Kelly who had bought a lime-coloured dress in Brown Thomas. Reports were that it looked a knockout. Kit hadn't killed herself getting this hotel off the ground just so that Philip's parents could sit back and take all the credit. She had wanted an arena, a public place to allow Stevie Sullivan to be seen to fall for her.

She needed to wipe the two mean little eyes of Anna Kelly and make her flee sobbing back to poor innocent Emmet, who would of course take her. Kit had made a promise that she was going to deliver. But now it was much more than that, it was something she wanted so much and so badly that it nearly hurt.

There was a sizeable crowd by the time that Kit made her entrance but Stevie and his clients had not arrived. Her eyes raked the room for them, but she couldn't see them. She went to where her father and Maura were standing with the Kellys. Maura was still wearing the little cape.

Lilian had admired it. 'Very smart indeed,' she had said, slightly enviously, Maura thought.

'Yes, I think I'll leave it on for a bit. I can't imagine the O'Briens having the place warm enough,' Maura whispered.

'I haven't seen you wearing it before.'

'Not much cause really,' Maura said. She had decided not to tell her sister that it had once belonged to Helen. And it was obvious that Lilian had never seen it before. What a strange woman Helen McMahon must have been to have had a lovely thing like this and never worn it.

'I wouldn't have believed the place, Kit.' Her father looked around him in amazement. 'I'll have to let you into the pharmacy next.'

'Fine, as long as you don't object to holes in the walls every two minutes like Mildred O'Brien did,' Kit whispered. 'Her bloody walls were falling down and great wedges of damp like lumps of penicillin and she says *not too many nails in the wall.*'

Mildred was standing like royalty near the fireplace accepting compliments from everyone. 'Well, the old place *does* have its charm,' she was saying modestly, as if it had looked like this all the time.

Then Kit joined Clio and the O'Connors. Clio wore a cream dress with a neckline of rosebuds. It was attractive but it wasn't startling. You wouldn't pick Clio out in the crowd like you would Kit in her scarlet dress. Or Anna in her bright lime colour. Clio seemed to sense it and the corners of her mouth turned down.

'Welcome to Lough Glass,' Kit said to the group.

'You look *terrific,*' Frankie Barry said.

'Thanks, it's very startling, anyway. If I were in London you'd think I was a pillar box.'

'Or a bus,' Clio said. Everyone looked at her, surprised. 'They're red too,' Clio said lamely.

'Yes, of course,' Kit said. 'Tell me, how was your trip to London?' she asked the O'Connor twins.

'Fabulous . . .' Michael said.

'No one there to hold a candle to you, Kit,' Kevin said.

Clio looked crosser than ever.

But Kit appeared not to notice. 'Tell me about your sister's fiancé. Did he turn out to be okay?'

Clio wished she had thought to ask. Kit was winning everybody there. She didn't even remotely *like* Kevin O'Connor, and yet he was hanging on her every word.

'He was okay,' Kevin said. '. . . like old and everything, but an all right fellow. You could see why she likes him. He drove us all round London in his car . . . down the docks, to Covent Garden . . . he was like a guide . . . in a way.'

'Did he not have to go to work?' Kit asked.

'Well, it was Christmas.'

'But isn't that the terrible thing about hotel work, we have to work at Christmas?'

Kevin looked at Michael '. . . that's true. I suppose he had time off.'

'I think he's left his hotel, you know, already. And they're getting married very soon. Real soon, wink, wink,' Michael said, nudging Clio.

Clio looked annoyed, but Kit was interested. 'And will you all be going over for the wedding again?'

'No, they're coming over here. It'll be in Dublin.'

Kit wanted to ask had they met his family, what had he been doing up to now. She wanted to get the two stupid, bone-headed O'Connor boys up against a wall and beat the answers out of them. Then she wanted to tell them that Mary Paula had got herself hooked to a liar and deceiver in the international league. She wanted to say that she could tell them a story about their future brother-in-law and his deceptions that would make their pale greasy hair stand on end.

'Clio, is that a new watch?' she asked.

Clio had been displaying her wrist in a way that simply called out for attention. 'Yes, Michael gave it to me.' There was a little simper.

'It's lovely,' Kit said and they all admired it.

Next year it would be the engagement ring. That's the way the mating dance worked. The watch was a preliminary. Kit looked at Clio with new eyes as if she had never seen her before. Clio was going to marry Michael O'Connor. She would soon be a sister-in-law of Louis Gray.

Mrs Hanley was loud in her praise of how well the young people had done. 'My Patsy was involved in it all,' she told Mrs Dillon from the newsagency. 'I'm surprised your Orla wasn't in on it from the start.'

'Well, of course Orla has her own life to lead, what with being married and living so far out in the country.'

'She won't be here tonight, will she?' Mrs Hanley asked.

'One never knows,' said Mrs Dillon distantly and moved away.

She had told her daughter Orla that there was no question of her turning up alone at the golf club dance. She either came with her husband and a family party or she didn't come at all. 'That crowd wouldn't know what a dance was,' Orla had said. 'And I'll go on my own if I like, there'll be plenty who'll dance with me.' Mrs Dillon, who feared greatly that Stevie Sullivan might dance only too much with her, had her mouth set in a grim line.

The buzz of conversation had become almost a roar when Philip and Kit decided that Bobby Boylan and his Band should begin to play. They hadn't wanted them to start until the noise level was already high.

'Something gentle without too many rat-tat-tats to start,' Philip had suggested.

'What does he mean – *rat-tat-tats*?' Bobby Boylan asked indignantly.

'I think he means reverberating drum sounds,' Kit said apologetically.

'He's got an odd way of putting things, your fellow.'

'He's not my fellow.' Kit didn't want even someone like Bobby Boylan, whom she might mercifully never see again, to go away with the wrong impression.

It was a five-piece band. They wore pale pink jackets, all of which must have been bought when the players were slimmer men, or else they had been borrowed from a skinnier band.

'"Red Sails in the Sunset" gentle enough, do you think?' Billy Boylan asked. He hated hotel dinners. He would like to have been in a big dance hall on New Year's Eve, but times weren't what they used to be. These days it was listening to children in jackets giving orders.

He sighed and waved his baton at the band that bore his name.

'How soon should we bring them in for the meal?' Philip asked Kit.

'They're all enjoying this bit, there's no one looking at their watches,' Kit said.

'Did Clio show you her watch?'

'She did. I thought she might want Bobby Boylan to call for a roll of drums and have it carried round the room.'

Philip laughed. 'It's good to know you can be bitchy like everyone else.'

'What, me? I'm hardly ever any other way. Let's wait another ten minutes anyway.' She had noticed that Stevie Sullivan and his party hadn't turned up yet. She didn't want to begin until the main star was there.

Anna broke off in the middle of a conversation. 'Excuse me, there's something I must do,' she said.

Kit's eyes followed her. Surely the decorations hadn't fallen to bits yet. But no, Anna Kelly had seen Stevie Sullivan arrive. She wanted to be there to greet him.

Kit looked at Anna's perfect skin, her blonde hair in curls down her back, little ribbons of precisely the same lime green as the dress threaded through her hair. She was like a vision.

Maybe Kit looked hard and tough by comparison. Perhaps scarlet had not been a good colour. Too fast. Too showy for Lough Glass.

Stevie Sullivan and his friends had been in Paddles'. They were all in very good form.

'By God, I wouldn't know this place,' said one of the car dealers. 'Used to be a place you'd be afraid to talk to anyone in case they keeled over and died at your feet.'

'And would you listen to the band, Stevie? You've got great class getting us into a place like this.'

They were red-faced men, bachelors maybe, people who had given big orders for tractors and vans and lorries over the years. They even bought a lot of their other farm machinery through young Stevie Sullivan, who acted as a broker but always got them a good deal and stood over whatever was delivered.

They were flattered that they should be invited to something with a name as fancy as the Lough Glass golf club dinner dance. It would not have been a place where they might normally have been invited.

Kit made a mental note to put extra warmed dinner rolls on their table. These were fellows who might eat the decorations if the food wasn't served quickly enough.

The names of the guests were in big writing on the tables. They didn't have to peer and fumble. Not a full seating plan, but just McMahon or Wall ... the groups arranged their distribution with a maximum of fuss and confusion. Emmet stood about watchfully; he was in charge of chairs. He would run for extra ones if they were needed or ease people into corners.

The baskets of warmed rolls were on the tables, served by the solemn girls from the convent, each one looking earnest with eyes cast down. Kit had forgotten that if she ordered no giggling she also seemed to have bought no smiling. She would know another time.

They had rehearsed so many times how the line would begin. Kit would urge those sitting at tables furthest from the buffet to come up first. It worked like a dream. Soon the entire company had got the picture on how it would work out.

And also the huge reassurance that there was going to be enough food. 'Please return as often as you like,' the sepulchral-looking girls in their white blouses urged.

Con Daly, the cook who was normally never seen anywhere in polite society, stood beaming at the door of the kitchen in his white outfit and chef's hat, as if he had been responsible for everything, rather than taking the most simple and basic directions from Kit and Philip.

Out of the corner of her eye Kit saw Orla Dillon – or Orla Reilly as she was now – arrive at the door. She looked small and shabby as if she had been in the rain for a while deciding whether or not to go in. Her dress looked limp, her hair lank. Years back they had all thought Orla a wild success, and had huge experience with men. Tonight she looked pathetic.

She was not on Mrs Dillon's table, that was obvious. There were six people there who didn't look at all as if they might be welcoming the wild girl who had left her family home in the mountains for a night of fun.

Kit moved over to her.

'Hello, Kit.' Her eyes looked dull.

'There you are, Orla. Are you with any particular group?'

'That's a gorgeous dress, did you get it in Dublin?'

'Yes.' Kit looked anxious.

'I'd love to go to Dublin. To work even.' She smelled of drink.

This was going to be awkward, Kit realised. She couldn't throw Orla out. But where was she going to seat her? She knew only too well of Orla's fling with Stevie Sullivan. That's probably why she was here. That was why she had come in from the back of beyonds, to have a little New Year's Eve magic.

'Well now, Orla, where did you plan to sit for dinner?'

'I heard it was a table where you went and helped yourself.'

'Well, yes, of course it is.'

'So what does it matter where I sit?'

'I wouldn't want you to be without a place to sit down.'

'Don't get your knickers in a twist over it. I'll find somewhere.'

This was all they needed, Kit thought. A drunk ex-girlfriend of Stevie's turning up. And for all they knew pursued by all her lowbred in-laws with hatchets.

Philip was at her side as Orla flounced off towards the food table. 'What's the problem?'

'Plastered,' Kit said succinctly.

'Jesus, what'll we do with her?'

'We could feed her more drink and she'd pass out and we could put her in a cupboard or something.'

He looked at her in gratitude; she wasn't making a drama out of it. 'Or we could give her to her mother, you know, that old saying, "To every cow its calf…"'

'It's not a saying Mrs Dillon might feel any way enthusiastic about. No, I think the thing is to see where she weaves and sort of settle her there. Emmet will get her a chair.'

They saw her weaving with a plate of food piled perilously high towards Stevie Sullivan's table. Emmet approached with an extra chair and hovered until he was waved forward.

'Well, at least she's sitting down,' Kit said.

She was so cross that this bit of Stevie's past had come back to haunt him. Yet she was nothing to be jealous of, poor Orla with the pinched face and the slurred speech. Except of course Orla had known Stevie in a much differerent way. Orla hadn't been Miss Prissy like Kit was being, she had been all the way.

'It's not fair on poor Stevie to let her land in on top of all his party,' Philip said. 'He's so decent, look at the crowd he brought.'

Kit felt a wave of guilt flood over her. If things went according to plan when the dancing began, she would be in Stevie's arms all night. Philip would not be referring to him as poor Stevie.

She saw Stevie go over to the table where all their own gang sat. She saw him speak to his brother Michael and hand him some car keys. Michael was nodding earnestly and bursting with importance. Then Stevie was back at his own table. The band played numbers that wouldn't disturb the digestive juices, the heavier dance beat would come later. Bobby Boylan and his band would have a recess later and be fed in another room.

'Philip, it's all fine,' Kit said. 'It's even better than we had hoped.'

'The first of many.'

'Isn't that what I said from the word go?'

They stood there proudly and watched. The unsmiling waitresses were beginning to clear the tables. As instructed, they did not scrape the plates there and then but piled them neatly and brought them to the kitchen. The desserts were being arranged on the long table. There would be no panic, everyone could see that bowl after bowl of trifle was lined up in readiness. Soon it would be time for the ladies to go and powder their noses, and the dancing to begin.

Kit told herself not to worry about Orla Dillon. Stevie Sullivan would cope with the sudden and unwelcome appearance of his past. He would know how to avoid a scene. Stevie Sullivan could cope with anything.

Michael Sullivan came up to Kit. 'I know I'm meant to be helping clear the dance floor space, but something's come up.'

'What exactly?'

'Stevie wants me to drive someone somewhere. Apparently she feels a bit sick.'

'And will he not be driving her himself?'

'No, I'm to say he will but he won't, if you know what I mean.'

'I know exactly what you mean,' Kit said, pleased.

It was done very cleverly. Stevie guided a weaving Orla to the door and whispered something in her ear. She went like a lamb out to his car, where his brother Michael followed.

'Where'sh Stevie?' Orla slurred.

'I'm to drive you there, it's more discreet apparently, and he'll meet you there.'

'Where'sh there?'

'We'll be off now, Orla,' said Michael Sullivan, and drove through the moonlit night over the roads with their great view of the lake.

He drove eleven miles until he came to Reilly's land and the house where Orla lived. There were sounds of a sing-song in her kitchen.

'Hey, this isn't where I want to go,' Orla said.

'This is what Stevie says is best. You're to say you went into town and bought a bottle of whiskey for the night that's in it.'

'But I didn't. I haven't got one.' Orla was frightened now.

'You did. Stevie's got one for you. I'm to wait, in case they think you were with Stevie or anything.'

'But they'll know you're his brother.'

'No they won't. I'm only a child in their eyes. I'm only a schoolboy, you wouldn't be with a schoolboy.'

'I don't know.' Orla looked at him. She got out of the car and walked unsteadily to the door. He prayed she wouldn't drop the bottle of whiskey.

One of the men opened the door. Michael could hear rough voices. 'Who have you out in the car?' the man said pushing past her.

'A child,' Orla said unsteadily.

The man came out to investigate.

'Good evening Mr Reilly,' Michael said nervously. 'The missus was getting you all a bottle of whiskey as a present and she had no lift back, so Paddles asked me to drop her out this way.'

'Why you?' the man said.

'I'm known to Mrs Dillon, the lady's mother,' said Michael.

'All right so, thanks.' The man was gruff.

'Happy New Year,' Michael called as he turned the car to get back on the road.

'And to you, young fellow,' he said.

Michael drove back to the party. Things were great. He had told Stevie he would do him the favour if and only if Stevie got him a car of his own, even the cheapest of things. Stevie had been desperate.

By the time Michael got back the dancing was in full swing. 'Did I miss anything?' he asked Emmet.

'Only lots of dragging tables and chairs out of the way. And the windows were opened to let out the smell of the people for a bit.'

'Did it?' Michael asked with interest.

'I hope so because it blew out all the candles which had to be lit again.'

Bobby Boylan asked everyone to come onto the floor for 'Carolina Moon'.

'Will you dance, Kit?' Philip asked.

It was the least she could do. They had worked together so happily over the weeks, and now it was a triumph. Already she had heard people saying that it would never leave the Central. She had been told by Kevin Wall's father that there was going to be a big dinner in which he was involved; they had written to the Castle Hotel for quotations but he could say categorically now that it would be held in the Central.

Dan O'Brien had shaken her hand and said that he felt she might have had some part in the organising of it all and he would like it to be known that he was not ungrateful. Through the convoluted speech with all its double negatives Kit could see that he was so pleased he hardly trusted himself to speak.

Orla's mother had clutched her in the ladies' room and said that she was a girl of great worth, and that her tact over poor Orla not feeling well would not be forgotten. 'It will not be forgotten,' Mrs Dillon said several times. Kit was mystified. She felt she had handled Orla's arrival very poorly, but it did appear that the girl had been driven back to her mountain men by Stevie's brother and that all was well.

Stevie. When would he speak to her?

As Bobby Boylan's band began to urge the Carolina Moon to keep shining, Kit and Philip took to the floor. They were the first out and as they began to dance their table stood up and cheered.

'Well done, Philip,' they called. 'Well done, Kit.'

Everyone else clapped. The pretty girl in the scarlet dress and the son of the house. Kit was stricken. Suppose Stevie thought she was doing it on purpose, looking for attention, spelling it out that she was with Philip. But there was nothing she could do except smile and acknowledge the cheers.

Outside the windows the moon had come from behind the clouds. It was making a long narrow silver triangle on the lake.

'Look at it, Philip. Isn't it like magic . . .'

In a way she pointed because it meant she could take her arms away from him. She knew Stevie was watching her. She didn't want to pull away from Philip too hurtfully. He looked. It was as they had hoped.

'Haven't you the most beautiful view in the world?' Kit exclaimed.

'We do,' he said simply.

'I'm so proud of Lough Glass tonight,' Kit said. 'I could shout it from the roofs. Usually I have to get ready for people to say Where? when I say I'm from here.'

'There's someone from the Castle Hotel ... they came to report apparently.'

'Well, they'll have a lot to tell.' Kit managed to get them back to talking as the friends they were rather than being draped around each other.

'He was interested in the summer-house ... said it was a real feature ... apparently they just knocked one down over there ... weren't we clever?' Philip said. They looked down from the big picture windows at the floodlit summer-house and the lake stretching away beyond it. 'You couldn't wish for a better setting to see in the New Year,' Philip said.

Kit looked at the clock, it was a quarter to eleven. She had seventy-five minutes to get Stevie Sullivan out on the floor kissing her and wishing her Happy New Year in front of the town. She could barely wait.

Maura and Martin danced to the music of 'On the Street Where You Live'. 'This must be the only place in the world where almost everybody does live on the same street,' Martin said.

'Didn't they do a great job? It's much better than up at the club, twenty times better.'

'You look lovely tonight, Maura.'

'And so do you, young and handsome.'

'No no, that's going too far,' he laughed at her.

'It's what I see.' Maura was transparently honest.

He held her a little closer.

Nearby, Peter and Lilian danced, stiffly and a little bit away from each other. It had all the hallmarks of a duty dance. Peter would go to the bar shortly.

Philip O'Brien was dancing with his mother.

He was a boy who knew how to do things right, Martin thought. Then he looked around for his beautiful daughter in her eye-catching scarlet dress. As he looked he saw her take the hand of Stevie Sullivan from the garage. Stevie looked like a film star, dark and brooding. As they began to dance Martin thought they looked very much as if they had been dancing together for a long time. Which was of course ridiculous; they hardly knew each other, those two.

'Not now, Emmet. I have to do the decorations,' Anna Kelly snapped at him.

'Absolutely.' He appeared not to see her rudeness. 'I just wanted to make sure I danced with everyone at our table. Patsy,' he raised his voice, '... will you do me the honour?'

Patsy Hanley's face lit up. She had a very presentable taffeta dress with a big broad sash. Her mother beamed proudly from another table as she saw her daughter walk to the floor with handsome young Emmet McMahon from the pharmacy.

This was a night Lough Glass would remember for ever. Kevin O'Connor was dancing with Frankie Barry. 'This is a great place, isn't it?' he said.

'Would you look at the view,' Frankie said. 'Philip O'Brien will be the biggest catch in Ireland with a hotel like this under his belt.'

'Play your cards right then, Frankie,' Kevin said laughing.

'No, I think he only has eyes for Miss McMahon . . . like the rest of you.'

'He'd want to be careful with Miss McMahon . . . she's the kind that could deal you a very sharp blow if you got out of order.'

'Yeah, well, that guy she calls the boy next door isn't getting kicked too far away is he?' asked Frankie.

And they looked at Kit McMahon and Stevie Sullivan, dancing as if there were no other people in the room, and no one had existed at any other time.

'You look great, Clio,' Michael said.

'Why did you say that?'

'Because you do.'

'And?'

'And because you're looking very glum.'

'And?'

'Because I want you to come up to the room with me now.'

'Now, in front of everyone? You must be mad!'

'This may come as a severe shock to you Clio, my dream girl, but nobody in this room is looking at us, or thinking about us . . . they've all got their own concerns.'

That was probably true. Clio looked at the dance floor. Kit must have gone quite mad. She was holding on to Stevie Sullivan as if she never wanted to let him go. Stevie Sullivan, who had been with everyone in the parish. She must have lost her mind.

'I'll go first as if I'm going to the Ladies'. You wait for three minutes. Okay?'

'Sure.' Michael had thought it would be more difficult.

Anna Kelly came back to the table at that moment. 'Would you like to dance?' she asked Michael.

'Later, okay?' he said. He saw her face flush a dark red.

'Not if you were the only man in the room with his own legs would I dance with you, Michael,' she said. Michael watched her flounce over to a table where a lot of men sat. 'I'm a great dancer,' he heard her say.

She was also a great-looking girl in that lime green colour. He wasn't surprised that about five of them rose unsteadily to their feet to compete for the honour. At least it had distracted her.

Michael slipped out of the room and upstairs.

'I've put on the electric fire,' Clio said. She was already in the bed, her dress hanging carefully on the back of a chair. He was about to follow her with speed. 'Lock the door, for God's sake,' she whispered.

'You're very experienced at this sort of thing,' Michael said in admiration.

Clio looked at him, alarmed. 'You know I'm not. There's never been anyone but you.'

'Aha, so you say.'

'You know that's true, don't you?'

'Whatever you say, lady.' He had his arms around her.

Clio's eyes were troubled. Suppose Michael really thought she might have been with other people, then that stopped her being special. 'I love you, Michael,' she said.

'Yes, and I love you too.' He spoke automatically, as people respond to a greeting. Wasn't it impossible to know if people really meant what they said.

The man dancing with Anna Kelly was a Ford dealer. He covered a big area and Stevie Sullivan was one of his best customers. The boy had a genius for knowing where the business was. He was definitely going places. Joe Murphy was delighted to be invited to this do tonight. Stevie had asked him did he want to bring his wife . . . but Joe thought no, there was no point in complicating things. Now with this little angel in his arms he was even more pleased he hadn't. There would have been great trouble getting someone to mind the children, and anyway Carmel was shy. She wouldn't mix well.

'You're a terrific dancer,' Anna said to him.

He held her tightly to him. This was a great place altogether. And to think that only this morning he had begun to think he was getting a bit old and fat, past the first excitement of youth. It had all been in his mind. 'Let me dance you off your feet,' he said to Anna as he did a tricky, showy sidestep. It was true what they always said about large men being light on their feet. She seemed delighted with him.

'Don't move away from me,' Stevie said.

'I think the music has stopped,' Kit told him.

'Well, that's only temporary.'

'I love you.' she said.

'People can lipread phrases like that.'

'So you're afraid of what people may hear or read on your lips?'

'No, I'm not afraid. I love you, Kit McMahon. I love you until my heart aches. I can't bear any time without you. You're my woman . . . and I *don't* mean that in some awful possessive way . . . I mean I'm your man. That's what I mean.' He smiled at her, a lovely crooked smile.

They were near a window. The music had begun again. There hadn't been a question of their separating.

'Look at that moon,' Kit said. 'It's as if we had arranged it with some electrician.'

'The lake looks lovely. Maybe we might go and have a walk down there later . . . you know, run down by the summer-house and on to the shore.'

'I think it's probably the worst idea in the world.'

'Yes,' he agreed. 'It is . . . I'd love to live down there, just beside the edge of the water . . .'

'Like Sister Madeleine used to.'

'Yes, we might have a little cottage, you and I, one day.'

'We'll not be together in a little cottage by the lake.'

'Why do you go and say that?' He looked genuinely upset.

'Because we're only fooling ourselves. But listen, enough of that.'

'A little cottage where the birds would come, where you could hear the water, like Sister Madeleine did.'

'I miss her,' Kit said.

'So do I.'

They were the two people in Lough Glass who might have been expected to resent the hermit. She had harboured the man who had injured their families. But they both knew it had been from a good heart.

'I wonder where she is tonight.'

'Oh, well tucked up in her bed in St Brigid's,' Stevie said.

'St Brigid's? You know where she is?' Nobody else knew. Her departure and her destination had always been a mystery.

'Yes, I've seen her, met her there.'

Kit could have fallen to the ground with astonishment. 'I don't believe it.'

'True. I was up there trying to persuade the Reverend Mother that if they bought a station-wagon for the old gardener to drive instead of a truck he could take them in to the station and do a whole rake of things. And I saw her, just standing there, the eyes as blue and strange as ever.'

'And did you speak to her?'

'Of course I did.'

'Stevie, you amaze me.'

'I'll bring you out there to see her one day, she'd love that.'

'Maybe she's hiding from people.'

'She may be, but not from us.'

She felt a shiver of pleasure the way he said us.

And the dances went on and on, Bobby Boylan and his band fuelling themselves with the pints that Philip thoughtfully provided at regular intervals.

The clearing up had been a dream of efficiency. Kit and Philip had insisted that the kitchen be scrubbed, that utensils be seen to have been cleaned by being turned upside down to prove that even the bottoms had been scoured. Dish-cloths and towels were hanging on a line. Food was either covered and put in the fridge or if it was for dogs or pigs it was in buckets out in a scullery, each one covered and labelled. Philip wanted to make sure that a few people were casually allowed to see the kitchen after the event, something that would never have been considered remotely likely up to now in the Central.

A certain level of democracy had been allowed. Con Daly, the cook, and the rest of the staff had been allowed to join the revellers. An extra table had been added for them near the kitchen door. In between serving drinks and cleaning tables the solemn waitresses and the more gleeful waiters would come and sit, to enjoy the first and finest dance they had ever seen.

'Could I have the next dance?' Kevin O'Connor approached Anna Kelly. She was really a beautiful girl. He didn't know why his brother referred to her as some kind of monster or a savage dog.

'I beg your pardon,' she said as if he had made the most incredibly obscene suggestion.

'I was just asking you to dance.'

'And what made you think I might dance with you?' Anna asked. She was still seething with indignation about Michael having refused her. His twin brother was equally horrible.

'Well, we are at a dance.' Kevin was uncertain of himself. 'I meant no offence,' he said humbly.

'I'm glad to hear it,' Anna Kelly said sternly and walked away.

Joe Murphy had been an unwise partner to have picked. He had let his hands roam around her in a very intimate way and even suggested that they go to his car, which was a brand new model he said, and there were only five of them in Ireland. She had found it necessary to lose him rather speedily.

But Stevie *had* seen her dance with him. She made sure Stevie saw her all the time. What was he *doing* with Kit, for heaven's sake. A duty dance was a duty dance, but this was ridiculous.

She looked around for her sister. Clio had been gone for ages. Then Anna's intelligent eyes noticed that Michael O'Connor wasn't there either. First she went to look for them in the summer-house. They had all said during the preparations that it would be an ideal place for courting couples; only the outside was lit up. Nobody could see what was going on inside. There was a long bench there with a long cushion. It would have been cold of course . . .

But Anna tiptoed around to peer in. There was no sign of her sister and Michael O'Connor. She paused to look out at the lake. It had never been more beautiful. Why was Stevie Sullivan taking so long to recognise that she was there, all dressed up, grown up, and waiting for him? He could be standing out in the moonlight with her now. Or in the summerhouse.

She was just about to move onto the path when she saw a shape. There were so many shadows here that she thought it was part of the hedge, but she realised now it was somebody crouching there. The shape stood up, it was a woman. A woman in a long woollen skirt and a cloak, a cloak that she pulled up over her face and head when she saw Anna could see her. Then she ran away, down the path that went towards the lake.

Anna got such a fright that she couldn't even find a voice to scream with. Her breath was gone. This woman must have been just beside her for about five minutes, and would have said nothing, shown no presence until Anna had gone back to the path. Who was she, and what was she looking at?

Probably one of the travellers. They were always stealing things, no matter what her father said. They might have come to see could they get at people's valuables. Fur coats and the like. Anna had thought Kit and Clio were stupid to insist that there be a proper cloakroom with someone to mind it. But now she realised they were right. Tinkers, travellers, whatever you wanted to call them, they weren't the same as other people. Imagine crouching in a garden instead of getting on with your life.

Her heart still pounding. Anna went back into the hotel.

Stevie was right in her path as she joined the dance. 'Don't you look lovely,' he said admiringly.

'Thank you Stevie, and you look very handsome. I've never seen you dressed up before.'

'Little Anna.' He was full of admiration for her.

'Not so little,' she was cross. 'And you brought an interesting party with you,' she said.

'Yeah, watch out for Joe Murphy though. He has a wife and family.' She was furious. Instead of being jealous he was just giving her a friendly warning.

'I'm sure he has, God help them.' Anna said loftily.

'I'm going to the bar to rescue some of my flock,' Stevie said. 'Otherwise I'd invite you to dance, but I have to make sure they're not disgracing me in there.'

'I don't have a free dance as it happens,' Anna said.

'Well then, isn't it all for the best,' Stevie said.

She wanted to pick up a nearby chair and hammer him to death with it.

In the bar Stevie found his cronies ordering large brandies and regaling Peter Kelly and Martin McMahon with their life stories. Joe Murphy was telling them about the car he had of which there were only five in Ireland. Harry Armstrong was telling them that he had been on a trip to Africa. It was the most interesting thing he had ever done in his life.

He kept stabbing Martin McMahon's chest. 'Have you ever been to Africa?' he asked. And no matter how many times Martin said no, the furthest he had ever been was England and Belgium, Harry Armstrong didn't seem to have received this information.

'Africa is the place,' he said over and over.

'What were you doing there?' Peter Kelly asked, hoping to lift the needle from the groove.

It was a complicated story, an opportunity that was meant to exist and hadn't turned out, a fellow who had a contact that hadn't materialised. Harry Armstrong hadn't given a fiddler's damn, he had enjoyed Africa, the whole fact of being there. And when he was down on his uppers he had gone and stayed with his Uncle Jack, who was a priest out there, nay, more than a priest, a bishop would you believe.

'That was a great thing, to be Bishop Armstrong in Africa.'

'Arse Armstrong?' cried Peter Kelly and Martin McMahon in one voice. 'You met Arse?'

'What? What?'

'You're a nephew of Arse?'

'I don't understand.' Harry Armstrong did understand something: that these two men who weren't at all interested in him and his travels before, were now fascinated by him.

'Large brandy for the nephew of Arse Armstrong,' Dr Kelly shouted.

Stevie shook his head in confusion. This seemed to be going fine for some reason that nobody could fathom, except perhaps it might have had something to do with the strength of the drinks being served.

Clio and Michael were still not at the table. Anna had now looked everywhere, they were not in the bar where her father seemed to be getting progressively drunker with some of Stevie's awful friends, they were not in the lounge where some couples were sitting talking. Clio wasn't in the ladies' room, she wasn't in the gleaming kitchen.

Anna Kelly, who should have been the belle of the ball in the dress that had cost a fortune in Brown Thomas, felt very sorry for herself. Stevie Sullivan had no eyes for her at all. Nobody else at the table had been in any way gallant. Her only conquest had been a fat married man with groping fingers. She had been frightened to death by one of the tinkers.

She felt like having a good cry. But not in the newly refurbished ladies' room where everyone would see her. There was a sofa up on one of the landings. She would go up there and sit for a while in the dark. Nobody would see her.

Anna sat and sobbed over the unfairness of life, the fickleness of men, the hopelessness of living in a goldfish bowl like Lough Glass where everyone knew everything about you, the vulgarity and cheap common red dress that Kit McMahon was wearing and how much everyone seemed to like it.

Nearby she heard a door lock open and her heart jumped again. This place was full of strange sounds and shapes and noises. Then through the light she saw her sister start to creep out. Anna gave a gasp. Clio had been in Michael O'Connor's room. They really had been doing it. Making love. My God. Her gasp must have been audible, because Clio went straight back into the room again. Anna crept to the door.

'There's someone out there, I tell you,' she was saying in a panic-stricken tone.

'Don't be ridiculous, who could it be?'

'I don't know. It could be anyone.'

'Who's the worst person it could be?' Michael asked. His voice was shaky too.

'My mother I suppose, or Mrs O'Brien. Mrs O'Brien, I think, because she'd tell my mother and she'd tell everybody and ... Oh Jesus, Michael, what'll we do?'

Anna giggled to herself for a moment, then she rattled the door imperiously and called out at the top of her voice: 'Open this door at once. This is Mildred O'Brien here, open this door or I'm sending for Sergeant O'Connor.'

The door opened and they stood there. Anna had to put her hand in her mouth she laughed so much. She went into the room and threw herself on the bed with mirth. Eventually she blew her nose and wiped her eyes and looked to see if the others were laughing.

They were not. But they had relaxed a little. Bad and all as it was being discovered by Anna there were worse things that could have happened.

'Very droll,' Clio said eventually.

'Wonderful to meet someone with such a sense of humour.' Michael had barely been able to recover his breath. 'If the performance is over perhaps we could go downstairs.'

'Oh, I've finished,' Anna said looking from one to the other. 'Have *you* though?' Then she got another fit of uncontrollable mirth.

They eventually managed to walk down the stairs, the three of them. There was safety in numbers. And they needed it. Mrs O'Brien was at the foot of the stairs. 'And where have *we* all been, might I ask?'

'I was showing a few people the lovely view from the corridor upstairs,' Anna said, cool as anything.

'It is a fine old place,' Mrs O'Brien said. 'Not everyone appreciated it but still we've always known.'

They were beginning to gather everyone together for the 'Auld Lang Syne'.

'Is it that time already?' Stevie said.

'I hope to God the place ran itself for the last few hours, I did nothing I was supposed to do,' Kit said.

'You did everything you were supposed to do,' Stevie said.

Bobby Boylan and the boys were giving little warning toots to tell people it was time to make the circle. The doors were opened so that they could hear the bells of the church ring out. Someone had the radio on to count down to twelve o'clock.

Stevie and Kit stood side by side as if they always had. Maura saw and her heart was heavy. Anna saw and knew she had lost the battle but maybe not the war. Clio saw and thought again that Kit needed her head examined. Frankie saw and decided that Kit had always fancied this guy since the world began and it had really taken off at that party in Dublin. Philip saw and knew that for him it was over.

And then they were all linking arms and crying out Happy New Year, the balloons were falling from the ceiling, the band was playing, the people were going out into the garden to call Happy New Year over the lake.

They could see the fires of the travellers over in the distance, across the lake. The place had never looked more beautiful.

Stevie Sullivan kissed Kit McMahon as if they were the only people on the earth. They stood in the garden of the Central Hotel with the lake in front of them and the path of moonlight which stretched out to the low hills and woods of the neighbouring county. This was their place and their time only.

They didn't see anyone else in the garden. Everyone was inside where Bobby Boylan had started a conga line snaking in and out of all the downstairs rooms. It was headed by Con Daly, the cook, who was being hailed as a chef of the century.

And as Stevie and Kit clung to each other they might have heard the sound of the lake lapping below them but they didn't hear the tears fall from the figure that watched them. The figure in the darkness who had sat watching all night.

Anna saw the way they looked at each other. It was like a knife. That's what it was, as if someone had put a sharp knife in under her ribs where her dress was at its tightest and most uncomfortable. She looked very woebegone.

Emmet was watching. This might be his time. Everyone in the town had seen how Kit had taken Stevie Sullivan as her own. He knew that his father and Maura would be cluck-clucking about it. He would never be able to thank Kit enough. If he couldn't make Anna come back to him now he never would.

'Do you know what I'd like to do?' he asked Anna.

'No.' She was ungracious, she was sure it would be to dance, to drink, to neck. She wanted none of these things, not with the broken heart.

'I'm tired of this, I'd love to go and sit in the summer-house.'

'And kiss and cuddle and take my dress off, I suppose.'

'Certainly not,' Emmet sounded shocked. 'Hey, you and I made a bargain. You love someone else but that will never stop us from being friends.'

'I don't think he loves me, I think your bloody sister managed to interfere there.'

'Well, that had nothing to do with me, or with you,' Emmet lied smoothly. 'We're friends, you and I, and I wondered would we go and read some poetry in the summer-house, like we used to do. Nobody reads poetry like you do, Anna.'

'Would you like that?' She was suspicious.

'I would, very much.'

'And when we get there it won't be all, now we're here we . . .'

'No, it's poetry, and I went and got a book in case.' They stood and looked at each other.

'Yes, let's do that,' Anna said. Anything would be better than witnessing the sickening failure of an evening that had gone so wrong.

Emmet had thought of everything. He had brought a rug so that they wouldn't be cold, he had a flask of drinking chocolate.

'Hey, this is nice,' Anna said, feeling good for the first time for hours. They had a poetry book but they didn't open it. They listened to the music thump out of the windows and across the lake.

'I just thought I'd say, speaking as a friend . . . that you look very beautiful,' Emmet said.

'Thank you.' Anna looked at him suspiciously.

'Not as a person about to make a lunge at you . . . just as an ordinary person . . . and the kind of thing a girl might say . . . the dress, it's just gorgeous. You look much better than a film star.'

'Well, that's very nice of you, I must say.'

'It would be a poor kind of friendship if I couldn't say what was in my mind,' he said eagerly.

Anna looked at him. There were tears in her eyes.

'You know what I mean,' Emmet said foolishly.

'Oh Emmet,' Anna Kelly cried. 'Emmet, I love you. I'm so blind and stupid, thank you for waiting for me, for understanding.'

And they held each other and kissed in the summer-house.

Watched a few yards away by a woman with a cloak over her head. A woman who cried too.

Kevin O'Connor and Frankie had discovered more about each other than they had ever known on this New Year Night. They looked at each other with new eyes. They went walking together by the lake shore, pausing for a bit of this and that. That's how they told it.

And when they were down near the boats they saw this woman, a woman with dark hair and a white blouse, sitting with her head in her hands crying as if her heart would break. It had been nobody who was at the dance.

Neither of them had ever seen anyone so upset. A great dark cloak lay beside her on the ground. When they came near her and spoke she picked up the cloak and flung it around her and ran, leaping over the mooring ropes of the boats. She ran away into the dark.

They told this to the others when they were back at the hotel. The older people were leaving, the young had gathered in the lounge unwilling to end the night. Kevin and Frankie were obviously startled by the encounter; it had been eerie.

'I saw her earlier,' Anna said. 'It was one of the tinkers. She ran in that direction when she left. She was crouching in the garden looking at the hotel, spying, seeing what she could see.' Emmet moved near her protectively as she shivered over the incident.

'No, it wasn't a traveller.' Frankie was very definite.

'No, I saw her face,' Kevin added. 'She had a different face.'

'And expensive clothes,' Frankie said.

'Did she say anything?' Kit asked, a nervous knot beginning to form in her stomach.

'No, nothing at all.'

'Would it be that ghost? Do you remember the woman years ago who was meant to have drowned herself in the lake and kept crying out . . .' Clio began. Then she saw the eyes fixed on her, Stevie's, Emmet's, Anna's, Kevin Wall's, Patsy Hanley's, all the children of Lough Glass who remembered who else had drowned in the lake. 'I didn't mean . . .' Clio began.

But Kit had broken away. She had run out the door down the path towards the lake. 'Lena,' she was calling, 'Lena, come back, Lena. Don't go again. Lena, come back, it's Kit.'

The others stood at the door and watched in horror as Kit ran into the dark night, shouting through her tears. 'Come back, Lena, come back.'

10

They talked about the dance for ages.

There were so many things to tell. Of the bold strap Orla Reilly and how she had been sent back where she belonged. Of the amount of food there was on the table – a banquet was all it could be called. The marvellous spot prizes – crates of brandy, whiskey and sherry seemed to have been donated, a turkey, legs of lamb, sides of beef, boxes of chocolates, tins of biscuits, fancy soaps, gents' scarfs, ladies' blouses (can be changed if size is inappropriate). Nobody in the town had held back when asked to contribute.

'Do you remember the moment the balloons came down?' people said. 'And Bobby Boylan's band playing like the pied piper as they all went through the kitchen. And wasn't the kitchen *shining*, it would put you to shame over your own place.'

And the fur cape that Maura McMahon wore, she was like royalty. And the great crowd of hard men that were guests of the garage, who slept in their cars and started drinking all over again in Paddles' the following morning. And the moonlight on the lake.

And Stevie Sullivan and Kit. The way they danced all night. And how she ran out of there when someone told a silly story of seeing a ghost at the lake, and she thought it was her mother's ghost. Poor girl, and she went out calling don't leave me, or something. Nobody could hear. And how she had run out in the cold in her red dress and stood down by the lake until Stevie carried her home.

There were so many things to tell.

'You know, Maura, you *can* leave Stevie in the room. I swear we won't take off our clothes and get it started immediately.'

'I didn't think you would.' Maura was indignant.

She had brought chicken broth for two days to a shivering Kit, without a word of remonstration about the strange way the night had ended. She had cleaned the mud off the red dress, waiting until it dried so that she could brush it properly.

She had been uneasy when Stevie Sullivan called so often to see the patient. She had found excuse after excuse to come back into the room. Kit reached out and held her hand. 'Maura, of course that's what you think. Hasn't Stevie been known for it with everyone in the county?'

'Well,' Maura reddened.

'But we've had plenty of places far more discreet and secluded than this, and if I didn't then, I'm unlikely to succumb in my own house. Come on, isn't that true?'

'I don't want you to get hurt.'

'I won't, I swear.'

Maura put her hand on Kit's forehead. 'I was given my orders by Peter to keep your temperature down. I think it's normal, but Stevie Sullivan's not going to be much of a help in that department.'

'I'd be worse without him, Maura.' Kit spoke as an equal.

Maura felt touched by this. 'I'll talk to your father.'

'He wouldn't understand unless you said it properly. I mean, I couldn't say to Father that Stevie and I haven't done it yet, and won't start under this roof.'

'I'll try to explain the situation a bit more diplomatically,' Maura said.

Nobody had asked Kit about her strange upset. Even Dr Kelly had said that it wasn't important. The story that the stupid girl from Dublin had told must have reminded Kit of the night her own mother disappeared. Nobody had told Dr Kelly that it was his own daughter Clio who had brought the whole thing to a head.

She lay there when there was nobody in with her, her hands gripping the sheets, her brain racing. It *must* have been Lena. Who else would have come and watched? She must have seen her son in the summer-house with Anna Kelly. She must have seen her daughter locked in Stevie's arms as they stood on the grass in the moonlight. She may have seen Maura Hayes wearing her little fur cape.

She saw a town lit up with life and banners and balloons and flowers. A town which had been grey and oppressive when she lived here. She knew that among the revellers were the O'Connor boys, young brothers of the girl that Louis would marry. A crowd of nearly two hundred people having a wonderful time while her own heart was broken. Standing on the edge of a place that believed her dead.

Now Kit was a prisoner here. She had caught a chill and she was ordered to stay in bed. There was never a time when people would leave the house, a time when she could ring Ivy to know had Lena returned. Ivy would know. But how could she get to talk to her?

Emmet sat on her bed. 'Are you all right, Kit? Tell me the truth.'

'Yes, I am. Didn't the dance go so well?'

'But afterwards?'

'Afterwards I got upset, I got a fright. I was all nervous and tied up inside and I had had nothing to eat with the fuss of it all.'

'You were wonderful . . . it all worked so well.'

'Yes.'

'I'll never be able to thank you.'

'I know a way,' she said.

411

'What? I'll do anything.'

She looked at him, his face eager to help, foolishly happy in love or what he thought of as the love of that dreadful Anna Kelly. In many ways he was still a child.

She just couldn't ask him to ring Ivy. She couldn't tell him everything. That his mother was alive, that she had come to look at them all, that she had run away again, run again towards the lake.

Clio came to visit. 'I could have kicked myself. I'm so thoughtless, why did I mention people in lakes, ghosts. I'm just so thick,' she said.

'No, it doesn't matter. I was nervous, I'd had three drinks, no food ...' This would be her excuse.

'Will you ever forgive me?'

'Of course.'

'You must be very seriously sick if you say that. Normally you never forgive me.'

'Oh, I forgive you this time,' Kit smiled wanly.

'It was terrific, the dance, wasn't it?'

'You didn't get caught?' Kit asked.

'No, only by Anna. Who, by the way, asked me to come and spy out the lie of the land here ... She wants me to find out all I can about you and Stevie Sullivan.' Clio giggled as she spoke.

'And she asked you to do it diplomatically?'

'Yes, she said I was to be discreet.'

'Oh, but you are,' Kit agreed.

'I don't want to give that ghastly Anna one scrap of information. But this is for me ... this is for myself ... Kit, what in the name of God Almighty were you doing? Were you really drunk?'

'Yes, probably, a bit.'

'You never saw anything like it. You were wrapped around him. All night.'

'I know,' Kit remembered.

'Listen, it's not the end of the world. They'll forget it, eventually.'

'Oh, I don't think so,' Kit said.

'They will, they'll know it was just part of the madness of the night.'

'Not when they see me glued to him for the rest of my life they won't.'

Clio's eyes and mouth were round. 'Kit, you're crazy. Stevie Sullivan, of all the people in the world.'

'Yes, of all the people in the world.'

'No Kit, he has a girl everywhere. He doesn't care who they are, married or single, fat or thin, you know what he's like.'

'I do. I love him.'

'You're still fevered, that's what it is.'

'You asked me, you wanted to find out the lie of the land. Now you've found it out.'

'Why did you tell me this ...? It can't be for real.'

'Because you're my friend. You tell me you love Michael O'Connor and you've been to bed with him and that you love it. We're friends, we tell each other things.' Her voice sounded a bit hysterical, Kit realised this as she spoke.

'But loving Michael is different, it's . . . well, it's what you'd expect. You can't love the fellow in the garage who's slept with every maid in the parish.'

'His past isn't important,' Kit said loftily.

'Ah don't be ridiculous, it's not his past. Didn't you see Orla Reilly turn up at the dance looking like a mad woman just wanting more of it with Stevie?'

'Didn't *you* see him sending her home?'

'You're serious,' Clio said in shock.

'You're the one who always said I was unnatural because I didn't love anyone. Now I do and that's wrong too . . .'

'Look, I'm going home . . . you're not well enough for visitors.'

'Okay, and tell Anna what I told you, that I'm crazy about him, and I won't rest until I get him.'

'I'll tell her nothing of the sort, I'll say you were so pissed drunk you don't remember dancing with him.'

'I'll tell her different and that'll get you into trouble for doing your jobs so badly.'

'I'll ignore you, you're quite mad. I came down to ask was there anything I could do for you, post letters, get you messages . . . but now I think I should get you a psychiatrist.'

'Thanks, Clio. You're a real pal.'

Kit realised that though she had known Clio as long as she could remember, it was an odd friendship. If Clio was the last person on earth she wouldn't ask her to ring Ivy and give a simple message. She couldn't say, Clio please ring this woman in England and ask her is Lena all right. No questions, just do it. Clio would want every detail and the whole country would know every detail.

'Are you too tired? I won't stay long.'

'No Philip, it's fine. It's great to see you. Wasn't it the best dance in the world?'

'Oh yes. I'll never be able to thank you.'

'For what, Philip? For making an eejit of myself . . . I just got upset when they started talking about ghosts.'

'Oh that,' Philip said.

'Sure, what did you think I meant?' Kit looked at him long and hard. 'How are your parents?' she said eventually.

'Oh, throwing out a new wing here and a new wing there. They think it was all their idea, can't understand why I never saw the potential of the place.'

His face was different. There was less dog-like devotion there now. It was as if the dance had managed to convince him that there would be no future for them together.

She could trust him to the end of the earth. But could she trust him to ring Ivy for her?

When Stevie arrived she was sitting up flushed and eager. 'Leave the door open,' she whispered.

'Why?'

'I want them to know we're not at it like knives on the bed.'

'Why did you suggest that? I'm just about able to control myself, if I think it's out of the question. Don't even joke about it.' His smile was broad.

'And I want to ask you something.'

'Anything.'

'I have it written down. I want you to do something, to make a call, but no one is to hear you.'

'Where is it to?'

'To London.'

'Sure.'

'Would Mona listen in on the exchange, do you think?'

'Not to me, I have too many boring calls to Dagenham and Cowley and places like that.'

'Not when Maura's there.'

'Understood.'

'It's the most important thing in my whole life. Could you do it now?'

'Straight away.'

'I've written it down for you.'

'Right.'

'No, it's not just an ordinary message, wait till you go through it . . .'

'Only Ivy, not her husband Ernest. Say you're my boyfriend, and that I've been sick and can't get to a phone . . . say I think I saw Lena here in Lough Glass on New Year's Eve. I want to know if Ivy's heard from her since then.' Tears began to fall down Kit's cheeks.

Stevie took a handkerchief and wiped them away tenderly. 'Will she tell me?'

'She might be worried, but you could say I trust you to ask the question but that you don't know anything else. You don't know the full story.'

He nodded as if he understood. He was so dear to her, his long dark hair on the collar of his scarlet jersey. She knew he had washed and changed his shirt just to cross the road and visit her. That made her feel so touched she could have cried again.

'I'll be back soon,' he said. 'Drink your soup, it's going cold.'

'Thanks, Stevie.'

He had gone, he would do it, he had asked nothing. Kit closed her eyes. She was absolutely certain she had done the right thing.

*

'How did you get home?' Ivy asked, taking the small bag from Lena's hand and removing the wet coat from her shoulders.

'Home?' Lena's face was blank.

'Well, back here to London?'

'I came by boat and train. It was easier. No talking to people, no booking ... no giving your name. You just get on.' The voice was flat and dead.

'You came by boat and train from Brighton?'

'I wasn't in Brighton.'

'Yes you were, Lena. I rang you there.'

'Oh then? Yes, that's right.'

'So where were you since?'

'Ireland.'

'Ireland?'

'Lough Glass. I went to see them.'

'I don't believe you.'

'Yes.'

'What did they say?'

'They didn't see me.'

'They threw you out?'

'No, they didn't know I was there.'

'Look, Lena, could I ask you have you had anything to eat ... ?'

'I don't know.'

'Suppose I were to make you something now ... what would you like? I won't offer you turkey ...'

'I don't mind, I haven't had any turkey this year.' A very wan little smile, but it was better than nothing.

'Well, soup and a turkey sandwich?'

'A very small one, Ivy.'

The phone rang. 'Wouldn't you know,' Ivy said. 'The operator said it was a call from Ireland.'

'Kit,' Lena leaped up. 'Give it to me.'

'No, we don't know ...' Ivy tried to take the phone back.

'Hello,' a man's voice said. 'Could I speak to Ivy please? This is Stevie Sullivan, I'm Kit McMahon's boyfriend.'

'This is Ivy,' Lena said.

'Well, it's about Lena. Kit wants to know is Lena all right? Has she phoned you?'

'Why isn't she phoning herself?' Lena wanted to know.

'She's sick and she's in bed.'

'Is she bad, too bad to phone?'

'No, I think it's a kind of secret and she's not meant to be heard phoning from home.'

'What do you mean you *think*? You must know if you're phoning. You must know everything.'

'Ivy,' the man said. 'I'm Kit's friend, she asked me to do this for her. She's distraught over someone called Lena. I *don't* know, truthfully I don't. But I want to go back across the street now and tell her if Lena's all right. Is she?'

'Yes,' Lena said slowly. 'Tell her she is.'

'Excuse me, but could I give her just a bit more information than that. I don't want to know who Lena is, but Kit was very ill and distressed the other night and she kept calling for Lena. I don't know what it is, but it's important.'

'Yes,' Lena said in a flat voice. 'It *is* important.'

'So?' he waited.

'So if you could say that Lena got home fine, by boat and train and that ... and that she's fine now and will write soon, a long long letter.'

'She's very upset, is there anything you could say that would sort of prove I've spoken to you?' He was going to do this right, he wouldn't go back to Kit unless he had a message to convince her.

Lena paused for a moment.

'You could tell her ... I suppose you could tell her that the hotel and the whole dance was a credit to her, that nobody could have believed the Central Hotel could look so well.'

'And that would prove that I talked to you?'

'Yes, it would, I think.' There was another pause before Lena spoke. 'You really don't know what it's about?' Lena asked.

'No.'

'Thank you,' she said.

'Thank you too, Ivy,' he said and hung up.

He ran across the road to tell Kit. He repeated the message word by word. When he told her about the praise for the Central Hotel she looked at him with two eyes as big as dinner plates.

'Say it again.'

He did.

'You weren't talking to Ivy. You were talking to Lena.'

She burst into tears.

Ivy helped Lena back to the table. 'Well now ... wasn't that timing? Suppose he had rung half an hour ago, I wouldn't have had anything to tell him.'

'Oh God,' Lena said.

'What do you mean?'

'She's confiding in him. She'll tell him and then she'll be in his power for ever.'

'What do you mean?'

'Stevie Sullivan will know her secret. He'll have total power over her from now on. He'll make her do whatever he wants with her. And however badly he treats her she'll have to put up with it, because she can never escape. He knows her secret, he'll always be able to hold that over her.'

'Why do you hate him so much?'

'I saw him, Ivy. I was as near to them as I am to you. I saw them kissing, I saw her eyes as she looked at him ...'

'She's going to fall in love ... you don't want her to be a nun?'

'No, but I saw him, Ivy.'

'And what's wrong?'

'He was Louis all over again. He could have been Louis' son. Or his younger brother. She's going to do what I did. Look at the legacy I've given the child. To love someone who's going to break your heart.'

'Jim, there's a letter from Lena,' said Jessie.

'Oh, thank God. I thought she'd abandoned us totally. What does she say?'

'That she's suffering from stress and her nerves, and that the doctor says it's overwork. And advised her to take some weeks off. She says she'll be back at the end of January.'

'Well, that's a relief that she goes to a doctor anyway.'

'And she does work too hard,' Jessie said.

'We've tried to stop her, get her to take time off.' Jim had, many times.

'She says she might go to Ireland for a while.' Jessie was studying the letter.

'That would be good. It's more restful over there. That's where they're from so they probably have friends and family.'

'She doesn't say anything about him.'

'Well, he'll probably go too.'

'She just says I all the time ... there's no We mentioned at all.'

Clio was having lunch with Michael O'Connor's family. They seemed to be very taken with her, accepting her into their number.

'You *will* come to Mary Paula's wedding?' Michael's mother asked Clio.

'Yes, I'd love to, Mrs O'Connor.' Things were going very well since New Year. Huge praise had been lavished on the festivities at the CHL, as it was now known between them all. The Central Hotel Lough Glass had done a great job.

Fingers O'Connor had been interested in every detail. 'And how did your stepmother enjoy the dance? Maura Hayes?'

'She's my aunt, actually,' Clio said.

'She's Kit's stepmother,' Kevin O'Connor said.

'And Kit is ... ?'

'Kit's the one I used to fancy,' Kevin explained helpfully.

'Well, how is she?' Fingers was persistent.

'I think she's losing her marbles actually. She's involved with the local rake.'

'Maura Hayes?' cried Fingers in disbelief.

'No, Kit,' they all said.

Fingers was going to get no more information about that nice plump woman he had always had such hopes of having a dalliance with.

Kit was back in Dublin. By an unspoken agreement Stevie Sullivan was not mentioned when she met Clio.

'Tell me about Mary Paula's wedding. Is it going to be a big one?'

'No, dead quiet.'

'That doesn't sound like the O'Connors.'

'Apparently the lovely Louis hasn't any family ... or any fit to field at a wedding.'

Clio sounded so snobby Kit hated her for a moment. Then she remembered who she really hated. 'So how are they going to do it then?'

'Not one of their own hotels. Marriage in University Church and sixteen people to lunch in a private room in the Russell. Just along St Stephen's Green.'

'The Russell! Lord, how posh.'

'I know. I don't know what I'm going to wear. You wouldn't tell me where you keep getting these gorgeous outfits.'

'You want to wear an off-the-shoulder scarlet evening dress to a lunch in the Russell?'

'Oh all right. I'll never know. There's so much I'll never know about you, Kit.'

'And me about you. Aren't we women of mystery?'

'You look very pale. Are you better from whatever it was?'

'Yes, I'm just a bit tired.' In fact she was awake all night waiting for the letter that Lena had promised to send. A letter explaining everything. But which hadn't arrived yet.

'Aunt Maura, it's Clio. Do you remember that lovely little fur cape you wore at the dance?'

'Hello, Clio. How nice to hear from you. All the way from Dublin.'

'Yes. Yes, well I can't talk long. But I was going to ask you a great favour.'

'What's that?'

'I was wondering would you lend it to me for a wedding I'm going to. I really want to look terrific and I think it would be smashing over my cream-coloured suit.'

'You're very young for furs, Clio. They're really for older women like me.'

'I know what you mean, but your one was particularly nice. It was really more suitable for a younger person altogether.'

'Oh, really,' Maura said.

Clio tried to retrieve it. 'What I meant was it looked so smart on you.'

'Good, I'm glad you liked it.'

'So I was wondering ...' Maura let the pause rest between them. 'I was wondering if you'd lend it to me. I'd be *so* careful of it ...'

'No, I'm sorry.' Maura's voice was cool. 'I'd love to be able to help, but that's a very special gift and I don't want to leave it out of my hands.'

Stevie came to Dublin four nights a week, and on every one of those nights he and Kit went out together. They agreed that they would meet out. The temptations of the bedroom, the quiet little bedsit where no one would notice who came into the building and who left, had too many dangers.

Stevie wanted to be true to his promise. If staying with Kit meant staying out of bed with her he said that was the deal; he wanted to be with her.

They sat in chip shops and held hands. They took the bus to Dun Laoghaire and walked along the pier in the wind and rain. They went to the pictures in the big cinemas in O'Connell Street. They met no other people. They didn't need anyone.

And who would they meet? Philip, whose face would break both their hearts. Clio, who thought that Kit was throwing her life away. Frankie, who was so wrapped up in Kevin O'Connor that she had time for no one else.

But they never tired of talking and touching and laughing. If anyone had asked her what they talked about, Kit thought one night, she couldn't tell. The time had flown, but she didn't know what they had spoken of. They didn't talk about his past. Or his wish to love her in a different way. As they never mentioned the woman that he had spoken to that day on the phone. The woman who remained a secret that he never wanted to know. One day Kit would tell him it was her mother, but not yet.

> My dearest Kit,
> I have tried so many times. There's a wastepaper basket full of pages torn up, screwed into little balls. I think I had a sort of breakdown. That's all I can say. I hope it's over. But it won't be over really until Louis marries. It's on 26 January in Dublin. When it's all over and done with then I think I'll be back to normal again. Please believe me, Kit. Forgive me in this as you have in so many other things. Tell me you are well and strong. That you are back at work.
> I talked to Stevie. He thought it was Ivy but you know it wasn't. He sounded very concerned about you. As if he loved you a lot. I'm saying this because I know you want to hear it. And also because I think it's true. This doesn't mean it's all for the best. I love you so much Kit. Whatever happens remember that.
> Your loving mother,
> Lena

Kit was very worried. Lena had used the word mother again in a letter. Did she really have a breakdown? What was her warning about Stevie? And most of all why was she warning her to remember that Lena loved her whatever happened? What could happen that hadn't happened already?

'Do you know what I'd *love* you to do?'

'No, I dread to think.' Kit said.

Clio's eyes were too bright. 'Could you pinch Maura's cape for me to wear, she'll not notice it's gone. I'd pay your fare down to take it back after the wedding.'

'Are you out of your mind?' Kit asked.

'That's my line to you. You're the one who's mad, not me. You're the one whose name is up with Stevie Sullivan all over the place. My mother was asking me what you were up to.'

'I don't give a damn what your mother thinks, asks, or says.'

'You've been saying that as long as I remember,' Clio said.

'I must have had some reason. You always quote her as if she knows everything and the rest of us know nothing.'

'Why are we fighting?' Clio asked.

'Because you were very rude and hurtful to me, as you almost always are.'

'I'm sorry.'

'No you're not, you just want Maura's cape.'

'For a loan. Look at the way we lend each other everything, shoes, bags, lipsticks . . .'

'But those were ours, not someone else's.'

'She won't know.'

Kit paused. Imagine the irony that she was being asked to lend someone Lena's cape for Louis' wedding. Maybe Louis had given that cape to Mother. Years and years ago. Father didn't remember buying it. You'd remember buying a fur coat, for heaven's sake.

Should she let Clio wear it? Startle Louis at his wedding with the memory of the gift he had given to Lena. But men were so hopeless. They remembered nothing. Suppose he remembered it, he'd just think Clio had another one like it. Clio watched her during the pause. It was as if Kit was deliberating. Deciding whether to give it or not.

'No,' Kit said eventually. 'Sorry for all the silly fighting and everything, but it's just not possible.'

'I wish the bloody wedding was over,' Clio said. 'Everyone's very tense about it. Except the bridegroom apparently. He's invited four people, and he's as happy as Larry. He's a real smasher, by the way, for an old man.'

'When did you meet him?'

'Oh he's here. They were having drinks at Michael's father's the other night. He holds your hand in a way that you think if things were different he might fancy you. Oh, and she's definitely preggers. You'd know by the way she stands.'

'Would we go to the North, you and I, next weekend?' Stevie asked her.

'No,' Kit said. 'I have to be in Dublin.'

'What for? I thought you'd like a nice drive. I've got a business meeting that will take about twenty-five minutes and then we could go and see a banned movie . . .'

'To drive me mad with lust . . . ?'

'No, just for fun, and we might drive up the Antrim Coast Road. It's meant to be gorgeous, like Kerry.'

'But we'd never do all that in a day.'

'We could stay the night. In separate rooms. Hand on heart, I swear.'

'No I can't Stevie, not this Saturday. I want to stay in Dublin really.'

'Why?'

'I'll tell you,' she said. 'I want to go to the church and watch Michael O'Connor's sister getting married to this man Louis Gray.'

Stevie looked at her. 'I was about to say what on earth for . . . but I won't ask you.'

'Thank you,' she said.

'But I am going to volunteer that if you're not going to come with me to the North, I'll be back that evening and maybe we'll go out.'

'I hope so.' Her face was serious.

'So will we?'

'Could you call round to the flat? If I'm there I'm there.'

'That's not much to drag a man a hundred and eighty miles back over long dark roads from the North on a cold January night,' he said.

'It's just that ... well it's just that I'm worried about something. I'm afraid something might go wrong.'

'Would you like me to stay with you, be here just in case?'

She was tempted for a moment. But eventually she decided against it. This trip to the North might be the beginning of big business. And anyway she was probably mad. Lena couldn't really be thinking of coming to Louis' wedding.

Louis Gray felt his years. He had spent too many evenings with the young members of the O'Connor clan trying to prove himself a satisfactory brother-in-law. Their capacity for pints was endless. His turn to buy came up with startling speed. Mary Paula had severe morning sickness and was in no mood to console him. He had to be particularly consolatory to her.

Which was difficult since he was staying in one of the O'Connor hotels and she was in her father and mother's house. He spent a lot of his time familiarising himself with the regime of the business he was about to join.

The staff were extremely respectful but Louis knew that this was because he was the prospective son-in-law of the chairman, and the heir apparent. These were not waiters, porters, desk clerks who would lavish such attention on the general public.

He found Fingers O'Connor, his future father-in-law, a difficult man, his wife a tiresome fusspot. There were many aspects of these crowded days which he found confusing. Like Mary Paula's brothers, two loutish lads; they seemed to be deeply involved in the affairs of Lough Glass of all places. They had hurried home from London in order to attend some function there in something called the CHL.

On Louis' many previous secret visits to Lough Glass there had been no such hotel, only a rundown flyblown place that you would be afraid to go into. But the O'Connor boys were saying that its Georgian frontage and old style charm might be the very thing that visitors to Ireland needed and looked for, rather than modern, purpose-built blocks. It sounded utterly right to Louis, who couldn't of course agree with this since his future was tied up in a very plain functional modern hotel block, the management of which was going to be his wedding present from Fingers O'Connor.

Louis had looked up old acquaintances in Dublin. He was always able to parry questions about himself, usually he used a rueful laugh. 'Ah, you don't want to be hearing all the mistakes I made, tell me about you now. Things going well?'

He had found a best man with no trouble. A man he knew in the retail business years ago. Presentable and unimaginative. Harry Nolan – a man who would think it reasonable that Louis Gray return to Ireland because he had managed to seduce the twenty-eight-year-old daughter of a wealthy hotelier and get a key management contract as a reward for making an honest woman of her.

Harry had many social skills, and like Louis was a better listener than talker. He was married but explained to Louis that his wife would not be a social addition to the scene so let the ceremony pass without involving her.

Ireland had changed, Harry assured his friend Louis. Business was business, people took chances where they could. Look at them both. They had been selling ladies' underwear once, now Louis was made, a hotelier of the future, Harry himself was the manager of a very important Grafton Street store and a man who moved in society.

Harry had been a perfect choice. The night before the wedding Louis and Harry had two drinks. Neither of them felt they could be confident of looking well after a batter, so the night was a moderate one.

Louis looked out over the Dublin roofs from his hotel room. He wished he could stop thinking about Lena, and where she was tonight. She had assured him she understood. Why was it so disturbing that she hadn't been seen at work or at home since?

He made one more call to Ivy. He disguised his voice and changed his name but he always felt she saw through him.

'I was wondering where Mrs Gray is? I've made many attempts to contact her at work,' he said.

'She's gone away,' Ivy's sepulchral voice replied. 'Nobody knows where or why. So I'm afraid I cannot help you.'

It was cold but fine. There was a thin winter sunlight when Harry Nolan and Louis Gray arrived at University Church in St Stephen's Green. The Saturday traffic passed by, people craning out of buses to see who was assembling at the smart church where wealthier people married.

'An hour from now the job will be done and we'll be in the Russell getting stuck into the gins and tonics,' said Harry.

Louis peered into the distance. He was jittery today. Everything seemed to have a resonance of some kind. It turned out that Mary Paula's brother Michael had every intention of marrying that pretty Clio, the doctor's daughter from Lough Glass. Someone that Lena probably knew well. He reminded himself that they all thought Helen McMahon was dead. Nobody would ever believe him if it were brought up that he had lived with her for so many years.

Then, as he stood there in the sunlight, he saw a woman across the road, a woman in dark glasses who reminded him so much of Lena that it made him feel weak.

'I don't suppose you brought any kind of sustenance,' he asked Harry.

'Yes, hip flask of brandy. Let's get inside the vestry before you attack it,' Harry said.

Fingers O'Connor helped his daughter out of the large limousine. The others had gone into the church ahead. 'You look lovely, Mary Paula,' he said. 'I hope he'll be good to you.'

'He's what I want, Daddy,' she said.

'Well then.' He sounded not entirely convinced.

'I don't look fat, do I?'

'No, of course you don't. Look at the people all admiring you.' A small crowd of passers by had stopped to smile at the bride. Some of them even went into the back of the church to watch the ceremony from a discreet distance.

Kit had her head in her hands as if she were praying. She wore a belted raincoat and a check headscarf. She was sure that none of the wedding party would see her. They were so far behind the action . . . those who had come to look on. But she wasn't praying, she was peering through her fingers. There were elderly people with their rosary beads talking silently but earnestly to God and His mother. There were a couple of students who were obviously killing time before lunch in Grafton Street. There were a couple of down and outs, a man in a sacking coat and a woman with five carrier bags.

She couldn't see Lena.

And then she saw a figure beside a confession box. A woman in a long dark woollen skirt, and a very smart military-style jacket. She had been wearing a headscarf and dark glasses, but she removed these and Kit saw her putting on a smart hat, a hat with a feather, a hat that had cost more than any headgear at this stylish but small wedding. The woman straightened herself up and prepared to join the body of the guests. She was going to sit on the groom's side.

Lena had done what Kit had hoped and prayed she would not do. She had come to Dublin and was going to break up Louis Gray's marriage day. She was going to lose anything she had left. Her dignity, her anonymity and possibly her freedom. She might well be about to attack the groom or the bride. Lena's eyes were wild, Kit saw. She could not be held responsible for what she did. She might spend the night and a great deal of life in prison.

The bride had gone up the church with her father and had been handed over to Louis, who stood there beaming.

Kit had only seen him once, but she remembered his smile. She even remembered how Clio had said that Louis Gray made you feel special. He made you feel that if things were different he might fancy you. She saw him there in front of everyone, like a handsome actor about to say his lines, and she realised that is all he had ever been and would ever be. Her wonderful mother could not, must not, lose anything over anyone as worthless as this.

Kit almost threw herself from one side of the church to the other. Nobody saw them, they were far too far behind the main action for anyone except the regular rosary sayers or scattered minds to notice them. She caught Lena's arm before Lena had time to get more than a few steps up the aisle.

'What!' Lena wheeled on her.

'Take me with you,' Kit hissed.

'Get out of here,' Lena said.

'Whatever you do, Mother, I'm going with you,' Kit said. 'If you drag yourself down by this you'll drag me too.'

'Kit, leave me, leave me. This has nothing to do with you.' They struggled in the shadowy part of the church, unnoticed by the congregation near the altar rails who had their backs to them.

'I mean it,' Kit said. 'If you have a knife or a gun I'm going with you, they can arrest me too.'

'Don't be ridiculous, I haven't anything like that.'

'Well, whatever trouble you're going to make I'll stand there too.' By this stage the sacristan and two of the altar boys had noticed some fracas and strained to look, but none of the guests turned. 'Believe me, I mean it,' Kit said.

'What are you doing to your life?' Lena said, her eyes wild with panic.

'I'm doing nothing to it, you're the one destroying it,' Kit said. It was a moment that went on for ever. Kit felt the arm loosen, the resolve go. 'Come out with me, come now.' Lena stood there. 'Mother, come with me.'

'Don't call me that,' Lena said.

Kit felt she was breathing normally. Things were back as they were. If Lena was prepared to retreat into the cover story again the crisis might be over.

Kit propelled her mother out into the open where it was crisp and cold. A wind blew along the street raising little bits of litter from the gutters. Soon the bride and groom would come out and people would throw confetti. They must be long gone by then.

Lena said nothing. Not a word.

'Are you tired, Lena?' Kit asked her.

'So tired I could lie down here on the road and sleep.'

'Come on, we'll go to the corner, there are taxis over there on a rank.'

Lena didn't ask where the taxi would take them. As they turned the corner a woman cried, 'Kit.' They both turned to see a smart woman in a swagger coat. It was Rita. Kit and Rita hugged each other. 'This is a friend of mine, Lena Gray, from England.'

'How do you do,' Rita said.

'Hello Rita.' There was too much warmth and pleasure in Lena's voice.

Rita's head snapped up to look at her again as if she recognised the greeting.

'Lena's been a great friend of mine and given me lots of good advice. She runs an employment agency,' Kit said desperately.

Rita was calm. 'Of course, and what a good business to be in these days. Young people need all the advice they can get. You must get a lot of satisfaction in your work.'

Lena said nothing.

'We've got to rush now,' Kit said.

'Great to see you, Kit.' Her eyes stayed long on Lena. 'And you too, Mrs ... Mrs Gray,' she said.

'She knew,' Lena said when they were around the corner.

'Of course she didn't,' said Kit. 'But let's get you away really quickly in case we meet anyone else. It could be Mona Fitz's day for a shopping excursion.'

The first taxi man looked at them expectantly. 'Where to, ladies?' he asked.

Lena looked blank. 'Will we go first and collect your case?' Kit asked. 'Case?'

'Suitcase, luggage, wherever you left it.' Kit tried to sound casual.

'I have no luggage,' Lena said.

Kit shivered. She might never know what her mother had intended to do at the wedding of Mary Paula O'Connor and Louis Gray. Lena had come to Dublin with no possessions, no plans of where she would stay at night. It was as if she had not expected to be a free agent by the time night fell.

'Will you come home and stay in my flat, rest now and stay the night?' Kit said. 'I've always wanted to have you to stay. And there's a nightie for you and a hot water bottle...'

'And will we fit in the bed?'

'I'll sleep on cushions on the floor.' There was a pause. 'I'd love you to come, Lena.' Another pause. 'I don't ask for much,' Kit said.

'It's very true, you don't,' Lena said.

Kit gave the taximan her address.

They climbed the stairs slowly. Lena said nothing when Kit opened the door. 'Well, say you like it. Say it's nice ... it's got character...' Kit was desperate. 'Say it's got possibilities even.'

Lena smiled at her. 'I've dreamed so often what this place would be like. I thought the window was on the other side,' she said.

'And what did you dream you might be offered for lunch when you came here?' Kit asked.

Lena saw on the little table beside the gas ring that there were four tomatoes and a loaf of bread.

'In my dreams I always had tomato sandwiches and tea,' she said.

After that it was all right. They talked to each other as friends.

And then finally, worn out, Lena went to sleep in the little single bed. It was only four o'clock in the afternoon. But Kit felt her mother might not have slept for many a night before now. Kit sat in a chair and looked out the window. She felt very empty. She wished that Stevie would come. The darkness came but she didn't put on a light.

About eight o'clock she saw Stevie's car. He paused to look up at her window. He had never been in this room. What a different way for him to see it from the way she had planned. With her mother lying in her bed.

She tiptoed to the door and beckoned him in. She pulled another chair to the window, a finger on her lips.

'She needs her sleep, don't wake her.' she said. 'It's Lena.'

'I know.'

They sat in silence. He had brought her a box of chocolate sweets that were only on sale north of the border. Things always seemed more exotic when you couldn't get them here. He stroked her hand.

'Was the trip okay?' she asked.

'Tiring,' he said. 'And the wedding?'

'Uneventful,' she said.

'That's what you wanted, wasn't it?' He looked at her, she could see his face in the street light.

She nodded. 'I'll tell you some time. I swear.'

'So do you want me to go now?' he asked.

Never had she seen such disappointment on a face. He had driven in the cold and rain all the way back and she was going to ask him to leave because of Lena, an unexplained woman in the bed.

'No, I'll write her a note, tell her we've gone to the Chinese, if that suits you?'

'I was thinking about sweet and sour pork since Drogheda,' he said.

'If she wakens up she might join us. But she'll know I'm coming back . . .'

'Can you see to write?' He stroked her hair as she bent over the table to write the note.

> Lena, you were sleeping so peacefully I didn't want to wake you. It's eight-fifteen now, Stevie and I have gone to the Chinese restaurant. I've left its little card to show you where it is. Please come and join us there. If not, I'll be back by midnight and will sleep on the cushions . . . but I truly, truly would love you to come and follow us there.
>
> Love always,
>
> Kit

Then they left the room on tip toe, pulling the door behind them.

Lena sat up when they were gone. She read the note and stood at the window watching them walk along the road, arms draped around each other. This boy did care for Kit, and cared a great deal. She agreed that he knew nothing of her circumstances, only that she was an unexplained friend, Lena from London.

And she also felt that he had every characteristic of Louis Gray. When he loved he would mean it at the time. But the time would not last very long in any given place. If only she could protect her girl from this.

Kit came back alone. She read the note.

> I did wake up, but forgive me, I didn't have the energy to come out and join you. I had some biscuits here and now I'm going back to sleep. Bless you dearest Kit, and see you in the morning.

Kit lay on the cushion and rugs on the floor. She felt certain that her mother's breathing was too even somehow. It didn't sound like the breath of a woman getting her first deep sleep in weeks.

'Let me take you round Dublin,' Kit offered.

'No, I'd better go back to London. The holiday is over.'

Kit hated the way she grimaced when she said the word holiday. She decided she would grasp it. 'Not much of a holiday, Brighton on your own, two quick visits here.'

'No, well. I'll organise it better another time.'

'I wish you'd meet Stevie. I want you to.'

'No.'

'You think he's unreliable.'

'He was only a child when I left, I rely on you for a definition of how he is.'

'I've told you everything about him, every single thing . . . if you're going to get so buttoned up on me and purse-lipped I'll have to stop telling you things.'

'I think you're just on the verge of stopping telling me things about him.'

'You mean that we're going to be lovers?'

'Believe me, I'm not criticising,' Lena said.

'So why don't you approve?'

'I think he'll break your heart.'

'So? It'll mend again.'

'If they're badly broken they don't.'

'Lena, I know you see . . . well, let's say some similarities . . .'

'If you see them then is it possible they might be there?'

'No, it's not.' Kit's chin stuck out defensively.

Lena pleaded with her. 'I know what's going through your head . . . you're going to say if only Lena had met Stevie a few months ago . . . suppose all this had happened when Louis was around . . . then she would have approved, understood, said you must follow your star.'

'And so you would,' Kit cried.

'I might not. I told *you* that it had been worth it. I mean, what would have been the point of anything if I hadn't believed I did the right thing? It would have meant I messed everyone's lives up for nothing, which is what I did. Every one, all because of me.'

'No, that's not so.' Kit was gentle.

'It is. I look around me and I see it.'

'But Father's all right, and Maura. And Emmet is happy, and I'm in love. And you and Louis . . . well, what you had was very bright, you told me that once . . . that it was better to burn brightly . . . it was very good . . .'

Lena looked very lost. 'In a way you're saying I didn't mess up people's lives, that everyone survived fine, including Louis. Only my own. I destroyed my own as surely as if I had drowned that day.'

'I certainly did *not* say that. Stop putting words into my mouth . . . I'm just saying don't feel so guilty. You've always been good for people, helping them, giving . . . not destructive.'

'If you hadn't been there . . .'

Kit would not allow them down this road. 'Tell me, what did you love most about Louis?'

'His face lighting up to see me, it was as if someone had turned on a switch . . .'

It was a funny phrase, Kit thought, especially when she had seen through

Louis at his wedding ceremony, an actor reading lines. Of course he could turn on a switch. 'And what was worst about him?'

'The way he thought I believed his lies. It made us both so stupid.'

'And why do you think it didn't last? What you and he had?' She was gentle but probing. She felt Lena wanted to answer. To think it out.

'I don't know . . .' Lena said thoughtfully. 'You tell me what do you think it was.'

'Maybe it was about not having children. If you had ever been pregnant . . .'

'I was,' Lena said. 'I was more pregnant than Mary Paula O'Connor. That's why I left you and Emmet and Lough Glass and Ireland. Of course I was pregnant.'

'And what happened?' Kit asked.

'I lost the baby. I lost it all over the train from Brighton and all over Victoria Station and in Earl's Court. That's where our baby is. Louis' and my child.'

Kit held her hand. 'And could you not have . . . did you never try . . . ?'

'He didn't want a child. He didn't want a child until I was too old to have one, but by then he wanted one with someone else.' Her face was in a hard white line.

Kit McMahon felt more troubled than she had ever been in her life.

They didn't speak of what had brought her to Dublin. Of what she might have done if Kit had not rescued her and taken her away in the nick of time. There would be another day when that could be talked about.

Lena was getting stronger by the hour. She was like a plant that needed water. Something was giving her back energy and hope and purpose. She was rapidly becoming the old Lena, full of plans and moving quickly. She had run to a phone box and found the times of planes. She had telephoned Ivy. To say she'd be back that night. And Jessie Millar to say she'd be at work next day.

'I'll come to the airport with you,' Kit said.

'No, we could meet a dozen more people we know.'

'I don't care. I'm coming.'

'What about Stevie? Suppose he turns up here?'

'I'll leave a note on the door for him.'

Lena looked at her thoughtfully. 'He doesn't have a key?'

'You know he doesn't.'

'Yes, I only meant maybe he should have.'

'But I thought you said . . .'

'I know you love him.' For Lena it was simple. Love was something that happened, you had no control of it. It took over.

Kit was bewildered. 'But what about everything you told me of all that happened to you, and how you didn't want it to happen again.'

'It's too late.' Lena was matter of fact. 'The only thing you must learn from me is not to take the safe option. Not to run away and marry a good kind man just because he *is* good and kind. That's not the solution.'

Kit thought of Philip. 'I don't think I'd do that,' she said slowly.

'You mightn't now, but if you were lonely you might. And it would be very wrong. Well, you can see how much hurt and wrong came out of it.'

Kit went back to what she had said earlier. 'You think I should give Stevie a key to . . . here?'

'I think you should ask yourself why you are putting off something you want so much.' They looked at each other in amazement. 'The only mother in Ireland today taking this side in the age-old argument . . .' Lena said, and they collapsed in laughter. Whatever madness had taken Lena over seemed to have gone, or to have been replaced with a different one.

Stevie knocked at the door. 'I'll only stay a moment,' he said.

'Come in and meet Lena . . .' Kit opened the door.

'How do you do.' She shook his hand firmly. 'I'm very sorry for messing all your plans up this weekend. Kit has been very good to me.'

'No, heaven, no.' His smile was warm. He was not awkward or ill at ease, which was remarkable, Lena thought, when he was in the middle of a situation he didn't even begin to understand.

'Anyway, the good news is that I'm off to the airport now. I'm trying to persuade Kit not to come . . . so you're the ideal excuse. Perhaps we could all walk down to Busaras where I could catch the airport bus.'

Before Kit could speak Stevie said: 'I have a car at the door. It would be my pleasure to drive you out there and I'll sort of circle a bit while you say goodbye.'

Lena accepted. Stevie looked around for her suitcase but didn't seem put out when he realised there wasn't one. Lena sat in the front of the car and Kit leaned on the back of the seat between them.

She pointed out landmarks. 'I can't remember – was Liberty Hall there in your time?'

'Not in my time as such.'

'Look, do you see this house on the corner? Frankie's grandfather lives there. He's as rich as anything and all the family keep calling on him and asking about his health. Imagine!'

'Does Frankie call on him?' Lena enquired.

'No, she's got more sense.'

'He'll probably leave her everything just to spite them,' Stevie said.

Lena looked at him with interest. Louis would have said that there was no harm in being nice to the old fellow, and you never knew the day nor the hour. She would have thought that Stevie Sullivan would have gone that route also.

He talked about things that could cause no frisson. He asked her nothing about where she had come from or why she was there. Instead he told her about planes and how he'd love to fly one. It must be great to soar up there and swoop and have miles of sky at your disposal, not just a straight road.

He had never been on a plane as it turned out. 'Real country hick, Lena,' he said with a grin. It was hard to believe that the son of dreary Kathleen Sullivan and her insane drunken husband could turn out like this. Handsome and confident, but not pushy.

Her fingers tightened on her handbag. She knew that her daughter had lost her soul to this man. Nothing she could say in terms of warning would do any good. All she could do now was hope and pray.

He was as good as his word about circling around. He said his goodbyes as he dropped her off. 'Come back and see us sometime,' he said, all warmth and invitation.

Lena responded in the same way. 'Or you two come over and see me. At least it would get you on a plane.'

Kit looked at her in delight. Stevie had been accepted. She could see that. Lena really did like him. She was overjoyed. As soon as he was out of hearing she clutched Lena's arm. 'I *knew* you'd like him,' she said excitedly.

'Of course I do. Who wouldn't like him?' Lena said.

She got out her wallet and paid for her ticket. She must have bought no return flight. What had she intended to do in Ireland, or had she not thought at all? She looked perfectly well now.

Kit walked to the departure gate with her.

'Soon, very soon, you'll come?' Lena's eyes looked deep into hers.

'Yes, as soon as you're settled back and settled in again. Of course I'll come.'

'Thank you, Kit. Thank you for everything.'

Kit didn't know what she was being thanked for. She had no idea what she had prevented. She was too choked to say goodbye so she just clung on to Lena for a long time and then ran back to the exit.

In the car she blew her nose loudly. 'Now, that's better,' Stevie said approvingly, as if he were talking to a toddler.

'It was very kind of you to drive her out.'

'Nonsense.'

'And thanks too for not asking and everything. Some time I'll tell you, but it's too complicated.'

'Sure. Would you like to go up the mountains?'

'Where?'

'You know, out in the Wicklow Mountains. We could just go where you'd see no houses or people or anything, sort of empty your mind a bit.'

'That would be lovely.'

They sat companionably, saying nothing but feeling no need of chat until they were beyond Glendalough, up in the Wicklow Gap. Then they parked the car and walked in the cold clear air past the gorse bushes and over the springy turf and rocky crags.

Stevie was right, it was as if the whole population had left. There was nothing to look at except what had been there when the earth began, trees and mountains and a river.

Kit felt her mind emptying. She took deep long breaths. They sat on a great big rock like a shelf and looked down at the valley below.

'It's a very long story,' she began.

'She's your mother,' Stevie said.

*

Ivy was overjoyed to see her.

'Come upstairs at once and see your new wallpaper,' she said.

The room looked totally different. Pink and white stripes from ceiling down to floor. A little stool at the dressing table covered with matching material. The position of the bed had been changed slightly and there was a pink eiderdown with a trim of the striped fabric.

'It's beautiful, it's utterly gorgeous,' Lena cried.

She could see the hours of time and work invested in this by Ivy. She could never thank her. But she knew that for Ivy to see her well again was reward enough.

'At least it's different,' Ivy said gruffly.

'It's very different. It doesn't look like the same place.'

'That's what I hoped.' Ivy was grim.

'No, it's all right. I'm fine now, I promise.'

'What were you doing in Ireland then?' Ivy wanted to know.

'I just went and saw it happen, saw with my own eyes that he married someone else. Now it's over.'

'You went to the wedding?'

'Just in the church, not as a guest . . .' she laughed lightly.

'You amaze me,' Ivy said. 'And do you want to talk about it or about him, or is it better if we don't.'

'I think it's better not. That way I get on with my life.'

Ivy seemed pleased. 'I'm sure that's the right way,' she said. 'Now, I suppose this means you might be able to eat again. Because I've got some steaks for the three of us.'

'A big rare steak . . . that's exactly what I was hoping you'd have,' Lena said.

Ivy trotted happily downstairs to tell Ernest that Lena was cured.

'Ah, women get over these things,' he said with the air of a man who understood the world.

Lena stood alone in the room where she had lived with Louis. She would speak of him no more, she would talk of him to nobody. But most of all she would think about him as little as was humanly possible.

She had seen him marry another woman. He had gone from her life. She was glad she had seen that, and been to the wedding. It finalised everything somehow.

It was a bit of a blur how she had got there and what she had intended to do. But that didn't matter, she had been and seen it. She had been so close to Kit and seen how she loved Stevie. Once this had frightened her. But now she felt there was no point in trying to fight it. It was just inevitable.

At work they were so pleased to see Mrs Gray back. There had been a few problems, naturally they hadn't wanted to interrupt her on her sick leave, but it was great to see her back.

'The Christmas party wasn't the same without you,' they said.

'The Christmas party!' How long ago that seemed now. She had forgotten she hadn't been there. 'Oh, I'm sure you managed,' she said.

'Not all that well. There was no spirit in it somehow ... Did you have a nice Christmas or were you still poorly?'

'I was still poorly, but thank heavens I'm better now.' Her smile was bright, her air was busy and let's get down to work. 'I'll be having a meeting tomorrow, when I've caught up with everything ... I am so sorry for leaving you all in the lurch but these things happen ... so I'll want you to let me know by the end of today any areas in your control where you feel any anxiety.'

Millar's gave a collective sigh of relief. Mrs Gray was back, all was well.

'James?'

'Is that you, Lena?'

'Yes, I was wondering if you were free for lunch any day?'

'Any day is exactly when I'm free. Today, tomorrow, every day in the year.'

'Very gallant indeed, James. Could we say tomorrow, same place as last time, one o'clock?'

'I'm looking forward to it very much,' he said.

Lena went through the papers, she saw where opportunities had been missed, contracts lost, unsuitable people given too much time. The normal monthly search through papers and publications trawling for possibilities had been poorly done. Even the office did not look quite as smart as usual. They were only small things but she noticed them.

There were wastepaper baskets not fully emptied, rings from cups left on desks, calendars not changed, flower water left to gather a little scum on it. She would have to be very diplomatic about all these things, make it appear that the staff had noticed them rather than she herself.

And also, she must smarten herself up as well as the office. She went to the salon after work. There were no questions from Grace West. But she was owed an explanation.

'He married a young girl who was pregnant. Her brothers are friends of my daughter. That's what Louis did next,' she said.

'Married? *He* got a quick divorce didn't he?' Grace said.

'No need, not an official marriage between us.'

'I'm glad you have a daughter,' Grace said simply.

James Williams was waiting at the table.

'You look so well,' he said.

'I feel well now,' she said.

'And I was so worried about you, I tried to get in touch.'

'I know,' she said.

'But why didn't you return any of my calls?'

'I wasn't well then, but I am now. So here we are.' Her face was bright and cheerful.

'A glass of wine?' he suggested.

'Yes, I need it.'

'I fired Louis,' he said. 'Did you know?'

'No, I didn't know that. I thought he stayed there until last week.'

'No, I couldn't bear to look at him after what he did to you.'

She was perfectly composed and calm. 'I don't know what I should say, I suppose I should thank you because you did it on my behalf . . . but the reason I asked you to lunch was to tell you that Louis has gone now out of my life. I won't be talking about him, thinking about him, or referring back any more . . .'

'Good,' he said approvingly.

'Yes, I went four days ago . . . that's all it was, and watched him get married. It's all gone now.'

'It won't last, you know. He'll cheat on her too.'

'You mean very well, James. But it's no consolation or help to me to know how well rid of him I am. These things only come from within.'

'I think you're perfectly right,' he said. 'His name will not be spoken between us again, but . . .'

'Yes?'

'I hope we'll be able to speak of other things like perhaps your coming to the theatre with me or to see an art exhibition or just to go out anywhere.'

She looked at him thoughtfully. 'From time to time I would love to go out with you as any friend, but that would be it. I don't want to anticipate anything on your part but I've learned that it's better to, should there be any misunderstandings . . .'

'Indeed,' he murmured.

'I mean it, James. I've had two marriages as I call them, two long relationships. I haven't an intention in the world of getting involved again.'

'I quite understand . . .'

'Not even a casual involvement. So if you'd like to be my friend and that we could buy each other the occasional lunch . . .'

'And dinner?' he said.

'And theatre ticket.' She entered into the spirit of the thing.

'And one could always live in hope?' he said.

'But an intelligent man like you would know that to live in an unrealistic hope is a very foolish way to spend a life.' She spoke with a steely edge to her voice. As if she knew that only too well.

He raised the glass to her. 'To our friendship,' he said.

Ivy watched her like a hawk.

Often she dropped in on her landlady. They had enlarged the room by knocking down a wall. Now Ernest sat looking at the television a distance away, shielded by a big screen.

It was a screen that Lena had found for them, in a secondhand shop, she said. In fact it was an antique. It was exactly right for the room. It also meant she could sit and talk to Ivy undisturbed.

Sometimes she had coffee, often Ivy persuaded her to take a sandwich. She was looking better, Ivy said approvingly. Her skin was firm and young again, she had put on those few pounds that made her look less anxious, less drawn. Kit's letters still came to Ivy even though there was no need. It was as if she sensed that Ivy liked being postman.

Sometimes Lena read her little extracts.

> We went to see Sister Madeleine. She's exactly the same in many ways. She works in the kitchen and in the yard. She has a pigeon with a false leg that she made herself. She has a hare, a poor old hare that sleeps in a box all day and eats cornflakes. It got hit on the head running away from something apparently and doesn't know where it is.
>
> She was so pleased to see me. She didn't ask about you by name of course and not in front of Stevie. But she did want to know if everything was fine over in London, and I told her it was. It's as if she were always there. If I tell her about people like Tommy, people she liked, she sort of looks vaguely away as if they were people she dreamed about once.
>
> I wonder was she ever married. Remember I told you that tale she told Clio and myself years ago, and we kept it as such a secret? I asked Clio the other day what did she think. Clio said she'd forgotten it. I can't believe she's forgotten. It was the biggest secret we ever had when we were young. But then Clio has her own secrets and problems these days. This time she's almost definite that she's pregnant. And she's terrified to tell Michael.

'Isn't it wonderful that she can tell you all these things?' Ivy marvelled.

Lena agreed. No mother could talk like this to a daughter. But there was something, she wasn't sure what it was, something about Stevie, that Kit wasn't telling. But she wasn't going to worry. She would tell one day . . . if it was important.

'I'm going to throw myself on your mercy,' Clio said to Kit.

'Don't do that. You'll only regret it.' They were in Kit's flat. Clio had called unexpectedly.

'I need help desperately.'

'You're sure then, you've had a test?'

'Yes, I sent a sample of urine into Holles Street under a false name.'

'And you still haven't told Michael?'

'I can't, Kit. It's too much for his father and mother. Two shotgun weddings in a few months.'

'But they won't have to pay for your one, your mother and father will.'

'Jesus, I know. Why do you think I'm so afraid? I have to tell them too.'

'Well, get it over with as quick as possible. Tell Michael today and I'll go home with you to Lough Glass and help you tell your parents. Now, will that do?' Kit looked at Clio expecting to be thanked. She was being very generous. Clio had been nothing but dismissive and downright hostile about Stevie. Kit felt saintly to be returning such good for evil.

'No, that's not the favour I want.'

'What else can I do?' Kit asked.

'I want to get an abortion.'

'You're not serious?'

'It's the only way.'

'You must be mad. Don't you want to marry him? Don't you keep saying that from morning to night? Now you have to. He has to.'

'He mightn't.'

'Of course he will. Anyway, you can't think of the other.'

'Lots of people do. If we only knew where to go . . . I wanted you to ask around.'

'Well, I'm asking nothing of the sort. Get a hold of yourself, Clio. This is the opportunity of a lifetime.'

Clio was sobbing. 'You don't understand. You don't know how awful it's going to be. You don't know what it's like.'

Kit put her hand on Clio's shoulder. 'Remember when we were younger we used to count the good points about things . . .'

'Did we?'

'Yes. Now let's see what are the phrases. He's respectable, your parents can't go berserk altogether as if it were someone like Stevie Sullivan.'

'That's true,' Clio said sniffing.

'You love him and you think he loves you.'

'I think he does, yes.'

'His family can cope with shotgun weddings. They've been through it, they know the sky doesn't fall on you.'

'Yes, yes.'

'You can ask Maura to help you, intercede for you. She's terrific about heading off rows, I've watched her.'

'Would she? I get the feeling she's gone off me.'

'I'll ask her to,' Kit said.

'But suppose, suppose . . .'

'And Maura could suggest you live in her flat, it's a great place. Michael could buy it from her, she was thinking of selling it. It's got a garden, it would be nice for a baby.'

'Baby!' wailed Clio.

'That's what you're having,' Kit explained.

'And will you be my bridesmaid?' Clio asked. 'Suppose it all worked out?'

'Yes, yes, of course. Thank you,' Kit said soothingly.

'And it needn't be big. Just a few of us . . . we could have it in the Central. Just Michael's family to come down, Mary Paula and Louis and . . .'

Kit's blood went cold. Louis Gray couldn't come to Lough Glass. She must think very fast. 'I don't know if it's a good idea to have it at home. You know the way half the town will be offended if they're not asked.'

'But if it's small . . .'

'They'll still be offended, the doctor's daughter and we weren't asked . . . you know how they are . . .'

'But where else?'

'Do you remember the place Maura got married? That was nice . . . and she'd be flattered if you asked her to try and set that up.'

'Kit, you're very devious, you should have been an international spy,' Clio said in admiration.

The Central Hotel, Lough Glass got four more bookings as a direct result of the New Year's Eve dinner dance.

Philip began to panic. 'We can't have Christmas candles all over the place.'

'No, your parents are going to have to bite the bullet and get the place decorated. We can't disguise the walls for ever. And suppose you had to have a lunch, something the light of day might shine on . . . then they'd see what it's really like.'

'Will you help me tell them?' he pleaded.

'Why me?' Kit felt she was involved with too much on too many levels.

'Because you sound business-like and calm, and you don't sound all up in a heap like the rest of us,' he said.

'Okay.'

The huge refurbishment of the Central Hotel began almost at once.

Even if Dr Kelly and his wife had wanted to hold the reception there they would not have been able. They were greatly helped over the whole distressing business by Maura.

'She's been so good to Clio,' Lilian said over and over. 'And I always thought that there was a bit of friction between them of late.'

'Goes to show how wrong we are,' Peter Kelly said. He was surprised at how strongly he felt about the news of his daughter's pregnancy. And at how casually it was being taken by Michael O'Connor, the young man responsible, and by Clio herself.

They all seemed to think that because Maura was selling them her flat that everything was falling into place. There was no mention of all the illicit sex that had led to this. Dr Kelly came from the generation where there *was* no sexual activity until you married. How had everything changed in his own family without his being aware of it?

'I'm sure you knew, Daddy. You must have known I was pregnant,' Clio asked him.

'No, no. I assure you it came as a very great shock to me.'

'But doctors often know,' she persisted.

'Not this one.'

For no reason at all there came to his mind a memory, a memory of the night a long time ago when he had seen Helen McMahon and realised she was pregnant. And then she had thrown herself in the lake. At least the world had changed in some respects for the better he thought to himself, and patted his daughter's arm.

'I'll tell you about what you'll wear as the bridesmaid,' Clio said. 'I'm going to talk to Mary Paula about it tonight, and we'll choose what everyone will wear.'

'No, that's not the way round it at all. I'll tell you what I'm wearing as your bridesmaid,' Kit said.

'What?'

'I'm wearing a cream linen dress with a jacket to match and depending on what you want, I'll either wear a big picture hat or some concoction of flowers and ribbons in my hair. It's three-quarters length. I am not wearing an evening dress to parade up an icy cold church, and I'm not dressing up in fancy dress outfits for whatever colour scheme you and Mary Paula think up . . .'

'I, I don't believe you,' Clio gasped.

'You'd better believe me, that's what you're going to get, or else change your bridesmaid.'

'I might easily do that.'

'It's your privilege, Clio. And please understand me that I don't mind at all if you do. There'll be no falling out.' In many ways it would be marvellous if they could fall out. Then she wouldn't have to go to a family gathering and meet Louis. Mother's Louis. But a serious falling out would cloud the day for too many people.

Kit sighed.

'I don't know what you're sighing about,' Clio said. 'I'm the one putting up with all this. I'm the bride, for God's sake. People are meant to be nice to me.'

'I *am* nice to you,' Kit hissed at her. 'I told you that clown would marry you, I told you about Maura as a middleman, about her flat, about the hotel in Dublin. Jesus, Mary and Holy Saint Joseph, how much bloody nicer could I have been?'

Her violent outburst made them both laugh.

'You win,' said Clio. 'I'll tell Mary Paula I've a mad bridesmaid. Just another cross to bear.'

Would you and Stevie come over to London – there's a special Car and Motor Show? *Lena wrote.* He'd love that and it would mean you and I could catch up on chat. Let me know if it's a good idea, and here's the fare anyway. I'm not paying for Stevie so that he'll have his pride, and he might use that as a real chance to see new cars and meet people.

Let me know what you think.

Kit rang Lena.

'I opened it five minutes ago. We'd *love* to come to London. Now, how about that for being eager.'

'And Stevie? He'd love it too?'

Lena's voice was light and happy that they were going to accept.

'He doesn't know yet but he's going to be thrilled. When I tell him.'

'You sound very sure of him,' Lena said.

'I'm very sure he'd like this,' Kit said.

'Where are you? Let me imagine where you are now.'

'I'm in the phone box outside my flat.'

'I remember, I can see you there now.'

'Well, you should see the big smile on my face.'

'I can imagine it. I can nearly see it,' Lena said.

Philip was walking along the road.

'*You* look very cheerful,' he said accusingly. It was so like something his mother would say.

She wondered did she have some of the same expressions as her mother. Perhaps everyone did. Take Clio – she said the same snobby things that Mrs Kelly did, and Frankie Barry was shruggy and couldn't-care-less like her mother.

Perhaps I really am going to live the same kind of life as my mother, Kit thought with a shock. She looked at Philip as if she had never seen him before.

'Hey, Kit, take it easy . . . I mean it's good to look cheerful,' he said.

'What?'

'Listen, are you awake yet? You're like someone sleep-walking,' Philip grumbled.

She linked his arm to College. They talked about things that they were not thinking about. Philip was wondering if Stevie Sullivan and Kit had gone all the way. Kit was wondering what Philip and all the O'Briens would say if she told them she was cheerful because her long dead mother had just invited her over to London.

I've booked you in a guest house near here. Two single rooms. You're my guests, you can make your own arrangements about the beds, *Lena wrote.*

No need for any arrangements, I told you I'd tell you if there is any of that, *Kit wrote.*

'I've friends coming over . . . I'll put the plan on hold for a couple of weeks,' Lena told the Millars at the Saturday lunch.

Their plan was to establish a branch of Millar's in Manchester. They had found the perfect woman to run it for them. Peggy Forbes was busy training with them in London. All that was needed was the right premises, the suitable staff and a big launch. There were so many applications from the North of England that it made sense to have a presence there. Peggy was a Lancashire woman herself. If all went well, and they were sure it would, they would make her a partner soon.

'I can't bear that you've been on a plane before me,' Stevie said as they checked in their bags in Dublin Airport.

'Oh, you've done a lot of things I've never done. Far too many in fact.'

He hugged her there and then. 'None of them were important,' he said.

'I *know* that,' Kit said loftily.

It wasn't a barrier between them, his wicked past and her virginity. It would sort itself out. Kit knew that Stevie had hopes it would sort itself out on this visit to London.

'Will you tell her I know?' he asked.

'Yes, I will. Though I think she probably guesses. We can read what isn't there when we write to each other. It's uncanny.'

'I won't try to please her, to impress her and pretend I'm good enough for you.' He spoke quite seriously.

'No, she'd see through you straight away,' Kit said as they walked through the Duty Free shop.

'I wonder what I'll get her.' He stopped and looked at the shelves of drink and cigarettes. He paused in front of the champagne. 'It doesn't matter whether she likes it or not. It's festive. It's celebration, that's what it is,' he said.

From everything Lena had told her, this is exactly what Louis Gray would have said and done.

Lena was there to meet them. Stevie marvelled at how well she looked. Her face had been gaunt two months ago, but now she was glowing with health and enthusiasm.

'I have a friend who insisted on driving me to meet you,' she said. 'We've got to meet him outside.'

'I know you'll be tied up with cars but if you've any time at all I'd be very happy to show you my neck of the woods . . .' James said. 'It's not that far out of town, and I'd love you all to come and stay in darkest Surrey.'

Kit saw Lena frown. 'Maybe on another visit, James,' she said. 'They don't have all that much time.'

He was relaxed. 'Certainly, but the offer's there. I'd love to show you. There are rolling green fields and parkland in England as well as Ireland.'

'Probably much nicer here,' Stevie said. 'Not covered in broken farm machinery and falling down cottages.'

They had a meal in Earl's Court and then James said goodbye. He was driving home tonight.

'All that way?' Stevie asked.

'It's about as far from here to there as Lough Glass to Dublin,' Lena said.

'Oh well, that's not too bad. I often drive that far four times a week, and back.' His eyes rested fondly on Kit.

'Isn't it known that you're a canonised saint?' Kit said.

Stevie took their luggage and said he'd leave them to talk. 'I'll put them in the right rooms, then I'll come back for you,' he said.

They held hands, Kit and Lena, after he went. Kit looked with delight into her mother's eyes. Everything would be all right.

'Lena, he knows,' she said, 'I didn't tell him, he just knew.'

'He's a bright boy, and he loves you very much. Of course he knows, we should have realised.'

'It doesn't matter, nothing will change.'

'I know.'

'I mean it. Who knows? Ivy does, Stevie does, in a sort of a way Sister Madeleine knows. Anyone else?' Kit looked at her mother.

'No, James doesn't know.'

'And none of these people are going to do anything that will upset us?'

'No, of course not. I'm glad Stevie knows. Glad for you, because it's a strain having to keep a secret.' Her face was thoughtful.

Kit realised that for years Lena had kept secrets. The letters first, and then the meeting. It must have been hard not to share that with someone you loved.

When he came back to collect them she stood up to kiss him. 'It's great to have you here in London, Stevie. Now take us both to our homes, will you?'

The weekend was magical. They went to Trafalgar Square and were photographed with the pigeons. 'Wouldn't Sister Madeleine go wild here?' Kit said.

'She'd have to hire a transporter to get them all back with her, she'd be afraid they didn't like traffic or the petrol fumes.'

They went to the National Gallery and wandered hand in hand around the pictures. 'I'm going to have to learn about an artist a month as well as reading a book a month,' Stevie said. 'I don't want you to be married to an ignoramus.' It was the first time he had said married. She looked at him sharply. 'Some day,' he said with his heartbreaking grin.

Stevie went and looked at cars a lot. He took Ernest with him one day and James another. Both of them said he was a knowledgeable fellow. There was nothing about the engine or chassis of a car he didn't understand.

Lena took Kit into her office. It was much larger and more splendid than Kit would have thought. And Lena was obviously the king pin.

'A friend of mine from Ireland' was the introduction.

People seemed interested. Lena Gray brought so little of her private life into the office with her. Her handsome husband had not been seen or heard of for a long time. But nobody had asked straight out.

'And this is my own little broom cupboard,' Lena laughed as she closed the door behind them.

Kit looked around her in amazement. The big carved desk, the pictures and certificates on the wall, the framed tributes and newspaper cuttings, the fresh flowers in a blue and gold vase.

Kit seemed at a loss for words.

'What are you thinking?' Lena asked gently.

'Well, oddly enough I was thinking that it's a great pity that people at home didn't know and will never know how well you did.' There was a catch in her voice.

'Sometimes I think that it's a great pity that nobody here will ever know how well I did in a different way ... they'll never know that you are my daughter.'

They were speaking seriously now. It was a different mood.

'Did you keep Louis very much apart from your work too?'

'Yes. Some kind of protection I suppose. I had to have an area I could control. Not that it always worked. One of the best girls we ever had working here was one of Louis' lengthy list of lady friends, it turned out. Dawn, Dawn Jones. I still miss her.'

'What happened to her?'

'I sacked her ... I couldn't sit and look at part of Louis' past every day,' Lena said.

'Half the country is part of Stevie's past,' Kit said ruefully. 'I'm having to put up with that.'

'Ah, but that's different,' Lena said. 'Past past is one thing, but when it's meant to be the present and these kind of people turn up, then that's not a good thing.'

'No, that's true. I wouldn't like that,' Kit said. She was biting her lip, Lena noticed.

'My mistake was that I looked the other way,' Lena told her. 'I think to be utterly unquestioning and forgetful about the past as I was, that's right. But I should have let him know that I knew about the present ... I think that was my mistake. I let him get away with everything just to keep him, or to keep some aspect of him.'

Kit's mind was far away. It was with Clio saying that everyone knew Stevie was still running after girls. That if Kit wouldn't go to bed with him then he wasn't going to be short of people who would. It was a worrying thought.

The airport terminal was just down the road from them in Cromwell Road. Lena came to see them off. 'James would have driven us, but you know ...'

'You don't want to be too beholden to him,' Kit suggested.

'Exactly. What a wonderful word.'

'I have to keep a dictionary beside me to keep up with her,' Stevie said.

'No you don't, Stevie. You don't fool me.'

'I'm not trying to sell you a car either, but why don't you have one? Kit said you had.'

'She's right. I gave it to Louis. Actually I bought it for him so I let him take it, that's a more honest way of describing it.' She spoke of Louis so casually to Stevie Kit was warmed by the sense of intimacy.

'You should have something, a little run-around that you could park easily. I'll think up what you should have and tell you when you come back.'

'Not easy to come back to Lough Glass.'

'I meant to Dublin.'

'I don't know, it's funny. I got a really stupid feeling when I was flying away over the city after you drove me to the Dublin Airport. I felt that this was the last time I'd ever be there.'

'That's a bit morbid,' Stevie said.

'No, I didn't mean it like that. I knew I'd see you both again and go on seeing you ... no, it wasn't to do with death or plane crashes or anything ... it was just I felt that was a period of my life that was over now. Like next time you come you could come to Manchester ... and see the set-up we have there ...'

'But Ireland's your home,' Kit's lip began to tremble.

'No, your home is your people, it's not a place. Believe me, that's true. I'll always have you, won't I?'

'Are you not coming back to Dublin because Louis lives there?'

'He doesn't live there, not in any sense for me. I swear to you it's as if he was on the planet Mars. No, it's just I thought you'd be coming here more and more . . .'

'And you'll come to our wedding? In a few years' time,' Stevie said.

'Well, well, well. I didn't know about this,' Lena said.

'Neither did I,' Kit said.

'Is it possibly an all time first for the West London Air Terminal, a proposal in the lounge?'

She was taking it lightly, so Kit decided to do the same. 'Listen Lena, don't mind him, by the time we get married, Stevie and I, you'll be so old you'll probably need a wheelchair. That's the kind of time scale we're working on.'

Their flight was called.

Stevie kissed her on both cheeks.

'I'll never be able to thank you for all the good times you gave us, and introducing me to all your nice friends.' Kit hugged her with tears in her eyes.

The crowd was filing out the exit and down to the buses. It was time to go.

Then suddenly Stevie turned and went back to hug her too. 'I'll look after her, please believe me I'll be good to her. If I thought I wouldn't, I'd go away now.' She was so surprised it nearly took her breath away.

When they were on the bus she asked him: 'Why did you do that?'

'I wanted to,' he said. Then after a pause: 'I got a funny feeling that I was never going to see her again.'

'Well, thank you very much,' Kit said in a fury. 'Jesus, that's a great thing to say. Which of you am I meant to be losing? Am I going to lose my mother or the man I'm going to marry?'

'Got you,' said Stevie happily. 'You've promised to marry me. Did you hear that?' He turned to an American tourist. 'Mary Katherine McMahon has agreed to marry me.'

'Think of the alimony,' said the man who looked as if he had had to think about a fair amount of it in his life.

*

Clio's wedding was going to be more difficult than Kit would have believed. And every detail of it apparently had to be discussed with her bridesmaid.

'I'll ask Stevie if you *insist*,' Clio said, 'but that means one more on Michael's side and he says he has it down to a bare minimum already and that if he has one more it will open the floodgates.'

'Stevie's busy anyway,' Kit said. He wasn't busy and she was deeply annoyed that he had not been invited. He would also have been such a helpful person there if only stupid Clio realised.

But then two days later there was an aunt of Michael's from Belfast who would be visiting Dublin. She would be included so Stevie could now come.

Clio grumbled about the hotel. It wasn't smart enough.

'You wanted it small,' Kit said.

'No, you wanted it small,' Clio said.

'Is Michael happy about the baby?'

'*Please* don't talk about the baby,' Clio hushed her.

'Look, I'm not going to get up at the wedding breakfast and make a speech about it, but I was just asking you if your future husband is pleased about fatherhood.'

'Well, he's not like Louis, if that's what you mean. Louis never has his hand off Mary Paula's stomach. He's so boring about it, he thinks it's kicking or twitching or something.'

'Yours is smaller, younger, it's not doing that.'

'Oh, shut up about mine,' Clio said. 'It's the honeymoon that's the problem now. Mr O'Connor thinks that Michael should do this kind of intensive course in book-keeping so that he can put him into one of the hotels.'

'Yes, well, that makes sense. He's not trained as an hotelier, he'll need some job.'

'We wanted to go to the South of France,' Clio complained. She looked like a four-year-old whose dolly has been taken away.

'Will you wear that fur cape that looked so well on you? It would be a nice thing for Clio's wedding,' Martin asked.

'No love, if you don't mind. I have a different outfit planned.'

'It really did look smart on you,' Martin said.

'I'll keep it and wear it at Kit's wedding,' Maura said.

'Don't tell me that's going to be imminent.' Martin McMahon looked alarmed.

'No, of course not,' Maura laughed. 'But she will marry one day and with luck you and I will be here for it.'

'She's very taken with Stevie.' He sounded worried.

'I know. I was alarmed in the beginning but he's a reformed boy. None of the lassies ringing him up. The only one he rushes out of the office to see is Kit.'

'I suppose there are men who can be reformed by a woman.' Martin McMahon was doubtful.

'Well, it's part of history certainly.' Maura was reassuring, hoping he wouldn't ask her what part of history. All she could think of was Helen of Troy or Cleopatra or Kittie O'Shea who had brought Parnell down, all of them troublemakers. She couldn't think of a single woman apart from in a wild western movie who had reformed a man.

It was curiously dispiriting, Clio Kelly's wedding day.

Any appearance of jollity and papering over pregnancy problems that the O'Connors had been able to muster had been used up. Fingers O'Connor had grasped Maura McMahon by the arm as soon as he saw her. 'Bad business this, bad business,' he said.

Maura removed his hand very deliberately. 'Perhaps if you had shown your sons some better example in the way to behave it might not have happened,' she said primly.

Lilian Kelly certainly never expected her first daughter's wedding to take place under such a cloud. Many times in her mind she had planned it. Always seeing it taking place in her own home town, with the reception in The Castle Hotel. This anonymous Dublin church and the same hotel as poor Maura had chosen all seemed very second rate.

Clio wore a white dress but Kit looked extremely casual in that outfit. The girl was pretty there was no gainsaying that, and her big soft white hat with the long ribbons was elegant.

It was some scant consolation to Lilian Kelly to know that Kit's disgrace was even greater than Clio's. All right, so everyone might suspect that Clio's wedding had been somewhat rushed, but at least she was marrying into the O'Connor family. Kit was hanging around with that Teddy Boy, the boy with the terrible reputation, son of poor old Kathleen and her mad drunken husband. That was a seriously unacceptable thing to do.

Stevie was a great addition to the wedding party, as Kit had known he would be. He talked to Michael's aunt about Belfast, told her of his visits there on motor related business, promised to look out for a good second hand Morris Minor the next time he was up there. He asked Mr O'Connor educated questions about the hotel business, promised Father Baily about the possibility of getting a car for a raffle. He spoke to Maura in such clear terms about the visit to London that she was reassured that there had been different rooms in the guest house.

'How did you find it?' she asked innocently.

'Oh, in this business you're always finding fellows who know places,' he said.

He spoke to Kevin about the great night on New Year's Eve.

He told Martin McMahon about his plans to expand the garage. 'I don't want to be ruining life for all my good neighbours if I do get more business ... I'll move down the town to more open space,' he said, allaying a worry Martin had been keeping to himself for some time.

And then he approached Mary Paula and Louis. Louis was so warm and easy-going Stevie felt a lump in his throat. It was for this man that Kit's mother left home, allowed a drowning to be believed. She had lived with him and with his betrayals for so long until it had almost cost her her mind.

Louis spoke of his own car, a Triumph Herald he got in London. He had it a while now but it still looked good and was no trouble. No, he had bought it new.

The bile rose in Stevie's throat as he heard the story unfold. How Mary Paula had first met him when he was driving it to a seminar. She had admired the man in the white Triumph. 'I said to him, "That's a nice car," he said to me, "Let's take it on a test drive then,"' and neither of them had gone to the seminar at all.

'Don't tell that to my father-in-law, though,' Louis whispered. 'He might think I was unreliable.' Mary Paula giggled.

'And you're not?' Stevie said stonily.

'No.' Louis looked alarmed. The boy was looking at him oddly.

Stevie moved away very quickly. Kit had been watching. 'Please,' she whispered in his ear. 'Please, for her sake, we must say nothing. For Father, for Maura.'

She looked across at Louis, her eyes full of hate.

Was he a moron that he didn't know who they all were? He *knew* that Lena was married to Martin McMahon, pharmacist from Lough Glass. He knew that Clio was from Lough Glass. Did he just not care? Was his life with Lena so much in the past that it didn't matter that her husband and daughter turned up at a festivity where he was with his pregnant wife?

Of course, he thought that they all thought Helen McMahon was dead, drowned in the lake and buried in the churchyard. But surely it must have cost him something to face these people.

Lena had never mentioned his name to Father. That much Kit knew. She had always said that she had loved another man. She had never pronounced his name because it made it too real. She had written it of course in the letter. But that was the letter Martin had never got.

There would be no sing-song, no extended drinking in the bar of this quiet hotel. The proceedings would end earlier than most enthusiastic Irish wedding guests would have expected. Clio went to change.

'That was wonderful,' Kit lied as she helped her friend out of the dress.

'It was diabolical,' said Clio.

'You're wrong, wait till you see the pictures.'

'Wait till I forget the look in everyone's eyes that's more like. Jesus, isn't Mrs O'Connor a pill. Her own daughter's pregnant and there's not a word about it. But I'm the one who led her son astray, it's written all over her.'

'Stop now. It was great,' Kit soothed her.

'Stevie certainly behaved himself.'

'Good,' said Kit in a clipped tone.

'He sort of moved round and talked to people as if he's used to it.'

'He probably is, in the car business.' Kit kept herself in control with dignity.

'No, I meant used to people like who were here.'

There would be no throwing the bouquet. Just a few more minutes showing off her going away costume and then Clio and Michael would leave. The rest would follow soon after.

Louis came over to join Kit, as she knew he would. He knew she was the daughter of Lena but he had no idea that she knew of any connection at all.

She wanted to be as far as possible from him, but it would be rude not to return his warm smile. 'Great day, isn't it.'

'Yes indeed.'

'But nothing between you and the best man? This won't be the making of another wedding, I'm not going to get another lovely sister-in-law?'

'No, no. Kevin's going out with my friend Frankie.' The words came out slowly, she felt very uneasy. She moved away.

Slightly at a loss, Louis turned to talk to someone else. Young women didn't normally walk away from him like that. Stevie had been watching; he saw the way Louis had laid his hand on Kit's arm with his easy familiar charm. It had made Stevie rage inside.

The crowd were gathering near the door to wave goodbye to the bride and groom. Louis and Stevie were on the edge of the crowd, 'You're from Lough Glass too, Clio tells me. It sounds a good place, we must go there sometime,' he said.

Stevie put his face very near him. In a slow and deliberate voice he said: 'You've *been* to Lough Glass.' There was a pause. And then with a heavy menace he said: 'And if you know what's good for you I wouldn't go again.' Then he moved away.

Louis had gone white. What did the fellow mean? He saw Stevie put his arm around Kit's shoulder and she held his hand tightly. Kit McMahon, Lena's daughter. And her boyfriend. But they didn't *know*, for God's sake. None of them *knew*.

*

Lena was in Manchester, she wrote. The people were so friendly and they seemed to have more time for each other than in London, they weren't always rushing off. And if you met someone you were likely to meet them again. More like Dublin really, though of course one met too many people in Dublin. Lena only vaguely remembered meeting Rita, but she knew Kit must have handled it. She wondered had she had a blackout or had she gone mad for a time.

It didn't matter now. All that mattered was that she be there for her daughter as much as Kit needed her.

Lena realised that she had to give up on Emmet. She had lost too much of his life to see him now. She had left when he was a child, a real child. Now he was old enough to hold a girl in his arms and tell her he loved her. There was no way she could come back into his life. She was finished with fantasy ... there would be none of that any more.

She was even going to get herself a small flat in Manchester. Peggy Forbes lived with her mother and anyway it would not be a good idea to share a flat with someone from work. Peggy was divorced, fortyish, wonderful with people. When next Stevie and Kit came to England they should come to Manchester. Peggy would show them all what life in the North was like.

Sometimes Kit showed parts of the letters to Stevie.

'I don't like reading what she's written to you, it's meant to be private.'

'I only show you bits, I keep the private bits.'

'Are they about me?'

'Sometimes.'

'Warnings like don't follow her down the primrose path?' He looked at her anxiously. He really wanted to know.

'They used to be. Not now.'

'When did she change?'

'When she met you.'

*

Clio and Michael moved into Maura's flat almost immediately after the wedding. The price had been arranged very quickly. Fingers had written the cheque without haggling.

'But Pa, I'm sure that's just the *asking* price,' Michael said. 'She'd probably come down a couple of hundred if you start to bargain.'

'We'll pay what's asked.' Fingers had had enough reproofs from Maura Hayes and her stepdaughter Kit to do him for a long time. There would be no haggling and drawing their wrath on him.

'You must come round and see it,' Clio said. 'You can even bring Stevie if you want to.'

'No thanks. I'll come round some evening he's not in Dublin.'

'Are there many of those?' Clio asked.

'Well, he *does* live and work in a place two hours journey away from here.' She knew she sounded defensive and sarcastic. Only Clio brought this out in her.

Clio was in very grumpy form the evening she did go around to the flat. 'Have you had your tea?' she asked ungraciously.

'Well, no. But I'm not hungry,' said Kit.

'I didn't think . . .'

'It doesn't matter.' Kit wondered how you wouldn't think, if you asked someone to visit you at six o'clock. Most people had *something* to eat in the evening.

Kit admired the place and the wedding presents. Some of them still not unpacked stood around in boxes.

'I think I'm getting *pre* natal depression,' Clio said. 'Did you ever hear of that?'

'No,' said Kit truthfully. 'I heard you were meant to be excited and thrilled and knitting things and getting dinner for your husband and your friends.'

Clio burst into tears.

'Tell me, tell me,' Kit said. She knew she was going to hear some story of woes. Should Clio be shaken until her teeth rattled? Should this have been done years ago? Dr Kelly and his wife had always let her get away with murder.

'Everything's absolutely *terrible*. Michael was out all night on Wednesday, there was a party up in the hotel where he's working and none of them got home. Louis didn't even go back to the house that he lives in beside the hotel. And Mary Paula's absolutely furious even though Louis gives her flowers every day. Michael's given me *no* flowers, he just says I'm a nag. Already! I'm only a few weeks married and I'm a nag.'

'Shush, shush. He doesn't mean it,' Kit said.

'And Daddy's no help, nor Mummy. I said I'd like to go down and stay a few days there and they said no. All this about making my bed and having to lie in it. And I *hate* this place, it has Aunt Maura written all over it . . . Everyone's in such bad tempers, Kit.'

'I'm not.'

'That's because you're being screwed silly by Stevie Sullivan and you can't think of anything else.'

'I'm *not* as it happens.'

'Well, maybe you should be.'

'Clio, *you're* the one who's upset. Talk to me. Let's look at the good points. Michael only stayed out one night and he was with . . . your brother-in-law, so you don't think he was up to no good.'

'I don't know,' Clio said darkly. 'Mary Paula told me there were other girls there, fast girls.'

Kit wondered wildly whether Mary Paula and Clio, who had both been pregnant brides in recent months, were actually in a position to be calling other girls fast. But she let it pass.

'What other good points are there?' Kit continued doggedly. 'You have a lovely home, Michael's got a job. You're going to have a baby.'

'Which means I can't have a job,' Clio complained.

'You didn't *want* a job. You said you were going to college to get a husband. Now you've got one.'

'Nothing's the same as it was,' Clio wept.

'No, it's different, but we've got to change too. I suppose that's it.'

'I wish we were young again, going to Sister Madeleine, coming home for tea.'

'Well, we're the ones who have to *make* tea nowadays. Will I go out and get some things?'

'Would you? I feel so awful and waddly, I can't move.'

'You're as bad as Mary Paula. When's her baby due?'

'This week, that's why it's all so awful about Louis and everything. And Michael's father has had a row with Louis about money. Apparently he just pockets his salary every month and didn't know he was meant to pay bills with it. There was an awful scene up there the other night.'

'Talking of money, I don't have much, if I'm to buy things for supper . . .' said Kit.

'Oh, there's a fiver under the clock.' Clio waved at it. The phone rang. 'Will you answer it Kit, please?'

It was Louis.

'That's not Clio,' he said.

'No, it's Kit McMahon. What can I do for you?'

'My wife's been taken into hospital and she's gone into labour.'

'Congratulations,' Kit said in a dull voice.

'No, wait. I was hoping Clio could ring her father-in-law and tell him.'

'Why don't you ring him yourself?'

'Well to be perfectly frank, I've had some words with him. I think he'd prefer to be told by another member of his family. I can't find Michael or Kevin anywhere.'

'Yes, I heard there was a problem with your father-in-law, all right.' Kit didn't know why she had said this. It was just the thought of the freeloader Louis sponging off everyone that made her feel sick.

His voice had changed. 'What do you mean you heard? Where did you hear this?'

'From Clio, who heard it from your wife.' She was brazen now.

'And is it any of your business?'

'No, none at all,' she agreed.

'So can you put me on to Clio?'

'She's not here.'

'Well, all right then.'

'Do you want me to ring Fingers?'

'What?'

'Fingers O'Connor. That's his name, isn't it?'

'That's an offensive nickname certainly. His name is Mr O'Connor.'

'Do you want me to ring him and tell him Mary Paula's in the labour ward? That you didn't want to tell him yourself?'

Louis hung up.

'What was that about?' Clio's mouth was open in astonishment.

'That creep Louis Gray, afraid to talk to your father-in-law.'

'Why were you so rude to him?'

'I hate him.'

'Why on earth do you hate him?'

'I don't know, irrational. Sometimes you get an irrational dislike.'

'Well, they're *my* bloody in-laws Kit. Don't work out your own hatreds on them just because things aren't going well with Stevie.'

'Who said things weren't going well with Stevie?'

'They can't be or else he wouldn't have been at that party up in the hotel where Louis and Michael were. The one on Wednesday night.'

Kit looked at her in disbelief. 'Stevie was there?'

'Yes, didn't he tell you?'

'You know he didn't tell me.'

Wednesday last ... he had told her that he had to go to a function in Athlone. God damn him and all other conniving handsome men to the pit of hell. Kit put on her jacket and went to the door.

'Kit, the fiver,' Clio pointed to the mantelpiece.

'Get your own tea, Clio,' Kit said and banged the door behind her.

She longed to write to Lena to tell her that Louis' marriage was in trouble only five months after it had taken place. She ached to put her arms around her mother and cry. To ask her should she tackle Stevie, ask him straight out had he been there? Should she check if the function in Athlone had existed?

Wasn't this the road her mother had gone down and lived to regret, the constant checking and then deciding to ignore it? She walked along looking at the other people whose lives were not in ruins, going about their business. Men coming home from work, wives opening doors, children playing in gardens in the June evening sunshine.

She must not tell Lena the news of Louis' fall from grace. Lena said her only peace was to know nothing of him. There was always the danger even at this late stage that Lena would take him back. Forget, forgive so much. After all what was a wife and baby to forgive when she had put up with so much?

Lena and Peggy Forbes were having supper in an Indian restaurant in Manchester after the official opening. Peggy was forty-three, blonde, well groomed. She had married very young and very foolishly, she said. A man who should have married a bookie. She had met him at the races, which should have given her some inkling but it hadn't. She had been divorced at the age of twenty-seven, after six years of a very unsatisfactory marriage.

She began to work then, very hard. She got a great deal of pleasure from it, she said. Not the money itself, she didn't regard wealth as a goal. She liked the people she met and enjoyed urging them on. She also liked the fact that she had some security and didn't need to fear that some man was going to sell the dining table and chairs as had happened to her on her twenty-fifth birthday.

Peggy said she didn't usually tell her whole life story to someone but since Lena was putting such faith in her she wanted her to know the background.

'I have a very confused background myself,' Lena said. 'I was married to two men, but neither marriage worked. I don't say anything at work about either marriage, in fact most people at work know nothing about my first marriage and think my second one is still in existence.'

Peggy nodded. 'It's better that way,' she said.

'The only reason I'm telling you,' explained Lena, 'is that I don't want to respond to your frankness with a blank brick wall.'

'I wouldn't have been upset.'

'That's because you're a practical woman, and you realise I'm the boss, but I would also like to be your friend.'

'I'm sure we'll be that.'

'And it would be very nice if we could go out sometimes here in Manchester, to the pictures or for a meal. Maybe I could visit your mother? But I'm not one for clubs or that kind of evening out.'

'Nor am I,' Peggy said. 'The younger girls I work with pity me, and they're always trying to get me out for what they call a good time.'

'I have that too,' Lena sympathised.

'The only thing I'm sorry about is that I didn't have children. I'd have liked a daughter, wouldn't you?'

Lena hesitated. 'I have a daughter, as it happens. But that's not known.'

'Don't worry, I won't talk about it,' Peggy said, and smiled a broad friendly smile.

'We're going to make this agency as big as the one in London,' Lena promised.

'We'll be calling you our Junior Branch in five years time,' said Peggy.

'I really think we made a great choice.' Lena was talking to Jim and Jessie Millar back in the London office. They were amused to hear they would soon be the Junior Branch.

'That's the spirit we need,' said Jim.

Lena smiled to herself thinking about how cautious he had always been at the start, and how every change no matter how minor had to be negotiated past him with care.

The receptionist came in. 'I'm so sorry Mrs Gray, but you know what you said about using your initiative?'

'Yes, Karen. Who is it?'

'It's Mr Gray. He says it's an emergency and he has to talk to you.'

'Use this room,' Jim Millar said, and he and Jessie got up to leave.

But Lena wouldn't hear of it. 'Take his number, Karen, and tell him I'll ring back in five minutes.'

She went to her office and looked at herself in the mirror. She was alive and well. She was sane. He would *not* upset her. There was no emergency in his life that could touch her.

She telephoned the Dublin number and they answered with the name of an hotel. Louis was ringing her from work. What else was new?

'It's Lena,' she said.

'Thanks for ringing back. I should have known you would, you were always so reliable.'

'That's true. What can I do for you?' Her voice was calm.

'Are you alone?'

'As alone as any of us are on these kind of lines. Why?'

'I'm in great trouble and so are you.'

'Why am I in trouble?'

'They know.'

'Who knows?'

'Everyone in Lough Glass knows.'

'What do they know, Louis?'

'They know about you.'

'I doubt that. Unless you told them.'

'I swear to God I haven't opened my mouth. Not to anyone. Up to now I haven't said a word.'

It was there, the threat. The blackmail in his tone. *Up to now.* 'And who in particular seems to know things?' she asked.

'A fellow called Sullivan. Do you know him?'

'I remember him. His people own a garage.'

'And Kit . . . Kit knows. She was so rude to me just yesterday. She bit the head off me.'

'I doubt that.'

'She *did*. She said she heard rumours of my having a fight with my father-in-law.'

'I'm sorry to hear you've fallen out with your relations.' Her voice was so hard she could hardly recognise it herself.

'Lena, cut this out. I'm in trouble too.' She waited. 'They expected me to have more cash than I have.'

'Yes?'

'And I was reading in the papers how you've opened a new office in Manchester . . . reading about the agency in the financial pages no less.'

'Yes. Aren't the Millars doing well?'

'I looked it up, Lena.'

'What?'

'I got someone to go to Companies House. You're a director.'

'So, Louis?'

'So you're a part of it. You're in a position to help me. I never begged in my life, I'm begging you now.'

'No, indeed, that's not what you're doing, you're trying to blackmail me.'

'I thought you were saying this might be an open line.'

'It's probably not at my end, who knows about yours.'

There was a silence. 'We parted friends, Lena, can we not remain friends?'

'We didn't part friends.'

'Yes we did. I remember the night.'

'We parted without a fight or a scene. I certainly wasn't your friend then, nor am I now.' There was a silence.

Lena spoke again. 'So if that's all, may I wish you well. And hope you get over this problem with your father-in-law. I'm sure you will, you're a man of great charm.'

'One payment, Lena. You'll never hear me asking again.'

'No, I hope you won't telephone me again. If you do, I shall ask the staff not to put your call through.'

'You're not going to get away with this high and mighty attitude. You don't know who you're dealing with,' he cried.

'A man who owes his father-in-law money, it would appear.'

'Not in any sense like borrowing or stealing. It's just he expects me to have private means.'

'Or to put your hand in your pocket sometimes.'

That was *exactly* the phrase Fingers had used. Louis had lied to him, he had said he was saving for the birth of his baby.

'I have a son,' he said.

'That's wonderful,' Lena said.

'No, I need some money to start a savings account for him. That's what I *said* I was doing, saving towards an account.'

'Goodbye, Louis.'

'You'll be sorry.'

'What can you do to me?'

'I can bring you down. Tell these country plodders, Martin and Maura and Peter and all, that you're *not* dead. You're living the high life of a director of companies over in England. By God, that'll get the fur flying down there in Lough Glass. Bigamous marriage, Maura a woman of easy virtue . . . Kit and her brother abandoned by their feckless mother.'

He didn't even know Emmet's name, Lena realised. 'Do that, Louis, and you go down further than you ever thought you could go down.'

'Easy threats,' he laughed.

'No, not at all. You made a great mistake by telephoning me today with this news. If you had sold your blood pint by pint to the blood bank, or done a smash and grab raid at a jewellers in Grafton Street, you'd have got your money quicker.'

'Lena . . .' he said.

But the line was dead.

She dialled Sullivan's garage. Maura McMahon answered the phone. Lena considered hanging up but time was of the essence. She disguised her voice in a poor imitation of a cockney accent. She asked to speak to Stevie.

'I'm afraid he's not available at the moment. Can you tell me who's calling?'

She had forgotten Maura's accent. The courteous tones, the soft voice. She felt even more determined than ever that this woman should not be disturbed in the even tenor of her life. Her happiness with Martin McMahon must not be overturned.

'It's really quite urgent. This is a guest house in London where he was staying.'

'Oh yes?' Maura sounded anxious now, alert . . .

'And you're sure he can't come to the phone?'

'Was there a problem with the bill or anything?'

'No, no. Nothing like that,' Lena knew her accent was all over the place but it was the best she could do.

'Well, can he return your call when he comes back?'

'When will that be?'

'Tomorrow. He's in Dublin.'

'Is there any way of contacting him there?'

'I'm afraid not. But if I could have your name and number . . .'

She gave Maura Ivy's name and telephone number. And then she put her head in her hands.

Stevie was her only hope.

Kit rang home that night and spoke to Maura.

'I hear Clio's an auntie-in-law,' Maura said.

'Oh, is that right?' Kit said.

'Yes, a little boy, so Lilian was telling me.'

'Super,' Kit said.

'So you've had *another* row with Clio?'

'This is the last one.'

'Glad to hear that.'

'No, I mean the friendship's over.'

'Kit, you're too old to think that. Friendships are never over.'

'If they weren't real they could be,' said Kit.

'Let's go on to happier subjects,' Maura said. 'Are you seeing Stevie tonight?'

'I don't know,' Kit said truthfully. The arrangement had been that if he was able to he would call to the flat at eight. She didn't know whether she wanted to see him or not.

'Well, if you do, will you give him a message?'

'Hold on.' Kit got out a notebook. 'Fire ahead, Maura.'

'He's to ring this guest house in London . . .'

'What?'

'No, it's not about a bill, I asked. But the woman was tight as anything, she wouldn't tell me. She wants him to ring her at this number . . .'

'I think I have the number,' Kit said.

'Let me give it to you anyway. It's Ivy Brown, and this is the London number.'

Ivy. Kit leaned against the side of the phone box. There must be something wrong with Lena. And it must be very bad if they asked Stevie to ring. Kit felt very weak indeed. What could have happened?

Wouldn't it be great to have enough money to make a call to London from a phone box just like that. Instead of keeping the coins aside for a couple of days to ring Lough Glass. She couldn't wait until eight o'clock, it was only six-fifteen now. She would go and borrow the money from someone.

As she left the phone box she saw Stevie's car pull up. He opened the boot and took out his good jacket. He often drove in his old one, he said for comfort. Imagine he still wanted to look good for her.

'Vain peacock,' she said, remembering the stories of Louis Gray's jackets hanging in Lena's cupboard. But she needed him now. She went over to him before he had put his old jacket away.

'You caught me,' he said.

'That's not something you'd mind being caught at surely?'

'What's wrong?'

'What do you mean?'

'You sound as if there was a list of other crimes I would mind being caught at,' he said.

'Aren't there?' she asked.

'No there aren't as it happens. What's wrong? You're white as a sheet.'

She told him about the call. 'It must be a message, a code.'

'I'll ring,' he said. 'Do you want to come into the box?'

'No.' She drew away from him. She didn't want the intimacy of the phone box, both of them pressed up together.

'All right so.'

She saw him talking on the phone for a while then hanging up and being phoned back. Whatever it was it must be serious. She walked around by the box, but his face didn't look shocked or distressed as it would if it was the news of an illness or an accident. He seemed very angry.

She opened the door of the phone box tentatively. She heard him say '. . . no, no. I won't tell her until it's sorted out. I quite understand. Yes, you can trust me. I'll ring you tomorrow. Goodbye.'

Then he came out.

'What is it?' she asked.

'You're mother's fine. I was talking to her, she's in perfect health and sounds very calm. She had something she wants me to sort out for her and I'm going to do it. But it's not something she wants you involved in.'

'I don't believe you.'

'Well, that's odd. If you told me something like that I'd believe you.'

'I can't trust you an inch,' she shouted at him. 'This is some other devious thing. You've used my mother in some awful way to give yourself a cover story.'

'Kit, you're going mad,' he said in a matter of fact way. 'You gave me the message, I rang the number, this is the way it's turned out. I don't know what you're talking about.'

'Yes you do, it's about last Wednesday. You want her to cover over for you.'

'Wednesday?' He seemed genuinely bewildered.

'Wednesday. Someone's told you the story was blown so you're hatching some deal with her because you think she likes you.'

'She does like me, I hope. And she certainly trusts me.'

'Stevie, you're a liar.'

'No,' he said quite simply, 'I'm not.' They stood for a long time looking at each other. 'Now, I'm not going to walk off on you over some misunderstanding. But I think you're too angry to explain it to me ... so what will we do, where would you like us to go?'

'I'd like you to go to hell,' Kit said.

'Why, why do you say that?'

'Because I'm my mother's daughter certainly, but I'm not going to put up with all she put up with in her life. And it's better you understand this now, than years down the line.'

'I have to go and do something now. Do something for your mother. I'd like to come back and talk to you.'

'You'll come back to a locked door,' Kit said.

'She particularly asked me to keep you out of it, but if you want to check up on me and add further grief and problems to her you can always telephone her yourself and check I'm telling you the truth. But then, what's the point?'

'What indeed?' Kit asked.

'I mean, if you don't believe me and have to check up on me you probably won't believe her, so save your money.' He got into his car and drove off very fast indeed.

She was awake for a very long time but he didn't come to the flat. He left no note, no message.

She was red-eyed when the morning came at last.

She met Philip in the college. 'Have you a cold, Kit? How are you?'

'A bit of a one, how are you?'

'Fine. Overworked. We have six tours booked in this summer. Kit, you wouldn't come and work in the hotel, would you? Have you a placement yet?'

'I don't know, Philip. This isn't a good day to ask.'

'I'll have to know some day soon,' he said.

'End of the week,' she promised.

'Oh, and Kit, Clio was looking for you.'

'When?'

'Just before I left my flat. She said if I saw you to ask you to ring her. It was very urgent.'

'It always is with her,' Kit said. 'She probably wants someone to pass her a handkerchief.' At noon she came out of a lecture room and saw Clio sitting in the hall. 'Aren't you afraid you'll get germs coming so far from your part of fashionable Dublin?' Kit said.

Clio was snow white. 'It was all my fault, Kit. I just said that to get even with you.'

'Said what?'

'About Stevie being at the party. He wasn't. I just made it up because you looked so smug.'

'So all right. Thanks for telling me now anyway.'

Kit's eyes danced, her heart was high. She should have *known* all the time that it was Clio's mean spirit. That Stevie wasn't telling her lies. Then she thought of last night's conversation at the phone box and shivered.

Clio was still looking at her.

'You needn't have come the whole way just to tell me,' Kit said.

'But I had to. After what happened.'

'What happened?'

'Stevie. He went up to the hotel and beat the living daylights out of Louis. He's lost three teeth and he has a broken jaw.'

'What?'

'He's in hospital. Mary Paula is nearly out of her mind. The christening is next week and Louis looks like something you'd pick up on the docks after closing time.'

'But why did Stevie do that?'

'I suppose he thought it was Louis that told you he was at the party.'

'I never *mentioned* the party to Stevie.'

'Well, someone else must have told him that Louis said it. Why else would he have gone to beat him up? Jesus, I'm so sorry, Kit. What awful things are happening these days.'

She had a lot to sort out. There was a message from Manchester. They hadn't known that there was an escort agency upstairs. People were getting the two agencies confused. It needed someone with huge diplomacy and even the cash to resettle the escort agency somewhere else and take over its premises. Lena said she would come up and see to it herself.

In the afternoon Louis rang. 'I see you haven't put my name on the blacklist yet. I got straight through.'

'What's happened to your voice, Louis? You sound different.'

'As if you didn't know. You sent a thug to beat me up.'

'No, I didn't. I sent a friend to reason with you.'

'He broke my jaw, I have a black eye and three teeth knocked out. I'm going to look a sight at the christening.'

'That's hard luck.'

'No, it's not hard luck, it's bad news for you. I'm going to sue him, and I'm going to explain in an open court why I'm doing it. The fellow has plenty of money, and of course you'll cough up if the award is bigger than we think.'

Lena laughed. 'You'd never do that. Throw away all you've got? A cushy job, a young wife and baby ... You won't let them know you've been shacked up with someone who ran away from her husband and children. No, I know you well enough to know you're bluffing.'

'I might have been until you sent the prize fighter in. Now everything's gone already. I've nothing to lose. Any credibility I have is gone. I am going down, but I'm taking you with me. I just wanted you to know that, in case you're having the luxury of sleeping well.'

'I don't believe you, and from now on you *are* on the blacklist. You'll never make a call to me again.'

'No, but you'll sure hear about me and what I've done to you, Helen McMahon.'

'Don't go tonight,' Jessie said. 'You've had a long day.'

'No, the sooner I'm there the better it'll be.'

'Take the train then, you can sleep on it.'

'I'll need the car when I'm there.' Lena had bought a Volkswagen Beetle on Stevie's advice. It had never let her down and she found it invaluable. 'I quite like being wrapped up in the car on my own, it's a little world that's different. I can think things out.'

'Don't think too hard,' Jessie said, 'and do pull in if you're tired, Manchester's a long way.'

'Oh, go in the morning,' Ivy said.

'Nonsense. Lovely long nights. It'll be daylight most of the way,' Lena said.

'Take a flask of coffee. I'll make it in two minutes while you're packing your overnight bag.'

'Right. Wait'll I get a little flat of my own there, and I won't have to pack a bag.'

'Talk about the jet set,' said Ivy.

She was well out on the A6 when she got that feeling, the one she had that time after New Year, when nothing felt real, and the floor seemed very far away and sounds were distorted. It went with a tightness in the chest, a fear she was going to faint or fall.

But this was idiotic. Here she was in her car, going at a perfectly normal speed. Should she pull in? She saw a place that was suitable and drew in to the side of the road. She sipped her coffee and then got out to stretch her legs. But that odd sensation returned of the ground being at a peculiar angle. She held the car to steady herself. Louis' face was everywhere around her, and his voice. 'I've got nothing to lose. I'll bring you down with me, Helen McMahon.'

She couldn't drive like this. But she couldn't stay here either. She should get back into the car. The seat and steering wheel would support her and it was just her mind playing tricks on her. After a while she moved out into the stream of cars heading north. She forced herself to think about the premises in Manchester. How had they not checked the other offices? Perhaps it was called something so respectable that no one would ever have known until the situation became apparent.

People had their lights on now. The road was˜shiny, it must have been wet, must have been raining here. Louis' face was coming back again. She couldn't imagine it as it was now, bruised, injured, teeth missing. She had asked Stevie to threaten him. Not to hit him. Perhaps she had not explained properly. But there it was again. His face, handsome, petulant, impatient, the way he was when he didn't get what he wanted.

'Get out of here, Louis,' she said aloud.

'I've nothing to lose now,' Louis said. 'I'll bring you down with me, you'll be sorry you didn't listen to me. I've nothing to lose.'

There was a huge truck. The lights of a truck and a terrible shattering of glass and . . .

Then there was nothing.

Peggy Forbes expected a call as soon as Lena checked into the hotel. It would be eleven p.m. at the latest. By midnight she was worried.

The hotel was also annoyed. 'We could have given her room away several times,' they said.

'I think the main thing is to find out whether Mrs Gray has had an accident rather than concentrating on room occupancy,' Peggy Forbes said.

They were very apologetic.

It was Ivy who heard at two a.m.

A young policeman came to her door. 'I wonder if I could come in,' he said.

'Ernest,' she called. 'Ernest, come quickly. Lena's dead.'

It was instantaneous, they told Ivy. She had crossed the road, into the oncoming traffic. She may have fallen asleep or lost concentration. The driver of the truck was not to be consoled. He was crying like a baby on the side of the road, said he'd never forget it to his dying day. He would like to tell her family how he couldn't have avoided it in a million years. Her car was out of control. But that was probably no consolation to her family, he said then.

'She has no family,' Ivy told the policeman. 'Her work and me, that's all she has. We're her family and I'll tell her work in the morning.'

'These are the only addresses given in her diary and wallet apparently,' the policeman said. 'Our people on the spot said that only you and Millar's were there as contacts, so I suppose that's in order then.'

'That's in order then,' Ivy said. 'Thank you officer, that's in order.'

*

Ivy went to Millar's at nine a.m. She dressed carefully in black. She had a list of things she would discuss with Jessie Millar. The police formalities and what they would involve, the undertakers, the funeral, the announcement in the papers.

Jessie Millar was griefstricken in a way that Ivy would never have believed possible. This wasn't a colleague, this was a true friend. When the weeping was over they settled everything.

'The question of Mr Gray is a delicate one, perhaps I could handle that,' Ivy suggested.

'Please, please. Come in and sit at her desk. Make whatever calls you like. Use the place as your own.'

Ivy had never sat in a posh office like this. She would have loved to talk to Lena about it, but instead she was sitting there arranging Lena's funeral with the undertaker. She would deal with Mr Gray next. She remembered the name of the hotel where he worked. She was unprepared for the violence of his response.

'This is some cheap, dirty trick, Ivy,' he said.

'Would to God that it were.' Ivy's voice was shaking.

'If she thinks she can get out of it by saying this, she has another think coming.'

'The funeral's next Thursday, Louis. It would be best if you were here.'

'Funeral! Don't make me laugh,' he said.

She gave him the name and phone number of the undertakers. She said she would confirm it in writing to him and mark the envelope personal. Again she said in a level voice, 'It would be best if you were there.'

Then she rang Stevie Sullivan. She spoke to the woman who must be Martin McMahon's second wife. 'This is Ivy,' she said.

'Oh we spoke before, you're from the guest house.' Maura was pleasant.

Ivy remembered the ruse. Imagine it was only a couple of days ago and Lena had been alive and well. 'Can I speak to him?' she asked.

'Certainly.' Maura was puzzled. This woman Ivy sounded totally different this time round.

'I have to go to Dublin, Maura,' Stevie said, throwing some papers into a briefcase and taking the keys of a car. 'It's sudden and important and I'll be gone a few days.'

'You have appointments, people to meet . . .'

'Cancel them if you would.'

'Any excuse?'

'No, not one I can give now. But you make one.'

'Can you tell me any more? Please, Stevie. I'm a little anxious, these calls from London . . .'

Stevie looked at her. 'Yes, I'm going to London actually. I'm stopping to pick up Kit. A friend of ours died.'

'But what friend . . . ?'

'Please Maura . . . I know you're worried but please. This is a bad time.'

'Her father will want to know what she's doing dashing off . . .'

'No, it's not dashing off. Now, I know you don't think I'm the most reliable man in the world but I'd die rather than let any harm happen to Kit. I think you know that. I haven't seduced her, I won't try . . . eventually in years and years from now I hope she'll marry me, but she may not. I can't tell you straighter than this.'

'Go and pack your things, Stevie,' she said. 'I'll sort it out.'

He took Kit from class. He held out both his hands to her. 'This is the second time someone has had to tell you this news, Kit,' he said. And she put her head on his shoulder and cried.

The body was released from the hospital and came to a funeral parlour in London. Stevie held Kit's hand as they went in. They stood together beside the casket. Lena looked as if she were asleep. Whatever discolouring and wounding there was in her forehead was hidden by her hair. Neither of them cried. They just stood there and looked for a long time.

Ivy asked them to stay in Lena's flat. 'That's where she'd want you to be,' she said. 'I've left it ready for you.' They went upstairs, limbs moving slowly as if in a dream.

'You've changed the wallpaper, she told me.' Kit said.

'After he left, to get the memory of him out of the place. I think it worked for a bit.'

'It sure did,' Stevie said.

'She had all her living ahead of her,' Ivy said, her face puckering. She turned away. 'I'll leave you here and come down if you need anything.'

'It's only got one bed,' said Stevie.

'We can survive that,' Kit said. She took off her dress, and her open-toed shoes. She stood in her slip at the handbasin where Mother must have stood so often and washed her face and arms and neck. Then she lay down on one side of the bed. Stevie lay on the other side, their hands held. And eventually he realised that she had gone to sleep.

'He won't come to the funeral,' Ivy said.

'Yes, he will,' Kit said. She was pale but calm.

'Maybe we're better without him. He caused all that upset,' Ernest said.

'I won't have her laid to rest without that bastard standing there watching,' Kit said. 'She deserves that much. She deserves him standing there with a black tie at her funeral.'

'But if he won't come?'

'I'll make him,' Kit said.

Louis Gray would not take a call from London from Kit McMahon. A secretary said she had instructions not to put Miss McMahon through. 'Give him a message from me please.'

'Certainly.'

'There's a certain gathering that he is expected at here in London, and I will need to know whether or not he plans to attend.'

'Hold on and I'll enquire.' She came back, 'I'm sorry the answer is regretfully no.'

'Then could you tell him that regretfully I shall have to come and collect him.' Kit hung up.

At the office she borrowed a hundred pounds from Jessie. She said it was for funeral arrangements. It was given willingly. Then she left a note for Stevie and went straight to the airport. The flight took an hour, the taxi to Louis' hotel another hour. She was calm when she asked to see him. He was in a meeting, they said, with Mr O'Connor senior and some of the board memebers.

'I have a taxi waiting,' Kit said, 'so I'd better go in and speak to him.' Before the receptionist could stop her, Kit was in the board room. 'I do beg your pardon for this, but it's an emergency,' she said.

Fingers recognised the girl who could and did cause so much trouble.

'Leave this minute,' Louis said.

'Louis, listen to her,' Fingers ordered.

Louis' hand was at his throat.

'I'm afraid that a great friend of ours in London has died and we all need you at the funeral. I wouldn't make such a drama out of it, but your presence is very much needed.'

'Who was this friend?' Fingers O'Connor asked, since Louis seemed to have lost his voice.

Very clearly Kit said: 'His name was Leonard Williams, a brother of James Williams, your previous employer. The family are most insistent that you come.' She looked directly at Louis as she spoke. She was telling him that she'd keep the secret, she would drop him in nothing if he came.

'That James Williams we met at the Dryden the first time?' Fingers asked.

'Yes, that Mr Williams. Can I say you'll be with me? I have a taxi outside.'

'They can't expect me to come *now*,' Louis gasped.

'It's a matter of being there as soon as possible.' Their eyes were still locked.

Louis knew that Kit would go the distance. That he had no option. 'I have to be back for the christening,' he said.

'In the midst of life we are in death,' Kit said. 'Christenings mercifully can be delayed but sudden death and funerals can't.'

'I'll go later tonight,' he said.

'You know where to go, to the house in West London. All the details are there.'

'Yes, yes. I know.'

'What's your involvement in this?' Fingers looked suspicious.

'The deceased was very very good to me, and good to all of us. That's why the people who were important in the deceased's life must be at the funeral,' she said.

The others in the room who didn't know what was happening, looked at each other in mystification. First, Louis Gray, the new hot-shot manager, was beaten up like someone after a bar-room brawl, now there were all these heavily loaded signals from some youngster to whom Fingers was listening with an uncharacteristic respect.

Louis Gray and his father-in-law left the room together and watched Kit getting back into her taxi. 'Better go, Louis,' Fingers said. 'If she has you by the balls like the rest of us, then we're all sunk.'

The day was too sunny for a funeral. London looked too well to be hosting something sad like this. Kit wore a plain black cotton dress and one of Lena's own hats. She carried a small black bag she had found in Lena's dressing-table drawer.

Ivy, Jessie, Grace West, old Mrs Park in her wheelchair, Peggy Forbes heartbroken from Manchester, came. The entire staff of Millar's, James Williams, all the tenants in the house, clients of the Agency, waiters from the local restaurants, clerks from the bank. There was a very large crowd in the Catholic church that Kit had found for the funeral mass.

As the priest read out the prayer about this night being in heaven and may the angels come to meet her, Kit held Stevie's hand very tight. They had both been in the parish church in Lough Glass when Father Baily had read this prayer for Lena before. But in those days the angels were being asked to meet Helen McMahon.

The priest had asked earlier if there was any particular hymn they would like. Kit couldn't think of any hymn. Not one. Something she might have sung at school, the priest prompted.

'Hail Queen of Heaven,' Kit had said.

It had not been a good choice. The organist began twice but the congregation, most of them Church of England, did not know this hymn to the Blessed Virgin Mary. Kit was not going to let it falter. She would sing it if nobody else did.

Hail Queen of Heaven, *she began, and Stevie joined in.*
The ocean star,
Guide of the wanderer here below.
Thrown on life's surge, we claim thy care
Save us from peril and from woe.

And then another voice joined in and they saw it was Louis Gray in his dark coat with his black tie, his face bruised and at an angle, his eye blackened. Most people thought he had been in the accident with her. He had a good strong voice and he helped Stevie and Kit along.

Mother of Christ, star of the sea,
Pray for the wanderer, pray for me.

The organist, pleased that someone had sung, struck up a second verse. They sang what had been sung already, all three of them. By the time it came to Pray for the wanderer Pray for me, everyone in the church had joined in. Kit and Stevie looked at each other. They had done Lena proud in London.

Only a few people went to the crematorium, that's what Ivy and Kit suggested.

Louis looked pathetically at Kit. 'Am I to go?'

'Yes,' she said.

It was so alien to anything that Kit had ever known; no coffin going into the earth, no sounds of spades and clay falling, just curtains parting and closing. It seemed unreal.

They stood outside the little chapel in the crematorium. 'When did you find out?' he asked Kit.

'I always knew,' she said.

'That's rubbish. The first Christmas she nearly died of grief because she couldn't ring you.'

'She wrote soon after,' Kit said.

'I don't believe you.'

'Suit yourself. I was the secret you didn't know about, you had many many that she didn't know about. Let's call it quits.'

'All right,' Louis said.

He looked old and tired. That was Kit's revenge.

They had to talk to a solicitor. Lena's entire estate had been left to Mary Katherine McMahon of Lough Glass. Apart from bequests to Ivy and Grace West, her quarter share of Millar's Agency now belonged to Kit.

'How will I arrange for it to be transferred to you after probate? We're talking about forty or fifty thousand pounds,' the solicitor said.

'I'll write to you about it later,' said Kit.

They hired a car, drove home through England. Through fields and woods and small towns, and then up through Wales. They would come back, they said, back to London to see friends like Ivy and Ernest and Grace and Jessie.

But now they wanted to go home.

'What'll I do with the money? I can't say I've been given fifty thousand pounds.'

'No,' Stevie was thoughtful.

'So what will I do? She wants me to have it . . . but I have to do it right. It would be terrible to blow the whole story at this stage.'

'You could give it to me,' Stevie said.

'What?'

'You could invest it in my business.'

'Are you mad?'

'No, I could transform the whole place, and when you marry me it'll all be yours anyway. Meanwhile I'll just look after it for you.'

'Why should I trust you?'

'Lena did.'

'That's true. But this would be sheer madness.'

'No it wouldn't. We could get a lawyer and do it legally. You could be a sleeping partner. Well, in that sense anyway.'

'I don't know, Stevie.'

'Think of a better idea,' he said and they drove along the roads of Wales. They stayed the night in Anglesey.

It was a lovely little guest house with a woman who had a sing-song accent. 'I have a beautiful room for you,' she said. 'A four-poster bed and you can nearly see Ireland from there.'

They were too tired to talk to her about the situation, or they each thought the other would. And anyway, they had slept blamelessly side by side in Lena's bed in London. They went upstairs and lay down. He looked so beautiful in the moonlight, with his long dark hair on the pillow. Kit reached out to him. 'If I'm going to be a sleeping partner,' she said, 'I suppose I'd better practise it properly.'

They stayed three days in Anglesey. And three nights.

And then they went home.

There were a lot of explanations but they didn't care. Kit agreed to work in the Central Hotel for the summer. Stevie told Maura that he might have an injection of money for the garage.

'I know where you got that money,' Maura said suddenly.

'Jesus, do you?' said Stevie.

'Yes, it was the greyhounds,' Maura said triumphantly. 'Was it? Tell me.'

'It was something like that,' Stevie said looking shamefaced.

'And you think I should regard you as reliable?'

'But you do, don't you?'

'Yes. Oddly, that day before you went off on your jaunt I knew you were telling me the truth about not seducing Kit,' Maura said.

Stevie hoped she wouldn't ask him again.

It was the shortest night of the year. They rowed out on the lake, Stevie and Kit.

Everyone was used to seeing them together now, wandering hand in hand by the lake. People didn't bother to gossip any more. Like Anna Kelly and Emmet, they had been together for as long as people could remember. And Philip O'Brien and the marvellous bossy girl who had come to work as a pharmacy student in McMahon's. Her name was Barbara and she was exactly the kind of girl Philip O'Brien was looking for all his life people said, and hadn't known it. People had forgotten Sister Madeleine, and Orla Reilly rarely came to town. Paddles' was full at night. Mona Fitz was in the sanatorium.

Life went on. And it was quite usual to see young people taking a boat out over the quiet water of the lake in Lough Glass at night.

Stevie and Kit took the little box of ashes and sprinkled it in the water. The moon was high in the sky and they didn't feel sad. It wasn't really a funeral. All that was over, in London and years ago ... the first time. This wasn't a sad thing, it was just the right thing to do.

As having a honeymoon in Wales had seemed the right thing to do. In years to come when people would look back on the history of the place and talk about the people who lived here, they might mention Helen McMahon who died in the lake. This way it would be true, her body was in the lake now, like so many who had gone before, but it had gone there peacefully.

It was strange this shorthand which meant that you didn't have to say things like that to each other. Stevie knew and Kit knew it. As they knew they would live on the lakeshore some day.

Some day when they were old enough to settle down.

Scarlet Feather

To my dearest Gordon, with all my love

New Year's Eve

On the radio show they were asking people what kind of a New Year's Eve did they *really* want. It was very predictable. Those who were staying at home doing nothing wanted to be out partying, those who were too busy and rushed wanted to go to bed with a cup of tea and be asleep before the festivities began.

Cathy Scarlet smiled grimly as she packed more trays of food into the van. There could hardly be anyone in Ireland who would answer the question by saying that they really and truly wanted to spend the night catering a supper party for a mother-in-law. Now that was the punishment posting tonight, feeding Hannah Mitchell's guests at Oaklands. Why was she doing it then? Partly for practice, *and* of course it would be a good way to meet potential customers. Jock and Hannah Mitchell knew the kind of people who could afford caterers. But mainly she was doing it because she wanted to prove to Hannah Mitchell that she could. That Cathy, daughter of poor Lizzie Scarlet, the maid who cleaned Oaklands, who had married the only son of the house, Neil, was well able to run her own business and hold her head as high as any of them.

Neil Mitchell was in his car when he heard the radio programme. It annoyed him greatly. Anyone looking at him from another car would have seen his sharp, handsome face frown. People often thought they recognised him; his face was familiar from television, but he wasn't an actor, he just turned up on the screen so often, pushing the hair out of his eyes, passionate, concerned and caring, always the spokesperson for the underdog. He had the bright burning eyes of a crusader. This kind of whining and moaning on a radio show really drove him mad. People who had everything, a home, a job, a family, all telephoning a radio station to complain about the pressures of life. They were all so lucky and just too selfish to realise it. Unlike the man that Neil was going to see now, a Nigerian who would give anything to have the problems of these fools on the radio programme. His papers were not in order due to bungling and messing, and there was grave danger he would have to leave Ireland in the next forty-eight hours. Neil, who was a member of a lawyers' group set up to protect refugees, had been asked to come to a strategy meeting. It could go on for several hours. His mother had warned him not to be late at Oaklands, it was an important party, she said.

'I do hope that poor Cathy will be able to manage it,' she had said to Neil.

'Don't let her hear you calling her "poor Cathy", if you want your guests to get any food,' he had laughed.

It was idiotic, this nonsense between his mother and his wife; he and his father stayed well away from it. It was obvious anyway that Cathy had won, so what was it all about?

Tom Feather was going through the property section of the newspaper yet again. A puzzled look was on his face. He lay across the small sofa – there was never room for his long limbs and big frame unless he draped himself somehow over the whole thing. If he could put a chair at one end for his feet to rest on, it was fairly comfortable; some day he would live in a place where there was a sofa big enough to fit him. It was all very well to have the broad-shouldered rugby-player's build, but not if you needed to sit down and study the Premises Vacant ads. He shook out the newspaper. There had to be something he hadn't noticed. Some kind of premises with a room that could be made into a catering kitchen. He and Cathy Scarlet had worked so hard to make this happen. Since their first year at catering college they were going to set up Dublin's best home catering company. The whole idea of serving people great food in their own homes at reasonable prices was something that fired them both. They had worked so hard, and now they had made contacts and got the funding, all they needed was somewhere to operate from. Cathy and Neil's little town house in Waterview, though very elegant, was far too small to consider, and the flat in Stoneyfield where he lived with Marcella was even tinier. They had to find somewhere soon. He was half listening to the radio programme. What would he really like to do on this New Year's Eve? Find the perfect place for their company to set itself up, and then he would like to stay at home with Marcella and to stroke her beautiful hair as they sat by the fire and talked about the future. No, of course that wasn't going to happen.

Marcella Malone worked in the beauty salon of Haywards store. She was possibly the most beautiful manicurist that any of the clients had ever seen. Tall and willowy, with a cloud of dark hair, she had that kind of oval face and olive skin that schoolgirls dreamed of having. At the same time, she had a quiet, unthreatening way about her that made older, uglier, fatter people take to her despite her beauty. The clients felt that some of her good looks might rub off on them, and she always seemed interested in whatever they had to say.

They had the radio on in the salon, and people there were talking about the topic. Clients were interested and joined in the argument, nobody really got what they wanted on New Year's Eve. Marcella said nothing. She bent her beautiful face over the nails that she was doing and thought how lucky she was. She had everything she wanted. She had Tom Feather, the most handsome and loving man that any girl could want. And even more, she had been photographed recently at two events with very good connections. A knitwear promotion and at a charity fashion show where amateurs had modelled clothes at a fund-raiser. This looked like the year it could all happen for her. She had a very good portfolio of pictures now, and Ricky, the photographer who had taken them, was giving a very glitzy party. A lot of media people would be there and she and Tom had been invited. If things worked well she would have an agent and a proper modelling contract, and she would not be working as a manicurist in Haywards by this time next year.

It would have been lovely for Cathy if Tom could have come with her to Oaklands. Moral support and company in that kitchen, which held so many bad memories for her, and also it would have halved the work. But Tom had to go to some do with Marcella, which was fair enough, it was going to help her career. She was so beautiful, Marcella, she just made people stop and look at her. Tall and thin, with a smile that would light up a night. No wonder she wanted to be a model, and it was amazing that she wasn't established as one already. But then Neil had said he would help and also they had hired Walter, Neil's cousin, to be barman. And she had kept it fairly simple, nothing too tricky; she and Tom had slaved on it all morning.

'It's not fair, your doing all this,' Cathy said. 'She's not going to pay us, you know.'

'It's an investment . . . We might make a rake of contacts,' he said good-naturedly.

'There's *nothing* in this lot that could make anyone sick, is there?' Cathy begged him.

She had a vision of all Hannah Mitchell's guests going around holding their stomachs and groaning with some terrible food poisoning. He had said she was getting sillier by the hour, and he must be mad himself to have such an unhinged business partner. No one would have lent them money if they realised how the cool-looking Cathy Scarlet was actually a bag of nerves.

'I'll be fine with real people,' Cathy reassured him. 'It's just Hannah.'

'Give yourself plenty of time, go there early, fill the van with swirling music to calm yourself down and ring me tomorrow,' he soothed her.

'If I survive. Enjoy tonight.'

'Well, it's one of those noisy things at Ricky's studio,' he said.

'Happy New Year, and say it to Marcella too.'

'This time next year – imagine . . .' he said.

'I know, a great success story,' Cathy said, looking much brighter than she actually felt.

It had been the way they got by. One being over-cheery and optimistic when the other was in any way down or doubtful. And now the van was packed. Neil wasn't home, he had to go to a consultation. He wasn't like an ordinary lawyer, she thought proudly; he didn't have office hours or large consultancy fees. If someone was in trouble, he was there. It was as simple as that. It was why she loved him.

They had known each other since they were children but had hardly ever met. During all the years that Cathy's mother had worked at Oaklands, Neil had been away at boarding school and then hardly home during his college years. He had moved out to an apartment when he was called to the Bar. It was such a chance that she should have met him again in Greece. If he had gone to one of the other villas, or she had been cooking on another island that month, then they would never have got to know each other and never fallen in love. And wouldn't Hannah Mitchell have been a happier woman tonight? Cathy told herself to put it out of her mind. She was still much too early to go to Oaklands, Hannah would just fuss and whimper over things and get in her way. She would call and see her own parents. That would calm her down.

Maurice and Elizabeth Scarlet, known to all as Muttie and Lizzie, lived in the inner city of Dublin in a semicircle of old, stone, two-storey houses. It was called St Jarlath's Crescent, after the Irish saint, and once the dwellings had all been occupied by factory workers who were woken by a siren each morning to get them out of bed. There were tiny gardens in front of each house, only ten feet long, so it was a challenge to plant anything that would look half-way satisfactory.

This had been the house where Cathy's mother had been born and where Muttie had married her. Although it was only twenty minutes from Cathy and Neil's town house, it could have been a thousand miles, and maybe even a million miles from the rarefied world of Oaklands, where she was going tonight.

They were delighted to see Cathy turn up unexpectedly with her white van. What were they doing to see the new year in, she wondered? They were going out to a pub nearby where a lot of Muttie's associates would gather. The men he called his associates were actually the people he met up in Sandy Keane's betting shop, but they all took their day's business very seriously and Cathy knew better than to make a joke about them.

'Will there be food?' she asked.

'At midnight they're going to give us chicken in a basket.' Muttie Scarlet was pleased at the generosity of the pub.

Cathy looked at them.

Her father was small and round, his hair stood in wisps and his face was set in a permanent smile. He was fifty years of age and she had never known him work. His back had been too bad, not so bad he couldn't get up to Sandy Keane's to put something on a cert in the three-fifteen, but far too bad for him to be able to work.

Lizzie Scarlet looked as she had always looked, small and strong and wiry. Her hair was set in a tight perm, which she had done four times a year in her cousin's hair salon.

'It's as regular as poor Lizzie's perm,' Hannah Mitchell had once said about something. Cathy had been enraged – the fact that Hannah Mitchell, who had expensive weekly hair appointments at Haywards store, while Lizzie Scarlet was down on her hands and knees cleaning Oaklands, should dare to mock her mother's hairstyle was almost more than could really be borne. Still, there was no point in thinking about it now.

'Are you looking forward to the night, Mam?' she asked instead.

'Oh, yes, there's going to be a pub quiz with prizes, too,' Lizzie said. Cathy felt her heart go out to her undemanding parents who were so easily pleased.

Tonight at midnight at Oaklands, Neil's mother would have a mouth like a thin hard line and would find fault with whatever Cathy produced.

'And have they all rung in from Chicago?' she asked.

Cathy was the youngest of five, the only one of Muttie and Lizzie's children still in Dublin. Her two brothers and two sisters had all emigrated.

'Every one of them,' Lizzie said proudly. 'We were blessed in our family.'

Cathy knew they had all sent dollars to their mother as well because they sent the envelopes to her address rather than to their parents' home. No point in driving their father mad with temptation, letting him see American money when he knew sure-fire winners were waiting up in Sandy Keane's betting shop dying to gobble it up.

'Well, I'd like to be with you tonight,' Cathy said truthfully. 'But instead I'll be disappointing Hannah Mitchell with whatever food I produce.'

'You took it on yourself,' Muttie said.

'Please be polite to her, Cathy, I've found over all the years it's better to humour her.'

'You did, Mam, you humoured her all right,' Cathy said grimly.

'But you won't start making a speech or anything, not tonight?'

'No, Mam. Relax. I agreed to do it, and if it kills me I will do it well and with a smile on my face.'

'I wish Tom Feather was going with you, he'd put manners on you,' Lizzie said.

'Neil will be there, Mam, he'll keep me in control.' Cathy kissed them goodbye and practised her smile as she drove to Oaklands.

Hannah Mitchell had contract cleaners these days, now that there was no more poor Lizzie to terrorise. Twice a week four women swept in, taking no nonsense from anyone, vacuuming, polishing, ironing and bringing their own equipment in a van.

They charged time and a half for working on New Year's Eve. Hannah had protested at this.

'Up to you, Mrs Mitchell,' they had said cheerfully, in the knowledge that plenty of other people would be glad to have their house cleaned on a day like this. She gave in speedily. Things were definitely not like they used to be. Still, it had been worth it, the house looked very well, and at least she wouldn't have to lift a finger. That Cathy with all her grand notions *was* in fact able to serve a presentable meal. She would be coming shortly in that big white deplorable-looking van: even the women who came to clean the house twice a week travelled in a far more respectable vehicle. She would come into the kitchen huffing and puffing and throwing her weight about. Poor Lizzie's daughter, behaving as if she owned the place. Which, alas, she probably would one day. But not yet, Hannah reminded herself with her mouth in a hard line.

*

Hannah Mitchell's husband Jock stopped on the way home from his office to have a drink. He felt he needed one before facing Hannah. She was always nervous and tense before a party but this time it would be magnified many times – she so hated having Neil's wife Cathy doing the catering for her. She had refused to accept that the couple were happy, well suited and unlikely to leave each other no matter how she schemed. Cathy would always be poor Lizzie's daughter, and somehow a villain who had seduced their son in Greece. She had always believed that the girl had got pregnant deliberately to trap him, and been most surprised when this had proved not to be the case.

He drank his single malt Scotch thoughtfully and wished that he didn't have to worry about this as well as everything else. Jock Mitchell had been severely disturbed by a conversation with his nephew Walter today. Walter, an idle layabout, the eldest son of Jock's brother Kenneth, had revealed that all was not well at The Beeches, his family home. In fact, things were very far from well. Walter said that his father had gone to England just before Christmas, and had left no indication of his whereabouts. Walter's mother, not known to be a strong character, was reacting to this turn of events by a heavy reliance on vodka. The problem was their nine-year-old twins, Simon and Maud. What was happening to them? Walter had shrugged; he really didn't know. They were managing, he implied. Jock Mitchell sighed again.

As she arrived at Oaklands, Cathy heard her mobile phone ring. She pulled in and answered.

'Hon, I'm not going to be there to help you unload,' he apologised.

'Neil, it doesn't matter, I knew it would go on a bit.'

'It's more complicated than we thought. Listen, ask my dad to help you in with all those crates, don't go dragging and pulling just to show my mother how wonderful you are.'

'Oh she knows *that*,' Cathy groaned.

'Walter should be there . . .'

'If I were to wait for Walter to help me unload and set up, the party would be halfway through . . . Stop fussing and go back to what you have to do.'

Cathy told herself that there were only six hours or so of this year left, only six hours or so of being nice to Hannah. What was the very worst that could happen? The very worst was that the food was awful and no one would eat it, but that could not happen, because the food was terrific. The second worst thing was that there wasn't enough of it, but there was enough in this van to feed half of Dublin.

'There are no problems,' Cathy said aloud as she looked down the tree-lined drive to the house where Neil had been born. A gentleman's residence, a hundred and fifty years old, square and satisfying somehow, with its four bedrooms above the large door and the bay windows on either side of it. Ivy and virginia creeper covered the walls and in front lay a huge gravelled circle where tonight twenty expensive cars would be parked. A house as different from St Jarlath's Crescent as you could imagine.

Shona Burke often stayed late in her office up on the management floors of Haywards – she had her own key and code to get in and out. She had listened to the programme on the radio and was wondering if she really and truly had a choice about how she would spend New Year's Eve. Long ago in a happier life there would have been a celebration, but not in the last few years. She had no idea what her sisters and brothers would do, and if they would go to the hospital. Shona would make the hospital visit out of duty, of course, but it was pointless, she wouldn't be recognised or acknowledged.

Then she would go to Ricky's party in his studio. Everyone liked Ricky. A pleasant, easygoing photographer, he would gather a lot of people and make a buzz for them all. There would be a fair crowd of poseurs and empty-headed types dying to see themselves in the gossip columns . . . She was unlikely to meet the love of her life or even a temporary soulmate, but still Shona would dress up and go there simply because she did not see herself as the kind of person who would sit alone in her apartment in Glenstar.

The question nagged her, what would she *really* like to be doing tonight? It was so hard to answer because everything had changed so much. The good days were over, and it was impossible to imagine doing something that would make her really happy. So in the absence of that, Ricky's would do fine.

Marcella was painting her toenails. She had new evening sandals which she'd bought at a thrift shop. She showed them proudly to Tom. They had been barely worn; someone must have bought them and found they didn't suit.

'They must have cost a fortune new,' she said happily, examining them carefully.

'Are you happy?' Tom asked.

'Very,' she said. 'And you?'

'Oh, very, very,' he laughed. Was that strictly true? He didn't want to go to this party at all. But just looking at her did make him happy. He couldn't really believe that such a beautiful girl, who could have had anyone she wanted, really found him enough for her. Tom had no idea that he was attractive, he thought he was big and clumsy. He honestly believed that all the admiring glances they got as a couple were directed at Marcella alone . . .

'I heard a radio programme saying people were never happy,' she began.

'I know, I heard it too,' Tom said.

'I was just thinking how lucky we were; poor Cathy and Neil can't do what *they* want tonight.' Marcella stood in her thong and picked up a tiny red garment from the back of a chair.

'Yeah, Cathy will be there now, at her mother-in-law's house, laying up the tables. I hope she keeps her temper.'

'Well she'll have to, it's work, it's professional. We all have to at work,' said Marcella, who had bent over too many imperious hands already in her life, and wanted her day in the sunshine, walking down the ramp as a model.

'Neil will be there and that pup of a cousin he has, so she should be all right.' Tom still sounded doubtful.

Marcella had put on the red outfit. It was actually a dress, short and tight, clinging to her and leaving nothing to the imagination.

'Marcella, are you really wearing that to the party?'

'Don't you like it?' her face clouded over immediately.

'Well of course I like it. You look beautiful. It's just that maybe I'd like you to wear it here, for us, not for everyone else as well to see you.'

'But Tom, it's a party dress,' she cried, stricken.

He pulled himself together at once.

'Of course it is, and you'll be the success of the night.'

'So what did you mean . . . ?'

'Mean? I meant nothing. I meant you were so gorgeous I didn't want to share you with people . . . but take no notice. I didn't really mean that at all.'

'I thought you'd be proud of me,' she said.

'I am so proud you'll never know,' he reassured her. And she *was* a beauty. He must have been insane to have had that sudden reaction.

Hannah Mitchell stood in her navy wool dress, her hair hard and lacquered from her New Year's Eve visit to Haywards. She always dressed as if she were going out to a ladies' lunch. Cathy never remembered her wearing a pinafore or even an old skirt. But then, if you did no housework, what was the point of wearing things like that?

Hannah watched Cathy carry in all the boxes and crates, one by one, standing in her way and fussing and blocking her journey. She offered to carry nothing at all. Instead, she was hoping the crates wouldn't mark the wallpaper, and wondering where would Cathy put the van so that it would be out of the way when people came. Grimly, Cathy marched to and from the kitchen of Oaklands. She turned on the ovens, laid her tea towels on the backs of chairs, placed her bag of ice in the freezer and began to sort out the food. It would be useless asking Hannah Mitchell to leave her alone, to go upstairs and lie down. She would stay put, fuss and irritate until the guests arrived.

'Will Mr Mitchell be home shortly?' Cathy thought she might ask him to help her unpack the glasses.

'I don't know, Cathy; really, it's not up to me to police Mr Mitchell about what time he comes home.' Cathy felt her neck redden in rage. How dare this woman be so offensive and patronising. But she knew she stood alone in this resentment. Neil would shrug if she told him. Her mother would beg her not to annoy Mrs Mitchell any further. Even her aunt Geraldine, who could normally be relied on for encouragement and support, would say what the hell. It just proved that Hannah Mitchell was an insecure nobody, not anyone to waste time worrying over. Cathy began to peel the foil from the dishes she had prepared.

'Is that fish? Not everyone eats it, you know.' Hannah had her very concerned face on now.

'I know, Mrs Mitchell, some people don't, which is why there's a choice, you see.'

'But they mightn't know.'

'I think they will. I'll tell them.'

'But didn't you say it was a buffet?'

'Yes, but I'll be behind it serving, so I'll tell them.'

'Tell them?' Hannah Mitchell was bewildered.

Cathy wondered was there a possibility that her mother-in-law was actually a halfwit.

'Like asking them would they like fish in a seafood sauce, or herbed chicken, or the vegetarian goulash,' she said.

Mrs Mitchell tried but found it hard to find fault with this.

'Yes, well,' she said eventually.

'So will I just get on with it now, do you think?' she asked.

'Cathy, my dear, may I ask who is stopping you?' Hannah said with her face hard and unforgiving at all this confidence in poor Lizzie Scarlet's girl.

Neil looked at his watch. Every single person in this room had some kind of New Year's function to go to except the student that they had all gathered to protect. They would be finished soon, but nobody must be seen to hasten away. It would be terrible for the man whose future hung in the balance if he thought that the civil rights activists, the social workers and lawyers were more interested in their own night's fun and games than they were in his predicament. He was trying to reassure this young Nigerian that there would be justice and a welcome for him in Ireland. Neil would not let Jonathan spend the dawn of a New Year on his own.

'When we're through here, you can come back to my parents' house,' he said. He was already late, but it couldn't be helped.

The big sad eyes looked at him. 'You don't have to, you know.'

'I know I don't have to, and a barrel of laughs it won't be, but my wife is doing the catering so the food will be good. My parents' friends are . . . well, how will I put it . . . a bit dead.'

'I'm okay, Neil, truly, you're doing so much for me and all this has delayed you from it already . . .'

'We'll go through it once more,' Neil said to the meeting, 'then Jonathan and I will go and party.' He saw them look at him in admiration. Neil Mitchell really went the distance. He felt a bit guilty at not being there to help Cathy as he had promised, but this was much more important – she'd understand. Cathy would be fine. His father and his cousin Walter would be there to help her by now . . . Everything would be fine.

Hannah still hovered, which meant that Cathy had to talk, answer inane questions, pat down unnecessary worries and even bring up topics of conversation, lest she be considered moody.

'It's nearly seven-thirty, Walter will be here any minute,' Cathy said desperately. She could have got things done far faster had she not been under the scrutiny of the most critical eyes in the western hemisphere.

Fingers could have been used more often than they were, things could have been flung into places rather than placed elegantly.

'Oh, Walter! Like all young people, I'm sure he'll be late.' There was a sniff of disapproval and resignation.

'I don't think so, Mrs Mitchell, not tonight. It's a professional engagement, he's being paid from seven-thirty until twelve-thirty. That's a five-hour booking. I'm certain he won't let us down.'

Cathy wasn't at all sure of this; she had no evidence that Walter Mitchell was reliable. But at least it was going to be known what his terms of business were. And if he didn't turn up, then his own relations would have been made aware of his shortcomings. She heard someone outside.

'Ah, that must be Walter now,' she said. 'I knew he'd be on time.'

It was in fact Jock Mitchell, who came into the kitchen rubbing his hands.

'This looks just great, Cathy. I say, Hannah, isn't this an amazing spread?'

'Yes,' said his wife.

'Welcome home, Mr Mitchell. I thought it was Walter. He's actually working for me tonight,' Cathy said. 'Did he leave the office at the same time as you, by any chance?'

'Ages earlier,' her father-in-law said. 'Boy keeps his own time. I'm getting a bit of stick from the partners over him, as it happens.'

Hannah Mitchell hated family business being discussed in front of Cathy.

'Why don't you come upstairs and have a shower, dear? The guests will be here in half an hour,' she said crisply.

'Fine, fine. Don't you want any help, Cathy?'

'No, not at all. As I say, my wine waiter will be here shortly,' Cathy said.

'And Neil?' he asked.

'At a consultation. He'll be along when he can.'

She was alone in the kitchen. So far she was surviving, but it was only fifteen minutes before eight o'clock. There were hours and hours to go.

Ricky's party was only starting at nine, and they would go much later, so Tom Feather had plenty of time to go up to his parents and wish them a Happy New Year. He caught the bus from outside the door of Stoneyfield flats, and it went directly to Fatima, his mother and father's house, weighed down with statues and holy pictures. He longed to call Cathy and ask how it was all going, but she said she had better not bring her mobile into the house – it seemed to irritate Hannah Mitchell beyond all reason. She would leave it in the van. Cathy would not appreciate being telephoned and called to the hall at Oaklands. He would have to leave it.

Tom sat on the bus, his heart heavy. He was so stupid to be upset by that skimpy dress Marcella was wearing. She was dressing up for him; she loved only him. He was so mean-spirited to grudge the hour it took to go and sit with his parents in their cluttered sitting room. It was just that they were so pessimistic, so willing to see the downside of things, while he had always been the reverse. He was a fool to be upset because they hadn't found premises for the new company yet. They would: it took time, that's what everyone said, and then the right place would come along.

Tom's mother said they had heard nothing from Tom's brother Joe, nothing at all even on Christmas Day. There were phones in London, he could lift one of them. Tom's father said that there was an article in the paper saying that the building industry was going to go through the roof, and yet Tom Feather was chasing after moonbeams trying to set up a catering company instead of entering a ready-made office. Tom was pleasant and cheerful, and talked on and on until his jaw ached, hugged them both and said he must go back.

'I don't suppose you'd make an honest woman out of Marcella next year. Could that be your resolution?' his mother asked.

'Mam, I wanted to marry Marcella about twenty-five minutes after I met her. I must have asked her at least a hundred times . . .' He spread his hands out helplessly. They knew he was telling the truth.

Walter Mitchell looked at his watch in the pub where a group of his friends were having a New Year's Eve drink.

'Shit, it's eight o'clock,' he said.

Cathy would be like a devil over this, but still, Uncle Jock and Aunt Hannah would stand up for him. That was the great thing about being family.

There was no sign of Walter, so Cathy unpacked the glasses, filled thirty of them with a sugar lump and a teaspoon of brandy and laid them on a tray. Later, once the guests arrived, she would top the glasses up with champagne. That boy was meant to be doing this while she got her trays of canapés ready. Cathy caught sight of herself in the hall mirror – she looked flushed and uneasy. Wisps of hair were escaping from the ribbon that tied it back. This would not do.

She went into the downstairs cloakroom and smoothed a beige liquid make-up over her face and neck. She dampened her hair and tied it more expertly back. This is where she needed Marcella, to put something magical on her eyes. Cathy hunted in her handbag. There was a stubby brown pencil, and she made a few stabs at herself with that. She put on her clean white shirt and her scarlet skirt. It looked a *bit* better, she thought. How wonderful if she got a lot of business for the company out of this party! But Cathy knew she must be careful. Any sign of touting for business, or giving a card, would be frowned upon by her mother-in-law. Please may it be a success, otherwise days and days of effort, and money they could ill afford, would all have been wasted.

Ricky's studio was in a basement, three rooms opening into each other, drink in one, food in another and dancing in a third. You didn't so much come in, you made an entrance by walking down a big staircase which was brightly lit.

Tom and Marcella had left their coats on the ground floor, and he felt every eye in the room was on Marcella in her little red dress as she walked gracefully ahead of him down the stairs, with her beautiful long legs and the gold evening sandals that she was so proud of. No wonder they looked at her. Every other woman seemed suddenly drab by comparison.

Marcella never ate or drank at these functions. She might have a glass of fizzy water. But she genuinely wasn't hungry, she said, with such sincerity that people believed her. Tom, however, was dying to see the food, to compare it to what he and Cathy would have done. For a party like this they would serve a choice of two hot dishes with a lot of pitta bread, something like the chicken in herbs and the vegetarian dish that Cathy was preparing at her in-laws' house. But Ricky's caterers seemed to have endless plates of insubstantial and tired-looking finger food. Smoked salmon already drying and hardening on bread, some kind of pâté spread sparsely on unappetising-looking biscuits. Cocktail sausages congealing and allowed to cool in their own fat. Bit by bit he tasted and examined, identifying a shop paste here and a bought biscuit base there. He ached to know how much they had charged a head. He would be able to ask Ricky eventually, but not tonight.

'Tom, stop tearing those unfortunate things to bits,' Marcella giggled at him.

'Look at them, will you – soggy pastry, far too much salt . . .'

'Come and dance with me.'

'In a moment. I have to see what other awful things are lurking here,' he said, poking around the plates.

'Would you like to dance with me?' A boy of nineteen was staring at Marcella in disbelief.

'Tom?'

'Go ahead. I'll come in and drag you away in a minute,' Tom grinned.

It was considerably later, and after three glasses of inferior wine, that he found his way to the little dance floor. Marcella was dancing with a man with a big red face and big hands. The man's hands were spread over Marcella's bottom. Tom moved up to them.

'I've come to drag you away,' he said.

'Hey,' the man said, 'fair's fair, find your own girl.'

'Oh, this *is* my girl,' Tom said firmly.

'Well have some manners, then, and let us finish the dance.'

'If you don't mind . . .' Tom began.

'Let's just finish this dance,' Marcella said. 'And then I'll dance with you, Tom, I *have* been waiting for you.'

He moved away, annoyed. Somehow it was now *his* fault that this lout had his hands all over Marcella. He saw Shona Burke, nice girl from Haywards, one of the many people in Dublin who had been asked to look out for premises for the new catering company.

'Would you like me to get you a glass of red ink and a piece of cardboard with a scrape of meat paste on it?' he offered.

Shona laughed. 'Now, you're not going to get anywhere by bad-mouthing the opposition,' she said.

'No, but this kind of thing really does annoy me. It's so shoddy,' Tom said. His glance went back to Marcella, who was still talking to and dancing with that horrible man.

'It's all right, Tom, she has eyes for no one except you.'

Tom was embarrassed to have been so obvious. 'I meant the food. It's really outrageous to charge Ricky for this. Whatever he paid he was robbed.'

'Sure you were talking about the food,' Shona said.

'Would you like to dance?' he said.

'No, Tom, I'm not going to be any part of this. Go and get Marcella.'

But by the time he came over, another man had asked her to dance and the man with the big face and the big hands watched her approvingly from the sidelines. Tom went off to have another glass of the unspeakable wine.

Walter arrived at eight-thirty, when there were ten guests already installed in the sitting room of Oaklands. He came in cheerfully kissing his aunt on both cheeks.

'Now let me give you a hand, Aunt Hannah,' he said with a broad smile.

'Such a nice boy, isn't he?' said Mrs Ryan to Cathy.

'Indeed,' Cathy managed to say.

Mrs Ryan and her husband had been the first guests to arrive. She was totally unlike Hannah Mitchell; a humble woman, who was full of admiration for the canapés and had plenty of small talk for Cathy.

'My husband will be annoyed that we were here first,' she confided.

'Somebody has to be first. I think it's nice to be one of the early arrivals.'

Cathy wasn't concentrating. She was looking at Walter, small and handsome like all the Mitchells, and she was trying hard to keep her temper under control. He was being praised and fêted by people like her mother-in-law and stupid guests for having turned up one whole hour late. She was barely listening to what the apologetic Mrs Ryan was saying about being a poor cook herself.

'One thing they always wanted was apple strudels, and I just wouldn't know where to begin.'

Cathy brought her mind back. The woman was having some business friends of her husband to coffee and cake next week. Was it possible for Cathy to deliver something to the house and not stay to serve them?

Cathy looked carefully as her mother-in-law left the room, then she took down Mrs Ryan's phone number.

'It will be our little secret,' she promised.

It was their first booking. Not even nine o'clock, and she had got a job already.

'Do you intend to stop dancing with strangers at all tonight?' Tom asked Marcella.

'Tom. At last,' she said, excusing herself with a smile from a man in a black leather jacket and sunglasses.

'But maybe I'm not good enough to dance with,' he said.

'Don't be such a fool, put your arms around me,' she said.

'Is that what you say to all the lads?' he asked.

'Why are you being like this?' She was hurt and upset. 'What have I done?'

'You've lurched around half naked with half of Dublin,' he said.

'That's not fair,' Marcella was stung.

'Well haven't you?'

'It's a party, people ask other people to dance, that's what it's about.'

'Oh, good.'

'What's wrong, Tom?' She kept glancing over his shoulder at the dance floor.

'I don't know.'

'Tell me.'

'I don't *know*, Marcella. I realise that I'm a spoilsport, but would you come home?'

'Come *home*?' she was astounded. 'We've only just got here.'

'No, of course. Of course.'

'And we want to meet people, be seen a bit.'

'Yes, I know,' he said glumly.

'Do you not feel well?' she asked.

'No. I drank too much very cheap wine too quickly and ate five strange things that tasted like cement.'

'Well, will you sit down until it passes over.' Marcella had no intention of leaving. She had dressed up for this; looked forward to it.

'I might go home a bit before you,' he said.

'Don't do that; see the new year in here, with all our friends,' she begged.

'They're not really our friends, they're only strangers,' said Tom Feather sadly.

'Tom, have another cement sandwich and cheer up,' she said to him, laughing.

Cathy tried to show Walter how to make the champagne cocktails. He barely watched her.

'Sure, sure, I know,' he said.

'And once they have started to drink the red and white with the supper, can you collect all the champagne flutes and get them into the kitchen. They need to be washed because champagne will be served again at midnight.'

'Who washes them?' he asked.

'You do, Walter. I'll be serving the supper . . . I've left trays out here ready for—'

'I'm paid to help pass things around, not to be a washer-up,' he said.

'You're being paid to help me for four hours to do whatever I ask you to do.' Cathy heard the tremble in her voice.

'Five hours,' he said.

'Four,' she said, looking him in the eye. 'You got here an hour late.'

'I think you'll find . . .'

'When Neil comes, I think you'll find that we'll discuss it with him. Meanwhile, please take this tray out to your uncle's guests.'

Cathy lifted the trays of food from the oven. This night would end, sometime.

Shona Burke watched Tom Feather standing moodily in a corner. She knew she wasn't the only woman in the room looking at him. But the place might as well have been empty for all that he saw of them.

'I think I'll go home,' he said aloud to himself. Then he realised that was exactly what he was going to do.

'Will you tell Marcella, if she notices, that I've gone home,' he said to Ricky.

'Not a lovers' quarrel on New Year's Eve, please.' Ricky always put on a slightly camp accent. It was part of the way he went on. Tonight it irritated Tom greatly.

'No, not at all: I ate five things that disagreed with me,' Tom said.

'What were they?' Ricky asked.

'Search me, Ricky, sandwiches or something.'

Ricky decided not to be offended. 'How will Marcella get home?'

'I don't know. Shona might give her a lift – that's if the man with his two big shovels of hands which he has all over her doesn't take her.'

'Tom, come on. It's under an hour to midnight.'

'I'm in no form for it, Ricky. I'm only bringing other people down. My face would stop a clock.'

'I'll see she gets back to you safely,' Ricky said.

'Thanks, mate.' And he was gone, out into the wet, windy streets of Dublin where revellers were moving from one pub to another, or looking vainly for taxis; where closed curtains showed chinks of light from the parties behind them. From time to time he halted and wondered was he being silly, but he couldn't go back. Everything about the party annoyed him; all his insecurity that he wasn't good enough for Marcella would keep bubbling back to the surface. No: he must walk and walk and clear his head.

Eventually Neil got away from his meeting. He and Jonathan drove through the New Year's Eve streets of Dublin and out onto the leafy road where Oaklands stood, all lit up like a Christmas tree. He saw that Cathy had tidied her big white van as far out of sight as possible. He parked the Volvo and ran in the back door. Cathy was surrounded by plates and glasses. How could anyone do this for a living and stay sane . . .

'Cathy, I'm sorry things took longer, this is Jonathan. Jonathan, this is Cathy.'

She shook hands with the tall Nigerian with the tired face and polite smile.

'I hope I'm not causing you additional problems by coming here,' he said.

'No, heavens no, Jonathan,' Cathy protested, wondering what her mother-in-law's reaction would be. 'You're most welcome and I hope you have a good evening. I'm glad you both got here, I thought I'd be singing Auld Lang Syne to myself.'

'Happy New Year, hon.' Neil put his arms around her.

She felt very tired suddenly. 'Will we survive, Neil, tell me?'

'Of course we will, we've covered all the options, they're not going to move on New Year's Day, are they, Jonathan?'

'I hope not, you've given up so much time for this,' the young man smiled gratefully.

Cathy realised Neil thought she had been talking about the extradition. Still, he was here, that was the main thing.

'Is it going all right in there?' Neil nodded towards the front rooms.

'Okay, I think, hard to know. Walter was an hour late.'

'Then he gets paid an hour less.' To Neil it was simple. 'Is he any help to you?'

'Not really. Neil, go on in and take Jonathan to meet people.'

'I could perhaps help you here,' Jonathan offered.

'Lord no, if anyone needs a party it's you, after all you've been through,' Cathy said. 'Go on in, Neil, your mother's dying to show you off.'

'But can't I do anything here for—'

'Go distract your mother. Keep her out of the kitchen,' she begged.

She could hear cries of excitement as people welcomed the son and heir of Oaklands, and told him they remembered him when he was a little boy. Neil moved around the room easily, talking, greeting and kissing here and there. He saw Walter having a cigarette by the piano and talking to a woman who was about twenty years younger than the average age.

'I think you're needed in the kitchen, Walter,' he said briskly.

'Surely not,' Walter said.

'Now, please,' Neil said, and took over the conversation with the vacant-looking blonde woman.

Tom Feather didn't go straight home to Stoneyfield flats. He walked instead up and down little streets that he had never walked before, lanes, mews and even backyards. Somewhere in this city of a million people there was a place which he and Cathy could find to start their catering company. All it really needed was someone with the patience and the time to go and look for it. And he had plenty of time tonight.

The phone rang in the hall of Oaklands.

Hannah Mitchell hastened out to answer it; she felt she needed time to collect her thoughts. She was so confused: Neil had brought this African man to the party without letting them know. She had nothing against the man at all, of course. Why should she? But it was annoying that people kept asking who he was, and she didn't really know. One of Neil's clients, she said over and over, adding that Neil was always so dedicated. But she felt she had been getting some odd looks. It was a relief to escape.

'I'm sure that's Amanda phoning from Canada to wish us a Happy New Year,' she trilled. Her face showed that it was not her daughter who had phoned.

'Yes, well, that's all very upsetting, but what exactly do you think . . . Yes,

I know ... Well, of course it is hard to know what to do, but this isn't a good time. Look, you'd better talk to your brother. Oh, I see. Well, your uncle then ... Jock, come here a moment.'

Cathy watched the little tableau.

'It's Kenneth's children, apparently they're in the house on their own tonight. You talk to them, I told them Walter was here but they didn't think he'd be any help.'

'Too damn right,' grumbled Jock Mitchell.

'Well, well, well, tell me the problem,' he said wearily down the phone.

Cathy moved among the guests, passing little plates of a rich chocolate cake and a spoonful of fruit pavlova on the side, giving them no time to dither and make a choice when everyone knew they wanted both.

She saw Jonathan standing alone and awkward at the window while Neil went around the room greeting his parents' friends. She spoke to him as often as she could without making it look as if she was trying to mind him.

'I could work in the kitchen, I'm good at it,' he said pleadingly.

'I'm sure you are, and it would probably be more fun, but honestly, it's not on – for my sake. I won't let Neil's mother say I wasn't able to do it by myself. I have to prove it – do you understand?'

'I understand having to prove yourself, yes,' he answered.

Cathy moved on and found herself within earshot of Jock on the phone.

'That's fine then, children, I'll put Walter on to you and I'll come round tomorrow. Good children, now.'

Neil had just managed to galvanise Walter into doing some work when Jock removed him from the scene again. Cathy listened as the boy talked to his brother and sister, who were over ten years younger than he was.

'Now *listen* to me, I will be home, I'm not sure what time, I have to go somewhere when I leave here but I *will* be there sometime, so not one more word out of you. Just go to bed, for heaven's sake. Father hasn't been there for ages and Mother never comes out of her room, so what's so different about tonight?'

He turned round and saw Cathy watching him.

'Well, as you will have gathered there's a crisis at home, so I'm afraid I'm off duty.'

'Yes, so I hear.'

'So suppose I just take what's owing to me ...'

'I'll ask Neil to give it to you,' she said.

'I thought you prided yourself on this being your own business?' He was insolent.

'It is, but Neil is your cousin, he'd know how much you're owed. Let's go and ask him.'

'Four hours will do,' he said grudgingly.

'You haven't even been here for three hours,' she said.

'It's not my fault that I have to—'

'You're not going straight home, you're going to a party somewhere. But let's not fight, let's ask Neil.'

'Three hours then, cheapskate.'

485

'No, that's what I am most certainly not. Come, let's not do it in front of the guests, come into the kitchen.'

Her heart sank when she saw the washing-up, including the champagne glasses that would be needed at midnight.

'Goodnight, Walter.'

'Goodnight, Scrooge,' he said, and ran out of the house.

Tom stood by the canal and watched two swans gliding by.

'They mate for life, swans, did you know that?' he said to a passing girl.

'Do they now? Lucky old them,' she said. She was small and thin, he noticed; a druggy prostitute with an anxious face.

'Don't suppose you'd like any casual mating yourself,' she said hopefully.

'No, no, sorry,' Tom said. It seemed rather dismissive. 'Not tonight,' he added, as if to say that normally he would be utterly delighted. She smiled a tired smile.

'Happy New Year anyway,' she said.

'And to you,' he said, feeling hopeless.

The doorbell rang at Oaklands.

Hannah teetered out on her high heels, wondering who else it could be, arriving so late. Cathy leaned against a table at the back of the hall to support her tired legs and to see what new confusion was arriving now. A late guest wanting a main course?

It appeared to be two children in a taxi which they didn't have the money to pay for. Cathy sighed. She almost felt sorry for Hannah. A Nigerian student, and now two waifs – what else would the night throw at her?

'Please get Mr Mitchell immediately, Cathy,' Hannah ordered.

'Is that the maid?' the little boy asked. He was pale and aged about eight or nine. Like his sister, he had dead straight fair hair and everything looked the same colour – his sweater, his hair, his face and the small canvas bag he carried.

'Don't say "maid",' the girl corrected him in a hiss. Her face was frightened and there were dark rings under her eyes.

Cathy had never seen them before. Jock Mitchell and his brother Kenneth were not close; the nearest they had ever come to solidarity was in the apprenticeship of Walter in his uncle's office, something that hadn't proved to be entirely successful, Cathy gathered.

Jock had come out anyway to see who was at the door. He was not enthusiastic at the sight of them.

'Well?' he began. 'What have we here?'

'We had nowhere to go,' the boy explained.

'So we came here,' said the girl.

Jock looked bewildered.

'Cathy,' he said eventually, 'these are Walter's brother and sister, can you give them something to eat in the kitchen?'

'Certainly, Mr Mitchell, go back to your guests, I'll look after them.'

'*Are* you the maid?' the boy asked again. He seemed anxious to put everyone in a category.

'No, actually I'm Cathy, married to Neil, your cousin. How do you do?' They looked at her solemnly. 'And perhaps you might give me your names?' Maud and Simon, it turned out. 'Come into the kitchen,' she said wearily. 'Do you like herbed chicken?'

'No,' said Maud.

'We never had it,' said Simon.

Cathy noticed them lifting some chocolate biscuits and putting them in their pockets.

'Put those back,' she said sharply.

'Put what back?' Simon's eyes were innocent.

'There'll be no stealing,' she said.

'It's not stealing, you were told to give us something to eat,' Maud countered with spirit.

'And give you something I will – so just put them back this minute.'

Grudgingly, they put the already crushed and crumbly biscuits back on the silver tray. Swiftly Cathy made them sandwiches from the cold chicken and poured them a glass of milk each. They ate hungrily.

'In your lives so far did anyone mention the words "thank you" at all?' she asked.

'Thank you,' they said ungraciously.

'You're most welcome,' she said with exaggerated politeness.

'What will we do now?' Simon asked.

'Well, I think you might sit here – unless you wanted to help me wash up?'

'Not really, to be honest,' Maud said.

'Should we be inside at the party, do you think?' Simon wondered.

'Not really, to be honest,' Cathy echoed.

'So will we sit here all night until we go to bed?' Maud asked.

'Are you staying here?'

'Where else would we go?' Maud asked innocently.

Hannah came into the kitchen, with her tottering, tiny steps which always set Cathy's teeth on edge.

'Oh, you're sitting here, Cathy, I think people's glasses need—'

'Of course, Mrs Mitchell, I'll go and see to it. Walter, who was meant to be seeing to glasses, seems to have disappeared, and I was, as you asked, giving supper to Walter's brother and sister . . .'

'Yes, well, of course,' said Hannah.

'So I'll leave you to make all the arrangements with Maud and Simon, then,' said Cathy on her way to the door.

'Arrangements?' Hannah looked alarmed.

Cathy paused just long enough to hear Maud asking in her bell-clear voice, 'What rooms will we have, Aunt Hannah, we've brought our pyjamas and everything . . .' Then she circulated the party refilling glasses.

'Are you finding it all insane?' she asked Jonathan.

He smiled his weary smile. 'At school I was taught by Irish priests. They told me all about Ireland, but I didn't expect New Year's Eve to be quite like this.'

'It's not meant to be, believe me,' Cathy grinned at him.

She moved on, topping up glasses here and avoiding people's eyes there. That nice Mrs Ryan had had quite enough already. To her surprise, she saw that Maud and Simon had joined the party easily as if it were their natural place.

Cathy worked and worked. She removed plates, picked up scrunched-up napkins, emptied ashtrays, kept things moving. Soon it would be midnight and things might begin to wind down. Most people here were in their late fifties and sixties; they wouldn't have the stamina to party on until dawn. She looked towards the window where she had left Jonathan to fend for himself. He was talking animatedly to someone. Cathy looked again. The twins were in deep conversation with him.

'Jock, *what* are we going to do with them?'

'Calm, Hannah, calm.'

'They can't stay here.'

'Well, not for ever, no, certainly not.'

'But for how long?'

'Until we get them settled.'

'And how long will that be?'

'Soon, soon.'

'So where . . .'

'Put them in Neil's and Mandy's rooms, or wherever. Haven't we a house full of bedrooms, for heaven's sake?' He was clearly irritated and wanted to get back to the party. Hannah went over to the ill-assorted group at the window.

'Now children, don't annoy Neil's client, Mr . . . um . . .' she began.

'Oh, but they're not annoying me at all – delightful company,' Jonathan begged. They were, after all, the only people who had talked to him normally all night. Certainly the only people he had ever met who had asked him whether or not his tongue was black and if he'd had a lot of slaves amongst his friends.

'Are you staying in this house?' Maud asked hopefully.

'No, no indeed, I was very kindly asked for supper,' Jonathan said, looking at the ashen face of Neil Mitchell's mother.

'Time for bed, anyway,' Hannah said.

'Can Jonathan come round for breakfast?' suggested Maud.

'I'm not sure that . . .' Hannah began.

'Very nice having met you both – we might meet again but sometime, not tomorrow,' Jonathan said hastily and the children left with reluctance.

Hannah ushered them up the broad, sweeping staircase of Oaklands before any more invitations could be issued; she showed them their bedrooms and said they were to remain there quietly in the morning, since the house didn't wake too early on the day after a party.

'Are your nerves bad? Like our mother's nerves are bad?' Maud asked.

'Of course they're not,' Hannah snapped. Then she recovered herself.

'Now it's all been very upsetting for you but it will get sorted out. Your uncle will see to that,' she said firmly, attempting to distance herself.

'Which is my room?'

'Whichever one you like.' Hannah pointed to the corridor where Amanda and Neil's old bedrooms still held souvenirs they had never collected for their new lives. There was a bathroom in between.

'Goodnight, now, and sleep well. We'll talk about everything in the morning.' She went downstairs with a heavy sigh. Her shoes were very tight, Neil had brought an African man and left him for everyone else to entertain and Cathy was being insufferable – who ever said it was easy giving a party? Even if you did have a caterer?

'Which room will you have?' Simon asked. They had done a complete tour.

'I'd like the one with all the coats in it,' Maud said.

'But she didn't say . . .'

'She didn't say *not* this one either,' Maud was determined.

'It could be their own bedroom, look, it opens into a bathroom, I don't think you should sleep here, Maud.'

'She said wherever we liked. We could put the coats on chairs.' They stood for a while in Jock and Hannah Mitchell's large bedroom.

'There's a television in this one.' Simon was sorry he hadn't found it first.

'Yes, but I have to move all these old coats and scarves and things.' Maud felt that made things equal. They pushed the coats on to chairs and, mainly, on to the floor.

'Look, she has all this make-up that Mother used to have on her dressing-table before her nerves got bad.' Maud picked up some lipsticks.

'What are the black things?'

'They're for eyebrows.'

Simon drew heavy dark eyebrows and then a moustache. The sudden ringing out of bells and celebratory shrieks startled him and the pencil broke, so he used another one. Maud put on a dark red lipstick and then used a pinker shade to make little spots on her cheeks. She picked up a cut-glass atomiser and began to spray.

'Hey, that got in my eye,' Simon said, picking up what looked like a large can of hair lacquer in retaliation. It turned out to be some kind of mousse. It went all over the dressing-table. 'What on earth is that?' he wondered.

'It could be shaving cream,' Maud thought.

'That must be it. Imagine her wanting that.'

There were long earrings which Maud tried on, but they were for pierced ears, so she went to the bathroom and found some Elastoplast. She admired herself. Simon had found a short fur jacket and put it on with a man's hat. They were bouncing happily on the two large beds with white counterpanes when two women came in.

They gasped when they saw the clothes on the floor; and one of them screamed when she saw Simon wearing her recently remodelled mink jacket. Her screams frightened Maud and Simon, who screamed back, and

Hannah and Jock came running up the stairs – followed by a small crowd – to find out what had happened.

Neil was in the kitchen.

'What in the name of God's that caterwauling upstairs?' he asked.

'Stay out of it, if you investigate, you'll only become part of it,' Cathy grinned.

'But listen to them!'

'Keep well out of it,' she warned.

'We'll give Jonathan a lift back when the time comes, okay?' Neil said.

'The time won't come for me until everyone else is gone. You should take him home yourself and let me come back under my own steam in the van.'

More voices were raised upstairs.

'I'd really better go and see what's happening,' Neil said, and he was gone.

Jonathan brought some ashtrays into the kitchen and wiped them.

'Terrible smokers, the older generation,' Cathy smiled at him.

'I'd like to slip away now, do you think I could get a taxi?'

'Not on New Year's Eve, but Neil's going to drive you home anyway.'

'I don't want to put him out any more.'

'It won't put him out at all, but he won't be able to go for a while. Do you want to use that bike out in the back?'

'Do you think I could?' His eyes were full of relief.

'Certainly. It's an old one. It used to belong to Neil. Go now, Jonathan, while the third world war is being fought upstairs.'

'I suppose I could make things worse and ask if I could have a bed for the night,' he said with a grin.

'Now, that's something I'd like to see,' Cathy said.

'Who are the children anyway?'

'A long story, cousins, children of Neil's very hopeless uncle and aunt. It's their first night here.'

'It could very well be their last.'

Tom walked on up from the canal, and over and through the Georgian streets and down a lane he had never been down before. And that's where he saw it. A wrought-iron gate leading into a cobbled courtyard, and what looked like an old coach house that had been converted for some business. He pushed open the iron gate and went up to the door where there seemed to be some kind of notice. It was a piece of cardboard where someone had written For Sale. There was a phone number to contact for details. Bells were ringing all over Dublin, it was midnight, a new year had arrived. Tom peered through the windows. He had found their premises.

Mrs Ryan told Cathy that she was a little the worse for wear. Cathy said the solution was three glasses of water and three small slices of very thin bread and butter, never known to fail. Mrs Ryan ate the bread and drank the water dutifully and pronounced herself fine. Cathy filled the champagne glasses for midnight, and as the bells rang over the city they all toasted each other and sang Auld Lang Syne. Hannah Mitchell looked almost pleased with it all. Cathy decided to let her have her moment, and moved quickly and quietly away from the circle of entwined hands.

She cleared and washed and dried in the kitchen, she packed crates and neatly arranged several little dishes of goodies for Hannah to discover the next day, in the refrigerator. She moved in and out between the kitchen and the van; the bulk of the work was done. Now all she had to worry about was serving more wine, and more coffee. She could scoop the coffee cups away later. She felt tired in every one of her bones. She heard the telephone ring, thank God. Neil's sister had finally called them. Then she heard Hannah say in tones of disbelief, '*Cathy.* You want to talk to Cathy?' She moved to the hall. Her mother-in-law stood there holding the receiver as if it might be transmitting a disease.

'It's for you,' she said, astounded.

Please let it not be bad news from home, Cathy prayed; may it not be her mother or father taken ill having chicken in a basket at the pub. Or some terrible phone call from Chicago where all her sisters and brothers had gone to live so long ago.

'Cathy,' said Tom, 'I've found it.'

'Found what?' she asked, not sure whether to be overcome with relief that it wasn't bad news, or with rage that he had phoned her here.

'The premises,' he said. 'I've found the place where Scarlet Feather is going to live.'

January

The year began in different ways in different houses.

Tom Feather woke in Stoneyfield flats with a pain in his shoulders and a stiff neck ... The armchair had not been at all comfortable. He got some cold orange juice from the fridge, and fixed a flower to the glass with some sticky tape. He marched straight into the bedroom.

'Happy New Year to the most beautiful, saintly and forgiving woman in the world,' he said.

Marcella woke and rubbed her eyes. 'I'm not saintly and forgiving, I'm furious with you,' she began.

'But you haven't denied that you are beautiful, and I have totally forgiven *you*,' he said happily.

'What do you mean? There was nothing to forgive *me* for.' She was very indignant indeed.

'Quite right, which is why we will say no more about it. I should thank you instead, because last night I found the premises.'

'You what?'

'I know it's all due to you: if you hadn't behaved so badly and forced me to leave that party, I'd never have found the place. I'll take you to see it as soon as you're dressed so drink up that beautiful elegant drink I've prepared for you and—'

'If you think for one moment that I'm going to leap out of bed and—'

'You're so right. I do not think that for one moment. Instead I think *I'm* going to leap *into* bed. What a truly great idea.' And he had his crumpled clothes off as he spoke.

In Neil and Cathy's house at Waterview the phone rang. 'It's your mother, saying all the guests are dead from salmonella,' Cathy said.

'More likely to be some shrink saying that you've been committed to a mental home for advanced paranoia,' Neil said, reaching over to ruffle her hair.

'I suppose we *could* leave it?' she said doubtfully.

'When do we ever?' Neil replied, reaching down under the bed where the phone was nestling. 'Anyway it's probably Tom.'

It wasn't Tom, it was about Jonathan. Neil was half out of bed.

'Tell them I'm on my way,' he was saying.

Cathy put on the coffee as he dressed.

'No time,' he was protesting.

'Listen, I've put it in a flask. Take it with you, you can drink it in the car,' she said.

He came back, took the flask and kissed her. 'I'm very sorry, hon. I *did* want to go and see this place with you this morning, you know I did.'

'I know, this is more important. Go.'

'And don't sign anything or accept anything until we've had someone take a look at it.'

'No, Mr Lawyer, you know I won't!'

'Now of course I *do* have the address in case this thing ends early. I could come straight there.'

'It won't end early, Neil, it will take all day. Go and save him before it's too late.'

Cathy watched him from the window. As he put the flask down on the frosty ground in order to open the car door, he must have known she would be watching. He waved up at her. Jonathan was lucky that he had Neil Mitchell in his corner. Neil would worry at the case like a dog with a bone, just as he would get a colleague to examine the title deeds of this place, which looked like the perfect premises at last.

JT and Maura Feather woke up in Fatima, a small red-brick house in a quiet road. They used to be workers' cottages, but the Feathers had noted with disapproval that a lot of trendy younger people were buying. Attracting burglars to the area.

'I never thought we'd live to see another year, JT. The Lord must have spared us for some purpose,' Maura said. She was a tall, thin woman with a long, sad face permanently set in the lines of a sorrowing Madonna bent low by the wickedness of the world.

Her husband was big and broad-shouldered, made strong by years of hard physical work in the building trade. His weather-beaten face had looked the same always.

'It's not that we're really all that old in terms of years, but I know what you mean,' JT agreed with her. He turned on the tea-making machine between their beds. It had been a gift from Tom. Maura had thought it was more trouble than it was worth, what with remembering to wash the pot and get fresh milk, but it was handy enough not to have to go down to the cold kitchen.

'Another year begun and not a sign of either of them wanting to do a hand's turn in the business,' he sighed heavily.

'Or settling down in marriage as God intended,' Maura sniffed.

'Ah, marriage is a different thing,' JT said. 'Anyone can marry or not marry, but no two other boys from this area have a ready-made business to walk into, and you have Joe making girls' dresses over in London and Tom making cakes and pastries. It would drive you to an early grave.'

Maura hated it when he got grey with worry. 'Haven't I told you to stop getting your blood pressure all het up over him,' she warned. 'He's like all young people, just looking out for himself. Just wait until he has a couple of children, then he'll be round to the door pretty fast wondering can he work in the business.'

'You may be right,' JT nodded, but in his heart he didn't think that he was ever going to see either of his boys ask him to put the words Feather and Son over his builder's yard.

Muttie Scarlet woke with a start. Something good had happened last night, and he couldn't remember what it was. Then it came back. He had drawn a horse in the pub sweepstake. That was all. Most people would be pleased about this. But to Muttie, who was a serious betting man, there was no skill or science in that kind of thing.

You just bought a ticket for a raffle and then twenty-one people got a horse, you couldn't even choose your own animal. He had something called Lucky Daughter. No form, nothing known about it, total outsider, probably had three legs. Lizzie didn't understand it at all. She had been pleased for him, said he'd have all the thrill of the race without having to put a week's wages on a horse.

Poor Lizzie. It was awful trying to explain anything at all about horses to her. And she was very sure that nothing *she* earned ever ended up at the bookmaker's. But to be fair, she *did* put the food on the table and didn't ask him for much from his dole money. Muttie hadn't known a week's wages for a long time. He had a bad back. But still and all, it wasn't too bad to get out of bed and bring Lizzie a mug of tea. She'd be going out to people's houses later to clean, to clear up their New Year's Eves for them. Lizzie was a great support to them all, the children in Chicago and to Cathy. Muttie smiled to himself as he often did over the fast one that their Cathy had done, grabbing Neil, the son and heir of Oaklands, Hannah Mitchell's pride and joy. Even if he hadn't liked the boy, Muttie would have been overjoyed at that marriage. Just to see the hard, hate-filled face of Hannah at the wedding was vengeance enough for all that she had put poor Lizzie through up in that house. But Neil himself, as it happened, was a grand fellow. You couldn't meet a nicer lad in a month of Sundays. It was odd the way things turned out, Muttie told himself as he went to make the tea.

Hannah and Jock Mitchell woke at Oaklands.

'Well,' said Hannah menacingly. 'Well, Jock, it's tomorrow now. You said you'd decide "tomorrow".'

'God that was a good party,' Jock groaned. 'I feel it not exactly in my bones, more in the front left-side of my head.'

'I'm not surprised,' Hannah was terse. 'But there's no time to talk about your hangover. We are talking about those children. They are not staying another night in this house.'

'Don't be hasty,' he pleaded.

'I'm not being hasty. I was very patient when you and Neil said they had to stay last night. I was a saint out of heaven, not breaking every bone in their bodies when I saw the wreckage they had achieved in here. That jacket of Eileen's will never clean, you know, never. God knows what they managed to smear into it . . .'

'Best thing if it doesn't. Makes her look like a vole,' Jock whimpered.

'You've done enough for Kenneth over the years . . .'

'That's not the point.'

'It is the point.'

'No, it's not, Hannah. Where else can they go? They're my brother's children. He seems to have abandoned them.' He winced with pain.

'It's too much,' Hannah protested. 'And they were very rude, both of them, no apology, saying I'd said they could have any room and they had chosen this one. Enough to crucify anyone at what was meant to be a party, a celebration.'

'You didn't over-indulge yourself?' He had a faint hope that she might also have a hangover, which might tolerate the thought of a Bloody Mary at breakfast.

'Someone had to keep an eye on things,' she sniffed.

'Well, didn't Cathy do that very well. I heard a lot of praise for—'

'What do men know of what needs to be done?'

'She left the place like a new pin.' He tried to defend his daughter-in-law.

'Well, at least some of the training I gave her poor mother must have paid off eventually.'

Hannah would say nothing good about Cathy. Jock gave up. Some things weren't worth fighting over, especially with this hammering in his head.

'True,' he said, feeling he had somehow let that hard-working girl down. But Cathy of all people would know how it was easier to take the line of least resistance with Hannah.

'And then running off at the end because she got some phone call in the middle of the night about premises for this crackpot idea of hers.'

'I know, ridiculous,' said Jock Mitchell, getting up to get a painkiller and feeling like Judas.

Geraldine had been up since seven o'clock. She had been alone in the Glenstar swimming pool: usually she would have had the company of half a dozen other Glenstar residents, who loved the amenity of their swimming pool. But New Year's Eve had taken its toll. Geraldine did her twelve lengths, washed her hair and went through the arrangements again for today's big charity lunch. She had advised a group to have their function on January the first, since it was often a flat day when people were eager to recover in company. And indeed, the response to the invitation list had been overwhelming. She had been wise to leave that photographer's party early last night. There had been nobody that interested her to talk to, a lot of them much younger than she was. She had slipped away quietly before midnight. She had seen Tom Feather and his dizzy girlfriend there but couldn't get to meet them across the room. Cathy and Neil would have been there, but of course Cathy had been catering the Mitchells' party last night; Geraldine hoped that it had gone well and that there had been a chance to make some useful contacts. Cathy hated that woman so much it was really important that the night had been some kind of success for her in terms of business. Geraldine wished they could find premises soon. She had agreed to back them for the loan when the time came, as had Joe Feather, Tom's rather elusive elder brother. All they had to do was find the place. And then brave, gutsy Cathy wouldn't have to nail a smile on her face and work in the kitchen of her mother-in-law's house, something she hated with a passion. One of the advantages of being single was that there were no mothers-in-law to cope with, Geraldine thought as she poured more coffee.

In a different part of the Glenstar apartments, Shona Burke woke up and thought about the year ahead. Many other women of twenty-six would wake today with a comforting body on the other side of the bed. In fact, she was sick of people asking her when she was going to settle down. It was so intrusive. Shona would not ask people why they didn't have a baby, or when they were going to have their facial hair seen to. She never queried why people drove a car that was falling to pieces, or stayed with a spouse so obviously less than satisfactory. How dare they speculate openly and to her face about why she hadn't married?

'It could be because you look too cool, too successful. Fellows wouldn't dare chat you up and go home with you,' a colleague had suggested helpfully.

Last night's party at Ricky's would have provided plenty of people who might have chatted her up and come back to the Glenstar apartments with her; in fact, she had had one very definite offer and two suggestions. But these would not have been people who would have stayed. Not anyone she could trust or rely on. And Shona Burke was not one to trust easily. She would get up soon, go out to Dun Laoghaire for a brisk walk with a neighbour's dog, come back and get ready for the charity lunch. Because she was considered the very public face of Haywards, she was often asked to such things. Haywards was *the* store in Dublin. It had survived takeovers, makeovers and the passage of time. And today it would give her the chance to wear the new outfit which she had bought at a discount in Haywards. Ridiculous to have so many nice clothes at twenty-six, and not enough places to wear them.

'Neil, is it all right to talk?'
'Not really, Father, we're in the middle of something . . .'
'So are we, we're in the middle of those two children taking the house apart brick by brick.'
'No, I mean what I'm in is really serious. I can't talk about Maud and Simon now.'
'But what are we going to do?'
'Father, we're going to look after them, it's as simple as that. We'll help you, Cathy and I, but now, if you'll excuse me . . .'
'But Neil . . .'
'I have to go.'
Jock Mitchell hung up wearily. The twins had unpacked all the desserts

Cathy had left in the fridge and eaten them for breakfast. Simon had been sick. On the carpet.

In a garden flat in Rathgar, James Byrne was up and at his desk. Ever since he had retired six months ago he had continued the routine and habits of working life. Breakfast of a boiled egg, tea and toast, ten minutes' minimal tidying his three-room apartment, and then a second cup of tea and twenty minutes at his desk. It had been such a useful thing to do when he worked in the big accountancy firm. Cleared his head, sorted his priorities before he got into the office. Now of course there *were* no priorities. He didn't have to decide whether or not to oppose some tax scheme on the grounds that it was evasion. Other, younger people made those decisions. There was less and less to do, but he could always find something. He might renew a magazine subscription, or send for a catalogue. To his surprise the telephone rang. Very few people telephoned James Byrne at any time, and he certainly hadn't expected a call at ten o'clock in the morning on New Year's Day. It was a girl.

'Mr Byrne? Is it too early to talk?'

'No, no. How can I help you?'

The voice was young and very excited. 'It's about the premises, Mr Byrne, we're so interested, more than you'd believe. Is there any chance we could see them today?'

'Premises?' James Byrne was confused. 'What premises?'

He listened as she explained. It was the Maguires' old place, the printing works they hadn't even entered since the accident. He knew that they had been listless and depressed. They had been unwilling to listen to any advice. But now, apparently, they had disappeared, leaving a For Sale sign on their gate and James Byrne's phone number. In years of business James had learned that he must never transmit any of his own anxiety or confusion to a client.

'Let me see if I can find them, Miss Scarlet,' James said. 'I'll call you back within the hour.'

Cathy put the phone down carefully and looked around her in Tom's apartment, where the little group had been following every word of the conversation. Tom leaning forward, like her father always did to a radio when he wanted to hear who was winning a race. Marcella in an old pink shirt of Tom's and black jeans, her dark eyes and clouds of black hair making her look more and more like the top model she yearned to be. Geraldine, crisp and elegant, dressed for her smart lunch but still giving time to be present for the great phone call and what it might deliver.

'He's not an estate agent, he's an accountant, he knows the people who own it and he'll ring us back in an hour,' she said, eyes shining. They could hardly take it in.

It felt like three hours, but Geraldine told them it was only thirty-six minutes. Then the call came. This time Tom took it. James Byrne, ex-accountant, had been in touch with his friends in England. They reported they really did intend to sell. They had made their decision over Christmas, and had gone away to England yesterday now that it had been made. James Byrne had been asked to set it all in train. And as quickly as possible. Cathy looked at Tom in disbelief. It really was going to happen, *exactly* the kind of place they wanted. And they were the first potential buyers, they were in there with a chance. Tom was thinking the same thing.

'We are very lucky that you made this enquiry for us, Mr Byrne, and now if you would like us to let you know—'

The voice interrupted him. 'Of course you will understand that my first loyalty lies with the Maguires who own the premises. They will have to be represented by a lawyer, an auctioneer, and I will have to try and get them the best price possible.'

'Yes, of course,' Tom sounded deflated.

'But I am very grateful to you, Mr Feather, for bringing this to my notice, otherwise it might have been some days . . .'

Geraldine was scribbling something on the back of an envelope and showing it to him.

'Is there any chance you could show us inside the place, do you think?' Tom asked.

There was a pause. 'Certainly,' the man said. 'That would be no problem. In fact, the Maguires were anxious to know what kind of people had discovered the notice so quickly; they only put it up yesterday before they went to the airport.'

'Yesterday?' Tom was astounded. 'But it looks as if the place has been abandoned for a long time.'

'It has; the family had a lot of trouble.'

'I'm sorry. Are you a friend of theirs?'

'In a way. I did some work for them once. They trusted me.'

It was a sober sort of thing to say. Tom hoped that they could get back to the bit about letting them in. Then Mr Byrne cleared his throat.

'Suppose we meet there in an hour?' he suggested.

The city was still partially asleep, but James Byrne was wide awake. Small and rather precise-looking, wearing a navy overcoat and gloves, with a silk scarf tied around his neck, he was a man in his sixties who might have been cast in a film as a worried bank manager or concerned statesman. He introduced himself formally and shook hands with everyone as if they were in an office instead of standing in the bitter cold on the first day of the year outside a falling-down printing business. At first Cathy was pleased to see him take down the ludicrous cardboard notice while tut-tutting at the amateur nature of it all, but then he explained again that the place would of course have to be sold professionally, maybe even at auction. It could still be snatched from them. They sensed somehow that he wasn't going to tell them anything about the Maguires and what sorrows or confusion there had been in their lives. This was not the time to enquire.

They walked through in wonder. The place that could be Scarlet Feather's new home. First home.

All this middle section could be the main kitchen; this would be the freezer section, that would be the staff lavatory and washroom, and they would have storage here. And a small room where they could greet clients. It was almost too perfect: everything was what they had hoped. And it was so desperately shabby and run-down; perhaps others might not realise the potential. Cathy was aware that she had clasped her hands and closed her eyes only when she heard James Byrne clear his throat. He seemed to be concerned that she might be too happy about it all, too confident. She knew she must reassure him.

'It's all right, James, I do know it's not ours. This is only the first step of a very long journey,' she smiled at him warmly.

They had been talking to this man for forty-five minutes, calling him *Mr* Byrne all the while. He was a stranger, twice their age and she had called him James. She felt a slight flush creep up her neck. She knew exactly why she had done this; subconsciously it was part of her wish never to feel inferior, never to crawl and beg. But perhaps she had gone too far this time. Cathy looked hard at him, willing him not to take offence. James Byrne smiled back at her.

'It might not be too long a journey, Cathy. The Maguires are very anxious to get all this over; they want a quick sale. It might move much more quickly than you all think.'

Cathy did not go home. She didn't want to sit alone in the house while her mind was racing – and there were very few other places she wanted to be either. Tom and Marcella would need time to be on their own together. She couldn't go to St Jarlath's Crescent and hear a detailed description of their night at the pub when she ached to tell them the excitement in her life. There was no way she would go near Oaklands. In that big house at this very moment, there would be a terrible war raging. Those strange children, with their solemn faces and total disregard for anyone else's property or feelings might well have wrecked the place by now. She knew very well that sooner or later she and Neil would have to take some part in their care; but for now it would seem the wisest thing to stay away from Oaklands.

Hannah Mitchell would be on the phone to her friends, laughing and groaning, or complaining to her husband that their daughter had not telephoned from Canada. She would not yet have discovered the neatly covered plates in her fridge with perfectly labelled chicken, vegetables and desserts. Cathy knew she would never be thanked for these. That wasn't part of any deal. The best she could hope for was that Hannah Mitchell would leave her alone.

No, that wasn't true. The very best thing would be if her mother-in-law fell down a manhole. Cathy was restless, she needed to walk, clear her head. She found that she was driving south, out of the city towards Dun Laoghaire and the sea. She parked the car and walked on the long pier, hugging herself against the wind. Many Dubliners with hangovers seemed to have had some similar notion, and were busy working up a lunchtime thirst for themselves. Cathy smiled to herself; she must be the soberest and most abstemious person here, one half-glass of champagne at midnight and nothing else. Even her mother who claimed that she didn't drink at all would have had three hot whiskeys to see the New Year in. It was probably wiser not to speculate on how many pints her father might have had. But there was nobody else walking this pier on this, the first day of the New Year who was nearly as excited as Cathy Scarlet. She was going to have her own business. She would be self-employed. Joint owner of something that was going to be a huge success. For the very first time since the whole thing had started she realised now that it was not just a dream.

They would paint the logo on the van, they would turn up in this funny mews every morning, the premises would have their name over the door. Nothing violent or loud that would be at odds with the area. Perhaps even in wrought iron? Already she and Tom had agreed that they would paint the two doors the deepest of scarlet red. But this was not the time for hunting down fancy door handles and knockers. No money could be spent on a detailed image at this stage. They had gone over so many times how much they could afford. They would not lose their business before it had even begun. One of those men at the Mitchells' party last night owned a big stationery firm; perhaps Cathy could go to him about a quote for printing brochures and business cards. They needn't accept it or anything, but it would remind the man and his rather socially conscious wife of their existence.

There were a million things to do; how could they wait now until they heard from these strange people who had apparently locked up a failed business and without making any arrangements about fixtures and fittings disappeared overnight? If it had not been for the calmer manner of James Byrne, Cathy would have feared that they were dealing with mad people who might never agree to the sale being closed. But there was something reassuring about this man. Something that made you feel safe, and yet who kept well at a distance at the same time. Neither she nor Tom had even dared to ask him where he lived or what company he had been with. They had his phone number from the strange cardboard notice, but Cathy knew that neither she nor Tom would telephone to hurry him up. They would wait until they heard his news. And in his perfectly courteous but slightly flat voice he had told them he was very sure that it would be sooner rather than later. Cathy wondered whether he had gone back to his house where his wife had prepared a lunch for him. Or would he take his family out to a hotel? Perhaps he had no family, and was a bachelor catering for himself. He had looked slightly too well cared-for: polished shoes, well-ironed shirt collar. It might take for ever to know such information about him. But after James Byrne had introduced them to the strange, elusive Maguires, then they would probably never see him again. She must take his address sometime, so that when Scarlet Feather was up and running she could tell him that he had been in there at the very start of it . . . It *would* be a success,

Cathy knew this. They hadn't spent two whole years planning it for it to end up as one of those foolish statistics about companies that failed.

And Cathy Scarlet, businesswoman, would be able to take her mother shopping and to lunch in a smart restaurant. And soon the consuming wish to kill Hannah Mitchell would pass, and she would be able to regard her as just another ordinary and even pathetic member of the human race. Tom Feather badly wanted it to succeed for all of his reasons, and she wanted it even more badly for all of hers. Which were very complicated reasons, Cathy admitted. Some of them very hard to explain to the bank, to Geraldine and even at times to Neil. There was a general feeling that life would be much safer if Cathy Scarlet was to bring her considerable talents to work for someone else. The someone else taking the risks, paying the bills, facing any possible losses. Usually, but not always, Cathy was able to summon up the passion, the enthusiasm and the sheer conviction that she was totally sane and practical. Cathy at top speed was hard to resist.

Sometimes during a wakeful night she had doubted herself. Once or twice when she looked at the opposition she wondered could she and Tom ever break into the market. At the end of long hours working in one of Dublin's restaurants, she was sometimes tempted to think how good it would be to go home and take a long bath rather than spend a couple of hours with Tom trying to work out what the food would have cost to buy, and how they might have cooked it better, presented it more artistically and served it more speedily.

But last night when she had seen the premises, and today when she had realised that they might possibly be within their grasp, she had no doubts at all. Cathy smiled to herself with all the confidence in the world.

'Well there's *someone* who had a nice New Year's Eve, anyway,' said a voice. It was Shona Burke, the very handsome young woman who was the head of Human Resources or whatever they called it at Haywards. Always very calm and assured, she was a friend of Marcella and Tom's and had been very helpful in trying to seek out contacts for them. She was being tugged by an excited red setter, who wanted to go and find other dogs or bark at the sea – anything except have another dull conversation with a human being.

'What on earth makes you think that?' Cathy laughed.

'Compared to everyone else I've met, you're radiant. They are all giving up drink for ever, or they've been abandoned by their true loves or can't remember where they're meant to be going for lunch.'

'They haven't begun to know hardship . . . They weren't catering a party for Hannah Mitchell.' Cathy rolled her eyes. Shona would know the dreaded Hannah, always the stalwart of fashion news and Valued Customer evenings at Haywards.

'And you're still alive and smiling.'

'I wasn't smiling over the party, believe me. You don't sell any untraceable poisons in that store of yours, I suppose? Where were *you* last night, anyway?'

'I was at Ricky's party. I met Marcella and Tom . . . Well . . . Tom just for a bit.'

Cathy paused. She would like to have told Shona their news, but they had all agreed nobody would know until there really *was* something to know. Geraldine and Marcella had agreed to be silent, so Cathy must say nothing. Nor did she ask why Tom had only been there for a bit.

'What was the food like?' Cathy asked instead.

'Not you too. Tom practically had a forceps and swab out examining it.'

'Sorry. I know we're very boring.'

'Not a bit, and the truth is the food was very dull. Not only did I ask them for a brochure which I'll send you, I also asked Ricky how much he paid them and you'll be stunned . . .'

'Stunned good or stunned bad?'

'Good, I imagine – I know what you two could do for that price. Sorry, this animal's going to have me in the harbour in a minute.'

'He's never yours, how do you keep something that size in Glenstar apartments?'

'No, I just borrowed him to get me out for a walk before lunch.'

Cathy realised that she knew nothing at all of Shona Burke's private life. Maybe everyone worked too hard these days to *have* a private life. Or more likely, maybe they worked too hard to have any time to speculate about anyone else's.

'I swear I'm keeping my eyes open for a place for you. You will find one when you least expect it, believe me.'

Cathy felt shabby thanking her. But a promise was a promise. She looked into the faces that passed her by. Some people might never be their clients in a million years, but others might well need Scarlet Feather some time in their lives. There would be birthdays, graduations, weddings, anniversaries, reunions – even funerals. People no longer thought that caterers were the preserve of only the rich and famous. They had given up the nonsensical superwoman image of pretending that they had cooked everything themselves while holding down a job, looking after their children and running a home. In fact, nowadays you were considered intelligent to be able to find someone else to take part of a compartment of your life. Some of these people taking a morning walk and watching the waves might well be sending for the brochure that she and Tom would soon get ready. The brisk couple with their two spaniels might well be booking a retirement party or a thirtieth wedding anniversary. The well-dressed woman who looked so fit might need to organise a ladies' lunch for fellow golfers. That couple holding hands might want a drinks party to announce their engagement. Even the man with the red eyes and white face, who was vainly hoping that fresh air might work miracles on whatever damage he had done to himself last night, might be a senior executive who was looking for a firm to run his corporate hospitality.

The possibilities were endless. Cathy hugged herself with pleasure. Her father used always to say that it was a great life just as long as you didn't weaken. Not that her father had ever shown much get up and go except to

Sandy Keane's, or Hennessy's the bookmaker's. Poor Da: he would fall down if he knew how much she and Tom Feather were prepared to pay for these premises. And her mother would go white. Mam would be apologetic to the end of her life that somehow the maid's daughter had snared the great Hannah Mitchell's only son. It had been a terrible crime – ten thousand times greater than taking a half-hour off for a mug of tea, a smoke and a look at a quiz show on television. There was no changing her. In the beginning, Cathy had tried to force the two women to meet socially but it had been so painful, and Cathy's knuckles would clench every time her mother leaped up from the table to clear away the dishes at Oaklands any time they were invited there, that she had given up the attempt. Neil had been relaxed and indifferent about it.

'Listen, nobody sane could get on with *my* mother. Stop forcing *your* unfortunate mother to do things she hates. Let's just go and see your family on our own, or have them to our house.'

Muttie and Lizzie were as welcome at Cathy and Neil's house as any of the young lawyers, politicians, journalists and civil rights activists who moved in and out. And Neil dropped in occasionally to see his parents-in-law. He would find something that interested them to tell them about. Once he had brought a young man that his own mother would have called a tinker but Neil called a traveller, to see the Scarlets. Neil had just successfully defended the boy for horse-stealing and asked him to come and have a pint to celebrate. Shyly the boy had said that travellers were often not welcome in pubs, and when no persuasion had worked Neil had said that he must come and meet his father-in-law: they would bring half a dozen beers and talk horses. Muttie Scarlet had never forgotten it, he must have told Cathy a thousand times that he was happy to have been of service to Neil in the matter of entertaining his prisoners. Cathy's father always called them prisoners, not clients.

Gradually her mother began to relax when Neil came to visit. If she started to fuss, throw out his cooling tea or sew a button on his coat, or, as she did on one terrible occasion, offer to clean his shoes, he just got out of it gently without the kind of confrontation that Cathy would have started. Neil found the whole scene seemingly normal. He never saw anything odd in the fact that he was having boiled bacon in an artisan's cottage in St Jarlath's Crescent with his in-laws, who were the maid and her ne'er-do-well husband. Neil was interested in everything, which is what made him so easy to talk to. He didn't show any of the fiercely defensive attitude that Cathy wore like armour. To him it was no big deal. Which, as Cathy told herself a hundred times, it was not. It was only her mother-in-law who made it all seem grotesque and absurd. Cathy put the woman out of her mind. She would go back to Waterview and wait until Neil came home.

Their house at number seven Waterview was described as a town house. A stupid phrase that just added several thousand pounds to the small two-bedroom house and tiny garden. There were thirty of them built for people like Neil and Cathy, young couples with two jobs and no children as yet.

They could walk or cycle to work in the city. It was ideal for Neil and Cathy and twenty-nine similar couples. And when the time came to sell there would be plenty of others to take their places. It was a good investment according to Neil's father, Jock Mitchell, who knew all about investments.

Hannah Mitchell had delivered herself of no view about Waterview, apart from heavy sighs. She had particularly disapproved of their having no dining room. Cathy had immediately decided that the room should be a study, since they would eat in the kitchen from choice. The study had three walls lined with bookshelves and one window looking out over the promised water view. They had two tables covered with green felt, and they worked on them in the late hours together. One would go and get coffee, then later the other would decide it was time to open a bottle of wine. It was one of the great strengths they had, the ability to work side by side companionably. They had friends who often sparred and complained that one or the other was working to the exclusion of their having a good time. But Cathy and Neil had never felt like that. From the very first time they had got to know each other out in Greece, when he had ceased to be that stuck-up boy at Oaklands whose mother had given everyone such a hard time ... When Cathy had stopped being nice Mrs Scarlet's brat of a daughter, they had had very few misunderstandings. Neil had understood that Cathy wanted to run her own business right from the start. Cathy had known that he wanted a certain kind of law practice. There would be no short cuts for Neil Mitchell, no ever-decreasing office hours like his father had managed to negotiate; no pretending that he was somehow doing business by being out on a golf course or in a club in Stephen's Green. They would talk late into the night about the defendant who had never had a chance because the odds were stacked against him, how to prove that he was dyslexic and had never understood the forms that were sent to him. Or they would go through the budgets yet again for Scarlet Feather, and Neil would get out his calculator and add, subtract, divide and multiply. Whenever she was downcast he would calm her and assure her that one of his father's partners, a man who lived and breathed money, would advise them every step of the way.

Cathy let herself into number seven Waterview and sat down in the kitchen. This was the only room where they could really see the pictures on the walls. There was no room for paintings in the study because of all the books, files and documents. The hall and stairs were too narrow, you couldn't really see anything they hung there, and the two bedrooms upstairs were lined with fitted wardrobes and dressing tables. So there was no room there.

Cathy sat at her kitchen table and looked up at their art collection. Everything there had been painted by someone they knew. The Greek sunrise by the old man in the taverna where they had stayed. The prison cell by the woman on a murder charge that Neil had got acquitted. The picture of Clew Bay in Mayo by the American tourist they had met and befriended when his wallet had been stolen. The wonderful still life by the old lady in the hospice who had an exhibition three weeks before she died. Every one of them had a history, a meaning and a significance. It didn't matter to Neil and Cathy whether they were great art or rubbish.

A telephone in a quiet house can sound like an alarm bell. Somehow, from its very tone, Cathy knew this wasn't going to be an easy phone call.

'Is Neil there?' her mother-in-law snapped.

'I'm afraid he's out with Jonathan. There was an attempt to hustle him out of the country this morning.'

'When will he be coming back?' Hannah's voice was a rasp.

'Well, when he's finished, he won't know when.'

'I'll call his mobile . . .'

'He turns it off at meetings like this, he couldn't . . .'

'Where *is* he, Cathy, he has to come here at once.'

'Has there been an accident . . . ?'

'There has indeed been an accident, and most of the kitchen ceiling has come down,' Hannah cried. 'They left bath taps running and the weight of the water . . . I need Neil to get those children out of here to wherever they're going to be sent. We haven't had a moment's peace – and as for you, Cathy, those children have eaten entirely unsuitable rich desserts and have been sick. I need to talk to Neil. Now.' Her voice was by now dangerously high and shaky.

'I can't contact him for you, I really can't. But I know what he'd say.'

'If you're going to tell me to calm down . . .'

'He'd say we'll take them here. So that's what we'll do.' Cathy sighed.

'Can you, Cathy?' The relief in Hannah's voice was clear. 'They've been allowed to run wild – they need professionals to look after them, to try to bring them back to normal. And I don't want Neil to say I put them on to you . . .'

'It won't be like that.'

'No. But get him to ring me the moment you can.'

Cathy smiled. She had now what her mother called her-meat-and-her-manners: she had offered and been refused – even if she had only offered because she could see it coming anyway. She dialled Neil's mobile phone to leave the message.

'Sorry to disturb you with trivia, but the twins have apparently brought down the ceiling in Oaklands. Ring your mother soonest. Hope it's all going well for Jonathan.'

Then she went to the spare room and made up two beds. The twins would be there before nightfall.

Tom rang to say he wanted to borrow the van and would that be all right.

'I want to go up into the mountains, I think. It's just I can't think or talk about anything else and I'm afraid I'll drive Marcella demented. Do you want to come? Is Neil bearing up?'

'He's still out fighting the good fight. I'd better not come with you, though, we have another horror-story brewing. Remember the twins from hell who turned up at Oaklands last night?'

'Have they burned the place down yet?'

'They might have by now. But they're probably packing their things and getting ready to come to Waterview as we speak.'

'Cathy, they *can't*!' Tom was aghast. 'You don't have room, apart from anything else.'

'Don't I know it, but as my father would say, even money we see them here tonight.'

'So what are you doing?'

'Nailing things down, mainly. Removing anything breakable. You know, the usual.'

'I'll just sneak into the courtyard and take the van away,' Tom said.

'Don't even look up at a window, they could fire something at you,' she said with a laugh.

'Just one word of warning Cathy, and then I'll shut up about it all. Don't let Neil take them on and then go off saving the world and leaving them to you.'

She sighed. 'And will you take one word of warning from me. Drive carefully, we haven't half-finished paying for that van and when you get excited you take your eyes off the road and your hands off the wheel.'

'When the business is successful, we'll get a tank,' he promised.

Cathy made yet another cup of tea and thought about Tom. They had met on her first day at catering college; with his shock of thick, light brown hair he had an artlessly graceful way of moving. His enthusiasm and the light in his eyes had been the keynote of their years on the course. There was nothing Tom Feather would not attempt, suggest, carry out.

There had been the time he had 'borrowed' a car from one of the lecturers because it had been left in the college yard for the weekend and Tom thought it could take six of them to Galway and back. Sadly, they'd met the lecturer in Galway and it could have been very difficult.

'We brought your car in case you wanted to drive home,' Tom had said, with such brio that the lecturer had half-believed him and almost apologised for the wasted journey since he had a return ticket and a girlfriend with him.

There had been the picnics and barbecues where Tom insisted they must be true to their calling and insisted on marinating kebabs when others would have been content with burned sausages. Cathy could almost smell those nights full of food and herbs and wine on the beaches around Dublin, and the winter evenings in the ramshackle flat that Tom shared with three other guys.

Cathy had envied him the freedom. She had to go back to St Jarlath's Crescent every night and, even though Muttie and Lizzie had allowed her a fair amount of freedom, it still wasn't the same as having your own place.

'You could come and live here,' Tom had told her more than once.

'I'd only end up doing their ironing and lifting their smelly socks off the floor.'

'That's probably true,' Tom had agreed with reluctance.

He had never been short of girlfriends but took none of them seriously. He had a way of looking at people that seemed to suggest no one else in the world existed. He was interested in the most trivial things people told him and he was afraid of no one. He was kind to his rather difficult parents but it never meant that he missed any of the fun. When they all wanted to go to a black tie event in one of the big Dublin hotels, none of them could afford to hire dress suits; but Tom had a friend who worked in a dry-cleaners. It had been dangerous and dramatic and at least four jobs were on the line, but as Tom said cheerfully, nobody lost and everybody won.

They had been talking about Scarlet Feather from the earliest days. No other form of catering had interested either of them; while their friends wanted to do hotel work, work on cruise liners, be celebrity restaurant chefs, write books and be on television, Tom and Cathy had this dream of serving top-grade food in people's homes. As Ireland became progressively more affluent, they felt sure this was the right way to go.

They worked together in restaurants to get the feel for the kind of food people liked. Cathy was amused at how casually Tom took the compliments and the come-on glances directed his way. Even the stern Brenda Brennan in Quentins was sometimes heard to say she wished she were twenty years younger.

Had Cathy fancied him herself in those days? Well, yes, of course, in a sort of way. It would have been impossible not to. And it might well have come to something. She smiled at the recollection.

They had planned to go to Paris on a very cheap flight. They had listed the restaurants they would visit: some to admire from the window, one to tour the kitchens because a fellow student had got a job there; and two where they might actually eat dinner.

They had never been to Paris before. They discussed it, heads close together over maps, night after night. Once they got there, they would walk here, take the Metro there; this museum would be open, that one closed – but it was mainly the food they were going to investigate.

They hadn't exactly said that this was the trip when they might become lovers. But it was in the air. Cathy had her legs waxed and bought a very expensive lacy slip. They had been all set to leave on a Friday afternoon and then that morning three things happened.

Lizzie Scarlet fell off a ladder in Oaklands while hanging Hannah Mitchell's curtains and was taken to hospital by ambulance.

Tom was offered a weekend's work at Quentins because Patrick's sous chef had let them down.

Cathy was called to interview for a job cooking in a Greek villa for the summer.

They told themselves and each other that Paris would always be there.

Cathy went to the Greek island to cook and met Neil Mitchell, a guest in the villa who kept putting off his return home to be with her.

And Tom met Marcella Malone.

And even though Paris was always there, it remained unvisited by Cathy Scarlet and Tom Feather.

She sometimes wondered about that weekend and what would have happened. But if they had been lovers, even for a short time, it would have been hard to forget once they were serious business partners in a thriving enterprise. And this way they brought no history with them. Nothing that could make either Neil or Marcella in any way uneasy.

Cathy heard a key turn in the door.

'Where are the twins?' she called.

'They're in the car,' Neil answered sheepishly. 'You knew they were coming? Mother said you did, but I didn't really believe her, to be honest.' His face was alight now, as if he had expected a protest. 'And you don't mind?'

'I didn't say that. But you had to bring them. How was Jonathan?'

'It looks as though it's going to be okay.'

'Well done.'

'It was a group effort, teamwork,' he said, as he always did. 'I'll get the twins — you're a hero.'

'For a few days I'll be one — they're not too easy to handle, are they? Did it get sorted out at Oaklands?'

'No way, a big shouting match with Mother before they left, right down to the "someone has to look after us" line, which is only too bloody true, poor things.'

'Wheel them in.'

She watched them coming up the steps, muttering to each other that it was a much smaller house, asking each other if Neil and Cathy had children, wondering was there a television in the bedroom. Cathy forced herself to remember that they were nine and frightened. They had been abandoned by their father, mother and brother, their aunt had thrown them out.

'This is the Last Chance Saloon,' she said pleasantly as they came in. 'You have one small bedroom between you with no television. We have a very stern policy on bathrooms here, leaving them clean but not overflowing for the next person, and there's an endless amount of please and thank you going on but apart from that you'll have a great time.'

They looked at her doubtfully.

'The food is terrific, for one thing,' she added.

'That's for sure,' said Neil.

'Did you marry her because she was a good cook?' Simon asked.

'Or did it just turn out that she was a good cook?' wondered Maud.

'And my name is Cathy Scarlet. I am married to your cousin Neil so from now on I won't be referred to as "she" or "her", is that very clear?'

'Why don't you have Neil's name if you're married to him?' Maud wanted everything cleared up.

'Because I am a woman of fiercely independent nature, and I need my own name for my work,' Cathy explained. This seemed to satisfy them.

'Right, could we see the room?' Simon said.

'I beg your pardon?' Cathy was icy.

He repeated it; she still looked at him questioningly.

He got it. 'I mean, please can we see the room. Thank you.' He looked pale and tired; they both did. It had been a long day: there had been nothing but dramas and recriminations. Their parents had disappeared, their future was uncertain, the boy had been sick all over the carpet in Oaklands, they had destroyed the kitchen ceiling and they would never be allowed back there again.

'Come on, then, I'll show you,' she said.

'How did you get on today?' Neil asked eventually when the children were asleep and they had time to talk to each other. She was by now almost too tired to tell him about it.

'It was exactly what we want – perfect place, perfect location, room to park the van . . . But we have to wait. Patience is what's needed apparently.'

The days crawled by after that. They waited and waited. And then finally, 'James Byrne here, Ms Scarlet.'

'Mr Byrne?' They were being formal; she was too nervous to call him James.

'I said I would try to come back to you within four days, and I'm very pleased to say that I have.' He sounded well pleased with himself.

'Thank you so much, but—'

'Mr Feather's answering machine was on, and you did say that it was fine to call either of you.'

'Please, is there any news?' Cathy wanted to scream at him for his slow, precise way of talking.

'Yes, I have been authorised to act for the Maguire family.'

'So?'

'So, they are going to accept your offer, subject to—'

'They're not going to go to auction . . . They might have got more at an auction.'

'They and I have discussed this, and with the estate agents too, but they would prefer an immediate sale.'

'Mr Byrne, what do we do now?'

'You'll tell Mr Feather, I imagine, Ms Scarlet, and then you both get your lawyer and your bank, and then we go to contract.'

'Mr Byrne?' Cathy interrupted.

'Yes, Ms Scarlet?'

'I love you, Mr Byrne,' Cathy said without pausing. 'I love you more than you will ever know.'

And everything began to move very quickly after that. Too quickly. Cathy looked back on the first three days of the year as if they had been in slow motion. Now she realised that there were not enough minutes in any hour to cope with all that had to be done. And she usually needed to be in three places at the same time. When she was sitting with Geraldine and the bank manager, she should have been meeting Tom and his father at the builder's yard. When she was making the four apple strudels for Mrs Ryan, the nervous woman she had met at Oaklands, she should have been having a medical at the insurance company, and when she should have been at the solicitor's going over every clause of the contract of sale, she was making spaghetti bolognese for Maud and Simon Mitchell, who were proving to be a nightmare.

At this of all times she appeared to have taken charge of a boy and a girl that she had never met before. Cathy, who knew all her uncles and aunts and cousins in great depth, barely had time to wonder why Kenneth and Kay weren't part of the extended family scene.

'He's got no visible means of support,' Neil said. 'He says he's in business, but no one quite knows what it is.'

'You mean like *my* father going to work, as he calls visiting the bookies, and meeting his associates, as he calls the others who hang out there?'

'No, nothing as straightforward as that, and I think she likes the vodka a little too much when he goes abroad. So that's the problem: no one quite knows where he is at present, and she's been taken away to hospital for not knowing where she is herself.'

He was unfeeling about the situation, not judgemental but not involved. Perhaps that's how you got to be a good lawyer.

It couldn't have happened at a worse time. *Why* had she agreed to take those monstrous children into Waterview for three nights because of some vague marital disharmony in their home? There was marital disharmony in every home in the Western world at the beginning of January. And suppose their father had gone walkabout and their mother retreated back into a psychiatric home, then why couldn't their big brother Walter look after them? Why bother asking that question? Walter wouldn't have known where to find their cornflakes in the morning, that was supposing he was ever home by breakfast. And Hannah had made it quite clear that her brother-in-law's children were finding no substitute home at Oaklands.

They were pale, solemn-looking children, who asked disconcerting questions . . .

'Do you have a drinking problem, Cathy?' Simon asked when they first came into the house.

'Only problem is getting enough time to drink these days,' Cathy said cheerfully. Then she remembered the danger of being ironic with children.

'Why exactly did you wonder that?' she asked, interested.

'You seem kind of anxious,' Simon explained.

'And there's a big bottle of brandy on the kitchen table,' Maud added.

'Oh! I see . . . No, that's actually calvados, it's for putting in Mrs Ryan's apple strudels and then glazing across the top, that's not for drinking. It's too dear. And anxious because I'm buying a business. I don't think it's all drink-related. But what do I know?'

'Why are you buying a business?' asked Simon. 'Doesn't Neil give you enough money?'

'Why don't you stay at home and have children instead?' Maud wondered.

Cathy paused and looked at them. With their pale, straight hair and pasty little faces they lacked their elder brother's charm, but they also lacked his selfishness. They did genuinely seem interested in her predicament, and she must answer them truthfully.

'Neil would give me half he has very willingly, therefore I'd like to have something of my own to share with him. So that's why I want a business,' she said.

They nodded. This seemed reasonable.

'And Neil and I may well have children sometime, but not just now because I'll have to be out so much and working such long hours. Maybe in a few years . . .'

'Wouldn't you be too old to have children then?' Maud didn't want any loopholes in the plan.

'I don't think so,' Cathy said. 'I did check, they say I'd be all right.'

'Suppose they came earlier, by accident. Would you give them away?' Simon frowned at the thought.

'Or worse.' Maud wasn't a fool about such things.

'We arranged that they won't arrive until we're ready for them.' Cathy had the bright strained smile of a woman who has a hundred things to do that are more important than this conversation.

'So you'd only mate about once a month, is that it?' Maud suggested.

'That's about it,' Cathy said.

Tom was sympathetic about the twins, but the day they were going to see the lawyers he became suddenly anxious.

'I wonder can we leave them anywhere else today, Cathy. I know you take them most places, but honestly . . .'

'Where, Tom, where? They're barred from Oaklands, Walter won't mind them. What can I do with them?'

'Could Neil . . . ?'

'No, he couldn't. Could Marcella . . . ?'

'No, she couldn't.'

'Jesus, Tom, I can't leave two defenceless children in a house on their own all day.'

'Are you suggesting that they come and negotiate some of the finer points of the contract with the solicitor?'

'Tom, stop picking on me. You're nervous, I'm nervous, it's too much money, it's too much risk. Let's take it easy.'

'I'm not nervous, and you're not nervous about it at all. The only thing that's causing any grief is those two time bombs you've installed in the van.'

'Where else can I take them?'

'Take them to your mother and father's.'

'And have my dad take their pocket money to put on something with three legs?'

'Tell them about your dad, warn them. Cathy, we *can't* take them to the lawyer. He's some posh friend of Neil's, believe me, they would not expect or appreciate those two with their sticky fingers all over the corporate furniture.'

'All *right.*' Cathy gave in. 'But remember, Tom, today is *your* tantrum for getting nervous; tomorrow or the day after is mine.'

'It's a deal,' said Tom.

*

'How are you, Simon?' Muttie gave a manly handshake.

'What's your name?' Simon was suspicious.

'Muttie.'

'Right how 'ya, Muttie,' Simon said.

'Or even Mr Scarlet, possibly,' Tom suggested.

'Muttie's fine,' said Cathy's father.

Simon looked triumphant.

'And this is Maud. You're very welcome, child.'

'All right, what are we going to do today?' Maud asked ungraciously.

Cathy thought to intervene but left it. It wouldn't be for long.

'I thought we'd take a little walk the three of us,' Muttie began. 'You see, I have one or two things to do, and maybe I could persuade you . . .'

'No, Da,' Cathy cried. 'And kids, remember what I told you, hey?'

'I know he's an addict,' Simon said.

Cathy closed her eyes.

'A what?' Muttie asked.

Simon was clear on his instructions. 'You can't help it, it's like being a drug addict. You think if someone has a pound you need it to put on a horse, and Cathy says we have to buy magazines or sweets as quick as we can if you suggest it.'

'Thanks, Cathy,' her father said.

'You know I didn't put it quite like that, Da.'

'Exactly like that, Muttie,' grinned Tom, who had always called him Mr Scarlet before but wasn't going to be outdone by young Simon.

'But on the other hand, if you think of anything lucky for *me* today, the day we sign the contract, then can you put this on his nose?' He handed Cathy's father a ten-pound note.

'You're a gentleman, Tom Feather, I always said it.' Muttie shook his hand warmly.

As they left for the lawyer's office Cathy heard Simon asking her father casually, 'Do you have an addiction to drink too, Muttie? My mother has, she can't help it, you see.'

Cathy leaped into the white van. 'I want to be out of here before we hear him inviting the twins down to a good pub on the docks to start the outing with a pint.'

'On balance, that would be better than having them in the solicitor's office.' Tom had reversed the van and they were speeding along to their appointment.

'Better for whom?' Cathy wondered.

It went so smoothly at the lawyer's that Tom and Cathy were worried. There should have been some hold-up, something unacceptable.

'The other side are being remarkably accommodating; they have given specific instructions for a quick sale, and so of course we need to do a very intensive search in case there's something to conceal.'

'Of course,' Cathy and Tom agreed through gritted teeth. Why couldn't barristers or solicitors ever believe that people might just be telling the truth, that these Maguires were so anxious for their money, and to forget their old life, that they wanted to sell? But they knew it had to be done by the book no matter how slow and laborious. There was one message each on their mobile phones when they got back to the van. Cathy was to ring her aunt Geraldine. Urgently. Tom was to ring his father. They stood at either end of the van, talking. They finished and came back to sit down, both in good humour.

'Well, you first, *was* it a crisis?' he asked.

'Absolutely not. It was great news, she knows a restaurant selling up a rake of kitchen equipment, cookers as good as new, an enormous chest freezer. We can go over there after we've visited *your* dad and look at them today.'

Tom said nothing.

'And you?' Cathy asked.

His father had agreed to do the building job but it involved putting someone else on hold. If Tom went round to sort that out and kept the name of Feather looking good, then it was a deal.

'He's around at the premises already, with two lads. There's an authorisation in from the Maguires; they want their equipment moved out and sold, so Da and the others are clearing the place. You can go there, can you?'

'Sure.' Cathy hoped they wouldn't mind talking to a girl about it.

'He thinks talking to me about building is *worse* than talking to a girl,' Tom said ruefully.

'But he needs you to do something more important?'

'Yes; talk nice to some architect and persuade him that my father and the team aren't a pack of cowboys.'

'What will you say?' Cathy was interested.

'I'll tell them the truth. It's amazing how often that works; tell them that the young Feather has a chance to do well. Might even pick up a bit of business for us – you never know.' He had such an engaging grin, Cathy knew it would work out.

JT Feather was a man very anxious that things should be done right. That no short cuts be taken, that the authorities never be offended in any way.

Cathy parked the van and noted with pleasure the way the place was being cleared out. The men had been working hard.

'You know it's very irregular, doing all this before the contract is signed.'

'You have their fax, Mr Feather. They want it this way.'

'But all my life I've worked on the principle that you don't touch a place until it is legally yours.' He frowned a lot.

'We're getting equipment this week; we have to have somewhere to plug it in.'

'Ah, not this week, Cathy, be reasonable. The floors have to be done, the walls hacked out and made good, there has to be a full paint job . . . There are a hundred details that have to be sorted out.'

'We'll talk about the details later. Tom told you, Mr Feather, we have to be up and running at the end of the month.'

'That boy was always a dreamer, will you look at the notions he had about this and that. You're never taking his timetable seriously, a sensible girl like you?'

'Oh, believe me, it's my timetable too, and we have a reception planned for the last Friday in January.'

'There's no rush, girl, the job must be properly done.'

'No, there isn't *time* to have it properly done. Three more catering firms will have opened and taken the business unless we get in there quick.'

'But the regulations, Cathy . . .' He was pale with anxiety.

Was this better or worse than her own reckless father, who would have put the deeds of the house on the next race if her mother hadn't kept them well hidden?

'I won't delay you, Mr Feather, I have to take some measurements for equipment that I'm going to buy today.'

'Today?' She could hear him gasp but she took no notice. Instead, she took out her metal measuring tape and moved past him into the room, which was looking emptier by the minute as the bulky machinery was being moved out into trailers. Cathy knelt down to see how much room there was for the freezer. Geraldine had said it was enormous but hadn't been specific. She was busy writing the measurements into her notebook when she saw Tom's father coming in, opening the top button of his shirt so that he could breathe more easily.

'Tell me they're not coming today.'

'Oh, not at all. I'm only going to *see* them today. The auction is tomorrow, they'll come at the end of the week. I'll have the details about where we'll need sockets before the day is over. Can you have the electrician here as early as he can make it tomorrow morning, do you think?'

'The world has changed totally,' said Tom's father.

'Tell me about it, Mr Feather,' said Cathy, and was gone.

Tom called. 'I daren't ask, but how are things going?'

'Not too bad. And your end?'

'I bought the time, told them we were wonderful and that we'd send them a brochure. Just give me the address again of that place with the freezers and cookers and I'll meet you there.'

Her friend June rang to know would they go to a wine bar.

'I may never go to a wine bar again for the rest of my life,' Cathy said, crawling out from behind a particularly complicated measuring job.

'Great load of fun *you're* going to be when you're a businesswoman,' June said sourly, and hung up.

Neil rang. 'How did it go with the lawmen?'

She told him there seemed to be no hitches or problems.

'There are always hitches and problems with the law. That's what most of them get paid for,' he countered.

'Well not so far.' She was anxious to believe that it might, for once in life, be plain sailing.

'Well, you're with the best people,' he said.

'What time will you be home?' she asked.

'Lord, I don't know. Why?'

'No reason. It's just with the kids . . .'

'Oh, God, I'd forgotten about them. Where are they now?'

'In St Jarlath's,' she said.

'You never left them with your parents!' He seemed astonished.

'I had to leave them *somewhere*, Neil. I couldn't take them with me to the solicitor's, could I? Or here, which is like a builder's yard full of rubble, and on to inspect appliances at an auction which is where *I'm* going now.'

'But Cathy . . .' he began.

'But what?'

'Nothing . . . nothing. See you later.'

There were very few people looking at the kitchen equipment. It was almost exactly what they wanted.

'Isn't it kind of sad?' Cathy said in a whisper.

'I know,' Tom agreed. 'I was just thinking that. Someone else's dreams gone up in smoke.'

'It won't happen to us.' She sounded braver than she felt.

And all day their mobile phones kept ringing. Something else the lawyers needed, some further problem JT Feather had unearthed, Marcella wondering would they all go to an early film, James Byrne looking for another detail. At none of the places they visited was there ever any proper parking. Nobody they called was ever at a desk or could be located. At four o'clock they were very hungry but there was no time to stop, so Tom got them two bars of chocolate and a banana each. Somehow they got through the day, and Cathy realised guiltily as she drove to St Jarlath's Crescent that she had left those children there for far too long, and that she hadn't bought anything for them to eat that night. They would pick up a takeaway on the way home. Fine way for a caterer to behave, she thought.

It was still an odd feeling to drive up this small street of two-up, two-down houses, where she had been born and brought up. Her father had always told her proudly how he had moved their belongings in using a handcart, and now Cathy would drive in casually in her white van or her husband's Volvo. Like looking at your past from a great distance, where everything had changed and yet in other ways nothing had changed at all. A place where her mother still strove to please the unpleasant Hannah Mitchell, even though she had long since ceased to work for her. Where her mother even at this stage would be in some kind of awe of these terrible poor children because their name was Mitchell. Oh, please may nothing awful have happened. May her mother not have cleaned their shoes, or her father cleaned them out of their pocket money.

The twins were alone in the kitchen, staring at the oven. The table and all their own clothes seemed to be covered with flour. They had made pastry, they said, because that was all there was to do here, and Muttie's wife had helped them make a steak and kidney pie which they were going to take home with them because the shoemaker's children were never shed.

'Shod,' corrected Cathy.

'Shed, shod, yeah, whatever,' Simon said.

'Did you enjoy it?' Cathy asked.

She had loved standing at that very table, helping her mother to cook.

'Not much,' Simon said arrogantly.

'He thinks it's not men's work,' Maud explained.

'It's just I didn't expect to be doing this. We don't do this at home,' Simon complained.

'It's always good to learn things,' Cathy said, wanting to slap him. Her kind mother had taught them to make a pie, and all he could do was complain. 'What did you learn today?'

'I learned you need sharp knives to cut up the meat. Have you got any sharp knives for your waitressing business?'

'Catering business, actually. Yes, I do have sharp knives, thank you Simon.'

'Muttie's wife has a great way to put salt and pepper in the flour,' Maud began. 'You shake it all up in a paper bag together, did you know that?' she asked Cathy.

'Yes, Mam taught me that too,' Cathy said.

'I never knew that before,' Simon said, as if it were somehow a suspect way of doing things.

'You never made pastry before until Muttie's wife showed us,' Maud said scathingly.

'Oh, for Christ's sake call her Lizzie,' cried Cathy, at the end of her tether.

'We didn't know her name, you see,' Maud explained, startled.

'She told us she used to work for Aunt Hannah as a sort of servant or cleaner or something,' Simon said. 'And we told her that we hated Aunt Hannah and that she hated us.'

'I'm sure your aunt Hannah doesn't hate you, you must have got that wrong,' Cathy murmured.

'No, I think she does, otherwise why would we be at Muttie and Lizzie's place making steak and kidney pie, instead of Oaklands?' Simon spoke as if the whole thing were totally obvious.

'Anyway,' Maud added, 'we told her that this is better in a lot of ways than Oaklands and we said that we could come again tomorrow.'

Cathy looked at them in disbelief. What amazingly self-possessed, confident children. They were sure of their welcome anywhere, free to criticise and comment. That's what being a Mitchell did for you. They watched her face as if trying to read her expression. She must remind herself that they were only nine, that their father had left home and their mother had been taken into a psychiatric hospital. Their brother was hopeless. This wasn't the best of times.

'We did say it to them,' Maud said.

'Say what?' Cathy asked.

'That we were going to keep coming here until things got back to normal at The Beeches,' Simon explained.

'And what did they say?'

'Muttie said that he didn't have any problem with it, and his wife Lizzie said that it would all depend on Aunt Hannah.'

'Where are they now?' Cathy asked fearfully. Was there any possibility that these two demented children had driven her unfortunate parents so mad they had left home?

'Muttie said he was slipping out to the shoemaker ...' Maud began.

'Bookmaker,' Simon corrected.

'Well, some kind of maker anyway, and his wife Lizzie is upstairs on the phone because her daughter telephoned her from Chicago.'

Cathy sat down in the kitchen. It could be a lot worse, she supposed.

'You must not interrupt us, we have to watch as it goes golden brown,' Simon said.

'Who is the bookmaker, and why was he never shod?' Maud wanted to know.

'Is he coming to dinner with us? Is that why we made the pie?' Simon wondered.

Cathy felt very, very tired, but she remembered asking her aunt Geraldine things years ago, and the really satisfying thing was that Geraldine had always tried to answer her.

'It's a sort of saying, really. What Mam meant was that in a shoemaker's house the man is making so many pairs of shoes for other people that he never has time to make any for his own children, and they go barefoot.'

'Why don't they get shoes in the shops?' Maud asked.

'But is he coming to dinner or is he not?' Simon insisted on knowing.

'Not tonight,' Cathy said wearily. 'Sometimes the shoemaker will come to dinner, I hope, but not tonight.'

Neil's court case was all over the papers; the fight had been won for the moment. Prominent civil rights leaders had come to court, there was talk of a big protest march, a stay had been given for three months, which was longer than they had hoped. Cathy had time only for a quick glance at the evening paper as she settled the children in the kitchen with instructions on how to set the table, and grabbed a shower. Neil had left a note saying he had gone out for wine and ice cream. She was just pulling on a clean T-shirt and jeans when he came into the bedroom.

'Those two told me they had made a pie – are they serious?'

'I think my mother made it, actually. Well done, I saw in the paper you're a hero. Was he delighted?'

'He was more stunned than anything else I think, but the great thing is we've mobilised a lot of support. It won't be so easy for them the next time, they can't bundle him out overnight any more.' Neil's face was animated and excited. He would have talked for ever. Cathy hung her head slightly. Her own day seemed suddenly very trivial in comparison.

He stroked her cheek. 'You look lovely, you know. What a pity we don't have time to . . .'

'I don't think we'll have time for that sort of thing in the foreseeable future. By the way, Maud told my mother that we mate once a month.'

'God, did she? What an extraordinary thing to say.'

'That's one of the mildest things they've said. Let's not even think about it, let's go and eat dinner and drink a great deal of wine and celebrate your win.'

Simon had the table set. 'Are we sure the shoemaker isn't coming?' he asked, slightly worried.

'The shoemaker?' Neil paused in drawing the cork from the bottle.

'Don't ask, please don't ask,' said Cathy.

'Were the cookers suitable?' Geraldine wanted to know next morning.

'Perfect, we're going to take two plus a fridge, a freezer, a deep-fat fryer and a lot of saucepans.'

'Great stuff, was Tom delighted?'

'Thrilled, we left bids on things, they'll ring tonight. I can't go today as I have to be with the electricians. Feather and Company finally found an electrician who gets out of bed before midday, so I'm meeting him there in a few minutes. Tom's out with other suppliers.'

'Have you time for lunch? You could come to the hotel, they have some foreign chefs doing a buffet, you could steal a few ideas.'

'I'd love it, Geraldine, but I haven't a minute, we have to meet the insurance broker again, fill in a planning application, change of nature of premises, and there's a good January sale on. I thought I might have a quick hunt for curtain material before we meet James Byrne again up at the premises.'

'You're killing yourself.'

'Early days, busy days.' Cathy sounded cheerful.

'And why are these awful children not going back to their own people?' Geraldine was disapproving.

'There *are* no own people, their father has been sighted in Leeds, and this has sent their mother back to the funny farm.'

'And what in God's name do my sister and her capable, energetic husband do with the twins from hell all day?'

'You know Mam, she'll get neighbours to keep them entertained when she's out working, and she's teaching them to cook.'

'That sounds sensible, they'll need someone to cook if they're to go back to that house,' said Geraldine.

'I *know*, Geraldine, but what can we do?' Cathy wailed.

'And what does Neil say? They're *his* responsibility.'

'He says we can't let them go into a home.'

'So they're in your mother's home instead.'

'And ours at night,' Cathy said with spirit.

'I bet that's a barrel of laughs,' Geraldine said.

'Neil finds it very hard to work while they're there. Don't worry, Geraldine; it's not going to last for ever.'

'Mr Feather not with you?' James Byrne asked when Cathy arrived to meet him, as agreed, on site in the late afternoon. The noise of drilling was loud in their ears.

'I wonder, could you call him Tom?' Cathy knew that she sounded tired, and hoped that the bright smile somehow compensated for it.

'Certainly, if you wish,' the voice was polite.

'It's just that we have so much on our minds that when you say Mr Feather, I immediately think you're talking about his father, who's inside worrying his guts out in case the Maguires will fly back from England in a helicopter and settle on his head with all kinds of restraining orders.'

'I have put his mind at rest about that.'

'How on earth did you do that?'

'I let him talk to the Maguires in person on the phone.'

This was more than Cathy and Tom had been able to do. But she knew better than to cross-question this strange, reserved man.

'Good,' she said briskly. 'That explains all the activity in the background. Now, would you like to see what we've done so far?'

'And Tom Feather?'

'Will not be here today. We have to divide the work up as we can't both be everywhere. Is it all right if it's just me?'

She looked tired and wan. Unexpectedly he leaned over and patted her hand. 'It's just fine, Cathy,' he said.

'Mam, I really owe you for this,' Cathy said, falling into a chair at the kitchen table in St Jarlath's Crescent.

'Not at all, they kept your father out of the betting shop.' Lizzie poured them mugs of tea.

'You mean he took them out for the day?'

'To the zoo, no less. They'd never been there, could you credit it?'

'And Da took them there with his own money?'

'There was a bit of a good flutter yesterday, apparently.'

'And do they have any more manners today?'

'Not really. But Cathy, you wouldn't need to go commenting on that in front of the Mitchells.'

'Where are they?'

'Drawing away, there's not a word out of them.'

Muttie had given them paper to draw their favourite animal at the zoo. Simon had ten drawings of snakes with their names printed underneath them. Maud had done six owls.

'Muttie says he sees no reason why we couldn't have an owl at home,' she greeted Cathy.

'He doesn't? Maybe he could explain it to your mother and father when they get back to The Beeches.'

'They might never be back,' Simon said cheerfully. 'But Muttie says that there might be more of a problem with snakes.'

'There might be, all right. But excuse me, what do you mean, exactly, they might never be back?'

'Well, there's no word of our father, and our mother's nerves are pretty bad this time, I think.'

'I see.'

Cathy went back to her mother in the kitchen. 'What am I going to do, Mam?'

'I'll tell you one thing, a couple of days here and that is fine, but long-term you're not doing yourself any favours taking those children in. Can't you see it's showing her up as well ... as well as everything else?'

'What do you mean, Mam? "As well as everything else"?'

'Well, you know I've said it a thousand times already to you, all this setting up a business. People like that, Cathy, you know they expect you to be grateful and glad you married so well. You should be staying at home and making Neil a good wife.'

'Oh, Mam, for God's sake.'

'No, listen to me for once, Cathy, I'm not as bright as you or as educated. I can't talk back to people like you do, but I do know them. I've cleaned their floors, yes, but I listen to them talking and they're not like us, we're not like them.'

'We are better than them, far, far better.' Cathy's eyes blazed.

'Now don't start ...'

'It's you that started, Mam. Tell me what's good about an old cow like Hannah Mitchell, pointing to the legs of chairs with her umbrella and making you go down on your hands and knees, throwing tea bags into a sink you had just cleaned, using good clean towels you had just washed and folded to mop up floors. Tell me what's good about her, one thing good about a woman who won't even take two unfortunate brats who are part of her husband's family.'

'Shush, Cathy, keep your voice down.'

'No I will *not* keep my voice down, I hate that woman for the way she turned her back on them and I despise her husband, they're his flesh and blood after all. I know they're monsters and they're both as daft as brushes but they're not the worst, and it's not *their* fault that everyone has abandoned them and nobody wants them.' She broke off because of the frozen look on her mother's face. It was indeed as she suspected. Simon and Maud stood behind her open-mouthed in the doorway, having heard every single word.

'Hi, Lizzie. It's Geraldine.'

'Sorry, Ger, she's just left.'

'Who?'

'Cathy. Didn't you want to talk to her?'

'No, I wanted to talk to you. How was she, by the way?'

'Terrible, she lost her temper with me and started giving out about the Mitchells in front of those two harmless children. They heard it all.'

'What did she say?'

'She said that she'd explain it all to them in the van going home. God alone knows what she'll explain, she'll make it worse you can be sure.'

'You're not taking them again tomorrow?'

'Of course I am, where else can they go?'

'And what will they do in your house, if I can ask?'

'They're going to bring their washing in a big bag and I'm going to show them how to use the washing machine and hang their clothes on the line . . .'

'You're not?'

'And then I'm working most of the rest of the day up in the flats, and they can have a swim in the pool. The place is empty in the day. I don't suppose you would—'

'No, I wouldn't do whatever you were supposing. I rang you about Marian.'

'Marian?'

'Listen Lizzie, have you gone soft in the head? You have a daughter called Marian, in Chicago, and she's coming to stay with you soon. She wants to know can she sleep with her boyfriend.'

'She wants to what?'

'You heard.'

'Why does she want my permission if she's going to? They all do what they like nowadays over there, anyway.'

'Not in Chicago, in Dublin when she comes to stay in your house.'

'She's ringing you from Chicago to ask *you* this?'

'She said I was to ask you tactfully if she and Harry could share a room in your house when they come over, so I'm doing that. Asking you tactfully.'

'I don't know, Ger, it's one thing turning a blind eye, it's another when it's in your own home. I don't know what Muttie would think . . .' She was riddled with doubt.

'Muttie will mainly be thinking of what to back at Wincanton,' Geraldine said.

'It's very blatant, isn't it?'

'Will I tell her yes, that of course they can have the room?'

'I don't know.'

'And that you don't know whether you're going to do it up in pale green, or a sort of beige pink?'

'What?'

'What colour? I think green myself, and I'll tell Marian to bring you a nice set of dark green towels to go with it. Americans love bringing towels as a gift, but they need to know the colour.'

'But Ger, who'd paint it? You *know* Muttie has a bad back.'

'Oh, yes, I know that, you'd paint it and I would, and if we still have that child labour force hanging around the place they could hold things and carry things for us, before we send them up and down the chimneys.'

'Ger, you're ridiculous.' But Lizzie was laughing. The battle was won.

The white van stopped for an ice cream. Cathy bought three cones and they settled down companionably to eat them in the van. 'I always think an ice cream is just as good in the winter,' she began.

'Why do you hate our father and mother?' Simon asked.

Cathy shrugged. 'I don't hate them at all, I've hardly met them. In fact, they didn't even come to our wedding.'

'So what were you shouting at Lizzie about?'

'You heard what I was shouting about. I hate your aunt Hannah. I don't hate your mum and dad, believe me.'

'Why do you hate Aunt Hannah?'

'You hate her too, you've often said so,' Cathy said defensively, coming down to their level.

'But you're not meant to hate her, and anyway, you're married to Neil.'

'That's the problem, she doesn't like my being married to Neil, she thinks that my family and I have no class. That annoys me, you see.'

'Do you want to have class?' Maud wanted to know.

'No, no way. I don't give three blind damns what she thinks about *me*, I've plenty of class. But she looked down on my mother, and I can't forgive her for that.'

'Do you want us not to tell?' Simon's eyes narrowed at the wonderful opportunities and power that lay ahead.

'Tell what?' Cathy asked, wide-eyed.

'All this about what you said, and about our father roaring round and our mother getting drunk to help her nerves.'

'But that's the way it is, isn't it?' Cathy looked from one to the other, bewildered.

'Yes.' Simon was on less firm a footing now. 'But do you want us not to tell about your hating Aunt Hannah?'

'Tell anyone if you want to, I don't tell her *you* hate her, it's just a matter of being polite, really. But it's not a secret, is it?'

Simon saw his vantage point disappear. He gave a last try. 'Suppose we told Neil?' he tried.

'Neil is sick of hearing it, Simon, but if you'd like to tell him again, please do. Now let's go and buy some supper, since you didn't make us a pie today.'

They finished their ice creams and drove off. Cathy allowed herself a small smile.

In the Chinese restaurant the children studied the menu carefully. 'Are you and Neil rich or poor?' Simon asked.

'Tending to be more rich than poor, but if you don't mind my saying so, it's not a question you ask people . . . Just so that you know.'

'But how would you ever find out, then?' Maud was interested.

'Sometimes we have to face it that we can't know everything.'
'I needed to know.'
'You did?'
'In order to know how many dishes we could order,' Simon said, as if it were the most obvious thing in the world.
'Oh, I see. Well, there's four of us.'
'We could have Imperial Menu A for five,' Maud said.
'Let's have it. I'd love Imperial Menu A.'
'Don't you want to check up the price of items first?'
'No, Simon, I don't.'
'You must be very rich indeed, richer than your father.'
'What?' she was exhausted.
'Muttie, your father. Do you hear things in your head, like he does?'
'I didn't know he heard things in his head.'
'Yes, all the time. The sound of hooves, thundering hooves.'
'Oh, like the races, I see.'
'He says they go at the same rhythm as your heart. Did you know that, Cathy?' Maud wanted to share any new things that she had learned.
'I'm not sure I did.'
'*And* Muttie says that the sound makes your blood run faster in your veins and gives you a better life.'
'Oh, it does? We must try that then,' she said as she grabbed the price list and ordered Imperial Menu A for five.
'I don't think it's something you try.' Simon was doubtful.
'You have it or you don't. We both have it, as it turns out,' Maud positively smirked with pride.
'I'm very sorry if you do, very sorry indeed,' Cathy said.
'Why?'
'Because you'll spend the rest of your lives deafened by the hooves, and have no time or money for anything else,' she said grimly.

Back at Waterview the twins set the table, washed their hands and sat down politely. 'Would you like a can of lager?' Simon offered.
'God, no. Thank you all the same, Simon.'
'It's just that Muttie says it relaxes him.'
'I'm totally relaxed as a matter of fact,' Cathy said.
The phone rang, it was Tom. 'All going okay?' he asked.
'I'm hanging in there, Tom.'
'Kids are still with you, I gather?'
'Absolutely.'
'So I won't ask you, did everything else go all right?'
'Amazingly it did, no problems at all. And at your end?'
'Good, tiring but no disasters,' he said.
'I'm sure it was,' she sighed.
'You'll have a day off next week, I'll organise it.'
'I know you will. Glad it all went well. Good luck, Tom.' She hung up and came back to the table.

'Is Tom doing a waitressing job tonight?' Maud asked.

'Catering,' Cathy corrected.

'Yes, is he?'

'Sort of, yes. What's the black bean sauce like?'

'A bit salty but okay. Can we finish this?' Simon was spooning it out of the containers.

'Sure, I've enough, and I've left Neil's in the oven.'

'And the shoemaker isn't coming?'

'No, Simon, he's not.'

'I hope he never comes,' said Simon. 'You always get upset when you talk about him.'

'They go back to school next week,' she told Neil that night in bed.

'Should make it a *bit* easier, I suppose,' Neil said.

'Tell me something, Neil.'

He put down the copy of the law reports he was reading and turned to face her. 'I know the question you are going to ask, and the answer is none.'

'What am I going to ask?' Cathy laughed.

'What plans did I make for the twins today?' he smiled ruefully. 'Honey, it was a desperate day.'

'I know; mine was fairly filled, too,' she said.

'I know, I know, and then I was late home, but Cathy, I can't work while they're here, I just sat in a café. It's terrible to be kept out of your own home because children keep asking question after question.'

'I suppose it's what kids do,' she said.

'I'm going to get them made wards of court,' he said simply. 'I'll start proceedings tomorrow.'

She looked at him, shocked. 'But they'd have to go into care, a home, a foster family, total strangers.'

'We were total strangers a few days ago . . .' he began.

'But they're family,' she said.

'Not yours and mine.' Neil was trying to sound firm and in control. 'I can't *have* this,' he said. 'I met that little shit Walter down at the Four Courts today, and he's as cool as a cucumber about it all. He has to work, he has to see people, he has to go skiing, there's nothing *he* can do.'

'Well, would you trust them to him for two hours?'

'But it's not just my work alone, it's your work too. I'm just not going to *let* this happen to us now. We've put too much in to let it be wrecked by children.'

'I suppose that's happening all over the world.'

'People's own children *might* be different, though I must say this has proved to me once and for all that we are totally right not to want them. Just looking at Maud and Simon makes me realise that very clearly.'

'Our children wouldn't look like Maud and Simon,' she giggled.

'We're not going to find out,' he said grimly. 'And truly, Cathy, I'll get them out of your hair. There has to be *some* money there, we'll mortgage

The Beeches, something to borrow against, we could still keep an eye on them.'

'You know we'd have no say in where they're sent. Leave it for a few days until we know more.'

He reached out for her. And she lay awake with her eyes open for a long time afterwards.

Geraldine still got to her office before eight o'clock. In the mornings, she herself handled only the public relations and publicity for the hotel group, but three others looked after the list of clients that she had built up when she opened a private company of her own. She flicked through the list of projects to see was there anything that might be channelled in Scarlet Feather's direction. Haywards the store were doing a fashion show some months down the line, but they wanted to book a hotel, nothing for Cathy there. Quentins the restaurant were doing a presentation of cookery prizes, but that was obviously in-house. Makers of garden furniture greatly wanted a presentation, possibilities there, but first she would have to examine the location, no point in sending those two into some awful place full of lawnmowers and rakes where nobody would see and appreciate their food.

By the end of the week, a lot of things had changed. The electrical appliances had all been installed, the shelves were painted and Tom and Cathy were waiting for the rest of the equipment. The window frames and door had been painted a vivid red. James Byrne had told them gravely, as if he were interpreting from some aliens on another planet, that the Maguires had professed themselves satisfied with everything. Tom and Cathy's solicitor said it was the nature of the law that things must take their time, but that nothing untoward was showing up in the search on the company title. Marcella was being supportive and begging to be allowed to help. Geraldine was already coming up with names of contacts for future events. Cathy and Neil had decided that there was now no way they could immediately abandon Simon and Maud, but that living permanently in Waterview was proving too much of a strain, and that they did need a bit of space from them. Lizzie and Muttie, on the other hand, seemed perfectly content with them, and found endless jobs for them to do around the house. Next week they would be going back to school. It was a compromise. Neil had told them that an unofficial carer's allowance had been arranged by his father. In fact, it was guilt money put up by Jock and Hannah until the situation sorted itself out. The arrangement was that Muttie and Lizzie would get a fixed amount for minding Simon and Maud in St Jarlath's Crescent after school, and they would sleep alternately in Waterview and St Jarlath's. Two homes instead of one. Maud and Simon said okay, it would suit them.

'Manners, Maudie,' said Cathy's father. There was a way that Muttie could correct the worst excesses of the twins without appearing ever to have taken offence.

'I'll never be able to thank you, Mam,' Cathy said to her mother.

'Don't go on like that, Cathy, doesn't it give Muttie some shape to his days. He's very fond of them.'

'He can't be, they're pig rude at times. Make sure they make their beds and wash up and everything. They left wet towels all over the floor of the bathroom in Waterview. Neil nearly lost his mind.'

'No, no, that's all fine,' her mother reassured her. 'And Neil is giving us so much money, I can give up Mrs Gray.'

'The one who's as bad as Hannah?'

'Oh, poor Mrs Mitchell was a walking saint compared to Mrs Gray,' Lizzie Scarlet said with a laugh.

Neil had been so good about going to St Jarlath's Crescent that Cathy felt she must visit Oaklands in return. Surely there must be other women in the world who had to sit down and think up a reason before calling to visit their mother-in-law? Cathy didn't want to talk about the excitement of the business, the way the premises were leaping ahead because Hannah was so obviously against the whole undertaking. Nor did she want to go into detail about the fact that Jock Mitchell's nephew and niece were currently residing partly in St Jarlath's Crescent with her ex-maid and what she always referred to as the unfortunate maid's ne'er-do-well husband. She couldn't say she had done those apple strudels for Hannah's friend, the nervous, edgy Mrs Ryan, because she would be accused of having touted successfully for business at the New Year's party. Mrs Mitchell showed no interest in what she and Neil had done with their house in Waterview, which was probably just as well, since she had done so little recently. Still, she owed it to Neil to keep the channels open.

She forced the white van up the drive of Oaklands at four o'clock one afternoon, knowing that Hannah's sniff of disapproval could be directed equally against her daughter-in-law or the vehicle. But Cathy was ready to ignore it and talk pleasantly for as short a visit as she could manage, without it appearing that she had just dropped by to deliver something. She brought her mother-in-law a sturdy-looking fern, one that couldn't die even in the tropical central heating of Oaklands, and knocked at the door.

'Cathy.' Her mother-in-law couldn't have been more astounded if a troupe of tap dancers stood on the step.

'Yes, Mrs Mitchell, I did send you a card saying I hoped to drop by and see you today?'

'Did you? Oh, you may have indeed . . .'

'But if you're with somebody?'

'No . . . no, it's amazing to see you, please come in.'

'I brought you this. It might . . .' Cathy handed over the little fern. The woman must be deranged, imagine saying that it was *amazing* to see your daughter-in-law, who had sent you an advance note about her visit!

'Thank you so much, dear.' Hannah Mitchell didn't even look at the plant, just left it on the hall table. 'Now that you're here, I suppose we should go into the kitchen, we'd feel more at home there,' she said, preceding Cathy down the hall.

Cathy seethed. And wondered if she could feel a tic in her forehead, or was she just imagining it? Mrs Mitchell rarely welcomed anyone into the kitchen. Guests, family, anyone at all who called would be received in the den. Cathy saw the subtlety and grinned at herself in the mirror. Her reflection startled her; she looked drawn and tired, her hair greasy and stuck behind her ears. When she got the show on the road she would really have to smarten herself up, she thought. She would frighten possible clients if she looked like this.

'You look very badly,' Hannah Mitchell said on cue.

'I think it's just one of those twenty-four-hour flu things,' Cathy said, saying the first words that came into her head. She saw Hannah physically draw away, as if fearing to catch some dreadful germ. 'Not contagious, of course,' Cathy said cheerfully. The conversation was painful. Cathy enquired about Amanda in Canada and heard there had been something wrong with the Ontario phone system, and Amanda worked in a really old-fashioned carriage-trade business that didn't have faxes or e-mail. Cathy allowed no muscle on her face to change as she listened. Either Amanda or her mother was spinning a story. Whichever one of them it was, the whole thing was just very sad. Remember that word 'sad', and she would survive.

Lizzie Scarlet, who had scrubbed this floor and the legs of the table for years was sitting at this moment in St Jarlath's Crescent serving a glass of milk and home-made shortbread to Simon and Maud, before helping them do their homework. Later they would play a game on the video, and tonight the children were going to learn ironing as a great treat. There would be speculation about whether this horse might be held back on Saturday to let his stablemate win, and there might be neighbours dropping in. There would be plenty of activity. Cathy knew that her aunt Geraldine was going to a dinner party at an embassy tonight, and had bought herself another stunning dress at Haywards. Her two married friends, Katy and June, had asked Cathy to a party they were having but she had said no, she wanted a proper dinner alone with Neil in Waterview, and they might even get a chance to mate more than once a month. Maud's definition of her sex life was looking uncannily prophetic. Shona Burke had a date with a man she met last week, a man that she thought would never call her again. Tom was also taking a night off from Scarlet Feather and was taking Marcella out to one of the clubs where she might get noticed. Ricky the photographer friend said there were a lot of big fashion-mag people in town. Mr and Mrs JT Feather were going to an Irish Tenor concert, and the silent James Byrne had mentioned that he was going to the theatre. And on this cold, wet January night Hannah Mitchell, patting her hair and smoothing her fine wool skirt, had no one to meet and nowhere to go. Cathy reminded herself of this as she forced the polite, interested smile to stay on her face.

Somehow a great many more things than they expected got done. They read all the hygiene regulations, put in an application to become regulated. They got the logo painted on their white van. One big, waving red feather. The name and phone number underneath. They went to a printer's to get the business cards, the brochures and the invitations printed.

'I know that address, it's where Maguire's the printer's used to be,' said the old man behind the counter when Tom and Cathy had gone to arrange the lettering.

'Yes, indeed, we've just bought the premises. Did you know them? Were they good printers?'

'Ah, the best at one time, but then everything changed, they didn't, and there was all that other business.'

'What other business?'

The man looked from one to the other and decided against it. 'I don't know, I can't really remember.'

'They're in England now,' Tom said helpfully.

'God be good to them wherever they are,' said the old man.

She was very quiet in the van. 'We'll never know, Cathy. Stop trying to puzzle it out,' Tom said.

'We knew there was something odd, and of course you'd never in a million years get it out of James.'

'It doesn't matter,' Tom said.

'Don't you want to know? Men are very incurious sometimes.'

'Practical, maybe. Let's go out tonight and have a coffee and make a list.'

They had taken to doing their Scarlet Feather work away from home. It wasn't fair on Neil to have his whole study commandeered, nor on Marcella to keep her out of her own sitting room or kitchen. It was not that Neil and Marcella had been in any way critical – neither of them had made a murmur of complaint – it was just that they hadn't any time to help. Neil was involved in committees and consultations almost every night of the week; Marcella had signed on for a fourteen-day course of aquarobics to tone up her already perfect body. They said they'd love to help if only there were time.

And indeed, one evening saw Neil up a ladder painting; and another evening Marcella helped hem the curtains. And then there was the evening Neil and Marcella had fallen about laughing over the ventilation regulations. Giggling over phrases like 'steam-emitting appliances' and 'mesh size 16 maximum pore size 1.2 millimetres essential to be fly-proof'. Cathy and Tom were familiar with such phrases from catering college, and just shrugged at all the mirth. And their main backers too had been very undemanding.

'If I didn't believe you could both do it, I wouldn't have invested my hard-earned money,' Geraldine said simply.

'How *did* she earn enough to be able to give us a whack like that?' Tom wondered.

'No idea. I used to think once that she was old Mr Murphy's fancy woman, but apparently not. Just invested it well, I think.'

'Up to now, anyway,' Tom had said, touching wood.

Joe Feather had written from London.

'Why does he never stay at home with your parents, they'd love to have him . . .' Cathy asked.

'I don't know,' Tom said. 'Selfish, I think.' There was something in the way he spoke that made Cathy look at him suddenly. The world was full of mystery, Cathy told herself sadly as they began to make the list for their launch party.

'Ricky knows good contacts,' Cathy began.

'I behaved like a horse's arse to Ricky on New Year's Eve,' Tom said sheepishly.

'If you did, and it's unlike you, I don't suppose he'll remember,' Cathy soothed.

'He might.'

'Go on, if I were the one that had said that, you'd tell me I thought the whole world revolved around myself.'

Tom laughed. 'Yes, you're quite right, of course we'll ask Ricky for contacts, and Shona, of course, and a couple of the guys we knew back at college. But mainly I think we should have friends and family, don't you?'

'Of course I do, though it has to be said hardly any of *my* family and friends will put any business our way, not much demand for caterers down on the morning shift in the bookies, with my dad's betting associates, as he's inclined to call them.'

'Nor mine,' Tom said. 'But that's not the point.'

'Can we do a quick deal, the pair of us? If you don't ask your in-laws, I won't ask mine,' Cathy pleaded.

'I don't *have* any in-laws, as you very well know, and you *have* to ask yours, as you also very well know.'

'It's just a wish,' Cathy sighed. 'She'll make it a misery for everyone there if she does come, and she'll sulk for six months if she's not asked.'

'And what does Neil say?'

'What do you think he says? He says it's up to me. As if that was any proper answer at all.'

'So we ask her?'

'I'm afraid so. Does Marcella have any hateful people who might destroy the evening for us?'

'No, not that she's mentioned.'

'Okay, then I'm the only one inviting a big bad wolf,' Cathy said. 'Let's get on with the list. Will we ask any famous people? They just might come.'

'Definitely let's ask famous people.' Tom was eager, and the shadow of Hannah Mitchell hung over them no longer.

'What will we do at the party?' Maud asked.

'I don't think you'll be there,' Cathy said.

'But where else would we be?' Simon asked, as if it were all arranged.

'You see, Simon, it's really for older people.'

'Yes, well, people of all ages I'd say.' Simon had thought about it.

'Sure, but not people who are just nine, actually,' Cathy said, trying to keep her voice steady.

'But where would we go? You're going, Neil's going, Muttie and Lizzie are going, Aunt Hannah and Uncle Jock. There won't be anyone left to look after us.'

'Muttie was saying when he picked us up from school that we'd be going.'

Cathy felt yet another urge to give her father a very hard kick for his helpfulness. But then she remembered that he did walk up to those school gates and wait for the children, which was more than any Mitchell seemed to be prepared to do. She must think, she must not panic.

'Walter, your big brother Walter will look after you.' Cathy felt very pleased that she had pulled this rabbit out of the hat.

'No, he's talking about going skiing,' Maud cried triumphantly.

'We could take the coats. Muttie thought that might be a good job for us,' Simon said.

'Did he now?' Cathy asked. 'And did he also by any chance suggest what I myself should do during the party, or was it only your work he had planned out?'

'No, he didn't say,' Simon answered solemnly. 'I think he thought you would probably *know* what to do, what with it being your own waitressing business and all.'

'Catering business,' Maud corrected primly.

And Cathy heard a sudden hysterical tinge in her own laughter.

The Feathers had wondered to Tom whether they should have replied formally to the invitation.

'Did you keep your temper?' Cathy was working on the choux pastry.

'With extreme difficulty,' Tom admitted. 'And it's so stupid, I could hear the sarcasm in my voice, asking them did they think they wouldn't be let in.'

'They're not used to parties, any more than mine are,' Cathy soothed.

'Well at least yours won't be fingering the walls and telling people that everything really needed another coat, but it was such a rush job that there wasn't time . . .' Tom wouldn't be consoled.

'No, but my mother wanted to wear a yellow nylon coat and wash up in the back kitchen. We've had three scenes about that, and my dad says that he's bringing his own beer because fancy wines give him a headache.' Cathy had finished the tray of little pastry cases and was setting the timer.

'But then you *have* got Geraldine working the room for us, and talking us up to everyone.' Tom was jointing the chickens expertly as he spoke.

'And you've got that sexy brother of yours to keep all the women happy. Let's hope he goes into one of his charm routines, I love to watch him in action, it's amazing the way they lap it up.'

'I was always afraid at the start that Marcella would fall for him when she met him, but mercifully she didn't,' Tom said.

'Marcella? Fall for Joe when she could have you?' Cathy laughed.

'He is very smooth, though.' Tom had a hint of worry.

'Very obvious, you mean, and your Marcella's too bright for that.' Cathy was confused by Marcella in these last days before the great launch. She had been extremely helpful behind the scenes, coming on from her work at Haywards, changing into jeans and taking out her rubber gloves to protect her hands: she did all the menial jobs anyone could give her. But she utterly refused to serve and help at the party. She had what seemed to her very good reasons.

'Listen, Cathy, you should understand about having a dream and a goal. You and Tom have got yours now. I haven't yet. I want to be a model. I know I can do it, I believe I'm as good as anyone else, I've spent a fortune on courses and portfolios. I just *can't* be seen in public as a waitress or that's all I'll ever be, a manicurist and a waitress.'

'You could be worse things.' Cathy had been curt.

'And you could have been a typist or a shop girl, but you wanted more,' Marcella had answered with spirit. She had refused to take the coats. She would be there only as a guest. She would work with them afterwards, clearing up, she promised, but her public face was to be an invited person. There was no moving her so Cathy didn't try. After all, she had yet to explain to Tom that the terrible twins might be part of the night. Partnership was all about give and take.

James Byrne said yes, he would come to the party. Cathy was somewhat surprised, but pleased.

'And of course if there's anyone else that you'd . . . um, like to . . . um, bring with you,' she said hesitantly.

'Thank you, but I'll come on my own.'

They were finally on first-name terms with each other, not that it seemed to sit easily with the older man. He was so courteous and old-fashioned. And so extremely reticent. The business with the Maguires seemed to be almost concluded now. Yet Cathy and Tom knew as little about the family of printers who had sold them the premises as they had known on New Year's Day. They did, however, know a little more about James.

He lived in what he called the garden flat of one of the big Victorian houses in Rathgar. He had been an accountant in a large provincial town for most of his life, and had only come to Dublin in the last five years. He was now retired. They couldn't ask him what he did all day, and if time was heavy on his hands these days. They didn't dare ask him had he any family. Their conversations, though warm and relaxed, were always professional. One day Tom had asked whether he might know someone who would act as a bookkeeper for them. They told him that they assumed that maybe one morning a week would be enough at this early stage, or possibly they didn't even need that. Perhaps he might have come across someone.

'I'd be very happy to do it,' he said.

'To find someone?' Cathy wasn't sure what he meant.

'No, I mean to act as your bookkeeper, if that would suit you. Two hours a week should be adequate at the start.'

'But Mr Byrne . . . I mean James . . . we couldn't ask *you* . . .' Tom began.

Cathy sensed he was lonely and had nothing else to do. 'But of course, if you would take us on a trial period we would be delighted,' she had said firmly. And an unaccustomed smile came across James Byrne's face, making him look handsome. Still grave, despite the smile, but definitely very handsome.

'I've got your mother a dress, *and* I've booked a hairdo for her,' Geraldine said.

'You'll be bankrupt,' Cathy protested.

'Not on the kind of place your mother insists on going to have her hair done in, that's when she does go at all.'

'But the dress?'

'It came from Oxfam.' Geraldine looked at her with clear, lying blue eyes.

'It didn't. It came from Haywards.'

'And what makes you think that?'

'Shona Burke told me she met you getting it.'

'Busybody,' Geraldine said, laughing.

'If my mother knew she was wearing a dress from Haywards she'd have to be in the next bed to my one in the nervous hospital, as Maud keeps calling it. Oh, Geraldine, *what* am I going to do with those children?'

'There must be someone in St Jarlath's Crescent, some neighbour.'

'Of course there are a dozen people, but Ma has reservations about all of them, and I don't want her like a hen on a hot griddle all night wondering are they all right.'

'All right, all right, give them to me,' Geraldine said. 'I'll get them into the child-sitting service at Peter's hotel.'

'What does that mean?'

'In their case, chicken nuggets and chips, suitable video and a swim in a heated pool if they want one.'

'Would you really?'

'Of course I would, and remember that I do have to protect my investment tomorrow night, don't I?'

'It's nothing to do with an investment, it's a lifeline that you've given us and always have,' Cathy said.

But Geraldine would hear none of it. 'It's just that you're overtired, but tomorrow will be a roaring success, believe me,' she said. 'And if the backers are confident, then everyone is confident. Take me through the menu again.'

'You're going to a hotel tomorrow evening,' Cathy told Simon and Maud.

'I'd be just as happy to go to the do,' Simon said.

'To help you,' Maud explained.

'I know, and I do appreciate it, but honestly there's not all that much room in the premises, and you'll have a great time there.'

'Is Walter going to your party?' Maud wanted to know.

'Yes, I think he is. He didn't reply, but I'm sure he will be there.'

'Will he be working for you and Tom?' Simon asked.

'Not if all the guests were lying writhing on the ground parched with thirst, pleading and roaring for a drink will Walter Mitchell ever work for me again,' Cathy said cheerfully.

'It doesn't sound much of a party,' Simon said to Maud. 'I think we'd be better off in the hotel, to tell you the truth.'

Neil was up and dressed when Cathy woke with a start. 'God almighty, what time is it?'

'Relax, it's not even seven yet.'

'Why are you up?'

'This is the big day,' he said.

Lord, she had forgotten. Today Scarlet Feather would be a reality, the launch party, the brochure out, the whole company up and ready for business.

'I know, I can hardly believe it.' Cathy stood there in her stripy nightshirt. She rubbed her eyes and shook her hair back.

'I know he's only a junior minister, but it's very big for him to come to the breakfast, and he's crazy about publicity so it'll give the whole thing some attention.'

She realised that it was a big day for Neil because a group of them had managed to get a government minister to meet them about prisoners of conscience.

'I hope it's a great success, anyway,' she said in a flat voice.

He looked at her, startled at the tone, but she said nothing by way of explanation. 'So I must run . . .' he said eventually.

'See you tonight,' she said.

'Oh yes, of course, the do. It will be great, honey, don't have a worry in the world about it.'

'No, of course not.' Still the same flat voice.

He came back and gave her a quick hug. 'I'm very proud of you, you know,' he said.

'I know, Neil,' she said. But she wished that it were much more important to him than a quick hug and a pat on the back.

Ricky sent one of his photographers down to the premises an hour before people were expected. Just to do a few food shots, to see the buffet before it got all clogged up with people. Cathy's friends June and Katy were well kitted out in their white shirts with the scarlet feather logo. They all posed beside the plates of dressed salmon, long, oval dishes of roasted peppers, colourful salads and baskets of bread.

One moment there seemed to be nobody except the staff standing around nervously, and the next the place was teeming with people. The front room, which would later be their little reception office, looked terrific tonight. How right they had been to have old-fashioned sofas and chairs. Their new filing system was cleverly hidden in elegant drawers. It was a peaceful place where they hoped that customers would sit and discuss menus. Nothing of the precision shining white and steel of the kitchens here: that was all beyond the door, and they had cleared spaces for people to stand and later to dance. Tonight the front room was acting as a cloakroom with two great rails. And a ravishing-looking redhead who worked in Geraldine's office but did not think helping at a party was beneath her gave people tickets for their coats and hung them neatly on the rails.

Then June and Katy, her two great friends through everything from schooldays long ago, stood with trays of welcoming drinks leaving Tom and Cathy free to greet and welcome and to listen to the praise and admiration for their new premises.

Neil was among the early arrivals. Cathy planned to place him very near to the door, so that he could cope with his mother whenever Hannah chose to make her entrance. Cathy's own parents were there, totally amazed by it all, awkward and out of place. Her father twisting his cap that he had inexplicably refused to surrender at the cloakroom, and roaming the room with his eyes looking for someone he might talk to. Her mother, in a soft, flattering green wool dress that had set her sister back a small fortune at Haywards and with her hair nicely styled, had no idea how well she looked. Instead, her eyes scanned the room for somewhere to hide.

'Mam, you look beautiful,' Cathy said, and meant it.

'No indeed I don't, Cathy, I'm a disgrace. I shouldn't be here with all these people at all. I wonder, is . . .' Why did they feel so ill at ease, as if somehow they were going to be found out, pronounced unacceptable and sent home? Cathy had been down this route, had asked herself these questions so often that she knew it to be totally fruitless. But of course Tom had to put up with it too. JT and Maura Feather didn't look as if they were having fun either. Now there was an idea. She excused herself from talking to a pleasant man who ran a house-cleaning service. They had been saying that there were ways in which they might well work together, one would recommend the other. Expertly Cathy made the introductions. In one way it didn't really work: instead of being moral support to each other, they made each other more nervous. But they each drew some strength and solidarity from realising that the other couple was also full of doubts. Tom's father said that if anyone wanted to know what he thought, then he thought that it wasn't worth spoiling the ship for a ha'porth of tar, and they should have given it more time. And Lizzie Scarlet said she was afraid they had bitten off more than they could chew. Maura Feather said there was a perfectly good living for Tom in his father's business and he needn't even get his hands dirty – he could have sat in an office and brought in clients. Like these people who were all dressed to kill, and would have plenty in the bank to build extensions and maybe even second homes. Muttie said that if his Cathy and their Tom were such great cooks, then if they went to work for other people without putting their money at risk they would save a small fortune in no time, but of course nobody ever listened to the voice of experience.

The mood was getting more relaxed by the moment. Cathy caught her aunt's eye and in seconds Geraldine was in there talking and enthusing and broadening the circle. The noise level was much higher now. Cathy noticed, and she allowed herself to take a couple of normal breaths and to accept that it was all going very well. She even looked around her at the guests. James Byrne had phoned at the last moment to say he couldn't come. Marcella looked just exquisite in a beautifully cut silk jacket and long black skirt. She wore no jewellery, even though anything at all around that long, slim neck would have looked good. Somehow she had great style the way she was. She was the centre of admiring glances, and Tom looked on proudly. Cathy was glad that this was not one of Marcella's rather over-sexy nights; she had seen Tom's face too often on such occasions.

In and in they came, and then she saw Neil's parents arrive. Jock with his handsome if marginally vacant face had the slightly affected manner of always appearing to think he should be somewhere else. Good-natured and bewildered, but not entirely convincing. And beside him was Hannah. She wore a harsh, dark purple dress that somehow drained the colour from her face. She looked affronted before she even came in the door. There was nothing here that she could fault, Cathy thought triumphantly. Nothing at all. There were even a few minor celebrities from the stage or television. But in general it was just a well-dressed, well-behaved crowd of people who might form a pool of future clients. She had, however, known Mrs Mitchell since her early childhood, for too long not to be able to read her face. The woman was spoiling for a fight. She would not have one with Cathy.

They all seemed to love the food: it had been worthwhile showing off their wares. Cathy noticed her father deep in conversation with a sports journalist, and her mother sitting happily with Mrs Keane, a neighbour of theirs from Waterview, on two chairs a little away from the general throng. To Cathy's surprise, Hannah Mitchell approached them.

'Ah, good to see you, Lizzie; give me that chair, will you, like a dear, and get me a plate of mixed bites, nibbles, whatever they call them . . .' She spoke imperiously, as someone who knew she would make it happen. And it would have happened, had Cathy not been near at hand. Poor Lizzie Scarlet stumbled to her feet and apologised. She was still Mrs Mitchell's cleaner, and she had been caught sitting down and talking in an overfamiliar way with the quality.

'Yes, Mrs Mitchell, sorry, Mrs Mitchell, what exactly would you like, a little of everything?' Cathy's resolutions were out of the window. She had never been so angry. This woman had now crossed over every boundary of behaviour and good manners. In an icy voice, she ordered her mother to sit down and not to abandon Mrs Keane in mid-conversation. Out of sheer shock Lizzie did just that, and with a combination of shoulder and arm Cathy moved and manipulated Hannah Mitchell to the other side of the room. Out of the corner of her mouth she hissed at June that she needed a stool, and at Kate that she wanted a plate with a small selection. Then she seated her mother-in-law in an area where she could see everyone.

'There was no need to push me across the room, Cathy, really.'

'I know, isn't it just terrible when places become so crowded? But you wanted a chair and I wanted to make sure you got one.' She smiled until the sides of her face hurt.

Hannah Mitchell was not fooled. 'I had a perfectly good chair where I was.'

'Sadly no, that was my mother's chair, but can I leave you for a moment? I do hope you like the premises.' And she was gone trembling and shaking.

Neil, who had noticed nothing amiss, was talking to his cousin Walter, jumpy and restless as ever. Cathy saw Joe Feather come in; he had brought them a kitchen clock with pictures of old-fashioned cooking utensils on it.

'Figured you didn't need any more food and drink in this place. What a great, great job – you've done it, I smell success everywhere.' Tom and Cathy beamed at him, he had such a knack for saying the right thing, and was a strange magnet immediately for people. He didn't even have to move towards them, they came to him.

They turned the background music level down slightly. It was time for the speeches. Tom and Cathy gave each other the thumbs-up sign. They had rehearsed these for ever. No long Oscar-style lists of thank-yous. No boasting of how successful they would be. Even before they had got the premises they had been trying them out on each other. It would be an absolute maximum of two minutes each, and then fade up the music. People could continue their conversations without feeling seriously interrupted, and it worked just as they'd planned. It was much too good a party to interrupt for more than four minutes, plus applause. When it was over, they looked at each other. Had they really said what they meant to? Neither could remember. They were congratulated on all sides, and could hardly take it in. Some early leavers were beginning to get their coats, but the hard core would be there for much, much longer.

'What a pity we didn't think of having a tape recorder!' Cathy said.

'I did.' Geraldine was beside her. 'And you were both brilliant.'

'Is Ma all right?'

'She is. Stop fussing.'

'You're lucky you can speak to Cathy like that, Geraldine. I try to, but she bites my head off,' said Tom.

'Ah, family gives you great privileges,' Geraldine said, and was gone.

Cathy saw JT and Maura Feather leaving. 'I don't think they've even *seen* Joe, he's been over on the other side of the room,' she began.

'Leave it, Cathy. Joe will find them if he wants to.'

'But wouldn't it be a shame . . .'

'It's always been a shame, but that's the way he is, he doesn't do anything that bores him and going to Fatima bores him, so he never goes.'

'He's going to meet them tonight,' Cathy insisted, and raised her voice loudly. 'Joe, I think your parents are leaving . . .' He had to meet them then. Cathy saw how their faces lit up with pleasure at the sight of their elder son. Joe put up a good show of being delighted and surprised to see them: he admired his mother's dress, praised his father for the work that had been done and swiftly he got them to the door. At no stage had Cathy ever seen such joy and enthusiasm on their faces when they were talking to their son Tom. Tom, who went to see them regularly and looked after their every need. But then, when had life been fair?

Geraldine had arranged a taxi, which would collect Muttie and Lizzie and take them to the hotel to pick up Simon and Maud. But by the time it came, neither of the Scarlets wanted to leave. Muttie was going to meet the sports journalist at the next big race meeting and was to be invited into the press box. Lizzie was going to visit Mrs Keane in Waterview to look at this new mop she had. Apparently you didn't need to kneel down on the floor nearly so much these days, and Lizzie's knees were a bit achy. It had begun as a conversation about cleaning equipment, but it was now almost a social visit. Cathy looked at her mother with a wave of love. The day would come, she swore it would, when Lizzie Scarlet would never again have to clean a floor for anyone other than herself. Just as the Scarlets had got to the front room, Hannah moved in on them again.

'There you are, Lizzie, get my coat for me, will you, dear?'

'Certainly Mrs Mitchell, is it your fur?'

'Of course not, Lizzie, to a place like this. No, it's my black cloth coat . . . Oh, but maybe you weren't with me when I got it. You might have left by then.'

'Do you have a ticket, Mrs Mitchell?'

'I don't have an idea what I did with the ticket, find it for me quickly like a dear, will you, I don't want to hang around here longer than I have to.'

Cathy moved in quickly. She nailed a smile to her face. 'Mam, your taxi is getting restless, I'll get Hannah's coat for her.' Together with Geraldine she got her parents into the taxi. Which was far from easy.

'And listen, thank you both for coming and for talking to everyone. You're marvellous, both of you, and thank you so much for looking after the little Mitchell children. I really don't know what they would all have done without you.' The last bit very loudly.

'Gently, Cath,' whispered Geraldine. 'You might need Hannah and Jock some day.'

'For what, exactly?'

'All right, but still gently.'

'Right, thanks Geraldine.' Cathy walked over to the gorgeous red-headed cloakroom girl and pointed out her mother-in-law's coat. 'That dame is pretending to have lost her ticket. Can I have that black one, please?' She held it open, but Hannah made no attempt to put it on. So Cathy laid it on a chair. They were alone in the foyer at this stage.

'You've gone too far, Cathy Scarlet. You'll regret your behaviour tonight, mark my words.'

'And I very much hope that you will regret yours, Mrs Mitchell, trying to humiliate my mother as a way to annoy me. Yes, it worked for you in that it *did* annoy me, but you couldn't humiliate her, it's impossible. She has a decent, generous soul, and because she took your money for years for hard, menial work she thinks she still owes you.'

Hannah was white at the insolence. 'Your mother, limited as she is, is worth ten of you.'

'I agree with you. And she's worth a hundred of you, Mrs Mitchell. I said it to her the other day. She wouldn't listen, of course, but it's still true.'

Hannah Mitchell gasped and Cathy went on. 'Believe me, I'm actually glad that we are having this conversation, and I want you to know that my days of being polite to you are over.'

'You were *never* polite to me, you common little ... little ...' Words failed Hannah at this point.

'When I was young and came to play in the garden, if Mam was working at Oaklands, I wasn't polite, that's true, but when I married Neil I was, I tried very hard. I didn't want to make things difficult for him and actually I was sorry for you. Yes, I was, because you were so very disappointed in the wife he brought home.'

'*You* were sorry for *me!*' Hannah snorted.

'And I still am in ways, but there will be no pretence any more. There's something you have not understood: I was never in my whole life afraid of you. You just don't have any power over me. Your day is gone, Hannah Mitchell. It's a new Ireland, a country where the maids' children marry who they bloody well like, and where the nobs like your brother-in-law, if he's aware of anything at all, are very glad to have Muttie and Lizzie Scarlet going down in a taxi to the best hotel in Dublin to pick up his children and take them back to St Jarlath's Crescent where it looks as if they might spend the next ten years—'

Hannah interrupted her. 'When you apologise, Cathy, as you will, I assure you, I am not going to forgive you or put it down to overexcitement because of all this ...' Hannah looked around her and sniffed.

'Oh, no, I will never apologise, believe me, I meant everything I said,' Cathy spoke icily. 'If you, on the other hand, apologise about the way you insulted my mother twice tonight, I will consider it and ask Neil what he thinks. Otherwise we will behave courteously to each other in public and communicate not at all in private. Now, you can either come in and join your husband or leave. Suit yourself.' And Cathy turned and went, head high, back to the party. Inside, she saw Geraldine looking at her anxiously.

'She still has a pulse, Geraldine, don't worry.' Cathy Scarlet had her first drink of the night. A very large glass of red wine. She realised now that Hannah had two ways to go. She wished for a moment her father were here to tell her the odds. But as Muttie often said, there are times when there are no odds, when you have to go by instinct. And her instinct was that Hannah would say nothing. Reporting the insolence of her daughter-in-law would mean putting the spotlight on her own behaviour. Hannah wouldn't risk it. So there would be no need for Cathy to explain anything at all. She smiled at the thought that she had won, she had really and truly won. It was somehow nearly as good as this launch.

'I don't like you sitting alone drinking wine and laughing to yourself,' Geraldine said disapprovingly. The music was louder. Tom moved to hold the beautiful face of Marcella in his two hands and began to dance with her. Cathy's two friends June and Kate were both quite reached by drink and dancing already. Dreamily, Cathy put out her hand towards Neil and they held each other tight. Over his shoulder she saw Jock Mitchell look around for his wife and eventually go out of the door to find her. She saw Joe

Feather leave quietly and watched Walter put a bottle of wine under his arm before leaving. And Cathy Scarlet closed her eyes and danced with the man she loved.

'What are you thinking about?' he asked her, but there were too many things even to begin to tell.

February

'Tell me that we cleared the place up,' Tom asked Marcella sleepily next morning. 'Tell me that we didn't just walk out and leave everything as it was.'

Marcella laughed. 'Surely you remember the way you said to everyone that you were calling two taxis in half an hour, and the place had to be perfect.'

'You know what? I thought I remembered that, but I was afraid I just dreamed it,' Tom said.

'You had us all running in and out like a fast-forward film, and by the time the taxis came everything was covered with cling film and put into the right places and the dishwasher was turned on.'

'I'm a genius,' Tom said happily.

'Of course you are. You did say, however, that there would be about a hundred more glasses to do, but you were very proud that all the litter bags were tied up and the floor was clean.'

'I really laid into the wine, I'm afraid.' He was contrite.

'Not until the end. You and Cathy must have drunk a bottle each in ten minutes and you deserved it, but you'd had nothing to eat or drink all day.' She stroked his forehead and began to get out of bed.

'You're never leaving me alone in the morning of my triumph and my slight hangover, are you?' He was very disappointed.

'Tom, it's my dance class,' she said.

'Of course.' He had forgotten. Marcella didn't need this two-hour class in movement every Saturday morning; she didn't need the other classes she took either. She was a lithe, gorgeous girl who turned heads. But she was convinced that these were all part of her apprenticeship, and worked hard for the extra money. She spent hours after work and early in the morning shelf-stacking in the Food Hall at Haywards. Only the staff saw Marcella Malone doing a menial job like that. And they didn't matter, as Marcella always said, because they were not the ones who were going to discover her and give her this break in modelling. The rest of the public saw her either as a beauty therapist in Haywards' salon, or as a beautiful party animal much photographed at press receptions and at the clubs.

Tom understood entirely why Marcella could never work as a waitress for them in Scarlet Feather. It would mean the end of the dream for her, admitting that there would be no starry future ahead. He wasn't totally sure that Cathy understood; sometimes he thought he saw a flash of impatience pass over his business partner's face when he said that his life partner would not be helping them out. Cathy's own husband Neil never minded carrying heavy trays or loading the van, if he was around. But then he seldom was, and anyway, he *could* do that because he was already somebody, a successful and known young barrister, his name and photograph often in the newspapers. He had already made his way. Marcella had yet to make hers.

Tom knew he should go into the premises and get the glasses done, check that the food really had been properly put away, but it was early still and they had been rushing so much in the run-up to last night, he deserved another cup of coffee. He looked out on the wintry scene, the leafless trees and wet courtyard surrounding Stoneyfield. Tom's father always said that it was a disgrace leaving that ground to go to waste when they could easily have fitted three more units into the space. It wasn't even as if it were a proper garden with lawns or anything. In vain would Tom try to tell him that the kind of people who came to live here had no time to mow lawns. But they did need places to turn and park cars, and for the athletic like Marcella, chain their bicycles in elegantly disguised sheds. JT Feather, builder, from an earlier time when more was good, would never understand it in a million years. Any more than he would take in the amount of their earnings that he and Marcella put into the mortgage. Better not to weigh his father down with details like that. As was increasingly becoming the case, Tom sighed to himself.

This thought led him to think of his brother. Joe had said he would call before he left for the airport, but then Joe was spectacularly vague about family. Tom dialled his hotel.

'You thought I'd forget to phone you,' Joe said.

'You? Forget to phone your family? Never.' Tom laughed at him good-naturedly.

'I would have, mainly to say that you've a great set-up there, it's very professional, really it is. Geraldine and I think our investment is one of the best we've ever made, we told each other several times.'

'She's a real looker that woman, isn't she? Loads of style. She's not there with you, by any chance?' Nothing was unlikely with his brother Joe.

'No indeed, she's not. Let's say *she's* not.'

'I don't know how you do it, Joe.' Tom shook his head. Imagine, Joe had picked up someone at their party last night and persuaded her to go back to his hotel!

'Only because I'm a sad old man without a lovely wife of my own like you have.'

'She's not my wife yet.'

'I know, but she might as well be for all the looks she gives towards anyone else.'

That pleased Tom, as Joe knew it would. 'Anyone I know from the party?'

'Aha,' said Joe.

'Is she there with you? Now?'

'In the bathroom at the moment. Any time for a drink before I get the plane?'

'I have to go round to the premises . . . I really do not want Cathy coming by and doing it.'

'Right, I'll see you round there in half an hour,' Joe said.

Tom was ready to leave in minutes. The van wasn't outside the door, it was in Waterview at Cathy's place. He'd get a taxi on the street. There was something he wanted to talk to Joe about too. Like was there any hope that he might actually *do* something in terms of their mother and father, come and see them even for very short visits. It would mean so much to them, and take so little out of Joe's lifestyle. And it would lift a great deal of the burden from Tom's back.

The van was there when he arrived. Tom was annoyed; not only had he not beaten Cathy to it but now he wouldn't be able to talk to Joe. Perhaps he could take him out for a coffee. He would make it up to Cathy later. Tom hoped that Neil would not be there, it would point up how much more involved the two of them were, Marcella at her dance class and Tom about to slip out with his brother. But no; Cathy was not with Neil. She was with those bizarre children that she seemed to have taken under her wing. Solemn-eyed, self-centred, intense and appallingly bad mannered, although there had been a bit of an improvement in their behaviour recently.

'You're late,' said Simon.

'Where's your girlfriend?' asked Maud.

Cathy came out and gave him a hug. 'Wasn't that a night to remember,' she said. Then, looking at the children, she said in an entirely different voice, 'Tom is not late, we are only here for two minutes, and his girlfriend Marcella is at her dance class, and what did I say about greeting people?'

They lowered their eyes.

'No, stop looking down at the floor. How do we greet people in a civilised society? Tell me this minute.'

'We say hallo and pretend to be glad to see them,' said Simon.

'We use their name if we know it,' added Maud.

'Okay. Sorry Tom, could you go out and come in again, it wasn't a civilised society for a moment but it will be when you come back.'

Tom went back outside, irritated. There was little enough time as it was, and now he was playing ridiculous games in a vain attempt to teach these monstrous children manners.

'Good morning,' he said as he re-entered.

Simon, with a nightmare rictus grin on his face, came out to shake hands. 'Good morning Tom,' he said.

'You are most welcome, Tom,' Maud said.

'Thank you . . . um . . . Maud and Simon,' said Tom, gritting his teeth at being welcomed to his own premises by these two children. 'Thank you so much, and to what exactly do we owe the pleasure of your company?' They looked at him without an idea of what he was talking about.

Cathy explained. 'My mother isn't all that well this morning.'

'Too much wine here last night,' Simon explained.

Cathy interrupted, 'And so I thought it would all be for the best if they came to help me here . . . And if you have no objections, they are about to unload and load the dishwashers very carefully now. *Now*,' she barked suddenly at the children, who scuttled away to get on with it.

'Sorry,' she whispered to Tom. 'I really had to. I've never seen my poor mother so shook. She never goes anywhere where there's drink, and it's all my fault. I hated that old bitch Hannah Mitchell so much I kept tanking poor Mam up so that she wouldn't hear your woman patronising her.'

'Cathy, whatever you want, believe me, it's just . . .'

'It's just what?' Her eyes were bright and searching his face for what he was trying to say.

'Well it's just that I don't seem to do as much as you do. I was going to meet Joe here and have a chat with him, so now we might slope off and that's not fair on you . . . And also it's just . . .'

'Oh, go on, say it Tom. Ask are they going to be living with us until Neil and I are old and grey, and the answer is I don't bloody know. I just know that we can't abandon them. And they will do this, you know, so go off with Joe and for God's sake stop saying you're not pulling your weight. You do far more than me.'

'It *was* a great night last night,' he said. ' I really do think we're going to be all right, don't you?'

'I think we'll be millionaires,' said Cathy, just as Joe came in through the open door.

'That's what I like to hear,' said Joe Feather. He took Cathy up in his arms and swung her round in a circle. 'Well done, Cathy Scarlet, you and my little brother here have really got the right touch.'

She was pleased, Tom noted, as every woman that Joe Feather looked at seemed pleased.

Maud and Simon peered out of the kitchen at the sounds. 'Good morning, I'm Maud Mitchell and this is my brother Simon. You're very welcome.'

'Would you like me to take your coat?' Simon asked.

'I'm Joe Feather. Delighted to make your acquaintance,' Joe said.

'Are you Tom's father?' Simon asked, interested.

Cathy's face fell.

'Not quite, more his brother,' Joe said agreeably.

'And do you have children and grandchildren of your own?' Maud wanted to be clear on everything too.

'No, I'm a bachelor, that's a man never lucky enough to marry,' said Joe as if he were being interviewed on radio. 'And I live by myself in London in an apartment in Ealing. I go to work by the Central line every day from Ealing Broadway to Oxford Circus, and I walk down to the garment district, where I sell clothes.'

Tom hadn't known any of this. He knew his brother's post code, but he hadn't known it was Ealing . . . He didn't know about the tube journey, either.

'Do you sell them in a shop or in a street?'

'It's more an office really. You see, they come in to me and then I send them out again,' Joe explained.

'Do you improve them before they go?' Maud asked.

'Actually, no. No, they go the same as they arrive,' said Joe.

'Terrible waste then, isn't it, them going to you?' Simon said.

There was a silence. 'I suppose it is in a way,' Joe agreed. 'But it's the system, you see. It's how I earn my money.'

There was another silence. 'Are we talking too much?' Simon asked Cathy.

'No, truly, but why don't you go into the kitchen again and sort the cutlery? Like now,' Cathy shouted so that they all jumped. Maud and Simon went out immediately.

'They're extraordinary,' Joe said.

'Mixed blessing,' Cathy said.

'Who are they?' he asked.

'You don't have time. Go off and have a coffee somewhere sane, and we'll do this place.'

Tom thought that Joe was reluctant to leave. His brother was such a womaniser and always had been. Tom hoped against hope that Joe hadn't suddenly taken a fancy to Cathy. Life was never uncomplicated, but all he needed now was something like this to happen, for his brother, who seemed to be able to get the entire female population of Ireland to fancy him, to move in on the happiest marriage in the Western world – that of Cathy and Neil Mitchell. Whatever else happened, this must not even be allowed to get to first base. 'Come on, Joe, we'll go to Bewley's,' Tom said, and they left.

'What does Geraldine do for a living?' Joe asked when they were seated with their sticky almond buns and coffee.

'She's got a PR agency, you know that.'

'No, I meant how did she get the money to set it up, and how can she match me pound by pound?'

'Funny thing,' Tom said. 'Geraldine asked Cathy the same question. She wanted to know where *you* got the money.'

'And what did Cathy say?'

'She said that she didn't know, and as far as she knew that I didn't know either.'

Joe said, 'So what do you want to know? Ask me, I'll tell you.'

'I suppose I don't know exactly what you do. You don't ever say.'

Joe leaned on the table and looked across at him without the usual jokey smile. 'God, you *know* what I do, Tom. I rent two rooms in the garment district in London. I get stuff made up out in the Philippines. I import it, I show it to retailers, they buy it and I get more stuff made up in Korea and I show it to more retailers and they buy it.'

'And that's it?'

'Of course it's bloody it. What did you think it was, stealing old ladies' pension books, selling hash in pubs?'

'No, of course not.'

'But what then? You know what I do. There was never any mystery. When you went to work in those restaurants I knew what you were at. I didn't say to myself, I wonder what Tom is doing in Quentins? I knew you were an apprentice learning how to cook with that chef Patrick, what's his name?'

'Brennan. Patrick Brennan.'

'Yes, I know. I often go in there, his wife Brenda is something else. When you went on the catering course, I knew what it was about. Ask me anything you like if you can't understand what it is I'm doing,' Joe grinned at him.

'I know, it does sound like the Special Branch. Sorry.'

'It sounds worse, it sounds like the Inland Revenue,' Joe said with a look of mock terror on his face.

'Talking about that, Joe, we have a very upright bookkeeper ...'

'I get your drift,' he laughed.

'No, I mean he really does ask toughish questions and, you know me, I like the canvas to be uncluttered with little problems.'

'I have one really spotless account, believe me. Any support comes from that one.'

Tom decided to go no further down the road on that one, in case he heard of accounts which were not spotless and learned more than he wanted to know. 'And do you ever go out to these places in the Far East to see them making your clothes?' he asked.

'As little as I can. I know you think I'm a capitalist pig but I actually can't bear to see how poor they are and how little they're paid, I just prefer to see stuff arriving in a warehouse.'

'Oh, I can't talk about people being capitalist pigs now, I've joined them,' Tom said ruefully.

'I know, the Feather brothers taking over.' Joe grinned at him.

'Talking of that ...'

'Yeah?' Joe was wary now, as if he knew what was coming.

'Joe, I don't want to preach but couldn't you just go sometimes to see Ma and Da. You *never* see them and I have to keep on ...'

'No, Tom, you don't have to keep on doing anything you don't want to. I met them last night, for God's sake.'

'For thirty seconds at a party.'

'You want me to spend hour after hour listening to Ma telling me I'll burn in hell because I don't go to Mass, Da complaining that my name isn't on the sign in the builder's yard ... No, Tom, I have a life to lead.'

'So do I, and I have to live yours for you too ... Where is he, why doesn't he stay in touch.'

Joe shrugged. 'Say you don't know.'

'I do say it, and it's the truth. I *don't* know. I don't know why you who are so good with people can't send them the odd postcard, make the odd call.'

'If I go to Manila I'll send them a card, is that a deal? Will you get off my back now?'

'A card from London would be exotic enough for Ma and Da,' said Tom, but he knew when he had to give up.

Tom and Cathy sat for hours dreaming up menus for the christening, the first night party and the business lunch. All of them desperately important in their own way. The christening would have a very flash, moneyed crowd at it, people who could spend. They would have to do it right, lay out a bit more on the actual presentation. The theatre party was on a very low budget; what they wanted was something much nicer than sausages and crisps but at the price that sausages and crisps would cost. It needed a lot of thought. If they got on well with the theatre crowd it would really stand to them, there would be contacts for all kinds of events from now on. Cathy had been endlessly patient trying to think of cheap food that would seem more upmarket. Crostini, maybe? And lots of dips and pitta. But since people actually *did* like sausages, maybe they should have some, with a redcurrant and honey glaze. She knew there would be no profit in it but that it was very dear to Tom's heart. So he wanted to help her also with the business lunch. Cathy's dream was that they would get into some of the banks or money houses in the financial centre, where they would serve light, exquisite lunches to the companies' clients as part of corporate hospitality, and have the ability to pick up further business at every meal they served. It would mean more daytime work, too.

Cathy had asked once if Marcella would consider helping to serve this first one, just to start them off. Nobody would ever forget Marcella pouring their mineral water and smiling her dazzling smile. Tom hated having to say no at the outset. He knew that Marcella just would not do it, and it would be unfair to ask her.

'She must have a stab at this modelling, you know, no matter how hard she pushes herself. I hardly ever see her.'

'I know what you mean,' she shrugged. 'But you're going to have to get used to it when she does become a model, because she'll be off at shows somewhere all the time.'

Tom realised with a shock that he had probably thought Marcella would never make it. He had somehow seen a future where Scarlet Feather became very successful and they could put in a manager. A future where he and Marcella would marry and have two children. But perhaps he was just fooling himself.

'Where will we be in ten years' time, do you think, Cathy?' he asked her suddenly.

'I'd say we'll still be here working out this bloody menu, and the child will be nearly grown-up and walking round a pagan because he never got christened at all,' she said. 'Come on Tom, let's cost it out, salmon *and* a chicken dish, they want it done right, and judging by your figures, they're not likely to have a big family and lots of other christenings to follow.'

'It'll be too dear, it's the rich who always carp about the prices . . . you know that,' Tom said.

They were back in business. Sitting arguing in their shiny new premises, drinking coffee from the marvellous mugs which said *Scarlet Feather*. A gift of six of them from Marcella, who had them painted specially. Cathy's friend June who had helped last night came in to say that she would love to do the odd night waitressing, and could they just show her a few of the finer points.

'I'm not sure we know them,' Tom said. 'But we'll try anyway.'

June was a small, jolly girl who had been at school with Cathy. She had got pregnant when she was sixteen and the great thing about that, she said, was that she had her family reared now and she was free to do what she liked. According to Cathy, she sometimes felt a little bit *too* free to do what she liked, or that's what her husband said, anyway. But June just laughed and said that she had to go dancing and to clubs nowadays: she had missed out on all that when she was seventeen and eighteen, pushing prams and minding babies.

'I'll try not to be too forward or anything,' she promised Tom, 'and if you tell me how to pronounce the things each time, I'll be great altogether. Well, I'll be cheerful anyway, and a lot of these ones you meet at functions look as if they have a poker up their arse.'

'Yes indeed,' Tom had said.

'But of course, if *they* fancy *me* then I can't help that.'

'No indeed,' Tom said.

'When's that brother of yours coming back to town? He's nearly as good-looking as yourself, but he's a real goer, isn't he?' June ate one of the crostini.

'June, stop that, you're eating the profits,' Tom said firmly. 'Oh, Joe comes and goes, he never stays. You just hear he's here, then you hear he's gone.'

'Dead exciting,' June said.

It flashed across Tom's mind that June could have been Joe's companion, the woman who had gone back to the hotel with him after the launch party. But no, surely not June. Her interpretation of having a bit of freedom could hardly have extended to staying out all night. She did have children at home. Then of course, he realised, it couldn't have been June, she had been here dancing at the very end, when Joe was long gone. But she could have gone on and joined him there later. Sexy little thing, in her way. Not something he would ask Cathy. What he really needed were those two Mitchell children. They'd get to the heart of any story. For some reason, nobody seemed able to refuse to answer their questions.

Cathy and Tom had been trained on the catering course to do their accounting very carefully, pricing their ingredients, labour and staff very precisely. They had to work out portion control in advance *and* take out the hours they worked afterwards. On the theatre job they lost a total of £76. Tom was shaken to the core.

'It's a one-off,' Cathy soothed. 'It's buying goodwill. We should put part of that under the promotional budget.'

'We don't *have* a promotional budget. The launch party saw to that,' Tom wailed in despair.

'It will lead to other things,' she pleaded.

'No, Cathy, it won't, it was to please my theatre friends, that's all. They asked half the audience in, so no future business in that crowd . . . and we were hours getting the place right.'

'*And* we had to send June home in a taxi, which was miles,' Cathy agreed.

'*And* we had to pay her two extra hours because she worked them. I had no idea it was going to go on so late.' Tom was contrite.

'Okay, three jobs this month and we lost seventy-six pounds on the first. I wonder what we'll end up losing? If we did it spectacularly enough they could use our books as an exhibit on some marketing course. How *not* to go into business.'

'We'll have to *get* bloody books, you know, otherwise we'll end up in jail as well as bankrupt. It all looked so simple in theory, didn't it?' Tom sounded less cheerful.

'What we need just now is one of those strokes of luck we kept saying that we were having,' Cathy said.

The phone rang. Cathy was nearer.

'Oh, yes, James, how are you?' Tom watched as Cathy frowned.

'Yes of course, James, it would be a pleasure.' She put the receiver down. 'You'll never guess what James wants.'

'Nothing would surprise me these days. It's not one of those strokes of luck we were looking for, is it?'

'I don't think so,' Cathy said slowly. 'He wants us to teach him to make a supper for two people, three courses. He says we are to buy the ingredients and come to his place. He's costing our time at fifteen pounds an hour. Minimum four hours, including the shopping.'

'When does he want it?' Tom asked. 'We're very busy this week, we're going to . . .'

'No, it's ages away, but he's going to pay us in advance to book us, he says it's proper professional practice and he insists upon it,' Cathy said, knowing well that James was only trying to put some money into their very meagre bank account.

'That's okay. Sixty quid will nearly make up the deficit on the theatre party.'

'Listen, he said fifteen pounds an hour *each*.'

'He's going to pay a hundred and twenty pounds to make a dinner? He's off his skull.'

'I suppose it's for some woman, he did say that discretion was to be a part of it,' Cathy said.

'Good. Then let's not let Simon and Maud know; they'd have it on the six o'clock news,' said Tom happily.

Once a month Neil and Marcella cooked a meal for them all. They were both utterly hopeless at cooking, and Tom and Cathy itched to get up and do it themselves. It would have taken half the time, and been so much better. But they had to sit through the endless fussing, sauces burning, meat shrivelling and salads being drenched in dressing. It was a ritual.

Tom thought to himself that if they were giving a lesson to poor James Byrne, perhaps they should include their partners as well. But it wasn't something you could suggest. It would look too critical of all that had gone before. But unexpectedly, it was Marcella who suggested it. When she heard about the lesson she said that she and Neil had been thinking of going secretly to Quentins restaurant to ask Brenda and Patrick for a lesson. Could this be the solution, here on their doorstep? A rehearsal for Mr Byrne? This month it was to be Stoneyfield in their own flat. Perfect.

'If you were as old as James and he was trying to seduce you, what would you like him to serve you?' Tom asked Marcella.

'She mightn't be old, she might just be a young one,' Marcella said.

'Well, what?'

'Oysters, grilled fillet of sole, French beans and fresh fruit salad with no sugar.' Marcella spoke with certainty.

'But that's because you've been on a diet since you were nine,' Tom complained. 'She might be a big fat lady dying for steak and kidney pie and apple pie to follow.'

'Yes, but she wouldn't like it on a date, she likes to be treated as if she were fragile, even if she isn't.'

Tom thought this was a good idea, and so did Cathy. 'We should put Marcella down as our group psychologist,' she said approvingly. And, as always, Tom beamed at the compliment for his girl. He loved people to praise Marcella, as he sometimes feared that they didn't know her well enough to realise how much she cared about the enterprise.

The cookery lesson was much discussed. Tom and Cathy had to accept that Neil and Marcella were even more hopeless than they had suspected. Everything was going to take three times as long as it should have; they would get flustered and confused. Even the very language of cooking, the simplest terms, seemed to upset them. Tom and Cathy had presented them with the instructions, which had proved far from clear. They didn't know what it meant to 'reduce' something. Neil was in a rush to leave, and he read the list briefly.

'I suppose reduce means you throw half of it away?' he said absent-mindedly as he hunted for his papers.

'I can't believe that anyone thinks you are an adult,' Cathy laughed. 'Of *course* it doesn't mean that, why would you make twice as much and throw half away?'

Neil shrugged. 'It's all very odd, anyway. See you tonight at their place.' He kissed her and was gone.

Cathy wanted to shout that he mustn't be late, Marcella was giving up a dance class to be there. But somehow it sounded trivial, so she didn't. Tom reported that Marcella thought to reduce something meant you had it wrong and should start again with fewer ingredients.

'We have an uphill job,' he said sadly.

Cathy drove past a house where she knew her mother would be working. Lizzie's face lit up when she saw her.

'Well now, isn't that a wonderful surprise,' she said, settling into the van. 'I feel like a great lady driving in this. I hope they all see me.'

Cathy looked at her fondly. She met so many people who would have looked askance at getting into a big white delivery van, but to Lizzie Scarlet it was a treat.

'Did the others like cooking at home when they were young, or was it only me?' Cathy asked.

'Marian was quite good. She's so efficient about everything she touches, it came automatically to her, but the others didn't have the feel that you do. They didn't have much time, really; they all left so young. What was there to stay for, when there was all that fortune to be made over there?'

Lizzie sighed. Ever since the first boy had emigrated to Chicago to his uncle's house, and told the youngsters about the wages that could be earned in Illinois, her children could barely wait to be eighteen and out at the airport. They had been amazed when Cathy had never shown the slightest interest in leaving. Her mother looked tired, as well she might after a day's cleaning.

'Are those kids too much for you, Mam?'

'No, I tell you, I like their company and your dad is great altogether with them. He'll take no guff from them. I'm inclined to be a bit more . . .'

'I know you are, Mam. You're too kind to everyone.'

'And it's *nice* having children around. I was always getting ready to look after babies again when you and Neil . . . that is, if you and Neil . . .'

'Mam, I told you lots of times there isn't any possibility of that, not for ages yet, if ever. We're far too busy now.'

'God be with the old days when you didn't have any choice in the matter,' her mother said.

'Now you sound just like Tom's mother, talking about the good old days. They were *not* good old days, Mam, you had eleven in your family and Da had ten in his. Where was the chance for any of you?'

'We did all right,' Lizzie's voice was small and tight and she had taken offence.

'Mam, of course you did, and you did so well by all of us, but it wasn't easy for you, that's all I'm saying.'

'Yes. Yes, I see.'

They had arrived at St Jarlath's Crescent. Her mother was still hurt by the thoughtless remark.

Cathy looked at her pleadingly. 'I don't suppose there's a hope you'd make me some tea?'

'Well of course, if you have the time.'

'And would there be any apple tart left, do you think?'

'Oh, come on Cathy, stop behaving like a five-year-old.' Lizzie was rooting for her key and dying to put the kettle on. Forty-five seconds, the longest sulk she had ever known her mother to hold. Cathy felt a prickle of tears in her eyes.

*

550

They gathered in Tom's flat in Stoneyfield. All the ingredients were out on the table and Marcella was looking at them doubtfully. There was no sign of Neil yet.

'Should we start?' Tom wondered. Neil and Marcella made such heavy weather out of everything, they might not eat until midnight otherwise. Patiently Tom and Cathy explained, and industriously poor Marcella struggled to follow their instructions. Then Cathy's mobile rang. Neil was tied up, he'd be there in an hour, could they start without him.

'Traitor,' called out Marcella from the other side of the room.

'Swear to her I'll be there and do my share,' he begged.

But Cathy had taken too many of those calls to make any such promise. They ran out of wine, and Neil, who was meant to be looking after that side of things, still hadn't turned up. Cathy knew he might easily forget so she called him. The background noise was a pub.

'Sorry honey, I'm on my way.' He sounded annoyed to be nagged.

'Just to remind you about the wine,' she said coldly.

'God, I'm glad you did. I forgot totally, can you open what you have there just in case . . .'

'We have,' she was brisk.

'All *right*, Cathy,' Neil said.

He was in Stoneyfield an hour later, exactly two hours after the time they were meant to start. He had brought a bottle of expensive wine which he opened and poured for them. Marcella had fumbled her way through a starter and a chicken with wine main course, and she was exhausted.

'You're to do the dessert, Neil,' she said, collapsing in a chair.

'Of course I will, *and* the washing up.' Neil smiled them all into good humour.

'Tell me what was this reducing business, anyway? I asked someone at the meeting and they thought it had to do with calories.'

They explained. 'Well why don't they use proper words like . . . well, make a concentrate?' Neil objected.

'Or like boil the divil out of it?' Marcella said.

Tom and Cathy took notes on the cookery lesson. It would have to be radically altered before they presented it to James Byrne. The salmon mousse was beyond them, they would have to take that off the list. The coq au vin was fine, but it took them all day and all night. The tiramisu looked and tasted disgusting. Tom couldn't see why, but it was soggy and bore no relation to what they had been asked to do. The food was terrible, but somehow the evening was not ruined. Cathy noticed that Marcella ate practically nothing and only sipped at her wine. Neil offered to keep his promise of washing up but Tom and Cathy knew they would be there until dawn if they let him, so they cleared the place up at high speed.

'Cleans up a treat, doesn't it?' Cathy admired their handiwork.

Tom looked around the flat. 'It's very practical, but I wouldn't want to live here for ever. It's like as if we're passing through without leaving any mark at all.'

Once he had mentioned it, the place did look very minimalist. Clean white walls and empty surfaces. No pictures on the walls, not many books on the shelf, no ornaments on the mantelpiece or window ledge. A little like a hotel suite, in fact.

'I know, I feel the same about Waterview sometimes. Move Neil's books out in one van load and it's just the way we got it. But then would you want it like St Jarlath's Crescent, where there isn't a space to put anything down?' she asked.

'Or Fatima. I know,' Tom agreed.

The happy medium was something that eluded the world, they all agreed.

They had no idea how hard it was to make contacts. People either didn't consider themselves in the league which hired a caterer, or if they did then they already knew someone who was doing just fine. Geraldine and Ricky gave them names, but they drew blank after blank. Tom was determined not to be downcast.

'Listen, we'll do leaflets and get some kid to deliver a thousand or two.'

If Cathy thought it was useless she didn't say so. Sometimes, after a fruitless day of searching for work, she would say that it was only Tom's enthusiasm that kept her going. And it was sincere, he really believed it. He wasn't just trying to keep her spirits up. They were so good, they had such imaginative ideas and worked so hard. It was only a matter of time until everyone realised this and recognised them for what they were. But Tom never sat back and just waited for things to happen: he was always on the move, looking, asking and hunting.

'I hate breaking into your time, Geraldine, but could I come and spend just thirty minutes going through your client list again? You *know* we're good, it wouldn't be compromising you to recommend us.'

'It does my street cred good to have a handsome young man like yourself come to the apartments,' Geraldine said. 'Come round on Sunday morning and we'll see what we can find.'

The Glenstar apartment block was immaculately kept. There was regular landscape gardening, all the outside woodwork was repainted every year, brass gleamed everywhere and a smart commissionaire stood in the hall. Tom wondered how much they paid a year in service charges. Then he reminded himself not always to think in terms of how much things cost and how much they might bring in. It was the way his parents went on, and he certainly didn't need that. It was just that these sessions with James Byrne had been exhausting and worrying.

He had organised a filing cabinet and installed proper ledgers for them, warned them thunderously about keeping every receipt, and details of every piece of equipment bought so that its eventual depreciation could be properly noted. He explained how they must bill separately for waiters or waitresses, asking clients to pay them directly; this way they avoided tax problems. It had been fascinating to hear James Byrne talk. It made Tom feel that anything was possible, and that they were safe from all the minefields of being prosecuted over VAT or any other kind of tax. Three jobs in February wasn't *too* bad. Was it? But he was out on the hunt for more work. And he had a Sunday-morning appointment with Geraldine O'Connor, so that she could go through her list of clients and decide who could be approached and with what angle. Geraldine looked magnificent: she wore a dark green velvet tracksuit, her hair was still slightly damp from swimming in the Glenstar pool. The smell of coffee filled her big sitting room. The Sunday papers were scattered over the big, long, low table in front of the sofas.

Geraldine got down to business at once, and they spent an hour at her dining table seeing where any opportunity might lie. 'Peter Murphy's hotel is useless, of course, since they have all their functions there and are catered by themselves. The garden centre never wants to spend any money, they serve thimbles of warm white wine and that's that.' The estate agents might, only might, let them send menus and a letter, saying how much it would enhance any future function to have unusual and memorable canapés served. 'Let's put it this way, it might give people *something* to remember from their dreary dos.'

Tom looked at her with admiration. She was afraid of nobody. Where had she got this confidence?

'But Tom, these now are a bit more lively . . .' She gave him the address of an import agency. 'They take a lot of clothes, even some from your brother, he was telling me the other night. The sky's the limit with these lads. And they're totally legal now, no more black economy. I'll tell them they should get better known. They need an upmarket party. I'll promise them buyers from Haywards if they come.'

'And Haywards themselves?' Tom said hopefully.

'No, not a chance. Shona Burke and I have talked about it over and over. She's done her very best but they have a café, you see, so it doesn't make any sense for them to bring in an outsider.'

'I know, that's true. It's just that it would have been such a feather in the cap for Scarlet Feather,' he said wistfully.

What Tom really meant was that it would have been good for Marcella too. If her fellow was doing the high-profile catering it would make her look good by association. But it wasn't to be. They went through the list of names. The pharmaceutical people possibly, the educational project no way, the people who organised the big literary competition were attached to a brewery and had their own contacts, the cross-border cooperation people had no money. Tom admired the matter-of-fact way Geraldine went about her business. She spoke affectionately, even discreetly about her clients, she emphasised to Tom that this was all in confidence, but she was in no way impressed by any of them. She told him that they had to have this conversation in her home rather than at her office as she would not want the staff to know she was divulging the secrets of the filing cabinet. She looked so at ease with herself, unlike any other woman he knew. Not like her sister, Lizzie, who worried and apologised; unlike Cathy, who was driven to show Hannah Mitchell that she was a career woman in her own right. Not like his mother, who saw only the bad side of everything and relied on the power of prayer. Not like Shona Burke, who always had this faraway, sad look on her face. He remembered Joe asking how Geraldine had got the money together to buy this agency, but it wasn't a question he would ever put to her, even though the great splendour of her apartment and her readiness to back them in this enterprise sometimes did make him speculate. But he frowned to himself. He would *not* become obsessed with money like so many people were nowadays.

'What on earth are you making faces about, Tom?' Geraldine didn't miss much.

'I was thinking about money, actually, and why it mustn't be a god itself but if you don't keep an eye on it you go down the tube,' he said.

'I know what you mean. Money itself is not important at all, but in order to make it and to get the life you want you have to pretend that it is for a while, just so as to keep it rolling on in.' Her face looked hard for a moment.

Tom said no more on the subject. He gathered up his notes to leave. When he took his coffee cup into the kitchen he saw ingredients for a lunch set out there. 'Have you a busy day?' he asked.

'A friend to lunch,' she said briskly. 'Which reminds me, find a few canapés that freeze well and give them to me, then I can talk you up all round the place.'

'Of course, but why don't you let us *do* a lunch for you, any time, it's the very least we can do.'

'I know, Tom, so Cathy already said. You're both sweet, but the kind of guys I entertain like to think that I cooked everything for them with my own fair hands.'

Shona Burke was getting out of her little car, and she called out to him as he left. 'Do you have your brother's phone number in London?' she asked.

'No, not you too. What do you all see in him?' he groaned.

'Purely business,' she said. 'Anyway, you're much better-looking than he is. They're doing a young people's promotion in Haywards in late spring, and he told me that he might just have a line of what he called fun clothes. Swimwear, lingerie, you know.'

'Sorry, Shona.' He took out a Scarlet Feather card and looked up Joe's London phone number for her in his diary.

'You don't know it?'

'Hey, no, I've no memory for numbers,' he said.

She nodded.

For some reason Tom said, 'Anyway, I don't call him that much or he me, I don't know why it is. Have you got sisters and brothers?'

Shona hesitated. 'Well, yes, in a way I do.'

It was an odd response but Tom let it go. Some people hated to be interrogated about their families; Marcella did. Her mother was dead and her father, who had married again, just wasn't interested, she said, and wanted it left like that. Cathy, on the other hand, had something to say every day about her parents: she loved Lizzie and Muttie, in spite of her mother's humble, grateful attitude to life. Cathy would also go on about her mother-in-law Hannah's innate viciousness, and about the sisters and brothers in Chicago, particularly Marian, the eldest, who had done well in banking but poorly in her love life until recently, and was now going to marry a man called Harry who looked like a film star. And look at his own brother Joe, who had not a family bone in his body. Tom got into his van waving her goodbye. She stood there taking no notice of the light rain that had begun to fall, not covering up her hair as most women would, still looking oddly lonely and vulnerable. She was a handsome girl, not strictly beautiful. Marcella always said that Shona Burke could look much better than she did if she wore more make-up and got her hair changed from that old-fashioned style. Her hair did look dull and flat. But she had a lovely smile. He wondered for a moment if *she* had been Joe's companion back in the hotel after the party. Why not? They were both free. She didn't have to tell anyone about it. Then he pulled himself together. He must stop speculating like this. She was saying something; he opened the van window to hear properly.

'I was only saying that you're very restful, Tom, a peaceable, handsome person,' Shona said.

'Not a word about the killer instinct that's going to make me a force in the land?' he called.

'Oh, that goes without saying.' She laughed.

Marcella came home from Haywards beauty salon the following evening and told Tom amazing news. This woman had come in to book a hairdo, manicure, a facial, the works, and said she was going to a drop-dead-cert smart christening party on Saturday, and she had actually said there were going to be fancy caterers at it. Tom could hardly believe it. Already people were talking about them and they hadn't even got properly started! He couldn't wait to ring Cathy. But tonight she and Neil were taking those children to see their mother in some drying-out place. He would tell her tomorrow.

'Will we celebrate?' he asked Marcella.

'Ah love, I'm just off to the gym,' she said.

'Couldn't you . . . Just for one night . . . To raise a glass to posh people in Haywards referring to us as fancy caterers?'

'Tom, we *agreed*. The subscription costs so much, the only way to make sense out of it and get any value is for me to go every day.'

'Sure,' he said, then knew he must sound a little warmer. 'You're absolutely right,' he said. 'And as soon as we really are a fancy caterers, then you'll come to every classy, fancy thing we do as a guest and get yourself photographed all over the place.'

'It will happen that you'll be a great big success . . . you do know that, don't you?' she said, and he thought he saw tears in her eyes. 'I'm not just saying that . . . you really know.'

'I know.' He *did* know. She had wanted the best for them from the start. 'Of course I know,' he said, and he held her close to him before she went to pack her leotard, trainers and body lotion. Tom looked out of the window until she waved up at him from the gates of Stoneyfield, as she always did. He wondered had she any idea how beautiful and endearing she was already, without having to punish herself with all this ruthless regime.

Ricky rang. He had the pictures they needed, six black and white arty studies of food which they were going to put up in the premises. He could bring them around tomorrow if the picture rail was up, and did Tom want the measurements. Tom did, and he got his paper and pencil.

'I was going to give them to you tonight at the do, but I figure it makes us look idiotic talking work at a party,' Ricky explained.

'Party?'

'Yeah, you know, the new club?'

'No, I never heard about it.'

'Well I told Marcella, she said you'd both be there.' Ricky was puzzled. Tom could feel his heart beating faster.

'Misunderstanding of some sort,' he mumbled.

'Sure. Now they're all portrait-format. I'll give you the top-to-bottom measurements first, then the side-to-side. Your father's getting a rail made, isn't he?'

Ricky went on and on with his specifications and Tom wrote down lists of numbers of centimetres on his pad, but his mind was on autopilot. He could not believe that she had just left pretending to go to the gym, and was in fact heading off to something without him. And how would she account for her late arrival home? He felt such a shock at the betrayal that he could hardly hear Ricky's words.

'Right, I'd better go and put on my going-out gear. Crazy idea having a party at this time. No one's properly awake yet. See you over at the HQ tomorrow, okay.'

'Okay Ricky, thank you a million times,' Tom Feather said to the cheerful photographer who had just broken his heart.

He needed to give his father the measurements. The pictures were to be suspended from a pole that would have grooves cut in it at a specific number of centimetres apart, and JT had been asking when anyone would inform him of what he had to do, so that it would not be yet another botched job. With fingers that seemed the weight of lead he dialled his parents' number, realising that first he must cheer him up before his father would agree to write down the measurements. Please may it be his da – he couldn't go through the whole cheering-up process twice if he got his mother.

But it was neither of them. It was a woman with a bark that nearly lifted him off the phone.

'Yes,' the voice said.

'Sorry,' Tom began, 'I've got the wrong number. I was looking for the Feathers.'

'This is the Feathers. Who's that?'

'Tom, their son.'

'Great bloody son you are, wouldn't you think you'd have left your number beside the phone for them?'

'But they *know* my number,' Tom cried, stung by the injustice of this.

'They don't know it now,' shouted the woman.

'What's happened. . . ?' This was a new kind of fear. Tom could hear voices in the background. Something must have happened. Eventually, and only when he had assured her that his phone number was at the top of a list in a plastic-covered notebook which for some reason his mother kept in the kitchen drawer, did the woman with the barking voice agree to tell him what was going on, and he learned that his father had chest pains and his mother had run out into the street to get help. Almost all the neighbours in the small street had come into Fatima, and someone had gone to the hospital when the ambulance came, and others had stayed making tea with poor Maura, who wasn't herself at all and couldn't cope with what was happening.

'Can I talk to her?'

'Why don't you just *get* yourself there?' said the woman with the unpleasant voice. Which made sense. He wished he had been nicer to his father, less impatient. Tom grabbed up his car keys and coat. He paused for a moment to consider writing a note. He and Marcella often communicated by letters left to each other on the table. But he didn't want to tell her about his father. And moreover, he couldn't forgive her for lying to him. And he knew she had. She had looked too excited going out to the gym, she smelled too well, there had been tears in her eyes over something. But then, she must not think he had run away either. 'My father's not well, gone to see him, hope you enjoyed the party,' he wrote. That would show her. He drove to the hospital.

Unless his father had another heart attack tonight the prognosis was fairly good, they told him in Intensive Care. Competent, calm young men and women his own age who knew about valves and arteries. A nurse asked him gently if he would perhaps like to take a seat outside. Tom realised that he must have been standing right in everyone's way.

'He's resting now, he's fine.'

'I know. Thank you,' Tom smiled.

She smiled straight back at him, a big, open smile. She was a square, freckled girl with a country accent and slightly messy hair. Tom recognised the look she gave him; it was the kind of look that almost every woman in Ireland gave his brother Joe. Interested, aware and slightly fancying. He looked back at her with a hollow heart. A perfectly nice girl, with a white cardigan over her uniform. But of course he could not fancy a woman like that in a million years. Compared to his Marcella, this girl was like something from a different planet. A totally separate species. He went out into the cold night to get some fresh air and telephoned his mother on his mobile.

'He looks fine, Mam.'

'What do you mean, he looks fine? Didn't I see him with my own two eyes clutching his chest, fighting for his breath?'

'But he's sedated now, Mam, he's breathing normally.'

She gave a whimpering sound and he heard her neighbours comforting her.

'I'll ring you in an hour.'

'Why?' she wanted to know.

'Just to tell you that he's still fine.'

'He's finished, Tom, you know he is. He shouldn't be up ladders at his age, he was just desperate to get that place right for you.'

'It has nothing to do with being up ladders, they said. It's looking good, everyone says that here.'

'Oh, so you know all about medicine, a boy who wouldn't even stay on in Sixth Year. Someone who couldn't go into business with his own father to help him out. You suddenly know what's causing heart attacks, do you?'

'Mam, I'll ring you back.'

It was freezing out here, but it was better than the heat and noise and medical smells of the hospital. He went to a bicycle shed and sheltered there against the wind, huddled in the corner, and willed his father to get well. And when he *was* well, he would talk to his father man to man, and not leave until the conversation had gone somewhere beyond a series of shrugs. He would from now on insist that his parents came up regularly to Stoneyfield to visit them. He would cook things *they* liked, roast chicken, shepherd's pie. He would beg Marcella to talk to them about things that would interest them. Marcella. He remembered with a shock. He stood and watched people arrive and leave in their cars from the big ugly-looking concrete car park. What a hideous place. But to be fair, if money were to be spent on hospitals he would prefer it spent on machinery that would monitor his father's heart than on attractive landscaping for the grounds. He saw someone very like Shona Burke locking a car and then walking purposefully towards reception wearing a raincoat and carrying a shoulder bag. It was Shona. He moved forward to talk to her, then he moved back. He didn't want to tell her about his father before he knew what there was to tell. Also, he didn't want her to ask about Marcella. It would be normal for someone's live-in girlfriend to be there when there was a question that his father might die. But then, what was normal with Marcella? But Shona had seen him and called out.

'You look shivery, Tom.'

'I know, but still it's too hot inside there.'

'Oh, don't I know all about it, I come here quite a lot . . .'

'I'm sorry, is it. . . ?'

'It's all right, Tom.' She spoke gently, letting him know that there would be no discussion on who she was visiting. 'But still, you look badly. Come on inside for a bit.'

'Right.' He walked in beside her.

At first, neither of them asked each other. Then she turned to him.

'Is it something bad?'

'I don't know. My father, chest pains, angina. It all depends on tonight – if he makes it through till tomorrow he'll have a great chance.'

'Poor Tom, when did it happen?'

'I just heard about it over an hour ago. All hell broke loose; my mother is so upset I think she should be in the next bed to him.'

'You mean you've only just heard?' Shona asked.

'Yes, it hasn't quite sunk in.'

'That means Marcella doesn't know yet, does she?'

'No,' his voice was flat.

'Oh, poor Marcella. I offered to drive her home from the gym but she said no, she was getting a bus, buying you a potted plant as a surprise.'

In front of everyone in the reception area, Tom Feather kissed Shona Burke and gave a whoop of delight. 'She was at the gym?' he cried. 'Tonight?'

'But you *know* that, Tom, she told me you wanted her to stay at home and celebrate that people were saying you're classy caterers.'

He drove home so fast he was amazed that there wasn't a police siren following him the whole way. He let himself in the door and she was sitting there at the table, a big fern in a pot beside her.

'Marcella!' he said.

'How is your father?' Her voice was icy.

'He'll be fine, it's all under control . . . You were at the gym?'

'As I told you I was going to be.' Her face was like a mask.

'Marcella, if you knew . . . you see, I thought . . .'

'What did you think, Tom?'

'I supposed you'd gone to a party, to a club . . .'

She put her head on one side as if asking a question.

'You see, Ricky said he'd asked you.'

'He did, yes. But I didn't want to go, because you're too busy and too tired, and I knew you'd hate it, so I went to the gym as I told you I was going to do.'

He couldn't stop the tears that came to his eyes.

'I'm so sorry. You see, I didn't think . . . I didn't think you could love me enough to give up something like that for me.'

'I did, yes of course I did.' Her voice was very level; she did not appear to see how upset he was.

'You do love me, I know it now.'

'No, Tom. I said I did, not I do.'

'It hasn't changed. Surely?'

She picked up the note and passed it to him. 'You are the most bitter, mistrustful man I ever met. How could anyone love you?' She stood up and went to the bedroom.

'Marcella, you're not leaving.' He was ashen-faced now.

'If you imagine that I could stay a night here with you when you think I'm a liar.'

He stood at the bedroom door looking at her.

She had taken off her clothes, and reached for one of those micro-skirts he hated her to wear. She picked dark tights from the drawer and moved towards the bathroom.

'Where will you stay?'

'I have friends. I'll find somewhere to stay.'

'Please, Marcella.'

She phoned a taxi to pick her up and then closed the bathroom door. Later, when she heard the doorbell ring, she came out.

'I am so sorry,' he said.

'So you should be, Tom, seriously sorry, because I have *always* told you the truth, and if you think it's possible to lie to anyone you love, then you're in deep trouble.'

And she was gone. Eventually the phone rang. It was his mother.

'You said you'd ring in an hour, I had to ring the hospital myself.'

'Is he all right, Mam?'

'A fat lot you care, Tom.'

'Mam, please.'

'He is for the moment. Tom, what will we do if he dies?'

'I'm coming round to Fatima, Mam,' he said.

Before he left he had two things to do. He rang his brother Joe in Ealing. He got an answering machine.

'Joe, this is Tom. Dad's had a coronary. I'll give you the number of the hospital. All you need to do is say you're his son and they'll tell you what's to be told. I hope you'll do something, Joe, but it's your life, not my life, so I'll just leave it at this.'

Then he sat down to write a note to leave on their table.

'I hope and pray you come back, and if you do, darling, darling Marcella, just know that I didn't know the meaning of love before I met you, and that I can't see much point in life without your love.'

Tom kept his mobile phone on all night, and not long after dawn he stopped at another builder's yard to make the pole with the notches to hang the pictures on, and drove to the premises. Cathy was there already.

'What does the other fellow look like?' she asked.

'What?'

'It's a joke, it's what you say to somebody who's been in a fight. You hope that someone else came off worse.'

He looked at her blankly.

'God, Tom, it was a joke. You're worse than Simon and Maud. Were you on the whiskey or something?'

'No, I've been up all night with my father. He had a coronary and Marcella has left me.' He said it in a very strange tone, as if he were just recounting two unimportant events.

Cathy looked at him, exasperated. 'What really happened, Tom?'

She was both kind and unbelieving at the same time. Tom was about to lose it, to break down and sob helplessly with his head on the table, when Ricky arrived with the pictures.

'Jesus but did you miss a wild night,' Ricky said, holding his head. 'You were the very wise one not to come along to that particular party, my friend.'

'That's me, Mr Wise Guy,' said Tom Feather sadly taking out the pole that his father had not been able to do because he had gone into heart failure before he got the measurements.

'You're nearly over twenty-four hours, Dad, so that means you're going to be fine,' Tom said to his father the next afternoon.

'If you knew what it was like, Tom, it was like two hands squeezing your ribs.' His father looked a lot better today. 'They tell me you were here all night?'

'Where else would I be?'

'But Marcella, you know?'

'She sent you her love, Da.'

'I know she did, and she's a grand girl, I heard from one of the nurses that the pair of you were hugging and kissing in the hall when you heard I was going to be all right, I'll never forget that.'

Tom looked at him blankly.

'Oh, that nice girl Catherine, she said she was very disappointed to know you had a ladyfriend. She was on duty and she told me everything.'

His father was patting his hand and Tom smiled at him. The nurse in the cardigan had seen him kissing Shona Burke when he had discovered that Marcella had really been to the gym.

The christening was what Cathy said should be called The Function from Hell. They had been asked to cater for fifty, but they could see as the room filled up that there were at least seventy people there. They hadn't cleaned the kitchen properly so Cathy, June and Tom had to spend the first twenty minutes wiping surfaces and putting down a disinfectant. When they opened the kitchen windows to let out the medicinal smell the baby's father came in and said the whole place stank like a urinal. When they tried to set up the buffet, the two small dogs of the house began a game of pulling the tablecloths.

'People who don't like animals are really not my kind of people,' said the baby's mother, who was three gins in before they had left for the church.

The ceremony had been forty minutes shorter than Cathy and Tom were told, so their bar wasn't ready.

'I was told you were top-drawer,' said the baby's father. 'We're in business just as you are, and we don't pay for what we don't get.'

They had ordered kedgeree served from a hotplate as a starter. It was a good choice, but before it got under way, the baby's mother began telling everyone, 'Don't bother eating all this rice and fish stuff, they have a proper roast coming later.' So a lot of people obediently put down their half-finished starters. Tom and Cathy looked at each other, wild-eyed, in the kitchen. Their only hope was that people would stock up on the kedgeree. Now they were waiting for the miracle of the loaves and the fishes.

*

'What in the name of God will we do?' Cathy asked him.

'Get them drunk,' Tom suggested.

'It's not fair on them, it means they will have to pay for all that extra wine.'

'What's fair, Cathy, tell me, what's fair about anything? What's fair about my father who worked hard all his life lying in hospital? What's fair about you having those kids that don't belong to you, ballsing up your life and your parents' lives? What's fair about that guy that Neil was trying to save being thrown out of Ireland? And what is fair about these two beauties telling us they were having fifty people when they have seventy-five? Get them drunk, I say.'

And they did. Spectacularly.

Before they started on their mission, Cathy Scarlet approached the baby's father firmly.

'Can I suggest something? Your guests seem to be enjoying themselves enormously, and you have chosen some particularly good wine.'

'Yes, yes, what?'

'And in case there's any doubt about the wine you would like us to serve, can I ask you to sign permission to bring out more?'

'We thought a half-bottle a person?' He was a small, fat man with small, piggy eyes.

'Yes indeed, that is what we suggested, but it's all going so well here, we would like your permission to bring out—'

'Do what you want.'

'And is it all to your satisfaction so far?'

'Yes, it's okay . . . just keep getting the drink round.'

'Thank you. You are a wonderful host,' Cathy said through tightly clenched teeth.

Nobody had ever told them it was going to be like this. Tom eased his way through the crowds of guests, smiling and telling them that the kedgeree was delicious.

'You're pretty delicious yourself,' said a woman with chocolate smeared over her face. She looked silly, and was about to become sillier. Tom thanked her for the compliment.

'You've got such a lovely dress,' he said. 'Is it from Haywards' designer room?'

'Yes, it is.' She was stupidly flattered.

'Come here to the mirror, you've got some kind of mark on your face.' He offered her a tissue, and she looked at herself. Then, appalled at the reflection, she wiped the smears away hastily.

'That was nice of you to do that,' Cathy said.

'Come on, Cathy, it's only those clowns giving the party who are the villains here. I wish I knew where I saw that guy before, he really annoys me. The poor eejit with the Walt Disney designs on her face isn't doing anyone any harm.'

'No, you're right. God Almighty, there's more of them arriving at the hall door. They'll be eating the wallpaper.'

'What does he do for a living? I've met him somewhere, I *know* I have.'

'Probably some bar we worked in once. Listen, give June a hand over there. I'll ring my father and get him to provide taxis.'

'Muttie? Taxis?'

'Have we time to start looking up taxis at this stage? Half the people my father bets with drive taxis.'

'You're brilliant, Cathy! Maybe there's something we can salvage from this after all. Listen, am I going mad or something, or is that man Riordan looking at me as if he's fallen in love with me or something?'

'Well you don't realise it, but you are quite good-looking. Why shouldn't Mr Riordan try his chances like everyone else?'

'Excuse me?'

'Yes, Mr Riordan?'

'Don't we know each other?'

'Well, Mr Riordan, I'm the caterer . . .'

'Stop pissing about, we met at a party a couple of months ago, New Year's Eve . . .'

'Oh, yes?' Tom wasn't really listening, he was watching the room, seeing where he was needed.

'I remember now. I just wanted to say that this sort of thing rarely happens, it was the drink, I felt very odd after it. I think they deliberately mixed the drinks there. Some photographer fellow, very irresponsible of him.'

Then Tom remembered him. He was the man who had been pawing Marcella at Ricky's party.

'Oh, yes, yes indeed, Mr Riordan, of course I remember you.'

'You did from the beginning,' Larry Riordan said.

'No, not until this minute.'

'Come on, you've had a load of attitude since you came in the door, you knew you had one over me.'

'I knew you had made a mistake about the number of guests you had invited. I didn't realise until now you were the happily married man I met on New Year's Eve,' Tom said. He seemed to grow taller and broader as he spoke. Larry Riordan shrank in front of him.

'The whole thing was a total misunderstanding, of course . . . due entirely . . .'

'We know what it was due to, Mr Riordan.'

'What I wanted to say was that if there was any offence . . .'

'Oh, there was great offence at the time.'

'But not now, I hope.'

'Now I shall continue to do this job professionally for you and your wife, with whom I have no quarrel. Despite the fact that you told us there would be fifty people and there are over seventy in the house.'

'That was also a misunderstanding.'

'There *have* been a lot of them . . . I *was* going to ask your wife . . .'

'No need to ask her anything. Just ask me.'

'Relax, Mr Riordan, I was only going to ask her did she think we should arrange some taxis for later; many of your guests will have to leave their cars behind.'

'Do whatever you like,' said the host, loosening his collar. 'But believe me, that was all totally out of order, that incident, and I hope it had no repercussions. I mean, that everything is all right in so far as . . .'

'Everything is fine, Mr Riordan.'

'Very fine, beautiful young lady . . . I apologise again.'

'Thank you, now if you'll excuse me there are quite a lot of people need attention.' Tom moved away. This man would never know that Marcella had left him.

Cathy had busily recycled the kedgeree, adding mushrooms and chopped potatoes. She told Tom that she knew all that crowd would need it later as blotting paper, and they certainly did. They gave everyone in sight their business card, and tidied the house to within an inch of its life. When those people woke up next morning, they would find their place looking immaculate. They would find one cold bottle of champagne and a carton of orange juice in their fridge. They lined the bottles up in the back garden in ranks like soldiers, so that there would be no dispute about the number ordered and drunk, and said they would collect them the following day when they called in the afternoon to present the account. Muttie had sent five taxi-driver friends to the scene. They did a shuttle service all evening, and were well rewarded for their efforts. Tom and Cathy paid June an extra three hours, and her taxi home, before they got back to number seven Waterview.

'Come in,' Cathy said.

'No, it's late, Neil will be . . .'

'Neil'll be one of three things: out, asleep or happy to pour us a drink,' Cathy said, and they went up the stairs.

Neil was sitting at his big table with papers all around. 'Oh, good, Cathy I . . .' Then he saw Tom, and momentarily his guard fell.

'Oh, Tom,' he said, disappointed, and then recovered quickly. 'How was the function? Come and tell me.'

'No, honestly Neil, it's late.'

'Come in now that you're here.'

He got three beers and they sat down.

'Tell me all about it,' Neil asked politely. His heart wasn't in it; Tom gave the briefest of descriptions and drained his beer. Before he could leave there was a tap on the door.

'Are you drunk?' Simon asked with interest.

'Not yet,' Tom said.

'Where's Marcella?' Maud wanted to know.

'Not here,' said Cathy.

'Should I not have asked? I was just being interested, as you said I should.' Maud was confused.

'No problems.' Cathy was tight-lipped.

There was a silence.

'Would you prefer us to go back to bed now?' Simon enquired.

'Yes. It is the middle of the night, actually,' Cathy said.

Maud and Simon departed swiftly, detecting a hint of steel somewhere.

Tom let himself into the van and drove home through the dark, empty streets. Those two really worked hard – few other couples were still earning a living at this time of the morning. And it couldn't be easy for Neil having those odd, awkward children there half the time. And your wife out all hours working as well. Cathy had been wonderful. She had asked everything about his father and nothing at all about Marcella, who had left him, had refused to accept his calls into Haywards and had not even come back to collect her clothes.

'Is there anything wrong, Neil?' Cathy said. 'Your mind was a million miles away when we were telling you about the party.'

'Sorry,' he said, 'but honestly, those children, I couldn't do a thing all night. They kept coming in, asking about this and that. Homework, and where they should do their washing.'

'Well that's an advance, when they first came they just threw it on the floor.'

'They can't keep coming here. We'll have to increase what Muttie and Lizzie get.'

'They don't do it for the money, we agreed to give them a bit of a break.'

'But who is giving *us* a break? There's so much to do and discuss, and we haven't one minute to talk.'

'Okay, we have a minute now.'

'No real time.'

'Well, okay, I'm happy to talk now, it's kind of unwinding, but if you're tired...'

'There's this job...'

'The big case next week...?'

'No, not a case. A job. I could... Now, it's not definite but I hear that I *could* be offered this amazing position...'

She looked at him open-mouthed as he told her about a committee that worked in connection with the UN Commission for Refugees.

'Now it's not an actual UN appointment, it's part of a group under the umbrella...'

She interrupted him. 'Sorry, I don't understand. Are you trying to tell me that you would consider taking a job abroad now?'

'Not immediately.'

'When then?'

'In about five or six months, I imagine. That's if it comes to anything, but it's only fair to tell you about it now.'

'Is this a joke?'

'No, I was amazed when I heard it myself. Usually you'd have to have much more experience, but they think that—'

'You're not asking me to throw up everything and follow you out to Africa because you got a *job* out of the blue?'

'It's not necessarily Africa. It could be Geneva, Strasbourg, Brussels.'

'You *have* a job. You're a barrister, that's your job. Defending people, rescuing them, representing them. That's your job.'

'But this is something—'

'That was never on the cards, Neil, never part of any plan.'

'You don't know anything about it yet. And you'd love it, you've never had a chance to travel.'

'Oh, but I have travelled. To Greece, didn't I, where I met you.'

'But that was only a holiday.'

'It may have been a holiday for you. It was a job for me. I was cooking in that villa.'

'Oh, but honey, that was only a Mickey Mouse summer job as a chalet girl,' he said.

Her face hardened. 'But I don't have a Mickey Mouse job now, I have a company,' she said.

'Yes, but you can't expect to think—'

'Think what?' she asked.

'It's not the right time to talk now, it's too late.' He stood up.

'One sentence isn't finished. You said I can't expect to think . . .' She looked up at him.

'Please, this is how fights start.'

'No, leaving sentences unfinished is how they start.'

'I didn't know how it was going to end,' he said, anxious to be out of it all.

'Well, will I finish it for you?' She sounded calm, too calm.

'No fights, Cathy.'

'Absolutely not. I think we'll end it like this: we can't expect to think that you'd ask me to give up my whole life's work and dream any more than I would ever expect you to. Was it something like that?'

'It needs a lot more thought and discussion,' he said.

'You're right,' she said, and they went to bed, where they slept so far from each other that not even a toe touched, and Cathy pretended to be asleep when he left Waterview early next morning having totally ignored his promise to take the twins to school.

At the premises Tom was in better humour – his father was definitely on the mend. His mother had apologised for her somewhat hasty words; it had been the shock. The Riordans sent a message that the account was all in order and the bill for the christening would be paid in full this afternoon. There had been a note from Marcella saying that Shona had told her of Mr Feather's heart attack, and she sent her sympathy and hoped that he was getting on well. All that news was good. The bad news was that Marcella had asked him please not to get in touch for the time being. There had been no word of response from Joe Feather, whose father could well have died and been buried. And when Tom told James Byrne that Mr Riordan, the baby's father, wanted to pay for the christening in cash, the accountant was not happy.

'Not good to hear,' James Byrne said crisply.

'I know this, James, but what do we do?'

'We present an invoice for *our* records, and receipt it when we get the money.'

'But suppose . . .'

'You're paying for my advice, so don't suppose,' James said.

'Mr and Mrs Riordan, I hope it was all to your satisfaction.'

'They loved it,' said the wife.

'Full of praise,' echoed her husband.

Tom didn't milk it, he did not want to make the man squirm any more.

'Our accountant actually prefers us to be paid by cheque.'

'Sure, it's sometimes that people like cash to avoid the tax,' said Larry Riordan.

'Which we wouldn't want to do.' Tom never lowered his gaze.

'No, of course.'

'Will we all go into the other room while I get my chequebook,' Larry Riordan suggested. He was obviously terrified to leave Tom alone for a moment, in case he began to tell tales.

Tom took out his calculator and his invoice book. 'The wine is all accounted for, the taxis and extras paid. It's just a small matter of . . . Are you sure you had the numbers right? You see, our waitress kept counting the plates and—'

'My wife says there was a mistake. She thinks we were well over fifty, actually.'

'How well over?' Tom's eyes were cold.

'Nearer to eighty, she thought.'

'Perfect,' said Tom, and signed a receipt for them.

Back in Stoneyfield he put on the Lou Reed record he loved because it showed other people had lives as confused as his own. There was a ring at the door. He answered it, and it was Marcella.

'You have a key,' he said quietly through the intercom.

'I wouldn't use it unless . . .' Her voice faltered.

'Unless what, Marcella?' He was still very quiet.

'Unless you wanted me to come in and talk.' He pressed the buzzer. But she didn't come in. 'I mean, really talk,' she insisted.

'Well, I've been just waiting for you all those days, hours, minutes, seconds, however long it's been,' he said.

'You know I know, come on, we both know how very, very long it's been,' she said simply.

'So, Marcella, are you going to come up here to me, or what?' He hardly dared to hope.

'Tom, I wanted to know how the christening went, and to tell you that I do know you love me, and that we both made silly mistakes along the way.' There was a silence. 'Would that let me come home, do you think?' He knew she was crying, and he didn't care if she knew that he was crying too as he ran down the stairs to bring her back home.

*

Next morning there was a call from the woman at the party whose face Tom had rescued. She said that she wanted to thank them for their courtesy and splendid food, and to book them for a silver wedding party weeks ahead. Geraldine booked them a lunch for a group of estate agents who wanted to get into the villa market, and would like a buffet with a Spanish theme. The hospital called to say that Tom's father was now well on the mend, and that Mr JT Feather would be going home today. There was a message from Joe in Manila saying that somebody had eventually caught up with him with the news about their father, and could someone now fax him back since he had to be in the Philippines for another two weeks. James Byrne left in a note confirming the date of his cookery lesson, and saying that he always paid in advance and always by cheque, being someone who disapproved strongly of the black economy. Cathy got an e-mail from her sister Marian in Chicago, asking Scarlet Feather to cater for a lavish Dublin wedding in August. The theatre wrote to say that there just *might* be another gig. Apparently everyone had been very pleased with the last one, they said with some surprise. They were sure Tom could oblige again. Cathy had received a letter from Hannah Mitchell marked 'personal', in which her mother-in-law had suggested a little lunch in Quentins to clear up any outstanding difficulties. And when Cathy rang Tom to tell him this last and most amazing of all the amazing pieces of information that day, the phone was answered by Marcella.

'Oh, Tom, you were so right to be optimistic. You just kept us all afloat. I'm so happy for you, so very happy,' Cathy said with a lump in her throat when Marcella passed the phone to him.

'I *know* you are,' he said, and he smiled at Marcella as he said it.

March

Cathy was early at Quentins.

'Coming to steal our ideas?' Brenda Brennan asked.

Both Cathy and Tom had worked as waiters and in the kitchen here, in what was often described as Dublin's best restaurant.

'Oh, we've stolen all those already,' Cathy admitted cheerfully. 'Those little tomato and basil tarts go down a treat.'

Brenda smiled, she had little to worry about in the way of competition from home caterers. People came to Quentins for the atmosphere as well as the food.

'Where will I put you, Cathy?' she asked.

'Where does my mother-in-law like to sit?'

'Nowhere very much, hard lady to please.' Brenda Brennan knew the score.

'Don't start me off, I'm trying to be nice today,' Cathy pleaded.

They chose the table least likely to annoy Hannah, and Cathy sat down to wait. She had told nobody about the meeting, not even Neil. They had an armed truce at home now, where normal conversation was carried on and meals were eaten, but the great thing that hung between them was only skirted around. They had agreed to give it a cooling-off period and then they would approach it in a saner way than at two-thirty a.m. in a small town house that was also home to Simon and Maud. Perhaps Hannah knew all about the job. But that was unlikely. She would wait until her mother-in-law showed her hand, and after all, the woman *had* put 'personal' on the envelope. Possibly Cathy's outburst had hit home, and Hannah really did want to apologise. If so then she should have the dignity to do so without thinking that there was an audience out there waiting to know the details. Perhaps it was about Maud and Simon? Apparently there had been some form of contact made with their father. Perhaps one of Hannah's friends might need a caterer? There had been some talk of Amanda coming back for a visit from Canada. Hannah might need a reconciliation just for appearances' sake? No point in speculating, Cathy told herself. She would know in just over an hour when the main-course dishes were cleared away, when they would both refuse dessert and ask for coffee.

*

569

In the private booth of Quentins James Byrne sat with his guest, Martin Maguire. The great thing about this particular table was that you could see out while others found it difficult to peer in.

'Lean forward just a little, Martin, and you'll see her. That's Cathy Scarlet on her own over there.'

The other man looked in the direction he had been shown, and saw the fair-haired girl reading the *Irish Times*.

'She's very young,' he said in a low voice.

'They all are these days, Martin.'

'No, she's never able to run a business, too much stress and strain.'

'She's about twenty-six, that's not young by today's standards.'

'That's almost the same age as Frankie.'

James Byrne looked at the tablecloth, searching desperately for words. Eventually he just said, 'Frankie's at peace.'

'How do we know?' asked Frankie's father.

'Because God is good,' James Byrne suggested.

The Riordans, who had given the christening party, recognised Cathy also.

'Didn't think they were up to this kind of place,' sniffed Molly Riordan.

'Well they sure as hell know how to charge. Why wouldn't they be able to afford it here?' asked the husband, who was still anxious that Tom Feather might blow the whistle on him.

At that moment Hannah Mitchell came in, hair freshly done, new heather-coloured wool suit, carrying parcels in Haywards bags, fussing about her fur coat, wondering very oversolicitously if the table was all right for Cathy. And eventually sitting down.

'God, that's Jock Mitchell's wife, they *do* move in high circles,' said the husband, very surprised.

'I've always wanted to meet her. Hannah Mitchell runs these charity bridge dos. They're always photographed in the papers and magazines. I might just drop past the table later,' said the wife.

'Oh, leave it out ... They're nobodies, those caterers. We don't need an introduction *that* badly,' said the husband, who greatly feared having to meet Tom Feather ever again.

'Mrs Mitchell, Ms Scarlet,' Brenda greeted them in her calm, measured way.

'You *know* my daughter-in-law?' Hannah asked, annoyed as always that she had not been able to make the introduction.

'It's always a pleasure to see both of you,' Brenda murmured as she left them the menus. She had not mentioned that Cathy had washed plates in the kitchen, served tables and was far better known in this establishment than the elegant Hannah would ever be. Mrs Mitchell was special only for habitually changing her table, sending food back or querying the bill. Cathy had carved for the entire restaurant the night that Patrick the chef had burned his hand. Cathy had found fifty pounds in the ladies' cloakroom and had managed to give it back to the woman who had left it there without letting her husband see. Cathy had been there the night the drains packed up. It was no contest as to who was the favourite customer.

'It is nice to have time to have a little chat like this,' Hannah Mitchell began.

'It's very kind of you, and a lovely break for me, certainly,' said Cathy, who had told herself twenty-five times already that there was no point in going to this lunch at all unless she remained calm and courteous. The shouting bit was over, the confrontation had taken place. She had not spoken to her mother-in-law for weeks until she had made the phone call to confirm this lunch date with her. She must listen now, listen and not react.

'Possibly you work too hard. You should have a few more breaks,' Hannah said.

'Possibly indeed.'

'So you agree you might be overworked, a little tense, ready to fly off the handle, then?'

Cathy saw now where her mother-in-law was coming from. She, Cathy, was going to be cast in the role of screaming neurotic, up to high doh over her little business, unable to control herself at functions. A-ha ... It was good to see the way the land lay.

'Funnily, Neil and I were saying this the other day, at our time of life we all have to work so hard running just to keep up, that by the time we get to your age and Mr Mitchell's, our life will be so much calmer.'

'You were saying that?'

'Yes. We were noting the way Mr Mitchell can spend so much time on the golf course, and you have all these hours to give to charity lunches. Our day, for all that, will come too.' Cathy smiled broadly.

Mrs Mitchell was put out. This was not the way she had intended the conversation to go. 'Yes dear, but don't you think you might be ... how shall I put this ... directing too much energy into one channel?'

Cathy looked at her, confused. 'One channel?' she asked.

'Well, this waitressing business.'

Cathy laughed aloud. 'Yes, that's what we call it too, like Simon and Maud. They *are* funny, aren't they. So solemn, and yet total babies at the same time.'

'I don't know what you mean.' Hannah was genuinely perplexed.

'I'm sorry, it's just that they call our catering company a waitressing business too because they don't understand ... I assumed you were quoting them.' Her eyes were hard and her voice harder still.

Hannah made a decision. 'Yes, of course I was,' she said.

'I knew you were, but to go back to your point, Mrs Mitchell, you're probably right. I am devoting a lot of energy to the new company, and so is Tom Feather, but that's natural. Once we get it off the ground we hope to relax a little more, have two or three nights properly off a week.'

'But my dear, that's ludicrous, isn't it? What about your life, your real life ... With Neil, for example.'

'Neil's working almost every night too, either at home or at some consultation. It's just the way things are.'

'I think it's just the way you've let things become, dear.'

Cathy remembered that tone. It was the way Mrs Mitchell had spoken to her mother. 'Sorry, Lizzie dear, I don't think we were terribly thorough cleaning the bath, were we?' Cathy had wanted to kill the woman then. The feeling was hardly less strong now. She crumbled some olive bread in her fingers and reduced the substance to a fine powder as she did so.

'Do explain what you mean, Mrs Mitchell.'

'It's just that I'm asking myself, *why* does Neil go out so much for work, why do you not have a social life, give dinner parties, go to clubs? I mean, are *you* a member of *any* clubs, tell me? It's just, I worry when a young couple don't have a healthy social life. One begins to wonder why.'

'We both work fairly hard, and I think we can safely say that Neil cares hugely about his clients and about justice being done, so this naturally takes up a lot of his time. I think that must be it, don't you?'

'Well, yes, of course, of course, that goes without saying, it's just that I wondered, perhaps if you were to ... Well if you were to try and ...' She seemed to lose the words.

'If I were to what, Mrs Mitchell?' Cathy was genuinely interested now. What on earth was the woman going to suggest? That Cathy should learn some new and devastating sexual techniques, or give dinner parties twice a week inviting politicians and the media? She waited with interest.

'Well, that you should smarten yourself up a little.' Mrs Mitchell was diffident. But once she had said it she was sticking to it. 'It's just that possibly you've been so busy with work and everything ... that you haven't had time to stop and take a good long look at yourself.'

Cathy did not know whether to feel humiliated or amused. It was so patronising for one woman to tell another that she needed to clean up her act. Yet this advice was being given by a woman aged sixty, with her hair scraped up into a style that was ten years out of date, squeezed into a wool suit one size too small, wearing a nail colour that had not been seen outside pantomime for decades. Hannah Mitchell, whose hard, over-made-up face and mink coat made her a caricature, was daring to offer Cathy advice.

'And where do you think I should start?' she asked in a level voice.

'Well, your hair, of course, and to show you how much I really mean it I've got you a token for Haywards.' Mrs Mitchell pulled out an envelope.

'I can't possibly accept this,' Cathy began.

'But you *must*. I don't think I gave you a proper Christmas present, and let this be it. You did such a delightful job catering for our New Year's Eve party, a lot of people have spoken of it so well since. The very least I can do is start you off on some kind of makeover.'

Cathy stared glumly at the envelope.

'And do get your nails done at the same time, have nail extensions maybe, won't you? There's a good girl. If there's anything a man likes to see on a woman it's long, groomed nails.'

'You know, Mrs Mitchell, I'll certainly think about the hairdo but if you don't mind, I think I'll pass on the nails. You see in our job nail extensions would be a bit dangerous – we could lose them making pastry, for example.' Cathy tried to be light-hearted. It was the only alternative to doing what she really felt like doing, which was standing up and pushing over the dining table into her mother-in-law's lap.

'Well.' Mrs Mitchell sounded sad and disappointed, as someone who had done her best but failed in the end, thanks to Cathy's gross stupidity.

'But truly I am grateful for your kindness, Mrs Mitchell. And for this lunch.'

They had just put the fish in front of them, and Hannah was looking at it suspiciously. 'Is it properly filleted?' she asked the waiter.

'I hope so, madam. Very often a tiny bone escapes, but I think you will find great care has been taken.' Cathy winked at the waiter as Hannah peered at her plate. She knew him well from her nights working here. He kept a solemn face. Brenda Brennan ran a tight ship at Quentins. He didn't want to be spotted mocking the customers.

James Byrne approached the table with an elderly man.

'Ms Scarlet, I wouldn't dream of interrupting you, but I hoped you might just meet Mr Martin Maguire, from whom you bought your premises. He is only in Dublin for a few hours.'

Cathy leaped up. 'I'm so pleased to meet you. Would you come round and meet Tom Feather there this afternoon? We'd love to show you how happily we've settled in, and excuse me, may I introduce Mrs Hannah Mitchell, who is taking me to lunch here?'

Hannah stared. She could never accustom herself to the fact that her maid's daughter introduced her with ease to two well-dressed men older than herself. Where had this confidence come from? Mr Maguire promised to come to the premises for coffee at four o'clock, and they were gone. Sensing the older woman's irritation, Cathy changed the subject.

'I must tell you that my sister Marian is getting married. Do you remember her at all from the old days?'

Hannah Mitchell's eyes narrowed as the old days were mentioned. 'No, your mother didn't bring any of the children except you.'

'Oh, Marian's the bossiest of us all.'

'Out in Chicago. That's where I think they went. I remember your mother saying.'

'They love it there. I've been out to visit. Have you been there at all, Mrs Mitchell?'

Before Hannah had time to shudder her disapproval of any city where poor Lizzie's children had ended up, Cathy saw that they were being approached again, and to her horror she saw that it was the terrible couple who had given the nightmare christening party. Again she made the introductions, but this time Hannah Mitchell offered some information.

'I'm actually Cathy's mother-in-law,' she said. This was a personal first.

'And is er ... Tom ... your son, then?' Molly Riordan asked, gushing.

'Oh, no, no, not at all. My son is a lawyer, a barrister actually,' Hannah said.

They left eventually, the couple having given their card to Hannah and assured her of substantial sponsorship at the next charity do.

'Sorry about that,' Cathy apologised.

'No, I'm amazed. If your poor mother could see you here with these people . . .'

'Mrs Mitchell, it's very, very good of you to take me to lunch here and to offer me this expensive hairdo, and I am touched and grateful, but can I ask you as a personal favour not to refer to my mother as my *poor* mother. She is far from poor, she is happy and content and has children and a husband who love her.'

'Yes, of course . . . I only meant . . .'

Cathy waited.

After a long time Hannah Mitchell said, 'I only meant she doesn't have your confidence.'

'Oh, confidence isn't everything, Mrs Mitchell.'

'It seems to get people quite far, though.' The mouth was narrow.

Cathy saw Geraldine being ushered to a nearby table with Peter Murphy, the managing director of the hotel where she did the public relations. Their eyes met, and Cathy gave a barely obvious shake of her head. Geraldine got the message and didn't acknowledge her. To be greeted by a third customer at Quentin's would put Cathy in an intolerable position. She had already shown her mother-in-law too much of this confidence thing. It was time to listen to the wisdom of having a regular facial and not let the muscles get saggy. Cathy listened, and wondered to herself as she had so often before how this empty, sad, envious woman and her pleasure-loving husband had given birth to Neil. Neil, who was at this moment fighting another no-hoper's case, Neil who would be mildly interested that she had met his mother for lunch but who would never understand in a million years how outrageous it was to be patronised like this. Cathy almost wished they could have gone back to the days of straightforward hostility. It was far easier to cope with.

Peter Murphy and Geraldine O'Connor saw them leave.

'God, isn't that a tiresome poor woman?' he said.

'She's pretty difficult as a mother-in-law, let me tell you,' Geraldine said.

'And how on earth would you know?' he asked.

'That's Cathy Scarlet, my niece, walking out the door with her. She has the bad luck to be in that role.'

'Yes, I *did* know that. She married the young lawyer, right?'

'*And* has set up a very good catering company I keep telling you about, which you keep telling me is of no interest to you.'

'No indeed, it is not of any interest only in so far as it's competition. She can't hate her mother-in-law so much if she's having lunch with her.'

'She does, believe me.'

'And why didn't you say hallo to them?'

'Cathy frowned at me not to,' Geraldine explained.

'I'll never understand women,' said Peter Murphy, who had nonetheless made considerable efforts to do so by having affairs with many of them. Including Geraldine, some years back. But that was all over now. Today they were just very good friends.

*

'I wish I hadn't agreed to go back to the old place,' Martin Maguire said to James Byrne as the two men strolled through Stephen's Green and fed ducks with the bread given to them by Brenda Brennan as they left Quentins.

'No, believe me it's a good idea. You'll remember it like this now, the way they have it all shiny, and different,' James reassured him. They watched in silence as a mother duck rounded up her ducklings for the new source of food.

'Look at that.' Martin Maguire was amazed. 'Look at the way they love their parents and trust them. It's not like that with humans.'

'Don't punish yourself. Please, Martin, there's no point.'

'There's not much point in anything. Are you sure you didn't tell them?'

'I told you I didn't.'

'They must have wondered why I was so eager to sell so quickly. They must have asked.'

'It's your story, your life, Martin. Of course I didn't tell them,' said James. 'Anyway, those two were so anxious to get their business up and running, they never asked. Believe me.'

'I can't go,' Martin Maguire said. 'It's as simple as that. Will you tell them, James?'

'Of course.' James Byrne nodded gravely.

'Imagine, she's their daughter-in-law and she's only got a real ordinary accent.' Molly Riordan was astounded.

'I could have told you that she wasn't married to that tall eejit Tom with the face like some kind of teenage idol,' said Larry, sounding aggrieved.

'I thought he was cute,' she said.

'Well I tell you, he's not going for a lady barrister. No, his line is a bit of stuff, believe me.'

'How on earth do you know?' Molly asked.

'I heard,' he nodded sagely.

Molly shrugged. 'Well, all our friends thought he was a doll. Why did you take such a dislike to him?'

The husband couldn't remember. Just one of those instant things, he thought.

Brenda Brennan was having a cup of coffee in the kitchen when lunch was over at Quentins.

'Patrick, we should try and put a bit of work in Cathy and Tom's way, it's very hard at the start.'

'What do you suggest?' he asked.

'You know the way people often ask us to do funerals . . . and we can't get away so end up sending them over a dressed salmon.'

'You're right, next one we'll recommend them. Get them to give us a card.'

'They already have,' said Brenda.

*

Tom and Cathy had coffee and shortbread ready at four.

'What were you doing at Quentins anyway?' Tom asked.

'Penance for all the many sins I committed in my life,' she said.

'What did you eat?'

'I can't remember. I was with Hannah.'

'Is there blood all over the place?'

'No, she just wanted to cut my hair,' said Cathy.

Tom found this increasingly puzzling. 'But she didn't?' he said eventually.

'She did.' Cathy tapped her handbag. 'She gave me a voucher for it, so I'll be in Marcella's domain one of these days. Tom, do I need my hair cut?'

'I don't know. Do *you* want to?'

'No, not particularly.'

'Then don't.' It was simple. Simple for men. Simple for anyone who hadn't taken Hannah Mitchell's money.

At that moment they heard James Byrne and Martin Maguire arriving.

'Remember, we must not sound as if we are too grateful or he'll take it back,' Cathy fussed.

'It's all signed and sealed, Cath, it's only a social call,' Tom whispered, and they opened the door. James Byrne was alone.

'I'm very sorry. He decided not to come after all, so I came along to give you his apologies.'

They were very disappointed. 'Whatever made him change his mind?' Cathy asked, and as soon as she spoke she knew that James Byrne would not tell her.

'I just said I'd tell you that he was sorry.' He looked sad himself.

'Well, maybe it was too soon for him; he might come another time,' Cathy said.

'He might indeed. He'll be glad to know that he didn't cause any fuss.' James Byrne left.

'We'll never know,' Cathy said.

'Nobody'll ever know our secrets from him either,' Tom said.

'We don't *have* any secrets,' she laughed. 'Though actually I do. I'm going to give this hairdressing voucher to June.' She waved it gleefully.

'How much is it for?' asked Tom and when she showed him he pretended to reel around the premises. 'Do people really spend that much money on hair?' he asked.

'Apparently.' Cathy laughed.

'Marian was on again about the wedding entertainment,' Cathy said to her mother.

'They get terrible notions over there,' Lizzie said.

'No, it's dead easy. Nothing we can't provide: *Ave Maria* and *Panis Angelicus*.' Cathy was casual.

'It's amazing you even know the names of the hymns, it's so long since you darkened a church.'

'Stop it, Ma, I tell everyone how tolerant you are...'

'How tolerant I *have* to be,' sighed Lizzie.

'They want a pageboy and a flower girl, Mam. That's a bit of a poser.'

'Well they can't have them,' Cathy's mother said. 'Marian's going to have to be told, it's not all posh Chicago notions here, we don't have anyone that age in the family.'

'We have Maud and Simon,' Cathy said thoughtfully.

'Oh, no, that wouldn't do at all,' Cathy's mother said immediately.

'Why not?' Cathy asked. 'If they're still here, and it looks as if they will be, then wouldn't it be nice for them? Marian would love them.'

'Cathy, stop filling their heads with such nonsense, you know *she* wouldn't stand for it, not for a moment.'

'Well *she* has nothing to do with it, Mam. Let's discuss it with Maud and Simon. They loved *Riverdance*,' Cathy said.

'Everyone loved *Riverdance*, but they won't learn something like that and anyway, I told you. She wouldn't hear of it.'

'Mam, *she* is not important. Let's ask the kids.'

'They're not here,' Lizzie said.

'Of course they're here, Mam, they're always here, listening, spying, stealing food. That's what they do all day, isn't it?'

'That's not fair, Cathy, you sound as if you hate them, they're only children who didn't have a proper home.'

'No, I don't hate them. I've got to like them a bit more recently. But they still steal food. It's because they're not sure they'll get any more. *And* they listen at doors. Don't you, Maud?'

'I was just passing by,' said poor Maud, and Simon raised his eyes to heaven.

'Tom, it's June. Can I ask you something?'

'Anything, as long as it's not asking to cry off the next job.'

'No . . . It's just . . . is Cathy sound in the head? She's given me *the* most amazing token . . .'

'Take it, use it, splash out with it.'

'But won't she be sorry?'

'No, it was from Neil's mother. She doesn't like the lady, so go get the hair done, Junie baby.'

'I was thinking of very bright purple streaks, highlights, you know, but they have to be well done otherwise they look a mess.'

'Go for them June,' said Tom, and he hung up.

There was just so much time you could spend talking about hairdos.

'I'm not being a pageboy at *anyone's* wedding,' said Simon.

'I'd like to have been a flower girl. I don't think anyone else would have let us be part of anything,' Maud said.

'Lots of people at school are learning Irish dancing, of course,' Simon said. 'It would be a way to learn it free.'

'How do you mean, free?' Maud wondered.

'Well, Father and Mother aren't there to pay for anything any more,' Simon said sadly.

'But Muttie hasn't any money to pay for lessons,' Maud protested.

'How do you know that?'

'Well, he has holes in his shoes, he hasn't a car or a chequebook or anything,' Maud said.

'So we won't get dancing lessons then.'

'Would you like them, Simon?'

'I wouldn't mind,' he said.

'We'll just wait and see. Let's wait for them to start talking about it again.'

'It's a pity they knew we took food,' Maud said.

'We don't from Muttie and his wife Lizzie now, only from Neil and Cathy, and that's because we weren't sure,' Simon agreed.

'I know, and Cathy *did* say she likes us more now.' Maud was always hopeful.

'Only a *bit* more, that's all she said.' Simon was more watchful.

'And what on earth is this,' Muttie said when they came in and saw a huge lump of pastry in the centre of the kitchen table.

'It's Beef Wellington,' Simon explained.

'Is it now, and where did it come from?' Muttie asked.

'I think Cathy nicked it for us from people who paid her in her waitressing business,' Simon was helpful.

'Stand up, Simon, and leave the room,' Muttie said.

'What did I say, Muttie? You asked, I told you.'

'That's not the truth. My Cathy never nicked anything in her life, in fact the only people that ever nicked *anything* in this house are you two, nephew and niece of the famous Mrs Mitchell that Lizzie spent her life cleaning up after. Those are the only thieves we ever had here.'

'Please Muttie, it was only four sausages and a couple of packs of cornflakes just in case,' Simon said.

'In case what?'

'In case there would be no more,' said Simon, ashen-faced, as Maud sat with the tears trickling down her cheeks.

'I had lunch with Cathy today,' Hannah said to Jock.

'That was nice, dear.'

'It was actually, much nicer than I thought.'

'Good, good.'

'She knew absolutely everyone at Quentins. Isn't it amazing, when you think of poor Lizzie.'

'But that was a different age, dear.'

'So it would appear,' she said.

'And what did she say about Neil's plans?'

'Plans? What plans?'

'No, no nothing dear, something else. You know my mind's always miles away.'

'Indeed it is,' Hannah said sadly.

'A quick yes or no: do you want the dancing lessons? Do you want to be part of this deal for Marian's wedding? Answer now,' Cathy said.

'It's a bit complicated,' Simon said.

'No it's not, it's very simple . . . It costs this number of pounds to get you taught three numbers to dance, it costs about twice that to pay real dancers to do it. But we thought you should make the choice.'

'Why?'

'Because you're family,' Cathy said simply.

'We're not really.'

'How often must I tell you, you live here in the house where Marian was born, you are the cousins of my husband. Just a yes or no, and we'll go ahead and book the real people.'

'Will we be coming to the wedding anyway, you know, as guests?' Maud asked.

'Doubt it,' Cathy said.

'But you said we were family,' Simon wailed.

'Not all that close, come to think of it.'

'Why are you being so horrible, Cathy?' Simon asked.

'Because *you* are both horrible. You told my dad I nicked that Beef Wellington, which I did *not*. I made it specially for him to thank him for looking after you, because you make Neil's life a misery and he can't get on with his work and because you have no manners and I wish your mother and father would come and take you straight back to The Beeches. Now is that a good answer?'

Cathy's mother came in at that point. 'We'd all like Mr and Mrs Mitchell of The Beeches to be well in themselves and run their own home again, but until that point Simon and Maud are very welcome here,' she said looking around her, 'and I hope that everyone here knows that.'

'I'm sorry Mam,' Cathy said later.

'Sure you should be, taking it out on innocent children.'

'Lizzie?' Simon knocked at the kitchen door. This was another great improvement; up to now they had stormed in everywhere. 'Lizzie, we'd like to do the dancing please,' he asked.

'It might not be possible, child. *She* might not like it.'

'She doesn't know us yet,' Simon complained. 'She can't hate us already.'

'She surely can't take against us without meeting us,' Maud protested.

'No, we're not talking about Marian, Mam is talking about your aunt Hannah, aren't you, Mam?'

'Well I was, Cathy, but not here, not like this, not in front of, can't you wait until. . . ?'

'It's all right,' Simon reassured her. 'We know all about Aunt Hannah, we know that Cathy hates her.'

'I don't any more,' Cathy said. 'I quite like her. I had lunch with her today, as it happens.'

'You never did.'

'I did indeed. We went to Quentins.'

'But why?'

'Search me, Ma, but it had something to do with cutting my hair.'

'I wish you'd be serious for a moment.' Cathy's mother beckoned her out to the scullery to get away from the twins.

'Is there any word on the children?' she whispered.

'She never mentioned them once,' Cathy said cheerfully, well aware that Simon and Maud had crept towards the door to listen.

'But talking about Marian,' Cathy continued, 'I think in a way I'm glad she wants child dancers. She might well go for it, she seems to be having the full works from what I hear. Fireworks, jugglers, lions and tigers.'

The children's faces lit up. 'Tigers at the wedding! Isn't that *great*,' said Simon. Again Cathy remembered too late her resolution not to be ironic in front of the children.

'I had lunch with your mother today,' Cathy said that evening when she got in to Waterview.

'Oh, good.' Neil didn't look up from his papers.

'Aren't you surprised?'

He was still reading a whole sheaf of something, but at her tone he looked up and kept his finger on the paper so that he wouldn't lose his place. 'What?' he asked.

'It's not a usual occurrence. I thought you'd wonder why.'

'Well, why then?'

'Don't know.' Cathy shrugged.

'Listen Cathy, you told me you had to work out a silver wedding menu and a Spanish buffet tonight, so I took all this stuff home . . .'

'What stuff? Is this about Africa?'

'No, of course not, I told you that all that about the job was on hold until we had time to talk about it seriously.'

'So?'

'So you said you were working, and I've two things to do here. I told them I'd get this paper together on a writer.'

'Sorry.'

'No, don't be like that.'

'I *am* sorry, you're quite right, I did say that . . .'

She meant it, she wasn't even sulking. They did tell each other in advance what their plans for the evening were. He was justified in being put out. Yet this was so huge a fact she had just told him, and he wasn't even mildly interested. His own mother, who had waged war on her for years, had invited her to Quentins for God's sake. Neil had not even registered it.

'No, I'm sorry I was a bit short with you . . . It's not just the unfortunate Nigerian writer. There's another bloody complicated thing, and we'll be in court over it tomorrow. I'm for the tenant who broke his back on a faulty stairway, and the landlords will have a top team saying they did all the proper repairs. Problem is, my fellow talks and looks like a gangster, and the landlord is mild and articulate and concerned, so it's all stacked against my client. I have to look up and list all these decisions . . .'

Cathy held up her hands. She really was contrite. 'I'm going out, anyway. I just came in to leave the shopping. I'll be back in a couple of hours and we'll have supper.'

'You don't have to, honey,' he said.

'I do,' she said, and she was gone.

Cathy hadn't intended to go out, she had planned to have a long bath and then sit down and go through some files and cookery books to think up dishes in a leisurely way. She had even thought about making a paella to rehearse for the Spanish buffet, but she knew the mood was wrong. Neil would just think she was killing time waiting until he was free. Better to pretend to be busy and go out. But where?

She couldn't go to Tom's; he and Marcella were going to the theatre tonight, a possible photo opportunity for Marcella since it was a first night. Cathy drove to Glenstar apartments and dialled Geraldine on the mobile phone from the van. The answering machine was on. Stupid to have come all this way without ringing first, Cathy thought, and then by chance she looked up at her aunt's flat and saw the curtains being drawn. There were two figures in the room. Geraldine was entertaining someone. A man. She was just about to pull out of the parking bay when she saw someone waving. It was Shona Burke from Haywards.

'I saw your van . . . Well, who could miss it?' Shona laughed. 'Do you want to come in for coffee?'

Cathy looked around as Shona got out the coffee machine. Similar to her aunt's flat, but not nearly as big and totally different furnishings. A lot of brightly coloured rugs and embroidered cushions. There were no family pictures on the wall, two shelves of books on management and business, a small, neat music centre and no television set. Cathy wondered what kind of people Shona entertained here, and how she could afford the rent or the mortgage. These apartments were not cheap. Of course Shona had a very good job at Haywards. Still. Perhaps she came from rich people. Shona Burke would never tell. She was very adroit at taking the conversation away from herself.

'You're very far away,' Shona said coming back to join her.

'I was thinking about Maud and Simon,' Cathy lied.

'Who are they?'

'Neil's cousins. We appear to have adopted them, my mother and I.' She laughed a little grimly and explained the background. To her surprise Shona didn't find any of it funny or endearing. Nor did she shrug at the hopeless inevitability of it all and praise them like other people did. She just listened, with no expression at all on her face.

'So that's it,' Cathy finished. 'Neil and his father got some kind of order, oh, I don't know exactly what, but it's about releasing money from trust funds, and some of that goes to my mam and dad, and I suppose some even comes to us if we need it.'

'And what about their social worker?'

'She's happy enough with the set-up, she knows they're well looked-after. The mother isn't getting any better, and the father isn't showing any signs of coming back home. We're holding the fort.'

'It's terribly unfair on the children,' Shona said.

'Life's unfair, Shona. Of course I'd prefer them to have a nice mummy and a nice daddy who knew who they were, and who read them bedtime stories and cared for them, but they don't, so we have to pick up the pieces.'

'And then they go back to hopeless Mummy and Daddy, and what then?' Shona asked.

'I wish I knew, but if I were Tom Feather I would say miracles happen, because he genuinely believes they do,' Cathy said wistfully.

Cathy drove home with a sense of depression that she couldn't quite shake off. She didn't know why it was there. She was not annoyed with Neil for being somewhat brisk with her – he was perfectly right, she *had* said she would be working. Her mother-in-law's crass criticisms hadn't the power to get beneath her skin any more, it wasn't that. Her own mother's craven humility was something Cathy had lived with for ever, this was nothing new. They had always *known* that Maud and Simon would have to go into care, that wasn't any great shock. Scarlet Feather was doing well these days, with lots of things booked ahead. Its books would look healthy enough at the end of this month to make James Byrne feel reasonably calm. Whatever it was it wouldn't lift.

At traffic lights on her way back to Waterview, Cathy was startled as two very dishevelled-looking people knocked urgently at her window. A man and a woman in their thirties, with empty eyes. Her first instinctive act was to make sure her door was locked. They looked rough and aggressive. Neil Mitchell would probably have pulled into the side and asked them what had happened. Tom Feather would have given them the price of a meal, and convinced them that good times were around the corner. Cathy felt ashamed that all she wanted was for the traffic lights to change and that she could be away out of there, away from their haunted, disturbed faces. She could hear them calling out. 'You have a good life, you have everything you want, please, *please*.' The lights were for ever red. She told herself that the social services were good these days, those people did not *have* to beg in the streets. There were centres, hostels, rescue teams on the streets. These must be winos, drunks or druggies. She must stare straight ahead as if she didn't see them, if she opened the window it could be dangerous. 'Please,' she heard the woman cry, 'you've got everything, a lovely van with a picture on it, a home to go to, just give us something.' It was the van with the picture on it that softened her heart. Cathy indicated and pulled to the side of the street. Out of her bag she took a ten-pound note. She opened the window a fraction and handed it to them. They looked at her in disbelief. It was five times what they might have hoped for. The woman looked younger close up, maybe younger than Cathy, her hair was matted and her face dirty.

'You deserve all your good luck, missus,' she said eventually.

'I don't,' Cathy said, grimly thinking, 'Nobody *deserves* good luck, it's just handed out. Very unfair, as a matter of fact.' The lights changed and she drove on. It was all such an accident, every bit of it when you stopped to think. Why was that girl standing there in the rain begging from cars at the traffic lights? Why was she, Cathy, driving a van with a picture on it to an expensive town house in Waterview? Why were Simon and Maud going to have to live with strangers? None of it made any sense at all. When she let herself into the house Cathy found a folded note. Her heart sank. He couldn't have been called out *again*. This was a workman's compensation case, for heaven's sake, not a political prisoner matter. She opened it and read: 'Sorry Cathy – back 11-ish, don't wait up.' She didn't.

Tom said that the whole trick for the estate agents' reception was setting up the Spanish atmosphere. Cathy said that was all very well certainly, but they must have a whole range of tapas to start. Followed by a knockout paella with all the right flavours. Tom was so busy chasing up Spanish hats, castanets, a guitarist and a flamenco dancer that he never seemed to have time to discuss the menus. Cathy worked out that they should have two paellas, one with shellfish and one less authentic one without. She knew how much the estate agents would love to see Marcella Malone moving among them, but she didn't even think of suggesting it to Tom. Instead, June was given instructions about hiring a Spanish outfit and learning to say 'arriba' at appropriate times. Cathy wanted little labels on the individual plates of tapas showing how typically Spanish they were; Tom begged her to believe that all they wanted was the feel that they were actually in Spain already which the sangria, Rioja and the click of the castanets would give them. They were showing off to potential clients and the press. But she wanted it to be right, there would be *some* people there, surely, who would know and recognise the real thing.

'Would it be educational for us to go to it, do you think?' Simon wondered the night before.

'No,' said Cathy briefly, and saw their two disappointed faces. 'Thank you for suggesting it, but actually it would be boring and depressing for you. Have I ever told you a lie?'

They paused to consider this question. 'No,' they said at exactly the same time. 'Will there be leftovers, do you think?'

'Not at St Jarlath's tomorrow, Maud. Your aunt Hannah is coming to Waterview tomorrow, tomorrow night, to supper with Neil and myself.'

'Are you going to poison her?' Simon asked.

'Of course not, I'm going to serve her and your uncle Jock some delicious Spanish food and try and make my hair look good.'

'Why would she want to see your hair?' Maud asked.

'Believe me, Maud, I'm not sure, but she does, and often when people want things that are quite easy it's probably best to do them, it saves trouble in the long run.'

'Where did you learn that ... Was it at school?' Maud wondered.

'No, my aunt Geraldine told me, years ago. It's a very useful piece of advice.'

The estate agents loved the lunch. None of them mentioned the food; they all talked about the atmosphere.

'Right again, Tom,' Cathy said, genuinely admiring. He got things so right, he had known all along they were selling the mood, not the gourmet dishes of Spain. A lot of these people wouldn't even venture into proper Spanish food when they bought their villas out there.

'They needed good food as a back-up. If it hadn't been as good as it was, we would have heard the complaints,' he reassured her as they packed up the leftovers. Some were going to Fatima, where Tom's father, now home from hospital was well on the mend. There had been a huge basket of fruit delivered there, courtesy of Joe who was still in the Far East. Tom didn't say much about it, but Cathy knew he was very pleased. Cathy was packing two separate boxes, a small one for the twins who would be hoping for something, and another to provide most of the meal tonight when the Mitchells were coming to Waterview. Please may Neil not be late again. Please may Jock not know any of the estate agents here today who might have mentioned they were at a Spanish lunch. And please may Hannah Mitchell not get into a temper because she hadn't used the hair voucher.

The Mitchells were in good time, and of course Neil wasn't home. Cathy had laid out little dishes of black olives.

'Thought we'd be getting these,' Jock Mitchell laughed his bluff, loud laugh.

'Ran into a couple of lads from the golf club and had a drink with them. They said you had done this slap-up Spanish meal, and I said to Hannah on the way over here, what's the betting we get the taste of old España tonight.'

Cathy's face took on a set look. 'Ah, but I hope you didn't have *real* money on it because you'd have been wrong, Mr Mitchell,' she said triumphantly. 'Just these lovely fat olives. I thought I'd save a few for you.'

He seemed disappointed. Hannah was busy hanging up her coat and looking around disapprovingly at their house, as she always did. She hadn't seen Cathy properly since she came in.

'Oh, dear, Cathy, no time to get the little job done on the hair yet?' she said, more in sorrow than in anger.

Cathy felt that she wanted to put on a raincoat and start running in any direction, miles and miles from these people.

'Alas no, Mrs Mitchell, but I have given it a lot of thought,' she said.

Neil came in at that moment. 'Hey, that smells good,' he began. Cathy put her finger over her lips and then spoke in a high, unnatural voice.

'Neil, *great* you're back. I have to do just five minutes' work and send something by taxi somewhere. Your parents are here, can you entertain them for just a minute?'

'Sure,' he said agreeably.

But before he went in she whispered in his ear, 'We are not eating Spanish food, not, repeat *not*.'

'Of course not.' He shrugged, puzzled.

She called her local taxi firm and wrote a note to Brenda Brennan at
Quentins.

'This is Last Chance Saloon. Can you send me with this taxi driver four
portions of anything at all on God's earth that I can give my bloody
mother-in-law. Only thing, *nothing* Spanish. I will pay whatever you want,
whenever you like or work it off for you in the kitchen. Love from a
distraught Cathy.'

Then she went back and talked nonsense and rubbish to them all for
forty-five minutes until the taxi returned with a wondrous steak and kidney
pie, a bowl of salad, mashed potatoes and garlic bread. She managed to get
it all on the table without any of them seeing, and called them in blithely to
their dinner.

'This is lovely,' Hannah said, and Cathy smiled serenely. 'I knew it wouldn't
be reheated Spanish food,' Hannah continued. 'Jock can be way off-beam
sometimes.'

'Sorry,' said Jock. 'Should have realised I was dealing with a professional.'

And Cathy knew she shouldn't be so pleased about it all, but there was no
way of hiding it. Afterwards when they were washing up she admitted it to
Neil.

'It was touch and go but it worked,' she said, delighted with the little
victory.

'Sure,' he said.

She knew that he was patting her down. 'But seriously Neil, wasn't it
brilliant?'

'It wasn't necessary, hon.'

'It was essential,' Cathy said with total conviction.

'What are you trying to prove?'

'That she hasn't won.'

'But you proved that, Cathy, long ago.'

'No I haven't.'

'I married you, didn't I? What other battleground has she got to fight
on?'

Tom was a great audience next morning when Cathy told the tale of the taxi
takeaway from Quentins. They sat companionably drinking mugs of coffee
and trying out his new date and walnut bread.

'Tell me how did they not see it coming in.' He sat like a huge child on
his high stool, wrapped in his scarlet apron.

'I put a big screen near the door.' She was gleeful about it all.

'And the containers, all the foil, didn't they notice?'

'No, Quentins sent proper dishes, all I had to do was put them straight
on the table.'

'And what did you do with the Spanish food?'

'I asked the same taxi driver to take it straight round to St Jarlath's. I
don't care *what* it all cost, it was worth it, Tom, it was so worth it.'

A pinger sounded on the kitchen wall, so Cathy reached into the oven to

•take out more bread and screamed with pain. Tom leaped up to take the tray from her.

'I've told you a hundred times to put on those long gloves,' he fussed.

'I know, it's just that I was trying to be quick.'

'That's what you always say, and is it any quicker? Here, let me see.'

He held her two arms under the cold-water tap and let the water flow over the red patches.

'It's nothing, Tom, stop clucking like a hen.'

'Someone has to cluck or you'll be as much use as the *Venus de Milo*.'

'What?'

'The one with no arms. It was a joke.'

'I know, you eejit, it's just that Hannah and Jock were only talking about it last night.'

'What cultured conversations you have with your in-laws.' He had patted her arms dry and was rubbing the cream in gently.

'I wish. It was an argument between Neil and his father. Jock had bought some sculpture for his office, Neil said it was showy and a waste of money. Jock said that if Neil got a present of the *Venus de Milo* tomorrow he'd only stick a pair of arms on it and sell it to raise funds for tinkers and foreigners. *That* kind of cultured conversation.'

Tom laughed as he stuck the gauze on loosely, leaving room for air to get into the burn, and put things away in their first-aid cabinet. 'And what did you and Hannah talk about?'

'My hair,' Cathy said simply.

To her rage, she felt tears in her eyes. Cathy didn't *want* to be as obsessed with her body as Marcella was, but she wanted to look well.

'Oh, Cathy,' he said.

'Tell me, Tom, is it stupid or something? I don't know.'

'Is this serious?' he asked, astounded.

'Of course it is. If that awful woman gave me a king's ransom to get it changed, then it must be frightening the dogs in the street.'

'But if Neil tells you it's lovely. . . ?'

'He'd say anything for an easy life.'

'No he wouldn't, and it's gorgeous.'

'What's it like? Go on, close your eyes, tell me.'

Tom closed his eyes. 'Let me see, it's fair, sort of honey fair, very thick and it's tied behind your back, and little bits curl over your ears and it smells of shampoo and it's just fine.'

Peter Murphy called Geraldine in the office.

'Awkward thing to ask you,' he began.

'My speciality, awkward things,' she said.

It was easy for her to sound so suave and cool. She knew already the awkward thing he was going to ask. Peter Murphy's estranged wife had died that morning, Geraldine had already been told this. It would be either asking her to attend the funeral or not to. It was a matter of indifference to her, whichever Peter wanted she would do. They were old history now as a couple; there had been many ladies in his life since she had been there. They were truly just good friends now. She listened and made what she hoped were the appropriate and non-committal sounds of regret, coming as they did from an ex-mistress. It turned out that Quentins wouldn't do the catering for the funeral, they were passing such work over to Scarlet Feather. Would this be embarrassing for Geraldine?

'Absolutely not, I'm just delighted they can help you, and I'm sure they'll do it very well,' she said, still in her concerned, sympathetic voice.

'It will be on Saturday morning . . . um . . . at what is . . . was . . . well, her house . . . The children . . . Her friends would expect . . .' Geraldine had never known Peter Murphy at a loss for words before. For years he had been able to live exactly the life he wanted to. Only by dying had the sad, rich, plain wife whom he had always managed to ignore satisfactorily even slightly inconvenienced him.

'Yes, Peter, and what would be best . . . ?' She waited. He was unwilling to decide, she would second-guess him. 'Perhaps I shouldn't come to the house. I didn't really know her personally, after all.' She could hear his sigh of relief, echoed by her own. Geraldine had no wish to be seen as a false sympathiser. Yet she *would* like to know who turned up. This way she could work behind the scenes, peer out and see everything without being seen herself.

'I've got a question for you, Simon,' Lizzie said.

Simon's face lit up. 'Is it about Muttie's Yankee today? Did it work, then?' He was very excited.

'Yankee?' Lizzie said.

'It's a bit complicated, it's a way of increasing your stake,' Simon explained helpfully.

'I know only too well what it is, thank you Simon, it's just that there was an agreement that such a thing as a Yankee was never, ever going to happen with household money.' Lizzie's face was thunderous.

'I'm sure it wasn't with household money,' Simon said swiftly.

'No, I'm sure it wasn't. It must have been from his own personal income, his stocks and shares and dividends,' she said vaguely.

'Oh, good, that's all right then,' Simon said, relieved.

Lizzie looked at him in despair. 'That wasn't the question,' she said. 'It's that you and Maud have to say yes or no to Marian's wedding today. If you say yes, then you get dancing lessons and outfits. If you say no then that's fine. It's got to be your decision, the pair of you.'

'Then I say no,' Simon said.

'Right.' Lizzie was leaving it at that.

'What do you mean, right?' Simon could be very imperious.

'Just that you got a choice, you said no. Maud will be disappointed, she said yes, she wanted to dress up.'

'Well I don't,' he said.

'Fine. Cathy will be relieved.' This was part of a plan.

'Why?' He didn't like playing into Cathy's hands.

'She says you'd have been no good. Muttie and I didn't agree, and it would have been a great day out but there, it's your choice.'

'I suppose I *could* do it, I mean, if Maud wants it so much.'

'Yes or no today.'

'Oh, all right then, yes.'

'And you do have to learn the dances and wear a kilt?' Lizzie was making sure there were no grey areas.

'Well, I suppose. There's not going to be anyone from school there, after all.' He was talking himself into it.

And then came the clincher. 'And of course the tigers? Will there still be tigers?' He had remembered Cathy's chance throwaway remark, just as he would remember Lizzie saying sourly that Muttie had stocks and shares.

'I don't think so, I think there was some kind of a problem getting the tigers into Dublin.'

'But *why*, Lizzie? Why?'

Lizzie finally spoke. 'I beg you, Simon, don't ask me the answers to any more questions. I don't *have* any answers. Why does Muttie throw away everything he gets? Why does Geraldine live like a millionaire? Why isn't Cathy grateful to Mrs Mitchell for everything that woman gives her? Why does Marian want some of the Mass to be in the Irish language at her wedding? Why do women I clean houses for leave such terrible rotting things in their fridges? I'll tell you, I really and truly don't know.'

'Do you know when the wedding is, Lizzie?' Simon asked in a level voice.

'Yes, it's in the summer,' she said glumly.

'I suppose we *could* learn to dance in four months,' said Simon, who had discovered that life threw something new at you all the time.

'Listen, can I help you out Saturday at the Murphy funeral? What I want to do is be in the kitchen out of sight, buttering bread and washing dishes.'

'Why?'

'Because you're a businesswoman. Where will you get a better offer, a pair of hands free for four hours?'

'No, you're doing this for some horrible reason.'

'Only pure curiosity. I used to have a fling with the grieving widower, as you well know. I'd like to see at first hand how many people turn up and who they are.'

'I'm not in favour of it,' Cathy said.

'I *could* approach your partner, Mr Feather.'

'How will we get you in?'

'I'll come in with you when they're all at the church.'

'The kitchen might not be big enough to hide you.'

'It is,' said Geraldine, who had after all been there when it was a joint family home, but when the deceased lady was not in residence.

This was their first funeral, and they must do it right. Brenda Brennan at Quentins, who had given them the job, said there was a lot of work in that area. You just had to be terribly nice and considerate to the family concerned, and keep everyone else fed and supplied with drink. The problem, of course, was that nobody could tell them how many people to expect. Certainly not Mr Murphy, who seemed highly embarrassed about it all.

They would cook two hams, Tom decided, baked and dressed, just produce one and carve it in the dining room, keeping the other in reserve. This way it wouldn't point it up if there was a very small attendance, much less than had been anticipated. They would have salads ready to make on the premises, a selection of Tom's breads ready to warm up in the oven, Cathy's home-made chutneys and pickles served in the big white pots with their Scarlet Feather logo. There would be warm asparagus quiches and big plates of Irish cheese served with apples and grapes. Desserts might make it somehow too festive and party-like. *Inappropriate* was the word they kept using to each other. And yet it was very odd and inappropriate to be looking for approval and new business and success just because some wealthy, unloved woman had died and her guilty, remorseful relatives were trying to give her a good send-off.

'Very big house, isn't it,' said Cathy as they climbed the steps with the first load of boxes.

Geraldine sniffed as if she could tell a lot of stories about this house but would not be drawn. June said that she might meet a rich fellow here today. Walter, who was being the barman once again, said it was ridiculous for one woman to have lived in a huge place like this on her own. Tom said it was great that there was lots of space, because he was so big he took up the whole kitchen in some houses. Cathy said nothing but just scurried back to the van for the next lot of trays. A lot of things were puzzling her. Why was Geraldine coming here, anyway? The place must have nothing but bad memories for her. Why was June talking about meeting a fellow? She had *met* a fellow years ago, for heaven's sake, and had two children with him. Why was Walter so bitter? He had everything going for him. All right, so two very dysfunctional and at present disappeared parents. But he had never been involved even when they *were* around. How could he resent anyone who had anything? Including a dead woman whom he had never even known. And lastly, how could anyone else on earth be so unfailingly optimistic as Tom Feather? They had three loose cannons on board with them today. They didn't know whether there would be thirty or two hundred people turning up today. And *still* he was able to see something good about it all, like he would have a big kitchen. She smiled to herself as she ran up the steps again.

'Don't get into a good humour on me, Cathy Scarlet . . . That's when you usually burn yourself or cut yourself,' he warned.

'Right,' she said. 'Grim-faced from now on.'

The family of the late Mrs Murphy were back at the house first. Cathy took their coats and hung them on her mobile coat rack which was set up in the back of the wide hall. Then Walter offered them a drink, and they moved into the big and seldom-used drawing room.

'Should we help with the food?' one of the daughters offered grudgingly.

'No, no, it's all under control, and you'll see we have set up a buffet here in the back room.'

They looked around. In all the years that she had lived here their mother would never have entertained like this. And the big rooms looked so well today; these caterers had added small touches, and certainly managed to show the place at its best. How sad that the first time their mother's house, their own family home, should be seen in its glory was at her funeral.

'It must be very poignant for you all,' Cathy said. 'So many memories all coming together.' They looked at each other, surprised. 'I'm sure she would have been very pleased that you opened up her lovely house to everyone . . . It will be a lovely way to greet her friends,' Cathy went on. She saw them relaxing, and yet again she blessed Brenda Brennan at Quentins saying that you can never be too sympathetic. Tom kept looking out of the window and giving a running commentary.

'They're coming very slowly, but I think there's just enough to take the bare look off the place. No, wait, there's three more cars pulling up outside, we might have a decent house after all.

'Oh, dear, there are people already checking their watches, they mightn't stay long. June, go in and take up your stand behind the buffet. Is Walter there, or has he gone off to have one of his fifteen-minute reads in the gents?'

'He's still in the hall. I've got my eye on him,' Cathy said.

'Geraldine, do we sympathise with Mr Murphy or not?'

Geraldine paused in her work, which was spreading pâté on small round biscuits, and garnishing each of them with a speck of tomato, parsley and crème fraîche. 'I think the words "Upsetting day for you" should cover it perfectly,' she said briskly, and peered again through the little service hatch. 'That's interesting, hardly anyone here from Peter's hotel, I don't suppose they know what the protocol is.'

The lunch party didn't last long, and soon people were saying goodbye to the daughters of the house. Peter Murphy had left, kissing each of his girls on the cheek. He didn't need to come into the kitchen; he never knew that Geraldine was there. The invoice would be presented to his hotel and the cheque in payment for it written immediately. Cathy wondered whether Geraldine was pleased or disappointed by the small turnout at the funeral of the woman whom she must have hated at one time. Geraldine had been involved with Peter Murphy for several years. But it was impossible to know: Geraldine gave little away, she just commented that the daughters had several of their friends there, but that there were hardly any of Mrs Murphy's own cronies out in that room . . .

'Possibly she didn't *have* many friends,' Cathy suggested as she counted the plates. They could only charge for forty-two people.

'Everyone has friends, specially if they live in a big house like this,' said June, as she packed the cutlery into the mesh baskets.

'Not necessarily,' Tom said, as he carefully wrapped up the unused ham.

'I think people get isolated in big places like this. Not that I know, or will ever know,' he grinned.

'It's got nothing to do with the house,' Geraldine said. 'She was in an impossible position. No man, so no escort, and people are afraid of women who lose their men, they think it's catching. And then no job either, nothing to talk about, so she must have been as dull as ditchwater.'

'That sounds very hard, Geraldine,' Tom said, wagging his head at her mock disapprovingly.

'Life *is* very hard, Tom, you had better believe me.' And it was as if a hard mask had come over her face for just a few seconds.

'Will we freeze the ham, or wheel it out again out for Mrs Hayes, do you think?'

Tom and Cathy had dropped Walter off at the top of Grafton Street, where he was going to spend his pittance, as he called his three hours' wages. They were driving June back with them to the premises. Her pittance was for five hours, since she was to stack the dishwashers and help tidy up.

'Mrs who?'

'The lady that had chocolate all over her face has given us a very nice job, as it happens, for her silver wedding, just because I rescued her.'

'Oh, yes, of course, you're great with the charm. No, let's freeze this fellow, I say. They want gooey things, lots of creamy sauces. A nice lean ham would be much too healthy for them.'

Cathy looked at him questioningly and he nodded. They were, as so often, in agreement; Tom had the label written and dated and the ham placed on the right shelf of the freezer. They turned on the answering machine: three requests for brochures, one girl asking if they had any vacancies, since she would like to pursue a career in catering.

'Pursue!' Cathy laughed. 'Why do kids talk like that?'

'Because they think it makes them sound as if they weren't kids,' Tom suggested.

Then there was a booking, a ladies' lunch for eight, just to deliver and leave for the Riordans.

'No address, no phone number. Great. Really, people are so thick,' Tom fumed.

'Come on, Tom, we *know* them. We've been there.'

'We have?' he looked at Cathy in puzzlement. They hadn't been to all that many houses. Not so many that he could afford to forget the names of clients.

'*You* know, we did the christening there, you kept referring to him afterwards as Mr Bloody Family Man.'

'Oh, *him*, yes indeed. I've blanked his name deliberately from my mind,' Tom said.

'Well mercifully we haven't blanked them out of the computer,' Cathy said. 'What will we give them?'

'A lecture on the subject that there ain't no good in men,' Tom offered.

'No, silly. To eat. And anyway, that's not true. There's plenty of good in men. My father's buying a puppy for the twins to keep in St Jarlath's Crescent, though he'll have to do all the work training it and cleaning up after it. My husband has got us two great tickets for the opera tonight, even though he doesn't really like it. James Byrne's going to give up his Sunday morning to do the books for us just because we couldn't meet him today. My business partner, also a man, is going to stay here and lock up on his own for me, so I haven't one thing against men at the moment,' she laughed at him.

'Why am I going to stay and lock up, remind me?' Tom asked.

'Because the love of *your* life is going to be at the gym all evening while the love of *my* life is busy thinking up reasons why we might not go to *Lucia di Lammermoor*, and I'd better be home to head him off at the pass.'

There was a note on the table. 'Now I *know* you'll think I'm trying to wriggle out of culture, but when you hear what's happened you'll agree . . .' A perfectly legal advice bureau was being threatened, and the solicitors said that the presence of a barrister would definitely make the authorities think again. There might even be a press conference . . . He was sorry . . . very sorry. He would make it up to her. The tickets were on the table. Could she find someone else? Cathy was furious. Could she find someone else to dress up and go to the opera with her at five o'clock in the evening? What world did he live in? She could feel the start of tears of annoyance and disappointment, but she fought them back. This wasn't a major-league thing. Not like all the real battlefields she had been on before . . . Not like the times that Hannah had sneered at her and said that she would only marry Neil over the dead bodies of herself, her husband, anyone who knew them. This wasn't as big as Hannah laughing loudly behind her back in a voice intended to carry, patronising her, saying she was the poor cleaner's daughter. This wasn't like wanting to take a job and live overseas. It was only about a night out.

However, who else could she ask at this late notice? June? At the opera? Forget it. Geraldine? Geraldine with her active social life was sure to have a date on a Saturday night. Cathy pulled the phone towards her. She'd call Geraldine.

'Geraldine?'

'You have another job for me, is that it?'

'Would you like to stand in for Neil at the opera tonight? I have a spare ticket.'

'I'd love it. Is it sad?'

'Pretty hopeless set-up, yes. Heroine marries a guy she doesn't love, she kills him. The guy she *does* love kills himself. That sort of thing, low in communication skills, fairly typical of opera.'

'Fairly typical of life, I'd say,' Geraldine said crisply.

'I'll take you to Quentins for supper afterwards.'

'It's a deal.'

*

They laughed with Brenda Brennan about the whole steak and kidney adventure. They saw Shona Burke having dinner with two of the senior Haywards people.

'I wish that girl would smile more,' Geraldine said.

'She's got quite a bit to smile about. Apartments at Glenstar don't come cheap; good job, good looks. Tom said he saw her up at the hospital visiting someone when his father had that heart attack. I did ask her about it, but she sort of clammed up on me.'

'She's good at her job but no warmth there,' Geraldine said. 'You did a fantastic job, today. I was very proud of you.'

'No, don't try to slip out of it. Were you pleased not to see a big crowd there, before?'

'No, I was indifferent really, just objectively interested, that's all.'

'But if you loved him once, you can't have been totally indifferent. You must have ... felt something.'

'I never loved Peter Murphy,' Geraldine said simply.

'But weren't you...' Cathy's voice trailed away.

'Certainly I was ... for over five years, but that doesn't mean I loved him.'

'At the time it must have seemed like love,' Cathy said.

'No, not for me.'

'Then what ... Why...' Cathy stopped again. 'I'm sorry Geraldine, it's none of my business.'

'No, I don't mind ... I was having a nice time with a pleasant companion who also introduced me to a lot of people and helped me build my business up. And why? I suppose I'd just say why not? *And* he got me the apartment in Glenstar.'

Cathy looked at her. 'He *got* it for you?'

'You're a big girl now, Cathy, you have your own business, stop being the round-eyed innocent with me.'

Cathy spoke with spirit. 'I'm not playing the innocent. I'm just surprised that you'd take a present, well, like a luxury flat from a man. That's all.'

'If people want to give me presents, I should throw them back?'

'Of course not, but a *flat*, Geraldine.'

'It was the same builder who was putting up Glenstar at the time as he was doing his hotel extension, and it didn't cost him as much as it would have cost other people. It was very generous, though, and as you know, we have always remained good friends.'

'But he doesn't think he can come round and...'

'No, of course he doesn't, Cathy. Please.'

'But wasn't it an odd thing for him to do? I mean, most men don't do things like that, do they?'

'I find that most men do,' Geraldine said, giving the matter some thought. 'People do give me things. I got the car as a present, and that CD player you admire so much.'

'You got all those things from different men at different times? I just don't believe you! You're having me on.'

'Not at all. Why would I make a joke about something like this? It's a fact. Do you think less of me?' Geraldine asked.

'No, *no*, of course not,' Cathy said emphatically. But she did. Greatly less. The aunt that she had so much admired, the gritty woman who had made it all on her own from a working-class background to a position of power and elegance turned out to be no more than what in the past was called a courtesan. She was getting presents for sex. It was one small step away from being paid for it.

'Good, I'd hate you to get all pious on me.'

'Me? Pious? Never,' said Cathy with a weak grin.

Geraldine had paid for a secondary education which Muttie and Lizzie thought to this day was a scholarship. Geraldine had bought the school uniform and listened sympathetically when Cathy said she wanted to learn the catering trade from the bottom up, and then provided the fees for the catering course when the time came. Geraldine had been her ally when she had come home from Greece with the amazing news that she was in love with Neil Mitchell, son of the hated Hannah, and had helped her calm Lizzie down . . . It was Geraldine who had been guarantor for the Scarlet Feather loan without hesitation. There was no way that Cathy was going to go all pious on her aunt. She sought to change the subject, and looked down at Geraldine's wrist.

'Hey, is that a new watch? It's gorgeous.'

'It *is* nice, isn't it.' Geraldine twisted it to make it catch the light. 'It's a lovely little setting, tiny seed pearls and a nice gold bracelet. That nice estate agent Freddie Flynn gave it to me last week. It was very sweet of him.'

'Was it good . . . all the screeching?' Tom asked early on Monday morning.

'What? Oh, great, just great.'

'And did Neil catch any sleep at all while he was there?'

'No, he wouldn't dare,' Cathy said. Why had she lied and pretended Neil had been there? It wasn't a lie exactly. It was more a matter of loyalty. It would have been very complicated to explain to Tom just how hard Neil worked, and how much he had regretted having to pull out of the opera. Easier to let it be. It was an unimportant white lie which would never come to light.

They had all the food they could freeze for the silver wedding ready.

'I might even buy you a beer just to get us out of here . . .' Tom began, as someone knocked on the door. He went out to answer it. It was Neil.

'I was in the area, so I thought if I offered my wife lunch she might forgive me for standing her up at the opera,' he called out.

Cathy came out to the front room.

'So will you forgive me?'

'There was nothing to forgive, I *told* you that. There wasn't even a row, Neil, none of this is necessary.' She was so mortified she could hardly speak.

'It *is* necessary. I promised something I didn't deliver. Can I deliver a lunch instead?'

'Go, Cathy. Go to one of the posher places and steal ideas,' Tom urged.

'See are there any exciting breads out there, ask to see the whole breadbasket and take one of everything, anything new, bring it back. Okay?'

She took off her Scarlet Feather overall, put on her jacket and got into the van.

'Won't we take the car, maybe?' he suggested.

'It's pure advertising, Neil, we can park it somewhere down near the quays where everyone will see it. See you, Tom.'

They sat opposite each other in a very trendy place. They only got in because it was a Monday, and gradually she got over her annoyance. It wasn't his fault. He really *did* feel badly about letting her down. She insisted that she had enjoyed her dinner with Geraldine.

'And now I get to have lunch with you as well, so I won out as it happens,' she said cheerfully.

'What did Geraldine have to say?' Neil asked.

'Not a lot, we just rambled on about everything.'

Cathy wondered why she hadn't told him about Geraldine's extraordinary lifestyle. Normally she told Neil everything. She decided yet again that it had something to do with loyalty. She wondered did this mean she would be lying constantly from now on.

'They've heard from the missing Uncle Kenneth.'

'I don't believe it, where is he?'

'On the high seas coming home, apparently.'

'And what about Aunt Kay in the funny farm?'

'Getting stronger by the minute, I hear.'

There was a lump of lead in Cathy's chest. 'It doesn't mean they'll be in any shape to take Maud and Simon back?' she asked fearfully.

'Well, not this very moment I'd say, but of course they will have to go back sometime, Cathy.'

Cathy was aware of her very mixed feelings. It would be wonderful not to have to worry about Simon and Maud any more. Yet these people were not going to look after their children properly. She had taught them some manners, some fear of upsetting others, her Mam and Dad had taught them love and friendship. It seemed a terrible waste to see it all washed away when Kenneth and Kay came back for whatever time suited them. The return of the prodigal parents had always been something for which she had devoutly hoped. Now that it was beginning to be a reality, Cathy was not so sure.

'They're okay, the parents, do you think?' she asked Neil.

'As good as can be expected,' he said. 'Anyway.' He was changing the subject. She looked at him. 'Anyway, none of that is really important. You and I have to talk about the job,' Neil said.

'Tom, it's Walter. Can I come in and have a word?'

Tom swallowed the sandwich he was eating and pressed the buzzer to let him in. The boy was basically harmless, Tom thought. No hard worker, a little over-swift to find his jacket at the end of a job rather than help carry the plates and glasses out to the van. A little snobby towards June and her pronunciation of words. Still, it suited them at the moment to employ him as a barman. He was reasonably personable, charming to the younger women and if he could only concentrate more, remembering who was drinking what, then he would have been fine. They had decided not to ask him to do the Hayes silver wedding. Instead they were going to try out a barman they had met, a red-headed boy called Con with a friendly smile, who managed to give the impression that he loved what he was doing.

'Cathy not here?' Walter looked around him, hand in pocket. Slightly quizzical, almost as if he had been let down. Tom remembered that he and Cathy had agreed in a whisper that Walter had this slightly annoying body language, as if he were conferring some kind of favour and wished the whole thing could be dealt with as quickly as possible.

'No, but she'll be back soon.'

'That's Neil's car in the yard?'

'Yes, he'll be back soon too. Can I do anything for you in the meantime?'

'This gig, this do ... whatever ... What time's it at?'

'I'm not with you,' Tom said.

'The big function on Wednesday. I want to know, is it dinner jacket for me to wear, and what time should I turn up?'

'I don't think we made any arrangement ...' Tom began.

'It's just that I was hoping you could give me something in advance now ... Towards getting geared up and all.'

Cathy would *not* have booked her husband's cousin without telling him. In fact, she had been more vehement against Walter than he had been. She had been quite outraged that he had called his wages a pittance. There had to have been a misunderstanding here. It was tempting to say that they should wait until Cathy came back to sort it out. But Tom knew he couldn't do that.

'We didn't book you for Wednesday,' he said, much more confidently than he felt.

'What?'

'Just that. We didn't book you, Walter, so there's no question of any advance, I'm afraid. I'm sorry if you got the wrong end of the stick.'

'Don't talk to me about wrong ends of sticks, you told me all about it, you spoke about it in front of me – what was I meant to think?'

'What are *we* meant to think, Walter? You describe the wages we give you as a pittance, you don't enjoy the work. How were we meant to be inspired with the idea that you want to work at the Hayes silver wedding?'

'Oh, this is what it's all about. It was a joke, it's what people do, they make jokes. They don't expect people to take a light-hearted remark seriously. But now I see it's a matter of bowing down to the ground and thanking you from the bottom of my heart for the privilege of being allowed to work with you.'

Tom thought that Cathy had been gone for an age, how long could one lunch take? Was she ever coming back?

*

In the restaurant, Cathy looked at Neil across the table.

'The job? The one they were going to offer you abroad?'

'Yes, and still are. You and I sort of got started on it the wrong way. I wanted to tell you what it's all about.'

'Do,' she said.

'No, not if you're going to put on that clipped tone with me.'

'Neil, I said tell me about it.'

'Please don't let's begin by being so hostile about it.'

'I have no idea how to ask you to tell me about this job without apparently insulting you or offending you, so why don't you just please *tell* me all about it?'

Just then, of course, they had to order. Neil was uncaring about what he ate, but Cathy wanted to taste different things, so she spent time making the choices.

'It doesn't matter,' he said when the waitress asked if they would like a cocktail.

'I'd love one of those silvery things over there with the frosting on the glass,' Cathy said.

'Why do you want that?' Neil was amazed.

'We're doing this silver wedding. You know, I told you all about it. This drink might be just the thing,' she said.

And she waited while he told her about the chance to change the whole thrust of immigration law. It was new and exciting, and it would be so great to be in on the ground floor when it was happening, and it mattered so much. And when all came to all there was only so much individuals could do on the ground in their own countries. What was needed was a proper policy up and running in the international institutions, not something that was controlled by politicians whose own interests could change, but by lawyers and social workers who cared. Cathy listened. Too often countries with perfectly good records on civil liberties looked the other way when there was oil involved, or if they were selling arms to the area, or if they were conscious of votes at home depending on the number of foreigners you let into your country. This agency would be above all that, it would be international, it would change the thinking of the world.

'Where from?' Cathy asked.

'Initially The Hague,' he said.

'You want us to live in Holland?'

'There will be travel, of course, and you can come with me, that's all agreed. You'll see places, Cathy, places that you never dreamed of.'

'What will you do every day, Neil? Try to give me a picture of how the day would break down.' Her voice felt disembodied; she needed to buy time to think about this. He really and truly did want to go, and expected that she would drop everything and go with him. She didn't listen as he struggled to paint a picture of how he saw their days shaping out. She wondered instead if anyone truly knew anyone else. This man opposite her who had defied his parents with icy indifference to their arguments when they had objected to his marrying her, now wanted to uproot her from the business she had slaved to form and take her away to be some kind of diplomat's wife. She heard words somewhere around her in the air as she tasted the bread which was ordinary and the tomato butter which was over the top. The silvery cocktail was a disaster – they would not even suggest it for the Hayes celebration.

'You're very quiet,' Neil said eventually.

'I'm thinking about it, letting it all sink in.'

'I knew you would, if we had time. Back in Waterview you had boxing gloves up in the air in confrontation, your-job-my-job sort of thing. It's not about that, it's about our life.'

'Yes, yes.' She spoke almost dreamily.

'What do you mean, Cathy?'

'Well, you're right, it is about life. Would you go without me, on your own, to live your life out there, just suppose I couldn't go?'

'But that's not what we're talking about. You can go if you want to,' he was bewildered.

'I'm trying to work out how you see your life. Would you go alone?'

'No, I wouldn't do that. You know that, don't you?'

'I'm just asking. So you'd stay here and go on with the way things are?' she insisted.

'Yes, but, well ... Yes, I suppose.'

'I see.'

'But it's not like that, Cathy. You can go, and believe me, I know you'll love it. They want you to come out with me for a week. Very soon, just to see first-hand where we'd be living and the kind of work that's involved. Cathy, you *love* a challenge, it's written all over you ...'

'We need a lot more discussion about this. A lot more,' she said, her voice still sounding unreal in her own ears.

'Of course we do.' He patted her hand.

Neil seemed to think the conversation had gone well. He called for the bill and they left. Cathy had parked the van precariously on a corner. She saw a traffic warden looking in its direction, and raced her to the vehicle.

'I won,' she laughed, clambering into the driving seat.

'What's Scarlet Feather ... is it a mattress?' the traffic warden asked.

'It's the best catering company in Ireland,' Cathy said, and got the van into gear and away from there at speed.

To their surprise, Walter was installed at the premises and Cathy noticed that Tom was looking hassled.

'Hey, are you better?' Neil asked Walter.

'Yeah, I'm okay,' Walter said, shrugging.

'What was wrong?' Cathy asked.

'He had a fall and hurt his back,' Neil explained. 'Dad was telling me this morning. He's been out of the office a week.'

Tom and Cathy looked at each other. They knew there had been no fall, but they said nothing. At that moment the phone rang. It was Mrs Hayes. They had decided they wanted two waiters for Wednesday. One to stay entirely behind the bar, the other to go round and refresh drinks. Would that be any problem?

'No problem at all, Mrs Hayes, it will be done straight away.' Tom hung up. He turned round to look at Walter. 'Usual pittance Wednesday, Walter, turn up here at six-thirty to help stack the van, no money up front, no need to hire a dinner jacket, you already have one. Okay?'

'Okay,' Walter said smiling. 'I knew you really meant me to work.'

'No we didn't, the situation just changed. We have Con, who is our waiter for Wednesday, you're just the back-up. That's if your own back will be all right by then?'

'Are you going back to the Four Courts?' Walter asked his cousin Neil. 'If you are, I'd love a lift.'

'Are you back at work then?' Neil was confused.

'No, but I have to see someone down that area.'

Tom was relieved that Walter was going to go. 'Did you two have a good lunch?' he asked.

'No. Breads we tried, and boy did we try them ... Weren't anything compared to yours, Tom,' Cathy said cheerfully. And Neil muttered agreement.

'Great news.' Tom was pleased. 'The show can stay on the road for another few weeks, then.'

When they were gone Cathy sat down and looked at him. 'Sorry, Tom.'

'About what? We know Walter's a little shit, but they *want* two ...'

'Not about that, about lying to you, about saying Neil *was* at the opera when he wasn't.'

'Oh, that ...' Tom appeared to have forgotten it totally.

But she went on. 'It was stupid, but you knew how much I was looking forward to it and I suppose I just ... didn't want you to think he'd let me down.'

Tom seemed to think she was making heavy weather of it all. 'Poor Neil couldn't face all the screeching when it came to it, was it? Can't say I blame him.'

Muttie had planned the surprise for weeks. And he wanted as many people to witness it as possible. So he asked Cathy and Neil if they could drop in about six o'clock on Tuesday, and Geraldine. It didn't really suit anyone, but they all made an effort. The little black Labrador puppy was going to be in the house already hidden on newspapers up in the bedroom. And then the conversation would be brought around gradually to dogs. Maud and Simon would say yet again how much they'd love a puppy, and Muttie would say excuse me, I think we *do* have one for you. Lizzie would say that it's nonsense, there couldn't possibly be a dog in the house without her knowing, and then Muttie would produce the little fellow ...

It didn't suit Cathy because she and Tom had to collect their dishes from the Riordan ladies' lunch in order to use them again for the Hayes silver wedding. Sometime they would have enough china and ovenproof dishes not to have to call everything in, but not yet. It didn't suit Geraldine because Freddie Flynn said he might be able to call round to the Glenstar apartment for an hour or two after work. But there was something magical about the thought of Muttie and this pedigree dog which had cost him over a hundred pounds. So they all tried to fit in. Lizzie would hurry back from her last cleaning job of the day. Geraldine told Freddie that she'd be a little delayed but would be back at the apartment by 6.45. Neil said he'd try to be there, but he'd have to be out of St Jarlath's Crescent by 6.30, just so long as everyone knew. Cathy said that she and Tom could call there for a while before they went to pick up the dishes at Mrs Riordan's.

'Is something happening?' Simon asked when they all sat down at the kitchen table.

'Why do you say that?' Lizzie asked.

'Well, everyone here's sort of waiting,' said Simon.

'No, Simon, we're sitting round a table having tea.'

Cathy continued her attempt to improve the twins' manners. 'And making general conversation rather than centring everything on ourselves. That's what people do, you see.'

'Is everybody all right for sugar and milk?' Maud said obediently.

Muttie cleared his throat. 'There's nothing better than a family sitting down round a table,' he began. 'All over Dublin there's people sitting down to their tea now, watched by their cats and their budgies and their dogs.' He looked around him proudly, as if this was a perfectly normal remark to make out of the blue ... He waited, but the children said nothing. They looked at him solemnly.

Tom felt he had to fill in the gap in the conversation. 'You've got a point there, Muttie, a family could be watched by all kinds of things, a hamster, a rabbit, well, from its hutch if the angle was right, and a dog, of course.'

Still not a word from Maud and Simon.

Muttie was desperate now. 'But there was never a dog in this house, of course, not having been in the past a family of dog lovers.'

'No, that's right,' Lizzie shouted as if reading lines from a play. Then the twins leaped up.

'It *is*,' cried Simon.

'I *knew* it,' shouted Maud, and they were out of the room in a flash and up the stairs towards the main bedroom. There were sounds of barks and screams and snuffles, and then they arrived carrying the puppy. It looked like a toy, all black fur and wagging tail and panting breath.

'It's beautiful,' said Maud.

'It's a he, I looked.' Simon was holding the puppy and looking again in case there should be any misunderstanding.

'Is it for us?' Simon asked, hardly daring to hope.

'It's for the pair of you,' Muttie said gruffly.

'To keep for ever?' Maud said, unbelieving.

'Sure, of course.'

'We've never had an animal, a real animal,' Simon said.

'There was a tortoise at The Beeches but he went away,' Maud said. 'And you know we were hoping you might get a dog. And only today...'

'We heard it whimpering inside the door,' Simon took up the story.

'And I said maybe it was a puppy.' Maud wanted to show how bright she had been in identifying the dog.

'And I said yes, Muttie *could* have got himself a puppy, but also it could be just some old person groaning and grunting on the floor of Muttie's bedroom and we'd better not go in.' Simon also needed praise for the great control that he had shown.

'But we never knew it was for us,' Maud said.

'For ever,' Simon said.

Cathy realised that this was the moment when the twins actually changed their personality. And everyone else seemed to think the same. The way they stroked it and laughed aloud at its antics would melt the hardest heart. They had the little animal on the table now, flopping about on its fat little paws. Tom put a newspaper under him, just in time, and people hastily took their cups of tea and biscuits away.

'He's just beautiful,' said Maud again.

'And he's very intelligent, too. Did you find him on the street or somewhere?' Simon asked innocently.

'Aw, well, I sort of went out and chose him, you see, he's yours now, he's for the two of you,' Muttie said, beaming all over his face.

'Dad went out to a kennels and bought him for you,' Cathy said proudly.

'And Lizzie went out to work so that she could pay for the vet's fees for injections and everything...' said Geraldine.

'And we'll show you now how to train him,' said Lizzie.

'You just keep pulling the newspapers nearer the door every day, well, that's what they used to do at Oaklands.'

'And what are you going to call him?' Tom wanted to know.

The puppy looked up as if interested to know as well. 'Hooves,' said Simon, and Maud nodded eagerly. There was a silence.

'Hooves Mitchell,' Maud elaborated, in case they hadn't understood.

'Yes Maud, but normally dogs don't get called by their surname, so he'll just be Hooves for most of the time, okay,' Cathy said.

'Okay,' said Maud.

'And ... umm ... why exactly did you think of this ... um ... interesting name?' Tom voiced everyone's thoughts.

The children were surprised that they didn't understand something so obvious. 'It's what Muttie always says is the best thing in the world ... the thundering hooves that match your heartbeat,' said Simon.

Muttie blew his nose very loudly.

'And when they're off...' said Maud, 'then the sound of those hooves touches your soul.'

Neil called Cathy on the mobile just as they were leaving.

'I'm so sorry.'

'It doesn't matter, Neil, nobody expected you to be there, and it was great, they just love the puppy...'

'That's what I was calling about, Cathy. They can't go on living in this fool's paradise. Uncle Kenneth is back cleaning up The Beeches, Kay is getting out of hospital at the weekend . . . This can't last here, all this make-believe.'

'It's not make-believe, it's a home. What kind of a home is that uncle of yours making for children?'

'According to Dad and Walter, who've been dragged in to help, not too bad a fist of it. Walter even suggested that they get some food from you for the freezer.'

'I'll tell them what to do with food for the freezer,' Cathy said.

'Cathy, please, we'll talk later.'

'Sure.'

Geraldine was leaving then too.

'Sorry I can't stay longer, Cathy, Freddie's coming round for a drink. I was going to cook an elegant dinner for him tomorrow night – he usually drops by on a Wednesday, but he has to go to some do, poor love.'

'No, *I'm* leaving too. Listen, do you want some posh canapés? I have a box in the van.'

'You're an angel, just the thing.'

Geraldine was gone in minutes, her smart red car taking the corner of St Jarlath's Crescent sharpish.

Tom came out then, and they got into the van. 'Wasn't it fabulous to see their faces,' he said.

'Yeah.'

'What is it?'

She told him.

'The courts, the social workers?' Tom began.

'Love the biological parents, apparently.'

'Even if they're fruitcakes?'

'So it seems.'

'You'll miss them,' he said simply.

'I'll miss them, certainly – but can you see Muttie walking that floppy hound called Hooves round for the rest of his life? He'll be devastated.'

'Won't they take it with them? The dog?'

'No – those two would freak if they had to cope with a dog as well as children.'

'But surely they'll go on visiting St Jarlath's Crescent a lot?'

'Kenneth Mitchell's son, going to a working-class area? Never! They'd be afraid they'd learn a common accent *and* get fleas!'

'It's just not fair,' Tom said. They were driving up to the Riordans' house as he said this. There were definite sounds of a party.

'There's another thing that's not fair,' Cathy said. 'They swore they'd be finished by five o'clock, *now* what will we do?'

'Leave it to me,' Tom said.

'Oh, I'll leave it to you willingly, but you're not going to go in and take Mr Riordan by the neck and shout at him about being Mr Family Man, are you?'

'No, this is a different task altogether. Stay in the van, have a sleep. It might take half an hour.'

She heard Tom rummaging in the back of the van for something and then saw him running up the steps with a package. Cathy closed her eyes. It had been a long, upsetting day and she was nervous about tomorrow's silver wedding. Still, this *was* her choice, she must never forget that.

Mrs Riordan came to the door. She looked at him guiltily. 'Oh, God, is that the time?' she said.

'Must have been a wonderful party.' Tom nailed his happiest, most enthusiastic smile to his face.

'What? Yes, they're all in good form.'

'Can I go in and say hallo to the ladies, I brought them a gift,' he beamed at her.

'What? Yes, of course, come in.'

'Good evening, ladies,' he said pleasantly to a group of eleven women who had drunk too much wine but who had also, he was pleased to see, eaten almost all the food provided. 'I thought you'd like . . .' he began.

'A stripper!' screamed one of the women happily.

'Sadly no,' he said hastily. 'I've hurt my back. I wouldn't be able to give you a proper performance at all, but I *did* come with a gift of petits fours and chocolates to thank Mrs Riordan for using our food . . . So here's a box to divide among you.'

They thought this was wonderful, and even though they said he was terrible to be giving them things that contained four hundred calories a bite, they ate them all the same.

'And while I'm here, why don't I give you more room to enjoy things?' Adroitly he started to clear the table. The women rushed to help him, and they scraped the plates. In the kitchen, they saw him begin to stack them in the crate.

'We must wash them first,' Mrs Riordan said.

'No, no, we do that back at base, all part of the service,' he said.

But they insisted. A sinkful of hot, soapy water, another for rinsing, two ladies drying. The party was in the kitchen now.

'Your back doesn't look all that bad to me,' said the woman who had hoped Tom was a stripper.

'Wait till I'm on real form,' he said to her roguishly, and she blushed with excitement.

They helped him carry the boxes down to the van, where Cathy leaped out in disbelief and began to stow them away. At that moment Mr Riordan's car came into the drive.

'Thank God the place isn't looking like a bomb-site, you're a pair of angels,' said Mrs Riordan, pushing two twenty-pound notes at them. 'Go on, go out and have a drink on me.'

Mr Riordan nodded at them. 'Looks as if it was all a good lunch,' he said grudgingly.

'Oh, the food was all right but I think they rather liked me as a stripper for most of the afternoon.'

'You're making this up,' the man spluttered.

'Well, you're never going to know, are you, Mr Riordan? After all, they're obviously going to say it didn't happen, aren't they?' Cathy and Tom laughed all the way to the city.

'Will we drop in on the reception after Neil's lecture? There'll be warm white wine and cold sausages provided by one of the faculty wives,' Cathy said.

'Sure, will I call Marcella? She should be home by now, we could pick her up on the way, she might like an outing too.'

'Great idea.'

They spent the forty pounds in a Chinese restaurant. Cathy noticed that Marcella had three prawns, no rice, no stir fry, no sweet and sour pork. Tom noticed that Neil was concerned because the Chinese waiters were probably not in trade unions. They told the story of Hooves.

'Isn't The Beeches a big house with a garden?' Marcella asked. 'They might be able to have it with them there.'

'Not until it's trained, it would run straight out on the road and be killed,' Cathy said.

'But maybe they won't be going back there for ages.'

Neil said that it would be much sooner than anyone thought; the law actually did move quickly in restoring children to their homes.

'It seems a pity if they're happy where they are,' said Tom, who had been touched by the family scene in St Jarlath's.

'That's not the point.' Neil was very strong on that. 'Years ago, children were always being taken from their homes and given to people who would so-called improve them . . . At least nowadays the importance of the birth parents is actually recognised.'

Cathy thought that this was being over-recognised in this particular case. But she said nothing. There were so many other things to be discussed with Neil, and a rare meal out for the four of them was not going to become a battleground over Simon and Maud.

The Hayes household was up to high doh when they arrived at six-thirty. Two discontented sons who lived at home were hanging around, unsure of what to do. An equally discontented daughter attached to what looked like a young man mightily disapproved of by her parents was saying that it was inconceivable and intolerable that there was no way she could use the ironing board in the kitchen, where it had always been used. Mrs Hayes said they were to call her Molly, and her husband was Shay. He was a plump, somewhat anxious man, who was obviously a hard taskmaster at the business he ran, and felt the need to bark out orders on this occasion as well.

'Shay, can I make us all a quick cup of coffee and briefly run through the agenda with you?' asked Tom.

Meanwhile, Cathy had switched on the kettle, asked June to help get the ironing board and iron up to the spare room, got the boys to put the two

Persian cats into a place with a litter tray and a bowl of food, a place from which they could not emerge and eat the trifle or shed hairs on the salmon. By the time the kettle had boiled Cathy had persuaded Molly that the main thing was for her to go upstairs and rest with her feet slightly raised. Cathy had even brought her a cold mask for her eyes, it worked wonders, she said.

'But setting everything up . . . ?' Molly begged.

'Is exactly what you are paying us well to do, and believe me we will do it,' Cathy said firmly.

She heard Tom telling Shay that they had a chain of command, a checklist, a routine to follow and it was wise if they were left to themselves to do it. He had always thought it good for the family to come down at seven-thirty, half an hour before the first guests arrived, so that they could examine everything and check it was all in order. Shay nodded, it made sense. And soon the Hayes family, fuelled with coffee, had all gone to their rooms. Tom and Cathy got into action, the food was unpacked, the conveyor belt for canapés was under way with June and her friend Helen. The buffet tables were set up. The ashtrays were placed in the conservatory where smoking was allowed, the cake was unwrapped and placed on a silver stand. The creamy dessert which needed to have the number 25 written on it with toasted almonds was produced, the salads were filling up the great glass bowls that had been rescued last night from the Riordans'. It was all going according to plan. At exactly seven o'clock the two barmen arrived. Con, the cheerful redhead they had spotted in a pub, and Walter, sulkier and moodier than ever.

'They'll be having champagne cocktails to start,' Cathy explained.

'How naff,' Walter said.

Cathy's face was hard. 'I'm never sure exactly what that word means. You know how to do them, and fill them up very shortly before the guests arrive with champagne.'

'Or what passes for champagne,' said Walter, lifting up a bottle and letting it slip back again into the case.

Cathy now addressed herself entirely to Con and not to Walter. 'I'd like you to get forty glasses ready in this way, and can you see that Walter opens twelve bottles of white and twelve bottles of red, the white goes into the big ice box outside the kitchen door, and after they're down to four then open the bottles in fours from then on, and . . .'

'Excuse me, Cathy, do you have a problem talking to me? Perhaps you don't want me here. Should I leave?' He looked so supercilious she wanted to hit him. He knew that she couldn't let him go now. Not just before the guests arrived. He could be as rude as he liked. Or could he? Neil was at home tonight – in a real emergency he would certainly come and help. She moved slightly away so that Con, the new boy, would not hear every word of the family row.

'Either change your attitude or get your coat,' she said crisply.

'I don't think you are in a position—'

'I'm in every position, I'm hiring you.'

'And where will you get a replacement at this hour?'

'Your cousin,' she said simply, and took out her mobile phone.

'Neil? You wouldn't.'

She began dialling.

'Okay, sorry, I was out of order.'

'No, I'm sorry, Walter, I can't rely on you. This is a big job for us.'

Suddenly he realised that she meant it. She really was going to ask Neil Mitchell the barrister to put on a dinner jacket and serve booze to these people. His uncle, who was also his boss, would kill him. His recent returned father, who was also his only other means of support, would kill him.

'I beg you, Cathy, you have my word,' he said.

'It had better be a very good word,' she said, and went and left him.

'Walter's actually doing some work for once,' Tom said admiringly, watching the wine bottles moving swiftly as requested.

'I put the frighteners on him,' Cathy said, with some satisfaction. 'The other boy's good, isn't he, we'll have him again. This is the last of Walter.'

'Will that not cause family strain?' Tom asked.

'No, probably prevent it, in that it will stop me killing Walter with my bare hands and messing up the kitchen,' Cathy said.

'Cooking is meant to have great elements of patience and calm about it,' Tom marvelled. 'You haven't a calm, patient cell in your body.'

'Cooking is also meant to have a certain fire about it, and I'm full of that,' said Cathy.

Just then the Hayes family all appeared downstairs. The fussing was going to start again.

'We have a little tradition, which is to take a family photograph before everyone comes, while the whole place is peaceful, and coincidentally when the food looks at its best,' said Tom, and he posed them next to the cake by the buffet table, accepting their first champagne cocktail of the night.

They saw the hosts beginning to relax, and by the time the first visitor arrived they had agreed that the house looked beautiful, and the food, and that it would be a good evening. Only an hour in they knew it was going to be a roaring success. Even Walter was moving swiftly from group to group, topping up drinks and talking pleasantly. 'Fantastic, these things,' said Shay to everyone about the trays of roast beef and Yorkshire pudding. It was in fact little choux pastries each filled with horseradish sauce and cream and a small slice of cold rare beef. People couldn't stop eating them.

'Did you invent these, Cathy?' a man asked her.

It was Freddie Flynn, her aunt's friend. Mrs Flynn was there, small and jewelled. Cathy looked at the woman's wrist; her watch was plain compared to Geraldine's. She smiled at them both.

'Mr Flynn, Mrs Flynn, thank you so much, no, alas I didn't invent them, but I did see them somewhere and remembered them! Is that as good?'

'Certainly,' he said. He had a nice smile. 'Darling, this is Cathy Feather, she's a sort of cousin of Geraldine, you know, who does our PR. Be nice to

Cathy and she might just do more work for us, and Cathy, this is my wife Pauline.'

'You might do *our* silver wedding when the time comes,' the woman said.

'Oh indeed, we'd be honoured. It was wonderful to meet you, now excuse me, I must see that everyone . . .'

She moved away, seething. He was darlinging his wife at every opportunity. They were going to have a silver wedding party. And according to Geraldine, this was meant to be a dead marriage. So poor Freddie was perfectly entitled to have his fun elsewhere, since there was nothing for them at home. God, it would make you sick.

The party went better than anyone could have hoped. Molly had said wistfully that she thought they would all feel too old to dance, but Tom had brought the *Best of Abba* for them just in case. First he put on Leo Sayer, 'When I Need You' and then 'Don't Cry For Me Argentina' and 'Mull Of Kintyre'. Nice and low but insistent in the background, and when he heard people humming and joining in the choruses and when the desserts had been cleared away, he let rip with 'Mamma Mia' and they were all on their feet.

Tom and Cathy paused to have a coffee in the kitchen. Around them the dishes had been collected and stacked. The two barmen had skilfully retrieved the Scarlet Feather glasses and replaced them with those that belonged to the house. Soon it would be midnight, time to pay them their five hours. Shay Hayes had also left an envelope for the staff, so there would be good pickings tonight. Cathy had brought a silver polish cloth with her to shine up the four solid-silver ladles that Molly Hayes had insisted on using. They had been a wedding present, she said, they must be shown off.

The van had been filled, the ashtrays had been emptied, open bottles left on the tables, the kitchen was immaculate and only a hard core of ten people remained to celebrate still further. Tom could pick up the CDs when he came round tomorrow to finalise things and present his account. Con asked if he could speak to Tom for a moment. The boy drew him away a little.

'Very awkward, this,' he began.

'What?' Tom hoped that Con wasn't going to ask for more money; he had been such a good waiter all night. They need never have that young pup Walter again.

'It's just that . . . This is a hard thing to say . . . but I think you should have a look at that sports bag over there if you know what I mean. God, I hate saying this . . . but I have to.' The boy looked really distressed. Without pausing to ask more, Tom unzipped the bag. There on top of Walter's sweater and jeans were four silver ladles, two silver cruets and an ornate photo frame. His throat constricted with fear.

'Thanks,' he said. 'You go off now, quick as you can. I found this bag myself, do you understand, and thank you again, we'll be in touch.'

'I'm sorry, Mr Feather.'

'So am I,' said Tom.

607

Cathy came back into the kitchen and took off her Scarlet Feather apron. 'Tom, you're a genius, how did you know that was the kind of music they wanted. It's working like a dream, look at them all leaping about to "Dancing Queen". God, I hope we'll be able to do that at their age.'

'Cathy, Walter stole the silver. His sports bag there, filled with their stuff, look for yourself.'

The colour left her face. He hated to do this to her, but there was no other way. He couldn't act until he knew what she would do. Walter was part of Cathy's family set-up, not his.

'Where is he?'

'Still in the dining room, chatting up Molly and Shay's daughter, being glowered at by the girl's boyfriend.'

Cathy took out her mobile.

'What are you doing?' he asked.

'Getting a taxi for June and Helen, there's a taxi rank a couple of minutes away, I took its number.'

'And then?'

'We sort this out here, get the guards if necessary, if he denies it.'

'What would Neil say?'

'I don't know, but I'll let Walter ring him, he's going to need a lawyer over this.'

'You're not going the distance on this?' Tom was amazed at her courage.

'If I can I will.'

'Walter, can I interrupt you for a moment? I need you in the kitchen.' Tom spoke in a low voice.

'Hey, my hours of servitude are over, I'm here on my own time now.'

'Straight away, please.'

When he saw the open bag, Walter began to bluster. 'How *dare* you root in my private things . . .' he began.

'An explanation, Walter.'

'I didn't put them there, *you* did. You both hate me.'

'We haven't touched them. The guards will be here shortly and will tell us whose fingerprints are on them.'

'You're never going to call the guards?' His face was white, but he still thought they were bluffing.

'It's what you have to do in a case of theft.' Cathy lifted her mobile phone again.

'You're going to call them now?'

'No, I'm going to wait for you to call your cousin first because you're going to need someone to speak for you, Walter. It might as well be Neil, that's if he takes you on.'

He looked at her, unbelieving.

'Go on, make the call.'

'I don't know the number.'

'It's pre-set. You just dial one.'

They sat and watched him as he waited until Neil answered. The kitchen door was closed; they could hear both ends of the conversation.

'Neil, sorry . . . sorry for ringing you, it's Walter.'

'What is it? Is Cathy all right, what has happened? Was there an accident?'

'No, actually I'm in a bit of trouble.'

'Where's Cathy?'

'She's here beside me . . . Do you want to talk to her?' Cathy shook her head. 'No, sorry Neil, I have to talk, apparently.'

'Talk then,' the voice said crisply.

'Well there was a bit of a misunderstanding . . . We're still at this house, you see, and Tom went rummaging in my private bag and he found or he says he found some silver there . . . belonging to the house, as it were . . .' Walter paused but there was no response so he had to go on again. 'And now, Neil, they're talking about calling the guards, Tom and Cathy are. Uncle Jock will kill me, you have to help me . . .' Still silence at the other end. 'What will I do?'

'Take off your jacket.'

'What?'

'Take off your jacket and hand it to Tom.'

'I don't think that's going to be any help. What's the point . . . ?'

'Do it, Walter.'

He did it. There was a rattle as he struggled out of his dinner jacket and passed it over to Tom. Tom shook it again. There were silver teaspoons in the pocket, a watch and a paper knife.

'Is it done?' Neil asked.

'Yes, there seem to be . . .'

'I was sure there might have been,' Neil said.

'What happens now?'

'Not up to me, I'm afraid.'

'Who is it up to?' Walter asked fearfully.

'Cathy and Tom and the people whose silver you stole. Do they know yet, by the way?'

'No, and I didn't really steal it, you know.'

'Of course not. Good luck, then.'

'What do you mean, good luck, aren't you going to help me?'

'No, I most certainly am not.'

'Neil you *have* to. I'm family.'

'No, listen to me . . . Cathy's your employer, you stole from her. You could have had her prosecuted, you stupid little shit.'

'Cathy's here, Neil, let me pass you over to her . . . Please, Neil, beg her, beg her.' There were tears running down his face.

'Cathy and Tom run their business, Walter. They had the bad luck to employ a thief. Anything they do is fine with me.' And he hung up.

Tom and Cathy looked at each other. 'Your trouser pockets,' Tom said.

There was a cigarette lighter and some more spoons. He wept and begged, but they spoke as if he weren't there.

'You call it, Tom.' She was very calm.

'No, I won't. I'm not taking on that emotional stuff. Truly I'm not. You wouldn't want to do it if he were Marcella's cousin.'

'That's fair.' There was a silence. 'I want him done for this, every bit of me wants that. There are just two things against it.'

'I'm family,' Walter begged tearfully.

'Shut your face about family,' Cathy said. 'It's that I don't want to spoil Molly and Shay's evening, and I don't want to look those children in the eye and tell them I was the one who put their brother in jail and added to all the problems the unfortunates already have.'

'So you'll not call the guards?' He grabbed at the lifeline he saw.

'Tom?'

'I'm with you,' Tom said.

'Give me back your wages,' she said.

Walter hurried to find them for her.

'No,' Tom said. 'Keep them, you did five hours' work, so you're being paid for it.'

'Thank you Tom,' he looked at the ground.

'Go now,' he said.

'I'm sorry, Cathy.'

'You're just sorry you were caught, Walter.'

'No, funnily enough I was beginning to enjoy it tonight for the first time, seeing the whole operation get under way.'

He spoke with an odd sincerity. 'Why did you do it, Walter? Jock pays you plenty.'

'I'm in debt,' he said.

'Well, look on the bright side . . . At least you're not in the Garda station,' she said.

'I'll never forget this, Cathy.'

'Sure.'

He left. Cathy sat there, very still.

'You were great,' Tom said. 'And Neil was great too.'

'I knew he wouldn't defend Walter,' Cathy said.

'I didn't.' Tom was thoughtful. 'I thought he'd see him as the underdog.'

'No, we were the underdogs, Neil could see that straight away. Our entire business could have gone under because of his little cousin.'

'He has an extraordinary sense of justice,' Tom said admiringly.

'So do you,' Cathy said. 'I'd never have given him tonight's wages, not in a million years. And yet you're right, he did earn them before he started nicking things.'

'Come on, let's go home,' he said, and they got into the van and drove back to the little town house in Waterview where Neil would be waiting up to talk over the night's events with Cathy. And then he would drive himself back to the flat in Stoneyfield where Marcella would also be waiting to know how this, their biggest booking ever, had gone.

'Do you get the feeling this night went on for days and days?' Cathy asked wearily.

'I do, weeks and weeks actually.'

They drove on in silence, then Tom said, 'But compared to a lot of the all-time losers we met tonight, I think you and I are fairly lucky. Or is that me being too over-cheerful?' he asked.

April

Molly Hayes said at lunchtime the next day that she had never enjoyed anything so much, and all her friends had rung to congratulate her. It had been an evening that could so easily have ended differently.

They had worked hard this morning, and it was good to have a little breathing space. They decided to visit Haywards mid-season sale. They found some white blinds with a discreet scarlet trim, and extra lighting strips. The preparations were all done for the two delivery jobs . . . a fancy bridge tea for twelve people, tiny sandwiches and little cakes to go to a private house. They had been ages working out how you put recognisable hearts, diamonds, clubs and spades on each as a motif, but between radishes and black olives as fiddly little decorations they had come up with something acceptable. They also had to sneak a supper to a woman who was pretending to her in-laws that she had cooked this meal herself. She had given them her own dishes, paid in advance – the only rule was that they just leave simple easy-to-follow instructions and never tell anyone that they had been. They would leave her a big jug of spinach soup, a slow-cooked casserole and a lemon tart. It was extremely puzzling to them, but then there was no point whatsoever in criticising her. She was part of the way they earned their living. They felt like children stealing time out of school as they sat down to have a coffee after their buying spree. Cathy saw Shona Burke, sitting alone and reading a book; she was eating a small salad and drinking something from the health juice bar.

'She's an odd mixture, isn't she . . . friendly one minute, shutting you out the next.'

'Yeah, maybe she has a sugar daddy tucked away,' Tom said.

'Why do you say that?'

'How else could she afford a flat in Glenstar?'

'It's only a studio flat, Tom, and they're all like little boxrooms; anyway she could be old money.' Cathy didn't want living in Glenstar being associated with sugar daddies or having gentlemen giving you gifts.

Shona looked lonely. And rather prim. She finished her lunch, closed the book, looked at her watch and was about to go back to her work when she spotted them. She looked a totally different person when she smiled.

'Aha, Scarlet Feather undercover in our café,' she said.

'Your breads are rubbish compared to mine,' Tom teased her.

To his surprise she nodded. 'You're absolutely right, that's what I was saying last Friday at a meeting, lovely soups and salads here but just the plainest and dullest of bread. You know, *that's* how I'm going to get you in here. They can put up a notice saying that the breadbasket is by Scarlet Feather. Listen, there's a meeting tomorrow at ten-thirty. Can you let me have a selection of your best, and I'll suggest it.'

They talked about prices and presentation and quantities and delivery. The enthusiasm was enormous. Shona became anxious about it.

'Don't be too disappointed if it doesn't work, I'll give it my very best shot for you both, I think it would be really good for the restaurant too.'

'You're a star, Shona,' Tom said, gathering up his bags of light fittings.

'Are you back to the kitchens to start baking now?' she laughed.

'No, now I'm going to see my father. I'll go into the premises tomorrow, early. You're not going to get one-day-old bread for your demonstration . . . It's going to be the real thing, fresh-baked, about five different kinds . . .'

'How *is* your father?' Shona always asked.

'Oh, he's fine thanks, Shona, you were very kind to me that night at the hospital. He's taking it a little easier, which is no harm. My mother thinks it's all to do with some prayer she said . . . A bit wearing, but if it works for her . . . why not?' Tom shrugged.

Cathy agreed. 'It's not doing anyone any harm, and she prayed like mad that our business would survive, so won't you be sure to tell her how well we're doing?'

'I will, of course. Listen, I'm going to run up to the salon and see Marcella for a quick word before we go.'

'Don't say anything yet about the bread business,' Shona warned.

'No, of course not. Cathy, will you pay for the coffee out of office funds, and I'll see you in the van in ten minutes.' He was gone. The two women watched him, and saw the admiring glances as he moved like an athlete through the tables, smiling his apologies if he had to push past people.

'He has absolutely no idea the effect he creates,' Cathy said. 'They're all mad about him wherever we go; the young ones are delighted to know that he's not attached to me, and of course all these old dears, they love him to bits and he just hasn't a clue.'

'When he and Marcella go anywhere together they're just like film stars, the pair of them,' Shona said, getting up to leave. 'Listen, let me look after your coffee for you.'

'No, no,' Cathy protested.

'Cathy, please. This time tomorrow you may well be official suppliers – you're certainly entitled to a cup of coffee.'

Cathy accepted, and as she picked up her parcels said, 'Tom said you had family in the hospital when he went to see his father?'

'Yes, that's right.'

'And is it all right . . . for them too?'

Shona looked at her. 'No, no, it wasn't all right, in this case she died.'

'Oh, I'm very sorry to hear that.'

'Thank you, Cathy.' Very flat, very unemotional.

'And was it anyone close?'

There was a pause. 'No, not close, not close at all.'

*

Marcella was sitting at her little table doing nail extensions for a very elegant woman who was busy holding out her hands and admiring them. She was delighted to see Tom, and jumped up to greet him. She looked so gorgeous in her short white uniform with the blue Haywards logo, her long slim legs in dark navy tights and her cloud of dark hair like a halo around her tiny face. Sometimes he could hardly believe how beautiful she was, and that she might love only him. He saw everyone in the salon admiring her.

'Will I get a video, or would you like to go out?' he whispered.

'There's a book launch,' she said.

'Let's hit that, then,' he said with a good-natured shrug. He knew not to ask Marcella whose book and on what topic. A book launch was a photo opportunity. Someone might take a very glamorous picture of Marcella, which could appear in the Among Those Attending column. It would be clipped from the newspaper and added to the growing file in the portfolio. He took the name of the bookshop and the time and said he'd see her there. No point in suggesting dinner afterwards. Marcella hardly ate dinner, and anyway, she'd be going to the gym.

'Could I drop you off at Fatima and then take the van tonight?' Cathy asked him when they had fitted the two blinds, and realised that the light installation needed an electrician. Tom said it was fine, he was meeting Marcella later in the city centre, he'd take a bus back in from his parents' house.

'Are you sure? I could go home and get the Volvo,' Cathy said.

'Where are you off to?'

'To see some of the further adventures of Hooves the wonder dog, and to try and reassure those two kids that their life isn't totally over if they do have to go back to their barking-mad parents.'

'But wouldn't you be a little bit relieved, in a way? Go on, be honest with me, I'm not family.' He smiled at her.

'I've never *been* more honest . . . I think it would be so wrong for them to have to go back to that set-up. We've just got some manners on them, some small appearance of normality, they have a dog, they have two happy homes to live in; what makes those selfish clowns think they can wake from their drinky, dysfunctional lives and take them straight back?'

'You won't be relieved then, I take it?'

'No, I'll be heartbroken, as it happens.'

'How 'ya, Dad?'

His father sat at the table reading an Irish Heart Foundation publication about avoiding stress.

'Tell me how on earth can anyone avoid stress? If you're in business you can't do it, that's what business is about. How do *you* avoid stress, Tom?'

'Well Da, there's a lot of people who say I never even achieved any stress, let alone have to avoid it.'

'Well it's true, you *have* had an easy business life compared to the building trade, but surely you must worry about . . . will this job do well, or will you get that contract?'

'Sure Da, every day. Today I'm worrying about whether the bread I make tomorrow will be good enough for Haywards to sell . . . I just try to put it out of my mind when I'm not actually doing it.'

His father grunted. 'Yes, yes, that's what they say here, but of course yours isn't really a business worry in the proper sense of the word.'

'No, Da,' said Tom, who wondered if his father had any idea at all of the years spent having to work night after long night in bars to make the fees for catering college, to borrow huge sums of money for the company, to ask people to be guarantors for the loan, to look at Marcella and know that she was the most beautiful person on earth, and surely someone with style and class would take her away from him. And his father still thought he knew no stress.

'Marcella sent her love,' he lied to his father.

'I know she did, a grand girl no matter what your mother says.'

'What exactly is she saying these days?'

'Ah, you know, the living as man and wife bit . . . the usual . . . nothing new.'

'Wouldn't you think she'd have got used to it by now, Dad?' Tom looked at him helplessly.

'People of your mother's frame of mind never get used to it, son, sure you only have to look at Joe to know that.'

'Joe? What do you mean?'

His mother came in just then. 'He's on the mend, isn't he, Tom? What were you saying about Joe just then?'

'I was saying it was nice of him to send Da that basket of fruit, that's all I was saying,' Tom said hastily.

'Huh,' said his mother.

'Marcella was saying it's a great present to send people, far healthier than sending them a bottle of wine or chocolates or something. Oh, and she sent you both her love.'

'Huh,' said his mother again in exactly the same tone.

'You must be delighted that Dad's so fit.'

'Well of course it's all thanks to Our Lady.'

'Sure Ma, and the hospital and everything.'

'The hospital could have done what it liked, it wouldn't have been able to cure your father if Our Lady hadn't intervened.' She nodded her head several times as if she were agreeing with other people who also held this view. Her husband and son looked at her at a loss. There was a silence.

'Was it the Thirty Days' Prayer?' Tom asked eventually.

'Fat lot you know about prayer. There wasn't *time* for the Thirty Days' Prayer, you eejit. I had to get something much quicker.'

'And she found it in the *Evening Herald*.' Tom's father knew what to say.

'Oh, laugh away, the pair of you.' She was huffed now.

'Maura! Am I laughing?'

'No, but you would if you had a mind to. It was a Never Known to Fail prayer, and all you have to do when you get your wish is publish it again in the paper so that someone else will see it and know how very powerful the Holy Virgin is in times of crisis, and . . .'

'That's pretty clever of the newspapers. It means they get columns of prayers in the classifieds,' Tom said admiringly.

Maura went on as if Tom had not spoken. 'And the other thing Our Lady asks is that we just sit down for five minutes with a non-believer and explain how her Son so loved the world that . . .'

'Yes, well, Mam, but I was only really dropping in to see how Dad was . . .'

'We could do it now, Tom.'

'But Ma . . .'

'Please son,' his father asked.

Tom sat obediently and listened while his mother told him of Our Lady's personal distress about a variety of subjects. 'Why can't you believe it, Tom? Just tell me,' his mother asked in the tones of one who would be able to sort it out immediately if she knew the exact point of disagreement.

'It's not that I *don't* believe,' he began.

'But what's the problem then?'

'Mam I've *told* you, it's not like that. I don't *not* believe things,' he began, imploring her to understand.

'But what *do* you believe Tom? What exactly?'

'Well, I believe there's something . . . something out there to make sense of it all.'

'But you know what's out there, Tom.'

His father's eyes were on him. 'I suppose I do, Mam.' He let his mind drift on to the kind of baskets he would use to present this bread tomorrow, and whether they should wrap them in the good Scarlet Feather napkins. He nodded gravely at everything his mother had said, and gave her longer than the five minutes she had sought. She was pleased now that the bargain with Our Lady had been kept. And went out to the kitchen head held high.

'Thanks Tom,' his father said.

'But Dad, *you* don't have to go along with all this . . .'

'I do, Tom, it's called give and take . . . Your mother gives a lot to me, so I give her this bit of listening, that's all there is to it.'

'No, there's much more to it, you have to put on a whole act about things you don't believe.'

'You'd do the same for Marcella now, son, wouldn't you?'

'Well, I suppose I go along with all these nights she spends at the gym when she's already perfect, but I wouldn't pretend to believe something I didn't believe. I wouldn't do that.'

'You might, you know,' his father said. 'In times to come you might well pretend just for an easy life.'

The twins were doing their homework in the kitchen when Cathy arrived at St Jarlath's. Her mother had begun making their wedding outfits, and had the sewing machine whirring away. Her father was out in the back painting the kennel that one of his pals from the bookies had made for Hooves. Another friend had given him an old horseshoe which he was going to nail over it for luck. The puppy sat on a newspaper quivering with pleasure in the warm kitchen.

'You're welcome, Cathy, but this is a house of hard industry at the moment. Everyone has to be kept at their work until after six-thirty, if you know what I mean.'

Cathy knew exactly what she meant. She meant that it was hard enough to get Muttie to paint and the children to do their school work without having a welcome interruption like a visit to cope with.

'I'm just going to do my accounts at the table,' she said quickly, and sat down opposite Maud and Simon. 'Hallo,' she whispered, as if she too were just a fellow hater of homework.

'Should we make tea?' Maud hissed hopefully behind her hand. Simon looked up eagerly.

'No, not until half past six,' Cathy whispered, and they all went back to work. She didn't even see the figures, they were just a blur. She had phoned Neil just before coming here. Simon and Maud's mother and father were very grateful to these people who had done so much when they were unavoidably absent, but everything was now fine again. They were looking forward to seeing their children again, and were expecting them to come home at the weekend. And tonight he was meeting someone who would let them know about the timescale.

'Timescale?' Cathy had asked.

About the job; apparently this guy knew how long it could be held open for Neil.

At half past six they all went on a tour of inspection of the snow-white kennel.

'It's beautiful,' Simon said with awe.

'A palace for Hooves,' said Maud.

'But of course he can't get into it until the paint is dried,' Muttie explained.

'Or he'll come out looking like a Dalmatian, all white spots,' said Cathy.

'Dalmatians are actually white with black spots,' Simon corrected her. Then he remembered that you didn't correct people. 'At least, what I meant to say was . . . that some of them are white with black spots. Of course, they *could* be the other way round, too.'

'Good boy, Simon,' Cathy said with sudden tears in her eyes. They had taught these children so much, they were almost human beings now, and for what? So that they could be sent back to these dysfunctional parents?

'Are you crying?' Maud asked with interest.

'Sort of. People of my age do cry sometimes, quite unexpectedly. It's a nuisance,' she said matter-of-factly and blew her nose.

'Our mother used to cry like that in the hospital, and she didn't know why either,' Maud said kindly, as a sort of reassurance.

'But in her case it was really due to her bad nerves.' Simon was anxious always to be fair.

She hadn't realised just how very much she was going to miss them. It was nonsense to say that they *belonged* with this ridiculous couple, Jock's brother Kenneth and his wife.

'Come on kids, let's take Hooves for a walk. I know he's not mine but I feel very close to him, even though I don't live here.'

'It won't be much of a walk, it's more a waddle,' Maud said, and ran for the lead. Up and down St Jarlath's Crescent they went, telling the people that they met about the puppy. They divided the time meticulously between them.

'I never thought we'd have a real puppy of our own, I thought we'd be able to play with someone else's, but not one of our very own, living in the house,' said Simon when it was Maud's turn to hold the lead.

'Sure, and he'll always be yours. The actual *house* where Hooves sleeps isn't all that important, not as important as the fact that he belongs to you.'

Simon looked up at her, troubled. 'Why do you say that?'

'Well, you know,' she shrugged vaguely.

'I know now,' he said. The old solemn look was back.

'What do you know?' she asked fearfully.

Maud had joined them, and was looking from one to the other.

Simon spoke very slowly and deliberately. 'Father has come back from his travels, Mother is coming out of the nervous hospital and we'll be leaving Muttie and his wife and we're going back to live with them and leaving Hooves behind us.'

Maud looked up, stricken, waiting to hear it wasn't true. 'We're to call Muttie's wife Lizzie,' she corrected. 'Remember.'

'Yes,' Simon said flatly. 'Sorry, I forgot. Yeah, it's Lizzie all right.'

There was a silence. 'It's your turn with Hooves,' Maud said to Simon.

'I don't want him, Maud. Thank you all the same,' Simon said, and walked ahead of them back home. His shoulders were hunched and his head was down. Cathy let him go. She knew that he was trying very hard not to show how upset he was.

'Are we really going to be leaving St Jarlath's Crescent and you and Neil, Cathy?' Maud's face was paler than ever.

'It's not really *leaving*, you know friends don't leave each other, you'll be coming back to us and to Dad and Mam and who knows, maybe things are much better now and you can take Hooves with you.'

'You didn't know Mother, did you?'

'No, not really *know*, so to speak.'

'Her nerves would never let her make a home for Hooves,' Maud said sadly.

Marcella was talking earnestly to Ricky, but her face lit up when Tom came into the bookshop.

'You'll never guess what Ricky's going to try and get,' she said excitedly.

'No, tell me.' Tom was tired. His mother had worn him out, the passivity of his father had depressed him, he feared they hadn't costed the breads right for tomorrow's demonstration. Cathy had rung him on the mobile to say that St Jarlath's Crescent was plunged into gloom and the only person giving her the time of day was the black puppy, who had peed several times into her shoe.

'I just wondered if you felt like a cheering drink,' she had asked.

'I'm on my way to have one, come and join us. We might make a pitch for the bookshop trade as well,' he offered.

'Will I get in? I wasn't invited,' Cathy wondered.

'I'd say they'll be out in the highways and byways dragging people in off the street,' he said.

'Tom, don't look now,' Marcella warned, 'but that woman over there in the hat ... She's the editor of the new magazine I was telling you about, well, Ricky thinks he could sell her a picture story. Big, hunky photos of you ... wearing a *much* classier sweater than that ... Huge publicity for Scarlet Feather, too ... you know, at home and at work or wherever.'

'Yeah, I mentioned it to her, she seems to be interested, but you know they never tell you yes or no. Still, I think she'll bite.'

'You do, Ricky?' Tom's eyes lit up. This would be truly wonderful. Everyone who was ever going to hire a caterer read this publication. He could see Cathy and himself taking the tray of bread into Haywards, the van with its jaunty little logo. Maybe they could give a recipe, and get a perfect picture taken of the completed dish. Like the scallops and ginger Cathy did so well, that would really show up well. They would never in a million years be able to get this kind of coverage. Wasn't Marcella *great* to talk Ricky into this. Ricky would persuade the woman in the silly hat.

'He's going to ask her to come over and meet you in a minute – give her your biggest smile,' Marcella begged. She looked so beautiful, but extra lively and happy tonight in a very smart short dark grey and white dress he had never seen before.

'New?' he asked admiringly.

'Tom darling, you are so wonderful but you know nothing about clothes. This would cost seven hundred pounds if you were to buy it.'

'So how did you ...'

'Joys of working in Haywards. Someone returned it to the designer room, a flaw in one of the seams or something. All I pay for is the dry-cleaning.'

She was like a toddler at a birthday party she was so thrilled with it all. Just then he saw Cathy. She looked bedraggled in her raincoat, and instead of a bright ribbon holding her hair back she had an elastic band. She wore no make-up, and she had lines under her eyes. He would not have noticed except that the room was filled with overdressed women and he had just turned away from the immaculately groomed Marcella in her designer outfit.

Cathy smiled. 'Lead me to the cheapest red wine and let me loose on it,' she said.

'Not if you're driving the company van, no way,' he said.

'No, I parked it up at the premises. It's all tucked up there waiting for the dawn baker to arrive.' She was as tired as he was. Where did all these other people get the energy to yap so much to each other?

'My God, look at Marcella! She's utterly dazzling in that dress. Bet it cost a few quid.'

'Don't ask,' he said.

'Oh dear, domestic rows on this matter?'

'No, I meant don't ask because it's off Haywards rail tonight and back tomorrow, I understand.'

'No harm done then.' Cathy was cheerful. 'Lord, but this is truly dreadful wine, I'll be glad when I've had enough!'

The woman in the silly hat approached and was introduced by Ricky. 'This is the celebrated Tom Feather I told you about,' Ricky said.

'Mmm,' she said, looking Tom up and down.

'I hear the magazine's doing really well,' he said.

'And your business too.' Again she seemed to let her eyes run all over Tom's body slowly and appreciatively.

'Yes, well, let me introduce you to the other half of the business, half of Scarlet Feather, Cathy Scarlet.'

'Great to meet you,' Cathy said pleasantly.

The woman looked somewhat puzzled. 'How nice,' she said.

'We'd be very happy to cooperate in anything . . . everything,' he said with his huge smile.

'Well *that* sounds like the best offer I've had all night,' she said. She had a strange manner, this woman with the hat. Full of innuendo, as if a very obvious pass was being made to her and she was being coy and flirtatious about it. Cathy thought she was grotesque. But she had gone now, so it was immaterial.

'Marcella . . . you look stunning.' She was genuine in her admiration.

'You're sweet, Cathy, it's just fine feathers, borrowed feathers actually.'

'Wait till you know what's going to happen, thanks to Ricky.' Tom couldn't wait a moment longer.

'What?' Cathy had rarely seen him so excited.

'That woman who looked as if she was wearing two building blocks stuck to a coat hanger on her head. She's the head of the new magazine we couldn't afford to advertise in, and wait for it, there's going to be a photo feature about Scarlet Feather in it.'

'Well, Tom . . .' Ricky began.

'*No!* You're not serious.' Cathy was utterly delighted but apprehensive. She was going to have to do so much, finally change her hairstyle, borrow some clothes, get a professional make-up . . . But it would all be worth it.

'When do they want to do it?' she asked, as excited as Tom was.

'Well you see, actually . . .' Ricky began looking ill at ease.

Marcella explained. 'Ricky was telling me she's a very difficult woman, she blows hot and cold, we won't really know when or what form it will take for quite some time.' She seemed to be looking very directly at Ricky as she spoke.

'Sure,' he said eventually. 'Marcella tells it as it is. Stay in this part of the room, honey. I'll get one of the guys from the Sundays to come over to snap you.'

'Photographers always use that word "snap" as a joke. It's like people calling the radio a wireless . . .' Marcella said.

'Why did Ricky change his tack so suddenly? A few minutes ago he was saying it was in the bag. I can't understand it.' Tom was puzzled and annoyed.

The woman with the hat was leaving. She waved at him. ''Night, Tom, be good now. We'll be in touch soon. Ricky knows everything,' she said and was gone.

'*Now*,' Tom was triumphant. 'I'm going to find Ricky and tell him.'

'Please Tom, don't.' Marcella spoke seriously. Cathy looked up at her tone. 'There's been a misunderstanding.' Marcella looked awkwardly from Tom to Cathy as if unsure where to start or which of them to tell.

'Go on Marcella,' Cathy was gentle.

'Ricky was selling her a feature for a kind of Glamorous Couples thing . . . you know, you the big, gorgeous gourmet cook, me the model, our home, pics of us coming out of Stoneyfield together, you serving a meal to me, me at the gym, you piping cream on a dessert . . . Me doing the charity modelling show for that children's home . . . That kind of thing . . . So you see . . .'

'It's not about Scarlet Feather at all.' He was bitterly disappointed.

'Well, of course it is in part . . . after all, it's going to say what you do for a living, people will get to know your name.'

'But it's all a fake. I don't cook you meals, Marcella . . . you don't *eat* any meals.' Tom's face was red with indignation.

'Oh, come on, Tom, I thought you'd be delighted. She said you were gorgeous-looking. She told Ricky that when he showed her a picture he had taken of both of us. This is the chance I need. Why are you being so difficult? They can't *have* a feature on the business alone, that would be just advertising and the other catering companies would all go mad.'

'And what about all the other models or future models, won't they go mad also if it's about you?'

'About *us*, Tom, not just me, it's you too, how else are you going to get Scarlet Feather mentioned? I thought you'd be so pleased.'

Cathy saw this argument going nowhere except sharply downhill. 'I think it's great, Tom, this is the very best way that we could get publicity you know, it's *exactly* what we want.'

Marcella looked at her, a quick, very grateful glance.

But Tom had yet to be persuaded. 'I think it's silly. I'm not a male model, strutting about for knitting patterns, dressing up in a posh sweater or serving something in a cream sauce that you wouldn't eat in a million years . . .'

'Tom, stop the dramatics. How else are we going to get Scarlet Feather that kind of publicity? Tell me.'

'*You're* not being asked to behave like an arsehole.'

'And neither are you . . . I'd do it for the company. I would in a flash if I looked the part, and if Neil's bloody job would let him take part. But you know the way those barristers go on . . .' She had defused it.

'So do you really think . . . ?'

'Well of course I think . . . But listen, in the end it's all up to you and Marcella to fight about it. I'll leave you now to get on with it. Just know that I put on the table the view that it would be great for business.' She turned to go away, and saw herself reflected in a glass door. Of course it had been ridiculous to think that a glossy magazine would have wanted her in it. She had been even more idiotic than Tom.

'Don't go, Cathy, you wanted a drink and to be cheered up.'

'Well I *am* cheered up, very.' Her eyes were very bright, over-bright. 'We've got a load of great publicity ahead of us and all you have to do is smile.'

'I'm sorry. I thought it was the two of us.'

'I'm not . . . I'm totally relieved,' and she was out of the bookshop.

'Do you think Mother will let us come back here to St Jarlath's?' Maud asked Simon hopefully.

'I don't think so, do you?' Simon had no idea.

'Not really. Her nerves might not be able to take it,' Maud said.

There was a silence. Eventually Simon spoke. 'I suppose it will be all right being back at home again. In a way.'

'Yes.' Maud was glum.

'At least we don't have to change schools again. Neil got that sorted for us,' Simon said.

'I suppose we'll just get ourselves home . . . I mean, Muttie and Hooves can't come and collect us any more.'

'No.' Simon was very sure on this.

'It's a pity Mother's nerves got better so soon in a way, isn't it?' Maud said.

'And that Father was found,' said Simon.

They looked at each other guiltily. But it had been said now, and it couldn't be taken back.

Cathy was around at the premises at dawn the next day.

'I'm not here to interfere . . . just to make coffee and tidy up after you . . . This is your show,' she explained.

Tom was overjoyed to see her. 'God, I'm glad to see you. I'm having awful second thoughts about the fruit and nutty bread.'

'But everyone loves that,' Cathy protested.

'They love it when they've paid for it in advance, when it's in their house and they can't give it back,' Tom wailed, 'but will they love it if they have to pay so much a slice and wonder why if it's sweet they aren't buying a slice of gooey gateau instead. I think it was a stupid idea.'

'It's in the oven, isn't it?' Cathy checked.

'Yes, but—'

'I think it's a great idea . . . Come on, strong, strong coffee and lots of backbone ... Which was Geraldine's great advice to me when I was a teenager. How's Marcella?' He had stopped worrying about the bread now.

'I proposed again last night. I said to Marcella that if we have to do this idiotic photo shoot let's make it an engagement celebration, but she won't hear of it.'

'Proper order. What an unromantic proposal!' Cathy said firmly.

'No, it's not that at all; she says she won't marry me until she's successful, until she believes that I'm getting as good a bargain as she is.'

'She's amazingly direct and straightforward, isn't she,' Cathy said with admiration.

'She is the only person I know in the whole world who has never told a lie,' Tom said.

'Hey, come on, what about me?'

'You lie from morning to night, as do I. We *have* to, we tell people their houses are terrific when they're terrible, we tell them this Chardonnay is better than that depending what price we get it for, we thank the butcher and tell him he's terrific to chop the meat for us even though he doesn't do it properly but at least he waves his cleaver at it. We're telling lies all day.'

There was a ping on the oven timer and the bread came out. It all looked perfect as it went onto the wire trays. Cathy shook Tom's hand formally. 'It's bloody great, Tom, I can't believe they won't take it. I *know* we're into Haywards today, I just know it.'

They delivered the baskets to Shona just before the big meeting. Shona looked so elegant in her dark suit and pale pink blouse, slightly severe but very much in control. You didn't stay in a senior job at Haywards just by looking pretty.

'It smells utterly magical, but you know it's not down to me. I can only hope for you,' she said, and she was gone.

They would meet in the café at noon to hear the result. They had the time planned down to the last second: they would go to the market to buy the ingredients for James Byrne's cookery lesson that evening. They would price little breadbaskets in the market too. Just in case they got the Haywards job ... They would check on a new laundry, what it would cost to do their tablecloths; they would walk around the new Eastern Delights delicatessen with notebooks at the ready, looking for more ideas. That would certainly fill up all their time until Shona was able to tell them the news.

Shona came running into the café, thumbs up in the air. Not only had they bought it as an idea, they had eaten it all at their coffee break. There had been little dishes of butter on the tray as well, to encourage them. They could start next week on a six-week trial period.

'Can we use our name?' Tom asked.

'Yes, but a bit smaller than you wanted ... They'd like "baked fresh every day especially for Haywards", and then your name ... But we can put your logo on, of course, and make it whatever size we like.' Shona was as eager as they were.

Cathy flung her arms around the girl. 'We'll never be able to thank you,' she said, her voice choked.

Then Tom folded Shona in a bear-hug. 'I swear I'll make it a success, for your sake as well as ours.' He was gruff with gratitude.

'You'll be responsible for putting two inches onto the hip measurements of Ireland,' Shona said. 'You should have seen the way they went at it, and they want double the order of the fruit and nut one.'

'And they accept the price?' Tom was beaming all over his face.

'Yes, they think it's fair, but don't be appalled when you see what *they* charge, they didn't get to be rich by having a small mark-up,' she apologised.

'We'd take you out to dinner tonight to thank you properly, but we have a job,' Cathy said.

'No need, believe me, I'm the flavour of the month after that feeding frenzy upstairs!'

Tom and Cathy looked at each other in disbelief.

'Back to the market,' she said.

'To buy the breadbaskets,' Tom said with a great whoop of joy that turned every head in his direction.

James Byrne had explained to them that he wanted three cookery lessons. And that he would need to master a starter, a main course and a dessert at each lesson. Then he could mix and match, and when the time came he could serve whatever he liked best or possibly whatever was easiest. They didn't ask him what was the time that was going to come. You didn't ask James Byrne anything personal like that.

It was a big house, back from the road, with a well-kept gravelled space for cars. The house was probably in four large apartments. James Byrne had said to ring the Garden Flat bell. It was a basement with iron bars on the window. Fairly typical of his cautious behaviour. Assume the worst. Be prepared for burglars, clients with laundered money, random tax inspections, people clamping your car, stolen credit cards. James Byrne was someone who did not automatically believe the best of people.

He opened the door to them and smiled his usual grave smile. Dressed formally – no sweater and sloppy corduroys for James Byrne at home. They carried in their bags of ingredients though a dark narrow hall. On the right was a sitting room, on the left a kitchen and straight ahead what must have been a bedroom and bathroom. It was mainly a dark muddy-brown colour, and even with the April sunset peeping through the dark curtains there was nowhere that the light seemed to land on a cheerful corner. The kitchen had various storage cupboards, all of different heights, and an awkward table, an old-fashioned oven, a sink that was impossible to reach and a fridge that took up a great amount of room, and which held a bottle of water, a carton of orange juice, half a litre of milk and a packet of butter. Cathy ached to get it all torn out. A phone call could have had two of JT Feather's men round in half an hour, then they could order fittings. She and Tom knew places who would deliver and install in a day. But this was not going to happen.

This man would live with these hopeless, outdated appliances for ever. How old was he now? About sixty-something. He had never said if he was single, married, divorced or widowed. His flat gave absolutely no sign of any lifestyle. You would not know what chair he sat in in the evening to watch television. Or if he ever did watch it. A small set stood at an inconvenient angle. A low table had a pile of neatly stacked newspapers and magazines on it. Were they waiting to be read, waiting to have things clipped from them, or just pausing before going to a waste-paper bank? Pictures on the walls were of mountains and lakes. Dull prints, no life in any of them. Old, inexpensive frames. Just two shelves of old books. They looked pretty undisturbed. A desk with some papers on it and an old-fashioned blotter, although nobody had written with ink for years. A plastic mug held all James Byrne's ballpoint pens. Cathy saw that Tom was looking around him, probably making similar judgements. She shook herself.

'Right. The lesson starts here, James: put on your pinny.'

'I don't think I have one . . .' he began.

'I didn't think so either, so I brought you one of ours!'

Triumphantly she produced a Scarlet Feather apron with its big red logo around the edge. He seemed bashful as he tied its strings around his waist.

'That was very nice of her, wasn't it, Tom?' he said. 'Trust a woman to have a nice little touch.'

'Not a bit of it, James; don't ever let the females think they have a monopoly on little touches. Look what I brought you, a great big oven glove so that you won't burn your arm to a crisp like some people I know.'

He was very pleased with this and tried it on, flexing his arm up and down. 'Looks as if it's all going to be much more intensive, not to say more dangerous, than I thought,' he said.

The conversation sounded so normal. Why did they feel they couldn't ask him why he was paying them all this money to learn how to make a meal? Who was he going to serve it to and why? But they knew that this was not a question that could be asked, nor would be answered.

They did a smoked mackerel starter in little ramekins. Cathy flaked the fish expertly and added the thinly sliced mushrooms and cream.

'The cheese for the top is nicer if freshly grated,' she said, 'but you could use a shake from the packet of Parmesan.'

James Byrne looked doubtful.

'I always use the packet myself for small things like this,' Tom lied.

'Oh, you do?' Cathy said, laughing.

'Indeed I do. Saves you that little bit of time just when you need it, I always say.'

'It seems a very easy thing to make.' James Byrne was suspicious.

'It tastes as if it were very difficult to make, I assure you.' Cathy patted him down.

'I've had it in restaurants, and you know I thought there was an awful lot of cooking in it, and now it's only tearing up a cold smoked fish and pouring cream on it.' He shook his head in wonder.

'Wait till we deconstruct chicken tarragon for you, James,' Tom laughed. 'You'll never trust a cook again.'

They sat and ate together, the three of them. Cathy had written out everything step by step. James said it was all quite delicious, and what's more, he thought he could do it on his own. They talked easily about the theatre, how Cathy and Tom had once seen every play that was on every stage in Dublin, and now they never made time to go at all.

'Do you go to the theatre much?' Cathy asked.

It turned out that James did, almost every week. Why did neither of them feel able to ask if he went with a group of friends or on his own or with a companion? They touched on a lot of subjects: politics, prisons, drugs and eventually opera. James said he used to go a lot to the opera when he was a student, but somehow since then . . . His voice trailed away. Neither of them asked why he couldn't go now. Or indeed, in the years in between.

'Do you listen to it here at home?' Cathy indicated the rather old-fashioned music centre.

'No, not for a long while. You have to be in the mood to set it all up.'

'No, James, of course you don't, you just put it on . . . it creates its own mood. I put it on doing the washing-up if I'm alone. Let's put on something when we're doing the washing-up here tonight.'

'No, please, I don't have anything suitable,' he said a little anxiously.

She drew back. 'Sure,' she said easily.

She had seen tapes of operas piled high in his sitting room, but he obviously didn't want to play them.

'Come on then, let's do the washing-up without an aria.'

'No, no, you must not feel . . .' he began.

'Rule one. *Never* refuse an offer of washing-up. Right, Tom?'

'Absolutely, and be quite sure to let your guest help do the washing-up if she offers,' Tom added.

'Why do you think it's a she?' James asked.

'Because a mere man wouldn't care what he was being offered if he came round to dinner, and probably wouldn't notice. Believe me, I've cooked for them, I know,' said Tom, cursing himself for being so tactless.

Cathy looked at him admiringly. 'Too true,' she said. 'No, James, the first thing is to have a dish of hot soapy water to stick the cutlery into after each course, and a place to scrape away the leavings. Then it will take two minutes.'

'I don't have a dishwasher, you know,' he said anxiously, in case there had been any misunderstanding.

Cathy looked around the kitchen that had no electric beater, liquidiser or proper chopping board. Of course the man wouldn't have a dishwasher. 'No need for one, hands are just as good. Take us five minutes at the outside, what do you say, Tom?'

'Six if we do it thoroughly,' Tom said, starting on the frying pan.

Joe rang at the door of Fatima. He carried a bottle of sweet sherry and a tin of fancy biscuits. He could hear his mother grumbling as she came to the door. 'It's all right, JT, I'm going to get it, whoever it is at this time of night.' It was seven o'clock on an April evening, hardly the middle of the night. He must not allow himself to become annoyed.

'How are you, Ma?' he said with false good humour.

His mother looked him up and down. She looked old and tired now, not like she had in January when he had seen her briefly at Tom and Cathy's launch party. Then she had worn a green tweed suit and a white blouse with a green cameo brooch at the neck. Tonight she wore a faded pinafore and shabby slippers. Her hair was flat, grey and limp. When he saw what women her age could do with themselves, Joe's heart felt heavy. Maura Feather must be fifty-eight at the very most. She looked as if she were well over seventy.

'And what brings you here?' his mother asked.

'I came to see you both, and to know how Da is getting along.' He kept the smile on his face.

'You know how he's getting along. We sent you a note to thank you for that basket of fruit.' His mother's face was hard.

'Yes, yes, indeed. It was a very nice letter.' Joe knew that Tom had written it, typed it, made it up for them. Anything to keep a lifeline open between them all.

'Anyway, now that I'm here, Ma . . .' He began to take a step over the doorstep.

'Who asked you to come in, Joe?'

'Well you're never going to send me away?' He held his head on one side, the way of pleading that rarely failed. But he was at Fatima now.

'What makes you think you're welcome in this house? You often come to Dublin, and never come to see us. I saw you one day myself out of a bus, laughing on the corner of a street. Why should we welcome you here?'

'I suppose any man who wants to see how well his father has recovered from a heart attack is welcome in his old home,' Joe said.

The legendary Joe Feather charm was not finding its mark with his mother.

'I've had to live with the results of your selfishness year after year, your father having no one to lift a hand to help him at his work.'

'Ma, I was never going to work in Dad's business, you know that.'

'I do not know it, and a fine example you were to your brother, too . . .'

'Tom was never going to work in it either, Ma . . .'

'Not good enough for you, only good enough to pay your school fees and buy you clothes and football boots and a bicycle, but not good enough—'

'Could I see Da, do you think?' Joe cut across her.

'What makes you think you can walk in here after all this time, and that your father will be pleased to see you?'

'I had hoped that you both would,' he said.

There was a tic in his forehead. Why was he doing this? One more refusal and he would leave, but he just had to see the old man before he went. He moved gently but firmly past his mother to the room where his father sat in the chair, straining to hear every word. The man looked white and papery.

But there was a welcoming light in his face that Joe hadn't seen in his mother's.

'Joe, good to see you, lad.'

'And you, Da, I know it's been a day or two but I wanted to make sure that you were as good as they say.'

'They?' His mother sniffed from the door.

'Well, Tom for one, Cathy Scarlet for another, Ned in the yard for a third. People who care about you.'

'Huh,' said Maura Feather.

'Look, I'm so glad to see you well, and you looking fine too, Ma. I'm just rushing through Dublin and I haven't been back here since you were in hospital, so I thought it would be good for us to meet just for a few minutes.'

'It is indeed, Joe.' His father reached out for Joe's hand.

Joe pretended not to see the gesture because he could sense his mother's hostility towards any hand-grasping.

'I brought us a quick small drink and a sweet biscuit, and maybe the next time I come Ma would make us a cup of tea and a scone . . .'

He didn't look at her, instead he opened the sherry and found glasses on the sideboard.

'I hope the next time will be soon. If you knew how tough it is over in London . . .'

'I can't remember anyone forcing you to go there.' Maura Feather was not won over yet.

'I liked it when I was young and foolish, Ma, everyone likes a big bad place then . . . But people aren't really happy there, like they're not in any big city.'

'What do you mean?'

'Well, you know yourself. You can see it in Dublin too, though of course London's much bigger. People are restless. They're looking for something to explain what it's all about . . .'

They looked at him blankly.

'You know, when I went to London first the churches were empty . . . Today there are people going into them at lunchtime, in the evenings looking up, everyone looking for answers.'

'How would *you* know?' Maura Feather asked.

'I know because I go sometimes, and into a temple or a mosque or a synagogue . . . There's not just one God, Mam, not like there was when we were young.'

'There's only one true God,' she snapped.

'I know, I know, but honestly nowadays it's much better than it used to be, isn't it, people respecting everyone's beliefs.'

'It's very little belief you respected, Joe Feather, when we last saw you.'

At least she had used his name. It was an advance. He poured the sherry and smiled at them. His professional smile. He didn't care for them himself – they were strangers, a weak man, a bitter woman. True, he had felt a tug of pity when he heard that his father had been fighting for breath in the hospital. Joe's own inclination would have been to continue sending the occasional long-distance gift. But he had promised Tom he would make the effort. And somehow he owed Tom.

Tom had been right, he hadn't helped the business of being a son of Fatima. He had been of little help in sharing what he saw as the burden of elderly and tiresome parents. He would keep smiling and talking about searching for more meaning in life and pouring sherry. He saw that his mother had relaxed and his father was touchingly pleased at his efforts. Joe thought he had put much, much more work than this into selling a line of coordinated tops and shorts to a tough Northern businessman. He would stay another half an hour.

The photo shoot was endless. Tom just could not believe that grown-up people spent such huge amounts of time doing something so trivial. Marcella had taken two days off work and arrived home with a selection of Haywards garments for both of them. The sweater and jacket she had chosen for him were astronomically expensive.

'It's all with Shona's blessing ... It's as good as an unpaid advertisement for them. And you are so gorgeous to look at I'm going to have trouble beating them all off you, the make-up artists, the hairstylists, the lighting people ... And that's only the men,' she laughed excitedly.

It was beginning to happen for her. The work dream coming true, as it had for him earlier this year. Tom would do his utmost to smile and look rugged, or whatever they wanted that would help Marcella's career.

The man who was meant to know the timescale of everything hadn't known it, according to Neil. It was a new posting, it was all up in the air, it was not fixed to any date. There was plenty of time to talk.

'Good,' Cathy said.

Muttie and Lizzie whispered in the dark bedroom.

'They'll be gone at the end of the week,' she said.

'I know, and I was just getting to like them,' Muttie said.

Neil said that Kenneth and Kay Mitchell were now installed, and everything was in place; they were ready and waiting.

'I told the social worker that it would be a bit hard on the kids to go straight back in, and she agrees entirely. She's very nice, by the way, you'll like her; her name is Sara. Anyway, Sara says that we should bring them to visit their parents once or twice before leaving them there. She'll come with us.'

Cathy felt an unreasonable twinge of jealousy. This was *her* call, hers and her kind parents, who had put themselves out for the children when nobody wanted them. Now it seemed that everyone wanted them – mad, runaway fathers, mad, drunken mothers, bossy social workers called Sara.

'Okay, I'll fix a time to take them over to the House of Horrors,' she said.

'Don't even whisper that name in front of those two. You know the way they pick up on everything,' he warned.

'You're right. I'll see when I can snatch an hour and take them.'

'Well, we'll have to coordinate when you're free, Sara's free and I'm free.'

'But Neil, that could be next year. This isn't a conference call that we're setting up, it's my taking those kids back to where they're going to be living from now on without frightening them to death. It's about putting some kind of mad appearance of normality on it, not about checking everyone's diaries.'

'Hon, I *know* what you're saying, but in these kind of things it's best to do it by the book, keep the social worker on board, then if anything goes wrong we're all in the clear.'

'But we know exactly what will go wrong ... Eventually Kenneth will hear the sounds of distant excitement in far-off lands and Kay will smell a vodka bottle and we're back to where we were.'

Tom had never seen Ricky at work before. He had only seen him as the relaxed man who watched everything and knew everyone. He had no idea of the preparation that went into taking what would result in five or six photographs in a magazine. Tom's face was a picture. He felt sure there had been some mistake, and that this was a multimillion-dollar movie that was being made in the small apartment in Stoneyfield. What he could not begin to understand was Marcella's sense of calm throughout all of this. She served endless coffee and ice-cold mineral water. When asked to smile, she did so with a radiance he could hardly believe. It didn't matter how many times she had to do it, the same smile was delivered as fresh as if it had come from the heart. She sat motionless as they applied yet more make-up, touched up the lip gloss and lacquered her already perfect hair. Tom, on the other hand, made jokes, clowned around, felt awkward, knocked things over and apologised again and again. He thought the day would never end. No night working in a noisy pub, no back-aching hauling of food up flights of stairs, no squeezing through tiny narrow corridors without upsetting trays of food had ever been half as exhausting as this. When they were finally alone in jeans and T-shirts, with all today's finery at the dry-cleaner's and tomorrow's hung up in readiness, Tom lay down on the sofa with his head on her lap. She stroked his brow. Still fresh as a daisy, and her eyes dancing with the pleasure of it all.

'Thank you, dear, dear Tom. I know you hated it,' she said softly.

'I didn't *hate* it, exactly, but it was very stressful. I was hopeless, I'm afraid.'

'You were wonderful. They all said so.'

'Marcella, how have you the patience?'

'I ask you always how have *you* the patience to do all that fiddly work. Those little perfectly shredded garnishes, and rolling up those tiny bits of sushi ... I would go mad rather than do it, I tell you.'

She stroked his brow and he wanted to go to sleep there and then. 'That's because you don't eat,' he said, smiling up at her. 'You've never had a lust for food like other fatter folk.'

'Oh, I might have had a lust for food once upon a time,' she said.

But he knew that she never had. Any of the few pictures of her childhood that he had seen showed a little waif-like girl. Marcella had never been a foodie.

'I have to go, alas,' he said, dragging himself up.

'Surely not? After all the work you put in already today?'

'We have a do. Cathy's been working on it all day while I've been posturing here. I have to go and help her serve it.'

'Sure you have to go. Though your posturing, as you call it, may well get you lots more business.'

'Marcella, be serious!'

'I was never more so. What is it tonight?'

'Our Lady's Ladies.'

'*What?*'

'I don't know. Some past pupils' group. They're all twenty years left school this year, and apparently two decades ago they swore a mighty oath that if they were alive today they'd have a party.'

'They're not really called that, are they?'

'Something like that. Anyway, off I go. Am I too casual, do you think?'

'I'd say Our Lady's Ladies will just about tear you to pieces,' said Marcella admiringly.

'Jesus, Cathy, what a day I've had: I'm so sorry for leaving all this to you.'

'No problem, Mister Cheesecake . . . I was glad to be distracted, I have to take those kids to meet some terrifying Nazi called Sara tomorrow, and ease them back to the madhouse . . . I preferred making salmon *en croute*.'

How they got through the night, they never knew. Tom, who was nearly dead from smiling at cameras for over seven hours and with the thought of the same thing again the following day, smiled and laughed and told the women that there must be some mistake, none of them could have left school twenty years ago. Cathy, who was nearly dead worrying about how to handle the horrific social worker Sara without putting anyone's back up managed to weave and duck around the room as the women shrieked and remembered funny things from years ago. Almost everyone had turned up, they told Cathy, only three had cried off. Janet who was in New Zealand, Orla who was in some kind of weird cult in the West of Ireland and Amanda who was in Canada running a bookshop with her lover. Was that Amanda Mitchell by any chance, Cathy had wondered, too much of a coincidence. Yes, it was, apparently! They were annoyed about Amanda, she always had plenty of money, her family owned that big house, Oaklands, so she could well have come back. It wasn't as if any of them were going to be worried one way or another about her lover.

'And who is he?' Cathy had asked politely.

'Aha, it's not a he at all, it's a she. Imagine! Amanda Mitchell is the only girl in a class of twenty-eight females who fancied a woman, what does that do to statistics?' asked the woman who had set up the party.

Cathy sat down in the kitchen. Her sister-in-law was a lesbian. What else would the day bring?

'They were a nice lot,' June said as she helped to pack the van.

'And they seemed pleased with it all,' Tom yawned.

'They gave me a good tip, too. And four of them asked me where I got my streaks done.'

'Did they like them?' Cathy was still doubtful about the startling violet sections of June's hair.

'They loved them, they were dead impressed that I could afford Haywards. Thanks again, Cathy, it was a great gift.'

'That bit was nothing, it's my hair we have to worry about with Hannah,' said Cathy.

They left June at a taxi rank. 'You know, I have a great life because of you two,' she said, and trotted off.

They drove in silence towards the premises.

'I didn't know it was all going to be so bloody exhausting,' Cathy said.

'Nor I. The food's no trouble, it's just the people who are a pain,' Tom agreed.

They spent one hour and forty minutes unpacking the van, loading the dish-washing machines, wrapping and freezing the leftovers and preparing the kitchen and ovens for the morning bake. They worked companionably, and didn't waste one unit of energy by speaking to each other. When they were through, Tom drove the van slowly out into the street.

'I'm like a zombie,' he said. 'Can you watch me in case I fall asleep?'

'Well, the very thought of you doing that might keep *me* awake, anyway,' Cathy said.

'It will be May next month,' Tom said.

'That's true.'

There was a silence.

'Why did you tell me that?' Cathy asked eventually.

'I can't remember,' Tom confessed.

'Are we becoming geriatrics, do you think? We don't actually *say* things any more.' Cathy sounded worried.

'No, there's not much to say except that my brother has turned into a major pain in the arse,' Tom said.

'And it seems that my sister-in-law is going to give a few people at Oaklands a few major surprises,' said Cathy. She looked at Tom's face. 'You don't need to know now. Anyway, as you say, it will be May soon. I've a feeling that this means something.'

'Something good or bad?' Tom wondered.

'Jesus, Tom, if I knew that . . . wouldn't I be able to run the world,' said Cathy Scarlet, who then fell asleep until Tom drove her into the courtyard of Waterview.

May

They told Hooves that they were only going out for a visit, and that they would be back later on.

'I know it sounds silly, but I think he does understand,' Maud said.

'Why wouldn't he understand? Isn't he a dog of pedigree?' Muttie asked.

'Do people have pedigrees too?' Simon wanted to know.

'No,' Cathy said, a little overemphatically. 'All people are born the same, they make their own pedigrees.'

She saw her parents looking at her and realised the futility of her statement. She could not accept that Neil was right to insist they be returned to their natural parents. Nothing would make her believe that this was the just or fair thing to do. But she had to go along with it.

'Come on, kids, into the van, and take me to see your house. I want to know where you were as babies.'

'Could Muttie and his wife come too?' Maud hung back.

'One day they'll come to see it, but today it's just us,' said Cathy, refusing to look at her parents watching the children leave.

The Beeches was in a road where a lot of other properties had been sold as apartment blocks, but it stood there in its own grounds ... A large, shabby, ill-kept house a hundred and fifty years old, a gentleman's residence which had seen better days. Not as imposing as Oaklands – there was no great sweep of a drive coming up to it – but attractive, with good proportions and creeper growing among the windows. A disused tennis court and a broken garden shed showed how grand it must have been at some stage. Before the parents of Walter, Simon and Maud lost interest in the business of keeping up a normal home. The children looked at Cathy anxiously as they drove in, watching her for a reaction.

'What a lovely house,' she said with a hollow feeling in her heart. 'It must have been a nice place to grow up.'

They looked at their home doubtfully. 'I'm sure St Jarlath's Crescent was nice to grow up in, too.'

These had been such horrible children, stealing food, referring to Cathy as a servant, throwing their clothes on the floor only a few short months ago, and look at them now! Cathy tried to keep the break out of her voice.

'It was indeed, Simon, thank you for saying that, it was a nice place to grow up. Now let's go and find your father and mother.'

Kenneth Mitchell welcomed them in as if they were the most honoured guests, rather than the two children he had abandoned and his nephew's wife whom he had never acknowledged before.

'How perfectly splendid,' he said as Cathy arrived with the children.

'Hallo Father,' Simon said.

'Simon, good chap. Good boy,' his father said, 'and Maud too, of course, excellent.' He looked at Cathy vaguely as if trying to place her. He was quite like his brother Jock in appearance, but he had not run to fat. Being on the road, or however he described it, meant that he had no paunch. There was no sign of his wife. She decided to address him by his first name.

'Well, Kenneth, as you say, it's all splendid. Shall we wait for Kay and Sara before we do the tour?'

'Tour? Sara . . . um, Kay?' He was bewildered.

It was now Cathy's turn to be bewildered. 'Kay, your wife?'

'Oh, yes, she'll be here in a moment, she's getting ready.'

No welcome, no warmth, and in the case of their mother, not even an appearance. Maud seemed to feel uneasy as well.

'What time is Sara coming?' she asked.

Kenneth Mitchell looked confused. 'Sara?'

'The social worker,' Cathy said in a level voice.

'But I thought *you* were the social worker,' he said.

'No, Kenneth, I am Cathy Scarlet, daughter of the people who have been looking after your children while you were abroad. I am also married to Neil, who is your brother Jock's son. The social worker is Sara, who is expected to meet us here . . .'

His embarrassment, if he had any, was spared by the sound of the bell ringing. They heard Kenneth out in the hall welcoming the social worker with great charm and even greater confusion. She looked as if she weren't seventeen or eighteen, a very tall, handsome girl with flaming hair and big laced boots. She seemed altogether too confident.

'Hi Maud, Simon, everything okay?' she asked.

'Well, Sara, you see . . .' Simon began, and Cathy felt a tug of jealousy.

'I mean, have you been to the bedrooms to check all your things are there?' She was so casual, so unafraid of Kenneth Mitchell, so out for the twins.

'We haven't been here very long, you see,' Simon said.

'We haven't even seen Mother yet,' Maud added.

'Okay, go and check the rooms and then come back to me.'

They scampered up the stairs obediently. Sara began to roll a cigarette.

'I'll smoke in the garden if you prefer, Mr Mitchell,' she said with such a threatening frown that Kenneth began to panic again.

'No, no, good Lord no, please, I mean, as you like . . .'

'How 'ya, Cathy. I believe you hate my guts,' Sara said companionably.

'I'm sure in your job you must know how kids exaggerate,' Cathy grinned.

'*And* your husband? He seemed to think you had problems with their returning home.'

'No, Sara, I don't think I have any problems with it at all.' Cathy's voice became serious. 'I brought them along here for a visit, their father, who is my father-in-law's brother, thought that I was the social worker, which was a little startling and their mother wasn't here to greet them, which I found odd.'

'Neil says that you and your family have bonded with them to an extraordinary extent.' Sara watched her carefully.

'*Someone* had to bond with them,' Cathy said, exasperated. 'Listen, I'm doing everything by the book. They're here for their visit. Why don't you go and inspect the visit and leave me out of it? I'm going to be out of it anyway when they come back here.'

Kenneth Mitchell had looked from one to the other as if he were watching a tennis match. When they had stopped talking he asked would anyone like tea, and seemed surprised by the abrupt refusal from Cathy and Sara.

'I did prepare a tray,' he said in an aggrieved tone.

'Very hospitable of you Kenneth,' said Cathy in a tone which made Sara look up again.

'And where is Walter?' Sara asked, looking at her notes.

'Walter?' asked Kenneth vaguely.

'Your son,' Cathy said helpfully.

'The whole family was meant to be here,' Sara said.

'I expect he's at work.' Kenneth looked anxious to be helping in an ever more confusing world. He was constantly being rescued by other people's arrivals. The children came in at that moment, holding their mother by the hand. Kay Mitchell looked frail and as if a wind would blow her away. She had a nice smile.

'Hallo, how nice to see you,' she said to Cathy.

'You look much stronger now,' Cathy said.

'Do I? That's good. Did you come to see me in hospital?'

'Yes, from time to time, but the important thing was the children's visit.' Cathy slid a glance at Sara, to hope that she was taking this on board.

'So much of it took place in a sort of fog, as if it were all happening to someone else.' She beamed around at them all.

'Any sign of your brother Walter?' Cathy asked the children.

'He sort of made the beds for us,' Maud said.

'But he didn't really, it was just the sheets and pillowcases left at the end of the beds, and actually . . .'

'They were very damp, so Mother has been helping us put them into the hot press,' Maud explained.

'That wasn't really work for Walter. Isn't there a Mrs Thing to make beds?' Kenneth was puzzled.

'Mrs Thing doesn't start until next week,' Cathy explained sarcastically.

'Mrs Barry, I see from my notes,' Sara corrected.

'So now it's only Walter we're waiting for, is that right?'

'He's meant to be here,' Sara said disapprovingly.

'I'm sure . . . There must be a misunderstanding, should he be telephoned, do you think?' Kenneth wondered.

'Might be best.' Sara wasted no words.

'Well, does anyone . . . I mean where . . . exactly?' Kenneth began.

'Your brother's office, Jock Mitchell's law firm.'

Cathy tried to hide the sarcasm in her voice. But Sara didn't miss it; there was a hint of a smile. Nobody helped with all the fumbling and looking up in the telephone directory. It turned out that Walter was on his way, he would be here shortly.

'And Walter lives here? This is his home?'

'Well, he's an adult man of course, he doesn't have to check in every night.'

'I see he sometimes stays with friends.' Sara was writing notes.

'But his room is here . . . For him, of course.'

'Locked,' said Simon.

'How do you know?' Sara was interested.

'We had a rocking horse and an old black and white telly. I thought maybe Walter had borrowed them when we were staying with Muttie and Lizzie . . . which would have been fine with us.' Simon's voice was straight and clear. He didn't want to get anyone into any trouble.

'Odd to lock a bedroom in a family home,' Sara said.

'When will we be coming back here for good?' Maud asked.

'Whenever you like,' her father beamed.

'The sooner the better,' her mother's smile was wide.

'When all the paperwork is complete,' Sara said.

'And Cathy, were you able to explain properly to Sara all about Hooves visiting, and the wedding of Lizzie's daughter to that man that she's sleeping in the same bed with in Chicago?'

'I say . . .' Kenneth began.

Yet again he was saved from having to say anything by the arrival of Walter. Dishevelled and out of breath, Walter had come on a bicycle.

'Hi kids, Mother, Father, Cathy.' He nodded to them all, then he put on the Mitchell smile.

'And you must be Sara? Aren't you terribly young and, um, gorgeous to be doing this job?'

Cathy looked at him in despair. *Please* may Sara not fall for it, the little-boy-lost bit, the hair in the eyes, the naked admiration.

'You were meant to be here forty-five minutes ago.' Sara was stern.

He tried to smile it away. 'But happily I'm here now,' he said.

Sara called the meeting to order with a cough. 'If Maud and Simon are coming back here to live, can we run through the arrangements, please?'

'Well, what arrangements exactly?' Kenneth was finding all this above him. 'I mean, I'm here, and their mother is here and these, er . . . kind people who looked after them when I was unavoidably away and Kay was ill have delivered them home. That's it, really, isn't it?'

'No, Mr Mitchell, it's not it. You know this. We've been down this road before, they are our responsibility, something which will not be given up until we know what's best for Maud and Simon and their future. So can we start with school.' Sara had her notes in order.

'Last September there was a problem with school for the twins. They needed to be driven there and people weren't really about to drive them. They missed a lot of days. But since they went to stay in St Jarlath's Crescent they have been doing well in their new school. You are content that they continue where they are, they have made friends and there is a bus journey if nobody can collect them.'

'Good to become familiar with buses,' said Kenneth.

'Quite. And meals. Will you do the cooking, Mrs Mitchell?'

'Well of course I will, and there's a Mrs ... Mrs ... Somebody who is coming to help with the awful things, isn't she?'

'Yes, a Mrs Barrington, darling,' Kenneth intervened.

'Mrs Barry,' Cathy and Sara said together with one voice.

'Silly of me, easy mistake.'

'Quite. Now about their sleeping arrangements. You say there are damp sheets on the beds.'

'Which will be aired, of course, by the time they come home,' Kay said.

'Yes indeed. And there's a matter of a missing rocking horse and a black and white television set.'

'I didn't say they were missing. They might be in Walter's room.' Simon wanted things to be clear.

'Which is locked,' Cathy added.

'I've every right to lock my room, everyone has.'

'Sure, but can we go and see if the kids' things are in it?' Cathy's eyes were narrow. She could sense his fear. There was something in that room that Walter didn't want seen.

'Excuse me,' he said, 'are you running this suddenly, Cathy? I thought it was Sara's job.'

'Do you know anything about a rocking horse and a television set?' Sara asked him levelly.

'Oh, those. They were very old and past their sell-by date. I gave them away to friends ages ago. Sorry, you're both much too old for a rocking horse. I didn't know they were still needed.'

Cathy knew he had sold them.

'We're not too old for a television set, though,' Simon said.

'And I liked the rocking horse, too,' Maud complained.

'Well, perhaps Walter has some gifts for you instead in his room ...?' Cathy suggested.

'Listen to me, Sara, is this a witch-hunt or what? You're here to make sure this is a fine family scene for Simon and Maud to come back to ... and then suddenly it's down to me to show off whether I've made my bed in my room or not. Now come on ...'

He looked so genuinely upset and put upon that Cathy could see that Sara was falling for it.

'Of course we don't want to examine your room, but we do want to know what contribution you can make to your brother and sister's return.'

Walter paused to give a slow, triumphant smile in Cathy's direction. There would be no inspection.

Then he turned to Sara. 'What I hope now that our family is reunited is that we should all get to know each other better. That I should learn about their interests and concerns . . . Like I don't want to go giving away rocking horses again. Do I, Maud?'

'Or television sets,' Maud said.

Cathy loved her with a passion at that moment. There were many more points also answered very vaguely by the children's parents, and with warmth and enthusiasm by their elder brother. Time now to take Maud and Simon back to St Jarlath's Crescent. There were no hugs; Kay kissed them both on the cheek and looked at them vaguely and proudly. Sara and Walter were outside, comparing bicycles. Sara's was the folding type.

'Handy for taxis when you get tired or drunk,' she explained.

'Why don't I give you a lift back to the office? I've got the van, your bike can go in the back,' Cathy said suddenly.

'Oh, I couldn't,' Sara said.

'She's not drunk yet,' Simon noted.

'No, but she could be fairly tired, and this way we can go by St Jarlath's Crescent and you can introduce her to Hooves.'

'I've seen St Jarlath's Crescent, and I am totally aware of the splendid care your parents have been doing as a stopgap,' Sara said.

'You haven't seen Hooves yet, Sara. Come on, and Simon and Maud would love to show you their outfits.'

'That's a great idea, Cathy,' Simon approved as they climbed into the van. 'This way she'll see the really important things.'

Cathy and Sara exchanged glances. And spontaneously they both started to laugh.

James Byrne's second cookery lesson was on Thursday.

'Did he say what he'd like?' Tom called out to Cathy in the kitchen of the premises.

'No, he's leaving it up to us. Oh, *shit*.'

'Have you burned yourself again?' He came running.

But this time she had cut her finger on the jagged edge of a can.

'Serves you right for using cans anyway. We're not meant to be a convenience-food outfit.'

'Tell me how to add tomato pureé to something without opening a can of it?' She held up her finger to be inspected.

'You don't need a stitch, come on and wash it. By using a tube and squeezing it, or if you have to have a tin, then by using the electric thing on the wall instead of going at it with a stone-age can-opener.'

'I was in a hurry.'

'Sure you were, and now you'll be wearing Elastoplast. Great advertisement for the company,' he grumbled to himself as he bound up her finger. 'Come into the front room and sit down to get over the shock,' he said.

'I'm not in shock,' Cathy protested.

'No, but I am. Come on.'

'There you go again, a broody old hen cluck-clucking,' Cathy said.

'You can stem your own pouring blood next time,' Tom said good-naturedly.

They loved a chance to sit down in their front room and relax in the big chintz sofas that Lizzie had covered for them. Cathy put her feet up on the low table with its elegant cookery magazines.

'Someday we'll have time to read some of these,' she said.

'Food will be out of date then,' said Tom.

It was pleasant to sit here and look up at the plates on the shelves, and see their discreet filing system looking for all the world like an elegant desk in a gracious home. Joe had found that for them at an auction, he said. They worried about it once or twice.

'I know he has a bit of an aversion to paying tax, but I don't think he deals in stolen goods,' Tom had said at the time.

'Of course he doesn't,' Cathy had stroked it lovingly – it was just right.

One of Muttie's associates was in carpet pieces, so they had got a perfect piece for the floor. It gave off such a good feeling when anyone came in to see them. If only a few more people would turn up, they would be less anxious about it all.

'What will we do with James?' Tom asked.

'We did smoked fish and chicken tarragon last time ... something redder, more violent this time, I think.' Cathy pondered.

'Parma ham and figs to start, fillet steaks in mushroom and cream sauce?' Tom wondered.

'He'll say the starter's too easy, and he'd fuss too much with the steak,' Cathy was shaking her head.

'No he wouldn't, he's much less of a fusser than he used to be since you told him you can always lift the pan off the heat. Apparently he never realised that before. Imagine.' Tom was amazed.

'I wonder did he ever have children?' Cathy said.

'Why do you say that?'

'I don't know, it's a funny thing but I get the impression that he's not doing this dinner for someone he fancies ... More for some young person that he wants to prove something to ...'

'I don't know where you get that notion. Perhaps you should bring a crystal ball to the next party we do.' Tom often thought women were complicated, but this was ridiculous.

'No, think about it. You know it's something like that, he's doing something to show someone he cares, which is hard for him because he's so buttoned up.'

'You're so non-buttoned up, why don't you ask him straight out?' Tom challenged.

'You know I can't do that, Tom,' she said. 'I think I've spent so long dinning politeness into Simon and Maud I've sort of caught some of it myself. I hope it's not destroying my personality.'

'No sign yet, I assure you. But I'll keep an eye out in case it does.'

'Eejit,' said Cathy. 'What will we give him as a pudding?'

'Brown-bread ice cream,' he suggested.

'Okay, now all I have to do is sell it to him.'

'Come on, Tom, injury time over, back to work,' Cathy said, and went back into the kitchen for the telephone.

James Byrne objected to every course, but they held fast.

'It sounds too simple, as if it were bought in a shop,' he complained.

'Listen, we have to show you how to cut the figs, how to arrange the ham.'

'But steak. It's too . . . too . . .'

'It's a huge treat, and you can have small steaks. Wait till we show you the sauce.'

'She'll think I bought the ice cream in a delicatessen,' he said.

At least they defined it *was* a she. That was some advance.

'Not when you can tell her how you made it, and honestly, it's great fun,' Cathy begged. She had a lot on her mind; she didn't want their accountant starting to grizzle about a perfectly reasonable menu. Her finger was throbbing, she was sick at heart about Simon and Maud, Freddie Flynn and his wife had asked them to do a dinner, she owed Hannah Mitchell a lunch. She had no idea what they were going to do as a great feast for her sister Marian's wedding in just over two months' time. She couldn't bear the thought of her poor father walking that hound to the betting shop every day and tying him up outside the door. Her hair looked awfully flat and dull. Hannah Mitchell had been right. She was not going to listen to one more word of James Byrne's fears that this was not a good dinner.

'James,' she said in a voice like the crack of a whip. Tom looked up from the dough in alarm. 'James. Do we question a balance sheet? No. Do we say that we don't think this input or output VAT return will work? No, we don't, we say James is the particular expert that we are paying for this advice. We are the particular experts that *you* have paid for our advice. Yes, good. See you on Thursday, James.'

She hung up with a loud noise. She knew without looking that Tom was looking at her open-mouthed. 'Well?' she asked belligerently.

'Well indeed,' he said.

'Meaning?'

'Meaning that you most certainly haven't altered your personality,' he said.

She laughed and he crossed the room to hug her. He was such easy company, and defused so many situations for them both.

'Tom, I need your advice.'

'Of course you do, you sound as if you actually need a heavy tranquilliser, but my advice will have to do.'

'How am I going to entertain Hannah? I'm trying to build a hedge of olive branches, but I'm no good at it.'

'What does Neil suggest?'

'He asks why bother? He shrugs. He's a man.'

'Big disadvantage, we know that. Right, is it just the two of you?'

'Yes. I can bear an hour and thirty minutes being patronised; I couldn't stand her doing it to someone else.'

'Do you want her to enjoy it, or do you want to show off to her?'

'Good question, but actually I'd quite like her to have a good time.'

'Okay, why don't you ask her here?'

'Here, to the premises?'

'Sure, ask her for lunch next Monday. We've nothing on, it will be nice and quiet. I'll serve you, then put the phone on answer and leave.'

'She'd think that very low-class.'

'No, she wouldn't: posh place that we are, nearly six months surviving. She gave it six days, I remember, the last time she was here.'

'Oh dear, yes, the opening. I sort of forgot the words we had then.'

'Bet she hasn't, though. Really, Cathy, this would be real olive-branch territory. Go on, ring her now. Ask her.'

'I'm not sure, Tom.'

'What did I just hear you saying about people taking professional advice? Ring her, Cathy.'

'You're not a professional in this area.'

'Like hell I'm not! We've been hearing you on the subject of Hannah Mitchell since we were at catering college. Call her now.'

'Absolutely fair. Pass me the phone.'

Hannah Mitchell accepted. It was a lovely idea. Quite a lot of her friends had heard of Scarlet Feather now. They would be very interested to hear what it was like inside.

'It looks as if Maud and Simon are going back to base next week,' Cathy said.

'Yes, thank God, what a terrible episode for everyone, and wasn't poor Lizzie wonderful to step into the breach so well.'

Cathy allowed the silence to last for many seconds. Long enough for Hannah to remember.

'Ah, yes, what I meant to say was wasn't it great that, er, Lizzie and, er, Muttie were so helpful when poor Kenneth and Kay had such problems . . . That's what I meant.'

'Did that go all right?' Tom asked.

'Yes, better than I dared hope.'

'Say thank you Tom, then,' he said eventually.

'Thank you Tom,' she said.

It was extraordinary not to be afraid of that woman after so many years.

Tom went to pick Marcella up from work.

'Your brother was in today,' she said.

'He's never back in Ireland twice in a few weeks. What's it all about?'

'He said he's setting up this show . . . Feather Fashions . . . He wants trade to come to it as well as the public. He's full of ideas, he's here to see Shona and I think he's going to meet Cathy's Geraldine about doing extra PR.' Marcella sounded very excited.

'Is he going to come and see *us* at all, do you think?' Tom felt an unexpected stab of jealousy that his only brother was in town contacting almost everyone except him.

'Of course he will, he just called to see me ... because ... Tom, you won't believe this, he's putting in a serious word that I should do some modelling during the show.' Her eyes were dancing.

Tom had said nothing in months that had pleased her as much as this.

'Just let me tell you that I hope and pray he gets you this job, with all my heart,' he said.

'I'm sorry I wasn't able to get up to The Beeches, the case went on for ever,' Neil apologised.

'No, that's okay, I didn't expect you.' Cathy was in the kitchen preparing supper. 'Things often turn up.' She spoke without any annoyance. In his life things *did* turn up. 'And anyway, you couldn't have done anything to help ... they behaved like the family from hell, but still they're getting the children back. That's showbiz and social workers for you.'

'Did you meet Sara, she's great, isn't she?' He sounded very enthusiastic.

'Yes, she is actually. I thought she was going to be boot-faced, but she doesn't miss much. Walter took her in, though.'

'I was very impressed with her, I must say, and she's going to help on this homeless project. It's good to have a social worker on the team, she has all the statistics from her end ...'

Neil was excited about it in a way that slightly turned Cathy's heart. She had been going to tell him all about Walter's locked bedroom, about her plans to entertain his mother at the premises, about the menus they were dreaming up for the Chicago-style wedding in July. But they all seemed very trivial and like tittle-tattle compared to the project for the homeless. The one where Sara with the big boots and the hand-rolled cigarettes was being co-opted onto the committee. A long time ago Cathy would have gone to those meetings, taken notes and typed letters; that was before she had a proper career of her own.

But by Saturday Cathy felt well cheered and able to cope with all that lay ahead, like taking the children back on a visit to their real home. She drove to St Jarlath's Crescent to collect them.

'Mam, how old is Geraldine this autumn?' Cathy asked when the children had gone out with Hooves, and so were way out of hearing.

'Let's see, I'm the eldest, and then ... Well now, she'll be forty next birthday. Imagine, the baby of the family forty!' Lizzie was smiling at the thought.

'I wonder, would she like a party?' Cathy mused.

'Don't you know her better than anyone, what do *you* think?'

'I don't know her all that well, Mam, I haven't an idea what she'd like in lots of areas. But would she like it mentioned that she was forty, that's what I don't know.'

'But aren't you in and out of each other's houses all the time?' Lizzie was surprised.

'Used to be, not so much these days. Mam, was she gorgeous-looking when she was young?'

'She certainly was, and wild! You wouldn't believe it . . . When we were married first Muttie and I couldn't come back into my mother's house without getting a list of complaints as long as your arm about Geraldine – she was out till all hours, never doing her homework . . . Dressed like a tramp . . . I wish my poor mother had lived to see the way she turned out in the end. The perfect lady, mixing with the highest in the land.' Lizzie spoke with admiration and amazement but no jealousy.

'And when did she change?'

'Oh, she had this fellow, I can't remember his name. Very posh anyway, and a good bit older; she began to smarten up her act to go out with him. Then after he was gone she went back to school again. My poor old ma used to think she was trying to educate herself so that Teddy – that's his name, Teddy – would think she was more top-drawer, but I said it was a bit late for that now. Anyway it didn't work out and there was no mention of him again. Teddy! I haven't thought of him in years.'

Cathy wondered if this was also true in Geraldine's case. She was going round there later, once she and Sara had made their second visit to the twins' family home. What she had said to her mother was true. There were many, many ways in which Cathy knew absolutely nothing about the glamorous, groomed, self-confident woman who took cars and jewelled watches and even an apartment from married men. She didn't even know whether Geraldine would want her fortieth birthday highlighted or buried.

This time the tea tray was on the table when they arrived. Kay poured from the heavy teapot with a frail, shaking hand. Kenneth seemed to be more aware of his surroundings and of the fact that his children, whom he had abandoned for months, were not automatically being returned to him. He knew that he had to put on some kind of a show.

'Two charming ladies *and* my beloved twins as well . . . Too much happiness,' he said.

The children looked at him, startled. This was even more effusive than last time.

Sara spoke first. 'Can we run through a few outstanding matters, Mr Mitchell,' she said briskly.

'My dear lady . . . anything, anything.'

Kay came running in at that moment. 'I made scones,' she cried triumphantly.

'But Mother, you don't . . .' Simon began.

Cathy frowned a terrible frown at him, and he stopped in mid-sentence. Cathy looked at the small shop scones which the woman had heated up in her attempt to make this look like a normal home. She felt a lump in her throat. Kay *had* given birth to Simon and Maud nine years ago. They must mean something to her, even in her confused state of mind. She had looked so poorly when they visited her in hospital; Cathy had never seen the day coming when she would be in charge of a home again.

'Your nephew Neil was telling me about your financial arrangements last night,' Sara said. 'Apparently his father has arranged for this house to be mortgaged and has set up a trust.'

'Very good of Jock, sorted it all out,' Kenneth nodded and beamed eagerly.

'He gave me these figures, and it's agreed that this proportion goes towards their clothes, school needs, books, bus fares, and so on, and that there was a figure towards the upkeep of the house, including Mrs Barry three times a week and a gardener half a day once a week to keep the place in check.'

'It all sounds wonderful,' Kenneth said.

'And how much do you think Walter will contribute to the household?' Sara's face was expressionless as she asked the question that she must have known was futile.

'Oh, poor Walter doesn't have any ready money,' his mother said with a little laugh.

'But his room and board? After all, he does go out to work and earns a salary,' Sara was dogged.

'He must be quite poor because he sometimes works in Cathy and Tom's waitressing, I mean catering, business as well,' Maud said helpfully.

'Not recently; he won't have that as a source of income any more,' Cathy said in a tone that left no doubt whatsoever.

Sara looked up with a smile. She was really pretty when she smiled. Her funny spiky hair and her big boots were outside the frame.

'You could of course let his room if he weren't here?' Sara's eyes were mischievous.

'Oh, no, it's the boy's home,' said Kenneth. 'By the way, he left you a note about his room . . .' He offered her a letter without an envelope, 'One that all were meant to see.'

Sara read it out. 'Dear Sara, sorry that I can't be here today to meet you. On your last visit my cousin's wife seemed to be suggesting that I was unwilling to show you my bedroom. I would hate it if my little brother and sister's return home were to be delayed by any misunderstanding over something so irrelevant. I have tidied it up, ready for inspection. Please feel free to go in as you please.'

They all listened as she read. 'No need to, of course, but very courteous of him,' Sara murmured.

'No need now,' said Cathy, half under her breath. Whatever Walter had been storing in his room, whatever stolen goods he was fearful that they should see, had been moved. They did a tour of the house, checked the bedrooms, saw that the linen had been aired, the bathroom properly cared for. Sara was very thorough; she checked that the washing machine worked and went through the food cupboard and examined the dates on items in the freezer. She asked practical questions about what work Mrs Barry would do, ensured that there were cleaning materials and even checked the garden shed.

'Nothing to cut the grass with,' she observed.

'We used to have a big motor mower,' Kenneth was startled. 'It was quite new, actually. Do you remember it, darling?'

Kay thought hard. 'Not really, not since last summer ... Children, do you remember a motor mower?'

'Walter took it to be mended,' Simon said.

'When was that, Simon?' Cathy asked.

'Ages ago, when we were living here,' he said. 'I think it was a secret.'

'Why do you think that?' Cathy was gentle.

'I don't know. I thought he had broken it himself, you see, cutting the grass, and he wanted to get it mended before Mother and Father found out.' Simon's face was so innocent that Cathy wanted to cry.

'When was this, can you remember at all?' Sara wondered.

'Oh, last summer, a long time ago,' said Simon, who had never wondered before why the machine had never been returned to the shed, and wasn't even particularly worried now.

'Will we wait until Neil gets here before we agree that they can come back?' Sara asked as she and Cathy walked through the wilderness of the garden.

'Neil?'

'Yes, he said he'd be here.'

'Oh, sure.' Cathy was actually sure that he wouldn't be here. She had left him back at Waterview still on the telephone about some other crisis.

'Walter sold the grass-cutting machine. And the kids' things,' she said.

'We've no proof whatsoever of that, Cathy.'

'Would you believe it if Neil said it?'

'But surely he doesn't think. . . ?' She seemed aghast.

'Let's ask him, Sara, when he gets here,' Cathy said.

In her heart she thought, 'If he gets here.' But she was wrong: when they got back to the house he was there, just as businesslike as Sara.

'Uncle Kenneth, have you been through the house to make sure that nothing went missing while you were away?' he asked crisply.

'But how could it have? I mean, Walter was here.'

'You know how hopeless young people are. Any items like clocks, or maybe any silver?'

'I did wonder had we put away the little carriage clock so carefully that we couldn't find it,' poor Kay trilled.

'And I can't seem to see those silver brushes I had,' Kenneth seemed puzzled.

'Maybe we should make a list,' Neil said.

'Oh, do you think so?'

'I do.' Neil was very firm.

'You see, when we were assessing the value of your estate, we took all the possessions into account. We'll have to assess downwards if some things turn out to be missing, and anyway we'll need to give a list to the police if you're to claim on your insurance.'

'And to show to Walter also, Neil,' Cathy suggested, 'because quite possibly he may have taken some of these items to have them mended.'

'Mended?' Neil asked.

'Yes, Simon here was telling us that Walter kindly got the new motor mower mended, took it off with him at the end of last summer . . . And it hasn't been mended yet, apparently,' Cathy said.

He nodded. 'You've understood all this, Sara?' he asked.

'Totally,' she said.

'Right, we'll go round the house and see what's not where it should be . . . Can you help, Maud and Simon? Your sharp young eyes will be terrific, and it will make it into a sort of game.'

'I think that the marble chess set isn't where it used to be . . . I can't see it, anyway,' Simon offered as information.

'Can I have a board like Sara's to write on?' Maud asked. 'Please, if it's possible, I mean,' she added.

Sara immediately ripped some pages off and handed the clipboard and pad to the child. Neil smiled at her in gratitude, and Cathy then saw the look that Sara gave him in return. It was naked admiration.

'Cathy, it's Geraldine.'

'People always say this, but I was just thinking about phoning you five minutes ago.'

'You weren't thinking about Sunday lunch tomorrow, by any chance?' Geraldine asked.

'No, but you're very welcome. It would force us to cook something instead of just picking, and we'd love to see you. That would be great.'

'I meant here, it's a working lunch . . . I really think it's time someone did something about Marian's wedding. Their hotel accommodation is booked, but nothing else . . . We should have a council of war.'

'Well, we have the hall. Should Tom come too, do you think?' Cathy asked.

She hated breaking into his weekend as she did into her and Neil's. There was so little free time for any of them these days. She was relieved when Geraldine said not to disturb him during his weekend.

'It isn't necessary now, not at this stage . . . This is really only talks about talks. Shona's coming, she's a great help at things like this, and Joe Feather will be here about something else, it's a fashion show he's setting up but he might have a few ideas about the Chicago party as well.'

Cathy felt tired. There was too much to think about. Her mind felt full of problems, like swarms of bees.

'That would be great, Geraldine. Can I bring something with me?'

'No, no.' It didn't sound convincing.

'I can go into the premises, take something out of the freezer,' she said.

'Well, if you did have a dessert . . . I certainly wouldn't say no.'

'Chocolate roulade?' Cathy suggested; she had plenty of those in the freezer.

'Great, see you tomorrow, notebooks at the ready.'

Cathy wondered whether Tom knew that his brother was setting up a fashion show, and more importantly, whether Marcella knew. But it was a Saturday night, let it go, let it go. Enough drama in her own family. Why get involved in other people's?

'That's twice in a month Joe came to see us, Maura, the boy's heart must be in the right place,' JT said as they had their Sunday lunch.

'I did offer him a dinner today, but he had somewhere fancy to go.' Maura was not yet totally won over.

'He's setting up a fashion show, Maura; he has to have lunch with the people who will help him.'

'They shouldn't be working on the Sabbath day,' she said.

'I don't imagine it's *working* as such, more talking, I'd say.'

'What would *you* know, JT, about fashion shows, and whether they're working or talking?' she asked.

'What indeed? But don't I have a proper life for myself, a great wife, a fine home, a decent business and a grand Sunday dinner on the table? Isn't that better than anything Joe has?'

He was rewarded. Maura returned to the kitchen and cut him an extra slice of beef off the very overdone roast which had been in the oven for several hours. She was gradually coming round to the son who had hurt her so much over the years by ignoring his family and abandoning his faith.

'No love, I can't go,' Neil said.

'Okay.'

'No, Cathy, don't be like that . . .'

'Neil . . . I said okay. I suppose I'm disappointed not to have you there, and I thought we might go to the pictures afterwards . . . But if you have too much to do then I understand.'

She called Geraldine to tell her there would be one less, but the number was engaged. What the hell, she'd tell her when she got there.

But when she got to the Glenstar apartment the table was only set for four.

'Joe not coming then?' Cathy asked as she placed the roulade on one of Geraldine's plates.

'No, he's on his way. It *is* set for four, isn't it?'

'Yes, of course.' Cathy was puzzled.

'You, me, Shona, Joe?' She came out of the kitchen and counted, and looked surprised that Cathy had thought it would be otherwise.

'Did Neil ring you then?' she asked, surprised.

'Neil? No, why?'

'To say he couldn't come. He was very sorry . . .'

'I didn't expect him to come . . .' Geraldine said.

'Well it turned out all right. My mistake, I thought . . .'

'Of course he was invited, but he never turns up at things, does he?' Geraldine said, going back to the kitchen.

'Ah, he does, Geraldine, he was marvellous out with the twins yesterday, you'd be amazed at him. He was just like a dog with a bone, nothing would deter him. He *does* go to things.'

'And if I wanted a lawyer for any cause whatsoever, he'd be first on my list, that's without a doubt.'

'But this wasn't a case, it was family.'

'*His* family, Cathy. He's too busy for other things.'

The buzzer went and Shona had arrived, followed minutes later by Joe. They were sitting down making plans. Cathy had to drag her mind back to the conversation. Why hadn't she forced Neil to come today? He would have if she had told him that she needed him. Cathy wondered was she getting flu; she had been feeling tired and slightly weepy for a few days now. Suddenly a terrifying thought came to her. There was no wild possibility that she could be pregnant? She grabbed her diary to see where she had put the little x's to show when she expected her period. It was three days late. But it often was, Cathy told herself firmly, and forced herself to listen to ways they could publicise a fashion show. As soon as this was over they would help her to organise her sister's wedding. And she'd think about the other thing later. There was no problem.

Hannah stood at the hall door of Oaklands and looked on with annoyance as Jock Mitchell put his golf clubs in the back of the car.

'I didn't know you were going to play on *Sunday* as well,' she complained.

'You haven't arranged anything?' he asked. Jock was a sociable man; he didn't like to think that guests would arrive at Oaklands and find him missing.

'No, but . . .' Hannah bit her lip.

'That's fine then. See you when I see you.'

'When will that be?'

'I wish I knew.' He was vague.

'But food, Jock? Will you be back for lunch?'

'Lord no, it's a competition. Sometime in the evening. Bye now, dear.' He was gone.

Hannah went back into the house. She would get the Sunday papers and sit in the garden and read. She got little joy these days from sitting under a tree on the well-kept lawn at Oaklands. She hated to admit it to herself, but she was very lonely. What had happened to this house where once Lizzie had been polishing and scrubbing, and Neil tumbling in and out with his friends, Amanda bringing girls home from school and all Jock's colleagues and friends dropping in for a drink? If she had invited people to lunch, Jock would not have run off to the club. But he wouldn't stay at home if it was only Hannah. Perhaps she should ask Cathy about simple things to have ready in the freezer. Yes, she'd do that tomorrow. She thought about Jock's brother Kenneth and his unstable wife. Hannah was glad that she had kept out of all their messy affairs. She could well have been landed with those children. She looked around the big, empty garden.

'Neil? It's Simon. Do we have any money of our own anywhere, you know, pocket money or anything like that?'

'Don't you get something every week?'

'Yes, but it's only a pound and that's not enough.'

'Enough for what, actually, Simon?'

'We wanted to buy a present for Muttie and his wife Lizzie to say thank you when we leave.'

'Oh, they don't want that at all . . .' Neil reassured them.

'That's not it, it's that we'd *like* to give them a present, they've been very nice and they bought Hooves and he cost real money, all Muttie's winnings one week.'

'Yes I know, but they realise you don't have any money . . .'

'We've got *much* more money than they do, haven't we got a huge house, Neil? And money in the bank and everything. St Jarlath's Crescent is very small.'

'Simon, you're not going to buy them a new house, are you?' Neil laughed.

'No, they like this house. We wanted to buy Muttie a good pen for his work at the bookmakers', it would be about two pounds, and we wanted to get Muttie's wife Lizzie leggings.'

'Leggings?'

'She has pains in her knees and she thinks it's the cold and damp, so if she had red woolly leggings they would keep her warm and stop the pains.'

Neil gulped a bit. 'The leggings cost four pounds, and then we'd like to get a present for Cathy too, she did an awful lot of driving us around. Maud says she needs hair lacquer, it's a kind of glue that holds your hair together. They're different prices. We'd like a kind of middle-price one, about two pounds.'

'So that's about eight pounds altogether. Is this what we're looking at?' Neil asked.

'About that, yes.' Simon sounded doubtful.

'You sound as if there's something more. Let's have it.'

'We'd like to leave a tin of dog food for Hooves, and to give you something too. I know you didn't do all *that* much, but we thought you should have a present, a small one.'

'Well, that's very nice indeed,' Neil said, trying not to be annoyed.

'So what do you think?' Simon wasn't going to lose the main clause.

'I think twelve pounds should see you right, with some over,' Neil said firmly.

'That sounds just right, thank you, Neil.' Simon, who would have settled happily for ten, was delighted.

'So it's a question of transferring the funds.' Neil took it all very seriously.

'What does that mean, exactly?'

'Well, you don't have bank accounts, so I can't send you a cheque. It will have to be a cash transaction, I'd say.'

'An envelope of money, do you mean, Neil? That would be great.'

'No problem, it's owing to you. I'll get it to you today.'

'Will Cathy drive it over? You see, we don't want her to know . . .'

'She's not here. I'll tell her nothing and I'll drive it,' he promised.

He hung up the phone and sat thinking about them for a while. They were funny little things, certainly, and Cathy had done wonders with them. But they were a full-time job. It had made them both realise what a wise decision they had made about their future. Be marvellous to other people's children, but don't have any of your own.

Joe Feather was very focused at the lunch. He never lost sight of what they were trying to do, not for one moment. He had a very quick mind, which was good in business but he said that he lacked broad sweeps of imagination, and also he was totally out of touch with the clothes scene in Dublin. First he needed to know the rivals in his field, then where they were succeeding and failing. He needed to identify trends in the ready-to-wear market, which might be different in country towns from Dublin. He wanted to be sure why Haywards thought it a good idea to go downmarket when they had designer rooms and a very wealthy clientele. He listened intelligently while Shona explained that Haywards was busy encouraging the younger shopper, women in their twenties who would buy three or four outfits for summer or a whole holiday wardrobe rather than those who paid a fortune for two items. Geraldine went through different types of PR plan, one very expensive indeed, involving lunches with fashion journalists and buyers and interviews with the financial press on the mechanics of getting the clothes to Ireland.

'Too expensive and too many awkward questions asked.' He grinned at her.

'You're right,' Geraldine agreed. 'But I had to show you what could be done. Right. This is what I suggest.' And she reeled through plans for a press party before the fashion show, advance photographs taken by Ricky and sent to papers and magazines so that each would have a different one, models, make-up, hairdressing. Joe Feather took quick notes, agreeing to this, arguing that. It took half an hour and one glass of wine each.

'You have my yes please on that at this moment, but I'm only a third of the company on this lot so could you bear to talk to my two partners if they were to call you?' Joe said.

'Of course I'll talk to them,' Geraldine said, 'but let me do out a proposal and e-mail it to them first so that we all know what it is we *are* talking about; it will take less of everyone's time. They'd have this tomorrow by eleven. Is that all right, Joe?'

'Super-efficient.' He raised his glass to her.

'Oh, and Joe, you should put yourself all out to talk to the press. Very difficult prima donnas, some of them are. A personable man like yourself, with an Irish accent and well able, would go down a treat.'

'Me?' He was genuinely surprised.

Cathy smiled. The Feather brothers had no idea how good-looking they were; it added to their charm.

'She's right, Joe, I don't go for your kind of looks at all, but you have that superficial, attractive charm that makes them fall off their branches and roll over for you,' Cathy said, laughing.

'Ah, Cathy, you wound me . . . I'm superficial . . . You don't go for my looks, what else are you going to hit me with?' He pretended to be offended.

They were unexpectedly helpful, it turned out, on the subject of the Chicago wedding. Cathy wished that Tom were here to share the ideas and the conversation that went backwards and forwards. Her hand raced across the notebook writing things down, as Joe had been doing about his fashion show earlier. Joe wanted to know all about the hall they had hired . . . It was an old church hall attached to a parish where James Byrne knew the parish priest. The priest had been happy with the thought of any money whatsoever for the parish, so the price was reasonable. Cathy and Tom had been to inspect it, and thought it was fine. It could be used as two areas, one for the reception and drinks and the other for the food, then the first one would be cleared for dancing. It would hold a hundred people comfortably, had fair kitchen space and cloakrooms. They could decorate it as they liked – Marian had suggested she would like an Irish-American theme, and maybe flags. Joe said that he thought it was over the top to drape the hall with US and Irish flags. Shona said it wasn't over the top at all, it was exactly what they would like. The Americans were travelling many thousands of miles for a ceremony; it must be marked. Geraldine asked was there a budget, and Cathy said yes there was, but of course they would go over it for Marian's sake. Joe debated buffets. He thought they were far better, you didn't get stuck with anyone. Geraldine said that the point of this was for people to get to know each other, and perhaps it should be a carefully thought-out seating plan. Shona said the thinking nowadays was not to mix up the families but let each side sit with its own. Geraldine had been at a smart wedding recently where everyone changed seats after each course – all the men moved to the next table – it meant that everyone got to know more people. Joe had been to a wedding where the receiving line was on a little stage surrounded with flowers. Cathy thought that Marian would prefer it to be as traditionally Irish as possible; people often thought like that when they had left home. Of course, it depended what you meant by traditional.

'You're the only married person at the table, Cathy,' Joe said. 'What would you like, what was your own wedding like . . . ?'

'You don't want to know about my wedding, oh, believe me, you don't,' Cathy said ruefully.

'It wasn't *that* bad,' Geraldine said.

'Well, that was only thanks to you,' Cathy said, grateful always to her aunt for having saved the day. 'We had the reception at Peter Murphy's hotel, lovely salmon I remember, my mother had to be sedated, my father bribed, Neil's parents stayed for thirty-five minutes. The priest we had was very decent, by the way. He said the right thing to everyone, it was just that no one was listening. Hannah's nose got further up in the air and my mother's head nearer the ground.'

The others laughed at the image, but Cathy was serious. 'No, if you only knew, it's quite true. We wanted to get married quietly, in London maybe, and go back to Greece, but we thought we owed it to them. Neil was the only boy in the Mitchell family and I was the only Scarlet left at home. We didn't want to short-change them. Boy, were we wrong!' Her face was set hard.

Geraldine lightened the mood. 'Well as far as we know Marian's doing what she wants, not what she thinks whole groups of the previous generation want.'

'But does she *know* what she wants? She thinks Ireland is coming down with Irish dancers leaping up into the air and that two of them are called Simon and Maud. She's probably told all the Americans that the place is like Maureen O'Hara in *The Quiet Man.*'

'Well give it to her,' Joe said as if it were obvious.

'The customer's always right,' said Shona.

'The atmosphere is more important than the food, I've always said that,' Geraldine said.

'Well thanks for the vote of confidence in the caterers,' Cathy laughed.

'No, silly, you know what I mean.' Geraldine was brisk. She summed up all the arguments for and against every suggestion they made. No wonder she had got on so well in business, she had a very clear mind. Cathy finally had a proper plan in front of her.

They cleared the table in minutes between the four of them and shortly afterwards, Shona and Joe left to go back to work. Cathy watched them from the window. Geraldine was sitting on one of the sofas when Cathy turned away from the window. She had poured two glasses of wine.

'I'm not sure . . .' Cathy began.

'Sit down please, Cathy.' The voice was firm; it wasn't an invitation, it was more a command.

'Sure.'

'What is it, Cathy? Tell me, please.'

'What do you mean?' she blustered.

'Don't insult me. I've known you since the day you were born, I skipped school and went in to see Lizzie in the hospital. You were already terrifying her with your roaring and bawling . . . So you won't go on pretending that everything's all right, we have been down too many roads together to lie to each other at this stage. It's one of two things: either I have offended you or annoyed you by something I did or said, or else it has nothing to do with me and you're in some bad trouble.' She sat there on her sofa, her legs tucked underneath her, looking ten years younger than her age. Always immaculately groomed, dressed today in a navy and cream outfit as if she were going to Quentins instead of hosting a working lunch.

'Which would you like it to be, Geraldine?' Cathy said eventually.

'Well obviously I'd prefer it to have been something I said or did, then I could explain it and apologise if necessary. Naturally that's what I'd want, rather than to think you had an illness or your marriage had problems.'

Cathy said nothing.

'So can I ask you again, which is it?'

'It's neither and both in a way.' Geraldine waited. 'All right,' Cathy said eventually. 'You're going to think this silly, but I was upset when you told me you took presents from men.'

Geraldine looked at her. 'You're not serious.'

'I'm very serious. It's only one degree away from taking cheques . . . it's so tacky, Geraldine. You don't need that. You're the icon for us all, you're the role model, for God's sake.'

'And you've changed your opinion of me since I told you that Freddie bought me this watch . . .'

'Well, yes, and that Peter gave you the flat and that someone else gave you that sound system, and the rug, and for all I know everything here.'

Geraldine's face was cold. 'You actually think less of me. Me, your friend, because I accepted gifts.'

'Yes, I do, it's so tacky, and it's so unnecessary. You don't love these men who fancy you, Geraldine, you haven't loved any of them, they're just . . . they're just . . . Well, I'd say a meal ticket, but you don't need a meal ticket, you have your own business.'

'Go on.'

'I shouldn't have started this, I feel much cheaper than I am accusing you of being, sitting here throwing back all your generosity to me and to my family . . .'

Geraldine just sat, calm and motionless.

'You forced me to say it. I see now why you didn't feel upset being in Peter Murphy's house . . . you never cared about them, not one little bit, it was all for this . . .' She made a sweeping gesture around the room and its style. Her face red and upset. Geraldine seemed unmoved. 'So what do you have to say to *me*? You said you wanted me to tell you and now I have. Is it going to be a stony silence?'

'No, Cathy, but nor is it going to be one word of apology, not one.'

'You're proud of all this?'

'I'm neither proud not ashamed, it's a way to live.'

'And you never loved any of them, that's right, isn't it?'

'I loved Teddy,' Geraldine said.

'Teddy?'

'Oh, I loved Teddy and he loved me, but not enough to leave his wife for me.'

'But that was back a long time ago. People didn't then.'

'It was twenty-two years ago, not the Dark Ages, and people *did* leave home and start again, as Teddy said he would, and as I believed he would, particularly when I was pregnant.' Cathy stared at her. 'But it turned out not to be the case.' The voice was very flat. Cathy hardly dared to move. 'And we agreed that the timing was all spectacularly bad, I can't remember what, one of his children going to school or leaving school or hating school or loving school. Some bloody thing. Does it matter?' Cathy took a sharp breath. This was horrifying. 'But it meant that there could be no baby.' A long pause. 'I *could* have kept the baby. But then I knew I'd lose Teddy, so I lost the baby instead. A friend of his was a doctor, not a great doctor, as it happened, and I had left it too late so that complicated it, and I don't think this doctor was entirely sober at the time. So after that, no more babies, ever.'

'Geraldine.' Cathy was stricken.

'So after that, as you can understand, I was a bit low, but I thought I'd have Teddy to comfort me, but as it happened I didn't. He was nervous. I had become a loose cannon on the deck, and he took his family and went abroad. So, Cathy, it sounds very dramatic but I didn't allow myself to wallow too much in the luxury of love after that. The men I've known since and who have been my friends like my company and conversation just as much as my bed and my wearing lacy underwear. I have not been dependent on *any* of them for *anything*. They can't offer me commitment or a home, so they give me watches and that silk rug on the floor in front of you. But I'm sorry if it *upsets* you and you think *less* of me and that it's, what did you say, *tacky*,' she repeated Cathy's accusations with great emphasis. 'That's all I can say. I'm sorry if it offends you, but it doesn't offend me, and it's my life.'

'I'm so ashamed I could die,' Cathy said.

Geraldine sighed. 'Leave it, Cathy. You had guts to say it, I give you that much. And what was the other thing that was upsetting you, the one that didn't have to do with me?'

Cathy spoke slowly. 'I don't suppose there could be any more inappropriate thing to tell you, but I think I might be pregnant, and it's the last thing on earth I want now.'

June

'What time is she coming?' Tom asked.

'Who?'

'Well excuse *me*, but I thought all this shining and polishing and getting out the best linen was to impress your mother-in-law,' Tom said.

'Oh, sorry Tom, I was miles away. Hannah's coming about half past twelve.'

'Let's get the skates on then, and go and make some soup,' he suggested.

Cathy leaped up guiltily. Tom had been here since five a.m., and she had been barely able to get in by nine. The bread had been delivered to Haywards, he had stopped at the fish shop on the way back, he had got all the vegetables and a huge lamb bone for a big soup order, he had already made her two cups of coffee and she had done nothing. Of course she hadn't told Neil last night. There had been no time. After the hours of crying in Geraldine's flat she had felt drained. Neil had been distracted, stuck in his books. And as Geraldine had soothed and consoled her over and over, it might be a false alarm. She must get a Predictor first, from the chemist, and then go to a doctor. Then and only then should she tell Neil.

'Tom, I'm so sorry. Here, pass me over the knife, I'll start chopping the basil and tomatoes.'

'She'll think it's tinned,' he objected.

'No she won't, so what, anyway?'

'*You've* got very courageous suddenly,' he said.

'No, I'm still terrified of her, but at least now I know there's no pleasing her, so that helps a bit.' Cathy's eyes were a little too bright.

'I don't think you should have a knife in your hand this morning,' Tom said. 'You'll be in ribbons by the time she comes. Leave the dangerous stuff to me.'

'Great. So what do I do?'

'Set the table, get some flowers.'

They had a great bank of flowerpots in a wheelbarrow in their courtyard. Whenever they wanted a table decoration they just lifted out a pot of primulas, pansies or begonias, cleaned it around the edges and placed it in a brass container. When the function or the need to impress was over, the plant went back outdoors.

'That doesn't sound very much,' Cathy said.

'And start practising your smile. Remember the last time Hannah

Mitchell was here? You were shouting at her like a fishwife about her coat and your mother and assorted other topics.'

'Oh, we've all mellowed since those days,' Cathy said loftily.

'I think we'd need to have,' said Tom, who had already got the stock into the soup saucepan and begun the work.

'Imagine, we'll be going home on the bus today,' Simon said to Maud.

'By ourselves, no Muttie,' Maud said.

'He said he might happen to be walking by the school sometimes, and he'd walk us to the bus,' Simon said.

'But he's probably going to the shoemaker's or the bookmaker's, it's not really on his way,' Maud worried.

'How else will we ever see Hooves?' Simon said, and they looked at each other in concern. It hadn't been actually said, but they knew that social visits to St Jarlath's Crescent were going to be very few and far between.

'You're a very sweet girl, you know, Geraldine,' Freddie said as they had coffee together in her office. He had called in to discuss the Italian villa presentation, which would be upcoming soon. But they were also talking about his own party, for which Geraldine's niece and her partner were going to do the catering.

'I know I am,' Geraldine said. 'I'm totally delightful, but in what particular way at the moment?'

'You're as anxious as I am that the party Pauline and I are having will be a success,' he said in some wonder.

'But why ever not, Freddie? I don't want anything from you except what I have, your company, your interest, your concern, your wonderful loving . . . Why *should* I not be interested and wish it all well?'

'You're amazing. You really mean it.' Freddie Flynn had not come across such women before.

'You know what the French used to say about a mistress. She must be discreet, and never, ever do anything that would upset the man's family, his children and certainly not his property . . .' She laughed engagingly at him.

'You ask so little, Geraldine,' he said in a throaty voice.

'But that's not true, and truly I have so much.' She waved her hand around the office, the business that was hers alone. The hand that she waved had a jewelled watch on the wrist.

'So Cathy will come round to the house and set it all up with Pauline, will she?'

'Yes, Cathy or Tom, they take it turn by turn. He's just as good,' Geraldine said.

She hoped it would be Tom that made the visit. The way poor Cathy was behaving at the moment, she wouldn't be able to keep her eye on the ball at all.

'Nice to see you, Mrs Mitchell, and don't you look well.'

'Thank you, Shona,' Hannah patted her hair. 'I've just had a glorious hour in the salon. I'm going to have lunch with Cathy, as it happens. I thought I'd buy her a little gift. What do you suggest?'

'Well, now, if it were anyone else I'd say a loaf of that delicious bread that Scarlet Feather does for us, but you'll be having that anyway ... Flowers are always nice, a fancy soap maybe?'

'The bread doing well, is it?'

'We can't keep it on the shelves or in the restaurant. I told Tom that we're going to have to make him an offer he can't refuse and come and work here full-time.'

'Imagine.' Hannah was surprised.

'Anyway, enjoy your lunch, Mrs Mitchell. Lots of people would envy you, you know.'

'Yes, I'm beginning to realise that,' Hannah said in a disapproving voice.

She still found it hard to accept that she was lucky to be getting a meal cooked for her by the maid's daughter. But she *must* not think like that, or else something would slip out as it so often did for absolutely no reason at all, and then everyone took horrific offence and Neil sighed and Jock sighed and Cathy went totally berserk. Don't say *poor* Lizzie. It was just an expression, but try telling that to Cathy Scarlet.

James Byrne had decided to cook a dinner that night. Not the real one, not the one he was rehearsing for, but just to see whether he could or not. And as it happened, Martin Maguire was going to be in Dublin. He would try it out on him. He took out Cathy and Tom's meticulous instructions – they had even typed out advice about the shopping. It was a Monday morning, he had nothing else to do with his time, he would go to the market that they had suggested with their list in hand. Martin Maguire would be very surprised indeed to be presented with such a gourmet meal. And it would be great practice for James. He had enjoyed those two evenings with Tom and Cathy enormously, and wished he could think of an excuse for more. But he must remember that this had been his undoing before. Becoming too fond of people, too dependent. It must not happen again.

'This house will never be the same,' Muttie said when the children had left for school. 'Those people won't get the children to do their homework the way we did.' He shook his head sadly.

'They'd know more than we do,' Lizzie said.

It had always worried her, looking after the children of the quality in her own home.

This was something that had never worried Muttie. 'It's a matter of discipline,' he said firmly. 'This house has proper rules and regulations.' And at that, he got out the paper and studied the racing pages, while Hooves laid his sad black head on his knee, and the woman that the children still called Muttie's wife got ready to leave a house that had proper rules and regulations to go out and clean the apartments and houses of the quality.

*

Joe Feather called his brother.

'Could I buy you a nice pint and a plate of sausages for lunch?' he offered.

'God, I'd love it Joe, but it has to be late. I'm setting up a lunch here for Cathy's mother-in-law!'

'Is it a big do?'

'No, only the two of them.'

'God, you've fallen on hard times, a lunch for two people. Have I invested in a Mickey Mouse company?'

'No, you fool, it's a social thing.'

They fixed a place to meet.

'Give Cathy my love. Thank her for everything yesterday.' Joe hung up.

'Hey, you didn't say you met my brother yesterday,' Tom said.

'Tom, I haven't said anything this morning. I'm like a zombie. I met him at Geraldine's, and he was a great help about the Chicago wedding. Actually he really was, I meant to tell you. I took lots of notes.'

'Geraldine's, no less?'

'Yeah, but they weren't thinking of withdrawing their funding or anything, it was about this fashion show he's putting on.'

'I know, Marcella's going to be one of the models, isn't it great?'

'Great,' said Cathy, wondering whether Tom knew that it was mainly lingerie that his girlfriend would be modelling.

'Come in, Mrs Mitchell.' Tom's smile rarely failed to hit its target.

'Oh, hallo, er ... Tom, isn't it?'

'It is indeed, Mrs Mitchell, and how well you're looking, if I may say so.'

She patted her hair again. It was so wise to go to a good salon regularly. Cathy was so foolish in this regard, as in so many things.

'I didn't know that we were all going to ... I mean ...'

'No, no, I'm just serving you and then making myself scarce.'

'I heard you do marvellous bread for Haywards.'

'Thank you so much, they're very kind about it. I've left you a little selection to try, and also a packet to take home.'

Eventually the Tom Feather smile had worked. Hannah Mitchell was smiling back.

'You are a kind boy,' she said, as so many middle-aged, middle-class matrons had said to him over the last few months.

Cathy stood waiting, in a pink and lilac summer print dress that did her no favours, her face as white as a sheet, her hair tied back with an elastic band.

'You're welcome, Hannah,' she said in a flat voice.

'It's a pleasure to be here, and my goodness doesn't the place look nice!'

She looked around, and Tom hoped that Cathy would respond warmly to her, otherwise all this would be in vain. To his relief, Cathy was smiling.

'This is our front room, where we sit clients down and persuade them to have much bigger parties than they intended,' she said.

'Very nicely done,' Hannah looked around her with grudging admiration. 'Nice colours, too.'

'My mother made the curtains and covers,' Cathy said proudly.

Hannah looked at them in disbelief. 'Oh, Lizzie was always . . . marvellous with her hands,' she said eventually.

Tom sighed with relief, poured them a sherry and went to the kitchen.

'Tom, will you either eat that sandwich or throw it away, but for God's sake stop analysing it,' Joe said, laughing at the way his younger brother was unpicking all the ingredients.

'Look at what they charge for that, Joe, no seriously, look at it. A tired tomato, a piece of plastic cheese, a dead leaf of lettuce, half a hard-boiled, discoloured egg . . . A smear of cheap salad cream . . . And they dare to call that a Summer Salad Sandwich. What do visitors to this country think, tell me what do they say . . . ?'

'Oh, shut up and eat something else,' Joe said good-naturedly.

'Like those cremated sausages you're eating? People have no standards,' he was still ferocious.

'What am I going to do about Ma?' Joe asked.

'What about her?'

'Well, I've been going up there a bit,' Joe began.

'I know you have, Joe, and honestly it does mean so much to them . . .'

'But they say you drop in every second day . . .' Joe said.

'When I'm passing I do, it's no trouble . . .'

'Come on, who ever passes Fatima on the way anywhere?'

'I've had to do it, Joe, it's no big thing.'

'I'm sorry I left it all to you.'

'Well, you were in London, and anyway you're doing your bit now, it lightens the load.'

'Okay, okay. So what'll I do about Ma? She wants to come to the fashion show.'

'Well, let her, can't you?'

'Of course I can't.'

'I'll keep an eye on her.'

'No, not that, the clothes. Ma can't see them.'

'But why not, she came to our launch party. I don't think she enjoyed it very much but she was glad to be there . . .'

'But Tom, the garments . . .'

'What about them?'

'It's swimwear, lingerie, half-naked girls all over the place . . . Mam would only drop stone dead.'

'It's not *all* that, is it?' Tom asked with a hollow feeling in his stomach.

'Most of it.' Joe looked at his brother's face. 'Marcella told you, didn't she?' he said.

Neil went into Quentins restaurant and sought out the elegant Brenda Brennan immediately.

'I'm having lunch with a real gangster, Brenda, he's going to try to get me drunk. Can you just put tonic at the bottom of my vodka glass each time ... so that he thinks I'm having a real drink?'

'It's not fair to charge him then, Mr Mitchell.'

'You'll manage something, take it off something else ... You know all the ways around things.'

'I've been long enough in the business for that, it's true, so perhaps, Mr Mitchell, if you'd like to keep your eyes down I'll lead you swiftly to a table without your having to meet your father, who will be exiting from a booth fairly imminently.'

Neil followed her as directed.

'You should run the world, Brenda!' he said, just glimpsing his father leaving with a blonde half his age.

'I often think I do,' Brenda Brennan sighed.

'That was delicious. That tomato soup, very sweet taste, and my heavens, that's good, that bread ... You hardly ate any,' Hannah said.

'Hannah, I'm eating it all day, and all night ... Tom is so proud of it, and olive bread isn't enough for him these days, you have to have green olive or black olive ... he's such a perfectionist ...'

'And what do we have now?'

Was there a time when she had dreaded this woman? How long ago it all seemed. 'It's monkfish, I think you'll like it, and quite a small helping to leave room for dessert ...'

'I brought you this.' Hannah spoke gruffly, and thrust across the table a gift-wrapped Haywards parcel.

Cathy knew she must open it, however ill-timed; the monkfish with its saffron sauce, the green beans with tiny lardons of bacon and toasted almonds, the potatoes and ginger were all wafting up their vapours at them. It was a time to savour the food, not to open presents. But she unpicked the elegant wrapping and opened the gift. From the paper came an overwhelming and pungent smell of incense. Cathy felt slightly weak.

'It's wonderful, Hannah, what exactly ... ?'

'It's one of those new very powerful aromatic oils for the shower, apparently young people like them ...' Hannah began.

It was too much, the heady smell of that and the food. Cathy clutched her stomach and ran from the table, and knelt vomiting into the lavatory pan. She heard her mother-in-law calling outside the door.

'*Cathy*. Cathy, let me in, are you all right?'

Marcella looked up from arranging bottles of nail colour and saw Joe Feather in the salon.

'You're very, very beautiful,' he said in an odd sort of voice.

'Joe?' she was alarmed.

'Sorry, I'm actually just saying this as a fact ... it *is* a fact ... but I sort of let slip to Tom that the lines you'll be modelling are fairly sexy ... And to be honest, I don't think he knew that.'

She looked at him, surprised. He began to wish he had never spoken.

'Now I'm getting out of it and letting you take it from here, Marcella . . . okay?'

'Sure.' She was very calm.

'It's just that he adores you . . . you see.'

'Of course.'

Joe shrugged. 'It's just, I don't honestly think Tom knew.'

'Thank you, Joe,' she said in a voice that made him feel small.

'I'm so sorry, Hannah, you'll have to forgive me, that's why I wasn't eating so much bread. You see, I've had an upset tummy.'

'But you should have said, you should have cancelled the lunch . . .'

'No, *please* Hannah, look, I'm fine now.' Cathy forked herself a helping of the monkfish, which tasted like soap in her mouth, and forced herself to swallow it. She had moved the heavily scented bath oil to another part of the kitchen entirely. Eventually she felt her stomach return to normal. The conversation wasn't exactly easy. Every subject had a background; any chance remark, a history. They talked about the twins returning to The Beeches and how genuinely *good* Lizzie had been. Good and generous, all the right words. Hannah remarked that Cathy hadn't found time yet to go to the Haywards salon, and Cathy looked her in the eye, promising that she would go soon. They talked about Neil and how hard he worked, and how lucky Cathy was that Neil did not play golf like his father, otherwise she would be a total widow. And suddenly out of the blue Hannah mentioned Amanda.

'Cathy, can I ask you something . . . Do you think Amanda has some reason for not coming home to see us?'

This was a moment where Cathy could do some good or some ill; she had to be very careful. She barely remembered Amanda Mitchell, two years older than Neil, bossy, distant and didn't come to their wedding, but had sent a really great present . . . a top-class atlas and an expensive radio that got all kinds of frequencies and wave bands and a card saying, 'May you see the world and love it.' Cathy had thought that lovely of her. Although it might have been rather over-prophetic, if Neil still had it in his head that they should set off to see the world and love it full-time. She had often asked about Amanda. Up to now, her mother-in-law had been vague and dismissive; Amanda was too busy, too successful in Canada to keep in touch with a new sister-in-law whom she barely knew. Neil had been no help about her either. Manda was great, he said, her own person, great, no, of course he wouldn't telephone her, what would they say? It seemed very distant not to want to talk to your only sister about *something* . . . Cathy would prattle non-stop about her sisters in Chicago at any time. Now that Cathy had heard fairly authoritatively that Amanda was in a gay relationship in Toronto, what did she say or do?

'Perhaps she's met someone over there?' she suggested.

'I don't think so. Amanda was never particularly interested in men, she didn't bring boyfriends home when she was here ... We always thought of her as a career woman.' Hannah was thoughtful.

'Maybe that's it, then, she's tied up in her career and the people she meets there, the other women who run the bookshop. Maybe that's her life now.'

It trickled away as other subjects of conversation had done. Soon Hannah made a move to leave.

'Won't you have more coffee?'

'No indeed, it was all quite perfect. I really enjoyed this lunch, and you look much better now, dear.'

'Yes, I'm so sorry ... And thank you again for the beautiful bath oil.'

Even remembering the smell of it made Cathy feel slightly nauseous again, but she held on. She watched as Hannah left taking small steps across the cobbled courtyard. In all those years of fighting this woman with the small, pinched face, she never could have envisaged a day like today. A day when she would stand at the doorway of her own business and might very well be, as it happened, pregnant with this woman's grandchild.

Simon and Maud couldn't believe it. Outside the school stood Muttie and Hooves, waiting for them as usual.

'I thought you'd need to be settled onto that bus,' Muttie said simply. They looked at him, delighted. 'For the first day anyway, until you got the hang of it,' he said, and the little group headed off happily to the bus stop.

Sara was sitting in the garden rolling a cigarette when Neil arrived. He went to join her on the old wooden bench.

'How does it look inside?' he nodded towards the house.

'Okay ... for the moment ... but you get the feeling that your uncle could be poised for flight at any time; he's fairly unsatisfactory about his plans.'

'He always was,' Neil agreed ruefully.

'I'll keep an eye on it,' Sara promised. 'Just because kids live in a lovely big house like this doesn't mean that they still don't need someone to look out for them.'

'They should sell it and move somewhere much smaller, more manageable, but they won't hear of it. All puff and style and grandeur and nothing to back it up,' Neil said.

'You don't approve of him,' Sara said.

'He's never done a proper day's work in his life. My father takes it all fairly lightly, but he *has* put in hours in an office. Anyway, I think it's ridiculous in this day and age, one family living in all these rooms,' Neil looked back up at the house.

'You and Cathy don't have a big house, then?' Sara asked.

'Lord, no. Small place in Waterview.'

'Oh, I know those, they're nice. Still, not a place for a family, though, not like this place here is.'

'We don't have children,' said Neil Mitchell, proceeding to take the papers out of his briefcase and tell Sara the social worker where they needed her help for a report on the homeless that was going to be presented by an umbrella organisation. They pulled the old garden table up to them and worked away happily. From inside the house, Kenneth Mitchell watched them absently from one window, only mildly interested in these people in his garden. Kay Mitchell watched anxiously from another. It was nearly time for the children to come home, she had asked Mrs ... Mrs Barry to make sandwiches for them. Mrs Barry wanted to know should the crusts be on or off; Kay decided eventually that there should be two plates, one with, one without.

'Please come in, Muttie,' Maud begged.

'No, child, honestly. Hooves and I will get another bus back.' He was very insistent.

'But we want to show you our house.'

'Another time, son, not the first day.'

'And Hooves could go for a run in the garden, our garden ... *please*, Muttie.'

But he was firm. It wasn't sensible, not the first day, there would be people taking notes, he didn't want it to look as if he and Lizzie were trying to muscle in, get more than their fair share of the twins.

'You mean, like ... everyone wants us to be with them.' Simon was puzzled at this possibility.

'Of course we do, but the best thing is that your own mam and dad are back to take care of you, now that they're in a position to do so,' Muttie spoke with a heavy heart. Nothing he had heard from Cathy made him think that this was any fit pair to be looking after the children.

'But you will come in *some*time, will you, Muttie?' Simon begged.

'Of course I will, son, when you're more settled, when Hooves is more acceptable.'

'And we're definitely coming to St Jarlath's Crescent at the weekend, that's agreed with Sara,' Maud said anxiously.

'Of course you are, child, and Lizzie and I are looking forward to it greatly, so we are.'

'I wish ...' Maud began.

'So in you go now, like a good girl,' Muttie said before anyone could say what they wished.

'Sandwiches!' Simon said, pleased.

'Thank you very much, Mother,' Maud said.

They sat down at the table and their parents watched them admiringly. Neil and Sara had come in from the garden.

'How many may we have?' Simon asked.

'Well, they're all for you, of course.' Kay Mitchell was proud to be seen to be such a provider.

'Yes, but won't it take our appetite away for tea?' Maud asked.

'Muttie's wife Lizzie always says only one biscuit each when we come in, otherwise it will spoil tea.'

'Well, this *is* tea,' poor Kay stammered.

'No, I meant *real* tea, you know, bacon and egg tea,' Simon asked.

'Or tinned beans or whatever,' Maud said in a small voice, as if realising that all was not entirely well.

Kay looked wildly from her husband to Sara. 'Nobody said anything about bacon and eggs, there was to be a tea ready and it's ready.' She looked about to cry.

'Well that's fine, Mother, we'll just eat them all now,' Simon said.

'It's enough for me, really,' Maud assured her.

Sara and Neil exchanged glances. Kenneth Mitchell looked out into the garden as if inspiration and solutions would come from the wilderness he saw.

'I had lunch with Hannah,' Cathy said to Neil that evening when they were both back at Waterview.

'Well done.' He went to the fridge to pour two glasses of Chardonnay.

'She was fine. She talked a lot about Amanda.'

'Sorry, she does drone on about her. Hey, have you gone all total abstainer on me? That's the second glass of wine you've waved away; you must be sickening for something.'

'I just don't want it now. Neil, did you know Amanda's gay?'

'No, I didn't. Did my mother tell you that? I just don't believe it.' He was open-mouthed at the very thought.

'Of course she didn't.'

'And since when?'

'I've no idea, but those women I did a reunion for the other day mentioned it, and I checked with another woman who knew her in Dublin when she worked in a travel agency, and this woman is gay herself and she said yes, it's true, and Amanda has this marvellous partner and they work in a bookshop together ...'

'Well, imagine that! Manda, who would have thought it? Good luck to her, I say.'

'And so do I, Neil, I say good luck to her, and all our friends will ... It's her mother and father who might not be so jolly about it.'

'No ... you speak only the truth,' he said, grinning ruefully.

'So anyway, I thought you'd like to know,' Cathy said.

'Cathy, how did you try to tell this news to my mother? I've pleaded some pretty impossible cases in my time, but this one I must hear.'

She laughed. 'No, I didn't even get to first base. Listen, are you going to sit down with that wine, or are you going to take it to work with you?'

'I'm taking it to work with me, by which I mean next door. I have a hell of a lot to finish on this homeless thing ... I met Sara today with the twins, by the way, and she's a lot of help ...'

'Oh, how did it all go? I'm dying to hear. Sit down for a minute and tell me.'

Neil sat down. 'It was amazing, she explained that there *is* funding, but that no one can really get at it. It needs the right questions to be asked at the right time ... She gave me lots of notes.'

'Funding?' Cathy was bewildered.

He explained at length about a European Union grant that might be available for the homeless, and how the ad hoc committee mustn't throw away this piece of information at once, they must keep it as a card to play later once they had got some muscle. Eventually, after a lot of listening to details of strategy, there was a moment when she could get in a word about Maud and Simon.

'Oh, they were fine,' he said, getting up to leave the table.

'No, sit down and tell me, Neil, did they have a welcome, any kind of a meal for them?'

'Yes, they had sandwiches.'

'Is that all?'

'The twins were so funny, they kept asking about their real tea. Sara took over, it's under control.'

And that was all she was going to hear. And it seemed it was not the night to tell him about anything else.

Tom was looking for the right way to mention the fashion show to Marcella. A way that would not reveal the sick feeling at the base of his stomach that she was going to be walking around half naked in front of strangers. He knew that this jealousy had nearly destroyed them before; he *must* keep it under control. She loved only him, he knew this, for heaven's sake. Why couldn't she just keep her clothes on and join him in the business? But he realised so well that this was destructive. It was impossible to fathom why someone as loving and happy in a relationship as she claimed she was still wanted to strut about in swimwear and lingerie. But he must be careful. This kind of suspicion and possessiveness was what had made her walk out before. He was walking on eggshells. To his surprise, she brought the subject up herself.

'You won't believe the colours that Feather Fashions have for the show, lime greens and fuchsias ... *nobody* could want to wear that kind of underwear.'

Tom let his breath out slowly. At least she was telling him that it was lingerie.

'No, give me basic black lacy stuff any day,' he smiled.

'Just so that you realise it's all a bit of fun?' she said.

'Of course.' His heart was heavy. She was preparing him. 'And the swimwear, what colour is that?'

She seemed relieved that he knew about that much, anyway. 'The same, mad, wild colours, almost luminous ... He either hasn't a clue what he's doing, or else he's got it just right ... There's a very fine line between the two.'

He stared at her. She really was obsessed by the whole fashion business. It didn't have anything at all to do with stripping off in public. He would be mad to let that thought settle in his mind.

*

'Darling, you'll never believe who was just on the phone!' Kenneth Mitchell said to his wife as he came back from the phone in the hall.

'Who was it, dear?'

'Old Barty coughed up out of nowhere.'

'Barty ... Our best man!' she cried, pleased.

'Yes, I told him he could stay. He's got a vintage car, or a veteran one, whichever ... He's going to take it to some show.'

'What did he cough up?' Simon asked.

'Sorry?' His father looked at him vaguely.

'Was it blood?' Maud asked fearfully.

'Or a pint of stout. Muttie coughed up a pint of stout once, his wife Lizzie was very annoyed.'

Their parents looked at them, confused.

'Anyway, old Barty says he'll take us all for a spin in the car, Saturday. You kids too.' He looked at them, proud of the treat.

'But on Saturday we go to St Jarlath's Crescent,' Maud said.

'To see Hooves and Muttie and Muttie's wife Lizzie.'

'No, darling, you can go another day. Those people won't mind,' their mother said.

'No, we can't go another day, honestly they'll be getting ready. They're making a proper tea and everything, we asked for sausages.' Maud was almost tearful.

'Well telephone them and say it's off, that's a good girl.' Her father was brisk.

'Why do I have to do it?' Maud was now mutinous.

'Because I don't know them, my sweet child, and you do.'

'Why can't Simon do it?' Maud complained.

'Girls are better at that sort of thing, darling,' her father said.

'They'll be so upset,' Maud said to Simon.

'And I'm upset too,' Simon said. 'I wanted to see Hooves. I have a new trick to teach him.'

'It's not fair,' Maud said.

'It's not,' Simon agreed.

They looked at each other.

'Let's ring Cathy,' they both said at the same time.

Cathy said they were to leave it with her, just say that they had telephoned and found Cathy there and spoken to her as her parents weren't in.

'But that's not exactly true,' Simon said. 'We *did* ring you at Waterview.'

'Yes, but I could have been in St Jarlath's Crescent. I don't think we should worry about it, do you?' Cathy was brisk.

'A white lie,' Simon suggested.

'Hardly a lie at all,' Cathy assured him.

'Neil, this is *not* going to happen,' she fumed at him.

'Hey, peace, peace ... I'm on *your* side, of course it's not going to happen.'

'So who rings your uncle and tells him, do you or do I?'

'I'll ring Sara,' he said. 'That's her job, and she'll tell them.'

'But she's not at work now, surely.'

'I have her mobile number,' Neil said, somewhat to Cathy's surprise.

As it happened, when old Barty turned up he didn't have his car at all, so the outing would never have taken place.

'Just as well the children went off to those people,' Kenneth Mitchell said.

'What people?' Barty asked as he sat down at the table and Kay fussed around vaguely, bringing in first a plate of bread, then a dish of butter, then removing the bread to toast it.

'Oh, some people who live up in some terrible place, but they've been very good to the twins . . .'

'Are they family?'

'No, or yes, in a way, through marriage. Very complicated . . .' Kenneth ended the discussion mainly in order to cover the fact that he wasn't entirely sure why his son and daughter had been looked after for months by a couple with the extraordinary names of Muttie and Muttie's wife.

'What did happen to your car, Barty?' Kay asked.

'Well, um . . . it's all a bit hard to explain . . . as old Ken here would say, it's all pretty complicated,' said Barty.

Kay went back to the kitchen to sort out what to do next. Barty explained to Ken in a low, urgent voice that he had actually lost the car in a card game, and wondered would his friend Ken help him win it back. Kenneth Mitchell explained in an equally low and urgent voice that things were not as they used to be. Today's world meant a budget, a tight budget worked out by Neil, that thin-faced nephew of his, and policed by people like this boy's wife and a social worker. Had to account for every single thing. His incomings, small as they were, from a couple of directorships and the rental of a property, went straight into some fund or trust, and a living allowance was paid out each month. Degrading to say the least. Old Barty hadn't given up hope. Could they borrow against next month's living allowance? Kenneth proved to be a changed man in this area . . . Things were too precarious, he said. Sorry, Barty old man, can't do.

'The dancing teacher's coming round tonight,' Lizzie told the twins.

'Oh, good, will we wear our costumes?' Simon wanted to know.

'No, I don't want them getting all messed up, I've made up cheap kilts and cloaks for you so you can get the swish of it all . . .' Lizzie's face was glowing with pride over it all. 'The teacher says you need a bit of practice; suppose you were to take a tape home with you and practise in your kitchen back there?'

'Yes . . . yes, we could I suppose,' Simon looked doubtful.

'Or would that not be too easy?' Muttie wondered.

Simon threw him a grateful glance. 'You see, it's Father . . . He can't understand fellows dancing, he says, and he doesn't understand it being a family wedding. I said it was for our cousins coming from Chicago, and he didn't understand that either.'

Simon looked embarrassed by having to explain all this, but Muttie hastened to reassure him. 'Oh, a man like your father, who'd have travelled and all, he'd not be in the way of knowing the way things have changed, fellows dancing and leaping all over the place there are nowadays,' he said cheerfully.

'But it *is* a family wedding, isn't it?' Maud was always anxious to have things straight.

'In a way . . . But of course . . .' Lizzie began. Humble again, and still not wanting to claim any kinship with the great Mitchells.

'It is *of course* a family wedding. Isn't Cathy the sister of the bride, and she's married to Neil, your first cousin. What on earth could be closer than that?' Muttie asked. This satisfied the twins totally, and they ran off to teach Hooves the new trick before the dancing teacher came.

Muttie and Lizzie looked at each other.

'We should never have taken them in,' Lizzie said.

'We should never have let them leave,' Muttie said.

Neil went into his father's office. The solicitors' firm was a busy one, long established and middle-of-the-road. They didn't send many briefs to Neil Mitchell, fiery defender of causes, but then he didn't need them. There was plenty of work coming in from elsewhere. Neil wasn't coming in about business; this time it was family. He saw Walter through an open door, and paused for a moment. By rights the boy should be brought in on it, but then he was much more likely to hinder than to help. Walter looked up.

'Neil?' he said without much pleasure.

'Glad to have the kids back at home?' Neil asked.

'What? Oh, yes, they're great,' Walter said unconvincingly.

'No problems with your parents or anything?'

'No, no, they leave me alone, I'm glad to say . . . and of course I'm not always there.'

'I meant with them and the twins,' Neil said coldly.

'I see. Of course. No, I don't think so. Should there be?'

Neil gritted his teeth. What a self-centred little monster Walter had become. He thought only of his own entertainment, his own good time. Neil remembered suddenly that he had lent the boy his very expensive binoculars recently to go to the races. He had asked for them back twice when he was at the house.

'By the way, Walter, do you have those field glasses I lent you? You told me they were at the office.'

'You came all the way in here to get them back?' Walter's face was a sneer.

'Do you have them, Walter, please?'

'Keep your hair on.' He got up and went to a drawer which he pulled, but it was locked and wouldn't open. 'See, I did my best.' He looked so supercilious and unrepentant that Neil felt his knuckles clenching.

'Lock your drawers in the office as well as your room at home, I see?'

'Can't be too careful, I say,' Walter said cheerfully and picked up the telephone to show the conversation was over.

'Dad, we're going to have to give some thought to Kenneth and the whole set-up there,' Neil said.

'Are we?' Jock Mitchell was disappointed. It was a sunny day, and he had been hoping to slip away from the office in a few moments. He had his golf clubs already locked into the boot of the car, and was just waiting until the coast was clear in order to leave.

'Walk down to the car with me, Neil, we'll talk as we go.'

'No, Dad, I want you to write him a letter on your office writing paper.'

'What about?' Jock was testy now. He had carefully organised his clients and his associates into line with his plans; all he needed was to be disturbed by his brother.

Patiently Neil explained that Kenneth Mitchell was in actual danger of losing his children into care. A foster home, or even residential accommodation might be found if he continued to break the terms of the agreement.

'He's not doing that already, surely?'

'Well yes, he is, he's reneging on everything: no homework supervision, forgot pocket money, tried not to let them go back to the Scarlets' on Saturday, Cathy says there's no proper food there at all, they live on crisps, cornflakes and sandwiches.'

'Is Cathy taking too much on, do you think?' Jock asked.

'No, I don't think that at all, *and* they're trying to take holidays at the time of this wedding when the children are doing a dance, they've been learning the bloody two-hand reel for months.'

'At Lizzie's daughter's wedding?' Jock asked.

'Yes, at my sister-in-law's wedding as it also happens to be, and they're not missing it. Believe me, they are not.'

'Hold your horses, Neil.'

'And that's another thing, that bloody Walter keeps his drawers locked in his office, why's that? He borrowed my binoculars to go and follow the horses six weeks ago and says he can't get them out of his file cupboards.'

'That's nonsense, Neil, everything's on computer these days, you know that. There are no locked drawers here.'

Neil saw his father checking his watch. 'If you dictated the letter now, Dad, and got it signed, then we could all go about our business, whatever that business is.'

Very grudgingly Jock Mitchell took notes and called in a secretary. 'Sorry Linda, my son insists,' he said.

Muttie brought the children back on the bus.

'I don't mind it, honestly. I like the journey, you see, and it makes us independent if we're able to go to and fro on our own without annoying Sara or Cathy or Neil,' he explained to them.

'If you had been a wealthy person would you have had a car, do you think?' Simon asked.

'Indeed I would, I'd have had a big red Beamer.' Muttie smiled at the thought.

'What's that?' Maud wondered.

'It's a BMW. But no, to be honest, I'd probably have had a station wagon, a great big thing half the length of the footpath outside,' Muttie said.

'But there's only the two of you,' Simon objected.

'Ah, but just stop and think of all the people in St Jarlath's Crescent who'd like a lift somewhere,' Muttie said.

'You are very kind, Muttie,' Maud said.

'You really *deserve* an accumulator,' Simon agreed.

Walter came home on Saturday evening and found that old Barty was still in residence. The introductions were vague. There seemed to be a bottle of good whiskey on the table which was causing his mother some distress.

'Father, don't you think ... I mean, weren't we meant to ...'

'Nonsense, Kay knows well that she's not drinking and I'm not wandering off, we're here to give you a home.'

His father sounded quite reached already.

'The children will be home soon. They might have their private army with them,' Walter warned.

'That's a good point, let's put this bottle on hold for a while.' Kenneth tucked it away out of sight. 'And Walter, since we have you, if you're going to be out and about I wonder could old Barty have your room? He's in the small room on the stairs, it's rather like a boxroom,' Kenneth began.

'Oh, no, heavens no, I'm just fine where I am,' Barty began to bluster.

'Sorry, Dad. I'll be here for a few days but then I was hoping to go off to England to the races, I'll have my room right for you by then.' He smiled his warm Walter smile. Barty said nonsense, he'd be well gone by then. Kenneth said nonsense, where could Barty go, he'd even lost his beloved car in a card game. Barty said that would all be sorted out soon, he had plenty of chances to win it back. And Walter pulled up a chair at the table with them to discuss how and when ... It seemed a subject very dear to his heart.

This time the twins persuaded Muttie to come in and say hallo, very much against his will. But he needn't have worried about being out of place. Kay Mitchell was already in bed, and the three men at the table looked up, mildly and politely interested.

'You've had supper at ... um,' Kenneth said.

And as Maud and Simon began to tell about all the extra things they had with their sausages, the flat mushrooms and the filled baked potatoes, Kenneth Mitchell's interest flagged.

'You're so kind to look after them so well,' he said to Muttie, and shook his hand firmly. Muttie opened his hand. A pound coin was there, less than his bus fare home. Muttie's face flushed a dark red, and the colour went right around his neck.

'Thank you very much indeed sir,' he said with great difficulty.

Simon and Maud looked on, stricken. 'See you next Saturday, Muttie,' Maud said. 'Thank you for a lovely time.'

'And for paying for the dancing lessons, Muttie, they can't have been cheap,' Simon added.

Muttie was backing out.

'Do you want to see our rooms, Muttie?' Maud asked.

'Another time, Maud, thanks all the same.'

'Or look at the garden where we could have a kennel if Hooves came to stay,' Simon begged.

'Honestly, next visit, Simon, thanks. Good luck to you all,' and he was gone.

The twins had thought they might do the reel tonight at home. They had a tape of the music with them. This would be a new audience. But they noticed a bottle of whiskey had come onto the table, and their father and brother and old Barty wanted to discuss something other than dancing. Everyone was waiting for the children to go to bed, on a bright summer evening when they had been hoping to be up for ages more. With brief goodnights the twins marched grimly upstairs. Mother's door was closed.

They missed sleeping in the same room as they had in St Jarlath's Crescent. Everything was different now.

Cathy said they couldn't possibly take on a sales conference lunch for thirty on the very same day as Freddie Flynn's party.

'It will be dead easy,' Tom pleaded. 'They're slave-drivers these people, no lingering and enjoying themselves for the employees, no drinking and getting messy like a real lunch. They'll be back working in that hall at two-fifteen and we'll be out in half an hour after that.'

'Stop smiling at me like that, Tom Feather, it doesn't work here,' Cathy said. 'We want to do the Flynn thing right, we're being silly taking on something else that might put it at risk.'

'And do we or do we not want to get this business up and running?' he asked.

'We do, but not by beating ourselves down onto our knees.'

'Aw, come on Cathy, I'll do the lunch with June and you and Con keep things ticking over here. We'll be back to you before three. Yes?'

'We're pushing ourselves,' she said.

'Stretching ourselves,' he corrected.

They looked at each other long and hard.

'It's easy money, it's a good contact,' said Tom. In his heart he was thinking that if he cleared a few pounds profit on this he'd take Marcella to one of those fancy hotels for a weekend, a place with a swimming pool and a health centre, a place she could dress up at night.

'We've always said people go under if they take on too much, their standards fall,' Cathy said. She was thinking that she truthfully could barely manage as things were, the nausea was still there, she didn't sleep properly and she still hadn't found or made the time to tell Neil. The Predictor from the chemist had said yes, but people knew they were often wrong, she had an appointment with the doctor next week. It might all be nothing, surely it was too soon to have morning sickness anyway, supposing it were true.

'Let's go to arbitration,' Tom said.

They took out of the drawer in the kitchen table the coin that they always used when they were at an impasse. Solemnly they watched as the coin spun round, and waited until it fell. Tom picked it up.

'So I won, but I promise you'll be glad.'

'Sure I will.' Cathy nailed the smile onto her face.

'Can we come to England with you on a holiday?' Simon stood at the door of Walter's bedroom.

'Of course you can't,' Walter said impatiently.

'But we'll have no holiday then,' Maud said.

'Aren't you back home . . . *and* you'll have no school, that's meant to be a holiday, surely?'

'Muttie was going to take us to the country when we were living in St Jarlath's Crescent,' Simon said mutinously.

'You weren't living there, you were only staying there,' Walter complained.

'It felt like living there,' Maud said.

Walter went on packing his case. The twins didn't move.

'Muttie has been to the country a few times, he said you wouldn't want to spend too long there, though,' Maud explained.

'He found it was desperately quiet, and that you could hear birds roaring at you from trees,' Simon said wistfully.

'Kids, I'm sorry, I have to get on.'

'Are you going today?' Maud asked, disappointed. It was marginally more lively here when Walter was around.

'Tonight or tomorrow. I have some work to do with Father and Barty.'

'But Father doesn't *have* any work.' Simon was remorseless about getting things straight.

'Of course he does, Simon,' Walter was annoyed. 'He has meetings and responsibilities.'

'With Barty?' Maud wanted to know.

'Not always, but today, yes.'

'So if Father's out and Mother's going to stay in bed . . . what will *we* do?' Simon and Maud looked at each other blankly. There had been so many things to do in St Jarlath's Crescent. And so many people, including Hooves, to do them with.

'You could get a job,' Walter suggested.

'I don't think we're old enough,' Maud said.

'No, doing kids' jobs: stacking shelves, collecting trolleys in a supermarket, tidying someone's garden . . . those kind of things . . .' said Walter vaguely, having never attempted any of them.

'We might be able to wash up for Cathy and Tom,' Simon said cheerfully.

'Hard taskmaster, that one,' Walter said.

'Still, it's worth a try,' said Maud.

'Imagine, no more school until September,' Cathy said when she saw the two faces arrive at the premises.

'I don't mind school too much,' Maud said. 'You wouldn't want to say it there, but I don't.'

'No, I didn't either,' Cathy said. 'I felt I owed it to Geraldine to do well, and I got great pleasure out of getting good results.'

'Why Geraldine?' they asked, and Cathy remembered that the twins produced every single piece of unwanted information at the wrong time. She was meant to have won scholarships, all through. Geraldine's generosity was never mentioned nor even known in Lizzie and Muttie's home.

'I meant she always encouraged me to study for the scholarships, you see.'

'Were you brilliant to have won them?'

'Not bad,' Cathy said modestly, feeling slightly ashamed. She racked her brains to think of something that the twins could do to help, where they wouldn't be in the way and they couldn't do too much harm.

'Polish glasses?' Con suggested.

'No, they'd smear them,' she whispered.

'Chopping anything . . . ?'

'They're worse than I am, the place would be running with blood. I know, they can shine up the silver and count the forks.'

Maud and Simon were installed in what was eventually going to be called the second kitchen but for now was the storeroom. They chattered on happily; sometimes Cathy leaned against the door and listened. There were bits about Father's business with Barty, and how good Sara was at getting Mrs Barry to do the shopping from a list. Sara knew a place where they could learn tennis, but Father said it cost too much. Whether Muttie would ever come to visit them at their home again after what Father had done. Cathy sighed. She had resented them so much a few short months ago, mainly because she knew they were being passed on by Hannah and Jock. But everything had changed so much. Who could have thought it? Again and again she went over when exactly it must have happened. Neil would be furious. Why did it feel different now? Once it would have been unthinkable to keep something this important from Neil. It was still unthinkable. She would tell him tonight.

Tom and June came back from the sales luncheon in high spirits. Fifty people, all of them as obedient as mice, start eating, continue eating, finish eating, if only the whole world was run like this.

'But how awful to be part of it,' Cathy said, shuddering.

'Ah, but it was so easy, Cath, you've no idea, they'd have eaten a paper plate smeared with jam, believe me.'

'They must have been *very* hungry,' Maud said, shocked.

'Well *hallo*, we have help.' Tom was surprised and pleased.

'And great help they are. Tell them you were joking about the paper plates and jam Tom, otherwise they'll tell everyone it's our signature dish.'

'You don't give them enough credit, you knew that was a joke, Maud, didn't you?' Tom said.

'I wasn't totally sure,' she admitted.

'Well it was, they'd never eat a paper plate, and what's more they wouldn't have a chance to. Why? Because we'd never serve anything on a paper plate, is that very clear?' He had a mock-ferocious face on. The children nodded furiously. It was clear, they said.

'We've been polishing your good silver,' Simon said.

'You could see your face in the punchbowl,' Maud said proudly.

'Well that's great, because everything we own, all the things we have been saving for are tied up in these four walls.'

'What, everything here is all you have?'

'Yes, our treasures are here, certainly,' Tom agreed.

'Is it all very valuable?' they asked.

June was stacking the dishwasher, and raised her eyes to heaven.

'Well, some of it is irreplaceable, like that punchbowl you just cleaned so beautifully,' Cathy said. 'I won that at a competition at college, it was first prize for a summer fruit punch, we use it everywhere now.'

'The Flynns don't want it tonight apparently,' Tom said thoughtlessly, after all Maud's hard work. 'Which means we have it ready shining and waiting for the next job, which is just *great*.'

Maud beamed with pleasure.

'And what's the next most valuable thing?' Simon wondered.

Tom, Cathy and June joked about whether it was the disk on the computer with all the recipes, the book of contacts, the double oven, or the chest freezer . . . They laughed as they listed all the things they had.

'We never thought we'd own such a huge amount of stuff,' Cathy said.

'Like Muttie thinks he'll never win an accumulator,' Simon said, eager to show he was on her wavelength.

'But he never will, Simon,' Cathy implored.

'People may well have said to you and Tom . . . that you'd never have any treasures,' Simon was fierce in his defence of Muttie's dreams.

'We worked for it, night after long night . . .' Cathy said.

'Muttie works at the bookmakers', he studies it, he learns about form and he lets the sound of hooves get in on his brain.'

'Of course he does,' Tom said gently.

'Are you insured, in case anyone came in and took all your treasures?' Maud worried.

Cathy made yet another resolution not to go down any road like this again with the children. 'Very well insured. James Byrne is like a clucking hen,' Cathy reassured her.

'What Cathy means is that James isn't remotely like a clucking hen: he is a marvellous man who made us take out a very big insurance policy.'

The twins seemed reasonably pleased with this, but Simon had one more worry. 'Do you lock up properly when you leave?' he wanted to know.

'Yes Simon, two locks, an alarm with a code and all.'

'And do you remember the code?'

'We had to make it simple for Tom,' Cathy said.

'Men find it hard to take complicated things on board,' June agreed.

'Do you have your birthday?' Simon asked. 'Or your lucky number?'

'No, they told us not to,' Tom said.

'So we have the two initials of Scarlet Feather instead.'

'Are you allowed to have letters?'

'No, the numbers, S is nineteen and F is six. If we forget, all we have to do is go through the alphabet. Even men can understand that, Simon.'

'I don't think that men are any more stupid than the rest of people, really,' Simon said thoughtfully.

'No, Simon,' Tom was contrite.

They agreed to drive the children back to The Beeches, since it was on the way to Freddie Flynn's house. Solemnly Simon and Maud watched as the alarm code was set.

'Brilliant idea,' Simon said.

'No one would ever think of that,' Maud agreed.

'Imagine, we're travelling with all the food for a posh party.' Simon was pleased.

'Yes, *and* all those nice shiny forks you polished as well.'

'Why do they not have knives?'

'Good question. They claim to have all the cutlery we need, but people never have enough forks. I went and checked; they don't have nearly enough forks.'

'You need to be quite intelligent for this work, don't you,' Simon said.

'You do,' said Tom as he counted and completed a checklist. 'It's all there, Cathy, ready to roll.'

'Okay Tom, okay June, ceremony of the keys.'

Simon and Maud watched fascinated as they hung the keys to the premises carefully on a hidden hook at the back of the van. 'Why do you put them there?' they asked.

'Whichever of us takes the van back needs to be able to open the place up, so we always have the ceremony of the keys . . .' Cathy explained.

They had arrived at The Beeches. The two children ran into the big house with the huge overgrown garden.

'Looks like a posh place,' June said.

'Yeah,' Cathy said, 'posh, dead sort of place.'

'They have to be with their own parents, their natural parents. Don't they?' Tom asked.

'To be honest, I've never exactly seen why,' Cathy said, and put the van into gear with a crash as they drove off.

Freddie Flynn was most welcoming when they got there. 'Now I know the drill, your aunt says you hate people saying to you this is the kitchen, this is the hot tap, this is the cold tap . . .'

'You wouldn't ever do that, Mr Flynn,' Cathy smiled up at him from under her eyelashes.

Tom let out a low whistle between his teeth when he'd gone. 'And you say that I put on the charm for the ladies . . . I never saw anything like that performance,' he teased her.

'I promised Auntie Geraldine he'd get the full treatment,' she whispered. 'Yeah, well.'

At that moment Freddie's small, plump wife Pauline came in. 'Freddie says I'm not to fuss, and I promise I won't, but somehow it seems like cheating to let you do it all,' she said.

Cathy felt a lump in her throat. This woman was being deceived by Frederick Flynn, important Dublin businessman, purchaser of diamond watches for Cathy's aunt. 'Not a bit of it, Mrs Flynn, you and people like you are providing Tom and myself with a generous living, we want to make it a huge success. Now your husband tells me you don't want anyone to take the coats. Have I got that right?'

'Yes, after all it *is* the summer, so they won't have that many coats . . . But you see, we got the upstairs all decorated, and I sort of hoped they might go up and see it so that I could show it off.'

'You are so right, let me see where I'm to direct them.' Cathy ran lightly up the stairs ahead of Pauline Flynn, and saw the magnificent bedroom which had been spoken of. It was in beautiful shades of pale green and blue, and there was an elegant white dressing table. It wasn't exactly a four-poster bed, but there was a ring with cascading curtains over the top; a white crochet bedspread and lace-trimmed pillowcases; doors opened on to a huge, luxurious bathroom with white fluffy towels alternating with others in baby blue. This place had all the appearance of an altar built to the god of pleasure. Cathy held her hand to her throat. Geraldine could not possibly know that Freddie's dead marriage involved this kind of decoration.

'Lovely room,' she said in a slightly strangled voice to Pauline Flynn.

'I'm glad you like it; I'm old and silly I know, but it's what I always wanted and Freddie seems to think it's nice too, and that's what pleases me most of all.'

Cathy ran downstairs quickly.

'Hallo Walter,' the twins were surprised. They thought he would have gone to England by now.

'Hallo,' Walter grunted.

'How was the business?'

'What business?'

'You said you were having a business meeting with Father and Barty.'

'Oh yes, I bloody was.'

'So it didn't work?' Simon was philosophical. 'Muttie always says that you win some, you lose some.'

'What does Muttie know about anything?' Walter asked.

'A fair bit,' Maud said. 'I think,' she added doubtfully.

There was a silence. 'We got a job like you said,' Simon said eventually.

'Good for you. Where?'

'With Cathy and Tom . . . They have a fortune in their premises, it's full of their treasures.' Simon wanted to impress his older brother.

'I'm sure,' Walter laughed.

'No, they do, all their worldly goods are there, they have two keys and a code lock in case anyone gets in.'

'Oh yeah, I bet the whole world is trying to get in there and steal catering plates and paper napkins,' Walter laughed.

'They have a solid-silver punchbowl, it's beyond price. They have loads of things,' Maud said.

'I'm sure it's very impressive, but do you mind moving off for a bit, I've a lot to think about now.'

'Okay,' Simon and Maud were good-tempered.

'And you're not whining for food or anything.'

'No. Cathy gave us something for the microwave.'

'What is it?' Walter asked with interest.

'Pasta. It will take four minutes on high,' said Maud. 'Do you want some? There's plenty for the three of us.'

'Thanks.' Walter was gruff.

They sat at the table, the three of them, Walter's mind a million miles away as the twins talked on happily about the party that Tom and Cathy were doing that night.

'They have money to burn, the Flynns do,' Maud said.

'I don't think they really *are* going to burn it though, I think it's only an expression that people use,' Simon explained.

'Yes, whatever.' She brought Walter into the conversation. 'Do you think we should get a burglar alarm here, Walter?'

'Nothing for a burglar to break in here for,' he said glumly.

'We could set it before we went out and disarm it when we got back.' Maud didn't want to let the notion go entirely.

'Yeah, can you see Mother and Father doing that? Can you see Barty coming to terms with disarming an alarm? It would be like a cops and robbers movie. We'd have the guards living here all the time.'

'But it's so simple,' Simon said. 'We know how to get into Cathy and Tom's premises just after seeing it once.'

'Sure, but do you have the keys?' Walter took his plate across the kitchen to the sink.

'No, but we know where they are,' Maud said.

Walter came back and sat down with them again.

The party up at the Flynns' was going very well. Twice Freddie put his head around the kitchen door to congratulate them.

'They're just loving it all,' he said. 'Well done.'

'Why is a nice man like that unable to look me in the eye and tell me he needs me to be a significant part of his life?' June wondered.

'Hard to know all right,' said Cathy as she piped out more crème fraiche on the little buckwheat pancakes that were disappearing with alarming speed from the platters.

'You'd never think that a woman like Mrs Flynn would be enough for him,' June said as she swept off with the new tray.

Tom and Cathy's eyes met. 'Funny old life, Tom, that's what I always say,' she grinned at him.

'Women are just riddled with intuition, Cathy, that's what *I* always say,' Tom replied.

Walter looked up the Flynns' address in the phonebook. It wasn't far away. He had been able to get the loan of a car from a night-owl friend for a few hours. He parked it beside the van and found the keys exactly where the twins had said. Through the windows he saw them all, Tom, Cathy, June and that creep Con moving about inside.

Geraldine moved restlessly around her apartment in Glenstar. Normally she never felt like this. She had been truthful in saying that she believed Freddie's private life was just that . . . private, and no concern of hers. It was just that . . . well, she hadn't planned to do anything tonight. She had taken work back to the apartment but she didn't feel like doing it, and there was nothing she wanted to see on television. In a million years she would not admit it, not even to herself. Geraldine was lonely. Then her telephone rang.

'I miss you,' he said.

She forced her voice to be bright. 'And I you. How's it going?'

'Fantastic. They're very talented, those kids, it's running like clockwork.'

'I'm so pleased for you, Freddie, truly I am.'

He hung up. A stolen moment away from his guests, his wife. It had always been like this, and this is what it was always going to be like from now on. So why was she complaining? Geraldine had known the score when she signed up.

Wearing black cotton gloves, Walter let himself in and used the code to disarm the alarm. Where were all these treasures the kids had talked about? He must be quick; he needed to get the stuff hidden in his garden shed, the key back into the van and the truck back to the friend who would be starting his evening at around ten p.m. It looked like it had always looked, a big ugly catering kitchen, a lot of stainless steel, coloured tea towels drying on the backs of chairs, shelves of inexpensive china, drawers of worthless cutlery. He pulled out possible items like a toaster, an electric grill, a microwave oven. But these things were peanuts. They wouldn't bring him a fraction of the money he needed. The money he had lost with that fool friend of his father's, old Barty, who knew a great game and had brought Walter along. On the table in the front room, he saw the big silver punchbowl the children had spoken of. It wasn't solid silver at all, and he pushed it aside in disgust. There were boxes of supplies, unopened steamers and saucepans in the storeroom; they might make *something* if he could just unload them on the right person. And he needed something, even if he got a couple of hundred quid it would be a start. He began to drag the items towards the front of the premises, and knocked over a tray of glasses as he did so. The splinters of broken glass were everywhere. They wouldn't like that when they got back. Something welled up in him, and he swooped an entire shelf of plates onto the floor as well. It was somehow satisfying. He would do more later.

He worked for forty minutes, unscrewing and transporting what might possibly change hands in an iffy market he knew about. Then, with his elbow, he raised the end of one of the china shelves so that all its contents went in a great crashing slide to the floor. He pulled out the plug of the freezer and tossed items out of it at random. He noticed with annoyance that they had a very poor stock of alcohol, and remembered that they usually arranged for a wine merchant to deliver straight to the venue. Still, there was a bottle of brandy and some other off-looking liqueurs; it would keep the guy who owned the car cheerful. He remembered one day how they had been going on and on for ever about what message to leave on the answering machine, so he wrenched it from the wall and stood on it. He hit the light bulbs with a stick and leaped aside as the shattered glass came tumbling down. He packed the car, taking the punchbowl at the last moment. He might get £20 for it anyway, and these days that couldn't be laughed off. What fools to tell the children that these things were treasure! They were so bloody smug, those two. This would show them.

July

Even if they hadn't had to tell the story two dozen times, they would never forget the return to the premises that night. They were high with the success of the party at the Flynns'.

'We've got so much better,' Tom said as he reached for the keys.

'I hope so. Sometimes I think we've just got more confident, you know, papering over the cracks,' Cathy said.

'No, we *are* better,' said June. 'I met the Riordans there, remember, the people who had the christening ... They said our food was in a different category altogether.'

Tom and Cathy loved the way June considered herself part of it all; even young Con was beginning to feel the same way. Then they opened the door. They had often heard that people who were robbed felt this strange sense of being violated. This was what it was like. When they walked into the front room, Cathy saw the clock Joe had given them lying on the floor inside the door, broken beyond repair. Tom saw the huge vase that Marcella had chosen with such care in three pieces beside the overturned table. And all their plates knocked from the shelves. June saw the drawers opened and their contents spilled and the telephone and answering machine dragged from the wall. Cathy saw that her punchbowl, the only prize she had ever won in her life, was gone from the table. They couldn't take it all in. Tom was the first to speak.

'Bastards,' he said. 'Total bastards. There's nothing to steal, and so they've destroyed everything we have ...' There was a catch in his voice which released the tears. He clung to Cathy and June.

The guards were mystified. No sign of a break-in, no forced entry, nobody else had access to keys. They had no idea of anyone who harboured malicious feeling towards them. Had they? They couldn't think of anyone at all. Rivals over work, possibly? No, they weren't in the business in a big enough way, they explained. One of the young guards who had already asked twice about insurance mentioned it yet once more to Tom.

'Yes, I told you,' Tom said a trifle impatiently. 'Our accountant insisted we pay what we think is a huge premium, but that's not the point ... That's not going to sort this out.'

'I know, sir. They can take it up with you themselves,' he said.

'Who can?' he asked.

'The insurance company, sir,' he said.

Neil was asleep when Cathy rang. 'Yes, Neil Mitchell,' he said sleepily.

'Neil, we've had a break-in.'

'Cathy?' He was mystified. He had thought she was beside him in their bed.

'Oh, Neil, burglars . . . the whole place is destroyed.' There was a catch in her voice.

'Anybody hurt?'

'No, but it's terrible,' she knew her voice was quivering.

She could see him swinging his legs out of bed as he had so often when phoned at night about a case.

'You'd like me to come in?' he said. His voice sounded resigned.

'The guards are here, it's very frightening, Neil.'

'I'll be there.'

'Do you mind?'

'Of course not.'

'Neil coming in then?' Tom said.

'Yes. Do you want to ring Marcella?'

'No, let her have her sleep, she'll know soon enough.'

Why had Cathy not done the same thing?

Neil arrived wearing a sweater and a pair of faded cotton trousers, but as full of authority as if he were wearing his full formal barrister's outfit and carrying a briefcase. The questions were endless and the leads seemed to be non-existent. The guards hadn't known of any gangs working in the neighbourhood, not anyone specialising in this kind of crime. Back and back they went to the keys and the access.

Finally the guard said, 'So all I can say is for you to take things up as best you can.'

'What do you mean, exactly?' Tom was barely paying attention. 'We *are* taking things up as best we can, aren't we?'

'With the insurance company,' the guard said.

'But what has this got to do with finding whoever did all this?' Tom waved his hand around despairingly.

Neil spoke suddenly in his crisp, barrister's voice. 'The garda is pointing out, Tom, that because there were no signs of a break-in or forced entry, the insurance company is going to have to look into the possibility of it being an inside job.'

There was silence in the room. Nobody thought that things could get any worse than they were, but they had now.

It seemed that all night they were cooking Tom's bread for Haywards partly in the small oven in Stoneyfield while Marcella helped and timed things and lifted out batches, and partly with the better facilities in Waterview with Neil and June helping.

'What will your Jimmy think about your being out so late?' Tom asked.

'He's had time to get used to it in the past; he'll think it's just another party,' June said succinctly.

The night ended, the bread was delivered and they were back at the premises.

Gradually and slowly they picked through the rubble, pausing to sigh or even cry over a broken treasure. Tom insisted that Cathy put on those big thick mittens they used to take things out of freezers.

'I can't feel anything with them on,' she complained.

'You'll cut your hands otherwise.'

'I won't.'

'Listen, Cathy, all we have left are your own good hands if we're ever going to get out of this mess,' he said.

The reality of it hit her. They might not get out of this mess. Whoever had done this to them had ruined their life's work, their dream, their one chance of running a business. She picked up a large, triangular piece of glass and took it to the heap outside. It had once been part of a corner cupboard in the front room. All the big coloured plates it had once held were broken, just as the ones from their old dresser had been flung to the ground.

She felt a great wave of sadness.

Good hands or no good hands they might never build this business up again; nothing would ever be the same. She wanted very badly to sit down and cry like a child.

They had fixed the telephone and it rang cheerfully from time to time, calls from people who had no idea into what devastation their call was being received. Molly Hayes wanted a supper for twelve. It was Shay's birthday.

'Can we come back to you on that one, Mrs Hayes, before the end of the day?' June asked in a bright, businesslike voice.

'Very busy, are you?' Molly asked.

'You wouldn't believe it, Mrs Hayes,' said June.

Cathy looked at June with pride. In six short months she had learned confidence and style as well as a lot of other little interests that her silent plumber husband would not have approved of. But she was no longer apologetic and afraid to tell the customers which was filo pastry and which was choux. June could discuss quail's eggs and langoustines with any of them now. And Cathy gulped thinking that June's career and future lay in ruins on the floor as well as their own. She watched Neil as he worked with them, helping with the clearing away: his face was grim at the outrage, his energy unflagging, even though he would have to be in court that morning. This was the man whom she had hoped to tell about the pregnancy, but that would have to wait. She paused and looked at him as he squatted in front of the cooker with Tom. They were trying to see how much of the actual fixtures and fittings had been destroyed. She couldn't hear what they were saying, but she saw him pointing and Tom pointing and the concentrated effort Neil was making to understand something unfamiliar to him.

Some of the frozen food still seemed very hard, but they couldn't take the risk of refreezing it. No one could know when the vandals had come in. It could have been any time after six p.m., and they hadn't discovered it for nine hours. By now the food might be twelve hours out of the freezer compartments. Impossible to know what to do.

When the rest of Dublin was beginning to wake up and go to work, they sent June home in a taxi; Marcella showered, changed and went to Haywards, put on her cool white coat and dealt with the nails of those with the money and time to pay for it. Despite the shocking events of the night, her heart was much lighter than usual. She wasn't going to be painting and shaping nails always. By the end of this month she was going to have had her first professional modelling work *and* an introduction to a model's agent. She could afford to smile and be charming to the customers. This life would not last for ever. Neil showered, changed, put on his lawyer's gear and went down to the Four Courts to represent two men in a wrongful dismissal case. Everyone said that he hadn't a chance, the two were troublemakers from way back, their case was full of holes. But Neil knew that the company who fired them was on very thin ice; it had an unhealthy history of being anti-trade union. He was going to win and confound them. Nothing to make legal history, and indeed his clients could well be described as highly unreliable, but it was the *principle* of the thing that mattered.

Back at the premises, Tom and Cathy looked at each other, red-eyed.

'They surely can't think it was an inside job?' she asked.

They had been asking each other this all the time.

'Apparently they could think we did it to get the compensation.'

'People would think *we* did this to *ourselves*?' She spread her hands out at the rooms.

'It's been done before, when companies were going down the tubes.'

'But we're *not* going down the tubes ... James could tell them that for one thing,' Cathy said.

James! They had forgotten about him. Was it too early to ring him? They risked that he would be up on a summer morning just before eight o'clock.

'James Byrne.' He was crisp and matter-of-fact when he heard the news. He asked questions, one after the other. The safe? Opened and papers scattered around. Yes. Yes. The guards? Any likely leads? No, no. The plant, cookers and freezers, would Scarlet Feather be able to continue trading? Hard to say. Quite, quite. The insurance? Yes, he assured them, it was all in order and would well cover losses. Then they told him that there had been no break-in, no forced entry.

'I see,' said James Byrne.

'But you know that it wasn't an inside job, James,' Tom cried.

'Yes, I know. Of course I know,' was the answer.

'But you mean they mightn't?' Tom was hardly able to say the words.

'Let's say it may just take longer for them to pay up,' said James Byrne. He was thoughtful and quiet. Last night by chance he had had a dinner with Martin Maguire, who had said that he wished those youngsters success in their premises, truly he did, but he felt that there was some kind of curse on the building. Something they would never be able to conquer and survive.

James didn't feel it necessary to report this conversation. Those two had enough to put up with already.

Shona Burke got them permission to use Haywards' kitchens from now on to do the breads; in fact it worked so well they said it could be permanent. Tom worked until the store opened, and assured the management that he would not use their ovens for his own work.

'Getting back to normal there?' the management at Haywards asked him sometimes.

'Absolutely,' lied Tom.

Nobody could be told of the shambles that was the kitchens of Scarlet Feather.

Cathy did the entire birthday party, including a chocolate birthday cake for Shay and Molly Hayes in her own house, and no one was any the wiser. No one but Neil, who was more or less dispossessed and had to step over crates and boxes everywhere if he moved, so much so that he set up a table and chair in the bedroom to do his own work.

'I thought a town house was small, but it seems to have become a bedsitter,' he grumbled. He was out almost every evening, so they could work on without fear of annoying him further.

They had forgotten how impossible it was to prepare food in such a small space. There was simply nowhere to leave anything down. Every single chair, stool and even suitcase had been pressed into service and used as a surface to store the plates that had been done, but they were always knocking them over. There wasn't nearly enough room in the freezer or the fridge; ice melted, cutlery fell on to the floor. Each day was more like a nightmare than the one that went before.

June and Cathy worked on and on as they had never worked before. They did a picnic for Freddie and Pauline Flynn; they did two First Communion buffet-lunch parties on the same day, shuttling from one to the other with Con. They left Tom to deal with the business of putting the pieces back together. And this, they all knew, was something that was sheer hell. Men from JT Feather's builder's yard came in to clear the premises, but only after James Byrne had insisted on photographs being taken and a representative of the insurance company coming to view the waste and destruction. It was going to cost over two thousand pounds to get the cooking under way again, and this was before they bought a single replacement item for the hundreds of pieces of china and glassware that would need to be replaced. The frozen food had been given away that morning or destroyed; long weeks of work thrown out at just a stroke.

Among the very first people that they should have told were Geraldine and Joe, their backers, the guarantors who had invested in their company. But neither Tom nor Cathy wanted to tell them until it was under control. Not until they knew they were going to come out of this horrible thing. They had the sickening feeling that they were going to go under. It was not a feeling that could yet be shared. Cathy didn't want to tell Geraldine. To ask her aunt to dig deep again into those pockets lined by wealthy men of whom Cathy had disapproved, and said so. She didn't want Geraldine to hand over more money. Cathy's pride had always meant that it was a debt of honour to repay Geraldine's investment with interest. The aunt who had given her so much, wanting nothing in return except the satisfaction of seeing her do well. The aunt whom she had insulted and criticised about her lifestyle. That was one aspect of it. Another aspect was that she feared Geraldine might say they should pack it all in now, since Cathy was pregnant; that the timing might have been in an odd way appropriate. There was a minefield that she didn't want to walk into yet.

'Do you mind if we don't say anything to Geraldine for a bit?' she asked Tom.

'That's funny, I was just going to say the same about Joe,' he said.

He didn't explain because they didn't have to tell each other everything. Joe was the last person he wanted to talk to just now. Joe who had given Marcella this chance to strut nearly naked across a stage in front of half of Dublin. Joe who had filled Marcella's head up with the chance of meeting some model's agent who could put her on his books and get her jobs 'across the water', as he called it. Tom hated the phrase – if he meant London or Manchester why couldn't he just say so? He couldn't bear to hear his lovely Marcella parroting it all and talking about the opportunity of modelling across the water. Joe who had been so good and generous with his funding; Joe who had obediently become a regular visitor to their parents at Fatima, thus halving Tom's own need to be present; Joe who somehow felt guilty about this fashion show, would dive into his resources and find funds for Tom as a way of buying himself out of any unpleasantness. Tom didn't want Joe to know how very near the ropes they were.

So if they didn't want Geraldine and Joe to know, that meant they couldn't tell a lot of other people either. Shona was sworn to secrecy, and June was asked to keep quiet as well – there was no problem there. They couldn't tell Muttie and Lizzie Scarlet, nor JT and Maura Feather. Cathy longed to tell her mother, to go to that familiar kitchen and cry while her mother stroked her hair. But if you told one you had to tell all. There were no accounts of it at all in the evening newspaper, nor did they go on the television programme which tried to get the public to solve a crime. James Byrne had urged caution as he always did, and Neil Mitchell had said the big multinational insurance companies would not be allowed to shelter behind a lot of pious phrases. It was an issue he felt very strongly about. He would fight for them against nameless bureaucrats who always kept the little people waiting for their money. He was already looking up precedents about it, and he wouldn't let them get away with it. He was being supportive, but Cathy wished more than anything that he had been a different kind of help. That he would take her head on his shoulder and stroke her hair. Tell her that he loved her and that they would get through this. And then she could tell him about the baby.

*

'Are we going to have tennis lessons?' Simon asked at breakfast.

'Tennis?' His mother looked at him vaguely as if she had heard the word before and with time would place exactly what it meant. She poured the cold milk out on the cornflakes, far too much of it so that the cornflakes were soggy and there wasn't any milk left for their tea. 'This is nice,' she said.

'Yes, Mother,' Maud said dutifully.

'Sara said there would be tennis lessons,' Simon said.

'Oh, Sara, yes, poor girl,' his father said.

'That the lady in boots and a cap on backwards? Dear, dear,' Barty said.

'I have her phone number. I could ring her,' Simon said. 'She'll know when and where.'

Kenneth Mitchell sighed. 'I have the address somewhere here, no need to ring her, I think just ring them and start the lessons off whenever you like.'

'And Father, when I do book the lessons, who shall I say is paying for them?' Simon was worried.

'Don't concern yourself with that.'

'I'll ring Sara,' Simon said.

'Damn it, boy, I'll pay for the bloody lessons. Stop driving everyone mad, will you, we have things to think about here.'

Kay Mitchell began to tremble. She hated seeing Kenneth upset.

'I'm sorry, Father.'

'No, no, that's all right, get your racquets out of the shed and start practising a bit here on the lawn.'

The twins lowered their eyes. This wasn't the time to tell their father that the shed was locked and they couldn't get into it.

'Cathy, could we come round to the premises to work today, to polish the treasures and things?' Maud asked.

'No Maud, sorry, today's not a good day.'

'We wouldn't want money or pasta or anything,' Maud begged.

'Sweetheart, if I could I'd say yes. We'll do it another time, okay?' She hung up.

'She hung up on me,' Maud said alarmed.

'Did she sound cross?' Simon wondered.

'A bit. What did we do?'

'Maybe we should have written to thank her for the pasta,' Simon said. 'It's very hard to know.'

'Sara, I'm ringing from a public phone on the road, it's Simon. Does Father pay for our tennis lessons?'

'Yes he does, he knows that.'

'I think he's a bit short of money.'

'Not too short for tennis lessons, it's part of his allowance ... Start whenever you like, I'll keep an eye on it.'

'It's just that, you know ... he gets a bit ...'

'I'll be very tactful,' Sara promised.

'And Sara, our racquets are locked in the garden shed.'

'Walter?' she asked.

'I suppose so, but they're all in such bad tempers if you ask anything.'

'You don't have to ask anything, I'll do it . . .' she said.

'Was *she* cross, like everyone else?' Maud wanted to know.

'Yes, she sounded cross, but not with us I think,' Simon said after some thought.

'Walter Mitchell? I'm Sara, Simon and Maud's social worker.'

'I know,' he smiled at her warmly. 'We don't get many like you visiting our house or our offices.'

But he was getting nowhere this time. 'Why have you locked your garden shed?' she asked.

'And what possible business is that of yours,' he said, smile now totally gone from his face.

'Look, I don't care if you have two thousand pornographic magazines stacked in there, just get those kids their tennis racquets.'

'You had to come all the way to my office to deliver that message? Why couldn't they just ask *me?*'

'Apparently everyone at the home I fought to have them rejoin is in a bad temper. They didn't want to make things worse.'

'So they rang you,' he sneered.

'Well at least I did something,' Sara said simply. 'Are you going to give me the key now, and I'll pick up their racquets for them, or . . .'

'I'll go back and get them,' he said.

'But your work?' she said.

'I'm my own boss. I can make my own decisions whether to go or stay.' He got up as if to leave.

'Thank you, Walter.'

'Don't mention it, Sara,' he said.

She noticed that he looked up and down the corridor as he left, and that he didn't go down in the main lift, but ran down the back stairs. Mr Walter Mitchell working in his uncle's office was not at all as secure as he would have people believe.

St Jarlath's Crescent had never looked so well. Smart new curtains, window boxes, the bedroom for the bride and groom filled with little touches.

'It's very empty, you know. I miss those children terribly,' Lizzie told her sister. 'And poor Muttie's distracted.'

'How often do they come over?' asked Geraldine.

'Every Saturday. They want to come more but it's not on, apparently.'

'Couldn't Cathy bring them over sometimes? She's able to get what she wants, and she's not afraid of any Mitchell,' Geraldine suggested.

'I haven't seen or heard from Cathy in days,' Lizzie said.

'I think she's got a lot on her mind,' said Geraldine, who wondered why Cathy hadn't phoned back to tell her about Neil's reaction to everything.

*

There was another rehearsal for the Feather Fashion show. Joe made it his business to talk to Marcella.

'Tom okay about everything? All this, you know . . .' He waved his hands at the half-dressed girls around him.

'Fine,' Marcella said.

'It's just that—'

'Just that what?'

'I haven't seen him recently, and I hope he's not pissed off with me for being part of all this.' He waved his hand around at the scene.

'No, no. Tom pissed off at you? Of course he's not, he's just very busy with everything, that's all. I hardly see him myself.'

'Hi Cathy, it's Geraldine.'

'Oh yes, Geraldine. Oh.' Cathy sounded distracted.

'Sorry, is this a bad time?'

It couldn't have been a worse time. The place was full of people and tension. James Byrne, Neil and the man from the insurance company were all walking in circles around the premises. She had been sitting with Tom and June going over it all for the umpteenth time.

'Not great. Why don't I call you?'

'I wonder.' Geraldine was terse.

'What?'

'I said, I too wonder why you don't call me, I've not heard from you since Freddie's do . . .'

'No, no.'

'And how did it go telling Neil the news?'

'I haven't.'

'But it's ages—' Geraldine began.

'Please, can I ring you back?' Her voice was near breaking.

'Certainly,' Geraldine said, puzzled, and sat and looked at the phone for a long time.

'It will be months before they pay,' Neil said when the insurance man had left. 'If we get it out of them by New Year we'll be doing well.'

'How much do we need, James?' Tom's face was hard.

'To get back to where you were when this happened, you need just under twenty thousand,' James said. 'Probably more because I'm basing that on a figure that's assuming you can get equipment marked down again, like you did before from the restaurant sale.'

'How much is that a week?' Cathy asked.

James Byrne told them what the repayments would cost at the bank. And that was if the bank were to give it.

'They'll give it because they know the insurance will pay in the end, and they'll get their money, but it's far too much,' Neil said.

'Neil, we wouldn't make half of that in a week, *and* we have all the other repayments, you know, on this place.' Tom's face was hard and sad.

James Byrne spoke. 'Before we make or reject any big decisions, will you give me twenty-four hours to prepare some figures, and then you really can see what your options are.' He seemed to know people wanted time to cool down; the hurt was too raw and the sense of failure too great for either Tom or Cathy to think rationally.

'I'm sorry, hon,' Neil said in the car as they drove home.

'Neil, are you going to be at home tonight?' She cut straight across him.

'You know I'm not, hon, you know I have to go to the homeless group, it will be the last and only chance to give them some points before I go to the conference.'

The conference! How *could* she have forgotten that Neil and four other lawyers were representing Ireland at an international forum on refugees, in Africa? He was leaving tomorrow evening.

'You can't go to that group tonight, I need to talk to you.'

'Talk to me in the car, hon, I can't let those people down.'

'Sara will explain to them, tell them what you want to say.'

'Cathy, be reasonable. Sara's a young social worker, she's not a lawyer.'

'What time will it be over?'

'How do I know, hon ... When it's over.'

'Don't go with them to some awful café talking and yammering all night, come back. *Please.*'

He was annoyed now. 'Cathy, I've spent all day, a day when I should have been getting my papers ready for the forum, down in your office sorting out the mess there. You know I'd do anything for you, but opting out of this thing tonight is not possible. And don't dismiss my work as going to some awful café yammering all night. I've never said anything like that about your work.'

'Neil!' she was aghast.

'No, I mean it, we made a bargain, we are partners in the very best sense of the word. We both care about the work we do and we help each other. In a few years' time we will settle down and take things more easily.'

'When?' she cried.

'Well, not tonight, obviously Cathy ... Not until you have your business up and running again ... Not until I have done something about all the things I wanted to do.'

'That could be five or six years,' she said.

'Well, that's what we always said, isn't it?' Neil Mitchell said.

There was a silence.

'I don't want to fight with you Cathy, specially not before I go away.'

'I don't want to fight with you either.' She spoke in a small voice.

'We're upset, that's all.'

'That's all,' she agreed.

'I'll try to get away as early as I can. Promise.' He smiled at her.

'Sure.' She forced a smile back.

'And listen, when I come back from Africa we'll go down to Holly's, that nice hotel in Wicklow where we once went to lunch, and we'll have dinner and stay the night.'

'Great,' she said.

When he came in that night, she was lying awake in bed. If he showed any signs of being alert she would get up and tell him. He couldn't go away for nine days and not know. Through her eyelids she saw him pull off his shirt with a weary movement. He went into the bathroom, and through the open door she could see that he barely brushed his teeth and ran a face flannel around his neck and under his arms. She saw his face; he was tired and strained. When he slipped into bed beside her, he spoke.

'Sorry, hon, there *was* a lot of yammering after it, as you forecast.'

'You don't feel like a cup of tea?' she offered.

'Believe me, I couldn't keep my eyes open long enough to get it to my lips,' he said, and he was asleep beside her. Cathy got up and went to the kitchen. As the dawn came up she still sat there, no nearer a solution. This was a good, strong marriage, a partnership in every way. Was she afraid to tell him? *Afraid* to give him the best news of anyone's life? She heard him moving about. He had slept for five and a half hours; she had sat at the kitchen table for all that time. Even if he did have an hour to listen now, which was unlikely, she was too confused and too weary to tell him properly. When he had gone to Africa she would go to a doctor and have confirmed what she knew to be true from her pregnancy indicator. What a terrible, terrible piece of timing.

'You two are so tiresome, you do know that?' Walter said when he got back home to the twins.

Simon and Maud were sorry. 'We thought it would be easier. She said in any difficulty to contact her.'

'But you weren't in any difficulty, you could have waited until I got back from work.'

'We thought you were going to England, you don't tell us what you do,' Maud said defensively.

'Not that you have to, of course,' Simon said.

'Oh, shut up, I'll get you the bloody racquets, then you can call her and say you're set fair for Wimbledon.'

'Can't we go with you to see if there's anything else we need from the shed?'

'No,' said Walter. 'Sit down and shut up.'

'But how will you know our—' Maud began.

'He'll take all the racquets and we can choose,' said Simon, who hadn't at all liked the look he saw on Walter's face.

'You're learning, Simon,' Walter said. 'Slowly, but at least you're learning.'

Martin Maguire had gone back to England without discovering the fate that had befallen his old premises. This time James Byrne had not pressed him to go and visit the couple who ran it nowadays. Martin Maguire had known so much sadness in that place he didn't think he yet had the strength to see two young people in such a desperate state.

*

Geraldine had to ring Joe Feather about his press conference at the end of the next week. She needed copies of his speech.

'I prefer to speak off the cuff,' he said.

'So do we all, but we have to have something that the journalists can write in their papers, some kind of statement of intent, policy, patriotism . . .'

'Oh, come on,' Joe laughed.

'I mean it. How you had to come back to Ireland, how you love Irish women, how much more adventurous they are nowadays, how well they dress . . . How great the government is, encouraging this and that . . .'

'Are you serious?'

'Never more so.'

'You wouldn't write it for me yourself, Geraldine, by any chance?'

'Not today, I have to go out. You have a stab at it, fax it to me, e-mail it, whatever you think, and I'll come back to you tomorrow morning.'

'Sure. By the way, have you seen anything of Cathy and Tom recently?'

'No, why do you ask?'

'It's just they seem to have vanished off the face of the earth. I've been trying to get hold of Tom. Marcella says he's fine, so why doesn't he return my calls?'

'If I find out I'll tell you,' said Geraldine, who then left her office and hailed a taxi. *She* was not going to hang about any longer. It was too much of a coincidence Tom not getting in touch as well as Cathy. Quite obviously something was wrong. She was going right up there to the premises to find out exactly what had happened.

The broken glass, china and woodwork had been cleared away. Well, more or less.

They were always finding some frightening reminder, like the broken glass at the back of the cutlery drawer. Like realising that the big platter they had thought was in good shape was cracked all over and disintegrated, taking with it an entire dressed salmon. It was all over the floor, nothing could be rescued; both food and china had to be swept into the bin.

'Hours of work,' wept June.

'We're getting there,' said Cathy in desperation.

But it had indeed been hours of work and now they were left with no main dish for a lunch party. Wearily, Cathy rang the fishmongers. Could they do one for her in two hours?

'It'll cost you, Cathy,' said the man apologetically.

'It would cost us more if we didn't deliver,' she replied. She saw Tom looking at her. They spent so much time cheering the others up, keeping the show on the road, they had hardly any time to talk to each other honestly.

'Will we survive, Tom? Will we?' she asked sadly.

'I know. There are times I think we won't, too,' he said. They looked at each other, frightened. If they were to panic, the lifeboat might sink. It was only their optimism that kept it afloat.

'Of course, it looks a lot better now than it did on Monday,' Cathy said.

'Even than yesterday,' Tom agreed.

The men from JT Feather's builder's yard had put a coat of paint on the place. Tom had told his father that it was very important that they told nobody about their misfortune; it didn't look good in business when a calamity like this happened. His father had nodded sagely and said he was right to keep his counsel. JT Feather never thought for one moment that it was a secret to be kept from Joe. When his elder son called to Fatima that afternoon, he got every last detail of the robbery.

'Why did Tom not tell me?' Joe was shocked.

'He said he wasn't telling business people because it looked badly,' JT said, shaking his head.

'I see.'

'But it's odd he didn't tell you, you're not business.'

'I suppose there's a way he thinks I am,' Joe said thoughtfully.

'What do you mean, son?'

'Nothing Da, I'm only rabbiting on to myself. Don't mention to him that you said a word; he'll tell me when he's ready.'

Geraldine got out at the end of the mews and walked slowly up. She let herself into the courtyard of the premises, through the gate she had oiled herself last January when they were frantically clearing everything up. There was nothing Cathy wouldn't have told her or discussed with her back then. How had it all changed? She looked through the window, where normally you saw the little square table with its silver punchbowl and flowers. The old coloured plates would look down from the wall, and the place was like a little haven before you opened the door into the bright, modern, busy kitchens. Geraldine had always admired how they kept the chintzy, welcoming feel with the deep chairs and sofa. Those two were very bright; they did a lot of things by pure instinct. Today it was totally different. There was nothing on the table, only a lot of broken implements like twisted egg beaters laid out in a line. Peering further in, she could see through the kitchen door that there seemed to be huge renovations going on inside. She couldn't see what exactly, but appliances had been pulled from the wall. What could have happened to this place since she had been here last? Tentatively she rang the bell and saw an exhausted-looking Cathy come to the door.

'Oh, Geraldine,' she said without enthusiasm, and with no attempt to invite her in.

'That's me,' Geraldine said, about to step inside.

'It's not a good time, as it happens,' Cathy began.

'It never is these days, which is why you always say you'll call me and never do.'

'Please, Geraldine, please. I'll come round to your place tonight and we'll have a chat. There's a lot to talk about.'

Geraldine looked past her. Everything seemed to have tilted somehow. And Cathy was doing everything except actually bar the door to her. Gently but firmly Geraldine pushed her way in.

'Excuse *me* Geraldine, aren't you the one who says nobody should ever invade anyone else's space . . . You said that. I was never to call into Glenstar without telephoning in advance . . . What's happened to all that now?'

It was too late, Geraldine was inside looking at the wrecked premises. 'Oh, my God,' Geraldine cried. 'Oh, my God, you poor child, you poor, poor child, who could have done this to you?' Cathy just looked at her, stricken. 'When did it happen? How long ago . . . ?'

'The night of Freddie's do.'

'He never said.'

'He doesn't know, Geraldine, no one does.'

'Why on earth not?'

'We have to sort out what to do first, then I was going to tell you.'

'But Cathy, I'm your friend, you have no closer friend than me.'

'I know.'

'So why couldn't you tell me about this terrible thing . . .'

'You know why . . .' Cathy hung her head.

'I *don't* know why . . . If someone had come in, done over my house or my office, I'd have told you immediately . . . not keep it all a stupid secret.'

'I didn't pay for your office, you did pay for mine,' Cathy said, still looking downwards.

'But that's got nothing to do with anything. Who did this, Cathy, who could it have been? Do they have any idea?'

'They think we did it, Geraldine, that's what they think. That we trashed this place just to get the insurance money.'

Marcella put some special oil in Tom's bath. It was meant to take the ache out of tired muscles and bones, she said; a lot of her customers swore by it.

'Most of them don't get up at five o'clock to make bread in Haywards, then spend the day shovelling away great sacks and boxes of broken things in their place of work,' Tom said grouchily. As he spoke he heard his own tones, whining and self-pitying, the kind of person he normally loathed. He felt Marcella recoil a little too.

'I know,' she said. 'It's very hard on you, but I thought it just *might* make you feel a bit better.' She had spent her hard-earned money on this gift for him, and all he had done was complain.

'Is there any hope you might massage it into a boy's shoulders?' he asked.

'Of course I will, but the boy is actually meant to lie for ten minutes soaking it up first.' She was all smiles now.

'I have no problem with that.' He smiled back at her, and went to lie down in the bath.

Marcella came in and sat on the edge of the bath to rub his shoulders. 'Now you've had a quarter of an hour it must have done you a lot of good,' she said, and he prayed she would never know that he had lain there clenched for fifteen long minutes, wondering how he was going to bear all that lay ahead in his home life and his work life without actually cracking up.

*

'I think you'd like tennis, Muttie,' Simon said the following Saturday.

'Tennis isn't for the likes of me,' Muttie said.

'But can't everyone do everything?' Maud asked.

'I'm not sure. They should be able to, but it doesn't always work out.'

'Cathy used to say it did,' Maud explained.

'That one thinks she can do anything, fly off the top of Liberty Hall,' said Lizzie disapprovingly.

'Sure Cathy could move mountains,' Muttie said.

'We think Cathy's cross with us,' Maud confided.

'What on earth would make her cross with you?' Lizzie said. 'Cathy's mad about you, didn't she bring you here in the first place?'

'But she never brings us anywhere now,' Simon said.

'It could be because you're meant to be above in The Beeches big house,' Muttie explained. 'They've laid down all kinds of rules and regulations about where you're to be and not to be, she doesn't want to butt in.'

'We never see her. I think we did something to annoy her,' Maud decided.

'We hardly see her ourselves these days, child,' Lizzie said. 'That job she's taken on is huge, you know, she and Tom will be worn to threads by the end of the year if they go on like this much more.'

'Joe, have you heard about this business in Tom and Cathy's?'

They were working on his press release.

'Well, I heard, yes, but I wasn't told, if that's what you mean.'

'Neither was I . . . I think it was something to do with not wanting to involve us any further. Financially.'

'Yes, I got that vibe too. But I'm perfectly prepared to go in with a bit more myself. Are you?'

'Certainly I am, but they're very prickly, both of them. I think we have to wait to be asked.'

'Cathy's always on an even keel; I don't see *her* as being prickly.'

'She has her own problems, Joe, believe me.'

'That's rather bad news, because my little brother is as high as a kite about Marcella in this show. Honestly, sometimes I wish I'd never put in a word for her with those guys at all.'

'You can't say that, isn't it her big break?'

'Big nothing, Geraldine. Marcella's twenty-five years of age. She's far too old now to be a model. If she were going to make it she should have been out there at sixteen.'

'Does she know that?'

'If she's got an ounce of sense she must.'

'Come in tomorrow and see a rehearsal, Tom,' Marcella begged.

'No, I don't want to be in the way,' he said.

'You wouldn't, lots of the other girls have their friends in to watch. Eddie and Harry think it's good for us to have an audience.'

Tom didn't want to go. It would be bad enough to see it all on the night;

he couldn't bear to go in and watch, an extra peep show. 'Love, if I can I will, but it's going to be a desperate day tomorrow.'

'But Tom, you'll actually be *in* Haywards anyway with the bread, all you have to do is come up to the fourth floor. I'd love you to be there.'

She was very anxious that he be a part of it. He was going to have to see it all on Friday next; why not please her? 'You're right, I'd love to get a sneak preview,' he said, and her eyes shone with the excitement of it all.

Shona came up to him next morning in the kitchen. 'Do you know that you really are Mister Popular here, Tom?'

'What did I do now?' Tom asked, alarmed, assuming that she was being sarcastic. But apparently not. The staff had been saying that it was great to get in to a kitchen that was already up and running each morning. Tom had coffee ready on the stove for them, and a loaf of his own bread to start their day. The restaurant staff had at first been a bit doubtful about letting an outsider into their territory, but it had worked out better than they could have dreamed.

'That's good to hear, Shona.' Tom's mind wasn't really on it; he knew he had to go to the fourth floor now and watch Marcella at what she saw as her new work. Shona hesitated.

'It's just that . . . Well, I don't know how to say this, but if you and Cathy sort of *don't* get back on the rails after this burglary, I thought you should know that there could well be a full-time job for you here.'

He swallowed hard before he spoke. Shona had no idea what she was saying. She was putting into words the great fear that Scarlet Feather might not survive. Something he and Cathy hadn't even dared to consider. And what was more, a lifeline was being thrown. Not to both of them, just to Tom. He scarcely trusted himself to answer.

'Shona, you are so good, and it would be a great honour, but you know how we're killing ourselves to try and get the show on the road back there.'

'And I'm sure you will,' she murmured diplomatically.

'You see, it's all to do with having this dream. I don't think you survive without one.'

'I don't know,' Shona said.

'Do you have a dream too?'

'I had once.'

'And did you get it?'

'Yes I did, I wished for my apartment in Glenstar,' Shona said in a small voice.

It seemed an odd, bleak thing to wish for. But then to other people his wish to run a catering company might not seem all that exciting either.

'And what about love?' he asked lightly.

'I gave up on that a long time ago,' she said equally lightly, but he thought she meant it.

A section of the fourth floor had been curtained off for the rehearsal. Tom hung around at the edge, unsure whether to go in. There were a lot of other people milling around equally vaguely. Some of them were involved in setting up lighting, a music track was starting and stopping, Ricky was there advising photographers about where to stand. There was no sign as yet of the girls or the garments. They must be in that area at the end, and would come out of that arched doorway each time. His stomach lurched again at the thought of his Marcella being part of this. He saw Joe in the distance but couldn't catch his eye. Then they were called to order for a run-through with music.

'We want a lot of hush now,' Joe was saying. 'It has to be timed fairly exactly, so if anyone falls or a light doesn't work just keep on going ... Right, we're going in ten seconds from now.'

Two men sat down beside Tom. He smiled and moved to make room for them. 'Thanks, mate,' said one. They must be Joe's associates from London, and there was also a man who owned a model agency who was looking in this week. Marcella had talked of little else. 'Mr Newton himself,' she kept saying, with a reverence that set Tom's teeth on edge. Maybe one of these guys with their London accents was Mr Newton himself. 'Mr Newton?' he asked. 'Over there, mate,' one of them said, nodding towards a small man leaning back in the kind of chair that movie directors used to sit in in studios over forty years ago. Tom Feather felt pleased to notice that Mr Newton himself looked like a disagreeable little pig. Tom sat and watched as one by one the girls came out, young and unformed many of them, almost schoolchildren in bathing suits. They danced along, hitting a beach ball one to another in time to the music, and there was Marcella bringing up the rear. Not dancing with the others, but walking haughtily through them as if she had tired of childish games. She wore a white bikini shaped like three shells, one cupping each breast and one as a tiny G-string. Her flat, tanned stomach and long, tanned legs looked so familiar and yet so alien in this setting. He wanted to do nothing as much as cry. She had told him that Joe insisted she should have a starring role, that she wasn't part of any chorus line, and this seemed to be true all right. When the halter-top beach dresses were shown, there were rainbows full of pastel shades for the line of dancing youngsters, but Marcella was there in black with a cleavage that came down to her navel. The men beside him seemed to watch her with admiration. Tom had to say something.

'I know her. She's good, isn't she?'

'Gorgeous,' said one of them.

'Some guys get all the luck,' said the other.

'Do you think she might make it, big time?' Tom asked, trying to keep his voice neutral. He wanted so very much for this to be a success for her; he wanted that much more than the base wish that she be a spectacular failure and give up the dream.

'Aw, she's not in this seriously, she's only doing it for fun,' said one of the men.

'She's a friend of Joe Feather, he got her the gig,' said the other.

'I think she's hoping to do it as a career,' Tom said.

They shook their heads.

'No way,' said one.

'She's far too old,' said the other.

'She's twenty-five,' Tom said.

'Exactly,' said the man, and looked back at the catwalk where the girls were coming out now in nightdresses. Marcella could not have looked more naked if she had stood in front of them without a stitch of clothing on. The wispy garment that hit and missed her artistically just pointed up all the beautiful parts of her, as if she had been coloured in with dayglo pen.

He left her a note saying that she was marvellous, the show was a winner and he was so proud of her. Then he drove the van to the canal and sat and watched two swans for about ten minutes as they sailed up and down and arched their long, beautiful necks. He didn't realise that he was crying until he went to start the van again, and felt his tears splash on his hand. He must be going totally mad.

At the premises he found that two envelopes had been delivered by hand. Geraldine had sent a letter to Cathy; it was short and factual. She wanted to make another investment in the company, and believed Cathy to be short-sighted and not looking after the good of the investors by refusing it. However, if that was her intent, she enclosed some details on renting equipment, china and cutlery. It would be expensive, but at least there would be no initial outlay.

Cathy rang her aunt and left a thank-you message on her machine. 'Tom and I both think that's a great idea. If we only have to rent it for a few months it will all make sense. Thanks again, Ger. You're great.'

The other was from Joe Feather to Tom. He had heard by devious means that they had had a break-in and he wished to offer his condolences and some cash in hand. This was not a time to be filling in forms and VAT returns. Take this thousand now, and of course he'd pay the bill for the catering for the press reception in the handy folding money too. Tom rang his brother and left a thank-you message on his machine.

'Cathy and I want to thank you from the bottom of our hearts, we will take that thousand pounds joyfully and lodge it as a further investment, but alas, everything else has to be done straight up, and right through the books. If you knew our accountant you'd realise we are more afraid of him than anyone on earth. Thanks again though, Joe, you're great. Oh, and I went to the rehearsal this morning, show looks really good.'

'Does the show look really good?' Cathy asked.

'Why do you ask that?'

'Well, everything else you said to him was lies, you're not afraid of James Byrne, it's just we don't want hot money floating around.'

'It was okay, the show,' Tom said slowly. 'That's what it was.'

'But presumably you found a better word to describe it to Marcella?' Cathy laughed.

'I did, a few,' he grinned ruefully.

'Listen, how in the name of God are we going to do that reception with no equipment?'

'We start renting,' Cathy said, phoning the company. 'This will be our first real do inside Haywards. We don't want to borrow a plate or a glass from them; we gotta show them.'

'Did you really think it was good?' Marcella asked when she got home.

They had been having drinks, Joe and his partners, about finer points, and Mr Newton had joined them.

'Was that Mr Newton himself?' Tom asked, regretting his sneer the moment he had said it.

Marcella however had noticed nothing amiss. 'Yes, he's as nice as anything, and very easygoing to talk to. When you consider all the kinds of people he has handled in his career! He's just very normal and ordinary, it's like talking to anyone.'

'Imagine,' Tom said.

'I know, and he was very praising of everything about the show. Joe was thrilled.'

'Good, great.'

'It's all kind of unbelievable to think that it's all going to happen on this very Friday,' Marcella said.

He looked at her, mute with the fear that those two business associates of Joe might be right, that Marcella was far too old even to think about beginning a modelling career. 'And there's a real possibility that Mr Newton might get you a contract?' he asked her.

'Well, I don't want to be too hopeful, but it looks like it. Still, he's only seen two rehearsals today, and apparently it all depends on how you do on the night . . . People can be fine in front of a handful of people and yet go to pieces in front of an audience.'

'You didn't go to pieces today, and there were lots of people there.' He was begging her to have confidence in herself.

'But there'll be three hundred and more on the night,' Marcella said, hugging herself. 'Still, I think I can do it, all those younger ones there in the group give me great confidence . . . It's been great working with them.'

'Are they younger than you, then?' Tom asked, wide-eyed.

'Oh, Tom, will you shut up. Of course they are, some of them are at least eight or nine years younger than me, stop playing the fool.'

'I didn't see that they were, you looked so much the best . . . But would Mr Newton not be looking for them, then, or are they too young?' he asked.

Marcella frowned. 'You know, I thought that too, that maybe he'd go for the younger ones for his books, but he said to Joe that he thought I'd be suited for a lot of stuff he has on hand.' Marcella hugged herself. 'It's all so wonderful, Tom, really, I can hardly take it all in.'

The letters, faxes and e-mails were coming in thick and fast from Chicago. Each one was headed simply *Wedding*.

'Nobody ever got married in the world before Marian Scarlet,' Cathy grumbled, looking at the latest message.

'So what are you complaining about? They want fancy, we give them fancy.' Tom was determined to be cheerful.

'No, wait till you hear.'

'Honestly, Cathy, it's just because she's your sister you're making all this fuss. That church hall where they've never had a wedding in their life, where you didn't want to have it, will become *the* place, believe me, Ricky's going to take pictures of it . . .'

'But you haven't heard . . .'

'The priest is delighted, and I think that we'll make a fortune out of it for us and for him too,' Tom said hastily. Cathy watched helplessly. 'My father's men have it all painted up already, the priest has got the parishioners to plant window boxes. It's going to look—' He broke off at the sight of her face. 'What is it?' Tom asked.

'They want a traditional Irish wedding, Tom, they want us to serve corned beef and cabbage.'

'What for, in the name of God?'

'That's what they think is traditional Irish food.'

'But Marian was brought up in St Jarlath's Crescent, she *can't* think that.' Tom was aghast.

'She's been a long time in Illinois,' Cathy shrugged.

'We are *not* going to serve them corned beef and cabbage,' Tom said.

'I know.'

'So who's going to tell her?' he asked menacingly.

'You have the better turn of phrase,' Cathy said.

'She's your bloody sister,' Tom answered.

'It's a question of what else we can persuade them is typically Irish.'

'But there are a thousand things, for God's sake. Wicklow lamb, Irish salmon, loads of lobster, mussels, we could have a centrepiece of Irish shellfish. I would have thought they'd have liked huge ribs of Irish beef. Isn't Chicago the sort of home of the stockyards and everything? They'd be used to big steer on their plates.'

'They don't want what they're used to. They want Irish dancers, shillelaghs, colleens saying top of the mornin' to them.'

'They don't?' Tom was aghast.

Cathy waved the letter at him again. 'Well it sounds very like it from this . . . All Harry's relations are so looking forward to the whole Irish experience, steeping themselves in another culture, experiencing the simple, unspoiled peasant cuisine.'

Tom put his head in his hands. 'Come on, Cathy, let's think what we'll offer them. Imagine, we once thought this was going to be an easy number.'

'There's no such thing as an easy number in this game,' Cathy said, with such a sigh that he looked up suddenly.

'Are you all right?' he asked, concerned at the expression on her face.

'Of course I'm not. We can't go on fooling ourselves. There's no way we can do this wedding.' She was bent double now, her head in her hands, her whole body shaking with tears. 'We can't possibly go ahead, it's ludicrous, we were mad to take it on . . .' she sobbed.

'Cathy, Cathy . . .' He got up from the chair in the front room and came to kneel down beside where she was hugging her knees and making no attempt to hide the tears or the fact that she had dropped her guard so completely.

'We'll think of something,' he said.

'But what is there left to think of,' she wept. 'Marian's gone mad, we should never have listened to one word she said, we should have told her we were done over and we couldn't cope, why do we have to keep on pretending and say that everything's all right when it's not.'

'Because that's the only way we stay in business.' He was very gentle and stroked her head soothingly.

'No, we don't have to pretend, we're finished, aren't we, we're never going to get back up and running . . .' She stood up suddenly, and looked at him, red-eyed and distraught. 'Can't you see we're only fooling ourselves, every step we take we're only sinking in further, it just makes it more difficult for us to get out, deeper and deeper in debt . . .'

Tom had stood up and now he pulled her to him in a big bear-hug.

'Now this is not going to go on, it's not, you have to help me. When I hear you saying all this, I half-believe you, do you hear?'

She cried in his arms as he stroked her hair over and over. It was a luxury not having to hold back, to keep a permanently false grin on her face in front of June and Con and anyone else who came in and out.

Her shoulders shook and he held her until the sobs died down. She mumbled something he couldn't hear into his sweater.

'What did you say?'

'I said it's over, Tom, we have to be strong and face it.'

'There's nothing strong about letting your sister down on the biggest day of her life.'

'Tell her to get some other leprechaun outfit.'

'There isn't one, we're the only leprechaun outfit in town.' He looked down at her face. It had worked a little. There was a half smile.

'You never thought of quitting?'

'No, not ever.'

'Right then.' She blew her nose loudly. 'Right then, if we're not quitting, then we'll have to redefine.'

'What, come up with something traditionally Irish that Scarlet Feather can actually live with?' He looked at her. She was better. They were back in business.

Their computer had escaped the vandalism by the sheer good luck of having been out for repair at the time. Cathy sat down in front of it.

'We'll send an e-mail, you come up with the creative, persuasive bit and I'll do the dear long-lost sister part.'

'We must make her think she's getting it just right,' Tom said thoughtfully.

'Whatever made us think that a catering business had anything to do with producing food?' Cathy laughed.

'It's only for the trade, Mam,' Joe Feather said to his mother for the twentieth time.

'But there was a thing in the paper saying it was for everyone.'

'Everyone in the rag trade, Mam, believe me I'd invite you if there was anything there you'd like to see.' He spoke the truth. His mother would not like to see her future daughter-in-law, of whom she already disapproved mightily, dressed in next to nothing. Nor would she like to see her son Tom's face as this was going on. Joe had seen him at the rehearsal, and had realised how hard he was taking the whole thing, and yet trying to face up to it as well. Which wasn't really necessary at all. Marcella hadn't a chance in hell of making it on the modelling circuit. Beautiful-looking woman, but wooden on stage and built so that you only saw her body, not the garments she was modelling. She wouldn't last five minutes in the big world out there. Surely Tom didn't take any of this business about finding work across the water seriously. Surely.

Cathy came back from the cash and carry and Tom helped her unpack the van.

'Just one message – Simon and Maud don't love you any more.'

'Simon and Maud? What have I done now?'

'It's what you've not done. They want to come and polish your treasures again.'

'But we don't *have* any treasures,' Cathy wailed.

'We never did, technically,' Tom said ruefully.

'They'll tell *everyone*, it's worse than having it on the nine o'clock news on television. They can't come here, they'll have Muttie and Lizzie up to high doh, the folks in Chicago will cancel, everyone would cancel if they knew what we were working out of.' She felt guilty about the twins, but she knew that she had total right on her side.

But Tom wouldn't let her get away with it. 'They think you've gone off them, they want to know what they've done.'

'Shit,' said Cathy. 'We don't need this now.'

Tom said nothing. He continued unpacking.

'All right, you win, to be fair they've enough to cope with, they don't need it either. I'll take them out somewhere.'

'I left their number there on the desk,' he said. 'Poor little devils, I'd say life is no bed of roses up in The Beeches.'

She went to the telephone.

The twins' father answered the phone. Cathy couldn't remember whether she called him Kenneth or Mr Mitchell.

'My name is Cathy Scarlet. I would like to speak to Maud Mitchell or Simon Mitchell, please.'

'Oh, yes indeed, um . . . er . . . we *have* met, if I'm not mistaken,' the voice said.

She could hear him saying 'extraordinarily rude woman' as he called the children. Cathy felt a moment of guilt when she heard their excitement.

'For us?' Simon was saying. Normally they wouldn't get any calls.

'Who is it?' Maud asked him, and got no reply, so she got to the phone first.

'It *is*, it *is*,' she called. 'It's Cathy.'

And Cathy felt a sudden rush of tears, which she beat back as she suggested they go on an outing.

'I thought we'd go to the cinema and have a burger, then I'll drive you home,' she offered.

'Will we come and pick you up at the premises?' Simon offered.

'*No*, I mean, no thanks, Simon, just get the bus in to O'Connell Street . . . and I'll see you there for the four o'clock show.'

'Come with us, Tom,' she suggested.

'No, only two days to the show. Marcella's nerves are frazzled, and she says she wants to talk this evening.'

'Right. I suddenly thought you could do with a relax too.'

'I could have,' he said. 'But these are stressed times, and you've not forgotten we're having a supper after the show?'

'No, indeed. Where are we going?'

'The little Italian place, Geraldine's coming. Ricky and Joe too, I think, if he can get away, Shona and half a dozen more. We'll be able to get away nice and early when the show is finished. No coming back here with the van or anything. Haywards says we can clear into their kitchens and just lock up. I'll cope with it when I get in to do the bread on Saturday.'

'You work too hard,' she said sympathetically.

'So do you. Was there a lot of standing and hanging around when you were up there at the cash and carry?'

She looked at him sharply. It had been exhausting, she had an ache in her back and some of the food she saw revolted her. She thought that the visit there would never end.

'Not too bad today,' she said. This would be another very hard conversation, the day she would have to tell him she would be taking maternity leave. But she would face it when she had to.

'And you're sure we didn't do anything bad?' Maud persisted.

They were having their burger after the movie.

'No Maud, remember what I told you about not being the centre of the world.'

'Yes, but we were afraid you thought—'

'I wasn't thinking about you at all, we've been very busy.'

'So how do you know when someone is really cross with you, or if they're just busy and not thinking about you?' Simon wondered.

'It's something that comes with time, you do get to know, Simon.'

'Were you older or younger than us when you got to know?' Simon asked.

'A bit older, about six months older, I think.' Cathy felt very tired.

The more the children talked on and on about some madman called old Barty and the strange food they ate, and Mother being in bed a lot during the day and Father out a lot at night, she knew it had been a great, great mistake to let those children go without a fight. Neil had given the wrong advice there. She knew it. It had nothing to do with flesh and blood. Muttie and Lizzie Scarlet sitting alone up in St Jarlath's Crescent would have made much better parents to these children than the ones who had actually brought them into the world.

'Why don't I take you up to see Hooves before we go home?' she suggested suddenly.

They looked at each other awkwardly. Embarrassed, Maud shuffled her feet and Simon looked out of the door of the restaurant.

'What is it?' Cathy looked from one to the other.

'Well, you know the bargain. We weren't to go back to St Jarlath's Crescent except on Saturdays,' Simon began.

'But the bargain was all about you being good children and going straight home from school. It's the holidays now.'

'Sara said it was the same term or holiday.'

'But it's just a drive, you're allowed to go out with *me*, can't I drive you where I want?'

'Better not, Cathy ... Sara said that Mother and Father are a bit jealous of what a good time we had at Muttie and his wife Lizzie's ... And they don't like us going back there ... in case it shows that it's where we prefer.'

'And is it?' Cathy asked.

'You told us not to say anything about preferring one place to another. You told us that would be bad-mannered,' Maud said, confused.

'Did I? I must have been very intelligent back then.'

'It's not all *that* long ago,' Simon said. 'You couldn't have lost a lot of intelligence in such a short time.'

'I love you, Simon,' Cathy said suddenly. 'And I love you too, Maud. Right, if everyone's finished I'll take you home to your parents' house.' Cathy busied herself about the departure so that she wouldn't have to see the looks of total shock on the twins' faces. Nobody had ever said I love you to them like that before. They hadn't an idea how to cope with it. Back at the house, she was about to drop them at the door.

'Please come in,' they begged.

'No, truly, it's better not.'

'But you're not afraid of them like Muttie is,' Simon cried.

'And we could do our dance for you,' said Maud.

'Certainly I'll come in,' Cathy said, and marched into the house purposefully. 'Kenneth, Kay, thank you for lending me your magnificent son and daughter, we had such a nice evening, or I think we did.' She looked at them, waiting for the polite, enthusiastic response she had taught them that people expected.

'Terrific film,' said Maud.

'And Cathy paid for two burgers each,' Simon said.

'So they won't need any supper.' Cathy looked around to see any signs that someone had been preparing a meal for the children at eight o'clock on a summer's evening.

'There's some ham in the fridge,' Kay said defensively.

'Oh, I'm quite sure there is, Kay, and that you would have made a lovely supper for them, according to all the agreement and everything, but tonight I don't think they'd be up for anything at all.'

'No indeed, thank you,' said Simon.

'Can we get our shoes and the tape recorder now?' Maud wanted to know.

The parents looked on in bewilderment as Simon and Maud waited, toes pointed, until the correct bar of the music, and danced solemnly up and down the kitchen. They had improved greatly since the last time Cathy had watched it, with her hand over her mouth to hide the nervous laugh and to beat back the feeling that her sister Marian would kill her dead for allowing them to get up in public.

'And this is for a wedding, apparently?' Kenneth Mitchell said, having clapped because his wife and Cathy had done so with such vigour.

'Yes, my sister's wedding next month ... They'll be the star turn.'

'It's just that I'm not really sure ...'

Cathy clenched her hands. This fool was not going to try to renege again on the wedding. 'Oh, you *are* sure, Kenneth, remember your brother Jock told you all about it, part of the terms of the agreement?'

'Yes, yes, of course.'

'And talking about the agreement, I want you to know how reliable Simon and Maud are about everything. You see, I had forgotten that you only want them to visit my parents' house once a week. I was going to drive them up there briefly to visit their dog ...'

'Well, come on now, it's not exactly *their* dog, is it?'

'Yes it is, very exactly their dog, my father bought it for them himself and looks after it for them with pleasure until their weekly visit, but you interrupted me. I was telling you how proud you should be of them; they reminded me of the agreement which I had forgotten. I think it's sad myself, but I do think they were splendid to be so up front about it all, since it's your wish.'

'Well ... um, yes, it ... of course ...'

'So I thought I'd mention that since they are being so generous and observing the letter of the law as regards your wishes, you might be equally generous next month and let them make a few extra visits around the time of the wedding, so that they can meet everyone properly.'

'Well, we'll have to see ...' Kenneth began.

'Of course you will, I knew you would.' Cathy beamed at the children. 'Your father is just as reasonable as I said he would be, and there will be no problem at all about the various wedding parties ... As soon as Neil is back from Africa, he and his father will be in touch to firm it all up.' The children looked at her, bewildered. 'Thank you all so much, it's been a very pleasant visit.' And then she was gone. She slowed down a little just to hear what Kenneth Mitchell would say.

'Extraordinary woman,' he said, and without looking, she could see him shaking his head from side to side.

*

'Love, before you even speak a word let me tell you that you'll be a sensation,' Tom said.

But her face was troubled, almost as if she hadn't heard him. 'Marcella, what are you worried about? *Tell* me, you look lovely, you knock the others off the stage, you are stunning – it's just actor's nerves, I know . . .'

'No, that's not the point.'

'But it is in a way. You tell yourself that in a day and a bit, tomorrow night at ten o'clock all this will be over and life goes on as normal.'

'But that's just it. I can't go back, not now.'

'What do you mean, go back?'

'To the salon to do nails.'

'But there'll be more jobs once people have seen you . . .'

'There will be no jobs unless I get an agent.'

'You said Mr Newton—'

'Paul Newton *is* interested in representing me and arranging for me to go over the water for some try-outs . . . But it's not definite . . . it depends.'

'I know you were saying you're afraid you won't be good on the night itself, but you will, I tell you, I can see confidence in every bone of your body.' He begged her to believe him.

'These are tough, selfish guys, used to getting what they want.'

'He'll see you perform tomorrow night, he'll *know* you're what he wants.'

'It's a bit different.'

'What do you mean?'

'It's all in their court, they can make or break you. If you play according to their rules, you get to be part of it all; if you don't, you're not allowed to join.' She was twisting her hands uneasily.

He had no idea what she was trying to say. 'So what's the problem? If you do right tomorrow on that catwalk, as you will, then you will be part of it, or whatever you say the expression is.'

'They say we have to go and party with them tomorrow night,' she said, looking at the floor.

'Party?'

'Yes, back at their hotel.'

'But we *can't*, you know I've set up a dinner in the little Italian place, everyone's coming. You'll have to tell them we can't make it.'

'Not you, just me.'

He assumed she was joking and laughed. 'And what do you do for an encore?'

'No encore. If I do that, then I'm on his books and that's it.'

He realised it wasn't a joke. She was actually telling him that this guy had made her such a gross proposition. You come round to the hotel and party, or you don't get on my books. It was laughable.

'It's just because you *do* look so lovely it makes men lose their senses and say such ridiculous things.'

'He means it.'

'Well he can mean what he likes. *I'm* telling Joe he's not to come near the place tomorrow night and upset you like this.'

Marcella allowed herself very few cigarettes a day; she knew they dulled her skin tone and discoloured her teeth. But she lit one now. 'Could you stop making gestures for a minute. There's no question of telling Joe anything of the sort. Joe needs people like Paul Newton to get his clothes shown, you're not going to say one thing that would upset that.'

'So what are we talking about?' Tom asked.

'We're talking about what Paul Newton suggested,' she said simply.

He looked at her in disbelief. And then he began to laugh. It was a real laugh, not a pretend one. She *had* to be joking. But why was she not laughing back? 'You're not remotely serious, are you?' he said suddenly.

'Never more so, that's what I wanted to talk to you about.'

'Stop it, you're unhinged, you're not some high-class tart he can buy with the thought of a modelling contract.'

'It's not the thought, it's the actual contract,' she said.

'And you'd screw him for that?'

'It won't come to that, you know it won't. Just a party with girls and champagne, that's what they like.'

'Give us a break, you nearly had me fooled.'

'I have never in my whole life told you a lie or done anything to deceive you, why would I do so this time?' She spoke in that strange, almost robotic voice she had used once before, that time when he had thought she had lied and gone to a party instead of to the gym.

'He's only calling your bluff, don't fall for it. You're too bright for that, for heaven's sake.'

'No, it's one or the other.'

'Well let it be the other, the decision that involves telling him to get lost.'

'It's my choice, my future, I'm the one who has to do it or not do it, to get onto a proper bona fide model agency's books or lose the chance for ever.'

He looked at her and realised that she meant it. 'So we're not discussing this at all, you're telling me what you're going to do. Is that it?'

'It's not like that.'

'What's it like, then?'

'It's like my never going behind your back as I could easily do, or could have done.'

'I wish you had.'

'You don't mean that. We swore that we would be honest with each other. I never knew that being honest would end up like this. It's meaningless, it's silly even thinking he's a hotshot.'

'Then why even contemplate it?'

'Because it's not meaningless to him. So where's the harm?'

'And you're telling me that you wouldn't mind, if for work's sake I were to do something similar?'

'We *have* to be nice to people in business. You do, every single day, and remember that awful woman who ran the magazine that did our photo shoot . . . She was making great signs of fancying you. I thought you might have to go off and have lunches and parties with her; if you had to, then you had to.'

Tom laughed aloud at the very thought of it. 'You see, you say something like that and I'm ninety per cent sure you must be winding me up about all this.' Again he got no answering laugh. 'So you admit he fancies you?' he said.

'He admires me, and I'm nearer his age than the teeny-tots are. It's just a party, Tom. I tell you again, I wouldn't have minded if you had to go to a party with that woman.'

'Not if my life depended on it, let alone just a career.'

'I'm sorry about the Italian place,' she said.

What he said and did now was very important. It would affect his whole life. He must be very, very careful. He stood in the little sitting room where Marcella still sat at the table. The picture imprinted itself on his mind. The table had a pink crushed velvet cloth which Cathy had given them last Christmas. There was a shallow white fruit bowl with peaches and black grapes. The evening sunlight came in and touched the edges of Marcella's hair, giving it that strange halo effect. As if she were some kind of saint. She wore a floppy black cotton sweater and blue jeans; she looked about eighteen. Her enormous eyes searched his face for the response he was going to give.

'So, Tom?' she asked.

'So, Marcella?' he said.

'So what are you going to say to me?' she asked.

'As you said, it's your decision, your choice, your career. Nothing I say will change that.' He spoke gently and held her hand.

'But?' she continued for him.

'But it would break my heart for you to leap to his command as a party girl, and it would lose dignity and respect for both of us, and despite what you say you *don't* need to do this. And under normal circumstances you wouldn't consider it, but these are not normal times, you're so nervous about tomorrow night.'

He looked at her waiting for her to throw herself into his arms and thank him for his insight and understanding. There was a long, long silence. 'So, then, my love, you'll come to our party with all your friends who will drink to your success?'

'Thank you for everything, for not losing your temper and getting those wild ideas that I'd tell you a lie.'

'No, no, I know you wouldn't,' he soothed. But she still hadn't said yes or no. He *must* let her work it out for herself. She didn't want to go ahead with this party, and he had spoken as honestly as he could without getting up and smashing his fist through the door, which was what he felt like doing. She came round to his side of the table, put her arms around him and drew him towards the sofa. And they sat there in the summer sunset, with her head on his shoulder, holding hands, for a long, long time.

*

A lot of the rented equipment had arrived, and was being installed at the premises. Men were backing in and out with the crates that held cookers and deep-fryers. The sheer volume of noise was frightening. Thinking about how much they were going to have to earn to pay for it all made Tom and Cathy feel weak. June and Cathy were supervising it while getting the finger food ready for the fashion show.

'Most of them won't eat at all, wannabe models like stick insects,' June complained.

'No, you're totally wrong, apparently people who are far too old and fat for the garments make up the main part of the audience. My mother-in-law will be there, for one.'

'And won't Hannah's eyes fall out of her head when she sees some of the items on display? Right, that's the second last tray – one more and I'll go out and start loading the van.'

'Okay, I'll get started on Mad Minnie,' June said cheerfully.

'Shush, June, one of these fine days she'll come in and hear you saying that,' Cathy warned.

Minnie was a woman whose husband thought she could cook, so every Friday she arrived for one fresh dish and five frozen suppers for two. Cathy had long ago offered to teach her to make the simple dishes she wanted, but no, she wanted them made for her in her own dishes. So every time they were making Beef Carbonnade or Chicken Provençale, they remembered to spoon two extra portions into Minnie's red or green containers.

'What a desperate life they must lead the two of them, never having anyone in or ever going out,' Cathy said sympathetically.

'Does she think there are six days in the week?' June wondered.

'No, they have fish and chips once a week, her husband's little treat to thank her for all this baking.'

'He must be as thick as a plank,' June said. 'She's better off not telling him anything, the less you tell men the better, I always say.'

'But what kind of communication is that, lying to him over something as basic as the fact she's not making his dinner?' Cathy asked.

'Believe me, I've been over the hoops longer than you two,' June said. 'Say nothing, do what you like, that's my motto.'

Tom carried the trays out grimly. There was some truth in what she'd said, he thought. Suppose Marcella had said that there was a training course or a business meeting in the hotel or something. Of course he'd have believed her, and he'd never have known the horror of last night and the lingering possibility that she might still choose Mr Newton's party rather than the one he had so lovingly organised himself. When he came back, Cathy was looking with some dislike at the food in front of her.

'What's this?' she asked June.

'God, imagine you asking me. They're poussins, baby chickens, I'm just doing them for Minnie, are you losing your marbles or something?'

'You take them over there to the other side, will you? I don't really like looking at them, they make me feel sick, they're sort of, I don't know, human-looking.'

'Sure.' June was cheerful as she prattled on. 'You know, I think we should try and get some kind of Christmas menu ready way in advance, a pack of things for eejits to have in the house like canapés, and teeny mince pies . . .'

'Like we could deliver them in the van?' Cathy sounded eager.

'I'd love that, going round to these houses saying Merry Christmas, like Santa Claus. But will you still be working at Christmas?' June asked casually.

'What do you mean?' Cathy looked alarmed.

'I mean, when will you be taking leave, and everything? We'd need to know, wouldn't we, Tom?'

'Of course we would,' Tom said, understanding nothing.

'And by the way, were you ever going to tell us about this baby? I mean, were we meant to wait until you asked us to boil some water and time the contractions?'

At Haywards things looked very busy. Tom's stomach felt sick about almost everything, and tonight the opinion that people had of Scarlet Feather's catering was way the lowest worry on the list. He helped Con, June and Cathy set up the press reception and then slipped away and left a small bunch of roses in a vase in the dressing room. He put a card saying, 'Beautiful, lovely Marcella. Good luck on your first night and always.' His hand trembled a little as he left it there. The girls were on stage for a photo call; they would come up and mingle with the press later. Tom hung around the dressing room. He knew in his heart that the whole thing had been brought on by nerves, and that she wasn't going to mention the matter again except with embarrassment. He just wished he could get that strange, dead, mantra tone she spoke with out of his mind. She had sounded like someone sleepwalking. Someone slightly out of control.

The press reception went very well, three journalists took the Scarlet Feather card as well as the Feather Fashions press release. The brothers were photographed together, arm in arm.

Cathy had been shocked by this morning's revelation. She had spun them a good story; the whole thing was something she hadn't realised at all herself. She had only just been to the doctor and confirmed it, and she had not been able to tell Neil before he disappeared to Africa. *Now* could they understand the need for discretion. Or a total news blackout. They had realised the urgency and backed off admirably.

'Well, we always wanted another pair of hands around the place. As long as the baby starts work at six months, we'll not mention the matter again,' Tom agreed.

'Sure,' June had said. 'Let's keep it really quiet, let's just tell Maud and Simon, is that okay?'

Cathy knew that she could rely on them, and that she could *just* get through today; the press reception looked as if it was motoring fine, then there was this show which was obviously cracking poor Tom up, then there would be the finger food afterwards, stack the dishes in Haywards' kitchen and then, as if the day had not been long enough, she would have to go to

the Italian restaurant to the party. Lucky old Neil with his bureaucratic red
tape and his composite resolutions at a conference under African skies. He
had nothing to worry about. He didn't begin to know what problems were!

Tom could hardly remember the show. He remembered a few gasps here
and there and a lot of applause. He saw Joe look across at him and put his
thumb up in the air a couple of times when Marcella was on stage; he forced
a smile onto his face. It only took him seconds to see where Paul Newton
was sitting, prime viewing area, without his cigar but sucking a pencil
instead. He felt such a loathing for the man that he almost fell over. Please
may Marcella stumble, he thought, or may she miss her cue, do it all wrong.
Then immediately he felt guilty: what a terrible thing to call down bad
spirits on someone's first night, especially the night of someone he loved.
And then there was the applause, and the buyers from different parts of the
country lining up for more details and information about stock in front of
Joe and his friends, Eddie and Harry, and a watchful eye on it all being kept
by Mr Newton himself. Tom worked like an automaton, passing filo-
wrapped prawns here and Thai fish cakes there. 'Delighted you like them,
we have a little recipe sheet there near the door if you're interested.' It had
been one of his own ideas, give them a list of how to make half a dozen
simple hors d'oeuvres that anyone could make really, and also add the
names of about twelve more that were complicated but part of the
repertoire. Phone, fax and e-mail of Scarlet Feather and you had a
wonderful advertisement – they were all tucking them into handbags. He
moved feverishly around the room, and felt a woman's hand on his arm. It
was the woman from the magazine that had done their photo shoot, the
hard-faced journalist fifteen years older than him, the one Marcella said
fancied him.

'Oh, hallo, I didn't see you at the press reception,' he said.

'You were looking out?' she asked.

He fled. And saw Marcella smiling and waving her glass across the room.
Would this evening never end? Gradually the crowd thinned.

'Don't fill their glasses any more, Con, they'll never go home,' he pleaded.

'Suits me, Mr F,' Con said, and began clearing up the empties.

'June, can you sort of amalgamate whatever food is left; the word's out
we're finishing up now.'

'Most of this won't survive, Cathy, we can't recycle it.'

'I don't care if we plaster the walls of the ladies' cloakroom with it, we're
not giving them any more,' Cathy said, with an insincere smile as she saw
her mother-in-law approaching.

'What a delicious spread, you really *have* come on in such leaps and
bounds.'

'Well, thank you so very much,' Cathy said, resisting with difficulty the
urge to knock Hannah senseless on the floor at Haywards, ensuring that she
and Tom never worked again.

'And a lot of my friends said so too, they said it was the only thing that
made the evening worthwhile.'

'You didn't like the show?' Her face was bland and innocent.

'Dear me no, tacky and tawdry, not Haywards at all. I must have a word with that nice Shona Burke.'

'Neil will be back on Sunday,' Cathy said, intent on changing the conversation. 'Apparently it's very interesting out there.'

'Such a pity you two don't ever manage to be in the same place at the same time at all.' Hannah Mitchell used to sing a very different tune. Times had changed.

The dirty dishes had been stacked in the Haywards' dish-washing machine, and trays of glasses rinsed for Tom to cope with next day. Con and June had seen to this as well as emptying ashtrays and taking every last sign of litter away from the salon. Tom was rounding the little group up for the restaurant. Joe had said that Marcella was terrific, star of the show and he would love to come to Tom's supper, but he simply had to stay with his colleagues.

After ages they were ready, the restaurant was only minutes away. Tom begged Cathy to take the others with her, to order the house Frascati and get it all started. They were flashing the lights on and off in Haywards, a definite sign that it was time to go. Security men and caretakers were going around checking the big solid ash-filled containers where cigarettes might not have been fully extinguished. Tom knew a lot of them by name from his early-morning bread-making visits.

'I'm just running up to the dressing rooms, Sean,' he said to one of them. 'Got to pick up Marcella.'

'Nobody there, Tom, lights all out, they're all gone,' said the man.

'No, Marcella went back to change. She must be there.'

'Honestly, not a soul,' the man said.

His job depended on it, Tom knew he was right. He went downstairs, mystified. She must be going straight to the restaurant, but why hadn't she said? And here was Shona.

'Come on with me; they must be all there in the restaurant already.'

'I was just looking for Marcella,' he said.

'Oh, she left half an hour ago. She left with Joe, and his pals Eddie and Harry and that Mr Newton. They all have to go to some do back in the hotel.'

He felt as if he were going to pass out. 'Sorry, they went where?' he said eventually.

Shona looked at him with concern. 'I said to her that I thought we were all going to the Italian to celebrate her night, and she said that you *knew* she had to go to this meeting. You did, didn't you?'

'Yes, deep down I did,' said Tom Feather.

August

Tom let himself into the flat with a heavy heart. How had he managed to keep cheerful all night, talking about everything under the sun except the fact that Marcella hadn't come to her own party? The others were supportive, too supportive. They had taken in the situation immediately. It was *Hamlet* without the prince; the beautiful model hadn't thought they were good enough to come and have dinner with afterwards, she had gone with the important people. They had all tried to behave as if it was an acceptable thing to do. Of course she had to, very difficult to get away, part of the job. He had wanted to cry so much that he was astounded he hadn't actually broken down. But no, they all went on, fussing about which pasta to choose. And he urged them to stay longer to have wine, he didn't want to go back to that empty flat and wonder when she would be home. He couldn't remember what he had eaten or how much he had paid. The evening was bitter in his mouth and heart.

Cathy said as he was leaving, 'She's probably at home already, furious that she couldn't be with us.'

'I'd say that's where she is all right,' he said with what he hoped was a grin, rather than the beginning of a howl.

Of course she wasn't at home. It was one a.m., and Mr Newton's party would only be getting going. He sat down and drank a lot of cold water to try to get rid of the taste of whatever he had been eating. He nodded off at the kitchen table. And woke suddenly to hear the phone ringing. It was twenty minutes after three o'clock.

'Tom?'

'Yes, Marcella?'

'Tom, the thing is . . .'

'Yes?'

'The thing is, the party is only just getting going here. So I wanted to say I'd be later, and I'm sorry, but you know the way these things happen.'

'Of course I don't know the way these things happen. It's nearly four o'clock in the morning. You're not coming home, is this what you've phoned to tell me?'

'Not immediately, and in fact some of the girls were thinking we should get a room between us and maybe stay . . .'

'Please stay, Marcella,' he said.

'It might be more sensible, what with taxis and—'

'Goodnight,' he said.

'Are you cross?'

'No, that's not the word,' he said.

'Tom, please, tell me you understand that it's all for the job.'

'Stay there, please, Marcella. Please stay.'

'Not in that cold voice, not making me feel—'

'Stay there,' he said, hung up and took the phone off the hook in case she called again.

It was an extraordinary Saturday morning. Tom was busy, saying nothing whatsoever about Marcella not having come home last night, or Cathy's pregnancy and all it would involve for the company. He couldn't believe that Neil was still in Africa knowing nothing of this news, and he didn't like the lines of anxiety in Cathy's face when she had told them this. Cathy was busy saying nothing whatsoever about not having spoken to Neil, or Marcella's non-appearance at the supper last night and all it might involve in Tom's life. She couldn't believe that Tom hadn't known until the last moment that there was a business do Marcella had to attend, and she didn't like the pale, waxen look on his face all evening. So they talked instead about the Chicago wedding, which was running into murkier waters all the time and was now under three weeks away. How had August 19th crept up on them so quickly?

'Is Marian like you at all?' Tom wanted to know.

'I've no idea, I've hardly seen her since I was a child. She left when she was seventeen, and I've been over once and she's only been back twice. And I don't know *what* Harry is like, so we can't get any clues to their character.'

'Do we know anything about the kind of people they'll be asking from Chicago?' he tried.

'No, not a notion.'

'And the Irish contingent?'

'A few of Mam and Dad's sisters and brothers, their children, a couple of cousins, all of them anxious to have the ties off, the shirts open and get stuck into the pints.'

'What would they like?'

'Prawn cocktail, roast chicken and ice cream with chocolate sauce.'

Tom groaned.

'And the message from Chicago sounded a bit pissed off about the typically Irish fare.'

'Yes, a huff has been taken, not to me personally mind, but behind my back to Mam, and to Geraldine . . . The "wouldn't you think Cathy would know what's expected" sort of thing. It would sicken you.'

'Do you think we should just *give* it to them, for an easy life?' Tom looked very tired.

Cathy wondered had he slept at all, they might have had words when they got home. 'I don't really, Tom. I know what you mean, we don't need all this aggravation, doing something right when they want a load of old rubbish.'

'But what about the customer being right? And another thing, there's not going to be anyone there who'd know us, that we'd feel ashamed in front of...'

Cathy frowned. 'I know there's truth in what you say, but honestly, I want it to be right for them, all this crowd are going to be eating in restaurants in Dublin the rest of the time they're here, they'll be having a rehearsal party in one hotel and a recovery party in another, they'll *see* that no one except on St Patrick's Day cards in New York eats bacon and cabbage. They'll all be at desperately expensive places. Places that will rob them blind.'

'Heigh-ho,' Tom said. 'Have they booked?'

'Well, I'd hope so, they've been talking about them for six months.'

'We'd better send another e-mail,' he said. 'Should we try pushing a choice of glorious Irish lamb and Irish salmon, we could even send them pictures of that dressed salmon we did a few weeks back, it was gorgeous.'

'It's not draped in shamrocks and Irish flags,' grumbled Cathy.

He was standing beside her cutting vegetables. They had exactly the same stroke, the same rhythm, it was as if they were rowing a boat together. There was something companionable and calming about it all. Even their conversation wasn't demanding, but it was enough to take their minds off their worries; they couldn't brood about Neil and Marcella if there was work to be done, food to be sent out, bills to be paid and the wedding of the century to organise.

James Byrne came in to go over the accounts.

'How did the fashion show go last night?' he asked politely, and was surprised at the curt response.

'Fine,' Tom said.

'Great,' Cathy said.

James Byrne asked no more. He went through the prohibitive cost of renting equipment, and noted the slow progress of dealings with the insurance company, which was really dragging its heels.

'When will Neil be back from Africa?' James Byrne asked innocently.

'Tomorrow,' Tom said.

'Monday,' said Cathy.

Both answers were barked out in exactly the same way as the previous ones. James Byrne looked from one to the other, and hoped that his friend Martin Maguire had not been right when he said that there was a curse on this place. These two, Tom and Cathy, used to be great friends, and the happiest of young people to work with. Today they were like wild animals waiting to pounce.

'The reason I said Monday was it's just that we're going to a hotel tomorrow night,' Cathy said. 'In case you were planning to talk to him about the insurance company.'

'Sorry,' said Tom. 'It's not my business when he comes back.'

James Byrne was mystified. He turned to a different and hopefully less tense subject. 'I want to check that you have work upcoming that will be paid at the time; we can't afford to give anyone ninety days' credit at the moment.'

'Yes, my brother paid half in advance, and when he gets the final wine list on Monday he'll pay at once,' Tom said.

James noted it down.

'And then there's my sister's wedding, they'll pay on the dot too,' Cathy added.

'You both have very admirable families,' James murmured.

'Haywards pays for the bread by the month,' Tom said.

'Mad Minnie pays by the week, but it's only tiny.'

'We'll be doing two jobs at the studio for Ricky, about three hundred pounds' worth; he'd pay on the night if we asked him.'

'There's a funeral next Wednesday; Quentins will get that money for us fairly quickly.'

'Good, good.' He nodded gravely at their list.

'Are you anxious, James?' Cathy asked suddenly.

'I'm always anxious,' he said with a weak smile.

'But no, is it serious, the cash flow, the situation?'

'Very serious,' said James Byrne. 'Very serious indeed.'

When Cathy got home at lunchtime there was a message on the answering machine saying that Neil's plane would be delayed on Sunday, but that he'd still love to go to the hotel in Wicklow. He'd ring from the airport when they got in, and he loved her.

When Tom got home at lunchtime there was an envelope on the mat. A note from Marcella saying she'd be back about noon, and maybe they might go out somewhere and have a nice cheerful lunch, that she'd ring him first. And that she loved him.

On Saturday lunchtime Geraldine got a phone call which was hard to understand.

'Hallo, is that the dry-cleaner's, it's Frederick Flynn here. I was meant to collect a jacket this afternoon but as it happens I won't be able to, I have to go away suddenly.'

'Freddie?' she gasped.

'Yes, thank you so much for understanding, can I ring you on Monday? Good, good, you've been most obliging.'

'What are you telling me, Freddie?'

He had been coming round in an hour's time. They were going to have two whole nights and a full day together. His wife was going to Limerick.

'Yes, thank you for making special arrangements for me, but I have to go to Limerick.'

'No, Freddie, you don't have to go, you said *she* was going.'

'Again, thank you for being understanding.' He hung up.

'Hallo, is that Mr ... er, Muttance Scarlet?'

'Muttie here. Who's that?'

'It's Mr Mitchell, actually.'

'Oh, is that Cathy's father-in-law?' Muttie asked.

'No, it's ... um ... it's ... er ... Simon and Maud's father.'

'Oh, good, how are you, Mr Mitchell? Lizzie and myself, we're here waiting for them to arrive any minute, but they're not here yet.' Muttie thought he wanted to speak to the twins.

'No, and they won't be there, I mean, they weren't able to go.'

'They're not coming?'

'No, I'm sorry, Mr Muttance. Very sorry.'

'And are they sick or something, Mr Mitchell?'

'Yes and no to that; let's say that their mother is not at all well, due to them, so they have to stay here and look after her.'

'And could I have a word with them do you think, Mr Mitchell?'

'That would not be at all appropriate.'

Walter came home to what he hoped might be a late lunch on Saturday. He saw his father sitting alone at the table.

'What's wrong, Father?'

'Just about everything, Walter.'

'Tell me.'

'Your mother's gone back on the drink, those twins have been dancing with things on their shoes all around the house all day driving her madder than ever before, old Barty got into another game and lost so much that he's gone into hiding.'

'But what had he to lose? Old Barty hasn't *got* anything to lose,' Walter said.

'Why do you think I'm so worried? I'm waiting for someone to come for the house,' said Kenneth Mitchell.

'No lunch?' Walter asked.

'Not unless you make some,' Kenneth said.

'Have the children gone out to those mad people in St Jarlath's Crescent?'

'No, I wouldn't let them go, it was their bloody tap-tap-tapping that sent your mother over the top.'

'So where are they?' Walter asked.

'Sulking in their room, I gather ...'

'Better be careful, Father, this army of women police will be after you if you break any of the rules.'

'They're my children, Walter. I've every right to say where they go for Saturday lunch.'

'Yes, Father.'

Walter looked pointedly at a kitchen table on which there was no sign whatsoever of a Saturday lunch being made for anyone.

Shona sat in her flat and read the letter for the thirtieth time. She was being invited to dinner on August 19th by someone she had never thought she would see again.

*

Lizzie said to Muttie that he must not disturb Cathy: the girl was the colour of a sheet these days. Muttie said you had to fight now or give up for ever. That man who had pressed a pound coin into his hand would walk over them unless they made a stand. Mark his words, the twins wouldn't be allowed to dance at the wedding if they gave in on this one. And the dancing teacher was waiting for them in the kitchen. He was going to ring Cathy this moment. She wasn't at Waterview, she wasn't on her mobile phone. He tried the premises.

Tom Feather had left Stoneyfield. He couldn't bear to stay there in case Marcella came back to check was he all right. He had to be out of the place immediately. He answered the phone. 'You missed Cathy, Muttie, she's taken herself off for the afternoon. On my orders; I told her that it had been too long since she had seen the sea, and she's never even visited James Joyce's tower, so I sent her out to Sandycove to see both and clear her head.'

'That was good of you. Lizzie's been saying she looks tired. It's just that I've a bit of a problem here.'

'Tell me the story,' Tom pleaded. Anything was better than being left with his own thoughts. He listened to the tale.

'I'll go and get them for you,' he said. 'Just give me the address.'

'We don't want to make any trouble,' Muttie said.

'Of course not,' Tom said.

'Good day, Mr Mitchell. I'm Tom Feather, come to collect the children to take them to St Jarlath's Crescent.'

'I'm sorry, I have no idea who you are.' He spoke arrogantly, and a small tic began in Tom's forehead.

'If your son Walter is here, he can verify who I am. I work with your nephew's wife Cathy. I'm sure my name has been mentioned to you, but in the meantime I'm collecting the children, their dancing shoes and their tape recorder as laid down in the terms of your agreement.'

'Agreement? We have no agreement with you, Mr ... er ...'

'With the courts, the social welfare department, with the Mitchell family.'

'I don't think this is any time ...'

'You're so right, there *is* no time, Mr Scarlet is paying the dancing teacher by the hour and there has been a delay already.'

'SIMON! MAUD!' he shouted.

The twins had been listening fearfully and came out into the hall. 'You should have been there ages ago,' he said, mock severely.

'But we couldn't go, we made Mother ill,' Simon said.

'By practising the dancing, you see,' Maud explained.

'Nonsense, of course you didn't. Right, get your shoes, hop into the van and we'll be off.'

'You have absolutely no right to barge into my house ...' Kenneth Mitchell began.

'Take it up with the social worker, and with Cathy and Neil when he gets home tomorrow. I'm only the driver,' said Tom, and slammed out of the house and into the Scarlet Feather van, which he revved up like a maniac.

He saw Walter looking at him from behind a curtain at an upper window. 'Hi, Walter,' he shouted. 'Always to the forefront when you're needed, as usual, I see.'

Walter disappeared. The twins were running out, excited but anxious at the same time. It was so cruel and unfair to treat children like this. When he and Marcella had children, they would be loved and praised. He remembered that Marcella had not come home last night. And suddenly there was a taste of bile in his mouth.

'Can I get anything for you, Tom? Tea, coffee, a drink, you're so good to get the children for us.'

'No, I'm just fine thanks, Lizzie, just wanted to do something to take my mind off things.'

'That work is just killing the pair of you, Cathy's pale as a ghost.'

'No, it's not that at all, we both love the work ... it's just ...'

He paused. There were so many things he couldn't say. Like why Cathy was so pale. Like why they had to work so hard because the premises had been done over. Like his own life being in tatters.

'It's just one thing, Lizzie, what time do they leave to go back to that place?'

'Muttie'll take them, it's only a couple of buses, they have to be back before eight.'

'I'll come and pick them up at a quarter to.'

'We can't have you traipsing all over the city with—'

'No, please, it suits me,' and he was gone.

She stood at the window and watched him leave.

'He's had a row with your one, you know, the beautician,' Lizzie said.

'How on earth do you make that out?' Muttie asked.

'Phyllis down the road, she was at the fashion show in Haywards, she said you wouldn't see it in an X-rated movie and that your one, Tom's girlfriend, had hardly a stitch on her.'

'I'm very sorry we didn't go, now that you come to think of it,' said Muttie reflectively.

'I asked Geraldine about it and she said to keep you under lock and chain and not let you near it, so I didn't,' said Lizzie with some pride.

Cathy thought that when Neil came home she would drive him straight down to Holly's hotel in Wicklow, and that they wouldn't stop at Waterview. She took down all Neil's messages for him on the answering machine, she packed him an overnight bag. Now he would have no excuse to pause at home and be distracted. She drove the Volvo to the airport and waited as the arriving passengers came though the gate. There he was: slightly tanned, so there must have been *some* free time. His handsome, animated face was full of the conversation he was having with one of his colleagues. He barely paused when he saw her.

She knew one of his companions, a very earnest man with no sense of humour but an ability to wear the other side down. She recognised another as a politician with an eye to self-advancement; the fourth was a tall, grey-haired man whom she didn't know.

'Good heavens, you're Scarlet Feather!' he said. 'We were at a do you did for Freddie Flynn, simply superb affair, we kept your card. Now this is just the prompting we need . . . Neil, why didn't you tell us you were married to this genius?'

'Because then you'd have taken your eye off the ball out there and talked about Cathy's food all the time,' he said. But he put his arm around her shoulder. He was proud of her, she could see. It would all be fine, she must not be so nervous about telling him. They walked hand in hand to the car park.

'I'm dying for a shower,' he said. 'We won't spend long at home though, we'll head straight down to Wicklow, a promise is a promise.'

Tom came out of one cinema in the big complex, went to the desk and bought a ticket for another. The blonde girl in the ticket office smiled at him.

'Glutton for the movies, aren't you?' she said.

'What?' Tom said, startled.

'That's the third you've got today. Are you catching up or something?'

He was so handsome, big shoulders, fair hair, a gorgeous smile. The kind of fellow you hardly ever met these days.

'Yeah, that's what I'm doing. Catching up,' he said.

She got the feeling he wasn't talking to her properly, that he couldn't really see her. She shrugged to herself. Maybe he was on drugs or something. When the cinema finally closed on Sunday there was still light in the sky. It must be the lights of the city causing a glow. Tom drove back to the premises and let himself in again. He wondered was the spy from the insurance company lurking somewhere, waiting for Tom to trash the place a second time. He wondered would he have anything to eat. After all, it was like a child in a sweetshop to be here. The rented freezers were stacked with food, or he could make a simple omelette. But food would taste like sawdust in his mouth. He sat down with his head in his hands. He lay down again on the sofa in the front office. He had slept here once before, in the run-up to the launch party last January. It had been cold then, and he had laid every coat he could find over him. Tonight was warm, and he needed nothing to cover him. He lay in the dark and looked at the ceiling. Soon he would sleep, and the awful, shocking hurt and jealousy would go away. But that hadn't worked at the cinema. The plots of all those movies had meant nothing to him. All he could see was Marcella. Talk to her, talk to her, he told himself. She might well be sitting up in Stoneyfield, anguished, waiting for him to come back. But what would be the use if they were not able to talk? What could he say, or she say that made any difference now? With horror Tom realised that there was nothing to talk about any more. They were way beyond that now.

*

'Any sign of Tom these days?' Joe asked his parents.

'Didn't you see him on Friday night at this trade fashion show?' Maura Feather sniffed. She still suspected that she had somehow been misled about the nature of that evening, and that neither of her sons had wanted her to attend.

'Yes, of course I did.'

'And isn't that only the day before yesterday?' his mother said.

'Is that all it is? How extraordinary.'

It seemed like a lifetime since the night his brother's great love Marcella had come back so unexpectedly to the hotel with Paul Newton to the party, instead of going to Tom's little dinner in the Italian restaurant. Joe didn't dare to think what Tom had made of it all.

Marcella telephoned four times on Saturday and was puzzled to find the answering machine on on each occasion. He had *known* she wasn't coming back on Friday night. She had *told* him, for heaven's sake. Why the sudden attitude? Maybe he was sitting waiting in Stoneyfield, brooding, sulking, looking like a little boy and needing to be cajoled and patted down.

'Tom,' she called as she went into the flat, but there was no reply.

The place was quiet, too quiet. Also tidy, too tidy. She realised at once that he wasn't at home. She looked around for a note, but there wasn't one. Marcella sat down and took out a cigarette. For a woman who claimed and believed that she didn't smoke, she was getting through rather a lot of cigarettes these days.

'I'm sorry if our dancing made you feel badly, Mother,' Maud said on Sunday.

'Dancing?' Kay Mitchell asked, confused.

'Father said the sound gave you a bad head and made you sick.'

'I don't remember,' she said.

'Could we get you a cup of tea or anything?' Maud wondered.

'That's very nice of you, dear, but why, exactly?'

'Well, you didn't come down for breakfast or lunch or anything, and we thought you might be hungry,' Simon explained.

'No, you are kind, but not at all,' she said.

Simon and Maud went downstairs. Their father was at the kitchen table in a very black humour altogether. Most of his rage was directed against old Barty, who had disappeared without trace, apparently. They knew from the past that it was unwise to ask about food when anyone was upset. So they took a tin of peaches and some bread out to the garden.

'Do you think they're sort of, you know . . . ?' Simon asked Maud.

'You mean, Mother's nerves getting bad and Father about to wander?' Maud spelled it out.

'Something like that,' Simon was upset.

'Don't let him see you crying. Let's go into the shed.'

'It's locked, isn't it?'

'No, Walter went out earlier and left it open. I went in to see was there a skipping rope.'

Simon scooped up the peach tin and scurried into the shed. His father's lectures on behaving like a man and to stop this very poofy dancing were becoming increasingly hard to take.

Tom tidied up the apartment at Stoneyfield meticulously. He packed an overnight bag for himself and put it in the back of the van. The phone rang just as he was leaving. He listened to hear who it was. It might just be Marcella. Or it might not. But he would not pick it up. After the click there was a hesitant intake of breath, and then whoever it was hung up. He played it four times to see what he could decipher. It was definitely Marcella.

She was shocked that he had left the phone on the machine. After what she had done, she had expected him to be waiting and ready.

He wondered where she was calling from. He wondered why he had never got that call identify gadget that Cathy had ... What would it have told him? It would have identified which hotel his brother had booked for this thug who had bought Marcella. Would it make it better if he could exonerate all the other hotels in Dublin and just blame one?

The phone rang harshly beside her. This would be Freddie now. She would be very cool. It wasn't Freddie Flynn, it was her niece Marian, ringing in floods of tears from Chicago. Through all the sobs she could only understand one word, repeated over and over, and it seemed to be the word 'men', then she heard how useless and unreliable and hopeless they were. Geraldine sighed a deep sigh. Harry was obviously as bad as every other man. They didn't breed them better in Chicago than anywhere else. But gradually it became clear, Harry had *not* run off with someone else and cancelled the wedding. The wedding was still very much on, it was just that Harry and his family hadn't booked the hotels for the rehearsal party and the recovery party, and they were now absolutely at their wits' end about what to do. Geraldine made soothing noises.

'Maybe Cathy will come up with something, she's there on the ground ... She won't have an awful lot else to do, will she?' Marian snuffled and wept.

'Stop crying, Marian, it will all be all right.'

'Geraldine, you're so good at calming people down, how did you get to be a member of our family, answer me that.'

Geraldine stared dumbly across her expensive apartment and wondered about this also.

He reset the machine and left the apartment. He would not come back tonight, he had packed gear that would take him through the weekend. He would not be here to listen to her explanations. He did not want to listen to the fact that it didn't matter that the party meant nothing, and that she was being so good and honest about having told him that she should be getting a pat on the back for it all.

*

It had taken Shona Burke twenty-four hours to know whether she would accept the invitation or not. She didn't want to go, but the wording was very hard to refuse. She wondered how long it had taken to write. Days, possibly. She could not be expected to respond instantly. She would write her letter carefully too. When other people were out enjoying a summer Sunday, Shona Burke would spend the hours composing her reply.

Geraldine was also in her apartment in the Glenstar building. She could not believe that Freddie had done this to her. Called her in front of his wife and told her that plans had changed. Pretended he was talking to the dry-cleaner's. She would not accept that. Not from anyone. No matter how tense the situation might be at home, no matter how great the pressure from his wife, and possible suspicion, Geraldine was owed more than a travesty of a phone call like that. When Freddie apologised, as he would, when he tried to explain how it seemed the only option open to him, she would listen to him coldly. As Geraldine had told him, she always behaved perfectly, she was the ideal mistress, she wished only the same consideration in return. She turned her wrist so that the jewels on her watch caught the light. Yes, of course he had been considerate to give her this and other gifts, but that wasn't the point. She needed respect as well.

'Ah yes, but a hijack is a hijack. They have showers in Wicklow too. My only hope to get you to myself is if we go straight there . . .'

'But hon, my messages . . .' he wailed.

'They're in the glove compartment, all of them, and you can't call anyone on a Sunday anyway,' she said.

And in the afternoon sunshine they drove down to Wicklow, and he told her tales of the conference and the people they met and what had gone well and what had been stymied as usual.

Tom went for a long run. It was a warm evening, and if he had been able to take in some of the things he saw he might have enjoyed himself. But he didn't see very much. He let himself into the premises. At first he thought he saw someone watching near the courtyard, but decided he must be imagining things. He went in and slept on the big chintz sofa. He slept badly, but had he gone back to Stoneyfield he would not have slept at all.

Holly's hotel did a big Sunday-lunch trade, it was just the right distance from Dublin. People brought grannies and mothers-in-law there. It always reminded them of their youth, some kind of continuity in a changing world. It had an old-world charm, a lot of chintz and the same waitresses year after year. They checked in at the big, old-fashioned desk with all the keys to the rooms hanging there with their coloured tassels. People were moving to and fro in the hall behind them. Among them, Molly and Shay Hayes. There was a lot of shouting about what a small world it was.

'Having a little anniversary, are you?' Molly wanted to know.

'No, Neil has just come back from Africa, he was at a forum on refugees,' Cathy explained.

'Hope you sorted them out,' Shay said glumly.

'Well, we did our best, Mr Hayes, but you know, there was so much red tape, and these things go so slowly.'

'Still, as long as you put the boot in, we've quite enough of our own in need here, without letting in a lot of people who don't know our ways . . .'

Neil's mouth was open in astonishment.

'We've got the room key, Neil, don't you think we should go on up?' Cathy said hastily.

'I don't exactly understand . . .'

'And neither do I, people speaking languages no one can understand getting free houses and filling up the place . . .'

'Mr Hayes . . . Molly . . . you'll have to excuse us, I haven't seen this man of mine for nine whole days. Do you mind if I drag him upstairs with me?'

'Not at all, I'm all for that sort of thing, there's not enough of it about these days,' Shay Hayes said approvingly.

They scampered up the stairs and burst into the big sunny room. Where they could let themselves laugh properly.

'He's a monster, that man . . . I don't know why we're laughing,' Neil said, almost ashamed of himself.

'Listen, you've met a thousand, I've met a thousand, but the hall in Holly's hotel isn't the place to fight it out,' Cathy pleaded. 'Forget him. Tell me all about it, I want to know what you did there from the moment you arrived.'

He sat down in one of their little chintz-covered chairs to tell her, the words tumbling out: the delegates who were expected and did not turn up, the surprise celebrities who came to give support, meetings that were cancelled, the others that started impromptu but grew to be more important. Cathy ordered a bottle of wine and a plate of sandwiches to be sent up to the bedroom as he told of what was being done and what an amazing amount there still was to do. Then he said he'd have the shower that had been promised.

He called out from the bathroom, 'Hardly any point my getting any of that clean gear on, is there? I mean, you'll only be tearing it off me, won't you?'

'Do put something on just for the moment,' she called back. 'And come and sit here, it's so gorgeous.'

He came out, damp and clean, glowing in the dark blue shirt she had packed for him. He was so attractive. No wonder they always wanted him on television as a spokesman. Neil Mitchell was so convincing about everything. She looked up at him as he came over to the table and poured a glass of wine for them both.

This was the time to tell him.

'There's something I want to tell you. I've been wanting so much to tell you.'

He came and sat opposite her and held her hand. He smiled at her. Perhaps he had guessed.

'What do you want to tell me?' he asked.

'Neil, I'm pregnant,' she said.

Neil looked at her stunned. 'Say that again.'

'You heard what I said.'

'You're not,' he said.

'Oh, I am.' She was smiling broadly but searching his face, wanting to see the answering smile and not finding it.

'How did this happen?' Neil asked.

'I think you know how it happened, like the way it always happens.' This wasn't the way she had thought the conversation between them would go.

'Don't play games, you know what we agreed.'

'Yes, I do.'

'So, then, how did this happen?'

'One night when I didn't put in my diaphragm. And when we thought it was a safe time of the month. We *did* discuss it.'

'Oh yes, I'm sure we did, long and logically.'

'Neil!'

'Sorry. I'm afraid that I just can't take it in.'

A small lump of fear began to grow in her heart. 'I thought you'd be pleased.'

'No, you didn't think that, this is not something we agreed.'

She was very frightened now. He had released her hands and pushed his chair back. He had got a great shock. Too great a shock. She knew she must be calm now, and speak in the same unemotional tones as he did.

'Some things are above and beyond agreement,' she said simply.

'No, that's not so.'

'It's the way it feels.'

'Not in an age when we can control fertility, not when two people agreed in Greece that we wanted to be together always, live our dreams despite any obstacles that would be put in our way and without children.'

'We never said permanently without children,' she said.

'No, you're right, but what we *did* actually say was that if we changed our minds we would discuss it, and we haven't discussed it,' he said.

'We are now,' she said, with a feeling of unreality.

He must come round to realising what was happening and how wonderful it was. He must.

'How far is . . .'

'About thirteen, fourteen weeks.'

'So there's plenty of time . . .' he began.

'For us to get used to the idea,' she finished swiftly.

'Why didn't you tell me sooner? You must have known a long time. Why didn't you say anything?'

'I wasn't certain . . .' she began.

'But even if you thought . . . ?'

'There was never time to talk. You always had to go somewhere, I always had to go somewhere . . .' She wanted to be sure to take equal blame for their having no proper time together in their marriage.

'But this is so big. You could have told me . . . surely?'

'I tried several times, but then we had the fuss about Simon and Maud, and you talking about this posting abroad, and then the break-in and all the hassle about that, then the night before you went away you had to go out ... no, you *had* to go, I know you had. So the days passed. I mean, was I to send you an e-mail about it?'

'Please don't be flippant, I beg you not to do that.'

'Oh, no, I'm not, not in the least bit flippant. Why do you think I got you down here to tell you? I wanted us to talk calmly. I was terrified to try and tell you at home with all that goes on, I needed there to be no interruptions.'

'So nobody knows? Your mother and father or my parents?' he asked.

'Of *course* they don't know,' she said truthfully.

He nodded as if ashamed that he had asked. 'I know. I'm sorry, I shouldn't have asked you that.'

She felt guilty that he didn't know that she had already told Geraldine and that Tom and June had guessed ... But it wasn't important, not nearly as important as the look on his face. She reached for his hand, but he moved away. Very slightly, but it was definitely withdrawing from her.

'It will take time to get used to it,' she pleaded.

'Time isn't necessarily something we have, hon.'

'What do you mean?' she asked in a voice that seemed to come from a thousand miles away; but she knew what he meant.

'Well, we have to make a decision, don't we?' He had never looked like this when he was facing the mighty Mitchells with the news that he was marrying the maid's daughter. He had never looked like this in the High Court.

'Decision?' she asked, to buy time.

There was a long silence.

'We agreed we wouldn't have children.' He was trying to sound calm.

'And we didn't intend to yet, but ...' she said.

'But fortunately there's time to reverse this.' He looked at her, his face drawn, his eyes cold.

'You want me to have a termination?' she said.

'I want us to discuss it, yes.'

'We marched together in the Woman's Right to Choose demo,' she said. 'Do you remember the day?'

'Of course I do, and that's exactly what I'm saying. It *is* a right to choose.' Neil believed this passionately.

'The *woman's* right,' Cathy said in a small voice.

The pause seemed very long. He looked at her, shocked. 'You mean, we're not in this together, suddenly it's all what *you* want, not what *we* want? Where's my right to choose whether or not to be a father, tell me that?' He was trembling as he spoke.

'That's not the way it is, Neil.'

'But it *is*,' he cried. 'We agreed that night in Syntagma Square, that night we decided to be together for ever that we would not have children ... We agreed it, nobody put a gun to anyone's head ...'

'We didn't mean never,' she pleaded. 'It just happened, that's it.'

'We have time, plenty of time to decide now, with total safety.'

'I don't believe you.' She was aghast.

'I'm not a monster, we were in this together, years ago, that would have been it, an accident, and of course I don't blame *you* for it . . . It was down to both of us . . . But there is a chance to alter that, rectify things, and then if we do want a child at a later stage, then it should be something we would plan for together and agree.'

'Aren't you at all glad? Aren't you in any way pleased that . . .' She didn't trust her voice to say any more.

She stroked her stomach and he leaped up and went to the window. 'It's not fair, Cathy, it's not fair, it's not our child yet. Don't talk of it like that. This is only something that could *become* a child, you *know* that.'

She couldn't say anything. The tiny mouthful of sandwich she had eaten ages ago seemed lodged at the base of her throat, as if it might choke her. She felt almost dizzy at what was unfolding before her. He didn't even want to discuss how they would manage with the baby. Neil didn't want the baby at all. There was going to be no discussion. He seemed to be saying that because she wasn't agreeing instantly to a termination, she had somehow broken a promise.

'Say something, please, don't just sit there, say something,' he asked with his back to her as he looked out on Holly's hotel where people were walking in the late afternoon sunshine. But there was too much to say, so she couldn't speak.

'You know that the job they're offering me was dependent on us not having children?' he said.

'I don't believe you, that's not a moral or legal basis on which to offer a job or to accept one. You would be the first to say that,' she said with spirit.

'Let's put it this way, I had already told them that children were not in the frame, and so that was a deciding factor in my favour.'

The silence was longer this time.

'I need some fresh air, I'm going out to the gardens for a while.'

'Don't go, please,' she cried.

'I tell you, my head is bursting. I need to be on my own and walk a bit, get something into my lungs. I feel like I'm choking.'

'Don't leave me, not now, not just now.'

'I'm not leaving you.' He was irritated. 'I need to breathe, that's all.'

He came towards her and stroked her cheek. 'I wouldn't leave you, it's just I've had a shock. I need time to think about it. I'm not running away. I'll be back.'

He was gone. She saw him walking along the paths, past the monkey-puzzle trees, his head thrown back, biting his lips, so striking and handsome, even though he always laughed that away and said he was too small to be good-looking. He went as far as the kitchen gardens, and she saw him in the distance bending over something to read a label. She sat in the bedroom, which had seemed so beautiful when they had come into it less than an hour ago. The ice chinked as it melted in the bucket under the bottle of wine, and the tears fell down her face. She had not believed that this would ever be possible, but she knew that no matter how many hours of discussion they might have tonight when he came back calmer and more reasonable, she would not choose to give up this child that she carried. It could not have appeared at a worse time for everyone, but that wasn't the point. It just wasn't a theory any more, not a case or a constitutional amendment. It was her baby.

It seemed a lot darker outside when she heard the door of the room open. But she had no idea how long he had been gone. He seemed different somehow. Not bewildered, not shocked any more. As if this were one of the many crises and dramas that formed part of his everyday work and the kind of practice he had chosen at the Bar. He sat opposite her at the little table, and though he smiled in an attempt at reassurance, she felt a little as if they were lawyer and client.

'Cathy, if you have the baby, who will look after it?' he asked. Gentle, but very deliberate.

'Well I will, of course.'

'But the business?'

'Well, of course I'll make arrangements.' She knew her voice sounded flustered.

'You can't take a baby into the premises to lie there all day in the middle of your cooking.'

'No, but there will be ways ... We'll find them.'

'What ways? A nanny?'

'Well, yes, if we can afford one.'

'And where would she sleep?'

'I don't know, you can get people by the day.'

'But as I see it, most of your functions will be in the evening, so what happens then?'

'Well, the odd time I suppose you could ...'

'How can I commit myself to doing that? I have to work at night, too.'

'We'll work it out when it happens.'

'We can't do that. We have to plan now. I'll be away from home a lot, more anyway. Apart altogether from the big job, I will have to go abroad quite a lot.'

'We'll manage.'

'Like you've managed up to now?'

'I don't know what you mean.' She was alarmed.

'Like the business is in great debt and danger, like you are already worked off your feet paddling to keep up, like there's a new crisis every day. What do we do if there's a child to consider?'

'So you're asking that there should be no child to consider?' She spoke carefully.

He answered just as carefully. 'That is most definitely *not* what I'm asking, Cathy. I have no right, no right whatsoever to deny you a child, and I will not dream of doing so.'

He was very calm, cold almost. This is what his walk among the roses, hollyhocks and lupins of Holly's hotel had achieved for him. The kind of honest clarity that always stood him in such good stead in every cause he had ever fought.

'So there will be no discussion about whether we have the child or not?'

'You obviously want to have the child, and I am not going to stand in your way. It wouldn't be a moral or right thing to do.'

Too measured, too calm. She felt frightened. 'Will it always be like this, do you think, where you will be putting up with the situation, and having our baby there will be something on sufferance?'

'I don't think it should be like that at all. But if we are going to have another person in the house we must prepare, we must make contingency plans.'

'You sound very distant. Very remote.'

'Believe me, that's not what I mean to be, it's just that we *must* go into this with our eyes open ... Yes, of course I wish it had happened at a time when we were ready in every sense to give a child a better welcome ... a better lifestyle, but it hasn't, so we must decide what to do. Like how much maternity leave will you take?'

'Three months, like anyone.'

'And will Tom agree to this?'

'It's the law, but he would anyway, I'm certain.'

'We'll have to move house. Waterview is so unsuitable for a child,' he said.

'Not yet, not for a baby ... it doesn't matter where a baby lives ... Later we might think ... ?'

'But I have committed myself to work in my area, I'm not taking big insurance cases or conveyancing just to make money.'

'We don't need all that much money. We don't need a big house like Oaklands, we don't want one of those gigantic prams like you were reared in, we don't have to go to a big expensive fee-paying school. Children don't need all kinds of luxury or royal treatment, they need to be loved.'

'We have had a good start. If we have a child, we must give that child a good start too.'

'My mam and dad raised six of us in St Jarlath's Crescent, and did so with no money and no problems.'

'Well, hardly with *no* problems,' he contradicted.

'What do you mean?'

'You are always railing that your mother had to go down on her hands and knees to scrub my mother's floors and put up with dogs' abuse while she did it.'

'But I won't have to do that, and neither will you.'

'I suppose I'm just not ready,' he said.

'Neither am I. But loads of people haven't been ready, and look at the great fist they made of it.'

'I'm not a monster, why am I being made to feel like one?'

'I'm not making you into a monster.' She was gentle.

'It's just ... it's just ...' He couldn't find the words.

She said nothing.

'Listen, I haven't even asked you anything about all this ... How do you feel? Have you been sick ... ?'

'It comes and goes ...'

'And what do *you* want to happen?'

'What's happening now, for us to talk about it calmly and sanely without getting upset.'

'What's there to talk about ...? I mean it.'

'What do you mean?'

'Let's be logical, we didn't want children, now you're pregnant.' It was very chilly, very clinical, the way he said it.

'We have been missing each other a lot recently ...' he went on. 'I misunderstood the depth of your feeling about the company, and I thought that you'd eventually see sense about it, come abroad with me because it was such a great posting ... and you misunderstood. Once you were pregnant, you thought that I'd automatically come round to being delighted to be a father. We both got it very wrong.'

Suddenly she couldn't help it any more, the remorseless logic, the working out where praise and blame were due. She felt the sobs coming on and couldn't stop them. He watched her aghast as her shoulders heaved with the misery that went right through her. It was impossible to hear what she was saying; the words were drowned with all the sobbing.

'Please, Cathy ...' He reached out to touch her. He hadn't expected this, he had been trying to sum it up as accurately as he could. He had been struggling not to blame her and say that he felt a sense of betrayal. He thought it was unjust that he had been somehow bypassed on their bargain, but the rights of a birth mother were obviously more important, so he had tried to concentrate on the practicalities, and now judging by her weeping that had not been right either. He wished he could understand what she was saying. And Cathy wept and wept, saying the same thing over and over. He didn't want the child. There was no instinctive, loving response to the thought of being a father. There was no way she could end this pregnancy, because even if she did, and suppose she got over it, she still would remember this day and how he had proved not to be a loving, caring, good person after all, only a selfish one determined to get all that he could achieve in his career. She wept more because she could not and would not believe this of Neil, the man she loved so much. He watched her, his eyes misting with confusion, he was doing his best for her, being as fair and just as anyone could be under the circumstances. His future was going to change because she had not kept faith and honoured straight dealing. He had agreed to go ahead with it, and then just sorting out a few details had reduced her to this state.

'I've never seen you cry like this before. Please, please stop,' he begged.

She made a great effort, and he passed her a box of tissues. She wiped her eyes and blew her nose.

'I'm not saying anything out of any badness, I just couldn't hear what you were saying,' he said. She blew her nose again. Tentatively he offered her some wine and she drank it. He moved her hair out of her eyes and put his arm round her shoulder.

'Cathy, hon?'

'Okay. I'm okay now.'

A determination as strong as she had felt all those years ago in Greece came over Cathy. They had been through too much, conquered so many problems, they would not fail now. Not now that the best part, a child, was on the way.

'When I told you I had something to tell you . . . what did you think I was going to say?' she asked, sniffing a bit.

'I don't know,' he was evasive.

'Please tell me.'

'Well, I think I believed you were going to say to me . . .' he hesitated.

'Tell me.'

'I thought you were going to say you'd decided to leave Scarlet Feather and come with me wherever I went,' he said.

And outside it was dark in the garden and the smells of cooking came from downstairs.

The man who was watching the premises thought that he had got lucky. The big guy who owned it was letting himself in. At this time of night, at a weekend. They had been totally right, it was, of course, all his own doing; he was going to do further destruction now. He crept up to the window to see it begin before he called for back-up. These insurance cases were all the same; they had to have heavy proof. He kept in the shadows; he wanted to watch it begin, but he didn't want to be seen himself and there might be more than one of them.

Marcella lay on the bed in Stoneyfield. He would have to come home sometime. So he hadn't wanted to go out to lunch; maybe she should not have suggested it to him. But he wasn't going to stay out all night, every night. This much she knew. Where would he go? He was too proud to go round to Ricky's studio apartment. He would never go to his parents in Fatima. He wouldn't want to go within a million miles of Joe at this time. He would come home. When she woke later and he still wasn't there, she began to worry. He was so headstrong, but he'd never have done anything foolish. Marcella couldn't sleep any more. She went out on the street and walked until she saw a cruising taxi. She asked it to leave her in a street near the premises, then she walked quietly down the lane and opened the gate into the cobblestoned yard. There was a man in a parked car outside, but he didn't seem to take any notice of her. She looked in at the window and, peering in the very early dawn, she saw a figure lying on the divan. Thank God. And how foolish of him. They would have to talk sometime; why keep putting it off? She rang the bell and he didn't stir. She could see that his eyes were open but he made no move. He must have known she was there.

'Tom,' she called. 'Please, Tom, don't leave me here. Tom, let me in.' He never moved. 'There was nothing else I could do,' she cried. And then finally, 'I never betrayed you. I told you everything, I was so honest with you. I can't understand why you won't talk.' After half an hour, cold and frightened, she left and got another taxi back to Stoneyfield.

The man who had been watching the premises was mystified. That big guy had not gone in to break the place up, he had gone in to sleep on a sofa, for God's sake. And what was more peculiar still was that one of the most beautiful women ever seen in Dublin had been hammering on the door trying to get in. Any normal man would have let her in straight away. This guy was weird.

Tom got up an hour later, went to Haywards and made the bread. Was it only two days since he had been in this building? Making the Saturday morning batch; clearing up after the fashion show while still half drunk and shell-shocked. It seemed like for ever, and yet he realised that he was only talking about a mere forty-eight hours. He was afraid that Marcella might try to confront him in the kitchen, but she wouldn't risk it. She couldn't afford a public scene so shortly after her triumph. It was strange, that whole business last night.

Back at the premises he was surprised to find Cathy already there.

'Was Neil delighted?' he asked.

'Yes I think he was,' Cathy said.

'Of course he was, anyone would be delighted to be having a baby with you,' Tom said.

'Yes, well, he was startled, that's for sure.' Cathy didn't catch Tom's eye.

It obviously hadn't gone well, this announcement. It was so much less than he had expected, Tom felt he should say something. 'I suppose it was a bit of a shock as well,' Tom was soothing.

She looked at him thoughtfully. 'Yes, it was a bigger shock than I realised.'

'But he'll be delighted when the shock bit dies down,' Tom reassured her.

'Of course he will,' Cathy said with a smile.

Tom might be right. Neil could well become excited about the baby. Eventually. He had been so kind last night in Holly's after her weeping fit, so gentle, and he had put away the interrogating manner. They had talked long and calmly last night, and got up very early to drive back through the sunshine of County Wicklow, getting to Dublin well before the traffic had started. Neil had driven, leaning over to pat her arm occasionally. Yes, when the shock died down, as Tom said, it would be fine.

'We decided that we wouldn't tell anyone about it yet,' she explained to Tom. 'So you see . . .'

He understood immediately. 'So the two clairvoyants you work with will keep quiet, is that what you're saying?'

'For a bit. I would be grateful. And Tom, thank you *so* much for sorting

Simon and Maud out on Saturday. Dad left a message on our machine about it; you really are a hero.'

'He's such a shit, that man Mitchell.'

'Oh, don't get me started on him, I've never wanted to hit anyone quite so much.'

'It's monstrous that they should have those children, but don't get *me* started on that either.' He paused, and she knew he was going to say something important. 'And since you don't ask, which is very good of you, I haven't seen Marcella since Friday and I might sleep here a couple of nights, if that's all right with the company.' He spoke lightly, but she could see his pain. Quietly, she put her arms around him.

Eventually, she said, 'That's fine with the company. Let's open up the e-mails and see what we've got.'

He moved away as she started up the computer, more grateful than he could ever say at her understanding and lack of questions at this raw time. Then he heard her scream.

'God Almighty, I don't believe this!'

'What is it?'

He came running. Together they read that Marian was throwing the whole wedding party on their mercy for a rehearsal and a recovery party because Harry and his stupid relations had not thought that you needed to book anything in Dublin. Sleepy little backwater Dublin, where nobody needed to make reservations. And they had to be booked into somewhere classy for a dinner and a lunch at the height of the tourist season, and they had to find the places in just under three weeks.

'It's impossible,' Cathy said. 'That's all there is to it. Great stupid eejits.'

'We'll have to cater them all ourselves,' said Tom. 'It's just as simple as that.'

'Now you're the one that's mad! We can't do that.'

'Why not? It'll make us some badly needed money, and it will take our minds off other things,' he said.

Walter was furious that they had played in the shed.

'It wasn't playing, it was dancing,' they said defensively.

'That's my shed, stay out of it,' Walter ordered.

'I didn't know it was your shed, Walter, honestly, I thought it belonged to all of us,' Simon said.

'Yes, well, you know now, and give over this dancing business, it's really annoying Dad. He might go away again.'

'Not over our dancing?' Maud was wide-eyed.

'No, but he keeps saying that old Barty's gone to England, and he might follow him.'

'And would he?'

'He just might.'

'And what about Mother?'

'Mother's been away with the fairies for days now, you must know that,' Walter said scornfully.

'And would her nerves get bad and she'd go to hospital again if Father went away?' Maud wondered.

'You can bet on it, so try to cut down on the dancing where anyone can hear you, will you? Okay?'

'Sure, Walter.'

'And no whingeing and whining to Sara, either. It was quite bad enough asking that Tom Feather to stick his nose in on Saturday.'

'We didn't ask him, honestly,' Maud said.

'Muttie rang Cathy and he took the message, that was all,' Simon said.

They were so obviously telling the truth that Walter left it. 'The only hope of keeping this place going at all is not to tell Sara long stories, do you understand?'

'Yes,' the twins said doubtfully.

Hannah Mitchell telephoned her daughter in Canada.

'No, Ms Mitchell has taken a long weekend with her partner.'

'Oh, she's a partner in the company. Now isn't that wonderful,' Hannah said.

'No, I mean she and her partner have gone to their chalet on the lake.'

'And when will she be back?' Hannah asked. She knew nothing of any chalet on any lake.

'Tonight I guess, tomorrow they're both back in the store.'

Hannah hung up, delighted with this news, and couldn't wait to spread it around. There had been so little about Amanda to boast about recently; in fact, so little communication at all.

Neil called into Oaklands on Monday at about six o'clock and told them about the conference in Africa. Hannah listened impatiently until she got a chance to deliver her own good news from abroad.

'Did you hear, Amanda has been made a partner in that bookshop,' she said.

'That's pretty big. When did that happen? Did she say?' Jock was pleased.

'Well, no, I didn't catch her herself, I called and they said she and her partner were taking a long weekend, and she must have got some kind of executive chalet by the lakes.'

Neil swallowed his drink hastily. He must head his mother off at the pass before she said anything further that would be seen as pathetic later. 'They're notorious in stores for getting things wrong. Let's wait till we talk to Amanda before we tell anyone,' he said.

'But the girl wouldn't have said—'

'You see, she might have meant with a partner, meaning her *partner*, a boyfriend, a girlfriend, you know the way people say partner nowadays.'

'But she meant in the bookshop ... I know she did.'

'She may have a partner *in* the bookshop.'

'But if Amanda had a boyfriend she'd have told us.'

'Not necessarily, Mother,' Neil said. 'You have to be sure in your own mind, you have to be sure that everyone's ready to hear.'

'Well I'm always dying to hear about any boyfriends or partners or whatever they're called now. Where's all the secrecy?' Hannah was annoyed.

'Let's wait, Mother, I feel sure it's best.'

He saw his father looking at him quizzically, but Jock asked no questions.

It took them all day to find what they kept calling Suitable Venues. For the rehearsal dinner they would have the basement in Ricky's studio. For the recovery lunch they would use Geraldine's apartment. They checked their watches: it was six o'clock. Good time to contact Chicago. They would send menus later, in a day or two, but for the moment Marian and Harry were to consider it done. They faxed it off and decorated the writing paper with wedding bells and horseshoes and good-luck charms to cheer the couple up. Marian phoned about five minutes later, in tears of gratitude. Cathy was an angel, a saviour, an uncanonised saint, and undoubtedly Marian's favourite sister, and Harry's family were just dying to see the menus so that they could make their choice, and truly money was no object, so don't hold back . . .

'Do you get any message from that conversation, Cathy?' Tom asked when it had been repeated to him.

'Yes I do, I'm afraid,' she admitted.

They looked at each other and laughed as they both chanted together: 'They want the menus *now*.'

At six o'clock on Monday Geraldine realised that she and Freddie Flynn were now finally over. He had not called at all during the weekend, after his hurtful and devious message letting her know that he would not be joining her. She had steeled herself not to call him all day. She had forced herself to believe that the best course of action would be to be pleasant, cool and have no screaming recriminations. To prove that she knew how to behave.

Freddie called into Glenstar and pressed the bell. Nobody ever had a key to Geraldine's place.

'Freddie?' she sounded pleased but surprised.

'I was wondering . . . ?'

'You didn't telephone.' It was an unbreakable rule.

'No, but this time I thought we might . . . I mean, if it's not convenient I could . . .'

'Certainly. Come on up, Freddie.'

He sat down and twisted his hands. Pauline had been told that he was seen holding hands with a woman, and she had been impossible to console. He just had to go with her to Limerick. Prove the gossipmongers wrong, for one thing; to reassure her for another. Geraldine nodded distantly and pleasantly as if Freddie were talking about a different species. And then it appeared that when they were in Limerick, Pauline had said she was lonely and frightened that he might leave her and she wanted him to come home early after work every day. Geraldine nodded graciously to this request.

'So you see . . .' he said.

'I see, Freddie, please believe me, I see.'

He sat there awkwardly in the silence. She made no mention of the watch. That had been given at a time when he had thought she was the loveliest woman in Ireland and would not have cared if his wife had discovered. It was a gift from a different part of their relationship. It would be crass and commercial even to *suggest* that it might be returned.

'I can't tell you how I'll miss you,' he said.

'And I you, Freddie.'

'You deserve much better than me, of course,' he began to bluster now, trying to joke his way out of the situation, which was that he was telling her the affair was over. She remained utterly cool.

'Now don't say that, don't sell yourself short, and you'll always, I hope, be a wonderful friend.' She uncurled her legs from the sofa and stood up . . . a sign for him to leave. Freddie Flynn moved to the door with an overpowering sense of relief that there had been no scene. She kissed him gently on the cheek.

'Good luck always, dear Freddie,' she said.

'You're a woman in a million, Geraldine. I just wish . . .'

'Goodbye, Freddie,' she said softly, and went in, closing the door behind her swiftly. She stood in her empty apartment, tense and taut with rage and annoyance. Of all of them, she had liked Freddie best. He wasn't as bright as Peter Murphy, or as sophisticated as some of the others, but he was fun to be with. She thought he would be there always. What had made Pauline confident enough to get him back on her terms? Pauline had a lot of family, brothers and sisters, and of course she had Freddie's children. Pauline had respectability; the future, the past. It was, in the end, better than having great legs, a big flat in Glenstar and designer clothes. Disappointing, but true.

So when Tom and Cathy had phoned asking whether they could stage the ridiculous Day After party or whatever it was in Glenstar, Geraldine said yes. It would serve a number of functions. It would please her niece Marian, who seemed to be having a nervous breakdown in Chicago. And it would take her mind off the faithless Freddie Flynn.

Marcella didn't know what to do after work on Monday. She delayed as long as possible in the salon, but then she had to make up her mind. She went back to Stoneyfield eventually and went through the whole ritual, telephoning in advance and getting the answering machine, ringing on the apartment intercom and getting no reply, then going into the flat. He hadn't been back. It was Monday evening, and Tom Feather had not returned to his own apartment. He must be going to live at the premises from now on. This was idiotic. This was *his* place, for heaven's sake, his flat, and he had just abandoned it. Her note remained untouched on the table, the same carton of skimmed milk stood in the refrigerator. It was a cold, dead place. She shivered a little, packed a grip bag with some of her essential things and wrote a second note. 'Tom, it's your place, stop sleeping on a sofa in the premises. Come home. I'll go away if you want me to; all you have to do is tell me why. Face to face. I love you. Marcella.' Then she dialled Scarlet Feather.

Cathy went back to Waterview that evening, her head swimming with arrangements and plans for the wedding. They had come up with such inventive ideas, she and Tom. Marian would be delighted with them. Neil was home.

'You can't keep working these hours, you're not able to do it,' he said. He was very concerned for her.

'No, I'm fine, nothing a big mug of tea won't cure,' she said.

'Okay, I'll make one. Do you have a pain in your back?'

'A bit now and then, not much. Why do you ask?'

'I read a bit about it in a book.'

Her heart soared. The shock bit was wearing off; the father bit must be starting now.

'I went to Oaklands today.'

'You didn't tell them, did you?' Telling Hannah was going to be something that had to be planned, if anything had to be planned.

'Of course not, but I was looking at those pictures Mother had on the piano, of Manda and myself when we were children. She had so much help in the house then, and no job, and look at all you have to do. It's just not fair.'

'It's not important what she had back then.' Cathy couldn't care less about the past.

But he was persistent. 'And it was easier for men, the way privileged people lived then too. When my father came home from work he could just close himself away in a study to work, and whichever baby it was was brought off to a nursery so as not to disturb him. I'm only saying it's just the system some people have, everything dead easy for them, and others just don't.'

'Stop trying to rewrite history, and anyway, your father was never home to go to a study or a nursery. Wasn't he out on the first tee two minutes after he left the office?'

'But it's the principle of it,' Neil insisted.

'And my father had six of us crawling over him in the kitchen and it never distracted his mind for one minute from what was running next day at the Curragh.' Cathy kept it light.

Neil made the tea, but he was still brooding. He talked on about his mother and father, how they were totally accustomed to their lifestyle and thought it their right, how his mother had misunderstood Amanda and her partner being at a chalet on the lake, how Sara had been on to say that some rich old man had died and left his Georgian house to an organisation for the homeless and all the neighbours were up in arms. The gross selfishness of this city was getting to him. Where he had been in Africa people had different priorities; he had come face to face with people who really did have generous and liberal attitudes and voted in socially responsible governments. There was this girl from Sweden he had met, and she would frighten you how she talked of how the rich paid taxes there to make sure that nobody would go without the best medical care ... She looked at him for a long time as he talked.

'Scarlet Feather,' Tom said.
  'Tom, don't hang up, please.'
  'Marcella.' His voice was flat.
  'Can I come round there and talk to you?'
  'No, I'm just going out actually.'
  'Are you going home?'
  'No.'
  'I've left you a note there, it's on the table beside one I left you yesterday.'
  'It doesn't matter, Marcella.'
  'But we can't leave it like this...' she said in disbelief.
  'Why not?' he asked, and hung up. He sat and looked at the phone for a long time. What on earth did she expect him to say?
  In Stoneyfield Marcella sat and looked at the phone. He'd have to talk sometime, even to say goodbye. Why couldn't he talk now?

'Geraldine, that never came from a charity shop?' Lizzie Scarlet held the brand new outfit from Haywards up so that she could look at it again.
  'It *did*, Lizzie,' her sister lied straight to her face. 'You just don't know where to look. These dames wear something once, they think their bum looks big in it or their girlfriend sniggered at it and that's it. Out.'
  'It's gorgeous,' said Lizzie, stroking the dress and coat in a dark grey silky material. 'I could be the bride myself in that, not just the mother of the bride.'
  'You might meet a rich American, Lizzie, and then we'd never see you again,' Geraldine teased her.
  Muttie looked up from his newspaper. 'Lizzie doesn't want a rich American,' he said firmly. 'She wants Hooves and myself in all our glory and with all our disadvantages, isn't that right, Hooves?' Hooves gave a bark of approval.
  'Hooves says you're quite right,' said Lizzie. 'He says what more could a woman want than what I've got?' And for the first time in her whole life Geraldine felt a pang of envy for the sister who had married a no-hoper and scrubbed floors all her life.

Tom and Cathy had worked very hard on the wedding plans. They now had three events to cater for, and had hired many more staff. The Friday night was going to be a theme party: Ricky's basement would be done up as a speakeasy in Prohibition times. They would paint bars on the windows and arrange that there was something that looked like a peephole, a little door you pulled back to see who was there. Guests would be given a password to let them in. Then Ricky had big developing equipment which could have labels stuck on saying Bathtub Gin; there would be Al Capone pictures on the walls and reference to the St Valentine's Day massacre; they would have the Chicago greats in jazz on the music centre and everyone would be so pleased with the way they had been made to feel at home. The food itself would be delicious ribs of beef, Chicago-style, and some kind of chocolate-mint ice cream that the recipe books said was a real favourite in that city. It was so hard to learn about Chicago food, because any recipe book or website they looked up seemed to say it was an ethnic cuisine with strong Polish overtones.

'Polish cooking's nice,' Tom said. 'Lots of red cabbage and sour cream. Should we try some of that, do you think?'

'Maybe they want to get away from it,' Cathy said. 'We'll check when they ring back later on.'

'They were a bit silent about the menus,' Tom said after two days had passed and there was no response from America.

Cathy agreed. 'And there was I being called a saint, an angel, a genius, but now they don't even bother to acknowledge all our hard work.'

'Should we ring them?' Tom wondered. 'We'll have to get going on the props as soon as possible.'

'I almost hate drawing them on us, I know it's silly. In more normal times I'm all for doing the hard thing first and dealing with it,' Cathy said.

'Listen, you're allowed to have silly feelings – at least you haven't been eating lumps of coal as we make the food,' Tom said.

'No, I mustn't get any special treatment, it's a natural process – women years ago had their babies and just got on with it, no one indulged them.'

'Maybe,' Tom said. 'All this male solidarity, going to the pub and getting drunk to stay out of the way . . .'

'Oho, you're all fine and noble now because you don't have to be there, wait until you're going to be a father, we'll have a reality check.'

He flicked a spoon of dough at her and she threw a handful of raisins back at him.

'Now look what you've done, I'll have to take them out of the tomato bread,' he complained.

'Could be the start of a world-class recipe,' Cathy laughed.

'Will Neil be at the birth?' Tom asked.

'Yes,' Cathy said firmly. 'Whether he knows it or not, he'll be there. Now which of us will ring Marian?'

'Since you're not having any special favours, then I think you should,' said Tom, picking the last raisins out of his mixing bowl and eating them.

Talking to Marian was like talking to an entirely different person than the one she'd spoken to two days previously. She was alternately tongue-tied, confused, hissing in a whisper, or else she was speaking in a false, high-pitched tone about how grateful they all were for all that was being done.

'Here, I can't make head nor tail of this,' Cathy said eventually. 'Tom, will you talk to her, please.'

Tom didn't do much better; he kept shrugging at Cathy. 'Is she drunk, or high, do you think?' he wrote down on a pad beside the phone. Cathy had to get up and move away to hide her fit of laughing at the very thought. Finally Tom had a brilliant idea. 'Could I talk to Harry about it all, do you think? Maybe he and I could sort it out, man to man.'

'Harry's here,' said Marian in her normal voice. 'He came into my office to discuss the situation, I'll put him on now.'

'Harry, I'm Tom Feather. I'm no relation of anybody. If you don't like our menus, you tell me now and we'll send you more. I was wondering about Polish food myself, big soups, dumplings. Just say it, Harry.'

'Tom, I'm going to say it: everyone here has had to go and lie down even at the thought of a speakeasy party, at the mention of St Valentine's Day, and the whiff of bathtub gin.'

'I see. We thought you'd love it.'

'No, it would be like having the worst theme party you could dream up ... something about the IRA with bombs and things.'

'Or corned beef and cabbage,' Tom said quickly.

'I hear where you're coming from, Tom.'

'So we trade over this, okay? No speakeasy, no corned beef.'

'It's a done deal,' said Harry.

Sara called quite unexpectedly, and did an inspection of the house. Eyes watched as she opened the refrigerator, the washing machine, looked at the food shelves and checked the laundry in the airing cupboard.

'Maud and Simon, can I ask you to go out into the garden and practise your tennis for a little bit? I see you have a net set up out there; you could get ready for your next lesson.'

'We don't have lessons now,' Simon said.

'They were too dear,' Maud explained.

'And I think the tennis teacher went away, didn't she?' Kenneth Mitchell said.

'No, just for a weekend,' Maud explained.

Sara's mouth was in a hard line. 'All the more reason to practise then,' she said, in such a falsely cheerful voice that the twins recognised the hidden threat it involved to everyone and scurried out into the garden. Sara called out after them. 'When I'm finished here, I'll come out and play each of you separately. We'll do the best of seven points. Do me good to have a little exercise. Okay?'

They thought that sounded great, and in the silence of the house Kay and Kenneth Mitchell sat and listened to the children laughing and groaning over shots missed and shots achieved, and to the pit-pat of the tennis ball on the dry, uncared-for lawn.

'Correct me if I'm wrong, but I don't think anyone invited you to play tennis with my children in my house,' Kenneth Mitchell said, deciding to attack first.

'Correct *me* if I'm wrong, but you don't seem to have the remotest idea of how serious your position is, and how you are both on the verge of losing your children. If the fears that I have about their welfare form a substantial part of my report and are accepted, they could be out of your hands by the end of the month.'

'Can we dance at all three parties, do you think?' Simon asked Muttie back at St Jarlath's Crescent later that day.

'I have nothing to do with the arrangements, son; as you get older you learn to stay out of all that side of things. It's a kind of thing men do.'

'We'd have to have separate dances for each one – it might be very hard. But I wouldn't want to let them down, the Americans.'

'It's probably the kind of thing Cathy would know about,' Muttie said thoughtfully.

'Sure. Muttie, do you know why we got to come here to St Jarlath's Crescent as often as we like?'

'I don't, and I tell you that another thing I never do is question anything at all that turns out better than you expect. Remember that day last week when I lost my concentration down at the office, and I put an each-way instead of a win? I was so disappointed, and I'd nearly thrown away the ticket, when didn't one of my associates down at the office remind me I'd done it for a place as well? I couldn't believe it but I never questioned it; I think that's usually the best way to go.'

Simon thought about it. 'You're probably right, Muttie; it's just that if you knew *why* people do things, you'd be in a better position to make them do them again. You see, Father suddenly changed his mind about everything. I'd love to know what it was that Sara said which made everything different.'

'We never know half the things that go on in the world.' Muttie shook his head.

'But honestly, Muttie, Father brought a tray with lemonade out to the tennis court for us and Sara, and Mrs Barry is back again, so she must have been paid, and the tennis lessons are on, and we are in charge of washing our own clothes in the machine but Mrs Barry irons them, and Mother gets up and gets dressed. And we can come here on the bus whenever we want, like whenever you're free, I mean, and Maud and I think we must have done something right to make it all good, but we can't think what it could have been.'

Shona came into the Haywards kitchen long before the store opened officially.

'You're spying on me and trying to steal trade secrets.'

'Lord no, little microwave meals for one, that's me.'

'I doubt it.' He concentrated on his work as he talked. 'Pour us a coffee, will you, Shona?' he called.

They talked companionably about a lot of things. But neither of them asked the question they wanted to ask. Tom didn't enquire whether Marcella still worked in the nail salon, or if she had already gone across the water to start working on this new modelling contract that she had earned herself. She had left one more note before moving her things from the flat in Stoneyfield. Marcella had left behind her a watch, a bracelet and a leather-bound book of love poems. Her note was short.

'I still love you, and I cannot believe that you will let four years of our life end without a discussion. But then I cannot keep asking you the same question every day. If you want to tell me why we can't talk . . . then we both work at the moment in the same store. You might be able to tell me there, if not here. You owe me that much. Just one conversation.'

But it wouldn't be a conversation, it would only be two people sitting there, one saying that something mattered and one saying that something didn't. As the days went by Tom had steeled himself not to call the salon and discover whether she was there or not. It had become a matter of pride with him that he must not enquire. Shona for her part wanted to ask Tom to tell her every single thing he could about Mr James Byrne, retired chartered accountant and present-day part-time bookkeeper to Scarlet Feather. She would like to have asked was he a cheerful person or very intense, did he love music and go to concerts? Did he have many friends, or was he alone? Had they ever been in his apartment? Did he live alone or with anyone else? But she had kept her own counsel for so long it was hard to ask anyone else about such private things. Even someone as open and approachable as that Tom Feather, who was obviously broken-hearted over his silly girlfriend Marcella.

'What are you going to wear at the wedding?' asked Geraldine.

'A huge maternity tent with a white collar and flat shoes,' Cathy said.

'No, be serious; and talking of being serious, when are you going to tell your mother that she's going to be a granny again?'

'Soon, soon, just let her get the wedding out of her hair first,' Cathy pleaded. 'And let me get through that too, as it happens. We have so much work on nowadays, you just wouldn't believe it. I'm afraid to leave Tom out of my sight in case he takes on another booking.'

'He's desperately anxious to make up the money, isn't he,' Geraldine was sympathetic.

'Yes, and to work himself into the ground so that he doesn't have to think about Marcella,' Cathy added.

'No change of heart there?'

'He never says a word. He's not sleeping at the premises any more, so I gather she's moved out of the flat.'

'Silly little girl in many ways,' Geraldine said.

'Yes, but he adored her; still does, I think. Who knows anything about men and what they feel.'

'Who does?' Geraldine was slightly clipped.

Cathy opened her mouth and closed it again. They had been in touch with Freddie Flynn about another Villa Abroad reception: the Spanish and Italian ones had been such a hit, and he wanted something in the same style only different, of course. Cathy had asked should they liaise through her aunt as before; there had been a pause, and then he had said it would be simpler to deal with him directly. Geraldine hadn't mentioned it; she was still wearing her watch. Cathy would say nothing until she was told. As she had so often said to Maud and Simon, it was all part of being grown-up.

'Are Mother and Father being invited to the wedding?' Simon asked Maud.

'No, and don't ask why,' Maud warned.

'Why?' asked Simon.

'There, you asked,' Maud cried.

'I was only asking why must I not ask why?'

'Oh, it's got to do with Muttie's wife Lizzie. She's afraid of Aunt Hannah, and they couldn't ask one without the other.'

'It's very complicated,' Simon said disapprovingly. 'Is Walter coming?'

'No, we're going to be the only Mitchells apart from Neil.' Maud was very well informed. 'And we're going to all three parties, but we're only dancing at the actual wedding day one to make that special for them.'

'I'd say we should bring our shoes to the recovery party in the big apartment where Lizzie's sister lives. In case they ask for an encore.'

Maud considered it. 'I think you're right,' she said.

James Byrne went in and out of his basement a lot, trying to see it through the eyes of a visitor coming here for the first time. It was very difficult to know what she would make of it. But it was important because it would also affect the way she was going to think about him. If she saw the place as severe and cold, that would confirm a lot of her opinions; alternatively, if she found it fumbling and overcrowded and messy, that would make her think that this is how he was, which was almost as bad. For the first time James Byrne realised why there were so many magazine articles and television programmes about decor. It was, when you came to think of it, more important than a lot of people ever believed.

'Will there be no Mitchells except us?' Simon wondered.

'Well, Neil will be there, of course,' Cathy replied.

'What about his sister, hasn't he a sister in America? Why isn't *she* coming over for a family wedding?'

'It's Canada she lives in, not the United States, and it's not exactly a family wedding for the Mitchells, you see . . .'

'Is she nice?'

'Yes, she's okay; she sent us a lovely wedding present,' Cathy said. For a moment she felt a wild urge to tell the twins about their cousin Amanda, to let them know she lived a happily gay life in Toronto with a woman called Susan. She would love to know exactly how much damage they could do with a piece of information like that. She smiled to herself.

'It's always dangerous when Cathy laughs to herself,' Muttie commented.

'What happens?' Simon asked anxiously.

'Anything could happen,' Muttie said. 'She could buy another building, a new van, take on more staff . . .'

The mobile phone rang. It was Tom. He had crashed into the back of some fool who had stopped without warning.

'Are you hurt?'

'No, but the bloody birthday cake I'm meant to be delivering is. I'm hopeless with cakes. Cathy, it looks like a bloody mess and I have to stay at the scene of the accident.'

'I'll get a taxi there. What should I bring with me?'

'Whatever you can lay your hands on: trays, cloths, icing sugar, cream, anything.'

'What! I'm meant to do all this, start from scratch in a taxi? Are you mad?'

'Well what am I to do, Cathy? It's running all over the van.'

'God,' said Cathy. 'Tell me where you are.'

They watched as she ran around her mother's kitchen, seizing this and that.

'Da, have you any very reliable associate who drives a cab, anyone who would like an exciting job for the afternoon?'

'Can we come? *Please,*' begged the twins when they heard what it was.

'Why not?' Cathy thought they couldn't make it any worse than it was.

They drove with Kentucky Jim, one of Muttie's very sound friends. He said he didn't believe that people got paid real money driving birthday cakes round to other people. It showed there was one born every minute.

'One what?' Simon wanted to know.

'A fool. They say there's a fool born every minute.'

'I wonder is there?' Maud said.

Cathy decided that she would never tell them that the philosopher Kentucky Jim had once owned a thriving business but his interest in Sandy Keane's betting shop had managed to reduce his circumstances to having a quarter share in a mini cab. It was doubtful if his views on fools being born every minute were necessarily very sound.

Tom was helpless when they found him.

'God, but you're a terrible driver, I've always said so,' she said, putting out a cloth and removing the silver paper-covered plinth and wiping it so she could reassemble the cake.

'Can you do it?'

'I'll have to do it, eejit. I brought the forcing bag so I could write the name again. Just as well, looking at what's left. Is this "Jackie"?'

'Yes, Jackie, that's right.'

'With an "ie" or a "y"?'

'Jesus, I don't know!'

'It's on the form, the order book, look it up!' Cathy cried as she glued back the crushed sides of the cake with a chocolate paste.

'You could ice in the two versions and eat one off when you find the right one,' Simon suggested helpfully.

'Shut up, Simon,' Tom and Cathy said together at exactly the same time.

'You're not turning my basement into a speakeasy after all?' Ricky said next day, and was disappointed. He had been looking forward to it.

'No, and Rick, be a mate and don't mention that little idea, will you? Real lead balloon *that* turned out to be.'

'Oh dear,' Ricky said.

'Anyway, it's all calmed down now.'

'Which is more than you have, apparently,' Ricky smiled at him.

'Not quite sure what you mean.' Tom was too nonchalant, he knew exactly what Ricky meant.

'Just, they all tell me you and Marcella haven't been seen together since her show. I just happen to think it's a pity, that's all.'

Tom said, 'Yes, well.'

'And if I am in touch with her, Tom, do you want me to say anything to her?'

'No thanks, Ricky, it's all been said.'

Ricky left it. He shook his head because he had heard in three different weeping fits from Marcella that nothing had been said, nothing at all.

Cathy saw James Byrne carrying parcels in Rathgar and tooted the horn of the van.

'Do you want a lift? Are you going home, James?'

'Ah, how nice to see you, Cathy. Yes, I'd love a lift.'

When they got to the elegant house he turned to her. 'Can I ask you something very personal?' he began.

Oh, please God may it not be that he too had guessed she was pregnant. 'Anything you like,' she said wearily.

'Will you just come in the door with me, just walk in and tell me what you see?' he asked.

Cathy's heart sank. All they needed now was for their sane, calm accountant to lose all his marbles and go mad. 'And what do you think I *might* see, James?' she asked fearfully.

'I don't know, Cathy, but you will be honest, won't you?'

'I'll do my very best, James,' said poor Cathy, dragging herself out of the van.

Tom was expecting Cathy back at the premises, so he just buzzed the door without looking up.

Someone stood at the door.

It was odd, Cathy usually rushed in through their front room and into the kitchen. Hoping nothing was wrong, he came out to investigate.

Standing with her back to the light was Marcella. The cloud of dark hair surrounded her like a halo; her face was anxious and upset. She began to speak immediately.

'It's not fair to tell Ricky that we've talked it all out; we've done nothing of the sort.'

'That didn't take long to get back,' he said.

'Do you hate me, Tom?'

'Of course not, of course I don't hate you.' His voice was gentle.

'But what you said to Ricky . . .'

He felt terribly weary, suddenly. 'No, Marcella, I didn't tell Ricky that we'd talked it all out, I said that it had all been said, that's quite different . . . I meant there was nothing more to say.'

'But I wouldn't have walked out on you without saying why.'

'You know why.'

'It was just a stupid party.'

'Yes.'

'You don't want to know about it, it was just messing. I *told* you it would be like that. You don't want to know about it.'

'You're right, I don't want to know all about it, and why you didn't come home that night.'

'I told you, Tom, in advance that it was all meaningless. Unimportant.'

'To you, Marcella, and I told you in advance that it was hugely important to me.'

'But you *knew* there was a party, and that I had to go.' She was weeping now. He stood there, his hands by his sides. 'I was so honest, I really was. You're never going to meet anyone as honest as I am as long as you live.'

'No, Marcella, you weren't honest. People who are honest wouldn't do that to each other.'

'I told you the truth,' she sobbed.

'That's not the same at all,' said Tom.

'I'll go in first, put these things away and then come and open the door for you when you ring it,' said James Byrne. Cathy sighed as she rang the bell. She made a mental note not to give anyone she knew a lift again for the next four years. James came to the door, and she entered the apartment where she had already given cookery lessons. 'Look everywhere. What do you see?' he asked.

'James, for heaven's sake, what am I meant to be looking for? Is this a game?' Her voice was short with him.

'What does it look like to you? Who would you think lives here?' His eyes were clouded, waiting for the answer.

'James, you'll have to forgive me but I've had a long day. I *know* who lives here. *You* live here.'

'No, I mean if you just came in the door . . . ?'

'Like a burglar, do you mean?'

'No, I mean like someone coming to dinner.' He was crestfallen now, and very vulnerable. The cool James Byrne was so ashamed of himself and his raw, nervous state.

'Oh, I see what you mean,' Cathy recovered. 'What you're trying to do is to see what someone's first impressions would be, is that it?'

'Exactly.'

'I'm sorry, I didn't quite understand.' She bought time looking around the dark, lifeless apartment with its lack of colour and spirit.

'No, I didn't explain properly,' he apologised.

'Listen, I don't want to be too inquisitive, but in order for me to answer this question properly I'd have to know what kind of a guest it is.'

'I beg your pardon?'

'Well, like a businessman, or a lady you were inviting on a date, or a long-lost friend or something.'

'Why did you say long-lost friend?' he asked anxiously.

'Because if it was a regular friend, then he or she would *know* what the flat looked like already.' Cathy spoke as she would to Maud and Simon, very clearly but as if talking to an imbecile.

He thought about this for a while. 'Long-lost friend is about the nearest,' he said.

'Age?'

'About your age, as it happens, that's why—'

'Man or woman?'

'Well, a woman, as it happens.'

'A few flowers. You can come and borrow some of our potted plants if you like. Some brightly coloured cushions ... and take all those papers off the desk there, and get your music centre out from under all those folded magazines or cuttings or whatever.'

'So what it needs is . . .'

'Some sense of colour, of light, a feeling of hope, of somebody actually living here.' She walked around the room as she spoke. Then suddenly realised what she had just said. How she had been so destructive about the way he lived. Tears came to her eyes.

'James, I'm so very sorry,' she said, coming over and touching his arm.

'No, please.' He moved away. 'I asked your opinion and I got it; what is there to apologise for?' He spoke stiffly.

'I have to apologise for that totally unnecessary harangue about your place, which is perfectly fine except that it needs a little more colour.'

'Yes, quite.'

'James, I'm so nervy and anxious that I have upset almost everyone I know these days. *Please* let me believe that I didn't offer you a lift and then come in here and add you to the list.' He lost his stiffness and relaxed his shoulders. 'Would you trust me to make us some tea?'

'I'd love that.'

'Is it any one big problem, or a lot of middle-sized ones?'

'It's a lot of very big ones actually, James, but do you know the way that if you don't admit them or acknowledge them they sort of go away ... Well, not really go away, but you know . . .'

'I know. They don't really go away but they do stay outside the door, at any rate.' He was sympathetic.

'You're very kind, James, a restful type of person to be with. I'm sure your dinner will be a big success.'

'I hope so, I really do. So much depends on it, you see.'

And they drank their tea peacefully, neither asking the other any more questions.

Back at the premises she found Tom curiously quiet. 'Anything more I should know about the wedding? Hit me with it if there is.'

'No.' He was far away.

'Right,' she said.

He didn't answer. It was very unlike him to be so taciturn. He had a lot of papers on the worktop.

'What are you working on?' she asked.

'This and that,' he said.

Marcella must have been in. She would go on as if nothing was wrong.

'I was talking to that priest who's going to marry them. He said we must never lose faith in prayer, even in the darkest hour.'

'Well let's hope he *would* say that; not much point in being in his particular line of business if he can't see a bit of light at the end of the tunnel.'

'No, you don't understand. He thinks *we* are the answer to his prayer.' Cathy laughed.

'Because we did up his mouldy old hall?'

'Exactly, he has an asset on his hands now: the community will get new life, money will roll in for good things.'

'Like statues, I suppose.' Tom was scornful.

'I think not ... He talked about old folks' outings, literacy classes.'

'Sorry,' Tom said.

'No, I'm just cheering myself up by saying that at least you and I are very important to *some* people, anyway.'

He understood. 'Yeah, let's list them: the dopey priest who didn't know he had a community hall until we showed it to him. That's one.'

'James Byrne is two. I had tea with him. The guest by the way is a woman my age, someone he hasn't seen for a long time.'

'Let's see,' said Tom. 'Mad Minnie, because we scrape bits of casserole into her dishes for her.'

'Nonsense, we give her gorgeous food and keep her marriage going, but you're right, that's three.'

'June. We keep her from killing Jimmy. Four,' Tom said.

'Con, or is that pushing it?'

'No,' Tom said, 'we are important to Con. That's five.'

'We could easily get to a dozen if we talked about satisfied clients. We could even get out a bit of paper and write them down,' Cathy said.

'Or we could do what you want me to do and get back to work,' he said with a laugh, and put the bits of paper away.

Cathy saw the words 'Dear Marcella' written on one of them. Things were very bad for poor Tom, much worse than they were for her. Without intending to, Cathy gave him a hug. She just came up behind him and threw her arms around his neck.

'See, we *are* important to lots of people,' she said.

To her surprise, he grasped her hands and held them to his chest.

'God, I hope so, Cathy, I hope so,' he said and his face moved around a little so that they were cheek to cheek.

*

Lizzie now had daily messages from Chicago about the upcoming visit and wedding. 'They sound very nice people, Harry's family. I hope they won't be disappointed in us,' she confided to her sister Geraldine. Apparently Marian had asked to see a video of the twins dancing. When she had asked for dancers she had really meant professional dancers, rather than children of Cathy's in-laws. She wanted to be sure that they were up to standard. Geraldine and Lizzie looked at each other in disbelief.

'Tell her they're brilliant and the video is on its way,' Geraldine said.

'But will we have to get one?'

'Certainly not, that's just today's worry. She'll have forgotten it tomorrow.'

'But suppose they're not good enough?'

'Lizzie, for God's sake, if they're like two blind elephants they're going to dance, you know that and I know it, and anyway Marian will be so crazed with excitement on her wedding day she'll think they're marvellous, believe me.'

'Cathy, you do realise you have taken on three weddings, not one, don't you?'

'It's under control, Neil.'

'It's not. If it were under control you would not be filling the freezer at eleven o'clock at night.'

'Only four more trays of these; I will rest when the wedding's over, I promise.'

'And the doctor, what does he say about it?'

'He's easy,' Cathy said, not exactly truthfully, but she *had* to do her bit; the others were working flat out.

Neil shook his head. 'Even Sara said you were doing too much in your condition.'

'You told Sara?' She was shocked.

'Hon, I *had* to tell her. She wanted me to join up for a big conference in England next year, I had to explain why I couldn't be a part of it.'

'Yeah, sure.'

'So she was concerned that you were working so hard.'

'What did she say when you told her the news?'

'She was very surprised, as it happens.'

'Why was she so surprised? It is something that happens to couples.'

'I know, Cathy, don't snap at me.'

'Sorry. It's just that I have to keep walking round you.'

'Oh, yes,' he moved slightly.

'Well she was surprised because I had told her a couple of weeks ago that we were never going to have children.'

'You talk about a lot of intimate things with Sara, don't you?'

'Not really, only when things have to be told, and talking about that, really, don't you think we should tell Mother and Father?'

'No, not until after the wedding, it's only a few days. Not until then, and ... Neil could you ever stand somewhere that's not directly in my path to the freezer, and if you do want to help, perhaps you could slide that in for me.' She smiled at him brightly. 'Thanks a million, this will speed us up no end,' she said.

'Drink that milk at your peril, Walter,' Kenneth Mitchell warned. 'Sergeant Sara could materialise at any moment to see if there's enough calcium in their diet.'

'Where are they?' Walter asked.

'Where do you think? Up with those people in that housing development, dancing like complete idiots for a crowd of halfwits.'

'Neil is going to make a speech at that wedding,' Walter said.

'Nonsense,' his father said.

'I'm only telling you what they said.'

'But what on earth would he be doing, visiting and speechifying with those Mutties and people like that?'

'They *are* his in-laws, I suppose.' Walter shrugged.

'She's a common, pushy girl that Cathy, not worth considering.'

'You shouldn't underestimate her, Father. Great mistake to underrate her because of her accent, believe me, I know.'

He did know. He had never believed that Cathy would go the distance that night when there had been the incident at the party. And he couldn't believe that her business was still up and running after his visit.

'Shona!'

'Lord, you look a busy shopper, Cathy. What have you got in all those bags?'

'You name it. Mainly material to make aprons; we're going to have to wear aprons with shamrocks on them, apparently; I keep waking up at night and seeing a great page of a calendar saying August Nineteen, August Nineteen in red neon lights. Will it ever be over, Shona, will it ever, ever be over?'

'August the nineteenth, you don't mean that you're going to be there?' She looked as white as a sheet.

'Of course I am, aren't I, cooking the whole damn thing.'

'He said there wasn't going to be anyone else, he wrote that he was cooking it all by himself.'

'Shona, what are we talking about?' Cathy asked her.

'What are *you* talking about?'

'My sister's wedding, three endless days of it. What were *you* talking about?'

'Sorry, I just thought for a moment ... No, it's nothing ... I've been invited out on August the nineteenth, and I thought you might be cooking for that.'

'Oh really, where?'

'No, just to a private house ... I thought that by some chance you might be doing the dinner.'

'No, I wish I were, it sounds nice and peaceful.'

'I wouldn't bet on that,' Shona said.

As Cathy left the store she wondered could Shona possibly be going to dinner with James Byrne? His party was on the nineteenth. He had said that his guest was about the same age as Cathy. But how could Shona be a long-lost friend? Anyway, this wasn't a village, this was Dublin, city of a million people. She was foolish to think that she knew everyone in the pond. And she had quite enough to worry about without drawing something still further on herself. Tonight, Wednesday, Marian and Harry were leaving Chicago, they would be here tomorrow morning. Their room was gleaming for them in St Jarlath's Crescent, Cathy remembered that nobody must sew the new aprons in front of them, or allow Simon and Maud anywhere near them. Tomorrow night, Thursday, the rest of the Chicagoans, dozens and dozens of them, were coming to various hotels near the city centre. They would all arrive on Friday morning. She felt dizzy thinking about it.

Harry was a small, round man with a head of dark curly hair and a great warm laugh.

'Muttie, I want you to know that I'm going to look after your little girl,' he said with a strong handshake.

'From all accounts you've been looking after her fine for a good while now,' said Muttie.

And the two men understood each other immediately. It turned out that Harry liked dogs and horses, and Muttie, who read more of the sports pages than people thought, knew all about the Chicago Bears. Marian was so excited she almost had to be tied to the table, she kept darting everywhere, saying she had no idea St Jarlath's Crescent was so small, so colourful, so elegant really. She couldn't believe the traffic, the number of posh cars parked outside the doors of the street where she had grown up. The fact that two of them, Geraldine's BMW and Cathy's Volvo, were connected with this house brought her further pleasure ... She was not at all the neurotic, hysterical sister who had plagued them for weeks and months by phone, e-mail and fax. Her wedding dress was unpacked and admired, her ring was tried on by all the women, her choice of husband praised to the skies.

'Where is he, by the way?' Cathy asked.

'He's gone off. Dad said he'd show him his office and get him a pint.'

'You know what your father means by his office.' Lizzie was still fearful of how all this would turn out.

'Oh, Mam, I've been away, that's true, but not so long that I don't know where my da's office is. Harry loves a bet just like the next man; he'd much prefer to be there than here talking about clothes.' Marian looked happy and relaxed; she looked younger than her thirty years, her hair was short, she was trim and fit, and her eyes were alight with happiness.

'Do you want me to take you on a tour, to show you where all the parties will be? Of course, they're not properly set up yet, but you'd get an idea,' Cathy offered.

'Not at all, Cathy, I can see you've got it all under control,' Marian said, and Cathy breathed normally for the first time in a few weeks.

*

'Tom Feather, my old friend, how are you?' Harry clenched Tom's hand at the pre-wedding party with a mighty grip.

'Look, not a sign of a speakeasy,' Tom hissed at him as he took the groom on a tour of Ricky's basement.

'And I got my folks to understand about the corned beef,' Harry whispered.

'Are there any pitfalls we should know about?' Tom asked him. He felt he could trust this man to the ends of the earth.

'My aunt over there, small, hatchet-faced, wearing purple – nothing has ever pleased her in this life . . . Nothing ever will . . . Oh, and Cathy's eldest brother Mike's been put off the sauce recently, finds it very hard.'

'Thanks a lot. Let me see what I can tell you. Lizzie's not used to too much sherry, Muttie likes pints, the woman in the cardigan is a plain-clothes nun. And don't let the kids dance tonight or the party will be over, tomorrow is quite enough.'

'Fine. My card is marked, and Tom, do you have a significant other here that I should meet?'

'No, I've just broken up with my significant other,' Tom said ruefully.

'I'm sorry. Her doing or your doing?'

'Have you three hours and I'll tell you,' Tom grinned. 'No, seriously, a bit of both, I believe.'

'Right, then you'll survive,' Harry promised.

And for the first time since the night of the fashion show, Tom felt that somehow he might.

They were back at the premises, and Neil apologised for not being able to come back to help. There was something tomorrow, papers he had to go through.

'Where's Marcella? She should be on board for something like this.'

'Marcella's not on board at all these days,' Tom said.

'I'm very sorry.' Neil looked at Cathy accusingly, as if to say he should have been told this piece of information.

'Yes, I'm sorry, I should have told you, Neil, but then I didn't know if it was going to be a long-term or a short-term break . . .'

'None of us knew that,' June interrupted cheekily. 'But it's been a few weeks now, and no sign of her, so we think he's on the market again.' She winked at Lucy, the student who was working with them that night. 'What would you say, Lucy?'

'Oh, definitely open season on Tom, I'd say,' Lucy said. 'Why else do you think I agreed to work here?'

And as they worked on companionably to get everything done in readiness for the morning, Cathy glanced at Tom from time to time. He did seem to be less drawn and sad. Perhaps he was getting over her. But maybe it was an act. People who were as involved as Marcella and Tom didn't just part without a great deal of heartbreak. Wherever she was tonight, the silly girl would be thinking of big, handsome Tom Feather with his warm, loving ways. Cathy was thinking that she had never come across anyone so perpetually good-natured when she heard him saying, 'I wonder, has that aunt of Harry's got any allergies? Maybe we could feed her nuts or magic mushrooms or something tomorrow, and kill her before she does any more damage.'

'She asked me to bring her up and out into the fresh air, and then to bring her back down again,' Con said.

'She told me I needed a good girdle . . .' said June.

'She's lonely, and old and frightened, just be nice to her,' Cathy said.

They all looked at her in amazement.

'Why are you taking that attitude?' June was astounded.

'Because Tom, for once, isn't, and *somebody* round here has to play the role of angel if we're going to keep this company on the road,' Cathy said.

The wedding day, August 19th, was a beautiful sunny day, which nobody could have guaranteed. The priest was warm and welcoming, which might not have been the case in every single parish church in the country. The congregation had assembled in plenty of time, and all the women wore hats in honour of the occasion. Harry stood there beaming as Muttie and Marian walked up the aisle. Slow, measured steps, not scuttling. It was a miracle. Lizzie looked like someone who could have been photographed at the races for the Best-Dressed Lady, in an elegant grey silk outfit and a smart black hat. Geraldine, who had hired hats for all of them, wore an apricot suit, and Cathy stood beside her in the silk dress she had bought the week before in Haywards.

Neil had his best appearing-in-the-High-Court suit on to impress the in-laws. Soon, soon they would be finished with all this. He would take a day or two off and they would rest and talk about the future. He had promised this. Just as soon as Marian's wedding was over. In spite of herself, Cathy felt the tears come down her face when she saw Maud and Simon walking as solemnly as if their very lives depended on it behind the bride and Muttie. They were *so* good. Why had she thought they might behave stupidly and let everyone down? Their hair shining, their little kilts immaculate, their ordinary shoes polished to the highest degree. And she sniffed seriously when she heard Harry and Marian, who had been living together happily in Chicago for ages now, exchange their vows. For the first time she wished that she and Neil had organised something bigger and more celebratory themselves for their wedding day. But at that time to get married at all had been such a victory.

The church hall where they had the wedding feast looked magnificent, draped in ribbons and greenery and flowers. When the church was emptied June and Con were sent in to bring the flowers out quickly from the altar to the top table. There was a glass of champagne offered as soon as the guests came in the door. Tom took charge of Mike, the brother who found being on the dry a problem.

'Hi Mike, I'm Tom Feather, your sister's partner.'

'I thought she was married to Neil.' Mike glowered at him.

'Sure she is, I'm her work partner. Be nice to me, I'm in charge of the food and drink.'

'Drink, huh?' Mike said.

'I've got something here you'd love. Low-cal cranberry juice with freshly squeezed grapefruit whipped up with a little sugar syrup and white of egg.'

'What's it called?' Mike was still unwilling to thaw.

'It's called, "Let's not show it to the others, let's find something bearable for ourselves",' Tom winked.

'You been put off alcohol too?'

'Hell, isn't it? Other people seem so stupid and go on so long and say the same thing over and over again.'

'And their elbows fall off tables,' Mike said in a fury.

'Oh, I know all about it . . .' said Tom. 'Still, we've got something here, you and I, that none of the others will have, and think how well we'll feel tomorrow.' Mike brightened up. 'And if *we* want to sing, we'll remember the words, unlike the rest of them.'

'Will there be singing?' Mike thought the day might not be so sepulchral.

'It's a wedding, isn't it? We have to sing the praises of My Kind Of Town Chicago Is, and then someone has to tell us about Dublin's Fair City, don't they?'

Mike was a much-cheered man when Tom left him. All Tom had to do now was make sure that there were a few singers in the hall. People who would be able to wrench the stage from Maud and Simon when their time came. There was a roar of conversation, and as they moved among the guests they realised that it was already a mighty success. The first of many weddings they would do in this hall. Next time, hopefully, wearing their smart Scarlet Feather uniform. Today, however, they were wearing their idiotic shamrock-decorated outfits which they had all finished sewing minutes before they put them on. They all reported conversations to each other as they flashed by in the kitchen, which was lit up by the late afternoon sun.

'Harry's aunt that you were being so nice about is fast asleep; that's how much she's enjoying it,' Tom said.

'I told them to let her sleep, not to wake her. It's jet lag. She can wake up for dessert and the entertainment,' Cathy said.

'Simon and Maud have asked us to hold their cake and ice cream, please, until after their dance,' June announced.

'Makes sense,' Con agreed. 'I'd hate to see them bringing up that lot on the floor, wouldn't you?'

In Rathgar, Shona stopped outside the house. She didn't have to go in. She had his phone number: she could call him now on her mobile and say that she didn't feel well. Which was actually true. She was an adult of twenty-eight years of age. She hadn't seen him for fourteen years. Nothing except a carefully written letter from an old man. Why had he said that he would cook for her? Somehow that had touched her. When she knew him almost a decade and a half ago, he couldn't cook. He had learned to cook especially to make her a meal, he said. It could be just a line he was taking in order to persuade her. But he had never been cunning enough or cared enough to do that in the past. Why should he begin now? And why on earth did he want to see her again? It was because she was so curious about this that she was here . . . And now that she was here, she would go in. Shona walked in and rang the doorbell of James Byrne's garden flat.

'Con, can you move that bottle of wine away from my mother and get my father another pint?' Cathy asked.

'They're devouring the salmon, will there be enough for second helpings?' Lucy asked.

'Yes, but fill the serving dish up with cress and dollops of sauce as well, to hide the fact that there ain't that much fish,' Tom advised, 'and carve another dish of lamb as well. Make it look nice; we can always use it again.'

And eventually there were the speeches, simple and straightforward, thanks being lavished everywhere and no awful best-man jokes. And finally, the moment was here for Maud and Simon.

Harry announced, 'When I first heard about this wonderful hospitable Irish wedding, I knew I would take my bride in my arms and dance around a flower-filled hall . . . I never realised how beautiful both would look, but there are so many wonderful surprises today, including being introduced to Maud and Simon Mitchell, who are cousins by marriage of mine, now . . . our beautiful flower girl and our elegant pageboy. Now they are going to dance for us, and I want you to give them the great big welcome they deserve.'

Maud and Simon strode out confidently in their cloaks, kilts and huge Tara brooches, as if they were totally accustomed to being greeted with such applause.

'My fellow guests at Marian and Harry's wedding,' Simon read from a piece of paper, 'I am Simon Mitchell. I want to welcome you all to Ireland, those who weren't here already, I mean. My partner Maud and I will dance a jig with the very suitable name of "Haste To The Wedding". Although in your case you're already here. *At* the wedding,' he beamed at them as an afterthought.

'Oh, loving God, let them start to dance before he thinks of any more asides,' Cathy breathed.

But she needn't have worried: Simon had nodded at the pianist, and they stood, arms high, hands joined and right foot pointed out until the introductory bars were played, and then they were away. There was thunderous clapping. And then Maud stepped forward.

'My fellow guests at this wedding, I hope you enjoyed the jig. Now my partner Simon and I will dance a reel with the name "Come West Along The Road". Which you haven't really done, since you came east to get here, but that's the name of the dance.'

She put away the paper and again they stood solemnly waiting for the music to start. They danced on, oblivious of the fact that the audience was fighting back tears at their eagerness and determination to explain everything and get it totally right, and fits of laughter at their pompous little ways. Cathy caught Tom's eye. He raised a glass to her. She smiled.

'You're smiling,' Tom said in mock surprise.

'I know, isn't it amazing? The muscles still work,' Cathy said.

'Come in, come in,' James Byrne fussed and led Shona into the room where he had carefully placed four brightly coloured cushions and two vases of flowers. She had brought him a bottle of wine. He made great play of looking at the label.

'My goodness, Australian Chardonnay, how wonderful. That looks very good, very interesting indeed.' He studied it as someone might look at a bottle of some vintage wine at a special wine auction. It set Shona's teeth on edge. It was a good, supermarket Australian white wine, no more, no less. Why did he have to keep taking off and putting on his glasses? Probably because he was nervous, she realised. As nervous as she was. Normally when you went into someone's place for the first time you found something to admire. Shona's eyes raked the room. She was at a total loss for words. She could see nothing she recognised, yet he could hardly have bought these things new. Perhaps it was just rented furnished accommodation. They sat down opposite each other, and she saw on the table the plate of fat olives plus a little basket of Tom Feather's bread. James Byrne was definitely making an effort. He had done all the talking so far . . . about the wine, the weather, whether she had found the house easily. It was now up to Shona to bring up some subject.

'When did you come to live in Dublin?' she asked.

'Five years ago,' he said. 'Just after Una died.'

'She died? I'm sorry.' But the voice was cold.

'Yes. Yes, it was sad.'

Shona did not ask what happened, had it been peaceful, had she lingered a long time. None of the questions you ask when someone tells you that a wife has died. The silence hovered between them. Shona steeled herself not to speak again. She had asked one question, the ball was in his court, this invitation had come from him, let James Byrne be responsible for directing the conversation. Eventually he spoke.

'Una was never strong, you know, she found ordinary things like going upstairs or making the beds very difficult. Would you have known that now, when you were with us?'

'No, I didn't. I suppose, since it was the only life I knew, I thought everyone's home was like that. I didn't know what other homes were like until I lost the one I had.'

He looked at her with a face as sad as a bloodhound's. 'She was never the same after you left,' he said.

'I didn't leave, I was taken away, sent away.'

'Shona, I didn't ask you here to go over a war of words that did nothing except tear us to pieces half your lifetime ago.'

'Why did you ask me, then?' She realised that since she had come in she had not addressed him by any name. But what name could she call him? Not Daddy, not Mr Byrne.

'I suppose I invited you because I wanted to tell you how great a gap you left in our lives, how nothing was ever, ever the same since the day you were taken away.'

'Since the day you handed me over without a struggle, saying it was the law,' Shona said, her face hard.

'But Shona, that's the terrible thing, it *was* the law,' he said with tears in his eyes.

In the church hall the pianist was playing the Anniversary Waltz and Harry led Marian onto the floor and everyone clapped.

'The bride will dance first with her father,' he announced.

Muttie, who had been explaining to his sons some of the finer parts of a horse that was going to make a killing next year, was startled. 'I'm not much of a dancer,' he whispered anxiously.

'Just relax, Dad, Marian will push you round as she does the rest of us,' they said to him.

They did two tours of the hall with everyone cheering them, and then the general dancing began. Tom had given the twins their cake and ice cream and a pound each, in return for their going to sit with the old lady in the purple suit and telling her about Ireland.

'What are *you* going to do, Tom?' Simon was suspicious.

'I'm going to circulate.'

'Does that mean dance?' Maud asked.

'*No*, just talk to people. I don't feel like dancing; anyway, what's all this after, you two?'

They were pleased. 'Would Marcella come back if you agreed to marry her, do you think?' Simon asked.

'No, I asked her lots of times and she wanted to have a career instead.'

'And did she have to choose? Couldn't you do both? Like Cathy, and Muttie's wife Lizzie?'

'There are women who can do both,' Tom explained, 'but modelling is a hard one, it involves travel.'

The twins shrugged. It was better that she went then. Tom said it was.

In the garden flat, they had managed to get to the point where a wooden and stilted conversation did manage to go backwards and forwards between them. He called her to the table and sat her down. She moved from being alternately touched at the trouble he had gone to, and enraged at the cold, clinical attitude to life that had guided him over years of silence and neglect. They talked of her school life after she had left the convent school in the country town. She spoke calmly about the home she returned to, the mother still lurching between drugs and rehabilitation, the father who had set up a new home with a more stable woman. Her older sisters who resented her return, claiming that she had been given airs and notions about herself. She told of her natural mother's death this year, and how she had dutifully gone to visit her in the hospital but felt nothing. He said that they had always known a foster child was only lent to them, and that if her home circumstances improved she would go back to them. They had unworthily hoped that this would never happen. He told of his wife's descent into the state of a permanent invalid, of the emptiness of the life they lived. He said it was impossible to stay in the house after her death, and he had come to Dublin and lost himself in work.

'Well I did that too,' Shona said as she finished the smoked fish and watched him put on his oven gloves to get the next course. 'I decided that work was the only answer, that and having something to show as a result. I wanted a place I could be proud of. Glenstar is far too expensive for me, but I like giving that address; I like coming home to a smart place like that each evening.'

'And what about love, Shona? Does that play any part in it?'

'No, I've never loved anyone.'

He smiled a little indulgently.

'Don't smile at me, James,' she said. 'The day you stood and let me go without telling me that you loved me and wanted me back, that day killed any thoughts of love that I would ever have.'

September

After the wedding, life had to return to normal. And normal wasn't always easy. Tom never finished the letter to Marcella. He had been right; there was no more to say. She didn't say goodbye when she went across the water. He heard during one of his early morning sessions at Haywards that she had left her job in the salon. Two of the kitchen staff had heard she was going to be a model. Geraldine read in the property pages that Freddie Flynn and his wife Pauline had bought a country house with twenty-four rooms and eight acres, outside Dublin. June's husband Jimmy had a fall at work, naturally on a cash-in-hand job with no insurance, and was lying in bed for the duration. Joe Feather gave a great deal of his merchandise to a wide boy who managed to sell it off to all and sundry before leaving the country, all bills unpaid. Muttie needed the money to pay a vet's bill for Hooves, and borrowed some of Lizzie's savings for a sure thing which turned out not to be sure at all. James Byrne berated himself a dozen times a day for not taking that hurt, withdrawn girl into his arms and crying over the time lost and the pain endured. He had been so afraid that she would push him away. Old Barty wrote to say that he was on his way back and hoped he could come and stay again for a few days. Kenneth Mitchell wrote him a cold note saying that times were difficult, and that old Barty had left last time owing a great deal of money, so a visit would not be possible. Kenneth got by return of post an even colder note saying that Barty had now recovered his fortunes, but if he were no longer welcome there then so be it. Walter Mitchell got what was defined as a final warning from his uncle Jock. One more late morning or early leaving and he was out. Jock's face made it look as if this time it was meant. Neil and Cathy put off telling Jock and Hannah about the baby for a few more days. And so they didn't tell Muttie and Lizzie either.

Unexpectedly, Hannah rang and said she would like to invite Neil and Cathy to Oaklands.

'That sounds nice, Hannah, anything in particular?'

'No, should there be? I mean, it is my own son . . . and his wife, no need for an occasion or an excuse.'

'Of course not,' said Cathy, who had never been invited socially to dinner there before.

'Oh, and Cathy, do you do foods which people just serve in their own . . . I mean, the leaflet does say . . .'

'Of course we do, Hannah, tell me what you'd like.'

Hannah wanted a pheasant casserole, because Jock had been given a brace. It took forever, and they all cursed her back at the premises. But some things were more important than others, Cathy said, and not being fazed by Hannah Mitchell was top priority.

'Do we put in an invoice?' Tom asked.

'No,' Cathy said. Con was delivering it in the van later that afternoon; it would be bubbling merrily at Oaklands when they got there. Next week Hannah would telephone and fuss and waste more of their time.

They sat around the table that Lizzie had polished so often, and almost always to the dissatisfaction of Hannah. Cathy wondered did Hannah still think back on those days, or had she moved on? She was certainly an easier person to deal with now. Cathy would never really like her, but the hate was gone. Sometimes little waves of annoyance came back. Like when Hannah wondered why it was that Cathy and Neil never took a holiday abroad together, like normal people.

'Neil has to travel abroad a lot on work,' she said.

'Cathy is very tied up in her business,' he said.

She saw the look of triumph on Hannah Mitchell's face. For once the combined forces of Neil and Cathy were not ranged against her. She had managed to divide them at last. Over this, anyway. Cathy warned herself that it must not happen again. One of the many reasons she wanted to save her marriage was to prove Hannah Mitchell wrong.

'Tired?' Neil asked her when they were in the car driving home.

'Not really, why?'

'You're sighing,' he said.

'I'm always sighing,' Cathy said.

'The food was nice,' he said.

'Thanks,' she said innocently.

'Did you do it . . . ?' he asked surprised.

She looked at him thoughtfully, one of the brightest young men at the Bar, but not a lot of practical sense. Of *course* she had done the food, that was why it was not over-done beef followed by ice-cream with liqueur poured over it. But there was no point in saying any of that now.

He told her about the project for the homeless. Something he and Sara were proposing which other people on the committee were resisting. Cathy let her thoughts drift away, and wondered should she give cookery classes at the premises when she was too pregnant to go out on jobs. It might be a good idea. Little groups of eight or twelve, rich, lonely women like Hannah who hadn't a clue. She wondered how James Byrne's dinner party had gone, but she would never ask. Neil was still talking on, Sara had said this, he had said that. He seemed to see an awful lot of Sara, but never reported anything back about the twins. Still, Cathy reminded herself that they were mainly involved in this committee now; Simon and Maud were only a small item on Sara's busy caseload.

*

Geraldine asked Scarlet Feather if they could cater for a spur-of-the-moment supper party at Glenstar.

'Any theme?' Tom wondered.

'She's looking for a new sugar daddy; we *could* think up a few sugar-based dishes.'

'You're awful about her,' Tom said.

'No, I'm not, those are her own words. Freddie Flynn's gone back to his wife full-time, have you noticed, he even took his account away from her PR firm, which is going a bit far.'

'Well, maybe his wife wouldn't trust him around Geraldine's long legs and flashing smile,' Tom said with a grin.

'She was pleased with how well Glenstar looked for the recovery party after the wedding. She's decided to capitalise on it.'

'She's not going to have the dancers as a cabaret, by any chance?' he asked.

'No, she's drawn the line there. Tom, are we taking on too much, do you think?' she sounded worried.

'No, of course not, we've a load of terrific stuff for a buffet in the freezer already, and I'd say she'd like shellfish, don't you think?'

'Yes, but getting it ready, setting it up, serving it.'

'Cathy, June and I will do most of it. Does she need a barman as well, do you think?'

'Yes, she does, whether she knows it or not.' Cathy wanted every hand on deck.

'Relax, Cathy, there are bound to be times you're tired. Accept it, will you?'

She smiled wearily. It was great not to have to put on a brave face all the time.

Freddie Flynn's next rented-villa reception went very well. This time they had rum punch served in coconut shells, Bob Marley on the record player and June wearing a garland of flowers around her neck, which was, strictly speaking, more Hawaiian than Caribbean, but nobody cared.

'How's that marvellous aunt of yours?' Freddie asked.

'Wonderful. Will we be seeing you at her big party next week?' Cathy asked with an innocent smile. It had the desired effect of catching him off guard.

'Er . . . um . . . no, come to think of it, I believe I'm away next week, yes, I am, so that must be it,' he said.

'Oh well, next time then,' Cathy said brightly.

Sara came to The Beeches to ensure that the back-to-school process was going as planned. Kay looked at her bewildered. Sara explained slowly. Textbooks, exercise books, uniform, shoes to the mender's, haircuts. The kind of things normal people understood.

'There's always so much to do,' Kay Mitchell sighed. 'It's all quite endless, really, isn't it, Sara?'

'Endless, Mrs Mitchell. Shall we make a list of what has to be done?'

*

When he was taking Hooves for a healthy walk, Muttie met JT Feather by chance.

'Desperate business about the vandals destroying Tom and Cathy's premises,' Tom's father said.

'Never heard one single solitary word about it,' Muttie said.

They agreed that children these days were secretive and devious, and took risks and wouldn't tell you about anything unless they had to.

'They had to tell me *something* to get my men to try and build the place up again,' JT said grudgingly.

'Well, you're streets ahead of me in information anyway,' said Muttie, which pleased the other man greatly.

'Why didn't you tell me?' Lizzie demanded.

Cathy was nonplussed. There were so many things she hadn't told her mother. Which one could her mother mean?

'About what?' she asked.

'About your premises getting broken into.'

'Oh, Ma, I didn't want you going on like you're going to go on now.'

'And do they know who did it?'

'Nope, not a clue.'

'And were you insured?'

'Of course we were, Mam.'

'So this isn't the reason why you're killing yourselves and you're looking like a long wet week?'

'Mam.' She felt a surge of gratitude to her mother. She'd tell her about the baby this minute if there was any point, but it would be just one more worry. 'No, Mam, we're absolutely fine,' Cathy lied straight into her mother's anxious face.

James Byrne had been to the premises today and said that the hopes of getting the insurance company to pay up in the foreseeable future were very slim. They would be renting this expensive stuff for months down the line. Working flat out, they would see no profit, and quite possibly a massive loss at the end of the year.

The room was filling up at Geraldine's apartment. From the kitchen, Cathy saw James Byrne come in, wearing his best suit, and trying to find a background to stand in.

'Hey, he isn't your speed,' she warned her aunt. 'I've been in his flat; nothing you'd aspire to at all.'

'If I didn't have so much invested in you, Cathy Scarlet, I'd throw you off my balcony this minute. Mr Byrne's here because he advises our Residents' Association about our service contracts. One of the ladies here knew him years ago in Galway, and now that he's retired he does several of these little jobs. Most helpful and courteous he is, too.'

Cathy was pleased to see him. When it got quieter she might ask him about how the dinner party went.

June went up to Peter Murphy, hotelier and great friend of Geraldine's. 'Lovely party, isn't it, Mr Murphy?' she said to him.

'It is indeed, my dear,' he said distantly, giving the air of never having seen her before in his life.

'I'm no hit with that Peter Murphy,' June complained to Cathy.

'I think he still fancies the hostess,' Cathy said.

'Well, why doesn't she go back to him now that his wife's gone to Holy God and the other fellow back to his wife?' June grumbled.

'I don't know. I did ask her, but she gave me some crap about never revisiting things. I haven't an idea of what's she's talking about.'

'Look who's here now,' June said, nodding to the door. Joe Feather had just come in.

'Oh, God almighty,' said Cathy. This would be the first time the brothers had met since the night of the fashion show.

Shona walked straight over to the window, to where James was standing.

'I'm very sorry, I didn't know you'd be here,' she said.

'And I didn't know you'd be here either,' he said simply.

'I'd like to return your hospitality sometime soon,' she began.

'Oh, please, don't think you have to do . . .' he stammered.

'I don't think I *have* to, I'd like to. Would you like to have lunch with me at Quentins one day next week?'

'But Shona, that's a very . . .' He spoke softly. But stopped. He had been about to say the restaurant was much too expensive. That might not have been tactful, or indeed sensitive.

She seemed to know what he had been going to say. 'I save my money to pay a posh rent and to have the odd meal in a posh place. I'd love you to be my guest. You pick a day.'

'I'd be proud and delighted to meet you there on Wednesday,' he said.

'I'll book the table for one o'clock,' she said, and left him.

'All right, Tom?' Joe said in a fake Cockney accent.

'All right, mate,' Tom answered in the same cheerful voice.

They looked at each other for a moment, not sure what to say next.

'Great place for a party,' Joe said eventually.

'Isn't it just? Have you a drink, or have you gone temperance on us?'

'I'm never going to drink again, Tom. Believe me.'

'Rough night, was it?'

'No, but I think I must have been drunk on the day when I gave that bloody gangster all that credit, he nearly wiped me out. Did you hear about it?'

'I heard something, yes.' Tom was vague.

'Listen, I won't interrupt you here at your work. Maybe we'll have a temperance lunch one day, and weep on each other's shoulders?'

'Okay, but I want somewhere with a pint, and I don't get to do any of the weeping, you do all that side of it. Okay?'

'Okay,' said Joe.

The telephone rang in Geraldine's apartment, and June answered.

'Please, June, could you put the call through to the bedroom, it's Frederick Flynn. Tell her I won't keep her long from her friends.'

'It's very busy here, Mr Flynn, do you think that you could—'

'Now, please, June,' he said.

Geraldine went into her bedroom and picked up the receiver. 'Yes, Freddie?' she asked pleasantly.

'I must have been mad. I tell you this, I must have been stark staring mad, I won't be without you, you mean too much to me.'

'I beg your pardon?'

'You heard me. I'm telling her.'

'What *exactly* are you telling Pauline?' she asked, her voice ice-cold.

'Well, I'm telling her that I have to spend some time in Dublin in the evening after work, that I can't be tied to coming home to the country every night, and ... you know.'

'Oh, don't do all that, Freddie, it will upset Pauline and it won't mean anything in the end.'

'What do you mean? I love you, Geraldine, you're an exquisite woman. I'm such a fool to have said I'd give you up.'

'You didn't say that at all, Freddie, we agreed it had run its course.'

'But it hasn't ... not for me.' There was a silence. 'Geraldine?'

'Yes, Freddie, I'm here, but I have people in so I must get back to my guests.'

'I *know* you have people in, half the bloody country, don't you think I want to be there too?' He sounded very upset. But she hardened her heart. He had made a decision. He had not called Geraldine with the news that he loved her so much that he would leave Pauline. Or even defy her. She was being asked to settle for a few more stolen nights until Pauline cracked the whip again. He had been the warmest, funniest of all her men, but still, he was a weak man, she wasn't going to get back into a muddled, uneasy compromise of a relationship where he would always be looking at his watch.

'You'll always be a special person to me, Freddie, but I have to go,' she said. She hung up, and straightened her bed. Geraldine went back to her party.

'Con, can you take this tray? I have to sit down,' Cathy said.

'Sure. You're very white, Cathy,' he said. 'Can I do anything for you, brandy, glass of water?'

'Yes, go and see which of Geraldine's posh bathrooms is free. I used to think she was mad to have two, but tonight we need one.'

He was back in seconds. 'The near one is free, lean on me, Cathy.'

'Thanks, Con, you're a trooper.' She went in and locked the door.

The first guests were beginning to leave. They had cleared a lot of things into the kitchen. June came in with a pile of plates.

'Cathy's in the loo, she doesn't look well,' Con reported.

'Right, you bring in the next lot of dishes, I'll go and check.' June went to the bathroom. 'Cathy, open up the door this minute.'

'June, go away, go to the other one.'

'I want this one, I'm going to keep knocking and shouting until you let me in.'

'You're mad, go away, get out of here.'

'CATHY,' June roared.

The bolt was drawn back, and Cathy sat there on the side of the bath, her face as white as the white porcelain around her.

'Go back, June,' she said in a weak voice. 'Go back, for Christ's sake, we can't afford to foul up on a good job like this, aunt or no aunt.'

'What's wrong? Just *tell* me,' June said.

'I felt a pain. Look, it's nothing, no bathroom full of blood, it's not a haemorrhage or anything, now will you go back.' She grimaced and held her middle.

'Have you passed any blood at all?' June snapped out the words.

'Literally a couple of drops, nothing you would notice unless you were looking for them.'

'You've got to lie down,' June insisted.

'Now? In the middle of the party? You're mad.'

'In the spare bedroom and now,' June said, scooping up all the towels she could see in the bathroom. 'Come on, Cathy, don't give me any trouble or I'll hit you in the jaw and knock you out.'

Cathy staggered to the spare room, very tasteful shades of lilac and mauve with a rich purple carpet and a wall-hanging in the same colours. 'Imagine, I'm probably the first person ever to sleep in this bed,' Cathy said dreamily as June put cushions under her feet and then went to collect what looked like an enormous amount of towels from the hot-press beside the bathroom.

June approached Peter Murphy. 'Mr Murphy, I'm June. I wonder if you could tell me quietly whether anyone in this room might be a doctor?'

'Has there been an accident in the kitchen?'

'A sort of crisis, yes; I don't want to disturb Geraldine . . .'

They both looked over to where Geraldine stood talking animatedly to a tall man who seemed very taken with her.

'I don't know half the people here,' Peter Murphy said. 'I was just leaving. Perhaps her new friend is a consultant or something; he certainly dresses like one.'

'Why are you looking for a doctor?' Tom had amazing ears.

'Cathy. She's in the spare bedroom.'

He was in there in a flash. 'Tell me quickly, Cathy, what do we do?'

'There's a bit of blood . . . Tom, I don't know whether it's better to try and get to a hospital or to stay still.'

'Jesus, why didn't any of us qualify as doctors? Have you got your mobile?'

'In my bag in the kitchen, but don't go just yet, Tom.'

June was back in the room. 'There *was* a doctor, she's coming in.' She was one of the residents at Glenstar, a small Indian woman with an easy smile. She took in the situation immediately, sat down on the chair that June offered her and held Cathy's hand.

'How many weeks?'

'Fourteen or fifteen, I think.'

'And the pain? The cramps? The blood?' She asked the questions without any sense of rush. And nodded, as if pleased with all the answers. 'We'll keep you here and make you comfortable for a while, and then we'll think again,' she said.

'Please go back to the party,' Cathy begged. 'I'm all right now, you can see that.'

'They're coping fine,' Tom soothed her.

'God, Tom, there's only Con out there, and you know the panic people get into when they think the party's about to end. Go out and give him a hand, both of you.'

'Calm, calm,' the doctor said.

'You might as well try to turn back the tides as ask her to be calm,' Tom said resignedly.

'Are you her husband?'

'No, no, I've rung Neil but it's the answering machine. I didn't want to leave a message that would alarm him. Can you give me his mobile number, Cathy?'

'Not yet, let's see what we have to tell him first. Now please go, all of you,' she begged.

They left, and tears rolled down her face in the darkened room with its graceful design. She noticed that the doctor, helped by June, had put still more big bath towels beneath her. The good news was that Geraldine's elegant counterpane would not be stained or marked. The bad news was that the doctor must be expecting to see a lot more blood shortly.

Geraldine knew that something was wrong but that it was under control. She bade farewell to Nick Ryan, who owned a chain of dry-cleaning firms around the city. She murmured that she must not monopolise him; he really should circulate and meet everyone else. He murmured that he hated to go, but really he had no interest whatsoever in talking to anyone else. That was about as strong an indication as he could possibly give that he found her attractive. Geraldine saw Peter Murphy looking at her. But she would not go back on her tracks. No revisiting, as she had often told Cathy, not that the girl ever listened to anything. And where was she, by the way? This party was so strange, in a way. James Byrne and Shona Burke knowing each other from way back. That very nice neighbour, Doctor Said, who had said that she would drop in just for an hour, still here with the hard core. Freddie ringing to ask her to go back to him. Peter Murphy being utterly jealous and possessive. Wasn't bad for a girl about to turn forty. Geraldine was about to congratulate herself, when she saw Doctor Said moving quietly towards the spare room, and she suddenly realised why she hadn't seen Cathy for the last hour or so.

Only when she got to the hospital did Cathy tell them Neil's mobile number. And by the time he got there it was all over.

Back at the premises Tom, June and Con unpacked the van, washed up, tidied and stored everything. Geraldine said she would call them there when there was any news. They sat and drank coffee on the big sofas in their front room. It was the first place they had insisted on repainting and doing up after the break-in. Otherwise they would have been too depressed to face a day's work. They were trying to be practical; they would get Lucy, that bright little student, in again, and she might even have a couple of friends. It often worked that way. Con had a pal who was a good, reliable waiter. Whatever the news, they knew that Cathy wouldn't be able to work for a while. If she had kept the baby, she might have to lie down for weeks.

'One thing is sure ... she's never going to recover her strength if she thinks *we* can't manage,' June said. What Cathy needed as much as any hospital care was the assurance that Scarlet Feather could survive her absence.

When the phone rang it seemed unnaturally loud. It was two in the morning and Geraldine was ringing from the hospital to say that Cathy had lost her baby. June sat there, and didn't even wipe away the tears. Tom and Con blew their noses loudly in great wads of kitchen paper. June, for the first time ever, rang a taxi and went without complaint or comment straight home to her husband. Con and Tom went to a club and had three Russian vodkas each.

'I thought it would make me feel better,' Tom said, disappointed.

'Me too, I don't even feel drunk,' Con said.

'What a terrible, terrible waste at those prices.'

'I know, we could have drunk vodka for free back at the premises, with no blaring noise and no strobe lights,' Tom said furiously.

And for some reason, they both found this funny, and they laughed as they headed for their homes. Con to the flat he shared with three other guys, who might still be up and playing poker. Tom to Stoneyfield to sleep for a full two hours before he got up to make the bread at Haywards.

Neil came in and sat beside the bed to hold her hand.

'Well,' she said to him in a very tired voice.

'They say you're going to be fine,' he said.

'Yes,' she said.

'That's what matters. You're very precious to me.'

'Yes,' she said again.

'And Cathy, I'm very, very sorry. It could sound a little hollow, but I know it's a huge loss, and I *am* sorry that this should happen.'

'Thank you, Neil,' she said.

He stroked her forehead over and over saying, 'Poor Cathy. You'll be fine.' Eventually she closed her eyes and he thought she was asleep. He kissed her and she heard him speaking to the nurse, saying he'd come back before he went to work the next morning.

'How many days will you keep her here?' he asked.

The nurse thought it might be two nights, but she couldn't say definitely. Neil said that was great, because he didn't have to go out of town for another few days.

'Very considerate man, your husband, some fellows who come in are all over the place,' the nurse said.

'That's right,' said Cathy, who realised that some fellows who came in here were heartbroken that they had lost an unborn child.

Cathy was adamant. She didn't want anyone else to know where she was. No point in telling four people that what might have been their grandchild had been lost. She knew too that she would have had to face the accusations that she had worked too hard, pushed herself too far. In other words, brought all this upon herself. Neil had been entirely supportive about this. It was her right to decide, he said, and only hers. Tom brought in a box of little home-made cakes for the nurses to have with their morning coffee.

Geraldine was also wonderful, she actually brought a file of work to Cathy's bed. 'Try to sleep, but I'm here if you want a chat,' she said.

It was very restful. Cathy dozed off several times, happy that Geraldine had plenty to do and didn't need to be entertained. Occasionally she would open her eyes and ask a question.

'Does Doctor Said like Ireland, do you think? When I'm better, Tom and I will make her a meal as a thank-you.'

'Was it a boy or a girl? In my mind I'll call the baby Pat, that could be either.'

'Do you really think I'm like you, Geraldine? You used to say I was once, but you haven't said it for ages.'

And finally, 'What would you do if you met that guy again, you know, the first guy, the one you really loved?'

She never stayed awake long enough to hear the bland, soothing answers that Geraldine murmured at her. But Geraldine thought about all the questions, and sat looking into the distance as Cathy lay there, white and weak, in the bed.

Neil drove her back to Waterview. He suggested that she go to bed; he would work and then bring her supper later. 'It's all right,' he reassured her. 'Tom brought round four little meals for two with instructions on them, so you won't be poisoned.'

The telephone rang. Cathy heard him telling someone that she wasn't there. They must work out a cover story for the next few days. She'd be on her feet again next week and back to work. But in the meantime, they must all say the same thing. Flu, virus or whatever.

'It was only Simon and Maud, some grouse, some whinge,' he said. 'I told them we'd ring in a couple of days.'

'Did that satisfy them?' Cathy asked.

'Satisfy those two? You must be joking, but I headed them off,' he said proudly.

'She *has* gone off us,' Maud said.

'But why? We haven't done anything. Not recently,' Simon said.

They went back over everything. Cathy had been great at the wedding, and had even said she was proud of them. Muttie and his wife Lizzie couldn't have told any tales. They washed all their own clothes, they kept their rooms tidy. They never complained when there was no meat or fish, only vegetables and rice. Sara had got them the money for school books. All they wanted to ask Cathy was could they do some more polishing for her at the premises because they wanted to earn some money for bus fares. Father had said that old Barty hadn't given him money that was owing, so there could be no pocket money this month.

'Miss Burke has booked a table for two,' James Byrne said as he came into Quentins.

'This way, Mr Byrne.' Brenda Brennan was always amazed by the strange way people in Dublin turned up with the most unlikely companions. Whoever would have thought that these two would have known each other?

'I thought we'd be less likely to get emotional and shout at each other here,' Shona said.

'Not a restaurant known for its shouting, I agree,' James Byrne said.

They chose from the set lunch menu, and ordered a glass of wine each.

'I shouldn't have said that you taught me never to love again, that was going too far,' Shona began.

'If it was what you felt, and I pray God it will not always be this way, then you were perfectly right to say it,' he replied.

'Can you tell me exactly what happened? I won't interrupt.'

And in a soft voice, without looking for pity, he told her the story. How he and Una couldn't have children. They had been for every kind of test. All the fertility treatment they had thirty years ago wasn't like it is nowadays. Nothing worked. And then this was the time that more and more girls who had babies outside marriage were keeping them, which, though very admirable and right, did mean that there was no pool of children for those who wanted to adopt them. However, the social services were always willing to help, and there was fostering. You were always told that your foster child was on loan. You had to understand that you were minding her until it was possible for her to be returned to her parents. There had been a problem in Shona's home. Her parents had come from Dublin to the West to make a fresh start, but it hadn't worked. Her mother had found suppliers and dealers there as well as in Dublin, and in many ways it was worse for her because now she had no extended family to fall back on. Shona's father had not been a tower of strength. The Byrnes had been given the toddler Shona, aged three and a half. Other relations had taken her sisters and brother. They had loved her, no one could have asked for a more wonderful child. They had always told her about her real mother and father. But they had seemed shadowy figures to her, people much less real and exciting than *Goldilocks* or the *Turf-cutter's Donkey* or the other stories they told her. And the years went on, Shona went to school and made lots of friends.

'Carrie and Bebe,' Shona said. Remembering.

And she turned out to be very bright at school.

'You sat for hours and taught me,' Shona said. 'I was never bright, Carrie and Bebe weren't, my sisters weren't either in the homes they were in; it was only because you spent such a time there, looking things up for me, explaining over and over.'

'You remember?' He was pleased.

'Some of it, yes indeed,' she said.

The waiter arrived with their first course. They stopped talking to smile their thanks at him, and when he had gone they continued. He told her of the shopping trips, how they often went out intending to buy a winter coat for Una or a pair of shoes for himself, and they saw something for Shona which they bought instead.

'I'm not trying to tell you how much we spent as if I want to be thanked for it; we had plenty of money. Just want you to know that you were the centre of our lives, and no decision in that house, from what kind of cornflakes we ate right up to where we would go on holidays, was made without thinking of you. It's not looking for thanks; we wished we could have done more . . . I just wanted you to know what a great hole you left in our lives when you had to go.'

The year they had to give her back, they had planned to take her to London to go to the Science Museum.

'I didn't know that,' she said. 'I've never been there.'

'It was to be a surprise, and well, obviously, when you had to go back we didn't tell you.'

'Did I really have to go back, James?'

'Oh, Shona, you did, and they told us that the best thing we could do for you was not to cry and tell you we'd miss you. They told us that you'd be with your family, and that it would be hard after ten years without us weeping and wailing and making it worse for you, so we were very strong and pretended that this was great news.'

'And I thought, always thought that you were relieved to be rid of me.' Her voice was flat.

'Ah, Shona, child, you *couldn't* have thought that. Not seriously?'

'What else could I think? No letters, I looked every day. You were both so good at writing to people, I couldn't believe you didn't write to me.'

'We were told not to, so as not to unsettle you.'

'I couldn't have been more unsettled than I was. I played it over and over in my mind that day. There were no tears when I went. I cried. I remember

I said I wanted to stay, and you stood there like two stones saying that this was what we all wanted, and I was to tell my mother and sisters that I was delighted to see them.'

'I'll tell you about that day, and then you tell me. The car drove off and we watched it go down the drive. You never looked back.'

'I hated you so much for handing me over.'

'And we went back into the house, and I wondered would we have a cup of tea and Una said, "What for?" And the words hung there. What *was* the point of putting the kettle on, or indeed getting up in the morning, when you weren't there to share it? So the day went on, and Una sat in the kitchen looking out in the garden, and I sat in the hall looking at the door, for I suppose half an hour. Then she came out to the hall to me and said, "James, something odd has happened, all the clocks have stopped. They stopped at a quarter to six." And I said, but that *is* the time, it *is* a quarter to six. And then she wanted to know was that the morning or the evening. And that was the beginning of it, Shona, her mind started to go that afternoon, she thought you had been gone for five or six hours, she thought it must be nearly midnight. I brought her out and showed her the sky, I turned on the radio. She said you had left hours ago, you weren't forty minutes out of the house, and her mind started to go.'

'And she was so clever, so well read and everything,' Shona sighed.

'The last conversation we had was the night before you left. She wanted us to run away with you, change our names, go to England maybe, start again. I had to tell her that we couldn't, we would have nothing, we'd be on the run and we'd have to give you up eventually.'

'She wanted to do that?'

'So did I, Shona, but how could I sell the house, get another job, do anything to provide for you if we had to take false names? They'd be looking for us everywhere, people that stole a child. And since we couldn't do it, what we wanted to do, that's why it seemed right to go along with what had to be done.'

'I see,' she said.

'And we were allowed to write back if you wrote to us, but you never did. Tell me how the day turned out for you,' he asked.

She paused for a while and he didn't hurry her. She remembered that from the past, too. Dad would always wait until you got your thoughts together.

'It was a summer day, and the light was behind us all the way as we drove to Dublin because the sun was setting in the west. And I was in the back of the car and they talked to each other, the two women, I didn't know who they were, or that they were social workers. I suppose they were nice enough. We stopped in a town on the way and they bought me a burger and chips, and even though I was hungry I threw it away. Anyway, I got back to the house and the woman they said was my mother looked desperate. She had long, straggly hair that she hadn't washed for weeks, and she smoked all the time. She looked at me and said, "Will you look at the cut of you." That's all she said, she hadn't seen me for ten years and that was her greeting.'

'What did you say to her?' James asked.

'I was fourteen. I said nothing.'

The silence rested there between them, but it wasn't awkward. He simply waited for her to speak again.

'And then in a few days I knew what I had to do, I had to get out, you didn't want me ... I thought, so I couldn't go back to you, I had to make my own way and maybe I could do it through school. So I began the life that I still lead, the life of a workaholic. My sisters were dossers, they did nothing except tell me I was full of airs and graces and I didn't like the milk carton on the table. "She wants a milk jug," they used to mock me. But I had great teachers. I told one, a Mrs Ryan, that things were bad at home, she was so nice. She said that things are always bad at home, that is the way the world runs, so I thought she had a lousy time too. It was only years later I learned that she had a great life. She taught me to type in lunch hours, and used to let me use the school machine to practise on. And there were others, too; it was a tough city school, so they loved someone who was making an effort to do something rather than shoplift or get pregnant at sixteen.'

'And when you left?'

'Ah, but before that I had to fight to stay and finish. They wanted me to work in the factory. I refused. I was sixteen. I wanted to get my Leaving Cert. and a life. My mother was using again, I didn't care any more. All I needed was somewhere to work, and I had my own room because the others left. I used to take a small amount of the welfare money every week, and tried to make an evening meal every night, potatoes, lentils, and you could get cheap, squashy tomatoes. Sometimes she was able to take a mug of soup, but mainly she didn't bother. And I'd love to have gone to university. I had enough points and everything, but the only way that I could get out of there was to get a job, so I went to work the day I finished my exams.'

'What did you do?'

'I moved out of home and worked in a travel agency as a junior. I learned everything I could in six months. I got a proper job in another travel agency. I got two holidays, one in Italy, one in Spain. The only holidays I ever had in my whole life. I've been to London on work a few times, but I never had another holiday. I remember the excitement of getting a passport. Then I worked in a dress shop, then a hotel and by the time the job came up at Haywards I was ready for it.'

'And your ... mother?'

'I went to see her every week ... You see, you did teach me manners after all. And how to behave. Sometimes she was so stoned she hardly knew who I was; other times she was depressed. I used to take her soup, some weeks she drank it, others I used to find it with mould on it. I wasn't the only martyr, my sisters went in too. We didn't fight, ever. They just sneered at me. Lady Muck, they called me in those early days. I said nothing; as time passed they got indifferent to me, as I to them. Now it's like meeting strangers. At the funeral I looked at them and I realised I knew nothing about them at all, or they about me.'

James took out a paper tissue and wiped his eyes.

'You finally realised you don't have to wash hankies. Mum and I used to say that you were the last of the folded-linen variety . . .'

She stopped suddenly. She realised that she had called his dead wife Mum after all these years. She held out her hand at the same time as he did.

'What a waste,' he said.

'Of so many lives,' she agreed.

'We must make very sure it doesn't happen any more, Shona.'

'I'm more grateful than I can say that you got in touch,' she said.

'Well. I learned how to cook three dinners; you've only had one, there are still two to go,' he said, wondering had he gone too far.

'Saturday?' Shona suggested. 'I don't know when I last had something to look forward to on a Saturday night.'

'I'm going back to work tomorrow,' Cathy said. She sat in her dressing gown at the kitchen table in Waterview.

'No, it's too soon.'

'But they said when I felt well, and I feel well now.'

'No, it's too dangerous . . . You're not fully better.'

'I've lost all I can lose. There are no bits of the baby left in there to lose any more.'

He winced at the phrase, the image. But she didn't mind. She wasn't going to pretend that this child had not existed.

'I still think you're not fully better,' he protested.

'I'm not fully better in my mind because I'm upset, but my body is fine and it needs to get back to working rather than sitting here all day on my own.'

'I'll be home early,' he promised.

'No, it's not that.'

'I know it's possibly not the right thing to say but in many ways—'

'Then don't say it.'

'You don't know what I'm going to say.'

'I do, and please don't say it,' she begged.

He laughed at her. 'You wouldn't get away with that kind of argument in court,' he said.

'We're not *in* court.'

'Please let me finish. I only wanted to say that in many ways all this sad business has shaken us up, made us have a proper look at ourselves and realise where we are going.'

'Yes.'

'And I will never assume again that you are willing to drop everything and follow me wherever *my* career takes me. Now that's all I was going to say. Is it all right?' He looked at her expectantly, waiting for a response.

'It's fine.'

'So after all you *didn't* know what I was going to say.' Again looking for the warm answer.

'Not precisely, no.'

'What do you mean?'

'I thought when you began you'd say it's all for the best, but you didn't, not in so many words.'

'I didn't say anything at all like that, and if you remember I called it a sad business. Where did I say it was all for the best?'

'But that's what you think, Neil,' she said sadly.

'So first I'm on trial for what I'm going to say and then when I don't say it, I'm on trial for what you believe I think.' He looked wounded.

'I'm sorry, Neil, when you put it like that, it sounds very harsh. I didn't mean to be that.'

'And neither do I mean to be insensitive. Rest more,' he said from the door.

Cathy wished things could get back to normal, but there seemed to be no way that she and Neil could talk about what had happened without her wanting to scream and rail. His cool, logical, lawyer's way of approaching it was driving her mad. She wanted them both to cry over the dead baby, to admit that it was a tragedy. But there was Neil going out purposefully to deal with other people's misfortunes, not realising that the biggest one was in his own home. If he could only give a tenth of that care and concern to the fact that they had lost a child, then it would be fine.

She mustn't sit around here indefinitely going over the same thing again and again. The only place things might be normal was back at work. She wouldn't even wait until tomorrow, she'd go today.

They were delighted to see her back, and made a great fuss. Nobody said anything about it all being for the best, they said how much they missed her and how hard they had worked.

'So what's new?'

'A couple aged about a hundred who want to get married next month and can't find a venue to suit them,' June said, taking out a file.

'How old are they really?'

'Ancient,' June said.

'Well, we can't all be seventeen-year-old brides,' Cathy laughed.

'Probably wiser not to be,' June sighed.

'How about the church hall?' Cathy asked.

'Too big for them, they don't know how many people they're going to invite. Fifty maybe; but they think it might only be about twenty-four.'

'They're not very flush with friends, are they?' Cathy asked.

'They were the nicest couple I ever met,' Tom said simply. 'They're coming in today, you'll love them.'

Tom was right. Stella O'Brien and Sean Clery were indeed the nicest people you could meet. Aged in their mid-fifties, they had met a year ago at a beginners' bridge class. They were both still utterly hopeless at bridge, but devoted to each other. There was a problem.

'Isn't there always a problem about a wedding,' Cathy said sympathetically.

This one centred around Sean's three children and Stella's two children. People who did not look forward to the nuptials. Stella's son and daughter assumed their mother would remain a widow, look after her grandchildren when they came along and leave them her house. Sean's three daughters had assumed that their father would remain a widower and would eventually move out of his house which could be sold and the money divided between the girls. They would move him from one of their homes to the other, none of them having him for more than four months a year. The couple didn't *tell* all this to Cathy, of course, it just emerged in the conversation. She nodded and listened and accepted what kind of places wouldn't do and why.

'This must seem very odd to you, Miss Scarlet. I mean, all you young people must live a normal, uncomplicated life where everything works like clockwork,' Stella apologised.

'Absolutely not, I didn't know on the morning of my wedding day if anyone except five friends and my aunt would turn up.'

'Tell us more than that did,' Sean begged.

'Yes, my mother and father came, and the few relations I had who didn't emigrate. Most of Neil's didn't, apart from his mother and father who were like two icebergs, but the friends made up for it. I look back on it and I think it was a fine day. You will too. Tell me where would you really *like* to have it, and we'll see if we can work out something around that.'

'Do you know Holly's hotel in Wicklow?' Stella began.

'Yes indeed,' Cathy said. It was where she had told Neil about the baby. What a long, long time ago that seemed now. 'They don't do weddings there, sadly, we did ask, but would you know somewhere a bit like that?' Cathy looked at Stella O'Brien, who had put a deposit on a dress at Haywards and who was so happy for the world to share her pleasure in meeting Sean Clery over a green-baize table. She looked at Sean Clery, who had bought her a gold ring with a Celtic design, and kept lifting her hand to admire it.

'I'll find you something like that hotel,' she promised.

'You are a very kind girl,' they assured her.

Cathy, who had shaken her head twice at the suggestion that she might talk to Maud and Simon on the phone, knew this wasn't true. A kind person would have spoken to those two children, but she really couldn't face them. Yet. She still felt a bit jittery, and wondered had she in fact come back to work too early.

'Anyone need the van for a couple of hours?' she asked.

She knew Tom's face so well, she could read on it that he was worried if she was fit to drive ... But if he thought it, he didn't show it.

'Sure ...' he said, and threw her the keys.

*

Cathy drove south to Wicklow. A beautiful autumn day, it was wonderful to get out of the city. She looked at the tape selection to see what was on offer. Pop groups she had never heard of, some Irish traditional music, a country and western tape and favourite arias. She put on the last one, and turned up the volume to lose herself and sang along to Pavarotti's swelling voice. The music made her sad. She thought again of the child who hadn't made it to getting born and the tears poured down her cheeks. Would she ever stop weeping? She sang louder to try and stop crying. At traffic lights, a man in the next car smiled at her.

'What are you singing?' he asked, looking at her admiringly.

'*Nessun dorma* . . . None shall sleep,' she said. 'Possibly too true in terms of my singing.'

'You're lovely,' he said. 'Fancy a drink in Ashford?'

'No thanks, but you are sweet to ask,' she said.

She felt fifteen years younger, like a kid out of school. She drove on to Holly's hotel.

'I can't do it, Ms Scarlet, we don't have the resources,' Miss Holly said.

'They're the nicest people you ever met. You and I have to deal with such awful people in our work.'

'I know, Ms Scarlet, but I have three waitresses who are as old as myself, we can't take on weddings.'

'Let me do it, Miss Holly. We'll rent the place from you, we'll be in and out, you won't know we were ever here.'

'Are they family, or are they blackmailing you?'

'I never met them until this morning, but to tell you the truth I've not been well. I had a miscarriage, and in fact today's my first day back at work and I'm feeling a bit vulnerable. They were so bloody nice, and they said they wanted a place as like this as possible . . . And you know I love it here, so I know what they mean.' She was afraid her voice sounded a bit choked.

'And you do like it here, you and your husband?'

'We love it, it's our great treat, it's a place that works magic for us.'

'It didn't last time,' Miss Holly said.

'What do you mean?'

'Last time you and your husband were talking about the baby at dinner. Betty, one of the waitresses, told me.'

'Yes, that's true, but we haven't actually told anyone else . . .'

'And neither have we. I'll let you have the place for the meal, Ms Scarlet.'

'You'll never regret it, Miss Holly.'

'Now all we have to do is think of the food for Stella and Sean,' Cathy said when she was back at the premises.

'What do you mean? We have to get a venue first, and it's so hard, given all the limitations.'

'Oh, that's all organised,' Cathy said, her eyes dancing.

'No, come on, I know you're superwoman, but we've been three days trying places . . . Nowhere suits.'

'Miss Holly said yes.'

'You drove down there today?'

'Yup,' said Cathy.

'I thought we could manage without her, Tom, but it turns out I was wrong,' said June.

'Are you going on a honeymoon?' Cathy asked Stella O'Brien.

'We hadn't thought of it. The wedding itself is such a big thing. Once we have that sorted . . .'

'I've sorted it all out, Stella. Miss Holly will let us do it in her place, so why don't you book in there for a honeymoon of three or four nights?'

'It's so peaceful, such a happy place to stay.' Stella O'Brien had tears in her eyes. 'It was a lucky day that we phoned your company,' she said.

'How *did* you hear of us, actually?' Cathy always liked to know.

'Last Easter I won a raffle at the school where I work, and the prize was to have a manicure at Haywards, and this very pretty girl said that her fiancé ran a catering company and gave me your card . . . So when Sean and I decided to get married . . . there you were in our address book. I'd really like to thank her.'

'Ah yes. Yes, indeed.'

'There's a problem about the girl, is there?'

'She and Tom aren't together any more . . . that's all. Now, what kind of music would you like?'

'I beg your pardon?'

'For the wedding. Will we have a pianist or an accordionist . . . Or would you prefer a music centre? Tom can organise that, no trouble, and put on all the CDs you want.'

Stella's voice dropped. 'I'm going to confide in you, I'd be afraid we might look silly if we had music. Sean had a very quiet wedding first time round, his wife was a kind of recluse I think. He's just dying for fun and excitement, he doesn't have an idea of how much his children resent us marrying. I don't think that any of those girls are going to come to the wedding.'

Cathy laid her hand on Stella's. 'They'll come just to see it. Believe me, they won't be able to let their father get married without coming to watch it. They'll be there . . . Will yours?'

'My son will be there. My daughter, I don't know.'

'Bet you any money she will,' said Cathy.

'Not a word from those children,' Muttie said.

'I suppose they have such a great life up at The Beeches, they wouldn't have the time for us any more.' Lizzie was both humble and philosophical.

'Cathy said you wouldn't ask an ordinary rat to live at The Beeches,' Muttie grumbled.

'Yes, but you know the way Cathy goes on about the Mitchells in general,' Lizzie explained.

'They didn't come last Saturday, and never a solitary word out of them,' Muttie said, very upset.

'Well, I rang Cathy and she said they were grown-up enough to make up their own minds,' Lizzie said.

'There was so much we had to do, to arrange,' Muttie said. 'I don't believe it was anything to do with being grown-up at all, I think they didn't have their bus fare, that's what I think.'

'Well don't go saying that,' Lizzie ordered.

'Of course I won't,' said Muttie, who then sat down and wrote a letter to Master Simon and Miss Maud Mitchell at The Beeches. 'Just in case there's a problem about transport between our residences, I enclose £5 (five pounds). We are always here ... M. and L. Scarlet.'

'Walter?'

'Yes, Father?'

'Has that ... er ... social worker been in touch about anything?'

'Don't think so, why?'

'I realise the twins didn't go up to Mr Muttie, or whatever he's called, at the Jarlath's place last Saturday.'

'Well, I suppose they got tired of it.'

'I don't think they had any money for the fare, as it happened.'

'Did they just spend their pocket money, Father? Was that it?'

'They didn't really *get* any pocket money, you see, old Barty actually left me a bit short.'

'Oh, God, Father, be very, very careful. That Sara and Cathy, those two are real ball-breakers.'

'I know. Let's keep a watch.'

Walter picked up the mail. There was an odd-looking letter from someone to the children. Walter opened it carefully. It might be something about this ridiculous arrangement, he and his father should be forewarned. He found the fiver and pocketed it. He put the letter and envelope into the fire.

Jock Mitchell called at The Beeches. The twins were doing their homework at the table.

'Where's your dad?' he asked.

They told him that Father's friend old Barty had rung up and sorted out an old quarrel, and so Father had gone off to meet him in order to celebrate the fight being over.

'And your mother?'

Apparently Mother had got upset when Father went to meet old Barty. And she had gone down to the shops. Jock Mitchell didn't like the notion of his sister-in-law going down to the shops. That's how the drinking had started before, she just went to one particular section of the supermarket.

'And everything all right here, is it?'

The twins looked at each other and nodded their doubtful agreement that everything was all right. Uncle Jock didn't come to see them often; he might not come again for months. No point in hoping he'd come in regularly, as someone to keep an eye on things.

'Did you come to see Father, Uncle Jock?'

'No, I came to see where Walter keeps his computer, actually.'

The twins supposed it must be in his bedroom. But that was locked.

'He says he uses it every night, that's why he took it from the office.'

Maud and Simon looked at each other. They had never heard the sound of any computer, nor seen one coming into the house. But they knew it was better to give no information at all, so they looked blankly at their uncle. They were funny little things. He wished Hannah had taken to them more. They could have come to Oaklands and played on the swings around the big trees ... It didn't look as if that hard-working son of his and his equally career-minded wife were going to produce any grandchildren for them in a hurry, and Manda had told them that in her case it wasn't a starter either. But no point in complicating things; Kenneth had always been an odd fellow, and his wife very unstable from day one. Wiser to stay well away from them and their children. Jock sighed: he had definitely failed to do this in the case of Walter. There was no way of getting him into any kind of shape in the office now. Neil, always the champion of the underdog, had unexpectedly advised him to throw the boy out. Jock suspected that Walter had stolen the computer and sold it. But he had no proof, and it didn't look as if he were going to get any this evening from his visit to The Beeches.

'Will we say you called to see Walter?' Simon asked.

'Or should we just say nothing at all?' asked Maud.

'I think we should say nothing at all,' Jock said.

He contemplated giving them a couple of pounds each, as one had done to children long ago. But maybe it was patronising nowadays, and there was in operation a very firm agreement about everything, including pocket money. Maybe it would just throw things out of kilter. So he just rattled the coins as the children looked at him hopefully, and then said goodbye.

Geraldine had dinner at Quentins with Nick Ryan. Brenda Brennan just nodded her head politely to her as they came in. No one would know that the women were friends. Some men felt threatened if they thought that their date was better known in the restaurant than they were. Geraldine admired that kind of professionalism. She practised it herself. Before this dinner she had read up a great deal about the dry-cleaning business in Ireland. He was a very pleasant man. Not afraid to pay a compliment. Also, he was upfront about everything, which she particularly liked. He said it was a treat for him to go out to dinner with a glamorous lady, normally at this time of the evening he was letting himself in the door at home and groaning to his wife about the day at the office and coping with two fairly difficult children. Geraldine nodded her understanding of this. *All* children were difficult, anyone who said otherwise wasn't a serious parent. This made him feel good, and also the way Geraldine seemed to accept the existence of a wife and family in the life of a man she was having dinner with. She looked, as always, perfectly groomed, and much younger than her years. She answered questions about herself in a practised, easy way, not giving very much away but still telling enough to make a picture of a woman with a working-class background who had worked hard to get where she had arrived. She made it very clear that she wasn't trying to get married and settle down. That she preferred a very independent life at this stage, and liked to see a great variety of friends.

'And you do have a lot of friends. I was very impressed at your party,' he said. 'Very pleasant gathering indeed.'

'I'm glad you enjoyed it, I hope you met a lot of people,' Geraldine said. It was far too soon in their relationship to tell him all that went on behind the scenes at the party, the bath towels, Doctor Said, Cathy being taken in an ambulance to the hospital.

'To be very honest, I wasn't all that interested in meeting other people,' he said.

'That's very flattering,' Geraldine said.

'And very sincere,' said Nick Ryan.

'I don't know how Geraldine does it,' Brenda Brennan said to her husband Patrick in the kitchen. 'She has yet another rich, handsome businessman out there purring at her and pawing the ground.'

'Ah, but she didn't get a safe and steady and reliable husband, like you did,' Patrick consoled her.

'I know.' Brenda's tone didn't seem to suggest somehow that she had won out in this comparison.

'Or a passionate, creative, temperamental chef like myself,' he suggested.

That was more like it. 'Indeed she did not,' said Brenda, pleased.

Mrs Barry wouldn't be at The Beeches for a while; she was going away to her daughter's for three weeks' holiday.

'The press is full of tins of things there for you, and the milkman is paid to the end of the month.'

'Thank you, Mrs Barry.'

'And you know . . . you know your mother's not well. She should have a doctor. I'll ring Sara and let her know.'

'No, Mrs Barry, we'll ring Sara,' Maud said.

'We have other things to tell her, so we'll tell her about Mother not being well.'

'Good. That's all right then, she'll be round to see to things.'

Maud and Simon didn't ring Sara. It only upset everyone when Sara came in; it was fine for five minutes, but when she left everyone and everything got worse. Better for her not to come at all. And when she called to know was everything all right, they said it was all just fine.

Sara met Neil at the big public lecture on homelessness.

'Glad it's all going all right at The Beeches,' she said.

'Oh, is it? Good,' he said.

'You haven't been there recently, then?' she asked.

'No; there have been a few other things on our minds. Listen, I have to tell you because you're one of the few people that knew she was pregnant; Cathy had a miscarriage.'

'Oh, I am sorry,' Sara said.

'Yes, but nobody, least of all the twins or any of the family knows a thing about it so, of course . . .'

'Of course not.'

'And in many ways, of course . . .' Neil began.

'I know, in many ways it could be for the best at this particular time, you could still take that job abroad now.'

'I may not go forward for it,' Neil said.

'Still, there's an awful lot of work to be done at home,' Sara said, pleased that he was not going away. She looked at him with undisguised admiration.

He smiled at her. It was nice when someone thought you were great.

Cathy was going to ring the twins. She actually got as far as the phone, but then she thought of having to talk to Kenneth Mitchell, and she changed her mind. She tried to think back to the first days of her engagement to Neil. Had she really tried to please awful people like that, had she tried to get Kenneth and Kay on her side in the battle against Hannah? She hoped that she had not. That whole battle seemed so long ago, and in many ways so unimportant. What did points scored over her mother-in-law *mean*, anyway? Neil had been right in that, and how silly Cathy must have been to hug those little hard-won victories over her mother-in-law as if they were trophies. She'd ring the twins when this wedding was over, when she had some time to give to them.

Simon and Maud sat at the kitchen table. They had eaten sardines and cold tinned beans, which went well together. They had tied up the rubbish and left it outside the gates of The Beeches; the binmen came tomorrow. They rescued a newspaper, in case they should clean their shoes for school. It was full of a race meeting coming up shortly. Muttie had said he was going to take them to that, so they would get the feel of a real country race meet. He had told them how great it would be, but now there was no mention of it. They supposed he had gone off them, as people so often did.

'I can't understand those children not getting in touch with us. They were all over us at the wedding,' Muttie said.

'Maybe they have no money,' said Lizzie, who didn't know about the fiver he had sent to them.

'They don't need any money to pick up the phone,' said Muttie, who had sent them the very fiver he could well have put on a horse that he had liked the look of but not the sound of. It had won at thirty to one.

Stella O'Brien's daughter came to visit Scarlet Feather. Tall, pale, mid-twenties, discontented, they didn't like her on sight at the premises. Like almost every woman who came into the place, she looked at Tom Feather with admiration and a sly little smile. It did her no good.

'Cathy is mainly dealing with this wedding, perhaps you should talk to her.' Tom got them coffee in the front room, and with some relief left them to it.

This girl Melanie looked full of grievance, and she hadn't begun yet. 'I hope you know my mother isn't made of money.'

'Nor are any of us, Miss O'Brien, but we did go over the costs very carefully, and she and her fiancé seemed very satisfied.'

'It's not the cost of what you're providing that's wrong,' Melanie said.

'So what is upsetting you then?'

'The numbers. My poor mother thinks that there are fifty people coming to see her marry that little fortune-hunter she met at a poker party . . . She's off her head and throwing good money after bad.'

'Well, she did say that there was a certain fluidity about the numbers; we've taken that into account.'

'Fluidity my foot, there's twenty-eight invited from our side, and I can tell you that a good twenty of them won't be there, only eight at the very most . . . I don't know how many he's fielding, but from what I hear his lot don't want it either.'

Cathy felt a great urge to stand up, lean over the table and slap Melanie O'Brien so hard across the face and so often that she would fall to the floor. But she held it back.

'Dear me! Mr Clery's family object, too?'

'That's what I heard.'

'Why don't you go and see them?' Cathy suggested.

'I don't want to go near them, have anything to do with them.'

'No, I was thinking of your mother's money. Well, if *his* family isn't going to come and yours isn't, then you're quite right not to let her put up that much outlay.' It was a heavy risk, but Cathy decided it was worth it.

'I don't even know where they live,' Melanie grumbled.

'I could give you Mr Clery's address and phone number from the files. I think one of his daughters lives with him, so you could find them that way.'

'That's very helpful of you, Miss . . .'

'Scarlet . . . Cathy Scarlet.' She had about another forty seconds of good temper left.

'It's just, I don't see why you want to do this.'

'I liked your mother, I wouldn't want her to pay out a lot of money for people who were not going to turn up, this way you'll be able to get me the exact numbers and we can run it past Mrs O'Brien again.' She had written down Sean Clery's address as she was talking, and then she ushered Melanie out of the door. Cathy came back into the kitchen.

'Give me something to punch quickly,' she shouted.

June found the clean laundry bag that had just come back. Cathy sank her fists over and over in the tea towels, tablecloths and napkins. 'That's much better,' she said at last.

'What was that about?' Tom asked.

'I was just rearranging Melanie O'Brien's face without having to go to jail for it,' Cathy said, pleased.

'And dare we ask what you actually said to her out there?' Tom asked.

'I took a risk, Tom, and if it doesn't work I promise that I'll take all the blame.'

'Could you give us a vague clue . . . just what area the risk was taken in?' He was laughing at her; he wasn't seriously worried.

But then he didn't know what she had done. 'You're better off not knowing,' Cathy said.

Joe Feather took out the backgammon set. 'Come on, Dad, I'm one up, so get your revenge.'

'It's a silly game, that one,' Maura Feather said. 'I don't know why you play it. It's just like ludo for children.'

'No, it's not, you have to be able to guess and second-guess and gamble. You'd be good at it, Mam.'

'I would not.'

'Come on here, and you play against Dad. I'll sit beside you and see how you fare.'

Grumbling, she sat down and got into the game. Joe's mind drifted away. It wasn't nearly as bad as he had thought it would be, helping out with the old folk at home. He had begun this regular visiting to help Tom, take some of the burden off him, and had continued it out of guilt over Marcella. But oddly, he didn't mind it at all these days. The time there didn't hang so heavy on his hands, and he wasn't being interrogated about his lifestyle. Which actually was fairly monastic these days, until he got all that money back from the guy who had conned him. He would do it one of these days. Joe Feather knew that he was not going to let that smart guy get away with it. Just as he knew there was no great news on the modelling scene from across the water. Someone had met Marcella, who was very anxious to come home.

Melanie arranged to meet Sheila, who was Sean Clery's youngest daughter. They were about the same age. They agreed that the marriage was ridiculous and gross, and had come about out of sheer loneliness.

'Why else would she have gone to that poker club?' Melanie asked.

'I thought it was a whist drive, but it's all the same,' said Sheila.

'Suppose we told them that we'd be around more, make them less lonely. Do you think that would work?' Melanie asked.

'Do you know, I think it's too late for that,' said Sheila.

'So will you go or will you not?' Melanie was looking to get the numbers.

'I don't know, honestly. I'm not sure. I'm not saying a word against your mother; I'm sure she's a perfectly nice person, it's just that my father is great, and I don't want to see him doing anything foolish.'

'So you might go, is that what you're telling me?'

'Well, if he's going ahead, and it would make him happy to see us there, then we might well go – not with a good grace, but we'd go. What about you?'

'I'm not going, and again, nothing against your father personally, but my mother doesn't *need* to marry again.'

'And your brother?' Sheila asked.

'A real mammy's boy, he'd do anything to get a pat on the head.'

'So he *is* going, you think?'

'Probably,' Melanie said unwillingly.

'Well, if her side are going, then to be honest we wouldn't really want Dad to be standing there by himself,' Sheila said.

'So you will come to this wedding, then?'

'I think rather than hurt him I would.'

Melanie looked glum. 'And of course if you go, then others will, like your aunts and uncles and everything.'

'Sorry, Melanie, but you did ask, and I don't think we're going to stop them getting married,' Sheila said.

Cathy went to The Beeches.

'There was nothing about this constant visiting in the agreement,' Kenneth Mitchell said.

'I came to visit my cousins, is that a crime?'

'They're not your cousins.'

'No, but they *are* my husband's cousins, which is more or less the same thing.'

'Entirely different,' Kenneth Mitchell barked.

'Suit yourself,' Cathy said. 'But I would like to see them.'

'You've missed them, I'm afraid.'

'Oh, really, where are they?'

'I have no idea,' he said.

Cathy's eyes narrowed. 'Now we really *are* talking about the agreement. You're meant to know where they are at all times.'

'All right. They've gone to see their mother in hospital.'

'*What*? She's back in hospital?'

'Only momentarily. She's coming home tomorrow. They were just bringing her some clean clothes.' Cathy got out her mobile phone.

'What are you doing?'

'What you should have done, notifying Sara.'

'You're totally overreacting.'

'Where's the hospital?'

'It's none of your business,' Kenneth blustered.

'I wasn't going to go over there and torture the woman. I wanted to pick up the children, that's all.'

'You needn't do that, I hear them coming in,' he said sulkily.

Cathy thought their greeting was a little cool. 'I'm sorry your mother isn't well,' she said.

'We didn't tell her,' Simon said, looking guiltily at his father.

'Not a word,' Maud confirmed.

'But you were *meant* to tell Sara or me when things change here, you're meant to be grown-up enough to understand the agreement.'

They hung their heads.

'If the children made no complaint, then they were perfectly happy with the way things were,' Kenneth said smugly.

'I still have to let Sara know. That was the *deal*, Kenneth,' she said.

'Interfering, meddling . . .'

The twins couldn't bear to hear this, so they went out to the garden. Cathy followed them. They sat on a little bench beside the garden shed.

'You see, it gets worse if we tell,' Simon said.

'And better if we don't really,' Maud added.

'Why haven't you been to see Muttie and his wife Lizzie?' Cathy smiled to herself as she used the same form of words as the twins always did. They looked at her guiltily. Eventually she got it out of them; they just didn't have the fare.

'Dad told me that he sent you a fiver. Why didn't you use that?'

'A fiver?' said Maud.

'We didn't get it,' Simon said.

They looked at each other. It was so much money for anyone to send them. Cathy knew without a shadow of a doubt that they spoke the truth. They had never got that fiver. She reached into her handbag. 'He wanted you to have it, it must have got lost.' They looked at her innocently. They were still at the age when they believed things got lost in the post.

'Aren't they such total clowns?' Neil said that night.

'Who this time?'

It could have been anybody. The government, the insurance company, the law library, the judiciary, the newspapers.

'The eejits up at The Beeches. Dad told me that Walter's nicked the computer from his office and hidden it there, and Sara tells me the twins have been getting nothing to eat and no pocket money, and that Kay's back in the funny farm.'

'Not quite as bad as that, it was a check-up. They think she's coming home tomorrow.'

'Still.' He was annoyed.

She badly wanted to remind him that it was he who had fought for these hopeless people to get their children back. It was Neil Mitchell who had said that they must be restored to their flesh and blood instead of living happily between St Jarlath's Crescent and Waterview, where everyone could keep an eye on them. But it wasn't something to go to war over. So she left it. However, she did tell him about Muttie's missing fiver.

'I suppose that fool Walter can actually feel money through envelopes. I imagine he took it,' Neil said casually.

She felt a sense of rage against Walter rise in her. Muttie's money taken by that young brat. Admittedly it wasn't money that Muttie had in any sense gone out and worked for, but Lizzie had earned that money house-cleaning. And that it should go to line a Mitchell's pocket. She actually felt herself give a gasp of indignation.

'Do you feel all right?' Neil asked.

'Sorry, it's nothing.'

'You went back to work too early.'

'I didn't. I like it there, it's very busy, it takes my mind off things.'

'And talking about things . . .' he began.

She must not let him annoy her now. He meant so well, but everything was driving her mad. He might ask diffidently if she felt ready to think about love-making again, and she most certainly did not. He might go on about her work and it being too tiring and that would drive her wild – only at work could she keep her emotions under control. Neil could say any of a dozen things which would upset her, none of them intentionally.

It never used to be like this in the old days.

'I must tell you about this wedding we're doing,' she interrupted. She didn't want any more Meaning of Life. Whatever he said would be wrong. Neil shrugged. Cathy went into the tale about Stella and Sean, but he wasn't listening at all. There was a polite, attentive expression on his face. But he had opted out of the story.

'So what do you think I should do?' she asked him suddenly. It was mean. But she had to know that he really wasn't listening.

'About what, exactly?' he asked.

'About the music,' she smiled. She hadn't mentioned music yet in the story.

'You'll know it when you hear it,' he said. No wonder he was such a good lawyer, so quick on his feet.

'You're right, and I think you're right too about my being tired, Neil, I'm going to bed now.' She lay there, eyes open, for a long time. No one had told her that it would be like this. So empty.

'Cathy's late this morning,' June noted.

'She's gone to look for music for the wedding,' Tom said.

'Isn't she incredible? I wouldn't know where to start.'

'I don't think she does either, she just says that she'll know it when she hears it.'

'It'll be great doing a job all the way down the country. I wish we could stay longer,' June sighed.

'June, you'd die. You're such a Dub you would perish like a rare bird out of its environment if you were to stay in the country.'

'No I wouldn't. Jimmy and I once thought of living right out in the country. Honestly we did.'

'For about three minutes, you did. How is he, anyway?' June's husband was housebound since his fall.

'Like a weasel,' June said easily. 'The sooner I find myself a new one, the better. He doesn't know if I'm there or I'm not, Tom. I said to him the other day that I could go off for a month and he'd just ask me if I'd brought back the sausages when I got home.'

'I'm sure that's not true,' Tom said.

'What would you know, Tom, you didn't marry when you were a schoolkid like we did. We've had no life, either of us, and now Jimmy has a busted back. At least I have a great career.'

Cathy walked down Grafton Street without seeing anyone or anything. She had woken this morning with a heavy feeling of guilt. And yet what had she to be guilty about? The miscarriage wasn't her fault. Of course it wasn't. So why did she feel that she was somehow letting everyone in her life down quite badly? She could put it all right if only she had more time. Like she would insist on Tom taking a couple of days off; he looked very weary sometimes. She would take her mother off in the van for a day's shopping in the markets. She would invite Geraldine to a four-hour lunch at Quentins. She would take the twins and Hooves for a weekend to Holly's; they had never stayed in a hotel, and Holly's had a guest-dog policy. And Neil? What would she do for Neil to make things better? It wasn't as easy as it was for everyone else. Then she heard the music, it was violins and accordions. Six men, a café orchestra playing on the street. They were refugees, they were collecting money. They would look perfect in the conservatory corner of Holly's hotel; they would be great for the party. She talked to Josef, the one with the best English, she explained everything, she wanted waltzes and old love songs.

'We do not have expensive clothes to play at a wedding in a hotel,' he said.

'That's not important. Do you know "A Kiss Is Just A Kiss"?' He said something to the group and they played it. And 'Smoke Gets In Your Eyes', and a Strauss medley.

'Would you have transport to Wicklow?' she asked, hardly daring to hope. It turned out that somebody had a van. 'You'll be perfect,' Cathy said. 'Where can I find you?' They gave her the name of a hostel, she gave them fifty pounds as a deposit.

'How do you know we may not take your money, pack our violins into their cases and go away before the wedding party?' Josef asked. 'Keep your fifty pounds.'

'No, how do you know that I'm not a madwoman and there's no wedding and no engagement at all? You must keep your fifty pounds.' She hugged herself and softly sang some of the songs they had played as she went down the street.

Shona called out to her, 'Hey, you're talking to yourself. That's a good sign.'

'Worse, I'm singing to myself. Better lock me up.'

Two days before the wedding, Melanie rang Cathy.

'My mother tells me you've booked a band, an entire band ... Is she paying for this?'

'She and Sean agreed that the group sounded exactly what they wanted.'

'She went to a refugee hostel to listen to some deadbeats playing . . . And you're charging her to let those people into—'

'Melanie, excuse me, there's someone at the door, back in a second.' Cathy got up and walked three times round the premises, then went over to Tom.

'Sorry, Tom, I'm going to blow this, there are some people I can't talk to. It's Melanie saying that the orchestra is far too dear . . . Can you talk to her?'

'*No, no, no,* Cathy.'

'Yes, Tom, I beg you. She needs your dripping sensuality down the phone. Just say something sexy, she'll be putty in your hands like they all are.'

'I hate you, Cathy Scarlet.'

'And I hate you a lot of the time, Tom Feather, but for the good of the company I put up with a lot of—'

'What did you tell her. . . ?'

'That I had to answer the door.'

He picked up the receiver. 'Melanie O'Brien, how *are* you?' he said. 'Cathy got tied up with someone at the door. Tell me what I can do for you, but before you tell me something, tell me you'll keep me a dance on Wednesday night?'

Cathy watched Tom make a gesture as if he were stroking a cat.

'Piss artist,' Cathy said to June.

'But desperately good at it,' June said shrewdly. 'She's not bellyaching about the cost of the bloody orchestra *now*, is she?'

On the Tuesday Maud telephoned Cathy.

'Excuse me, I don't want to delay you,' she began.

'Good girl, Maud, I am quite busy,' Cathy said.

'It's just that you know you said we should be grown-up.'

'And you are being grown-up by saying we mustn't delay, so what can I do for you, Maud?'

'You don't want any treasure polishing, you say?'

'No, not at the moment, thank you.'

'But Cathy, when you gave us that fiver from Muttie, we went up to Muttie and his wife Lizzie, and they told us that some of your treasures were stolen . . .'

'Yes, but don't worry about that.'

'No, it's just I remember how much you liked the silver thing you called a punchbowl.'

'Yes, Maud?'

'Are they very dear?'

'I don't know, Maud, honestly, and if there isn't anything else . . .'

'It's just I saw one in our garden shed. It's usually locked, but I went in today and I thought maybe it might be nice for you instead of yours, and I could ask Father—'

'Don't ask anything for the moment, Maud, I beg you, we're up to our tonsils here and we'll get back to you.'

'You said that before, Cathy, and you never came back at all.'

'Jesus, Maud, don't nag, please, please don't nag, if you *knew* the kind of day we're having here.'

'Sorry.'

'And after we've done this wedding tomorrow, I really *will* come and see you. Promise. Okay?'

'Who was that?' Tom asked.

'Maud. I wasn't as patient as I might have been, but she was going on and on about some punchbowl.'

'What?'

'She says there's one hidden in their garden shed up at The Beeches.'

Suddenly they looked at each other.

'Oh, my God.' Cathy put her hand over her mouth.

'Walter,' said Tom.

It was a day when everything seemed to take twice the length it should have. They just didn't have the five minutes they needed to talk about the possibility of Walter being responsible.

'I can't believe he did all that damage,' Cathy said.

'You'd understand him nicking things, it's in his nature.'

'Maybe whoever was with him.'

'But how did he get *in*?' Tom worried

And that was it. They had to concentrate on the news from the fishmonger's that the catch had been bad last night and the fish they had ordered just hadn't turned up. So the platter that would have looked so well as a starter had to be rethought. Tom had forgotten to ask the butcher to cut and cube the meat, that meant another half-hour with knives. Cathy had arranged the wedding cake, but the confectioner didn't deliver to Wicklow. Yes, they delivered, they had snapped on the telephone, but to Dublin, not the wrong side of the moon. Con had a toothache and needed to go to the dentist. June said her husband Jimmy was behaving like a madman and insisting she be home by midnight, could Tom or Cathy ring him and tell him how far Wicklow was and how unpredictable the time a wedding ended. Lucy said she had had a row with her parents, who had asked were they paying university fees for her in order that she become a waitress. There had been a very firm demand that she spend more time at her lectures and less time working for Scarlet Feather. People who never rang them decided to call today. Joe Feather had rung to know would Tom come round tonight and help him beat the daylights out of the guy who had taken all his merchandise. Lizzie rang to say the photographs from Marian's wedding had arrived and they were beautiful. Did they want her to bring them into the premises? James Byrne rang about a final demand for a bill they thought they had paid, and they had to look up the records. Neil wanted to know which night could they invite this guy from Brussels to dinner. Cathy wondered would they maybe eat out, she didn't say since she was cooking all day it might be a treat. She hadn't time to tell him about Walter and the punchbowl.

Tom went ahead to Holly's with the others, and on the way dropped Cathy at the church. She wore a hat borrowed from Geraldine to honour the day, and a spray of flowers on her lapel. It didn't look promising, the gathering. Two very separate groups standing heads close together outside the church, each darting glances over at the other from time to time. Cathy went to the group that did not have Melanie O'Brien in. This was the family of Sean Clery on his big day, whispering and heads shaking. She introduced herself cheerfully and held a few names in her head, then she more or less backed over to the other group and made some introductions. Both sides were resisting it, but there was little they could do when this woman in the hat was more or less forcing them to shake hands. Then Sean arrived. There were no hugs from his family. Just a shrugging acknowledgement of his great beaming smile as he hurried into the church. Cathy felt an urge to kick them all. Then Stella arrived; she looked lovely in a blue and silver dress and jacket. She wore a little blue hat and huge silver earrings. Cathy felt a lump in her throat at the sight of this generous woman who wanted to spend her savings entertaining friends and family. Cathy looked over at the sour Melanie, who had barely bothered to wash her face or change her cardigan for the celebration, and she swore to herself that she would do everything in her power to make this day a great one, a memorable one for Stella and Sean.

Tom had everything under control when they got to Holly's. Trays of champagne greeted the guests as they came in.

'What was it like at the church?' Tom hissed.

'A bit grim. Is the orchestra here?'

'Yeah, they're a bit way-out-looking.'

'You haven't heard them play,' she pleaded.

'No, well, nobody might, go and talk to them, will you? I keep hitting on the ones that can't speak English.'

'Racist, how much of their language do you speak?'

'I don't know, what *is* their language?' Tom said with spirit.

'No idea, I'll go and talk to Josef,' she said cheerfully.

'And Cathy?'

'What is it now?'

'Take off your hat, put on your pinny, you're meant to be working here,' he laughed.

Josef understood weddings: in another life he had worked in a hotel, he said.

'Do you know what I mean when I say this one needs quite a lot of attention?' she asked.

'Like that music will be needed to replace conversation at the beginning?' Josef suggested.

'Let's hope and pray that it's only needed at the beginning,' said Cathy.

Because of the uncertainty as to who would or would not attend, they had arranged a buffet with open seating. All Sean's side sat at one end, all Stella's at the other. Lucy and Con poured the wine as liberally as they could, but reported a lot of hands placed firmly over glasses. They had even heard one of Sean's daughters saying she wouldn't give the other side the satisfaction of letting them see her drunk. The food went down well, they got some grudging compliments and plenty of requests for second helpings, The mazurkas and polkas and whatever else Josef's people were playing did indeed disguise the fact that this was not the most relaxed and happy of gatherings. Stella and Sean were so happy that everyone had come after all, they didn't seem to take in the degree of resentment around them. They were simple enough to believe that everyone had turned up today to wish them well. Lucy reported from the ladies' room that some of them were saying they'd try to escape before the speeches. So Tom nudged them towards the cake, and Josef's troupe gave a fanfare of anticipation. And Sean cleared his throat.

'When my wife Helen died, and when Stella's husband Michael died, we both thought our lives were over. And then we got a second chance. It's not going to be the same. Nobody can replace Helen and Michael, and no one is trying to, but we want to thank you for coming out with us this day to celebrate the happiness we had in the past and the happiness we hope is waiting for us in the future. This day would be nothing to Stella and myself if Helen and Michael's children and relations and friends didn't come to wish us well, so can I ask you to drink one toast to friendship and the future, and then to join us on the dance floor.'

They staggered to their feet and muttered the words. Josef struck up with a slow waltz, and turned round to beckon with flamboyant gestures that the group should dance. Sean led Stella onto the floor. It was a time when people should have applauded and looked at each other with warm smiles. But nobody joined them on the floor. Stella tried to encourage people.

'Don't beg them, don't beg them,' Cathy pleaded. She didn't realise she had spoken aloud.

'Take off your pinny,' Tom ordered.

He was ripping off the Scarlet Feather sweatshirt he wore over his ordinary white shirt. Then he dragged her out onto the dance floor. Josef and his friends had been playing something which might have been 'Tennessee Waltz', and now had turned into something that might have been 'Sailing Along On Moonlight Bay'. Cathy had never danced with Tom before. She had forgotten how very big he was; her head was way beneath his shoulder. When she danced with Neil they were the same size. Tom smelled of soap.

'I'm afraid to look, is anyone dancing?' she muttered into his chest.

'Con has Lucy out there, but I think it's time to change partners.' He released her suddenly and walked purposefully towards Melanie O'Brien. 'Now Melanie . . . you *promised*,' he called to her.

Melanie stood up and accepted his hand. Cathy had pulled a red-faced friend of Sean's from his group, June had joined in and got Stella's son on his feet, Con and Lucy had split up and asked other people. It was done with such authority that nobody could refuse. It happened very gradually, but it happened. They had got them on the dance floor. Tom danced with the bride. Stella smiled up at him.

'I'll simply never be able to thank you,' she said. 'Better than any son and daughter could have been. *My* wish is that you two will be blessed with your children in the future.' She looked over to where Cathy was dancing animatedly with the red-faced man. Like so many people, she assumed that Tom and Cathy were a couple.

'Cathy's married to a lawyer, and I'm, well, I'm still looking,' Tom said.

'I hope you find someone wonderful,' she said.

'I hope I'm as happy as you and Sean . . . Whenever I *do* get married, I'll think of this day, but I'm going to give you back to him now and go back to work.'

He passed round the cake, topped up the glasses and noticed that there actually *was* some conversation going on as well as dancing. It could never be voted the Party of the Year but the terrible freeze, the chilling silence when the bride and groom had danced alone was gone. He heaved a sigh of relief. If people started to go now it wouldn't be embarrassing. But of course, perversely, nobody now had a notion of leaving. They felt that they had to increase the sum they were giving Josef and his orchestra, since they were now an hour over the time agreed. They did their usual discreet clearing up, removing paper napkins, extra cutlery and coffee cups but without exactly wresting the glasses from people's hands. And soon the guests began to drift home. Tom decided to move the van nearer to the kitchen door of the hotel. It wouldn't start. Not a sound from the engine. They tried jump leads, without success. There wasn't a garage for miles. He moved quickly; Josef and his orchestra would drive June home.

'All my birthdays at once, I get to go home with the band,' June said, overjoyed.

Con could give Lucy a lift on the back of his motorbike, which she liked as an idea too. Miss Holly was hovering in the background supervising the departure, clucking with admiration at the spotless kitchen, thanking them for the gifts of food covered with cling film and neatly stacked in the hotel refrigerator. He made sure that the bride and groom knew nothing of what was happening. They sat down in the kitchen to have a badly needed glass of wine.

'You two are an example to the whole catering trade,' Miss Holly said approvingly. 'And if ever there's a chance of another wedding, I'd really be most anxious to do it, I can't tell you how—'

'Hold the praise, Miss Holly,' Tom said. 'We can't get the van to start, we have to stay the night here. I'm terribly sorry, it's never happened before . . .'

'Don't worry, you're in the right place, there are plenty of rooms free. Just take the keys from the rack in the hall.'

It was a feature of Holly's hotel, that old-fashioned key rack with the big tassels in different colours.

'Will you join us in a nightcap, Miss Holly?'

'No, I'm overexcited already by all this, I must go to bed. Stay as long as you like; you need to unwind,' she said, and went to her own quarters.

*

Tom and Cathy relaxed in the kitchen of Holly's. They talked on and opened another bottle. They could really expand once they had a place like this to do weddings; they must get Ricky to photograph it before the leaves had all left the trees. They talked about giving cookery classes on Wednesday afternoons back at the premises, about freezer packs for sale at the premises or even through stores. Tom would ring Haywards early tomorrow morning to get his emergency breads released from the freezer. How wise he had been to set up the system. 'I must ring Neil now,' Cathy took out her mobile. Tom made a move to give her some privacy, but she waved him back to sit down. It was only the answering machine.

'Neil, you'll never believe it but the van broke down, so I'm going to stay the night here at Holly's. I don't know what time we'll get it on the road tomorrow, but I'll give you a ring in the morning. Hope you're all right, *you're* out late but I expect the meeting went on a bit. The wedding down here went fine, by the way. I love you. Bye.'

'You're very independent, both of you.' Tom admired the way they could lead separate lives.

'It works, it usually works, but at the moment it's a bit up and down. He thinks I should go on a holiday with him.'

'Well go,' Tom said.

'I most certainly will not. What have we just been discussing? This is our very busiest time upcoming. I want *you* to take a couple of days off soon, but I'd be very pissed off if you decided to go off on a real holiday somewhere just now.'

'All right, I won't,' he grinned.

'We'll have one more glass of wine, Tom.'

'Sure, and a hangover, but why not.'

'Let's take it upstairs,' Cathy said.

They took one of the tasselled keys, and giggling like schoolchildren they went to open the bedroom door. Cathy picked one of the beds, kicked off her shoes and lay down, looking at him.

'We really should have a notebook to write all these things down. We won't remember anything tomorrow.'

'Write what down?' Tom sat on the other bed and poured the wine. 'Don't spill it, Cathy, you're very drunk.'

'Unlike you, who are stone-cold sober. Write down the ideas, the Wednesday cookery classes, the freezer-fillers, whatever.'

She put the glass down beside her and went straight to sleep. Just like a two-year-old would, or a puppy dog. One minute she was awake and talking about notebooks, the next she was fast asleep. Tom covered her with an eiderdown. He considered going down and getting a second key and finding another room. But they were talking about four hours, really. He lay down on the other bed and was asleep a few minutes later.

Walter Mitchell couldn't sleep. Those *stupid* twins had actually telephoned Cathy Scarlet and told her that half her stolen stuff was still in his garden shed. He couldn't believe it. Maud had been rooting around when he discovered her. Some cock and bull story that Cathy was going to call round after a wedding today and see them, and she wanted to see if there was anything else useful in the shed. Poor Cathy and Tom had this terrible burglary where vandals had got in and . . .

'I told you *never* to go into my shed, you promised me you wouldn't, but you are such liars, no wonder no one wants you.'

'People do want us,' Simon said.

'Name one.'

'Muttie does and his wife, that's two,' Simon said.

'They don't want you anywhere near them,' Walter said.

'They do, Cathy said that. He even sent us a five-pound note for bus fares, but it never got here.' Maud was stung. 'And Muttie is taking us to the races for our birthday.'

'And did you tell Cathy that you were rooting in *my* shed?'

'I told her that there was a punchbowl there like one of her treasures.'

Walter went white. 'And what did she say, tell me, you little halfwit, before I have to beat it out of you.'

Maud was terrified. 'She didn't say anything, Walter, she only said she was busy but she'd come round after the wedding.'

'Go to your bedrooms at once,' he ordered.

'What are you going to do?' Maud asked.

'I'm leaving this house. I can't bear the sight of you, either of you, liars, messers, meddlers. No wonder nobody wants you anywhere near them.'

'But—'

They didn't wait. They peered out and saw him packing a suitcase in his bedroom, and then he went out to the garden. Out of the window they saw him filling black sacks full of things from the shed, then a taxi came and he stacked all the bags in it. He really was going. Father rang and said he had met old Barty, and wouldn't be home until very late tonight or possibly in the early morning, so not to send out a full-scale alert for him.

'You will be coming home tomorrow?' Simon asked.

'You really are the most tiresome child I ever met in my whole life,' Kenneth Mitchell said, and hung up.

'Walter's right,' Simon said. 'Nobody does want us. Nobody at all.'

Next morning Kenneth Mitchell came home at dawn from old Barty's club, where he had dozed in an armchair for a few hours and felt much revived. He found a note on the kitchen table. 'We are leaving home. Goodbye, Maud and Simon.'

He called his brother Jock. Jock was not well pleased to be woken at seven o'clock in the morning.

'Talk to Neil and Cathy, they'll know,' he said, and hung up.

Neil listened with no pleasure to the confused story.

'Shouldn't you ring Sara?' he suggested.

'I thought I'd talk to the family first,' Kenneth said.

'Okay, I'll contact Cathy for you. Doesn't Walter know anything?'

'He doesn't appear to be here either,' said Kenneth Mitchell.

Betty was on duty at Holly's hotel. She was full of praise for the way those young people had left the place, and treats in the fridge as well. The phone rang and she went to answer it. Very early for Holly's hotel. It was that nice young Neil Mitchell, looking for his wife. Apparently the van had broken down and she had stayed the night.

'I couldn't understand why that big van was still here. Hold on a moment, Mr Mitchell, she must be in Room Nine. I'll put you through.'

Neil waited, and then the phone was answered.

'Hallo,' the voice said. It was Tom Feather.

'Hallo?' Neil said again, puzzled. 'Is that Room Nine?'

'Yes, it is. Who's that?' Tom had a headache, he had woken an hour later than he intended to, he had to find a car mechanic, mend the van and get back to Dublin. Who was this ringing him and annoying him?

'I was looking for Cathy,' the voice said.

It was Neil. Tom was awake immediately. 'My God, Neil, what bloody bad luck we had last night, the van was dead as a dodo . . .' As he spoke, he began to shake Cathy into wakefulness in the next bed.

'Yes, I know, Cathy left a message. Where is she, by the way? I asked for her room.'

'Oh, she's down sorting out the van. I just came up here to her room to get her mobile for her, I think she was going to ring you on it.'

'I tried that first. She has it turned off.'

'No, I think the battery's dead, anyway, will I tell her to ring you on a real phone, a hotel phone I mean?' He was playing for time. Cathy had by now sat up, straightened herself and realised where she was.

'No, there's a bit of a crisis here. Will I hang on, or can you transfer me back down to the desk?'

'*No*,' Tom shouted. 'No, Neil, hang on, I see her coming up the stairs. Cathy, Cathy,' he shouted loudly. 'I found your phone here in your room, but the battery's down, but Neil is here on the hotel phone, come and speak to him.'

Cathy had understood much more quickly than he had thought she would. 'Sorry, Neil, I'm out of breath running up the stairs. Everything okay?'

He told her. 'Neil, I'm in the heart of the country with no transport, can't you ring Sara?'

'What about your parents?'

'They'd have phoned someone if the kids had turned up at St Jarlath's Crescent, but ring them anyway, please, Neil.'

'And of course no sign of Walter, the one time you'd need him.'

'*Neil*! Neil, I hadn't time to tell you. I think Walter was one of the vandals who broke into the premises. Something Maud saw in the shed, you must check the shed, they might be hiding things there. Listen, I'll charge this phone up and ring you later to know is there any news.' She hung up. They looked at each other.

'Quick thinking,' she said to him.

'Quickly taken up,' he praised her back.

'It wasn't really necessary, you know, we could have said what happened. Neil would have understood.'

'I know, but this way was easier,' he said.

'You're right. Less explaining. God, I feel terrible,' Cathy said, and went into the bathroom. 'And I look worse,' she screamed when she saw her reflection in the mirror.

'What's happened to the children?' Tom asked.

'They've run away. Of all the days out of the three hundred and sixty-five, they chose today.'

But the day was only beginning. When they had tidied up and splashed enough water to make themselves a bit respectable, they opened the door of the bedroom. Betty was in the corridor, bringing a breakfast tray to the newly-weds in Room Twelve. She paused to look at them. Betty, who had seen Cathy in the hotel just over a month ago telling her husband that she was pregnant, was utterly shocked. Miss Holly also seemed a lot less cordial today. She must have been informed.

It was an endless morning of negotiating with garages. The fault was identified, the part was found. She phoned Neil at the law library.

'Nothing at all, Sara's really worried. Can you call her? She wants to talk about Walter, apparently.'

'Do Mam and Dad know?' Cathy asked.

'They have the whole of St Jarlath's Crescent out with sticks beating bushes by the canal.'

'Not really?'

'No, but nearly. Are you all right, Cathy? You sound very ropy.'

'I have too much to do.'

'We choose our lives, Cathy. I've offered you a holiday.'

'We've been through that . . .'

'No, we've been through one poorly thought-out—'

'Neil, I'll ring you later,' she said.

They got back to Dublin in the early afternoon, in no humour to hear of June's fun with the orchestra, nor of Lucy's argument with her parents about her coming home on a motorbike with a man. They had no time for James Byrne about the final demand, Hannah Mitchell wittering on about a letter from Canada, or Peter Murphy who wanted to have a cocktail party to annoy Geraldine. They didn't want to hear where Freddie Flynn had bought villas nowadays, nor to discuss a Hallowe'en extravaganza with Shay and Molly Hayes. But they had to do all those things because that was what work was about. When the day was finally drawing to a close, two phones shrilled. Cathy looked at Tom with big, tired eyes.

'Why do I feel these are things we don't want to hear?' she asked him, and picked up the one nearest to her.

'Don't hang up on me, Cathy, it's Marcella, please try to get Tom to talk to me, *please.*'

Tom answered a call from Sara, saying it was all in the hands of the guards now and Maud and Simon were assumed to have spent one night sleeping rough and were heading into a second. Everyone was very worried indeed.

October

Simon and Maud discussed telephoning Muttie and his wife Lizzie. If they really *had* sent a five-pound note that went astray, then they might not be as hostile as everyone else. They got Lizzie on the phone; she was cagey about Muttie's whereabouts, he had gone away for a day or two. This was puzzling. Muttie never went away anywhere. And what about the birthday treat?

'He's not refusing to talk to us or anything?' Maud asked.

'Child, aren't you the most extraordinary little thing, why would he do that?' Lizzie said. It sounded reassuring, but it wasn't a yes or a no.

Simon thanked her for the five-pound note. 'It was very kind of you, it's made a lot of difference,' he said.

Lizzie said they must be thinking of the wrong people; she and Muttie had sent no fiver. They explained how it had got lost in the post, and how Cathy had taken one from her handbag.

'Ah, there must have been some mistake.'

'I'm sorry, Lizzie,' Simon said politely. '*Do* you know when Muttie will be back?'

She sounded guarded. 'Hard to say, a day or two I think.'

'She's lying,' Maud said afterwards.

'Muttie never goes anywhere . . .'

'Except the races.'

Muttie Scarlet had spent a night in hospital . . . an embarrassing matter of his private parts being examined by young doctors and unmentionable things being put into them. He wanted it neither discussed nor known. Lizzie was under strict instructions to say that he was away on business. He came home to find all hell had broken loose. The twins had disappeared. Sara, their social worker, was going mad and interrogating Lizzie. Poor Lizzie was going over every word of the conversation.

'I didn't know they were contemplating anything like this . . . How was I meant to be inspired? They always said they were fine, I thought they were tired of coming here . . . They didn't sound upset at all, they were full of old rubbish, thanking me for a fiver that we never sent them.'

It had been an endless day, with people going back over things, fruitlessly examining the note left in the kennel: 'We have taken Hooves with us.' It seemed somehow a very bleak little letter, giving no information, not even a hint of where they were heading. A search of possible places led nowhere:

friends at school could reveal nothing. Kenneth had pulled himself together sharply and revealed with every sentence he spoke how little he knew of the life that went on at The Beeches. There seemed to be no trace of Walter. He had not shown up at work, so it was quite possible that the twins were with him. Kay, now frightened into sobriety by the amount of activity in the house, said no, that Walter had left earlier, in a taxi with a lot of black bags. But since she was not considered a reliable witness, nobody took much notice of this memory. By the time the guards had been called and Maud and Simon were officially declared missing, Muttie had alerted many of his associates who said they would help to search for the children, who must have been in the neighbourhood of St Jarlath's Crescent at any time after ten p.m. when Lizzie went to bed. Neighbours who knew the children were drafted in. Every time the phone rang, everyone in St Jarlath's Crescent jumped. This time it was Cathy – she was on her way over to them. Muttie relaxed for the first time that day. Cathy would get it sorted.

'I have to go over there,' Cathy said.
'Go straight away, take the van.'
'Could you ring Marcella?' she said, too casually.
'What?' He sounded shocked.
'I've written down her number here, she's waiting by the phone.'
'Thanks, but I'll pass on that.'
'She was crying, Tom, I said I'd do my best.'
'And you have.' He was cold.
'I can't leave her standing in a phone box waiting for you to ring,' Cathy begged.
'Thanks, Cathy, take the keys and stop worrying. They'll turn up, those two, with some amazing explanation.'
'In the middle of a street in London, Tom, she deserves more than that.'
He turned away. Cathy dialled the number.
'Tom!' The excitement in Marcella's voice was almost hurtful to hear.
'No, Marcella, I'm sorry, it's Cathy again. I told him, and he's not going to phone you. No, I don't know why, but I didn't want you standing there waiting.'
There was a silence. 'Why won't he even talk?' Marcella sobbed.
'I'm so very sorry,' Cathy said, and she hung up and left the premises without even catching Tom's eye.

'It's all my fault, I was so short with poor little Maud,' Cathy wept at the kitchen table. 'I kept saying things like Hurry up, and If that's all, Maud . . .' Everyone was startled. This wasn't the Cathy they knew. Lizzie, Geraldine, Muttie and Sara all looked at each other helplessly. 'And the awful thing is that she was being so kind, she was trying to get me a punchbowl from the shed and she didn't even realise that it was stolen by her little shit of a brother.'
'Simon?' Muttie asked, totally bewildered.
'No, Walter, he has a shed full of things from our premises, I gather.'

Sara looked up sharply. 'You think Walter was your burglar?'

'Yes, he must have been. Maybe this has something to do with the children running away,' she said anxiously.

'Have you reported any of this?'

'No, I only heard yesterday or the day before, and I've been up to my tonsils in a wedding in the country.'

Sara seemed to think this was odd. 'But if you thought that, surely you'd have told Neil?'

Cathy took no notice of her disapproving tone. 'Did you say that Walter has gone from The Beeches?'

'Yes, his mother thinks he went last night in a taxi . . . carrying a lot of bags,' Sara said somewhat doubtfully.

Then suddenly Sara and Cathy looked at each other as the implication became clear. Sara took out her mobile phone and called the guards again.

At The Beeches, Kenneth and Kay waited for the guards to arrive. There was no news, but the guards needed to look in the garden shed and in Mr Walter Mitchell's bedroom. They said that Ms Cathy Scarlet would be joining them shortly.

'What does she want?' Kenneth asked.

'She is the daughter of the couple whose house the twins visited last night to collect their dog.'

'They don't *have* a dog,' Kay said.

'They think they do, madam, and Ms Scarlet is also married to your nephew, so could be considered family. I believe her husband is also joining her here.'

'Huh,' Kenneth said.

'Mr Neil Mitchell is a barrister, sir; if you have any objection to our looking though the house, please state it now.'

'And what would you do if I objected?' Kenneth asked.

'We'd get a search warrant,' the young guard said simply.

'I'm not saying he *did* steal the things, I'm only saying it's a pretty odd coincidence,' Cathy said to Neil as they drove to The Beeches.

'We must be very careful not to go in hurling accusations,' Neil warned. 'Dad did tell me that he nicked a computer from work *and* didn't turn up today, so it looks as if you're right, but . . .'

'And your drinky aunt thinks she heard him leaving with a lot of black plastic bags in a taxi last night . . .'

'I know. And if he took them, Cathy, no mercy, you understand?'

'No, I don't believe you, in the end you'll say he was a victim, he deserves our concern.'

'What have I done, hon? Why are you fighting with *me*?' Neil asked, aggrieved.

'I don't know, Neil, I really don't. I want to kill Walter and I want to kill myself. If I had only been just a bit nicer, those two foolish children wouldn't have run away.'

'You're working too hard. You just didn't have the time,' he said.

'No, Neil, I just didn't *make* the time, that's different.'

'But I have a surprise for you. I wasn't going to tell you before, but I think you need it now.'

'A surprise?' she looked at him warily.

'You *are* very tired, hon. I talked to Tom about it; he can spare you, he says, and I've booked us a week in Morocco!'

He waited to see her pleasure, but he was disappointed. 'Neil, it's kind of you, but no.'

'It's booked!' he said.

'I can't think of anything now except those children, and I don't really want to go away at all, we're too busy.'

'Tom said . . .'

'Tom is a kind man, he says what he thinks people want him to say. Most of the time,' she added, thinking of Marcella weeping down the phone. 'Can we talk about it another time, Neil?'

'Whenever you feel you'd like to give the time,' he said huffily.

'Well, not *now*, when we're worried sick about the kids.'

'Not any time, Cathy. There's no time to talk to you these days, and no way of talking to you, either.'

'I don't know what you mean.'

His face was very hard.

'If I talk about the miscarriage, I'm saying the wrong thing and upsetting you. If I don't talk about it I'm hard and unfeeling and I've forgotten it.'

'It's not like that.'

'Well, that's the way it looks from here. And when I do something, get us away from here for a bit of peace . . .'

'It's not peace trekking through Morocco seeing would I like Africa . . .'

'Oh, *shut up*, Cathy, there's no pleasing you. If I suggested a holiday on the Isle of Man you wouldn't want it either.' His face was set in a look she hadn't known before. He was very, very angry.

She spoke slowly. 'I would be perfectly happy to go on holiday but only if we discuss it, not when you *tell* me you've booked something . . .'

'Don't worry, a holiday with you is the last thing on my mind,' he said and they drove to The Beeches in silence.

The punchbowl was gone when the guards searched the shed, but there were a lot of other things that they asked Cathy to look at. At first she thought that she could see nothing that belonged to them. Then she saw some salad servers and a linen tablecloth.

'The salad servers were a present from Neil's parents last Christmas, the cloth has our laundry mark on it,' she said in a small, flat voice.

Neil nodded gravely. The guards seemed entirely convinced. It would nail Walter when they found him.

Neil's father made a statement to the guards about the missing computer. 'And I want you to know that nephew or no nephew, we intend to go the distance on this one.'

They nodded, satisfied. 'Do you have any explanation of why he might have taken the children, sir?' The guards had long decided that there was little future in talking to the children's parents. They had higher hopes of Jock Mitchell, who seemed normal and articulate and capable of understanding that two nine-year-olds had left a note and vanished from their home.

'I can't understand it at all,' Jock Mitchell said. 'He never mentioned them at all, and if I ever asked about them he was vague, as if he really didn't know anything.'

'He didn't know they were there,' Cathy said. 'He never took them with him, I know that much for a fact. He high-tailed it out of here on his own because he thought we were onto him.'

'But it's too much of a coincidence that they should all go on the same day,' Neil argued.

'Neil, you never listened to him. I swear they didn't figure in his life, he didn't kidnap them or take them as hostages or anything.'

'I say,' Kenneth said disapprovingly, as if this kind of chat was going too far. They all looked at him, waiting to know what he was going to say. But he said nothing. 'Sorry,' he said eventually.

'They could still get in touch,' said Jock hopefully.

'But who would they ring?' Cathy asked. 'That's the thing that's breaking my heart, they rang everyone, and none of us listened.'

'They could be anywhere,' Muttie wailed.

'They're only nine, people will look at two kids and a dog and question them. And they're so distinctive, the guards will find them in no time,' Geraldine soothed them as best she could.

'No, the guards haven't a clue where they are, they keep asking us to think of likely places and known companions, and none of us knows anything about their lives, poor little devils. Why couldn't they have left them here with us instead of transplanting them to The Beeches?'

'They had to go,' Lizzie said because she believed it.

'And didn't they do really fine there,' Muttie scoffed. 'They did so fine that they ended up having to run away, come here by dead of night and take Hooves and head off the Lord knows where.'

'Do you remember them at Marian's wedding, they were so proud of themselves,' Lizzie said.

'And their speeches,' said Muttie, blowing his nose heavily.

'Oh, they're not *dead* for God's sake!' Geraldine said. 'Really and truly Lizzie, get a hold of yourself, those two are well able to look after themselves.'

'No, they're not, they're real babies,' Lizzie said.

'Wherever they are now, they're terrified,' said Muttie.

Tom was restless. He could settle to nothing. The idea of Marcella on a London street crying in a phone box wouldn't go away. He had been right not to speak to her; there were no more words to be said, only a circular argument going nowhere. But he wished that she hadn't called, she must have been desperate, particularly to admit it and plead with Cathy. Marcella was always so anxious to preserve an image of herself as confident. If he had answered the phone himself, would it have been different? Perhaps he could have said in his own normal voice that it hurt him too much to talk about what could not be changed. Then she might not have been left crying in a phone box. He could concentrate on nothing because of that image. He decided to go and see his parents. JT and Maura Feather were sitting at the kitchen table playing three-handed bridge with Joe. Joe looked as if a wall had fallen on him, his left eye was closed, his lip was swollen and part of his head had been shaved where he had stitches.

'Jesus!' said Tom.

'Wasn't it dreadful?' Maura Feather said. 'Poor Joe reversed into a wall, and it was the direct intervention of God that he didn't do himself any serious damage.'

Tom looked at the injuries which were obviously not the result of reversing into a wall.

'Was it the right wall?' he asked.

'Yes, it was,' Joe nodded painfully.

'And what happens now?' Tom asked.

'Bills are going to be paid,' Joe said with satisfaction.

'At some cost, though?' Tom looked at his brother's injuries sympathetically.

'No cost at all, considering,' Joe said.

And Tom realised that Joe the businessman had suffered much more by being cheated than he had in a fist fight. His street cred was now restored, and to Joe that meant the injuries were irrelevant. His father frowned as if the conversation should change channels. So Tom told them that the twins had run away, and nobody knew where to start looking for them.

'Those two would be well able to speak up for themselves, aren't they Mitchells when all's said and done,' Maura sniffed.

'I'm worried about them, Mam, they're very odd, quaint kind of children, they take everything literally, anything could happen to them.'

'And tell me, is Marcella still on her holiday in London?' Maura asked.

'It's not a holiday, Mam, I told you that she's got contacts there and she wants to be a model, so she has to be in London for that.'

'And is it going well for her over there?' JT Feather asked kindly.

'I think so, Dad, I hear she's doing fine.'

'That's funny,' Joe said, 'I hear the very opposite.'

'No word?' Tom asked.

Cathy shook her head. 'No, and that's two nights out on their own somewhere; it's serious, and they all think that Walter has something to do with it, which is utter nonsense.'

'They'd only slow him down,' Tom agreed.

'It's some damn thing that they took literally, you know, like they thought that I was coming to see them on the night of the wedding, apparently I said, "after the wedding", I didn't mean that very day.'

'Would Muttie have said anything to upset them?'

'No; he was so embarrassed about having to go to hospital with his prostate, he hasn't said anything to anyone for days.'

They went through all the things it could be; some dancing engagement they thought they had got, some school project – a quest to find another punchbowl? Those two were so strange, they could have flown to Chicago. They jointed chickens and made sauces as they talked about the children. They never got around to mentioning the hunt for the man who had stolen their belongings and vandalised their premises. Or indeed, the confusion of spending a night, however innocently, in the same room. And just because that night wasn't mentioned, it seemed to take on a greater significance. The fact that Tom had lied to Neil on the phone. The knowledge that it had been seen and completely misconstrued by the hotel. It could easily have been one of the many things they laughed about, but because of the children they lost the moment, and now it was too late to go back to it.

Walter's friend Derek with the sports car wouldn't let him stay. 'You're too much trouble, Walter, and now you say the law is after you, I can't afford to have any policemen poking round this flat.' There was a fair chance they might find cocaine if they did, and black sacks of goods from the shed at The Beeches.

'Can I leave the stuff?'

'No, you can't ... Take it up to the market,' Derek advised. 'You can unload it there in no time.'

'For peanuts.'

'Well, take the peanuts then and put them on a horse, *then* you're in the clear,' said Derek, who wanted Walter Mitchell miles from here.

Sara was tireless in her efforts to find them; she reread her notes over and over in case they might offer a clue. She came round to Waterview to ask Neil and Cathy what kind of interests the twins had.

'Well, they loved that dog, which is why they went and took him,' Cathy said.

'When they were here, what did they do in the evening?'

'We used to make them do homework for a bit, and they liked jigsaws ... I don't know what else, Neil, do you?'

'Not really, they kept asking questions all the time ... How much do you earn, how often do you mate.'

'Sara, nobody could have murdered them or anything?' Cathy's face was very anxious.

'She's very overwrought,' Neil said. 'Honestly, Cathy, you can't go on like this.'

'No, of course not,' said Sara, but her voice was shaky.

Cathy's eyes filled up and, unexpectedly, she leaned over and patted Sara on the arm.

'They'll be fine, they're a real pair of survivors, those two,' she said, consoling the white-faced social worker.

'Well, you'll be glad of the holiday,' Sara said.

'Holiday?'

Neil interrupted quite quickly. 'That's postponed now,' he said.

Cathy was annoyed. He should *not* have told Sara all about the holiday as if it were settled before he had checked it with her. It wasn't important now, but it was very, very irritating all the same.

Geraldine couldn't settle down to work, thinking about the twins. There were two important jobs on hand, *and* her upcoming date with Nick Ryan. But the strange, troubled, pale faces of those children wouldn't go out of her mind. They had been so funny in her flat on the day of the recovery party, doing their encore because they thought people would expect it. She had kept cheering the others up, and mocking them for fearing the worst. But in her heart she was very worried. Two odd, unworldly children, and you heard the most awful things. Every day in the papers there was some horror. Geraldine shook herself firmly. She had a rule to stop herself brooding about things. When you can, you must concentrate feverishly on work, and if that doesn't work, concentrate feverishly on sex and social life. Geraldine and Nick Ryan were planning an evening which was going to involve his staying over at Glenstar. Both of them knew this, though neither of them had mentioned it. It was an elaborate ritual about the difficulty of finding somewhere they would like for a late dinner after the theatre. There were endless problems. Places to park, driving after a couple of glasses of wine, noisy people at other tables when you were trying to talk. Possibly they could bring some smoked salmon back to Geraldine's apartment. Indeed, what a good idea, and she had some of Tom Feather's wonderful bread in the freezer. And Nick would love to bring a bottle of wine. And did Nick have to leave at any specific time after the meal? Not at all, the night was his own, her own, their own. It was set up. The affair had begun.

Muttie went in just from sheer habit to Sandy Keane in the betting shop. 'Don't feel like having a bet today, my mind's distracted,' he said.

'Suit yourself, Muttie, but that was a nice little windfall you got yesterday,' Sandy said dourly.

'Yesterday, I didn't have a bet yesterday, I was preoccupied,' said Muttie.

'Internet Dream,' said Sandy.

'Never heard of it,' Muttie shrugged.

'Well, you won seventy pounds on it yesterday morning, which is good for a horse you never heard of,' Sandy said.

'Is one of us losing our minds, I wasn't near here yesterday.'

'I know, Muttie, they told me.'

'Who told you?'

'The twins,' said Sandy.

'Oh, my God, what time?'

'First race at Wincanton,' Sandy said.

'Can I have your phone? I must ring the guards.'

'You're going to bring the guards in here and tell them that I took a bet from minors? You're off your head, Muttie.'

'They won't be interested in that.'

'They won't like hell!'

'No, Sandy.' Muttie had begun to dial. 'You don't understand. The guards are out looking everywhere for these children. They've been missing for two days.'

It didn't in fact bring them very much further down the line. So the children had hung around the St Jarlath's Crescent area for the night with the dog, until the bookie's was open for bets.

'I feel a bit better that they had seventy pounds rather than just a fiver,' said Cathy.

'But it does mean they can stay away longer, like now they won't have to come home out of desperation,' Muttie said, biting his lip.

The hunt centred much more around St Jarlath's Crescent than The Beeches. This is where the children had been happiest, where they had collected Hooves and written their last note. Lizzie looked through the pictures she had of Maud and Simon. The guards had asked for a recent picture, which they would use if there was no news by tomorrow. They had obviously given up on the notion of getting anything helpful from Kenneth and Kay. Lizzie took out a big box; there were some lovely ones of them from Marian's wedding. But maybe they should use the one of the twins with Hooves. She must not let herself think that anything had happened to them. This was Ireland, not some dangerous place; nothing bad could happen to them here.

'I mean, nobody would *hurt* children, or anything?' she asked the guard fearfully as she showed him an endearing picture of Maud and Simon in their kilts outside the church at the wedding.

The guard looked at the two serious little faces and cleared his throat. He hated cases about children. 'We have to hope not, Mrs Scarlet.'

She had seen in his face the possibility that it might not end well, and the tears came down her face again. 'You see, you'd really have to know them to realise that they're such an odd little pair, not in the real world at all. They just get notions and follow them anywhere.'

'And would they trust strangers, do you think?' The big guard gave Lizzie a paper handkerchief.

'Of course they would, they'd go off with Jack the Ripper if he came to the door with a plan.' She put her head down on the table and wept aloud.

Muttie came and patted her shoulder awkwardly. 'If we could just think what mad thought was going through their little minds the moment they took off, then we'd find them in no time,' he said, shaking his head again and again.

All over Dublin people were trying to think what might have been going through their minds. To little avail. Maud and Simon, left so long surviving in a strange, troubled and changing lifestyle, had invented a little world of their own where no one could follow them.

'You know it will all be so obvious when we find them,' Cathy said to Neil.

'*If* we find them,' he said.

'Come on, you don't mean it. Why say something so frightening?'

'I'm only saying what the guards are saying, they don't like it at all,' he said.

The twins had no idea of the drama they had created. To them it had been utterly simple. Muttie had promised to take them to the races for their birthday. To hear the real thunder of hooves. *That's* where he had gone, to the country, to the races, and his wife Lizzie didn't want to admit it. And so they made their plans. They would go to the races and confront Muttie. Ask him straight out what they had done to annoy him. They had five pounds and eighty-three pence. It was a lot of money, but would it take them the hundred miles to County Kilkenny? They stayed up all night discussing it. There was nobody to object. Father was out with old Barty, Mother didn't get up these days at all and Walter had left home. They packed a plastic carrier bag each to take with them, extra shoes, a big sweater, pyjamas, a pot of jam, a loaf of bread and two slices of ham. There was an animated discussion about soap. Simon thought there might be soap already wherever they were going; Maud said that since they were going to be sleeping in sheds and barns and in fields it might be mad to think there'd be any soap in those places. They took a small piece, just in case. Then shortly after dawn when the first bus passed the end of the road the twins ate into their savings and made their way to St Jarlath's Crescent. They weren't leaving without Hooves. Five pounds wouldn't take them to Kilkenny.

'What do people do when they need money desperately?' Maud wondered.

'They earn some or they steal, or they win the Lotto.'

'The Lotto isn't until Saturday,' Maud said.

'There's Muttie's office,' said Simon.

After that it had all been simple. They studied the paper for a long time before they went in, and they wrote out a slip of paper. Mr Keane knew them well.

'How's tricks?' he said, as he always did.

They told him tricks were great and placed the bet. Two pounds to win on a horse called Internet Dream.

'I break every rule in the book for the pair of you,' said Mr Keane. 'I let minors into my establishment and a small four-footed beast as well.'

'Muttie asked us to put it on for him.'

'Where's the man himself, he wasn't in yesterday either.'

They had planned for this one, too. They couldn't say he had gone to Gowran Park race meeting in Kilkenny, otherwise he should be putting on his own bets there.

'He has a whole lot of tiring things to do for his wife Lizzie today, so he asked us to put the bet on for him,' Simon said.

Sandy Keane nodded; this seemed entirely reasonable.

'And may we wait here to bring his winnings back to him?' Maud asked politely.

'Would you mind waiting outside, you're too young to be seen in here, strictly speaking.'

'It's cold outside, Mr Keane.'

'All right, but sit somewhere out of sight.'

They sat as quiet as mice until the race. Internet Dream won at thirty-five to one and they had their fare to Kilkenny. Hooves loved the train journey; he socialised with some of the other passengers by laying his head in their laps, and they seemed delighted with him.

'What will we do if he wants to pee?' Maud whispered.

'What do other people do with dogs on trains?' Simon whispered.

They looked around them. Nobody else had a dog.

'Maybe he'll know you can't go on a train,' Maud said optimistically. Hooves saw a nice leather briefcase and was about to relieve himself against it. Simon and Maud jumped up horrified and alerted the owner of the briefcase, who was reading a newspaper.

'Could you take it away? He thinks it's a lamp-post.'

'Easy mistake, often made,' the man said.

'Where should I take him? I can't hold him out the window,' Simon asked.

'Just out there where the two carriages sort of join, and look away as if you have nothing to do with it,' the man advised.

They came back and sat down to talk to him since he was so pleasant, and told him that they were going to the races.

'Aren't you a bit young to be going on your own?' he said.

'We'll be meeting a grown-up there, of course,' Simon said.

'Is that your dad?'

'Yes,' said Simon.

'No,' said Maud at the same time.

'Sort of stepfather, foster father really.'

'And does he have any tips for today?'

'No, but he'll have been studying form all morning,' Maud explained.

'Great. The important thing is to feel lucky.'

'We've been quite lucky already today, we had Internet Dream,' Simon said proudly.

The man looked at him with more interest. 'You had? What odds?'

'Thirty-five to one,' Maud said.

'Well, maybe I should stick with the pair of you. How did you pick Internet Dream, anyway?'

'The name,' said Simon, as if it were self-evident.

'And who put the bet on for you?'

'We did it ourselves.'

'By God, I'll certainly stay with you, you could be the making of me,' said the man, who said his name was Jim, known to his friends as Unlucky Jim, and he'd be taking a taxi to the races if they'd like a lift.

'Thank you very much, Unlucky,' Maud said. 'But you know, all this business about not going in cars with strangers . . .'

'And we think there's going to be a bus to the racecourse anyway,' Simon said.

'Perhaps Unlucky could come on the bus with us?' Maud didn't want to let him go, they might need him to help them find Muttie.

'I don't think his name is Unlucky, I think it's Jim,' Simon whispered.

'Which is it?' Maud wanted a ruling.

'I think for a day at the races it had better be Jim,' the man said, bewildered.

Unlucky Jim came on the bus with them to the races. 'Where are you meeting your father?' he asked.

'Father?' Maud said alarmed.

'Muttie,' Simon hissed.

'Oh, just round and about, he'll be looking out for us.'

They realised that they must lose Unlucky Jim now. He was asking questions that were hard to answer.

'I think we'll take Hooves for a bit of a stroll before we go in,' Maud said.

'In case he tries to pee on someone else's briefcase,' Simon said.

'Have you the price of getting in?' Jim asked.

'Of course we do, we have a fortune,' Maud explained.

'You've been very good company. I wonder, would you let me buy you a drink after the third race, the bar beside the Tote? Your father too, if you've made contact.'

'We will, of course,' said Simon, as if at the age of nine he were used to travelling down the east coast of Ireland in a train and being invited to have a drink in the bar near the Tote.

Simon and Maud searched everywhere for Muttie, but with no success. They went in and out of bars, they stood near the winning post for one of the races, they went to the parade ring. If Muttie were here, then surely this is where he'd be. After the third race they went to meet Unlucky Jim.

'Did you have any winners?' they asked.

'What do you think? I'm here depending on you both.'

'We haven't studied form yet,' Maud said.

'And what about your da, did he come up with anything?'

'Not really,' Simon said.

They decided they would pretend they had met Muttie; people hated it if they thought you were on your own and lost or something. Better let people think they were being looked after.

'Where is he now?'

'He said he might drop in.'

'What do you fancy in the next one?' Jim asked.

'We're not experts, Jim,' Maud admitted.

'Well, you couldn't do worse than I've done.'

They looked at the race card carefully. 'Lucky Child,' said Maud.

Jim peered at it for a while. 'It hasn't much going for it.'

'Look at the weight, and it didn't do badly last time out.' Muttie had taught them to read the vital signs.

'You're right, I'll put fifty each way on it,' said Unlucky Jim.

Maud and Simon went down and willed Lucky Child forward. It was a near thing, but he won.

'Thank God,' said Maud devoutly.

'It's very easy really, isn't it? I wonder why Father and old Barty and people who have money troubles don't do this all the time,' Simon said.

'I think they *do* do it all the time, which is why they have money troubles,' Maud said.

'You may be right.'

'Still, it's a pity we didn't put ten pounds on Lucky Child ourselves, look at what we'd have won.'

'But if it hadn't won we'd be in desperate trouble,' said Simon, who still had no plans on where they would stay for the night.

Unlucky Jim searched the place to give the twins a share of the biggest win he'd ever had. They were such quirky little things, dragging that dog round with them, so serious about everything and carrying stuffed plastic bags with them. He'd like to meet up with them again, and not only to mark his race card. Tipsters who could land Internet Dream and Lucky Child in one day were very few on the ground. Then he realised that he didn't even know their names.

'A lot of people don't come the first day, they come the second day,' Simon said wisely.

'Did Muttie *say* which day he had planned to take us?' Maud was tired, and a little worried about the night ahead.

'No, but if he's not here today he'll be here tomorrow.'

'So what do you think, should we try to sleep here in the racecourse, it would save us having to pay to get in again?'

'No, they must go round looking otherwise everyone would stay the three days,' Simon said.

So they got a bus back to Kilkenny. They walked and walked to find a suitable place, and then just by pushing a door they found it. It was a big shed with some broken agricultural machinery, tractors and things in it.

'It's like someone's boxroom,' Maud whispered.

It was ideal for them; there would be no problem with Hooves, and there was even a car seat ripped from some vehicle that they could sleep on. They gave Hooves one slice of ham, shared the other and had bread and jam. Tomorrow they'd find Muttie, no problem.

They slept very well because they were so tired, and woke only at the sound of Hooves barking. They had tied him to the door since he might well have found his way back to St Jarlath's Crescent. Maud looked around her. They had been sleeping in a shed full of broken machinery. She had hardly any clean clothes, they had stale bread and over half a jar of jam. They had to go out and find Muttie today.

Simon woke and rubbed his eyes. 'It's nearly ten o'clock,' he said.

'Do we have enough money for a breakfast?'

'You mean, go into a place and pay for it at a table?' Simon was horrified.

'We could have bacon and egg,' Maud said.

Simon was counting the money, they'd have to be very careful, he said, there was the bus to pay for, the entrance again, and then of course if they didn't find Muttie, the train fare home.

'But we're not *going* home, are we?' Maud asked.

Simon agreed this was so, and that under the circumstances they should go out and look for breakfast. Somewhere that would let Hooves in. They felt a great deal better after breakfast. They tidied themselves up as best they could and set off for the races again.

Unlucky Jim said to himself that he had never won so much money before as he had on Lucky Child. Perhaps there was a message here for him. Like quit when you're winning. Jim had never lived by this philosophy. He wondered should he try to do so now? But then he had never met two such odd children. Travelling on their own to the races, rescuing his briefcase, near-psychic powers about forecasting winners. There was something about that story of going to meet a father or a foster father that didn't sound right. Jim rang his wife and said he was coming home from the races.

'It's only day two,' she said in disbelief.

He alarmed her still further by suggesting that they go out for a meal somewhere posh tonight. She spent most of the day wondering what he could have done to make him feel so guilty.

The racecourse was becoming familiar to them now. They wondered if they would meet Unlucky Jim again. They realised and were almost ready to admit that they didn't really know *what* kind of a place they'd find Muttie in. Where would he be studying form? Would it be in a bar, or talking to the bookies? Up to now they had only seen him at work in what he called his office, Mr Keane's betting shop.

Maud sat down. 'I'm tired of looking,' she said.

'You can't be tired, you had an expensive breakfast,' Simon said.

'Suppose he's not here,' Maud said.

Now it was out in the open. Now it had been said and could never be taken back. Simon got such a shock that he let the lead go, and Hooves took off at a great rate through the crowds. The children were aghast. Hooves was a dog that could be allowed off a lead in a field or a park or on the beach, but never where there were crowds of people. He would do terrible damage out of sheer fright and a sense of unfamiliar freedom. They could hear him barking as he pushed his way through the crowds. They pushed their way after him . . . People had staggered back as Hooves had come at them, bewildered and hysterically barking his head off. They saw him break for some space. The horses had left the parade ring and were lining up.

'Please, Hooves, please don't go on the racecourse, help, help, he'll be killed,' Maud cried, and fell over flat on her face, getting two very badly grazed knees and a cut forehead. But she picked herself up and ran on.

Simon was nearer. 'Please stop the dog,' he shouted.

From every side they were getting looks and indeed shouts of annoyance, no place to bring a dog, the horses might get frightened and rear up . . . who let those children in here anyway with their damn dog? Hooves had decided against the actual racetrack and swerved to a reasonably empty area where there were some cars and horseboxes . . . He looked around him, his eyes wild, and then ran straight under the wheels of a jeep that was reversing. The driver couldn't possibly have stopped in time. But the twins saw it all as if it were in slow motion. The way that Hooves was thrown right up in the air and then fell to the ground. He was very still when they got there.

Muttie was having a pint with some of his associates, and opinion was divided about Sandy Keane; should he have taken the children's bet? How could he have refused it? Might he not have thought something was amiss? Where *was* Muttie, anyway, for the last couple of days? That's what they'd all like to know. Muttie was vague about his overnight stay in hospital, and glossed over it easily. They couldn't live for ever on seventy pounds, they'd have to come out sooner or later. They could hardly go round all the betting shops in Dublin putting two quid on outsiders, or to a race meeting.

'Oh, my God,' said Muttie. 'I told them I'd take them to Gowran Park for their birthday. They could have gone there.'

Walter was going up to the bookmaker with the pittance he had got in the marketplace. He saw some disturbance in the distance, but didn't investigate what it was. The odds on Bright Brass Neck weren't good enough, he'd move around, get something better further down the course. Always stupid to put it on at the first place, and he had really good hopes of this one. He'd walk away today with a lot of the debt paid, not all, but a fair whack. And all the other things could then be sorted out. Walter was good at explaining.

Maud had fainted when she saw the accident, and a crowd had gathered. The children were taken into the offices. They were told that the dog was being looked after.

'Is he dead?' asked the boy with the tear-stained face.

'What's your name?' they asked him.

'Hooves,' said Simon.

They were bewildered, but they could get no more from Simon: he was too shocked to talk. Maud's cuts had been cleaned, she had been given hot sweet tea but she wouldn't stop shaking. Eventually they had managed to get the children's first names and an announcement was made.

'We have two children here at the information office in a state of considerable distress. Can the adults accompanying Maud and Simon please present themselves? They are particularly anxious to meet a Mister Muttie.

The information office, please, as soon as you can. The children are very upset.'

Walter had gone down a line of bookies, there were better odds now on Bright Brass Neck than there were at the start. He had been wise to know they would lengthen. Then he heard the announcement. He couldn't believe it; those two devil children had followed him here. But they couldn't have. He had hitched in three stages. So what *were* they doing here? Then, beside him, he heard someone say that must be the same children who were in the accident with the dog and the jeep. Could he wait for a few minutes and go to the information office when he had placed his bet? There was the usual last-minute crowd around the bookies' stands, and the announcement was made again with a greater sense of urgency. Walter went to the information office.

Everything happened then at the same time. The guards in Kilkenny had heard from Dublin that there was a good chance of the missing children turning up at the race meeting. The race committee and its security staff, which were beginning to despair of ever discovering who these children were, were relieved at this news, which cast them all in the role of heroes. One of the many vets at the races said that Hooves would live. He would be lame and might have to have one paw amputated, but he would definitely live. The young woman who had been driving the jeep was comforted with so many brandies that she eventually couldn't drive at all and had to be taken home. Maud and Simon, already overjoyed with the good news about Hooves, could hardly believe it when Walter came to rescue them. Their faces lit up with delight because they knew now that they had been forgiven for all the awful things they had done: they hugged him tightly, and for the first time in his life he actually felt cheap and shabby.

'Are you Mr Muttie by any chance, sir?' one of the guards asked Walter.

Walter looked sadly at the guard's uniform.

'That's Walter, he's our brother,' said Maud proudly.

'He came to find us,' Simon said, pleased.

'There is a call for Simon and Maud, Mr Scarlet is on the line.'

'Muttie!' they cried in delight.

And outside, where the races still went on, the tannoy announced that Bright Brass Neck had won at eleven to one.

Muttie was being considered the hero of the hour, but he thought of himself as the villain. Of course he had told those children he'd take them. It was all his fault from start to finish. But he wasn't allowed to take the blame. Cathy insisted it was all *her* fault, she just hadn't realised how dependent they were on people, she should have let them into the vandalised premises, she should have given them a precise date when she was visiting them after the wedding rather than letting them sit there waiting, disappointed. How mean to break a promise to kids who had so little. And to forget their birthday was unforgivable. Neil said a lot of it was down to him, he had believed his father's brother and he really *had* thought

the principle of blood being best was right. Sara said they were all mad, she
had just lost the plot on this one, she had been too involved in the
campaign for the homeless to see what was straight in front of her, the fact
that Simon and Maud, who were her direct responsibility, had no home to
speak of. Kenneth Mitchell said little. He had been told that his elder son
was most probably guilty of a serious crime, of vandalism and theft. And
that the relations intended to prosecute. Kay said even less than her
husband did, she had been drinking vodka all day from a bottle which she
claimed to be mineral water. Soon somebody would find out. But it didn't
really matter because quite obviously Kenneth would be going on his travels
again. And this time it might all be over and The Beeches would be sold.

Geraldine brought Nick Ryan back to her flat for the little supper, which
would be much more convenient than going to a restaurant, mainly because
it would let them start their affair nice and easily. She sat down while Nick
opened the bottle of wine.

'You're a very restful person,' he said.

Geraldine thought about it. That's probably what she was, restful. Not
making demands, not whining. Never seen in a dirty pinafore, or over a
sink of dirty dishes. A woman who had time to listen, a woman who,
because she wouldn't see him again for three or four days, had time to rest
and go to the gym and restock the fridge and the bar. Not someone who
had to bring up his children, entertain his boring work contacts, keep his
house the way *he* liked it.

'Restful, that's a nice compliment,' she said, 'but will you excuse me until
I see if there's any news of the children?' There was a message waiting. They
had been found, safe and well. Lizzie and Muttie had been driven down to
Kilkenny to retrieve them. She closed her eyes with the relief of it all. You
heard such terrible stories, anything could have happened to them. She
came back to join Nick. 'Good news, they're on the way home,' she said,
and then talked no more about it. Men didn't like people prattling on
endlessly about people they didn't know. Geraldine knew a lot about men.

Sara drove Muttie and Lizzie down to collect the children.

'And you're sure the Mitchell family won't mind if they stay the night
with us?' Lizzie asked fearfully. 'The agreement, and everything.'

'No, Mrs Scarlet, they'd be very pleased. All of them.'

'It's just, we don't want to make any trouble,' Lizzie said.

'And we're so sorry,' Muttie added.

'But no, there's nothing for *you* to be sorry about, and it all ended well,'
she reassured him.

'Except for Hooves,' Muttie said.

'They're very pleased he's not dead,' Sara said.

'I know,' said Muttie.

'Simon has a theory that if we got him a roller skate for his bad foot, he'd
be as good as new.'

'You love them, don't you?' Sara said suddenly.

'Ah, well, doesn't everyone love children, all of ours went off to Chicago apart from Cathy so we've nobody here, it was great to have children around the place again.'

'You must have been very upset after Cathy's news, then,' Sara said.

'What do you mean?' Muttie asked.

'If you love children so much.'

'What news?' Lizzie said.

With a feeling of lead in the bottom of her stomach, Sara realised that they didn't know about the miscarriage. Neil had told her it was low-key; she hadn't realised just how low.

'I thought it was Cathy who gave you the news that Maud and Simon were found,' she said helplessly.

'No, Muttie was there when the guards phoned,' Lizzie said.

'And why would we be upset? We were overjoyed.' Muttie was confused.

Sara bit her lip and told herself that she must be the worst social worker in the western hemisphere, as she drove on through the twilight to collect her charges.

'Cathy?' The call was late. Cathy was reading in the kitchen, Neil was working at his big table.

'Yes, who's that?'

'It's Walter.'

'Oh,' she said. The story that she heard had not been entirely clear, but it did appear that Walter had on this occasion managed to behave normally and had gone to the help of his little brother and sister.

'I'm still down here, they sort of thought I should wait until Maud and Simon were collected.'

'Good.' She was crisp.

'It's just, I was wondering, who is collecting them, you know...'

'My mother, father and their social worker.'

'And will there also be ... do you think?'

'Yes, I think there will...'

'I see,' he said. There was a silence between them. Then he spoke again. 'It's too late, I suppose, to ask you to—'

'Much too late, Walter, it's all in hand, your parents have been informed.'

'I see,' he said again.

'Would you like to talk to Neil, or will I just say goodbye, then?' she asked.

There was a pause. 'Goodbye then, Cathy,' Walter Mitchell said.

Tom Feather had been so pleased to hear the good news that he made a cake and delivered it round to St Jarlath's Crescent. He had attached a card with the words 'Happy Birthday and Welcome Home to Maud and Simon and Hooves' on it, and left it with Muttie and Lizzie's neighbours. He was delighted they had been found safe. Such funny little things. He had once said to Marcella that he hoped they'd have children like that one day, real individuals with their own personality through and through. He remembered she had smiled indulgently, as if he was saying that one day he'd fly his own spaceship to Mars. Perhaps Marcella had never intended to have children. He had been sorry to hear Joe's cryptic remark that things were not going well in London for her. He guessed that this must be so after her phone call to Cathy. It was not what he wanted to hear. The only thing that made sense out of all this hurtful, tragic business was if she got what she wanted by doing what she had done. If she hadn't got a modelling career, then what on earth was the point of the whole thing?

Neil had wanted to make love that night, but Cathy said she was too tired.

'Well, now. Tired, is it?' he repeated.

'I *am* too tired actually, I have to get up very early, I'm going to pick up the kids from Mam and Dad's and take them to school, everyone thinks they should go straight back, it would cause the least disruption.'

'Certainly, whatever madam the educationalist thinks,' he said, hurt and annoyed at her rejection.

'Don't be so sneering and bitter,' she said.

'I'm not.'

'You're making fun of me,' she said, 'mocking me.'

'And you're keeping me at arm's length.'

'Goodnight, Neil,' she said.

And it was one of those increasingly frequent nights where they slept as far from each other as possible.

Nick Ryan left Glenstar discreetly half an hour before Geraldine did the next morning. It had been a memorable evening, 'a delightful and important evening,' he said. Geraldine murmured her agreement. Nick Ryan obviously felt slightly uneasy about the situation, and the fact that he would not be free to come back to this welcoming flat that evening.

'I really wish . . .' he began.

Geraldine stopped him. 'Let's not waste any time wishing,' she said as she poured the excellent coffee into beautiful china cups. 'Let's just look forward to another lovely evening, whenever it turns up.'

She knew when he left that he was already besotted with her. For all the good that that would do in the long run. She sighed and went to phone Lizzie. Everything was wonderful in St Jarlath's Crescent. The twins were going to stay there for the time being, Cathy was coming round to drive them to school, the dog's paw didn't need to be amputated, only a splint. And Sara, the nice social worker, who had been kindness itself, said that Muttie and Lizzie should apply to foster the children. She thought that they might have a very good chance of getting them.

Shona Burke rang James. 'Great news, those children have turned up.'

'I *am* pleased to hear that,' he said. 'Where are they now?'

'With Muttie and Lizzie Scarlet.'

'Well, please God that's where they'll stay,' James said, very aware of the issue that hung between them.

Simon and Maud were just ten. They were nearly five years younger than Shona was when the law said she must leave the place where she was happy.

'Please God indeed,' Shona said.

'The world is a saner place nowadays, Shona,' he said. There was a silence. 'Let's hope Muttie Scarlet has a lot more courage than I did,' James said.

'Let's hope he has just as much love as you did,' Shona said gently.

James Byrne felt better than he had done for a long time. A few minutes later, he got a call from Cathy.

'Good news for once.'

'I've just heard about the twins, isn't it wonderful?' he said.

'No, this good news is actually about their brother. The guards are looking for Walter Mitchell, they've retrieved enough items from The Beeches and they know now that he did the break-in.'

'I don't want to add a sour note . . .'

'But?' Cathy said.

'It wasn't technically a break-in, that has been the whole problem with the insurance company.'

'Well, that's what he did,' Cathy said impatiently.

'No, Cathy, look at it from their point of view . . . Your husband's cousin let himself in to your premises with a key. It won't make them think any less that the whole thing was an inside job.'

She thanked him politely and said goodbye. Then she crashed the receiver back and shouted at the phone. 'Thanks for ruining our day,' she yelled in a rage.

'Who did you just slam the phone down on *now*?' Tom asked mildly. She told him.

'Walter's so slippery, he might even *say* that we were in on it all for the insurance money.' She sounded very upset.

'No, he's too stupid, he'd never think that one out for himself,' Tom soothed her.

'But much, much more serious is how *did* he get the keys?'

'He might have seen us doing the ceremony of the keys in the van and crept along to pick them up,' Cathy said.

'I've been over that, we didn't start doing it until Walter was sacked,' Tom said.

'You mean *you* thought they'd still think it an inside job even though we'd found the thief?'

'It's just bad luck his being a cousin,' Tom said.

'I know,' Cathy sighed. 'Oh, I really wonder where cousin Walter is, now this minute?'

Cousin Walter had made three phone calls since all the confusion at the races. There was the one to Cathy; then he phoned his father to say that he was sorry but the heat was on and he might not be home for a while.

'I know, I heard,' his father said gloomily.

'Still, it's good no harm came to the children,' Walter said.

His father was strangely distanced from this. 'They've brought all hell down around our ears over it all, social police, real police walking in and out of The Beeches as if it was their office, and that dreadful girl your cousin married, claiming you robbed her premises and getting people to search your room. And other people asking your mother how much she drinks really and truly.'

'I know, Father.'

'No, don't tell me about innocent, blameless children, they went to a licensed bookmaker and put on a bet at their age, they brought that Muttie's dog to a racecourse, the last place you should bring a dog, they all nearly got killed and somehow it's turned out to be *our* fault. Why they couldn't have stayed here like normal children is beyond me.'

Walter's third call was to Derek, to say that the guards would probably land there anyway, so to make sure there was no substance in the house that shouldn't be.

'Don't mind about that,' Derek said, 'I'm not going to be done for your stolen goods, am I?'

'No, it's all out of there.'

'And what are you doing?'

'I'll stay away for a few weeks until it all dies down. See you then, back in Dublin.'

'Take care of yourself, Walter, you're not the worst,' Derek said a trifle guiltily.

Walter caught the tone and went for a last throw. 'Oh, Derek, in about five hours' time you could report your credit card missing,' he said.

'You never took my credit card?' Derek roared down the phone.

'No, but I know its number and I'm going to book myself a one-way ticket.'

'To where?' Derek asked in a panic.

'Relax, just to London, I'll be out the other side of Heathrow airport in five hours, so that's when you call them and notice it's missing.'

'Walter, that's not fair.'

'Not fair, not fair? Just one measly air ticket? When I'm facing jail? Get real, Derek!'

'Okay, five hours from now I get a new credit card number, and it had better only *be* the air ticket,' said Derek.

Sara seemed very ill at ease when Cathy went to see her.

'You know your parents want to foster the twins?'

'Yes, and I want to know what are the chances of Muttie and Lizzie getting them. Realistically. They just adore them, I don't want them to have to go through all this again.'

'You know we're talking about fostering, not adopting.'

'I know that. Poor people foster, rich people adopt,' Cathy said cynically.

'That's actually not true, and you know it's not, it's because Maud and

Simon's parents are alive and could easily put up a case to have them back, and the law says . . .'

'The law doesn't know its arse from its elbow about things like this,' Cathy said.

'Believe me, I'm with you on this, my work every day is saying what you just said, but not as succinctly.'

'I know you are. You are tireless about things, just like Neil. Did he tell you, by the way, that he will be free after all to go with you to that conference next February? Remember when I was pregnant, he told you that he couldn't?'

'But won't you be gone by then?' Sara asked.

'Gone?'

'By February?' Sara was surprised.

'Gone where?' Cathy asked. Sara made a big production out of looking for her mobile phone. 'Gone where?' Cathy repeated.

'No, I'm mixing it up with someone else who was going away to . . . um . . . to England around then. Take no notice of me, I'm in pieces these days.'

Cathy looked at her thoughtfully. Sara had gone quite pale.

She was very tired from the finicky work they had to do for Peter Murphy, a cocktail reception at his home with top-drawer finger food. The crème de la crème was there, he assured Cathy several times, and that she must tell her aunt. Cathy didn't believe people ever used phrases like that any more.

'He still fancies your aunt, you know!' June said. 'I hope we'll have as many people lusting after us when we turn forty.'

'I know it's not what you want to hear, but your husband is pretty anxious to put a stop to your gallop in the lusting department . . . He was on to Tom this morning to know what kind of a do this was.'

'Don't mind him, he's mad.'

'He loves you,' Cathy said.

June laughed. 'God, he may have once for about twenty minutes when I was sixteen.'

'Don't put yourself down June, he *must* love you. Why else would he care and ring up about you?'

'I don't know, but I wouldn't put any money on it,' said June. 'Are you going straight home yourself when we're through?'

'Yes, tonight it's Tom and Con's turn to unload the van; you and I get home to our fellows.'

'Well you'll be delighted to see your fellow, and he'll be delighted to see you, there's the difference for a start,' June said. 'Be sure and keep a few of these prawn in filo pastry things for him, those will soften his cough.'

'I couldn't bear to look at any more of them, June.'

'But *he* hasn't been looking at them all day like we have,' June said with remorseless logic.

*

'Was it tiring tonight?' Neil asked.

'No, fine, sorry for grizzling about being tired last night.' Cathy was bright and cheerful.

'What are these?'

'I thought you'd like a few special prawns.'

He seemed pleased with them on their little plate. 'They're great, so light ... Did you make them?'

She felt a great urge to say no, they had picked them up in a takeaway, what did he think she *did* for a living? But she smiled and said that she had.

'They're really great.' He didn't ask about the do tonight, he never asked about any do, whether it was Peter Murphy's cocktails, a fashion show, a wedding or a funeral. It was always still Cathy's funny job.

'You met Sara today,' he began. He seemed uneasy.

'I wanted to ask about the twins. Like whether there was a real chance of Dad and Mam fostering them full-time.'

'And what did she say. . . ?'

'Well, she told me that the law might come down heavy because of them being old and working-class, but I told her that was balls and she more or less agreed.'

'But did you talk about anything else?'

'Is this a guessing game, or what?' Cathy asked.

'Okay, straight out, she rang me and said she had put her foot in it.'

'About what?'

'You know, now it's you who's playing guessing games.'

'I *don't* know, tell me.'

'She said that she had let it slip to you that I was still interested in the refugee job.'

'Well of course you are,' she was perplexed. 'I assumed you wouldn't have thought of it so seriously and then suddenly just let it slip out of your mind, I supposed you'd be thinking about it, yes.'

'The thing is, they've put the offer to me again, with different terms.'

'And you're going to take it.'

'Of course I'm not going to take it just like that, but we need to talk about it seriously.'

'Meanwhile you talk to Sara about it seriously.'

'Cathy!'

'I'd love a nice long bath,' she said.

'Please don't be like that.'

'Look, Neil, of course we'll talk about it seriously, but not at this time of night. Now I'm going off to lie there and think about the world, and I'd prefer to do so as your friend than somebody having a silly pointless argument with you.'

'Enjoy your bath, friend,' he surrendered.

Tom Feather invited Shona Burke out to dinner. He meant it as a combination of a work dinner and a thank-you gesture. He took her to a small French place.

'I promise I won't spend the time examining and criticising the food,' he said with an apologetic smile. 'People tell me they see me cutting up things, analysing them and they spot me as a rival from a mile away.'

Shona said that she was exactly the same, she kept looking out for something that would be useful to her at work. And took notes. One man thought she was writing down what he was saying.

'And was he saying anything he didn't want written down?' Tom asked. He had been talking about motorcycles, apparently, and Shona had been writing down the name and address of an efficient air-conditioning system. 'And did you see him again?' Tom wondered.

'No, but I did learn something from the experience – I don't take my notebook on dates any more.'

'Very wise, I'd say. But then, what would I know. I haven't been out on a date myself for so long.'

'Do you miss her a lot?'

'Marcella?' he said, surprised.

'Sorry Tom, it's your business. I don't usually pry into other people's lives.'

He didn't seem offended. 'Well, the answer is yes and no. I miss what I thought we had rather than what we really had. Maybe that's the way it always is when something's over.'

After dinner, Tom took Shona back to Glenstar and refused coffee on the grounds that he had early-morning bread to make and needed his sleep. He drove home to Stoneyfield. As he parked he could see someone sitting on the steps outside in the cold night air. It was Marcella.

November

'Come in, Marcella,' he said wearily.

They walked in silence up the stairs to the flat where they had lived together so happily once. She looked around her as if seeing it for the first time. Neither of them had spoken yet. Tom sat down at one side of the table, which still had the pink velvet cloth on it. And with his hand, made a gesture for her to sit at the other. There had never been any point in offering Marcella food or drink, she had taken none of it, so he didn't start now. He looked at her as he waited for her to speak. She looked very tired, beautiful, of course, with the tiny face and all that dark hair. She wore a black leather jacket and a white sweater, a red scarf tied around her long, graceful neck. She carried only a small leather handbag on a chain; she hadn't brought any luggage with her.

'Thank you for letting me in,' she said.

'Naturally I'd ask you in,' he said.

'But you don't talk to me on the phone?'

'It's late, I'm tired, I have to get up very early to bake bread, you and I don't want to go through it all again, now do we?' He spoke gently, trying to be reasonable rather than showing the hard, hurt side of himself as he must have done before.

'I just want to tell you something and then I'll go.' She sounded very beaten and down. Not pleading or sobbing, but just as if all the life had gone out of her.

'Then tell me,' he said.

There was a silence. 'It's quite hard. Do you think I could have a drink?'

He went to the kitchen and looked around him, confused about what to offer her. 'Anything at all,' she said. He took a can of lager from the fridge, picked up two tumblers and brought her an ashtray as well. She seemed to take ages lighting her cigarette. Eventually she began to speak.

'Paul Newton *does* have a model agency, and I know he does have quite well-known models that go through it. It's well established over there. But it wasn't what was going to work for me. It didn't work at all, not at all, not even from the start.'

She looked so bleak and sad that Tom felt he had to say something. 'Well you *tried* it, that's what you wanted to do.'

'No, I never got a chance to try. He didn't want me for that kind of modelling, not for shows and what I thought . . . Only glamour modelling.

First he sent me to people who did lingerie pictures for catalogues . . . and they wanted what they called glamour shots, which is topless.' There was such shame and sadness in the story, Tom closed his eyes rather than see her face. 'It was terrible, so I said to them there had been a mistake, that I was a real model on Mr Newton's books and they only laughed, saying I could take it or leave it.' There was a silence. 'I left it, of course, and went back to Paul Newton to tell him. I thought that he'd be furious with these people.' She paused to sip the lager that he had never seen her touch before. 'He was very busy that day. I waited ages to see him. I remember all the people coming in and out, all the kind of people I had wanted to meet all my life, stylists and designers and other models. And then after a long time I got in to see him, and I told him and he said . . . he said . . .' She stopped, hardly able to repeat the words. 'He said what else did I expect at my age . . . and I said that he had promised to have me on his books as a model, and he got really impatient and said he *had* done that for God's sake, so what was I complaining about? And do you know what happened then? Joe called him about something and obviously asked after me, and Paul Newton said that not only was I fine but I was right here in the office, finding it all a bit strange in the beginning but getting to know the ropes.' Tom drank his beer in silence; he could sense how hurtful it must have been. 'Anyway, he finished with Joe and he said to me that now I must be a big grown-up girl, act my age and get on with it . . . But I said, "You promised," and then he got really annoyed. "I told you the truth," he said, over and over . . .' Tom looked at her. 'And suddenly it was just like my sitting talking to you, where I told you that I had told you the truth but you said it wasn't the same as being honest, and that there was a difference. I didn't see it until then.'

'Oh, Marcella.'

'Yes, so anyway I had enough money for a month's rent, and then I didn't have any more. I took my portfolio around, and when I showed them the pictures of you and me that we did for Celebrity Couples, people asked what I was doing over there when I could be here. And I had no answer. And then the next month I didn't have the rent, so I did the topless pictures, and oddly enough it wasn't as disgusting as I thought. Everyone was quite professional and got the job done as quickly and as high-quality as possible, they were all quite respectful in an odd sort of way. And the money went through Paul Newton's office. I collected it at the end of each fortnight. I never saw him, except, except for the day . . . the day that I rang you . . .'

'What happened . . . tell me?' Tom asked.

'He was at the reception desk when I was picking up my envelope, and he asked me to come in. He said he was sorry we had parted bad friends, and that I was very good at what I was doing, and now he had something else to offer me. I was pleased because I thought he had a real job for me at last. And first he showed me magazines with me in them topless, I'd never seen the pictures before, and I felt upset when I saw them and then he said I didn't have to do this kind of thing all my life. I waited and he said that if I wanted to I could earn real money, and he showed me other magazines, hard-core porn ones, and I felt so sick when I saw where he thought my future lay.' She stopped again, shaking her head in memory of the shock. 'He said that these people were very detached about their job, and there would be no pawing or anything, that wasn't the way it was done, it was just a day's work for everyone in the end, and I thanked him and said I'd call him the next day and I moved flats and never saw him again.' A long pause. 'And then I came home.'

'And where. . . ?'

'I'm staying at Ricky's for the moment. I clean the place and help him around the studio. I've worked in bars a couple of nights too, and in a sandwich bar at lunchtime. You know that I'd be a real asset nowadays to Scarlet Feather?' The longing in her voice was almost too much to bear.

But he said what had to be said. 'No, believe me, this is not spite, nor sulking, but it's no.'

'I'm not saying we should get back together immediately . . . I'd go on living at Ricky's for a while . . .'

'No.'

'I'll ask you again, it's all I want to do. Be back the way we were. Suppose it were *you* that had made the mistake, and had upset me by stretching too far in some direction. And just suppose you realised it was the most stupid thing and begged me to start again, wouldn't you like me to say something hopeful rather than a cold, blank no?'

'It's not a cold, blank no, believe me it's not. There's nothing I'd like better in many ways than to wipe the past bit from our minds and start again . . .'

'Then why can't we . . . ?'

'It's just not the way things are. It would all be a pretence, an act, like playing at being in love again. Maybe I'm shallow and you're better off without me. I've told you that before.'

'I didn't believe it then, or now.'

'But I don't love you any more. I'll never forget all we had together, and if I do ever love someone else, that will always be special . . .'

'Love me again, don't look for someone new. Love *me* all over again.'

He felt no desire for her, no memory of a love shared in this very flat. He felt nothing but pity. 'It wasn't a great summer for me, and after you left a lot of things went wrong and I was very unhappy,' he began. 'But compared to yours, mine was nothing. I'm more sorry than I can say.'

'You must be pleased that you were right,' she said.

'No, I was right about nothing. I didn't have an idea all this was going to happen to you, I thought you'd be a great success, you were, and are, so beautiful. And truly I hoped you would because you wanted it so much.'

She picked up her handbag. 'I'll always be here, always around, if you change your mind,' she said.

'No you won't, not a treasure like you.' He tried to make her smile. But her face was sad. 'Come on, I'll drive you back to Ricky's,' he said.

'Will we be friends from now on, anyway?' she asked.

'We'll be much more than friends; weren't we together for four years?' he said.

'That's true, and there's so much I want to know.'

But though he wanted to tell her all the adventures and dramas, and about the twins going missing and the guards looking for Walter for the break-in, he felt it wasn't the time for small talk, so they drove though the dark, empty, wet streets in silence.

'If you won't come on a holiday with me, will you come away for a weekend?' Neil asked.

'Sure, that would be nice,' Cathy said.

She didn't really like the sound of a weekend away. It sounded dangerously like a honeymoon and she wasn't ready for that yet. The doctor had said that Normal Married Life would of course resume, it took different people different times. But Cathy thought that in her case it might take a long time. It wouldn't really be fair to go away with Neil unless she felt ready. Then again, it wasn't something she could easily discuss.

If she said to him that she wasn't ready for love-making yet, he would reasonably say that he hadn't suggested it, he was only thinking of a weekend away. And in many ways a weekend would be nice. She would think about places to suggest to him. Not yet. In a few weeks' time.

They had fallen into a disconcerting habit of one being out when the other was in. Breakfast was the only meal they shared, and even at weekends they were both out a lot of the time. Cathy was cooking less at home in Waterview now during the day, since the facilities had much improved back at the premises. In fact, she often spent time there in the evening, and found herself sitting to read and relax in the big comfortable sofa rather than going back home. If Tom noticed, he said nothing; sometimes he was there himself, other times out. Cathy knew that he occasionally took girls out on dates, but rarely anyone a second time. She knew that Marcella was back in town and staying with Ricky; that's all he had told Cathy. June, however, who heard everything, had it that Marcella had totally changed and was doing all kinds of jobs she would have turned her nose up at, and was aching to get back into Scarlet Feather. She had told someone that she would wash dishes all day if she could come back.

'Will he take her back, do you think?' June's eyes were round with interest.

'She never worked here to be taken back,' Cathy said defensively.

'No, stop playing games – you know what I mean.'

'He never, ever talks about it.'

'You surprise me. The pair of you have been through so much together, I thought he'd weep on your shoulder.'

'No, I think there's too much shoulder-weeping in this business as things are.' But she also knew that they needed their space from each other. She had been tempted to tell him how much Neil had upset her over the whole pregnancy thing. But she didn't even want to acknowledge it openly. And anyway, a lot of that hurt seemed less sharp now. She and Neil *did* get on very well on many levels. Only this morning he had said how he wished she were free to come to the big demonstration for the homeless, but he knew she had to work.

'Good luck, Neil,' she said. 'I hope you get a good crowd.'

'You never know, mid-week.' He sounded worried. 'But then, if it does take off it really will focus serious attention on everything.'

He had sounded so concerned, she was glad again that she hadn't decided to tell a whole self-pitying tale about him to Tom. Poor, tired Tom who had promised himself a nice quiet day at the premises when they were all out on this job.

'Oh, June, how are we going to get through this lunch today, this woman's a monster.'

'You say that about them all, and they turn out to be pussy cats.'

'Not this one: we are to use the back entrance to the house, and take the van and park it somewhere so the guests won't see it and be offended by it; we all have to have house shoes, which we put on when we come in the back door, only that way will she know that muck has not been walked in.'

'Oh, well, if it keeps her happy.'

'Wait till she sees your hair, June.'

'What's wrong with it?' June looked in the mirror and patted her head. She had never again been able to afford the outrageous purple streaks that she had got with the Haywards token, and they had grown out, leaving her with a slightly piebald appearance.

'Oh, Mrs Fusspot said that she hoped the staff would be decorous, because some of the guests are embassy wives.'

'Decorous? I wonder,' June made faces at her reflection.

'But if we're really good, then we might well get into a lot of embassies, that's what we must think throughout.'

Tom wasn't coming on this one, there would be Con as barman, June and Cathy to prepare and serve the lunch. He urged them to leave in plenty of time, the lady seemed to think punctuality was highly important.

'Cathy, stop calling her Mrs Fusspot, will you? You'll say it to her face when you're there.'

'No I won't.'

'Do you know where the place is?'

'Yes, I looked it up just now.'

'Have you got your mobile?'

'*Yes* Tom, and let me tell you, *you* are rapidly becoming Mr Fusspot, perhaps the two of you are well met.'

He laughed and patted the van. 'Good luck,' he called after them.

The phone never stopped ringing.

'Hi Tom, Neil here, have I missed Cathy?'

'Yes, but she's got her phone in the van.'

'No, it's okay, just tell her I've booked us into Holly's for the weekend after next, that will cheer her up.'

*

'Simple question, Tom: I met Marcella, she said she'd like me to take her up to Fatima to see Mam and Dad, that you and she were good friends now. I just wanted an update.'

'She never wanted to go to see them in Fatima when she lived with me,' he said simply.

'You'd prefer not, then?'

'She must go where she pleases.'

'She's very broken, you don't know the kind of time she must have had over the water, she doesn't talk about it but it can't have been great.'

'No, and I do wish her well, and I really hope she finds happiness like I would for any friend.'

'Right Tom, matter dropped.'

'Tom, it's Muttie here. You see, the twins are making an Irish stew for Lizzie as a treat tonight, and they gave me a list . . .'

'You'd like us to make it for you . . . Okay, Muttie . . .'

'I beg your pardon, they wouldn't *hear* of you making it. This is to be all their own work. I have all of the lamb and carrots and onions, but it's just that it says stock on the list. What's that?'

Tom told him what little cubes to ask for in the local supermarket, and what they looked like. Cathy's mother probably had plenty of excellent stock in her freezer, but this was no time for opening the wrong things.

'Is that Tom Feather? Nick Ryan here, I want to have a surprise birthday party for Cathy's aunt at her apartment, and for you both to cater it.'

'You know, Mr Ryan, we have a policy on surprise parties . . . we don't usually do them. They can go so very wrong.'

'But not with Geraldine, surely . . . she has so many friends?' He sounded uncertain.

'Could Cathy come back to you on this one? Please.'

'Well, all right then, I thought you'd be glad of the business.' He sounded huffy now.

'And indeed we are, Mr Ryan, as I say, Cathy will sort it all out as soon as she can.'

'Yes, well.'

'Tom?'

'Cathy, there's telepathy, I was just going to ring you.'

'Tom, have you her letter and the map there?'

'You mean you aren't *there* yet? Oh, my God!'

'Don't you panic, you're the one on dry land with the map, I've been to number twenty-seven, they never heard of Mrs Fusspot.'

'Well, if you called her—'

'Of course I didn't call her that, Tom, quick, will you.'

He ran to the desk and took down the file with that week's bookings in it. He came back to the phone and read out the address.

'That's where I am.'

'Well, it's on her writing paper printed there in front of me.' He read it aloud again, this time with the name of the suburb.

'*What?*' she screamed. There were two streets with the same name. People should be hanged for allowing this in any country. She was on the wrong side of Dublin.

'Tom, what will I do? If I ring her now she'll go to pieces. Tom, speak to me.'

'Just get there. I'm much nearer, I'll ring her and go round in a taxi with champagne and smoked salmon and hold them at bay until you get there. Drive carefully, don't take any risks. I don't want the entire company dead on arrival.'

He had a fairly horrific phone conversation with Mrs Fusspot, where he had to hold the mobile far from his ear. The taxi man looked at him sympathetically.

'You know your job is nearly as bad as mine,' he commented, when Tom had put the phone down, exhausted.

'I don't think it's always as bad as this, but give me yours today, I beg you.'

'Not today, you wouldn't want it,' the taxi driver said gloomily. 'There's some kind of protest in the centre of Dublin, people marching from O'Connell Street to Stephen's Green. We'll be all day and all night getting to your one on the phone, and the one you were talking about with the van of food will be lucky to get there by next weekend.' Tom lay back and closed his eyes. He must stay calm. Somebody somewhere in this city must be calm.

Mrs Frizzell was around fifty, tiny in an unwise emerald-green wool dress. She had black hair scraped up into an angry-looking chignon and was very bad-tempered when he arrived. He saw with relief that there were no other cars, and noted from the high volume of abuse with which she greeted him that she must be alone, and that he had at least made it ahead of the guests.

'There, there, there.' Moving quickly into the kitchen and finding suitable glasses, he said, 'You see, I told you, the traffic was terrible, they'll all be delayed, it's exactly the same for everyone.' He hadn't said anything of the sort, but he was picking up what the taxi driver had said. 'I think it's some kind of protest march, Mrs Frizzell, it has totally disrupted the traffic and some streets are closed.' Her face was stony. Tom opened one bottle expertly and stood it in ice, then he swiftly arranged the smoked salmon pieces on the buttered brown bread, found a sharp knife and cut them into tiny pieces.

He had grabbed lemons and parsley to take with him, but he needed a plate. He looked around for one.

'I thought you said you provided all your own—'

'And indeed we do, and our china is on the way, it's just as I told you, the transport has been unavoidably delayed in this protest march.'

'Protest,' she scoffed.

'I know, it *is* inconvenient, but still, it's good that we live in a democracy, isn't it, and people can make their views known.'

Mrs Frizzell did not appear to think it was particularly good to live in a democracy, nor may ever have thought so. Meanwhile Tom had spotted a plain white platter. 'Let me use your lovely white plate, I'll take great care of it,' he soothed her, and produced in seconds an entirely acceptable dish of canapés. He noticed her beginning to thaw slightly.

'Let me take you back into the very nice sitting room I saw briefly on the way in, and give you a glass of champagne while you wait for your guests. They too will be anxious, being so late for you,' he said.

The guests were in fact not late at all, and to his annoyance he saw a big black car coming up the drive. He settled her down and ran back to the kitchen opening cupboards, fridges, drawers, anything to see was there any raw material from which he might make up a lunch, supposing Cathy never turned up. He did find a bottle of cheap brandy, and decided to add a few drops quietly to every glass of champagne he served. This was going to be the longest pre-luncheon drink in the history of catering: they might as well enjoy it.

'I don't *believe* this,' Cathy cried when the guard on traffic duty told her that the roads were closed. 'Has there been an accident?'

'Oh, no, it's only the homeless and those who care about them to the point of closing the city down,' he said, casting his eyes up to heaven. He was a weary man and he had little sympathy for those who made his job more difficult than it already was. 'Are you conjurors, the lot of you?' he asked them, interested. They had such a funny van with a red feather on it; they might be children's entertainers.

'*No*, Guard,' said Cathy before doing a perilous turn. 'But we may have to become conjurors before this day is over.'

'Who could have got them to close the streets?' Con asked in amazement.

'My husband,' Cathy said grimly.

Most of the women were very much at ease the moment they came in the door. They all signed a book on the hall table so that Mrs Frizzell could show her husband who had turned up . . . Tom moved among them, easily smiling, reassuring that there were *no* calories in smoked salmon. He fought down his own panic. There were twelve women, two of the four bottles of champagne he had brought were empty, the plate of smoked salmon was nearly finished. It would take an hour to set up the table and serve the lunch, and there was no sign whatsoever of the van.

The television cameras covered the march, which was all the more impressive for being done in heavy rain. The banners were held high and the people were of all ages.

'I can't believe it, Neil,' Sara said. He squeezed her hand; it was better than any of them had ever believed possible. He wished Cathy could have come, but he'd tell her about it tonight, and some of the speeches might even be on the nine o'clock news.

Tom ripped open three tins of sardines, drained them and squeezed lemon juice and ground fresh black pepper into the mixture, and then like lightning he spread it over the contents of a packet of biscuits he had also unearthed.

'Very nice,' one woman said. 'What are they called?'

'Sardines au citron,' he said.

'They're good.' She smiled into Tom's eyes.

He smiled nervously and moved away.

He kept topping up the champagne with further drops of brandy, but never Mrs Frizzell's own glass, as he didn't want her to know why her guests seemed so animated. Tom tried to keep a mental note of all he had taken from Mrs Frizzell's stores; if this day ever ended he would have to restore as well as half a bottle of brandy many more items. He had opened jars of gherkins, chopped a cucumber and made a little bowl of dip out of various yoghurts he found in the fridge. Oh, please God, remember that Mrs Maura Feather of Fatima prayed night and day to Him, and surely there must be some credit in the prayer bank now which God could use to make the van turn up.

'I'm afraid to go in,' Cathy said at the gate. 'They're here; and the place is full of cars. God, there are even chauffeurs.'

'Drive in, Cathy,' said June.

'Will I ring first?'

'Drive in,' Con begged.

Cathy drove right up to the front door, then remembered and reversed to go to the back door. Tom saw them coming, and thanked God and his mother for having answered the prayer.

'I've seen her somewhere before. I know her, and that dress,' Cathy said.

'Of course you haven't, you're hallucinating . . .' Tom hurried them on.

'Cold canapés of any kind – no time to heat anything, I have the ovens on, just fling the main course in,' he hissed to Cathy.

'And open more champagne, Con, they've drunk my lot. Quick, June, start the tables.'

There were twelve in total: she was going to have two tables of six, do her best. Cathy went into the dining room, stunned that Tom had been able to make these people stay so long without anything to eat. She urged them to have the little asparagus tips with Parma ham, and insisted that Mrs Frizzell have just one of the tiny caviar and sour-cream blinis . . . All the other guests seemed to be enjoying them. To her amazement, Mrs Frizzell said she was very sorry about those dreadful protesters who had delayed her; a lot of the guests had been upset by the traffic diversions too. Mr Feather had explained all about the march and had been marvellous. Cathy said she was delighted to hear it, and scooped up some really revolting-looking things on plates which were on the tables and the piano.

'God, what on earth are these?' she said scraping them into a bin.

'Those were my best efforts, and they loved them until you arrived with the cavalry,' he said. 'I'll go home now, and leave you to cope.'

'You *can't* go.'

'But there's three of you here!'

'Tom, our nerves have gone, you *must* stay and help.'

'Of course I won't, I'm off now to lie down for a month.'

'You don't understand, they love you, they can't stand the rest of us, you *have* to stay and help us get on with it.'

She saw he had only been joking. 'Of course I'll stay, you clown, anyway, I don't have the strength to walk down that avenue. I have to get a lift home in the van.'

And so it all went into its well-tried routine. They all moved around the kitchen, helping each other, passing things, getting rid of rubbish, totting up the number of wine bottles on the calculator, covering little delicacies in some of Mrs Frizzell's dishes for her to discover later in her fridge. Con gave them the word, the ladies were leaving, the van was loaded. Three of the eleven guests had been interested enough in the food to ask for cards. They were ready to roll. Tom had listed the sardines, brandy and other items he had taken, so there would be no misunderstandings. Mrs Frizzell thanked them grudgingly. It had, of course, been very distressing that everyone was so late, and extra precautions really should have been taken on a day when everyone knew that the city traffic would be difficult.

'Ah, but *did* they know,' Tom said. In about eight minutes they would be out of here. Cathy had promised to buy them all a pint to apologise for having got the address wrong.

'Well, apparently they did, or should have; some of the ladies were telling me that that good-looking lawyer son of Jock and Hannah Mitchell you always see spouting on about causes was on breakfast television this morning warning everyone, so really you should have known. Still, in the end it had turned out all right, and you needn't pay for the items you used, just regard that as a tip.'

'You know the Mitchells then, Mrs Frizzell?' Tom said innocently.

'My husband plays golf with Jock. We were at their house once. Oaklands – big place, very nice.'

Cathy remembered her then, and the dress, from New Year's Eve. But mercifully Mrs Frizzell had no similar memory. They smiled until their faces hurt, until they got in their van. Then when they had driven out through the gate they played the scene out over and over for Con and June.

'. . . that good-looking lawyer . . .' Tom said.

'. . . spouting about causes . . .' Cathy giggled.

They told Tom that the guard had thought they were conjurors. And Tom said if that guard had seen him scraping Mrs Frizzell's bits and pieces onto biscuits he would know that conjurors was exactly what they were. He told Cathy she was to call Nick Ryan sometime about a surprise fortieth birthday for Geraldine.

'That's a non-starter, she'd flay us alive,' Cathy said. 'Anything else happen when I was driving the wrong way round Dublin?' she asked.

'Yes, the handsome spouting lawyer rang and said he'd booked you both into Holly's the weekend after next.'

'Well, that's another non-starter for a variety of reasons,' said Cathy, looking straight ahead and not catching Tom's eye as he drove to the pub.

Neil came home just in time for the news.

'It was a huge success, I gather,' Cathy said.

'Yes, people can't pretend any more that they don't know about the problem, and that's good.'

'Let's turn on the television and see what they say.'

She handed him a glass of wine and put a plate of warm Stilton tartlets on the table between them.

'These are nice,' he said. 'Leftovers?'

She was annoyed. She had saved them specially for him in waxed paper. 'Well, I suppose they are in a way, but I didn't see them like that.'

'Stop being prickly, hon.' She shrugged. The news hadn't yet begun. 'How did it go anyway, *your* do?'

'Fine. She knew your parents, as it happens . . .'

The signature tune for the news came on. 'Shush. Here we go,' he said. The march got very full coverage, and there were aerial pictures too of the way Dublin transport had been brought to a halt. Somewhere in that television footage was the Scarlet Feather van, turning and twisting like a wounded animal. She half hoped they would see it. It would be hard to miss with its distinctive logo. Instead they saw Neil. About twenty seconds' worth of him, young and eager, his hair blowing in the wind, his face wet from the rain, but there as always with the one short, telling phrase.

'Thank you for coming out on the streets today to say that in a country of plenty we are ashamed that people will sleep without a home tonight.' He looked straight at the camera. 'Let nobody's conscience feel easy by saying that the homeless have sought out their lifestyle. Which one of us here would choose to spend this November night in a doorway or under a bridge in the cold and rain?'

As he got down from the platform, supporters grasped him and hugged him in solidarity. One of the people reaching out to him was Sara. Cathy watched wordlessly.

And then the report went on to a politician saying what was being done, and a member of the opposition saying that not nearly enough was being done. Neil had stood out above them all. These were just grey people in a studio, without the passion of the young man standing in the rain.

'You were great,' Cathy said admiringly. And she meant it.

'It just might help to change things.' He was talking about the whole demonstration, not about his own little excerpt. 'It was great out there, Cathy; I *wish* you had been able to come, be a part of it.'

Cathy thought how she and June and Con had sat for what seemed like hours in their van, and cursed him to the pit of hell. 'In a way I *was* a part of it,' she said.

And then the phone began to ring. People congratulating him, further tactics to be agreed, newspapers and radio programmes wanting him to do more interviews. He was adept at passing the requests on to other people. He was only one person of a very big committee, and perhaps they should talk to this person or that; he could give them a phone number, an e-mail address. Neil knew too well the pitfalls in being seen as the only voice; he made sure that there was no danger of his taking the whole thing over. When people called him on his mobile, Cathy answered the ordinary phone. She was indeed kept fully busy for the evening as the assistant and helpmate he wanted her to be.

'Cathy, it's Sara.'

'Oh, Sara, good to hear from you. Did it all go well?'

'Well, sure it did, didn't you see, don't you know?'

'I haven't had time to ring my mam yet, but I hear that they're making an Irish stew to mark the day.'

'Who are? I don't understand.' Sara sounded totally confused.

'The twins, you know, all their belongings have gone into a lock-up shed, my dad told me all about it. The Beeches is being boarded up today.'

'Oh, the *twins*,' Sara said. Cathy was silent. 'Sorry, Cathy, of course you meant the twins. Sorry.'

'And *you* meant the march?'

'Yes, I was walking a bit of the way with Neil. Wasn't he wonderful on television!' Sara said.

'He was indeed, will I put you on to him?' and she passed the phone to Neil. Cathy felt very tired, and out of things. In fact, she wanted to go to bed. These calls could go on all night. Yet it looked dismissive and cold to Neil on his big day to show so little interest. In something that meant so much. She would have been very happy to curl up on a sofa and hear all about it. But these weren't sofas you could curl up on; slim, clean lines, and there wasn't any chance of hearing anything except one end of a telephone conversation. A few months ago she would have told him all about Mrs Frizzell and they would have laughed at his being called a spouting lawyer. Tonight it would have been out of place. Things had changed a lot. They really did need to spend some time away from everything. Which reminded her that she must tell him that she wouldn't go to Holly's with him, but tonight was not a night for a row so she would leave that until tomorrow. So Cathy sat there, listening enthusiastically to Neil's side of phone calls. He waved away any offers of food, the adrenalin was enough. 'It will be real food, not leftovers,' she said. And immediately wished she hadn't.

'Oh, Cathy, you *are* getting very petty about a silly remark. Sorry if it offended you, anyway, I don't want any more, thanks all the same.'

The phone rang again and he seemed to take the call with some relief. Well why not? Cathy asked herself. The rest of Ireland thought he was a hero. His wife just made petty remarks about leftovers. Which would anyone prefer?

*

Next morning Neil was rushing, he had to get into the radio studio to do an interview on *Morning Ireland* before anything else. Cathy didn't tell him about Holly's then. It seemed inappropriate.

'See you at eleven,' she called as he was leaving. 'You'll knock them dead on the radio.'

'Eleven?' he said.

'Remember, the meeting.'

'Meeting?' He looked blank.

'Oh, Neil, at our premises, the bad guys are coming, and James.'

'God yes, of course, I'll be there,' he said.

James Byrne had asked for another meeting with the insurance company. He had been told that the position was still very unsatisfactory; apparently a cousin of one of the partners had let himself into the premises and destroyed everything for no apparent reason. This said cousin had now disappeared, and the insurance company was expected to pay up as if this in fact had been a de facto breaking and entering by criminals who were strangers. Neil hadn't turned up at eleven when they were meant to begin. Coffee was served in the front room, the phones put on the answering machine and James began. He would like the representatives of the company to look around the place, which had shown all the signs of two people trying to get their business back to where it had been. And until Neil Mitchell, barrister-at-law, who was advising them arrived . . . perhaps James could step in and bring them up to date with the way things were progressing. He showed them the meticulous books he kept, the receipts for the equipment they rented, the ongoing calendar for work planned and booked. He explained that they were now not in any position to take on a job that meant large financial outlay, they didn't dare to accept anything which would not be paid for within the traditional ninety days that big companies insisted on. He painted a picture of a decent, hard-working, struggling pair who were anxious only for what was theirs by right and law.

'Law has to be interpreted, defined,' one of the insurance men said.

Cathy wished with a passion that Neil was here to answer him. *Why* did he have to be late on this of all days? Then her mobile rang.

'Neil?'

'Sorry, hon, you've no idea the impact all this has made, I'm literally besieged . . .'

'They're here for the consultation, and we need you . . .'

'I'm really sorry, and please give my sincerest regrets to—'

'*No* Neil.' Tears had sprung to her eyes. He did this too often. Everyone had been looking at the door for the last half an hour waiting for him, and now it turned out that he wasn't anywhere near them.

'If I could . . .'

'They've just said law has to be interpreted and defined, you *should* be here to do that for us.'

Tom and James started to talk loudly, at exactly the same moment, to gloss over what was obviously a husband-and-wife quarrel and the slightly humiliating non-appearance of their legal adviser. But Cathy had turned her phone off.

'Neil wasn't able to make it, he said to apologise to you all, so even though I'm furious with him for not being here, I'm passing on his regrets.'

Tom let his breath out. Slowly. She was in control again. They pointed out that Walter was not Cathy's cousin, merely a cousin of her husband, that they were most certainly not in touch with him, the guards believed that he was in London, and they had no idea where. The fact that Cathy's parents were hoping to foster Walter Mitchell's brother and sister did not mean a close and continuing relationship. Walter had nothing to do with anything at all. The meeting ended indecisively, the insurance men left saying that they would not come to another meeting or consultation until there was something new to put on the table. Meanwhile, investigations and negotiations would go on at their usual pace.

Tom, James and Cathy sat in silence after they had left.

'I could kill him,' Cathy said.

'Don't,' said Tom. 'We're in enough trouble already.'

'We are in trouble,' James said. 'Unless the insurance pays before Christmas, you won't be able to carry on.'

Sandy Keane wouldn't let those two children near his betting office again, so Simon and Maud had to wait outside when Muttie went to his office to meet his associates there.

'I'm calling the guards if they come in the door,' he said.

'You're a very extreme person, Sandy,' Muttie said.

'You're not the one who got grilled by the entire Garda station . . . They said a man who could take a bet off children under ten years of age was capable of doing anything, even abducting them.' Sandy shivered at the memory.

'Well why *did* you take their bet then?' Muttie wondered. 'I'd never sent them in before with money to you.'

'But you weren't there, you hadn't been seen for two days. Where were you, anyway?'

'I was about my business,' Muttie said. He wanted no mention or indeed memory of the hospital examination.

'Muttie, you don't *have* any business except coming in here tormenting me,' cried Sandy in despair.

There was a loud knocking on the door. The twins stood outside.

'No,' cried Sandy.

'We're not coming in, thank you, Mr Keane, it's just to tell Muttie that Cathy came by in her van and is going to take us for a drive, and as we were getting a bit wet out here . . .'

'Good, good, go on the drive, goodbye,' he shouted.

'We didn't want Muttie to think we'd gone missing again.'

'No, we'd all hate that,' Sandy Keane said drily.

'Thank you, Mr Keane,' Maud said.

Muttie came out to them. 'Man has a head like a block of wood. What harm on earth would two well-behaved children and a pedigree Labrador do to his betting shop? They'd raise its tone. He has no judgement whatsoever.'

Cathy brought the van up beside them. 'I needed a bit of nice company, so I thought of Hooves, and of course that means taking Simon and Maud too.'

'That's a joke,' Maud said to Muttie.

'Cathy was always a great one for the jokes when she was young,' Muttie said. 'She used to come home from school with a new one every day.'

'You don't have many jokes nowadays, Cathy,' Simon said.

'Oh, I'm full of them,' she said.

'When do you tell them and laugh at them?'

Cathy paused to think. She had laughed properly in the van when they were coming away from Mrs Frizzell's house. 'At work, at home, everywhere.'

'Does Neil like jokes?' Maud asked.

'He loves them. Dad, we can't tempt you . . . ?'

'No, I have a lot of work ahead of me. Will see you at supper, maybe; there's still some of that great Irish stew the twins made.'

'We made far too much, I'm afraid,' Simon said.

'No, you can never make too much, that's what God invented freezers for . . .'

'But God didn't actually . . .' Simon began. 'I see,' he said.

They went to an Internet café and the twins sat at a machine, while Cathy drank too much coffee and planned what she would say to Neil tonight. His presence there today would have alerted those people; things might have been moved forward. He must be made to understand that. Without nagging, whingeing and being . . . what was that word he used about her recently? Prickly. And even though she hated doing it, she felt it only fair to tell him about James's very dire forecast. Perhaps it might make him feel more guilty about letting them down today. And of course she hadn't had time to tell him that she wouldn't go to Holly's. It would be a conversation with very few jokes in it, she realised. At that moment Simon came back from the computer.

'We've found a really good website, Cathy, could we have another half an hour of it, or is that greedy?'

'No, that's fine.' She gave them the money.

'It's not too dear, is it, what with you being poor again after the robbery?'

So far the twins didn't really understand Walter's part in it all, and she kept it from them. Their mother and father had abandoned them yet again; there was no point in taking away the only remaining member of their immediate family, the one who *had* stood by them that time.

'No, we can afford another half an hour, and don't forget, you might well get a computer at Christmas. You'd never need to come to a place like this again.'

'Imagine, having it at home.' Simon's eyes were shining.

Cathy had arranged that Jock and Hannah give them this as a present. She would arrange for a good basic computer to be delivered to St Jarlath's Crescent. Neil had said that strictly speaking, since it was educational, the funds should come out of whatever trust there was for the twins. He might talk to Sara about it all. Cathy had sighed.

'Let your parents do something for them, Neil, they did so damn little that they were full of guilt. This will get them off the hook.'

He had been startled, but agreed.

'And you don't mind sitting here?' Maud asked.

Cathy didn't. She was in no hurry to go back to Waterview.

There was news when they got back to St Jarlath's Crescent. Marian had been on the phone. It was early days, but she and Harry were expecting a child, wasn't it wonderful? They would have the christening in Chicago in April, and everyone must come over.

'Do they dance at christenings?' Simon asked.

And Cathy found herself reaching out to squeeze her mother's hand at the same time as Lizzie reached for hers. Neither of them trusted themselves to speak.

Cathy was still putting off going home. She went to one of the new places hidden among the foodie streets in Temple Bar for a snack. Neil wasn't eating these days, it appeared, and there were plenty of what he called leftovers to offer him. To her great surprise she was served by Marcella. She looked very beautiful in a smart black trouser suit and a red necklace around her throat. They stared at each other in disbelief.

'You look lovely, Marcella, but then you always did.'

'For all the good it did me,' Marcella said. There was a sudden awkward silence. 'Are you meeting anyone?' Marcella asked.

'No, I was . . . Well, I just wanted a glass of wine and something small.'

'We have a lovely plate of mixed tapas,' Marcella suggested.

Cathy nodded dumbly. 'That would be fine,' she said in a choked voice.

'And Cathy, I'm just on my break now. Would it annoy you if I sat down with you for ten minutes? I'd love that.'

'So would I,' said Cathy insincerely. Please may Marcella not want to cry and tell the whole story about just wanting to talk to Tom all over again. But in fact it was quite different. Marcella asked about Scarlet Feather and what had happened since she left. There was a lot to tell. Cathy told her about Marian's wedding, and her own pregnancy and miscarriage; she told about the twins' disappearance, about June's husband Jimmy being housebound, about Geraldine's new chap, how Con was now working almost full-time with them and about Walter being the thief. She left some things out. Like their very poor financial future. Like Tom looking like a ghost for so long that they all worried, and just now beginning to show signs of recovery. She didn't tell either about having grown so distant from

Neil that she dreaded going home to see him tonight. Which was why she was sitting here eating tapas.

'I've been rabbiting on about myself. You can tell me or ask anything you like, Marcella, Tom and I never talk about personal things at all, it's just like an unwritten rule.'

'Do you think there's a chance he'd have me back?' It was so naked, humble and sad.

'I haven't an idea, Marcella, I really don't. I know one side of him so well, and nothing at all about the other.'

'And does he have anyone in particular . . . ?'

'No, no one in particular. I know he does take girls out, but I don't hear anything.'

'Thank you, Cathy.' She looked at her watch and got up.

'I'd better go, too.' Cathy took out her wallet.

'On me, Cathy.'

She knew that the wages in these places were not good, and there would be no tip. But dignity was also important. 'Thank you. It was delicious, and I'll send people here.'

A group of people had just come in. Marcella went to greet them, tall and beautiful, with that assured smile.

She called Neil at the town house. He wasn't home yet. She didn't want to sit there waiting. Where else could she go? It was eight o'clock on a winter's evening. It was tempting to go and sit in the premises for an hour, put on some music, sit in one of those deep sofas and close her eyes. But she might fall asleep. She would go back to Waterview. Funny how she hardly ever called it home now. Just Waterview.

They arrived together, her van pulling in beside the Volvo.

'There's timing,' he said, pleased. He had a lot of documents under his arm and a briefcase over his shoulder. He walked ahead of her and looked at the number of times the little red light flashed. 'Only three messages. Good,' he said.

'Leave them, Neil.'

He laughed. 'What on earth are you talking about, hon, you don't have a message machine, unless you want—'

'Please leave them. If you listen to them, you'll have to do something about them,' she said.

'Ah, Cathy, what *is* this?'

'An attempt to talk before we are both too exhausted and have to crash into bed,' she said simply.

'I *told* you, I booked us into Holly's. We'll talk all weekend there.' He was moving towards the phone.

'I'm not going to Holly's with you,' she said, her voice unexpectedly loud.

'You really are coming on very strong. You won't come on the holiday which I cleared with Tom, I told Tom how tired you were and he said they'd cover for you, I took the time off myself which was hard, cancelled a whole lot of things I now have to refix. Then you agreed to go to Holly's, now you change your mind. Honestly . . .'

'I said I'd like a weekend, I didn't ask you to go ahead and book it without discussion.'

'But you *like* Holly's.'

'I don't want to go there,' she said.

'Why on earth . . . ?' he looked at her, bewildered.

'The last time you and I went there I was telling you about how we were going to have a baby. You don't think I want to go back there again, Neil?' She felt guilty as she said it. It was valid, but only half the reason. Still, she had nothing to be ashamed of, no real secret. She would have told Neil that she had fallen asleep in Tom's room, had she been given a chance.

He looked at her, embarrassed. 'I'm afraid I didn't think of that. I'll book us somewhere else tomorrow.'

'Or maybe we could do it after some discussion between us,' she said.

Neil gave up thoughts of checking the telephone. 'Is this what this is about? My not running everything past you before we do it? Is that it?'

'No, it's about much, much more. It's about your not turning up today when we really needed you so badly,' she said.

He had forgotten. It had been such a busy day for him. If they turned on the nightly current affairs programme he would be mentioned in it. How could he have thought to recall a conference with some insurance people, long agreed and then totally abandoned? 'Look, I told you at the time . . .' he began.

'You weren't there, Neil.'

'You knew how much in demand I was today after the march, for God's sake, you were there last night when the calls came in.'

'Then you should have cancelled our meeting.'

'But Cathy, it wasn't . . .' he began.

This time she didn't interrupt him, she waited. He said nothing. 'It wasn't what, Neil?' she asked, almost defying him.

'It was a matter of priorities,' he said eventually. 'We all have to make decisions every day about what to do and what not to do.' He was still calm, reasonable.

'And you decided at the last minute not to come to a very important meeting about your wife's company? Leaving the three of us looking so foolish you wouldn't believe it?'

He stopped being calm now. 'Cathy, please. There were things that had to be done, a joint committee is being set up, they needed someone to advise about the terms of reference . . .'

'*We* needed you at the premises, you had promised to come. You don't know what happened, they ran rings around us, they were supercilious and . . . And you won't believe this, but if they don't pay up in time we could be out of business before the New Year.' She waited for the shock on his face, but it wasn't there yet. 'Like go out of business, permanently cease trading,' she said, afraid that he hadn't understood.

'Cathy, I know this is a blow for you and Tom, and I'm sorry of course, but seriously, in terms of what else is going on . . . It's not something I could run away from everything else for. It's only a business, after all, it's only a small business, cooking food for rich people, giving them upmarket food.'

'What?' She looked at him astounded.

'You know I've always been very proud of you, and you've done very well. Very well . . .' He paused.

'Sorry, I don't understand. This is my job, Neil, this is what I do.'

'I know, hon, but you can't compare what you're doing . . . You know, all these discussions about canapés and finger food, with what I had to do today.'

'There were no discussions about finger food today, there were people, big companies whose job it is not to pay up until they have to. You told me that yourself when we had the robbery.'

'I know, I know.'

'So what are we talking about then? Tell me, Neil, tell me now why we, who had booked you for a consultation, couldn't have you, couldn't rely on your being there as you had promised?'

'That is such a grossly unfair—'

'Tell me.'

'Because it was not as important as the setting up of a joint committee. Don't get carried away with the importance of a business, Cathy. They come, they go.'

'Even if you've slaved for them and played everything by the book like we've done all the way?'

'What are we talking about . . . You despise these people, you just make money out of them, I've heard you over and over groaning and pouring scorn on them, but you still take their fees.'

'And is that immoral, to do a service and get paid for it?'

'No, Cathy, it's not, but it seems to me that you are trying for a very high moral ground saying that I should have given up good work in defence of the homeless in order to protect what we all agree is something which in the end is fairly unimportant.'

'Just say that again, Neil.'

'Stop playing games, you heard me.'

'You think Scarlet Feather is unimportant.'

'Not in itself. It is filling a need, but in terms of—'

'Did you always think this, like, say, a year ago when I was so busy setting it up?' she asked. He sighed heavily.

'I need to know.' She was calm.

'Well, I thought it pleased you, you know, because of all this nonsense about your mother and mine, which never mattered to anyone.'

'It mattered to everyone except you,' she said.

'So you say . . .'

'So you always thought it was a fairly trivial enterprise, something that started and could close.'

'That's what happens to businesses.' He shrugged. Uncaring.

'So why did you even bother to get involved when we had a break-in . . . a robbery that was actually masterminded by your own first cousin, as it happens?'

'I wondered when we'd get to that,' he said.

'No, Neil, why did you bother taking it up if you weren't going to follow through?'

'I was going to follow through, and I am going to, but today was not the day. Anyone in Ireland could have told you, I had other things to do today.' He looked very hurt.

'But you thought it a Mickey Mouse, rich people's enterprise. Why then did you bother at all ...'

'It was the principle of the thing, they should not be allowed to get away with it,' he said. There was a long silence. 'Cathy?'

'What?'

'Do you ... um ... um ...' he asked.

She looked at him for a long time. 'Do I think you should listen to the phone messages now? Yes, I think that's a great idea,' she said.

'Don't piss me about.'

'I'm not. Believe me.'

'You wanted to talk,' he said.

'And we did,' she said.

'Is there anything I could say or do to make you feel better?' he asked.

'No, no, there's not, Neil.'

'I know I'm very insensitive, like that thing about Holly's hotel.'

'Again, I tell you, it's not important, believe me there, too.'

'I love you,' he said.

'Maybe, Neil.'

'No, really and truly, and we have always been honest with each other, always.'

'Yes,' she said thoughtfully.

'And I don't want anyone else in the world but you. So yes, I annoyed you today and maybe also a bit over the past months by not being here enough. I admit this. But I've come to a decision.'

'Yes?' She looked at him.

'I honestly didn't realise how much that whole baby thing meant to you.' He leaned forward and held both her hands. 'Cathy, I want to say it straight out. If you'd like us to try for another child, then I wouldn't mind, I really wouldn't mind at all.'

December

One of Muttie's associates went to have acupuncture and his back straightened up; in fact he wondered had he been to Lourdes, so great was the transformation. Cathy told June about it just in case it would help her husband.

'Nothing will help Jimmy, he's like Interpol these days, what time did the job end, why was I so long coming home. It would drive you right up the walls and down again.'

Cathy took Jimmy's side. 'To be fair, now you gave him a bit of reason to be jealous ... going off to parties and clubs.'

'I never slept with anyone else since I married him a hundred years ago, more than you can say for most people, but there's no telling him that. He's put a halt to my gallop recently, and me the only blameless soul left in Dublin.'

Cathy wondered was that right. Were most people unfaithful? She never had been. And Neil? Hard to know, very hard to know nowadays. The thought shocked her, that he could be in bed with red-haired Sara, for example, saying the same things that he said to her, doing the same things. It was unthinkable. But then, so were so many other things.

'*Cathy*. You've put seventy into that box, not sixty...' June snatched it from her. They were doing their Christmas freezer order, flat boxes of canapés. Sixty per box.

'You're miles away,' June grumbled.

'You're right.' She pulled herself together sharply. 'And we must finish quickly because we're having Power Elevenses, remember?'

'All right, I'll speed up if you put your mind on them.'

'All right. I'll keep my mind on them if you give Jimmy the name of the acupuncture man. He deserves a crack at it.'

And with that they went into fast mode, laughing as they bumped into each other, but the boxes got filled and labelled and filed deep in the heart of the rented freezers. By eleven o'clock Tom was well back from Haywards and the cash and carry. Con and Lucy had turned up as requested to, and they were all sitting in the front room, five Scarlet Feather mugs of coffee and a plate of shortbread on the table that used to hold Cathy's beloved punchbowl.

'Now this is like a council of war. Cathy and I thought it only fair that you all realise how near the edge of the precipice we are. Our only hope is to work the arses off ourselves this month. There will be nothing whatsoever to do in January, there will be no money out there, so our only hope is in the next four weeks. Now what we have to do is to know how many days and nights we can all work, otherwise we'll be taking on more than we can handle and we'll fall on our faces.'

'I can work every night except Christmas Day,' Con said.

'But Con, the pub?' Tom gasped.

'I've asked for the day shifts there. I prefer it. Anyway, it's messy in December.'

'If you're sure?'

'I'm sure. I'm going skiing with a bird in January, so I need all the dough I can get.'

'And you, Lucy?'

'Any night except Christmas Day, most lunchtimes too.'

'Lucy, have you given up university?'

'No, but there's not much on between now and February when we have to put our heads down and study; anyway, I'm going skiing with a fellow so I'll need to buy a few clothes.' She laughed conspiratorially with Con.

'June?' Tom said.

'Every night including Christmas night,' she said.

'But Jimmy?' Cathy began.

'Isn't bringing in any money, and will be glad of my wages.'

'Cathy?' Tom asked.

'Any night, obviously, and any day. This is our last throw.'

'But won't you have to . . . ?'

'No,' she said.

'The holiday, the weekend?' He was mystified.

'Won't happen. I'll be here for the duration.'

'And I'll be here all the time, so there was hardly any need for a Power Elevenses at all.' The team would be there, every one of them, every night. They were going to do it, all five of them; they would see that Scarlet Feather didn't go under. All they had to do now was go out and get the bookings.

It was a matter of leaflets; they'd put them up everywhere, in Lucy's university, in Con's pub, on the food counter in Haywards, in Geraldine's friend Mr Ryan's chain of dry-cleaners. Geraldine and Shona would deliver them around Glenstar, Lizzie would leave them in the apartment blocks where she cleaned. Stella and Sean, still starry-eyed from their wonderful wedding, would give them out in their area. Tom was to go to the printer's that morning. Cathy would go to the market and see if any of the stallholders might put them up. Geraldine was on the phone; she was delighted to hear they were all so enthusiastic, she would call in a favour from Harry, a journalist she knew, and ask him to give Scarlet Feather a mention in one of those Countdown to Christmas columns. They agreed to report progress to each other before the day was out.

*

Their progress was strange. When Tom went to the printer's the man remembered him.

'You lot were in a year ago, you bought Martin Maguire's place.'

'That's right.' Tom was surprised.

'Any word on how the poor divil is getting on these days? Terrible business that was, terrible.'

'I think he's fine. Cathy, my partner, met him during the summer; he was going to come and see us, but at the last moment he didn't.'

'Ah, you couldn't expect the man to set foot in that place again after all that happened in there.'

'I'm afraid that I don't know. What *did* happen?' Tom said eventually.

'Don't mind me, I talk too much,' the printer said.

'Please tell me.' Tom was gentle but insistent.

'His son Frankie went and hanged himself there, right in the premises. They never did another day's work in that place.'

Cathy went to the market, it was gearing up with Christmas gifts, and there would be huge crowds passing through. But most of the stalls and stands didn't look suitable places to advertise their party service. Perhaps there was a community noticeboard on that building at the end; she walked towards it, and on her way she saw a bric-a-brac stall, and noticed a silver punchbowl just like hers. She picked it up and looked at the base.

There it was. 'Awarded to Catherine Mary Scarlet for Excellence.'

'How much?' she asked the stallholder in a whisper.

'Not sterling silver or anything, but a nice piece.'

'Please?' she asked again.

'Thirty?' he said doubtfully.

'Twenty?' she suggested, and got it for twenty-five pounds.

'It doesn't matter to me in the slightest, but would you have any idea where you got it?' she asked.

'Not an idea in the world,' he said.

'It's not important now,' she said, and totally forgot about finding a place for their advertisement.

Geraldine dropped into the newspaper and gave in the little piece about Scarlet Feather that she had typed out. It was ready to run. Harry was an old mate. She had known him for ever, and had recently given him the telephone numbers of two politicians, so he owed her.

'Will you come and have a drink, Ger, it does me good to be seen with a young dishy piece like yourself, makes my street cred go up.'

It was flattering to be called a dishy young piece, but then Harry was considerably older than she was. Everything was relative.

'I won't, Harry, thanks all the same, I've a lot to do.'

'Pity, I'm a bit down. I needed to be cheered up.'

'I'm sorry, what has you down?'

'All my old friends dying off like flies, poor Teddy's the latest, I suppose you heard.'

Geraldine had heard not a word about the one man she had ever loved, the man who had left Ireland for Brussels with his wife and family twenty-two years ago. She felt faint, but she hid it. 'I heard something,' she murmured. 'But tell me . . .'

'Oh, the usual, he's not going for the chemo this time. Wants to come back to Ireland to die. Funny, he hardly came back at all over all that time, and he must be gone about fifteen years.'

'Longer, I think,' she said.

'Maybe. Did you know him at all back then?'

'A bit,' she said, and got out into the fresh air before her legs went from under her in the warm office.

'Do you get enough money to make it all right for us to live here, Muttie?' Simon asked.

'Cathy said you're not to ask people about what money they get,' Maud was reproving.

'I didn't ask how much Muttie got, I just wanted to make sure it was enough.' Simon was outraged to be misunderstood.

'We have plenty, son, we lack for nothing,' Muttie said.

'You lack a good coat, Muttie, yours is very thin.'

'But I have a great thick jumper,' Muttie said cheerfully.

'Father always had a good coat with a velvet collar, and I'm sure they got a lot of money for The Beeches.' Simon was distressed at the unequal nature of things.

'Ah, but now remember, your poor father lost his house and your mother lost her health, so not everyone has everything, that's the most important thing to remember,' Muttie said.

'There are new people going into The Beeches after Christmas,' Maud said.

'Will that upset you, child? Will you miss the place?'

'No, Muttie, I mean there's no one there any more, Mother's going to be in a home mainly, Father's travelling with old Barty and Walter's gone away. There's no one there any more to miss.'

'And this is your home for as long as you like. For ever, really. I know it's not a grand place like you are used to, but we'd miss you to bits if you weren't here . . . We did, you know.'

'We know you did,' Simon reassured him. 'Didn't you come all the way down to Kilkenny to find us?'

'I wonder where Walter is,' Maud said. 'He never sends a postcard or anything.'

'I'm sure he will one day,' Muttie reassured them.

'I hope he has a good job,' Maud said. 'He was so nice to come and find us too, the day you did; I didn't expect him to.'

'No, I thought he wouldn't bother with us, but he must have been worried about us,' said Simon.

'We thought he had gone away himself that night, I don't really remember it all clearly,' Maud said with a troubled face.

Muttie decided it was time to change the subject. 'They always say you should never look back. Do I look back to the day I meant to put the tenner on Earl Grey, and I wasn't seeing things clearly, so didn't I mix up the names and put it on to King Grey instead? A dark day that was, but do I look back on it? I do not.'

'Tom, don't hang up, it's Marcella.'

'I'm not going to hang up,' he said.

'Listen, I can't talk long, there's this television game giving dream prizes, you know, a flight in a helicopter, someone to cook a dinner party for you . . .'

'I know.' Tom sighed. 'Geraldine tried to get us in there, but . . .'

'I'm having dinner with the director, I'm actually at Quentins with him now. Why don't you and Cathy get down here, and I'll introduce you, and Brenda will praise you to the skies. Wouldn't it be a great chance—'

'You're very good to think of it, but . . .'

'But what, Tom, it's eight o'clock at night. I'll be here with this guy for at least another hour and a bit. Go on, get Cathy, I bet she'd think it was worth it.' She was gone.

They met at Quentins. Tom was wearing a dark suit and white shirt.

Cathy looked at him with admiration. 'You scrub up very well,' she said. She wore her blue velvet trouser suit, and her hair hung loose on her shoulders.

'And you've put on make-up!' he said.

'Let's only have a starter, we can't afford a whole meal,' she said, looking at the menu anxiously.

Tom was looking over at Marcella, smiling up at a square-jawed man with glasses. The director who had the power to make Scarlet Feather's name. He realised with a sense of loss that he really didn't love Marcella any more.

Brenda came to the table. 'I know what this is about,' she said. 'They're having their coffee now, don't order anything yet and they can sit with you for five minutes on their way out; you don't want the table covered with food.'

'You're a genius,' Cathy whispered.

'No, it's just that I love these kind of dramas, trying to change people's lives, it's what makes the business worthwhile. You should know, you do it yourselves.'

It worked like a dream. Marcella showed surprise to see them, Tom begged them to sit down for five minutes. Douglas, the director who seemed a nice sort of fellow, the only one in the dark about the whole thing, talked easily. Nobody mentioned the television show.

'What are you doing nowadays, Marcella?' Tom asked.

'I hope she'll decorate our television programme as one of the prize-givers,' Douglas said, smiling.

At that point Brenda arrived and congratulated Douglas on having discovered Scarlet Feather, the best-kept catering secret in Ireland. 'Patrick and I always quiver when they come in here, they have such high standards,' Brenda said.

'Tell me, what kind of a dinner party would you cook for eight people . . . ?' Douglas began. And they knew it was theirs. Under the table, they squeezed each other's hands very tightly.

Kay Mitchell was in a nursing home. It was thought that she would never be able to look after herself fully; sheltered accommodation was mentioned as a long-term plan. The nursing home had been chosen with a view to easy access for the children, who could get there on one bus journey from school or from St Jarlath's Crescent. There was a cheerful sitting room where she could come and meet them every week. And would, of course, meet her husband Kenneth if he ever came back from his travels with old Barty. And Walter, if anyone could tell her where he was and when he was coming back. Sometimes she asked the twins, but they didn't know. Sometimes she forgot that The Beeches had been sold and asked about the garden. There were even days when she wasn't sure who Maud and Simon were, exactly. But the twins remained good-tempered throughout.

'I expect if you've got bad nerves people sort of slip out of your mind like down through a grating,' Simon said as they went home after a visit where their mother had constantly asked them who they had come to see.

'And then when the nerves get better, she finds them again,' Maud agreed, as they went back to the comfort of St Jarlath's Crescent, where everyone knew who they were and welcomed them home for supper.

Geraldine did not take long to find which hospital Teddy was in, and learned that he had a private room. Twice she went to the hospital with the intention of visiting him, twice she left without doing so. She had even got as far as the corridor and seen that there was nobody else with him . . . But still something stopped her. Why had he come back to Ireland? He hardly knew anyone here now, his family had grown up in Brussels, he wasn't close to his brother and sister. Did she want to see him now, when he was so very ill? Did he want her to see him this way? Was there a wild possibility that now, in this last part of his life, he had wanted to see her again, but did not dare to ask her to visit? On her third visit she was determined not to run away. The door of his room was slightly open; she could see the end of a bed and a nurse talking to him. But still she couldn't go in. She had the phone number of the hospital and her mobile . . . She moved further down the corridor and made the call; they put her through to his room. She could hear the phone ringing beside his bed and then he answered.

'Teddy, it's Geraldine O'Connor,' she said.

'I'm sorry?' His voice was frail, he sounded confused.

'You know . . . Geraldine,' she said, and paused.

'Have you got the right person?' he asked.

'Teddy, it's Geraldine, for God's sake, Geraldine.' She moved nearer to the room. He was not going to forget her or pretend that he had forgotten her. This was not going to happen. She had behaved so well for over half of her life, she only wanted to say goodbye, tell him that she had never stopped loving him.

'I'm sorry,' he apologised. 'I'm on a lot of medication and I'm afraid I don't recall everyone's names.'

'So why did you come back here, then, Teddy, if you don't remember anyone?' She knew her voice sounded hard.

'Please forgive me,' he said, and put the phone down.

She saw the nurse moving around his bed. Geraldine didn't go into the room. She stood without moving in the corridor and watched the pleasant-looking girl go back to the nurses' station at the corner. Geraldine didn't know how long she stood there. One or two people asked her if she was all right, and she must have answered satisfactorily. She saw people going into the various rooms, but nobody went into Teddy's. Eventually she turned away and went to the elevator. She was too shaky still to drive her car, so she had a cup of tea in the restaurant downstairs. It was all for the best, she told herself. What could she have talked about with him, anyway? How he had ruined her life, how his doctor friend had ruined her chances of ever having a child? Would she have told him about all the men who had replaced him in her life, but none of them loved as he had been loved? A man about to die would not want to hear such tragedy. She wiped away the tears that were falling into her cup of tea. It had all been for the best that he hadn't remembered her.

It had been such a wonderful night at Quentins that Tom had not wanted to darken the mood by telling the story of young Frankie Maguire, who had killed himself at the premises. Sometimes he looked around wondering which room it might have happened in. But it wasn't something Cathy had to know now, nor indeed any of the others. And anyway, there wasn't a free moment for anyone to tell anything. The television dinner party was on . . . Tom and Cathy would be in the studio . . . The leaflets were beginning to yield some results, the five of them worked non-stop, cooking, packing and unpacking the van, delivering, serving and clearing up, taking more bookings. So much was happening that Tom couldn't sleep. It was no effort to get up and go to bake bread at Haywards at a time when most people were asleep.

Shona wasn't asleep; she was letting herself in at the same time.

'I'll make you breakfast,' he offered.

'Done.' She came and sat in the kitchen and watched as he got the place to life, prepared his doughs and got them both coffee and toast.

'What on earth has you in so early, Shona, they work you too hard?'

'No, this is my own life. I'm in because I want an uninterrupted hour on the Internet. I'm the one in charge of booking a holiday and I'm not very used to it.'

'How many of you are there going?' Tom asked absently.

'Two,' she said.

He looked up with a smile. 'That's nice,' he said.

'Not what you think, Tom.'

'Nothing's what you think,' he said. 'The older I get, the more I realise that.'

Cathy went into the hairdressing salon at Haywards. 'I want a totally new image for a television show tomorrow,' she said.

'What kind of an image?' asked Gerard, the senior stylist.

'I want to dazzle everybody,' she said.

Gerard had been given better guidelines in his life. 'What will you be wearing?' he asked.

'A red T-shirt, black trousers and a white pinafore. I have to have my hair sort of hidden in a hat I think, or something to make it look as if it isn't falling onto the food.' Gerard asked not unreasonably why, if her hair was going to be hidden by a hat, she needed a new hairstyle or any hairstyle, in fact. Maybe it was a hat she needed, a smart, white hat. 'I have to have a nice hairstyle because months ago my mother-in-law gave me a token here,' she said, as if it was the most obvious thing in the world.

'What did you do with it?'

'I gave it to my friend June who got purple streaks,' Cathy said.

'I see,' said Gerard.

'And I only have three-quarters of an hour, Gerard, so could you think of something quick.' Gerard sent down to the store for a white hat so that they could examine the situation more clearly. 'This will take for ever!' Cathy wailed.

'You're a pro and I'm a pro. You wouldn't let your food go out looking like swill. I don't want you going on the television with my hairdo looking like a bird's nest after a party.'

Cathy saw the point; he had to protect his reputation too. Gerard fixed on the white cap at a jaunty angle, and then proceeded to cut her hair to just above her shoulders.

'I look like a simpleton in a pantomime,' Cathy said, staring at herself.

'Thanks a bundle, and I bet your food tastes like shit too,' said Gerard, insulted.

They caught each other's eye in the mirror, and both began to laugh. The sedate clientele of Haywards was startled to see the near hysteria as Cathy and Gerard laughed until they thought they would never stop.

'Tom, you know we wouldn't annoy you in a million years,' Maud said on the telephone.

'I *know* that, like you know I wouldn't offend you in a million years, but it's just that we're so busy now, you wouldn't believe it.'

'I would believe it. I heard Muttie tell his wife Lizzie that the two of you will be in your coffins before St Patrick's Day with the amount of hours you're working . . .'

'He said that?' Tom reached over and grabbed a saucepan just before it began to burn.

'He did, he said if ever he got a lot of money that he'd go out and he'd invest it in your company.'

'Well, that was very kind of him, Maud, and it *is* nice to have a chat from time to time, but—'

'We have a day off school on Friday, we wondered could we come and polish your treasures, we want to earn money to buy Muttie a coat.'

'I don't think you'd earn enough in an afternoon, to be honest.' Poor Tom was desperate.

'There's a coat in the thrift shop for three pounds,' said Maud.

'Oh, well then, we'll see you Friday,' Tom said, and hung up.

'I don't believe you,' Cathy said.

'I had to,' Tom said. 'You would have had to if you'd been here. Well, come on, take off your hat. Let's see the new you . . .'

'I look like a plough boy with a straw in his mouth,' Cathy said.

'I know, you've always looked like that, but let's see the hair.'

'Come on,' June said. 'Why else do you think I hung about?'

'Did Jimmy go to the acupuncturist?' Cathy fought to buy time.

'We've had this discussion, he did and he feels a bit better, now let's see your hair.' June was giving no quarter.

She took off her hat. Unlike other women who cared about their appearance, she didn't go to a mirror to fluff it up, and explain that it was probably a bit flat by now.

Tom, June, Lucy and Con looked at her in silence.

'Oh, Jesus, is it as bad as that?'

'You look beautiful,' June said simply.

'Beautiful,' Tom agreed.

Con and Lucy clapped and beat saucepan lids on the work surfaces.

'That's enough, I will not be mocked,' she threatened them. But they could see she was pleased, and when she got a chance she went into the cloakroom and looked at it herself. It wasn't at all bad; it looked as if it were meant to be that way. It was shiny and sort of glamorous, not scraped back out of the way as if it were an embarrassment. She must send a postcard to Gerard to thank him. Now all she had to do was cook a dinner in front of half a million people.

The day in the studio passed in a horrible blur. Hot lights melted things, the food had to be pinned together eventually, sprayed with a terrible kind of starchy substance so that it would keep a shine. Over and over they were told that it didn't *matter* what it tasted like, the audience was not going to eat it, only to see what Tom and Cathy could prepare for the winner. They had to unpack things from refrigerated boxes so that the viewers could imagine them turning up in simple kitchens anywhere in Ireland and producing this gourmet meal. Douglas, the director, looked not at all hassled in the studio. Tom and Cathy watched him admiringly; they had never been so alarmed and so self-conscious, yet this man was as cool as anything. Oddly, he seemed equally admiring of them that they could cook under such circumstances.

'You're naturals,' he said. 'I wouldn't be at all surprised if you are invited back. Nice little earner that, the new celebrity cooking couple. Have you been long together?'

'We've been working together as Scarlet Feather for a while, but we've only had the premises for under a year,' Cathy said.

She knew he thought they were a real couple, as so many people did.

'I bet your guests get well fed in your home,' he said.

They hadn't the energy to disabuse him. They nodded glumly as the make-up girl came to powder their faces again.

'She's a lovely girl, your friend Marcella, isn't she?' Douglas said.

Tom and Cathy's eyes met.

'Lovely,' Tom said. 'Very special.'

'She's been a friend of ours always,' said Cathy.

And then they were back into countdowns, and settle down studio and good luck everyone for the final rehearsal before they went out live.

The phone hardly stopped ringing the next day. In the front room Lucy sat coping with the requests, taking details and sending out brochures all morning. It had done exactly what they had hoped – brought them right out there into the public eye.

'You'll never be able to thank Marcella enough,' June said.

'I'm going to send her a bunch of flowers from all of us,' said Cathy. 'Here's the card, let's all sign it now and we'll get it delivered round to Ricky's.'

They let Tom be the last to sign before it went into the envelope. He wrote, 'Marcella, you have been a very generous and good friend, love from Tom.'

Cathy noticed that Lucy was stretching her muscles. 'Here, I'll take over the phone for a while, go and move around the kitchen for a bit,' she said. It was peaceful there in the front room. Her punchbowl back on the table, a little Christmas tree in the window, their coloured box files filling up with more and more addresses, contacts, customers. And it was quiet. It gave her a chance to think between calls. Think about Neil. Last night when she got home, Neil had been working as usual. He had smiled, glad to see her. And then suddenly a look of guilt came over his face.

'Oh, my God, it was tonight, the television thing.'

'You didn't see it?'

'I'm so sorry...'

'Or record it...?'

'I can't tell you...'

She had gone straight to bed. And she had left this morning before he had got up. Things had never been so bad. He would call sometime today to say he was sorry; she needed time to think what she would say. It wasn't a matter of sulking or refusing to forgive him. Because in many ways it didn't really matter all that very much. Not in itself; more what it seemed to say about them both.

'Geraldine, Neil Mitchell here. Did you by any chance make a video recording of Cathy's thing yesterday?'
    'Yes, I did, wasn't she great? They were marvellous, the pair of them.'
    'Could I see it?'
    'You don't have one yourselves, there's casual,' she laughed.
    'Can I have a loan of it please, Geraldine?'
    'No, sorry, I gave it into a place to adapt it for America, you see, I thought Cathy's sister Marian would like—'

'Muttie, did you see Cathy last night on the television?'
    'Wasn't half St Jarlath's Crescent in here watching.'
    'Do you have a video of it?' Neil sounded urgent.
    'Neil lad, the children took it to school today.'
    'What in the name of God for?' He sounded almost angry now.
    'For a project, they have a project every Thursday where the children have to stand up and present something. So Simon and Maud are going to show seven minutes of Cathy and Tom, then they're going to talk about the food industry. Aren't they gas little tickets,' Muttie said proudly.
    'Gas tickets, yeah,' said Neil, and hung up.

'Mother, did you record Cathy last night on television?'
    'No dear, why should I?'
    'I just thought you might. Did you see it?'
    'Yes, they were surprisingly good, don't you think?'
    'Yes, yes, very,' Neil said.
    'I'm delighted she finally did something about her hair, used that token I gave her, makes a lot of difference, don't you think?'
    'Great difference, goodbye, Mother,' Neil said.

Sara rang him to arrange about a meeting later in the day. 'Hey, wasn't that a great plug for Scarlet Feather?' she said.
    'You saw it?'
    'Well, of course I did.'
    'But how could you have seen it, you were in the café with us all when it was on.'
    'I know, but I videoed it.'
    'You did? That's great. Can I have the video?'
    'No, I've recorded over it, a horror film later last night.'
    'Sara, was Cathy's hair different?'
    'Yeah, I hardly recognised her,' said Sara with her usual tact.
    'What?'
    'Well, I don't mean that, but it's pretty good, you have to admit.'
    'I didn't notice it,' he said.
    'Really?' Sara said, her spirits lifting.

*

Some of the calls that came in were of congratulation, clients who were proud of them, the Riordans, Molly Hayes, Stella and Sean, Mrs Ryan who had the apple strudels way back, even Mrs Fusspot. June's husband Jimmy rang to say they had been stars, and that he was also dead grateful about the acupuncture, some mad heathen kind of superstition but you wouldn't believe it, it seemed to be working. And then Neil rang.

'There's nothing I can say except I am so ashamed.'

'It's all right, Neil,' she said wearily, and she actually meant it. It *was* all right. Compared to the much bigger picture, the fact that the programme had slipped his mind was no big deal.

'Look, I know lunch wouldn't make it all right.'

Cathy wasn't going to keep up the dark mood. It was no life living in a perpetual sulk. She knew he was devastated.

'I don't have time for lunch today, Neil, I'm not being cold, it's just a fact. The phone is jumping off the hook – you wouldn't believe it.'

'Congratulations, I'm very proud of you. I'll try to see it today.'

'No, don't, honestly, you're too busy, we'll get a copy of the video from Mam and Dad later on. Leave it, Neil, it's all right, believe me.'

'And your hair, Cathy?'

'Yes?'

'It's very nice.'

'You told me that.'

'When did I tell you?'

'On Tuesday. I asked you did you think it suited me, and you said yes.'

'And I do,' he said. 'When will you be home if you don't want lunch?'

'About seven,' she said. 'But you're going out.'

'I won't tonight,' he promised. 'I'll cancel that meeting.'

Shona Burke was having lunch with James in his flat. He had discovered that soups were very easy to make; he didn't know why nobody had ever told him this before. They talked about the great television programme, and how it could be the turning point for them.

'If only the insurance would pay up,' James said. 'I don't want to be the spectre at the feast, but it's serious, you know. How did that horrible boy gain entrance? We need to know, and he's unlikely to tell us.'

'There's five of them working flat out there today. I called in to congratulate them on my way here . . .'

'What do they think of us going to Morocco for Christmas?' he asked.

'I didn't tell them.'

'Why ever not?'

'Well, you're such a private person, you never talk about your own business. Neither do I. I didn't think you'd want them, or indeed anyone, to know . . . about us having found each other and everything . . .' she looked awkward.

'I used not to be a private person, Shona, I used to tell everyone everything, I brought your essays to the office to show my colleagues, that's how outgoing I used to be, once.'

'Me too. I just learned to be private. But I suppose we could unlearn it. Will I tell them, or will you?'

'We could even tell them together,' he suggested.

Cathy came in at exactly seven o'clock. She looked tired, he thought, and her hair was beautiful, very soft and feminine; how had he failed to notice it before, or admire it only in a perfunctory way on Tuesday night?

'I have turned the answering machine down, we won't even *hear* anyone if they call.' His infectious smile didn't get a response. 'I got oysters,' he said. 'To try to make amends ... They aren't open. I don't know how to open them, actually, but I thought you might like ...'

'To come home from eleven hours in a catering kitchen and open oysters?' she asked.

'No, perhaps not. Not a great idea.'

'It's beyond gestures now, isn't it, Neil?'

'What do you mean ... ?'

'We're much too far apart, there's nothing left. Weekends, feasts, surprises, talk, oysters ... It would only be acting.'

'It's a bad patch, certainly ... We are missing each other a lot in a way that we never did before, but I *did* say that I was perfectly willing to try for another child.'

'That's the one thing that has driven us further apart than anything else.'

'What do you mean?'

'Neil, you can't say you'll *give* me a baby and *put up* with a baby just to shut me up.'

'I never used any of those words, nor felt them. Don't put things into my mouth.'

'It's what you were offering me as a last chance.'

'You're imagining it,' he said.

'You and I used to be able to talk about everything. It was the greatest thing in the world.'

'We can get it back, can't we?' He sounded unsure of himself.

'I don't think so.'

'You're not serious,' he said.

'I am. What you want is a different kind of wife entirely. Someone who idolises you, someone who will stay at home with you and have nice dinner parties for your colleagues ...'

'I never said ...'

'No, you didn't, and I'm not saying it's wrong to want that, but you don't need someone independent with a career, you need someone who will throw up everything and follow you. I'm not that person, but there are many of them out there. Sara, for example.'

'Sara? What are you talking about?'

'You have that ability to talk with her that you and I used to have once.'

'Sara ... you're not suggesting?'

853

'I'm just saying she's very young, she hero-worships you . . .'

'She's very concerned . . .'

'She's got a crush on you, but that's not the point, that's not what we're talking about.'

'What *are* we talking about?'

'I suppose about what we do now.' She felt exhausted and fatigued, almost defeated. Somehow once she had said the words they seemed less frightening. It was out in the open. They were admitting that things between them were very bad indeed.

'You still care about what I do, the work that has to be done, don't you?'

'Yes, I do, I really do. But I think you've forgotten about you and me in the whole thing. We don't talk . . . It's not that we have no time, it's just that we make no time. And much as I admire you, it seems to me that you bleed for everyone in the world and for big global problems, but you can't see the hurts and hopes and dreams on your own doorstep.'

'Now that's not really fair, you *said* you supported the same things as I did, then you suddenly went off on a tangent trying to be the world's biggest caterer. You *said* that you didn't want children, just like me, and then you got pregnant and I was the worst monster in the world because I wasn't suddenly delighted. Then you *said* you were sad and lonely and tired, and I said okay, let's have another baby, and apparently that was the worst thing I ever said in my whole life. So don't throw all the accusations at me.'

Cathy looked at him as if for the first time. He really and truly felt that she had totally misjudged him in all this. They were further apart than she had thought.

'I don't want a slanging match, Neil, I just said that you are so involved in everything else you don't see what's happening to us. There's nothing out there that you wouldn't fight for, but we are missing each other every step of the way.'

'No, that's not so, I won't have this. I've done everything I can, you're trying to put a label on me – it's not fair to say I'm Mister Rent-a-Cause. I just won't accept it.'

'What will you accept then?' she asked. 'Are you going to accept that things are very, very bad between us?'

'I can't believe this is happening,' he said, shaking his head as if to get a buzzing noise out of his ears.

She sat very still and said nothing.

'This is all a total mess. It's brought about by us both working too hard,' he began. 'Cathy, don't let us lose it, it's up to us . . . you know that . . . If we want something we can get it. We did it before.'

She was about to say that she thought it was too late, but the words didn't come out.

'Listen to me, Cathy, we can start again, leave here, leave all the pressures, start all over. I'll take the job, we can go away, put everything behind us, we'll have space and peace to work everything out, have our baby when we want to. We can put all this unhappy year behind us.'

She looked at him open-mouthed.

'That's what we'll do, they're on to me every day to make up my mind. We'll tell them that we'll go. We'll go together.'

'Please, Neil, no, please.'

But she couldn't stop him, he was in full flight now.

'It's what we've needed, to get out of here . . . People do get bogged down by things, you're right, we have been missing each other. What with rushing between the twins and the break-in and your parents and my parents and the American wedding and the insurance and the late nights and the never having time to talk . . .'

'It's got nothing to do with all that,' she attempted.

'It has everything to do with it. Once we're on our own far way from everything here . . .'

'There is no way that . . .'

'We've been working too hard, we haven't given ourselves time to pause and think . . .'

'No, Neil.' Suddenly she snapped.

'Will you stop shaking your head at me and talking like a nanny. Honestly, even my mother wasn't as certain and definite as you are. I'm offering us the chance to save our marriage, we love each other. We fought hard to get each other, against a lot of opposition, we're not going to throw it all away just after one bad year, are we?'

She said nothing.

'Are we? Don't just sit there looking at me reproachfully as if I were Maud and Simon. This is serious, this is our future for God's sake.'

'It's your future.'

'I want it to be ours, I want us to do it together . . .'

'But . . . ?' she said.

'But I don't know what you want, I really don't. If I did know what you want, I'd try to do it.'

'I've always wanted the same thing,' she said.

'No, that's not true, you want to be out all hours with stupid, vain, rich people making them ever more ludicrous food.'

'I see.'

'It's not a life, it's not a way to live. This was never our plan. Come away with me, come on, we can make it work.'

'No.'

'You're just being stubborn, you're making a point.'

'Not true.'

'We've been through this over and over. This is important. I am at the point that I can't bear us to go on having these endless rows. I'll go without you if you won't come. I mean it. They're on to me every day. I've only been stalling them for you. Now if you're not going to come, what's the point of stalling them any more?'

'No point,' she said blankly.

'I don't want to go without you.'

'No, no I see that.'

'But I will, I mean this is what I've always wanted. I thought it was what we had always wanted. I would turn sour, be very bitter, we'd have nothing left at all if I were to stay.'

'You have a very good career at the Bar, you do a lot of good for a lot of people, people like Jonathan.'

'I can do more on a bigger canvas.'

'And you'll go alone?'

'Yes, if I have to. I'm going to go now, before Christmas if I can, and leave it open for you to join me.'

'That's a non-starter. You know that. I know that. You can't railroad people into things.'

'Would you ever have come with me?' he asked.

She thought for a while.

'I might have, but not until the business was up and running, I had paid back my debts, found someone to replace me.'

'It mattered as much as that?'

'Did you think it was a game?'

'I thought it was something to show my mother you could be a person in your own right. I never thought you needed to prove that to anyone, but honestly, that's all I thought it was.'

'We'll have to tell her, you know.'

'Tell her what?'

'That your plans have changed, that you'll be abroad – we were going there for Christmas.'

'Yes, I suppose so.'

'Funny, I think that's something that's going to stick in my throat badly, the fact that she was right all those years ago when she said I wasn't right for you.'

'Cathy . . .'

'If you don't mind I won't stay for us both to get more upset. We can talk better in the daylight.'

'Please don't go,' he begged.

'It's for the best,' said Cathy Scarlet as she packed a bag and left.

She knew Tom was out with Con doing a rugby club party. There were kitchens at the club, so they would not be coming back here tonight. Before she lay down on the chintz-covered sofa, she left a message on Tom's phone back at his flat.

'Hope the company doesn't mind, I'm spending a couple of nights on its sofa.'

Then she went to sleep. When she woke to get a drink of water in the night she saw that a fax had arrived. It said simply, 'The company wishes you sweet dreams.' She knew he would never ask her a question any more than she had ever asked him. Somehow it was very restful.

She had every sign of her overnight stay carefully removed before anyone came. And as she knew there wouldn't be, there was no comment from

Tom Feather. Once or twice he lifted a pot for her, or passed her oven gloves as if he feared she would do herself an injury.

'Shona said that she wanted to come and have coffee this morning,' she said. 'James will drop by too, and it won't take long.'

'God, what a morning to choose, we have the heavenly help force with us today.'

'What?'

'Had you forgotten? A team of highly skilled polishers have a half-day from school and are heading in this direction, on the invitation of someone who is Just a Boy Who Can't Say No.'

'Oh, God, Simon and Maud.' She had forgotten.

'Doesn't matter, the day will end sometime.'

The twins arrived early. They were wearing their oldest clothes, they said, and could do heavy work. Muttie's wife Lizzie had given them wire scrubbing pads and old toothbrushes for getting into the crevices of things which might have legs.

'I didn't know what she meant, exactly,' Simon said. 'Like chicken carcasses or something.'

'No, like sauce boats or the handles of things,' Cathy explained.

'Oh, look, you've got another punchbowl,' Maud said, pleased.

'It's the same one, actually, look, my name is on the bottom,' Cathy said.

'How did you find it?' Simon asked. 'Was it here all the time?'

'No, no, it made a weary journey around the place from black plastic bag to garden shed to one market stall and then another. I bought it back.'

Then she remembered the twins didn't know of Walter's part in the burglary. She hoped they hadn't made the connection between the garden shed and their brother storing things there. But they were too happy and eager to start their work to notice anything at all. Cathy told them their duties, and stressed the need to keep out of people's way in the kitchen because there was a rush on.

'Do we have the relaxing hot drink and a scone like we had before when we came?' Simon wondered.

'Why not?' Cathy said. 'Come on, Tom, let's take five minutes to relax with Maud and Simon.'

The four of them sat in the front room while the twins told what a success the project had been at school. Everyone loved it, and was very impressed that Cathy was their cousin. Cousin! She would not be their cousin for much longer, when she and Neil divorced. The thought hardly seemed real; she had to run it past herself again. The children chattered on.

'Do you still have the same code to get in, nineteen and then six?' Maud asked.

'How on earth did you know that was our code?' Cathy asked, quietly.

'You told us. Remember, one day when you were driving us back to The Beeches in the van. You were doing a party, and you told us about the ceremony of the keys. What you did each time in the van and where you put them.'

Cathy could hardly breathe.

'And did you tell anyone else about it, do you think?'

'I don't think so,' Simon said. 'No point in telling your code to everyone we meet, some of them might be robbers and come in.'

'We did tell Walter that night,' Maud said.

Tom and Cathy let their breath out very slowly.

'You did?' Tom said, in a deceptively light tone.

'Yes, you see we had been telling him all about your treasures and polishing them and things, and he said we knew nothing about your business, so just to show him . . .' explained Maud.

'It doesn't matter, does it?' Simon felt uneasy.

'No, it doesn't matter,' Cathy said. 'In fact, it's very good to know that, because a lot of things fall into place.'

'No, Cathy, you can't ask them,' Tom began.

'We can, we'll explain,' she said.

'It's too tough on them. Leave them something to hold on to.'

'Do you think Walter was your burglar?' Simon asked suddenly.

'And then that really was your punchbowl in our garden shed?' Maud said, horrified.

'But Muttie said everything was all broken into little pieces, why would Walter do that?' Simon said.

'Do you think he did it, Cathy?' Maud asked straight out.

'I do, yes, Maud.'

'Why?' she asked.

'I don't know, maybe he was short of money.'

'He was always very nice to us, except when we were stupid,' Maud said.

'I know, I know,' said Cathy.

'And he did come to find us that time.'

'Of course he did.' They must be allowed to believe that, at least.

'Are you very cross with him?' Maud asked.

'No, not now, but there *is* something which would help us a lot without getting Walter into any more trouble.'

'What's that?' They looked at her with anxious eyes.

Gently Cathy explained that the guards already knew Walter had taken the goods, but didn't know how he had found the code and the keys.

'You won't get into any trouble,' Tom promised. 'It's my fault, I didn't tell you it was a secret.'

'And Walter isn't in Ireland anyway, so they can't find him, but it will mean that the insurance company might pay us. Do you mind doing that, telling people? If you do mind, then we'll leave it, but it would be such a great help.'

They looked at each other. 'We'll tell,' they said.

And in the middle of one of the busiest mornings that Scarlet Feather had ever known, hours were spent while Maud and Simon Mitchell told James Byrne, then the guards and then an insurance official about the night they had wanted to prove to their brother they knew all about the business. And everyone softened at the obviously true story and the mixed feelings about their big brother, who had crossed Ireland to find them because he knew they were in trouble.

'It's going to help a great deal, believe me, this is what we needed,' James said.

'What were you going to tell us, Shona?' Tom asked.

'James?'

'Hold on a minute. Simon, Maud, do you want to make an extra pound? Could you go down to the newsagent, it's at the end of the street, and buy me an *Irish Times*?'

'A whole pound?' Simon said.

'Should I go on polishing, do you think?' Maud wondered.

'No, go with him for company,' James said.

When they were gone, Shona spoke immediately. 'When I was young I was fostered with James and his wife Una in Galway, but I was taken away and brought back to my own home when I was fourteen. We've only just got to know each other again.'

Cathy and Tom exchanged glances. What else would this day throw at them?

James spoke in a different voice than usual. 'We were told it was for the best that we didn't make contact. I didn't question it; that's what I blame myself for, not questioning something that felt so wrong, like letting the child we loved go away without begging to have her back.'

'So now we're making up for lost time, meal after gourmet meal . . .' She laughed at the teachers who had taught her lost father to cook.

'And we're going to go away together for a three-week holiday,' James said proudly.

Tom blew his nose loudly. 'If I hadn't another ten hours' work ahead of me today, I'd say that we all went out and got drunk on this.'

'In the New Year,' promised James. 'You come round to my flat, I'll cook a Moroccan speciality for you.'

'Oh, be sure to buy those Tajine dishes and we'll make chicken and prunes and almonds,' Cathy's eyes danced at the thought.

'Weren't you and Neil going to go there?' James asked.

'No, that's not going to happen now,' Cathy said, and at that moment the children came back with the paper.

'Mam, can I have my Christmas dinner here?' Cathy asked.

'Well, of course you can, but I thought the pair of you were going to Oaklands.'

'Neil is, Mam, I'm not.'

'Ah, now, don't tell me you've fought with Mrs Mitchell again, that is very silly at this season of the year.'

'Mam, sit down, I have to tell you something,' Cathy said.

'Geraldine, will you be coming to Mam and Dad's on Christmas Day, as usual?' Cathy asked.

'Yup, that's what us naughty ladies never get to have, Christmas Day with a man. They have this habit of going back to base for the turkey.'

'I'll be joining you there on my own, and I'm relying on you to keep it all going.'

'A bad row?'

'No, a separation. Oddly enough, there have been very few rows.'

'Well then, why in the name of God? Why don't all those men I know who are in the middle of perfectly dreadful marriages not break up? Why leave it to you and Neil, who fought everything to get married and are so suited in every way.'

'Not any more, Geraldine. I need him to care about home and us and having a child and about Maud and Simon, and about maybe a dozen or two dozen people; he wants me to care about millions of people and principles and . . . issues.'

'You can do both.'

'Not the way we've been going at it, Geraldine.'

'Do you love him?'

'I thought I did, but I don't really. I'm very fond of him, though.'

'And is there someone else?'

Cathy laughed aloud. 'Me? I don't have enough time to keep one relationship going, how would I have time for two?'

'I just wondered.'

'Well, you wondered wrong.'

'You're being dangerously calm about it all,' Geraldine said. 'When I think of how you fought Hannah Mitchell and the world to marry Neil.'

'I know, I think about that too; it's hard to explain, but I get the feeling that I loved the idea of him rather than him himself. Does that make any sense at all?'

'I know exactly what you're talking about, as it happens.' Cathy looked at her doubtfully. 'You remember the man I told you about, the man from long ago?'

'Yes?' Cathy said.

'He doesn't remember me.' She told the story.

'Of course he remembers you,' Cathy said defensively. 'He just pretended, that's all. How could he not remember you at eighteen, and what happened? Tell me where he is. I'll go in and see him, beat the truth out of him.'

Geraldine's face was very sad. 'No, dear Cathy, thank you for the vote of confidence. I've said all that to myself over and over. But the truth is he doesn't. I was loving the idea of him, not the reality. I've thought about him for twenty-two years, and he must have hardly thought of me at all.'

'We'll help each other through Christmas Day,' Cathy promised.

'Not that it will be hard with that cast,' Geraldine said.

It wasn't really all that much easier to talk in the daylight, but then Cathy had never really thought it would be. Yet they managed a very creditable performance between them. They spent a few hours sitting peacefully in Waterview and made a list of who would take what.

'Live here, if you won't come with me. Stay here, it's your home.'

'It never felt like home. I have too much of St Jarlath's in me to like it. It's too minimalist.' She smiled ruefully when she said it, and so did he.

In so many ways it seemed quite natural to be sitting there, talking, making mugs of tea. But there was nothing natural, it was like reading lines in a play. They decided to put the house on the market in January; that would give them plenty of time to find a destination for the furniture they wanted. Neil said that there would be no problem in putting his share in a warehouse. Cathy said she would have found somewhere to stay by then. They looked at the pictures. There was the one they'd bought in Greece.

'Please take it,' she said.

'No, it was painted for you,' he said.

'Let's neither of us have it,' she said and it went into the great number of personal items which would find a home with neither Cathy nor Neil. He promised to finish off the insurance business for them and she assured him she didn't want the Volvo, the van was fine. Neither one of them could believe it was real sometimes. Yet they knew that there was no going back.

'Have you told many people?' Neil asked.

'Just my mam and Geraldine really,' she said. 'And you?'

'Nobody.'

'The one thing we should really do together is go and see your parents. We owe it to them,' Cathy said. 'I'd really like to go tomorrow evening, about six.'

'That's fine for me. I will be there, I promise,' he said.

But of course he wasn't. They had arranged to call in for a visit at six o'clock the following evening. At five, she got a call to say that the meeting was going on.

'We can't have them sitting there wondering what it is,' she said.

'You don't have to go today, you can wait until I'm able to come with you.'

She hung up. She saw Tom looking at her.

'Thanks,' she said.

'What for . . . ?'

'You know what for, for not asking.'

'Oh, *that's* no trouble,' he said, smiling at her. 'You know how dim men are, they wouldn't even know if there was anything to ask about.'

'Oh, you came in the van,' Hannah said as she answered the door.

'Neil has the Volvo, he's been held up,' Cathy said, walking straight in the hall door, leaving her scarf and gloves on the hall table and hanging up her coat. She moved into the den, where Jock and Hannah had been sitting.

'Ah, Cathy, a drink?'

'Yes please, Jock, a small brandy would be nice. Lovely fire, it's very cold out.'

'And is Neil not with you?'

'No, you know the way he always gets tied up at things. Well, today there's a meeting and he sent his apologies.'

Hannah rushed to defend him. 'He has *so* many responsibilities, he couldn't drop them for a social call.'

'It's more than a social call, Hannah, we had something to tell you, but now I'll tell you myself.'

Jock looked alarmed. 'Nothing wrong, is there?' he asked suddenly.

Hannah's hand went to her throat. 'I know what you're going to tell us, you've come to tell me that you and Neil are going to have a baby!'

Walter rang the premises, and Tom answered.

'Er, it was really Cathy I wanted,' he said.

'I'm sure she'll be overjoyed that you called, Walter,' Tom said. 'But sadly she's not here.'

'Stop pissing about, Tom, this isn't a joke.'

'You'd better believe it isn't a joke, Walter.' Tom looked around the premises that the boy had so nearly permanently destroyed.

'I wanted to ask her a couple of things.'

'Ask away,' Tom said agreeably.

'Can you put me on to her?'

'No, she's not here.'

'Has The Beeches been sold?'

'Yes. What else did you want to ask?'

'The twins, are they okay?'

'Much more okay than when they had you to keep an eye on them.'

'Are they with Cathy's parents?'

'Why?'

'I wanted to send them a Christmas present. I didn't know the address.'

'Send them to this address, this is one address you certainly know.'

'You think you're a comedian.'

'No, I think I'm a poor fool who actually goes out and works for a living to be able to buy Christmas presents, rather than steal and smash places up for them.'

'Tell Cathy I rang, anyway.'

'I will. I don't suppose you'd like to leave a number where she can call you back?'

'She and half the guards in Ireland,' Walter said.

'Could happen,' Tom said agreeably.

'Wise guy,' said Walter, and hung up.

Cathy sat for a moment and looked at her parents-in-law. It wasn't fair to keep them dangling, waiting about something as big as this.

'It's nothing like that at all. I came to tell you that Neil and I will not be spending Christmas here. He is taking this overseas job that he mentioned to you before and I'm not going with him, so he won't even be in Ireland for Christmas and under the circumstances I will go to my parents in St Jarlath's.'

They looked at her open-mouthed.

'Are you serious?' Jock asked eventually.

'I'm afraid so. Neil promised he would be here to tell you with me, but it hasn't turned out that way. It's a matter of us both wanting different things . . .'

'Well, by heavens, you wanted him badly enough some years ago when we all told you that you were different people with different backgrounds.'

'I don't think the background has anything to do with it, it's more the future. Neil wants to go abroad and has his mind on a big job in Europe. I don't want to leave my business . . .'

'But surely your business isn't as important as . . .' Hannah began.

'Unfortunately, Neil didn't think it was important either, so we differed about that too.'

'A bit drastic, isn't it?' Jock said. 'It sounds a bit more like a tiff to me.'

'No, it's much, much more than that.'

'So what's going to happen?' Hannah asked. She didn't look triumphant and superior. She actually looked frightened. A now familiar world was changing.

'We're taking it slowly.'

'Have you someone else?'

'I have nobody else in my life, Hannah.'

'You're not suggesting that Neil does, I hope? Does poor Lizzie know about all this?'

'Yes Hannah, *poor* Lizzie knows.'

'You're so quick to take offence, you always were, when there's absolutely no need.'

'Well I'm sure you'll be glad that you were right about me all along,' Cathy said.

Jock interrupted. 'Now none of that, we're both very shocked at your news. It's out of the blue.'

Hannah spoke slowly. 'And no matter what you think, I am *not* pleased. I think you did make Neil happy. I get no joy of saying I told you so, no joy at all.'

'I've made your Christmas cake and plum pudding. Con will deliver them whenever it suits, and anything else you want, of course.'

'And when will Neil come and tell us all about it, what time will his meeting end?' Hannah looked bewildered, a little lost.

Cathy spoke gently. 'I really don't know, you see, he doesn't have to tell me his plans, his schedule any more. I know he'll come and tell you everything, I know he will.'

'It's really all very sad,' Hannah said flatly.

There was a silence. And then Cathy got up. 'You'll want to talk, and Neil will get in touch with you. I'll go now. You can always get me at work, and I've left the number I'll be staying at for the next three weeks, it's at Glenstar apartments. I'm minding Shona Burke's flat.' She paused at the door of the den. 'I'll see myself out, I don't think there's any real etiquette over all this, except to say that I hope we can always keep in touch. I really mean that. Even if Neil is abroad, we might meet through Maud and Simon.' And she left them to digest the news that they would have loved to hear half a decade ago. That she and their son might not have a future together.

'Ricky's having people in on Christmas Day, buffet all afternoon,' Marcella said to Tom.

'I know, we gave him a load of stuff for his freezer,' Tom said, pleased.

'At least they'll get something to eat. It's mainly for people who are on their own, people who don't want to sit down to endless turkey.'

'I'll be up in Fatima for the day,' Tom said.

'There's no strings attached, just a lot of nice people.'

'I know, but I'm still going to be in Fatima.'

'You're very stubborn, can't Joe go for once?'

'He'll be there too,' Tom said.

'And I don't suppose that . . .'

'I know, I don't suppose that either of us will stay awake for the whole afternoon, but it's something we've agreed to do, to have just the four of us,' he said, intent on heading her off at the pass. He knew Marcella wanted to come to Fatima. But it was too late for her to visit there now. He thought back on all the times he would have loved her to have been there.

On Christmas Eve they opened a bottle of champagne at the Scarlet Feather premises. And then another and another. It was a celebration that they had done what they hoped.

The insurance had paid up, they had been booked to do another television show, there was vague talk of a whole series of thirteen programmes. Between them they had worked all day and all evening for twenty-four days. Even James Byrne had begun to smile before he went off to Morocco. So they deserved a party. Jimmy was there, his back magically straightened by the man with all the mad needles. Geraldine sent her apologies, she was having a little drink with Nick Ryan as he made the excuse of last-minute shopping. Lucy's mother and father were there, disapproving at the start and thawing out gradually. Con was there with his mother, who watched Lucy steadily for the first two drinks and then relaxed considerably. Muttie and Lizzie came with the twins. Only Tom and Cathy had no one to field.

'There's a parcel for you two,' Tom said cheerfully to the twins.

'Is it from you?' they asked.

'No, my present is under your tree in St Jarlath's Crescent.'

They asked could they open it, and Lizzie thought definitely they could.

They tugged at it and produced two watches. Watches that you could use underwater, watches that would give you the time in America if you wanted it. They immediately worked out Chicago time, and set the little dial for that. They had never seen watches like that before. The card said, 'Love from Walter.' This was greeted by a total silence.

'Very nice of him,' Cathy said loudly, and they all murmured that it was.

'Hot?' Tom whispered to her.

'As the hob of hell, I imagine,' she said.

'But we'll leave it, won't we?' he pleaded.

'Of course we will, eejit.' She smiled at him.

'Will you come to Christmas dinner in St Jarlath's Crescent tomorrow, Tom?' Simon offered graciously.

'Thanks, but I have to arm-wrestle my mother over the turkey, she's inclined to put packet stuffing in it and burn it to a crisp if I'm not there to fight her all the way.'

'It won't be very much the season of peace and goodwill, will it?' Maud said, worried.

'He's joking, Maud,' Cathy said.

'Not altogether,' Maud said.

'Sharp girl,' Tom said.

They were all off now until New Year's Day, when there was a big lunch and the team would gather again, but the main thing they were celebrating was that they had refused eleven bookings on New Year's Eve. They wanted to consider it an anniversary . . . one whole year since they had found the premises. Everyone went home. Tom and Cathy insisted that they do the clearing up.

'It's only putting things in a machine, don't our arms do that automatically?' Tom said.

The twins were going back to the best Christmas of their lives.

'Have you got a present for Hooves?' Maud asked Cathy.

'Would I forget Hooves?' asked Cathy, who had.

'I didn't see it under the tree,' Simon said.

'That's because he might have smelled it under the tree,' Tom intervened.

Their eyes lit up.

'She's got him a *bone*!' Simon said, excited.

'Or something in that area,' Cathy said.

They went off down the lane from the premises arm in arm with Lizzie. Tom and Cathy waved them goodbye.

'Get me something out of the freezer for Hooves, for God's sake. You're an utter genius, did you know that?' Cathy said.

'I could thaw a fillet steak if you like,' he suggested. 'We froze them in threes, remember. Well, I might eat one myself, I'm not going anywhere,' Tom Feather said.

'Neither am I,' said Cathy Scarlet.

The day passed as Christmas Day passes for so many people, in a sea of paper and presents and fuss about cooking.

Maura Feather asked them all to kneel down for the papal blessing, and to please her they did because she had given in on everything else, including the turkey.

*

Neil had an awkward lunch at Oaklands, where nobody was able to talk about the situation, and where Amanda rang from Toronto to wish them all well. It seemed very artificial.

Muttie was delighted with his new red overcoat that they had got him in the thrift shop, and said he would wear it everywhere. Including tomorrow, when they watched the races on television. He said that he had the accumulator of a lifetime on tomorrow at the races, everything he won on the first race would go onto this horse in the second race, and all the way through the card. It could be millions. And for a very small stake.

Simon and Maud planned spending the millions. They would get their mother a dressing gown like another lady had in the home. Mother hadn't known it was Christmas Day. It had been a bit sad, but Lizzie had said that the poor lady was in a bit of a dream and she was quite happy. Father had sent them five pounds to buy gifts, and said he and old Barty would be home to see them sometime. And of course Walter had sent them the marvellous watches. They could hardly believe that Uncle Jock and Aunt Hannah had given them the computer of their dreams. They had been sure that Aunt Hannah hated them. Neil had left presents under the tree for them: they were marvellous computer games.

Cathy had got Hooves a wonderful steak wrapped up in silver paper with a big pink bow, and she even cooked it for him herself. She was smiling a lot, even when there was nothing particular to smile at. They had been warned by everyone to be particularly nice to her because of this separation thing. But she hadn't been cranky at all. It was a mystery.

The next day, as he sat in his new red coat in front of the television, Muttie's first horse won and so did his second. They were all standing behind his chair watching the television, willing the horses to win for him. When the third horse won they all began to get chest pains. Even Hooves began to howl at the tension in the air. Geraldine's face was contorted by the time the chosen horse started to pull away from the rest in the fourth race.

'I didn't know the meaning of the word stress until this moment,' she said in a strangled voice.

Lizzie said over and over that he should have done the races individually, then they'd have been fine. *Why* had he to do it this way and give them all heart failure? They were fairly short odds, some of them were even favourite, and his associates said he was as mad as a hatter, but Muttie said he had been studying form seriously. This time he really knew what he was doing, Sandy Keane up at the bookie's wouldn't know what hit him this time. The phone rang just as the fourth horse won. Tom answered it. It was Marian from Chicago. He spoke in clipped tones.

'Marian, no one in this house is able to speak now, including myself, so just hang up will you, like a good girl, and we'll call you back later.'

Then he left the phone off the hook. During the fifth race he had his arm so tightly around Cathy's neck she thought she was going to choke. When it won, they all leaped up and hugged each other; only one race to go.

Lizzie said, 'If he hadn't included the last race he'd have walked away with ten thousand pounds, Mother of God, imagine putting ten thousand pounds that would have solved our problems for ever onto a horse. Muttie, *nobody* puts that kind of money on a horse . . . I can't believe this is happening.'

'Lie down, Mam.' Cathy got her a footstool and a cold towel for her forehead. Hooves, sensing illness, laid his head in her lap . . .

'What are the odds on the next one?' Maud and Simon were screaming with excitement as they tried to work it out.

Tom got Muttie a glass of water, he got Geraldine a whiskey and then he drew up two chairs for himself and Cathy – they no longer had the strength to stand. Muttie's face was ashen, it was within his grasp. Tom and Cathy clutched each other's hands like people on a life raft. The horse was in the last three. One of the others fell.

'I can't *bear* it,' screamed Geraldine.

'Come on, Muttie. Come on, Muttie,' shouted the twins. There had been so many horses to cheer for in the afternoon, they had forgotten the name of this one.

'Listen, God, I'll give you another try if it wins,' Tom said.

'Please, please horse, win for my dad, please win for him, he's never done a bad thing in his life,' Cathy begged the horse, with tears streaming down her face.

'Ten thousand pounds that could have set us up for life thrown away on a horse.' Lizzie had her eyes closed, so she didn't see Muttie's horse, the only long shot on the list, come in at thirteen to one.

'That's thirteen thousand pounds, not bad for a day's work,' said Muttie with a beatific smile on his face, well satisfied with his efforts.

'No, Muttie, it's a hundred and thirty thousand,' said everyone in the room, except Lizzie and Hooves, at exactly the same time.

Nobody remembered much about what happened after that. Tom reminded them to ring Marian, and they told her that they would all be over for the baby's christening. Muttie took some of his associates for a drink, and told them firmly that the money would be invested by Lizzie, who was good at this sort of thing, and he would still get an allowance, though perhaps an increased allowance. All things considered. And some of the savings would be used to go to Chicago, and some to help finance Scarlet Feather, and some to buy a second-hand van in case Lizzie and himself wanted to go on outings or take the children somewhere educational.

'And what about yourself, Muttie?' everyone asked.

'Haven't I got everything a man could want?' Muttie would say with such sincerity that people got an odd feeling in their noses and eyes.

Tom said he'd drive Cathy back to Shona's apartment in Glenstar. Geraldine was going to stay the night in St Jarlath's Crescent; she said that someone had to mind this family, which had now gone totally insane.

She kissed Cathy goodnight. 'What a year,' she said.

'It had its moments, certainly.' Cathy tried to be light; then she saw Geraldine's face and remembered that Teddy had died, Freddie Flynn had gone and the future with Nick Ryan was uncertain. Cathy had been trying to put a brave face on it for herself and all that had happened to her.

'Next year will be better for all of us, I have a real feeling about that,' she said as she got into the van.

Just before the turn to Glenstar, Tom said, 'You know we never had any Christmas cake tonight.'

'After all the trouble we took icing it,' Cathy said.

'We could drop by the premises, maybe, and have tea and a slice of cake there?'

She thought it was a great idea. Neither of them wanted to go home to empty flats, but it hadn't been their custom to invite the other in at night. The premises had always been neutral ground.

They settled into the front room, drank their tea, and talked about Muttie's win.

'I think he's more pleased about beating Sandy Keane into the ground than actually getting the money,' Cathy said.

'I know, it's personal. We can't take any of his money though,' Tom said.

'We can let him invest,' Cathy said. 'At least that way it's here, rather than in Sandy's hot little hand.'

'I do wonder which is the sounder investment,' Tom said.

'Stop that at once, Tom Feather. We won. We've had a hard year, but in terms of the business, anyway, we won, didn't we?'

'Sure we did. It was a worse year for you than me, but we did win in the end.'

The phone rang.

At this time of night?

'Leave it,' Cathy said.

'I hadn't a notion of answering it,' he said.

They listened as the twins spoke their message. They were thanking them for the best Christmas ever. It had been magic, they said, pure magic. And Muttie's wife Lizzie, and Lizzie's sister Geraldine had said they could stay up until they were so tired that they fell down.

Tom and Cathy sat side by side on the sofa and listened while the twins talked on. They moved very slightly closer to each other and realised that they were holding hands. It seemed very natural so neither of them moved away.

'Goodnight, Tom. Goodnight, Cathy,' the twins said eventually when they thought the tape might be running out.

'They knew we were here,' Cathy said in surprise.

'Imagine,' said Tom Feather as he stroked her hair.

Quentins

To my dear good Gordon.
Thank you for a lifetime of generosity,
understanding and love.

Part One

1

When Ella Brady was six she went to Quentins. It was the first time anyone had called her Madam. A woman in a black dress with a lace collar had led them to the table. She had settled Ella's parents in and then held out a chair for the six-year-old.

'You might like to sit here, Madam, it will give you a full view of everything,' she said. Ella was delighted and well able to deal with the situation.

'Thank you, I'd like that,' she said graciously. 'You see, it's my very first time here.' This was in case anyone might mistake her for a regular diner.

Her mother and father probably were looking at her dotingly, as they always did. That's what all the childhood pictures showed, anyway ... complete adoration. She remembered her mother telling her that she was the best girl in the world, and her father saying it was a great pity he had to go off to the office every day, otherwise he would stay at home with the best girl.

Once Ella asked why she didn't have sisters and brothers like everyone else seemed to. Her mother said that God had only sent one to this family, but weren't they lucky that it was such a wonderful one. Years later, Ella learned of the many miscarriages and false hopes. But at the time the explanation satisfied her completely, and it did mean that there was no one she had to share her toys or her parents with and that had to be good. They took her to the zoo and introduced her to the animals, they brought her to the circus whenever it came to town, they even went for a weekend to London and took her picture outside Buckingham Palace. But somehow nothing was ever as important as that first visit to a grown-up restaurant, where she had been called Madam and given a seat with a good view.

The Bradys lived in Tara Road, in a house which they had bought years ago before prices started to rocket. It was a tall house with a big back garden where Ella could invite her friends from school. The house had been divided into apartments when the Bradys bought it. So there was a bathroom and kitchenette on every floor. They had restored most of it to make it a family home but Ella's friends were very envious that she had what was like a little world of her own. It was a peaceful, orderly life. Her father Tim had a twenty-two-minute walk to the office every day, and twenty-nine minutes back on the return journey, because he paused to have a half-pint of beer and read the evening paper.

Ella's mother, Barbara, only worked mornings. She was the one who opened up the solicitors' offices right in town near Merrion Square. They trusted her utterly, she always said proudly, to have everything ready when the partners arrived in at 9.30 a.m. All their mail would be on their desks sorted for them. Someone to answer early-morning phone calls and to imply that they were already at work. Then she would go through the huge collection in what was called Barbara's Basket, where they all left anything at all to do with money. Barbara thought of herself as a super-efficient book-keeper, and she controlled the four disorganised, crusty lawyers she worked for with iron rules. Where was this receipt for transport undertaken in the course of a case? Where was that invoice for the new stationery that someone had ordered? Obediently, like small boys, they delivered their accounts to her and she kept them in great ledgers. Barbara dreaded the day when they would all become computerised. But it was still far away. These four would move very slowly. They would have liked the quill pen to work with had they been given a choice!

Barbara Brady left the office at lunchtime. At first she needed to do this in order to pick Ella up from school, but even when her daughter was old enough to return accompanied only by a crowd of laughing girls, Barbara continued the routine of working a half-day only. Barbara knew that she achieved more in her four-and-a-half-hour stint than most others did in a full day. And she knew that her employers realised this too. So she was always in the house when Ella returned. It all worked out very well. Ella had somebody at home to provide a glass of milk and shortbread and to listen to her colourful account of the events of the day, this drama and that adventure. Also, to help her with what homework needed to be done.

This system meant that Tim Brady had an orderly house and a good cooked meal to return to when he got back from the investment brokers where he worked with ever-increasing anxiety over the years. And when he came home every evening at the same time, Ella had a second audience for her marvellous people-filled stories. And the lines of care would fall gradually from his face as she followed her father around the garden, first as a toddler then as a leggy schoolgirl. She would ask questions about the office that her own mother would never dare to ask. Did they think well of Daddy at the office? Was he ever going to be in charge? And later, when it was clear to Ella how unhappy her father was, she asked him why he didn't go somewhere else to work.

Tim Brady might have left the office where he was so uneasy, and gone to another position, but the Bradys were not people to whom change came easily. They had taken a long time to commit to marriage, and an even longer time to produce Ella. They were nearly forty when she arrived, a different generation from the other parents of young children. But that only deepened their love for her. And their determination that she should have everything that life could possibly give her. They did their basement up as a self-contained flat, and let it to three bank girls in order to make a fund for Ella's education. They never did anything just for themselves. In the beginning a few heads were shaken about it all. Was there a possibility that they did too much for the child? some people wondered. That they would spoil her totally? But as it happened even those who had forebodings had to agree that all this love and attention did Ella no harm at all.

From the start she seemed able to laugh at herself. And everyone else. She grew into a tall, confident girl who was open and friendly and who seemed to love her parents as much as they loved her.

Ella kept a photograph album of all the happy events of childhood, and wrote captions under the pictures – 'Daddy and Mam and the Chimp at the zoo. Chimp is on left' – and would peal with laughter at it every time.

Even at the age of thirteen when other children might have wriggled away from scenes of family life, Ella's blonde head pored over the pictures.

'Was that the blue dress I wore to Quentins?' she asked.

'Imagine you remembering that!' Her father was delighted.

'Is it still there?' she asked.

'Very much so, it's got smarter, more expensive, but it's certainly still there and doing well.'

'Oh.' She seemed disappointed to hear it had become expensive. Her parents looked at each other.

'It's a long time since she's been there, Tim.'

'Over half her lifetime,' he agreed, and they decided to go to Quentins on Saturday night.

Ella looked at everything with her sharp young eyes. The place looked a lot more luxurious now than the last time. The thick linen napkins had an embroidered Q on them. The waiters and waitresses wore smart black trousers and white shirts, they knew all about every dish and explained clearly how they were cooked.

Brenda Brennan had noticed the girl looking around with interest. She was exactly the teenage daughter that Brenda would have loved to have had. Alert, friendly, laughing with her parents and grateful for being taken out to a smart place to eat. You didn't always see them like that. Often they were bored and sulky and she would tell Patrick later on in the night that possibly they had been lucky to escape parenthood. But this one was every mother's dream. And her parents didn't look all that young, either. The man could be sixty, he was tired and slightly stooped, the mother in her fifties. Lucky people, the Bradys, to have had such a treasure late in their years.

'What do most people like best to eat, are there any favourites?' the girl asked Brenda when she brought them the menu.

'A lot of our customers like the way we do fish . . . we keep it very simple, with a sauce on the side. And of course many more people are vegetarian nowadays, so Chef has to think up new recipes all the time.'

'He must be very clever,' Ella said. 'And does he talk to you all normally and everything while he's working? I mean, is he temperamental?'

'Oh, he talks all right, not always normally; then of course he's married to me, so he has to talk to me or I'd murder him.' They all laughed together and Ella felt so good to be treated as one of the grown-ups. Then Brenda moved on to another table.

Ella saw both her parents looking at her very intensely.

'What's wrong? Did I talk too much?' she asked, looking from one to the other. She knew she was inclined to prattle on.

'Nothing's wrong, sweetheart. I was just thinking what a pleasure it is to bring you anywhere, you get so much out of everything and everyone,' her mother said.

'And I was thinking almost the very same thing,' her father said, beaming at her.

And as Ella went on to high school she wondered if it was possible that they might care too much about her. All the other girls at school said that their parents were utterly monstrous. She gave a little shiver in case suddenly everything went sour. Maybe her parents wouldn't like her clothes, her career, her husband? It was going dangerously smoothly so far. And it continued to go well during what were meant to be the years from hell, when Ella was sixteen and seventeen. Every other girl at the school had been in open warfare with one or both parents. There had been scenes and tears and dramas. But never in the Brady household.

Barbara may have thought the party dresses Ella bought were far too skimpy. Tim may have thought the music coming from Ella's bedroom too loud. Ella might have wished that her father didn't turn up in his nice safe car and wait outside the disco to take her home at the end of an evening, as if she were a six-year-old. But if anyone thought these things they were never said. Ella did complain that her father fussed over her too much and that her mother worried about her, but she did it lovingly. By the time Ella was eighteen and ready to go to university, it was still one of the most cheerful, peaceful households in the Western Hemisphere.

Ella's friend Deirdre was full of envy. 'It's not fair, really it isn't. They haven't even got annoyed with you for doing science. Most parents refuse point-blank to let you do what you want.'

'I know,' Ella said, worried. 'It's a bit abnormal, isn't it?'

'They don't have rows, either,' Deirdre grumbled. 'Mine are always on at each other about money and drink ... everything, in fact.'

Ella shrugged. 'No, they don't drink, and of course we rent out the flat so they have plenty of money ... and I'm not a drug addict or anything, so I suppose they don't have any worries.'

'But why are they all on red alert about everything in *my* house?' Deirdre wailed.

Ella shrugged. She couldn't explain it ... it just didn't seem to be a problem.

'Wait until we want to stay out all night and go to bed with fellows, then it will be a problem,' Deirdre said with her voice full of menace.

But oddly when that happened it wasn't a problem at all.

In their first year at university, Ella and Deirdre had made a new friend, Nuala, who was from the country and had her own flat. Right in the centre of the city. So whenever anything was going to be too late or too hard to get home from, the fiction of Nuala's flat was used. Ella wondered if her parents were truly convinced, or did they suspect that she might be up to some adventure? Perhaps they didn't want to know about any adventures, so they didn't ask questions to which the answers, if truthful, might be unacceptable. They just trusted her to get along with everything as they always had. Occasionally she felt a bit guilty, but there weren't all that many occasions.

Ella never fell in love during her four years at university, which made her unusual. She did have sex, though. Not a great deal of it. Ella's first lover was Nick, a fellow student. Nick Hayes was first and foremost a friend, but one night he told Ella that he had fancied her from the moment she had come into the first lecture. She had been so cool and calm while he had always been over-eager and loud and saying the wrong thing.

'I never saw you like that,' Ella said truthfully.

'It's got to do with having freckles, green eyes, and having to shout for attention as a member of a large family,' he explained.

'Well, I think it's nice,' she said.

'Does that mean you fancy me a bit too?' he asked hopefully.

'I'm not sure,' she said.

He was so disappointed that she couldn't bear to see his face. 'Couldn't we just talk a lot instead of desiring each other?' she asked. 'I'd love to know about you and why you think science is a good way into film-making, and, well . . . lots of things,' she ended lamely.

'Does that mean that you find me loathsome, repulsive?' he asked.

Ella looked at him. He was trying to joke, but his face looked very vulnerable. 'I find you very attractive, Nick,' she said.

And so they became lovers.

It was less than successful. Oddly they weren't either upset or embarrassed. They were just surprised.

After a few attempts they agreed that it wasn't all they had expected it to be. Nick said that it was his first time too, and that perhaps they should both go off and get experience with people who knew all about it.

'Maybe it's like driving a car,' he said seriously. 'You should learn from someone who knows how to do it.'

Then she was fancied by a sporting hero, who was astonished when she said she didn't want to have sex with him.

'Are you frigid, or what?' he had asked, searching for an explanation.

'I don't think so, no,' Ella had said.

'Oh, I think you must be,' said the sporting hero in an aggrieved manner. So then Ella thought it might be no harm to try it with him, since he was known to have had a lot of ladies. It wasn't any better than with Nick, and there was nothing to talk about, so it was probably worse. She had the small compliment of being told by the sporting hero that she most definitely wasn't frigid.

There were only two other brief experiences, which, compared to Deirdre and Nuala's adventures, were very poor. But Ella wasn't put out. She was twenty-two and a science graduate; she would find love sooner or later. Like everyone.

Nuala found love first. Frank, dark and brooding. Nuala adored him.

When he said that he wanted to join his two brothers in their construction business in London, she was heartbroken.

This called for an emergency dinner at Quentins. 'I really and truly thought he cared, how could I have been so taken in, so humiliated?' she wept to Deirdre and Ella when they settled at their table.

It was meant to be an Early Bird dinner, where people came in at six-thirty and left by eight. It was intended for pre-theatre goers, and the restaurant hoped to be able to have a second sitting for the table. But Deirdre, Ella and Nuala showed no signs of leaving. Mon, the lively little blonde waitress, cleared her throat a couple of times but it was no use.

Finally Ella approached Mrs Brennan. 'I'm very sorry. I know we are meant to be Early Bird and the cheaper menu, but one of the birds at our table has a terrible crisis and we are trying to pat down her feathers.'

Brenda laughed despite herself and despite the people waiting in the bar for the next sitting.

'Go on then, pat her down,' she said good-naturedly.

'Send them a bottle of house red, with a note saying: "To help the crisis",' she told Mon.

'I thought we were meant to be dislodging the Early Birds,' Mon grumbled.

'Yes, you're right, Mon, but we have to be flexible too in this trade,' Brenda said.

'A whole bottle, Mrs Brennan?' Mon was still confused.

'Yes, a very poor wine, one of Patrick's few mistakes, sooner it's drunk the better,' Brenda said.

They were overjoyed at the table.

'As soon as we get some money, we'll eat here properly,' Ella promised.

And they settled down to the plan of war. Should they just murder Frank now, or go to his house and threaten him? Should Nuala find another lover in the next two hours and taunt Frank about it? Should she write him a hurt, sad letter that would break his heart and unsteady his hand for the rest of his working life? None of these things proved to be necessary, because Frank came into the restaurant looking for Nuala. He was greeted with a great deal of hostility by the three girls. He seemed very bewildered. Yet they were ranged against him and there was no way of talking to Nuala alone.

'All right, then,' he said, with his face red and almost tearful. 'All right, it wasn't what I had planned, but here we go.' He knelt down and produced a diamond ring.

'I love you, Nuala, and I was waiting for you to give me an indication of whether you would mind coming to England with me. When you were so silent, I thought you wouldn't come with me. Please, do please, marry me.'

Nuala stared at him with delight. 'I thought you didn't love me, that you were leaving me,' she began.

'Will you marry me?' he said, almost purple now.

'Frank, you see, I thought you wanted a career more than . . .'

A vein was moving dangerously in Frank's forehead.

'I was so upset I had even been looking up jobs in London . . .'

Ella could bear it no longer. 'NUALA, WILL YOU MARRY HIM . . . YES OR NO?' she shouted, and the whole restaurant watched as Nuala said that of course she would, then everyone cheered.

Deirdre and Ella were to be the bridesmaids three months later.

'Maybe I might meet my own true love at Nuala's wedding,' Ella said to her mother. 'I'll certainly be hard to miss in this awful tangerine-coloured outfit she has insisted we wear.'

'You look well in anything,' Barbara said.

'Come on, Mam, please. We look like two things dressed up to sell petrol in a garage or to give away sweets for a charity.'

'Nonsense, you're much too hard on yourself . . .'

'Deirdre was saying that again only the other day, she says you both give me everything I want and praise as well, that I'm a spoiled princess.'

'Nothing could be further from the truth.'

'But Mam, you don't even nag me about not going to Mass.'

'Well, I will if you like, but what good would it do? Anyway Father Kenny says we should look after our own souls and not everyone else's.'

'It's late that Father Kenny and the Church have decided that, what about the Crusades and the Missions?'

'I don't suppose you're going to tell me that you think poor Father Kenny was personally involved in the Crusades and the Missions,' Barbara said with a smile.

'No, of course not, and I will be polite and respectful all during the wedding ceremony, though I think Nuala's crazy to go for the whole church thing.'

'So when the time comes for you, we won't have to alert Father Kenny?'

'No, Mam, but by the time the time comes for me, it could be the planet Mars that might be the in place to get married.'

Ella didn't meet her true love at Nuala's wedding, but Deirdre did meet and greatly fancied one of Frank's married brothers, who had come over from London for the wedding.

'Oh, Deirdre, please don't. I beg you, put him down,' Ella had said.

'What on earth do you mean?' Deirdre's eyes were wide open with innocence.

'I'm worn out covering for you and that fool of the first order, delaying photographs and everything until the bridesmaid comes back dishevelled with one of the ushers, what *are* you thinking of?'

'It's okay, it's a bit of a laugh. Nuala would laugh too – will laugh, in fact.'

'No, Deirdre, you've got it so wrong, that's her brother-in-law now. Someone she'll be seeing with his wife twice a week in London. Nuala won't laugh, and what's more, she won't know.'

'Oh, God, you're so disapproving! That's what people *do* at weddings, that's what weddings are *for*.'

'Adjust your dress, Deirdre, more piccies to be taken.' Ella had a voice like steel.

'What do you mean, adjust my dress?'

'Well, pull it down at the back, it's all caught up in your knickers.' Ella had the satisfaction of watching Deirdre's worried face as she beat around hopelessly at the back of her dress, which was, as it happened, not caught up at all.

At the wedding, Ella met Nuala's cousin, a woman she had not met for years. She was just about to leave her job as a science teacher; did Ella know anyone looking for a job?

Ella said she'd love the job herself.

'I didn't know you were going to teach,' the woman said, surprised.

'Neither did I, until this minute,' said Ella.

Her parents were very surprised at the news also. 'You know you can go on at university and take more degrees, the money is there for you,' her father said, nodding towards the downstairs flat, where the three women bankers were happy to pay for the privilege of living in a good address like Tara Road.

'No, Dad, really, I've been to the school, they're nice. They don't mind I've no experience. They seem to think I'll be able to manage the kids; well, I'm tall physically . . . that's a help, if it comes to arm wrestling,' Ella said with a smile.

'You got a good degree as well,' her mother reminded her.

'Yeah, well, that helped, I suppose – anyway I just have to do this teaching diploma, which means lectures in the evenings . . . and since the school is over that way near the university, I was thinking . . .' She wondered how to put this to them. That it was time to leave home. They took it very calmly.

'We had wondered if you'd like to live in the basement flat eventually?' Her father was tentative.

'You'd be free to come and go like the bank girls there are,' her mother said. 'Nobody to bother you or anything.'

'It's just the distance, Mam, it's not about people bothering me. You never have.'

'You know, days could go by without your having to see us, just like the tenants. And there are big, strong walls . . .'

She knew this was their last plea, then they would give in. 'No, I'm not worried about your hearing my wild parties, Dad. Honestly, it's only to make it all quicker and easier. And I'll be at home often, even staying for whole weekends if you want me.'

The deal was done.

'I don't believe you, your own place *and* a room at home, that's pure greed. Why should you get it all, Ella Brady?' Deirdre said.

'Because I'm reliable, that's why,' Ella replied. 'I'm no trouble. I never have been. That's why I have such an easy life.'

And it all did go easily. Ella liked the school, the other young teachers warned her of the pitfalls, the staffroom bores, the danger of getting sucked into campaigns, how to cope with parent–teacher meetings, how to lobby for better equipment for the lab. She liked the children and their enthusiasm. It seemed only the other day that she was in a classroom on the other side of the desk. The lectures were easy too, and she found herself a flat in a leafy road only five minutes from the school.

'I feel free here somehow, independent,' Ella explained to Deirdre.

'I don't know why you bothered, you got your meals served to you back in your parents' place, and it's not as if you ever brought a bloke in here, by the looks of things.'

'How do you know?' Ella laughed.

'Well, have you?'

'No, as it happens, but I might.'

'See?' Deirdre was triumphant. 'I don't know why you feel so free and independent, I really don't.'

And in a way, neither did Ella know. She thought it had something to do with not having to think about her parents' marriage. They were old now, in their sixties, and they still clung to work rather than retire like other people of their age did. They could sell that big house in Tara Road for a fortune and buy a much smaller place. Then Mam would not have to go in anxiously to the law firm where she suspected that she was being kept on from kindness. Dad would not have to go to what he saw as a changing world of money men.

They got on well together. Surely they did? As she had so often told Deirdre, they never had rows. Suppose they were to turn the house back into apartments, then the rent that would bring in would mean they could retire. She would say nothing yet, just let the idea develop.

She went back home to see them for supper at least once a week and every Sunday as well, but she never stayed over. She said she studied better in the flat. Some months later, she made the suggestion that they should let her room.

Never had anything fallen on such unresponsive ground. They were astounded that she should even think of it. They didn't want to retire. What would they do with their days?

Suddenly Ella's legendary laughter left her. She saw a very bleak future ahead. Imagine what desperate lives people must lead if these two, who were meant to be Happily Married, couldn't even bear the thought of being side by side at home instead of going to jobs which they found tiring and anxiety-creating.

'I'd prefer to be a nun than have a dead marriage,' Ella told Deirdre very earnestly.

Deirdre worked in a busy laboratory where she knew a great many men.

'You might as well *be* a nun, the way you live,' Deirdre said. 'In fact, I think you are one in plain clothes.'

And as time went by Nuala still kept in touch from London. She had decided not to get a job after all, but instead to work in the company as a receptionist. Frank said it was better to keep all the family secrets within the family, she wrote.

'What family secrets does she mean?' Deirdre wondered.

'Probably that her brothers-in-law are screwing everything that moves in there,' Ella suggested.

'Very droll.' Deirdre still wondered what they could be hiding.

'Oh, for heaven's sake, Dee. Remember them at the wedding in their sharp suits and their eyes never still, moving around the room? Those fellows have never known what it is like to keep proper books or pay proper tax in their lives.'

'You think all builders are unreliable, that's your prejudice.' Deirdre was spirited.

'No, I don't, look at Tom Feather! His family are above-board. Lots of them are. It's just Frank's lot make me shudder.'

'If you're right, do you suppose they have our pal Nuala drawn into it all?' Deirdre wondered.

'Poor Nuala. I'd just hate to be wrapped up with that lot,' Ella said.

'Now funnily enough, I'd find being wrapped up with Eric, that eldest brother, no problem at all,' Deirdre laughed.

'You might get your chance, they're going to have a family gathering here in Dublin for Frank's parents. We're invited,' Ella read at the end of the letter.

'Great. I'll get one of those suspender belt things.'

'No, Deirdre, you won't, it's only three years since the wedding, they won't have forgotten you. We'll keep well away from Frank's family.'

The party was very showy. There were even columnists and photographers at it. Frank and his three brothers posed endlessly as an Irish success story. They were photographed with politicians, celebrities, with their parents and their wives.

'It's very fancy for a fortieth wedding anniversary, isn't it ... all this razzmatazz. I think that the old folk look a bit bewildered,' Deirdre said.

Ella pushed her sunglasses back on her head to study the party more seriously. 'No, they're well able for it, the mam and dad, for them it's a triumphal celebration. It's "Look at what a success Our Boys have made in life".'

'Why don't you like them, Ella?'

'I don't know, I really don't, to be honest.'

'Do you think Nuala's happy?'

'I think so, a bit hunted. But she got what she wanted, so I suppose that's happy.'

Ella always remembered that remark because just as she was saying it a man beside them was jostled against her by a press photographer. 'Please, Mr Richardson, can we have you in the group?'

'No, thanks all the same, but this is a family party. It's not appropriate.'

'It would make sure we got it in the paper?' The cameraman was persuasive, but not enough.

'No, thanks, as I said, I'd really much prefer to talk to these two lovely ladies.'

Ella turned at the calm, very forceful voice. And she looked at Don Richardson, Financial Consultant, whose picture was indeed often in the newspapers. But they had never done him justice. He was good-looking certainly – dark curly hair, blue eyes – but he had a way of looking at you that excluded everyone else in the room. Ella knew she hadn't imagined this because out of the corner of her eye she saw Deirdre shrugging slightly and moving away. Leaving her alone with Don Richardson.

Ella had never been able to flirt. Her friend Nick said it was a weakness in a woman. Men just loved that come-on look from under the eyelashes. Ella was too up-front he said, lessened the magic somehow. She wished she had listened to Nick. Now for the very first time she wanted to know how to do it.

Even if she had five minutes with Deirdre – but her friend had gone to hover in the danger area of Frank's brothers.

It turned out not to be necessary.

He held out his hand to her with a great smile. 'Ella Brady from Tara Road, how are you? I'm Don Richardson. It's such a pleasure to meet you.'

'How do you know my name?' she croaked.

'I asked a couple of people, Danny Lynch, the property guy, he told me. He lives near you, apparently.'

Ella heard herself saying, 'Yes, well, near my parents, actually. I've moved out of home, you see, and I have my own place.'

'Why am I very pleased to hear that, Ella Brady?' he asked. He hadn't stopped smiling and he hadn't stopped holding her hand.

2

Ella got home from the hotel somehow on her own. She thought afterwards that she must have taken a taxi, but she didn't remember it. She sat down and looked around her for a long time before she took stock of it all. This was not happening to her. This was the stuff of silly movies or magazine stories, which had to have the love-at-first-sight theme running through them. Don Richardson was just a known charmer, a professional who made his money by saying Trust Me to people, by holding their hands for a little too long, by letting his eyes lock into theirs. There was obviously a Mrs Richardson in the room tonight, maybe a history of several of them. There were little Richardsons at home, all of whom would need quality time. Ella Brady was *not* going to go down this road. She had mopped the tears of too many friends who had told her fantasy tales of men who were going to leave their wives. She would not join their number. Women had an amazing capacity to fool themselves, Ella had seen it over and over. She would never be part of it.

He was waiting outside the school next morning. Sitting in a new BMW and smiling as she approached. Ella wished that she had dressed better. But he didn't seem to notice.

'Are you surprised?' he asked.

'Very,' she said.

'Can you sit in for a moment? Please,' he asked.

'I have to get to class.'

She sat in his car. She wanted to make some kind of joke, some wisecracking remark that would disguise how nervous and excited she felt.

But she decided to say nothing at all. Let him explain what had to be explained.

'I'm forty-one years old, Ella, married for eighteen years to Margery Rice, daughter of Ricky Rice, who is theoretically my boss, or at any rate the money in our company. I have two sons aged sixteen and fifteen. Margery and I have a dead marriage – it suits both of us to stay together, at the moment anyway. It certainly suits her father and it suits our two sons. We share a home out in Killiney, by the sea. I also have a business flat in the Financial Services Centre.

'Margery spends most of her day golfing or running charity events. We live entirely separate lives. You would be breaking up nothing, nil, zilch, zero, if you were to say that you would have dinner with me tonight in

Quentins at around eight.' He put his head on one side as if waiting for her argument.

'I'd like that, see you there,' Ella said, and got out of the car. She felt her legs shaking as she went into the staffroom. Ella Brady, who had never taken a class off in her teaching life, went straight to the principal and said she had to leave the school at lunchtime, it was an emergency. She booked a hairdo, a manicure and a leg wax. She bought fresh flowers for her flat, changed the sheets and tidied the place, examining it with a critical eye. It was probably a wasted effort. But it was wiser to be prepared.

'You got your hair done,' he said as she joined him in one of the private booths at Quentins.

'You went home and changed too. Long trek out to Killiney and back,' Ella said, smiling.

'Separate lives, Ella, either you believe me or you don't.' Don had an extraordinary smile.

'Of course I believe you, Don. Now that that's out of the way, we never have to mention it again.'

'And do I have to get anything out of the way? Long-term loves, jealous suitors, possible fiancés in the wings?'

'Nothing at all,' she said. 'Believe me or don't.'

'I totally believe you, what a wonderful dinner we are going to have,' he said.

The evening passed too quickly. She reminded herself over and over that there must be no brittle jokes about it being time to send him home.

He had dealt with that side of it already. They were meeting as free agents or not at all. He told her about a lunch they'd had in the office today with outside caterers for the first time, and how it must be the hardest job on earth preparing and clearing up after businessmen who all wanted endless vodka and tonics without letting their bosses see just how much they were knocking back.

They were marvellous kids, he said, ran the thing like clockwork, he'd get them more work. Didn't even want to be paid in cash, said they had some accountant who went ballistic over VAT and everything. Ella said that she thought everyone did.

'Sure they do, of course they do. I was only trying to give these two at Scarlet Feather a break.'

'Oh, Scarlet Feather, I know them! Tom and Cathy, they're great people,' Ella said, pleased they had someone else in common.

'Yes, they seemed fine. I'd hire them again. They're not going to get rich quick, but that's their business.'

He seemed for a moment to think less of them because they weren't going to get rich quick. A shadow came over it all. Maybe Rice and Richardson only liked people who made lots of money.

'How do you know the builders, Eric and his brothers?' she asked.

'Oh, business,' he said quickly. 'We handle a few investments for Eric and the boys. And you?'

'My friend Nuala is married to Frank, the youngest brother,' she said.

'Some small city. Imagine you knowing that catering couple as well. Anyway, Angel Ella, now tell me about your lunch.'

She told him about the elderly teacher who was afraid they would all get radiation from the microwave, and the sports teacher who had lost his front tooth biting into a hard French roll. She told him about the Third Years sending up a petition about school uniform being a danger to girls as they were maturing, since it made them objects of ridicule. None of these things had happened today because Ella had been racing around getting her flat cleaned and her body prepared for what might lie ahead. But as stories they were real incidents from other lunchtimes in the staffroom, and they made him laugh. And with Don Richardson it was going to be important to keep him laughing.

If you wanted to be his friend or whatever there would be no place for moody.

No place at all.

He drove her back to her flat.

'I enjoyed this evening,' Don Richardson said.

'Me, too.' Her throat was tight and her chest constricted. Did she ask him in? They were free agents. Or was it sluttish? And why should it be sluttish for the girl, not the man? She would wait and take her timing from him.

'So, since I have your telephone number, maybe we can go out again, Angel Ella?' he said.

'Yes, please.' She kissed his cheek and got out of the car while she still had the strength to do so.

He waved and turned the car.

She would not spend *any* time wondering would he drive eleven miles south to Killiney and the dead marriage or one mile north into the city to the bachelor pad.

She let herself into the flat and looked accusingly at the vase of expensive fresh flowers she had arranged before she had left.

'Fine lure you were to get him back here,' she said.

The flowers said nothing.

Maybe I should get myself a cat or a dog, something that might grunt at me when I come back here alone, Ella thought. But then she might not always be coming back here alone.

It was her father's birthday next day. Ella had bought him a gift voucher for a hotel in Co. Wicklow. An old-fashioned place with a big, rambling garden. When she was a child, they sometimes drove down there for Sunday lunch. He used to point out the flowers to her and she would learn the names. Ella remembered her mother smiling a lot there, sitting and pouring out afternoon tea in the garden.

Maybe it would be a nice peaceful place for them to go and stay. The voucher covered dinner, bed and breakfast. It could be taken up any time in the next month. Surely they would like that?

They loved the idea, both of them. Ella felt tears at the back of her eyes to see such gratitude.

'What a wonderful gift, just imagine it,' her father said, over and over.

Ella wondered why had he never thought of such a thing himself if it was so great. Her mother was delighted too.

'The three of us all going down to Holly's *and* staying the night!' she said.

Ella realised with a shock that they thought she was going with them as well.

'So when will we go?' Her father was excited now like a child.

'A Friday or a Saturday?' she suggested. She couldn't ruin it all now by explaining that she hadn't meant to come with them.

'You choose,' Father said.

Don wouldn't ask her out on a Saturday, that would surely be family time.

They fixed to go the following Saturday. Just as Ella was about to call the hotel and make the booking her mobile phone rang.

'Hallo,' Don Richardson said.

She noted that he hadn't said his name. It was arrogant in a way to assume that she knew who it was. But she was no good at playing games.

'Oh, hallo,' she said pleasantly.

'Is it okay to talk?' he asked.

'Oh, it's always okay,' Ella said, but she got up and moved out towards the spiral steps down to the garden at the same time. She gave an apologetic shrug to her parents as if this were a duty call she had to take.

'I wondered if you'd like to have dinner Saturday?'

She looked behind her into the sitting room. Her parents were examining the brochure for Holly's as if it were some kind of map of a treasure trove. She could not cancel it now.

Ella held on to the wrought-iron rail. 'I'm so sorry, but I've just arranged something, literally in the last few minutes, and it would be a bit difficult, you see, to . . .'

He cut her off.

'Never mind, it was on the off chance, there'll be other evenings.'

He was about to go. She knew she must not begin to burble at him but she was so very anxious to keep him on the line.

'I *wish* I didn't have to . . .'

'But you have,' he said crisply before she could cancel her parents' outing and go with him wherever he suggested. 'So catch you again.' And he was gone.

All during dinner her heart felt like a stone. And later, she helped her mother with the washing up and they had the most extraordinary conversation.

'Ella, you couldn't have done anything that would please your father more, it's just what he needs. He's been very pressured at work.'

'Then why didn't *you* take him to Holly's, Mother?' Ella hoped her tone was not as impatient as she felt inside. Her mother looked at her, amazed.

'But what would we have done there together, just the two of us looking at each other? We might as well just stay here looking at each other if there was to be just the two of us.'

Ella looked at her mother in shock. 'You can't mean that, Mam?'

'Mean what?' Her mother was genuinely surprised.

'That you don't have anything to talk about with Dad.'

'But what *is* there to talk about, haven't we said it all?' Her mother spoke as if this were the most glaringly obvious thing in the world.

'But if that's the way it is, why don't you leave him, why don't you separate?' Ella stood with the dinner plate in her hand. Her mother took it away from her.

'Oh, Ella, don't be ridiculous, why on earth would we want to do that? I never heard of such nonsense.'

'People do, Mam.'

'Not people like me and your dad. Come back inside now and we'll talk about this great visit to Holly's.'

Ella felt as if a light warm woollen blanket had been put over her head and was beginning to suffocate her.

She went to the cinema with Deirdre and for a drink afterwards. They talked normally as always. Or so Ella thought. Then Deirdre ordered another drink and asked Ella, 'They're serving sandwiches. Do you want one?'

'What?' Ella said. 'Oh, yes, whatever.'

'I'll get you one with mouse's dirt and bird droppings in it, then,' Deirdre said cheerfully.

'What?'

'Oh, good. Welcome back, you're awake again,' Deirdre laughed.

'I don't know what you mean.'

'Ella, you saw none of the movie, you haven't said a word to me, you've bitten your lip and shuffled about. Are you going to tell me or are you not?'

She had told Deirdre everything since they were thirteen, but she couldn't. It was odd, there was too much to tell and too little. Too much in that she had fallen in love with an entirely wrong man *and* that her own parents' thirty-year marriage, which she had always thought was very happy, was fairly empty. And yet too little to tell. To Deirdre it would all be simple. She would say that Ella should go for the man, married or not. Take what she wanted and not get hurt. And Deirdre would say that everyone's parents had rotten marriages, it's just the way things were.

'Nothing, Dee, just fussing, ruminating, being neurotic . . . that's all it is, honestly.'

'That's all it ever is, honestly, but you always tell me,' Deirdre grumbled.

'You've got such a great, uncomplicated way of looking at things. I'm envious.'

'No, you're not, you think I'm sexually indiscriminate, that I have a hard heart . . . come on, you're not envious.'

'I am. Tell me of your latest drama, whatever it was.'

'Well, I had a great session with that Don Richardson, you know, the consultant guy you see all over the papers. *Very* good he is too, insatiable nearly.'

Deirdre held her head on one side and watched Ella's face. After a few seconds she was contrite. 'Ella, you clown, I was just joking.'

Ella said nothing. She had both hands on her head as if trying to clear it.

'Ella! I didn't, I never even met him, you silly thing, I was only on a fishing expedition to see if that's who you fancied.'

Ella took her hands away from her face.

'And it seems as if I was right,' Deirdre said.

'How did you know?' Ella's voice was a whisper.

'Because I'm your best friend, and also because you couldn't take your eyes off him when he came up to you at Nuala's do the other night.'

'Was that only the other night?' Ella was amazed.

'Will I get a half-bottle of wine?' Deirdre suggested.

'Get a full bottle,' Ella said, some of the colour coming back to her face.

The next Saturday the Bradys left Tara Road in the middle of the afternoon so that they could take a tour of Wicklow Gap before going to Holly's. Ella was determined to do it well if she was doing it at all. Give them a day and night out to remember. Oddly, Deirdre had seemed highly approving that she had refused the date with Don for Saturday night. To have agreed would make Ella too available. He would call again, mark Deirdre's words, she knew about such things. Ella had brought a flask of coffee and three little mugs and they stood in the afternoon sunshine to admire the scenery. There was bright yellow gorse on the bare hills, and some flashes of deep purple heather. Here and there a thin vague-looking sheep wandered as if bemused that there wasn't more green grass for them to eat.

'Imagine, you can't see a house or a building anywhere and yet be so near Dublin, isn't it amazing?' Ella said.

'Like the Yorkshire Moors. I was there once,' her father said.

Ella hadn't known that. 'Were you there too, Mam?'

'No, before my time.' She sounded clipped.

'It's a bit like Arizona too, all that space, except it's red desert over there,' Ella said. 'Remember the time you gave me the money for the Greyhound Bus Tour? When Deirdre and I went off to see the world.'

'You were twenty-one,' her mother remembered.

'And you sent us a postcard every three days,' her father said.

'You were very generous. I saw so much that I'll never forget, thanks to you. Deirdre had to work for the money and borrow some, I don't think she's paid it all back yet.'

'Why have a child if you can't give her a holiday?' Barbara Brady's lips were pursed with disapproval of those who didn't take parenting seriously.

'And what is money when all is said and done?' said Tim Brady, who had spent all his working hours, weeks and years advising people about money and nothing else.

Ella was mystified. But she remembered Deirdre's advice about not killing herself trying to understand them, there was probably nothing to understand.

Holly's Hotel was buzzing with people, most of them having driven from Dublin for dinner. But the Brady family had their rooms, time to stroll in the gardens, have a leisurely bath and then meet in the chintzy little bar for a sherry while looking at the menu.

'I must say, this is a marvellous treat,' her father said over and over.

'You are such a thoughtful girl,' her mother would murmur in agreement.

Ella told them that she loved looking at people in restaurants and imagining stories about them. Like that couple near the window, for example, they were drug pushers back in Dublin, just come for a nice respectable weekend to know what the Other World was like.

'Are they?' Her mother was alarmed.

'Of course not,' Ella said. 'It's only pretend. Look at that group over there – what do you think they are?'

Slowly her parents got drawn into the game. 'The older couple is trying to get the younger ones to go halves in buying a boat,' said Tim Brady.

'The younger couple is telling the older ones that they're bankrupt and asking for a loan,' said Barbara Brady.

'I think it's a group sex thing, they all answered one of Miss Holly's ads for wife-swapping weekends,' Ella suggested.

And they were all laughing at the whole crazy notion of it in this of all places when Ella looked up and saw Don Richardson and his family being ushered from the bar into the dining room. He looked over and saw them at that moment. It would be frozen for ever in Ella's mind. The Bradys all laughing at one table and Don at the door holding it open for his father-in-law, his sons aged sixteen and fifteen, and his wife Margery who only lunched for charities and otherwise played golf. Margery, who was not large, weather-beaten and distant-looking, but who wore a smart red silk suit and had one of those handbags which cost a fortune. Margery, who was petite, smiled up at her husband in a way that Ella would never be able to do since she was exactly the same height.

Ella's father was very engaged by the menu. Would smoked trout salad be too heavy a starter if he was going to have Guinness, steak and oyster pie?

Ella wondered if she might possibly be going to faint. Was this a sign that since she had refused to go out with him Don had decided to play the rare role of family man? Was this self-delusion of the worst kind? Did he think less of her for being with her parents? Or quite possibly more? Would he acknowledge her in the dining room? Ella ordered absently and chose the wine. It was too late now to ask if they could eat upstairs in the bedroom. She had to face it.

In the dining room they were quite a distance from the Richardson party and it was the two teenage boys and their grandfather who faced them, the couple with the dead marriage had their backs to the Bradys.

Ella's parents were still playing the 'let's imagine' game about people. The two women over there were planning a shoplifting spree, her mother thought, or they were discussing putting their father into an old people's home. Ella's father thought they had hacked into a computer and made a fortune and were wondering how to spend it.

'What do you think, Ella?'

She had been thinking about the body language of Don and Margery Richardson as they sat together easily. They were not stroking each other or hand-holding but they didn't have that stiffness that couples often have when there is a distance. Like her own parents had. Every night except tonight when they seemed to be very relaxed.

'Go on, Ella, what do you think they are?'

She glanced briefly at the two retired women who obviously treated themselves out to a meal and a gossip twice a year.

'Lesbians planning which of them should be inseminated this time,' she said, forgetting she was talking to her parents rather than to Deirdre. To her surprise they thought it was very funny and when Don turned around slightly to look for her as she had known he would, there they were all laughing again. Ella felt a touch of hysteria. She wanted to stand up and scream to the whole restaurant that at best life was just one ludicrous, hypocritical façade. But you'd need to be a brave person to lose control at Miss Holly's. Ella thought that he would say hallo, stop by the table and say something smooth and pleasant. Just be prepared for it and behave accordingly. Nothing glib or too smart.

Her father removed his glasses and seemed pleased to be able to identify at least one of the fellow diners. 'My goodness, that's Ricky Rice, of Rice and Richardson Consultants,' he said.

'Oh, do you know them, Dad?' she asked, her mouth hardly able to form the words.

'No, no, not at all, but we all know of them. Dear Lord, do *they* have clients,' he said, shaking his head with envy.

'How did they get such great business, do you think?' Her mother was peering over at the table.

'Know all the right people apparently,' her father shrugged, his face defeated and sad.

Ella was determined to raise the mood. She asked them about property prices in Tara Road. One house there had sold for a fortune recently.

'Didn't you do well to buy a house there, Dad?' she said.

'We wanted a place with a nice garden for you to grow up,' her mother said. 'And wasn't it marvellous? Still is, of course.'

'But you don't live there any more,' her father said.

'No, Dad, not full-time, but I'll come back and see you as I will always do while you're there, or wherever you are.'

'What do you mean, wherever we are?' Her mother sounded very anxious.

Please, please, may he not look around again now and see them all frowning and anxious. 'I meant, Mam, that some day you'll want to sell Tara Road and buy a smaller place, won't you? Won't you?' She looked from one to the other eagerly.

'We hadn't ever thought . . .' her father began.

'Why should we leave our home?' her mother said.

'You know that guy Danny Lynch who used to live in Tara Road? He says this is the time to sell.'

'Well, he left his wife and children – he's no role model,' her mother said.

'No, but he is an estate agent.'

'Not any longer.' Her father spoke gravely. 'Apparently he and his partner got into a lot of funny business,' he said very disapprovingly.

'And anyone who would cheat on his wife like he did isn't worth listening to on any subject,' Ella's mother said.

There was a movement two tables away. Ella saw him stand up. She knew he was coming over. Make them laugh, she told herself.

It was a tall order. She had about thirty seconds.

'Don't mind me, Deirdre says that I'm obsessed by property. That's another game I play, I pretend houses aren't what they seem to be. Apart from Holly's Hotel here being the wife-swapping centre of Europe, I think Mam's law office is money laundering big time. And wait till I tell you what I think Dad's firm is up to . . .' She stopped just as he arrived at the table. It had worked, they were both looking at her with eager smiles to know what she would say next.

'Hallo, I'm Don Richardson. We met at Frank and Nuala's party this week.'

'Oh, that's right. Don, these are my parents, Tim and Barbara Brady.'

His handshake was so firm, his tone so warm, she felt nothing but gratitude to him. He was being so genuinely pleasant to two strangers. He was not speaking to this couple as a man who was about to seduce their daughter, betray his wife; she saw him as someone who had come to rescue the conversation. She explained it was her father's birthday; he explained that it was a celebration because his son had scored a winning goal in a match. In the few short moments that he stayed he managed to discover the name of, and praise, her father's firm, he even knew of the office where her mother worked when it was mentioned and said they were highly respected lawyers. And then he was gone.

They spoke of him admiringly.

'Very hard-working man. That's why he got where he is. People used to say it was all his father-in-law but the firm was nothing until he got into it,' her father said.

'And very easy with people too,' her mother said.

Ella felt it was very foolish to be as pleased as she was that they liked him. And she felt very pleased indeed at the way he smiled at her as he left the dining room. She knew he was going to call her again soon. But she hadn't known that he would call her at midnight.

'I hope I didn't wake you,' he said on her mobile phone.

'No. I was reading, there's a kind of window seat here, I was actually looking at the shapes of the bushes and flowers more than reading.'

'Bushes? Flowers? Where are you?' He sounded confused.

'How quickly men forget. I'm in Holly's, we met here about four hours ago.'

'In Holly's?' He sounded very disappointed.

'Don, you know I am. Is this a game?'

'If so, I've lost,' he said.

'Where are *you*?' she asked.

'I'm parked in your road. I was hoping you'd ask me in for coffee.'

'So your son's celebration is over?'

'And your father's continues?'

'That's life, I suppose.' She was smiling now, he was outside her door back in Dublin. He had not gone back to his Killiney home with the wife in red silk. His ties to his home must be very loose, as he had said. He had driven all the way in to Dublin on the off chance of seeing her. He *must* fancy her.

'You could come in for coffee another night. Like tomorrow,' she said.

'Tomorrow's bad for me – a big political fund-raiser – I have to be there glad-handing people.' He sounded regretful.

'Oh, well.' She made herself shrug.

'Monday night?' he offered.

Deirdre had told her not to be too available. 'Bad for me, Tuesday or Wednesday are fine, though.'

'Tuesday then, I suppose, since it can't be earlier. Suppose I brought a bottle of truly lovely wine, would you cook me a steak?'

'It's a deal,' said Ella, who wondered how could any human get through the number of hours between now and Tuesday at eight o'clock.

They had the Full Irish Breakfast, and Miss Holly came to talk to them. 'Nice to meet Don Richardson last night.' Ella's mother wanted to show that they were anyone's equal.

'Ah, yes, wonderful family man, Mr Richardson,' said Miss Holly, nodding in approval. 'You see it all in this business, Mrs Brady, believe me, so many of our so-called business leaders don't have the same standards as they used to, no indeed.'

'Brings his family here a lot then, does he?' said Ella in a strained voice, stabbing at the sausage on her plate as if she wanted desperately to kill it.

'Well, no, he works so hard, you see. Usually it's just his wife and her father and the children, but Mr Richardson always rings and orders them some special wine, and when he can he's with them.'

'That's nice,' said Ella, suddenly feeling a great deal better.

She kissed them goodbye at Tara Road and refused to think about the fact that they might spend a lonely wordless afternoon now that she was no longer there to be the central point of their life. She had done her best to get them to sell this big place. To liberate some money so that they could go on a cruise, get a better car or whatever they might like. She knew that it wouldn't matter where they lived or how much money they had, they were not going to take their future in their own hands and make the best of it. Which was what she, Ella, was going to do. She was going to get involved with this dangerously attractive man, no matter how many turnings there would be in the road ahead. And if she got hurt then she got hurt, that's all there was to it.

Her phone rang. She pulled in to the side of the road but it wasn't what she had hoped. It was Nick, her old mate from college.

'Oh, Nick,' she said.

'Well, I've had warmer receptions,' he said.

'Sorry, I'm coping with traffic,' she lied.

'No, you're not, you fibber, you've pulled in, I'm in the car behind you.'

'Is this a police state or what?' she said and leaped out of the car to give him a hug.

'I saw you ahead of me and I wondered if you'd like a late lunch.'

'Like it? I'd love it, Nick.'

They sat companionably as he told her all about the dramas in his life and she told him nothing about the dramas in hers. Nick was such an easy person to talk to, such a friend. No need to explain anything or wonder about what he was thinking. It was all there on his handsome, freckled face and in his big green eyes. He was wearing a black leather jacket and sunglasses on his head. It would have been so uncomplicated to love someone like this instead of what she had got herself into. She looked at Nick affectionately. He would never know what she was thinking.

When they had last met he had just set up a small independent film production company called Firefly Films with two others and they were doing quite well. Much better than they had hoped. They still did a fair bit of bread and butter work like videos of weddings and advertising things, a lot of word of mouth. That's what it was all about in Dublin today – Nick had been able to point a job to Tom and Cathy who ran a catering company called Scarlet Feather. And apparently it had gone well so now Tom and Cathy in return had got him a job to film and edit a big fund-raising event tonight. Huge money, the guy wanted to pay in cash but, hey, that was okay too.

'Tonight?' Ella's eyes were dancing.

'Yeah, he wants a nice, neat fifteen minutes of the highlights showing as many celebs as possible and literally just the best sound bites, no long tedious speeches ... we could do it in our sleep.'

'Nick, can I come with you? To help. Please.'

'Hey, Ella, you don't want to be involved in any of this kind of business!' Nick was startled.

'Please. I beg you. I'll get you coffee, I'll carry your bags.'

'Why?'

'I just want to, we're friends. You wanted to have lunch with me and I said yes, why can't I say I want to go on this gig with you tonight and you say yes?'

'You'd be bored.'

'Please, Nick.'

'Okay, but you do get to carry my bags, do you hear?'

'I love you, Nick.'

'You love someone certainly; you're as high as a kite,' he said. 'But it's not me.'

She met them outside the hotel later in the evening. She hardly recognised Nick, he was so businesslike and efficient.

'This is Ella. She knows nothing but she's here to help,' he said casually. Ella grinned. 'I always wanted to be in movies,' she said, joking.

'Well, you picked the wrong team, tonight's only video,' said a small, earnest-looking girl who did not at all like the tall, blonde Ella coming in on the act.

'Look, I promise I won't be in the way.' Ella concentrated on the girl, the two men were no trouble and couldn't have cared less about her. 'Just tell me what to do or to get out of the way and I'll do it.'

'Well, okay, thanks then.' The girl was gruff.

'What's your name?' Ella asked.

'Sandy.'

'Well, Sandy, I mean it, anything I can do?'

'Why are you here?' Sandy was blunt. She fancied Nick greatly and probably in vain. But as far as she was concerned, Ella was a threat.

'Because I'm keen on someone who's going to be here and it was the only way I could get in.' There is never anything as good as total honesty.

Sandy believed her immediately.

'And is he keen on you?'

'Not enough,' Ella answered, and they were friends for life.

She tidied away their gear into corners, got a pot of coffee from the kitchen, asked the office to let them have three photocopies of the seating plan rather than the one they had been given. And was in fact quite useful and helpful until she saw Don Richardson come in with Margery on his arm.

This time she wore dark green silk and what looked very like real emeralds. She knew everyone and they were all kissing her on the cheek. Today was a Sunday yet she looked as if she had come straight from the hairdresser, she must have somebody come to her house. She was like a little porcelain doll. Ella felt tall, ungainly, sweaty, and out of place. From behind a pillar she watched as Don spoke swiftly to Nick telling him what needed to be done, where to position himself. And then she did no more to help anyone in Firefly Films, she stood there twisting a table napkin around in her hands and watching Don Richardson. He had said tonight was bad for him to meet her because he had to do a lot of glad-handing.

She wasn't even sure what the words meant.

Now she knew. It was shaking hands and at the same time gripping the other person's arm firmly above the elbow. It was looking into their eyes and thanking them for their support. It was turning to introduce them to other people with a fixed smile of gratitude. And Don Richardson did it very well.

Ella had no idea how long she stood there while others in the great dining room ate through a five-course meal. But Don didn't sit down either, he moved from table to table, talking here, laughing there, always nodding imperceptibly at Nick if he wanted him to turn the camera on groups. Margery sat at a table and talked easily with politicians and their wives. Margery's eyes never roamed the room looking for him, wondering was he hesitating too long at this table, laughing too animatedly with the two bosomy women who did not want to let him go. Was this because she knew how to play it? Giving him a long lead meant he always came home? Or had he been telling Ella the truth, that they really did lead separate lives?

There was dancing now, but Firefly Films' work was over. Don Richardson hadn't wanted to film any red-faced groping on the dance floor. The party supporters would want to see a video of themselves looking decorous, mixing with the party leader, with cabinet ministers and celebrities. That's what Nick and Ed and Sandy were going back to the office to do now, edit the video and copy it for Don Richardson. It had to be in his office next day by lunchtime. It would mean working all night.

'I don't suppose you're going to come and help us some more back at base, Ella,' Nick said, without any hope.

'I'd love to,' she said guiltily. 'It's just I have school tomorrow morning, you see.'

'Why did I know you were going to say that?' Nick gave her a brotherly pat on the behind.

Sandy wasn't jealous any more. As they packed away the equipment, she whispered to Ella, 'Did you see him?'

'Yes, I saw him.'

'Did he see you?' Still a whisper.

'No, no he didn't.'

'Are you glad or sorry you came?' Sandy had to know. Again total truth is very satisfying.

'A bit of both, to be honest,' Ella Brady said, and slipped out the back way before she might see Don Richardson hold out his hand and ask his tiny, emerald-wearing, estranged wife to dance.

She got a taxi home and stayed awake until 5 a.m. After two hours she woke groggy and bad-tempered. And when she got to her class, she didn't feel any better. 'If you know what's good for all of us, you lot must be no trouble today,' she warned the Fifth Years, who were inclined to be difficult.

'Was it a heavy night, Miss Brady?' asked Jacinta O'Brien, one of the more fearless troublemakers.

Ella strode so purposefully towards the girl's desk that the class gasped.

Miss Brady couldn't be about to hit a pupil, surely? But that's what it looked like. Ella stood, her face inches from the child's. 'There's always one in every class, Jacinta, one smart-arse who goes too far and ruins it for everyone. In this class you are the one. I was going to treat you like adults, tell you the truth – which is that I didn't sleep and don't feel too well. I was going to ask for your co-operation so that I could give you as good a lesson as possible.

'But no, there's always the smart-arse, so instead we will have a test. Get out your papers this minute.'

Ella gave them four questions, and then she sat there trembling at her outburst. She had said smart-arse. Twice.

This wasn't the kind of school where you said that.

She had meant to say smart aleck. Oh, God, why couldn't it be Tuesday? Then she could see Don Richardson that night.

But she got through the day and was relieved to get home.

'I understand you've started stalking him now,' Deirdre said on the phone that night.

'How did you hear that?' Ella gasped.

'It was in one of the gossip columns. I can't remember which,' Deirdre said. As usual Ella fell for it.

'What?'

'Oh, shut up, Ella, you eejit. I met Nick. He told me you wanted to crash Don's big fund-raiser with him.'

Ella began to breathe again.

'Some capital city this is, you can't do anything,' she grumbled.

'Well, you haven't *done* anything, have you?' Deirdre reminded her.

'No. Tomorrow night,' Ella said. 'It would have been tonight, but I remembered what you said about not being too available.'

'Can we meet lunchtime Wednesday?' asked Deirdre.

'No, that's my short lunch . . . it will have to wait till after work.'

'Early Bird Quentins? My treat?' Deirdre offered.

'Early Bird starts at six-thirty. I'll be there,' Ella promised.

There was an old clock on a church tower near Ella's flat. It was just striking eight when he knocked on the door. 'I'm boringly punctual,' he said. He carried a briefcase, an orchid and a bottle of wine.

'I'm just delighted to see you,' Ella said simply. There was something about the way she said it that made him put down everything on the table and take her in his arms.

'Ella, Angel Ella, I'm never going to hurt you or be bad for you in any way.'

There was a catch in his voice as he spoke into her hair. 'Nothing bad is ever going to happen to you, believe me.'

And as she looked at him before she kissed him properly, Ella knew this was true.

They put the orchid in a long narrow vase, and got about the business of preparing dinner. He sliced the mushrooms, she made the salad. They had a glass of cold white wine from her fridge. And he opened the bottle of red he had brought before they sat down in the most normal and natural way, as if this was where they had always lived. She didn't ask him would he stay the whole night because she knew he would. They talked easily. He said he had enjoyed meeting her parents.

'They liked meeting you, too, but I expect everyone does,' Ella said.

'Does that mean you think I'm putting on some kind of an act?' he asked, hurt.

'No, I don't think it does, you do like people, and you make them feel as if there's no one else in the room. It's just the way you are . . . even now.'

He looked round her flat. 'Come on, there is no one else in the room!' he said, laughing.

'No, it's a way you have, I expect you were great at the fund-raiser thing on Sunday.' Her eyes were bright.

'I don't know,' Don Richardson said thoughtfully. 'People had been generous, I was just thanking them, making them feel that they weren't being taken for granted, that the Party appreciated them. It wasn't meant to be all smarmy, just gratitude.'

'Glad-handing,' she said, remembering his words.

'Yes, I was sending myself up when I said that, it's just that I would have preferred to be with you.'

'You were very good at it, I saw you,' Ella said suddenly. She didn't know why she had made this admission. Possibly because she wanted no lies, no pretending. To her amazement he just nodded at her.

'Yes, I saw you, too,' he said.

She felt her face redden with shame. He had actually spotted her stalking him as Deirdre described it.

'Nick, the guy who did the video, he's a mate of mine. He wanted some help.'

'Sure.'

'Actually he didn't want any help, I just asked if I could come along too.'

'Did you, Ella? Why?' His hand rested on top of hers, lightly.

'I just wanted to see you, Don, I was very sorry too that we weren't meeting that night, to go to the do was the next best thing.'

He stood up and held her face in his hands and kissed her. 'I didn't dare to believe that might be true, Ella. I've thought about it over and over since then and prayed it was true.'

'And would you ever have said that you'd seen me?'

'No, it was your business that you were there, I'd never interrogate you. Never.'

'You were very good, Don, you were tireless.'

'No, I was very tired, I drove past this house on the way back to my flat, I saw your lights on and realised you were home ... but ...'

'But what?' she asked.

'But our date was for tonight. I didn't want to look foolish and over-eager.'

Her eyes had tears in them as she led him away from the table and to the bedroom. And it was everything that it had never been before, with Nick or with the sporting hero or the two one-night stands. Ella lay in his arms long after Don had gone to sleep. She was the luckiest woman in the world.

Next morning, she just offered him coffee and orange juice, and didn't fuss about breakfast. He seemed to like the lack of fuss. Possibly Margery and the boys made too much noise and crowded him out. Ella would never be like that.

She picked up a package of papers to take to school.

'What are they?' he asked, interested.

'Oh, I gave the Fifth Years a test yesterday. The good side of that is you have forty minutes' peace while they do it, the bad side is you have to mark thirty-three extra papers.'

He kissed her on the nose.

'I know nothing of your life, Ella Brady,' he said.

'Probably better to keep it that way, in case you keel over and die of boredom,' she said.

'You couldn't bore me.' He sounded very serious. 'May I come back tonight, a bit late-ish?'

'I'd love that,' Ella said. She had been forcing herself not to ask when they would meet again.

'I'm not tying up your evening on you?' He was solicitous.

'No, I'm meeting Deirdre for an early supper at Quentins. I'll be back by nine. Does that suit?'

'I'll be here around ten, I'll have eaten a very dull and sober dinner . . . a financial committee. I have to take notes and be alert so maybe I could drink a glass of wine or two with you?'

She gave a little shiver. Don Richardson who had homes in Killiney, in the Financial Centre and in Spain, was going to stay in her little flat two nights running. Last night in bed he had told her he loved her. It looked as if he meant it.

Ella managed to get through the day, and when she arrived at Quentins, Deirdre was waiting.

'Are you going to tell me everything?' Deirdre demanded before Ella said hallo.

'Not as much as you'll want to know, but I'll tell you a fair bit.'

'Tell me the main thing, the only thing, is he coming back for more?' Deirdre asked.

'He's going to stay the night tonight as well, yes.'

'He stayed the whole *night.* Oh my God!' cried Deirdre in such a loud voice that everyone in the restaurant looked over at their table.

'Thanks, Dee,' hissed Ella. 'Why didn't you ask for a microphone, then even the faraway tables could have heard you.'

'No worries.' They were consoled by Mon, the young waitress whom they both knew and liked. She had told them in the past about her unerring bad taste in men back in Australia, and how she had lost her heart and all her savings to a fellow in Italy. Deirdre and Ella had been sympathetic and said that it was pretty much a global problem. Men were the cause of most of the unrest and unease on the planet.

Mon had recently found a new love, she had confided. He was older and wiser and trustworthy. His name was Mr Harris.

Had he a first name? they wondered. He had, apparently, but Mon liked to think of him as Mr Harris at the moment.

'I hope your Mr Harris isn't here to be shocked by my loudmouth friend Dee,' Ella said in a low voice.

'No, he's not, and he wouldn't be shocked, but tell me, did that guy with the gorgeous smile and the dark blue eyes really stay the whole night?' Mon whispered.

'Dee, I will stab you very hard with something,' Ella said.

'No, don't stab her. No one heard except me and, anyway, the others are all tourists. It doesn't matter if they did,' said Mon cheerfully.

*

Don stayed that night and the next. On Friday morning he said he was going to Spain for a few days.

'I wish I didn't have to.'

'Enjoy it,' Ella managed to say. She didn't ask if it were business or family. She didn't want to know. But he told her.

'I look after a lot of property interests out there. I need to go out at least once a month, not a hardship posting, I agree. Sometimes the boys come if it's half-term or when they can get a day or two off school. But not this time. Still, I'll be back next Wednesday and maybe we can go out for a meal. I don't want you getting tired of cooking for me.'

'I enjoy it, Don, truly I do, and perhaps, you know, it's wiser not to be out in public in the circumstances.'

He looked surprised. 'Honestly Angel, I told you there's no problem, it's separate lives.' He said it so often it had to be true.

But the next day some torment made her call the Richardson home in Killiney and ask to speak to Mrs Margery Richardson. She was prepared to hang up when the woman came to the phone.

'I'm afraid she's not here,' said the housekeeper. 'She's gone to Spain. She'll be back on Wednesday.'

'Nick? It's Deirdre.'

'Oh, I know, Deirdre. You want to join Firefly Films,' he said.

'No, I don't, but I'm worried about Ella.'

'Join the club.'

'No, seriously. She's not herself, Nick.'

'When are any of us ourselves?'

'Stop being flippant, it's not funny. This guy Don Richardson, where is he at the moment?'

'He's gone to Spain. He ordered another dozen videos, to be ready when he gets back. Main thing, he seemed pleased with them.'

'That's not the main thing, Nick, the main thing is . . . Ella is miserable. Did he say it was business or going with the family?'

'How would I know? And what difference does it make?'

'So why is Ms Brady throwing herself off O'Connell Bridge?'

'No!' Nick cried.

'It's a figure of speech, she just won't be consoled.'

'Oh Jesus, this love business is terrible,' Nick said sympathetically.

'Tell me about it, Nick! I'm so glad I never bought into it myself,' said Deirdre.

'It's wonderful that Ella came to us for a whole long weekend,' Tim Brady said. 'Imagine, she's going to stay here until Tuesday.'

'Yes,' said his wife.

'Aren't you pleased, Barbara?'

'I'd be much more pleased if she hadn't asked us to say she isn't here and we have no idea where she is,' Ella's mother said.

'She says she wants to cut herself off a bit from the world, have a rest.' Her father believed the story.

'Yes, but some man has rung four times. He says her mobile is turned off, he's getting anxious and annoyed.'

'Trust Ella, it may just be some fellow she doesn't want to encourage. Does he say who he is?'

'No, and I don't ask him,' Barbara Brady said.

On Sunday the man on the phone did say who he was. 'Mrs Brady, it's Don Richardson here, we had the pleasure of meeting briefly in Holly's Hotel last week . . . I am most anxious to talk to Ella. I wonder if you could ask her to call me? I can give you the number.'

'Oh, yes, of course, Mr Richardson, I remember. Nice to talk to you again.'

'Yes, so if she's there . . . I wonder . . .'

'No, unfortunately she's not at home.' Barbara Brady hated telling lies. She knew she wasn't very good at it either.

'But she will be back sometime, won't she? I mean, you will see her, won't you?'

'Oh, yes, of course,' Barbara Brady said too quickly.

He dictated his telephone number and thanked her.

'Ella?' Barbara Brady knocked on her daughter's bedroom door. 'May I come in?'

'Sure, Mam.'

Ella sat hugging a cushion and rocking to and fro. She was red-eyed, but not actually crying.

'Don Richardson called again.' Her mother's voice was clipped. 'This time he left his name and number. He said that he was in Spain and I told him that I would give you the message and the number.'

'Thanks, Mam.'

'And are you having any supper?'

'No, Mam.'

'Or any plans to tell your father and myself what's going on?'

'None at all, Mam.'

'I'll leave you to your thoughts then.'

'I love you, Mam.'

'Three easiest words to say in the whole world, "I love you".'

'But I do!' Ella was stung.

'We will be downstairs when you love us enough to join us,' her mother said with her mouth in a very hard line.

'I don't suppose she could be involved with this Don Richardson?' Barbara said to her husband in a low, frightened voice.

Ella's father was shocked. 'He's a married man, Barbara, married to Ricky Rice's daughter.'

'Of course, she couldn't be so foolish.'

Ella had come to the top of the stairs and heard this. She went back to her room and stared ahead of her for a long time. It was inconvenient keeping her mobile phone turned off but she didn't want to get any messages from him, and she kept the phone in her flat off the hook, too. She had forgotten about the school. There were two dozen red roses for her there on Monday.

'Stop hiding, I love you,' was the message.

Everyone in the staffroom had read it before she did. Their eyes were on her as she looked at the card.

'Oh, I never knew the Fifth Years cared so much,' she said with a laugh.

As she left the room Ella heard them talking about her. 'They must have cost a fortune, seventy to eighty euros,' said one. 'Bet he's married, otherwise he'd have put his name on the card,' said another.

Ella gritted her teeth and got down to work. She wouldn't have to think about him until Wednesday night. If he showed up.

He knocked at her door at 8 p.m. on Wednesday. He had no flowers, no wine.

'Hallo Don.'

'What's all this about?'

'I don't understand,' she said.

'Neither do I. I said goodbye to you here on Friday morning, I told you I loved you, you told me you loved me. Then I went to Spain on business and suddenly you won't take my calls and get your mother to lie for you. What's going on, Ella?'

'I don't know. What *is* going on?' she said.

'You tell me. I've been straight up all the way, you're the one playing games.' He looked very angry.

They were still on the doorstep.

'You have not been straight. You didn't tell me you were taking your wife to Spain.' Ella let the words tumble out.

'I took "my wife", as you call her, nowhere!' he shouted.

'Your wife is what she is,' Ella cried.

'I don't care. I will go the distance here on the doorstep, but on mature reflection, as they say, you may prefer to do it indoors,' he said.

Wearily she opened the door.

He marched into her sitting room as if he owned it and sat down. 'Okay Ella, tell me,' he began.

'No, you tell me. You said you were going to Spain on business and then I hear that you took your wife.'

'And how do you hear this, Ella?'

'It's not important, you did take her.'

'I did not take her, she decided to come at the same time, she owns half the house.'

'But you didn't tell me that she was going.'

'I didn't bloody know until she said she was going and anyway, it's not important. I don't have to tell you, you agreed to accept that we lived separate lives. You told me you agreed, that you believed that.' He looked bewildered and upset.

'Huh,' she said.

'What does that mean?'

902

'I don't know,' Ella said truthfully.

'You said it, so you must know. What do you mean? What are you asking me?'

There was a silence.

'What do you want to know?' he asked again.

Another silence and then she spoke. 'Did you sleep with her? Do you still have sex with her?' Ella's voice was low.

Don Richardson stood up. His face was working, she had never seen him so upset. 'I'm sorry, Ella, I'm really sorry. I thought I had made it all clear, I really thought I had come and told you the whole situation outside your school that day.'

'Yes, but . . .' she began.

'And I thought you said that you understood.'

'I thought I did but . . .'

'But you don't understand at all, you actually think that I could love you and have sex with Margery, you really do think that, don't you?'

'I think it's possible, yes.'

'Then you and I, we haven't much more to talk about, Ella, my angel, have we?' he said sadly.

'Do you?' she asked.

'Do I what?'

'Do you have sex with her?'

'Goodbye, Ella,' he said, moving towards the door.

'So it's yes,' she said in a heavy tone.

'It's no actually, but it doesn't matter. I won't stay where there's such suspicion. Someone must have hurt you very badly somewhere along the line to make you feel hurt and anxious like this.'

'Bullshit, Don Richardson, nobody hurt me before, nobody touched me before, I never loved anyone before. There's no mythical villain. You tell me it's a business trip and then I hear your wife is with you, what's so abnormal about being upset? Don't make me into some kind of freak.'

'And how exactly did you hear, might I ask?' His voice was ice cold.

It was the end. Ella knew it. 'Not that it matters, but I called your house, and I was told that the lady of the manor was in Spain.' Another silence.

'Thanks, Ella, thanks for everything, thanks for coming to spy at the fund-raiser, thanks for calling to check on my family's movements, thanks for jumping to conclusions, and most of all thanks for not believing me when I say I love you. I'm sorry – but then what exactly am I sorry for?'

She looked at him in horror as he stood there saying goodbye.

'Why should I apologise for being utterly honest from the start, telling you the score, telling you the truth, coming to meet your parents, calling them to say I was worried that you didn't answer your phone? Are these the actions of some kind of shit? No, I think they're what a man who loves you might do.

'But you know better. You have some different standard. I truly hope you find what you're looking for. You are a lovely girl, Ella. An angel in fact, and I'll always wish you well.'

He was nearly at the gate when she caught him, held his arm and pleaded with him to come back. People walking their dogs on the leafy road saw the blonde girl in floods of tears pleading with the tall handsome man.

'I'm sorry. Forgive me. I want just one more chance. I'm such a fool, Don, it's only because I love you so desperately. I'm just afraid to believe you love me. Come back, please, please.'

And if they had continued looking they would have seen the man leading her back into the lighted hall with his arm around her.

'Does all this mean he'll be moving into your place now?' Deirdre asked some days later.

'Of course not, don't be silly,' Ella said.

'Why is it so silly? It would save the rent on the place in the Financial Services area.'

'But he has to say he's somewhere. He can't say he's here,' Ella said as if it were totally obvious.

'No, of course not,' Deirdre said, confused.

'Why can't he say he's shacked up with Ella if it's a dead marriage?' Deirdre asked Nick later.

'Don't ask,' Nick said. 'I've found it much easier not to bring up cosmic questions like that.'

3

The pattern of their life began then, at least three and sometimes five nights a week together. Ella saw no other friends in the evening because she was never sure whether Don might suddenly be free.

There were lunches, of course. Deirdre would voice the questions that Ella never spoke aloud. 'Is he going to leave her for you? He's practically living with you, for God's sake.'

'He can't leave, because of his father-in-law. I told you that.'

'Ricky Rice lives in the modern world. He's heard of divorce, he knows Don isn't in the family nest every night.'

'Why rock the boat? We're fine as we are.'

'And your parents, what do they think?'

'They're fine with it,' Ella shrugged.

'No, Ella, they are not. Nobody's fine with their little girl being the plaything of a tycoon.'

Ella pealed with laughter. 'I don't know why I have you as a friend. You try to unsettle me and you use ludicrous phrases. "Plaything". "Tycoon". For heaven's sake! You're so old-fashioned, so utterly disapproving.'

Deirdre took a sip of wine, and spoke in a rare serious moment. 'Actually, no, I'm not. I'm envious if you must know. I'd really love to be as absorbed and obsessed as you are.'

Ella said nothing for a moment. It wasn't like Deirdre to be so utterly honest. It demanded a similar honesty in response. 'Well, okay, if you must know, it's not at all fine with my parents.'

'How could it be?' Deirdre was sympathetic.

'Well, it could be if they allowed themselves to move into this century, Dee, if they just looked at the calendar and checked that it's not nineteen twenty-something.'

'They're no worse than anyone else of their generation.'

'Oh, but they are, even at school they don't go on that way.'

'Well, you can hardly tell the nuns you have a lover that lives in half the week.'

'There are hardly any nuns left, only a few old ones doing the accounts or the garden or something.'

'But isn't it called a convent?' Deirdre protested.

'Oh, they're all called convents, but that's not the point. Some of the staff are ancient, but they don't go round frowning and fretting.'

'Do they know, though?' Deirdre persisted.

'They don't *not* know. They don't ask, they don't mutter and have suspicions.'

'Well, they aren't your parents.'

'But they're in this century. It's all changed. You know when we were at school they used to say "Ask your mummy and daddy this" or "Tell your mothers and fathers that"? We don't say that any more. It's just not relevant. You can't assume that everyone has one daddy and one mummy at home.'

'So what *do* you say?' Deirdre was interested.

'We say: "Ask them at home." Can they have a dictionary, an atlas, sheets of graph paper. Whatever. Even the geriatric teachers accept that it's not magic happy families for everyone these days.'

'Still, you can't blame people for wanting the best for a daughter,' Deirdre said. She was worried about her friend.

'If I had a daughter, I'd want her to be happy, not respectable. That's the best anyone can have, to be happy, isn't it?'

When there was no reply, Ella spoke again. 'Deirdre! It's what you just said a minute ago! You said you envied me because I was so happy.'

'I said obsessed,' Deirdre said.

'Same thing,' said Ella.

Don brought some clothes and arranged them neatly in Ella's wardrobe. He used Ella's washing machine and ironed his own shirts. Sometimes he ironed her things for her too. Ella's father wouldn't have done that in a million years. 'Why not? I'm at the ironing board anyway,' he would say with a grin that melted her heart.

Every two weeks or so she invited her parents for a meal in her flat, always on a night when she knew he would be busy elsewhere. She didn't even have to ask him to move his clothes from her wardrobe and his electric razor from her bathroom shelf. He just put everything into a suitcase and covered it neatly with a rug. It was never mentioned, even when he was unpacking the case, when he would return late that night after her parents had left.

He always sounded interested in them and what Ella had to report. He remembered everything she told him. Even small, unimportant details. That her father liked seedless grapes because he was afraid of appendicitis. Don would buy some when her parents were expected. He remembered that her mother liked a particular perfume and he bought it in the airport in time for her mother's birthday.

'I'd like to meet them socially, you know,' he had said more than once.

'I know, Don, and they'd love you, but it's easier this way,' she would say.

'Is it all easy and happy for you, Angel?' he asked.

It was happy, yes, but easy, no. They asked too many questions.

'Ella, your father and I wouldn't dream of interfering in your personal life.'

'I know you wouldn't, either of you. What about more Greek salad?'

'But we do wonder: do you have enough friends and go out? I mean, if you are going to live in this kind of monastic seclusion here in this flat . . . then why don't you live at home and save the rent?'

'What your mother is saying, Ella, is that we'd love you to have a home of your own.'

'And I do, Dad, and we're in it, having supper,' she said, eyes too bright.

'Your father and I were just hoping . . .'

'Oh, we all live in great hope. Look, I'll clear this away. I have a lovely cheese and grapes. No seeds, Dad. No pips.'

It was getting harder and harder. She wished they could just meet Don. Socially. Without any statement being made.

It happened on a Sunday not long after that. Don was to go out to Killiney for the day. Margery's father had taken his grandsons out shooting. They had some pheasant and they were going to cook them.

'Savage kind of thing to do, going out killing small birds for fun,' Ella had commented.

'I agree with you. I never go shooting, as you may have noticed.' He held his hands up in surrender.

'You haven't time,' she laughed at him.

'Even if I had. Anyway, they say they're shooting them for food, and they are eating them,' he said as an excuse.

'Okay, peace, peace. I don't suppose that the chicken that ends up in the *coq au vin* for Sunday lunch enjoyed it all that much, either. Will you be late? I only ask because I was going to take my parents for an Irish coffee in that new hotel in town, in case you think I'd abandoned you.'

'Great idea. They'd like that,' he said. 'No, I won't be late as it happens, and I'm too arrogant to think you'd abandon me.'

In the new hotel she was pointing out some of the features to her parents, the paintings of politicians on the walls, the very expensive carpeted area which had been closed off from the public by a silk rope, when she saw Don. He had come in from Killiney by himself. He was looking for her, he was going to engineer a social meeting with her parents. She sat back and let it happen.

'We did meet in Holly's, didn't we? How are you both?' He looked from one to the other with pleasure. 'And Ella, great to see you again.'

She smiled and let him carry the conversation. Had they ordered? No? Good, then let him get them something. What about an Irish coffee?

Her parents looked at each other in amazement. That's exactly what they were going to have. How had he guessed?

Ella wondered what would happen if she said he had guessed because she had told him about it in bed that very morning. Nothing good would happen, so she didn't. She watched him move the conversation from himself to getting her parents to talk. He was alert and attentive to everything they said.

Ella watched him objectively. She let her mind wander. It was not an act, he did like these people just as he had liked the people at the fund-raising dinner, just as he liked the people in Holly's Hotel, at Quentins, and presumably everywhere. It was a wonderful gift and he used it well.

She tuned in again as he was talking to her father.

'I agree with you entirely. You can't ask people to buy stock that you would not buy yourself. That way you lose your integrity.'

'But, Mr Richardson, you wouldn't believe how greedy and impatient young people are these days. The old, safe options aren't good enough ... they want something fast, something now, and I have a terrible time urging a bit of caution.' His face looked sad and complaining, as it often did of late.

Ella heard Don speak in a slightly lowered voice. 'It's the same for all of us, Mr Brady. They all want the new car, the boat, the second home ...'

'Ah, but it's different for you over there in Rice and Richardson. You have high fliers going in to you, people who already have money.'

'Not so. We get all sorts of people who hear that we're good. It's a lot of pressure to be good every week. You're talking to someone who knows about it.'

Don Richardson was making himself the equal of her timid father.

'I think that every Monday morning,' Ella's father said sadly.

'Well, speaking about tomorrow, let me share something with you that I'm going to do myself first thing in the office ...'

Their voices were really low now. Ella heard mention of a building firm which just might be going to get a huge contract. It would be the nearest thing to a safe bet that they could offer to their demanding high fliers. 'If it's only a might ...?' Ella heard her father say fearfully.

'I wouldn't steer you wrong.' His warm voice was so strong and reassuring. Don wouldn't steer anyone wrong or lie to them. It wasn't in his nature. Please, may Dad be strong enough to take his advice. If Don said these builders were going to get the contract, then he knew they were. Don knew everything.

Naturally, the builders got the contract. And, amazingly, her father had actually passed on the tip and he was much more highly regarded in his company than before. Her father told her happily that it had been a real act of kindness of that man to give him the word. And Ella forced herself not to sound too pleased.

Her mother said that the partners in the law firm where she worked couldn't believe that Rice and Richardson had recommended them to do some work. Nothing complicated, just run-of-the-mill testamentary and probate work, but it had done her no end of good. People used to think that it was almost time for her to retire, but not any more. Ella said it was only her mother's due.

Nick told Ella that Don Richardson must have a filing system in his head. At least twice a week they got a call from someone saying that Don had given them the name of Firefly Films. It was like a seal of approval.

And finally, the last citadel fell, and Deirdre said she liked him. 'You don't have to tell me this, Dee. I'll survive even if you don't,' Ella said with a laugh.

But no, Deirdre wanted to make her position clear. She had been in a trendy nightclub and Don had come up to her. 'Very far from all your domestic fronts tonight,' Dee had said to him.

'I know you disapprove of me, Deirdre, and in many ways I respect you for looking out for a friend. All I can say is that I love her, but I wouldn't be helping anyone or anything by leaving Margery and the boys now. Ella knows everything there is to be known.'

Deirdre looked almost embarrassed. 'I believed him, Ella. I bloody believed him. I even believed him when he told me he was entertaining people from Spain and they had insisted on coming to the nightclub. He does love you. You do have everything.'

'Not everything, Dee. Not the home and the babies,' Ella said.

'Don't worry about it. Women can have babies at sixty these days,' Deirdre had said cheerfully. 'You have over thirty years before you need to start getting broody.'

As the months went by, Ella felt she had known no other life. Soon those boys would grow up and they could think again seriously. But now? It was all fine, so why upset what was working well?

Don's part of the study was as tidy as he was. He used a mobile phone and got in the habit of moving out into the hall when he answered a call. The reception was better and he didn't interrupt the television or the music that they listened to. He had a few books on the wall shelves, and business magazines in the rack, but everything else was in a small laptop.

'Suppose you lost it?' she teased him once. 'Suppose we had burglars, or it was snatched from you in the street?'

'Backup,' he said simply. 'House rule: we all copy every single thing from that day's transaction on to a disk every evening.'

'And what do you do with the disks?' She was interested. 'Surely you could lose a disk just as easily?'

'What have we here, Ella? An investigation, a tribunal?' He laughed, but his eyes weren't smiling.

Ella was annoyed with him and showed it. 'Sorry, Don. Didn't know the little woman wasn't allowed to be interested. Forget it. Forget I even spoke.'

'Hey, Ella angel, you're being a little bit heavy,' he began.

'No, I'm not. If you asked me a question about school, I'd think you were interested and I'd answer you. I wouldn't accuse you of being part of a Department of Education hit squad.'

'I apologise.'

'No need to. Message received. Don't ask Don about his work. Okay, I'll remember.'

'You're very hurt,' he said.

'No, just a bit pissed off. I'll get over it.'

'Come here, please ... I beg you.' His eyes were pleading.

'What?'

He opened his little computer. The one that fitted in his briefcase. 'First my password. I want you to know that.' His face was very serious.

'Don, this is silly.'

'My password is "Angel". It has been since I met you.' He typed it in and the program sprang to life. 'Please, Ella, look at the headings. My life is your life. You are welcome to look at any of these at any time.'

'That wasn't what I wanted ... you were short with me, that's all.'

'See, here's Killiney, all the details about bills and expenses are there. Here's the boys' school fees and trust funds under their names, James and Gerald ... and here's travel, and here's Ella.'

'You have a file on me?' Her voice was a whisper.

'Angel, of course I have.' He pointed to a file called 'Brady'.

She was in tears now, but he took no notice. He was determined to explain everything, show her how open he was being with her.

'These are the day-by-day transactions in these files. These are the ones we put on disk, and since you wanted to know what we do with the disks, we post them back to the office. We all have little ready-stamped envelopes. Now, Ella, you know the password, anything you want to know is there, but don't ever tell me again that I am secretive. That's the last thing I am.'

'How can I tell you how sorry I am?' she asked through tears.

He stroked her hair. 'Angel Ella, I'm the one to be sorry if I sounded sharp to you. I get people asking me questions day and night. It's such a relief to be with you, you don't.' His face was full of remorse.

'I'm such an eejit,' she sniffed.

'I love you, Ella.'

'I know,' she said. 'I don't deserve you.'

'Your father wouldn't dream of asking you, but then you know me. I'm such a busybody, Ella. It's just that we wondered, do you see a lot of that Don Richardson?' Barbara Brady's voice trailed away with the enormity of her intrusion into her daughter's life.

'Oh, I run into him a lot around the place, yes. Any problem with that?' Ella looked a long, clear look at her mother.

'No, no, none at all. It's just that he is married, and all that sort of thing.'

'What sort of thing exactly?'

'Well, married, I suppose, and with children. Two sons, I heard.'

'Ah, that's nice for him then.'

'Ella, you know we want the best for you.'

'As I do for you and for Dad, too.' Ella's smile was radiant.

'Will you come to Spain at half-term?' Don asked her.

'I'd love to, but won't it be ... difficult?'

'No, not remotely. I'd love to show you the coast.'

'I'd love to see it. I pay for my own ticket, though.'

'That's silly, Angel. I have a ticket for you.'

'Leave me my pride and dignity. Won't I be staying in your house? Isn't that enough?'

'Well, no, I thought we'd stay in a hotel. Easier.'

'Sure.' But Ella was quiet.

'I chose it for you in case you were uneasy about staying in what is in many ways a family house.'

'No, I mean it, sure, that's very sensitive of you, but I have my own money, Don. I'd prefer to pay for the ticket.'

'Fine, Angel,' he said.

'How many days?'

'You said you had six days. I booked for that.' He smiled at her.

'God, I love you, Don Richardson,' she said.

The airport was crowded with families, couples, lovers, groups of girls on package tours. None of them were remotely as happy as Ella. She had six days here. Like a honeymoon.

She almost hugged herself at the airport as they came out among the other passengers into the sunshine towards all the hoteliers and travel agents waving banners and shouting out names.

Don had booked a car in advance.

'Sit here, Angel. I'll go and do the boring bit,' he urged. So Ella sat minding their cases and Don's briefcase. She admired him as he walked relaxed and easy to the car desk, his jacket over his arm.

She thought she saw him paying in cash. He seemed to have a fistful of notes. But that was unlikely. Maybe he was just changing money. He was coming back to her, smiling.

'Enjoy your vacation, Señor Brady,' the man at the car desk called to him.

'I put your name on the rented car too. He obviously knows who is the important one here,' Don said with his arm around Ella's shoulder.

She was childishly pleased. 'I've never driven on the wrong side of the road,' she began.

'A bright girl like you, of course you can do it,' he teased.

'It's very good of you, Don.'

'Not a bit of it. Anyway, nice for you to have the car if I have to do a little work. Come on now, let's go find it and we'll toss a coin for who drives.'

'I think we've tossed it and you won,' she said, laughing and taking him by the arm.

It was a very luxurious hotel. They had a huge balcony, where room service delivered their meal, lit candles for them, and gave Ella a great big white orchid, which she put in her hair. 'I'm so happy here,' she said.

'Tomorrow I have to trek off and meet people, do things, set up things. Will you be all right on your own?'

'Of course I will. I'll just lie out here and read. And get sun-tanned. And maybe trip up and down to the pool.'

'Good girl. I'll be back by seven at the latest.' He smiled lazily at her over his Spanish brandy.

'Will you take the car?' she asked innocently.

She saw his eyes narrow momentarily. 'I might, Angel, I might not. I'll see, okay?'

'Sure. I didn't want you to tire yourself out, that's all.'

He relaxed.

Next morning she watched from the balcony as he went off on his list of meetings. A woman picked him up in the forecourt of the hotel. A woman who looked very like his wife Margery.

The day seemed endless. There were just so many times you could swim up and down a pool. The thriller she had bought at Dublin airport didn't hold her attention. She wasn't hungry enough for the hotel buffet.

She took a taxi into town to the harbour and had a glass of wine, some cheese and olives as she looked at the boats bobbing up and down and the tourists walking up and down. She would not ask him. It could have been anyone. She would not call Margery Richardson's house back in Killiney. What would it prove if she were not there? Either you trusted someone or you did not. It was as simple as that. And she must have been mistaken, he would have told her if Margery were in Spain. But suppose just for a moment that Margery were here. After all, she was still involved in her father's business. She had a right to be here. The marriage was over. How often had he told her this? He had taken her on this magical holiday because he loved her and wanted to be with her ... Wouldn't Ella be very silly to make a big scene about it? However much it cost her, she would say nothing.

It was very hard not to ask innocent questions that could sound like an interrogation. So when he returned in time for a swim in the sunset, Ella asked nothing. He was very loving. She had been insane to imagine that he had met up with his ex-wife or estranged wife or whatever she was. Nobody who loved her the way Don did, so passionately, could have spent the day with another woman. Then he said he had to do a bit of work, check that he had all the notes of today's work in his computer, and make the backup disk. She sat and watched him dreamily.

'Order up some supper, Angel. I'll be through in half an hour,' he said.

She ordered asparagus and a plate of grilled prawns to follow.

'Was it a tiring day?' she asked.

She had considered the remark for a long time. There was surely no way he could take offence at that.

He looked at her and took her hand. 'It was, Angel, very tiring. People are very greedy, you know. A lot of my clients want the sun, moon and stars, and then some more. They think they own me.'

'You don't need them that badly, do you?'

'We do, really, Angel. Ricky always says that they are the most demanding, the ex-pats, they have nothing to do all day except play golf, swim and read their portfolios.'

'Why can't they come back to Dublin to see you?' she asked innocently.

'Why do you think?' His face was hard.

She realised that a lot of them were tax exiles; some of them might have an even more pressing need to stay away.

'Sorry,' she said.

He got up and went over to kneel beside her. 'No, I'm the one that's sorry. One of these guys just insists I spend a couple of nights in his *hacienda*, as he calls it ... He won't let me stay all alone in a hotel.'

'No!' She was shocked.

'Yes, I'm afraid I have to. What do I tell Ricky? That I won't go out to a huge place with two swimming pools, billiard room, and the works...'

'He can't eat into your private time, Don...'

'He doesn't see it as private time. Please don't make a scene, Ella. I'm so upset myself already, I couldn't bear it if you...'

'No, of course I won't.'

'Thank you.' He kissed her on the forehead. Then she saw him moving towards the big carved chest of drawers.

'Not tonight, Don?'

'He insists. I'm so very sorry. You know how little I want it. This was meant to be our time.' He said it with his hands spread out in mystification.

She must be very careful not to upset him, but she was so annoyed she could barely speak. Imagine her sitting here like a fool in a big posh hotel, while Don played billiards and swam with some tax dodger, or worse. To please his father-in-law.

'Don't be silent on me, Angel.'

'No, of course not. Let's get you packed. The sooner you're gone the sooner you're back.'

He looked very relieved. A row averted.

She watched him pack. Don Richardson, the fastidious man who was going away for three days, took one shirt, one change of underwear. And his laptop computer.

She told him she would be just fine and that she would dress up and cruise the swimming pool and find a new companion. She would have forgotten his name when he got back.

'Don't forget me, Angel. I am the great love of your life. As you are of mine. One of the reasons I'm doing all this nonsense is so that we can be free to spend long years together, in places like this where I can throw the laptop out into the sea and we never have to go and be nice to boring old clients who are semi-crooks. Do you believe me?'

Ella did. Why else would he have taken her out to Spain if he didn't love her?

It was a long two and a half days, but she kept busy. She went on a bus tour of the area. They passed a cluster of very wealthy homes.

'They all have two swimming pools and billiard rooms and mountain views from one side and sea views from the other,' the guide said proudly. 'Mainly English and Irish people, who come very often here,' he added.

It could be the very place where Don was playing billiards to please his father-in-law, Ella thought. She noted what it was called: *Playa de los Angeles*. Place or beach of the Angels. How ironic it would be if he had to leave his own Angel for a place with the same name.

*

'Did you find a new love?' Don asked when he came back, two and a half days later.

'No, did you?' she laughed.

'No, but I'm weary. Can our vacation begin now, Angel?'

So she knew there would be no chat about the client who'd insisted on taking up all his time and wrecking their holiday.

Don spent a lot of time at the laptop, more than she would have liked. When she woke he was tapping away. Often, after they made love in the evening, he slipped from the bed and seemed to come to life again at the little screen. That's today's world, she told herself. He is doing it so that we can have all these years together when the time comes.

'Will we go through separately?' Ella asked at Dublin airport.

'Why?' Don was mystified.

'Well, in case anyone sees us,' Ella said.

'Like who?'

'Like Margery,' she said.

'But how could she see us? Isn't she still in Spain?' he asked, confused.

So she had been right. Margery had been in Spain after all.

'Ella, it's your mother,' Don called out.

Usually he didn't answer the phone in her flat, but he had been waiting for an urgent call and had given the number.

'Thanks, Don. Hi, Mother.'

'Oh, Don is there, I gather.' Her mother sounded both doubtful and disapproving.

'Yes, we were just about to go out to a reception together. He said he'd pick me up. Well, what's new?'

'When will you be on your own?'

'I beg your pardon?'

'Can I talk to you when you are alone?'

'Talk away, Mother.'

'Call me back when you are free to talk.' She hung up.

'Shit,' Ella said.

'Something wrong?' Don raised his eyes from the computer.

'No, just a mad mother. You don't ever talk about yours.'

'Nothing to say. She's quiet, lives her own life. Lets other people live their own lives.'

'How admirable of her!' Ella began dialling her mother. 'Listen, Don's gone out to get his car. What did you want to say?'

'Have you seen tonight's evening paper?' her mother asked in clipped tones.

Ella pretended she needed to get some milk and coffee. She went around to the convenience store. The evening paper had a big gossip column spread over two pages, and specialised in lots of photographs. 'Who is the blonde on Don Richardson's arm as he comes back from Spain? The tycoon from the troubled R and R firm doesn't look as if he is suffering any of the anxieties that their customers report. R and R need not mean Rice and Richardson, maybe Rest and Relaxation.' There was a picture of Ella and Don laughing happily together at Dublin airport.

Ella felt the energy drain out of her as she leaned against the doorway of the shop. She read the whole paragraph again.

She was there in full view of the whole of Dublin described as a blonde in the same tone as you might say she was a tramp. What would people say or think?

But more frightening than any of that, what did it mean that Rice and Richardson was a troubled firm? Could they seriously be in any financial difficulty? Could Don be in danger? The newspapers always exaggerated about things but surely it was dangerous to imply that a company was in trouble unless it were true? The newspaper could well be sued.

When she got back to the flat, Don was still bent over the computer. She laid the newspaper on the table and went into the kitchen. She needed tea or coffee, something to stop her trembling.

'Anything you'd like, Don?' she called, forcing her voice to sound normal.

'Oh, peace of mind would be nice,' he said with a hollow little laugh.

'Two of those on toast then!' she said, trying to laugh. But she wasn't laughing at all.

He left the computer and came across to the table where she put a large whiskey and the paper folded in front of him so that he could see the picture and caption.

'This is what caused the alarm bells with your mother, I suppose?' he said.

'You've seen it?' she said, shocked.

'Yeah, Ricky got an early copy.'

'Why didn't you tell me?'

'I told you before, Angel. Let me worry about the work side of things.'

'But this isn't about the work side of things,' she said, bewildered.

'What else is it about, Ella? Once clients read that other clients have reported difficulties, there'll be a run on the place. Ricky and I have to get our strategy right.'

She looked at him, dumbfounded.

'What is it, Ella?'

'The picture, the picture of you and me.'

'That's not important.'

'What?'

'I mean, compared to all the rest that could be going down.'

'But your wife, your father-in-law, my parents, everyone ...' Her voice was shaky.

'Listen, Angel, believe me, that's the least of our worries.' His face was white and strained. He looked really ill and it alarmed her. So, it was true. Something was wrong. What was happening? But Don was so on top of everything.

'Don, you are going to be able to sort all this out, aren't you?'

'Oh, yes. There's always plan B.' He gave a mirthless little laugh.

'What's plan B?'

'It's an expression. If this plan isn't working we have to turn to another. It's just a phrase.'

'Do you have a plan B?' she asked.

'There are loads of plans, but I didn't want to have to change to one of them. I like things the way they are.' He looked around the room almost wistfully.

Ella felt herself shudder for no reason.

He downed his drink and became all businesslike. 'I have to go out to Killiney.'

'I thought you said she was in Spain.'

'I go out there for a lot of other reasons than to see my ex-wife, as I tell you over and over, Angel.'

'Will you be coming back tonight, Don?'

'No, but I tell you, I'll take you to a big treat lunch tomorrow in Quentins.'

'We can't, not after the picture of us . . .' She indicated the evening paper.

'Nonsense. Everyone will have forgotten that – yesterday's news. Once they know their money's safe, they won't mind how many blondes parade through airports with Ricky and myself.' He saw her face. 'Joke, Angel.'

'Sure.' She saw he was packing his few things in a suitcase. 'Getting rid of the evidence?' she said, and wished she hadn't.

'Should be ready for whatever hits the fan.' He smiled. 'Please, Angel, I'm stressed out enough as it is. Tomorrow, Quentins, one o'clock. I'll tell you everything then.'

He was rushed and fussed. Calm, cool Don Richardson, who always moved languorously, wasn't moving like that now. Twice he put down his briefcase, his coat, his overnight bag, the evening paper. Twice he picked them all up again. She must not allow him to leave thinking she was in a sulk.

'Come over here and kiss me goodnight then, if I'm not to have the pleasure, the great pleasure, of you tonight.' She ran her hands all over him and he began to respond.

But he pulled away. 'No, Ella angel, that's not fair, that's using weapons that haven't been invented yet . . . Let me get out of here before we end up in the sack.'

'Nothing wrong with that,' she said into his ear. But he escaped her clutches and ran out of the door.

Then suddenly with a shock she saw his briefcase. He had left his laptop. Did that mean he was stressed or what? He never parted from it for a moment. But at least it meant he was coming back. She had been so nervous when she saw him packing his things and looking wistfully around the room.

Ella wasn't hungry. She put away the food she had been about to cook. She called her mother and said that it was idiotic to get into a tizzy about what a stupid paper wrote. And that it was just a picture of friends who had met at the airport or on the plane or whatever.

'Or on a holiday in Spain,' her mother said.

'Or that,' Ella said.

'Your father and I wondered.'

'It's a mistake to wonder too much,' Ella said.

'Don't be offensive, Ella.'

'I'm sorry, Mother. I'm just worried about something else, as it happens.'

'Is he still there? In your flat?' her mother whispered.

'No, Mother, I'm all on my own. Come round and check.'

'I only want what's best for you. We both do.'

'We all want what's best. That's the problem,' Ella said with a great sigh and hung up.

Then she phoned Deirdre. It was an answering machine. 'It's Ella, Dee. Be very glad you're not at home. I was going to groan and grumble and complain for a bit at you, but, well, now I can't. You must have seen the paper. It's not as bad as it looks. Don is very confident about it all, and I'll know much more after tomorrow lunchtime so I'll tell you everything then. Do you remember when we thought that life was a bit tame and dull? Wasn't it nice then?'

She hung up and sat at the table for a long time. She knew she wouldn't sleep, but she had better go to bed and try.

At three she got up despairing, and made tea. At four she opened the laptop computer. She typed out the word 'Angel' that he had said was the password. It didn't come to life as it had when he typed it. It just said Password Invalid. She closed the machine and waited until dawn. Then she dressed carefully and went to the school. She supposed that she must have taught her students normally, on some kind of autopilot. But she couldn't remember a word she had said. Then it was lunchtime, and she drove to Quentins.

4

Mrs Brennan ushered her to a table for two. 'Will you have a drink while you're waiting, Ms Brady?'

'No, thanks. I have to teach this afternoon. Better not be breathing fumes over them. One glass of wine with lunch will be my limit.'

Brenda Brennan laughed. 'They're not all as wise as you are, Ms Brady. They often go back to run big companies or indeed the country after considerably more than one glass of wine, I tell you.'

'You'll have to write your memoirs,' Ella said.

'No, I want to go on serving meals for a long time. No point in closing us down.' She moved on to other tables, always a pleasant word here and there, never staying too long anywhere. She was amazingly elegant, Ella thought, and gracious. No wonder the place was so successful.

Brenda Brennan could make generalised remarks, but she would never say anything specifically indiscreet. Brenda would have realised that Ella was meeting Don Richardson, known family man. She might even have seen the photo in yesterday's paper. But she would give no hint. Of course, she had an easy life, Ella thought enviously. She was married to the man she loved, the chef Patrick Brennan. Lucky Brenda, she had no nerve-racking lunch ahead of her.

Ella wondered if she should order a brandy, but decided against it. Whatever he said, Ella would take it. She would not be like she was last night, whimpering and talking about herself and her picture in the paper. Clearly he had his problems. She could have kicked herself for behaving so badly when he needed her most.

At one-fifteen he wasn't there. It was very unlike him. At one-thirty she began to worry. Quentins was not the kind of place that hurried you or told you that the kitchen would be closing. But at twenty minutes before two, Ella went to the ladies' room. Brenda Brennan hated mobile phones at the table and she had to try and phone him.

There was no reply from his mobile. And no message recording service. This was very unusual. She would order something to eat. Or should she call the school first? Or should she telephone the house in Killiney? Or the office of Rice and Richardson? 'Don't fuss, Ella,' she spoke to herself aloud. She decided she would order food, something cold for both of them, and then when he eventually arrived there would be something to eat.

As she returned to her table, she noticed that Brenda had ordered her things moved to a private booth. Her book and glass of mineral water were there, waiting for her. Also, what looked like a small brandy.

Ella looked around her in surprise. Mon, the waitress, was nearby.

'Here you are, Ella. Much more cosy set-up if you're meeting a fellow.' Mon had a huge smile and two jaunty little bunches of hair which stuck out at angles from her head.

'Yes, but . . .'

'Listen, compared to most that come in here, Ella, you don't have anything to worry about. That fellow's mad about you, we often say it behind your back, so why not to your face?' Mon was eager and reassuring.

'Did Don ring and ask to change the table?' Ella asked Mon.

'No idea.' Mon was cheerful. 'Mrs Brennan said do it double quick, so it's done.'

Ella felt a great sense of alarm. Whatever he wanted to tell her must be terrible if it had to be told in a secluded booth. Then she noticed Brenda Brennan slipping in opposite her. She carried an early copy of the evening paper for today.

'Ella,' she said urgently.

What had happened to all the 'Ms Brady' bit of an hour ago? 'What is it?' She was full of fear.

'One or two customers recognised you. I thought best you be in here.'

She opened the paper, and there it was again – the picture of Ella laughing up at Don at the airport. But why had they printed it a second time?

'When he comes in, he'll explain.'

'He's not coming in, Ella. It was on the news at one-thirty. We heard it in the kitchen. He's gone to Spain. He left on the first plane this morning.'

'No!' Ella cried. 'No, he can't have gone away.'

'He has, apparently. He was out there setting it all up. He has his wife and children there already, his father-in-law went yesterday through London . . .'

'How do they know . . . ?'

Brenda's voice was just a whisper. 'When all the clients went around to the office today to check on their assets, they couldn't get in. The place was locked up. They called the Guards and the Fraud Squad . . . and apparently he was on the eight a.m. plane.'

'This is not happening.'

'I took the liberty of getting you a Cognac.'

'Thank you,' she said automatically but she didn't reach for it.

'And I could call the school for you if you gave me the number and told me who to call.'

'That's kind of you, Mrs Brennan, but I actually don't believe any of this. Don is coming in. He keeps his word.'

'It's important how you behave now, for your own sake. You don't want to be running into a rake of journalists and photographers.'

'Why would I?'

'This idiotic paper said he had a love nest with you in Spain. Gives your name and where you work.'

'Well, see!' Ella was triumphant. 'They know what you don't, that he'd never leave without me, never.' Her voice was getting high, shrill, and very near hysteria.

Brenda caught her by the wrist. 'The news programme on the radio knows what this crowd in the newspaper didn't know. They spoke to neighbours in Killiney about the house being closed up. They spoke to Irish people living in Spain, who were all very tight-lipped, as you might imagine.'

'He couldn't, he couldn't.' Ella shook her head.

Brenda released the girl's wrist. 'There's an explanation. He'll get in touch, but the main thing is to get you out of here before someone sneaks a call to a journalist.'

'They wouldn't!'

'They would. Don't go home and don't go to your school.'

'Where will I go?' She looked pitiful.

'Go upstairs to our rooms. We live over the shop. Drink that down, write out the name and number for your school, and then go straight over to that green door there near the entrance to the kitchen . . .'

'How will you know what to say to the school?'

'I'll know,' Brenda said. She didn't add that it would hardly be necessary to say anything. They would all have read the paper and heard the lunchtime news. They would not be expecting Miss Brady back to classes this afternoon.

Ella was surprised to see the big, handsome brass bed with the frill-edged pillows and rose-pink coverlet. It looked too luxurious, too sensual, for this couple, somehow. She took her shoes off and lay down for a moment to get her head straight. But the sleepless night and the shock worked more than she believed they would. She fell into a deep sleep and dreamed that she and Don were carrying a picnic up a hill, but everything was in a tablecloth and getting jumbled together. In the dream, she kept asking why did they have to do it this way, and Don kept saying, 'Trust me, Angel, this is the way,' and all the time there was a rattling of broken china.

She woke suddenly to the sound of a cup and saucer being placed beside her by Brenda Brennan. It was almost six o'clock. There was no picnic. She couldn't trust Don Richardson any more. Was there the slightest possibility that he might be back in her flat waiting for her? She began to get out of bed.

Brenda said she was going to have a shower. Perhaps Ella might like to look at the six o'clock news on television. 'I'll be in the bathroom just next door if you need me,' Brenda called.

Ella turned on the TV and found the news. She watched without thinking until the story came on. It was worse than she thought. Don had gone. That much was certain. And he had been out in Spain last week setting it all up. There were interviews with people who had lost their life savings. A man with a red face who had given money to Don Richardson every month so that he could buy a little retirement home in Spain, because his wife had a bad chest and needed good weather. 'We are never going to see Spain now,' said the man, twisting his hands to show how upset he was.

There was a tall, pale woman who looked as if she were too frail to stand and talk to a man with a microphone. 'I can't believe it. He was so charming, so persuasive. I believe he will be back to explain everything. They tell me I don't own any apartment in that block. But I must. He showed me pictures of it.'

Mike Martin, a man she knew, a friend of Don's and described by the newsreader as a financial expert, came on next. Ella had had a drink with him several times. He knew all about her. Don had said he was a bit of a smart aleck, always in something for what he could get out of it, but not the worst. Mike looked horrified by it all and said that it couldn't have come as a greater shock. Don and Ricky were such a pair of characters, of course, and everyone who flies near the sun gets their wings burned now and then.

But then he went on: 'It looks as if they must have known for about six months. But I still can't believe it. Don Richardson is such a decent fellow, he'd help anyone, you know, fellows on the street, people he met in bars. He was always generous with advice. Other guys in his line of business would say: "If you want my advice, come into the office and consult me." But never Don. I can't imagine him spending months plotting this runaway life, knowing he's leaving people in the lurch. He cared about people. I know he did.'

Ella watched, open-mouthed.

The interviewer asked: 'And will he miss people, friends, a lifestyle that he had in Dublin, do you think?'

'Well, of course, when all was said and done he was a family man, he loved his wife and boys, they went everywhere with him.'

'Wasn't there a rumour that he had this blonde girlfriend, a teacher, who was photographed with him?'

'No. You better believe one thing,' Mike Martin said. 'I may not know a lot about Don, and I sure as hell didn't know what he's been up to in the last six months in terms of his clients . . . but one thing shines out. He never looked at another woman. Come on, now. If you were married to Margery Rice, would you?'

And then they cut to a picture of Margery Rice presenting prizes at a youth charity, very tiny and immaculately groomed, watched by her husband with pride.

Ella put the cup down.

Brenda came back into the room in her slip and put on a fresh black dress and arranged a lace collar in position.

'He knows about me and Don,' she said. 'I've met him many times.'

'Well, isn't it just as well he kept his mouth shut?' Brenda said.

'No, it's not, it's better people know the truth. Don loves me. He told me so last night.'

'Listen to me very carefully, Ella. I have to go down and serve a room full of people who will be talking about nothing else. I will have a polite, inscrutable smile on my face. I will say it's hard to know and difficult to guess and a dozen other meaningless things. But I know one thing. Only you must survive this, you must call your parents, tell them you're all right, decide what to do about your job and then go and find some of your friends, your own friends, not his. He only has business friends.'

'You don't like him, do you?'

'No, I don't. My very close friends have lost their savings. Thanks to Mr Charming.'

'He'll give them back,' Ella cried.

'No, he won't. Fortunately it's not very much. She and her fellow don't have very much, but they were saving hard and Mr Richardson told them how to double their money. They believed him.'

'He often said people were greedy,' Ella said.

'Not these two, if you knew them. But that's neither here nor there. Survive, Ella, and rejoice that he may have loved you – well, at least enough not to let you or your family lose any of your savings in his schemes.'

'No.' She stood up. Her legs felt weak.

'What is it, Ella?'

'It's just my father. He's always going on about ideas Don gave him, hints here, a word there . . . he wouldn't have been so foolish . . .'

'When were you talking to your parents?'

'Yesterday, but they said nothing. They were going on about my picture in the paper. If there was anything to say they'd have said it then.'

'Nobody knew the extent of the scandal then. People only began to know it this morning.'

They looked at each other in alarm.

'Ring them, Ella.'

'He couldn't . . . he didn't.'

'You heard what they said on the television . . .'

Brenda Brennan pointed to the white phone beside the bed.

Ella dialled. Her mother answered. She was in tears. 'Where *were* you, Ella? Your father thought you'd gone to Spain with him. Where are you?'

'Is Dad all right?'

'Of course he's not all right, Ella. I have the doctor here with him. He's ruined.'

'Tell me, tell me, what did he lose?'

'Oh, Ella, everything. But it's not what we lost that matters, it's what the firm lost. What his clients lost. He may have to go to gaol.'

That was when Ella fainted.

Mrs Brady hadn't hung up. That was something. At least Brenda could keep her there for long enough to get her address. She held Ella's head downwards so that more blood would flow towards the brain.

'I have to get home to them,' Ella said over and over.

'You will, don't worry.'

'Your restaurant – won't you be needed downstairs?'

'Head *down*,' Brenda insisted.

Then she summoned Patrick's younger brother, Blouse. 'You know where Tara Road is?'

'I do. I often deliver vegetables to Colm's restaurant if he's short.'

'In about fifteen minutes, when she's up to it, drive her there, will you, Blouse?'

'Where are the car keys?' he asked.

Brenda turned out the contents of Ella's handbag. The keys were all on one ring.

It had a cherub on it.

'Angel,' said Ella weakly.

'Yes, we have the keys.' Brenda crammed everything back into the handbag, pausing only a fraction of a second to glance at a picture of Don Richardson smiling at the girl who had loved him. Ella's eyes were open and she was watching. Otherwise, Brenda would have torn it into a dozen pieces.

Ella gave Blouse directions to her parents' house. When they arrived, Ella's mother ran to the car. 'I suppose you're one of his friends,' she said when Blouse helped Ella from the car.

'I'm not really anyone's friend, Madam. I'm Brenda's brother-in-law. She asked me to drive this lady home.'

'From where, exactly?'

'From Quentins Restaurant,' he said proudly.

'Leave him, Mam. He's got nothing to do with anything.'

'What do we know what has to do with anything?' Her mother looked as if somebody had given her a beating.

'Where's Dad?'

'In the sitting room. He won't go to bed. He won't take any sedation. He says he has to be alert if the office rings him.'

'And have they rung him?'

'Not since lunchtime. Not since we learned that Don has left the country. There's no point in anyone ringing anyone now, Ella. It's all gone. All gone.'

'I can't tell you how sorry I am,' she said.

'Well, I'll be off now, then,' Blouse Brennan said.

'Thank you very much, and will you thank your sister?'

'Sister-in-law,' he corrected.

'Yes, well, say I'm very grateful.'

'It's nothing,' he said.

'How will you get back?' Ella's mother realised that he had left the car keys on the table.

'Which end of Tara Road is shorter to the bus?' he asked cheerfully. He was so unconcerned, he lived in a world where you drove people home in their own cars and took a bus back to a kitchen or scullery or wherever you worked. A world where people weren't greedy and didn't win and lose huge sums of money over business deals. He would never know anyone who lied and lied and lied like Don Richardson had lied. Even to people who loved him. Particularly to people who loved him. But Ella was too tired to care any more. All she wanted was to reassure her father that the world hadn't come to an end. She wanted to look him in the face and tell him that it would be all right. It was just that with every passing second, it seemed so unlikely that this was true.

He looked like an old man, a paper-thin old man whose skeleton was covered with a very fine parchment. When he smiled it was like a death mask. 'I didn't know, Dad. I didn't have any idea,' she said.

'It's not your fault, Ella.'

'It is. I introduced him to you. I made you think he was my friend. I thought he loved me, Dad. He told me last night that he loved me. You see, I was sure he did.'

She knelt beside him. Her mother watched from the door with tears on her face.

'Dad, I'm young and I'm strong, and if I have to work day and night to make sure that you and Mother are all right, I will never take a day's holiday until I know I've done all that can be done.'

'Child, don't upset yourself.' His voice was very hesitant, as if he were having trouble breathing.

'I'm not a child, Dad, and I will be upset, very upset till the day I die that this should happen, because I made such a stupid, stupid error of judgement. But you know, Dad, even at this late stage, there *could* be an explanation. Perhaps it was all his father-in-law's doing.'

'Please, Ella. Everyone trusts people when they love them,' her mother said.

Her mother? Instead of bawling her out, she actually seemed to understand.

'No, I couldn't be like ordinary people, normal people like you and Dad, who found someone decent to love. I had to find a criminal, someone who ruins people and steals their livelihood and their savings.'

'I don't mind losing the savings, Ella, that was just greed. I wanted to make a profit so that we could buy you a little house.'

'A what? But I don't want a little house.'

'But we knew you weren't ever going to come and live here, so we wanted you to have a small place with character, and what with property being so dear, you'd never get that on a teacher's salary . . .'

'Father, what did you lose? Tell me.'

'But I don't *mind* about what we lost. It's the office. He had been so helpful, you know, always seemed to be in the know.'

'Yes, he was in the know, all right.'

'And those first bits of advice that I gave people went down so well . . . I took risks, Ella. I can't blame anyone but myself . . . it's just, it's just . . .'

'Just what, Dad?'

'Just that two weeks ago, he said it would be easiest and quickest if I gave him the money direct to invest for a few of my clients. I'd never done it before. You know the laws and rules there are about that . . . but Don made it all sound so normal, somehow. He said he was going out to Spain. He could invest it there and then save time, cut a few corners. Why not? That's what he said, and you know I did think . . . why not?'

'I know, Dad. Who are you telling?' She stroked his hand. But her mind was far, far away. It was in Spain. The bastard. He had conned her father out of money which he had spent in that hotel. Don had spent the money that he pretended to be investing for her father's clients in shoring up his love nest for himself, wife and kiddies. While the daughter of the victim lay in the hotel swimming pool, waiting for him. Was there anything in the whole history of faithless love as sick and pathetic?

'Dad, you won't really have to go to gaol?'

'I will certainly have to go to court,' he said.

'But wasn't Don a legitimate adviser? You know, with a licence and everything . . . surely *you* can't be held responsible?'

'All that would have helped if my clients were his clients, but they weren't. I only took his advice, his tips, his hints, as hearsay.'

'Dad, your bosses, they know . . .'

'They know me for what I am, a weak, foolish old man,' he said, and then for the very first time she began to cry.

She would recover. She knew that sometime in the future she might get over it and over him. But her father never would. That's why Don could never be forgiven.

Everything passes, even scandalous stories like the disappearance of Ricky Rice and Don Richardson, and soon the front pages had other stories to tell. There was an official inquiry announced, of course, and people became much more cautious about investing anything anywhere. There had been much speculation about whether the family was really in Spain or had gone further afield. After all, there were extradition laws in Europe now. People could not hide in one member state from the law they had broken in another. Perhaps they were in Africa or South America.

Ella had been questioned by detectives. Did Mr Richardson say anything about any plans to relocate in Spain when he and Ella had been on holiday there? Ella told them grimly that she knew of no such plans. The pain in her face seemed to convince them. She was as much a victim as many others had been.

Then the interest died down. In the media, if not for those whose hearts had been broken. The man with the red face, who had put all his money in a retirement villa for his wife, didn't forget. Nor did the pale woman who thought she had made a wonderful investment and owned an apartment in the south of Spain. The friends of Brenda Brennan, who had saved money for a wedding party, decided to laugh and make the best of it. They were people of middle years. Maybe fate was telling them they would have been foolish to have had a big celebration. Possibly a plate of sandwiches would do them fine.

Tim Brady took early retirement from his firm and spent his days filling out forms and dossiers about how and why he had given advice based on the casual snippets of information he had heard from a man he hardly knew. Barbara Brady offered to take early retirement from her firm of lawyers saying that she didn't want to embarrass them by staying on. Delicately, they managed to convince her that nobody knew who she was and it didn't matter anyway, and possibly theirs was a household that might need a little money coming in.

And Ella? Each day seemed to be forty-eight hours long. And no day seemed different from any other day nor any night from the one which followed.

It was just that the nights were worse.

Sleep would vanish. She would get up and pace around her room looking up at the shelf where she had hidden his briefcase and the laptop it contained. A hundred times she had wanted to take it to the Fraud Squad, say she had found it. They might be able to track down some of the money and rescue people like her father, like Brenda's friend Nora whose wedding savings were gone, like the man with the red face buying a villa, so he thought, for his wife who had a bad chest, like the pale woman on the television interview who said she knew she owned the flat because Don had shown her a picture of it.

But she couldn't do it.

He had trusted her, he never left that briefcase behind him, she used to joke that it was chained to his arm. She had delayed him by kissing him when he was leaving her flat in a rush that day but he hadn't worried or panicked. He hadn't called her or got anyone else to. He knew she would keep it safe for him.

And, in spite of all the evidence, she knew he would be coming back for her.

Anyway it was all down to Ricky Rice, he ran the whole show. Everyone knew that, people just did his bidding. Indeed, the very fact that Don had left the computer with her was some kind of message. Why hadn't she thought of that before?

Of course he would just come walking back into her life to tell her that it had been sorted. A love like theirs wasn't the ordinary kind of affair that people thought it was.

He was just sorting things out.

At night it seemed clear and certain.

She just had to wait for it to happen.

It was during the days that it seemed unlikely. There was no message from Spain, no call on the mobile, no text message. And then one day there was the request for a meeting by the Fraud Squad. Did Ella have anything pertinent to their enquiries? Like a list of files?

Ella looked the two men straight in the eye and said no, she had no files and no knowledge of anything that would help them.

'He didn't give you anything to look after for him, Madam? Any records, that sort of thing?'

She wasn't quite sure why she said no. Strictly speaking it was true. He hadn't asked her to look after anything for him. But of course she was lying to them and she knew it. Why? she wondered. Why had she wrapped Don's laptop in a great amount of padding and put it deep in her suitcases of clothes that were on the way back to Tara Road? If they had a search warrant they would have found the little machine and she would have been in real trouble. But in a mad way she felt she owed it to him not to hand over something he had left in her care. And of course he knew she had it, so he might well get in touch with her about it.

It was a very unreal time. She would have been lost without her friends. Deirdre had been there day and night whenever she was needed. Sometimes they said nothing, they just listened to music. Sometimes they played gin rummy. Deirdre helped her to pack up all her things in the flat and move them back to Tara Road. Ella wanted to burn the sheets on the bed. Deirdre said this was no time for dramatic gestures; she would take them to the laundry and then give them to a charity shop.

It was Deirdre who explained to the landlord that Ella would not be in a position to pay any more rent, and could they cut the agreement short? Deirdre often made sure she was there in the evening, about suppertime, so that the family would have to give the appearance of normality and sit down and have something to eat.

Sometimes Deirdre asked her, 'Do you still love him?'

Always Ella answered, 'I don't know.'

Deirdre asked would she take him back suppose he did ask her? Ella took the question very seriously. 'I think not, and when I look at my father's face, I think surely I'd never be able to look at Don again. But then I keep hoping there's some other explanation for the whole thing, which of course there isn't. So, crazy as it sounds, I must have some feelings for him still.'

And Deirdre would nod and consider it too. Deirdre had insisted on only one thing: that she go in to the school and face them immediately. So Ella went to see the school principal.

'I'll leave whenever you want me to,' she said.

'We don't want you to.'

'But where's the bit about us giving a good example to the little flock?'

'The little flock would buy and sell us all, Ella, you know it, I know it.'

'I can't stay, Mrs Ennis, not after this scandal.'

'What did you do? You were taken in by a man. You won't be the first or the last to have that happen to you, let me tell you. You're a good teacher. Please don't go.'

'The parents?'

'The parents will gossip for a couple of weeks and the kids will make jokes, then it will be forgotten.'

'I don't know if I can face it.'

'What's to face? You have to look at people whatever job you do. And presumably you have to earn a living.'

'Oh, I do, Mrs Ennis, I do.'

'Then earn it here. Go on just to the end of the school year anyway. See how you feel then.'

'I might want to get out of teaching entirely, you know, try something different.'

'If you do, then do it, but not in mid-year. You owe us this, and you owe it to yourself not to run away, like he did.'

'You've been very understanding. Imagine an Irish convent school allowing a scarlet woman to stay on.'

'You're not very scarlet, Ella, just a bit pink-eyed at the moment. Get back into those classrooms. The one thing we can all say about teaching is that it's demanding enough to take your mind off other things.'

'Thank you, Mrs Ennis.'

'Ella, he won't get away with it totally, you know. Even if he doesn't get a gaol sentence. He'll get some sort of punishment.'

Ella shrugged. 'Whatever.'

'He will. He can't swan around here any more, go to golf clubs, yacht clubs, be recognised in restaurants.'

'They've all those things in Spain, too.'

'Not the same at all. Anyway, none of my business. Hang in there for the rest of the year, will you, and then we'll talk again.'

'You're very kind, very understanding.'

'Well, we've all been there, Ella, and just between us, the late Mr Ennis, as he is often respectfully called, is not late, he's just out of the frame. He had a different view of his future which involved my savings account and a girl young enough to be his daughter, so of course I understand.'

For days afterwards, Ella wondered whether she had imagined this conversation. It seemed highly unreal as did everything else these days. It was as if she were watching all these conversations on a stage rather than taking part in them.

First Sandy phoned. She still worked with Nick in Firefly Films.

'I just rang to say that if you were looking for extra work, there's always a bit of night work going here.'

'Thanks, Sandy, that's very nice of you. Nick okay with this?'

'Yeah, but you know the way he is. He didn't want to ask you in case you thought he was patronising you or patting you on the head or something.'

'I wouldn't think that.'

'Men are complicated.'

'Tell me about it, Sandy.'

'What'll I tell Nick?'

'Tell him I'd love it, anything at all.'

And Brenda Brennan offered her work when Ella had telephoned to thank her for all the kindness. 'If you want any weekend work here in Quentins, just ask. I know it's only a few euros when what you need is thousands, but it might be a start.'

'Half the city wants to work in Quentins, you can't let me waltz in there ahead of the rest.'

'There's a bit of solidarity among women, Ella. You got a punch in the face and now you need a hand up as well. You'll find a lot of people will offer one.'

'Ella Brady?'

'Yes?' She always sounded jumpy and nervy on the telephone now. It was a bad habit and she must get out of it.

'This is Ria Lynch from down the road.'

'Oh yes, indeed.'

There had been a time when this woman, rather than Ella, had been the subject of gossip all over Tara Road. Her husband had left her, and in a very short time Ria had taken up with Colm, who owned the successful suburban restaurant. The place had buzzed for a while, but now they were as settled and staid as any regular married couple. What could she be calling about?

'I heard you were badly hit by Don Richardson, and I want to give you some advice. I thought I'd talk to you rather than your parents.'

'Yes?' Ella had been a little cold. Unasked-for advice wasn't too welcome these days.

'Don't let your father sell the house to raise money. Change it into four flats; they were flats already – you're halfway there. You'll get a fortune for renting them. Then take your garden shed, make it bigger and live in it for a couple of years.'

'Live in the shed?' Ella wondered if the woman was deranged.

'Look, it's enormous. All it needs is a couple of thousand spent on it, put in plumbing, and it can be made into two bedrooms, and a living room with a kitchenette.'

'We don't have a couple of thousand.'

'You would have in weeks if you let your beautiful house. I'll take you and show you Colm's old house if you like. It's a gold mine. Everyone wants to live in this road these days, and there's so much money about.'

'Why are you telling me this, Ria?' Ella had hardly ever talked properly to this woman before.

'Because we've all been through this – bankruptcy, a fellow not being what he said he was.'

Ella wondered if this was true. Had half the country been cheated and duped?

One night she dreamed that he had sent her a text message on her mobile phone. Just two words: Sorry Angel. It was such a real dream Ella had to get up in the middle of the night and check her phone. There was nothing there but a message from Nick.

'I really need your help for a competition . . . Say yes.'

She phoned him next morning. He brought a sandwich up to the school and they had lunch in her car. His enthusiasm was as boyish as ever. There was going to be a film festival on a theme. Some aspect of Dublin life which would illustrate all the changes there had been in the city over the years.

'What kind of change do you mean? Architecture or something?'

'No, I don't think everyone will go for that,' Nick said.

'Well, what then? The growth in Irish self-confidence?'

'Yes, but we can't just make a film saying everyone's becoming more confident. Lord, just look at those confident faces passing by . . . there has to be something that binds them together, some theme.'

'And if we found one, what do we do next?'

'Go to New York and sell it to this fellow there who has a foundation. The King Foundation, to help young people in the arts. If we made this film, Ella, and won a prize at the Festival, we'd be made. Made, I tell you. Something that gives a picture of Dublin changing ... Can you think of anything that sort of sums it all up?'

'Sorry to ask, Nick, but would there be money in it? You know we're cleaned out.'

'I sort of heard,' he said, looking away.

'So is there?'

'Yes, there would be, if we got the right idea.'

'And when would it need to be done?'

'We need to be ready to pitch in three months' time.'

'That would work out all right. I could work during the day, once we get school holidays from here in two weeks from tomorrow.'

'Do you have any ideas at all?' he asked.

She was silent for a moment. 'Quentins,' she said eventually.

'What do you mean?'

'Do a documentary about the restaurant, the changes in people's aspirations, their hopes and dreams, since it was founded about forty years ago.'

'It's never been there that long.'

'Well, it was a totally different kind of café in the sixties and early seventies, until Brenda and Patrick took it over. It was really only watery soup and beans on toast before then, you know.'

'I didn't know that.'

'Well, that's what people wanted then. And look how different it all is nowadays. You could tell the stories of the kinds of people who come there ... how it's all changed since the days when it was full of people with suitcases tied with string come in for tea and a couple of fried eggs before they took the emigrant ship.'

'It was never like that, surely?'

'It was, Nick. They have pictures of it all up in their bedroom, a whole history waiting to be told.'

He didn't ask how she had been in the Brennans' bedroom. Nick was very restful sometimes. But he didn't buy the idea. 'It would just be a plug for them. It would be like a commercial for the restaurant.'

'They don't need it. Aren't they full all the time? No, it wouldn't be done like that ... it could be a series of interviews with people remembering different times ... you know ... oh, all kinds of things – the way First Communions have changed, stag party dinners, corporate entertaining. It sure tells the story of a changing economy better than anything I know.'

He was interested now. 'Other restaurants are going to be full of grizzles and complaints about why we didn't pick them.'

'Deal with that when it happens, Nick.'

He looked at her admiringly. 'You're very bright, Ella,' he said.

'Where did it get me?' she asked.

'You asked about money,' he said, changing the subject. 'Well, this is what I suggest. If you help me develop this and sell it to Derry King, I'll pay you a proper wage for five weeks. Suppose I said eight hundred euros a week?'

'That's four thousand euros. Fantastic,' she said, delighted.

'What do you need it for so badly?'

'To do up the garden shed for my mother and father, because thanks to my lover, they are going to have to leave their own house.'

He laughed first and then stopped. 'You're bloody serious,' Nick said, shocked.

'Yes, I am.'

'I can give it to you now, tomorrow.'

'No, you can't, Nick.'

'I can. Let's say I can get my hands on it easier than you can.'

'You're not to go into debt.'

'No, but we've got to get the Bradys a henhouse or whatever to live in.' He grinned at her.

Wouldn't it have been much easier if she had loved Nick, Ella thought.

They made an appointment with the Brennans the next day. Nick and Sandy and Ella sat in the kitchen of Quentins at five o'clock and told them about the project. Brenda and Patrick were doubtful at first. They listed their reservations. It would be too much upheaval, it would get in the way of their main business, which was to provide food. They didn't need the publicity. Perhaps some of the customers might not like to be interviewed.

Slowly they were worn down. Soon they began to think of the positive side of it. In a way, it would be some kind of permanent proof of what they had done. It would be exciting to be considered part of the history of Ireland. Customers who didn't want to be interviewed need not be approached. They had huge amounts of memorabilia. Both of them were magpies who collected things and refused to throw them away. And then the most compelling reason of all ... Quentin would surely love it.

'Quentin?' Ella said. 'You mean, there really is a living person called Quentin?'

'Oh yes, indeed there is,' said Patrick Brennan the chef.

'Yes, he would,' Brenda said slowly. 'It could be a sort of monument to him.'

'Could you tell us some of the stories about the place?' Ella asked, and as she turned on the tape recorder she realised that for the past hour and a half she had not thought about Don Richardson once. The pain that was like something sticking into her ribs was not nearly so sharp. Still there, of course, but not like it had been earlier.

Quentin's Story

Quentin Barry had always wished that he had been called Sean or Brian. It was hard to be called Quentin at a Christian Brothers school in the 1970s. But that was the name they had wanted, his beautiful mother Sara Barry had wanted, she who had always lived in a dream world far more elegant than the one she really lived in.

And it was what his hard-working father Derek wanted too. Derek, who was a partner in Bob O'Neill's accountancy firm. He had always seen the day when his son's name would be on the notepaper too. That had been very important to him. Bob O'Neill had no son to succeed him. If people saw the name Quentin Barry on the office paper as well as Derek's, they would know who was important.

Since his earliest days, Quentin knew that he was going to work in his father's firm. It was never questioned. He even knew which room he would work in. It was across the corridor from his father's. At present, it was a storeroom and his father was keeping it that way until it was time for Quentin to take over.

The other lads at the Brothers didn't know what jobs, if any, they would get when they left school. A few of them might go to university. Some might go to England or America. There would, of course, be a couple of vocations to the priesthood or the Brothers.

Quentin used to pretend that he too had a choice in it all. He said that he might be a pilot or a car mechanic. These were things that sounded normal and masculine. Not like his name, not precious, like his lifestyle as an only child with a mother who looked like a film star and talked very fancy when she drove by school to collect her son in a cream-coloured car.

Sometimes Quentin felt able to tell his mother about his doubts about his future career. 'You know, Mother, I might not be a good accountant like Dad is,' he would begin nervously.

'Quentin, my sweet one, you are twelve years old!' she would say. 'Don't get involved in the awful world of business until you have to.'

He loved to help in the home, choosing fabrics for the sitting room, making table decorations for dinner parties.

His father frowned on this kind of activity. 'Don't have the lad doing girly things like that,' he would say.

'The lad, as you call him, likes to help, which is a blessing since all you do is sit down, put your elbows on the table, and eat and drink what's put in front of you.'

Quentin wondered did other people's parents bicker as much as his did. Probably. It wasn't something they talked much about at school. He knew one thing, which was that the other boys' mothers did not talk to them like his mother did.

Sara Barry always called him her Sweet One, and the Light of her Life. Or something else very fancy. Other boys' mothers called them great galumphing clods and useless good-for-nothings. It was very different. And although his mother loved him to bits, she was always saying it, she never took him seriously about not wanting to be an accountant. 'But my sweet boy, you are only twelve.'

Or thirteen or fourteen. By the time he was sixteen, he knew he had to say something.

'I do not think I'm cut out for accountancy, Dad.'

'No one's cut out for it, boy. We have to work at it.'

'I won't be any good at it, truly.'

'Of course you will, when you're involved. Just concentrate on getting your exams like a good lad.'

'I'm way behind at Maths, and honestly, I'm not going to get any good exam results in anything. Isn't it better to be prepared for that now rather than it coming as an awful shock?'

'Do you study, do your homework?' His father's frown was mighty.

'Well, yes, I do, but . . .'

'There you are. It's just nerves. You're too like your mother, highly strung, not a good thing for a man to be.'

Quentin failed his exams quite spectacularly.

The atmosphere at home was very hostile. It made it worse that his parents blamed each other much more than they blamed him.

'You upset him with all that pressure that he has to be a dull boring accountant and fill your shoes,' Sara Barry hissed.

'You fill him up with nonsense, mollycoddling him and taking him shopping with you like a poodle,' Derek Barry countered.

'You don't care about Quentin, all you care about is having two Barrys in that plodding office to annoy Bob O'Neill,' Sara snapped.

'And what do you care about, Sara? You only care that the dull plodding office, as you call it, makes enough money for you to buy ever more clothes in Haywards.'

Quentin hated hearing them shout over him. He agreed to repeat the year and have extra tuition. Derek Barry was glad that he had never mentioned any actual timings to Bob O'Neill.

One of the Brothers up at the school was a gentle man with a faraway look. Brother Rooney was always to be found in the school gardens, digging here, planting there. He used to teach a long time ago, but he said he wasn't good at it, he would drift away and tell the boys stories.

'That would have been nice,' Quentin said.

'It wasn't really, Quentin, it was no use to them. I was meant to be putting facts into their heads, getting them exams. So I sort of drifted out to the garden, which was where I wanted to be in the first place, and I'm as happy as Larry now.'

'Aren't you lucky, Brother Rooney? I don't want to be an accountant at all!'

'Then don't be, Quentin, be what you want.'

'I wish I could.'

'What do you like? What are you good at?'

'Nothing much. I like food. I love beautiful things and I like helping people enjoy themselves.'

'You could work in a restaurant.'

'With *my* parents, Brother Rooney? Can you see it?'

'Well, it's good, honest work, and they'd get used to it in time. They'd have to.'

'And what about the bit where God says, "Honour thy Father and thy Mother"?' Quentin smiled at the older Brother.

'It only says honour them, it doesn't say lie down like a doormat and go along with any of their cracked schemes.' The old man with the gardener's hands and the faded blue eyes looked as if he was on very safe ground.

'Is that what you did, Brother Rooney?'

'I did it twice, boy, first to get into the Order. My parents wanted me to work on the buildings in London and bring in big money, but I wanted peace, not more noise and bustle. They were very put out, but I never raised my voice to them, and it worked. Eventually. And then when I was in here I had to fight again to get out of the classroom and into the garden. I explained over and over that I couldn't hold the children's attention, couldn't make them understand things, but I'd love to make the garden bloom, that I could serve God best that way, and that worked. Eventually.'

'I wonder how long is eventually.' Quentin sounded wistful.

'You'd be wise to start at once, Quentin,' said Brother Rooney, picking up his hoe and getting at some of the hard-to-reach weeds at the back of the flowerbed.

'Eventually is now, Father, Mother,' Quentin said that evening at supper.

'What's the boy talking about?' His father rattled the paper.

'Derek, have the courtesy at least to listen to your son.'

'Not when he's talking rubbish. What does that mean, Quentin? Is it something you got from one of your loutish friends up in the place we thought was going to make a man of you and give you an education? Nicely fooled we were, too.' Derek Barry snorted.

'No, Father, I don't have many friends as you may notice. I'm not interested in football or drinking or going to the disco, so I'm mainly on my own. I was talking to Brother Rooney, who does the gardens up in the school.'

'Well, you might have tried talking to one of the more educated Brothers, one who would tell us what on earth we are to do with you, my darling.'

This time it was Quentin's mother's turn to look sad and impatient with him.

'You see, I'll never be an accountant. I'll never get the qualifications to get me taken on to study as one. We will all understand and accept that eventually. So why don't we accept it now?'

'And you'll do what with your life, exactly?' his father asked.

'I'll get a job, Father, go out and get a job like everyone else.'

'And what about the place in my office I was keeping for you?' His father had lines of disappointment almost etched into his face.

'Father, I'm sorry, but it was only a dream, your dream. We'll all understand that eventually. Can we not understand it now?'

'Oh, stop repeating that gardener's mumbo-jumbo.'

'I can't bear telling Hannah Mitchell. She's so proud of her son going to do law like his father.' Sara Barry's pretty face pouted. Ladies' lunches didn't look so good from this viewpoint.

'What kind of job?' Derek Barry said.

And Quentin knew that Brother Rooney had advised him well. Eventually was now.

He worked first in a seaside café south of Dublin, then an Italian restaurant in the city. Then he got a kitchen and bar job in one of the big hotels. This meant antisocial hours, so he moved out of his parents' home and got a bed-sitter. His father didn't seem to notice or care. And his mother was vague and confused about it all.

And eventually he went for an interview in Haywards store where they needed someone in their restaurant. He was interviewed by Harold Hayward, one of the many cousins who worked in the family firm. This was much smarter than the other places he had worked. More like home, in fact, where he had loved helping his mother with her dinner parties.

And this is exactly what Quentin Barry did, imitate his own mother's stylish presentation. Soon there were heavy linen napkins, good bone china, and the best of silverware all on display.

He suggested special afternoon teas, with warm scones dripping in butter, served with little bowls of clotted cream and berries to spread on top . . .

He presided over it all as if he loved being there and as if it were his own little kingdom which he had created.

His mother was not best pleased. Quite a lot of the ladies she lunched with went to Haywards. None of *their* sons worked at tables.

'You could tell them I'm serving my time until I open my own place,' Quentin suggested.

'I could, I suppose,' his mother said doubtfully.

He was shocked. He had been making a joke, and she took it seriously. What was so awful about doing a job he liked? Good, honest work. Sitting around over coffee afterwards, discussing how to make the place even better. His beautiful mother did not call him the Light of her Life or Sweet One these days. Possibly he had given all that up when he had passed on being an accountant.

From time to time, Quentin went to see Brother Rooney back at his old school. He brought the man a packet of cigarettes and they would sit on a carved wooden seat or in the greenhouse. The old man with the pale, watery blue eyes would point out proudly some of the changes there had been since Quentin's last visit. The dramatic difference it had made cutting that hedge right back; there were magical things under it that no one had ever seen and now they were flowering away once they had been given the light.

'Did you miss girls when you came here?' Quentin asked him one day.

'Don't they have girls now?' The school had become co-educational in the last couple of years. It had been a big change.

'No, I meant girlfriends. Did you miss that side of things?'

'No, not at all,' Brother Rooney said. 'Funny, but it never bothered me at all. I never had a girlfriend, couldn't take to it.'

'Would you have preferred fellows, do you think?' Quentin knew the old man wouldn't be offended.

'Divil a bit of it, neither one nor the other, a kind of a eunuch, I suppose. But you know, Quentin, that's not as big a loss as people might think.'

'I suppose it's a positive benefit, if you're in a religious order and have taken a vow of chastity,' Quentin smiled at him.

'No, I didn't mean that at all. I meant like if you're not taken up by desire for people then you can see beauty more around you. I see all kinds of colours and textures in flowers and trees that I don't think other fellows see at all.' He seemed pleased with himself over the way attributes had been handed out. Some got this, some got that.

'You're one of the happiest people I know, Brother Rooney.'

'And if you won't be offended and take it the wrong way, I think you're quite like me, Quentin. You see beauty in things too, and you have great enthusiasms. It does my heart good to hear you talking about that restaurant you run.'

'Oh, I don't run it, Brother. I only work there.'

'Well, you sound as if you did, and that's a great thing.'

'Will you come in and see me there one day?'

'I'd feel out of place in a fancy restaurant like that. They'd be looking at my nails and everything.'

'They would not. Come in and see me one day.'

But Quentin knew that Brother Rooney would not make the journey from the garden where he lived and would probably die without ever visiting him. He wondered, was the old Brother right about Quentin being like him? A eunuch, interested in neither men nor women? It could very possibly be true. Anyway, there was no time to think about it today. The restaurant was full.

The legendary afternoon teas were a huge success; tiny warmed scones with a serving of cream and raspberry jam were disappearing rapidly from trolleys. There was hardly room for all the customers.

'Move that old tramp on, Quentin, will you?' Harold Hayward the manager said with a wave at a shabby man in the corner.

'He's not a tramp. He's just a bit untidy,' Quentin protested. Perhaps

Brother Rooney had been right and this was not the place for a man with grimy hands.

'Move him on anyway. He's only had a pot of tea in the last hour and there's a line forming at the door.'

Quentin went to the table. The man looked up at him from a sheaf of papers. A near-empty teapot sat on the table. Harold the manager had been right. This was not a customer from whom they would make much money this afternoon. But it didn't seem a reason to move him on.

Quentin smiled apologetically at the man, who was in his sixties. 'I'm sorry to inconvenience you, sir, but as you can see, people are standing in a long queue waiting for tables.'

'Are you asking me to get out?' He had bushy eyebrows, a red weather-beaten face and a slightly Australian accent.

'Certainly not! I just wondered, would you mind if I helped you move your papers so that we could let other people share your table?'

'He asked you to move me on, didn't he?' The old man jerked his head at where Harold Hayward stood watching.

'Now we have room for those two ladies who both have walking sticks. They will appreciate it. May I bring them over?' Quentin was charm itself. He replaced the teapot with a fresh one at no extra charge.

The old man outstayed three sets of people who were brought to his table. At the end of the day he asked Quentin if he was part of the Hayward family himself.

'Alas, no,' he smiled apologetically. 'Just a labourer in the field, as they say.'

'Why do you say "alas"? They can't be any great shakes as a family, judging by the face of the guy who looks as if he swallowed four lemons.'

Harold Hayward did indeed look a bit sour.

'Oh, I suppose I meant it would have made life much easier for me if I could have joined the family firm. My father is an accountant and he had my name on a door in his place, but I couldn't face it. At least Harold's family are pleased with him.'

The old man came in regularly after that and he always sat at one of Quentin's tables. His name was Toby, shortened to Tobe. He had travelled the world, he said, and seen wonderful things. 'Have you travelled?' he asked Quentin.

'No. My problem was that since I decided not to go in with my father, I was so determined to make a living, I never gave myself time to go anywhere. I'd love to see the colours in Provence or in Tuscany, and I'd love to go to North Africa. One day, maybe,' he smiled sadly.

'Don't leave it too late, Quentin.'

'Eventually should be now,' Quentin said, thinking of old Brother Rooney.

'There was never a truer word said.' Tobe nodded his head vigorously.

There was no doubt that he looked a lot shabbier than the rest of the clientele. Sometimes Quentin would tell him there was this miracle stain remover he had discovered, and when Harold Hayward was not looking, he would attack a particularly noticeable stain on Tobe's chest. Once he handed him a comb and another time he gave him elastic bands to hold back his frayed cuffs. He didn't know why he did this, probably because he wanted to prove Harold Hayward wrong in his attitude. Also, he knew he wasn't offending Tobe, who was totally unaware that he looked rather eccentric and was perfectly agreeable to being brought courteously more into the mainstream.

And work was becoming Quentin's life. He still had few friends apart from the pleasant and casual relationships with those he worked with and served.

His kindness did not go unnoticed. Even his fellow staff were aware of how well he got on with the customers.

'You're very warm to people,' Brenda Brennan said to him one day.

She was one of their part-time staff, but a superior girl, cool and elegant, calm in a crisis and always perfectly capable of dealing with whatever the day might pitch at them.

He wished she would take a permanent job there but she told him that she and her husband had dreams of owning their own place.

'That was a nice gesture,' she said to him when she had seen him give the odd refill to Tobe without charging.

'Lord, Brenda, it's only hot water and a teabag,' Quentin said. 'He's happy here watching people come and go. I like his company. You should hear him talk about those orange and purple sunrises they have out in Australia.'

'I wonder what sent him out there all those years ago,' Brenda said.

'Probably his family.' Quentin was thoughtful. 'He never talks about them and it's our families who usually upset us most.'

His own father and mother barely spoke to each other now. On the few occasions when he went there to try and cook a lunch, the atmosphere was intolerable. Tobe may have gone through something like that years ago. Quentin wondered where he ate when he did eat. He obviously couldn't afford the prices in Haywards.

One night by accident he found out. There was such a bad mood in his family home, with his mother retiring to bed and his father sighing and saying he would go to his club, that Quentin had left quietly.

He didn't think that either of them were really aware that he had left. He went to a café called Mick's on a corner where he often bought chips on his way home from the cinema, but had never sat down to have a meal.

Beans on toast, fried eggs and chips, two sausages and a spoon of mashed potatoes and peas. That was the choice at Mick's. The place smelled of cooking fat, nobody wiped down the tables, the lino on the floor was torn and yet something about the place itself was enchanting. It was very handy to get at on a corner of a busy street but a little oasis when you went into its cobbled courtyard and closed the door. It was as if the world slowed down there.

Quentin saw Brenda the waitress and her husband Patrick, a serious guy, deep in conversation over their beans and toast. Then he saw Tobe with his plate of sausages, egg and chips.

Tobe waved him over. 'If you're not meeting anyone . . . ?'

'No, indeed, I'd be happy to have your company.' Quentin sat down with the older man and they talked about this and that. Neither asking the other what they were doing there. 'See you tomorrow at Haywards,' Tobe said.

He paused for ten seconds to greet Brenda and her husband, enough to show them he had noticed them but not enough to intrude on what looked like a very private conversation.

So the weeks went by, and every now and then they met in Mick's for eggs and beans, and Quentin said what he would do with this place if it was his and he had a backer, and Tobe said that his visit was nearing its end and he was going back to Australia.

Quentin told him how his parents would be so much better in two small separate establishments, but that neither of them would budge. Tobe told Quentin that for forty years in Australia he had wondered about his Irish family. Now that he had discovered them he would waste no more time, not one second, wondering about them, they simply weren't worth it.

'You can't have spent much time with them, Tobe. Weren't you in Haywards all day and at Mick's Café all night?'

'I saw them all right, and I didn't like what I saw. Have you made your plans to travel, Quentin?'

'Yes, I have got as far as enquiring the price of off-peak travel, it's still very dear. But Tobe, are you changing the subject away from your family? I'll probably never see you again after next week when you go back. I'll go mad wondering what you said to your family and they to you. Can't you tell me?'

'Not yet. I have something to think through. But I'll tell you next week, in Mick's. Would Thursday be all right, do you think?'

At Mick's on Thursday Tobe looked different, more together somehow. 'Come on, Quentin, my treat. We'll lash out and have beans *and* egg *and* sausages.'

It was hard to put a finger on it, but it was as if Tobe had suddenly taken charge. 'It's been a great pleasure meeting you. It made my visit to Dublin worthwhile and helped to clear my thoughts. Will you come and see me in Australia in a few years' time?'

'Look, Tobe, I'm having difficulty getting the money to go to Italy or Marrakesh, for heaven's sake. How could I get to Australia? Even if I do want to see the purple and orange sunrises.'

'You'll be able to afford it,' Tobe said, quite calmly, as if he knew it would happen.

'Oh, I wish,' Quentin said, pushing his hair back from his face.

And then Tobe told him the story.

Beginning with his name, which was Toby Hayward.

He was the cousin who didn't fit in, the remittance man who got an allowance as long as he stayed out of the country and far away. He had come back to see the Haywards, but since they didn't know him, he thought he would observe them a bit first. He had seen nothing in their store that he liked, nothing except Quentin. Tobe had done well in Australia, better than any of the Haywards had ever known. It wasn't their business, so he hadn't told them.

And now that he had seen haughty Harold in the restaurant, and arrogant George Hayward in the furniture department, sour and prissy Lucy Hayward in the silver department, he realised they were not people he wanted to be involved with.

Quentin, on the other hand, a boy with a dream who wanted to run a restaurant. Now that was something different. That was what he could pay back to Ireland, the land where he had been born. Quentin would come to a solicitor tomorrow morning with him and then be in a position to buy Mick's Café that afternoon.

'This doesn't happen in real life,' Quentin said.

'But you believe me, don't you? You believe I have the money and I'm giving it to you. I'm not out of the funny farm or anything.'

'Yes, of course I believe you want to do this, and I know I would do the same myself if it were me, so I understand. But it won't work, Tobe.'

'Why not?'

'Your family?'

'Don't know I'm home. I'm just the shabby old person they move from section to section of their store.'

'They might feel they have a prior claim ... family money.'

'No, I made this money. I worked and invested, and I worked day and night and invested more.'

'Maybe you should give it to a charity.'

'I've given plenty to charity. I'm just giving you enough to buy this place.'

'Maybe Mick won't sell.' Quentin was afraid to let himself believe it would happen.

'How much do you think would be a fair price, Quentin?'

Quentin told him.

'Give him half as much again, he'll sell, he'll run out of the place.'

'And then?'

'And then you'll call in sick to Haywards tomorrow and we get the money organised.'

'This doesn't happen,' Quentin said for the second time.

'Mick, could you come over here for a minute, mate?' Tobe called.

And Mick, who was tired and wanted nothing more than to be able to take his wife and handicapped daughter down to the country to live, was summoned to the table to hear the news that would change his life.

Brenda's Decision

Brenda and her friend Nora had been inseparable during catering college. They made plans for life, which varied a bit depending on what was happening. Sometimes they thought they would go to Paris together and learn from a French chef. Then they might set up a thirty-bedroom hotel in the countryside, which would have a waiting list of six months for people trying to come and stay.

In reality, of course, it was slightly different. Shifts here and there and a lot of waitressing. Too many people after the same jobs, plenty of young men and women with experience. Nora and Brenda found it hard going at the start.

So they went to London, where two things of great significance happened. Nora met an Italian man called Mario who said he loved her more than he loved life itself. And Nora certainly loved him as much, if not more.

Brenda at the time caught a heavy cold, which turned into pneumonia, and as a result lost her hearing for a time. She regarded this deafness as a terrible blow. She who could almost hear the grass grow, before her illness.

'I was never sympathetic enough to deaf people,' she wept to the busy doctor who gave her leaflets on lip-reading classes and told her to stop this self-pity, her hearing would return in time.

So Brenda went to the classes, mainly much older people, men and women struggling with hearing aids.

She learned how to practise on a VCR machine. You watched the news with the volume turned down over and over until you could guess what they were saying, and then you turned it up very high to check if you were right.

Miss Hill, the teacher, loved Brenda as she was so eager to learn. Brenda learned to study people's faces as they spoke, trying to make sense of what she couldn't hear. She understood that the hard letters to hear were the ones in the middle of a word. Most people could read the word 'pay' or 'pan', for example, but it was much harder to see a hidden consonant like an l or an r in the middle of a word. 'Pray' or 'plan' were much more difficult to work out. You had to do that from the meaning of the sentence.

Brenda had taken to it all so much, she hardly realised when her normal hearing returned. By this stage she could read conversations across a room.

Nora and Mario were very impressed. 'If all else fails, we can put you in a circus,' Nora cried, delighted.

'And I will sell tickets outside,' Mario promised.

But they all knew this wouldn't happen. Mario was going back shortly to Sicily to marry his fiancée, the girl Gabriella who lived next door to him back there.

Nora knew this too, but she just would not accept it. She was not going to stay in London without Mario, or go back to Ireland to cry over him there. She would follow him to Sicily and all it would bring.

Brenda was lonely in London when her friend had gone. She was bewildered by a love so great that it could withstand such humiliation. In her letters, Nora wrote of how she lived in a bed-sitting-room in the village that looked down on Mario's hotel. How she saw his wedding and the children's christenings and was slowly becoming part of the life of the place.

Brenda could never have loved like that. Sometimes she wondered if she would ever love at all. She came back to Dublin, but it was the same there. Nobody filled her days and nights with passion like Mario had been able to do for Nora O'Donoghue. Everyone said that Brenda was cool and calm in a crisis, a great reliable person to have around if someone spilled the gravy or dropped a tray. Brenda wondered was she going to be like that all her life, look calm and unflappable? Never in love like the couples she served at table, never upset and aching like the colleagues she consoled in kitchens when their love affairs were shaky. Never to marry even as two of her younger sisters had married, with huge drama and great expenditure of nerves. Brenda had been there, cups of tea, aspirins and calm advice at the ready.

She didn't know why she went to the dance that night. Possibly to have something to write to Nora about. It was for past pupils of their catering college. Maybe she hoped she might hear of some job opportunities.

She wore the new dress she had bought for her sister's wedding. It was very dressy, cream lace with a rose-pink jacket. It looked well with her dark hair. She thought that she got many admiring looks, but perhaps she was only imagining it.

Across the room she suddenly saw Pillowcase. Now she couldn't remember why she and Nora had called him that, an over-serious fellow, head in his books, barely any time to socialise. She heard he had gone to some high-flying place in Scotland, that he had been with a pastry cook in France. What was he doing back here? And even more important, what was his name? Paddy ... Pat?

She looked over at him. As clearly as if the words were written like subtitles, she read his lips and heard him say to the man he was with, 'Will you look at that. It's Brenda O'Hara from our year in college. Isn't she a very fine-looking girl? I haven't seen her in years. Very classy, altogether.' He seemed full of admiration.

The man he was with, a loudmouth whom Brenda knew around town, said, 'Oh, you'll get nowhere there. Real ice maiden, let me tell you.'

'Well, I'll go over and say hallo. She can't take offence at that.' He walked towards her.

Sometimes she felt a little guilty at having advance knowledge because of her extra hearing due to the lip-reading. Why hadn't the other eejit said his name, so that at least she'd know that much?

Pillowcase approached her with a broad smile. He had smartened himself up. He looked taller, or else he didn't crouch over so much.

'Patrick Brennan,' he said as he shook her hand.

'Brenda O'Hara, delighted to see you again.' She must beat the silly nickname out of her mind.

'Don't I remember you and Nora O'Donoghue very well, and is she here tonight as well?'

'Sometime when you have an hour, remind me to tell you what happened to Nora,' Brenda laughed.

'I have an hour and more now, Brenda,' he said.

Would she have seen the admiration in his face anyhow, or was it because she had lip-read his praise of her that Brenda turned her charm on Patrick Brennan?

Whatever it was, she saw him most evenings for the next two weeks. He seemed pleased that she still lived with her family. 'I'd have thought a glamour girl like you would have gone off with a rich man long ago,' he teased.

'No, no, I'm an ice maiden, didn't they tell you that?' she teased him back.

'I think I heard it said.' He shuffled awkwardly.

She wrote about him to Nora.

He's still very serious about work. He'd rather do nothing than work for a place that he doesn't think is worth it. He says I'm wasting myself doing waitress shifts here, there and anywhere. He'll do construction work or delivering cases of wine rather than work in a kitchen which would give him a bad name. But I don't agree. It's all work. You're learning all the time and anyway, he's a man who doesn't even have a flat of his own. He sleeps on people's sofas or floors. He doesn't notice.

He told her about the small farm in the country where he grew up; how his younger brother, who wasn't exactly simple-minded but not far off it, lived there still. She told him about the corner shop where her father had worked so hard to make a living. They went to the cinema and sometimes she paid if Patrick had no money. They went to Mick's Café for old times' sake.

One lunchtime as she unpacked their sandwiches to eat by the Grand Canal, she said to him firmly that she had her own plans as to how they would spend the evening.

'I live at home, Patrick. For over a month now I've been going out every single night with you.'

'Yes?' He looked anxious.

'So I'd like to let them see you, know the kind of person I'm meeting.'

'Sure.'

'No, you don't understand. It's not for them to inspect you. It's not a gun to your head. It's common courtesy.'

'No, I agree entirely. I thought you were going to say you were tired of going out with me. When we have a daughter won't we feel the very same way about her, want to know her friends?'

'What?' said Brenda.

'When we have a daughter. It's not the same with sons.'

'But what are you saying, exactly?'

He looked at her, bewildered. 'When we're married. We will have children, won't we?' He was genuinely concerned.

'Patrick, excuse me. Did I miss something here? Did you ask me to marry you? Did I say yes? It's quite a big thing. I should have remembered it, I know I should.'

He held her hand. 'You will, won't you?' he begged.

'I don't know, Patrick. I really don't know yet.'

'What else would you do?' he said, alarmed.

'Well, a number of things. I might marry no one. Or I might marry someone else as yet un-met. Or I might marry you in the fullness of time when we know that we love each other.'

'But don't we know now?'

'No, we don't. We haven't talked about it at all.'

'We haven't stopped talking about what we'll do,' he said.

'But that's work, Patrick, what jobs we'll get.'

'No, it's about what kind of life we'll live. I thought it was about our life together.'

'This is nonsense, Patrick.' She stood up, upset. 'You can't take us for granted like that. We're not even lovers.' She was very indignant.

'It's not for want of trying,' he protested.

'Not on the sofa of some ghastly flat with half of Dublin about to walk through the door with cans of Guinness any minute.'

'So what do you want, Brenda? A night in a B & B and for me to go down on one knee? Is that it?'

'No.' She was hurt and angry. 'Not that at all. It sounds ludicrous. I *do* like you, Patrick, you fool. Why else was I inviting you home? But I wanted love and passion and desire and all those things too. Not a casual munching on a sandwich and talking about our daughter as if it were all planned.'

'I'm sorry I did it wrong,' he said.

'If I thought you loved me and would take any kind of job like I do while saving for a home, and if you talked more rather than having glum silences about your future. And if you asked me properly and . . . well, if you desired me . . . I can't think of a better word, then I would strongly think of marrying you, and sooner rather than later. But it's useless now, because if you do all those things it's only my having written the script and my having fed you the lines.'

'So I can't come to supper? Is this what you're saying?' he asked.

'No, you clown, come to supper,' she said, and went away fast before he could see the tears in her eyes.

That night she reassured her mother that there was nothing in it. 'He's just a friend, Mam, a quiet friend without much to say for himself. Can't anyone of your sex-mad older generation realise that people in their twenties can be friends these days?'

At supper, Patrick Brennan brought flowers to her mother and sat down to have chicken and ham pie. And from the moment he came in the door, he never stopped talking. He praised the lightness of the pastry and flavour of the sauce. He admired the cushion covers which Mrs O'Hara had embroidered. He begged to see the wedding albums. He asked Mr O'Hara where he got fresh vegetables and told him of a cheaper place. And when they were all worn out trying to get a word in edgeways, he told them all, her two younger sisters included, that he loved Brenda but up to now had no prospects and no hope of being able to make a home for her. But suddenly on the canal bank he had got enlightenment and he realised it was a matter of any old job in catering until they had a home and could go and build their dream.

The O'Haras were astonished at him. Brenda was dumbfounded. When he left, they said he was a very nice fellow indeed, gabby though, very over-talkative, hyper almost. Hadn't Brenda said he was quiet?

'I got it wrong,' Brenda said humbly.

In weeks he had found them a job together, Patrick as chef and Brenda as front-of-house manager.

'You despise this kind of place,' she said.

'What does it matter, Brenda? A month's salary and we'll have our bed-sitter,' he said.

'We can have it now, from my savings,' she said.

They found one that day, and they practised passion and desire that night and found it fine.

They were married very shortly after that, a simple wedding with just cake and wine. It was a beautiful cake made and iced by Patrick and much photographed.

There was a series of jobs, none of them really satisfactory, none of them giving scope to what they thought they could do. But they had no money, no one to back them, to set them up in a place where they could make their mark.

And as time went by there was no sign of the daughter they had spoken of, or the son. But they were still young and perhaps it was better that they didn't have to worry yet about raising a family.

They worked in a place which only served food smothered in batter. In another where there was after-hours drinking and people wanted omelettes way into the night. They tried to take over an office canteen but were given so little money, it was impossible to present decent food. Finally, they were in a place where they realised that tax avoidance and cutting corners were going to have it closed down. This last place began to break their hearts.

Particularly since the management was supercilious and snobbish and made the guests feel uneasy.

'We'll have to leave here,' Brenda said. 'If you saw how they humiliate people in the dining room.'

'Don't let's go until we have somewhere else,' Patrick begged.

The very next night Brenda saw the nice boy Quentin Barry, whom she often met when doing extra afternoon shifts at Haywards. He was with his mother and had chosen a quiet table far across the room from her.

It was a quiet night. She had served her tables. Quietly she took off her shoes as she stood behind a serving table with its long tablecloths hiding her indiscretion from the restaurant. Her shoes were tight and high and she had been on her feet since 8 a.m. It was bliss to be in her stockinged feet.

She looked across at the mother and son talking. Very alike in blond and handsome looks, but not in manner. Mrs Barry was fussy and very self-conscious. Quentin was gentle and a listener. But not tonight. He was telling his mother about something that seemed to astonish her.

Automatically, Brenda tuned in. She didn't have any sense of eavesdropping, to her this was as if they were speaking at the top of their voices.

'You only get peanuts, working as a waiter,' Sara Barry was saying.

'I got enough working there to keep myself for several years.' Quentin was quiet.

'Yes, but you can't *buy* a place, Quentin. Be serious, sweetheart. You're not the kind of person who can buy a place and make a restaurant out of it.'

'It's not very smart now. In fact, Mick's Café, well, it's very down at heel, but if I get the right people . . .'

'No, darling, listen to me. You know nothing of business. You'd be bankrupt in a month . . .'

'I'll get people who would know, people who were trained, who would do it right.'

'You'd tire of it every day. The anxiety . . .'

'I wouldn't be there. I'd be travelling.'

'I feel quite weak, Quentin,' Sara said.

'No, Mother. Don't feel weak. I just wanted you to know how happy I am. I haven't been happy for a very long time. You used to tell me I was the love and the light of your life. I thought you'd be pleased to know I am so happy.'

Brenda then for the first time realised she was in a private conversation and looked away. She put on her shoes, walked to the kitchen on unsteady feet.

'Patrick,' she said, 'could you pour me a small brandy?'

'You look as if you've seen a ghost.'

'I've seen our future,' she said.

And in a matter of days it was sorted out.

It would be their future to turn Mick's Café into the restaurant they had always dreamed of.

'What will you call it?' they asked Quentin.

'If you don't think it's too arrogant, I think my own name,' he said shyly.

'And now can I ask you one thing, how did you hear I was buying Mick's place? I know he didn't tell anyone, and I didn't tell anyone. So it's a mystery,' he smiled.

Brenda paused. 'I don't put it on my CV. It's not a nice quality. But I lip-read. I heard you telling your mother.' She looked down.

'It's a good quality to have when you run a restaurant,' Quentin said. 'I bet we'll be glad of it through the years.'

Blouse Brennan

No one could remember why he was called Blouse Brennan. No one except his big brother Patrick.

Blouse was a bit slow at school, but he was very willing so they didn't make fun of him. The Brothers liked him, Blouse was always there to do a message, run down town and get them a pack of cigarettes, and the shopkeepers never minded giving them to Blouse though he was well under-age, because you'd know they weren't for himself.

The other boys decided that Blouse was not to be tormented because of his brother Patrick. Patrick was built like a tank and you'd be a foolish lad to take him on. So Blouse lived a fairly peaceful life for a guy who couldn't play games properly, who stumbled over his shoes and couldn't remember more than two lines of poetry no matter how long he studied.

When Patrick left school to serve his time in a hotel, Blouse worried. 'They might beat me when you're gone next term,' he said fearfully.

'They won't.' Patrick was a man of few words.

'But you won't be there, Patrick.'

'I'll come in once a week until they understand,' Patrick said. And true to his word, he was there on the first day of term walking idly around the schoolyard, giving a cuff here, a push there to establish a presence. Anyone who had even contemplated picking on Blouse Brennan had a severe change of mind.

Patrick Brennan would be back.

Patrick came home every weekend and always took his brother out for a run. The boy could talk to him in a way he didn't talk at home. Their parents were elderly and distant. Too absorbed in making a living from the smallholding with its few animals and its rocky soil.

'Why do they call me Blouse, do you know, Patrick?'

'Sure, they have to call you something, they call me Pillowcase at work.' Patrick was shruggy about it all.

'I've no idea how it all came about,' Blouse said sadly.

Patrick knew that it had all started when the lad had been heard calling his shirt his blouse years back and some of the kids picked up on the name.

For some reason it had stuck. Even the Brothers called him that, and half the people in the town. His mother and father called him Sonny, so hardly anyone knew that he had been baptised Joseph Matthew Brennan.

*

Patrick worked very hard in the hotel business. He rose from scullery helper to kitchen hand, he did stints as a porter and at the front desk, and went to do a catering course where he eventually met a girl called Brenda and brought her photograph home for inspection.

'She's got a lovely smile,' said Blouse.

'She looks healthy enough,' his father admitted grudgingly.

'Not a girl to settle in the land, I'd say,' his mother complained.

'Well, that's also for the best then, since Brenda and I haven't a notion of running this place, Blouse will be in charge here in the fullness of time.' Patrick spoke very definitely.

The parents, as was their custom, said nothing at all.

And that was the day Blouse got his great bout of confidence. He was fourteen years old, but one day he would be a landowner. That made him superior to nearly everyone else in his class at school. He made the mistake of telling Horse Harris who was a bully, and Horse mocked him and pushed him around. 'Squire Blouse', he kept calling him.

Patrick made one appearance in the schoolyard and rearranged the nose of Horse Harris. Nothing more was said, the word 'Squire' was never mentioned again.

One day Patrick bought Blouse a pint and said that when he and Brenda married, he would like Blouse to be their best man.

'Imagine, you a married man with a home of your own,' Blouse said.

'You're always welcome to come and see us, stay the night, even a weekend.'

'I know, but I wouldn't have much call going to Dublin. What would a fellow called Blouse be doing in a big city?' he asked.

Patrick brought Brenda home for a visit.

Very good-looking, Blouse thought, and confident. Not like people round here. She was very polite to his mother and father, helped with the washing up, and didn't mind the big hairy dog pawing her smart skirt.

She explained to Blouse and Patrick's mother that the wedding would be performed by her uncle who was a priest, and she reassured their father that it would be a very small affair, only twenty people at the most. They were going to have a beautiful wedding cake and bottles of wine.

Wouldn't people think it off not to have plates of cold chicken and ham? Blouse's mother wanted to know.

Apparently not in Dublin, where people were as odd as two left shoes.

There was a lot of groaning and grumbling when the day came. Blouse drove his parents to the railway station and Patrick met them in Dublin. Blouse wondered how anyone could live in a place as full of noise and strangers as Dublin, but he said nothing, just smiled at everyone and shook hands when it seemed the right thing to do.

He thought the meal was extraordinary all right, no bit of dinner, but the cake was a miracle. Imagine, his own big brother had iced it and done all those curly bits himself and the pink writing too with the names and the date.

He was taking his parents home on the five o'clock train. There had been no question of an overnight in Dublin. It would have been too much for them.

Brenda, his new sister-in-law, had been very kind. 'When we get a place with more room than just the floor, Blouse, you'll come and stay with us. We'd like that and we'll show you Dublin.'

'I'll do that one day, maybe even drive the whole way in the van,' Blouse said proudly.

It would be something to think about, look forward to. Something to say around the village. 'My sister-in-law in Dublin wants me to go and stay.'

His father got a pain in his chest and died three months after Patrick's wedding. His mother seemed to think it was just one more low in life, like the hens not laying properly or the blight in the apple trees. Blouse looked after her the best he could. And time went on the way it always had.

There weren't any girlfriends because Blouse said he wasn't really at ease with girls. He never understood what they were laughing at, and if he laughed too they stopped laughing. But he wasn't lonely. He even went to Dublin to see his brother and sister-in-law. He drove the van the whole way.

Brenda and Patrick worried about how Blouse would cope with the traffic, but it wasn't necessary. He arrived at the house without a bother.

'I meant to tell you about the quays being one way,' Patrick said.

'That wasn't a problem,' Blouse said. He sat eagerly like a child waiting to be entertained.

They talked to him easily and told him how they were hoping to get a job running a really classy restaurant for a man called Quentin Barry.

'It has all been due to Brenda,' Patrick said proudly. She had managed to find them this opportunity just at the right time.

Quentin Barry had come into some money, bought Mick's Café and wanted to set up a restaurant. He needed a chef and manager.

If this were to happen!

If they got this place going properly they were made, because the man would hardly be back at all, they could put their own stamp on the restaurant.

Blouse wasn't a drinker, but he had a glass of champagne with them to celebrate. When he got home, his mother said that Horse Harris had been around to talk business about the farm.

'What did Horse want to know?' Blouse was worried. Horse had never been good news. Apparently he had talked business with his mother. That was all she would say. Blouse wondered should he tell Patrick all about it, but no, they were too busy and excited. They had got the job working for this man Quentin who was going to let them set up their own class of a place. It wouldn't be fair, boring them with matters like Horse Harris coming to the farm and Mam's refusal to talk about it all.

Brenda wrote a note every week as regular as clockwork, and Patrick wrote a few lines at the end.

'I don't know what it is that has her writing all that nonsense every week, and putting a stamp on it,' Mrs Brennan said. 'Too little to do, that's her problem.'

But Blouse liked it. He told Horse one day that he got a letter every week from Dublin.

'Don't bother your barney replying to those two, they're after the place, that's all,' Horse had said scathingly.

Blouse went to take his mother her mug of tea and found her dead. He knelt down beside her bed and said a prayer, then he got the doctor, the priest and Shay Harris, the undertaker. When he had everything organised he phoned Patrick and Brenda.

There were a respectable number of people there.

'You're very much liked here, Blouse,' Patrick said to him.

'Aw, sure, they all liked Mam and Dad,' Blouse said.

Shay Harris asked if Patrick was going to take his things with him when he was going back to Dublin.

'What things?' Patrick asked.

And they learned that Shay's brother Horse had bought the little farm. His money was in the bank safe and sound, it was all legal and documented. Blouse would have to leave in a month.

Patrick was incensed but, oddly, Brenda didn't agree. 'He'd be far too lonely here on his own, Patrick. He would become a recluse. Tell him to come and live with us in Dublin.'

'Blouse would be lost in Dublin,' said Patrick.

Blouse couldn't believe it all. 'I'm too stupid to live anywhere,' he said sadly. 'I should have told you about Horse coming round here, but I was afraid you'd think I wanted you to come down and hit him for me again.'

'My days of belting people are over, Blouse,' Patrick said.

'You'll come and be near us,' Brenda said. 'You'll have your own money from the sale of the farm, so when you want to find a place for yourself you can, and you'd be a great help to us.'

'What could I do? I only dig fields and mind sheep and collect eggs from under the hens.'

'Couldn't you do that for us in Dublin too?' Brenda suggested.

Patrick looked at her, bewildered.

'Well, maybe not the sheep, but we could get an allotment.'

'A what?'

'Allotment. You know, Blouse. They must have them in country towns too. Big bits of waste ground and everyone rents a patch and grows their own things on it, digs and plants and harvests.'

'And who would it belong to?' Blouse was confused.

'Well, whoever owns the bit of ground, I suppose. I'll bring you and show you. They have little sheds and huts to put your shovels and forks in and big fences of wire to grow things up against, and what you grow you keep.'

Even his brother Patrick seemed to think it was a good idea. 'We could put that on the menu . . . organic vegetables, fresh free-range eggs,' he said.

'But where would I live?' Blouse began.

'There are plenty of places letting rooms near here. I'll ask around and find out,' Patrick said.

'And you could eventually come and live with us, of course,' said Brenda. 'There's a warren of old rooms in the back and upstairs. They're in the most desperate state at the moment but it will all look fine in time. We've done our room upstairs so when we have time to get the rubble cleared out, we'll paint one of them for you. You could help choose the paint and all.'

His mother had never asked him what colour room he'd like. Blouse had always wanted yellow walls and a white ceiling. He had seen a room like that in a magazine and thought it would be very cheerful with a tartan bedspread. And now he was going to have one of his own.

'I'd love to see the place and have a vision of it,' he said.

There was something about the way he said 'vision' that made Brenda and Patrick feel choked up.

They had a million other things to do which were higher priority than finding Blouse somewhere to stay but that's not the way it seemed now.

'Come on and we'll take you to see where you might live,' Brenda said.

Once they arrived at the shambles that was going to be their beloved restaurant they found themselves leading Blouse off to the storehouses, outhouses and falling-down rooms that formed the back of Quentins.

Blouse found a room that suited him well. He was not one to sit down and talk about things. 'Will I start on it now, do you think, Brenda?' he asked with his big, innocent smile.

She seemed to have tears in her eyes when she said that would be great, but he might have imagined it.

He got a wheelbarrow and got rid of the rubble. Blouse wanted the room to be nice and empty when they brought up all the furniture from home, from the little farm that Horse Harris had bought. They would bring the bed he had slept in all his life and the grandfather clock.

'Maybe I'll clear out a few other rooms for you,' Blouse offered. 'We have a lot of furniture coming up from home, and if in the future you could offer the staff living accommodation you might get them cheaper.'

They looked at him in amazement. It was all coming together. Thanks to Blouse. And it was arranged much more speedily than anyone could have believed.

Patrick managed to call and see Horse Harris before they left the town with every stick of furniture on board a huge rented van.

'Glad there are no hard feelings,' Horse said with the horrible smile of a man who knew he had beaten the slightly simple Blouse Brennan and his smart-arse brother.

'None at all, Horse,' said Patrick, giving him a handshake that could have broken every finger in Horse's hand and a twist of the wrist that could have and did twist the muscle.

Horse had no grounds to complain.

Blouse worked hard on the allotment. He drove there every day in the old van that had belonged to his parents. He learned about new vegetables that had never been part of his life back home. He had two dozen Rhode Island Reds who laid big fresh eggs and he was planning to get two dozen more.

Some evenings he helped behind the scenes in the restaurant. Blouse never minded what he was asked to do. Take out the rubbish, stack the dish-washing machines. He moved out of Patrick's house and got himself a little place near the allotment so that he could keep an eye on the hens. He had a lock on their coop at night, but it was nice to be near them.

A young, businesslike woman called on him one day. She said she was Mary O'Brien, and she had been given his address by Mrs Brennan in Quentins. She was anxious to do an article in a magazine about keeping hens and growing vegetables and she wondered if she could discuss the finer points with him.

They sat and talked, and he stroked the feathers of the hens as he spoke, and he picked out seedlings to show her how they should be planted.

Mary said she hadn't enjoyed herself so much for ages, and now could he show her where to get the bus back to the office?

'Don't you have a car?' Blouse thought she was a smart kind of person who would definitely be driving an office car and changing it every eighteen months.

'I'm afraid to drive. I've tried lessons, but I always panic,' she admitted.

'Ah no, it's very simple,' Blouse explained. 'When you panic you just indicate and pull in, that's what I always did for years and I drive now like as if I had wings.' He gave her a lift back in his battered van, and pretended he was anxious now and then.

'I don't like the look of that big bus bearing down on me. I see a place on my side so I'll indicate and move in until we catch our breath and then we can go.'

Mary O'Brien looked at him with amazement. 'Would you teach me to drive?' she begged.

'Oh, no, I'm not qualified. I'm only an eejit. You have to go to a professional, they wouldn't want a half-wit like me to be taking away their living.'

She shook his hand and said she'd send a photographer out to his allotment. 'You're no eejit, don't put yourself down. I really hope I'll see you again,' she said.

Blouse felt terrific. He knew she meant it. 'If you got a nice driving teacher, maybe he'd let me sit at the back of the car as a kind of support,' he said.

'I think that wouldn't be a problem,' said Mary O'Brien.

They were loath to part.

'You'll be famous after this article, Blouse Brennan. Self-sufficiency guru, they'll call you. Well, I'll call you that anyway, and then other people will.'

'Imagine,' he said.

'Oh, by the way, about your name ... your brother said your real name was ...'

'I'm happy with Blouse,' he said quickly.

'I think you're right. If I had a name like that, I'd keep it,' Mary O'Brien said wistfully.

'I'll give you a ring when the photographer has been and gone,' said Blouse Brennan, who had never had his picture taken professionally and never telephoned a girl before in his life.

Longings

Brenda had been very sure that she would conceive quickly. Her mother had given birth to five daughters and there were hints that there would have been many more had not great abstinence been practised. Two of her sisters had what were called honeymoon babies, and apart from her friend Nora out in Italy, everyone else that she knew had children. In fact, there were times when she feared that pregnancy might come too early and leave her unable to cope. In those years she had thought about it from time to time. But now, with the eighteen-hour days they often worked at the setting up of Quentins, in those early, exhausting months dealing with builders, planning the layout of the kitchens and the dining area, the setting up of suppliers, it was the furthest thing from their minds.

When it got a little calmer, after the opening of the restaurant when Quentin had gone away with an easy heart to Morocco to leave them totally in charge, Brenda began to think about it all again. They had been many years married now, both of them apparently fit and strong.

'About us having children?' she began one evening when they were sitting with mugs of tea in the kitchen they had insisted on having in their upstairs flat. Even though they would live over one of the best kitchens in Dublin, they didn't want to go down there if they needed a scrambled egg.

She saw Patrick's eyes light up and he reached for her hand. 'Brenda, no?' There was such hope in his voice and face.

'No, sadly no.' She tried to keep her own voice light and not to dwell on the sense of loss she had just noticed.

He got up to try and hide his face. 'Sorry, I just thought when you said about us having children,' he muttered away from her.

She sat still. 'I know. I want it as much as you do, Patrick. So don't you think we should talk?'

'I didn't think that's how you got children, by talking,' he said in a slightly mutinous way. He didn't usually have a tone like that. She decided to ignore it.

'No, I agree with you, but we do a fair amount of what does get children as well and it's not working, so I wondered, should we go and get ourselves looked at, if you know what I mean?'

'I know what you mean,' Patrick Brennan said. 'And I'm not crazy about the sound of it.'

'Me neither, a lot of legs in stirrups and things,' Brenda said. 'But if it works, then it will have been worth it.'

'When you think of what you read in the papers, half the country seems to get pregnant after one drunken fumble on a Friday night,' Patrick grumbled.

'So will I make an appointment for us with Dr Flynn?' Brenda asked.

'Does he see us both together, do you think?' Patrick wondered.

'Probably for a chat, I'd say, and then he sends us off for tests.'

They both thought about the whole undertaking ahead with no pleasure at all. They didn't book the appointment that week, because it was the week the inspectors were coming to check the ventilation. Nor the next because there was the huge excitement that Blouse Brennan and Mary O'Brien announced they would marry. Nor the week after, as there were several intense social visits with the O'Brien family, who had to be convinced that a man called Blouse was the right match for their daughter.

And then there were the meetings with Quentin's accountants, with the bank, and with lawyers. Even the meeting with the sign painter, who was coming to put their name up, took far longer than it should have. It was in heavy gold paint on very dark rich green: a huge Q in front and a hanging sign with the name on the side. They looked at it in disbelief. The whole word ran into one; the painter had put no apostrophe after the name.

'But we showed you, Brian, look at the drawings, we agreed.'

'I know, it's a mystery all right.' Brian scratched his head.

'Brian, we could have had really good painters like the Kennedy Brothers and instead we took you to give you a start, and what happens? We're the laughing stock of Dublin, that's what. We can't spell the name of our own place. That's what people will say.'

Brian saw the two upset faces looking up at the sign. 'I'll give it to you for nothing. Can't be fairer than that, can I?' he asked.

They asked Quentin on his weekly phone call.

'I was never one for punctuation. I'd prefer it the way your painter did it,' he said.

So week after week went by without Brenda and Patrick Brennan thinking they had the luxury of an hour or two to visit the doctor about something which was not after all a serious illness.

And often at night, after their long, busy days, they reached for each other in their big double bed with the white lace curtains around it. If they thought that maybe the whole matter would right itself before they needed to discuss it with Dr Flynn, neither of them said anything about it at all.

Blouse and Mary had a small wedding and a week's honeymoon on an organic farm in Scotland. They came home full of further ideas of what they could grow. Blouse was a married man now. No more living in a shed up beside the allotment. No, indeed. They had transformed the small room at the back of Quentins, taking in other storerooms, and made the whole thing into a perfect little apartment.

Mary got herself a regular column in a newspaper where she became highly respected as an adviser on growing your own vegetables in a small space. She even appeared on television programmes as an expert on the subject, her wonderful red curls bobbing and her eyes dancing as she spoke of her husband Blouse, without any self-consciousness about the name but with huge pride in the man.

Blouse grew more confident every day and no day did he seem more happy and self-assured than the day he told Patrick and Brenda that they were expecting a child. Four months married, and now this great news.

They managed to show their enthusiasm and hide their jealousy until they were alone that night in their bedroom. They tried to be generous but it was hard. The sense of unfairness was all around them. Although they sat side by side there was a huge gulf between them. Their shoulders didn't even touch.

'It will be all right,' Brenda said.

'Of course it will,' Patrick said.

'I'll ring Dr Flynn tomorrow,' she promised. 'To wave his magic wand.'

When they got into bed, she put her arm around him. At bad times they were a great consolation to each other. So often making love had washed away the cares and anxieties of the day.

But not tonight.

'I'm tired, love,' he said, and turned on one side away from her.

Brenda lay awake all night looking at the walls covered with pictures and memories. Even though her limbs were aching with fatigue, she couldn't find any sleep.

Dr Flynn was pleasant and technical and made them feel that he was not sounding overly intimate when he asked questions about whether full penetrative intercourse had taken place. He then sent them both to a hospital for a series of tests and asked them to come back in six weeks.

It was a strange time in their lives. They made love only twice and a third time, when it had seemed likely, Patrick said there was no point as it was the wrong time of the month for Brenda, nothing would come of it.

And during all this time, Mary patted her small bump proudly and Blouse talked about the responsibilities of fatherhood ahead of him.

Every woman Brenda met seemed to be talking about children, for good or evil. Either they were such darlings and so wonderful that the women couldn't bear to go out to work and leave them. Or else they were as troublesome as weasels, snarling and ungrateful, and if their mothers could get rid of them legally they would.

And Brenda listened and smiled.

The only person who understood was her friend Nora, miles and miles away in Sicily. Nora who could never tell the village that she loved Mario, even though many of them may have suspected. Sometimes people then said to Signora, which was what they called her, not Nora, that she was lucky to be childless, not to have the problems they had. But Nora would sit at her window and watch Mario playing in the square with his boys. How she yearned for a little dark curly-haired baby of his to hold in her arms.

She longed with such an ache that she nearly convinced herself he might leave Gabriella and his other children and stay with her if she were to produce a baby for him.

But fortunately she had never tested the theory.

Brenda wrote to Nora as she could write to no one close. She wrote one night as Patrick slept on deeply on his side of the bed:

He doesn't love me as me any more. He will only consider touching me when I am meant to be most fertile. The tests showed that there is nothing preventing us conceiving. I ovulate normally. Patrick's sperm count is normal. They keep telling us we're not ready for fertility drugs yet. Patrick just keeps wondering how old do we have to get? I don't know any more, Nora, I really don't. You keep hearing of people having eleven embryos with fertility drugs. Then Mary and Blouse will have their baby next week. And I have to be glad and delighted and thrilled. I feel so mean-spirited not to be.

Patrick didn't want to talk about it. 'What do you mean, how do I *feel* about Blouse being able to father a child when I'm not? How do you think I feel?' he snapped.

'I didn't put it that way.' Tears of hurt sprang in Brenda's eyes.

'It's what you meant, though, Brenda. The fool of the family is able to get his girl pregnant but you can't say the same for the elder brother.'

'I will not have you speak of Blouse that way, Patrick. You never did before. You never let anyone else do so. He told me you used to go to his schoolyard and fight battles with anyone who made such a remark, and now you're doing it yourself.'

He felt ashamed, she could see it, his head hung down. 'I'm sorry. I don't know what came into me.'

'What came into you is what's in me too, a longing, a longing to have a child of our own, no wonder it unbalances us, Patrick.'

'You're not unbalanced about it. You're very calm,' he said.

'No, that's my way of coping, pretend everything's normal and it may become normal.'

'I'm sorry, Brenda. It's hard on you too. I'm not trying to excuse myself for anything. It's just sometimes when I'm as tired as a dog at the end of a day I wonder what it's all for.'

'All what?'

'All the hard work. What are we doing it for, exactly?'

Brenda thought they were doing it for themselves, for each other, for the shared dream. But she knew she must speak very carefully. 'I know, I feel the same,' she said slowly.

'You do?' He seemed surprised.

'Well, of course I do, Patrick. What do you think I feel?'

'It's just that last month you said . . . when we realised once more that it hadn't happened . . . you said maybe, just maybe, it was all for the best for the moment.'

'What would you have preferred, that I would have opened my mouth and howled out from the bathroom in front of everyone, the suppliers, the customers, Blouse and Mary, anyone else passing through, that yet again we had failed to make a child? Should I have sobbed and upset everyone? You tell me, so that I'll do it right next month.'

He put his arms around her and she cried into his chest for about fifteen minutes before her shoulders stopped shaking. Then he held her away from him and he looked at her tear-stained face. 'Come on, now, put on your face for both of us, brave Brenda Brennan,' he said, and kissed her for the first time in a long time.

Mary and Blouse had a little boy. They called him Brendan Patrick. He was perfect.

Brenda went in to see him every day. His little fingers tightened over hers. He smiled sleepily up at her. He would stop crying when she held him. She was good with children. One day she would have one of her own.

She rang Dr Flynn and said yes to any fertility drugs available, including experimental ones. He urged caution and waiting. She said there wasn't any question of that any more.

She kept the smile of welcome and delight about little Brendan Patrick nailed to her face. She was sure that nobody saw in her face the yearning, the longing for her own child. Then one day her lip-reading skills showed her a conversation between Blouse and Mary.

'Isn't it great that Brenda loves him so much?' Blouse was saying.

'Yes, but I think we shouldn't boast about him so much,' Mary said.

'Boast? Doesn't she admire him and talk about him just like us?' Blouse was astonished.

'It's just that she might have wanted one of her own,' said little Mary O'Brien with the red curls and the perfect new baby.

There were reasons why the drugs didn't seem to suit. High blood pressure, allergies, contra-indications. In vitro fertilisation had a very long waiting list. Brenda never really understood what each problem was because the shroud of disappointment was so great, and the hard lines of Patrick's face more firmly etched.

Dr Flynn tried to explain it to them. He got the feeling he was talking to two brick walls. He talked about resuming and keeping up the active happy sex life they had told him they had before. He mentioned adoption tentatively. Very often this was a wonderful thing, not only in itself but it had the additional side effect of leaving the parents more relaxed and therefore having a successful conception.

They said nothing.

Dr Flynn said that adoption wasn't as easy as it used to be, too many people chasing after a small pool of babies. The days were gone when single girls gave up their babies to orphanages or for adoption. Very much healthier attitude, of course, but not helpful when you were looking for a child.

And of course there was the age factor, nobody over forty was really in with a chance of adopting, so it would have to be speedy if they wanted to try and apply.

To the outside world, nothing had changed, but for the great team that had been Brenda and Patrick Brennan, something had. Only those very close to them guessed that there was anything wrong at all. Blouse and Mary thought the couple were very overworked, that they didn't seem to laugh as much as they had in earlier times. Brenda's mother noticed nothing except that any time she was unwise enough to enquire about the patter of tiny feet, she got a very short answer.

Quentin Barry noticed in his weekly phone call that the same spark wasn't there in Brenda.

He put it down to strain and rules and regulations and anxiety. 'Don't kill yourselves,' he wrote kindly. 'I know that we won't be trading at a profit for quite a long time. My accountant barks much more loudly than he bites. Together we will have something marvellous, don't lose your passion and fire over this.'

If Patrick and Brenda had both read his instructions about not losing fire and passion with a wry laugh they said nothing to each other. They had been serving food and changing everything restlessly for months now.

There were so many teething troubles. Who would have known ... that parking would be such a nightmare. That taxi firms would be so likely to let them down. That the fish catch would be so unreliable at times. That well-known people would have used-up credit cards. That people would steal ashtrays and linen napkins. They learned, slowly and sometimes bitterly. This was the first time they had run their own place. Or Quentin's place. He had told them to think of it as theirs.

But when Brenda saw Patrick sighing, she remembered how he had asked, 'What's it all for? What am I doing all this for?' Her heart was heavy.

By the time the end of their first year approached, Brenda had lost a great deal of weight and looked very tired. Mary, Blouse's wife, who looked blooming in motherhood, was also, it appeared, able to hold down a series of jobs as well. Through her contacts she had arranged huge publicity for the first anniversary party.

Three nights before the event, when every catastrophe that *could* have happened *had* happened, Patrick and Brenda were still in the restaurant kitchen at 3 a.m. They had lived through a day when a car had reversed into one of their windows, leaving broken glass and a whistling wind until the whole thing could be boarded up and made to appear like a bomb site. Then there had been a gas leak, a shelf containing a lot of valuable produce collapsing, and a lavatory in the ladies' room overflowing. Somebody had sent back the fish because it tasted 'funny' and everyone else felt uneasy about their portions, which had tasted fine up to then. One of the waiters had left because he said, frankly, the place was a shambles and would never take off as a top-class place to work.

'What are we doing it for?' Patrick asked again.

'Sorry, Patrick?'

'You heard me. What's it *for*? I'm bloody exhausted. You're like skin and bone. You've aged twenty years. We were mad to try to do all this. Crazy, that's what we were . . .'

'Would it have been worth it if we had a child or even the prospect of one, do you think? Would it have made sense out of a day from hell like today?'

'You know it would.'

'No, I don't. We would have been just as tired, even more so.'

'You know what I mean. There would have been some sort of purpose to it all. Something at the end.'

'And there's nothing now, no purpose in anything, is this what you're saying?'

'You're picking a row, Brenda. It's far too late.'

'You're right. Why don't you go on up to bed?'

'Aren't you coming?'

'In a while. Please go on up.'

Patrick dragged himself to the door and climbed the stairs.

Brenda looked around the place where she had soldiered since 7 a.m. Twenty hours. She walked thoughtfully over to a mirror they had put strategically for staff to give themselves a quick glance before going into the dining room. Skin and bone, he had said. Aged twenty years, he had said.

She wrote a short note to Patrick.

I'm sorry, but I don't feel like sharing a bed with you tonight. Not if you think I'm old and sad and wretched-looking. Not if you see no hope, no purpose in anything. I'm going to a friend for the night, or what's left of it. But whatever I am, I am a pro. I'll be back tomorrow, 12 noon for the photo call Mary has arranged, and for my lunchtime shift. I don't feel the need to say anything about this to anyone, so you needn't either.
    Brenda

She left it on the table beside where he slept in a deep sleep, arm thrown across to her side of the bed as he had done for years. She took her coat, a change of clothes and some washing things, and let herself out into the early morning of Dublin City.

She took a taxi to Tara Road where Colm ran a restaurant. He was a recovering alcoholic, a man who slept lightly. He too lived over the premises. They had always joked about being rivals, but his restaurant in its green suburb catered to an entirely different clientele from Quentins' city-centre trade.

She rang the bell and he answered in a wide-awake voice. 'Brenda Brennan? The very person.'

'Colm, could I have a bed for the night, what's left of it?'

'Sure. Will you have tea and toast or do you want to sleep straight away?'

'Tea and toast will be fine,' she said.

He never asked her what it was about and she went to bed half an hour later in Colm's spare room, where she slept until 10 a.m.

'Do I look skin and bone and twenty years older, Colm?' she asked at a breakfast of melon, champagne and orange juice, and a freshly baked pastry.

'No, and only an overtired husband in a blind panic over his restaurant would have said that. Are you going back to him?'

'Of course I am. I'm a professional.'

'And you love him?' he pleaded.

'Maybe.'

'No, definitely,' he said.

'Anyway, Colm, could you get me a taxi, and know you are the truest friend anyone ever had?'

The taxi came in five minutes. Eleven minutes into the journey the taxi was hit by a large truck. It came from the side where Brenda was seated. The blow to her head knocked her unconscious at once. She knew nothing at all after the impact.

Brenda had never been late for anything. Patrick began to be seriously worried. She had said she would be back. He knew that she would. He wondered what friend she had gone to see. He wished that he hadn't been so sharp-tempered. Why could he not have given her a hug and said that when the world settled down they would talk? Brenda was never moody. She wouldn't make a scene like this on such a very important day.

When she hadn't turned up for the photo call, he became seriously alarmed. He had tried to reassure everyone else, insisted that Blouse and Mary be included in the pictures as well as the newly recruited staff. He said there were a million last-minute things that each of them had to see to.

They served a lunch short-handed, every moment he expected to see her come in to the kitchen and slip her coat off. But lunch was over, and there was still no sign.

The afternoon didn't bring her, either. He was now getting really worried. By six o'clock he was ready to call the Guards. They were not helpful. A domestic incident at 3 a.m.! They were sympathetic, but they had better things to do with their time. Most missing people came home, they said. Try her friends, they suggested.

He had no idea who to call. He slapped the food on to plates for the dinner with no idea what he was serving.

She would *not* have left him like this.

In hospital, they searched for any identification which would tell them who the dark-haired woman was. All they had was a set of keys and some bank notes in her pockets, a change of clothes in an overnight bag. No hint at all about whom they might contact.

During dinner Patrick went upstairs again. He saw Brenda's handbag on the floor beside the dressing table. She had gone away without anything. It wasn't possible that she had gone away to kill herself. He didn't want to involve Blouse and Mary. Blouse was so simple and innocent. But by eleven o'clock that night he had to tell them.

He was sitting crying in the kitchen and they demanded to know why.

'We'll call the hospitals,' Mary said.

They took six of the major places and tried two each.

Blouse found her on his first go.

'Long, straight, dark hair usually tied up in what is called a French pleat,' he said, proud of having got it all together.

Patrick wondered if he would have been able to give such a good description. He grabbed the phone. 'Is she alive?' he sobbed. 'Thank God. Thank God.'

She had come round for a moment, spoken in a garbled way of Patrick and Quentin but they had no idea what she meant. They were letting her sleep now.

Blouse got out of the van. Patrick sat inside holding his head. Had he really said to this wonderful, strong, loyal woman that there was no hope, no purpose in anything? Could he have driven her out into the night because she couldn't bear to lie beside him? The only thing that mattered was Brenda, he knew it somewhere inside. Why could he not have admitted it, and said it to her? Please, please God, may there be years and years ahead when he could tell her.

He sat by her bed all night and stroked her thin, pale cheek. He half-remembered people telling him about the accident and the taxi and the truck. She had been on her way home to him and this had happened.

Then at dawn she woke and he laid his head on her chest and sobbed as if his heart would break.

There was no concussion, very little bruising, just great shock. She had been lucky. The taxi driver had been lucky. Everyone was all right.

'I think I'll make it for the party after all,' she said.

'You're everything in the world to me, Brenda. You're enough, do you hear what I'm saying? You're more than enough. I love you so much, we have huge hope, a huge future together, you and I.'

Everyone was there that night at the anniversary party of Quentins, which was as glittery a do as Dublin had seen for a long time, and they would always remember one particular moment.

It was when Patrick Brennan took his wife's hand in his and held it very tight. He looked around the crowd and lowered his voice slightly.

'Brenda and I have a wonderful baby to rejoice over with you tonight. The baby is one year old and we have all of you here to celebrate the fact we have a restaurant which survived a year and where we hope to make friends and strangers alike welcome and happy with us. It's not as wonderful as a real christening with a real baby, but for us it's everything that a real christening is, with a sense of fulfilment and hope and a future ahead of us all. So will you drink to our baby, Quentins, and wish us all well in the adventures that the rest of life will bring to everyone in this room?'

Even hard-bitten media people and professional first nighters were silent as Patrick Brennan kissed his thin, elegant wife Brenda. As the years went on, people said that Brenda Brennan never cried, they must have imagined it. But those who were there knew that they hadn't imagined it. And it wasn't only the Brennans who had cried. Everyone in the room seemed to have been affected, too.

Part Two

5

There were so many stories about Quentins, it was hard to sort out which they could use and which to throw away. Setting up a movie seemed to cost a great deal of money. They pored over their budget with anxious faces. Sandy had some money in a savings account which she willingly put into the fund. Nick mortgaged his flat and raised a reasonable sum. But, of course, if they were going to make a film that would win prizes and awards, they would have to have high production values and it would mean asking for serious finance from the King Foundation. They had received their application form and took great care over filling it in.

'I'll have to work much harder than you two because I have nothing to invest,' Ella said. 'So today I brought us a bottle of champagne that a customer gave me in Colm's last night. Imagine, he said he didn't want to insult me with money! If he only knew how ready I was to be insulted with money.'

They laughed as they got great tumblers and poured it out. They toasted Firefly Films, Quentins, and the King Foundation in New York.

When they had finished the bottle of champagne, Nick had said they must be realistic. They were looking for something that was way out of their league. 'It's not Mickey Mouse money this time,' he said, frowning.

Sandy tried to make light of it. She hated to see Nick frown. 'Don't knock Mickey Mouse. He made a lot of money for Walt Disney in his time,' she said.

He grinned feebly. 'Sandy, I'm only saying aloud what we're all thinking. Maybe we can come up with another terrific idea. Ella got us this far. All we need is another leap now.'

Ella saw the shadow pass over Sandy's face. 'I didn't get us very far. It was Sandy who wrote out the whole proposal that won the pitch. And in addition, as soon as this champagne's finished I'm going to have to leave you and look for more paid work with other people. I hate to do it, but you know the scene.'

'Are your parents in the shed yet?' Nick asked.

'Yes, we all are, but we actually call it the Annexe, to make ourselves feel better.'

'Is it very cramped?' Sandy wanted to know.

'Not too bad, amazingly. Colm knew some builder in the early days, and they do each other favours. Anyway, this fellow built us a grand place with lots of windows in the roof so at least there's plenty of light coming in and there's a whole bank of storage lock-ups so that my mother can keep things for when we get out of debt again. I even put my things in there.'

'And will you? Ever get out of debt?' Nick was blunt.

'I don't know. I wouldn't think so, but it's a start, and my father's calmed down again. For a while I thought he was going to be in a mental home. People know he's doing his utmost to pay them back and that's a help. And two of the flats are already occupied in what we now call the Main House; two more ready by the end of next week. That's not a bad recovery.' She forced her voice to sound cheerful.

Sandy and Nick nodded with respect. Compared to what the Bradys were going through, their own problems were small. They would find the money for their project, or they wouldn't – at least they didn't owe real money to anyone.

'What work are you going to do?' Nick asked.

'Deirdre's got me a part-time job up in her lab. I've got two nights a week waitressing in Colm's, two nights a week for Scarlet Feather – you know, your pals Tom and Cathy – weekends in Quentins and, wait for it, two hours a week teaching a pair of twins maths and basic science. They're something else, those two. They keep asking me am I part of the New Poor. I don't know where they heard the expression, but they love it.'

'Doesn't sound as if there's much time for a social life,' Nick said.

'Oh, Nick, I've had as much social life in the last two years as any girl needs,' she laughed wryly.

'Was it as long as that?' He seemed disappointed that her affair had gone on for such a time.

'Give or take a bit,' she said. 'In my case, mainly give, but who's counting?'

Afterwards Sandy asked her very confidentially, 'Do you think Nick likes me at all, Ella, or am I just wasting my time?'

'Oh, I think he likes you a great deal, Sandy. But I beg of you, don't listen to me, what do I know about men and what they like and don't like? Nothing, that's what I know.'

Deirdre said that Nuala was coming over next week. 'Great, let's get a bottle of wine each and entertain her,' Ella said. 'But wait, it will have to be after midnight or between four and six Wednesday and Saturday.'

'Oh, God, I can't wait till you're back in teaching and have normal hours again.'

'I'm not going back,' Ella said.

'Of course you are.'

'I can't afford to,' Ella said simply. 'Why don't we say we'll have a picnic in Stephen's Green? Nuala would like that, then I can get back to Quentins at six.'

'I'll check it out,' Deirdre said.

*

'Bad news, Ella. I'm going to give it to you straight. Nuala doesn't want to meet you in Stephen's Green.'

'Okay, where does she suggest?'

'This is the hard bit. She doesn't want to meet you at all.'

'I don't believe you.'

'It's what the lady says.'

'Has she gone soft in the head or something?'

'It's to do with Don. Her husband and his brothers lost a lot of money because of Mr Richardson. Apparently she's feeling a bit sore about it.'

'Well, I'm sure she is, and so are a lot of other innocent people, but why doesn't she want to meet *me*? I haven't got her bloody money.' Ella was hurt and angry.

'Oh, I don't know, some garbled thing about you having a fine time out in Spanish hotels with Frank's money.'

'Isn't she a weak slob? Couldn't I do the same to her, moan and groan and say that it was at her awful in-laws' party that I met Don and ruined my life?'

'Leave it, Ella. She's not worth it.'

'But you're still going to meet her?'

'Not if you don't want me to.'

'Oh, meet her, for God's sake. What do I care?'

'Ella, come on now!'

'No, I don't care. What does one more small-minded, petty self-seeker matter?'

'She used to be our pal.'

'She's forgotten that pretty quickly.'

'I'll tell you what she says,' Deirdre sighed.

'If you must.'

'I'll take her to Quentins, some time you're not working there.'

'Yeah, make sure I'm not working when she's there. I've a neat way with very hot soup straight into someone's lap,' said Ella.

It was Ella's weekly lunchtime lesson with Simon and Maud. They lived with their grandparents in St Jarlath's Crescent. They were bright enough, but had missed out on some mathematics teaching. They were some kind of cousins of Cathy Scarlet. Ella had learned never to ask for too much detail. But then, she had never met children like Simon and Maud before. They insisted on telling her their whole life story and that they were really related to Cathy's ex-husband, the lawyer Neil Mitchell, but that through a lot of adventures and eventually court orders, they were now living with Cathy's mother and father, Muttie and Lizzie.

They had a dog called Hooves, who had a limp. They had a brother who was on the run from the police in several countries. They had their own passports, which they had needed because they'd been to Chicago to dance at a christening party. On the plane, they had been allowed up to the flight deck. In Chicago they had . . .

'Sure, but I think we'd better get down to the algebra before I hear any more.'

'Are we boring you?' Simon asked very earnestly. 'People say we go on a bit.'

'No, you're not boring at all,' Ella said truthfully. 'It's just that I am being paid proper money to teach you, and I don't want to cheat your grandparents or whatever.'

'Strictly speaking, they're not *our* grandparents,' Simon began.

'So I brought this book. It's simpler than the one you have at school, but I thought if we went through it first, then when it was all a bit clearer, we could look at your book.'

'And can we have real conversation with you when we've understood it?' Maud asked.

'Certainly,' Ella said, flattered.

'It's just that we were told not to be asking you questions about your sad life, but we wanted to know all the same,' Simon explained.

Ella put her hand up to her face to hide the smile. 'I'll give you blow-by-blow details if you can get your heads round these equations,' she promised.

'You're not going to spend the whole lunch looking at me as if I'm some kind of criminal?' Nuala said.

Deirdre shrugged. 'No, because I'm sure you have some very good reason for behaving like a prize arsehole.'

'Deirdre, please, there's no call for that kind of language.'

'There's every call. Ella's had enough worries. She was looking forward to seeing you, and you as good as spat in her face.'

'But, Dee, she knew what she was doing, going on luxury holidays all on Frank's money and his family's investments. You have no idea the mess that Don Richardson left behind him.'

'She spent one long weekend with him, her half-term from school, she bought her own ticket, you fool.'

'I heard . . .'

'You heard what you wanted to hear, Nuala. I know what went on, including the fact that the man she met at your party lied to her, betrayed her, humiliated her, left her father without a name, house or reputation to call his own. I don't care what you know or think you know. Let's look at the facts: Ella is working sixteen hours a day to make up what the bastard took from her parents . . . and she doesn't even have the comfort of having a picnic lunch with someone she once thought was a friend.'

There was a great silence.

'Why did *you* come then, if this is the way you feel?' Nuala said in a very small voice.

'To tell it to you straight.'

'Please tell her I'm very sorry. I didn't think it through.'

'No, I'll tell her nothing, you know her phone number. Tell her yourself.'

Nuala began to take her phone out of her handbag.

'Not here, it's not allowed,' Deirdre said.

Nuala went to the ladies' room. Brenda Brennan asked was everything all right.

'Yes, Mrs Brennan.'

'Correct me if I'm wrong, but isn't that the young lady who got proposed to here in this restaurant?'

'The very one.'

'And did it all ... er ... work out ... all right and everything?' Brenda Brennan could sense the tension.

'Yes, I suppose it did, he's a greedy money-mad pig of a man, but he's reasonably faithful to her and she seems content enough. The only problem in paradise is that they were burned badly by Don Richardson, of course.'

'They're not alone there.'

'No, but she had the nerve to imply that Ella had gained something out of it all.'

'Everyone knows that's not the way things were. I thought she and Ella were friends?'

'So did Ella,' Deirdre said.

'Well, thank heavens Ella has at least one good friend in you.'

'And in you, Mrs Brennan. She's very grateful to you.'

'She's working too hard, that's my only worry. She's white as a sheet. Patrick and I worry about her health, and whether she'll be able to carry on. She's taken on far too much for any one woman.'

They saw Nuala coming to the table and Brenda nodded and left to talk to another customer.

'She had her mobile on answer,' Nuala said.

'Yes, well, she'll be working, trying to pay back what that bastard stole from her father and his clients. Working while we have lunch here in Quentins.'

'Don't make me feel worse, Deirdre. Life isn't actually a bed of roses with me either, you know.'

'It never is, Nuala,' Deirdre sighed. 'Come on, let's have the pasta starter and the seared tuna for main course, and you can tell me what Frank's been up to now.'

'How on earth did you know he's been up to something?' Nuala was stricken.

'Your face, Nuala. It's written all over it. You have suspicions, isn't that it? You think he's looking at some woman over there in London in a certain way.'

'Oh, Dee, you can read minds,' Nuala said.

'There's probably nothing in it at all.' Deirdre began giving the speech that Nuala wanted to hear. 'After a few years, all couples go through this. It's only we, the old maids, who get to hear about it. They don't tell other wives.'

'But it's been going on a bit.' Nuala was doubtful.

'It could have been going on a bit just in your mind, you know. Frank is like his brothers, charming to everyone. It could be a matter of nothing,' Deirdre said.

Nuala's eyes were shining. 'That's exactly what Frank says. He says it's all in my mind.'

'Well then, there you are,' said Deirdre wearily.

There was a very positive letter from the King Foundation. The application had been read and had been moved on to a shortlist. There were various other technical details to attend to, and criteria to meet, but in general they had met all the main requirements and they were on to the next level. The letter was signed 'Derry and Kimberly King'. Nick and Sandy wished that Ella were there to share it with them, but she was giving private tuition to these extraordinary twins. They would celebrate with her later. Meanwhile, they held hands and rejoiced at having got so far.

'If we do get it made and it goes to festivals and we get known and have plenty of money, what would you do with it?' Sandy asked suddenly.

'What would *we* do with it, you mean?'

'No, I mean you, actually.'

He looked at her, dumbfounded. 'We'd get better premises, wouldn't we? New equipment. Take on someone full-time, have a honeymoon of some kind, get a really good, glossy brochure out. Isn't that what you'd do?'

'Yes,' she said, her cheeks getting pinker. He had actually said honeymoon.

'You'd do all that too?' Nick teased her.

'I would, yes.' She didn't look at him.

'But there's one thing, Sandy. We can't have a honeymoon without getting married first.'

'I know,' she said.

'So are you going to ask me to marry you?' he went on.

'Doesn't the man do that?' Poor Sandy was still not sure if he was teasing her or proposing.

'Not always. The better decision-maker usually does it. You're the better decision-maker in our company.'

'And should I wait until we got rich, do you think?' Her anxiety was so obvious now he couldn't bear to let it go on any longer.

'I'd love if we got married, rich or poor,' he said.

'Oh, Nick.' Her smile was so broad, he picked up a Polaroid camera. 'I want to show this to our grandchildren some day, tell them what you looked like the day you proposed.'

The phone rang just then. It was Mike Martin, a friend of Don Richardson's in the past, he had put some work their way. Nick was surprised to hear from him.

'It's not a job, alas, those are thin on the ground these days with the climate we have now.'

'That's for sure,' Nick agreed sadly.

'It's more of a personal favour. You know Ella Brady, I believe.'

'Yes.' Nick was cautious.

'Well, you remember a friend of hers. Someone who no longer lives in this land – who went to Spain?'

'Do you mean Don Richardson?' Nick asked baldly.

'Yes. Well, I was trying to be more discreet.'

'I have no need to be discreet. That was his name. This isn't a police state. We can say people's names, surely?'

'No, but the guns are out for him, Nick. You know that.'

'The guns may well be out for him, but they are hardly tapping my phone about him.' Nick felt very annoyed with this man.

'Did you lose money, Nick? I know for a fact that Don is doing his level best.'

'I'm sure he is, his very level best. No, I didn't lose anything, but I have great friends who were ruined.'

'And believe me, they will be recompensed, compensated.'

'That's not what we read in the papers.'

'What do journalists know? And it's actually about that I'm calling. Is this a convenient time?'

'Yes. You interrupted a marriage proposal, but it can be continued when we've finished talking.' Nick leaned over and stroked Sandy's face.

'I never know whether to take you seriously or not.'

'I know, it's a worry.'

Nick let a silence fall.

'Anyway, our friend hasn't been able to contact Ella.'

'I think Don probably knows Ella's phone number.'

'It's not as simple as that.'

'It probably is, or he could send a letter, a postcard, an e-mail.'

'I'm going to cut to the chase, Nick. You're not being as co-operative and understanding about the problem as we'd hoped.'

'We?'

'Um ... Don and I.'

'You're with him as you speak?'

'That's neither here nor there. What I was going to do ...'

'... was cut to the chase. I heard you.'

'There's this briefcase with a laptop computer.'

'I'll bet there is.'

'Which Mr Richardson inadvertently left in Ms Brady's apartment ...'

'That must have been a day or two ago.'

'I beg your pardon?'

'Don Richardson ran out of here four months ago. He must have missed his briefcase before now.'

'Now is when he's looking for it, Nick.'

'Well, he can come home and pick it up, can't he?'

'He can't find Ella. She's not in that apartment. She's not in the house in Tara Road.'

'And I imagine he knows why. They had to sell everything, give up everything, because of him.'

'I don't think he sees it that way ...'

'You do surprise me!'

'I'd like to give you a phone number. Please give it to Ms Brady and ask her to call Mr Richardson.'

'I wouldn't hold your breath, Mr Martin.'

'I'll dictate the number, and I'm sure you'll be responsible enough to pass it on.'

'I'll take lessons in responsibility from your pal Don, will I?'

'Have you a pen or pencil?'

'Yes, but what's to stop me giving this to the newspapers, the authorities, or some of the people he robbed blind?'

'I'm sure you'll do the right thing, Nick,' said Mike Martin, and read out a number. Then they both hung up.

'What was that all about?' Sandy asked, round-eyed.

'About a tactless oaf who interrupted you when you were about to kneel down in front of me . . . wait, wait . . . and meet me kneeling down in front of you, and we were going to ask each other the most important question of our lives.'

'And that guy in Spain?'

'Can wait his turn like everyone else,' said Nick, kneeling down on the floor.

Barbara and Tim Brady were having a late lunch in the little bit of garden they had kept for themselves beside their Annexe. Through the bamboo hedge they could see the Main House, where they had lived until three months ago. All of it now let at astronomical rents. Oddly, they didn't miss it nearly as much as they had thought they would.

Looking back on it now, they realised it had been too big for them. And lonely, too. Somehow, since they had come here, it was much more companionable, and they saw so much more of Ella as she dashed in and out and grabbed cups of tea. Her friend Deirdre called a lot, which was nice. They still had a great deal of anxiety and the nightmare about the debts they owed and the people in Tim's office who had lost money. But all in all, it was a happier time, a better quality of life. They hardly dared to admit it to anyone except each other. And they were able to talk to each other these days. Which was another change for the better.

6

'It's not too hard, when you put your mind to it,' Simon said.

'That's what I've always found,' Ella agreed.

'But of course, there's no real point to it,' Maud said.

'I don't know. There's a sort of a point, like it's a principle, a formula. When you know how to do it once, you can always apply it again.'

'But when would you ever want to apply it again?' Maud wondered thoughtfully.

'For exams, I suppose,' Simon said. 'Do we really need to do that whole page of problems before next week?'

'Yes, you do if I'm to be sure you've understood it and can move on to the next thing.'

'Nobody else at school has to do a page of problems,' Maud said with a slightly downturned mouth.

'I know, Maud. Aren't you lucky that they're paying extra for you to learn more?' Ella said.

Maud was debating this when Ella's phone rang. It was Nuala. She was in tears. She was so sorry, she was such a fool, she had quite rightly had the head bitten off her by Deirdre. She'd love to talk to Ella. That is, if Ella would ever forgive her.

'Sure, I'll forgive you,' Ella said. 'That bastard upsets everyone, makes them behave out of character, that's all.'

Maud and Simon exchanged glances.

'But Nuala, I have to go. I'm at work at the moment.'

'Dee says you never stop.'

'No, I'm fine. I'm entering the social phase of work now. Isn't that right, Maud and Simon?' she said to the children.

They looked at her, startled.

'What on earth does that mean?' Nuala asked with a giggle.

'It means that Simon and Maud are going to put away their books, get me a huge mug of tea, and I'm going to tell them all about my very unhappy life,' Ella said.

'You sound absolutely unhinged, Ella, but I'm so glad you forgive me. You can behave however you like. I'll call you tonight.'

'Not between six and midnight,' Ella said cheerfully and hung up her phone.

She had just got to telling the twins the bit of her very unhappy life where she hadn't been chosen for the hockey team.

'It doesn't sound *terribly* unhappy,' Maud complained.

'No real, awful things,' Simon added.

'If you wanted to be on the First Eleven, and should have been, then that's pretty terrible,' Ella protested.

Her phone rang again. This time it was Nick. She listened and her face got red and then white again. The twins watched her with interest. 'The bastard,' she said eventually. 'The class-A bastard.' She took down a number on the back of her notebook. 'Thanks, Nick, I'll get back to you on this.' Her voice was slightly shaky, but a promise was a promise.

Those children had got their heads around quadratic equations. Now she had to tell them the story of an unhappy life. 'So the day of the school's hockey final approached . . .' she began.

'Could you tell us about the bastard, please?' Maud asked politely. 'It sounds much more interesting.'

All evening she thought about that slimy Mike Martin, out there in Spain with Don, after telling the television cameras that he couldn't understand the disappearance, the flight, the whole thing. He had told the nation that Don Richardson adored his wife, the lovely Margery Rice. Now he was contacting Ella, the mistress, and looking for a computer.

The only thing this proved was that there was something in the laptop that they didn't want found. Now that was interesting. Very interesting. And also a little frightening. It was only a matter of time before they found where she lived. Someone would tell Mike Martin that they lived in the garden shed on Tara Road. And then surely he would come to collect the computer that belonged to the great Don Richardson, and presumably must contain some of his secrets. Ella had assumed that Don must have deleted every file in it, and that was the reason why his password, 'Angel', didn't work.

It was packed with her things in storage at the Annexe in Tara Road. She hadn't thought about it in weeks. She wouldn't think about it now, she was working too hard. And also because she did not want to believe that it had not been left there purposely. And so he would not be coming back for it himself. Ever.

'God, Ella, you look dreadful,' Nick said when they met down by the Liffey for coffee.

'Thanks, Nick, and I always think you look very handsome, too,' she said.

'No, you look as if you've been on a ten-day binge. You've got huge dark circles under your eyes.'

'Yes, Nick. Sorry, Nick. Now tell me, is there any good news on the search for investors?'

'There's other news first . . . Sandy and I are going to get married,' he said sheepishly.

She flung her arms around him. 'I'm so pleased. You'll be very happy, both of you.'

'Why do you say that?'

'Because you're such friends. That's a huge start.'

'Weren't you and Don friends?'

'No, as it happened, it didn't seem to matter at the time, but looking back on it, of course that was the huge gap in it all.'

'What are you going to do about his bloody computer?'

'I gave it away,' she said, looking straight at him.

'No, you didn't, Ella.'

'Why should I keep it?'

He looked at her, his head on one side. 'I know you, for heaven's sake. You didn't give it away. Who would you give it to, for one thing?'

'I don't have it.' She looked mutinous.

'You *do*, Ella. You're talking to me, your friend. I know you have it and you must give it to the Fraud Squad as quick as possible and don't have these goons coming after you. Give it in, be done with it, I beg you.' His face was troubled.

'There's nothing in it, anyway.'

'So what's the problem then?'

'It's not something you do, informing, sneaking, getting people into trouble.'

Nick looked at her in disbelief. 'Listen to yourself speak for a moment. What has *he* done, Ella? Think for a moment. Just because you loved him doesn't make you remotely his sort of person. We're just not the kind of people who do everything under the table and run like rats when it all goes up in flames.'

'Okay, Nick, don't go on.'

'I have to go on. You seem to have lost your marbles on this one, Ella. You did not give it away. If you had, he wouldn't be looking for it all over the place.'

'There's nothing on it.'

'There must be some information in there. Why do you think he's set Mike Martin on to you? Saying give us a number to phone. Or else.'

'He didn't say "Or else", did he?'

'No, but it was in Martin's tone.'

'What do you think I should do, Nick?'

'If you won't give it to the police then go away,' he said.

'I can't go away. You know that. This isn't the time for a holiday. My head would explode.'

'It wouldn't be a holiday. It would be work, paid work.'

'Where?'

'New York City! We've had more good news. The King Foundation says we've got to the next level. We're on the shortlist.'

'Nick, that's great. Why didn't you tell me?'

'There were bigger things to talk about. But this is great, and one of us has to go, so it's perfect timing. Go on, Ella. It would solve everything.'

'I can't leave all my jobs.'

'We've asked round. They'll all let you go. Tom and Cathy, Quentins, Colm's and Deirdre's laboratory. The only parties having any problems with this are Maud and Simon, who have learned whatever it is you asked them to and fear they might have forgotten it when you come back.'

'You asked them without telling me ... you dared to do this on my behalf?' Ella was incensed.

'We had to prove to you that you could go, before we bought the ticket.'

'Ticket?' she said.

'Yes, yes. You need a plane ticket to get to New York. Go, Ella.'

'Make the call,' she said suddenly. 'I'll go out and look at the river.'

'I'll tell him you are away and it will be true,' Nick said.

Mike Martin answered the phone.

'I went to find her,' Nick said slowly.

'And?'

'And she's not here, apparently.'

'Not here? What does that mean?'

'What it says. She's gone away. No one knew where.'

'Who did you ask?'

'Her various employers. You can check with them.'

'She'd be wise not to play around with Don.'

'Oh, I'm sure she knows that now, but at the time she probably thought it was a good idea and that he meant what he said and that sort of thing.'

'You're a smart-arse, aren't you, Nick?'

'No, I'm relatively simple, but I was pleased that Ella is away, as it happens, and hope that she's strong enough to face you all when she gets home.' He hung up, shaking.

Ella came back from the river.

'They believe you've gone, Ella, so now let me brief you properly on Derry King.'

'On what?'

'A very rich guy indeed. He set up a foundation to help artists and film-makers. More strong black coffee. All the hopes and the entire current assets of Firefly Films are going into this trip.'

'You can't do this to me, Nick.' Ella was alarmed.

'We have to. It's our only hope.'

'I'm fragile. You said yourself I look like shit.'

'You have two and a half days before you meet him. You could paint your face or something.'

Her parents were pleased with the news. 'It will get you out in the real world again,' her mother said.

'Lord, I don't think staying in a Manhattan hotel and trying to get a man to invest in a tiny Irish company is exactly what you'd call the real world,' Ella said.

'It's a change,' her father said.

'There's one thing I have to tell you. Otherwise I can't go. You know that man, Mike Martin? He's often on television.'

'I know him,' her father said.

'Well, he's a friend of Don's, apparently, and Don is looking for a laptop machine he left in my flat. So Mike Martin might just possibly come and ask you about it. Suppose he does come and enquire. Can I ask you to say you have no idea where I am, but you know I took a laptop with me? I hate the lies, more lies, but it's nearly true. I am taking it with me, and you won't know where I am every hour of the day.' She looked from one to the other pleadingly.

'That's fine. We'll say it just like that,' her mother said.

'You never tell us your movements, that's what we'll say,' her father agreed.

'And you won't let them browbeat you or anything?' She was looking at her parents fondly.

'Browbeat ... what a marvellous word. I wonder what it means.' Her father was smiling a less papery smile than he had some months back.

'Let's look it up, Dad.' She went for the dictionary. It wasn't all that helpful. It meant to bear down on someone sternly, to bully them.

'We knew that already,' he said.

'It's from Old English, "bru",' Ella read.

'A lot of help that is,' her mother laughed.

They were much more like a happy family out there in the shed than they had ever been before.

Ella called in briefly to the twins in Muttie and Lizzie's house.

'Hallo, Ella. We heard you weren't coming. We were just talking about you.' Simon sounded pleased.

'You were?' Ella was apprehensive.

'The man who rang and said you're not coming for two weeks, was that the bastard?'

'No, no it wasn't at all. It was Nick, a very nice man.'

'Is he part of your future?'

'No, Simon, he's not, as it happens.' Ella had a nearly irresistible urge to say that Nick was part of her distant past, the first man she had slept with, in fact. But not with those two, never wise to let them have any real information at all.

'I'll tell Maud. She's making fudge in the kitchen.'

'Simon, I'll be posting a letter in the mail to you. We were meant to be doing some geometry this week...'

'But we don't have to work if you're not here, surely?'

'You don't *have* to, but wouldn't it be nice if when I got back you had both studied this nice, easy explanation that I've written out for you about circles?'

'Oh, they're too hard. We couldn't understand those at all. One thing was the radius and then they called it the diameter and then they called it the circumference ... no, that's too hard on our own.'

'Not if you read it in the simple way I explain it, it isn't.'

'It *is*, Ella.'

'But you're going to do it. And you're going to know acute angles and obtuse angles. Believe me, you are.'

Simon had a conference with his sister in the kitchen. 'Maud wants to know, do you get paid for this?'

'Yes, your grandparents give me money.'

'They're not exactly our grandparents.'

'So when this letter arrives ... you are both to take it seriously too.'

'Why can't you send it by e-mail, it would be quicker?' Simon countered.

'I can't do that.'

'Don't you have a computer?' He was scornful.

'Yes, I do, actually. But the password is jammed, I can't get into it.'

'I could do that in a minute,' Simon said. 'Do you have it with you in your bag?'

'Yes.' Ella wasn't sure.

'Simon is terrific at computers,' Maud said reassuringly.

'It's just that it's not mine. It's a friend's. He asked me to open it for him.'

'Well then, Simon, help her pull it from the briefcase.'

'What do you think the password is?'

'I thought it was "Angel". I saw him type it in,' she said. Her heart was thumping. Was she really insane enough to share this with these two children?

'No, it's not Angel.' Simon had tried it expertly. 'It often is something just like that.'

'Cherubs,' Maud said. 'Feathers? Wings?'

'Don't think so,' Ella said.

'Is he in America?' Simon asked.

'No. Why?'

'It could be something like Los Angeles.'

She remembered the blue and white tiles on the white walls of the resort of Playa de los Angeles. Playground of the rich, criminal or famous. The hiding place full of billiard rooms and swimming pools. *That* must be where Don lived. That could be the password. She wrote it down with a trembling hand.

Simon entered it and the screen sprang to life. List after list of initials and numbers, column after column of them.

'It wasn't hard,' Simon said loftily.

'No, no indeed.' She closed it down. 'Thank you both very much. I'll bring you a present from ...'

'From where?' Maud asked.

'From where she's getting her head stuck together,' Simon explained.

It was midnight. She would be leaving Dublin at noon the next day. She was sitting drinking coffee in Deirdre's flat. Ella needed her wits about her. Deirdre and Nuala were drinking a great deal of wine and laughing a lot. It was as if there had never been any coldness. But they had agreed not to tell

Nuala about New York, just that Ella was heading off somewhere to get her head together.

Ella was trying on Deirdre's clothes. 'I think I'll take this red jacket, and the black dress, definitely,' she said.

'Yes, I'll be walking to work in my knickers,' Deirdre said. 'Take the red and black scarf too, while you're at it.'

'Imagine going off to wherever you want to.' Nuala sounded envious. 'It's years since I've been able to do that.'

If the others thought that Nuala's husband Frank was always able to do just that, they didn't say it.

She hadn't slept at all by the time she got on the plane. Her only expense at the airport was a fairly heavy-duty makeup. And something the assistant recommended, which was an under-eye concealer.

On the plane she studied the brief that Sandy and Nick had prepared for her. There was an entire folder of clippings, photographs and a biography of the man she was going to meet. She looked at the pictures first. Pleasant enough face, square-shaped, his hair short, thick and coarse, like a brush with bristles. In most pictures he appeared to be peering, almost squinting, at something, causing very exaggerated smile lines at his eyes. His nose was quite snub, but his chin was strong. It was hard to see if he was tall or small. He dressed formally. He was rarely photographed without collar and tie even at a young film-makers' gathering, where everyone else was much more casual. Either he had many tuxedos or he got the same one cleaned regularly, since he always looked smart at the many functions where he was captured. There were no pictures of his home surroundings.

She wondered how old he was, and began to check up. He was born forty-three years ago in New York, the son of an Irish father and a Canadian mother. The eldest of three sons, he described himself as self-educated. Yet some of his citations included honorary degrees from universities, so he must have done a good job educating himself. She read how he had worked in many different aspects of the stationery trade and eventually set up a company specialising in office equipment. It had become a market leader, with branches all over the United States. She read many company profiles, trying to analyse its success and its award-winning status. Nobody seemed to be able to pinpoint the exact reason it had gone on when so many had fallen by the wayside. Any more than anyone had been able to define Derry King, the Chief Executive Officer and Chairman. He was described as hard-working and easy-going, and said to be determined but not ruthless.

Ella got the feeling that he had been courteous to those who interviewed him, but not greatly forthcoming. He gave no details about what he did for breakfast or how he spent his leisure time. He gave hardly any information about his taste in books, music or theatre, saying apologetically that he had worked so hard in his youth that he had never known the luxury of losing himself in music, drama or literature.

But he did love the visual arts. When he was nine, he had a very inspiring teacher at school who told the children that they could all paint and all find beauty inside and around them if only they looked. This had been a great surprise to the young Derry King. He said that he never claimed to have any artistic talent himself, but it had certainly opened his eyes to the beauty around him, which is why he sponsored so many art competitions among the young in the inner cities.

One of the many jobs he took in order to pay his school fees was that of cleaning and tidying up in a cinema. It meant he saw many movies free. It had left him with a love of the film world all his life. No, he had never been tempted to sink his considerable fortune into a studio or a production company, but had tried instead to encourage young people in various aspects of film-making.

When asked about his typical day, Derry King gave no little human glimpses of himself reading the stocks and shares over a plate of fruit or visiting a personal trainer, or any minimal insight into his family life at home. Either he did not know how to manage publicity or else he knew how to manage it very well. Ella wasn't sure.

He emerged as a philanthropic benefactor who gave to charities across the board. Always he was interested in causes that helped young people, and advanced funds to those who had not been given an easy start in life. You had to read very hard between the lines to work out what he was like and so far he sounded quite staid, Ella thought.

But that didn't matter. She was coming to New York, on Nick and Sandy's hard-earned money, to be entertained and fascinated by this guy. It was her job to make him interested in their project. To sell it as well as she possibly could. There was not a great deal of publicity about his foundation. It was as if he didn't want to be thanked in public for doing good. She could have done with more information.

It was in many ways a bald file. No pictures of him in a penthouse suite or in a Malibu Beach home. On a ranch at weekends. There was mention of a wife, Mrs Kimberly King, a leggy number, very possibly a trophy wife. In one interview he said they had no children. In another he said that both his parents were now dead. Nowhere did he say anything about his Irish ancestry. Twice in the clippings he mentioned happy childhood vacations in Alberta, Canada.

She looked long and hard at his picture again.

A man of forty-three, the same age as Don Richardson, who had worked hard all his life. She learned little from his picture. But then she had learned little of Don after two years of loving him. This Derry King looked older than Don. Perhaps his life had been harder. He might not have had all the perks and pleasures that Don had. And, indeed, probably continued to have.

7

The hotel was a small, inexpensive but chic place off Fifth Avenue in midtown Manhattan, far from the boarding house in Queens where she and Deirdre had stayed that time so many years ago when they had come to New York. It was a place owned by someone's brother who was meant to give them a great deal but there had been a great misunderstanding. He had thought they were coming out to his place to give him the trade, not the other way round looking for a bargain. She had been so young then, Ella thought. Imagine them getting upset by that! If she had known what upset was really like!

Anyway, no point in brooding. She must enjoy the days in the hotel to the full. She had said she didn't really need to spend all this time in New York, but they had insisted. Nick and Sandy had said it was essential that she should be on the spot and available, in case Derry King needed to rethink something through with her.

Deirdre had said that it took everyone at least fourteen days to get a head together, especially since Ella's head had been so battered and then tried to cure itself by overwork. Brenda Brennan said that she should make the most of it. New York City in autumn was everyone's dream. She must not think of running back. Her father and mother said she must write down some of the things she saw, they'd love to hear all about it when she came back. She realised that they were all afraid for her. They were afraid of Don Richardson and what he might do when he came back.

Ella shared a taxi into town with a small, plump Dublin woman who knew every angle there was in the world. She was a dealer, she said proudly, had travelled over with four empty suitcases. She was going to buy stuff in bargain basements for the next four days, fantastic stuff you didn't see at home at all, slippers with pink fur on them, black underwear with red feathers. She'd sell it all at three times what she paid. She did it every year. She could not understand to save her life why there weren't more people in on it. It was the easiest money she'd ever made, and believe her, she had made money in many different ways.

She asked Ella what line she was in herself.

'I'm trying to raise money to make a film,' Ella said.

The woman said her name was Harriet, and that if ever Ella was lonely, give her a ring at her hotel and they'd go out for a few drinks.

Ella tried to cover her amazement that Harriet named a very expensive, five-star hotel. There must be good money in importing exotic lingerie. Or was it smuggling? The lines were getting more and more blurred. If you could afford a hotel like that, why were you bringing over four empty suitcases to buy cheap gear? Why were you sharing a taxi with someone into town? Then again, maybe that kind of economy was exactly *why* Harriet could afford the five-star hotel she was staying in.

She settled into her own hotel and had a long bath. Deirdre had given her a very expensive oil, 'to put you in a good mood'. Its scent seemed to seep into every part of her body and all around the room. Ella didn't really believe that these unguents and lotions did any good, but she did feel a lot better. And maybe looked a little less drawn.

Then she called the hotel beauty salon to make an appointment for the next morning. She had promised Nick and Sandy that she would have her hair done before she met Derry King. On behalf of the company they said she had to do this. They didn't want her frightening him away before the negotiations started. And then she found herself wandering around the room, pacing like an animal in a cage. To her amazement, she felt restless and edgy. In need of company, any company. It might be midnight back home, but it was only 7 p.m. here. Outside her windows, a New York evening was just getting under way. If only Deirdre were here. They would have great fun. Or Nick and Sandy, she enjoyed their company. If they were here now, with a bottle of inexpensive wine that Sandy would have found in some liquor shop, they could sit and plan their strategy.

Or anyone else she liked. Brenda Brennan from Quentins, for example. She was surprisingly good fun when you got to know her.

She looked over at the laptop. No, she would keep her promise to herself. Don't look into all it contained until she had dealt with Derry King. There would be plenty of time later. And now at last she knew how to unlock its secrets. She really owed young Simon for that.

Deirdre called around to the Bradys for solidarity. 'It will do her no end of good, this trip,' she said.

'I'm very anxious, Deirdre, our daughter to be running away from someone like as if we were all in gangland! Couldn't she have given the laptop to the Guards and be done with it?'

'She will do that when she comes back, I'm sure of that,' Deirdre murmured. 'She'll do the right thing. It will just take her a little time.'

'Deirdre, I've been phoning you all night.'

'I was out, Nuala. But now I'm home. What is it?'

'Listen, Frank got a message from Don.'

'He never did.'

'Yes, late this afternoon. I've been trying to find you.'

'And what did he have to say to Frank?'

'Apparently a lot of it was completely wrongly reported.'

'Yes, I'm sure.'

'No, really, he explained it was all taken out of proportion.'

'Is this why you rang me, Nuala?'

'Well, yes and no. You see, Frank was wondering whether Don might contact Ella?'

'Why in the name of God would Frank think that?'

'Well, I said that she went off somewhere today and she didn't tell any of us where she was going.'

'So?'

'So Frank thought she might still be carrying a torch for Don.'

'Carrying a torch!' Deirdre screamed with laughter. 'A torch, no less. What a ludicrous thing to say. Is Frank losing his marbles? If she was carrying a torch anywhere near him, she would gouge his eyes out with it. She hates him, Nuala, you know that.'

'Love and hate aren't all that far apart,' Nuala said prissily.

'I don't think so in this case, and did Frank get this idea out of the air or did you sow it in his mind?'

'No, I didn't sow it in his mind, but after he was talking to Don, he seemed to think it was a possibility.'

'And he's all buddy-buddy with Don now?'

'I told you, there was a misunderstanding. Don has sent a sum of money to a PO box, one of Frank's brothers picked it up.'

'So Frank has forgiven him.'

'He's listening to him anyway.'

'And what does he hear?'

'That Don wants to make it up to Ella. He'd like to know where she is.'

'Well, I have no idea. She went to clear her head and I don't want to talk about it any more.'

Deirdre sent up a silent prayer of thanks that they had told Nuala nothing. Suppose they had innocently said where Ella was going? One of Don's henchmen could have been waiting for her in the New York hotel this very minute.

Nick and Sandy were just going to bed when Deirdre rang. 'I know it's silly, but I'm just sitting here on my own worrying. She *is* all right, isn't she? It's just that Don's getting Frank and his desperate brothers to use Nuala to get to Ella. He even paid them the money they lost.'

'Do you think we should tell her?' Nick asked.

'I don't know. Part of me thinks we should, but then it's your pitch. I don't want her to go to pieces on you out there.'

'The job's not as important as her being all right. Look, I'll discuss it with Sandy and then we'll give her a call.'

'Think about it, Nick. If she's on her own out there, it might be worse for her to know.'

'Go to bed, Deirdre. Don Richardson can't ruin every night's sleep in the Western world.'

*

They called Ella's hotel, but she was not in her room. Nor was she in the hotel dining room. 'It's one in the morning,' Sandy said disapprovingly.

'It's only eight p.m. there. We're not her mother and father.'

'Still, who does she know there? Where can she be?'

Ella was at a party in Harriet's suite, drinking cocktails and meeting some of Harriet's contacts. They were mainly women in their fifties, scouts that she had sent out looking for supplies. Some of them were younger and wearing a lot of jewellery and expensive jackets. Harriet had not been at all surprised that she phoned and had welcomed Ella warmly. Everyone was interested for a moment when she was introduced as a movie-maker, but they lost interest when they heard it was a documentary.

Harriet's contacts had brought her samples. Ella examined yellow negligees with rhinestones, scarlet thongs and black panties with pink lace rosebuds on them. Had Ireland changed a great deal? Or did everyone else at home wear underwear like this and Ella was the only one left out?

'You can buy anything you need at cost,' Harriet said to her kindly.

'Thanks, Harriet. I don't have much of a sex life going at the moment. I think I'll pass, if you don't mind.'

'Fine-looking girl like you, you do surprise me,' Harriet said.

Some of the contacts seemed to suggest that owning a proper wardrobe of what was on display was the surefire way of restoring a good sex life fairly speedily.

Ella had eaten nothing and was beginning to feel a little light-headed. 'Well, if I thought they'd help sell my film idea to Derry King,' she said, pretending to consider one of the little corsets.

'Not *the* Derry King!' said one of the contacts.

'You've heard of him?'

'There was a big piece about him in the paper today . . . but what was in it?'

None of them could remember.

'I hope he hasn't gone bankrupt,' Ella said. That would be all they'd need. But it appeared that it had something to do with rescuing a dog shelter. Derry King had not only given the place the funds it needed, but he had marched with the protesters personally and raised their profile considerably. 'A dog lover, I see,' Ella noted. It hadn't mentioned that in any of the files. 'Then I'll buy that jewelled dog collar for him,' she said.

'It's a bit flash, Ella. I mean, it's only five dollars. It's for guys to give their girls who have silly bow-wows.' Harriet didn't want to steer her wrong.

'No, what's more, I'll buy two. I know a dog called Hooves back in Dublin who'd absolutely love it.'

She had three more cocktails, went back to her own hotel, and fell into sleep without even listening to her voice-mail on the telephone.

This was meant to be her day off. Her whole day to relax and get ready for tomorrow to meet the great Derry King, investor and apparently a dog lover. And now she had the most unmerciful hangover. Slowly she got herself into the day. The woman at the beauty salon suggested a facial. It was very expensive, but what the hell? She would pay Firefly Films back one day. That's what she was going to spend the rest of her life doing anyway, it seemed. Paying people back.

'Sorry, Nick, I was out last night. I forgot to check my messages,' she said when she found the winking light and called him back.

'Great, Ella. You're really on top of things over there,' he said.

'No, I'm fine. I have such hair and such skin you just wouldn't believe it.'

'Terrific.'

'What were you on about anyway?'

He told her briefly about it all, how they were all a little bit worried in case Nuala might just have got any of it right.

'Not very likely, based on previous performance.' She was brisk.

'Don't be flip, Ella. We're your friends, okay?'

'Sure, sorry, it's just that I'm a bit frail. Nuala's half-wit take on everything doesn't seem real from here.'

'Why are you frail?'

'Hung over. Mixed cocktails.'

'Jesus, Sandy, she's been spending our money on cocktails.'

'No, they were free. I met this woman on the plane . . .'

'I don't want to hear about it . . . listen, Ella. It could be serious. He's paid off Frank and his brothers simply because he's married to a friend of yours and hopes she knows where you are.'

'No, he doesn't want to contact me,' she said.

'Why do you say that? Hasn't he got Mike Martin and Frank sending out feelers?'

'If Don really wanted to talk to me, he'd find me.'

'And would you talk to him?' Nick asked fearfully. He had a sinking feeling why Ella had kept the laptop. She wanted Don to get in touch with her.

'Probably.' She sounded very far away.

'But you can't. Not without someone else being there.'

'This is costing you a fortune, Nick. Thanks for being involved, I mean it, and thank Sandy and Dee for me. But I'm fine.'

'You're okay, really?'

'Really I am. And I can't wait to meet Derry King. I bought him a jewelled dog collar, by the way.'

'I ask myself over and over if we did the right thing, sending you to New York,' Nick said.

Harriet rang to know had she survived.

'Yes, just about. Sorry for laying into your booze so heavily.'

'Not at all. It's just that . . . I don't know, those dog collars are a bit tacky. You know, if you really do want to impress him that might not be the right way to go.'

'Thanks, Harriet. I'm meeting him tomorrow. I'll see how it goes.'

'Anyway, who am I, talking to someone like you . . . you're well able to look after yourself.'

'I wish.'

'I recognised you as that money broker's girl, the one they thought he had run off with.'

'Oh, you did.' Ella's voice was dull. She often wondered if people recognised her. Now that the months had gone by very few remembered her, but of course she had to meet someone who did.

'Only because a mate of mine, a real nice woman, Nora O'Donoghue, she lost her wedding money to him.'

'I know Nora. She works in the kitchen of Quentins sometimes. She's very nice.'

'She lodged with my sister once in Mountainview and she's getting married to this teacher. Apparently he was giving Latin lessons to Richardson's sons . . . anyway, they lost their savings . . . that's why I'd remember.'

'A lot of people lost their savings, my own parents did,' Ella said.

'And no one knows where he is?'

'Well, we think he's in Spain. He must have been setting up a different name and home when I was with him. It all seems so long ago.'

'You know, I half-wondered when I saw you if he was out here. New York would be a good place to hide, and maybe you were coming out to meet him. And I said to myself it might be dangerous for you.'

Ella felt a sudden shiver of fear. It was probably the hangover, she told herself firmly. But two people within five minutes of each other warning her on the telephone was hard to take.

'No, truly, Harriet. He's long gone out of my life.'

'So good luck with the film anyway, and remember what I said. Think carefully about the dog collar.'

'Good luck, Harriet, and thanks for everything.'

'There'll be other fellows, there always are.'

'Oh, I'm sure of it. It's just that I'm not ready for one yet.'

'They turn up when you least expect them.'

'Did someone turn up for you, Harriet?'

'The nicest fellow that ever wore shoe leather. Married to a right bitch. She pushed him too far one day and he came over to me with a suitcase. That's ten years ago.'

'And why isn't he here with you?'

'He's terrified of planes and big cities.'

'And what'll he do while you're here?'

'He'll cook grand things like chicken pies and spaghetti sauces and label them and put them in the freezer. And he'll talk to his pigeons, and he'll go and have a pint with his son, and he'll be at the airport in a van to lift me and the bags home.'

'Good luck to you,' Ella said.

'And to you, Ella, and you know that no one blames you for that bastard. But I'd love it all to come out about your family and everything . . .'

'One day,' Ella promised as she looked over at the laptop computer on her desk.

It was such a lovely day. No blustery wind to blow her new hair-do away, so she went for a long walk down Fifth Avenue.

New York was full of energy. Ella felt a new spring in her step as she walked. She called into St Patrick's Cathedral and longed to have enough faith to pray to God and ask for the meeting with Derry King to go well. But it wouldn't be fair. And it wouldn't work anyway because God knew that she didn't really believe.

So instead she told God that if He still happened to be listening to sinners, and there were no strings attached, she'd like to remind Him that thousands of films got made every year and it wouldn't upset anyone if theirs was one of them next year.

She looked at florist displays. She read the menus on windows. She admired the uniforms of doormen. She strolled through the atriums of office blocks. She watched the office workers coming out into the street to smoke or grab sandwiches in a deli. She wondered what it would be like to work in this huge, exciting city where nobody seemed to know anyone like people did in Dublin, where you were always nodding at people and saluting each other.

A tall man passed by and looked at her appreciatively. Ella felt alarmed. Suppose Harriet had been right about New York being a good place to hide. Possibly Don *was* in this city. She might meet him at the end of this block, at the next traffic lights. But she must not give in to silly fears. This was the way madness and weakness lay.

'You've got to have courage,' she said aloud suddenly.

'Right on, lady,' said a man at a news-stand who was the only one who had heard her.

Ella hugged herself. She liked New York, she was as safe here as anywhere. She would walk until she was too tired to walk a step further, and then she would take a taxi back to her hotel.

She slept for fourteen hours and got up feeling better than she had felt for ages.

'I thought you'd be older,' Derry King said as he shook hands with her in the foyer of the hotel.

'I thought you'd be older too,' Ella said with spirit. 'But here we are, babes in a big business world, so can I offer you coffee?'

He smiled.

He had a good smile for a square-built man with a very heavily lined face. She knew to the day how old he was, and yet he didn't look it. Forty-three-year-old New Yorkers wore their years better than most Dubliners of the same age.

'I'll drink coffee, sure. Do you want us to talk here, or should we talk in your suite?'

'We are a small outfit, Mr King. I have a bedroom, not a suite. I think we'd be much happier here.'

'And I'd be happier if you called me Derry. I prefer the first-name thing.'

'Fine, Derry. I brought you a present,' she said.

'You did?' He was surprised.

'I heard you loved dogs, so I got you a nice dog collar.' She produced it from her handbag.

'It's horrific! Where on earth did you get it?' he laughed.

'It's not horrific. It cost me five dollars from a dealer who comes to New York every year to buy really tasteful gifts for the Christmas market back home,' Ella said defensively.

'You and I are going to get on fine, Ella Brady,' he said, and her churning stomach settled down.

He was right. They would get on fine.

8

'Do you think she's seriously going to give him a dog collar?' Sandy asked Nick.

'Nothing would surprise me,' he said gloomily.

'Of course, it may work out very well. He may fall in love with her.'

'Jesus, I hope he doesn't. He has a wife called Kimberly who owns half the business.'

'Does Ella know that?' Sandy sounded fearful now.

'Oh, definitely, she's read the file. But the presence of a wife didn't exactly stop her before, if you know what I mean.'

The man who came to ask the Bradys about renting a flat in Tara Road was very polite. He admired their garden residence, as he called it, and said he loved a place with photographs. It made a house into a home.

'Is that your daughter, and isn't she a very handsome girl?' he asked, looking at a picture of Ella.

'That's right,' Barbara said.

Ella had told her to be cautious and she would be, but this well-dressed man couldn't be in any way sinister. He was so courteous and he wanted an apartment for a colleague who was coming over from the UK in a few months' time.

'Does she live with you?' He was still looking at the picture of Ella.

'Oh yes, in and out.'

'And is she here at the moment?'

'No, she's gone off ... the way they do at that age.'

'Has she gone abroad, do you think?'

Ella's mother was frightened now. This was no courteous man looking for an apartment for a colleague. It was someone looking for Ella.

'Do young people ever tell you where they're going these days?' She laughed nervously.

'Oh, I know, but doesn't she have to work? I think you said she was a teacher.'

They hadn't said Ella was a teacher.

'She does a bit of this and a bit of that ... it's easier to get time off.'

'Maybe she went out to the sun, to Greece or Spain?' the man suggested. 'Lots of people go out there in September.'

Barbara Brady directed her firmest gaze on her husband. 'She didn't say anything about going to the Continent to me, did she mention it to you, Tim?'

'Not a word,' he said. 'Somewhere down in Kerry or West Cork, she said. It could be that she's got herself an extra little job. She ran into a spot of bad luck earlier in the year, and she's desperately trying to gather some money together.'

'So anyway, to go back to the flat . . .' Barbara began.

But the man had lost interest in the flat in Tara Road.

'We're back here for a few days. Will you have lunch with me, Deirdre?'

'No, Nuala, thanks, but I can't.'

'You didn't even wait to hear which day,' Nuala complained.

'I can't any day. There's a crisis at work. We're all on short lunch hours,' Deirdre lied.

'Are you annoyed with me about something, Dee?'

'No, I'm annoyed about having to eat into my lunch break. Why would I be annoyed with you, for God's sake?'

'You seemed pissed off when I asked you where Ella was. It's just that I have to know. Frank keeps going on at me. He says it's the one thing I might be expected to know and I don't even deliver on that.'

'Real charmer Frank turned out to be,' Deirdre said unsympathetically.

'No, they're frightened. His brothers too, all of them.'

'I thought they got their money back in a brown paper bag?'

'That was just a little to show that they *could* get it back if . . .'

'If what?'

'I suppose, if they played ball . . .'

'And handed Ella over, is that it?'

'I don't think it's quite like that.'

'So it's just as well that neither of us knows where she is, then, isn't it, Nuala?' Deirdre was brisk.

'You know, Dee.'

'I wish I did.'

'Advise me. Help me, *please*.' Nuala was desperate.

'I don't suppose it's the kind of thing you'd get the Guards in on,' Deirdre said.

'Not really. Frank and his brothers always steer clear of police and lawyers,' said Nuala.

Patrick and Brenda Brennan were going to bed. It had been a long, busy night. 'I ask myself, do we need this documentary? Every table was full tonight,' Patrick said.

'I know, I've thought that too. We'd have to consider expanding.' Brenda was frowning.

'Which would change it all.' Patrick frowned too.

'Still, it's not meant to be just an advertisement,' Brenda cheered up. 'It's more like a history of Dublin, isn't it, as seen through the changes in one place.'

'Now you're beginning to sound just like young Ella Brady,' he said, yawning.

'I wonder how she's getting on out there,' Brenda said as she sat at her dressing table and took off her makeup.

She couldn't hear what Patrick said, since he was under the duvet and mumbling into the pillow.

'I do hope she's all right. She's been through a really terrible summer,' Brenda said to herself as she creamed away the last traces of the stylish makeup that always took ten years off her age.

Derry King was right. They did get on well together. Ella told him no lies, and exaggerated no aspect of Firefly Films.

'What's in it for me?' he had asked early on, and she had tried to tell him as truthfully as she could. He would be part of something fresh and new, made with high production values, which could well win prizes at film festivals, that would be shown on television in many lands.

'How is it new and fresh?' he wanted to know.

'It's not going to be full of shamrockery,' she said and he had laughed.

'What's that?'

'Oh, you know, the how-are-things-in-Gloccamora, top-of-the-morning approach. There's nobody doing leprechaun duty on this movie.'

He was interested. 'Warts and all, then?'

'Well, yes . . . we'd want to make fun of everything pretentious,' she said.

'Give me an example.'

'Patrick's very funny about the way Irish people often pretend they know things when they don't, like they don't want to look foolish. He says that you should never drink the second cheapest wine on the menu. It could be any kind of old rubbish, because it's the one people go for so they don't look cheap or shabby by buying the very cheapest on the list.'

Derry was smiling at her. 'And he'll say all this?'

'Certainly.'

'Not afraid of losing his clientele?'

'No, he'll walk a fine line. You'll like him when you come over. I'm actually amazed you were never in Quentins when you were in Ireland before,' Ella said.

'I was never in Ireland,' Derry said flatly.

'I'm sorry?'

'I was never there,' he said, and though his smile did not leave his face, his eyes looked hard. 'And I never intend to go.'

Cathy Scarlet and Tom Feather had only lost a small sum when Rice and Richardson had gone to the wall. Compared to others, they had been very lucky. Only an outstanding bill for 700 euros: one catered function unpaid for.

It was the one afternoon a week when Maud and Simon were in to polish what were called Tom and Cathy's 'treasures', and to discuss in detail the forthcoming baby. What would it be called? Where would it live? Would it be grown-up when Tom and Cathy finally got around to getting married? Could they teach the baby to do step-dancing?

It was almost a relief when the bell rang in the front office and they could escape the children's questions for a few minutes. It was someone enquiring about brochures and price lists. He was a well-dressed man who didn't seem to have any precise idea about what he wanted. There was something about the vagueness of his request that made them suspicious.

'I believe you know Ella Brady,' he said, out of the blue.

'Yes,' Tom said, giving nothing away.

'Slightly,' said Cathy, making sure that she was even more distant. They knew where Ella was, but that it had to be kept a secret.

'Would you have any idea where she is now?' he asked politely.

'None at all, I'm afraid,' Tom said.

'Not a clue,' Cathy said.

'Now, that's a pity . . . I've been asked to give you some money for a debt that was overlooked. Inadvertently, of course. Around seven hundred euros, I think.'

Tom and Cathy looked at each other, astounded. 'You're from Rice and Richardson?' Cathy said, stunned.

'No, alas, I'm not, but let's say I'm a friend of one of the people involved, and he felt bad that there had been this misunderstanding and shortfall.'

'I'm sure he did,' Cathy said.

The man opened his wallet. 'He asked me to get it to you personally. He's not a man who likes to leave bills unpaid.' The man paused as he laid the seven notes on the small table. 'And he'd be very grateful if you could ask Ella to call him at this number.'

'Well, this is great to get the money,' Tom said. 'But we don't have any idea where Ella is.'

'So if one depends on the other,' Cathy began, 'then we shouldn't take the money.'

'No, keep it. It might remind you of where she is.'

'We know where she is,' came a clear voice. Tom and Cathy looked in horror at Maud.

Was there a possibility that Ella might have been so foolish as to mention anything to those children?

'Go back to the kitchen, Maud, *please*,' Cathy begged.

'You don't know anything about Ella's whereabouts,' Tom said.

Simon was stung by the unfairness of this. 'We do know,' he said mutinously.

'And where is that, exactly?' the man was interested.

'She's gone to hospital,' Simon said triumphantly.

'She's having a piece of her head put back on,' Maud added. 'It will take two weeks, altogether.'

The man looked at Tom and Cathy as if for confirmation. They both shrugged.

'Could be, I suppose,' Cathy said.

'Quite possible,' Tom agreed.

The man turned and left without saying a word. As he went down the cobbled lane they saw him pause and take out his mobile phone.

'I guess he's calling Spain,' Cathy said.

'Is that where the hospital is?' Simon said. 'I thought it might be in America, from something Ella said.'

Tom let his breath out slowly. 'And why didn't you share that view with the gentleman when he was here?'

'I wasn't sure. It's just she said something about spending her last dollar on something but it could have been just an expression.'

'It could,' Cathy said, holding Tom's hand in relief.

'Will you be mating again when the baby is born?' Maud asked.

'Probably. If we have the energy,' Cathy said.

'Does it take a lot of energy?' Simon was interested.

'Back to the kitchen, everybody,' Tom suggested.

From the corner of the road, the man phoned Don Richardson. 'I'm not having much luck, Don. Nothing from the film-makers, her parents, that restaurant; and nothing the caterers.'

He listened for a while and then nodded. 'All right. Plan C then, as you say.'

Ella looked at Derry King open-mouthed. 'You're never going to Ireland!' she said, astonished.

'Not if I can help it, no.'

'Then what are you doing, talking about making a movie there?'

'I'm not making it, you are.' He spread out his hands to show how simple his argument was.

'But what have we been talking about if you don't . . . if you never intend . . . I'm sorry, Derry. I don't understand.' She looked hurt and annoyed.

'I don't have to *love* Ireland to invest in a movie about it. Anyway, from what I see it's not a hymn of praise to the place . . . it's showing up all its weaknesses, all this new money, greed, so-called style.'

'We didn't say that . . .'

'Well, that's what it came over like, people imitating Europeans.'

'But we *are* Europeans!' Ella cried.

'No, you said it was warts and all . . . just a minute ago.'

'Derry, there's something very wrong here.' She looked down at her notes. 'I've been talking to you in this coffee shop for hours and I must have been giving you completely the wrong message.'

'I have, for personal reasons of my own, no love for Ireland,' he said. 'The legacy of my father is not one that would make me go and look for my roots. I was interested in this project because I thought you were sending them up.'

'But you have the initial notes from Nick.'

'He said it would be frank and groundbreaking. That's why I'm here . . . to learn how.'

'And what have you learned so far?' Ella felt a cold lump of disappointment in her chest.

'I've learned that we have stayed too long in this coffee shop. We should have a break now, then I'll send a car for you and take you to a meal. All this talk about food has made me hungry.'

She was afraid to let him out of her sight. 'They have a restaurant here . . .' she began.

'No, they don't, not a real restaurant. Car will be here for you at seven. Okay?'

'One thing before you go.'

'Sure, fire away.'

'I'll be talking to Nick. Will I say it was all a misunderstanding, the whole thing?'

'Why would you say that?'

'From what you said, I thought that it had been.'

'Hey, we're only into talks about talks so far. The real talks are way down the road.'

'But I couldn't betray this restaurant, none of us could. I mean, we'd have to cancel the project if that's what you wanted.'

'I understand, and I respect you. Seven p.m.'

It was an awkward telephone conversation. 'I'm not getting the whole picture,' Nick said.

'Neither am I, to be honest. Could I leave it that we're in talks about talks?'

'Not really, Ella. We've invested all we can in this; we're both in a bit of a panic.'

'That makes three of us, or possibly four. Derry could be in a bit of a panic as well. It turns out that he hated his father and he hates Ireland.'

'I don't believe you.'

'That's what he told me. Will I ring you when I get back? It will be about three or four a.m. your time.'

'Don't bother, Ella. Leave it till tomorrow.'

Ella wore Deirdre's black dress and red jacket. She had taken a large handbag, which was big enough to hold papers and photographs without looking like a briefcase. A chauffeur collected her.

'What restaurant are we going to?' Ella asked chattily.

The chauffeur pronounced the name of the place with awe, and as if it were the only possible place to go if you were the guest of Mr King.

He was waiting at the table. He wore a dinner jacket. In a way he looked quite as formal as he did in the photographs in those clippings she had read so carefully on the flight over to New York. Yet those interviews and articles told very little about him. They gave no hint of his enthusiasm and willingness to work at something until it was achieved. They didn't speak of how his face lit up when he thought they were getting somewhere. He was a very keen businessman, out of her league.

Suddenly Ella felt a wave of inadequacy. 'I hope I'm dressed enough,' she said.

'You look very nice,' he said.

'Your wife was not able to join us tonight?'

'Not for many nights,' he smiled.

'Sorry, that's another thing I got wrong,' she apologised.

'No, you looked up your files perfectly correctly. You just didn't get to the bit where it says "Marriage Dissolved".'

'Was that a long time ago?' Ella tried to be as cool as he was being.

'Oh, ten years, I'd say, but it's hard to remember because we meet every week at the foundation, you see.'

'Does that work? Well, obviously it does because otherwise you wouldn't both be able to do it.'

'It does work, remarkably well as it happens, and Kimberly is remarried and goes out a lot at night. I don't, so we rarely meet in the evenings. But we met this afternoon. She was most interested in the project, and she will join us tomorrow.'

'There will be a tomorrow, then?' Ella was almost tearful in her gratitude.

'Of course there will, Ella. Now look at this menu and tell me. Do your pals in Quentins match up to this place?'

'I wish they could see me now. I wish everyone could see me now.' She looked confident and happy for the first time since she had come to New York.

Kimberly looked as if she were twenty-two, but Ella knew she must be almost forty. With a perfect, glossy hairstyle that had to be freshly done at a salon every day, a perfect smile with even, white teeth, a pale, peach-coloured designer outfit and high black heels, she was dazzling. She was also as smart as anyone Ella had ever met. She was totally on top of the project, and realised what Firefly Films was trying to do. She told them of other movies they had underwritten, one about a young songwriter who had believed so mightily in her own career that she overcame all the rejections and obstacles en route. Another was about a woman who arranged a social club for mentally handicapped children to give their parents a break, but was closed down by the authorities because she did not have the necessary official qualifications. There was another about the stress of being police wives, and another about a woman who had kept a cat for thirteen years in a No Pets Allowed condominium without anyone finding out.

Ella couldn't find any common thread amongst them. Derry and Kimberly seemed pleased. They didn't want to be predictable. Tomorrow they would get down to the nitty-gritty, Kimberly said, and plan out a tour for Derry to make when he got to Ireland.

Ella looked up, startled. 'But I didn't think you were going to Ireland, Derry?'

'Of course he is. That's only nonsense,' Kimberly said.

'No way, Kim, forget it.' Derry smiled lazily.

'Would you come instead, Kimberly?' Ella pleaded.

'Yes, Kim, you'd love it.' He was teasing her.

'Derry knows I am not going to stir from New York and leave my very young and suggestible husband to all the temptations of this city.'

'Oh, Lorenzo wouldn't stray,' Derry said. 'Not in a million years.'

'His name is Larry, Ella, which Derry very well knows, and he is not being left alone to test out any theory.'

Ella looked back at Derry. He didn't seem at all annoyed.

'It will all be sorted out eventually. Kim likes to play games. Always her little weakness.' He spoke without malice, affectionately in fact.

'Lord, someone has to play games around this place,' she laughed, ruffling his hair.

'Now less of this wasting time doing a re-run of an old argument.'

'Derry has to go to Ireland sooner or later. He will leave when he's ready. Why don't you tell us your stories, Ella? Tell us all about these people who will make up the movie.'

It was time now, time to convince them that this restaurant was filled with people's lives. She took out her notes and began to tell the stories.

The Short Fuse

Martin went back to sleep after he had switched off his alarm. He dreamed a troubled, complicated dream about having the wrong change and being refused service. He woke shaking with irritation about it all and became even more annoyed when he realised it was seven o'clock and that he would now be twenty minutes late for work. Today of all days. He tried to hurry and naturally that made him slower than ever. He got into a shower that was too hot and had to leap out again, knocking down the contents of a shelf. He lost a button off his best shirt, spilled the orange juice in the fridge. He remembered that he had intended to drop clothes off at the dry cleaners, now there would be no time. This meant that he would not have a freshly cleaned suit for tomorrow. It was the day to put out the rubbish and he had literally no time. He ran out and realised it was raining, went back for an umbrella, and heard the phone ring. Before eight o'clock in the morning, it must be urgent. He answered it and discovered to his great irritation that it was his son.

'Hi, Dad, it's Jody. Just wanted to make sure you hadn't forgotten.'

Why did the boy think that he might have forgotten a lunch arrangement made over a month ago?

'It's just that you're always so very busy. It could have slipped your mind.'

'No, Joseph, believe me, busy people don't forget things like longstanding arrangements. I'm afraid that the luxury of forgetting is only for those who are not busy, don't have anything important to do. Those who have nothing important in their lives.'

Why did he do it? Anger the boy further, widen the gulf between them still more. Delay himself still further. And now Joseph was twittering on about the menu, saying his father must choose whatever he wanted to eat. 'Yes, yes, I think that's what one usually does in restaurants,' Martin snapped.

But Jody heard no coolness in his father's tone. 'I just wanted to make sure you knew you didn't have to keep to the fixed menu or anything,' he tried to explain.

'Joseph, I have to go.' Martin hung up. Outside in the wet street, everyone else had managed to put out rubbish. Other people had got up in time and gone to their dreary little jobs and yet he, Martin, hadn't managed it. Martin, who ran the biggest advertising agency in the city, a man known all over the country. Today they were making a pitch for the biggest corporate client ever. Something they had been preparing for three months and now that the day was here, he had to have this tedious anxiety dream and go back to sleep. There were other things that had to be done today too. Kit Morris, his secretary, must be smartened up. She was too old for the job, her face didn't fit and she wasn't up to speed on all the new technology. Perhaps he should put off talking to her until much later in the day. The thing about Kit was that she never watched the clock, she worked very hard. She had been with him a long time. Probably had no other life outside.

On any day of the week it wasn't going to be easy telling her that she didn't give the image he wanted by appearing in a shapeless skirt and long cardigan. But today was a tense day and it wasn't going to be an early night, either. They were having a reception for their American partners at 5 p.m. with dinner to follow. The timing could not have been worse. If they didn't get the new corporate account, they would not feel at all like entertaining the Americans.

Martin sighed as he hastened along the slippery pavement. This of all days to have to meet Joseph for lunch. But the boy had been adamant. It was the anniversary of Rose's death. His wife had been dead for fifteen years. Martin had thrown himself into work since it happened. But tragedies affect people in different ways. Joseph had dropped out of school only weeks after the funeral. It had been impossible to talk to the boy about anything since then.

Martin arrived wet, out of breath and bad-tempered at his office.

'They're waiting for you,' Kit said cheerfully.

'Please, Kit, don't come at me with profound wisdom. Not today.'

Kit was not at all put out. 'It's all right, Martin. I've given them coffee and your apologies. I told them you'd had a power breakfast you couldn't cancel. Actually it might work to your advantage.' She smiled at him reassuringly.

Martin squared his shoulders and began his morning.

He wasn't to know it, but other people's mornings were difficult too. His son Jody had paced and paced around a small bed-sitting-room rehearsing over and over the speech he would make at lunchtime in Quentins Restaurant. Would it come out as he intended it to? The more often he said it, the less likely it seemed.

In the restaurant, under the watchful eye of Brenda Brennan, the Breton waiter Yan was polishing the cutlery on each table with a soft cloth and having a bad morning. There had been a letter from home with vague mentions of his father going to Concarneau to have tests in the hospital. Nobody said what the tests were for. Should he go home and find out? It would be useless to telephone, they would only tell him not to waste his hard-earned money.

Kit Morris was not having a good day either. It didn't help that Martin was behaving like a spoiled child. She had her own problems. Like how the future was going to work out for her elderly mother. She was no longer able to cope on her own. It would be coming to live with Kit or going into a home. There were no other options, her married brothers had made that clear. Kit needed some time to think it through. She had been going to ask Martin for a few days' leave. But today was not the day to ask him.

Martin sat at his table in Quentins, drumming his fingers. One of his colleagues had driven him there. The man had patronisingly urged Martin to have a good relaxed lunch, noting that he was on a fairly short fuse today. So now he was fifteen minutes early and of course that boy would be late as he always was. Martin went over the meeting in his mind. The people had been very cagey, they had not said yes or no to the pitch that had been made. They would let him know later in the day. Most things had gone well.

What he needed was a good stiff drink. The waiter, foreign of course, didn't manage to catch his eye. The boy did look over once, but his eyes were vacant, so Martin clicked his fingers to attract his attention. Something happened to the boy's face then. A veneer of coldness came over it. It was so deliberate that Martin could not believe his eyes. The young pup was not even going to acknowledge him. This was not good enough, it simply was not. This was a top-class restaurant with standards. He clicked his fingers again and the boy's face was like stone. Martin felt a nerve beginning to tic in his forehead. He stood up and was just about to approach Brenda Brennan to complain in the most forceful of tones when there was a sudden power cut. Every light in the place went out. In a dark, heavily curtained restaurant on a wet, overcast day, it was astonishing the effect it caused. The place seemed to be in complete darkness. For a moment, Martin thought that he had been having a blackout and was greatly relieved to hear fellow diners gasp, laugh and make remarks about the incident.

Holding the table for support, he eased himself back into his seat. Brenda had organised her troops with candles on every table within minutes. She moved amongst them all, assuring everyone that they cooked by gas as well as electricity. So there would be no problem and she insisted that everyone have a drink on the house by way of an apology.

'That's if you can get anyone who will serve you one,' Martin grumbled.

'I beg your pardon, sir?' Brenda Brennan was startled.

'Well, that Latin Lover over there seems to have been stricken with deafness and blindness even at a time when the lights *were* on,' Martin said.

'Yan is one of our best waiters, so you do surprise me, but let me please serve you, sir. What would you like?'

He saw her speaking to Yan while the boy tried to explain something. He was being very definite about whatever it was he was saying. Martin couldn't hear, but he saw Brenda seem to console him and place her hand on his arm. And then she was back with exemplary speed with his vodka and he tried to relax. Eventually the waiter approached to leave him the menus. Martin had not yet succeeded in relaxing.

'Oh, I see you've noticed me at last,' he said.

'I'm sorry, sir,' he said.

'Don't even try to tell me that you didn't see me,' Martin began.

'No, sir, I did see you. I am sorry for not coming over.'

'And why didn't you?'

'You made this sound with your fingers.' Yan did that click.

'Yes, because I wanted to get you to see me.'

'I trained with a *maître d'hôtel* who said we must develop a diplomatic blindness if such a thing happened, and not to serve the person. Ever. But Mrs Brennan, she has just explained this is not the policy here, so I apologise.'

'Things like that might work in France...' Martin began.

'I am from Brittany, sir,' Yan said. His face looked pale and anxious. Possibly Brenda had threatened to sack him. The boy did not look well.

'Are you all right?' Martin asked unexpectedly.

'Thank you for asking me. Just I'm a little worried in case my father might be ill and if I should be beside him.'

'Are you close to your father?' Martin asked.

'No, he is far away in Brittany,' Yan explained.

'I meant, can you talk to him, do you like each other?'

'No father can really talk to his son, no son can really talk to his father, only the very lucky ones. But I care very much, yes.'

At that moment, Martin saw his own son being shown to the table. The familiar surge of annoyance filled him. Joseph ... or Jody as he insisted on calling himself ... wore a torn anorak and grey faded sweater underneath. He looked so shabby, so out of place, yet his smile was confident and happy.

'Dad, I'm so sorry I'm late. The buses were full because of the rain, and I was so anxious to get here because...'

'It's all right, Joseph. Give the waiter your order for a drink. It's free because the electricity has failed.'

'Has it?' Jody looked around in amazement. He said, 'I didn't even notice.'

Martin looked very impatient. The boy was showing himself to be almost an imbecile.

'Please, Joseph, get some grip on reality,' he began.

'But Dad, I was so excited coming to see you to tell you the great news, great, great news.'

'You've got a job?' his father asked.

'I've always had a job, Dad,' Jody said.

'If you call sweeping up leaves a job.'

'It's gardening, Dad, but that's not the point. The point is that...' Jody stopped, hardly able to speak for the magnitude of what he was going to say. 'The point is, Dad, I spent two whole mornings wondering how to tell you and now I wonder why, why was I rehearsing it?'

'Rehearsing what?'

'I saw you, Dad, as I came across the room, talking to the waiter...'

Jody indicated Yan, who had not left but was looking from one to the other as if he were at a tennis match. 'And you looked so kind and concerned, like an ordinary person, not a great businessman ... so I said to myself, why do I have to wait until it's a good time to tell you? We are going to have a baby, Jenny and I ... we are so excited, I can't tell you how pleased and happy we are. Imagine, a son or daughter of our own. A new person!'

The hint of tears was in his eyes, the eagerness that had never died. The optimism that even his father's cool dismissive attitude had never managed to quench shone out of him.

At that very moment Brenda came over with an envelope for Martin. 'Your secretary delivered it by hand. She said she knew you would not like to be disturbed by the telephone.'

Kit had chosen this moment of all moments to bother him with some office business. He barely looked at it but tried instead to think of a response to his son. Before Martin could speak, Yan had taken Jody's hand. '*Mes félicitations* . . . I mean, my congratulations, what a wonderful piece of news. You must be happy, you and your wife.'

'Jenny and I aren't married . . . we never saw the need . . .' Jody began.

'No, no . . . in French it is the same word, wife and woman.'

'So it is,' Jody said, but his eyes were on his father. 'Do you want to open your message from the office, Dad? It might be important,' he said humbly.

Martin was almost too choked to speak. 'Nothing is as important as this,' he stammered eventually. 'I'm so very pleased for you both, and for me, and maybe . . . maybe . . .' his voice broke, '. . . maybe there's even a way your mother might know.'

'Of course she does,' Jody beamed.

Yan stood back as if he expected the two men to stand up and embrace . . . and with one movement they did. Something they had never done before. Almost embarrassed, they sat down and looked at each other.

'Now, please, Dad, open the message. It's making me nervous,' Jody said.

Kit had written to say that they had got the corporate contract and she had taken the liberty of ordering champagne to celebrate with the American partners. 'Everyone is so pleased, Martin,' Kit wrote. 'You've made this place much more like a family than a workplace. Well done from all of us.'

Martin felt almost weak as he read these words.

What had he been *thinking* of to want to change Kit?

She was utterly essential to the office the way she was.

Thank God he had said nothing to her, it would have been unforgivable.

Jody talked on about names and plans and how he would look after the baby as much as Jenny would.

'I wish I had done that with you,' Martin said slowly.

'I asked Mother about that, but she said you had far too short a fuse for minding a child,' said Jody, who didn't seem to have an ounce of resentment in his body.

'When I say goodbye to the people in the boardroom this evening, can I come around to you and Jenny to celebrate?'

Jody looked at him in amazement. His father had never been to his flat. Perhaps the short fuse wasn't as important for grandfathers.

Serious Celebration

When Maggie Nolan did so well in her Leaving Certificate, her father said it was something that called for a Serious Celebration. The Nolan family were going out to have dinner in a hotel.

This had never happened before. They had never even been in an ordinary restaurant, let alone a hotel restaurant. Other people went to the Chinese or the Italian – the country was becoming cosmopolitan. Well, some of it was.

But not the Nolans.

There was never the money to spare. There was so much to pay for and so many calls on their time. Mrs Nolan's mam lived with them, for one thing, and Mr Nolan's dad had to have his dinner cooked for him and taken over to his flat every day.

Mr Nolan worked in charge of the bacon counter at one of those old-fashioned grocery stores that people said were on the way out. He was very happy and well-respected there but, of course, if the store really were on the way out, it would be hard for Mr Nolan to get another job.

Mrs Nolan worked as a cleaner in the hospital. She was very popular with the nurses and with the patients, but the hours were long and tiring, her veins were bad, and she hoped she would be able to continue working until all the children had been accounted for.

Maggie was the eldest of five. The others were all boys who wanted to play for English soccer teams. They had no interest in their studies and were utterly amazed that their big sister had got enough marks in exams to make people talk seriously about her going to university. They were even more amazed that their father was going to take them to the big posh hotel where nobody they knew had even been inside the door.

But he kept saying Maggie's marks would mean nothing unless there was a Serious Celebration.

'Will it be just the three of you – Mam, Dad and Maggie?' they wanted to know.

'A family celebration,' he insisted.

'Will Grandma come?' they asked.

Grandma Kelly was inclined to take her teeth out in public. The money would not extend to Grandma, it was explained firmly. Grandpa Nolan said that he wouldn't cross the door of such a place on principle. He said this

1004

before anyone had invited him, without explaining what the exact principle was.

But that still meant seven people going to a preposterously expensive hotel.

'We can't do it – it's ludicrous, Mam,' Maggie said. Her mother looked tired after a long day pushing a heavy, awkward cleaning trolley around the wards.

'Listen, child, we are so proud of you, and what has your father been in there slicing bacon for, year after year, if he can't take his family to a posh place when the eldest turns out to be a genius?' Maggie's mother's eyes were bright as they shone in her weary face.

So this stopped the discussion. There could be no more protesting.

Maggie went to her room.

She was eighteen. She knew that the celebration dinner would cost a fortune, maybe two weeks of her father's wages. He would have to borrow from the Credit Union at work. Maggie would have much preferred them to have had chicken and chips and for her father to have given her fifty pounds towards books for university.

But she listened to her mother. This Serious Celebration at the best restaurant in Dublin would give some meaning to a lot of lives. Not only her father's – her mother, too, would like to walk around the ward mentioning casually what was on the menu at the dinner party last night.

Her two difficult grandparents would rejoice as much as if they had been there. Her four younger brothers would think it was a great adventure. And if they could perhaps be persuaded not to peel the potatoes with their nails . . .

Mr Nolan made the reservation.

'Did they need a deposit?' Maggie's mother wondered.

'Indeed they did not. They asked for a phone number and I gave them the bacon counter extension,' he said proudly.

The boys became very annoyed about the amount of washing and scrubbing and clean shirts involved in it all. Maggie's mother said that she had told the matron where she was going and the matron had kindly lent her a stole. Maggie's father had told the general manager where he was going and the general manager had insisted that he would phone ahead and offer them a cocktail before dinner with his compliments.

And eventually the evening arrived.

Maggie had not thought a great deal about it because there was so much else to think of, like the fees for university and how to fit in her studies with all the hours that she would have to work earning the money. The night out in the posh restaurant, the Serious Celebration, was only one more crisis along the line. Since the Nolans didn't have a car they took two buses to get there. Mr Nolan had the money in an envelope in his inside pocket. He patted it proudly half a dozen times on the journey. Maggie felt an urge to cry every time she saw this but she kept cheerful and said over and over that she couldn't believe they were all going to this restaurant. Her friends would be so envious, she said over and over. And she was rewarded by her mother hitching her borrowed stole higher, and her father saying that the general manager was altogether too good to arrange the cocktails.

They arrived at the door and the place seemed enormous and intimidating, nobody wanted to be the first up the steps.

They felt nervous and out of place once in the restaurant. Mr Nolan wondered, should they have the cocktails in the lounge or at the table? Maggie, who thought that the boys might do less damage if corralled into just one destination, was in favour of the dining room, but her mother thought that Mr Nolan might like to see the lounge as well.

There was endless confusion when Mr Nolan mentioned the general manager's name. There had been no message about cocktails. Apparently nobody had phoned ahead with any such order.

'Just as well, Da, we'd have all been on our ear if we had them,' Maggie said, and tried not to watch the waiter wince as he overheard her remark.

They decided to study the menu and bypass the cocktails.

The menu was in French.

'Can you translate it for us, please?' Maggie said to the scornful waiter.

She was maddened with grief that the Serious Celebration was somehow going to be dimmed.

The waiter translated, under duress; Maggie remembered what everything was. She decided that her father was going to have the steak, her mother the chicken, and that she and the boys would have well-done lamb chops. Nobody would have any starters, she said, but they would all have dessert, she promised the sneering waiter.

The boys were so shocked and overawed by it all that for once in their wild lives they agreed with her.

She had never felt so angry and upset in her whole life. The look on her parents' faces was like a knife sticking into her. They were embarrassed and ashamed – after all their borrowing and planning it had not been a good idea.

'This is something I will always remember, Mam, Dad,' Maggie said truthfully. She would remember it every day of her life, when she was a high-flying lawyer, when she was confident enough to know every dish on the menu and to be known with admiration by every one of the hotel staff here.

'Maybe it wasn't quite . . .' Dad began.

Maggie felt faint, quite literally, as if she were going to fall over. He had wanted so much for this outing to be a success for her. The more she protested, the worse it was going to get, and the more pathetic she would make him seem.

A waitress was setting up the table with the appropriate cutlery. An elegant, groomed woman, aged around thirty, she wore a white lace collar and she was probably as horrible, snobbish and dismissive as the rest of them. Maggie burned with rage at it all.

But this woman somehow managed to catch her eye with a look of understanding. This woman seemed to know it was a special occasion.

'My name is Brenda Brennan, and I'll be serving at your table. Might I enquire if this is a special family celebration?' she asked.

'My eldest – you wouldn't believe, Miss, the marks she got.' Poor Da was bursting with eagerness to tell someone, anyone, what it was all about.

'Well, I'll tell this to Chef. He just loves to hear that we have academic people in. Usually it's only people on expense accounts,' the woman called Brenda said.

Maggie wanted to get up and hug her. But she knew that she must not do that – there was a role to be played.

'Thank you so much. When you're qualified and on your way, Chef Patrick and I will have our own restaurant,' the woman called Brenda said.

Maggie's father's face was glowing red with pleasure.

'You will leave us your name, won't you, sir, so that we can keep you on our lists?' she asked.

The scornful waiter was surprised when Patrick, the tall, dark and moody chef, said he was doing a special dessert, free, for everyone in the Nolan party.

He piped the name 'Maggie' on it in chocolate and asked for it to be brought out and photographed. He posed beside it, wearing his chef's hat, with his arms around the family.

The supercilious waiter sniffed. Imagine making a fuss of riff-raff like these people . . .

The Nolans went home on the bus with half the cake. It had been a seriously good celebration.

Maggie looked out of her window that night and thought of the length of time it would take her father to pay it all back.

By the time she was a qualified lawyer and received her Parchment as a solicitor, four years had passed. And a lot of things had happened.

Her father's company had sold out, as had been predicted, but he had been taken on by the new buyers and he wore a straw hat and striped apron at the bacon counter, which pleased him a lot.

Maggie's mother had had a successful operation on her varicose veins and felt like a new woman. She had been made supervisor of cleaning. One of Maggie's brothers had, in fact, gone to train with a big English soccer team, though the others were going nowhere fast.

Her grandmother went to a day centre now; things for old people had vastly improved. She loved it there, where she could terrorise everyone happily all day.

Maggie's grandfather, who when he was seventy couldn't cook his own lunch, met when he was seventy-two a tough woman who taught him to cook everything, married him and turned round his life.

Maggie won the Gold Medal in Law and was in a position to choose from any law firm in the country.

She knew her father wanted to take her back to the dull, snobbish restaurant, which had by now become totally *passé*. She couldn't tell him that the place had fallen from grace and that no one went there now.

She didn't need to tell him.

Once Maggie's Gold Medal was announced in the papers, an invitation arrived at her father's house. Brenda and Patrick Brennan, who were now managing the magnificent Quentins Restaurant, hoped the family would join them for a Serious Celebration. They wrote to say that their luck had turned on the night they met the Nolans. It was only fitting that they all mark this in a special way.

Maggie's father was a generous man. He had no idea that Quentins was the last word these days.

'Well, I'd like to have got you the best, Maggie, but seeing as these people did well, it would seem to be ungracious not to go, don't you think?'

'You've never been ungracious, Da.'

'And you know it's not just to have a free dinner? I have the money saved to go back to that smart place,' he said, anxious there should be no misunderstandings.

They went to Quentins by bus, but they would go home by taxi – this was going to be Mam's treat. Maggie's brothers were not overawed this time. They were four years older for one thing; but the place didn't try to put them down.

Maggie recognised the woman. Everyone was greeting her, trying to catch her eye. Brenda Brennan was warm to everyone but dallied at no table; she was always on the move.

'We can never thank you enough for this,' Brenda began.

'And do you run this place yourself, Miss? I must say, it's very respectable-looking,' Da interrupted.

Brenda said she did run it, and that Chef Patrick this time had a cake with a gold medal on it for Maggie.

It was ten times as good a meal as the one they had had four years ago, they all agreed.

Mam's taxi arrived to take them home and they were getting their coats.

'Why did you do it for us, Mrs Brennan?' Maggie asked quietly as they were leaving. 'All that business about pretending that your luck changed the night we met you . . .'

'But that was true,' Brenda said. 'That was the night we realised we could not go on working for a place like that, no matter how good it looked on a CV. Supercilious, snobbish people, no welcome, no warmth, no love of food . . .'

'How do you remember it was the night we were there?' Maggie wanted to know.

'You were real people, honest people having a celebration. They treated you like dirt. We couldn't bear it. We talked about you for a long time that night. The evening seemed to sum up how degrading it was to work for a place that treated its visitors so badly. And as it happened I came across some information the next night, sort of heard, you might say, that they were looking for people to run Quentins. And because of your family we somehow found the courage. We gave in our notice – and, as you see, it worked out rather well.'

Maggie knew Mrs Brennan wasn't an emotional person. Not someone you might hug. But Maggie still put a hug in her eyes. And saw it had been received. The woman swallowed and spoke slowly.

'In fact, Maggie, as you must realise, I'm very much understating it – it's a habit you get into at work. It all worked out better than we could have dreamed. It's we who owe you – that's why you were our guests tonight and you must come again.'

'When my parents are twenty-five years married, maybe?' Maggie said with a smile.

Brenda Brennan agreed. 'That, or when your brother gets picked to play soccer for Ireland. My brother-in-law out in the kitchen recognised him – he wants his autograph. Would it be all right if he asked your brother for it, do you think?'

'I think it would make this into the most Serious Celebration this family has ever known,' Maggie said.

Change of Heart

Drew had never been to Ireland in his life. And had never even considered going there until the company announced that the sales conference would be held in Dublin. Moira said it would just be a piss-up, an excuse to waste even more money than usual. 'The company is paying for it all,' Drew protested.

'Not for everything,' Moira said. She knew that there would be pints and outings and items that no company would pay for.

Drew and Moira had been going out together for three years. A lot of things were agreed between them but nothing was settled. They loved each other, that was agreed, and they would marry and have two children one day, that was agreed. But when this would happen was not settled.

Moira wanted them to get a house, which meant having a deposit. Drew wanted them both to move into his flat which was cheaper than Moira's. Moira wanted them to have a big wedding with all their friends and relations. Drew wanted them to have six people at the Register Office with pints and sandwiches afterwards.

Moira thought you only had one crack at life and you should give it your all, like putting away a certain amount of money each week. Drew thought you had only one crack at life and you should enjoy yourself first time round.

Moira realised that there was no way Drew would not go to a sales conference in Dublin which he insisted on thinking of as a freebie outing but she knew would cost money. Drew realised that he was going to have to come to some decision about all this very soon. He had given up the Friday night out with the lads, and he had given up the thought of ever having a decent new jacket. Now it looked as if he were going to have to give up the notion of having any extras while he was on this great trip.

When he kissed her goodbye before the conference, they both knew that something would have to be settled by the time this meeting was over. They were nervous because they didn't dare to say it to each other. It was too big, too important, in their lives.

When they got to Dublin they stayed in a big, modern hotel. The first night, Drew told his colleagues that he was way behind with his figures. He'd love to come out with them on the town but seriously now, they'd have to forgive him this time. They accused him of being over-eager and ambitious. He was going to be a tycoon, they said, a captain of industry.

Drew grinned weakly. He was trying to save the twenty pounds he would have spent in the pubs and more, much more, if they had gone on to a nightclub. He saw there were tea-making facilities in the hotel, so he would have tea and biscuits and look at what was on television. He might even do what he had said and look over his sales figures, examine some trends.

If only he got a promotion, then he and Moira would not have to set aside an amount that meant they literally had nothing to spend on fun any more. He yearned to talk to her, hear her say something loving, to remind himself why all this self-denial was necessary. But as they had to pay for their own calls, phoning Scotland would have been a huge extravagance.

The Irish Lottery was on. That's what he needed, win that and come back a millionaire. But it was too late. If only he had bought a ticket on the way in from the airport. He saw later that there had been six lucky winners. He could have been one of them with never a financial worry again. But it hadn't happened.

Drew began to feel unreasonably irritated with those six lucky winners. What had they done after all, except have the time to buy a lottery ticket? But he tried to get this very useless and destructive envy out of his system. He reminded himself that people made their own luck and created their own chances. He had read enough of this in management books to believe it might even be true.

The next chance he got he would take. There were many chances that he could take now, this very minute. He would just learn the names of all the senior people who would be addressing them tomorrow and study the little biographies that were among the papers they were all meant to look at.

Maybe he might look brighter than he was. Possibly someone could pick Drew for a promotion. It happened all the time.

Next day, he did seem to be brighter than the others, mainly because he had been asleep some four hours before any of them. And he hadn't discovered how much better Guinness tasted when drunk by the River Liffey in great quantities. So this was possibly why he was among twenty of the group chosen to go to dinner at Quentins.

Drew found out that not only was the company paying, but they would all go there and back in taxis, so this was another huge saving.

Quentins was certainly very elegant. You had to ring at the door to get in. They had a notice saying that they did this, as they liked to welcome their guests. Drew decided they probably also liked to keep out unsuitable people. He must remember the details of it all to tell Moira.

Moira worked as a waitress and would love to move to a classier place. She would even press her face to the windows of smart restaurants at home to get the feel of smart places. She would love to be walking in by his side tonight, to a place like this.

Would it ever happen? Or would he put so much in his savings that there would be nothing left for him ever to have a treat like a night out in Quentins or somewhere of its class?

Some of the lads he had been at school with were into great schemes for making money. One of them had a big line in issuing fake certificates for old motor cars.

Drew would have been able to do this and square it with his conscience. People spent far too much time and bureaucracy on cars anyway. But of course Moira wouldn't hear of it. Only Crims did that she said. Moira and her family had a great fear of criminals and what they called the Crim mentality.

Sometimes it would have been much easier not to love Moira, she was so unbending in her ways. Not flexible like other girls he had known. And she didn't understand how hard it was to go on a trip like this and be thought tight-fisted. She would say something stupid about the bosses watching him and how impressed they'd be.

That wasn't the way it happened in the real world. The boss class often spent more than anyone else.

Still, here he was now on a real fancy night out and he was going to enjoy it. Maybe they might give away little boxes of Irish chocolates and bits of Irish glass as well, then he'd have a present for Moira and for his mother's birthday.

Drew thought to himself that it would be nice not to have to be so obsessed with money and the price of things. Not to be looking at the floor endlessly in case someone had dropped a wad of notes. Would he give it in to the authorities if he found one? Oh how he would not!

When they were all in the restaurant they were shown to two round tables for ten. The young waiters and waitresses were Europeans from different lands, all smartly dressed in their dark trousers and white shirts.

Around them moved an elegant woman, Mrs Brennan, apparently, who put everyone at their ease, translating the names of dishes casually as if they had all easily known them already. She had a way of explaining how they were made as if it were peculiar to the restaurant. She even said in a conspiratorial whisper to Drew and his end of the table that they must be very highly thought of indeed, since the best of wines had been ordered and no effort was to be spared.

His mind wandered back to the unfairness of life. Why could some people have this lifestyle all the time, and for others like himself must it be a one time only that he would describe to Moira at second hand.

He didn't even need a whole sixth of the lottery. Just a few hundred pounds would be fine.

He dragged himself back to the conversation the others were having. It was about a girl with big sad eyes sitting at the next table. The table was set for two but she was alone.

Some of his mates thought she might be persuaded to join them. Drew had his doubts. Quentins didn't look like a place where you could pick up a bird at a nearby table. And she looked tearful. Quite possibly having drunk a little too much. Much wiser to leave her where she was. 'Aw, don't mind Drew, he's in love,' someone said.

He was, he knew it, but unless he had some more money soon, he might not be and that was very frightening. Drew decided to think about something else.

Nobody was talking to Mr Ball, the Head of Department, an anxious, uncommunicative man with no small talk whatsoever. But it was either talk to Mr Ball or think about Moira. And the same Moira had often said that everyone was interesting if only you could find their subject.

'Are you a golfer, Mr Ball?' Drew asked desperately.

'Oh no, Drew, never saw the sense of it, actually,' Mr Ball said, closing the door to any more talk of that.

Drew wasn't giving up. 'But you look so fit, Mr Ball, I thought you must do some sport and I know I once asked you, did you play football, and you said no.'

Mr Ball looked left of him and right of him and then he told Drew in endless detail about his visits to the gym. There was no point in going once or twice a week, he said. You had to go five days a week. Fortunately, this hotel here in Dublin had a reasonable workout room. Had Drew seen it? No? Well, Mr Ball would show him round it tomorrow.

'I'm sorry to drone on about money, Mr Ball, but is that gym you go to back home expensive?'

Mr Ball mentioned the annual figure and saw the look on Drew's face.

'Of course, when you get to the next level in the firm, if you're promoted, the company will pay for your subscription. It's in their interest to have fit personnel,' he said. In truth, he had never thought of Drew as on the fast track.

'And tell me about your programme, Mr Ball,' Drew said in desperation, nailing on to his face a smile of interest as he heard about muscles and movements and routines. He nodded and shook his head as he heard of machines that did all they promised and those that did not. He got an ache in his face but Mr Ball thought that Drew was fascinated. Drew saw that Mr Ball was loath to leave the conversation and only had to do so out of a sense of duty.

Drew joined his own colleagues again. They were still talking about the girl and speculating about whether she might be an available companion for the evening.

'Get sense,' Drew advised them. 'She'd be no fun at all. Look at her, she's crying. Didn't any of you notice?'

At that moment, Mrs Brennan the manageress woman had arranged that the customer with tears in her eyes be helped to the door gently and discreetly by one of the young waiters. The taxi had already been phoned for by the restaurant. Possibly she was someone who ate here regularly and maybe drank a little too much. Someone worth looking after. It was all done with great dignity, Drew noticed. Then he saw the wallet on the floor.

He leaned back and put it into his pocket. Nobody had seen. He went to the gentlemen's cloakroom. Inside the cubicle he opened it. A big, black, soft leather wallet. It had credit cards, receipts, tickets for a theatre and a letter.

It also had plenty of cash.

Silly girl, drunk on her own, leaving without checking. She could have lost it in the taxi. Or on the pavement while getting into the taxi. Or getting out of the taxi.

He would take the cash and tomorrow he would mail the wallet back to the restaurant anonymously.

He never knew when he decided to read the letter. He wasn't a criminal, just someone taking a chance. She was called Judy and she wrote to some guy saying she was sorry to plead and beg with him to have this last dinner with her, but she had so many things to tell him – how much she loved him and how nothing else mattered. And she had to tell him that she was pregnant, but she would be noble about it and never tell his wife.

And Judy would not ask him for child support. She wanted nothing from him, except the memory of their love and the hope of their child in the future. She would have this last dinner, leave early and hand him this letter and then go out of his life. She wanted only that he would know how much he had been loved.

Drew sat there and thought about love and deception and how some people had it really very, very difficult indeed.

He left the men's room and went straight to Mrs Brennan.

'I found this under a table,' he said.

'Yes, I sort of noticed you did,' she said.

She wasn't disapproving or anything.

'Did you know anything about the . . . um . . . the situation?' he asked.

'A little. It was not a happy one, but I don't think I want to go into any of that . . .'

'It's just, I'm from miles away. I'll never be here again. I wondered should anyone tell him she's pregnant?'

If Mrs Brennan was startled that he revealed this to her, admitting that he had read a private letter, she made no criticism.

'I don't think that will change anything at all one way or the other,' she said reflectively.

'But shouldn't a man know that he was going to be a father? She intended giving it to him tonight but he didn't show up.'

'He's quite good at not showing up, it never stops the ladies.' She shook her head at the folly of people and their relationships.

'So he'll never know?' Drew was astounded.

'Or maybe care,' Brenda said.

'That's hard to believe,' he said.

'For a nice young man like you and a decent, hard-working woman like me it is, but not for people like the no-show tonight.'

'I'm not a nice young man,' Drew said. 'But it's all there, every penny of it.'

'I'm sure it is,' Brenda Brennan said with a smile.

'Why are you sure?' He was puzzled. She was serene and she was non-judgemental.

'Because if it wasn't all there, then you'd just have kicked it under the table when you had a change of heart,' she said simply.

'A change of heart!' he said, surprised at her accuracy.

'Sure, that's what it was. Can I offer you a dinner here some evening, another time, you and a friend?' she suggested.

'It would mean getting back here all the way from Scotland,' Drew said.

The others were all getting up to leave now, and asking about nightclubs.

'Not for me, alas,' Drew said. 'Too old and staid. I'm heading off in my Head of Department's taxi for an early night.'

'I've a feeling it will stand to you,' Brenda Brennan said.

Drew saw her talking to Mr Ball, but he knew that she wasn't telling tales, that he had almost stolen a wallet.

He only discovered next day what she *had* been saying.

That he was a remarkable young man, who had not only rescued a wallet for another customer and handed it in, but who had been caring enough to be concerned over the woman's distress.

Mr Ball felt the very same about Drew. A boy who might have been overlooked before.

But once he had discovered Drew's interest in the gym and his obvious sense of disappointment that he couldn't afford to join one, Mr Ball, too, had a change of heart. He would recommend the boy's promotion the moment they got back to Scotland.

Brown Paper Cover

Mon often wished that she was back in Sydney, Australia. On a day like today, she could go out to the beach and lie there with her friends. In Ireland it was what they thought of as summer, but truly it was not a day for the sand. She would be blown to death by the wind, heartbroken by the small tidal ripple instead of the rollers she knew and loved back home, frozen by the ice-cold water if she ever dared get into it.

Still, she hadn't come to Ireland looking for a life of surf. She had come as part of a great world tour. Oddly, there had not been all that much of a tour. It was meant to start with a week in Rome, and then a week in Dublin and six weeks hitchhiking around the rest of Ireland, then a dozen other lands before going back to the rest of her life. But something strange had happened – after the week in Rome she had arrived in Dublin totally broke.

It wasn't exactly that her money had been stolen or lost or anything. It was just that she had managed to spend in one week almost all her two years' savings on a man called Antonio. It was hard to realise quite how, but this had somehow happened.

And so, on her first day in Ireland, she needed a job.

There was an advertisement in the newspaper that she read on her way in from Dublin airport and she had phoned for an interview, got the job in Quentins. Somehow the time had passed.

'You've fallen in love, that's why you're still there,' her mother accused her by e-mail. But it wasn't true.

'There must be a crazy scene with those Irishmen,' her friends wrote. But that wasn't true either.

What had happened was that Mon, or Monica Green (as she was never called), had settled in. She had worked in eleven different jobs since she left college, but for some reason she could never understand, Quentins was the first place she really called home. Patrick Brennan, the chef who taught her how to cook when things weren't too busy, his younger brother, called Blouse for some reason, who was a little less than intelligent but certainly not a fool. Patrick's cool, unflustered wife Brenda, who seemed to know everyone in Dublin. She felt as if she was some kind of a younger sister, part of the family. Mon was part of this team and she liked it. No need to move on. For the moment.

'We'll have to find you a fellow,' Brenda Brennan said unexpectedly to Mon one morning.

'Why?' Mon was genuinely surprised.

It wasn't the way Brenda usually talked. She must have a reason for saying it. And indeed she had.

'You're very good, the customers like you, Mon, you'll go on somewhere else unless you get caught up in some complicated messy romance like they all do.'

Brenda smiled as she spoke, as if she alone knew the ways of the mad world they lived in.

'Any advice and help always welcome,' Mon said.

'Someone once said to me that I should keep my heart open as well as my eyes. It worked.'

Mon gasped – immaculate, ice-maiden Brenda telling her this. Maybe she was right. But after that amazingly foolish and romantic adventure with Antonio in Rome, Mon was being cautious. Perhaps she had swung too much to the other side. Maybe she should keep her heart more open. Or a fraction more open anyway.

Mon went through the restaurant before lunch as she did every day, checking that everything was in place on every single table. Mr Harris from the bank next door came in, to eat his lunch alone as he did three days a week. Dull man with nothing to say. His head always in a book, usually with a brown paper cover. Once Mon had laughingly asked him if it was pornography and his eyes had been cold. She made no more jokes. Her cheerful Aussie humour had been very unsuccessful.

'Miss Green,' he nodded at her.

'Mr Harris,' Mon nodded back.

But Brenda had insisted on unfailing politeness and charm, even to those who did not return it. So Mon nailed on her smile as she handed him the menu.

'Chef has done a really beautiful monkfish today, Mr Harris. I think you'd like it.'

It was hard to know what the man would or would not like. He seemed to eat without noticing. None of them liked serving him.

About thirty-five, fortyish. Must have some big job in the bank, since he could afford to eat in Quentins so often. Never a guest or companion, never a newspaper or magazine, never a smile to left or right of him. Just studying books covered in brown paper.

Mr Harris said he would try the monkfish and as Mon leaned over to pour him a glass of water, she accidentally knocked against his book, which fell to the ground and the cover came off.

It wasn't pornography, but it was something equally surprising. Pop psychology. A book offering twenty ways to a woman's heart. A Never Known to Fail guide to making any woman love you.

Mr Harris and Mon Green looked aghast at each other and the book revealed in all its humiliating pathos.

Someone had to say something.

'Does it work, do you think?' Mon asked as she handed it back to him.

Mr Harris had a face like thunder. 'Why do you ask?' he wondered.

'Well, over a year back, when I was in Rome, I met this guy, Antonio, and well, I'd have read anything to get him, and they have that kind of guide for women too, to get to fellows' hearts, and you see, I couldn't find the bookstores that sold English books and then it was too late . . .'

She knew that she was burbling on and on, but she couldn't stop.

'Too late?' Mr Harris looked interested. 'How did you know it was too late?'

'Well, Antonio had gone, and all my money. You see, I was going to invest in a sandwich bar with him . . .'

'He took your money?' Mr Harris was horrified.

'Yes, well, that wasn't the worst bit . . . actually none of it was too bad, but I'd sure like to have known the Way to his Heart,' Mon admitted.

Mr Harris was looking at Mon as if he had never seen her before. 'You mean, women actually read these books too?'

'You bet they do. Maybe the person you fancy is reading one wherever she's having lunch today.'

'I don't think so.' Mr Harris shook his head sadly.

'Mr Harris, would you like to have a drink with me about six o'clock this evening and we could sort of pool what we think we know about the opposite sex?' Mon heard herself say.

Brenda Brennan was, of course, passing the table at that moment. She slowed down slightly so that she could hear Mr Harris saying that nothing would give him more pleasure, and where would Miss Green suggest?

And for weeks they went out and sought manuals on how to be appealing to the opposite sex, which mainly involved being thoughtful and considerate and tactile.

Everyone knew that they fancied each other long before Mr Harris and Miss Green did. Their faces lit up when they saw each other. The six o'clock drinks turned into dinners, and theatre visits. And when the annual Bank Dinner Dance came round, Mon was surprised that everyone in the restaurant knew that she was going to go as his guest.

They thought for a considerable time that they were only exchanging helpful books with brown paper covers. But it turned out, of course, that they didn't need these books at all. Mr Harris and Miss Green had well found the way to each other's hearts long before either of them realised it.

The Special Sale

The January Sales started earlier every year. Most of the big stores opened the very day after Christmas. A lot of people protested and said it was ruining family life. But secretly they were often relieved. Family life could often be overrated. Patrick Brennan said they should cash in on it, serve a comforting lunch to take the weight off the weary shoppers' feet.

'And what about the weary staff's feet?' Brenda asked. But she knew that he was right. People would love it. It would take the effort out of shopping if people knew that they could hand their parcels in to Quentins' big roomy cloakroom and sit down to a lunch where cold turkey would make no appearance.

'We won't force anyone to work unless they want to. We wouldn't need the full team.'

Patrick's brother Blouse and his wife Mary would help. There was no way they could open their organic vegetable shop that day. On the day after Christmas people wanted to buy digital cameras, copper saucepans or designer shoes. They did not want Blouse and Mary Brennan's parsnips, guaranteed free from pesticides.

They put a discreet little notice on each table in the restaurant advertising a Special Sale Lunch with a limited but interesting menu on 26 December. Early booking was essential. The menu was not, strictly speaking, limited, since they planned to serve Patrick's legendary steak and kidney pies, rack of lamb and a fiery bouillabaisse.

Yvonne booked a table for four as soon as she heard about it. It was the ideal choice for her boss Frank. He could take his three children to lunch there as a treat, something totally different on this, the first Christmas that he would spend away from his home. Frank's difficult wife, Anna, who had laid down so many ground rules and made things so awkward, would not object to this. It was quite extraordinary, Yvonne thought, that Anna, who had left Frank for another man, was still calling the shots. She still lived in the family home, and she had the children for Christmas. Frank was altogether too easy-going. He said that there was no point in upsetting little Daisy, Rose and Ivy still further. The whole thing wasn't their fault. He seemed to imply that it was nobody's fault. Anna had suddenly fallen in love with this other man, Harry, and there was nothing anyone could do about it. Everyone at the office was furious with him. Some even went so far as to say that if he were as passive as this then perhaps Anna had a case for leaving him.

But Yvonne knew better. Frank was a loving husband and father who put in long hours in computer sales so that his family could have a holiday abroad, a new carpet, add decking in the garden. Yvonne knew how he worried about these expenses. She saw him sigh and frown when he thought that no one was looking.

Yvonne was always looking at Frank, but he never saw. Why should he see her? The small, dumpy assistant in the sales department. Yvonne lived with her handicapped mother. Yvonne, who had no style or love of her own. A million miles from the tall, blonde Anna, who only had to smile and everyone did what she said.

She told her mother about it.

'And will you go too?' her mother asked eagerly.

Sometimes Yvonne despaired. She would love to have had a great lunch on the day after Christmas in a smart, buzzy restaurant with Frank and his three children. Love it more than anything, but it would have been entirely inappropriate and intrusive. The only part she could play was to call his attention to the lunch and make the reservation for him.

'Oh, no, Mother,' Yvonne said. 'That wouldn't do at all.'

'You must go out yourself over Christmas, Yvonne,' she said. 'I'm fine here on my own with my thoughts and my television.'

'I know, Mother, but there's really not all that many places I want to go.' Yvonne looked into the flames and thought about being thirty-six, the same age as Anna. Even Mother, who was in a wheelchair, had once had a life and a love and a child. Wasn't it odd the way the world turned out for people? Frank reported that Anna had been highly approving of the lunch-in-Quentins idea. She had even praised him for thinking of it.

'I'm afraid I didn't say it was your idea,' he apologised. She wanted to lean over and stroke the side of his face. But she restrained herself. He would have been horrified and embarrassed and eventually the nice, easy friendship they had would have disappeared.

Christmas Day was cold and windy in the city centre. Brenda Brennan cooked a turkey for Patrick, Blouse and Mary. And the new baby Brendan. Mon and her fiancé were with them.

Yan the Breton waiter telephoned to send them greetings and to say that his father was now fully recovered and home from hospital. Mon's family called from Australia to say they had been sunburned at the beach and to know if Mon's Mr Harris was still on for the wedding. Or had he seen sense?

Mr Harris, flushed with port, told them all that he just adored Mon and he didn't care who knew it. They ate in the kitchen of Quentins and played Country and Western music all day long.

'I hope we'll all think it's worth opening tomorrow,' Patrick said.

They reassured him. 'Isn't the place going to be full, and we don't get that every Tuesday,' Brenda said, ever practical. Blouse said he loved the thought of being a waiter for the day, all dressed up and people thinking he was the real thing.

'You *are* the real thing,' they all said to Blouse at the same time. They talked about the bookings they had taken. Blouse had taken one from a woman in a wheelchair who had never been there before. She had been very anxious for a table where she and her companion could be seen by everyone. Brenda had booked a table for a young man who was going to propose to his girlfriend and wondered could they have champagne on ice ready. And if it were not needed he would let them know. They all agreed that there was no other job quite as interesting as watching the human race at feeding time.

Christmas Day was cold and windy outside the big house where Anna and Frank's three little girls opened their presents. Harry stood watching.

'It's a bit rough on Frank that he's not here to see it,' he murmured to Anna.

Her blue eyes were sad. 'We have to start as we mean to go on,' she said, 'and he does get them all day tomorrow.'

Frank didn't notice the weather as he sat in his sister's home playing with her children instead of with his own. Trying all the while to avoid everyone's pity for him and their rage at Anna.

Yvonne and her mother sat together as they had for many a year. Yvonne's mother was resplendent in the fine wool stole with a soft lilac colour which had been Yvonne's gift. Yvonne was sitting speechless, looking at the invitation for two to lunch at Quentins the following day, which had been her mother's gift to her. There was no way she could return or refuse to accept a present like this. She would have to go through with it.

Frank called for the girls at ten-thirty. Anna looked beautiful as she always did. Harry looked a bit embarrassed, not sure how to play it. The girls were excited, they dragged him over to the Christmas tree to see what Santa Claus had brought. All of the gifts were exactly what they had been hoping for. And Mummy had given them each a new velvet dress.

'What time would you like me to deliver everyone home?' he asked mildly.

Anna gave a tinkling laugh. 'Frank, honestly, you don't have to ask, you are their father. We aren't the kind of people who have court rulings. Keep them all day until they're tired. Right, girls?'

Right, they said, pleased that there was no row. Daisy was nearly nine and almost grown-up, so when the others weren't listening she whispered some of her theories about Santa Claus to her father. Frank listened thoughtfully and said it was hard to know all right and we should all keep an open mind on things.

'Do you mind about Harry being here, Dad?' she said.

'No, darling, not if it makes your mother happy.' He tried to read her face, but wasn't sure if he had given the right answer or not.

*

The shops were crowded. It was hard for six-, seven- and eight-year-olds to make decisions. The little legs were tired when they got to Quentins, the first guests.

'You're welcome,' the waiter said. 'Can I take your parcels for you, ladies?' Daisy, Rose and Ivy giggled at being called ladies.

'How will you know which are ours?' Ivy asked.

'You'll give me your names and I'll write them down,' he said.

'What's your name?' Daisy asked.

'Blouse Brennan,' the man said.

'Why?' Ivy asked.

'When I was a young fellow I called my shirt my blouse. I forgot all about it, but no one else did.'

'Well, a shirt *is* a sort of blouse,' said Daisy.

'That's what I always thought,' Blouse said, pleased.

Frank looked at his eldest daughter with pride. The restaurant filled up, mainly families, the odd twosome. Even though he felt a deep sense of loneliness not to be part of a proper family, Frank thought from time to time that he got envious glances with his three beautiful daughters. Alert and smiling and interested in everyone.

'Look at that couple kissing,' Rose said as a bottle of champagne was opened at a nearby table.

'Does that woman have any legs?' Daisy said in her bell-like voice.

The woman in the wheelchair turned round with a smile. 'I do, dear, but they're not any use to me, so the waiter wheeled me in up the ramp. He was very helpful.'

'I saw you come in. That was Blouse that wheeled you in.'

'Blouse, is it? A very nice young man,' the old lady nodded.

Finally her companion looked up from staring at the floor. It was Yvonne from work.

Frank was amazed and pleased. 'So you decided to come yourself, too,' he said happily. 'Isn't it great! I must introduce you to my daughters.' He brought them over to Yvonne's table where they all stood in everyone's way until Blouse Brennan suggested that he merge the two parties to save on space.

Yvonne's face was scarlet. 'I can't tell you how sorry I am, Frank. This was all my mother's idea,' she hissed at him.

'But I can't tell you how delighted I am . . .' he began.

They could hear the children talking to Yvonne's mother, asking her how her legs had decayed, and did she bother wearing stockings, and what would happen if the restaurant went on fire? 'Blouse would push me down the ramp,' Yvonne's mother said.

'Indeed I would, Madam,' he said as he tied Ivy's table napkin around her neck, the way the French do.

'What lovely dresses you have.' The old woman felt the coloured velvet frocks.

'They're from our mother. She doesn't live with Dad any more, you see, so that's why she's not here.' Daisy seemed to have a mission to explain today.

'So you must remember it all to tell her. She'll want to know what you did because she loves you so much, like your father does. He must love you a lot to think of taking you to a very high-class restaurant like this.'

'Is it high class?' Rose was interested.

'The highest there is.' Yvonne's mother was firm on this.

'It's a pity they're not both here together,' Daisy sighed.

'Oh, I don't know . . . you can have better times separately. Like Yvonne's father and I. We loved her to bits, but we changed in loving each other, and she was always happy with both of us, weren't you, Yvonne?'

'Yes, I was, indeed,' Yvonne said, astounded.

'So her dad loved someone else eventually, and I loved someone else, but it didn't take away one bit from loving Yvonne. *Isn't that right?*' she barked at her daughter.

'Oh, absolutely right, Mother. Like as if your heart got bigger or something and there was more love in it,' Yvonne said, wild-eyed at the whole thing.

Frank patted her knee and stroked her hand. 'Yvonne, I wish you knew how much this means . . .' he began.

But Yvonne was listening to what her mother might be up to now. It was reasonably harmless. She was asking her new best friend Blouse Brennan for some bread that they could throw to the ducks in St Stephen's Green.

'Can we come too?' Rose asked.

'Please,' Frank begged. '*Please.*' And it was arranged. There would be time later, much later, when she would tell him that her mother and father had never separated, and he had died fifteen years ago and her mother had never looked at another man. This was not the time to do it. The Special Sale Lunch was nearly over, the rain had stopped and it was time to go and feed the ducks.

Part Three

Part Three

9

Ella looked up when the stories were told. As far as she could see, they had gone well. At least she had managed to hold their interest. She must leave them now and give them a chance to talk about it all. She moved swiftly. No, no, she would get herself a taxi, she pleaded. It was part of the excitement of being in New York. Please let them not see her out, she would much prefer them to stay and discuss what she had told them.

And then she escaped. Down in the lift, out of the quiet building into the amazingly noisy traffic. And then she got to her little hotel, which was beginning to seem like home, and up to her room.

Now she could do what she had been putting off until she got her work settled. She sat down and opened up Don Richardson's computer.

It got dark in New York as she trawled through the computer. Bank account numbers in the Isle of Man, in the Cayman Islands, in Switzerland. None of it made any sense, since the names were in some kind of code.

She recognised property agreements there, but none in Don's name or in his father-in-law's. Then she saw the file with her own name and her heart leaped. Maybe he *had* made an investment for her as he had once told her he would. Something to provide for her after his time. She gulped in case he really had done that. He must have loved her at one stage. But it didn't seem likely. It wasn't Ella Brady. This Brady family, a family of five, a man, his son, the son's wife and two children, and they were living in Playa de los Angeles. There were letters about them to banks and from banks. Whoever they were, these Bradys had plenty of money. And a lot of it deposited very recently. By far the largest sum had been the week that she had been in Spain with Don. When he had been away from the hotel. When his wife Margery Rice, mother of his two children, was there. Suddenly she realised that not only had he taken everything else she had but he had also taken her name.

There were so many things she could do. She could find the number of the Fraud Squad in Dublin and tell them the machine was ready for collection. She could contact an Irish television station. She could telephone Don now; the Brady family had a phone number and were listed in his machine. She could tell him that if he restored all that her father had lost, she would hand him back the computer, no questions asked. She could contact one of the various insurance companies involved and offer to give it to them. She realised that this was a decision she had to make entirely on her own. Everyone's judgement would be partisan. They would want to do what they thought was best for her or for them or for somebody. Why did she not give it straight to the police? That was what a normal citizen would do.

She opened the mini-bar in her room and took out a miniature Jack Daniel's and drank it from a tooth mug. It made nothing clearer. It did nothing to sharpen the blurred edges. If you had loved someone, slept with him, shared everything with him for month after month, you didn't hand over the files without a backward glance. There was some kind of mad nobility about it . . . Even if *he* behaved like a bastard, she was not going to. This was just one more test of her loyalty.

There was a way she wanted to show him that not everyone sold out their friends and lovers. She didn't want to talk to Deirdre about it, or Nick or Sandy or anyone. She had to make up her own mind what to do. In some crazy way she wanted to talk to Don. Well, that was an option too. Mad as it sounded. There were so many things she wanted answers to. Like had he always known he was going to call himself Brady or was it because of her? Like how could he have planned everything so meticulously and then left the machine in her flat? Did he intend to or was it an oversight?

And if he had always loved Margery, why had they lived such totally separate lives? And did he have any guilt, or could he live with it all, saying it was just showbiz? In some insane way, she could imagine the conversation. But she would not have it from here. She had been alarmed to know that he was now looking for the machine and sending messengers around the place trying to track her down. It had been a bit frightening.

But she hadn't felt frightened before. In fact, having the laptop made her feel in some odd way more secure. And as long as she had this computer in her possession, he might get in touch. She realised now that this was why she had never let it go. It was her last link with him. For four months it had been a sort of comfort to her to know that it was there physically. Some solid reminder of all they had.

But things were suddenly very different now. She could no longer tell herself that Don knew nothing of all that had been going on. That he had been swept along somehow in his father-in-law's plans. That there was going to be a perfectly innocent explanation.

Having opened the lid of the laptop, she could no longer tell herself this. It was beginning to dawn on her that Don Richardson was deeply involved. For the very first time she realised that she might indeed be in real danger and she had no idea what to do. She was so tired she couldn't think.

She would do nothing tonight. There was no need. After all, the briefcase containing the computer had been in her possession for over four months. If she had been going to turn him in, he could well assume that she would have done it by now. He must think that she had never got into it and had decided not to hand it over to those who would be able to learn what it contained. He should be feeling safe and secure now, so why on earth was he suddenly getting jittery and sending her messages about it? Maybe he really wanted to see her.

*

A man went up the lane behind Tara Road and put a letter into what they called the Annexe of what used to be the Bradys' house. It was not in an envelope, just folded in half. It had been sent by e-mail and printed out, but with no name or identifying marks at the top.

Barbara and Tim Brady didn't hear it coming through the letterbox, because they were asleep. They didn't see it until the next morning at eight o'clock, when Barbara was going out to work. And she did not read it then because the hall was dark and she was running for the bus. She let herself out by the wooden door into the lane behind the house. The garden didn't belong to them any more. It never would again.

In New York, Ella was in bed. Not asleep but resting. No pressure, no hurry, she told herself over and over.

She had to be at Derry and Kimberly's office tomorrow at nine. She must sleep well.

There was a system on the hotel telephone where you could switch it to automatic voice-mail. She switched it over. That meant if someone called in the night it wouldn't wake you. Not that she was expecting a call, but she had to be alert tomorrow, no matter what happened. No pressure, no hurry. He doesn't know you've opened it.

She had a long, warm bath, went to bed, and fell asleep with a television chat show blaring away.

So she missed the series of phone calls that began at about ten minutes after 3 a.m. New York time, just after everyone in Ireland had come to grips with the 8 a.m. news there. She didn't look at the little winking light until she was dressed and ready to leave the room. Hoping it wasn't a message from either Derry or Kimberly about the meeting, Ella dialled the number to retrieve the messages.

She sat in horror on the edge of her bed as she heard Nick and Deirdre and her father tell her what had happened.

These were the only households who knew where she was staying. Nothing they said made any sense. It was like words that were all jumbled, strung together, not proper sentences.

Only one more person knew her address and that was her new friend Harriet, the dealer who had sold her the dog collar. She had called also. Because Harriet's voice was less shocked, less horrified and sympathetic than the others, it was the only message that Ella understood.

'Listen, Ella. In case nobody's told you, he's killed himself out in Spain. He was scum. He wouldn't even stay and face what a mess he'd got everyone into. Probably half the country's already told you, but just in case, I wanted you to be warned. You're worth twenty of him, so don't weep over him, Ella. He's not worth it.'

When she got her breath back, she played the first three messages again. Now she understood what they were saying. It had to be true. They couldn't all have imagined it. Who should she phone first? Ella didn't want to talk to any of them.

She looked across at the computer. It really didn't matter any more. He had taken a boat out to jagged rocks and ended his life. She wondered had he choked or suffocated to death, or had his body been dashed against rocks? Had he any last-minute regrets and tried to survive? Don dead. Because of other people's money? Because of failure? Because he couldn't get his hands on that briefcase? *Why* hadn't she given it back to him? She hadn't even known what to do with it herself. If she had called him and said he could have it, then he would still be alive. She would call up the Irish newspapers on the Internet and see what they said. Before she talked to anyone, she needed to know more.

Don Richardson's handsome face looked out of every newspaper in Ireland and even some in England. He was described as a disgraced financier. The newspapers congratulated themselves for having correctly speculated that he had been in hiding in Spain. It was reported that his small boat had foundered on rocks at a particularly dangerous Spanish headland. A place where nobody took any kind of craft. Certainly, an experienced boatman like Don Richardson would have been aware of its perils. His body had not been found. The tides in this area could have carried it far out to the Atlantic.

He had parked his car on a nearby pier and left several envelopes on the front seat. The contents had not been made public, but it was understood that the letters were in the nature of an apology and an attempted explanation. Sympathy and concern had already been expressed by many of the business community in Ireland. Shock and disbelief had been registered by those of his family and former friends when they had been contacted. Of his immediate family there was no information. Some papers thought that they were co-operating with the authorities. Others said there had been no trace of them. One newspaper, in an article called 'Darling Margery', claimed that one of his letters had been to his wife, urging her to bring up the children in dignity. But since that newspaper was also one which in the past believed it had interviewed extraterrestrials and women who had been born with four legs, it was not given a lot of credence.

She telephoned her father first, but his phone was engaged. So she called Deirdre on her mobile.

'I know there are ways it's sad for you,' Dee said, 'as well as being a terrible shock, but honestly there are ways it's for the best.'

'That someone should kill himself, that's somehow the best?'

'I'm thinking of you, Ella. That's all I'm doing. You can get on with your life now.'

'I'm getting on with my life fine. I've been doing that since he walked out on me months ago. It's he who's not getting on with his life. Can't breathe or talk or know what day it is today.'

'I'm not making light of it. I thought in a way it kind of ended all the stress . . . somehow.' Deirdre was backtracking now. She had most definitely said the wrong thing.

'What stress did I have that has ended? I still know he never loved me. I still have to work to pay off the debts he left my family with. What's better about his being at the bottom of the ocean?'

'I'm so sorry, Ella, so very sorry,' Deirdre said.

'I know you are, Dee. Just don't go round thinking it's all for the best, will you?'

Deirdre made a quick call to Nick. 'She's probably trying to get through to you now. Whatever you do, walk on eggshells. She doesn't see it all as the great relief that we do. I opened my big mouth and felt a right eejit.'

'Thanks, Dee. I'll warn Sandy.'

'Heavy on the sympathy, that's where I fell down,' Deirdre said ruefully.

'You're a good friend. She'll know that.'

'I hope.'

'Hi, Nick.'

'Ella, poor, poor Ella.'

'Why am I poor Ella, Nick? He never loved me. He stole everyone's money. I was just saying to Dee, nothing's changed. That's all the same as it was. He's dead, that's all. I just wanted to talk to you about this meeting today.'

'You're going to it?' He was astounded.

'Well, of course I am, isn't that what I'm here for?'

'But maybe not today, Ella. I could call them and explain.'

'This is my job, my pitch. Don't dare interfere. The thing I wanted to talk to you about was these clearances they talk about so much here. Our usual form which people sign agreeing to let us use the interview ... that's enough, isn't it?'

'Those forms are fine. You can reassure them I checked all that out,' said Nick, who decided that women were so unpredictable there was no point in trying to understand them any more.

'Dad?'

'Oh, Ella, thank God you rang.'

'You're not to get upset, Dad. He was a grown man. He knew what he was doing, he must have.'

'No, it's not that.'

'And people say you should remember the good, there was some good, Dad. I had a bit of a time trying to drag it up but I have, so ...'

'Ella, stop. Let me speak.' His voice was like a cry.

She paused.

'He sent you a letter.'

'What?'

'A letter was delivered here last night by hand.'

'No, Dad, it can't be from him ... he was drowned out in Spain. How could he have ...'

'It was an e-mail, put through the door by someone when we were asleep.'

'But how do you know it's from him?'

'It was open, not in an envelope.'

'It's not from Don. Dad, there's a mistake.'

'I don't know what to do, Ella. I've told your mother. She didn't read it on her way out . . . she said I could take it to her office and she would fax it to you.'

'Is it long, Dad?'

'No, it's quite short.'

'So could you read it to me?'

'But perhaps you wouldn't want me to . . .'

'You've read it already, Dad, and you've read it to Mother. Just once more. Please.'

She could hear him putting on his glasses and rustling the paper. It probably took a couple of seconds. It seemed like infinity.

'"Dearest Angel,"' he read. '"By the time you get this it will all be over. Maybe you won't care at all. You refused to get in touch with me through the many, many messages that I sent you, so perhaps you never cared. But I can't believe that. I can't believe those hours and hours of love meant nothing to you. So I want to say a special goodbye and a great thank you for making my life so happy, and to tell you three things.

'"There was room in my heart for you all, you and my family. I couldn't leave them when the crisis hit. I was always trying to come back for you, too, but you wouldn't listen. The briefcase doesn't matter now. I won't be there to face what it reveals. If you have the generosity to throw it away on the grounds that I trusted it to you and that you would like to show me some trust too, then that would be great. But it's up to you. And lastly, I really liked your father and I know he lost clients' money because of my advice. I arranged some bank drafts, things that can be easily cashed. It's to say sorry to him and to you. This is the number of the deposit box. I wish I could give everything back to everybody. But then I wish a lot of things, mainly that I had years ahead with you, Angel Ella. You made me feel young and happy, you made my heart sing. Please know I loved you. Don."' Her father's voice trembled as he came to the end. There was a silence.

'Thank you, Dad.'

'I wish you weren't so many miles away, Ella. We wish you were at home.'

'I'm better off working hard, Dad. Believe me, I'm fine, and tell Mother, won't you?'

'He did love you, Ella.'

'Of course he did, Dad.'

She sat for a while and looked at her reflection in the mirror. None of this was happening. She would wake up soon back at a time before she had even met Don Richardson. When conversations like she was having this morning were totally impossible. But meantime she had to get on with what the rest of the day was going to throw at her.

She went down to the lobby and asked for a taxi to Derry and Kimberly's office. She was shown into their boardroom, where they sat close together at the far end of a table. They jumped up when she arrived.

'Ella!' Kimberly said as if surprised.

'You're here?' Derry was definitely surprised.

'We did say nine o'clock, didn't we?' Now Ella felt suddenly anxious. Maybe the shock had wiped everything out. They reassured her, that was what they had said. There was something odd about the way they looked at her, as if they hadn't expected her to make it. Had Nick disobeyed her and told them? No, he wouldn't dare.

She sat at the table and Kimberly poured coffee for them all.

'Have you been on to Dublin ... um ... this morning?' Derry began.

'We were just wondering if you'd been able to talk to anyone back there,' Kimberly asked.

They did know something. But how?

Ella was determined not to weaken or to put her head down on the shiny table and cry her heart out to these people about her dead love. The man who had written her a letter and e-mailed it some hours before he killed himself.

'I spoke to Nick,' she said brightly. 'He said to tell you that those clearance forms are standard.' She looked from one to the other. They didn't seem to be listening to her. 'So if that's all right, then ...' She waited for them to get on with the meeting.

'You know, if you don't feel like working or concentrating today, then that's fine, there are many other days.' Derry's eyes were very kind and he actually patted her hand in a gesture you don't see outside the movies.

Kimberly was offering the same kind of sympathetic reassurance. 'No need to force yourself,' she pleaded. 'It can be done when you're feeling more up to it.'

'You know,' Ella said slowly. 'Someone told you about me and Don and what happened.'

'We always knew about you and Don from the outset,' Derry said simply. 'We just read what happened to him this morning.'

'How did you know?' She felt cold.

'Same way as you knew I liked dogs. We looked up the files.'

'That's different. You're a public person. There's no file on me,' Ella said with spirit.

'There's plenty of information. We're not going to take up with a tiny outfit like Firefly Films, make a movie about a place we never heard of called Quentins, unless we have someone on the ground to advise us.'

'And who did you ask to advise you?'

'A lawyer. Nice guy. He marked our card, everything you said all checked out. This is about four months ago, remember, so you were a bit in the news.'

'And he bothers with tittle-tattle like that!' Ella was stung.

'To be fair to him, I think he was just letting us see everything that was on the table about everything. It has never had the slightest relevance to anything, only today we wondered ...' Derry's voice trailed away.

'You know Don seems to have been thorough to the end,' Kimberly said.

Ella wondered how they could work together so amicably after a long spell of marriage. Once there must have been a time when they had both wished for years ahead together . . . and, what were Don's words, when they had felt young and happy and made each other's hearts sing.

Ella tried to lift her coffee cup but her hand was shaking so she put it down again. She *must* pull herself together, banish the sound of his voice. She must. But at this point she could almost hear Don saying, 'I want to say a special goodbye, a special goodbye, special goodbye . . .' It was booming through her head.

She gripped the sides of the table very hard, but she felt herself falling down. Right down into a great black pit with the voice still there in her ears. When she saw shapes they were vague shapes first, then they turned into legs. They were legs of chairs, and Kimberly's amazing, shapely ankles in their high dark shoes, and also legs in brown trousers, and eventually she saw Derry King's face only inches from her own. The square, lined face that gave nothing away. Except now it was worried and full of concern.

'She's coming round, Kim,' he said with relief.

'Keep her head down. You're meant to let the blood flow to the head.' Kimberly was authoritative.

'We'll have to lift her back on to a chair then, to get her head down.'

Gently they did that, and she actually did feel something happening to her head as if everything really was sliding back into place.

'What happened?' she began, but by the time she asked the question she knew the answer. She had fainted. She struggled to sit up, but she could feel Derry's hand on her neck and she could hear his voice speaking urgently.

'You're just fine. Keep your head down. Breathe deeply, you'll be okay in ten seconds.'

Ella counted to ten and then sat up. They were both looking at her anxiously. She managed a weak grin. 'Textbook lesson on how not to present your case,' she said feebly.

'We've all the time in the world. Stop fussing,' Derry said.

'You've had a shock,' Kimberly said.

'But I was fine and suddenly everything tilted.'

'Could you be pregnant?' Kimberly asked.

Derry seemed startled by her question, but Ella wasn't at all put out by it. 'No, when you consider all the disasters that have happened . . . and there have been many . . . that's not one of them.'

'Maybe you had no breakfast?' Derry wondered.

'I can't really remember if I had or not, but that wouldn't be it.'

'Your colour is coming back a little,' Kimberly said. 'Have a glass of water.'

'You're both so kind.' She sipped the water.

'Would you like us to contact a doctor for you?'

'No, Derry, thank you. It was just a silly faint. Just nerves, I imagine. At all this. And how much depends on me.'

'You're not nervous, Ella. We were saying that about you just as you came in. You have no real film-making experience, yet you're very confident and calm . . .' Kimberly was admiring.

'I hope I didn't pretend to have more experience than I do . . .' Ella began.

'No, indeed, you've been very open and frank, but you didn't come over as nervous to us,' Derry said.

'I was fine yesterday,' she said without meaning to.

They looked at each other as if unsure what to say. 'And now?'

'And now, if you'll forgive me for collapsing on your floor . . . I'll try not to do it again . . . now I'll try to get back to where we were.' Ella's eyes were very bright.

'We don't have to . . .'

'But we do have to, Derry, or I have to. This is my chance. There will be others who will get their time. Others who won't waste it by fainting on the carpet . . . so I must tell you.'

'Slowly, Ella, catch your breath,' Kimberly laughed gently.

Ella's face was agitated. 'No, there's no time for me to go slowly. I've talked to Nick about those release and disclaimer forms you spoke of. He's on top of all that. Apparently they have the same legal standing as here. And I have my notes all here, all ready when you are.' She opened her file with shaking hands. She could see them watching as she tried to pull the right piece of paper out. It was protruding from the others but it still wouldn't come out properly. It seemed to take for ever.

Eventually Derry leaned over gently and took it out for her. He placed it on the table. 'It's all right, Ella,' he said. His voice was very gentle.

So was Kimberly's voice when she said, 'Ella, you've got it, you've convinced us.'

'What?' She was confused.

'It's all right,' Derry said. 'No more pitching, we're going to give you the grant. All we do now is talk about how we make the film.'

She looked at them wildly. In the middle of all this terrible nightmare, one thing had turned out as she had hardly dared to hope. 'Seriously?' she checked as if they might only be teasing her.

'Very seriously,' he said with a smile.

It was the smile that did it. She put her head down on the table and cried until they all thought her heart would break.

10

Ella could barely remember how she got back to her hotel. She knew Derry and Kimberly stood together smiling at her from the foyer as the yellow cab pulled out into the New York traffic. Somewhere she heard a bell ring. Or a clock strike. It was only ten o'clock in the morning. She got to her room and called Firefly Films.

'How did it go?' She could hear the raw anxiety in Sandy's voice.

'It's over, Sandy,' she said. 'It's finished. Would you believe it?'

There was a silence and then she heard Sandy speak to Nick. 'Okay, Nick, she did her very best but it didn't work. She says it's over. Nick, she gave it all she could.'

Kind, good Sandy, so loyal and supportive. Trying to say something to take the bleak look off the face of the man she loved.

'*No*, Sandy ... *no* ... We got it, they're giving it to us. We won, we won the grant.'

Ella could hear the gasp and then the phone was handed over. 'Is this possible?' Nick's voice was shaking.

'Open up the e-mail in half an hour. They're sending you a confirmation, Nick.'

'I don't believe you were able to go out and pitch today with everything ... with all you had to cope with. You're a hero, Ella, a bloody hero. How did you do it?'

'Don't ask too much about it. Let's just thank the Lord or someone that it worked out.'

'What did you say to them, Ella? Tell us, we want to know every word, every heartbeat.'

'You don't want to know.'

'But we do. We've been sitting here rigidly for the last hour and a bit ... now she's going in. Now she's saying this, now that.'

'Yes.'

'Ella, *please*, we're only here in a panic, you're there on the spot. You've done it! Tell us!'

'I fainted on the floor first, and then they lifted me back into the chair, and then when I was starting the pitch proper they said we'd got it and I cried for what seemed like an hour but may only have been fifteen minutes ...'

'She's totally unhinged,' Nick explained to Sandy. 'Probably drunk as well. We're going to get nothing out of her until she calms down.'

'Brenda?'

'Is that you, Ella? Everything all right?'

'Yes, fine . . . I just rang . . .'

'I'm so sorry about Don. It must have been a terrible shock to you.'

'Yes, it was.'

'And of course people who do something as terrible as that don't really know what they're doing . . .'

'No, he knew exactly what he was doing, but that's not what I'm ringing about . . .'

'Are you in . . . well, where you went?'

'Yes, I'm in New York. It doesn't matter anyone knowing now. He can't send anyone after me. Actually of course he never would have.'

'No, of course not,' Brenda murmured reassuringly.

'It's just that we've got the funding. We can go ahead with the project now,' she said proudly.

Brenda seemed astounded that she could speak of such things. 'Well, now. That's wonderful. Well done. And thank God you got it over before you had all this other thing to upset you.'

'Well, in fact, I didn't. I did it this morning, just after I heard about Don. I told you I'd call the moment I knew.'

'You are remarkable, Ella. That's all I can say.'

'No, I'm only hanging in by a thread, if you must know.'

'None of us knows what's in people's minds.'

'No, I'm okay, because I do know what was in his mind. He loved me. He really did. You know, he wrote me a letter just before he died. Imagine, Brenda!'

'That's . . . that's . . . extraordinary,' Brenda stammered.

'It's amazing,' Ella said and hung up.

'I think she's having a nervous breakdown,' Brenda said in a low voice.

'Well, she's certainly right about the documentary,' Patrick replied. 'Sandy was in half an hour ago to get me to sign some forms. It's all going ahead.'

'But she couldn't suddenly think that guy could have loved her,' Brenda said. 'She spent over four months getting over him. She can't possibly believe he had a change of heart two minutes before he killed himself. It seems too simple, too easy. And not a word about what happened to Margery and the children, not to mention Ricky Rice.'

'I sound more like my old father every day, but it's not over by a long chalk,' Patrick said.

'Deirdre, she got us the funding,' Nick said. 'She'd have called you from New York but it's too expensive.'

'Proper order,' said Deirdre. 'If you're going to be tycoons, first step: you must become as tight as ticks with money.'

'Very funny. Anyway, she may be home earlier than we thought. There's no need for her to be in hiding any more if the guy is dead.'

'*If* he's dead,' Deirdre said.

Tim and Barbara Brady got a three-minute call from Ella. 'I can't speak long, but the *great* news is that the movie is up and running.'

'Well done, Ella,' her mother cried.

Ella's father sat there in his chair. It had not been a good day. The death of Don Richardson had drawn a final line under the hopes that some of his clients might have nourished about ever seeing any of their money again. Several had been in touch with him. They had not been easy conversations. He watched his wife's pleasure as she told him with delight how Ella had managed to make the King Foundation underwrite the project. And now that Don was no longer a threat, she was going to come straight home. Rather than hiding out in New York.

'Why aren't you cheerful, Tim? It's wonderful news,' Barbara complained.

'It's great news,' he said, forcing a smile on his face. Quite a few of the people he had talked to today had expressed the view that Don Richardson might have faked his suicide. By the following morning, the newspapers had begun to express the same doubts. They reprinted stories of those who had folded their clothes, left farewell notes on beaches and had turned up in different countries with different passports years later. But then, the Richardson family was already in a different country at the time of the drowning. There were a lot of things that didn't quite fit together, causing a great deal of vague and uninformed speculation in the various feature articles of the newspapers.

What had happened to his family? The wife, sons and father-in-law whom he was meant to adore? They had not come out of hiding to mourn his death. Why had Don Richardson left his wallet and documents to be readily found in a car that he had only rented that morning? What had happened to the missing money? He must have used an alias for the past four months. Were his family still living in this disguise? And if the family still had the embezzled funds, then what did Don Richardson's suicide actually achieve? It hadn't restored any livelihood to those who had lost it.

The press carried on for a few more days. The mystery of the months spent in Spain. The possible lifestyle the Richardsons might have lived on what was once called the Costa del Crime. The whereabouts of the grieving family. As always, Spanish authorities said they were co-operating closely with the Irish law forces to track them down. Efforts to find the family had been intensified among British and Irish expatriates in the area of the drowning tragedy. They had led to nothing. Nobody had ever heard of this family. There had been no trace of any of them since that morning four months ago when they had arrived in Spain using their own passports, and simply never been seen again.

And gradually, as other things happened, the story and speculation about Don Richardson disappeared from the papers. And public opinion began to revert to the thinking that he really had drowned. Brenda noticed from hearing people talk in the restaurant that the pendulum had swung back to where it was before. There had been no sightings of Don back in Dublin. And surely, if he had staged his own suicide, it would have been to get away from the mindless anonymity of being in a Spanish resort, back to where he had been king of everything. To Dublin, where he was a somebody. Don the great risk-taker would have known enough people who would have hidden him. And yet there had not been a whisper.

Ella was in control again. She was alert and interested when Derry had introduced her to some of his financial people, the section where Firefly Films would direct their final budgets. She concentrated hard so that she would be able to put a face to each name.

Kimberly suggested she see some films already made on similar themes, and got her in touch with a viewing theatre. It was all very simple, if you had an introduction through the Kings. Ella realised more each day how important they must be and was glad she had not really understood this at the outset.

Most evenings she ate in a restaurant with Derry. He chose all kinds of different places for her, and seemed pleased with her company. He said he hated to eat alone in restaurants and usually wound up with take-out and ate at home, so she was saving him from indigestion. They talked easily. She never asked him why a man so wealthy, so single and obviously very eligible managed to escape the New York prowling ladies. She told him tales about her childhood, and though she mentioned that they lived in what had been a garden shed next to their old house, she never said why.

Derry told her tales of holidays in Alberta when he was a child; the three children went to their Canadian grandparents for the whole summer. Five years they had done that, it had always been magical. He never said why his mother had not gone with them, and she never asked.

She told him about Deirdre who had been her friend since she was ten and how Nick and Sandy were going to get married. She said she missed teaching, but that she had needed to leave herself free to make money this summer.

He seemed to think that this was a perfectly normal thing to do. He himself had left school at fifteen and had worked in a variety of jobs. When he was twenty, he realised he'd need qualifications if he were to try to give his brothers any kind of start in life. So he got a job as a cleaner/janitor in a college and arranged his hours so that he could do business studies as well. It hadn't been easy, of course, mopping the floors and clearing the litter bins when other kids were going out to ball games or bowling alleys. But then nobody had it easy all the time, and he got a few good night-watchman stints too, which of course made it very easy for him to study. So he had done well in his examinations and won scholarships. And he had got his brothers into college as well.

So Ella didn't ask questions. She told how she would have loved brothers and sisters, but Deirdre had said that they were vastly overrated and that rabbits were a much better idea.

He had laughed. 'She sounds like a character, this Deirdre.'

'Oh, you'll meet her in Dublin.'

'I'm not going to Dublin, Ella,' he said.

'Sorry, I forgot.'

Ella had decided not to push it. And maybe it would be much better if he didn't come. They would be freer to get on with things.

He very rarely talked about his work as the head of a hugely successful office supplies company, one of the biggest in the United States. He said it was a team effort, that he had been lucky to identify a need at the right time, something that wouldn't change every few hours as computer software seemed to do. Kimberly had been brilliant on the marketing side, and almost everyone had been there from Day One, so in many ways it ran itself without his having to be there every day. That's what gave him so much time to deal with the Foundation, which was what he really enjoyed.

Yes, of course he had to be ruthless sometimes at work, make decisions that he hated in his heart. When he had to close down a division of his company he made sure the employees were retrained or given early retirement. He was indeed easy company. Kimberly must have met someone very special in Larry if she were able to walk out on Derry King.

Every night when she came back from her dinner with Derry King, Ella sat down at the computer and looked up the Irish papers of the day. She read with horror how there had been a thought that Don was not really dead. If only this were true. If only it were possible. She would go to any part of the earth to tell him she loved him. That she understood why he had to do what he had done. But she knew that he was dead. He had written to her to say goodbye.

Then she would read about Margery and the children. And where they could be in hiding. Only Ella knew where they were. In Playa de los Angeles, using her name. Calling themselves Brady. It was strange to think that she could lift a telephone and give their address to the authorities. But she would never do that. Don deserved better than a girlfriend who would blow everything. He had looked after those who needed to be looked after. His children and their mother and their grandfather.

And Ella. He had sent her those bank drafts, which she could cash and get her father out of trouble with. Oh, if only he were alive, even for an afternoon, she would tell him how glad she was that he had loved her after all.

The emptiness of the last four months had been filled by something strange like a curious sense of peace.

And eventually the formalities were all done. Ella had booked the Thursday night plane home. 'I'm going to miss our suppers,' Derry said.

'Me, too, but you won't come to Ireland and continue them, so what can we do?' she said.

'So if tonight's going to be the last night, then let's make it in my place,' he said.

'That would be great.' Ella was pleased. She wanted to see his duplex apartment that she had read about long before she met him. Full of paintings by young people. Many of them now valuable since the artists had been on the way up. Some of them by people who had never made it. But Derry King bought what he liked, not what he thought would appreciate in value.

Kimberly too seemed sorry she was leaving and asked her for a last lunch.

'You even get to meet Larry,' Kimberly promised. 'And that's not given to every looker that comes across my path.'

'Oh, I'm not a looker,' Ella laughed. She meant it, too. Since she had come to New York she realised how unglamorous she looked, so shabby and ungroomed.

'Oh, you are a looker, Ella Brady,' said Kimberly, and she meant it, too. So much so that Larry was only going to join them for a cocktail.

He was handsome with longish dark hair and a designer suit, sunglasses which he took off at once, very assured and confident. Slightly showy, with large gestures, holding Kimberly away from him so that he and everyone could admire her grey silk outfit. Then a long, admiring look at Ella and a light stroke of her long blonde hair.

'Perfect,' he said as if he had been asked for an opinion by a judging panel. 'Just perfect.' And then to the waiter: 'Am I not a lucky guy, having cocktails with not one but two beautiful women?'

'Very lucky gentleman,' said the Chinese waiter, who had taken in the whole situation at a glance and knew that the lady in grey silk would be the one with the credit card.

Larry spent thirty over-excited minutes with them. He told them about various dramas and screaming matches back at the showrooms. How this buyer had threatened to burn the place down unless she got her order and that designer had said he was leaving for the Islands before he had finished his spring collection.

'Which islands?' Ella asked with interest.

'Oh, who knows, who cares, Ella. He won't go there, it's only a cry for attention,' Larry explained.

He asked nothing about Kimberly's morning, which had been spent meeting their advertising agency. He asked nothing about what Ella was doing, with her long blonde hair and Irish accent, in New York. But he was very excited about a reception they were going to later. It was an art exhibition and it was so far uptown they were thinking Albany. But they *had* to go, and Kimberly must leave time to go home and change, and if she was tempted to eat pasta carbonara for lunch, then she must remember the zipper of the new dress was notoriously sticky and had to be fastened so maybe she might think twice about carbonara!

And he was gone, with a flurry of goodbyes, secure in the knowledge that everyone in the bar saw him go.

'Isn't he something else?' Kimberly said proudly.

Ella struggled to agree.

'Very different from Derry, as you can see,' Kimberly said.

'Oh, indeed, yes, totally.'

Ella had just been thinking that and wondering what kind of madness had made Kimberly King attracted to Larry. Maybe being a part of the fashion world appealed to her. But to give up Derry King, with his crinkly smile and his ability to understand what you were thinking before you said it . . . for this guy. A man who looked at himself in mirrors, for God's sake. It was beyond comprehension.

'Larry makes me feel young again, you see.' Kimberly answered the question Ella had not asked aloud.

'He's full of excitement, isn't he, and totally gorgeous looking.' Ella hoped there was enough enthusiasm in her voice to match the look of adoration there had been in Kimberly's eyes when she spoke to Larry.

'He certainly keeps me on my toes. I had indeed been thinking of pasta before he reminded me of the new dress.' Kimberly gave a little giggle and picked up the menu to choose the salad with no dressing which she ordered instead.

'I'll have the same,' Ella said.

'No, you like your food, have what you like,' Kimberly pleaded.

'I'm having dinner with Derry tonight. I'll have plenty then,' Ella explained.

'Where's he taking you?' Kimberly had a huge interest in good restaurants, although she had rarely eaten three hundred calories' worth of food in any of them.

'At his place. I'm looking forward to seeing it.'

'Well, be prepared for a two-hour tour of child art first. He's kept all kinds of rubbish as well as the valuable stuff. Oh, and remind him to call the take-out early on. Often he leaves it too late.'

'You and he are wonderful together. Kind of jokey, but no bitterness.'

'What's to be bitter about? Derry's a great guy. He gave me half of everything. That's how I set up the business with Larry. And he's so practical, he said there was no use trying to hang on to me if I wanted to go. I would have done that for him too, if he had been the one to fall in love with someone else. It's crazy to try and kick life into something that's over.'

Ella thought of Margery Rice. Suppose she had thought like that? Would everything have been different? She could have had half of what Don had. More. She would have let him go. Don would not have taken all those risks. He would have been alive today. And he and Ella would have been together. For one moment Ella almost told Kimberly the whole story.

She was a good listener. Her perfect face was alert and interested but not eager. If Ella wanted to talk, she would have had a sympathetic audience. For a moment she was tempted. But then she decided against it. It was her last day in New York. Tomorrow she would go back to Ireland and whatever was going to happen now. All the decisions that had to be made. About the bank drafts in a safe deposit account. About the knowledge of where Don's family lived. It would take a lot of working out. An emotional lunch was not what she needed just now.

'I'll never be able to thank you both for such solidarity. It was exactly what I needed.' She was closing the door very politely.

Kimberly understood. 'Sure, well, we were there if you needed us, still are.'

'I know one thing I did want to talk to you about, if it's not indiscreet. Is Derry really dead set against going to Ireland? It would be marvellous for us if he came.'

'Utterly. His father was a wife-beater and a drunk and an all-round bad guy. And Derry simply blames it on his being Irish.'

'So it's really deep. I won't try any more.'

'I wish you would try. It's exactly what he needs, to go there, to get the monkey off his back or whatever the expression is.'

'You think it would help?'

'It might make him normal. That's his problem, you see, these demons he has about Ireland. It was part of our difficulties, part of everything for him. He had to damn a whole country because of his father.'

'But why did he choose an Irish project to support?'

'He thought it was going to send the place up, make it all look very foolish.'

'But he doesn't now. I explained all that at the first meeting.'

'He's honourable enough to go along with something once he's into it, in order to be fair. He wouldn't raise your hopes, get you over here, and then because of his prejudices pull the plug. But you asked why he chose it in the first place, and I told you. He thought it was going to be a hatchet job.'

'He seems so calm and in control.'

'And he *is* calm and in control. He looked after his whole family. He raised his brothers, they adore him. He wanted to get his mom a nice home back in Canada where she grew up, couldn't understand that she had lived so long in New York that she is a New Yorker now.'

'So she didn't go?' Ella asked.

'No, she had all her friends in the neighbourhood, she even had some happy memories of her husband. Derry couldn't see any of that. His father is his one blind spot. He can't go into an Irish pub, hear Irish music, says they glorify drink and violence. He's never going to change unless he got back there to Ireland and saw they were all as normal as anyone else. Just getting on with their lives.'

'Have you been to Ireland, Kimberly?' Ella asked suddenly.

'Why do you ask?'

'Just the way you said that made me think you had.'

'You're right. When we were first having our problems I went there. I even went to see his relations. Perfectly ordinary people. I didn't tell them about Derry, just asked around a bit. He has two cousins who started as house painters, run their own business now. They are so like him in many ways. But he'll never get to know them.'

'Did you tell him?'

'Tried to, but no use. Then I met Larry, so I had other things on my mind.'

'How long have you and Larry been married?' Ella asked.

'Eighteen months. I hope it lasts.' She laughed a very brittle laugh.

'You are very hard on yourself, Kimberly. He adores you. Anyone can see that.'

'Aha, I wish I had your faith and optimism.'

'Oh, but he does. You saw him. And so does Derry. He looks at you as if he still loves you a lot.'

'No, Derry doesn't love me. He's my great friend. He looks out for me. He keeps a quiet eye on some of Larry's worst extravagances. He doesn't think I know. And I care for him too, as a friend. Were you and this Don Richardson friends?'

'What?'

'I know you loved him, but were you friends?'

'No, no, he went away and left me. He wasn't a friend in that sense. But he still loved me, he wrote to me to tell me that the night before . . . the night before it happened.'

Kimberly looked as if she were struggling to find something to say. Ella rescued her. 'It's all right. Everything changed then. I can do anything now that I know he really loved me.'

'I can see by your face that's true,' Kimberly said truthfully. Ella's face did look serene and calm. Whatever this guy had said to her, she believed it and it was doing her good.

The tour of the artwork was leisurely. They walked, glass of wine in hand, while Derry King explained about the young people and their sense of vision. Some of the artists were from inner-city schemes, where their brothers and neighbours were mainly into gangs and drugs, yet they saw beauty in everyday life.

And Derry King didn't send out for a take-away, either. Instead, he took Ella into his state-of-the-art kitchen and said he was going to make a stir-fry in a wok. He had asked the butcher to cut up the meat into tiny strips, the vegetables were chopped and prepared too. 'It's probably not so much making it, more assembling it,' he said apologetically.

'Oh, no. I'd definitely consider it was making it,' Ella reassured him. 'You went to the butcher's yourself, and you don't have a fleet of staff serving it.'

'Did you expect that?' Derry still had the habit she had noticed the first time she met him of asking simple, direct questions that made you reveal much more about yourself than you intended to.

'Well, I suppose I know you're very wealthy. This is an extremely classy building. I suppose I thought people opening your door for you and cooking your meals might go with the territory,' she admitted.

'Is that what you'd have?'

'No! I'd hate it. If I had a place like this, I'd well look after it on my own, no matter how much money I earned.' She stared around it admiringly.

'I do have a team that comes in three times a week when I'm not here. They clean and iron, and I have to admit that today I called them and asked them to do the vegetables. Was that cheating?' He had a very infectious smile.

'I bet they're mad about you,' she teased.

'Oh, I doubt it. One more job in a long day of hauling cleaning stuff around Manhattan.'

'You're probably their only client who has that much sympathy for them.'

'I have admiration for them too. They saw a niche in the market and went for it.'

'Did you find them, or did Kimberly?'

'I did. Kim liked to have someone live in. It was a different kind of life, kind of place entirely.'

'So you and she didn't live here then?'

'Lord, no. Kim thinks this isn't a home. She thinks it's a school project room. No, her place, and indeed our place when we were together, was a matter of one drawing room opening into another ... perfect for entertaining. I don't do much of that ... as you can see ... so all this suits me better.'

And then it was as if he had very politely pulled down a shutter. It was as if he were saying, This is as far as you are going to go today, Ella Brady, no more personal questions ...

She took the message on board. She told him about her plans for the next day. She had a small sum of money kept aside to buy gifts if her mission had been successful, and now it was, so she would go shopping.

'Women love that,' he said, almost wistfully. 'I can't get a kick out of it myself, clothes are just to keep you warm and decent.'

'Oh, I won't be shopping for clothes. I'm talking about trinkets. You know the kind of thing ... joke clapper board for Nick and Sandy to show they're really in the big time now, some big paper sunflowers for my mother, a football hat for my father, a frilly nightie for Deirdre, a book of table decorations for Thanksgiving for Brenda and Patrick in Quentins. Oh, I've got another dog collar for Simon and Maud, like the one I gave you that horrified you so much.'

'It did *not* horrify me. It touched me to the heart,' he protested.

'Now, Derry, I want to leave this country while still continuing to respect your honesty,' Ella laughed.

'Then look at this.' He opened his wallet and took out a Polaroid of a lopsided puppy with a hopeless grin wearing the twinkling, bejewelled collar.

'You actually did put it on an animal! Aren't you just marvellous!' she cried.

'That's not an animal, that's no ordinary dog. I'll have you know you're looking at Fennel.'

'Well doesn't Fennel look just fine in his new collar!'

'He loves it, apparently. They tell me at the kennels he won't have it taken off. He pines until they put it back on. Maybe you know more about dogs than I do.'

'He lives at a kennel?'

'He has to live somewhere. He can't live here. He followed me home one night. I couldn't leave him.'

'Maybe he belongs to somebody.'

'Fennel never belonged to anybody. He was born in some alley. His mother may have been killed. He lived by his wits until he found me. He's a survivor, Fennel. He found one of the few men in New York who would look him in the eye and then pay for him to live in luxury for the rest of his life. I take him for walks in the park. We get some very odd looks, thanks to that collar ... but what do I know? Maybe the other dogs are drop-dead envious.'

'You're a very kind man, Derry King,' Ella said.

'And you're a kind girl, Ella Brady, going off to stores getting gifts for all your friends when your heart is broken,' he said.

Then everything changed a little, as if they had been old friends for ever.

She helped him to make the salad and told him about Don quite calmly, from the very first day she had met him, right down to the letter that had been delivered to her parents' house.

He asked questions that never seemed intrusive, but which carried the story along. 'Did he seem sad when you were in Spain together?'

'Yes, he did, sometimes. I didn't realise that it was worry because he was preparing a hiding place. I thought it was because he wanted it to go on for ever ... the two of us there.'

'Perhaps it *was* that,' Derry suggested.

And then, later, she was telling him about the numbing shock of reading in the newspapers that he had left people without their life savings. Story after story unfolding of loss and deceit.

'What was the very worst bit?' Derry asked.

'At the start, the worst bit was the papers talking about him and his wife, this close couple which I knew they were not. That hurt a lot. But the very worst bit was my father trying to be brave. My poor, decent, hard-working father, who would never cheat anyone in his life, ending his career in disgrace because *my* boyfriend gave him some false leads. It was bad enough for him to know that I was having an affair with a married man, that alone was enough to upset him and my mother. But the other. That was unbearable. I literally could not bear to think about it, which was why Nick and everyone got me involved in this project, so that I wouldn't have to think any more.'

'And look what you did with it!' He was admiring.

'Ah, that was due to everyone else, and now finally to you helping me. But what thanks do you get? A dog collar for Fennel. And here I am, sitting blubbing away about it, hour after hour.'

'No, you're not. In fact, you're remarkably calm.'

'I am because he loved me. I know that now. For some months I thought that maybe I had only imagined it. Invented the whole thing for myself.'

'But he's dead, Ella. You'll never see him again. Isn't that very bleak for you?'

'It's a waste, a desperate waste. But it's what happened and we have to get on with life.'

'And when you get back . . .'

'I'll be so busy with the Quentins project, I promise . . .' she smiled at him.

'No, I don't mean that. You will have four major decisions to make about all this and quite soon.'

'Four decisions?' She was surprised that he was so precise.

'One . . . whether you'll cash the bank drafts for your father. Two . . . whether you'll hand over the laptop to the authorities. Three . . . if you *do* give it over, will you erase the information about where his wife and family live? Four . . . if you *don't* hand it over, what will you do with it, throw it away or hang on to it?'

'No wonder you did well in business, Derry. You have a very sharp mind. You can get down to the bones of something in seconds.'

'Yes, but those are, as you say, just the bones. You have many other things to think about. It seems that you have good friends. They'll help you.'

'I'll keep you informed, Derry.'

'You don't need to. There's something sacred about confidences, part of that is you need never follow up unless you want to.'

'That's true, but part of a confidence, if it is to be sacred, means that the listener must give as well as the talker.'

'What do you mean?'

'I've told you my whole heart and life story,' she said.

'You know mine.' He tried to be light.

'I don't, really. What is so terrible out there that you can't face visiting the country where your father was born? He's dead and as you said to me about Don, you'll never see him again.'

'We're not talking the same planet here, Ella.'

'I know it's not bleak for you and a waste, like it is for me. For you it's probably a good thing, because you can only hate him and what he did in retrospect. But he had to be born somewhere, and he happened to be born in my country, and that, whether you like it or not, makes you part-Irish.'

'You don't understand.'

'Well, *tell* me then.'

And slowly he told her. The life of disappointment that this big square man had lived. The blame that he sent in every direction. Towards his native country for not giving him a living back in the early 1960s. To his new country for not giving him streets paved with gold as he had been led to expect. Towards his gentle, hard-working Canadian wife because she looked wistfully backwards to the peace and tranquillity of her country home. Towards his three sons who were never good enough for him, and then too good for him. Derry told the stories of the beatings and how his mother would neither leave him nor report him. His mother believed that if you said 'for better or worse', then it was easy to stay when it was better, the only testing ground was when it was worse. And that was when you really *did* have to stay.

His face was sad and twisted when he spoke of her. 'She preferred to stay in that run-down place, that place where he disappeared for days, where he had burned her with a saucepan of hot soup.'

'Maybe she was just afraid to go back to her own small town in Canada.'

'She'd have had nothing to fear there. She would have had peace, respect, roots ... far away from all he had put her through.'

It was clear to Ella that this woman must have had some happy times with her husband. It had not all been misery. There must have been times of hope ... hope that they would turn a corner. She wished that she had Derry's clear mind, that somehow she could reduce it all to four main points. But it was more complicated than that. It was a lifetime of hatred and regret.

'So I have no wish to set foot in Jim Kennedy's birthplace and see all the great sights he talked about when he was drunk.'

'Jim Kennedy?' she asked.

'My father. You don't think I kept his name, do you? He gave me nothing else. Why should I take his name? I changed it when I was old enough. And amazingly you are old enough to change your name quite early in life. I've called myself Derry King since I was fifteen. Since the day I went out to work.'

'We were asking Ella what you'd call the baby when it gets born,' Maud said to Cathy Scarlet.

'Were you, now? And did she know?' Cathy smiled.

'She said we were trying to get her mind off all the equations,' Simon said.

'And was she right?'

'Sort of, but we were wondering. We've thought of some great names ourselves.'

'I'm sure you have, but it's an oddly personal thing, Simon. Tom and I will think nearer the time.'

'You'd want to think soon,' Maud said reprovingly. 'You never know the day or the hour.'

'Well, we know vaguely the day and the hour, and it's not for another two months,' Cathy said. 'But the day and the hour that Ella is coming here again for a lesson is in two days' time, so I hope you've done all those problems she left you.'

'Her head got mended very quickly,' Simon grumbled.

'I don't think it was broken at all, to tell you the truth,' Maud agreed with him.

Cathy wondered whether to tell them to go easy on her when she came back. The girl had had terrible news while she was away. But that wasn't the kind of information anyone would ever put in Maud and Simon's direction. Ella would be worse off if the twins had been warned to treat her gently.

Ella's mother couldn't sleep. And she couldn't talk to Tim about it, either. Only the three of them knew the contents of the letter. Ella had said nothing on the telephone about Don's offer to give back what he had taken. Tim said he couldn't take those bank drafts to clear up his own and his clients' debts. It wouldn't be fair. There were too many other demands on the assets of Rice and Richardson. But if Ella cashed them and gave him the money, then he would *have* to take it. Barbara Brady prayed that she would manage to keep out of it, as her husband had pleaded that she should. It was just so hard looking at his frailty and realising that it was in Ella's power to sort all that out.

'I wish he'd come over with her, could you credit him having an allergy to coming near the place,' Nick complained.

'Ella says she has pages of notes,' Sandy consoled him.

'And the whole thing about your man has died down,' Nick said thoughtfully.

'He was never *my* man, thank God,' Sandy said.

They sat easily together in the huge apartment, looking out at the lights of New York. Their conversation was as intense as either of them had ever known, yet there were no tears or signs of upset. At no stage did they reach out to console each other. At no stage did they feel they had to backtrack on what they said, explain or apologise.

'I got us green figs as dessert ... would you like those?' Derry said.

'Love them, thank you,' Ella said.

They had drunk very little wine. She noticed that he rarely had more than one glass throughout an evening. The reaction to his father must have been very deep-seated.

'Cream with them?' he called from the kitchen.

'Please.'

She thought suddenly of Kimberly's handsome Larry telling her not to eat a fattening pasta. Possibly Derry had never served figs and cream to his beautiful wife. She wondered, had he been able to talk to her like they had talked together tonight? But she could ask him anything.

'Did Kimberly help you over any of this?'

'Immensely,' he said. 'You can see how good she is with people, and how smart. She said it was holding me back as a person, and she's right, of course. She even went to Ireland to find my roots for me, but I handed them back to her. I prefer the hate, you see. I don't want Jim Kennedy to be an ordinary, decent man who took to the hard stuff. I did all I did, and denied myself so much, just because he was a monster.'

She listened to him and was silent for a moment. 'I see – you don't want him to be normal, with normal relatives who work hard like you do. You don't want him to have an ordinary background. You want him to have come straight out of the pit of hell, all steaming and hissing.'

'Something like that,' he agreed ruefully.

They finished the figs.

'It's really your story we should be telling in a movie, isn't it,' she said with a smile.

'Oh, no, they don't make movies like that. They make them where the son goes home and everyone loves him and drinks themselves senseless and dances jigs. Then the guy goes to his father's birthplace and weeps and begs his dead father to forgive him for not talking to him more. That's what would sell.'

'I wish you were coming back to Dublin tomorrow with me, in many ways. Not for you but for me,' Ella said suddenly.

'You do? Why do you say that?' He was gentle as he always was, interested but not invasive.

'It's funny. I've only known you for just over a week, and yet I feel very safe talking to you. When I step off the plane in Ireland, I'm back in a land where anything could happen, anything *did* happen. I have to go to a city where I know Don Richardson will never walk or breathe again. That's hard. All these decisions you identified . . . I have to make them but I may do it all wrong. It would be much easier if you were there. That's all I'm saying, I suppose.'

'Very well,' he said.

'What?'

'I'll come with you,' Derry King said simply.

'You can't, not just like that?'

'But you just asked me to.' He seemed surprised.

'Yes, but why?'

'If you have to face all that and get through it, then surely I can face a few old memories,' he said.

And he took away the plate that had held her figs and cream before it fell on the floor.

11

It had never occurred to Ella that Derry King's office would have booked him first class to Dublin and neither of them discovered this until they were at Kennedy airport in New York. 'Dumb of them not to check,' he said, and went to change.

'No, please, you *must* have your comfortable seat,' Ella begged him. It was quite bad enough that he was coming to Ireland on a whim without him turning up with backache and stiff legs from travelling at the back of the bus.

But he wouldn't hear of it. 'It's only a few short hours. It would be highly antisocial and, alas, first class is full, or we'd upgrade you,' he said.

Ella began to panic. What would she talk to him about for six hours, knowing all the time that he could have stretched his legs out in comfort and watched a movie of his choice?

They heard the over-hearty laughter of a group on the other side of the departure lounge. They were rather red-faced and might have had a couple of cocktails to speed them on their trip. Ella listened to them carefully and then identified American, rather than Irish, accents.

'Yours, I think,' she said to Derry.

'What do you mean?'

'You have me so sensitive and quivering now about the Irish being loud and drunk that I'm very relieved to say that those people over there aren't my lot, they're actually yours.'

'Oh dear, that's a pity. I thought that we might keep score and tick them off,' he mocked her.

He was easy company on the plane as he had been everywhere else. Talking some of the time, reading a magazine or even sleeping a little. When the trolley passed along the aisle selling duty-free goods, the stewardess asked, 'Do you want to wake your husband in case he wants to make any purchases?'

Ella didn't correct her about the relationship. 'No, he doesn't want any, nor do I, thank you.'

She would have bought Deirdre a bottle of duty-free gin, under normal circumstances. But these were far from normal times.

Why had she said she would like him to come to Dublin? Now she had to look after him, make sure he liked the place. Confirm that he had done the right thing in lending the Foundation's name and support to this venture.

She had to draw him into her life, introduce him to her friends and family. Yes, it would certainly take her mind off Dublin now being a city without Don, but she wanted some time on her own to think about that too. Time to mourn him, without having to plunge into all this. And to decide what to do.

But to be fair, he hadn't asked her to make any arrangements for him. His office had booked his hotel, and a limousine would meet them at the airport. He said that he realised she would have to get back to work. He knew she would not be free to dine with him every night because she would possibly be working in the very restaurants where he might want to go and eat. In Quentins itself, and in Colm's restaurant up in Tara Road. It would be very different from the life of a lady that she had been leading in New York.

She looked at him as he slept. This was a man who had worked all his life. He would understand she had a living to earn.

She fell asleep herself. And dreamed a troubled dream, where Don Richardson was waiting for her at the airport, saying that he had come back from the next world for twenty-four hours to give her a message, but he had now forgotten what it was. In her dream, Ella had clutched the computer harder and harder.

She woke just before they were making their approach to Dublin in the pink Irish dawn. She heard the stewardess asking Derry King to make sure his wife's seatbelt was fastened, and he had not bothered to correct the relationship either.

She realised that there would be no Don at the airport or anywhere ever again. She bit her lip to hide what she feared might be a look of upset on her face. If he noticed, Derry said nothing. He just looked out of the window at all the green. It was hard to read his expression.

Then the plane landed, and there was no time to discuss anything.

She had never come into the city any way except the bus. It was curious to see the road from the back of a big black Mercedes. The chauffeur asked Derry which route he should take. Ella began to protest that she should be dropped at Derry's hotel in St Stephen's Green, and that then she would find her own way home from there.

Derry took no notice. 'Tara Road first, please,' he said simply, and there had been no argument.

Neither of them commented on the city that they were both looking at with new eyes. Ella was glad to see that the weather was good. It was a crisp, late-autumn day. The early-morning rush hour had not yet begun. The streets looked as if they had been cleaned by a recent shower of rain.

He could not find this place repulsive at first glance. He had to see it as a gracious city.

Derry was pleased to see some colour return to her face. She had looked very pale as they had landed. It was a series of hard things for a girl to have had to face over a period of four months. The loss of the man she considered her true love, the financial ruin of her family. And then the second loss of the suicide. Not easy for her to come back, but at least she had friends in this place. She would survive.

They made arrangements for her to pick him up at his hotel that night for an early dinner.

'This is a beautiful street,' he said when they came to Tara Road.

'Yes, but I'm round at the tradesmen's entrance these days,' she said with a bright little smile.

'Not for ever, Ella,' he consoled her.

'Well,' she shrugged.

'Shall I take the car up the lane, Madam?' the chauffeur enquired.

'No, it would get stuck, I'm afraid. Just leave me at the corner, if you don't mind.'

The chauffeur was about to carry her case but she wouldn't hear of it.

'See you tonight at six, Derry.' She ran off before anyone could say more, down the narrow lane behind the big houses of Tara Road to where her parents would be waiting, up already for hours, and peering out the windows of what used to be the garden shed.

Ella couldn't sleep. She tried, but it didn't work. Her mother had gone to work, her father sat at the kitchen table moving papers around him. The huge, paper sunflowers looked cheerful in the window as she had known they would. She looked across at the house where her parents had lived since their marriage until this summer. She remembered Derry King saying that this situation would not be for ever. Maybe a man thought differently, in that he would work and scheme and slave to get it all back. While Ella would lose it all and more on top of it if she only thought she could see Don just once more. She wished she could sleep because she felt a great weariness and sense that life was going to be so empty from now on, it didn't really matter what happened.

In his hotel room, Derry King paced up and down. He had a stiff neck from the plane journey. His eyes felt heavy. In theory, he should be able to sleep. In the past, when he had criss-crossed the United States to go to conventions, meetings, sales conferences, his ability to snatch sleep had been legendary. He would wake refreshed and ready for everything.

But it was different here. These were the streets that Jim Kennedy had walked when he was young. This was the land that had not given him a living or an understanding, the city he had fled to find a better and brighter life. Jim Kennedy would not have been welcome in a hotel of this calibre. He would not have been allowed past the door. But those small bars they had passed on the journey from the airport, places with family names over the door, that would have been his territory. And in the telephone directory there were people who could tell Derry about it all.

But he didn't want to ask and learn. He didn't know what he wanted to do. For years he had steeled himself against useless regrets and time-wasting, wishing himself elsewhere. There had been too much maudlin 'if only' in his father's conversations. Derry King would be no part of it. He would spend no time wondering why he had decided to come to this place. Nor wishing that he had stayed where he was and taken Fennel for a three-hour walk every day in Central Park. He was here now and he would make the best of it. And if sleep would not come, then he must go out and walk in that park across from his hotel.

Brenda Brennan's friend Nora was working in the kitchen. She knew that the American was in town. The one who would provide the money to make the film about Quentins.

'Will he sneak in to have a look at the place, do you think?' Signora asked as she expertly cleaned and diced vegetables that Blouse Brennan produced triumphantly in ever more earth-covered trays.

'No, I think he's too smart for that,' Brenda said thoughtfully. 'He'll have to meet us sooner or later, so he doesn't want to be unmasked as someone having a private peek.'

'That's true, but I bet he has a private peek through the window sometime today, don't you?' Signora said.

'Oh, definitely,' Brenda laughed.

Patrick Brennan looked at them. Women's friendships were amazing. Brenda and Nora O'Donoghue had been so close since they had all met at catering college. Even the years Nora had spent in Sicily didn't seem to have broken it, they wrote each other long letters all that time. It didn't matter that one of them ran the restaurant and the other was scraping vegetables in it. They were still equals. Still like girls, giggling over whether a rich American would come and peek in the window. Patrick wished that men had friendships like that, where there were no secrets, where nothing was hidden.

'Would he be the kind of fellow that would fall for me, do you think?' Deirdre asked in the café at lunchtime.

Ella had begged her to have a quick lunch and they were having a sandwich near Deirdre's work.

'No, I don't think he would. He's too interested in work, more work and art and brooding and more work and homeless dogs to have any time for you,' Ella said.

'Hey, I could be interested in all those things too if I wanted to,' Deirdre protested.

'Well, your powers are extraordinary, Dee. We all know that . . . and what do I know? When you meet him, you might start to sing arias at each other.'

'And will I meet him?'

'Of course you will. I'm just trying to work out where. It can't be Quentins. That has to be formal and work and everything . . . we haven't room to swing a cat at our home these days, otherwise I'd have a Sunday lunch for him to meet my friends . . .'

'I could have a Sunday lunch in my place if you like,' Deirdre offered.

'Would you, Dee? And we could ask Nick and Sandy.' Ella was pleased.

'Your parents could come, and Tom and Cathy,' Deirdre said.

'Oh, Dee, what would I do without you?'

'Nuala is back in town, but I think not, don't you?' Deirdre said.

'I think very much not.' Ella was reflective.

'Sorry for bringing her up,' Deirdre said. 'But you might just run into her or Frank of the one-track mind.'

'Now that Don's dead, do you think he'll shut up about it all, and let him rest in peace?'

'Are you asking me for an honest answer?'

'Of course I am.'

'Then I don't think that people like Frank and his brothers would let anyone rest in peace while they think that someone owes them a sum of money.'

'Oh well, welcome back to the real world, Ella,' she told herself ruefully.

'You never left the real world, Ella! You're terrific to cope with all that's being fired at you. Truly you are.'

'No, you're right, I'll survive.'

'I'm only babbling on because I honestly don't have the words to tell you face to face how sorry I am about what Don did. It's a nightmare for you, and I just want you to understand that I know this.' Deirdre's eyes were full of tears.

'Let's think of what we'll eat on Sunday,' Ella said. She could cope with anything but sympathy just now.

Tom and Cathy were delighted with the invitation to lunch. Something they didn't have to cook and serve themselves. It was heaven. But there was a problem which they had to work around.

'Deirdre, we'd just love to come to lunch, and we'll bring you a really luscious dessert from the freezer,' Tom offered.

'You don't need to do that. I'd love it, but you don't need to . . .'

'We do.'

'Why?' Deirdre was suspicious.

'Because we're going to ask you if we can bring the twins. We're meant to be looking after them that day. Muttie and Lizzie are going on an outing. We said we'd take the kids. They're so mad and awful really we thought if we gave you a roulade *and* a pavlova it might sort of make up.'

'How mad and awful?' Deirdre asked.

'Just desperately curious and inquisitive, really. They ask all kinds of intimate questions without realising it. They might offer to dance, but we can close them down on that.'

'No, we might need it if it's all a bit sticky. Ella says they're great value. Of course they can come and I get two puddings as well.' Deirdre sounded well pleased.

'What's the worst Maud and Simon could say to this rich American guy, do you think?' Cathy asked Tom.

'They're very into mating conversations just now. They could ask him about his sexual habits, I suppose,' Tom suggested.

'Oh, yes, they'll definitely want to know about who he mates with. I was wondering if they want parts in the film or anything, you know how much they like to belong,' said Cathy.

'I'm sure he'll be able to deal with them.' Tom hoped he sounded more certain than he felt.

Ella called in to Firefly Films. They weren't expecting her. They hadn't their response ready.

'It's all so unfair, Ella,' Sandy began.

'People put too much pressure on him,' said Nick, who used to say that there was no pit of hell deep enough for Don Richardson.

'Yes, when Derry King's gone back to New York, I'll cry on your shoulder, believe me I will, but now we have to work out how to make the best of his sudden decision to come here. I'm meeting him tonight to go over our notes.'

She saw their faces lighten. This was exactly what they had hoped for, but they didn't want to appear crass by not acknowledging that the love of her life had first left her and then killed himself. They sat down to plan the campaign.

Nick and Sandy looked at her with admiration as she pushed the hair out of her eyes. She took out an armful of files, some with coloured stickers on them.

'There are so many different ways we could go. In a way it will depend on who talks best. But come on, let's have a look at the stories anyway.'

Starters

Derek Barry was entertaining a couple of wealthy clients to lunch. He didn't actually know them. But Bob O'Neill, his partner, had been most insistent.

They put plenty of work through the books of Barry and O'Neill Accountants, and they were threatening to move elsewhere.

All they needed was some stroking and patting and reassurance. Bob had intended to take them himself, but his plane was delayed in London and he couldn't get back. Derek must hold the fort.

There had been hardly any time to check them out. All he knew was their bank balance. That and the fact that Bob O'Neill, the senior partner in the firm, said that it was a Must Do.

So, Derek sighed and booked a table in Quentins.

That was one advantage of being the father of the restaurant's owner. He always got a table there. He arrived early.

'Where can I put you, Mr Barry?' Brenda Brennan was always outwardly polite, but he felt she didn't like him.

'It doesn't really matter, Brenda. I'm meeting a pair of clients, Bob's, not mine, loads of money, dot-com millionaires or something. Complete nobodies.' He shook his head disapprovingly.

'Well, I hope they'll enjoy their lunch, Mr Barry.'

She was too cool. He didn't like it. She was, after all, an employee of his son Quentin, and so was her husband, that fancy chef Patrick. Derek Barry, small and self-important, sat down at his table, bristling with a sense that he wasn't being treated with enough respect.

The couple were shown to his table. In their late thirties, he decided, big, both of them, far from elegant, cheap, ill-fitting clothes. The woman carried a shabby handbag, the man wore a loud jacket. They looked out of place in this quiet, smart restaurant, decorated for Christmas, but not garishly so. Little Christmas trees with small white lights dotted around.

Still, Bob O'Neill had been adamant. These two were to get the treatment. They paid big fees for the firm's services. Derek Barry was to make sure that they were happy and continued to be so.

'Mr and Mrs Costello, what a pleasure,' he said, standing up. 'I'm Mr Barry.'

'Bob O'Neill's not coming to the dinner?' the woman said, surprised that the table was set only for three.

'Er . . . no. Mr O'Neill sends his best regards but you know the pressure of business ... he was delayed in London. And as one of the senior partners myself, I thought it was time for us to get to know each other.' Derek hated her calling lunch 'dinner', and in a place like this.

'Well, I'm Jimmy and my wife is Cath,' the man said.

'Ah,' Derek said.

'What's your first name?' Cath asked.

It was ignorant rather than impolite, Derek thought, just a woman with no social graces. He wished he had made the time to find out exactly what kind of business they were in.

He told them his name.

'So you drew the short straw, Derek,' said Jimmy, settling in and looking at the menu.

Flinching at the way his first name was being used so easily, Derek asked nervously what that meant.

'Well, I suppose it means that Bob O'Neill sent you to this dinner to do his dirty work,' Jimmy explained cheerfully.

'Like, so that you'll be blamed when we take our business away from you,' Cath added. 'Do they serve draught beer here? I'd really love a pint.'

Derek Barry felt dizzy. Things were moving out of control. People calling lunch 'dinner' and wanting pints in Quentins. These two people talking casually about moving their business away from the firm.

'Well, well, whatever we must be, we must not be hasty,' he said.

'No haste at all, Derek,' Jimmy said good-naturedly. 'We'll just come back to the office with you after our dinner and collect the papers.'

Derek Barry felt a slow anger begin to burn inside him. Had Bob O'Neill realised how serious the situation with these people was? Probably not. Jimmy and Cath Costello were not the kind of people Bob would have known socially. But he would have known that something was wrong. That was why he had made Derek the fall guy.

Cath was deep in the menu. 'Are we all going to have starters?' she asked, almost childlike in her enthusiasm.

'I don't know what any of them are,' Jimmy said, examining the list.

They were about to lose wealthy clients, and this woman with her tight perm and her nylon scarf twisted around her neck was proving to be far too confident in a restaurant of this standing.

The waitress said her name was Monica, Mon for short, and she was delighted to help. This one was quails' eggs, tiny little things, in a bed of pastry with a gorgeous sauce served on the side. This one was kidneys with a mustard sauce on toasted scone.

'I never had a quail's egg,' said Jimmy. 'But I'd love kidneys in mustard sauce. I'm in a lather of indecision.'

'I'm the same way myself, Jimmy. We'll have two starters, that's what we'll have.'

'I don't really think ...' Derek began. But he stopped. There was something about Cath's expression that he didn't like. It was as if she could see right through him, could read his embarrassment and snobbish feelings about her earthy way of going on.

'Are you going to have starters and mains?' she asked Derek with interest.

He tried not to shudder and show how little he liked every phrase she uttered. These vulgar people were important to his company. Bob had said only this morning that they couldn't afford to lose their business. So Derek knew he must turn on his charm.

'Before I decide what to eat, why don't you let me get some drinks in, Cath and ... er ... Jimmy, and then you'll tell me what it is you actually do.'

'But you know what we do,' Cath said simply. 'You are our accountants. You must know what we do.'

'Well, you see, as you said, it's really Bob O'Neill who deals with you ... very big firm, lots of clients nowadays, many different aspects, the whole problem of expanding ...' He looked at them helplessly.

'Then why did you ask us to dinner?' Jimmy asked, tearing his bread roll apart as if it were a killer fish which he had to demolish first.

'Bob couldn't make it himself this once. So he asked me to stand in at the last moment ...'

'And you never looked us up?' Jimmy said. 'Lord, I wouldn't last one day if I didn't know about the people I was meeting.'

Derek looked miserable. 'I'm sorry, Mr Costello – I'm sorry, Jimmy. You're right. It was a courtesy and I did not have time. I didn't make time. I apologise. Can you tell me about yourselves? Now?'

'What do you want to know, Derek?' Jimmy asked.

Derek wondered what to ask them. 'Do you have children?' he heard himself ask. He wondered why he had said it. Normally he never asked about people's families.

'Do you?' Cath asked in a level voice.

'Yes, just one son. He didn't follow me into the business, as I had hoped he would. I even had a room ready for him, but I'm afraid he didn't take to the accountancy business.'

'Imagine!' Cath said. 'And did he do all right on his own?'

'Very well. This is his restaurant, as it happens.'

'Well, you must be delighted with him,' Cath said, her eyes far away.

'And your children?' Derek asked. 'Did they go into your business with you?' Again he didn't know why he wanted to know. He was not one for the personal question.

'No, we went into it for them, really,' Jimmy said.

There was a silence. Derek knew that he must smile and be charming. Tomorrow he could rail at Bob O'Neill for landing him in all this so very ill-prepared. Today, he had to get these people on his side.

'So? Your actual day-to-day work?' he said, his face nearly splitting with a smile.

'Takes up about sixteen or seventeen hours of the twenty-four,' Cath said, in a matter-of-fact way.

'Starting at six in the morning and ending at ten or eleven with a pint before closing time,' Jimmy explained.

'But surely you don't need to work that hard?' he said, appalled.

'Oh, we do,' Cath said.

'But Bob O'Neill told me that you were very financially secure.' Derek was bewildered. 'Why do you work so hard?'

'To forget,' Cath said simply. 'To take our minds off the children.'

'The children?' He looked from one to the other.

'Bob didn't tell you?' They couldn't believe it.

'No, he told me nothing.' Derek was ashamed.

'We had three children who died in a fire ten years ago. We nearly went mad, but someone told us that if we worked and worked it would make it better.'

Derek looked at them wordlessly.

'So we did just that,' Jimmy said.

'Hour after hour, year after year,' Cath said. 'It wasn't great, of course, but I think it would be worse if we hadn't. We've no way of knowing, but I think I would have been worse if there had been time to think.'

'I suppose it gave you a comfortable lifestyle, anyway,' Derek said. He didn't know how to sympathise. Better to look on the bright side.

They looked at him, speechless.

'What do you actually do for a living?' Derek asked eventually.

'Fund-raise,' Cath said. 'Didn't you know? Doesn't Bob tell you anything at all?'

'I'm beginning to think he doesn't,' Derek said. 'He told me you were very wealthy people.'

'Worth a dinner?' Jimmy said.

'Worth a dinner, yes.' Derek felt ashamed.

'And you didn't even know that we're leaving your firm?' Cath asked.

'No, not until I met you. No. And of course nothing is definite yet . . .'

'He's an odd kind of partner then, Derek,' Cath said.

'I don't really know the whole story,' Derek blustered a little.

'We went to your firm because you were respectable and well thought of. If we could put your name on the bottom of our notepaper it gave us a bit of standing. People couldn't think we were just two yobbos . . .'

'I'm sure they wouldn't have thought . . .' Derek began to protest.

Jimmy interrupted him: 'Of course that's what people would say. Two poor, mad yobbos who can't see straight because of their own tragedy. Why should anyone give us money and believe that we'd spend it right? That's why we needed people like you. Or thought we did.'

'Oh, but you do . . .' Derek began again.

'No, we don't. We realised this. You see, we said to Bob that we thought the fees were a bit steep . . .' Cath said.

'Not that we thought you should work for free or anything, just because our work is for charity . . .' Jimmy said.

'But it turned out that he didn't really care at all about what we were doing. He just looked at a file and said there seemed to be a very healthy profit balance and he didn't know what we were complaining about.' Cath was indignant.

'He said there are sort of fixed rates an hour,' Jimmy said.

'Which there are, of course,' Derek said. 'But I imagine we could discuss . . .'

'No, that's not it. You see, he didn't even care that we are a charity,' Cath said.

'Oh, come come come . . . of course he does. Of course the firm realised you were a charitable . . . organisation, but . . .' Derek said with a little laugh.

'You didn't,' she said simply.

It was unanswerable.

Brenda Brennan was at their table supervising the serving of a second starter. She also handed Cath an envelope.

'Mrs Costello, everyone in the kitchen was so impressed when they heard you were both here, they made an immediate collection for your children's fund. Every single person contributed.'

'How did they know we were here?' Jimmy wondered.

'I'm afraid we recognised you from television. Believe me, Mr Barry was very discreet about you. Gave us no information at all about you, concealed your identity even.' Her eyes were hard and cold.

Derek remembered how he had described his guests. He flushed darkly to think about it.

Jimmy got out a postcard and wrote a thank-you note to the people in the kitchen. Cathy took a receipt book out of her big, shabby handbag. They counted the money and sent a receipt to the kitchen staff as well.

Two honest people maddened with grief over lost children, people who had now been ignored and patronised by his own accountancy firm. He longed to reach out and touch them and hold their hands, beg them to tell him what had happened the night their children died. He wanted to take out his chequebook and give them a donation that would stun them. He could have told them that not everyone has it easy. Take Derek's own life, for example. His wife had left him for a few years. She came back remote and distant. His son lived abroad and kept in very little contact. He felt he could talk to these odd people about it, and he would see they got not only vastly reduced fees, but that they also got a sponsorship as well.

These thoughts welled up, but Derek was a man used to thinking long and carefully before he spoke, so he said nothing. And he missed the moment where Cath had seen some softness in his eyes, and where Jimmy had thought for a second or two that Derek might not be a bad old skin.

Instead of speaking with his heart, Derek spoke with his accountant's mind.

And, as the three of them left Quentins to go back to the firm where they would pick up their papers and he would face the wrath of Bob O'Neill, Derek saw people from other tables smile at them and even clasp their hands as the Costellos walked with him.

Nobody greeted Derek Barry, partner in the accountancy firm and father of the proprietor of Quentins.

The world had changed, and not for the better.

The Independent Streak

Laura Lynch was forty when her husband left home. There had been no row. He just said it had been an empty, shallow, one-way relationship. She had not grown or developed within the marriage while he had and bettered himself.

Laura had been so dependent, so lacking in get-up-and-go, so he could no longer stay in something that was making neither of them happy. And he left with a much younger colleague, who had no problem at all in getting up and going. He had been coldly and clinically fair in the division of property, and even given her some unasked-for advice.

'If I were you, Laura, I would develop an Independent Streak,' he said quite seriously, as if he had not insisted that she be a stay-at-home mother for their children.

And in the twenty years since he left, Laura Lynch did indeed develop an independent streak. She needed one since it was hard work, turning what had been the family home into a guest house. The children were fifteen, fourteen and thirteen at the time of the break-up. All of them much more like their father in personality. Independent to a fault, Laura sometimes thought.

It was never a house of hugs and spontaneous gestures. They showed no need for any emotional exchanges or confidences. So Laura learned to be independent. She learned not to be needy and never to allow herself to feel disappointed and let down over things.

She had hoped that she might meet someone and marry again, but it did not look likely. She managed her money well, and once she had sold the guest house to buy a small garden flat, she made a sort of social life with friends of her own choosing. There were bridge lessons, and theatre groups, and creative writing classes. No empty evenings to sit brooding and wondering why she heard so little from the two daughters and son and four grandchildren that she loved so much. She must indeed have been a very dull and dependent woman as her ex-husband had said.

Amazing that she had not resented his cold parting words, but had actually heeded them instead.

It was great that Mother had such an independent streak, they told each other. A lot of their friends had the most dreadful problems with clinging mothers, interfering mothers, critical mothers. They were indeed blessed with their own.

The Lynch family often told each other this when they met once a month in Quentins for Saturday lunch. It was a tradition they enjoyed: Harry Lynch and his sisters, Lil and Kate. No spouses, just the three of them, twelve times a year they kept up with each other's lives, unlike many families they knew who just lost touch.

Lil looked forward to these Saturdays. She got her hair done and went to the charity shop. Lil's husband, Bob, was careful about money. He said that anyone with a good eye could pick up the most marvellous stylish bargains there. And he was right, Lil said defensively, as she often did. Her sons had Saturday jobs, their father didn't believe in letting young people idle about.

Kate loved the family lunch, too. Weekends were often lonely for her, since Charlie went back to his wife and children for the weekend to keep stability in the family. Charlie was so wonderful to her brother and sister: he admired Lil's crazy 1980s jackets and always asked about Harry's endless garden work.

Harry enjoyed the lunch meeting. He found Lil's Bob rather trying, telling him how to save money on phone calls, and there was something phoney about Kate's Charlie, who appeared to be running two establishments quite cheerfully. Nice to see his two sisters on their own, and tell them about the new pergola and how well the azaleas had done when repotted. He would talk too about Jan and the girls, who always spent Saturdays at the gym and didn't know where Harry had his lunch or even if he had his lunch.

Brenda Brennan wondered how long they had been coming in, these Lynches. Must be nearly fifteen years now, or was it more? From time to time she had seen Kate in here with that Charlie, the man about town who usually brought his wife here for anniversaries or birthdays. Still, people made their own arrangements, Brenda shrugged – as she often did about the way her customers lived their lives. She knew that Lil was married to a man who had a very good job.

Bob often brought big groups to Quentins for very pricey meals. He always checked and sometimes queried the bill. Maybe that's why his wife dressed in other people's cast-offs. Harry Lynch was a dull bank clerk, whose eyes only lit up when he talked to her about growing vegetables. It was fairly easy for Brenda to talk about vegetables, since Quentins prided themselves on their homegrown organic produce. But how did people in the bank react, she wondered. But this was not her business.

Her husband said that she got far too involved in people's lives. 'Just serve them, Brenda,' Patrick would plead.

But there was no life in that sort of thing, and anyway, part of Quentins' success was due to the fact that she remembered who people were and all about them. She knew that the Lynch family always chose pasta, so she came armed with information about the really good pesto. Contained pine nuts of course, just in case anyone was allergic, but a very distinctive flavour. They would have one glass of house wine each, and Kate would stay on to read her paper and have a second and third glass on her own. There was not much that escaped Brenda.

'I see that there's a booking for twelve, under the name of Lynch, for Mother's Day. Is that your family?' Brenda asked brightly. The moment she had asked she regretted it. They were bewildered, looking at each other in surprise.

'Mother's Day. No, that's not us. We usually just give Jan a bunch of flowers from the garden,' Harry said.

'My boys wouldn't be able to afford this . . . and Bob, well, he doesn't like big gatherings,' Lil said.

'A lot of these Mother's Days and other things are just purely commercial,' Kate said with her brow darkening. Charlie's wife would undoubtedly get the full works.

Brenda recovered herself. 'You're so right, Kate, it only benefits us and the florists and of course the card manufacturers. Still, we are happy to see it! That's commercialism for you, of course!' She laughed easily and moved back to the kitchen, mopping her brow.

'Sometimes, not all the time, Patrick, but sometimes I think you're right about not getting involved in their lives,' she said ruefully.

'What have you said now?' he laughed affectionately.

'I just thought that the Lynches at table nine might have booked to take their mother out for lunch a week from tomorrow, but the thought had never crossed their little minds.'

'We don't need any more bookings. We couldn't cope with them. We're full.' Patrick was mystified.

'That's not the point. They have a mother, they haven't booked her in anywhere at all.'

'Leave it alone, Brenda,' Patrick said, shaking a spoon at her.

'Do you think she might have meant had we booked for Mother?' Kate asked.

'But we never did anything like that. Mother wouldn't have expected it. Nor wanted it,' Harry said. He would have to do a lot of persuading to get Jan and the girls to go along with such a scheme. Sundays were for long healthy walks, not for sitting down and ingesting calories.

'And even if we were to ask Mother out to lunch, it couldn't be a place like this,' Kate said. Kate had a particular distaste for those kinds of wives and mothers who wanted a silly expensive fuss made over them, just to reinforce their status.

'And she's so independent,' Lil said. 'She's always doing something whenever you want to see her.'

'Yes, I suppose so,' Kate said.

'I see her very often,' Harry protested. 'We have coffee quite a lot, as a matter of fact.'

'Only because she goes to the garden centre on late-night opening to meet you there,' Kate said.

There was a silence. Harry seemed put out. 'At least I do see her, and as Lil said, she has a fiercely independent streak. When do you see her?'

'I often ring her and suggest that we go to the cinema on the spur of the moment. Half the time she's doing something else,' Kate said. She knew that the others would realise that she only rang her mother on the nights when Charlie was unexpectedly unable to meet her.

'It's a long way for her to get into town to meet you,' Lil said.

'So what do you do for her, Lil?' Kate asked, stung.

Lil paused to think. 'When we go to the market and get vegetables in bulk, we often drop in. You can only buy things in huge quantities, and this way it works out cheaper for Mother, you know . . .' Her voice trailed away.

'She's got loads of friends,' Harry said defensively.

'And would hate waste.' Lil was very definite on this.

'I suppose she would consider it a waste?' Kate had done the unforgivable. She had introduced some doubt about Mother's independent streak, the one solid pillar that had given them all the freedom to get on with their slightly complicated lives without considering the needs of a sixty-year-old woman, whose husband had left her two decades previously.

Lil and Harry were uncomfortable. Kate was sorry she had spoken. Their pleasant lunch was turning to ashes on them and it was all her fault. Kate needed her brother and sister rather more than they needed her. After all, they had the fairly unsatisfactory Bob and Jan, plus, of course, their children. Kate had nothing but the part-time attention of Charlie.

'Look, why don't I phone and ask her out somewhere? That would cover it.'

'We don't want to leave it all to you . . .' Lil protested very feebly.

'I mean, perhaps we could . . . I mean . . .' Harry said very unconvincingly.

'No, honestly, I'll do it. I know that dragon lady, Brenda Brennan, hates mobile phones, but if I whisper, she can't complain.' Kate saved the lunch for them.

Mother thanked her and said it was sweet of Kate, but she and a group of friends had already planned to go out that day. But she really did want to thank Kate. So they looked at each other with relief. The day and the ritual of their monthly lunch was secure again. Silly of Kate to have thought Mother, who was so independent, might be at a loose end.

Laura Lynch sat very still for a while. This was the first time that any of her children had offered to celebrate Mother's Day or acknowledged it in any form other than a small, dutiful card.

How odd that she hadn't even been tempted to accept Kate's offer. But there wasn't a question of it. She would so much prefer the previous engagement.

As part of her Independent Streak, Laura had created an annual outing. It was called the Chickless Mothers. Women like herself, who did not have loving or demonstrative families. Women for whom there would be no breakfast in bed and huge fuss made. They knew the expression 'a motherless chick' – it was in some song. But the opposite held good too. The only rules for the outing were that they enjoy themselves, they did not speak disparagingly of their thoughtless young, nor were they allowed to make defensive speeches excusing them. It had worked very well for the past years, and on each occasion they chose a different restaurant.

This year it would be Quentins.

And the twelve Chickless Mothers would certainly enjoy that.

The Molluscs

Patrick Brennan was very annoyed when the message came. His routine prostate examination required him to return to the district hospital for some more tests.

Probably nothing at all to worry about, he had been told by the cheerful young woman from the hospital – a woman who was maybe fifteen years younger than him and who would never have to have a prostate examination herself anyway. Easy for her to say there was nothing to worry about.

'It's all your fault for making me have this checkup,' he grumbled to Brenda. 'One of the busiest weeks in the year, and I have to be out of the restaurant having bits of me poked at and frightening myself to death.'

Brenda ignored him. She was consulting her big contacts book. She would find someone who could cover for him in the restaurant. Patrick knew this.

'If I died, you could just look up that book and replace me in six months,' he said.

'Why should I wait six months?' Brenda asked, absently. 'We'll ask Cathy Scarlet or Tom Feather. One of them will do it for us.'

Anyone she suggested he would object to, and they both knew it.

'They have their own business to run,' Patrick complained. 'They can't abandon that and come in to run our kitchens because some fool in the hospital couldn't do proper tests on me first time round.'

'We helped them in the past, Patrick, and they'll do it. After all, you're only going to be out for three days.'

'That's what they say.' Patrick's voice was sepulchral.

'Oh, for God's sake, will you stop upsetting yourself. And me, Patrick. You're going to be fine and those two will be delighted to come in. Either of them could cope with anything.'

'Don't tell them what is ... what's wrong with me,' Patrick said.

'No, Patrick, I'll just say it's a mystery illness ... some kind of plague originating in our kitchens. Would that satisfy you?'

He smiled for the first time. And stretched out his hand to her.

'It's just that I was worried, if you get my drift,' he began hesitantly.

She squeezed his hand very hard. 'My drift is the same, Patrick my love, but we're both mad to be worried. Instead we should be delighted that we live in such modern medical times.' Brenda blew her nose. 'Now can I ring these two and get us sorted?' she said, briskly.

'You never said yes? Not this week, when we have so much on?' Cathy Scarlet's mouth was a round 'O' of horror and amazement.

'What was I to say? The poor guy has to go back for more tests. Obviously he thinks he's for the high jump.'

'It's probably just routine.'

'Yes, for you and me it looks like routine because it's happening to someone else. Suppose it were us?' Tom Feather's handsome face was upset.

'I know.' Cathy did know. She would have responded exactly the same way.

'So we do it?' Tom checked.

'Of course we do. I was just having a grumble. But don't forget we have that awful family with their graduation party.'

'I know, but we can use Quentins' kitchen to do some of that work there. Brenda said we can use the place as our own.'

Tom had learned that it was often wiser to tell Cathy the good news and let the bad news creep up on them. So he didn't tell her that Brenda said there was going to be a shellfish banquet organised by a company who were really and truly the People From Hell. That would be faced later.

Blouse Brennan drove his brother to the hospital. 'Should I say we'll manage fine without, or should I say we'll be lost entirely?' he asked, innocently.

Patrick managed a weak smile. 'Say you'll manage fine without me for three days but after that you'd be lost entirely,' he suggested.

'I'll make sure the vegetables are top class,' Blouse said soothingly.

'This is the week when I wish you grew oysters, scallops, clams and mussels in that garden of yours,' Patrick said.

'Molluscs,' Blouse said, proudly.

'That's right.' Patrick was surprised. His young brother had been a slow learner at school and to this day frequently read instructions on a packet by putting his finger under each word. Imagine him knowing a word like mollusc!

'The very thing, Blouse.' Patrick tried to keep the amazement out of his voice.

'I'm interested in them. They have no say in anything, did you know that, Paddy? They're just swept along by the tide and stick to rocks. They never make a decision of any kind. Isn't it a queer sort of life?'

'Well, I suppose it is, but no worse than for a lot of sea creatures,' Patrick said, mystified.

'Aw, no, Paddy, a crustacean has legs after all, or claws, and a lot of them even have a jointed shell. They've got a load of choices where to go. Not like your poor mollusc.'

Patrick Brennan took his small suitcase out of the car and went into the hospital. While he was waiting to check in, he thought about the conversation with Blouse.

He would tell Brenda about it when she came to settle him in for the night.

Brenda admired the way Tom and Cathy got down to business and how well they got on with the waiters. Monica, the Australian girl, Yan, the Breton, and Harry, a new boy from Belfast, listened intently as Tom explained how the dishes would be cooked.

'Stay up at the hospital for longer, Brenda,' Cathy pleaded. 'I can do your front-of-house bit for one night. I've seen you do it often enough. Just go through the bookings with me first and then tell me if there's anything I should know.'

From Brenda's face it looked as if she were going to agree.

After all, there was a very solid team already in place.

Mon was a great sunny waitress. Nothing could go wrong with her tables.

Yan the handsome Breton boy was charm itself.

Even Harry the newcomer was showing signs of being a reliable lad. He had the huge advantage of realising that he didn't know everything and the ability to ask when in doubt.

But even though she was tempted, Brenda said that Patrick would never get better if he thought there was nobody minding the shop. So she waited until the dinner was well under way before she got her coat and left them to return to Patrick. 'Save your strength for the real horrors ahead on Wednesday,' she said as she left.

'What real horrors?' Cathy asked Tom when Brenda had gone to the hospital.

'Oh, you know, just the usual Wednesday people,' poor Tom stammered.

'Tom. You are the worst liar in the world. Tell me what's happening on Wednesday or else I shall take out both of your eyes with the melon baller.'

He told her about the shellfish banquet for this hated public relations company.

'A seafood buffet?' she asked.

'No, specifically shellfish, the guy said. Not salmon, not smoked salmon, not trout. Unless the thing lives in its shell it doesn't get on our table.' Tom tried to make light of it.

'We can't do it,' Cathy said, grimly.

'What do you mean? We have to.'

'Listen, Tom, I've been doing the fish-buying for the last couple of weeks. The catch is very small. There were practically no prawns, the lobster cost a fortune, and the oysters had all gone to France.'

'But they'd have contacts . . . I mean, this is Quentins. They wouldn't be Mickey Mouse like us . . . they must spend a fortune on fish, for God's sake . . .'

'Well, let's pray they do,' Cathy said.

'We've a lot of stuff frozen back at the premises. We could give them that.'

'We can't. We thawed the lot today for the Demon Graduation Party.'

'Oh, God, please, please, nice God, won't you be very good to us and let us lay our hands on some shellfish?' Tom prayed.

'Tell me more about this job on Wednesday,' Cathy asked Brenda when Quentins had closed. They sat in the kitchen rubbing their ankles and drinking great mugs of tea.

'Something we should never have taken on. He's the most disgusting man. He fights every bill, upsets the staff . . . It has been a bit slow recently, so I thought it would be worthwhile. But I fear we have a few problems.'

'Like?' Cathy said, although she knew the problem only too well.

'Like a grave shortage of shellfish. No joy from the usual sources, I'm afraid. I've been on to them all.'

'He'll have to take salmon like everyone else. We'll tell him, Brenda, he can't expect someone to do a quick miracle these days. Those times are long gone.' Cathy spoke firmly as if to encourage her own flagging spirits.

Brenda looked up. Her face was white and drawn. 'I wish you hadn't said that. I was sort of relying on the thought that there might be a few miracles still hovering around.'

The Tuesday seemed to be ninety hours long for everybody. For Patrick, in hospital, the time crawled. He forced himself not to look at his watch again. They would have to come for him sometime soon.

Back at Scarlet Feather's premises, Tom, busy dressing the lobster for the Graduation Lunch, feared catching sight of the clock in case he would panic at how behind they were. They really needed Cathy today, but she was down at Quentins.

Cathy was purple in the face trying to rescue cream sauce that had unaccountably curdled. Brenda showed the guests to their tables with her usual polite, welcoming smile. Inside she was churning. It was lunchtime – surely the doctors must have seen Patrick by now. And if they had, why hadn't she heard? Her friend among the nurses promised to call as soon as the test results came through. Please, please, may it not be bad news.

Tom phoned when the pressure in Quentins Restaurant was at its height. Sorry, sorry, he knew this was the worst time, but the Graduation Party had hit another low. Could someone, anyone, come over with a big bowl of tomato salad? The Graduate's mother was now losing what remained of her senses and was weeping over something that had never been ordered. Was there a chance? If they only knew what it was like here!

'If you knew what it's like here!' Cathy said. She had the phone clamped against her ear while she mixed more sauce and issued directions to the waiters. Brenda's strained face moved in and out of the dining room. She didn't need another crisis.

'I'll send Blouse,' Cathy said. 'Give him the address, will you, and get off the phone quickly in case the hospital rings.'

*

At half-past two, Patrick was told he had the all clear. Could he get back to the restaurant? he asked. Apparently not, still a few formalities to go through. And rest. He must rest. But he could leave tomorrow.

Three minutes later, he was on the phone to Brenda. Cathy handed her a paper towel to wipe the tears from her immaculately made-up face. The staff looked away so as not to catch Mrs Brennan with her guard down.

'Where's Blouse?' she wanted to know.

'Don't ask,' Cathy pleaded. But she wondered where on earth he actually was. It was an hour and a half since he'd left in a taxi. Please may there not have been yet another disaster to drive them mad. Had he found the right house? When she next had two seconds, she would call Tom.

But Tom called first. 'Can you talk?'

'Sure. Great news. Patrick's okay. And he'll be back tomorrow.'

'Good news here, too . . .' Tom began.

'Listen, I'm sorry for interrupting you, but have you any idea where Blouse is?'

'He's here, saving our lives.'

'The tomato salad?' she asked, bewildered.

'No, nobody's eating that, like I told them.'

'So what's he doing, then?' Nothing would surprise Cathy by this stage.

'There are about fourteen horrific children, monsters all of them. Anyway, they were annoying everyone, breaking things, sulking. Blouse has them all down at the bottom of the garden. He's running a herb competition.'

'What?'

'You wouldn't believe it. He has them captivated. They all have little yoghurt pots or cream cartons. And he's talking about lovage and verbena.'

'What about the Graduate's mum?'

'Mrs Dracula is fine. She's my new best friend, as it happens.'

'Oh, tell me about it. You turned on the charm. Maybe you could charm some shells out of the rocks for us for tomorrow here?'

'That not sorted yet?'

'No, but we're on the case.'

From his hospital bed, Patrick Brennan was also on the case. And the news was very bad. Not a prawn or lobster to be found. Patrick rang the PR man.

'Why does it have to be shellfish . . . please, just tell me?'

'It's an image, a concept – the whole idea of sticking fast. We've used it in our literature just to attract this client's account. You're not telling me you're going to go back on the agreed menu . . .'

'I'm not telling you anything. What are you advertising?'

'It's no business of yours . . .'

'What is meant to be sticking to what? What's the concept about? Can't you tell me? We're doing the bloody presentation for you,' Patrick roared.

'All you were asked to do was to provide a shellfish buffet.'

'It's in your interest to tell me,' Patrick lowered his voice impressively.

The PR man eventually gave in and told him it was a new insurance company that stuck with you through thick and thin.

'In that case you don't need shellfish, you eejit. You need molluscs.'

'I need what?'

'Prawns and lobsters don't stick to things, you clown. They walk all over the ocean floor. Your clients would drop you as soon as look at you. What you want is molluscs. Why didn't you tell me before?'

He hung up and called the restaurant. 'I need Blouse urgently,' Patrick begged. He was told he would have to wait in line. 'We have to find him quickly, Cathy. Tomorrow we're doing molluscs.'

'Doing what?'

'Didn't they teach you anything at that catering college? Molluscs. Single shell, double shell. There's thousands of them out there, stuck to rocks. All we have to do is get them to the table.'

'Do you mean things like mussels or whelks or cockles?' Cathy felt dizzy.

'Yes, and everything else ... clams, razor shells, limpets ... Blouse will know where to find them. Where is he, anyway?'

'I'll get him to call you in the hospital, Patrick,' Cathy sighed. The restaurant must be in a poor position if Blouse Brennan was going to be sent off to scrape limpets off rocks.

Tom rang again. 'The party's over but the children won't go home. They wouldn't even come up for the group picture with the Graduate. Blouse has them hypnotised, he's like the Pied Piper. I wouldn't be surprised if they followed him back to Quentins.'

'Yeah, well ask him to break off just long enough to call his brother in the hospital. Patrick wants him to do the Pied Piper thing along the shore tomorrow to collect limpets.'

'Isn't this a totally crazy life?' Tom said, with the tone of a man who would never live any other kind of life.

Cathy felt the same. But with one proviso. She wished mightily that tomorrow night was over. She couldn't see one redeeming feature that would save them. But she had reckoned without Blouse and his newly found self-confidence.

And the next night they all watched, astounded, as the boy they had all considered slow, pointed out, with an elegant cane, the variety of shellfish displayed on what he called the Mollusc Medley. The limpet, the cockle, the whelk and the winkle ... all of them praised for their qualities of constancy. The oyster, the scallop, the mussel likewise. These were loyal invertebrates, Blouse told the group earnestly. Like the insurance company they were here to honour, these magnificent molluscs were noted for their sticking power in a world where, alas, not everything could be relied upon.

Patrick Brennan sighed a very great, long sigh. His early release from the hospital had been justified. The PR man was as delighted as the Graduate's demon mother. The PR company he ran was booking further spectaculars, but only if Blouse could be part of the package.

'He doesn't come cheap, of course,' Patrick heard himself saying. His voice sounded weak. It had taken hours to persuade Blouse not to stress the lonely, futile and pathetic lifestyle of the mollusc. He hadn't been sure if Blouse had grasped it until the very last moment. But there were lots of things he wasn't sure of any more. Like how Blouse had found all those children to help him get buckets of those terrible things to the restaurant. They kept coming in all afternoon and all they needed for payment was an ice-cream.

Best not to question good news, Patrick always believed, like the look of love and huge relief in Brenda's eyes as she reached out her hand and stroked his through the most extraordinary – and successful – evening that Quentins had known so far.

Carissima

When Brenda's great friend Nora had lived all those years in Italy, she had written long, long letters. Always she began with the word '*Carissima*' ... It sounded a bit fancy, Brenda thought, a little over the top, but Nora had insisted. She spoke Italian, she dreamed Italian now. To say 'Dear Brenda' would sound flat and dull.

Carissima ... dearest ... was a better way to begin.

And Brenda wrote back faithfully. She charted a changing Ireland for her friend, for Nora who lived in the timeless Sicilian village of Anninziata. Brenda wrote how the waves of emigration were halted, how affluence came gradually to the cities, how the power of the Church seemed to slip away and change into something entirely different.

Brenda wrote that young people from different lands came to find work in Ireland now, girls who found themselves pregnant kept their babies instead of giving them up for adoption, young couples lived together for six months or a year before their marriages.

Things that were unheard of when Brenda and Nora were young.

Nora wrote about her friends in this village. The young couple who rented the pottery shop. Signora Leone. And of course Mario.

Mario, who ran the hotel.

Nora never wrote of Mario's wife Gabriella or their children. But that was all right. Some things were too huge to write about.

Brenda wrote about a lot of things, how she had met this guy they used to call Pillowcase, but was most definitely called Patrick Brennan these days, how they had fallen in love and worked in many restaurants. She told how the good fortune of running Quentins had fallen into their lap and they were rapidly making a great name for themselves. She wrote about the people who came and went, staff, and those like Patrick's brother Blouse, who had stayed and flourished there.

But Brenda only once told the deepest secrets of her soul, their great wish to have children, the long, often humiliating and eventually disappointing road of fertility guidance. That was too hard to write about.

Brenda was very helpful in that she acted as a spy for Nora O'Donoghue by going to see Nora's family. Hard, unforgiving people, who regarded her as a sinner and a fool, someone who had disgraced them by running off after a married man.

They were so uncaring about Nora's life that Brenda urged her friend to forget them. 'They have forgotten you unless it suits them,' she had written to Sicily. 'I beg you, don't listen to any pleas they may have when they are older that you should return and be their nurse.'

'*Carissima*,' Nora had written, 'I will never leave this place while there is a chance that I can see my Mario. I wish they could share my happiness. But perhaps one day they will be able to.'

Nora's Mario died, killed in an accident on the mountain roads which he drove across so fast. The village implied that the Signora Irlandese should now leave and go home.

Brenda would never forget the day Nora had appeared at Quentins, long dress, wild hair, her face mad with grief for the only man she had ever loved. She still called Brenda '*Carissima*'. They were still best friends. The long years apart, well over two decades, had changed nothing between them.

And when Nora found a new love, Aidan, the teacher up in Mountain-view School, she and Brenda clutched each other like teenagers. 'I'll dance at your wedding,' Brenda promised.

'Hardly, there is the little problem of his first wife,' Nora had giggled.

'Come on, Nora, drag yourself to the present day ... there *is* divorce since 1995.'

'I managed for well over twenty years without marriage first time round. I can do it again.' Nora wasn't asking for the moon and stars.

'You do what you like, but I'm not giving up on it,' Brenda threatened.

Patrick said that it was amazing they found so much to talk about. He was never jealous of their friendship, but often said that men just didn't have conversations like that about every single aspect of life.

'You are the losers,' Brenda said.

'I agree, that's what I'm saying,' Patrick said unexpectedly.

Nora went every week to the hospital where her elderly father lived in the geriatric ward. Rain or shine she wheeled him in the grounds. Sometimes he smiled at her and seemed pleased, other times he just stared ahead. She told him about any happy things that she remembered about her childhood. Often these were difficult to dredge up. She didn't tell him about Sicily because already it was fading in her mind like a highly coloured photograph left in bright sunlight. So she told him about Aidan Dunne and Mountainview School and the Italian classes. And she talked pleasantly about her sisters Rita and Helen, and her largely silent brothers, even though she hardly saw them at all.

The news that she had moved into a bed-sitting-room with a married Latin teacher had horrified them all over again. Really, Nora seemed to be a scourge sent to lash their backs.

Nora called to see her mother every week. Age had not improved her mother's temper or attitude, but Nora was determined to remain calm. Years of practice had given her a skill at being passive. And it was easy to call in for an hour and listen to her mother's list of complaints if she could go back on the bus to good, kind Aidan, who was so different and saw nothing bad in the world.

The day of her father's funeral was bleak and wet. Brenda and Patrick came but they decided against letting Aidan take part. He might be like a red rag to a bull.

Some of her students from the Italian class came to the church, an odd little group which certainly helped to boost the numbers.

'I'd ask you back, but I don't honestly think that my mother would be able to . . .'

No, no, they insisted, they had just wanted to pay their respects. That was all.

Nora's mother found fault with everything. The priest had been too young, too swift, too impersonal. People hadn't worn dark clothes. The hotel they had gone to for coffee, just the family, had been entirely unsuitable.

She brooked no conversation at all about Father. Did not care to hear that he had been a kind man and that it was good that he was at peace. Instead there was a litany of his mistakes which were apparently legion and the main one was his never having taken out a proper insurance policy.

'And now of course you'll all go off to your own homes and leave me alone for the rest of my days,' she said.

Nora waited for the others to speak. One by one they did. They told Mother that she was in fine health, that a woman in her seventies was not old these days. They reminded her that her flat was very convenient for bus stops, shops and the church. They said that they would all come to see her regularly and now that there was no longer a matter of visiting Father, they would take her on different outings.

Their mother sighed as if this was not nearly enough. 'You only come once a month,' she said.

This was news to Nora. It had always been implied that the visits from her sisters and sisters-in-law were much more frequent. It meant then that she, with her weekly visit, was indeed the best of them all.

She noted it without allowing her face to change.

Rita and Helen were quick to explain. They were so *busy* and, honestly, others must remember how hard it was with *families* and running *proper homes*.

The implication was that Nora had all the time in the world and no responsibilities so should play nursemaid and be glad to do so. Nora, who worked harder than any of them, Nora, the only one of them without a car who did the awkward shopping, and visited four times as often as the others did, always bearing something she had cooked for her mother.

It was grossly unfair of them to make her of all people feel guilty. And she had promised Brenda Brennan that she would never weaken. But Nora had also promised herself that she would be polite and courteous to the family, she would not return their hostile, bad-mannered attitude.

So she blinked at them all pleasantly as if she hadn't understood the direction of their conversation. She could see it driving them all insane. Still, what the hell, she was not going to lose her dignity on the day of her father's funeral.

And after all, she had Aidan to go home to after all this. Aidan, who would make her strong tea, play some lovely arias in the background as they talked, and want to know every heartbeat of the day.

Then tomorrow she would meet *Carissima* Brenda and tell her the story again.

She looked at her sisters, brothers and their spouses. Not one of them had a fraction of the happiness she had.

This gave Nora great confidence and strength and made it easy to put up with their taunts and very obvious suggestions that she abandon everything and go and look after her mother full-time.

'I'll come round to see you tomorrow,' Nora promised as she left. She kissed the cold parchment of her mother's cheek.

Did this woman miss the man they had buried today? Did she look back at times when there was passion and love? Maybe there had never been any passion and love.

She shuddered at the thought. She who had found it twice in one lifetime.

She saw Helen and Rita looking at her oddly. She knew that her sisters often talked about her with their sisters-in-law. It didn't matter very much.

'Will you be round at Mother's tomorrow also?' she asked them pleasantly.

Helen shrugged. 'If you're going, Nora, there's not much point in us all crowding in,' she said.

'And anyway I'll be there next week,' Rita snapped.

But she could still hear them reassuring their mother, 'Nora'll be in tomorrow.'

'Aren't you going to be fine tomorrow, Nora will do any jobs for you.'

'Nora has nothing to do, Mam, she'll do all the shopping for you when she comes to see you.'

It would be like this always. But it didn't matter. None of the rest of them had known happiness like Nora had. It was only fair that she should give something back.

'Did you end up paying for their coffee and sandwiches yesterday?' Brenda asked her friend Nora.

'Brenda, *mia Carissima* Brenda, don't you always have the hard word?' Nora laughed.

'That means you did,' Brenda cried triumphantly. 'Those four kept their hands in their pockets and you, who have no money at all, paid.'

'Don't I have plenty of money thanks to good people like you?'

She went on washing and chopping vegetables in Quentins, where she was paid the hourly rate.

'Nora, will you stop and listen to what you're saying? We pay you a pittance here because you insist it will all mount up to take Aidan and yourself to Italy, and then those selfish pigs make you spend your few pounds on their bloody sandwiches. It makes my blood boil.'

'Brenda *Carissima* . . . you of all people must not boil. You know they call you the ice maiden, you know you must be cool and calm. To boil would be a great, great mistake.'

Brenda laughed. 'What am I to do with you? I can't make it up for you which might stop me boiling. You won't take what you call charity.'

'Certainly not.'

'Well, swear one thing. Now. Swear here and now that you won't listen when they tell you that she needs a full-time carer and that you are it.'

'They won't!'

'Swear it, Nora.'

'I can't. I don't know the future.'

'I know the future,' said Brenda grimly. 'And I'm very sad that you're not going to swear.'

It happened sooner than even Brenda could have believed. Only weeks after her father's funeral, Nora found herself being told that her mother had failed terribly.

They didn't get in touch with her at home because the little flat she shared with Aidan Dunne was still out-of-bounds territory for her brothers and sisters. Some of the letters were sent to Mountainview School, some care of her mother. Helen directed hers through Quentins Restaurant, which was why Brenda became suspicious.

'Tell me, I demand to know what are they asking you to do now,' she begged.

'You are really a very difficult friend, *Carissima*,' Nora laughed as she polished the silver, another little restaurant job she had managed to wangle to help top up the Italy fund.

'No, I'm so helpful and so good for you. Just tell me what they want.'

'Mother is walking around in the night. It came on her suddenly. She can't bear being on her own, apparently.'

'Your father was in hospital for over three years, she had some time to get used to it.'

'She's old and frail, *Carissima*.'

'She's seventy-five and as fit as a flea.'

They looked at each other angrily.

'Are we having a fight?' Nora asked.

'No, we couldn't have a fight, you and I. You know all my secrets, where all the bodies are buried,' Brenda said ruefully. 'But believe me, I tried to persuade you not to run after Mario, and as it turned out I was wrong. You had the life you wanted. However, I'm not wrong this time and that kind of pressure was nothing to what I'm going to put on you now. Before I have to shake it out of you, what have they asked?'

'That I spend some nights in Mother's place,' Nora sounded mutinous. 'It's not much to ask. I mean . . .'

'How many nights?' Brenda's voice was like steel.

'Well, until they get full-time help . . .'

'Which they won't . . .'

'Oh, they will eventually, *Carissima* . . .'

'Don't *Carissima* me, Nora. They've asked you to go in every night, haven't they?'

'For a very short time . . .'

'And Aidan?'

'He'll understand. I'd want him to do it if it were one of his parents.'

'Listen. That man had one class-A bitch of a wife already. Don't let him have a second wife who turns out to be as mad as a fruitcake.'

'We owe it, we have so much happiness, and isn't it like a bank? You have to give something out if your account is overflowing.'

'No, Nora, that's not the way it works.'

'It is for me and for Aidan too. I know it will be.'

There was a silence.

Nora spoke again. 'It's not that I don't have the guts to refuse them. I do, plenty of guts. I know my mother disapproves of me, and my brothers and sisters do, but that's not the point.'

Brenda knew with terrible clarity that this was indeed the point. This family wanted to destroy Nora's happiness.

Nora had spent too many years in the hot sun of southern Italy. It had affected her judgement, softened her mind. It was going to lose her the love of that good man Aidan Dunne.

'Will you promise me one thing . . .' Brenda began.

'I can't make any promises.'

'Just do nothing for a week. Say nothing to anyone for one week. It's not long.'

'What's the point if I'm going to do it anyway?'

'Please. Just to humour me.'

'*Bene Carissima* . . . just to humour you, then.'

Brenda Brennan called a friend who was a matron in a hospital. 'Kitty, can I ask you a very small favour? There's a nice bribe of dinner for two in the restaurant.'

'Who do I have to assassinate?' Kitty Doyle asked eagerly.

'Do you like having me around your flat, Mother?' Nora asked.

'What kind of question is that?'

'I just wondered. You don't smile. You don't laugh with me.'

'What's there to smile and laugh about?'

'I tell you little jokes sometimes.'

'Ah, don't start going soft in the head, Nora. Really now, on top of everything else.'

'On top of what else?'

'You know.'

'Can I bring Aidan to meet you, Mother? I've met all his family.'

'You haven't met his lawful wedded wife, I'd say.'

'I have, actually. I met her up at Mountainview School and I met her up at her house. You know, where Aidan used to live. I painted the Italian room so that she could make it into a dining room when she sold the house.'

Her mother showed not the slightest interest.

'Would you like me to paint the kitchen here for you, Mother?'

'What for?' her mother asked.

'No, let's leave it,' Nora said.

'Your mind is a million miles away, Nora,' Aidan said that night. 'Is something worrying you?'

'Not really.'

'Tell me.'

'I'll tell you in a week,' she said.

'There's nothing wrong, Nora? I can't wait a week. Tell me, tell me.'

'No, it's no illness or anything. It's just a problem. I promised I'd wait a week. You sometimes wait before you tell me things. Believe me, it's nothing sad,' she said, her hand on his arm.

'I love you so much, my beautiful Nora,' he said, tears in his eyes. 'And I too will have news for you in a week.'

'I'm not beautiful. I'm old and mad,' Nora said seriously.

'No, you foolish love, you are beautiful,' said Aidan, and he meant it.

Back in her mother's flat, Nora assessed how much she needed to bring with her. Sheets, a couple of rugs that could be easily stored when they were not in use on the sofa.

She would have to have a sponge bag, a change of shoes and some underwear that she could store in the bathroom cupboard. She must get a stronger electric light bulb. Maybe she could do some embroidery at night when Mother was asleep.

It would be so lonely without Aidan, and he would be lonely too. But there was no point in trying to get him under her mother's roof. The protest was too strong.

Brenda had been to see Nora's mother yesterday.

As always, Mrs O'Donoghue sighed and said it was such a pity that Nora hadn't turned out like her friend. Properly married, earning a decent living.

'Very selfish, of course, she and her husband not having a family just so that they could get on in their careers.'

'Perhaps they tried and the Lord didn't send them any children,' said Nora, who knew just how hard they had tried.

Her mother sniffed.

'And I hear Helen was here.'

'She hasn't been here for days,' Nora's mother said.

Hard to know which of them to believe.

Helen had said she was leaving a letter for Nora on the dresser. Nora read it. The usual stuff about how Mother was failing every day, some accommodation must be reached, the rest of them had proper homes and families . . .

There was also another couple of letters. They were about Mother's health. Nora took them down to read. One was a typed letter from a Ms K. Doyle, matron of a large hospital, responding to a request to know about the availability of in-home carers.

Nora's heart soared. She always knew that her sisters must have planned for her mother's care. But it was good to see it proved.

Ms Doyle had offered them several options but suggested first that their mother's health should be properly assessed so that her needs could be established. Then, oddly, there was a photocopy of the letter that Helen must have sent back.

Nora stood there reading.

Thank you for your concern. I am at a loss to know exactly who it was that contacted you, possibly my sister Nora who has been abroad a lot and is very unbalanced. She doesn't realise that our mother is a very strong, fit, seventy-five-year-old, well able to look after herself. Like all elderly people left on their own, she sometimes suffers from the need for company. But now that Nora has, we think, returned to Ireland permanently, she might well spend overnights with my mother which would get her out of another unsuitable situation and kill many birds with one stone. So there is no question of us needing any help now or in the foreseeable future.

I am sorry that you have been bothered in this regard by my sister, who undoubtedly meant well but who, as you can see, has little grasp of the situation. I am surprised that she asked you to reply to me, but glad that I was able to set you right on this.

Nora has always been a great problem to this family. We don't suggest that she live full-time with our mother as Nora has no social skills and is unable to be a companion for anyone. Still, the night-time company should surely benefit both of them.

Thank you again for your courteous and helpful letter.

Nora sat for a long time with the letter in her hand. Surely her sister had not intended her to read it. It must have been sent in error. It *must* have been. Helen would surely not want her to see what she had written. That Nora was unfit, without social skills, that Mother was fit and strong, needing no caring, that the family was trying to rescue Nora from an unsuitable situation.

But if Helen had not left her this letter on the high shelf of the dresser, then who had?

For a long moment Nora thought about her friend Brenda, dear, dear, Brenda *Carissima*, who had been so loyal over the decades, and who had asked her to wait a week. Just one week. But even Brenda couldn't have set this up.

This was a real person . . . Ms K. Doyle, her name was on the hospital's letterhead. This was Helen's handwriting. Not even wily, cool Brenda could have accomplished this.

Nora went back home to Aidan.

'My week is up, so I'm telling you that I'm going to spend every single night with you until I die,' she said.

'This was what was worrying you?' Aidan was puzzled.

'Yes, I thought I might have to spend every night on my mother's sofa.'

'We'd have been very uncomfortable on a sofa,' he agreed.

'No, you'd have been grand, you'd have been here,' Nora said, stroking his face.

'I wouldn't have been at all grand without you,' he said softly.

'What was your news for me?' she asked.

'I saw Nell about the divorce. She said fine, but that we're far too old to be getting married at our age, but fine.'

'She is right, of course,' Nora said thoughtfully.

'She is *not* right. We will be married, you and I, with all our friends there to celebrate our good luck and happiness,' said Aidan with spirit.

'Aidan, you're wonderful but we can't think of it, we haven't any money, and I've been saving for it all the time.'

'But I'll have the money.'

'How can you save, Aidan?'

'Well, this man Richardson, whose kids I teach. He's a big financial adviser and he told me what to do with my money. In fact, I don't take my fee at all from him. Now each week he invests it for me and it's well over doubled. Imagine that.'

'Imagine!' She looked at him with great love.

'And now about you. Was this big decision about your mother's sofa easy to make?'

'In the end it took about ten seconds,' Nora said. 'I have to tell just one more person, *Carissima*.'

'Will she be surprised?'

'You have no idea with Brenda Brennan,' Nora said. 'She'll be pleased, but I will go to my grave wondering whether or not she's surprised.'

Homecoming

'Why did you call the place Quentins?' Mon asked one morning at coffee break.

'That's his name, the guy who owns it.' Brenda was surprised that the young Australian girl didn't know this. She was so bright, so quick.

'I thought you two owned it.' Mon was very confused. 'You mean, you could be given the push, just like me?'

'Oh, very unlike you,' Brenda laughed. 'He knows we are reliable. You're still proving it.'

'Does he know about me?' Mon wanted to be part of the team.

'Not too much detail, but yes, he would know that we hired you and we're pleased. Now is that all right?'

'Does he ever come over and see the place?'

'No, hardly ever, once he got us in to run it. Sometimes he sends friends and then lets us know that they thought it was all going fine.'

'He must trust you utterly.'

'Well, we send him the accounts regularly, but you know, I think he hardly reads them,' Brenda said wonderingly. 'And I haven't heard from him in a long time. I think I'll send him a cheery message if there's time today.'

'What makes you think there's going to be time today? There never is any other day.' Mon rinsed her coffee cup and went out to check the faultless dining tables in Quentins Restaurant.

By chance, Quentin's father came in to lunch that day. He had now retired from the accountancy practice where he had always hoped that his son would succeed him. Distanced and confused by the boy's wish to go abroad and paint, he was grimly pleased that the dream of being a great artist had somehow eluded his son.

'Do you hear any news from Morocco?' Brenda asked quietly as she settled the older man at his table.

'You'd hear more than I do,' Quentin's father grunted.

'Absolutely not. He's the employer you dream of. Not a word except a raise at Christmas, no wonder we get arrogant, Patrick and I, and think we own it ourselves.'

'By rights you should own it. Didn't the pair of you make it what it is?'

'No, your son had the dream, the idea. We just helped him carry it out.'

Brenda and Patrick never would have been able to raise the capital to buy the place, but it didn't matter. As long as Quentin lived his peaceful life in the hills of Morocco and let them at it, they had no worries. Sometimes they wondered what would happen if Quentin should die suddenly. Still, every day they worked there, their reputation increased. Brenda and Patrick Brennan would not be long unemployed in Dublin.

'My son gets many compliments for this place, but they should all be addressed to you and your husband,' the old man said gruffly.

'They are, Mr Barry, and you are kind enough to send us a lot of marvellous clients . . . so please know we are very grateful.' She moved away gracefully.

Over the years she had learned just how much people like to be recognised, acknowledged, but not monopolised by restaurant staff. She wished that Quentin would come back just for a week, sit at the discreet table in the booth and see how the restaurant that bore his name carried on while he lived and painted in the hot African sun.

She would telephone Quentin now, this very afternoon. She needed to keep him up to speed about the documentary anyway. She had written when it was first suggested and asked his permission but as they had expected he wrote back to say that the matter was entirely in their hands, he knew they would make the right choice.

She reached for the telephone.

He was having his early-evening mint tea served in a glass held by a metal container. One of the little boys in Fatama's corner shop brought it along at five-thirty every evening. Like the people who sent him bowls of vegetables scrubbed clean to make soup, or baskets of luscious fruit wiped lest an insect or a bruise appear. They were so good to him. Quentin could have never asked for kinder people, but he had an urge to go home. Just to see was it home or another country, a different world? That was the moment she rang. The cool unhurried voice of Brenda Brennan.

They had just served 120 spectacular lunches, his father had been in, and one of the staff, Mon, a laughing young waitress, could not believe that they didn't actually own the place themselves, and that there *was* a Quentin.

'Did you tell her I'd be no good to her?' he laughed as he always did about his sexuality.

'No, I did not. You are good to her providing her with a great restaurant to train in. Anyway, she doesn't want you, she's landed one of our most prestigious customers from the bank next door.'

He didn't ask why Brenda called. She would come to it.

'I was thinking, would you like to come back for a visit, Quentin? Just sit and observe us secretly. We'd love to show off for you.'

'You're psychic . . . I was just thinking of it.'

They fixed a date. It was for a few weeks ahead.

'I'll leave it to you to tell your father about your plans.' Brenda was diplomatic.

'Thank you. I'll take my mother to choose a hat one day and I'll probably call Father the day before I leave. Less is best. Do you feel that too about families?' Quentin was always polite and never intrusive. Nobody minded answering any of his direct questions.

'Well, my parents are mainly fine, but then I always had plenty of sisters to share them with, unlike you. Sort of shared the load.'

'Yes, there was just me, a big disappointment to them both.'

'Your father's in here very regularly, Quentin. He can't be all that disappointed in you. In fact, he boasts of being your father.'

'Imagine.' There were very bitter tones in his voice.

'Will it just be you?' Brenda asked. Once there had been a delightful young man, Katar.

'I'll be on my own,' he said.

'I'll make sure Patrick has something from our poor imitation of Moroccan cuisine when you come,' she promised. 'We do a nice orange and cinnamon salad with a chicken *tajine,* but it's not quite exotic enough.'

'Probably quite exotic enough for Dublin,' Quentin laughed.

'You have been away for a long time,' she said.

She talked to Patrick about it that night.

'You should have said a couscous,' he complained. 'He'd know we were trying, at least.'

'He's not coming home to examine the food,' Brenda said.

'What for, then?'

'I don't know.' She didn't know. It seemed too odd to say she thought he was coming home to say goodbye.

He came in exactly on time and smiled warmly as he was introduced to the staff. A tall, slight man, forty-something, still handsome, tanned, but tired-looking.

'Where did he get the money to own a place like this?' Mon whispered to Yan.

'I heard it was from some inheritance,' Yan said.

'But who? Not his awful father, for sure.' Mon shook her head. 'Look at his face. He looks like a sort of saint really, doesn't he?'

You couldn't speak softly enough to avoid detection by Brenda Brennan, who could, after all, lip-read. 'Quentin's not exactly a saint,' she said to them pleasantly. 'But he came by the place legally. From an old friend.'

She watched their mouths drop open with the shock of being overheard and smiled to herself. It had been so useful, that little trick, she'd learned so very much over the years. Quentin saw her smile when she came back to the table.

'I'd love to know what you're thinking,' he said gently.

'I might even tell you later. Now I have to get the show on the road.'

Brenda made sure that Quentin had two kinds of bottled water. She sensed he would not drink wine. She ordered a tray of appetisers. Something he could pick from. She had seen enough people come and go to know that he was not going to eat very much. Quentin Barry was a sick man.

*

He ate in the booth and watched his mother come to lunch with three of her friends. Sara Barry had aged in a way that she would not have enjoyed had she been able to observe it properly. She looked puffy and rather silly. He would have advised her against the light pastel colours and the fussy jewellery.

Quentin's mother had no idea that she was being closely watched from the discreet little booth across the restaurant. All she cared about was that the four women at her table realised just how much she spent on clothes. She talked to them about the wisdom of having an account at Haywards store, it saved so much trouble in the end. You just waved your card and that was that, they were so obliging.

Quentin felt sorry for her. The staff in Haywards would be equally helpful and obliging had she waved a credit card, a chequebook or a fistful of notes. He had worked there for long enough to know. All those years before his luck had changed. He knew Mr George, Mr Harold and Miss Lucy and how little respect they had for card holders above anyone else.

And he thought back on how his future had been written for him through the generosity of Mr Toby Hayward, who still wrote to him from Australia and who had given him this strange, unexpected start and a chance to own his own restaurant.

It had all been so mysterious. Quentin had been told that his best policy was to ask no deep questions.

Katar had said the restaurant had been given to him by God, some vague Irish god who knew Quentin was unhappy and wanted him to have a business that would eventually give him the funds to go out to Morocco. But then, Katar was the sunniest person Quentin ever knew.

Ever had known.

Impossible to believe that he would never hear that laugh or see those dancing eyes again. He had brought Katar to this very table once. Quentin smiled as he remembered the occasion.

'I would like to run around and tell them all at every table that this is ours, ours. Then I would like there to be a trumpet sound . . . ta-ra, ta-ra . . . and you would stand up and we would all sing . . . "For Quentin, he ees the jolly fine fellow".'

Katar would have liked that, and would have seen nothing silly or inappropriate in it. Only a celebration, like his whole happy life had been. Even the last months of his illness.

'It's so good for me, I have you to look after me, to tell me stories in the dark night. Who will do the same for you?'

'Ah, there are plenty who will.' Quentin had put cold rose water on Katar's hot brow.

'Well, you must go and find them, be ready to ask them, let them know you need help. Not the false braveness, swear to me. I will know, I will be looking at you.'

'I swear, Katar,' Quentin had said. 'No false braveness.'

But oddly, when the time did come, Quentin didn't need any friend. He just looked at the beauty of the hot country he had come to think of as his own. Lying calmly and resting there brought him peace. Life didn't seem so huge and important somehow. You were just part of a process, like mountain ranges and sandstorms and the blossoms that came in springtime. Next week he would be back there and he would wait. It would not be frightening. But first, he had decisions to make here.

About his father and mother there would be few problems. They had already said goodbye to him in a meaningful sense, long, long ago.

'Mother, can I take you out and buy you a hat?' Quentin asked on the phone.

'I'm not going out to some awful souk in Marrakesh.'

'I'm in Dublin, Mother.'

'That's good.' She didn't sound excited or pleased.

'So?'

'So, of course I'd love a hat,' Sara Barry said. She didn't say she would love to see her son, but then she didn't know he was dying.

'Did you know that Quentin's in Dublin?' Sara asked her husband that night.

'No, but he'll call from the airport before he leaves, that's what he usually does.' Derek Barry barely looked up from his newspaper.

'That's because you have nothing to talk to him about,' she criticised.

'Yes, that's true, unlike you who can compare shades of lipstick with him after all.' Derek spoke bitterly.

'See what I mean, ready to pick a fight where none exists.'

'Oh, my fights with Quentin are long over,' Derek Barry sighed.

Quentin had one more decision to make.

The restaurant. The place that bore his name.

He had asked Tobe Hayward his thoughts, but the old man had said quite simply, 'Believe me, when it comes to your time, you will do something worthwhile.'

That's all Tobe Hayward could come up with. But he also reminded him that everything was in Quentin's name.

Quentin had always supposed that he would know what to do when the time came. But he had not known how soon the time would come. How ridiculously early in fact. Still, he felt in his heart that everything was clear now, as Tobe had forecast it would be. He knew what should happen next.

For now he would get to know the staff and talk to them.

The beautiful Mon who told him every heartbeat of her romance with Mr Clive Harris, and how she didn't give a damn about the Italian who had sweet-talked her out of all her money. He was welcome to it.

He heard from Yan about how his father back in Brittany wanted to put money into a small restaurant there for him. And how Yan didn't know how to tell him he was having too much fun in Ireland to leave.

He discovered that Harry had thought working in Dublin, the heart of the Republic of Ireland, would be a misery that he was prepared to endure in order to get a good training. But in fact he was never happier, and all his friends came down to Dublin for the weekends now. Times had changed, he explained to Quentin.

Quentin got to meet some of Brenda and Patrick's friends. The extraordinary woman who called herself Signora, who chopped vegetables, cleaned brasses, spoke flawless Italian, was going to marry a divorced man at her age, and confided to Quentin that she had the happiest life of any human on the planet.

The man she was going to marry had apparently lost money to some financier. They had been planning to have a wedding party with it but they could well survive without a party. And anyway maybe they were too old for one.

He met Blouse Brennan, brother of Patrick, so proud of his red-haired wife Mary and their little son. Blouse confided that, compared to a lot of the fellows he had been at school with like Horse and Shay Harris, he had done very well. And no one would have expected it at the time.

Quentin met all kinds of people that he never knew existed in the old Ireland. There were Ella Brady and Derry King, who were going to put together a documentary about the place. His restaurant! Quentin made a note to write to Tobe about that.

And their colleagues in Firefly Films, Sandy and Nick. Utterly dedicated to their job.

Were there people like that around when he was young, full of courage and determination? Quentin wondered. There was no one to ask. Brother Rooney wasn't there to visit any more. He had gone to some big garden in the sky.

There were Tom and Cathy, who ran a catering service. Sometimes they did outside catering for the restaurant's clients, so they were in and out of the place a lot. They were expecting a baby, and there was a lot of kissing and hugging and wishing them good luck about that from time to time.

Quentin saw the sad look on Brenda's face one day when they had gone. 'Was that something you would have liked?' he asked gently.

'Oh yes, so much. And Patrick would have been a wonderful father.'

'Still, there have been compensations?' he asked hopefully.

'This restaurant is our baby,' Brenda said, looking around the place very proudly.

He smiled and suddenly she realised that perhaps she had been presumptuous. 'I didn't mean to suggest anything except that we have loved working here,' she said, flustered.

'Did you wonder why I came back, Brenda?' Quentin asked her gently.

'Why shouldn't you come back to see how well it's all going? I told you we wanted to show off.'

Her eyes were too bright. She knew all right.

'I'm dying, Brenda,' he said.

*

'I brought those dates and nuts over to the booth like you asked me,' Blouse Brennan explained to his brother. 'But Brenda and Quentin were crying, so I decided not to interrupt them,' he said.

'Crying?' Patrick was surprised.

'Yes, Brenda was using the starched napkin to wipe her face.'

'That's serious crying. You were right not to disturb them,' Patrick said. 'Any other dramas out there?'

'I was afraid to look,' Blouse admitted. 'It's safer in the kitchen.' And he went back to the vegetables with Signora, the two of them chopping contentedly and expertly. It was good to be far away from All Human Life, which seemed to be fairly volatile out in the dining room.

'What about your friend, Katar?' Brenda asked, unaware of her tear-stained face.

'He went before me, last year,' Quentin said. 'Thank you for remembering his name.'

'Who would forget him? He was charming and so full of life ... to say something which is foolish, because it's no longer true.'

'He liked it here. We sat at this table and Katar said that if the poor and the sick could only eat great food like this, they would surely get well ... or at any rate, they would die happy.'

They laughed at the memory of the handsome laughing Moroccan boy, unafraid to face death, full of optimistic philosophy to the end.

'Well, that's what you could do, Quentin. Sell this place as a going concern and with the money you get set up a kind of charity ... very high-quality food for those who would not have been able to afford it.'

'I can't sell this from over your heads ... you and Patrick have made it what it is,' Quentin protested.

'We'll get employed, our name is good ...'

'But it's like your baby, you said.'

'There are other babies, Quentin.'

'But Blouse and Signora and everyone ...'

'Will also survive.'

'Isn't there enough in the business to do both ... keep this place going and the other?'

'Of course there could be, do you ever read those accountants' reports? They are always saying you should expand ... but you will want money for medication, for clinics, for whatever ...'

'No, no, I will go back to the house where Katar and I lived, that is best.' And his face looked much more peaceful as they talked about practical things. Blouse brought them dates, honey and nuts. Figures were written down on paper.

'And this film documentary, do you not want to be any part of it?' Brenda asked.

He shook his head gently. He wanted nothing at all to do with it but was happy if it went ahead.

Now he wanted her to listen carefully.

Quentin Barry was selling his enterprise to Brenda and Patrick Brennan, who would pay him a small, once-only payment, and then a share of their profits would be paid every year to a company called The Kindness of Katar. They would cook gourmet food for those who were terminally ill.

'We'll need a lawyer,' he said. 'I don't want my father's stuffy old friends.'

'I know the very girl. Maggie Nolan. She was partly the cause of our coming here. It would be a nice way of rounding it off.'

He loved the story of Maggie's eager family and wiped his eyes. 'Katar said I cried very easily. If he could see me now,' he said.

At the end of the week, Maggie and her colleagues had been in and out of the private dining booth several times and everything was signed.

Quentin Barry had bought his mother an elegant hat and told her that she had the finest cheekbones in Dublin. He had taken his father for a long walk out by the sea and commented on the elegant boats and the good state of the Irish economy. He held their hands a little longer than usual when he said goodbye, but not so much longer that they might get suspicious.

And when he left the restaurant, he hugged Brenda and Patrick as if he never wanted to get into the taxi. If anyone was close enough, they would have heard him say that he too had a baby and that he was leaving it in good hands.

Part Four

12

Tim and Barbara Brady had soup and toast for a late lunch, as they did most days. 'She didn't go to bed at all?' Barbara asked.

'Apparently not. She made a few calls on her mobile. Then she went out.'

'And did you talk about anything . . . you know?'

'No, Barbara, I said nothing about anything that was in a private letter for her, one which we were never meant to have read.'

'I'm not sure, it was open . . .'

'Anyway, we didn't discuss anything, nor, as I told you, will I bring the matter up. And she called back to ask us to go to a brunch at Deirdre's on Sunday, so that we can meet the millionaire.'

'Good, that's something,' Barbara said.

'I don't know,' Tim Brady said gloomily. 'I've had it up to here with millionaires, if you must know.'

'Apparently, your friend Ella was in America, and it didn't take her long to pick up a sugar daddy there,' Frank said to his wife Nuala.

'I don't know what you're talking about.'

'And you sure don't know much about your so-called friends. They were spotted getting off the New York flight and into a limo this morning. So can you get on to her sharpish?'

'I can't, Frank.'

'Why not? You're always bleating on about what friends the two of you are.'

'Not since you said I shouldn't be friends with her any more. She didn't take well to that.'

'Call her sometime today, Nuala,' Frank said firmly.

'He's dead, what does it matter now?'

'Today, Nuala.'

Ella was early for their meeting, but Derry was there already waiting for her in the bar. It had only been ten hours, yet it seemed much longer since they had been together.

'I had an odd, restless day, how about you?'

'Odd and restless. That covers it,' he agreed.

'Did you sleep?'

'Not a bit. And you?'

'Not a wink. So I don't think we should go to Quentins tonight. We're both so jet-lagged we might fall asleep the moment we got in the door.'

'So what would you suggest?' He was agreeable to whatever she came up with.

But she felt at a loss. If she still had her own flat, she could have made him supper. 'Do you know, Derry, I haven't any idea,' she said honestly.

'Great pair of movie-makers we are,' he laughed. 'We spent day and night in New York talking about this city of Dublin and how to tell its story, and now that we're here, we don't even know where to begin.'

They both began to laugh with a slightly hysterical tinge to the laughter. They agreed to go to the restaurant in the hotel. But just as they got up to move, a man approached them.

'Ella Brady? I'm Mike Martin. Remember we talked before about the late Don Richardson . . .'

'Yes, I was very sorry to hear of his death.' She kept moving but the man moved with them and Derry steered her to the lift.

The man positioned himself between them and the door, and spoke again. 'I know he tried to get in touch with you before he died.'

'I must go now.' She looked at Derry for help.

Very quickly Derry put his large, square frame between them.

Mike Martin reached around behind Derry. 'Please, Ella . . . it was important to him.'

'Excuse me,' she said, and made for the lift.

Derry was behind her. He turned around to the man who was still trying to catch Ella's arm. 'I think you heard the lady,' he said.

'Don't you obstruct me,' Mike Martin began.

Derry King was very swift. He was into the lift before her and then pulled Ella in with him. She was shaking and he put his arms around her to calm her down as he pressed the number of his floor. It was a bear hug, a brotherly gesture. The kind of hug he could have given to anyone who had been through a shock. It only lasted a few seconds. Then the lift stopped.

In the suite he opened a miniature brandy. 'Medicinal. I'll split it with you,' he said.

She swallowed and stopped trembling.

'Who was that?' he asked.

'A henchman,' she said.

'What a great word! What does it mean?'

'You know,' she said.

'Well, I imagine that it means a timeserver, a sidekick, a supporter. But what's a hench exactly?'

'It's okay, Derry. No need to fuss over me. I'm fine now.' She managed a watery smile.

'No, I'm interested. I'll go look it up.'

'You may find a Gideon's Bible, but I don't think they run to dictionaries,' Ella said.

'I never travel without one.' Derry went to a table where he had unpacked some books and papers. She watched, amazed, as he looked it up.

'Apparently it comes from some Old English word and some Old German word meaning a horse! Horseman! Isn't that absurd?' He was shaking his head with annoyance.

'It's not a very *big* dictionary,' Ella said.

'No, but it's a very good one. I look up ten words every day, always have.'

'Why on earth?'

'If you leave school at fifteen, it gives you a complex,' he said.

'I don't buy that. You went *back* to school, for heaven's sake!'

'Yes, but they never catch up on what you should have been learning earlier.'

'This isn't a real conversation,' she said suddenly.

'No, but it will do until we get over that guy downstairs.'

Ella agreed easily. 'I'm sorry for involving you,' she said in a low voice.

'You didn't,' Derry said.

'He's nothing. He's not important. It's not serious.'

'You know that's not true.'

'Why do you say that, Derry?'

'Because he pushed right up to you in a public space, talking about private things which he's not meant to know about in front of the whole of Dublin. He's come out of hiding, Ella, and he doesn't care who knows it. He shoved me. He was going to grab at you. It's very damn serious and you know it.'

She stared at him.

'And if it's not serious, why did you bring that laptop computer with you in that shoulder bag? I'm not a fool. You were afraid to leave it at home, Ella. So can you just stop telling me that people aren't important, that things aren't serious? Give me some credit for something, will you?' He looked angry and upset.

'All right, I'll tell you. I got a call from Nuala. Remember her in the saga?'

He nodded.

'She said she called to see how I was, but I know her husband and his brothers are very anxious indeed to find me. I'm not sure why. But I got scared and brought the laptop with me. I was hoping you might not notice . . . but you have very sharp eyes. And I'm really very grateful to you for getting me out of all that business downstairs.'

'Yes, but what about tomorrow and the day after?' he asked. 'Who'll get you out of it then?'

'I'll have to think, Derry.'

'Do you trust me?'

'You know I do.'

'Then why don't we look at it together?' he said.

'What?'

'You could go phone us up some coffee and sandwiches, and we'll open it up and decide what to do.'

There were tears of relief in her eyes as she reached over to the telephone and called room service.

*

'*No*, Nuala, I don't know where Ella is tonight,' Deirdre said.

'You must know, you're her friend.'

'And so were you, until you started behaving like some kind of security firm trying to get her to talk to Frank.'

'It's not Frank, it's his brothers,' Nuala whined.

'Well, whoever it is, they have no sense. Ella is in bits over Don being dead and they don't have a word of sympathy for her. They just go on behaving like tracker dogs snuffling round to see does she know anything about Don's business affairs. No wonder she doesn't return your calls or speak to you or anything.'

'She *did* speak to me. She just said she was going out. I assumed it was with you.' Nuala was very plaintive.

'It wasn't, Nuala, so leave her alone, will you?'

'I'm just telling you this, they'll find her.'

'And I'm telling you this too. I don't like your tone. It sounds like a threat.'

'It's not a threat, it's just that I'm worried about Frank's brothers.'

'With every reason, and if you come at me again about them, I'll sing loud and clear about what I got up to with Eric, one of the said brothers, on your wedding day. So think carefully before hounding Ella any more. Do you get my drift?'

Deirdre hung up the telephone and took down the recipe book.

'What's that whole series of numbers there?' Ella asked Derry, pointing to a section of figures as they sat looking at the screen.

'It's like a series of routings. Someone bought a property here, sold it on there, it was sold again, the money invested here, the money taken out and put into something else.' He shrugged as he spoke.

'And could you work out where something went? Suppose you ran this program?'

'Yes, but there's no proof that it would all be in the same name, the same ownership, as it started out with at the beginning, if you see what I mean.'

'And I suppose that ordinary people don't keep records in this very complicated way.' Ella looked at him.

'No, not unless they want to obscure things.'

'And can you tell if it had been going on from the very start?' Her voice was very small.

'It goes back a fair number of years, certainly, since they set up this particular program and way of keeping records.'

'It's not a last-minute panic, then?'

'Afraid not, Ella.'

'I suppose I wanted to think they were clean at the start, but you say they were hiding things all along.'

'Perhaps they were doing it with the knowledge of clients who might have wanted to hide things also.' Derry King struggled to be fair. 'But from the sound of things, the clients were not informed of these routings.'

'I think not. So they always planned it, Don and Ricky Rice.' She shook her head in disbelief.

'About this Ricky Rice . . .'

'His father-in-law. He pulled all the strings, made all the decisions. He dragged Don into it all. He was struggling to get out.'

'Sure.'

'No, I know I sound as if I'm defending Don. But Ricky Rice was the brains of it all. He ran it with an iron fist. They all had to make disks of their negotiations each day and mail them to Ricky personally. That's how much control he had.'

'Yeah.'

'What are you saying? You're just answering me in grunts, Derry. What is it?'

'There's no mention of Ricky Rice in here, none at all. That man could walk back into this country without a fear in the world. His name is on nothing here, nothing at all.'

'What do you mean?'

'There's nothing to tie him in with any of it. The entire thing was engineered by Don Richardson.'

'Any luck finding Ella, Nuala?' Frank said when he came in.

'No.' She was sullen.

'Well, you can thank your stars that someone's prepared to go and look for her. Mike Martin phoned. He's found her, wining and dining in Stephen's Green with an American. Staying with him in the hotel there, even. Didn't take long for her to get over her grieving.'

'Frank, listen to me.'

'No, why should I? You listen to me. My brothers asked you to do a simple thing and you wouldn't do it. You *know* how much we owe them and this was one occasion when you could have done a little digging . . .'

'I did do a little digging, and they won't like what I found. Not one bit. And if we don't stop hounding Ella everyone will know. Including Carmel, for God's sake.'

'Know what?' Frank was confused.

'Know what your beautiful brother has been up to . . .'

'You mentioned Carmel.'

'Yes, I mentioned Carmel, because your brother Eric, if you remember, is her loving, faithful husband. She would be most interested in knowing what he was up to on our wedding day. Our own wedding day, I tell you, Frank.'

She saw from his face that the escapade with Deirdre did not come entirely as a bolt from the blue to Frank. 'Oh shit,' he said.

'Precisely. And you knew, you *knew* about it, didn't you? Very funny, all lads together. Well, let's see what Carmel says.'

'You're not going to tell her?' Frank was fearful now. Carmel was the most fearsome of the sisters-in-law.

'I hadn't intended to, but believe me, Deirdre will if anyone goes near Ella.'

'It will implicate Deirdre too, of course,' Frank began to bluster.

'She doesn't give a damn if she's implicated or not. And indeed if I thought that this is the kind of thing that *you* go along with, I'd damn well tell Carmel myself.'

'Nuala,' he begged. 'You know I've never looked at another woman in my whole life. You know that, don't you?'

'No, I don't know, but I'm sure your brother will know and will tell me all about it when he has had to face Carmel in full flow,' Nuala said.

Ella tried to take it all in. No mention of Ricky Rice in the company that bore his name. 'Is there something missing, something we just haven't been able to access?'

'I can't see it.'

'But the very name of the company even? Somewhere in there it must show it belonged to Mr Rice.'

'That's all here. Look,' Derry said, scrolling down. 'Three years ago there was a deed transfer. Rice gave it all to Richardson. It was witnessed. It's registered. The entire company belonged to Don Richardson.'

'But why did his father-in-law run away with him, then?' Ella felt her head spinning.

'Maybe it was a set-up. If it all hit the fan, the father-in-law could run with them. If it cleared, well and good, and the father-in-law could walk home free as a bird. An older man, he might have stronger roots in Ireland.'

'And his daughter, didn't she have shares?' Ella could barely speak.

'Not that it shows here.' Derry shook his head.

'So they can all come home now? Now that Don's dead.'

'Well, Lord, Ella. I'm no expert on all this, but it appears to me from reading this for the last two hours that they could. In terms of not being held responsible.'

She was silent.

'They may not want to, of course,' he said hesitantly.

'Derry, I don't feel very well. I don't think I could go back to Tara Road tonight. Would you mind very much if I stayed here?'

'Not at all. I was going to suggest something along the same lines,' he said.

'You were? Good. Then I must ring my parents. Do you mind?'

She spoke in a matter-of-fact voice to her mother. She was going to spend the night in the hotel. There was a lot of work to be done.

'Your mom okay with that?'

'She hasn't been okay with anything I've done for two years, but she didn't make any fuss,' Ella said.

'That was Ella,' Barbara reported. 'She said we were not to wait up for her. She's going to stay the night in the hotel. They have a lot of work to do, apparently.'

'I see,' Ella's father said.

'Don't be like that, Tim.'

'I'm not being like anything. She's a grown-up woman. She's free to do whatever she wants to.' But he sounded tight-lipped.

'All I'm saying is that if you'd been talking to her, you'd have felt the same. This isn't anything like the last time. It's not a romance. I have an intuition about it.'

'I'm sure you're right. Neither of us had much intuition about anything last time round.'

'Should we order more coffee and maybe some dessert? You know, to keep us going while we work things out.'

'Yes, that sounds fine.' Ella sounded vague and distant as if she had forgotten what coffee was. 'What things do we have to work out, exactly?'

Derry walked around the room for a bit, trying to find the words. For the first time since she'd met him, he seemed unsure. When he was speaking about his Foundation, about Kimberly, about his work, about his hatred for his father, he had been definite. But now he was searching for a way to say what had to be said.

'Like whether you take the bank drafts for your father. Like whether you should hand this machine in.'

She watched him objectively. A big, square man in his shirtsleeves. Someone so well-known that even Harriet and her friends had heard of him. Tired now, much more tired than he had been earlier. Those lines etched on his face, as if they would never leave.

'What do you think I should do, Derry?' she asked.

'No. No way. It's your call, Ella. I only skimmed the surface, to identify what you have to do.'

'Do I have to do these things now?' She knew she looked piteous, putting off the decision.

'Sooner rather than later, I'd say, since you asked me.' His face was worried.

'Why? It's been going on for months. Why can't we wait a little longer?' She looked at him hopefully.

'Because of that guy down in the bar pushing us around, for one thing. Because of your friend with all the brothers-in-law, for another. Because people know you have this and they want to know what's in it, and to get their hands on what they can.'

'I'm not ready yet to make up my mind,' she said.

'As I said, it's your call.'

He went to the phone and ordered the coffee. She sat there and watched the traffic of Dublin swirl around Stephen's Green.

And then they talked about other things. She told him about her driving test and how she must have been the only person in the world to drive into a motorbike three minutes after she set off. The examiner had said it was entirely the biker's fault and that Ella had been cool and responsible throughout.

Derry said he didn't remember how he learned to drive. Possibly when he was about twelve. It could have been a friend of his father's who taught him. He had often driven his father's van home when the man had passed out.

He asked Ella what else had happened in her odd and restless day. She told him about her lunch with Deirdre, and about the planned lunch party to meet him on Sunday, and the news that the marvellous twins from hell would be there.

He wondered were there any hints about handling them.

'Tell them nothing about yourself,' Ella warned him.

'I'm good at that,' he admitted.

'You are, too,' she said, smiling at him.

'I'm sorry. Does that make me some kind of a pain?'

'No, not at all. We're all so blabbermouth here ... telling everything. You're a refreshing change, keeping yourself to yourself.'

'Ask me anything, Ella, and I'll answer.'

'No, of course I won't.'

'I want you to. I want to be free and open and say what I mean. I've not been that for a long time.'

'Can it be about me and not about you?'

'Anything you like.'

'All right, Derry, if this isn't cheating ... What would you do about all this if you were me?' With a sweep of her hand, she pointed to the laptop computer.

He paused, but she didn't rush in. She knew that he was going to answer. Eventually he spoke. 'I'm not you, Ella. But I promised you that I'd answer and therefore I will. I would take the bank drafts for your father, but I know you are not going to do that. And I know without your telling me that he wouldn't take them, either.'

She blinked with amazement at his understanding.

'And about the rest of it, I would hand it over. That's what I, Derry King, would do, but I don't know what you, Ella Brady, should do. If it were my own land and my fellow citizens, I would have to do that. I would think it was illegal to sit on such information and say nothing. But here it could be different. And I know how much you loved this guy, and don't want people's heavy boots walking around in his business. So this is possibly not an option for you at all. And may never be. Now, Ella, is that up-front and blabbermouth or what?'

She looked at him with such gratitude she could hardly speak. 'Thank you, Derry,' she said eventually.

'No, it doesn't hurt to be challenged.'

'You've been a very good friend to me,' Ella said. 'I'd like to do the same for you.'

'Maybe you will,' he said.

'You're right about one thing. I'm not going to take those drafts. There were people who were left much worse off by this whole disaster than we were. And you're right too that my father wouldn't want them, either.'

He nodded.

'But the truth is, I don't know what I'm going to do about all this mess here in the computer. You're right, it will have to be sooner rather than later. But there's something else, just one thing I have to do first.'

He put his head on one side to listen to her.

'Could I talk to you about that tomorrow?' she asked him.

'Whenever, Ella,' he said.

'Thanks, Derry.'

And they sat there as old friends do when they are tired, when there's nothing that has to be said because everything is understood.

They made plans for their Saturday. Derry was to take a bus tour of Dublin. Ella would go to Quentins and get things moving. They would not meet again until they went to Deirdre's apartment, at noon on Sunday.

'What shall I bring?' he asked.

'Wine,' Ella said.

'How much wine?' he wondered.

'Relax. I know this is Ireland, but just one bottle. White or red.'

'Thanks for marking my card,' he said.

'Thanks for giving me a place to sleep,' she said, taking off her shoes.

'Now please. I am a gentleman, in my heart, anyway. Please have the bedroom,' he begged.

'Out of the question, Derry. I sleep on this lovely sofa. Put that rug over me, will you? I'll be out of here before you wake.' She gave him a big, cheerful smile.

'You're a great girl, Ella, and it's a pleasure to be working with you,' he said as he tucked her feet in.

'You're a sort of hero,' she mumbled.

'What?' he asked.

But she was asleep.

At 9 a.m. Derry woke to the phone. It was Kimberly. 'God, you were asleep! I'm just so sorry,' she said. 'I was wakeful, I thought I'd call you.'

'No, I have to get up, it's fine,' he said.

'All I want to know is, did you survive?' she asked.

'I think so. I haven't seen much of the place yet.'

'But no dramas, no scenes, no regrets?' she wanted to know.

'No, none of those things, Kim,' he said.

He looked at the door to the sitting room, which he had left open. Was Ella awake? Listening? He had better go and see. 'Hold on, Kim,' he said, and walked next door. The sofa had a folded rug on it and beside it was her computer. With a note on top.

You are a generous man, Derry King. I will never forget your kindness to me last night. Please, can I leave this machine with you to look after for me? I will have made my decision about what it contains by Sunday night, and I so appreciate your help.
  Love, Ella

He went back to the telephone. 'Sorry, Kim. I thought it was room service.

No, everything's fine here, as you said to me years ago. It's an ordinary place, not full of dragons, as I thought it might be.' He heard her breathe more easily.

'Thank God, Derry. That's what I wanted so much for you. You deserve it,' she said.

He sat for a while thinking about their conversation. In his whole life he had never lied to her so much. Everything was *not* fine here. He had not been checking room service. There were more dragons in this place than he had encountered for a long time. None of them having anything to do with him but everything to do with Ella Brady.

13

'I'm sorry for staying out all night,' Ella said. 'I hope you weren't worried or anything?'

'No, not when you called, of course not,' her father said.

'I meant worried that I was going to start yet another unsuitable affair.' She managed a slight smile.

'No, heavens, no,' he protested.

'Derry's not in the same league at all, totally different. He's all work, no time at all for relationships of any kind. Anyway, you'll meet him tomorrow at Dee's place.'

'And is he enjoying Dublin?' Ella's mother asked.

'Hard to know. He plays it very close to the chest.' Ella's face was thoughtful. She seemed miles away.

'Will you be at home today?'

'No, Mother, I've a lot of things to sort out.' Again she was distant. 'I want you to think about something very seriously,' she said eventually. 'All the money you lost because of Don, it's there, you know, in this safe deposit box, banker's drafts, cash, bearer's bonds, whatever. You've read the letter. You know where it is. I haven't looked, but I know it's there. If you want to take it, I'd be happy for you to do that.'

'Now, Tim,' Barbara said in triumph, 'I *knew* she would feel like this. Your father said not to mention it to you, but I said you'd see sense about it all. After all, it was his last wish that you should be seen all right and not have to work like a dog.'

'Oh, I'm not taking one euro of it, Mother, but you and Father, that's different. It's your choice.'

'And of course, if we don't take it, then it just lies there,' Barbara Brady was almost pleading.

'Or we could give it to others who were defrauded,' Ella said crisply.

'We don't want it,' her father said.

'Tim!'

'Discuss it today. Tell me what you come up with tomorrow. Oh, and there's another thing, Dad. In your talking to people, did you think that Don or Ricky was the brains of the outfit?'

'Ricky Rice, they said, but Don injected all the charm and the sort of razzmatazz into it,' Tim Brady spoke ruefully. A man reduced to living in a wooden house in his own garden because of someone's charm and razzmatazz.

'Would it surprise you to know that Ricky Rice owned nothing, that it was all in Don's name? Ricky is free to come back here any day he wants to and may well do so now that Don is dead.'

'He'd never have the gall. He couldn't face people who've lost money,' Ella's father said.

'If he wasn't a part of it, then why did he flee?' Ella's mother was practical.

'I don't know. I've been thinking about that all night,' Ella said.

'They were always together, he and Don, and he was crazy about his grandchildren. Maybe he couldn't bear to let them go.' Tim Brady tried to work it out.

'But why wasn't his name on things?' Ella wondered.

'There must have been a good reason,' Tim Brady said.

Ella drove down to the Liffey and parked her little car. She walked around the apartment blocks where Don Richardson had had his little hideaway, the place he was meant to be living when he stayed all that time with her. They were small and purpose-built. Not much movement around the place on a Saturday morning. Perhaps people would come out later and buy papers and milk for their coffee. She must enquire what had happened to his little flat here. Who had bought it, who lived a life in those four walls now.

Then she drove back to look at her own flat. The place where she had been so happy with Don. It was rented now by two girls who worked in the television station down the road. Ella had found them in twenty-four hours, once she decided to move. She had slaved to leave the place looking perfect, and even donated some of her own possessions. Like the duvet. She could never sleep under it again.

She parked across the road and looked at the place thoughtfully for a long time. If it had not been for meeting Don Richardson, she might be living there still to this very day. Her garden was shabby. Had she ever noticed that before? She longed to go over and tidy it up a bit, take away some of the autumn leaves and dead stalks of flowers. But what would they say if they had seen her, the women who worked in the television station? They had already thought her eccentric. After all, the time they met her she was famous, her photograph every day in the evening newspaper, usually beside the words 'love nest'. If they were to spot her back months later, kneeling in their garden, then they really would be alarmed.

She drove past the school where she had taught. She had been happy there too, before Don Richardson had been part of her life. The kids had been mainly great. She wondered how the new teacher was getting on. Was she able to cope with loudmouths like that brassy Jacinta, who always answered back and went as far as she could get away with? Still, no point in sighing over them. Kids would learn with whoever was put in front of them. They were very resourceful.

Which reminded her about Maud and Simon, who were coming to lunch tomorrow. She must find out how they were related to Tom or Cathy, whichever it was. They kept saying that Cathy's parents were not really official grandparents, but then they got everything so confused. Dee said she did hear once, but it was all so complicated and far-fetched that you'd be asleep by the time it was explained.

She drove south of Dublin, then through the suburbs and by the sea to Killiney, where Don and Margery had their elegant home. Where his sons had played tennis, where his father-in-law had visited so often it was like his second home. Ella knew the address but she had never seen the place. Today she needed to look at it.

It said Private Road, but there was no gate keeping you out. Just the words and the size of the house would do that, keep you away, unless you had business there. She drove slowly along, noticing the gardeners here, the window-cleaners there, the activity of an autumn Saturday morning in a wealthy area. She saw the big cars parked in the driveways, the women who dressed to go to the supermarkets and shopping centres, the expensive security systems. This was where Margery Rice had lived for years with her father, husband and sons. Yet she must have lived a lot of the time on her own. Her sons had been at school, her father out working, her husband in the arms of Ella Brady. And today Margery was calling herself Mrs Brady and living in Playa de los Angeles, in Spain. Did she want to be back in this splendid house with the immaculate green grass? Had it been sold, or did they rent it out? Would Margery and her father, if they were so blameless about everything, come home and take up where they had left off?

She got out of her car, went to lean on the gate. She had to study this place and see if it told her anything at all about what might have happened.

A woman came out to speak to her. She was about twenty-five, with jeans, untidy hair, and a two-year-old by the hand. 'Can I help you at all?'

'No, I'm just looking at these lovely homes. I used to know people who lived here, the Richardsons.'

'Oh yes, indeed.'

'Did you know them?' Ella asked.

'Only knew *of* them. I'm sort of house-sitting this place. My uncle rented it after they left. He was a great friend of theirs.'

'He must have been very cut up when Don died.'

'Yes, I think he was,' the girl said, rescuing the child who had run away.

'He's sweet, isn't he?' Ella said when the child had been retrieved.

'He's Max. He's a handful. It makes it difficult to go out and work, so that's why it was wonderful to get this place right out of the blue. My name's Sasha, by the way.'

'I'm Ella.'

'Would you like to come in and have a coffee?'

Ella thought for a moment. The name Ella hadn't rung any alarm bells, reminding the young woman of love nests. So why not then? She followed Sasha into Don and Margery's house.

It was fully furnished. There were paintings on the walls by artists she knew Don liked. There were Don's kinds of books. Nothing could have changed. This house was as they had left it the day they disappeared.

'I'd have thought it would be ... you know, more bare.'

'So did I when my uncle approached me. You see, Max doesn't have any father on the scene, if you know what I mean, and I'm a bit of a family problem one way and another!' She smiled engagingly. She was an attractive person. She showed Ella how she had covered a lot of the good pieces with sheets so that Max wouldn't get his sticky fingers all over them. There was a view of the sea from one side of the house and of the countryside stretching down to the Wicklow Mountains from the other. It was a dream house. No wonder Sasha felt she had fallen on her feet to get to stay there.

'And does your uncle stay here too?'

'He comes and goes, but he travels a lot. Mike's not someone you'd pin down.'

'Mike?'

'That's my uncle's name. Mike Martin. You must know him?'

'I've seen him on television, certainly,' Ella said, looking around her nervously. 'And are you expecting him today, do you think?'

'Oh, he never says, just turns up.'

Ella put down her coffee and said she had to go.

Sasha was disappointed. 'To be honest, I was hoping you'd stay. They're all so old round here, and desperately rich. You're more normal.'

But Ella moved very quickly. Mike Martin was the man who was looking for her and the laptop.

'You didn't say how you knew the family,' Sasha said as she came to see her off.

Ella thought for a moment. Sasha would tell Mike anyway. No point in hiding anything now. 'Actually, I'm a bit of a problem in my family too, Sasha. The reason I knew them was that I was in love with Don Richardson. I was mad about him, and my heart is broken because he's dead. I just wanted to see where he lived when he was alive.'

'Oh my God,' Sasha said.

'So perhaps if you didn't tell your Uncle Mike, it might be better. For all of us.'

Sasha nodded vigorously, and Max held out a face covered in ice-cream for a goodbye kiss.

Nothing would be said about her visit.

For the moment.

Ella had bought a sandwich and a carton of milk. She drove up to Wicklow Gap, where you could sit and see nothing but hills and sheep and rocky paths down to a river in a valley. She always loved it here, and somehow things seemed clearer.

She took the rug out of the car and sat for a long time with her eyes on the quiet scene around her. Sometimes cars passed by and once or twice they parked nearby to look at the view from this vantage point. But nobody bothered her, and she wasn't really aware of them. And eventually the place worked its magic as it always did, and she got back into her car and drove home.

Her parents were anxious to discuss money, but Ella told them there was no need. 'Just listen,' Barbara Brady pleaded. 'Your father won't take it and therefore I have agreed.'

'But not with your heart, Mother.'

'My heart's not important in all this. He's right. There are people worse off than we are, and it wouldn't be fair.'

'I don't have to do anything about it until tomorrow night. You can have more time,' Ella said.

'And what are you going to do tomorrow night?' her mother asked fearfully.

'I'm not quite sure, Mother. That's the truth. I think I know, but I'm not totally certain just yet.'

Deirdre said she'd have everything ready by noon, and that Ella should collect Derry from the hotel and bring him along early so that he didn't have to come into a room full of strangers.

He was horrified when he saw that Ella was driving. 'Somehow I never thought of myself as trusting my life, what's left of it, to you.'

'I take deep offence at that. You drove me around New York and I put up with that,' she said, avoiding a bus neatly.

'Are there any traffic cops here at all?' he asked through his fingers, hiding his eyes.

'Don't be silly, Derry. It's easy today. You should see a crowded weekday at rush hour. Thing to remember is that no one indicates left and right.'

'Including you?' he asked.

'I don't want to confuse them,' she grinned.

'I'm going to change the habit of a lifetime and have a stiff drink,' he said when they got to Deirdre's.

'Thanks be to God,' Deirdre said. 'Ella said you sipped at one white wine for three hours and I was wondering what we'd do with you, especially when you meet everyone. Maud and Simon came an hour early to set up their puppet show.'

'It's all very different,' said Derry King as he sat down and allowed the panic he had felt over Ella's driving to subside.

14

'Ella says you and your wife were very good to her when she was in New York,' Barbara Brady said.

'My former wife Kimberly talks very highly of Ella, and so do I. You have a very bright daughter, Barbara.'

'We love to hear that, any parent does. Do you have children, Mr King?' Ella's father was more formal.

'Oh, call me Derry, please. No, no children. I wish we had. We are an unusual couple in that our separation did not make us enemies. We would have shared children quite amicably. I really do wish Kim well, and she me. I was resisting coming to Ireland for a lot of personal reasons from the past. Kim is delighted that I faced up to it at last.'

'And are *you* delighted?' Ella's father was sharp, observant.

'I'm not sure yet, Tim. It's early days.'

'You and she might get back together one day,' Barbara suggested.

'Oh, no, that's not going to happen. Kimberly has a new husband. They are very happy together.' He spoke simply, as if stating a fact.

Just then Brenda Brennan came in. He recognised her at once from the photographs in the Quentins file he had studied so carefully in New York. They didn't need to be introduced, but talked together easily. She was as he knew already very groomed and in control. But warm as well. She seemed genuinely interested in the things they had talked about, and anxious that his stay in Ireland would be a good one.

'We'll want to keep you here in Dublin all the time, but you'll want to travel, maybe go to the west. It's not a big journey by American standards.'

'A perilous one on these roads, I'd say.'

'Not at all. Grand, big, wide motorways nowadays. You should have seen it back when,' she said proudly. 'Where are your people from, by the way?'

'I have no people.'

'I'm sorry, I misunderstood. I thought Ella said you had an Irish background, as so many Americans coming here do, you see.'

'I do have an Irish background on one side of my family, but no people.'

'So you won't be looking for roots then?'

'No way.' Derry realised he sounded sharp and short. He had better say something that made him seem less abrupt. 'But as it happens, my father's people did come from Dublin.'

'Great. I like to hear of Dubs doing well. My husband is from the country, you see, and he says that they are the lads who succeed abroad.'

'I wouldn't say my father did well.' Derry's eyes were bleak.

Brenda Brennan had had a lifetime of reading faces and moods. 'No? Well, his son doesn't look too much like a loser to me,' she said with a bright smile. She was rewarded. He smiled back. 'Let me introduce you to a couple of people,' she said efficiently. 'These are Ria and Colm. They run a magnificent restaurant on Tara Road, which you must visit while you're here and drop little cards advertising Quentins on each table!'

'As if she needed it!' Ria was small, dark and curly-haired with a huge smile. Her husband was handsome and thoughtful-looking.

Derry saw Ella looking over to see that he was all right. He raised his glass to her. He felt for a moment as if he belonged here in this easy place where no demands were being made on him. He must beware that feeling. It was probably brought on by the strange, strong drink he had taken to recover from Ella's driving. He would have no more. In fact, this moment he would ask for an orange juice.

Beside him, the small, earnest face of a blonde girl aged ten or eleven appeared. 'May I refresh your glass?' she asked.

'That's very good of you ... um, do I know your name?'

'You might have been told about us. I'm Maud Mitchell. My brother Simon and I are providing the entertainment this afternoon.'

'Oh, isn't that splendid. I'm Derry. Derry King.'

'And what do we call you? Simon and I, we're always calling people the wrong thing.'

'Derry,' he said.

'Are you sure? You're much older than we are.'

'Yes, but I want to feel younger than I am, you see.'

Maud accepted this as normal and suggested that he have a grapefruit juice mixed with a tonic. It was meant to be refreshing. Of course, strictly speaking, it was actually two drinks, but since he was the guest of honour, it would probably be all right.

'Am I the guest of honour?' he asked.

'Yes, because we have to check with you about the entertainment. We can't dance because there isn't a proper floor, only an old carpet. We brought a puppet show but Tom and Cathy think it might be too long. We were going to sing, and with you being an American, we were going to sing awful things like "When Irish Eyes Are Smiling" and "Come Back To Erin", which is what they all loved when we were in Chicago.'

'Are they awful things?'

'Well, they wouldn't sing them here, if you know what I mean. And then we were told you didn't want any of that stuff, you weren't a normal American.'

'No, no, that's true.' Derry was delighted with the child. 'And what would they sing here, do you think, given your choice?'

'Well, "Raglan Road", "Carrickfergus". I'll ask Simon. He's better at judging, but the main thing is that we're not to bore you by singing too long. That's what we do sometimes, go on too long. The puppet play is seven minutes, so if we sang two songs, would that be fair?'

'That would be great,' he said. 'Will you start now?'

'You must have very funny parties in America,' Maud said. 'Of course we can't start now, we have to wait until they're all sitting down with their puddings and cups of coffee.'

'Ella, I'm desperately sorry about the twins monopolising Mr King,' said Cathy. 'I've tried to break them up half a dozen times, but he says he's enchanted with them. He won't talk to anyone else.'

'Don't worry, he really is enjoying them. I've never seen him so happy.'

'It's a great party, Dee,' Ella said.

'Nick and Sandy are a little disappointed they can't talk to him more – he's spending all his time with those kids.'

'He keeps shunting people away when they try to rescue him,' Ella said. 'I wish I knew what they were talking about.'

'Brenda Brennan can actually lip-read,' Deirdre said. 'I'll ask her later.'

The twins were busy explaining who they were. 'You see Cathy over there with the big stomach? It's a baby actually, but that's not the point.'

'No,' Derry agreed.

'Well, she's the daughter of Muttie and Lizzie, his wife. And we once went to live with Cathy and the husband she had then, who was Neil Mitchell, and he's our cousin. Neil's father and our father are brothers. So that's it!' Maud was triumphant.

'But you live with Muttie?'

'Yes. And his wife Lizzie.'

'Good. But why, exactly?'

'Father and Mother aren't able to have us. They'd like to, but they're not able to so we go and see them on weekends to say hallo. Muttie drives us in his van.'

'And why can't your parents have you?'

'Mother has bad nerves and then Father goes travelling. It's better we stay with Muttie and his wife Lizzie.'

'Nerves?'

'Yes, she gets worried about things and then she drinks lots of vodka and doesn't know where she is any more.'

'And why does she do that? Drink the vodka?' Derry asked.

'It helps her nerves. It's like a magic potion. She forgets whatever was upsetting her. The trouble is that she makes no sense and falls down and everyone gets cross with her,' Maud said.

'But if she stopped, then you could both go and live with her, couldn't you?' Derry was unforgiving about a woman who could leave such marvellous children with strangers.

They explained that they had a brother, but he had done some crime, he was never spoken of, and he didn't come home. One time he used to work in Neil's father's office with Uncle Jock, but he didn't any more and he had gone away. 'Are we talking too much about ourselves?' Maud wondered. 'We haven't asked you any questions so that you could have a bit of talking.'

'Not much to know about me. My father had bad nerves too. He used whiskey as a magic potion to make them better. Lots of it.'

'And did it work?' Maud asked.

'No, not at all. It made him worse.'

'And did your mother go wandering off on travels like our father does?' Simon was so innocent it nearly broke Derry's heart to see children accepting this intolerable state of affairs.

'No, she couldn't. She had to raise her children, and raise us without any money or support.' His face was hard now.

The children noticed. Maud spoke gently. 'But if his nerves were bad, what could anyone do about it?'

'He could have tried to stop drinking. He could have kept a proper tongue in his head to my mother.'

'But he didn't mean all those things,' Simon explained as if to a simpleton. 'When Mother has been drinking she tells Father terrible things like that he has other ladies, and that we are monsters and sneak money from her purse. None of us take any notice.'

'What?' Derry was amazed.

'Well, you *can't* take any notice, they don't mean it. Wouldn't they much prefer to be living a nice, peaceful life like everyone else?'

'And you don't hate them both?'

Simon and Maud looked at him as if he were from another world. 'Hate them? Your mother and father? Nobody could do that. It isn't possible.' They spoke every second sentence.

He was silent for a while. The twins looked at each other. He looked as if he might be going to cry.

'Are you all right, Mr Derry?' Maud said.

'Did we talk too much?' Simon wondered.

Derry King shook his head.

'Do you think we should do the entertainment now?' Simon asked Maud.

'Maybe it mightn't be right for entertainment, Simon, you know the way it sometimes just isn't and everyone expects us to know.'

'I could check with Cathy,' Simon agreed.

'But we don't want to leave him all upset,' Maud said.

Derry still had said nothing. His face was working as he tried to hide his emotions.

'Maybe, Mr Derry, you could go behind the sofa and have a big cry if you want to about your father's nerves and then you'd feel better. Often when we go to see Mother, afterwards we have a big cry to think of all she missed. Would you like to do that?'

'No, but I might have one later,' he stumbled out the words.

'Yes, I bet you will.' She patted him consolingly on the hand in the shared friendship of those who were children of the nervy.

Brenda Brennan, who was lip-reading, reported the conversation to Ella. 'Maud is urging him to go behind the sofa and have a big cry.'

'Jesus, Mary and Joseph. Is he going to?'

'He says he'll have one later.'

'And what's the boy saying?'

'He's wondering whether they should get on with the entertainment,' Brenda reported.

'I think they should start it almost at once, don't you?' said Ella.

Cathy announced that the puppet play, which was about seven minutes long, was called 'The Salmon of Knowledge', but the salmon puppet itself had been damaged in transit and had lost some of his scales, so everyone was to imagine it more scaly. The audience cheered it to the echo, Maud and Simon took several bows. They asked if there were any requests for songs. They were allowed to sing two, they said, looking eagerly around the room, sure of the delighted enthusiasm they would receive.

Derry King couldn't bear them to wait one more second. He heard himself calling for a song. 'Carrickfergus'. He didn't know it at all, he just remembered the name the twins said people liked.

They had true little voices and stood very still, side by side, singing the song of lost love and dreams.

> The seas are deep, love, and I can't swim over
> And neither more have I wings to fly
> I wish I met with a handy boatman
> Who'd ferry over my love and I . . .

Derry felt a very unaccustomed prickling in his nose and eyes. He *hated* this kind of music, glorifying loss and building up a sentimental image of the Old Country. He was not going to let two simple children who had seen no violence in their home make him change his own attitudes. Jim Kennedy was a violent man who had made life hell for everyone around him. There was no way Derry was going to go all soft on him now. There was just some small seed there that made him think he understood why his mother forgave him so often. It must have been some kind of belief, like these children had said, that Jim Kennedy like any other drunk would have preferred a different life, but it had somehow escaped him. Was that in his mother's heart as she insisted on staying in the home that Derry had been urging her to leave?

They were at the last verse now, and generously allowing the audience to join in. Even encouraging them by raising their arms.

> I'm never drunk but I am seldom sober
> A handsome rover from town to town
> Ah, but I'm sick now and my days are over.
> Come all you young men and lay me down.

They all clapped and praised Maud and Simon. The twins were busy trying to decide what their second and last song should be.

'Do you know, that was so terrific, I wonder if you'd consider quitting when you're winning?' Cathy suggested.

It was not a concept that the twins grasped easily. But Maud glanced over at Derry King. He was the guest of honour, the man they had been asked to entertain. She saw what the others had already noticed. That tears were falling unchecked down his face.

'You're right, Cathy. I think we should leave it. Not always, but just this once.'

'Love you, Maud, and you, Simon,' Cathy said.

'Everyone's getting very odd round here,' Simon said, annoyed that they hadn't been able to sing 'Low Lie The Fields Of Athenry'.

'You don't have to be quiet just because I cried, and you don't have to drive at five miles an hour because I dared to criticise the mad speed you went at on the way here,' Derry grumbled.

'Lord, but there's no pleasing you today,' Ella said with a sigh.

He was contrite. 'There *is* pleasing me as you put it. I did so enjoy that lunch. Everyone was so welcoming. Thanks, Ella.'

She smiled at him. 'Go on, they were delighted with you. All of them.'

'Were they?' He was childishly pleased.

'Oh yes, and Brenda says now that she's met you, she has less anxiety about the project. My parents don't think that you're a big bad dangerous Yank. My mathematics pupils love you to bits. You did yourself a lot of good!'

'I had a happy day.'

'So did I. Which is just as well, because I have a lot ahead of me,' Ella said.

'You do?'

'I do, Derry. I want to sort this whole thing out about Don's computer. Finish it, once and for all. And I wonder if I can do it from your suite in the hotel.'

'Sure.'

'You're very restful, do you know that? You don't say big long sentences when one word will do.'

'Good,' he said with a smile.

'I wouldn't be able to do this without you, Derry,' she said.

She was grateful that he hadn't asked her what she was going to do, but then Derry was a practical businessman. He knew he'd find out just as soon as he got to his suite.

'Why don't you make Muttie and Lizzie some sandwiches?' Cathy said as she let the twins off in her old home in St Jarlath's Crescent. 'I'll leave them some pavlova as well. Apparently Dee is on a diet and won't allow it to stay in her house overnight, in case she eats it.'

'Did you ever hate Muttie and his wife Lizzie?' Maud asked Cathy in her normal conversational tone.

'No, Maud, never. Did you?'

'Of course not.'

'Then why do you ask?'

'Something Derry said. He said he hated his father.'

'He said that?' Cathy was shocked.

'Not exactly, but nearly. He has cousins here, but he's not going to look them up,' Simon confirmed.

'They're called Kennedy and they're house painters here in Dublin,' Maud said, proud to have got the information.

'I know them,' Cathy said. 'They work with Tom's father.'

'Will we have a surprise party and bring them all together?' Maud suggested.

'No, Maud. I know I'm a dull stick, but believe me, that's not a good idea,' said Cathy, who decided she must ring Dee and tell her at once.

Ella and Derry made a pot of tea from the little tray in the room. 'First I'll call my parents, ask them if they're sure they don't want to take the money and run.' She made the call swiftly.

They wouldn't be happy to be paid off in this way, they told her.

Yes, of course, if there was compensation, if insider trading could be proved, then they'd be happy to have a share, but not this way.

'We liked Derry King,' her mother ended.

'And he you, Mother.'

She sat very still for a long time after that.

Derry sat equally calm, sipping his tea.

'Right,' she said eventually.

'Tell me what you're going to do.'

'I'm going to call his wife. Ask her what she intends to do. Does she want to have a life in Ireland again, does she own that place in Playa de los Angeles? It's the only one that's not owned absolutely by Don. Maybe he wanted that as a home for her and the children. Maybe he left her a note, too.' She was very calm.

'And then?' Derry King said.

'And then, depending on what she says, I will most probably call the Fraud Squad here and ask them to come to the hotel lobby and collect the laptop.'

'And what might she say that would change your mind?'

'If she says she will have nowhere to live and she can't bear the shame, I'll ask you to help me erase the stuff about her home.'

'Very generous of you.'

'I owe him that.'

'You owe him nothing. We've been through this.'

'Then you'll remember I want to behave perfectly.'

'He's dead, Ella. He doesn't know how well and perfectly you'll be behaving.'

'Please, Derry, help me.'

'How?'

'Sit beside me while I make the call.'

'You've thought it all out then?'

'Yesterday, all day. I made a tour of the past, pulled it all together. This is what I want to do.'

'Right, I'll sit beside you,' he said.

The phone only rang six times, but it seemed like ages. A man answered.

'Can I speak to Mrs Margery Brady, please?' Ella felt her voice faltering. Derry squeezed her for solidarity.

There was a pause. 'Who?' the man asked.

'Mrs Brady. Margery.'

'Where did you get this number?'

'Is this 23 Playa de los Angeles?'

'Yes, but ... this is not a number that anyone has ...'

The voice sounded familiar. Terribly familiar.

'Don?' Ella gasped.

'Angel? Ella, is that you? Angel?'

She couldn't find the breath to say a word.

Derry had an arm around her shoulders and was offering her a sip of water. She pushed the water away but held his hand very tight.

'Don, is that really you? You're not dead?'

'Where are you, Angel?' His voice was insistent, very anxious.

'You told me you were going to die, kill yourself,' she said, shaking her head in disbelief.

'I *was* going to, but in the end ... No good at finishing anything, me.' He gave a hollow little laugh. The laugh he gave when things were very serious.

'I thought you were dead, Don. Dead, you know, at the bottom of the sea. I wept over you everywhere, that you would never see this lovely autumn with the leaves changing, with the sun coming through the trees. I even wept for your sons, that they wouldn't know you ... and you never died ... you never died at all.'

'But that's good, Angel Ella, isn't it? We'll be together once I sort out this mess.'

'You never loved me, Don.'

'Of course I did ... do.'

'What had you intended to do, Don?'

'Wait until I could get the laptop so that we could sort it all out. Get our life together.'

She was silent.

Derry squeezed her hand harder. She had been holding the receiver so that he could hear what was being said.

'Ella. Ella Angel, are you there?'

'You never loved me at all. Was it just sex? Was it because I was young? What was it?'

'We'll meet. Bring me the laptop. I'll tell you everything then.'

'I can't do that, Don.'

'Why not?' He sounded weak.

'Because I gave it to the Fraud Squad.'

'And the money for your parents? I can prove you took that.'

'No, I gave that back too.'

'I don't believe you.'

'Why not?'

'There would have been someone on to me by now.'

'There will be, Don, there will.'

'When did you give it to them?'

'An hour ago,' she said, and hung up the phone.

15

It all took much less time than they thought.

The detectives came to the hotel. Two quiet, unassuming-looking men, one a tall, dark man she had met before when she had lied about the computer.

'So it turned up eventually?' he said, looking at her.

'It did,' she said simply.

'And you are . . . ?' he asked Derry.

Derry handed him a business card. 'Derry King, friend and business partner of Ms Brady.'

'And this is . . . ?'

'A ticket and key for a safe deposit box. Don Richardson claims he left bank drafts or certified cheques there for me.'

'And you haven't opened it?'

'No.'

'If they were for you . . . ?'

'He defrauded my father of money. They were a sort of apology, or that's what I thought.'

'All the more reason to take them, then . . .' The detective never finished a sentence, just left it hanging there and someone finished it for him.

This time it was Derry. 'Ms Brady and her parents, being very moral people, decided they couldn't just take money like that and say nothing. They are returning it to you.'

'Quite so. Very admirable.'

'And the password to the computer is Playa de los Angeles, like the city Los Angeles.'

'Ah, you just guessed this . . . ?'

'Not exactly . . .'

'So Mr Richardson told you . . . ?'

'Not exactly that either. He told me ages back that it was "Angel" and when I tried it recently it wasn't, so I tried words a bit like that and it opened.'

'Well done, Ms Brady.'

'But that's not the main thing . . .' she said, her words tumbling out.

'It's not?'

'No, the main thing is he's not dead. He's alive. I spoke to him this evening. He never killed himself at all.'

She looked from one face to the other to see the shock register. But to her surprise there was nothing at all.

'We never really thought he *was* dead,' said the detective. 'Didn't fit the pattern. Made no sense for him to kill himself.'

'I thought he was dead and I used to know him very well indeed,' Ella said.

'Yes, I'm sure.'

'You might have told me,' she said with tears in her eyes. 'Saved me all that heartbreak.'

'We didn't exactly see you since it happened. We asked you to keep in touch in case his briefcase turned up and you didn't ... so how could we have told you?'

Derry intervened. 'But now the briefcase *has* turned up and Ella *has* been in touch, so is that everything?' His voice was smooth but with authority.

The two men responded to him. They stood up and shook hands. They thanked them for the co-operation and asked if Ella, and indeed Derry if he wished, would accompany them to the safe deposit box, so that the hand-over of what it contained could be authenticated.

'His name and address and contact numbers are all there,' Ella told them. 'He calls himself Brady, of all names. Isn't that a really nice bit of a laugh for all of us?'

There was real sympathy in the faces of the detectives. The whole thing was over in an hour.

Ella called her mother. 'It's done. It's given back. Well, given to the Guards, anyway,' she said in a dull tone.

'Well, I'm sure that's right. Thank you, Ella.'

'No, thank you, Mother, and Dad, too, for being nice and normal and believing someone I introduced you to. I will make it up to you if it's the last thing I do.'

'Stop, Ella.' Her mother noticed that the voice on the phone was shaking and tearful.

'And one more thing, Mother ...'

'You're not coming home tonight?' her mother guessed.

'That's it. You're psychic,' she said.

'Don't get too upset, Ella. That's all I ask. The man is dead now, let him rest. We have no way of knowing how sorry he may have felt at the end. His mind disturbed and everything. We can't judge the dead.'

'The man is not dead, Mother. He's alive and well and living with his family in Spain.'

'No, Ella. He was killed in that terrible boat tragedy ...'

'He faked it. He's living out there on Dad's money, and do you know what? He's calling himself Brady, Mother. That's what he's doing.' She sounded quite hysterical.

'Is Derry there?' her mother asked.

She handed him the phone. Ella could only hear his end of the conversation.

'Well, of course I will, no, have no worries. Certainly I will. No, she's actually much calmer than she sounded to you. I think it's just saying it for the first time to someone is the hard bit. No, she's in no danger, Barbara, believe me, she's not. And I too. Goodbye.'

She sat there unseeing. They were talking about her as a parcel. A package of nerves and reactions. Not a person.

'Do you know, Derry, the only thing that will hold me together over all this is very hard work,' she said.

'Good. I was hoping you'd say that.'

She was surprised. 'I thought you'd say talk, examine it, analyse it.'

'No, there's no point. We won't get to first base now, analysing what makes that guy tick. You've done all you said you would from this end. Now get on with your life.'

'And I can stay here?'

'Of course. Let's get down to work straight away.' He pulled a second chair up to the desk. 'Let's look at some of these stories. See how we could tell them ... should it be table by table ... have Mon and Mr Harris sitting down side by side, explaining how it all began at one table, then move to another and get another story ... Or we could do it as an hour-by-hour thing ... like the restaurant starts to stir at about five a.m.'

Ella laughed. A real laugh. 'I don't think *anything* stirs in Dublin at five a.m.'

'Now we're changing roles. You've been busy telling me how modern it all is here.'

'Make it seven and we're more realistic.'

'Nonsense, Ella. Think about the garbage being collected, the stuff coming in from market. It *has* to be earlier.'

'It would be interesting to see. We'll ask Brenda and Patrick tomorrow night,' she said. 'Meanwhile, we'll go through the best stories and the ones that will be hard to tell.'

'The guy from Scotland, Drew, he's not going to tell his own tale, is he? Show himself up as a would-be thief?'

'Apparently he is, his luck turned that night, his fiancée admired him so much for resisting temptation. Brenda says he's only bursting to tell his story.'

Derry shook his head in amazement. 'Aren't people here quite extraordinary?' he said in wonder.

'No, they're not. It's not just Ireland. It's the same everywhere, in England, in the US, all dying to tell their story and have their fifteen minutes of fame.'

'There's a danger that people will exploit them,' he said.

'Of course there is, but we're not that kind of business. Derry, you're not having second thoughts on me, are you?'

'No, of course not. But talking about second thoughts ...?'

'Yes?'

'I just wanted to say when your anger dies down, you'll probably be relieved that he's alive. Don, I mean. It's only natural. You loved him and he loved you. It has to be better that he's alive, not dead at the bottom of the ocean. So, if you have second thoughts about him and are glad he's still around, then that's normal. That's all I wanted to say.' He looked oddly uncomfortable, as if he didn't really believe all this, but felt that it should be said from a fairness point of view.

'No, I won't ever be glad about anything connected with him. Whether he is alive or dead doesn't really matter to me. I think I preferred him dead. I certainly don't love him or anything about him. So there'll be no second thoughts. But I'm not going to spend my life consumed with hate, either. That would really make me the loser.'

She thought he looked very pleased, but maybe it was just his pleasant smile.

When she awoke on the sofa yet again there was a note.

> I've already gone to investigate this early-morning Dublin. See you tonight at Quentins, 7.30. Call my mobile anytime if you need me.
> Love, Derry

Ella spent the day at Colm's restaurant on Tara Road.

'I don't know why you should think I should help you boost a rival restaurant,' Colm grumbled.

'Because I'm a neighbour's child, because you're not remotely in competition with me, and you love to talk about your pride and joy. I just want to know what's a typical day?'

'As if there ever was one. Come on in and have coffee and I'll walk you through it.'

By lunchtime, she thought she had understood the routine. It would be very visual. Derry would like it. Patrick and Brenda wouldn't object, their place was immaculate and all that backstage stuff would be something to be proud of.

'You look tired, Ella. Stay and have lunch. You've seen it all being cooked. Enjoy it.'

'No, I have a lot of things to do. I have to tell several people something but I want to rehearse on you, Colm. Just to make sure I can do it without crying.'

'Fire ahead.'

'Don Richardson's not dead. I spoke to him yesterday. He's in Spain, on the run.'

'Is it a secret?' Colm asked.

'No, not now.'

'Good. I'll tell Ria's ex-husband Danny that he might go out and kill him for all of us. Would that help?'

Ella laughed nervously. 'No, not really, but it did make me laugh. I don't suppose everyone else will be as practical as you are, Colm.'

*

She told Deirdre. Deirdre sat and listened with a stony face. 'Mother of God! Why couldn't he have done it properly? Did he wash up somewhere?'

'No, I don't think he tried it at all,' Ella said.

'And now of course you're taking him back?' Deirdre was anguished.

'*No*, Dee, I'm only telling you in case it was in the papers.'

'No! You are taking him back or going out to him, I know you are.'

'Oh, Deirdre, shut up. You're meant to be cheering me up, telling me some old song like "There Ain't No Good In Men". Not telling me I'm going back to him.'

'I wonder if Nuala knows,' Dee said.

'Let's tell her, then,' Ella said, her eyes dancing. And for a glorious moment Deirdre thought maybe it was going to be all right. That the one great love of Ella's life might not be able to seduce her back in again.

'Nuala! It's Dee.'

'No, Dee, I'm not going to talk to you. Last time you frightened me to death – I've had to blackmail them all with the threat of telling Carmel about your disgraceful antics with Eric to get them off Ella's back. Fine pair of friends you both turned out to be.'

'Shut up, Nuala. I told you if we had anything to tell you we would.'

'Did you?' Nuala was confused.

'Yes, and now we have. I have Ella here and now we do have news for Frank and his brothers.'

'You do?'

'Will I put Ella on?'

'Well, not if she's going to be cross with me,' Nuala said.

'Not at all. She won't be cross with you. Here's Ella now.'

'Hi, Nuala.'

'Oh, Ella, I'm sorry. I don't think Dee explained it all properly at the time.'

'No, Nuala, I'm sure she didn't. Have you got pen and paper?'

'Yes, I have.' Nuala sounded very nervous.

'Write this. It's Don's telephone number in Spain. Oh, and he's not dead, by the way. That was a mistake. He's alive, but he calls himself Mr Brady. I know, isn't it a scream? No, I'm not drunk, Nuala. That's the number and the other thing is that the Fraud Squad has his computer, with all the details, everything it contains. Oh, and the last thing is that Dee would have gone the distance and told Carmel every last detail. She's been a marvellous friend.'

'Ella,' Nuala's voice was hoarse with fright. 'They're going to be in terrible trouble if it all gets out. Not only will they have lost money and property but there's a matter of tax, you see.' She ended in a near whisper.

'Oh, there often is, Nuala. Anyhow, we're all fair and square now.'

Ella hung up and they giggled as they had done for so many years.

'What I've been saying is getting easier to say as the day goes on,' Ella said as she walked into Firefly Films.

'I hate mystery statements,' Nick said.

'Don Richardson's alive and presumably coming back to this land in leg irons,' Ella said.

'You're not serious? Sandy and I once wondered if he might have staged it,' Nick said.

'You were right,' she said crisply.

'How did you find out?' Sandy asked.

'I spoke to him on the phone,' Ella said, and it didn't make her feel even slightly tearful. 'I spoke, and he called me Angel as he always did, and he had never died at all. Imagine.'

'Are you okay?'

'Yes, I'm fine, I'm fine, but I need to be kept very busy. Could I work here this afternoon until we all go to Quentins? I'm just a bit jumpy and I need to be with people.'

'Why did he ring you?' Nick asked.

'He didn't. I rang him, or rather his wife. I didn't know he was still alive.'

'And are you glad?' Sandy asked.

'I don't care, really and truly, I don't. Too much has happened to care.'

They believed her, got her a sandwich, and sat her down so that she could write out a type of running order that they might go through at tonight's meeting at the restaurant.

They watched her through the glass door, her head down over the paper as she planned out a very rough shooting schedule.

'Do you think she'll go back to him?' Sandy wondered.

'With any luck he won't be in a position to ask her.'

Cathy and Tom at Scarlet Feather heard from Ria and Colm that Don Richardson was still alive. Nora O'Donoghue heard it from them because she had gone into their premises to book a little wedding party. Nora was busy costing out the possibility of having canapés and wine in the back of a bookshop, which would let them have the premises free. There wouldn't be a huge number, but they had really very little money. Still, some things called for the equivalent of fireworks.

Cathy knew that the discussions were irrelevant since Brenda and Patrick had planned to give them a wedding present of a reception in Quentins. But they were only being told this much nearer to the time. Nora had been pushing Cathy for details of how many canapés each there would be for so many euros.

Then this news came suddenly out of the blue.

'I knew he wasn't dead,' she said calmly.

'How on earth did you know that, Nora?' Tom was sceptical.

'I saw him this morning,' she said simply, 'getting out of a taxi in Stephen's Green.'

Tom and Cathy called Deirdre to alert her.

'Is she sure? She can be quite odd, Nora O'Donoghue.'

'No, she's fine, she saw him, she said nothing and was going to say nothing because of Aidan, this guy she's going to marry, he was the one who knew him, taught Don Richardson's kids, and was conned out of money by him, she didn't want to upset him coming up to the wedding.'

'Thank God she mentioned it to you,' Deirdre said. 'Now we can alert Ella.'

'And maybe the Guards as well,' said Cathy.

Ella's mobile number was engaged. So Deirdre rang Nick at Firefly Films.

'Don't panic, it's okay, I can see her, she's in the next room talking away on the phone.'

'She's not talking to him, is she?'

'He doesn't have that number. It's a new phone.'

'What will we do, Nick?'

'Why don't you find Derry somehow. I'll tell her parents. It's not as if he's going to do anything in broad daylight.'

'It's just so that he takes nobody by surprise. Will you tell her, Nick? Gently, you know?'

'Sure thing, Dee,' he said. 'As soon as she gets off the phone.'

Ella was phoning Sasha, the girl who was now living in the Richardsons' Killiney house, the girl with Max the lovely baby, and whose uncle Michael Martin was a great friend of Don's.

'Do you remember me, Ella Brady? I came to visit you on Saturday,' she began.

'Well, am I glad you called.'

'You are?'

'I was looking everywhere for anyone who might tell me where you lived.'

'But why? What for, Sasha? I was just going to tell you that . . .'

Sasha interrupted. 'He's not dead, he never died. It was all a pretend suicide. He's alive, and he's coming back to look for you.'

'No, he can't, the police know, he wouldn't dare to come back here.'

'Well, he left his home in Spain last night. He'll be here today. He says if he can get to you first you won't sell him out.'

'But I've done it. I've given everything to the police.'

'He doesn't believe it.'

'Who told you all this, Sasha? Who says he doesn't believe it?'

'Michael Martin, my uncle. He told me to pack up everything of mine and Max's to have the place looking perfect in case Mr Richardson wants to stay here.'

'In his own house? But he's wanted for huge frauds. He wouldn't go there in a million years.'

'I know. That's why I wanted to find you. It's obvious he's not coming here, he's going after you.'

Derry King had begun his day at 5.30 when he walked to Quentins Restaurant to see if there was any sign of life and indeed he was proved right.

Eight large rubbish bags stood in bin containers, each bag tied and labelled. A private rubbish collector was removing them to a truck. The empty bins were left in the alleyway behind, some on their sides.

Derry nodded with satisfaction. This was one point he could score over Ella. She said no one was awake then.

She was such a courageous girl. She had faced everything so bravely. And there had been a lot to face. The only good thing was that this guy Don Richardson could not come back to Ireland now. It would be far too dangerous for him. So at least Derry didn't have to worry about Ella being in any danger. He went to get himself an early mug of tea. A small café not far away obliged. It was at times like this that Derry longed for a New York diner. Still, it wasn't too bad.

He nodded at the men sitting there. 'You're up early,' Derry said pleasantly.

'Big rush job, office block over there. We get treble time before seven o'clock in the morning,' one of them said.

'Nothing wrong with that kind of money. Did it take much negotiating?'

'No, Kennedys are tough but they're fair. If you do the work right, paint well and put in the hours, then you go home with a decent pay packet at the end of the week.'

'Kennedys?' he asked.

'That's us, well, that's the bosses.'

'Two guys called Sean and Michael?' Derry enquired.

'The very ones.'

'Well, isn't that a small world.'

'You know them?'

'No, my ex-wife met them a few years back, said they were good guys.'

'They're not bad at all.'

'Will they be round during the day, do you think?'

'Bound to be, they usually come in round seven when we're meant to be clearing out of the place. Will I tell them who was looking for them?'

'No, it's okay. I'll come back and tell them myself.' He had no intention of coming back. It was such an extraordinary coincidence that he should walk into his father's family by accident. What was anyone doing, calling this place a city? They were mad. It was a village.

Sandy called Tim and Barbara Brady to tell them that Don Richardson had been seen in Dublin.

'Thank you, Sandy. As it happens, Mr Richardson is here with me at this very moment. I'm telling him that we have no idea where Ella is and that you don't either.'

'She's here, Mrs Brady, don't worry. We'll get the Guards,' Sandy whispered.

The phone was hung up.

'Ring them again, Nick, quick, tell them he's in Tara Road.'

'They're not taking it as urgently as I thought,' Nick said. 'They seem to think it's all a matter for Fraud, they don't think she's in any danger.'

'Well, can't we speak to Fraud?' Sandy said. 'They may think differently.'

'They've passed my message on,' Nick said. 'But I'll ring again saying where he is now.'

'We didn't expect to see you again, Don,' Barbara Brady said when she got over the shock of seeing him on her doorstep.

'I know, I know. But you *did* know I was alive? Ella must have told you.'

'Yes, she did, last night. She was very startled, shocked.'

'Is your husband at home, Barbara? I'd like a quick word with you both. It won't take long.'

'Tim isn't here. He's at the doctor. He doesn't sleep at all well, and there's a matter of his getting counselling.'

'I can't tell you how sorry I am.' Don looked sun-tanned but thinner than he had before. He had lost his lazy, easy confidence and his eyes darted around all the time.

'Yes,' Barbara Brady said bleakly.

'I have had so many regrets in this sad business. I truly did enjoy talking to him. He was a man of such integrity and a, well, a man of faith in a way.'

'He's not that now,' Tim Brady's wife said, looking around the small house they lived in, her face showing just how disturbed and upset the man of integrity and faith was these days.

'I did everything I could to make it up to him. I sent money. Ella surely told you that?'

'We couldn't take that,' Barbara said as if it were obvious.

'May I sit down, please?' Suddenly the great Don Richardson looked tired and even a little frightened.

'I'd prefer if you didn't, Don, it would be hypocritical to pretend that you are welcome here.'

'Ella?' he asked.

'I don't know, I really don't. She didn't come home last night.'

'Please.'

'I can't tell you what I don't know.'

'I'll only talk to her for ten minutes, in front of you and Tim if you like, or here in the house. Please, I have to ask her something.'

'I think you asked her enough over the years.'

'No, I'll tell you what it is. I know her. I *know* her, for God's sake. When I was talking to her last night, she said she had given in the laptop. She wasn't telling the truth. All I have to do is meet her and tell her how much she can save, for everyone, if she doesn't give it in. I can get it back together, that's what I'm trying to do. I can rescue people's investments, your Tim's, too.'

'I don't think she cares about the computer,' Barbara said.

'I agree with you and I don't believe she's handed it in.'

'She told me she had given it back.'

'She said given it *back*?'

'Those were her words. Then she said, "Well, to the Guards anyway".'

He was thinking hard. 'I still don't believe she would have done it. I know her voice, you see.'

The telephone rang. 'Can you answer it? It just might be her,' he pleaded. But it was Sandy at Firefly Films.

He stood listening.

'Who was that?'

'Just friends concerned for her.'

'So they know I'm back, you can see I haven't much time.'

'Do you know that I don't give a damn how much time you have, Don Richardson, or how little? Our only daughter had the misfortune to love you and she has ended up a hurt, damaged girl as a result. She lives with a sense of guilt and shame on account of you, and the fact that her father is a shell of a man, disgraced and empty, and that I live in a prefabricated hut instead of that house over there. She has wept oceans over your leaving her to live in a marriage that she thought was over. She wept further oceans when she thought you were dead. *Now* do you understand how little I care about how much time you have or don't have? I do *not* know where Ella is, and if I did know, then by God I wouldn't tell you.'

'I'll go now, Barbara, and I won't say any more. I urge you not to, either. Remember, there is still the possibility that Ella may forgive me and come with me. I don't want her to feel that the door to her mother and father is closed.'

He was gone and Barbara Brady stood in her doorway shaking at the courage she had shown and her fear that Don Richardson might be right. Was it possible that, after everything, Ella would go back to him again?

Derry walked by Quentins again. This time there was activity inside. He knocked at the back door. 'I'm Derry King. I'll be meeting you tonight,' he said.

The tall dark man dusted the flour and sugar off his hands and gripped Derry's warmly. 'Brenda told me all about meeting you at lunch. I couldn't be there. Someone had to run the shop.'

'And it's an elegant shop I hear from all.'

'Well, thanks to you we're going to make it more widely known, certainly. Come on in, won't you?'

If Patrick Brennan was the slightest bit surprised to see a caller at 6.30 in the morning, he showed no sign of it. He was always here at this hour to do the pastry cooking. He was bad at delegating, he admitted, and just couldn't hand it over to someone else. This was his real skill, and what he enjoyed most. Today he had to make two lemon tarts, a chocolate roulade, a chocolate mousse, a tray of poached pears, a great bowl of chocolate curls, two litres of praline ice-cream and a raspberry coulis.

'But do you have to start so early?'

'Well, I do, really, you need constant exact temperatures for desserts. Later in the day the ovens are always opening and closing. It's not as good.'

And before the city woke up properly, Quentins seemed to be buzzing. A lad called Buzzo came in to hose out the dustbins in the lane and line them with heavy-duty rubbish sacks. He scrubbed out the kitchen and made a note of supplies needed.

'My brother used to do this at the start,' Patrick explained. 'But he's a family man now and he'll be going out to get us the vegetables, so we hired Buzzo. Poor divil, it's his only way of having a proper breakfast, getting a few euros together and still getting to school by nine a.m. He gets the money in his hand from me. I don't really approve, but if you had Buzzo's family . . .'

'Drink, I guess?' Derry enquired.

'Oh, no. Drink they could cope with. Drugs, I'm afraid. Lives in a bad area. All his brothers are addicts and his father's a dealer.'

'His mother?'

'Away with the fairies, spaced out for years now.'

'No hope for the kid then?'

'He's survived so far. He's very bright, you see, so a few of us just make it easier for him to get by without having to be tempted by the drug money. Soon he'll be old enough to have a place on his own. He's gone down now to make tea and tidy up a bit for Kennedy's men, who are doing a job down the road.'

'Are they a good firm?'

'About the best. They did our last repaint job and I couldn't praise them enough.'

There was the sound of a horn outside.

'It's the linen, Mr Brennan. I'll take the sack down to them now,' Buzzo called out.

Yesterday's dirty tablecloths and napkins went off at speed down the lane and Buzzo returned carrying a large box of folded replacements. This had just been placed in what was called Brenda's cupboard when the meat arrived.

By now the chef trainee had arrived, so he took over and Buzzo, with his folded banknote in his pocket, was heading off for the second job of the day. It reminded Derry so much of his own early years, finding any job that was going and nailing it down. He wished he could tell Buzzo how well it had turned out for him, but kids hated these preaching speeches, so he would say nothing.

The trainee, who was called Jimmy and was a bit slow for Patrick's liking, was being hastened through his coffee. His job now was to cut up the meat and have it ready for Chef to cook when the time came. At the same time he was to make a stock with the bones, chicken carcasses and vegetables that were in the cool room all tied up in plastic bags.

And then Blouse Brennan appeared to check the list of what they needed. 'I'll have to buy courgettes. My own are ludicrous,' he apologised.

'That's all right, Blouse, a lot of places buy all their vegetables,' Patrick assured him.

Then the fish box came, from the fishmonger, and then boxes of wine from the supplier and the cheeses.

The assistant chef, Katie, said that there were three new cheeses today. She laid them out expertly on a marble-topped trolley in the cool room. 'That's three more to teach the waiters how to explain and pronounce. I'll have to ring up the cheese man and check myself first. We don't want to look like eejits.'

Derry smiled at her. If she were to say that to the camera, it would be very endearing. Ella had been right. Following a day in the restaurant was a good way to let the story unfold.

Ella! She was going to be fine. She had promised to ring if she wasn't.

Ella wanted to be alone. She needed to think. She did not need endless helpful voices of friends telling her she was all right and that it was all right and everything was going to be all right. None of these things was true.

Don Richardson was coming after her. Or was he?

Could she take Sasha seriously? She needed to talk to somebody. It wasn't fair to wear Derry down with it all again. Perhaps Don would go to her parents' house.

She called her mother. And discovered that he had just left.

'How was he, Mother?'

The question seemed to upset Barbara Brady. 'He was . . . well, he was all right.'

'No, Mother, I mean it.'

'Well, what do you want to know? He wasn't pale or anxious . . .'

'I mean, was he sane or did he look as if he were going to come after me with a cleaver?'

'He thinks he's coming after you with an offer you can't refuse. He thinks you're going back to him.'

'Then you've answered my question, Mother. He's far from sane and we must bring in the cavalry.'

She phoned the Fraud Squad. They had heard. He would be in custody by evening.

Dee wasn't able to come to the phone, her message said. Ella saw Nick and Sandy watching her covertly through the glass door . . . she couldn't wait like this in a trap until he arrived. She had to get out. But she knew they wouldn't let her.

Leaving her jacket over the back of her chair and her handbag on the desk so that they would think she was coming back, she took her telephone and her wallet with her. She slipped out to the bathroom and to the side door into the lane. They would be annoyed, but she had to be alone. She hailed a cab and asked to be taken to Stephen's Green. From the back of the cab she dialled directory enquiries and got Michael Martin's number. She got through straight away.

'Yes?' he said crisply.

'Tell him to stop looking. I'm on my way to Stephen's Green. I'll be beside the duck pond. I'll see him there.'

'Yeah, you and half the Guards in Ireland.'

'If they're there it's not because I'll have brought them,' she said and hung up.

'You okay?' the driver asked, looking at her in the mirror.

'I don't know,' Ella said. 'Why do you ask?'

'You're shivering. You've no coat. You look worried.'

'All of these things are true,' Ella agreed.

'So?'

'So I have to do something I don't want to do and I'm a little bit afraid,' she said.

'Take someone with you,' the driver suggested.

'I can't.'

'You've got a phone. Then tell someone where you're going.'

'But I don't want anyone coming in and interrupting it.'

'You're in a mess then, aren't you,' the driver said agreeably.

'I am indeed,' she said.

Derry King walked back to the building where the major painting job was taking place. He saw the professional sign for the painters. His father could have been part of this firm, lived in this city. Derry could have grown up here. But then, if he had, he might well have been like that boy Buzzo, cleaning out dustbins, making tea on sites before school. Like his own childhood in New York.

He saw two men walking towards a van with the name Kennedy on it. They stood discussing a sheaf of papers, some attached to clipboards. He watched them for a long time with a lump in his throat. They were square men like himself, same bristly hair, a little taller than he was, but they had the same lines coming out like stars around the eyes. You would not need a college degree in genetics to know that these were his relations.

He should be their friend. They were, after all, the sons of brothers. But there was so much to regret. To try to forget. He would walk away.

At that moment they looked over. He couldn't run.

'Sean? Michael?' he said.

'Well, Derry, you came to see us at last,' said one of them.

'You knew me?' He didn't know whether to be pleased or outraged.

'Of course we did.'

'Kim, I suppose?' he said.

'Well, she did show us a photo of you when she was here, but that was a while ago, and anyway, aren't you the spit of us?'

'That's right.'

Derry still seemed uneasy.

The bigger man said, 'Now it's easy for us to know you. There's only one of you. You don't have an idea which of us is which. I'm Sean and this is Michael, the brains of it all, and can we buy you breakfast?'

'I've been eating breakfast for hours,' he said with a half-smile.

'It's the one meal you can't overeat on, they say.' Sean was eager. Touchingly eager to treat the cousin who had ignored them for decades.

He looked from one to the other. 'You don't seem surprised to see me,' he said.

'Kimberly sent us a message saying you might be here and to look out for you,' said Michael.

'And one of the painters said there was a Yank who was the dead image of us, asking about us in the café,' added Sean.

And they laughed like old family friends as they went to Derry's third breakfast of the day.

Possibly ducks were not as content as they looked. Maybe they were up to their little feathered armpits with worry, but they looked fairly sound, Ella thought. As if they had it sorted.

She looked around. There was no sign of him yet.

She sat down on a bench and found a paper bag with the remains of someone's breakfast croissant. Normally she would have been appalled at the Dublin litter problem. Now she could give it to these quacking ducks as she pleased. Maybe it was what they called an Act of Random Kindness to leave the bag there.

She saw people moving around, some of them hurrying, others idling. None of them was Don. And yet she knew he would come. He had moved so quickly from Spain. He must be desperate to find her. Perhaps he had thought she was lying when she spoke to him last night about having given the laptop in already. He must have flown out of Spain immediately, gone by London possibly. What passport had he used?

Suddenly she felt frightened. Why had she arranged to meet him here?

She dialled the number of Derry King's mobile. It was up on the screen, but she needed to press the green button for it to start ringing. Before she could do that she saw Don. He was moving towards her, arms out.

'Angel,' he cried. 'Oh, Angel, nothing matters now. I'm just so glad to see you again.'

Derry didn't know how the day passed, so much happened, so much was seen and noted. Even in his busiest days setting up his own business in the USA, he had not met so many people in the space of one day.

His cousins brought him back to their headquarters and explained the business from the ground up. How it had seemed such a great idea to hire themselves out to builders as master painters, to put a seal on their work as it were. But there were problems.

They told him unemotional stories about their own father, now dead, and their mother, who was in an old people's home and would love to see him, but maybe in another visit, not this one. They pushed him not at all and he felt he had known them all his life.

He went back to Quentins to follow how the day was unfolding there. He met the staff, saw them learning the names and nature of the new cheeses, watched the clever switching of tables as bookings changed minutes before lunch was served. And noted the clockwork precision of the kitchen, where everything had its own rhythm.

Derry saw Brenda on the phone and she told him she had just heard that Don Richardson was in Dublin.

'Does Ella know?' he asked immediately.

'Apparently so, she's safe at Firefly Films. With Nick and Sandy.'

'He didn't waste much time,' Derry said.

'No, I suppose he thought he'd better run in before the Guards got their paperwork ready,' Brenda said.

'If he sees her . . .' Derry began.

'He won't.'

'No, but if he does, do you think she might go back to him?'

Brenda noticed what she thought was more than a professional interest in the question. His face was very concerned. Wishing she believed what she was saying, she assured Derry that there wasn't a chance in hell that Ella would look at that man again.

'Hallo, Don.' Ella's voice was flat.

'Oh, my darling Ella.'

'No, Don, none of that.'

'But nothing's changed. There's been such hell and I know that I put you through it, but I had to. So that in the end we would be . . .'

'No, Don, you didn't. You didn't *have* to do anything.'

'It's going to be all right now, Angel. You and I can go away now. We'll get that money your mother and father wouldn't take, that will get us abroad anywhere, then with the computer we can get everything sorted out.'

She looked at him in disbelief. He really meant it. He thought it was possible that she would drop everything and run away with him.

What did he think her life had been like for all these months, what kind of grasp on reality did he have?

She looked at his face, wondering how he could be so confident and loving. He really did think she was going with him.

'I can't believe that you're here, Don, walking right back into the lion's den . . .'

'You didn't give it to them, Ella. I know your voice. I know everything about you, honestly I do. I know what you're like asleep and awake. I think of you all the time. I know every heartbeat. I can tell when you're lying, when you're frightened. I never knew anyone as well as I know you. I know every breath you take.' He was shaking now, trembling, and there was a heavy sweat on his forehead.

Suddenly she got frightened. She pressed the green button on her phone, which was behind her. She could hear the number being dialled. Please God, may Derry be there. Please may he hear me.

'Don, believe me, I'm not going away with you,' she began.

'You are of course, Angel Ella, and we'll be together as we were always meant to be.'

She could hear something click on the phone behind her. May it be Derry picking up.

'I didn't come out to meet you in Stephen's Green to talk about this, Don,' she said.

'Why *did* you come then, if you don't love me, want to go away with me to have a life together? Why else did you come?'

'To say goodbye and to say sorry, I suppose.'

'Sorry? You're not saying sorry for anything, Angel. You haven't given anything to anyone. It's all somewhere waiting for us to collect.'

'No. I gave it in.'

'Before or after you talked to me?'

'After,' she said, looking at the ground.

He smiled almost dreamily. 'I knew, I was right about that, that I could tell when you were lying.'

'Well, can you tell now? Can you tell that this much is true ... that as soon as I put the phone down I rang the Fraud Squad and they came round and took the laptop. And we went and got the bag from the safe deposit. And they took that too.'

She looked at his face. He did believe it now.

'Why did you do this to me?'

'To have the courage to look you in the face and say it's over and you should give yourself up. Say you're sorry. Put your hands up. There has to be *something* that can be rescued. Do your time, give the boys some dignity in their father. And your wife, too, for that matter.'

His face seemed contorted now. 'Will you shut up. Do you hear me? *Shut up*, mouthing these pious wishes. Are you going to come in and visit me in the gaol for twenty-five years and wait until you are an old woman?'

She was very scared of him now, afraid that he would hit her. 'I'm only just up the road from you,' she shouted over her shoulder, hoping it would reach the phone behind her.

'What are you talking about?' he cried.

'I'm saying where I am to stop myself being frightened of you, Don, and the horrible look in your eyes. I'm in Stephen's Green beside the ducks. That's where I am, and I'm not afraid. It's the middle of Dublin City. You're not going to add to all you've done by hurting me.'

'Hurt you, Angel? Are you mad? I *love* you,' he cried.

'No, you never loved me. I know that now.'

'I came back for you ...'

'You came back for your computer,' she said.

His eyes seemed very mad. Had they ever been like this before?

'Go away, Don,' she said in a weary voice. 'Please, go away.'

'Not without you.'

'You don't want me any more. I've given away what you thought I had. You should never have come back.'

'You are such a stupid, stupid fool, Angel.'

'Oh, yes, Don, I was, I know that now.'

He was very near her and he looked totally out of control. 'You could have had everything, Angel, anything you wanted.'

'I want you to go. Maybe you might even get away. Escape before they catch you. You've plenty of friends who'll hide you.'

'Not so many nowadays, Angel. Not without the computer.'

Then she saw people moving towards them. Out of the shadows, behind the trees and bushes of the park. The mother duck had taken the little ducklings away from the scene as if she knew it wasn't the place for them to be. A place where a grown man sobbed like a child to policemen and howled out, 'I did it for you, Angel. I did it all for you.'

And here Ella Brady trembled and shook in the arms of Derry King, who held her as if he was never going to let her go.

16

The meeting in Quentins that night was cancelled. There had been too much drama. No one could concentrate on a possible film documentary when real life itself had been so full of passion and fear. Over and over, people told each other the events of the evening. Nick and Sandy told Deirdre how they had run out to get a taxi to Stephen's Green when they heard from Derry what was happening. Brenda and Patrick told Tom and Cathy how Blouse had been crossing Stephen's Green on his way back to the restaurant and had seen it all. There was Mr Richardson crying out and roaring like a child.

Barbara Brady told anyone who would listen that she had finally found her courage and her voice possibly when it was too late. But she would remember for ever that she stood up to Don and told him she didn't care what happened to him in the future.

Sasha was told by her uncle Mike Martin that she was to unpack at once and re-establish herself in the Killiney house. Mike Martin himself was going abroad. Mr Richardson would not be coming back, and the best move was to establish squatter's rights immediately.

Nuala rang Deirdre to say that two of Frank's brothers had been in Stephen's Green also, in case the laptop was being handed over. They had been phoned by Mike Martin as a last-ditch stand. They had been horrified by Don's behaviour, and said that Ella had hired an American lawyer to protect her interests.

Square kind of a fellow called King.

There were photographs in the morning's paper of Don Richardson in custody and some eye-witness accounts of the scene. But there was one picture of Ella captioned 'woman being consoled at the scene'. Only those who knew her recognised her. Neither the press nor the public made any connection with Love-Nest Ella of many months back. Except Harriet, who had met Ella on the plane to New York. She might get a couple of hundred euros if she rang a newspaper and tipped them off. But still, Ella was a nice kid. She deserved a break.

And there were so many other ways of making money. The sharp-eared witnesses who were meant to have heard everything said that Don Richardson had called out over and over: 'I did it all for you.' This was hard to interpret.

Some of the feature writers said that he may have been calling out to his beloved wife who, it was understood, was still in Spain but expected imminently in Ireland. Some thought to stand at her husband's side. Others thought to answer charges.

Since the long-planned dinner in Quentins was postponed until everyone was calm enough to deal with things, everyone seemed to assume that Ella would go back to the hotel with Derry.

'I don't suppose there's a way you'd like to try the bed tonight?' he said.

'Jesus, no, Derry. I've been through enough today without considering that side of things,' she said.

'I didn't mean in bed with me in it, I meant you have the bed with me on the sofa.'

'Oh, I see,' she said. 'Sorry.'

And for some reason they found this very funny, and laughed all through the ordering of smoked salmon and scrambled eggs.

They played a game of chess as they had often done. They talked not at all about Don Richardson, where he would be tonight and what would happen to him. They didn't talk about Quentins either. In fact, they hardly talked at all.

And by the time Ella lay down on the sofa, which she insisted felt like home to her now, her eyes looked less frightened and her voice sounded much less shaky.

'I don't want to delay you in Dublin, Derry. We really *will* get down to work tomorrow.'

'I'm in no hurry to leave. There's a great deal to be done here,' he said as he kissed her lightly on the forehead and spread a rug over her.

'But America?' she said drowsily.

'Will survive for a bit without me,' Derry King said.

What could have happened in that week that made everyone change their minds about the documentary? And where did it start first?

Possibly in the kitchen of Quentins.

Blouse Brennan was going through the boxes of fruit. Expertly he was dividing them into the areas where they would be needed: limes and lemons at the bar, fresh berries over at the pastry table so they could be dusted with icing sugar and added at the last moment to desserts.

'I bet you they'll film you doing that, Blouse. You look very graceful,' Brenda said admiringly.

Blouse reddened. 'They won't have *me* in their pictures,' he said.

'Of course they will, Blouse, and out in the vegetable garden and with the hens, aren't you the most colourful part of it all?' Patrick reassured his brother.

But Blouse didn't respond to the flattery. 'I didn't think it would be nice to be in it as, well, I don't want people looking at me.'

'They'll be nice people, you know most of them, Nick and Sandy and Ella,' Brenda pleaded.

'No, I don't mean them.'

'Well, Mr King was in here, and he was the nicest man you could ever meet.'

'No, I mean real people, outside people looking at it. People like Horse and Shay back home. The Brothers who taught me, fellows who work on the allotments. I don't want them seeing me and knowing my business,' Blouse said, flushed and upset.

They knew not to let him get more distressed.

'Well, there's no question of you being in it if you don't want to, Blouse,' Patrick said.

'It would be a great loss, but it's your choice, no question of that,' Brenda agreed.

'Thanks, Brenda, Patrick ... I don't want to let you down or anything.'

'No way, Blouse,' Patrick said through gritted teeth.

Or it could have been in Firefly Films. They got the offer they had dreamed of from the day they started: to film one of Ireland's greatest rock bands all the way through from composing and rehearsing the songs up to a huge rock festival. They would be made if they could do it, but they would need to start almost immediately.

Nick was about to refuse. They were committed to Quentins.

Sandy said they should stall them for a week, a lot could happen in a few days and Derry King could easily change his mind.

Or it could have been Buzzo. He said he couldn't be seen in the film because nobody at school knew he worked here, and that his brothers would take any money off him if they knew he had it.

And Monica said that her husband, Clive, though the greatest darling who ever walked the earth, had been having second thoughts about their telling their love story. People were odd in the bank, no sense of humour. They might think less of Mr Clive Harris if they knew he had read books covered in brown paper about how to be attractive to the opposite sex. Regretfully, they would have to pull their story out.

Someone had told Yan the Breton waiter that if this film was successful, it would be shown everywhere, even in his homeland. Then his father would hear him saying for all the world to hear that they had not got on well as father and son. It was a very enclosed community. In his part of Brittany, people didn't air their problems in public. A million pardons, but he wouldn't be able to contribute.

And then Patrick Brennan finally had his annual checkup. He did all the stress tests on the treadmill and the exercise bikes. Then he sat down, still sweating mildly, to talk to the counsellor as part of the checkup.

'It's a stressful job, running a restaurant, of course, but once we get this documentary out of the way, we should be fine. We've promised to take time off together, delegate more.'

'When will that be?'

'Oh, a few weeks' time, I gather. It will be hell keeping the show on the road until then, but we have to do it.'

'Why, exactly?' asked the counsellor.

*

Brenda's friend Nora O'Donoghue was in the kitchen chopping vegetables. Brenda looked at her affectionately. She was such a handsome woman, with her piebald hair and her long, flowing clothes. She had no idea that she was striking and wonderful. Even there, as she washed the vegetables in a sink, laid them out on cloths to chop and dice, she looked like some happy goddess from a classical painting.

'I wish you'd stop that and come and talk to me, Nora.'

'Listen, I'm doing three hours' work for your husband, if not for you. Come and talk to me here while I work.'

Brenda pulled up a chair. 'Do you mind them filming you doing this?' she asked.

'They wouldn't want me, for God's sake, a mad old woman.'

'Oh, they would, Nora. You look lovely. I was just thinking it. Would you mind?'

'Not at all, if it's any help to you and Patrick. I'd be honoured.'

Brenda looked at her with a lump in her throat. What a generous-spirited person she was. She didn't care if her mother and awful sisters, if the students in the Italian class she taught, if Aidan's colleagues, saw her scrubbing vegetables in a kitchen. What a wonderful way to be.

'You're tired, Brenda.'

'Which means, You're ugly, Brenda.'

'No, it means, You're worried, Brenda.'

'All right, I am worried. Worried sick about this documentary and that we get it right.'

'You don't need to do it,' Nora said.

'If we are to amount to anything, then let us leave some kind of legacy after us.'

Nora carefully put down her short, squat, but very sharp knife and laid her hand on Brenda's. 'You? Amount to anything? Legendary, that's what they call you two already. How much more do you want to amount to? You've been giving legacies into people's lives and will continue to do so for ever.'

'You're kind to think we amount to a lot, Nora, but I don't see it that way. I thought this would sort of define us in a way.'

'Brenda, you have each other and all this marvellous place. In the name of God, woman, don't you have enough?'

Ella ran into Mrs Ennis, the school principal, in Haywards Café.

'I can't tell you how pleased I am to see you,' Mrs Ennis said.

Ella was surprised. She had left Mrs Ennis slightly in the lurch by leaving the school so quickly. Then Mrs Ennis, too, might have regretted her indiscretions about her own private life which she told to cheer Ella up.

'I was going to ask you, did you want any part-time work? I did try to call you, but none of your phone numbers worked.'

'Oh, I went into hiding for a while,' Ella admitted.

'But I gather from what I read in the papers that you're out now.' Mrs Ennis was matter-of-fact.

'Yes, that's right, I am.'

'Does teaching still interest you? You were good. The girls liked you.'

'I did like it, very much. It was more solid than anything else, in a way.'

'But maybe solidity isn't enough.'

'I think it is now. But I have to make a film documentary first.'

'How long would that take?'

'A few weeks, Mrs Ennis. I won't be part of the editing.'

'What's it about?'

'It's about a day in the life of a restaurant.'

'Why?' Mrs Ennis asked baldly.

Ella looked at her for a moment. 'Do you know, I'm not quite sure why. A dozen reasons along the line, partly as therapy for me at the start, I know that. Then a lot of other people got drawn in.' She seemed confused, thinking about why they were doing it.

Mrs Ennis was brisk. 'You know where we are, Ella. Ring us within a week if you'd like to come back to us. We need you.'

'You're very kind.'

'And the other business? All right about that?'

'Oh, yes. It's as if it all happened to someone else, not me.'

'Good, then you're getting better,' Mrs Ennis said.

Ella hadn't talked to Derry properly for three days. He was with his cousins morning, noon and night.

'You haven't had a fight with him?' Barbara Brady asked.

'You couldn't fight with Derry,' Ella said. She remembered his ex-wife Kimberly saying something similar.

When he rang later that day, he asked to see her. 'We have to talk, Ella. Can we have dinner at Quentins?'

'Will I get Nick and Sandy to come?'

'No, just you.'

It turned out that he had been eating there every evening with his cousins. Sean and Michael knew the place already and had come for special treats.

'I'm sorry you're going to turn all this into a sort of circus,' Sean had said bluntly as he looked around him.

'What do you mean?' Derry wondered.

'Well, when you have all these people appearing on television, they'll become celebrities and folks will come in to gawp at them. They won't be able to get on with their job like they did before. Before they became actors, I mean.'

'Ah, now, Sean, don't go discouraging Derry. This is his work, his business. You wouldn't like it if he were to go telling you how to paint a house,' Michael said.

'I wouldn't mind if he had anything interesting to say.' Sean was honest.

And that night, Derry told Ella all this. How the brothers had opened up his eyes about so many things. Filming wasn't his business, he assured them, selling was his business, creating needs for people, then filling them. That's what he was good at. He had spent time in their business and told them about ways they could expand. Sell paint as well as doing the job. Set up an advisory service after hours, in the evenings or Saturday mornings. Draw in the young couples, give them colour charts, do and don't lists. Make them your friends. You weren't doing yourself out of a market. There were two different worlds, those who painted and those who didn't.

And then, he said to Ella, he had listened to them as well. And understood what they were saying. He had grown to love Quentins, there was a possibility that a fly-on-the-wall would destroy it and the hard-working people there. He felt clear in his head about it. Now the only problem was to explain all this to Ella and to everyone else. He was amazed at how easy that turned out to be.

The only person who was confused and annoyed in the end was Deirdre. 'For week after bloody week I've been talking, sleeping, dreaming, breathing this documentary. It was going to be the making of everybody. And now suddenly, out of a clear blue sky, I'm meant to be overjoyed that it is *not* happening. No, Ella, give me some sense of being something rather than a nodding dog.'

'*You*, a nodding dog, Dee! Please!'

'No, I'm serious. It's all ludicrous. What happens when you go back to teaching, your man goes back to America, your other man goes to gaol, Firefly Films become rock groupies, Quentins misses out on immortality? Where's all the joy in that?' Deirdre was great when she grumbled. Which was never for long.

'Listen, cheer up. You're invited to a big party to celebrate.'

'God, what a mad crowd you are. Celebrating! Anyone else would be in mourning.'

'No, Dee, you eejit, it's for lots of things . . . the new company, Kennedy and King. Derry's going in with his cousins. It's for Aidan and Nora's wedding party. It's for Nick and Sandy's new contract. It's for my getting exactly the job I want, part-time teaching, and I'm going back to university to do a doctorate as well, and it's for my father going to have a job as a financial adviser in Kennedy and King. And for so many other things . . . if you can't celebrate all that, then you're only a miserable old curmudgeon.'

Deirdre threw her arms around Ella. 'I never saw you so happy. So that maybe is a reason to get a new party frock. Will there be anything there that I could get my nails and teeth into?'

'Lord knows, there might be,' said Ella. 'It's shaping up as a very unusual party.'

'Yes, Mrs Mitchell. I know it's inconvenient. Perhaps you could choose another night.'

'But my daughter-in-law . . . well, my ex-daughter-in-law, tells me she's going to Quentins on Saturday night . . . tomorrow.'

'But as I'm sure she told you, it's a private function, Mrs Mitchell.'

'Well, I had thought there might be exceptions for regular clients.'

'No, we *have* had this notice on the tables for three weeks, Mrs Mitchell, and in the newspaper.'

Brenda came off the phone and rolled her eyes up to heaven. 'Amazing how Cathy didn't kill that one dead. She's the most trying woman in Dublin.'

The next call was from Nora's mother. 'I don't know what you're thinking of to imagine that I and my family are going to a surprise party for Nora. I never heard such nonsense, and at her age. And at such short notice.'

'We had to keep it at short notice in case they heard about it.' Brenda's eyes rolled further around in her head.

'But I thought that this ceremony was going to be in a bookshop. That's what Nora said, and we wouldn't have gone to that either.' Mrs O'Donoghue sniffed.

'We so much hope you'll be here tomorrow. It will be a great feast and every woman wants her mother there at a wedding party.'

'Huh, as if it were a proper wedding.'

'It will be a marvellous wedding. I'm one of the witnesses. So can I hope you all will come, or is this a definite no?'

Nora's appalling mother didn't want to rule herself out of what was being described as a feast. 'I can't say yes or no.'

'Well, we hope that's a yes. Meanwhile, not a word of any of this to Nora and Aidan.'

Brenda knew that the old bat would try to ring them and spoil it, but it was impossible now; Nora was staying in Quentins for the night and Aidan was at his son-in-law's house. Mrs O'Donoghue would not be able to find them now, no matter how hard she tried.

Maud and Simon were told that Hooves, their dog, could *not* come to the party no matter how rejected it made him feel. He had a collar the same as Derry King's dog had in America, but even that didn't get him in. They were warned by Cathy that two songs was the maximum, and could they be love songs?

Simon thought of 'Please, Release Me, Let Me Go'. But that was not suitable for a wedding, apparently.

Neither was 'Young Love, First Love, Is Filled With Deep Emotion', which they knew, because the couple were not in the first flush of youth.

'Love,' Cathy said. 'You must know *some* song about love?'

They said they would do some research.

'Nothing to be sung without consulting me,' Cathy said. 'That's an order.'

Sean and Michael Kennedy were the first arrivals. They were trying out the canapés and looking at the banners on the wall. The menu was engraved for Aidan and Nora as it should be with wedding bells attached, but there was a banner for Kennedy and King too, and one for Firefly Films, and one for Ella's degree.

The sign writer had been busy tonight.

At the piano, two earnest-looking blond children sat beside an old man as he picked out the notes of a song and tried to teach it to them.

'We'd better write it down, Muttie,' the boy said.

'Everyone knows the words,' the old man protested. 'They're not words you'd be able to write down like, they're not in English.'

'Then why are we singing it?' the girl asked.

'Because Cathy says they must love it. She said it was a pity you didn't know it but you will if you concentrate.'

They concentrated heavily.

Derry came in a car to collect the Brady family.

'We're not really much for parties,' Tim protested, but Ella noticed he had dressed up smartly all the same.

'Can't have a party without my financial adviser there. I might revert to my father and get drunk and silly,' Derry said.

Ella smiled at him. He was able to make a remark about it, a joke even. At last.

'We wouldn't miss it for the world, Derry,' Ella's mother said.

Ella looked at the streets around her as they drove to Quentins. This was her world. There was no other and there never would be again.

Patrick made an appearance at the party in full chef's gear. 'Brenda is with them. She's taking the little party, just Aidan, his daughters and the son-in-law, down to Holly's for afternoon tea and they think they're going to the bookshop afterwards.'

'Wouldn't they be afraid Nora would get a heart attack when she finds the place closed?'

'No, don't worry.'

The registrar was a kind man. He knew when he saw a party of only six people, a bride and groom tending towards middle age rather than extreme youth, that a ceremony of great dignity was called for. He looked from one to the other and stressed the importance of the day and the decision they were making in front of all present.

They thanked him profusely and asked him to join them for afternoon tea in Holly's. He was often invited to join the festivities, but never accepted. Today for the first time he was tempted. They were so touchingly happy, it made him blow his nose quite a lot. They had obviously travelled a long road to get to this day.

They drove to Holly's and got a great welcome. Photographs were taken in the garden under the huge trees. Tiny sandwiches and little cream cakes were served. Everyone was very relaxed. But the bride had her eye on her watch.

'We must be in time for the bookshop,' Nora said.

Brenda was delaying them. 'Ah, don't worry. It will start without us ... they'll know we're on the way.'

'How many will there be altogether?' Aidan's daughter Brigid asked. She was in on the whole thing and thought it was so cool. In fact, totally cool.

'There will be fourteen altogether. I'd have loved to have asked more, but you know . . .' Nora said.

'It's the fourteen important ones anyway, and the others will understand. Don't start fussing, Mrs Dunne.' Aidan looked at her with great affection.

'Oh, God, you put the heart across me, Aidan. I thought your first wife had materialised down here in Wicklow.'

Nick, Sandy and Deirdre arrived together. They had been firmly instructed by Brenda to move among the guests talking and introducing. There were people from a lot of different worlds here tonight, and they needed someone to keep them together. Brenda would have done it effortlessly, but she was needed elsewhere.

Nick, Sandy and Deirdre got their first drink and began doing their duty, moving around and bringing the little groups together. Getting names and giving them.

'Aren't you a very lovely person? Are you an actress or a film star?' a man asked Deirdre.

'No, I'm not. I work in a lab and I'm as cross as a bag of weasels,' Deirdre said.

'And what has made a gorgeous girl like you cross?'

The man was well-dressed, with bristly hair like Derry King's. Of course, it must be one of the painter cousins.

'Are you Sean or Michael?' she asked.

'I'm Sean. Imagine you having heard of us.'

'Everyone's heard of you. I'm Deirdre.'

'And what's upset you, Deirdre?'

'I paid four hundred euros for this dress and I look like the wrath of God in it.'

'You do not, you look lovely.'

Deirdre moved and examined herself in the mirror. With a very disappointed face.

A woman with the most amazingly brassy hair came over and watched her. 'It needs a scarf draped over it, something that picks up the colour,' she said.

'A lot of use that is to me to know that now. It looked fine in the shop.'

'Bet they draped a scarf over it for you?'

'They did, as it happens. I'm Dee, by the way, Ella's friend.'

'I'm Harriet, Nora's friend, and Ella's too. We met when she was going to America.'

'Oh, yes, she told me about you. You sold her a dog collar.'

'I can sell you a scarf now, if you want one. Just wait and I'll get you a selection. I checked my bag in to the cloakroom.'

In minutes Deirdre was transformed.

'I'll leave you now. He's one of the best catches in Dublin,' Harriet whispered.

'Who?' Deirdre felt disconnected from everything.

'Sean Kennedy, rolling in money and he's drooling over you.'

'I'm really meant to be mingling,' Deirdre said.

'I'd say you've mingled enough,' advised Harriet.

When they saw the notice on the door, Nora felt the tears coming down her face. 'Oh, Aidan, isn't that desperate? *What* could they mean, unforeseen circumstances?'

'They were so sure.' Aidan's face was bleak. 'And what did they do with the wine and the canapés?'

'Does it say anything else?' Nora wept.

Then they found a second note.

'It says the Dunne reception has been transferred eight doors down the street.'

'Which direction?' she sniffed.

'It says to Quentins,' Aidan said.

They looked at the others, who were beaming with delight.

'But we can't go to Quentins, not on a Saturday night. No, *Carissima* Brenda, even for a wedding. We can't do that on you.'

Now Brenda had tears in her eyes.

'I've a feeling it's going to be perfectly fine,' she said, and led the newlyweds eight doors down the road to Quentins.

Brigid Dunne had run ahead and when they came in the door, a man at the piano struck up with 'Here Comes the Bride', and after that everyone they could ever have wanted to see at their wedding appeared, to hug them.

Nora's hair was a triumph and her lilac-coloured dress with the dark royal purple chiffon sleeveless coat looked astounding. Harriet had got an immense bargain for her somewhere. No one would ever know how immense, not even the man whose lorry it was meant to have fallen off.

The twins approached. 'We are only allowed to sing two songs. Will we sing them now?'

'Of course.' Nora could hardly speak.

Simon and Maud liked things announced.

'The bride and groom have connections with Italy, what with the bride having lived out there for a long time and her teaching Italian here, so we thought they'd like "Volare".' Everyone in the room seemed to know it and joined in the chorus.

Maud announced the next song. 'It doesn't matter what age you are when you get married, your wedding day is meant to be your best day, so for this couple we are going to sing "True Love".'

The twins knew all the words, even the bit about the Guardian Angel on High with Nothing to Do. They looked round proudly as they sang. They were making a fine job of this, unlike 'Volare', which wasn't even English and everyone had drowned them out. So when they were doing it so well why was everyone weeping unashamedly? Simon and Maud found life more impossible to understand every day.

*

'Those two are extraordinary, they break people up all over the place,' Cathy said to Tom in the kitchen.

She had come in to sit down. Three times in the last two weeks she had gone to the hospital, certain that the baby's birth was imminent. Three times they had sent her home saying that there was absolutely no sign of anything. So she hadn't taken much notice of the pains earlier on today. She was so anxious to be at the reception. And she knew the hospital would only send her away again, but there was this pain, well, it wasn't a pain, more a downward dragging feeling. It had come on quite suddenly.

'Cathy, are you all right?' Tom asked suddenly.

'I must be, I have to be, but . . .'

'But what?' He was ashen.

'But I think the baby's coming, Tom,' she said.

Blouse and Mary saw first what was happening. And knew there was no time to get an ambulance or to move them upstairs.

They moved instead to the storeroom and sat her down in a big armchair. Mary ran to her own quarters for sheets and towels. Blouse ran into the dining room to get Brenda and Patrick.

Ella came into the kitchen that moment and took everything in. 'Well done, Cathy,' she said. 'We'll be absolutely fine.' Her voice calmed the two, who were holding hands so tightly it looked as if they would never be prised apart.

'Couldn't be a better place, plenty of boiling water,' she soothed. 'Tom, get Derry to point out a Brian Kennedy to you. He's actually a doctor. You couldn't be in better hands. Quick now, but don't alarm them.'

Cathy's face was terrified. Mary and Ella calmed her. 'You couldn't be safer, Cathy,' they begged her.

Brenda was with them and then they began to believe it might be true. They leaned over her.

'Push, Cathy,' they all said. The baby's head was there.

Dr Brian Kennedy said by the time he came in, it was all over. The baby was born. Tom and Cathy had a son.

That was when Derry had come into the kitchen to find Ella. And the moment was frozen for ever in everyone's lives.

There should have been the noise of the kitchen, the ovens, the humming of the various appliances. There should have been the sounds of the party in the next room. They definitely should have been heard.

But they all remembered a moment of total silence before the little lungs of the boy who was going to be called James Muttance Feather gave a cry to say he was safely in the kitchen of Quentins and the world.

'I love you,' Cathy said to Tom.

And Mary said it to Blouse.

And Patrick Brennan said it to Brenda.

And Derry and Ella said it to each other at exactly the same time.